The Barsetshire Chronicles

Volume One

By

Anthony Trollope

ISBN: 978-1-78139-550-9

Contents

THE WARDEN

BARCHESTER TOWERS

DOCTOR THORNE

FRAMLEY PARSONAGE

THE WARDEN

Chapter I

HIRAM'S HOSPITAL

The Rev. Septimus Harding was, a few years since, a beneficed clergyman residing in the cathedral town of ——; let us call it Barchester. Were we to name Wells or Salisbury, Exeter, Hereford, or Gloucester, it might be presumed that something personal was intended; and as this tale will refer mainly to the cathedral dignitaries of the town in question, we are anxious that no personality may be suspected. Let us presume that Barchester is a quiet town in the West of England, more remarkable for the beauty of its cathedral and the antiquity of its monuments than for any commercial prosperity; that the west end of Barchester is the cathedral close, and that the aristocracy of Barchester are the bishop, dean, and canons, with their respective wives and daughters.

Early in life Mr Harding found himself located at Barchester. A fine voice and a taste for sacred music had decided the position in which he was to exercise his calling, and for many years he performed the easy but not highly paid duties of a minor canon. At the age of forty a small living in the close vicinity of the town increased both his work and his income, and at the age of fifty he became precentor of the cathedral.

Mr Harding had married early in life, and was the father of two daughters. The eldest, Susan, was born soon after his marriage; the other, Eleanor, not till ten years later.

At the time at which we introduce him to our readers he was living as precentor at Barchester with his youngest daughter, then twenty-four years of age; having been many years a widower, and having married his eldest daughter to a son of the bishop a very short time before his installation to the office of precentor.

Scandal at Barchester affirmed that had it not been for the beauty of his daughter, Mr Harding would have remained a minor canon; but here probably Scandal lied, as she so often does; for even as a minor canon no one had been more popular among his reverend brethren in the close than Mr Harding; and Scandal, before she had reprobated Mr Harding for being made precentor by his friend the bishop, had loudly blamed the bishop for having so long omitted to do something for his friend Mr Harding. Be this as it may, Susan Harding, some twelve years since, had married the Rev. Dr Theophilus Grantly, son of the bishop, archdeacon of Barchester, and rector of Plumstead Episcopi, and her father became, a few months later, precentor of Barchester Cathedral, that office being, as is not unusual, in the bishop's gift.

Now there are peculiar circumstances connected with the precentorship which must be explained. In the year 1434 there died at Barchester one John Hiram, who had made money in the town as a wool-stapler, and in his will he left the house in which he died and certain meadows and closes near the town, still called Hiram's Butts, and Hiram's Patch, for the support of twelve superannuated wool-carders, all of whom should have been born and bred and spent their days in Barchester; he also appointed that an alms-house should be built for their abode, with a fitting residence for a warden, which warden was also to receive a certain sum annually out of the rents of the said butts and patches. He, moreover, willed, having had a soul alive to harmony, that the precentor of the cathedral should have the option of being also warden of the almshouses, if the bishop in each case approved.

From that day to this the charity had gone on and prospered—at least, the charity had gone on, and the estates had prospered. Wool-carding in Barchester there was no longer any; so the bishop, dean, and warden, who took it in turn to put in the old men, generally appointed some hangers-on of their own; worn-out gardeners, decrepit grave-diggers, or octogenarian sextons, who thankfully received a comfortable lodging and one shilling and fourpence a day, such being the stipend to which, under the will of John Hiram, they were declared to be entitled. Formerly, indeed,—that is, till within some fifty years of the present time,—they received but sixpence a day, and their breakfast and dinner was found them at a common table by the warden, such an arrangement being in stricter conformity with the absolute wording of old Hiram's will: but this was thought to be inconvenient, and to suit the tastes of neither warden nor bedesmen, and the daily one shilling and fourpence was substituted with the common consent of all parties, including the bishop and the corporation of Barchester.

Such was the condition of Hiram's twelve old men when Mr Harding was appointed warden; but if they may be considered as well-to-do in the world according to their condition, the happy warden was much more so. The patches and butts which, in John Hiram's time, produced hay or fed cows, were now covered with rows of houses; the value of the property had gradually increased from year to year and century to century, and was now presumed by those who knew anything about it, to bring in a very nice income; and by some who knew nothing about it, to have increased to an almost fabulous extent.

The property was farmed by a gentleman in Barchester, who also acted as the bishop's steward,—a man whose father and grandfather had been stewards to the bishops of Barchester, and farmers of John Hiram's estate. The Chadwicks had earned a good name in Barchester; they had lived respected by bishops, deans, canons, and precentors; they had been buried in the precincts of the cathedral; they had never been known as griping, hard men, but had always lived comfortably, maintained a good house, and held a high position in Barchester society. The present Mr Chadwick was a worthy scion of a worthy stock, and the tenants living on the butts and patches, as well as those on the wide episcopal domains of the see, were well pleased to have to do with so worthy and liberal a steward.

For many, many years,—records hardly tell how many, probably from the time when Hiram's wishes had been first fully carried out,—the proceeds of the estate had been paid by the steward or farmer to the warden, and by him divided among the bedesmen; after which division he paid himself such sums as became his due. Times had been when the poor warden got nothing but his bare house, for the patches had been subject to floods, and the land of Barchester butts was said to be unproductive; and in these hard times the warden was hardly able to make out the daily dole for his twelve dependents. But by degrees things mended; the patches were drained, and cottages began to rise upon the butts, and the wardens, with fairness enough, repaid themselves for the evil days gone by. In bad times the poor men had had their due, and therefore in good times they could expect no more. In this manner the income of the warden had increased; the picturesque house attached to the hospital had been enlarged and adorned, and the office had become one of the most coveted of the snug clerical sinecures attached to our church. It was now wholly

4

in the bishop's gift, and though the dean and chapter, in former days, made a stand on the subject, they had thought it more conducive to their honour to have a rich precentor appointed by the bishop, than a poor one appointed by themselves. The stipend of the precentor of Barchester was eighty pounds a year. The income arising from the wardenship of the hospital was eight hundred, besides the value of the house.

Murmurs, very slight murmurs, had been heard in Barchester,—few indeed, and far between,—that the proceeds of John Hiram's property had not been fairly divided: but they can hardly be said to have been of such a nature as to have caused uneasiness to anyone: still the thing had been whispered, and Mr Harding had heard it. Such was his character in Barchester, so universal was his popularity, that the very fact of his appointment would have quieted louder whispers than those which had been heard; but Mr Harding was an open-handed, just-minded man, and feeling that there might be truth in what had been said, he had, on his instalment, declared his intention of adding twopence a day to each man's pittance, making a sum of sixty-two pounds eleven shillings and fourpence, which he was to pay out of his own pocket. In doing so, however, he distinctly and repeatedly observed to the men, that though he promised for himself, he could not promise for his successors, and that the extra twopence could only be looked on as a gift from himself, and not from the trust. The bedesmen, however, were most of them older than Mr Harding, and were quite satisfied with the security on which their extra income was based.

This munificence on the part of Mr Harding had not been unopposed. Mr Chadwick had mildly but seriously dissuaded him from it; and his strong-minded son-in-law, the archdeacon, the man of whom alone Mr Harding stood in awe, had urgently, nay, vehemently, opposed so impolitic a concession: but the warden had made known his intention to the hospital before the archdeacon had been able to interfere, and the deed was done.

Hiram's Hospital, as the retreat is called, is a picturesque building enough, and shows the correct taste with which the ecclesiastical architects of those days were imbued. It stands on the banks of the little river, which flows nearly round the cathedral close, being on the side furthest from the town. The London road crosses the river by a pretty one-arched bridge, and, looking from this bridge, the stranger will see the windows of the old men's rooms, each pair of windows separated by a small buttress. A broad gravel walk runs between the building and the river, which is always trim and cared for; and at the end of the walk, under the parapet of the approach to the bridge, is a large and well-worn seat, on which, in mild weather, three or four of Hiram's bedesmen are sure to be seen seated. Beyond this row of buttresses, and further from the bridge, and also further from the water which here suddenly bends, are the pretty oriel windows of Mr Harding's house, and his well-mown lawn. The entrance to the hospital is from the London road, and is made through a ponderous gateway under a heavy stone arch, unnecessary, one would suppose, at any time, for the protection of twelve old men, but greatly conducive to the good appearance of Hiram's charity. On passing through this portal, never closed to anyone from 6 A.M. till 10 P.M., and never open afterwards, except on application to a huge, intricately hung mediæval bell, the handle of which no uninitiated intruder can possibly find, the six doors of the old men's abodes are seen, and beyond them is a slight iron screen, through which the more happy portion of the Barchester elite pass into the Elysium of Mr Harding's dwelling.

Mr Harding is a small man, now verging on sixty years, but bearing few of the signs of age; his hair is rather grizzled, though not gray; his eye is very mild, but clear and bright, though the double glasses which are held swinging from his hand, unless when fixed upon his nose, show that time has told upon his sight; his hands are delicately white, and both hands and feet are small; he always wears a black frock coat, black knee-breeches, and black gaiters, and somewhat scandalises some of his more hyperclerical brethren by a black neck-handkerchief.

Mr Harding's warmest admirers cannot say that he was ever an industrious man; the circumstances of his life have not called on him to be so; and yet he can hardly be called an idler. Since his appointment to his precentorship, he has published, with all possible additions of vellum, typography, and gilding, a collection of our ancient church music, with some correct dissertations on Purcell, Crotch, and Nares. He has greatly improved the choir of Barchester, which, under his dominion, now rivals that of any cathedral in England. He has taken something more than his fair share in the cathedral services, and has played the violoncello daily to such audiences as he could collect, or, *faute de mieux*, to no audience at all.

We must mention one other peculiarity of Mr Harding. As we have before stated, he has an income of eight hundred a year, and has no family but his one daughter; and yet he is never quite at ease in money matters. The vellum and gilding of "Harding's Church Music" cost more than any one knows, except the author, the publisher, and the Rev. Theophilus Grantly, who allows none of his father-in-law's extravagances to escape him. Then he is generous to his daughter, for whose service he keeps a small carriage and pair of ponies. He is, indeed, generous to all, but especially to the twelve old men who are in a peculiar manner under his care. No doubt with such an income Mr Harding should be above the world, as the saying is; but, at any rate, he is not above Archdeacon Theophilus Grantly, for he is always more or less in debt to his son-in-law, who has, to a certain extent, assumed the arrangement of the precentor's pecuniary affairs.

Chapter II

THE BARCHESTER REFORMER

Mr Harding has been now precentor of Barchester for ten years; and, alas, the murmurs respecting the proceeds of Hiram's estate are again becoming audible. It is not that any one begrudges to Mr Harding the income which he enjoys, and the comfortable place which so well becomes him; but such matters have begun to be talked of in various parts of England. Eager pushing politicians have asserted in the House of Commons, with very telling indignation, that the grasping priests of the Church of England are gorged with the wealth which the charity of former times has left for the solace of the aged, or the education of the young. The well-known case of the Hospital of St Cross has even come before the law courts of the country, and the struggles of Mr Whiston, at Rochester, have met with sympathy and support. Men are beginning to say that these things must be looked into.

Mr Harding, whose conscience in the matter is clear, and who has never felt that he had received a pound from Hiram's will to which he was not entitled, has naturally taken the part of the church in talking over these matters with his friend, the bishop, and his son-in-law, the archdeacon. The archdeacon, indeed, Dr Grantly, has been somewhat loud in the matter. He is a personal friend of the dignitaries of the Rochester Chapter, and has written letters in the public press on the subject of that turbulent Dr Whiston, which, his admirers think, must well nigh set the question at rest. It is also known at Oxford that he is the author of the pamphlet signed "Sacerdos" on the subject of the Earl of Guildford and St Cross, in which it is so clearly argued that the manners of the present times do not admit of a literal adhesion to the very words of the founder's will, but that the interests of the church for which the founder was so deeply concerned are best consulted in enabling its bishops to reward those shining lights whose services have been most signally serviceable to Christianity. In answer to this, it is asserted that Henry de Blois, founder of St Cross, was not greatly interested in the welfare of the reformed church, and that the masters of St Cross, for many years past, cannot be called shining lights in the service of Christianity; it is, however, stoutly maintained, and no doubt felt, by all the archdeacon's friends, that his logic is conclusive, and has not, in fact, been answered.

With such a tower of strength to back both his arguments and his conscience, it may be imagined that Mr Harding has never felt any compunction as to receiving his quarterly sum of two hundred pounds. Indeed, the subject has never presented itself to his mind in that shape. He has talked not unfrequently, and heard very much about the wills of old founders and the incomes arising from their estates, during the last year or two; he did even, at one moment, feel a doubt (since expelled by his son-in-law's logic) as to whether Lord Guildford was clearly entitled to receive so enormous an income as he does from the revenues of St Cross; but that he himself was overpaid with his modest eight hundred pounds,—he who, out of that, voluntarily gave up sixty-two pounds eleven shillings and fourpence a year to his twelve old neighbours,—he who, for the money, does his precentor's work as no precentor has done it before, since Barchester Cathedral was built,—such an idea has never sullied his quiet, or disturbed his conscience.

Nevertheless, Mr Harding is becoming uneasy at the rumour which he knows to prevail in Barchester on the subject. He is aware that, at any rate, two of his old men have been heard to say, that if everyone had his own, they might each have their hundred pounds a year, and live like gentlemen, instead of a beggarly one shilling and sixpence a day; and that they had slender cause to be thankful for a miserable dole of twopence, when Mr Harding and Mr Chadwick, between them, ran away with thousands of pounds which good old John Hiram never intended for the like of them. It is the ingratitude of this which stings Mr Harding. One of this discontented pair, Abel Handy, was put into the hospital by himself; he had been a stone-mason in Barchester, and had broken his thigh by a fall from a scaffolding, while employed about the cathedral; and Mr Harding had given him the first vacancy in the hospital after the occurrence, although Dr Grantly had been very anxious to put into it an insufferable clerk of his at Plumstead Episcopi, who had lost all his teeth, and whom the archdeacon hardly knew how to get rid of by other means. Dr Grantly has not forgotten to remind Mr Harding how well satisfied with his one-and-sixpence a day old Joe Mutters would have been, and how injudicious it was on the part of Mr Harding to allow a radical from the town to get into the concern. Probably Dr Grantly forgot, at the moment, that the charity was intended for broken-down journeymen of Barchester.

There is living at Barchester, a young man, a surgeon, named John Bold, and both Mr Harding and Dr Grantly are well aware that to him is owing the pestilent rebellious feeling which has shown itself in the hospital; yes, and the renewal, too, of that disagreeable talk about Hiram's estates which is now again prevalent in Barchester. Nevertheless, Mr Harding and Mr Bold are acquainted with each other; we may say, are friends, considering the great disparity in their years. Dr Grantly, however, has a holy horror of the impious demagogue, as on one occasion he called Bold, when speaking of him to the precentor; and being a more prudent far-seeing man than Mr Harding, and possessed of a stronger head, he already perceives that this John Bold will work great trouble in Barchester. He considers that he is to be regarded as an enemy, and thinks that he should not be admitted into the camp on anything like friendly terms. As John Bold will occupy much of our attention, we must endeavour to explain who he is, and why he takes the part of John Hiram's bedesmen.

John Bold is a young surgeon, who passed many of his boyish years at Barchester. His father was a physician in the city of London, where he made a moderate fortune, which he invested in houses in that city. The Dragon of Wantly inn and posting-house belonged to him, also four shops in the High Street, and a moiety of the new row of genteel villas (so called in the advertisements), built outside the town just beyond Hiram's Hospital. To one of these Dr Bold retired to spend the evening of his life, and to die; and here his son John spent his holidays, and afterwards his Christmas vacation when he went from school to study surgery in the London hospitals. Just as John Bold was entitled to write himself surgeon and apothecary, old Dr Bold died, leaving his Barchester property to his son, and a certain sum in the three per cents. to his daughter Mary, who is some four or five years older than her brother.

John Bold determined to settle himself at Barchester, and look after his own property, as well as the bones and bodies of such of his neighbours as would call upon him for assistance in their troubles. He therefore put up a large brass plate with "John Bold, Sur-Surgeon" on it, to the great disgust of the nine practitioners who were already trying to get a living out of the bishop, dean, and canons; and began house-keeping with the aid of his sister. At this time he was not more than twenty-four years old; and though he has now been three years in Barchester, we have not heard that he has done much harm to the nine worthy practitioners. Indeed, their dread of him has died away; for in three years he has not taken three fees.

Nevertheless, John Bold is a clever man, and would, with practice, be a clever surgeon; but he has got quite into another line of life. Having enough to live on, he has not been forced to work for bread; he has declined to subject himself to what he calls the drudgery of the profession, by which, I believe, he means the general work of a practising surgeon; and has found other employment. He frequently binds up the bruises and sets the limbs of such of the poorer classes as profess his way of thinking,—but this he does for love. Now I will not say that the archdeacon is strictly correct in stigmatising John Bold as a demagogue, for I hardly know how extreme must be a man's opinions before he can be justly so called; but Bold is a strong reformer. His passion is the reform of all abuses; state abuses, church abuses, corporation abuses (he has got himself elected a town councillor of Barchester, and has so worried three consecutive mayors, that it became somewhat difficult to find a fourth), abuses in medical practice, and general abuses in the world at large. Bold is thoroughly sincere in his patriotic endeavours to mend mankind, and there is something to be admired in the energy with which he devotes himself to remedying evil and stopping injustice; but I fear that he is too much imbued with the idea that he has a special mission for reforming. It would be well if one so young had a little more diffidence himself, and more trust in the honest purposes of others,—if he could be brought to believe that old customs need not necessarily be evil, and that changes may possibly be dangerous; but no, Bold has all the ardour and all the self-assurance of a Danton, and hurls his anathemas against time-honoured practices with the violence of a French Jacobin.

No wonder that Dr Grantly should regard Bold as a firebrand, falling, as he has done, almost in the centre of the quiet ancient close of Barchester Cathedral. Dr Grantly would have him avoided as the plague; but the old Doctor and Mr Harding were fast friends. Young Johnny Bold used to play as a boy on Mr Harding's lawn; he has many a time won the precentor's heart by listening with rapt attention to his sacred strains; and since those days, to tell the truth at once, he has nearly won another heart within the same walls.

Eleanor Harding has not plighted her troth to John Bold, nor has she, perhaps, owned to herself how dear to her the young reformer is; but she cannot endure that anyone should speak harshly of him. She does not dare to defend him when her brother-in-law is so loud against him; for she, like her father, is somewhat afraid of Dr Grantly; but she is beginning greatly to dislike the archdeacon. She persuades her father that it would be both unjust and injudicious to banish his young friend because of his politics; she cares little to go to houses where she will not meet him, and, in fact, she is in love.

Nor is there any good reason why Eleanor Harding should not love John Bold. He has all those qualities which are likely to touch a girl's heart. He is brave, eager, and amusing; well-made and good-looking; young and enterprising; his character is in all respects good; he has sufficient income to support a wife; he is her father's friend; and, above all, he is in love with her: then why should not Eleanor Harding be attached to John Bold?

Dr Grantly, who has as many eyes as Argus, and has long seen how the wind blows in that direction, thinks there are various strong reasons why this should not be so. He has not thought it wise as yet to speak to his father-in-law on the subject, for he knows how foolishly indulgent is Mr Harding in everything that concerns his daughter; but he has discussed the matter with his all-trusted helpmate, within that sacred recess formed by the clerical bed-curtains at Plumstead Episcopi.

How much sweet solace, how much valued counsel has our archdeacon received within that sainted enclosure! 'Tis there alone that he unbends, and comes down from his high church pedestal to the level of a mortal man. In the world Dr Grantly never lays aside that demeanour which so well becomes him. He has all the dignity of an ancient saint with the sleekness of a modern bishop; he is always the same; he is always the archdeacon; unlike Homer, he never nods. Even with his father-in-law, even with the bishop and dean, he maintains that sonorous tone and lofty deportment which strikes awe into the young hearts of Barchester, and absolutely cows the whole parish of Plumstead Episcopi. 'Tis only when he has exchanged that ever-new shovel hat for a tasselled nightcap, and those shining black habiliments for his accustomed *robe de nuit*, that Dr Grantly talks, and looks, and thinks like an ordinary man.

Many of us have often thought how severe a trial of faith must this be to the wives of our great church dignitaries. To us these men are personifications of St Paul; their very gait is a speaking sermon; their clean and sombre apparel exacts from us faith and submission, and the cardinal virtues seem to hover round their sacred hats. A dean or archbishop, in the garb of his order, is sure of our reverence, and a well-got-up bishop fills our very souls with awe. But how can this feeling be perpetuated in the bosoms of those who see the bishops without their aprons, and the archdeacons even in a lower state of dishabille?

Do we not all know some reverend, all but sacred, personage before whom our tongue ceases to be loud and our step to be elastic? But were we once to see him stretch himself beneath the bed-clothes, yawn widely, and bury his face upon his pillow, we could chatter before him as glibly as before a doctor or a lawyer. From some such cause, doubtless, it arose that our archdeacon listened to the counsels of his wife, though he considered himself entitled to give counsel to every other being whom he met.

"My dear," he said, as he adjusted the copious folds of his nightcap, "there was that John Bold at your father's again to-day. I must say your father is very imprudent."

"He is imprudent;—he always was," replied Mrs Grantly, speaking from under the comfortable bed-clothes. "There's nothing new in that."

"No, my dear, there's nothing new;—I know that; but, at the present juncture of affairs, such imprudence is—is—I'll tell you what, my dear, if he does not take care what he's about, John Bold will be off with Eleanor."

"I think he will, whether papa takes care or no; and why not?"

"Why not!" almost screamed the archdeacon, giving so rough a pull at his nightcap as almost to bring it over his nose; "why not!—that pestilent, interfering upstart, John Bold;—the most vulgar young person I ever met! Do you know that he is meddling with your father's affairs in a most uncalled-for—most—" And being at a loss for an epithet sufficiently injurious, he finished his expressions of horror by muttering, "Good heavens!" in a manner that had been found very efficacious in clerical meetings of the diocese. He must for the moment have forgotten where he was.

"As to his vulgarity, archdeacon" (Mrs Grantly had never assumed a more familiar term than this in addressing her husband), "I don't agree with you. Not that I like Mr Bold;—he is a great deal too conceited for me; but then Eleanor does, and it would be the best thing in the world for papa if they were to marry. Bold would never trouble himself about Hiram's Hospital if he were papa's son-in-law." And the lady turned herself round under the bed-clothes, in a manner to which the doctor was well accustomed, and which told him, as plainly as words, that as far as she was concerned the subject was over for that night.

"Good heavens!" murmured the doctor again;—he was evidently much put beside himself.

Dr Grantly is by no means a bad man; he is exactly the man which such an education as his was most likely to form; his intellect being sufficient for such a place in the world, but not sufficient to put him in advance of it. He performs with a rigid constancy such of the duties of a parish clergyman as are, to his thinking, above the sphere of his curate, but it is as an archdeacon that he shines.

We believe, as a general rule, that either a bishop or his archdeacons have sinecures: where a bishop works, archdeacons have but little to do, and *vice versa*. In the diocese of Barchester the Archdeacon of Barchester does the work. In that capacity he is diligent, authoritative, and, as his friends particularly boast, judicious. His great fault is an overbearing assurance of the virtues and claims of his order, and his great foible is an equally strong confidence in the dignity of his own manner and the eloquence of his own words. He is a moral man, believing the precepts which he teaches, and believing also that he acts up to them; though we cannot say that he would give his coat to the man who took his cloak, or that he is prepared to forgive his brother even seven times. He is severe enough in exacting his dues, considering that any laxity in this respect would endanger the security of the church; and, could he have his way, he would consign to darkness and perdition, not only every individual reformer, but every committee and every commission that would even dare to ask a question respecting the appropriation of church revenues.

"They are church revenues: the laity admit it. Surely the church is able to administer her own revenues." 'Twas thus he was accustomed to argue, when the sacrilegious doings of Lord John Russell and others were discussed either at Barchester or at Oxford.

It was no wonder that Dr Grantly did not like John Bold, and that his wife's suggestion that he should become closely connected with such a man dismayed him. To give him his due, the archdeacon never wanted courage; he was quite willing to meet his enemy on any field and with any weapon. He had that belief in his own arguments that he felt sure of success, could he only be sure of a fair fight on the part of his adversary. He had no idea that John Bold could really prove that the income of the hospital was malappropriated; why, then, should peace be sought for on such base terms? What! bribe an unbelieving enemy of the church with the sister-in-law of one dignitary and the daughter of another— with a young lady whose connections with the diocese and chapter of Barchester were so close as to give her an undeniable claim to a husband endowed with some of its sacred wealth! When Dr Grantly talks of unbelieving enemies, he does not mean to imply want of belief in the doctrines of the church, but an equally dangerous scepticism as to its purity in money matters.

Mrs Grantly is not usually deaf to the claims of the high order to which she belongs. She and her husband rarely disagree as to the tone with which the church should be defended; how singular, then, that in such a case as this she should be willing to succumb! The archdeacon again murmurs "Good heavens!" as he lays himself beside her, but he does so in a voice audible only to himself, and he repeats it till sleep relieves him from deep thought.

Mr Harding himself has seen no reason why his daughter should not love John Bold. He has not been unobservant of her feelings, and perhaps his deepest regret at the part which he fears Bold is about to take regarding the hospital arises from the dread that he may be separated from his daughter, or that she may be separated from the man she loves. He has never spoken to Eleanor about her lover; he is the last man in the world to allude to such a subject unconsulted, even with his own daughter; and had he considered that he had ground to disapprove of Bold, he would have removed her, or forbidden him his house; but he saw no such ground. He would probably have preferred a second clerical son-in-law, for Mr Harding, also, is attached to his order; and, failing in that, he would at any rate have wished that so near a connection should have thought alike with him on church matters. He would not, however, reject the man his daughter loved because he differed on such subjects with himself.

Hitherto Bold had taken no steps in the matter in any way annoying to Mr Harding personally. Some months since, after a severe battle, which cost him not a little money, he gained a victory over a certain old turnpike woman in the neighbourhood, of whose charges another old woman had complained to him. He got the Act of Parliament relating to the trust, found that his *protégée* had been wrongly taxed, rode through the gate himself, paying the toll, then brought an action against the gate-keeper, and proved that all people coming up a certain by-lane, and going down a certain other by-lane, were toll-free. The fame of his success spread widely abroad, and he began to be looked on as the upholder of the rights of the poor of Barchester. Not long after this success, he heard from different quarters that Hiram's bedesmen were treated as paupers, whereas the property to which they were, in effect, heirs was very large; and he was instigated by the lawyer whom he had employed in the case of the turnpike to call upon Mr Chadwick for a statement as to the funds of the estate.

Bold had often expressed his indignation at the malappropriation of church funds in general, in the hearing of his friend the precentor; but the conversation had never referred to anything at Barchester; and when Finney, the attorney, induced him to interfere with the affairs of the hospital, it was against Mr Chadwick that his efforts were to be directed. Bold soon found that if he interfered with Mr Chadwick as steward, he must also interfere with Mr Harding as warden; and though he regretted the situation in which this would place him, he was not the man to flinch from his undertaking from personal motives.

As soon as he had determined to take the matter in hand, he set about his work with his usual energy. He got a copy of John Hiram's will, of the wording of which he made himself perfectly master. He ascertained the extent of the property, and as nearly as he could the value of it; and made out a schedule of what he was informed was the present distribution of its income. Armed with these particulars, he called on Mr Chadwick, having given that gentleman notice of his visit; and asked him for a statement of the income and expenditure of the hospital for the last twenty-five years.

This was of course refused, Mr Chadwick alleging that he had no authority for making public the concerns of a property in managing which he was only a paid servant.

"And who is competent to give you that authority, Mr Chadwick?" asked Bold.

"Only those who employ me, Mr Bold," said the steward.

"And who are those, Mr Chadwick?" demanded Bold.

Mr Chadwick begged to say that if these inquiries were made merely out of curiosity, he must decline answering them: if Mr Bold had any ulterior proceeding in view, perhaps it would be desirable that any necessary information should be sought for in a professional way by a professional man. Mr Chadwick's attorneys were Messrs Cox and Cummins, of Lincoln's Inn. Mr Bold took down the address of Cox and Cummins, remarked that the weather was cold for the time of the year, and wished Mr Chadwick good-morning. Mr Chadwick said it was cold for June, and bowed him out.

He at once went to his lawyer, Finney. Now, Bold was not very fond of his attorney, but, as he said, he merely wanted a man who knew the forms of law, and who would do what he was told for his money. He had no idea of putting himself in the hands of a lawyer. He wanted law from a lawyer as he did a coat from a tailor, because he could not make it so well himself; and he thought Finney the fittest man in Barchester for his purpose. In one respect, at any rate, he was right: Finney was humility itself.

Finney advised an instant letter to Cox and Cummins, mindful of his six-and-eightpence. "Slap at them at once, Mr Bold. Demand categorically and explicitly a full statement of the affairs of the hospital."

"Suppose I were to see Mr Harding first," suggested Bold.

"Yes, yes, by all means," said the acquiescing Finney; "though, perhaps, as Mr Harding is no man of business, it may lead—lead to some little difficulties; but perhaps you're right. Mr Bold, I don't think seeing Mr Harding can do any harm." Finney saw from the expression of his client's face that he intended to have his own way.

Chapter III

THE BISHOP OF BARCHESTER

Bold at once repaired to the hospital. The day was now far advanced, but he knew that Mr Harding dined in the summer at four, that Eleanor was accustomed to drive in the evening, and that he might therefore probably find Mr Harding alone. It was between seven and eight when he reached the slight iron gate leading into the precentor's garden, and though, as Mr Chadwick observed, the day had been cold for June, the evening was mild, and soft, and sweet. The little gate was open. As he raised the latch he heard the notes of Mr Harding's violoncello from the far end of the garden, and, advancing before the house and across the lawn, he found him playing;—and not without an audience. The musician was seated in a garden-chair just within the summer-house, so as to allow the violoncello which he held between his knees to rest upon the dry stone flooring; before him stood a rough music desk, on which was open a page of that dear sacred book, that much-laboured and much-loved volume of church music, which had cost so many guineas; and around sat, and lay, and stood, and leaned, ten of the twelve old men who dwelt with him beneath old John Hiram's roof. The two reformers were not there. I will not say that in their hearts they were conscious of any wrong done or to be done to their mild warden, but latterly they had kept aloof from him, and his music was no longer to their taste.

It was amusing to see the positions, and eager listening faces of these well-to-do old men. I will not say that they all appreciated the music which they heard, but they were intent on appearing to do so; pleased at being where they were, they were determined, as far as in them lay, to give pleasure in return; and they were not unsuccessful. It gladdened the precentor's heart to think that the old bedesmen whom he loved so well admired the strains which were to him so full of almost ecstatic joy; and he used to boast that such was the air of the hospital, as to make it a precinct specially fit for the worship of St Cecilia.

Immediately before him, on the extreme corner of the bench which ran round the summer-house, sat one old man, with his handkerchief smoothly lain upon his knees, who did enjoy the moment, or acted enjoyment well. He was one on whose large frame many years, for he was over eighty, had made small havoc;—he was still an upright, burly, handsome figure, with an open, ponderous brow, round which clung a few, though very few, thin gray locks. The coarse black gown of the hospital, the breeches, and buckled shoes became him well; and as he sat with his hands folded on his staff, and his chin resting on his hands, he was such a listener as most musicians would be glad to welcome.

This man was certainly the pride of the hospital. It had always been the custom that one should be selected as being to some extent in authority over the others; and though Mr Bunce, for such was his name, and so he was always designated by his inferior brethren, had no greater emoluments than they, he had assumed, and well knew how to maintain, the dignity of his elevation. The precentor delighted to call him his sub-warden, and was not ashamed, occasionally, when no other guest was there, to bid him sit down by the same parlour fire, and drink the full glass of port which was placed near him. Bunce never went without the second glass, but no entreaty ever made him take a third.

"Well, well, Mr Harding; you're too good, much too good," he'd always say, as the second glass was filled; but when that was drunk, and the half hour over, Bunce stood erect, and with a benediction which his patron valued, retired to his own abode. He knew the world too well to risk the comfort of such halcyon moments, by prolonging them till they were disagreeable.

Mr Bunce, as may be imagined, was most strongly opposed to innovation. Not even Dr Grantly had a more holy horror of those who would interfere in the affairs of the hospital; he was every inch a churchman, and though he was not very fond of Dr Grantly personally, that arose from there not being room in the hospital for two people so much alike as the doctor and himself, rather than from any dissimilarity in feeling. Mr Bunce was inclined to think that the warden and himself could manage the hospital without further assistance; and that, though the bishop was the constitutional visitor, and as such entitled to special reverence from all connected with John Hiram's will, John Hiram never intended that his affairs should be interfered with by an archdeacon.

At the present moment, however, these cares were off his mind, and he was looking at his warden, as though he thought the music heavenly, and the musician hardly less so.

As Bold walked silently over the lawn, Mr Harding did not at first perceive him, and continued to draw his bow slowly across the plaintive wires; but he soon found from his audience that some stranger was there, and looking up, began to welcome his young friend with frank hospitality.

"Pray, Mr Harding—pray don't let me disturb you," said Bold; "you know how fond I am of sacred music."

"Oh! it's nothing," said the precentor, shutting up the book and then opening it again as he saw the delightfully imploring look of his old friend Bunce. Oh, Bunce, Bunce, Bunce, I fear that after all thou art but a flatterer. "Well, I'll just finish it then; it's a favourite little bit of Bishop's; and then, Mr Bold, we'll have a stroll and a chat till Eleanor comes in and gives us tea." And so Bold sat down on the soft turf to listen, or rather to think how, after such sweet harmony, he might best introduce a theme of so much discord, to disturb the peace of him who was so ready to welcome him kindly.

Bold thought that the performance was soon over, for he felt that he had a somewhat difficult task, and he almost regretted the final leave-taking of the last of the old men, slow as they were in going through their adieux.

Bold's heart was in his mouth, as the precentor made some ordinary but kind remark as to the friendliness of the visit.

"One evening call," said he, "is worth ten in the morning. It's all formality in the morning; real social talk never begins till after dinner. That's why I dine early, so as to get as much as I can of it."

"Quite true, Mr Harding," said the other; "but I fear I've reversed the order of things, and I owe you much apology for troubling you on business at such an hour; but it is on business that I have called just now."

Mr Harding looked blank and annoyed; there was something in the tone of the young man's voice which told him that the interview was intended to be disagreeable, and he shrank back at finding his kindly greeting so repulsed.

"I wish to speak to you about the hospital," continued Bold.

"Well, well, anything I can tell you I shall be most happy—"

"It's about the accounts."

"Then, my dear fellow, I can tell you nothing, for I'm as ignorant as a child. All I know is, that they pay me £800 a year. Go to Chadwick, he knows all about the accounts; and now tell me, will poor Mary Jones ever get the use of her limb again?"

"Well, I think she will, if she's careful; but, Mr Harding, I hope you won't object to discuss with me what I have to say about the hospital."

Mr Harding gave a deep, long-drawn sigh. He did object, very strongly object, to discuss any such subject with John Bold; but he had not the business tact of Mr Chadwick, and did not know how to relieve himself from the coming evil; he sighed sadly, but made no answer.

"I have the greatest regard for you, Mr Harding," continued Bold; "the truest respect, the most sincere—"

"Thank ye, thank ye, Mr Bold," interjaculated the precentor somewhat impatiently; "I'm much obliged, but never mind that; I'm as likely to be in the wrong as another man,—quite as likely."

"But, Mr Harding, I must express what I feel, lest you should think there is personal enmity in what I'm going to do."

"Personal enmity! Going to do! Why, you're not going to cut my throat, nor put me into the Ecclesiastical Court!"

Bold tried to laugh, but he couldn't. He was quite in earnest, and determined in his course, and couldn't make a joke of it. He walked on awhile in silence before he recommenced his attack, during which Mr Harding, who had still the bow in his hand, played rapidly on an imaginary violoncello. "I fear there is reason to think that John Hiram's will is not carried out to the letter, Mr Harding," said the young man at last; "and I have been asked to see into it."

"Very well, I've no objection on earth; and now we need not say another word about it."

"Only one word more, Mr Harding. Chadwick has referred me to Cox and Cummins, and I think it my duty to apply to them for some statement about the hospital. In what I do I may appear to be interfering with you, and I hope you will forgive me for doing so."

"Mr Bold," said the other, stopping, and speaking with some solemnity, "if you act justly, say nothing in this matter but the truth, and use no unfair weapons in carrying out your purposes, I shall have nothing to forgive. I presume you think I am not entitled to the income I receive from the hospital, and that others are entitled to it. Whatever some may do, I shall never attribute to you base motives because you hold an opinion opposed to my own and adverse to my interests: pray do what you consider to be your duty; I can give you no assistance, neither will I offer you any obstacle. Let me, however, suggest to you, that you can in no wise forward your views nor I mine, by any discussion between us. Here comes Eleanor and the ponies, and we'll go in to tea."

Bold, however, felt that he could not sit down at ease with Mr Harding and his daughter after what had passed, and therefore excused himself with much awkward apology; and merely raising his hat and bowing as he passed Eleanor and the pony chair, left her in disappointed amazement at his departure.

Mr Harding's demeanour certainly impressed Bold with a full conviction that the warden felt that he stood on strong grounds, and almost made him think that he was about to interfere without due warrant in the private affairs of a just and honourable man; but Mr Harding himself was anything but satisfied with his own view of the case.

In the first place, he wished for Eleanor's sake to think well of Bold and to like him, and yet he could not but feel disgusted at the arrogance of his conduct. What right had he to say that John Hiram's will was not fairly carried out? But then the question would arise within his heart,—Was that will fairly acted on? Did John Hiram mean that the warden of his hospital should receive considerably more out of the legacy than all the twelve old men together for whose behoof the hospital was built? Could it be possible that John Bold was right, and that the reverend warden of the hospital had been for the last ten years and more the unjust recipient of an income legally and equitably belonging to others? What if it should be proved before the light of day that he, whose life had been so happy, so quiet, so respected, had absorbed eight thousand pounds to which he had no title, and which he could never repay? I do not say that he feared that such was really the case; but the first shade of doubt now fell across his mind, and from this evening, for many a long, long day, our good, kind loving warden was neither happy nor at ease.

Thoughts of this kind, these first moments of much misery, oppressed Mr Harding as he sat sipping his tea, absent and ill at ease. Poor Eleanor felt that all was not right, but her ideas as to the cause of the evening's discomfort did not go beyond her lover, and his sudden and uncivil departure. She thought there must have been some quarrel between Bold and her father, and she was half angry with both, though she did not attempt to explain to herself why she was so.

Mr Harding thought long and deeply over these things, both before he went to bed and after it, as he lay awake, questioning within himself the validity of his claim to the income which he enjoyed. It seemed clear at any rate that, however unfortunate he might be at having been placed in such a position, no one could say that he ought either to have refused the appointment first, or to have rejected the income afterwards. All the world,—meaning the ecclesiastical world as confined to the English church,—knew that the wardenship of the Barchester Hospital was a snug sinecure, but no one had ever been blamed for accepting it. To how much blame, however, would he have been open had he rejected it! How mad would he have been thought had he declared, when the situation was vacant and offered to him, that he had scruples as to receiving £800 a year from John Hiram's property, and that he had rather some stranger should possess it! How would Dr Grantly have shaken his wise head, and have consulted with his friends in the close as to some decent retreat for the coming insanity of the poor minor canon! If he was right in accepting the place, it was clear to him also that he would be wrong in rejecting any part of the income attached to it. The patronage was a valuable appanage of the bishopric; and surely it would not be his duty to lessen the value of that preferment which had been bestowed on himself; surely he was bound to stand by his order.

But somehow these arguments, though they seemed logical, were not satisfactory. Was John Hiram's will fairly carried out? that was the true question: and if not, was it not his especial duty to see that this was done,—his especial duty, whatever injury it might do to his order,—however ill such duty might be received by his patron and his friends? At the idea of his friends, his mind turned unhappily to his son-in-law. He knew well how strongly he would be supported by Dr Grantly, if he could bring himself to put his case into the archdeacon's hands and to allow him to fight the battle; but he knew also that he would find no sympathy there for his doubts, no friendly feeling, no inward comfort. Dr Grantly would be ready enough to take up his cudgel against all comers on behalf of the church militant, but he would do so on the distasteful ground of the church's infallibility. Such a contest would give no comfort to Mr Harding's doubts. He was not so anxious to prove himself right, as to be so.

I have said before that Dr Grantly was the working man of the diocese, and that his father the bishop was somewhat inclined to an idle life. So it was; but the bishop, though he had never been an active man, was one whose qualities had rendered him dear to all who knew him. He was the very opposite to his son; he was a bland and a kind old man, opposed by every feeling to authoritative demonstrations and episcopal ostentation. It was perhaps well for him, in his situation, that his son had early in life been able to do that which he could not well do when he was younger, and which he could not have done at all now that he was over seventy. The bishop knew how to entertain the clergy of his diocese, to talk easy small-talk with the rectors' wives, and put curates at their ease; but it required the strong hand of the archdeacon to deal with such as were refractory either in their doctrines or their lives.

The bishop and Mr Harding loved each other warmly. They had grown old together, and had together spent many, many years in clerical pursuits and clerical conversation. When one of them was a bishop and the other only a minor canon they were even then much together; but since their children had married, and Mr Harding had become warden and precentor, they were all in all to each other. I will not say that they managed the diocese between them, but they spent much time in discussing the man who did, and in forming little plans to mitigate his wrath against church delinquents, and soften his aspirations for church dominion.

Mr Harding determined to open his mind and confess his doubts to his old friend; and to him he went on the morning after John Bold's uncourteous visit.

Up to this period no rumour of these cruel proceedings against the hospital had reached the bishop's ears. He had doubtless heard that men existed who questioned his right to present to a sinecure of £800 a year, as he had heard from time to time of some special immorality or disgraceful disturbance in the usually decent and quiet city of Barchester: but all he did, and all he was called on to do, on such occasions, was to shake his head, and to beg his son, the great dictator, to see that no harm happened to the church.

It was a long story that Mr Harding had to tell before he made the bishop comprehend his own view of the case; but we need not follow him through the tale. At first the bishop counselled but one step, recommended but one remedy, had but one medicine in his whole pharmacopoeia strong enough to touch so grave a disorder;—he prescribed the archdeacon. "Refer him to the archdeacon," he repeated, as Mr Harding spoke of Bold and his visit. "The archdeacon will set you quite right about that," he kindly said, when his friend spoke with hesitation of the justness of his cause. "No man has got up all that so well as the archdeacon;" but the dose, though large, failed to quiet the patient; indeed it almost produced nausea.

"But, bishop," said he, "did you ever read John Hiram's will?"

The bishop thought probably he had, thirty-five years ago, when first instituted to his see, but could not state positively: however, he very well knew that he had the absolute right to present to the wardenship, and that the income of the warden had been regularly settled.

"But, bishop, the question is, who has the power to settle it? If, as this young man says, the will provides that the proceeds of the property are to be divided into shares, who has the power to alter these provisions?" The bishop had an indistinct idea that they altered themselves by the lapse of years; that a kind of ecclesiastical statute of limitation barred the rights of the twelve bedesmen to any increase of income arising from the increased value of property. He said something about tradition; more of the many learned men who by their practice had confirmed the present arrangement; then went at some length into the propriety of maintaining the due difference in rank and income between a beneficed clergyman and certain poor old men who were dependent on charity; and concluded his argument by another reference to the archdeacon.

The precentor sat thoughtfully gazing at the fire, and listening to the good-natured reasoning of his friend. What the bishop said had a sort of comfort in it, but it was not a sustaining comfort. It made Mr Harding feel that many others,—indeed, all others of his own order,—would think him right; but it failed to prove to him that he truly was so.

"Bishop," said he, at last, after both had sat silent for a while, "I should deceive you and myself too, if I did not tell you that I am very unhappy about this. Suppose that I cannot bring myself to agree with Dr Grantly!—that I find, after inquiry, that the young man is right, and that I am wrong,—what then?"

The two old men were sitting near each other,—so near that the bishop was able to lay his hand upon the other's knee, and he did so with a gentle pressure. Mr Harding well knew what that pressure meant. The bishop had no further argument to adduce; he could not fight for the cause as his son would do; he could not prove all the precentor's doubts to be groundless; but he could sympathise with his friend, and he did so; and Mr Harding felt that he had received that for which he came. There was another period of silence, after which the bishop asked, with a degree of irritable energy, very unusual with him, whether this "pestilent intruder" (meaning John Bold) had any friends in Barchester.

Mr Harding had fully made up his mind to tell the bishop everything; to speak of his daughter's love, as well as his own troubles; to talk of John Bold in his double capacity of future son-in-law and present enemy; and though he felt it to be sufficiently disagreeable, now was his time to do it.

"He is very intimate at my own house, bishop." The bishop stared. He was not so far gone in orthodoxy and church militancy as his son, but still he could not bring himself to understand how so declared an enemy of the establishment could be admitted on terms of intimacy into the house, not only of so firm a pillar as Mr Harding, but one so much injured as the warden of the hospital.

"Indeed, I like Mr Bold much, personally," continued the disinterested victim; "and to tell you the 'truth,'"—he hesitated as he brought out the dreadful tidings,—"I have sometimes thought it not improbable that he would be my second son-in-law." The bishop did not whistle: we believe that they lose the power of doing so on being consecrated; and that in these days one might as easily meet a corrupt judge as a whistling bishop; but he looked as though he would have done so, but for his apron.

What a brother-in-law for the archdeacon! what an alliance for Barchester close! what a connection for even the episcopal palace! The bishop, in his simple mind, felt no doubt that John Bold, had he so much power, would shut up all cathedrals, and probably all parish churches; distribute all tithes among Methodists, Baptists, and other savage tribes; utterly annihilate the sacred bench, and make shovel hats and lawn sleeves as illegal as cowls, sandals, and sackcloth! Here was a nice man to be initiated into the comfortable arcana of ecclesiastical snuggeries; one who doubted the integrity of parsons, and probably disbelieved the Trinity!

Mr Harding saw what an effect his communication had made, and almost repented the openness of his disclosure; he, however, did what he could to moderate the grief of his friend and patron. "I do not say that there is any engagement between them. Had there been, Eleanor would have told me; I know her well enough to be assured that she would have done so; but I see that they are fond of each other; and as a man and a father, I have had no objection to urge against their intimacy."

"But, Mr Harding," said the bishop, "how are you to oppose him, if he is your son-in-law?"

"I don't mean to oppose him; it is he who opposes me; if anything is to be done in defence, I suppose Chadwick will do it. I suppose—"

"Oh, the archdeacon will see to that: were the young man twice his brother-in-law, the archdeacon will never be deterred from doing what he feels to be right."

Mr Harding reminded the bishop that the archdeacon and the reformer were not yet brothers, and very probably never would be; exacted from him a promise that Eleanor's name should not be mentioned in any discussion between the father bishop and son archdeacon respecting the hospital; and then took his departure, leaving his poor old friend bewildered, amazed, and confounded.

Chapter IV

HIRAM'S BEDESMEN

The parties most interested in the movement which is about to set Barchester by the ears were not the foremost to discuss the merit of the question, as is often the case; but when the bishop, the archdeacon, the warden, the steward, and Messrs Cox and Cummins, were all busy with the matter, each in his own way, it is not to be supposed that Hiram's bedesmen themselves were altogether passive spectators. Finney, the attorney, had been among them, asking sly questions, and raising immoderate hopes, creating a party hostile to the warden, and establishing a corps in the enemy's camp, as he figuratively calls it to himself. Poor old men: whoever may be righted or wronged by this inquiry, they at any rate will assuredly be only injured: to them it can only be an unmixed evil. How can their lot be improved? all their wants are supplied; every comfort is administered; they have warm houses, good clothes, plentiful diet, and rest after a life of labour; and above all, that treasure so inestimable in declining years, a true and kind friend to listen to their sorrows, watch over their sickness, and administer comfort as regards this world, and the world to come!

John Bold sometimes thinks of this, when he is talking loudly of the rights of the bedesmen, whom he has taken under his protection; but he quiets the suggestion within his breast with the high-sounding name of justice: "*Fiat justitia, ruat cœlum.*" These old men should, by rights, have one hundred pounds a year instead of one shilling and six-pence a day, and the warden should have two hundred or three hundred pounds instead of eight hundred pounds. What is unjust must be wrong; what is wrong should be righted; and if he declined the task, who else would do it?

"Each one of you is clearly entitled to one hundred pounds a year by common law": such had been the important whisper made by Finney into the ears of Abel Handy, and by him retailed to his eleven brethren.

Too much must not be expected from the flesh and blood even of John Hiram's bedesmen, and the positive promise of one hundred a year to each of the twelve old men had its way with most of them. The great Bunce was not to be wiled away, and was up-held in his orthodoxy by two adherents. Abel Handy, who was the leader of the aspirants after wealth, had, alas, a stronger following. No less than five of the twelve soon believed that his views were just, making with their leader a moiety of the hospital. The other three, volatile unstable minds, vacillated between the two chieftains, now led away by the hope of gold, now anxious to propitiate the powers that still existed.

It had been proposed to address a petition to the bishop as visitor, praying his lordship to see justice done to the legal recipients of John Hiram's Charity, and to send copies of this petition and of the reply it would elicit to all the leading London papers, and thereby to obtain notoriety for the subject. This it was thought would pave the way for ulterior legal proceedings. It would have been a great thing to have had the signatures and marks of all the twelve injured legatees; but this was impossible: Bunce would have cut his hand off sooner than have signed it. It was then suggested by Finney that if even eleven could be induced to sanction the document, the one obstinate recusant might have been represented as unfit to judge on such a question,—in fact, as being *non compos mentis,*—and the petition would have been taken as representing the feeling of the men. But this could not be done: Bunce's friends were as firm as himself, and as yet only six crosses adorned the document. It was the more provoking, as Bunce himself could write his name legibly, and one of those three doubting souls had for years boasted of like power, and possessed, indeed, a Bible, in which he was proud to show his name written by himself some thirty years ago—"Job Skulpit;" but it was thought that Job Skulpit, having forgotten his scholarship, on that account recoiled from the petition, and that the other doubters would follow as he led them. A petition signed by half the hospital would have but a poor effect.

It was in Skulpit's room that the petition was now lying, waiting such additional signatures as Abel Handy, by his eloquence, could obtain for it. The six marks it bore were duly attested, thus:

his	his	his
Abel X Handy,	Greg^y X Moody,	Mathew X Spriggs,
mark	mark	mark

&c., and places were duly designated in pencil for those brethren who were now expected to join: for Skulpit alone was left a spot on which his genuine signature might be written in fair clerk-like style. Handy had brought in the document, and spread it out on the small deal table, and was now standing by it persuasive and eager. Moody had followed with an inkhorn, carefully left behind by Finney; and Spriggs bore aloft, as though it were a sword, a well-worn ink-black pen, which from time to time he endeavoured to thrust into Skulpit's unwilling hand. With the learned man were his two abettors in indecision, William Gazy and Jonathan Crumple. If ever the petition were to be forwarded, now was the time,—so said Mr Finney; and great was the anxiety on the part of those whose one hundred pounds a year, as they believed, mainly depended on the document in question.

"To be kept out of all that money," as the avaricious Moody had muttered to his friend Handy, "by an old fool saying that he can write his own name like his betters!"

"Well, Job," said Handy, trying to impart to his own sour, ill-omened visage a smile of approbation, in which he greatly failed; "so you're ready now, Mr Finney says; here's the place, d'ye see;"—and he put his huge brown finger down on the dirty paper;—"name or mark, it's all one. Come along, old boy; if so be we're to have the spending of this money, why the sooner the better,—that's my maxim."

"To be sure," said Moody. "We a'n't none of us so young; we can't stay waiting for old Catgut no longer."

It was thus these miscreants named our excellent friend. The nickname he could easily have forgiven, but the allusion to the divine source of all his melodious joy would have irritated even him. Let us hope he never knew the insult.

"Only think, old Billy Gazy," said Spriggs, who rejoiced in greater youth than his brethren, but having fallen into a fire when drunk, had had one eye burnt out, one cheek burnt through, and one arm nearly burnt off, and who, therefore, in regard to personal appearance, was not the most prepossessing of men, "a hundred a year, and all to spend; only think, old Billy Gazy;" and he gave a hideous grin that showed off his misfortunes to their full extent.

Old Billy Gazy was not alive to much enthusiasm. Even these golden prospects did not arouse him to do more than rub his poor old bleared eyes with the cuff of his bedesman's gown, and gently mutter: "he didn't know, not he; he didn't know."

"But you'd know, Jonathan," continued Spriggs, turning to the other friend of Skulpit's, who was sitting on a stool by the table, gazing vacantly at the petition. Jonathan Crumple was a meek, mild man, who had known better days; his means had been wasted by bad children, who had made his life wretched till he had been received into the hospital, of which he had not long been a member. Since that day he had known neither sorrow nor trouble, and this attempt to fill him with new hopes was, indeed, a cruelty.

"A hundred a year's a nice thing, for sartain, neighbour Spriggs," said he. "I once had nigh to that myself, but it didn't do me no good." And he gave a low sigh, as he thought of the children of his own loins who had robbed him.

"And shall have again, Joe," said Handy; "and will have someone to keep it right and tight for you this time."

Crumple sighed again;—he had learned the impotency of worldly wealth, and would have been satisfied, if left untempted, to have remained happy with one and sixpence a day.

"Come, Skulpit," repeated Handy, getting impatient, "you're not going to go along with old Bunce in helping that parson to rob us all. Take the pen, man, and right yourself. Well," he added, seeing that Skulpit still doubted, "to see a man as is afraid to stand by hisself is, to my thinking, the meanest thing as is."

"Sink them all for parsons, says I," growled Moody; "hungry beggars, as never thinks their bellies full till they have robbed all and everything!"

"Who's to harm you, man?" argued Spriggs. "Let them look never so black at you, they can't get you put out when you're once in;—no, not old Catgut, with Calves to help him!" I am sorry to say the archdeacon himself was designated by this scurrilous allusion to his nether person.

"A hundred a year to win, and nothing to lose," continued Handy. "My eyes! Well, how a man's to doubt about sich a bit of cheese as that passes me;—but some men is timorous;—some men is born with no pluck in them;—some men is cowed at the very first sight of a gentleman's coat and waistcoat."

Oh, Mr Harding, if you had but taken the archdeacon's advice in that disputed case, when Joe Mutters was this ungrateful demagogue's rival candidate!

"Afraid of a parson," growled Moody, with a look of ineffable scorn. "I tell ye what I'd be afraid of—I'd be afraid of not getting nothing from 'em but just what I could take by might and right;—that's the most I'd be afraid on of any parson of 'em all."

"But," said Skulpit, apologetically, "Mr Harding's not so bad;—he did give us twopence a day, didn't he now?"

"Twopence a day!" exclaimed Spriggs with scorn, opening awfully the red cavern of his lost eye.

"Twopence a day!" muttered Moody with a curse; "sink his twopence!"

"Twopence a day!" exclaimed Handy; "and I'm to go, hat in hand, and thank a chap for twopence a day, when he owes me a hundred pounds a year; no, thank ye; that may do for you, but it won't for me. Come, I say, Skulpit, are you a going to put your mark to this here paper, or are you not?"

Skulpit looked round in wretched indecision to his two friends. "What d'ye think, Bill Gazy?" said he.

But Bill Gazy couldn't think. He made a noise like the bleating of an old sheep, which was intended to express the agony of his doubt, and again muttered that "he didn't know."

"Take hold, you old cripple," said Handy, thrusting the pen into poor Billy's hand: "there, so—ugh! you old fool, you've been and smeared it all,—there,—that'll do for you;—that's as good as the best name as ever was written": and a big blotch of ink was presumed to represent Billy Gazy's acquiescence.

"Now, Jonathan," said Handy, turning to Crumple.

"A hundred a year's a nice thing, for sartain," again argued Crumple. "Well, neighbour Skulpit, how's it to be?"

"Oh, please yourself," said Skulpit: "please yourself, and you'll please me."

The pen was thrust into Crumple's hand, and a faint, wandering, meaningless sign was made, betokening such sanction and authority as Jonathan Crumple was able to convey.

"Come, Job," said Handy, softened by success, "don't let 'em have to say that old Bunce has a man like you under his thumb,—a man that always holds his head in the hospital as high as Bunce himself, though you're never axed to drink wine, and sneak, and tell lies about your betters as he does."

Skulpit held the pen, and made little flourishes with it in the air, but still hesitated.

"And if you'll be said by me," continued Handy, "you'll not write your name to it at all, but just put your mark like the others;"—the cloud began to clear from Skulpit's brow;—"we all know you can do it if you like, but maybe you wouldn't like to seem uppish, you know."

"Well, the mark would be best," said Skulpit. "One name and the rest marks wouldn't look well, would it?"

"The worst in the world," said Handy; "there—there": and stooping over the petition, the learned clerk made a huge cross on the place left for his signature.

"That's the game," said Handy, triumphantly pocketing the petition; "we're all in a boat now, that is, the nine of us; and as for old Bunce, and his cronies, they may—" But as he was hobbling off to the door, with a crutch on one side and a stick on the other, he was met by Bunce himself.

"Well Handy, and what may old Bunce do?" said the gray-haired, upright senior.

Handy muttered something, and was departing; but he was stopped in the doorway by the huge frame of the newcomer.

"You've been doing no good here, Abel Handy," said he, "'tis plain to see that; and 'tisn't much good, I'm thinking, you ever do."

"I mind my own business, Master Bunce," muttered the other, "and do you do the same. It ain't nothing to you what I does;—and your spying and poking here won't do no good nor yet no harm."

"I suppose then, Job," continued Bunce, not noticing his opponent, "if the truth must out, you've stuck your name to that petition of theirs at last."

Skulpit looked as though he were about to sink into the ground with shame.

"What is it to you what he signs?" said Handy. "I suppose if we all wants to ax for our own, we needn't ax leave of you first, Mr Bunce, big a man as you are; and as to your sneaking in here, into Job's room when he's busy, and where you're not wanted—"

"I've knowed Job Skulpit, man and boy, sixty years," said Bunce, looking at the man of whom he spoke, "and that's ever since the day he was born. I knowed the mother that bore him, when she and I were little wee things, picking daisies together in the close yonder; and I've lived under the same roof with him more nor ten years; and after that I may come into his room without axing leave, and yet no sneaking neither."

"So you can, Mr Bunce," said Skulpit; "so you can, any hour, day or night."

"And I'm free also to tell him my mind," continued Bunce, looking at the one man and addressing the other; "and I tell him now that he's done a foolish and a wrong thing. He's turned his back upon one who is his best friend; and is playing the game of others, who care nothing for him, whether he be poor or rich, well or ill, alive or dead. A hundred a year? Are the lot of you soft enough to think that if a hundred a year be to be given, it's the likes of you that will get it?"—and he pointed to Billy Gazy, Spriggs, and Crumple. "Did any of us ever do anything worth half the money? Was it to make gentlemen of us we were brought in here, when all the world turned against us, and we couldn't longer earn our daily bread? A'n't you all as rich in your ways as he in his?"—and the orator pointed to the side on which the warden lived. "A'n't you getting all you hoped for, ay, and more than you hoped for? Wouldn't each of you have given the dearest limb of his body to secure that which now makes you so unthankful?"

"We wants what John Hiram left us," said Handy. "We wants what's ourn by law; it don't matter what we expected. What's ourn by law should be ourn, and by goles we'll have it."

"Law!" said Bunce, with all the scorn he knew how to command—"law! Did ye ever know a poor man yet was the better for law, or for a lawyer? Will Mr Finney ever be as good to you, Job, as that man has been? Will he see to you when you're sick, and comfort you when you're wretched? Will he—"

"No, nor give you port wine, old boy, on cold winter nights! he won't do that, will he?" asked Handy; and laughing at the severity of his own wit, he and his colleagues retired, carrying with them, however, the now powerful petition.

There is no help for spilt milk; and Mr Bunce could only retire to his own room, disgusted at the frailty of human nature. Job Skulpit scratched his head;—Jonathan Crumple again remarked, that, "for sartain, sure a hundred a year was very nice;"—and Billy Gazy again rubbed his eyes, and lowly muttered that "he didn't know."

Chapter V

DR GRANTLY VISITS THE HOSPITAL

Though doubt and hesitation disturbed the rest of our poor warden, no such weakness perplexed the nobler breast of his son-in-law. As the indomitable cock preparing for the combat sharpens his spurs, shakes his feathers, and erects his comb, so did the archdeacon arrange his weapons for the coming war, without misgiving and without fear. That he was fully confident of the justice of his cause let no one doubt. Many a man can fight his battle with good courage, but with a doubting conscience. Such was not the case with Dr Grantly. He did not believe in the Gospel with more assurance than he did in the sacred justice of all ecclesiastical revenues. When he put his shoulder to the wheel to defend the income of the present and future precentors of Barchester, he was animated by as strong a sense of a holy cause, as that which gives courage to a missionary in Africa, or enables a sister of mercy to give up the pleasures of the world for the wards of a hospital. He was about to defend the holy of holies from the touch of the profane; to guard the citadel of his church from the most rampant of its enemies; to put on his good armour in the best of fights, and secure, if possible, the comforts of his creed for coming generations of ecclesiastical dignitaries. Such a work required no ordinary vigour; and the archdeacon was, therefore, extraordinarily vigorous. It demanded a buoyant courage, and a heart happy in its toil; and the archdeacon's heart was happy, and his courage was buoyant.

He knew that he would not be able to animate his father-in-law with feelings like his own, but this did not much disturb him. He preferred to bear the brunt of the battle alone, and did not doubt that the warden would resign himself into his hands with passive submission.

"Well, Mr Chadwick," he said, walking into the steward's office a day or two after the signing of the petition as commemorated in the last chapter: "anything from Cox and Cummins this morning?" Mr Chadwick handed him a letter; which he read, stroking the tight-gaitered calf of his right leg as he did so. Messrs Cox and Cummins merely said that they had as yet received no notice from their adversaries; that they could recommend no preliminary steps; but that should any proceeding really be taken by the bedesmen, it would be expedient to consult that very eminent Queen's Counsel, Sir Abraham Haphazard.

"I quite agree with them," said Dr Grantly, refolding the letter. "I perfectly agree with them. Haphazard is no doubt the best man; a thorough churchman, a sound conservative, and in every respect the best man we could get;—he's in the House, too, which is a great thing."

Mr Chadwick quite agreed.

"You remember how completely he put down that scoundrel Horseman about the Bishop of Beverley's income; how completely he set them all adrift in the earl's case." Since the question of St Cross had been mooted by the public, one noble lord had become "the earl," *par excellence*, in the doctor's estimation. "How he silenced that fellow at Rochester. Of course we must have Haphazard; and I'll tell you what, Mr Chadwick, we must take care to be in time, or the other party will forestall us."

With all his admiration for Sir Abraham, the doctor seemed to think it not impossible that that great man might be induced to lend his gigantic powers to the side of the church's enemies.

Having settled this point to his satisfaction, the doctor stepped down to the hospital, to learn how matters were going on there; and as he walked across the hallowed close, and looked up at the ravens who cawed with a peculiar reverence as he wended his way, he thought with increased acerbity of those whose impiety would venture to disturb the goodly grace of cathedral institutions.

And who has not felt the same? We believe that Mr Horseman himself would relent, and the spirit of Sir Benjamin Hall give way, were those great reformers to allow themselves to stroll by moonlight round the towers of some of our ancient churches. Who would not feel charity for a prebendary when walking the quiet length of that long aisle at Winchester, looking at those decent houses, that trim grass-plat, and feeling, as one must, the solemn, orderly comfort of the spot! Who could be hard upon a dean while wandering round the sweet close of Hereford, and owning that in that precinct, tone and colour, design and form, solemn tower and storied window, are all in unison, and all perfect! Who could lie basking in the cloisters of Salisbury, and gaze on Jewel's library and that unequalled spire, without feeling that bishops should sometimes be rich!

The tone of our archdeacon's mind must not astonish us; it has been the growth of centuries of church ascendancy; and though some fungi now disfigure the tree, though there be much dead wood, for how much good fruit have not we to be thankful? Who, without remorse, can batter down the dead branches of an old oak, now useless, but, ah! still so beautiful, or drag out the fragments of the ancient forest, without feeling that they sheltered the younger plants, to which they are now summoned to give way in a tone so peremptory and so harsh?

The archdeacon, with all his virtues, was not a man of delicate feeling; and after having made his morning salutations in the warden's drawing-room, he did not scruple to commence an attack on "pestilent" John Bold in the presence of Miss Harding, though he rightly guessed that that lady was not indifferent to the name of his enemy.

"Nelly, my dear, fetch me my spectacles from the back room," said her father, anxious to save both her blushes and her feelings.

Eleanor brought the spectacles, while her father was trying, in ambiguous phrases, to explain to her too-practical brother-in-law that it might be as well not to say anything about Bold before her, and then retreated. Nothing had been explained to her about Bold and the hospital; but, with a woman's instinct she knew that things were going wrong.

"We must soon be doing something," commenced the archdeacon, wiping his brows with a large, bright-coloured handkerchief, for he had felt busy, and had walked quick, and it was a broiling summer's day. "Of course you have heard of the petition?"

Mr Harding owned, somewhat unwillingly, that he had heard of it.

"Well!"—the archdeacon looked for some expressions of opinion, but none coming, he continued,—"We must be doing something, you know; we mustn't allow these people to cut the ground from under us while we sit looking on." The archdeacon, who was a practical man, allowed himself the use of everyday expressive modes of speech when among his closest intimates, though no one could soar into a more intricate labyrinth of refined phraseology when the church was the subject, and his lower brethren were his auditors.

The warden still looked mutely in his face, making the slightest possible passes with an imaginary fiddle bow, and stopping, as he did so, sundry imaginary strings with the fingers of his other hand. 'Twas his constant consolation in conversational troubles. While these vexed him sorely, the passes would be short and slow, and the upper hand would not be seen to work; nay, the strings on which it operated would sometimes lie concealed in the musician's pocket, and the instrument on which he played would be beneath his chair;—but as his spirit warmed to the subject,—as his trusting heart looking to the bottom of that which vexed him, would see its clear way out,—he would rise to a higher melody, sweep the unseen strings with a bolder hand, and swiftly fingering the cords from his neck, down along his waistcoat, and up again to his very ear, create an ecstatic strain of perfect music, audible to himself and to St Cecilia, and not without effect.

"I quite agree with Cox and Cummins," continued the archdeacon. "They say we must secure Sir Abraham Haphazard. I shall not have the slightest fear in leaving the case in Sir Abraham's hands."

The warden played the slowest and saddest of tunes. It was but a dirge on one string.

"I think Sir Abraham will not be long in letting Master Bold know what he's about. I fancy I hear Sir Abraham cross-questioning him at the Common Pleas."

The warden thought of his income being thus discussed, his modest life, his daily habits, and his easy work; and nothing issued from that single cord, but a low wail of sorrow. "I suppose they've sent this petition up to my father." The warden didn't know; he imagined they would do so this very day.

"What I can't understand is, how you let them do it, with such a command as you have in the place, or should have with such a man as Bunce. I cannot understand why you let them do it."

"Do what?" asked the warden.

"Why, listen to this fellow Bold, and that other low pettifogger, Finney;—and get up this petition too. Why didn't you tell Bunce to destroy the petition?"

"That would have been hardly wise," said the warden.

"Wise;—yes, it would have been very wise if they'd done it among themselves. I must go up to the palace and answer it now, I suppose. It's a very short answer they'll get, I can tell you."

"But why shouldn't they petition, doctor?"

"Why shouldn't they!" responded the archdeacon, in a loud brazen voice, as though all the men in the hospital were expected to hear him through the walls; "why shouldn't they? I'll let them know why they shouldn't; by the bye, warden, I'd like to say a few words to them all together."

The warden's mind misgave him, and even for a moment he forgot to play. He by no means wished to delegate to his son-in-law his place and authority of warden; he had expressly determined not to interfere in any step which the men might wish to take in the matter under dispute; he was most anxious neither to accuse them nor to defend himself. All these things he was aware the archdeacon would do in his behalf, and that not in the mildest manner; and yet he knew not how to refuse the permission requested.

"I'd so much sooner remain quiet in the matter," said he, in an apologetic voice.

"Quiet!" said the archdeacon, still speaking with his brazen trumpet; "do you wish to be ruined in quiet?"

"Why, if I am to be ruined, certainly."

"Nonsense, warden; I tell you something must be done;—we must act; just let me ring the bell, and send the men word that I'll speak to them in the quad."

Mr Harding knew not how to resist, and the disagreeable order was given. The quad, as it was familiarly called, was a small quadrangle, open on one side to the river, and surrounded on the others by the high wall of Mr Harding's garden, by one gable end of Mr Harding's house, and by the end of the row of buildings which formed the residences of the bedesmen. It was flagged all round, and the centre was stoned; small stone gutters ran from the four corners of the square to a grating in the centre; and attached to the end of Mr Harding's house was a conduit with four cocks covered over from the weather, at which the old men got their water, and very generally performed their morning toilet. It was a quiet, sombre place, shaded over by the trees of the warden's garden. On the side towards the river, there stood a row of stone seats, on which the old men would sit and gaze at the little fish, as they flitted by in the running stream. On the other side of the river was a rich, green meadow, running up to and joining the deanery, and as little open to the public as the garden of the dean itself. Nothing, therefore, could be more private than the quad of the hospital; and it was there that the archdeacon determined to convey to them his sense of their refractory proceedings.

The servant soon brought in word that the men were assembled in the quad, and the archdeacon, big with his purpose, rose to address them.

"Well, warden, of course you're coming," said he, seeing that Mr Harding did not prepare to follow him.

"I wish you'd excuse me," said Mr Harding.

"For heaven's sake, don't let us have division in the camp," replied the archdeacon: "let us have a long pull and a strong pull, but above all a pull all together; come, warden, come; don't be afraid of your duty."

Mr Harding was afraid; he was afraid that he was being led to do that which was not his duty; he was not, however, strong enough to resist, so he got up and followed his son-in-law.

The old men were assembled in groups in the quadrangle—eleven of them at least, for poor old Johnny Bell was bed-ridden, and couldn't come; he had, however, put his mark to the petition, as one of Handy's earliest followers. 'Tis true he could not move from the bed where he lay; 'tis true he had no friend on earth, but those whom the hospital contained; and of those the warden and his daughter were the most constant and most appreciated; 'tis true that everything was administered to him which his failing body could require, or which his faint appetite could enjoy; but still his dull eye had glistened for a moment at the idea of possessing a hundred pounds a year "to his own cheek," as Abel Handy had eloquently expressed it; and poor old Johnny Bell had greedily put his mark to the petition.

When the two clergymen appeared, they all uncovered their heads. Handy was slow to do it, and hesitated; but the black coat and waistcoat of which he had spoken so irreverently in Skulpit's room, had its effect even on him, and he too doffed his hat. Bunce, advancing before the others, bowed lowly to the archdeacon, and with affectionate reverence expressed his wish, that the warden and Miss Eleanor were quite well; "and the doctor's lady," he added, turning to the archdeacon, "and the children at Plumstead, and my lord;" and having made his speech, he also retired among the others, and took his place with the rest upon the stone benches.

As the archdeacon stood up to make his speech, erect in the middle of that little square, he looked like an ecclesiastical statue placed there, as a fitting impersonation of the church militant here on earth; his shovel hat, large, new, and well-pronounced, a churchman's hat in every inch, declared the profession as plainly as does the Quaker's broad brim; his heavy eyebrows, large open eyes, and full mouth and chin expressed the solidity of his order; the broad chest, amply covered with fine cloth, told how well to do was its estate; one hand ensconced within his pocket, evinced the practical hold which our mother church keeps on her temporal possessions; and the other, loose for action, was ready to fight if need be in her defence; and, below these, the decorous breeches, and neat black gaiters showing so admirably that well-turned leg, betokened the decency, the outward beauty and grace of our church establishment.

"Now, my men," he began, when he had settled himself well in his position, "I want to say a few words to you. Your good friend, the warden here, and myself, and my lord the bishop, on whose behalf I wish to speak to you, would all be very sorry, very sorry indeed, that you should have any just ground of complaint. Any just ground of complaint on your part would be removed at once by the warden, or by his lordship, or by me on his behalf, without the necessity of any petition on your part." Here the orator stopped for a moment, expecting that some little murmurs of applause would show that the weakest of the men were beginning to give way; but no such murmurs came. Bunce, himself, even sat with closed lips, mute and unsatisfactory. "Without the necessity of any petition at all," he repeated. "I'm told you have addressed a petition to my lord." He paused for a reply from the men, and after a while, Handy plucked up courage and said, "Yes, we has."

"You have addressed a petition to my lord, in which, as I am informed, you express an opinion that you do not receive from Hiram's estate all that is your due." Here most of the men expressed their assent. "Now what is it you ask for? What is it you want that you hav'n't got here? What is it—"

"A hundred a year," muttered old Moody, with a voice as if it came out of the ground.

"A hundred a year!" ejaculated the archdeacon militant, defying the impudence of these claimants with one hand stretched out and closed, while with the other he tightly grasped, and secured within his breeches pocket, that symbol of the church's wealth which his own loose half-crowns not unaptly represented. "A hundred a year! Why, my men, you must be mad; and you talk about John Hiram's will! When John Hiram built a hospital for worn-out old men, worn-out old labouring men, infirm old men past their work, cripples, blind, bed-ridden, and such like, do you think he meant to make gentlemen of them? Do you think John Hiram intended to give a hundred a year to old single men, who earned perhaps two shillings or half-a-crown a day for themselves and families in the best of their time? No, my men, I'll tell you what John Hiram meant: he meant that twelve poor old worn-out labourers, men who could no longer support themselves, who had no friends to support them, who must starve and perish miserably if not protected by the hand of charity;—he meant that twelve such men as these should come in here in their poverty and wretchedness, and find within these walls shelter and food before their death, and a little leisure to make their peace with God. That was what John Hiram meant: you have not read John Hiram's will, and I doubt whether those wicked men who are advising you have done so. I have; I know what his will was; and I tell you that that was his will, and that that was his intention."

Not a sound came from the eleven bedesmen, as they sat listening to what, according to the archdeacon, was their intended estate. They grimly stared upon his burly figure, but did not then express, by word or sign, the anger and disgust to which such language was sure to give rise.

"Now let me ask you," he continued: "do you think you are worse off than John Hiram intended to make you? Have you not shelter, and food, and leisure? Have you not much more? Have you not every indulgence which you are capable of enjoying? Have you not twice better food, twice a better bed, ten times more money in your pocket than you were ever able to earn for yourselves before you were lucky enough to get into this place? And now you send a petition to the bishop, asking for a hundred pounds a year! I tell you what, my friends; you are deluded, and made fools of by wicked men who are acting for their own ends. You will never get a hundred pence a year more than what you have now: it is very possible that you may get less; it is very possible that my lord the bishop, and your warden, may make changes—"

"No, no, no," interrupted Mr Harding, who had been listening with indescribable misery to the tirade of his son-in-law; "no, my friends. I want no changes,—at least no changes that shall make you worse off than you now are, as long as you and I live together."

"God bless you, Mr Harding," said Bunce; and "God bless you, Mr Harding, God bless you, sir: we know you was always our friend," was exclaimed by enough of the men to make it appear that the sentiment was general.

The archdeacon had been interrupted in his speech before he had quite finished it; but he felt that he could not recommence with dignity after this little ebullition, and he led the way back into the garden, followed by his father-in-law.

"Well," said he, as soon as he found himself within the cool retreat of the warden's garden; "I think I spoke to them plainly." And he wiped the perspiration from his brow; for making a speech under a broiling mid-day sun in summer, in a full suit of thick black cloth, is warm work.

"Yes, you were plain enough," replied the warden, in a tone which did not express approbation.

"And that's everything," said the other, who was clearly well satisfied with himself; "that's everything: with those sort of people one must be plain, or one will not be understood. Now, I think they did understand me;—I think they knew what I meant."

The warden agreed. He certainly thought they had understood to the full what had been said to them.

"They know pretty well what they have to expect from us; they know how we shall meet any refractory spirit on their part; they know that we are not afraid of them. And now I'll just step into Chadwick's, and tell him what I've done; and then I'll go up to the palace, and answer this petition of theirs."

The warden's mind was very full,—full nearly to overcharging itself; and had it done so,—had he allowed himself to speak the thoughts which were working within him, he would indeed have astonished the archdeacon by the reprobation he would have expressed as to the proceeding of which he had been so unwilling a witness. But different feelings kept him silent; he was as yet afraid of differing from his son-in-law;—he was anxious beyond measure to avoid even a semblance of rupture with any of his order, and was painfully fearful of having to come to an open quarrel with any person on any subject. His life had hitherto been so quiet, so free from strife; his little early troubles had required nothing but passive fortitude; his subsequent prosperity had never forced upon him any active cares,—had never brought him into disagreeable contact with anyone. He felt that he would give almost anything,—much more than he knew he ought to do,—to relieve himself from the storm which he feared was coming. It was so hard that the pleasant waters of his little stream should be disturbed and muddied by rough hands; that his quiet paths should be made a battlefield; that the unobtrusive corner of the world which had been allotted to him, as though by Providence, should be invaded and desecrated, and all within it made miserable and unsound.

Money he had none to give; the knack of putting guineas together had never belonged to him; but how willingly, with what a foolish easiness, with what happy alacrity, would he have abandoned the half of his income for all time to come, could he by so doing have quietly dispelled the clouds that were gathering over him,—could he have thus compromised the matter between the reformer and the conservative, between his possible son-in-law, Bold, and his positive son-in-law, the archdeacon.

And this compromise would not have been made from any prudential motive of saving what would yet remain, for Mr Harding still felt little doubt but he should be left for life in quiet possession of the good things he had, if he chose to retain them. No; he would have done so from the sheer love of quiet, and from a horror of being made the subject of public talk. He had very often been moved to pity,—to that inward weeping of the heart for others' woes; but none had he ever pitied more than that old lord, whose almost fabulous wealth, drawn from his church preferments, had become the subject of so much opprobrium, of such public scorn; that wretched clerical octogenarian Crœsus, whom men would not allow to die in peace,—whom all the world united to decry and to abhor.

Was he to suffer such a fate? Was his humble name to be bandied in men's mouths, as the gormandiser of the resources of the poor, as of one who had filched from the charity of other ages wealth which had been intended to relieve the old and the infirm? Was he to be gibbeted in the press, to become a byword for oppression, to be named as an example of the greed of the English church? Should it ever be said that he had robbed those old men, whom he so truly and so tenderly loved in his heart of hearts? As he slowly paced, hour after hour, under those noble lime-trees, turning these sad thoughts within him, he became all but fixed in his resolve that some great step must be taken to relieve him from the risk of so terrible a fate.

In the meanwhile, the archdeacon, with contented mind and unruffled spirit, went about his business. He said a word or two to Mr Chadwick, and then finding, as he expected, the petition lying in his father's library, he wrote a short answer to the men, in which he told them that they had no evils to redress, but rather great mercies for which to be thankful; and having seen the bishop sign it, he got into his brougham and returned home to Mrs Grantly, and Plumstead Episcopi.

Chapter VI

THE WARDEN'S TEA PARTY

After much painful doubting, on one thing only could Mr Harding resolve. He determined that at any rate he would take no offence, and that he would make this question no cause of quarrel either with Bold or with the bedesmen. In furtherance of this resolution, he himself wrote a note to Mr Bold, the same afternoon, inviting him to meet a few friends and hear some music on an evening named in the next week. Had not this little party been promised to Eleanor, in his present state of mind he would probably have avoided such gaiety; but the promise had been given, the invitations were to be written, and when Eleanor consulted her father on the subject, she was not ill pleased to hear him say, "Oh, I was thinking of Bold, so I took it into my head to write to him myself, but you must write to his sister."

Mary Bold was older than her brother, and, at the time of our story, was just over thirty. She was not an unattractive young woman, though by no means beautiful. Her great merit was the kindliness of her disposition. She was not very clever, nor very animated, nor had she apparently the energy of her brother; but she was guided by a high principle of right and wrong; her temper was sweet, and her faults were fewer in number than her virtues. Those who casually met Mary Bold thought little of her; but those who knew her well loved her well, and the longer they knew her the more they loved her. Among those who were fondest of her was Eleanor Harding; and though Eleanor had never openly talked to her of her brother, each understood the other's feelings about him. The brother and sister were sitting together when the two notes were brought in.

"How odd," said Mary, "that they should send two notes. Well, if Mr Harding becomes fashionable, the world is going to change."

Her brother understood immediately the nature and intention of the peace-offering; but it was not so easy for him to behave well in the matter, as it was for Mr Harding. It is much less difficult for the sufferer to be generous than for the oppressor. John Bold felt that he could not go to the warden's party: he never loved Eleanor better than he did now; he had never so strongly felt how anxious he was to make her his wife as now, when so many obstacles to his doing so appeared in view. Yet here was her father himself, as it were, clearing away those very obstacles, and still he felt that he could not go to the house any more as an open friend.

As he sat thinking of these things with the note in his hand, his sister was waiting for his decision.

"Well," said she, "I suppose we must write separate answers, and both say we shall be very happy."

"You'll go, of course, Mary," said he; to which she readily assented. "I cannot," he continued, looking serious and gloomy. "I wish I could, with all my heart."

"And why not, John?" said she. She had as yet heard nothing of the new-found abuse which her brother was about to reform;—at least nothing which connected it with her brother's name.

He sat thinking for a while till he determined that it would be best to tell her at once what it was that he was about: it must be done sooner or later.

"I fear I cannot go to Mr Harding's house any more as a friend, just at present."

"Oh, John! Why not? Ah, you've quarrelled with Eleanor!"

"No, indeed," said he; "I've no quarrel with her as yet."

"What is it, John?" said she, looking at him with an anxious, loving face, for she knew well how much of his heart was there in that house which he said he could no longer enter.

"Why," said he at last, "I've taken up the case of these twelve old men of Hiram's Hospital, and of course that brings me into contact with Mr Harding. I may have to oppose him, interfere with him,—perhaps injure him."

Mary looked at him steadily for some time before she committed herself to reply, and then merely asked him what he meant to do for the old men.

"Why, it's a long story, and I don't know that I can make you understand it. John Hiram made a will, and left his property in charity for certain poor old men, and the proceeds, instead of going to the benefit of these men, go chiefly into the pocket of the warden and the bishop's steward."

"And you mean to take away from Mr Harding his share of it?"

"I don't know what I mean yet. I mean to inquire about it. I mean to see who is entitled to this property. I mean to see, if I can, that justice be done to the poor of the city of Barchester generally, who are, in fact, the legatees under the will. I mean, in short, to put the matter right, if I can."

"And why are you to do this, John?"

"You might ask the same question of anybody else," said he; "and according to that the duty of righting these poor men would belong to nobody. If we are to act on that principle, the weak are never to be protected, injustice is never to be opposed, and no one is to struggle for the poor!" And Bold began to comfort himself in the warmth of his own virtue.

"But is there no one to do this but you, who have known Mr Harding so long? Surely, John, as a friend, as a young friend, so much younger than Mr Harding—"

"That's woman's logic, all over, Mary. What has age to do with it? Another man might plead that he was too old; and as to his friendship, if the thing itself be right, private motives should never be allowed to interfere. Because I esteem Mr Harding, is that a reason that I should neglect a duty which I owe to these old men? or should I give up a work which my conscience tells me is a good one, because I regret the loss of his society?"

"And Eleanor, John?" said the sister, looking timidly into her brother's face.

"Eleanor, that is, Miss Harding, if she thinks fit,—that is, if her father—or, rather, if she—or, indeed, he,—if they find it necessary—but there is no necessity now to talk about Eleanor Harding; but this I will say, that if she has the kind of spirit for which I give her credit, she will not condemn me for doing what I think to be a duty." And Bold consoled himself with the consolation of a Roman.

Mary sat silent for a while, till at last her brother reminded her that the notes must be answered, and she got up, and placed her desk before her, took out her pen and paper, wrote on it slowly:

PAKENHAM VILLAS
Tuesday morning

My dear Eleanor,   I—
and then stopped, and looked at her brother. "Well, Mary, why don't you write it?"

"Oh, John," said she, "dear John, pray think better of this."

"Think better of what?" said he.

"Of this about the hospital,—of all this about Mr Harding,—of what you say about those old men. Nothing can call upon you,—no duty can require you to set yourself against your oldest, your best friend. Oh, John, think of Eleanor. You'll break her heart, and your own."

"Nonsense, Mary; Miss Harding's heart is as safe as yours."

"Pray, pray, for my sake, John, give it up. You know how dearly you love her." And she came and knelt before him on the rug. "Pray give it up. You are going to make your-self, and her, and her father miserable: you are going to make us all miserable. And for what? For a dream of justice. You will never make those twelve men happier than they now are."

"You don't understand it, my dear girl," said he, smoothing her hair with his hand.

"I do understand it, John. I understand that this is a chimera,—a dream that you have got. I know well that no duty can require you to do this mad—this suicidal thing. I know you love Eleanor Harding with all your heart, and I tell you now that she loves you as well. If there was a plain, a positive duty before you, I would be the last to bid you ne-glect it for any woman's love; but this—; oh, think again, before you do anything to make it necessary that you and Mr Harding should be at variance." He did not answer, as she knelt there, leaning on his knees, but by his face she thought that he was inclined to yield. "At any rate let me say that you will go to this party. At any rate do not break with them while your mind is in doubt." And she got up, hoping to conclude her note in the way she desired.

"My mind is not in doubt," at last he said, rising. "I could never respect myself again were I to give way now, because Eleanor Harding is beautiful. I do love her: I would give a hand to hear her tell me what you have said, speaking on her behalf; but I cannot for her sake go back from the task which I have commenced. I hope she may hereafter acknowledge and respect my motives, but I cannot now go as a guest to her father's house." And the Barchester Brutus went out to fortify his own resolution by meditations on his own virtue.

Poor Mary Bold sat down, and sadly finished her note, saying that she would herself attend the party, but that her brother was unavoidably prevented from doing so. I fear that she did not admire as she should have done the self-devotion of his singular virtue.

The party went off as such parties do. There were fat old ladies, in fine silk dresses, and slim young ladies, in gauzy muslin frocks; old gentlemen stood up with their backs to the empty fire-place, looking by no means so comfortable as they would have done in their own arm-chairs at home; and young gentlemen, rather stiff about the neck, clustered near the door, not as yet sufficiently in courage to attack the muslin frocks, who awaited the battle, drawn up in a semicircular array. The warden endeavoured to induce a charge, but failed signally, not having the tact of a general; his daughter did what she could to comfort the forces under her command, who took in refreshing rations of cake and tea, and patiently looked for the coming engagement: but she herself, Eleanor, had no spirit for the work; the only enemy whose lance she cared to encounter was not there, and she and others were somewhat dull.

Loud above all voices was heard the clear sonorous tones of the archdeacon as he dilated to brother parsons of the danger of the church, of the fearful rumours of mad reforms even at Oxford, and of the damnable heresies of Dr Whiston.

Soon, however, sweeter sounds began timidly to make themselves audible. Little movements were made in a quarter notable for round stools and music stands. Wax candles were arranged in sconces, big books were brought from hidden recesses, and the work of the evening commenced.

How often were those pegs twisted and re-twisted before our friend found that he had twisted them enough; how many discordant scrapes gave promise of the coming harmony. How much the muslin fluttered and crumpled before Eleanor and another nymph were duly seated at the piano; how closely did that tall Apollo pack himself against the wall, with his flute, long as himself, extending high over the heads of his pretty neighbours; into how small a corner crept that round and florid little minor canon, and there with skill amazing found room to tune his accustomed fiddle!

And now the crash begins: away they go in full flow of harmony together,—up hill and down dale,—now louder and louder, then lower and lower; now loud, as though stirring the battle; then low, as though mourning the slain. In all, through all, and above all, is heard the violoncello. Ah, not for nothing were those pegs so twisted and re-twisted;— listen, listen! Now alone that saddest of instruments tells its touching tale. Silent, and in awe, stand fiddle, flute, and piano, to hear the sorrows of their wailing brother. 'Tis but for a moment: before the melancholy of those low notes has been fully realised, again comes the full force of all the band;—down go the pedals, away rush twenty fingers scouring over the bass notes with all the impetus of passion. Apollo blows till his stiff neckcloth is no better than a rope, and the minor canon works with both arms till he falls in a syncope of exhaustion against the wall.

How comes it that now, when all should be silent, when courtesy, if not taste, should make men listen,—how is it at this moment the black-coated corps leave their retreat and begin skirmishing? One by one they creep forth, and fire off little guns timidly, and without precision. Ah, my men, efforts such as these will take no cities, even though the enemy should be never so open to assault. At length a more deadly artillery is brought to bear; slowly, but with effect, the advance is made; the muslin ranks are broken, and fall into confusion; the formidable array of chairs gives way; the battle is no longer between opposing regiments, but hand to hand, and foot to foot with single combatants, as in the glorious days of old, when fighting was really noble. In corners, and under the shadow of curtains, behind sofas and half hidden by doors, in retiring windows, and sheltered by hanging tapestry, are blows given and returned, fatal, incurable, dealing death.

Apart from this another combat arises, more sober and more serious. The archdeacon is engaged against two prebendaries, a pursy full-blown rector assisting him, in all the perils and all the enjoyments of short whist. With solemn energy do they watch the shuffled pack, and, all-expectant, eye the coming trump. With what anxious nicety do they arrange their cards, jealous of each other's eyes! Why is that lean doctor so slow,— cadaverous man with hollow jaw and sunken eye, ill beseeming the richness of his mother church! Ah, why so slow, thou meagre doctor? See how the archdeacon, speechless in his agony, deposits on the board his cards, and looks to heaven or to the ceiling for support. Hark, how he sighs, as with thumbs in his waistcoat pocket he seems to signify that the end of such torment is not yet even nigh at hand! Vain is the hope, if hope there be, to disturb that meagre doctor. With care precise he places every card, weighs well the value of each mighty ace, each guarded king, and comfort-giving queen; speculates on knave and ten, counts all his suits, and sets his price upon the whole. At length a card is led, and quick three others fall upon the board. The little doctor leads again, while with lustrous eye his partner absorbs the trick. Now thrice has this been done,—thrice has constant fortune favoured the brace of prebendaries, ere the archdeacon rouses himself to the battle; but at the fourth assault he pins to the earth a prostrate king, laying low his crown and sceptre, bushy beard, and lowering brow, with a poor deuce.

"As David did Goliath," says the archdeacon, pushing over the four cards to his partner. And then a trump is led, then another trump; then a king,—and then an ace,—and then a long ten, which brings down from the meagre doctor his only remaining tower of strength—his cherished queen of trumps.

"What, no second club?" says the archdeacon to his partner.

"Only one club," mutters from his inmost stomach the pursy rector, who sits there red-faced, silent, impervious, careful, a safe but not a brilliant ally.

But the archdeacon cares not for many clubs, or for none. He dashes out his remaining cards with a speed most annoying to his antagonists, pushes over to them some four cards as their allotted portion, shoves the remainder across the table to the red-faced rector; calls out "two by cards and two by honours, and the odd trick last time," marks a treble under the candle-stick, and has dealt round the second pack before the meagre doctor has calculated his losses.

And so went off the warden's party, and men and women arranging shawls and shoes declared how pleasant it had been; and Mrs Goodenough, the red-faced rector's wife, pressing the warden's hand, declared she had never enjoyed herself better; which showed how little pleasure she allowed herself in this world, as she had sat the whole evening through in the same chair without occupation, not speaking, and unspoken to. And Matilda Johnson, when she allowed young Dickson of the bank to fasten her cloak round her neck, thought that two hundred pounds a year and a little cottage would really do for happiness; besides, he was sure to be manager some day. And Apollo, folding his flute into his pocket, felt that he had acquitted himself with honour; and the archdeacon pleasantly jingled his gains; but the meagre doctor went off without much audible speech, muttering ever and anon as he went, "three and thirty points!" "three and thirty points!"

And so they all were gone, and Mr Harding was left alone with his daughter.

What had passed between Eleanor Harding and Mary Bold need not be told. It is indeed a matter of thankfulness that neither the historian nor the novelist hears all that is said by their heroes or heroines, or how would three volumes or twenty suffice! In the present case so little of this sort have I overheard, that I live in hopes of finishing my work within 300 pages, and of completing that pleasant task—a novel in one volume; but something had passed between them, and as the warden blew out the wax candles, and put his instrument into its case, his daughter stood sad and thoughtful by the empty fire-place, determined to speak to her father, but irresolute as to what she would say.

"Well, Eleanor," said he, "are you for bed?"

"Yes," said she, moving, "I suppose so; but papa—Mr Bold was not here tonight; do you know why not?"

"He was asked; I wrote to him myself," said the warden.

"But do you know why he did not come, papa?"

"Well, Eleanor, I could guess; but it's no use guessing at such things, my dear. What makes you look so earnest about it?"

"Oh, papa, do tell me," she exclaimed, throwing her arms round him, and looking into his face; "what is it he is going to do? What is it all about? Is there any—any—any—" she didn't well know what word to use—"any danger?"

"Danger, my dear, what sort of danger?"

"Danger to you, danger of trouble, and of loss, and of—Oh, papa, why haven't you told me of all this before?"

Mr Harding was not the man to judge harshly of anyone, much less of the daughter whom he now loved better than any living creature; but still he did judge her wrongly at this moment. He knew that she loved John Bold; he fully sympathised in her affection; day after day he thought more of the matter, and, with the tender care of a loving father, tried to arrange in his own mind how matters might be so managed that his daughter's heart should not be made the sacrifice to the dispute which was likely to exist between him and Bold. Now, when she spoke to him for the first time on the subject, it was natural that he should think more of her than of himself, and that he should imagine that her own cares, and not his, were troubling her.

He stood silent before her awhile, as she gazed up into his face, and then kissing her forehead he placed her on the sofa.

"Tell me, Nelly," he said (he only called her Nelly in his kindest, softest, sweetest moods, and yet all his moods were kind and sweet), "tell me, Nelly, do you like Mr Bold—much?"

She was quite taken aback by the question. I will not say that she had forgotten herself, and her own love in thinking about John Bold, and while conversing with Mary: she certainly had not done so. She had been sick at heart to think that a man of whom she could not but own to herself that she loved him, of whose regard she had been so proud, that such a man should turn against her father to ruin him. She had felt her vanity hurt, that his affection for her had not kept him from such a course; had he really cared for her, he would not have risked her love by such an outrage. But her main fear had been for her father, and when she spoke of danger, it was of danger to him and not to herself.

She was taken aback by the question altogether: "Do I like him, papa?"

"Yes, Nelly, do you like him? Why shouldn't you like him? but that's a poor word;—do you love him?" She sat still in his arms without answering him. She certainly had not prepared herself for an avowal of affection, intending, as she had done, to abuse John Bold herself, and to hear her father do so also. "Come, my love," said he, "let us make a clean breast of it: do you tell me what concerns yourself, and I will tell you what concerns me and the hospital."

And then, without waiting for an answer, he described to her, as he best could, the accusation that was made about Hiram's will; the claims which the old men put forward; what he considered the strength and what the weakness of his own position; the course which Bold had taken, and that which he presumed he was about to take; and then by degrees, without further question, he presumed on the fact of Eleanor's love, and spoke of that love as a feeling which he could in no way disapprove: he apologised for Bold, excused what he was doing; nay, praised him for his energy and intentions; made much of his good qualities, and harped on none of his foibles; then, reminding his daughter how late it was, and comforting her with much assurance which he hardly felt himself, he sent her to her room, with flowing eyes and a full heart.

When Mr Harding met his daughter at breakfast the next morning, there was no further discussion on the matter, nor was the subject mentioned between them for some days. Soon after the party Mary Bold called at the hospital, but there were various persons in the drawing-room at the time, and she therefore said nothing about her brother. On the day following, John Bold met Miss Harding in one of the quiet, sombre, shaded walks of the close. He was most anxious to see her, but unwilling to call at the warden's house, and had in truth waylaid her in her private haunts.

"My sister tells me," said he, abruptly hurrying on with his premeditated speech, "my sister tells me that you had a delightful party the other evening. I was so sorry I could not be there."

"We were all sorry," said Eleanor, with dignified composure.

"I believe, Miss Harding, you understand why, at this moment—" And Bold hesitated, muttered, stopped, commenced his explanation again, and again broke down.

Eleanor would not help him in the least.

"I think my sister explained to you, Miss Harding?"

"Pray don't apologise, Mr Bold; my father will, I am sure, always be glad to see you, if you like to come to the house now as formerly; nothing has occurred to alter his feelings: of your own views you are, of course, the best judge."

"Your father is all that is kind and generous; he always was so; but you, Miss Harding, yourself—I hope you will not judge me harshly, because—"

"Mr Bold," said she, "you may be sure of one thing; I shall always judge my father to be right, and those who oppose him I shall judge to be wrong. If those who do not know him oppose him, I shall have charity enough to believe that they are wrong, through error of judgment; but should I see him attacked by those who ought to know him, and to love him, and revere him, of such I shall be constrained to form a different opinion." And then curtseying low she sailed on, leaving her lover in anything but a happy state of mind.

Chapter VII

THE JUPITER

Though Eleanor Harding rode off from John Bold on a high horse, it must not be supposed that her heart was so elate as her demeanour. In the first place, she had a natural repugnance to losing her lover; and in the next, she was not quite so sure that she was in the right as she pretended to be. Her father had told her, and that now repeatedly, that Bold was doing nothing unjust or ungenerous; and why then should she rebuke him, and throw him off, when she felt herself so ill able to bear his loss?—but such is human nature, and young-lady-nature especially.

As she walked off from him beneath the shady elms of the close, her look, her tone, every motion and gesture of her body, belied her heart; she would have given the world to have taken him by the hand, to have reasoned with him, persuaded him, cajoled him, coaxed him out of his project; to have overcome him with all her female artillery, and to have redeemed her father at the cost of herself; but pride would not let her do this, and she left him without a look of love or a word of kindness.

Had Bold been judging of another lover and of another lady, he might have understood all this as well as we do; but in matters of love men do not see clearly in their own affairs. They say that faint heart never won fair lady; and it is amazing to me how fair ladies are won, so faint are often men's hearts! Were it not for the kindness of their nature, that seeing the weakness of our courage they will occasionally descend from their impregnable fortresses, and themselves aid us in effecting their own defeat, too often would they escape unconquered if not unscathed, and free of body if not of heart.

Poor Bold crept off quite crestfallen; he felt that as regarded Eleanor Harding his fate was sealed, unless he could consent to give up a task to which he had pledged himself, and which indeed it would not be easy for him to give up. Lawyers were engaged, and the question had to a certain extent been taken up by the public; besides, how could a high-spirited girl like Eleanor Harding really learn to love a man for neglecting a duty which he assumed! Could she allow her affection to be purchased at the cost of his own self-respect?

As regarded the issue of his attempt at reformation in the hospital, Bold had no reason hitherto to be discontented with his success. All Barchester was by the ears about it. The bishop, the archdeacon, the warden, the steward, and several other clerical allies, had daily meetings, discussing their tactics, and preparing for the great attack. Sir Abraham Haphazard had been consulted, but his opinion was not yet received: copies of Hiram's will, copies of wardens' journals, copies of leases, copies of accounts, copies of everything that could be copied, and of some that could not, had been sent to him; and the case was assuming most creditable dimensions. But, above all, it had been mentioned in the daily *Jupiter*. That all-powerful organ of the press in one of its leading thunderbolts launched at St Cross, had thus remarked: "Another case, of smaller dimensions indeed, but of similar import, is now likely to come under public notice. We are informed that the warden or master of an old almshouse attached to Barchester Cathedral is in receipt of twenty-five times the annual income appointed for him by the will of the founder, while the sum yearly expended on the absolute purposes of the charity has always remained fixed. In other words, the legatees under the founder's will have received no advantage from the increase in the value of the property during the last four centuries, such increase having been absorbed by the so-called warden. It is impossible to conceive a case of greater injustice. It is no answer to say that some six or nine or twelve old men receive as much of the goods of this world as such old men require. On what foundation, moral or divine, traditional or legal, is grounded the warden's claim to the large income he receives for doing nothing? The contentment of these almsmen, if content they be, can give him no title to this wealth! Does he ever ask himself, when he stretches wide his clerical palm to receive the pay of some dozen of the working clergy, for what service he is so remunerated? Does his conscience ever entertain the question of his right to such subsidies? Or is it possible that the subject never so presents itself to his mind; that he has received for many years, and intends, should God spare him, to receive for years to come these fruits of the industrious piety of past ages, indifferent as to any right on his own part, or of any injustice to others! We must express an opinion that nowhere but in the Church of England, and only there among its priests, could such a state of moral indifference be found."

I must for the present leave my readers to imagine the state of Mr Harding's mind after reading the above article. They say that forty thousand copies of *The Jupiter* are daily sold, and that each copy is read by five persons at the least. Two hundred thousand readers then would hear this accusation against him; two hundred thousand hearts would swell with indignation at the griping injustice, the barefaced robbery of the warden of Barchester Hospital! And how was he to answer this? How was he to open his inmost heart to this multitude, to these thousands, the educated, the polished, the picked men of his own country; how show them that he was no robber, no avaricious, lazy priest scrambling for gold, but a retiring, humble-spirited man, who had innocently taken what had innocently been offered to him?

"Write to *The Jupiter*," suggested the bishop.

"Yes," said the archdeacon, more worldly wise than his father, "yes, and be smothered with ridicule; tossed over and over again with scorn; shaken this way and that, as a rat in the mouth of a practised terrier. You will leave out some word or letter in your answer, and the ignorance of the cathedral clergy will be harped upon; you will make some small mistake, which will be a falsehood, or some admission, which will be self-condemnation; you will find yourself to have been vulgar, ill-tempered, irreverend, and illiterate, and the chances are ten to one, but that being a clergyman, you will have been guilty of blasphemy! A man may have the best of causes, the best of talents, and the best of tempers; he may write as well as Addison, or as strongly as Junius; but even with all this he cannot successfully answer, when attacked by *The Jupiter*. In such matters it is omnipotent. What the Czar is in Russia, or the mob in America, that *The Jupiter* is in England. Answer such an article! No, warden; whatever you do, don't do that. We were to look for this sort of thing, you know; but we need not draw down on our heads more of it than is necessary."

The article in *The Jupiter*, while it so greatly harassed our poor warden, was an immense triumph to some of the opposite party. Sorry as Bold was to see Mr Harding attacked so personally, it still gave him a feeling of elation to find his cause taken up by so powerful an advocate: and as to Finney, the attorney, he was beside himself. What! to be engaged in the same cause and on the same side with *The Jupiter*; to have the views he had recommended seconded, and furthered, and battled for by *The Jupiter*! Perhaps to have his own name mentioned as that of the learned gentleman whose efforts had been so successful on behalf of the poor of Barchester! He might be examined before committees of the House of Commons, with heaven knows how much a day for his personal expenses;—he might be engaged for years on such a suit! There was no end to the glorious golden dreams which this leader in *The Jupiter* produced in the soaring mind of Finney.

And the old bedesmen, they also heard of this article, and had a glimmering, indistinct idea of the marvellous advocate which had now taken up their cause. Abel Handy limped hither and thither through the rooms, repeating all that he understood to have been printed, with some additions of his own which he thought should have been added. He told them how *The Jupiter* had declared that their warden was no better than a robber, and that what *The Jupiter* said was acknowledged by the world to be true. How *The Jupiter* had affirmed that each one of them—"each one of us, Jonathan Crumple, think of that!"—had a clear right to a hundred a year; and that if *The Jupiter* had said so, it was better than a decision of the Lord Chancellor: and then he carried about the paper, supplied by Mr Finney, which, though none of them could read it, still afforded in its very touch and aspect positive corroboration of what was told them; and Jonathan Crumple pondered deeply over his returning wealth; and Job Skulpit saw how right he had been in signing the petition, and said so many scores of times; and Spriggs leered fearfully with his one eye; and Moody, as he more nearly approached the coming golden age, hated more deeply than ever those who still kept possession of what he so coveted. Even Billy Gazy and poor bed-ridden Bell became active and uneasy, and the great Bunce stood apart with lowering brow, with deep grief seated in his heart, for he perceived that evil days were coming.

It had been decided, the archdeacon advising, that no remonstrance, explanation, or defence should be addressed from the Barchester conclave to the editor of *The Jupiter*; but hitherto that was the only decision to which they had come.

Sir Abraham Haphazard was deeply engaged in preparing a bill for the mortification of papists, to be called the "Convent Custody Bill," the purport of which was to enable any Protestant clergyman over fifty years of age to search any nun whom he suspected of being in possession of treasonable papers or Jesuitical symbols; and as there were to be a hundred and thirty-seven clauses in the bill, each clause containing a separate thorn for the side of the papist, and as it was known the bill would be fought inch by inch, by fifty maddened Irishmen, the due construction and adequate dovetailing of it did consume much of Sir Abraham's time. The bill had all its desired effect. Of course it never passed into law; but it so completely divided the ranks of the Irish members, who had bound themselves together to force on the ministry a bill for compelling all men to drink Irish whiskey, and all women to wear Irish poplins, that for the remainder of the session the Great Poplin and Whiskey League was utterly harmless.

Thus it happened that Sir Abraham's opinion was not at once forthcoming, and the uncertainty, the expectation, and suffering of the folk of Barchester was maintained at a high pitch.

Chapter VIII

PLUMSTEAD EPISCOPI

The reader must now be requested to visit the rectory of Plumstead Episcopi; and as it is as yet still early morning, to ascend again with us into the bedroom of the archdeacon. The mistress of the mansion was at her toilet; on which we will not dwell with profane eyes, but proceed into a small inner room, where the doctor dressed and kept his boots and sermons; and here we will take our stand, premising that the door of the room was so open as to admit of a conversation between our reverend Adam and his valued Eve.

"It's all your own fault, archdeacon," said the latter. "I told you from the beginning how it would end, and papa has no one to thank but you."

"Good gracious, my dear," said the doctor, appearing at the door of his dressing-room, with his face and head enveloped in the rough towel which he was violently using; "how can you say so? I am doing my very best."

"I wish you had never done so much," said the lady, interrupting him. "If you'd just have let John Bold come and go there, as he and papa liked, he and Eleanor would have been married by this time, and we should not have heard one word about all this affair."

"But, my dear—"

"Oh, it's all very well, archdeacon; and of course you're right; I don't for a moment think you'll ever admit that you could be wrong; but the fact is, you've brought this young man down upon papa by huffing him as you have done."

"But, my love—"

"And all because you didn't like John Bold for a brother-in-law. How is she ever to do better? Papa hasn't got a shilling; and though Eleanor is well enough, she has not at all a taking style of beauty. I'm sure I don't know how she's to do better than marry John Bold; or as well indeed," added the anxious sister, giving the last twist to her last shoe-string.

Dr Grantly felt keenly the injustice of this attack; but what could he say? He certainly had huffed John Bold; he certainly had objected to him as a brother-in-law, and a very few months ago the very idea had excited his wrath: but now matters were changed; John Bold had shown his power, and, though he was as odious as ever to the archdeacon, power is always respected, and the reverend dignitary began to think that such an alliance might not have been imprudent. Nevertheless, his motto was still "no surrender;" he would still fight it out; he believed confidently in Oxford, in the bench of bishops, in Sir Abraham Haphazard, and in himself; and it was only when alone with his wife that doubts of defeat ever beset him. He once more tried to communicate this confidence to Mrs Grantly, and for the twentieth time began to tell her of Sir Abraham.

"Oh, Sir Abraham!" said she, collecting all her house keys into her basket before she descended; "Sir Abraham won't get Eleanor a husband; Sir Abraham won't get papa another income when he has been worreted out of the hospital. Mark what I tell you, archdeacon: while you and Sir Abraham are fighting, papa will lose his preferment; and what will you do then with him and Eleanor on your hands? besides, who's to pay Sir Abraham? I suppose he won't take the case up for nothing?" And so the lady descended to family worship among her children and servants, the pattern of a good and prudent wife.

Dr Grantly was blessed with a happy, thriving family. There were, first, three boys, now at home from school for the holidays. They were called, respectively, Charles James, Henry, and Samuel. The two younger (there were five in all) were girls; the elder, Florinda, bore the name of the Archbishop of York's wife, whose godchild she was: and the younger had been christened Grizzel, after a sister of the Archbishop of Canterbury. The boys were all clever, and gave good promise of being well able to meet the cares and trials of the world; and yet they were not alike in their dispositions, and each had his individual character, and each his separate admirers among the doctor's friends.

Charles James was an exact and careful boy; he never committed himself; he well knew how much was expected from the eldest son of the Archdeacon of Barchester, and was therefore mindful not to mix too freely with other boys. He had not the great talents of his younger brothers, but he exceeded them in judgment and propriety of demeanour; his fault, if he had one, was an over-attention to words instead of things; there was a thought too much finesse about him, and, as even his father sometimes told him, he was too fond of a compromise.

The second was the archdeacon's favourite son, and Henry was indeed a brilliant boy. The versatility of his genius was surprising, and the visitors at Plumstead Episcopi were often amazed at the marvellous manner in which he would, when called on, adapt his capacity to apparently most uncongenial pursuits. He appeared once before a large circle as Luther the reformer, and delighted them with the perfect manner in which he assumed the character; and within three days he again astonished them by acting the part of a Capuchin friar to the very life. For this last exploit his father gave him a golden guinea, and his brothers said the reward had been promised beforehand in the event of the performance being successful. He was also sent on a tour into Devonshire; a treat which the lad was most anxious of enjoying. His father's friends there, however, did not appreciate his talents, and sad accounts were sent home of the perversity of his nature. He was a most courageous lad, game to the backbone.

It was soon known, both at home, where he lived, and within some miles of Barchester Cathedral, and also at Westminster, where he was at school, that young Henry could box well and would never own himself beat; other boys would fight while they had a leg to stand on, but he would fight with no leg at all. Those backing him would sometimes think him crushed by the weight of blows and faint with loss of blood, and his friends would endeavour to withdraw him from the contest; but no, Henry never gave in, was never weary of the battle. The ring was the only element in which he seemed to enjoy himself; and while other boys were happy in the number of their friends, he rejoiced most in the multitude of his foes.

His relations could not but admire his pluck, but they sometimes were forced to regret that he was inclined to be a bully; and those not so partial to him as his father was, observed with pain that, though he could fawn to the masters and the archdeacon's friends, he was imperious and masterful to the servants and the poor.

But perhaps Samuel was the general favourite; and dear little Soapy, as he was familiarly called, was as engaging a child as ever fond mother petted. He was soft and gentle in his manners, and attractive in his speech; the tone of his voice was melody, and every action was a grace; unlike his brothers, he was courteous to all, he was affable to the low-ly, and meek even to the very scullery-maid. He was a boy of great promise, minding his books and delighting the hearts of his masters. His brothers, however, were not particular-ly fond of him; they would complain to their mother that Soapy's civility all meant something; they thought that his voice was too often listened to at Plumstead Episcopi, and evidently feared that, as he grew up, he would have more weight in the house than either of them; there was, therefore, a sort of agreement among them to put young Soapy down. This, however, was not so easy to be done; Samuel, though young, was sharp; he could not assume the stiff decorum of Charles James, nor could he fight like Henry; but he was a perfect master of his own weapons, and contrived, in the teeth of both of them, to hold the place which he had assumed. Henry declared that he was a false, cunning crea-ture; and Charles James, though he always spoke of him as his dear brother Samuel, was not slow to say a word against him when opportunity offered. To speak the truth, Samuel was a cunning boy, and those even who loved him best could not but own that for one so young, he was too adroit in choosing his words, and too skilled in modulating his voice.

The two little girls Florinda and Grizzel were nice little girls enough, but they did not possess the strong sterling qualities of their brothers; their voices were not often heard at Plumstead Episcopi; they were bashful and timid by nature, slow to speak before company even when asked to do so; and though they looked very nice in their clean white muslin frocks and pink sashes, they were but little noticed by the archdeacon's visitors.

Whatever of submissive humility may have appeared in the gait and visage of the archdeacon during his colloquy with his wife in the sanctum of their dressing-rooms was dispelled as he entered his breakfast-parlour with erect head and powerful step. In the presence of a third person he assumed the lord and master; and that wise and talented lady too well knew the man to whom her lot for life was bound, to stretch her authority beyond the point at which it would be borne. Strangers at Plumstead Episcopi, when they saw the imperious brow with which he commanded silence from the large circle of visitors, chil-dren, and servants who came together in the morning to hear him read the word of God, and watched how meekly that wife seated herself behind her basket of keys with a little girl on each side, as she caught that commanding glance; strangers, I say, seeing this, could little guess that some fifteen minutes since she had stoutly held her ground against him, hardly allowing him to open his mouth in his own defence. But such is the tact and talent of women!

And now let us observe the well-furnished breakfast-parlour at Plumstead Episcopi, and the comfortable air of all the belongings of the rectory. Comfortable they certainly were, but neither gorgeous nor even grand; indeed, considering the money that had been spent there, the eye and taste might have been better served; there was an air of heaviness about the rooms which might have been avoided without any sacrifice of propriety; col-ours might have been better chosen and lights more perfectly diffused; but perhaps in doing so the thorough clerical aspect of the whole might have been somewhat marred; at any rate, it was not without ample consideration that those thick, dark, costly carpets were put down; those embossed, but sombre papers hung up; those heavy curtains draped so as to half exclude the light of the sun: nor were these old-fashioned chairs, bought at a price far exceeding that now given for more modern goods, without a purpose. The breakfast-service on the table was equally costly and equally plain; the apparent object had been to spend money without obtaining brilliancy or splendour. The urn was of thick and solid silver, as were also the tea-pot, coffee-pot, cream-ewer, and sugar-bowl; the cups were old, dim dragon china, worth about a pound a piece, but very despicable in the eyes of the uninitiated. The silver forks were so heavy as to be disagreeable to the hand, and the bread-basket was of a weight really formidable to any but robust persons. The tea consumed was the very best, the coffee the very blackest, the cream the very thickest; there was dry toast and buttered toast, muffins and crumpets; hot bread and cold bread, white bread and brown bread, home-made bread and bakers' bread, wheaten bread and oaten bread; and if there be other breads than these, they were there; there were eggs in napkins, and crispy bits of bacon under silver covers; and there were little fishes in a little box, and devilled kidneys frizzling on a hot-water dish; which, by the bye, were placed closely contiguous to the plate of the worthy archdeacon himself. Over and above this, on a snow-white napkin, spread upon the sideboard, was a huge ham and a huge sirloin; the latter having laden the dinner table on the previous evening. Such was the ordinary fare at Plumstead Episcopi.

And yet I have never found the rectory a pleasant house. The fact that man shall not live by bread alone seemed to be somewhat forgotten; and noble as was the appearance of the host, and sweet and good-natured as was the face of the hostess, talented as were the children, and excellent as were the viands and the wines, in spite of these attractions, I generally found the rectory somewhat dull. After breakfast the archdeacon would retire, of course to his clerical pursuits. Mrs Grantly, I presume, inspected her kitchen, though she had a first-rate housekeeper, with sixty pounds a year; and attended to the lessons of Florinda and Grizzel, though she had an excellent governess with thirty pounds a year: but at any rate she disappeared: and I never could make companions of the boys. Charles James, though he always looked as though there was something in him, never seemed to have much to say; and what he did say he would always unsay the next minute. He told me once that he considered cricket, on the whole, to be a gentleman-like game for boys, provided they would play without running about; and that fives, also, was a seemly game, so that those who played it never heated themselves. Henry once quarrelled with me for taking his sister Grizzel's part in a contest between them as to the best mode of using a watering-pot for the garden flowers; and from that day to this he has not spoken to me, though he speaks at me often enough. For half an hour or so I certainly did like Sammy's gentle speeches; but one gets tired of honey, and I found that he preferred the more admiring listeners whom he met in the kitchen-garden and back precincts of the establishment; besides, I think I once caught Sammy fibbing.

On the whole, therefore, I found the rectory a dull house, though it must be admitted that everything there was of the very best.

After breakfast, on the morning of which we are writing, the archdeacon, as usual, retired to his study, intimating that he was going to be very busy, but that he would see Mr Chadwick if he called. On entering this sacred room he carefully opened the paper case on which he was wont to compose his favourite sermons, and spread on it a fair sheet of paper and one partly written on; he then placed his inkstand, looked at his pen, and folded his blotting paper; having done so, he got up again from his seat, stood with his back to the fire-place, and yawned comfortably, stretching out vastly his huge arms and opening his burly chest. He then walked across the room and locked the door; and having so prepared himself, he threw himself into his easy-chair, took from a secret drawer beneath his table a volume of Rabelais, and began to amuse himself with the witty mischief of Panurge; and so passed the archdeacon's morning on that day.

He was left undisturbed at his studies for an hour or two, when a knock came to the door, and Mr Chadwick was announced. Rabelais retired into the secret drawer, the easy-chair seemed knowingly to betake itself off, and when the archdeacon quickly undid his bolt, he was discovered by the steward working, as usual, for that church of which he was so useful a pillar. Mr Chadwick had just come from London, and was, therefore, known to be the bearer of important news.

"We've got Sir Abraham's opinion at last," said Mr Chadwick, as he seated himself.

"Well, well, well!" exclaimed the archdeacon impatiently.

"Oh, it's as long as my arm," said the other; "it can't be told in a word, but you can read it;" and he handed him a copy, in heaven knows how many spun-out folios, of the opinion which the attorney-general had managed to cram on the back and sides of the case as originally submitted to him.

"The upshot is," said Chadwick, "that there's a screw loose in their case, and we had better do nothing. They are proceeding against Mr Harding and myself, and Sir Abraham holds that, under the wording of the will, and subsequent arrangements legally sanctioned, Mr Harding and I are only paid servants. The defendants should have been either the Corporation of Barchester, or possibly the chapter of your father."

"W-hoo!" said the archdeacon; "so Master Bold is on the wrong scent, is he?"

"That's Sir Abraham's opinion; but any scent almost would be a wrong scent. Sir Abraham thinks that if they'd taken the corporation, or the chapter, we could have baffled them. The bishop, he thinks, would be the surest shot; but even there we could plead that the bishop is only a visitor, and that he has never made himself a consenting party to the performance of other duties."

"That's quite clear," said the archdeacon.

"Not quite so clear," said the other. "You see the will says, 'My lord, the bishop, being graciously pleased to see that due justice be done.' Now, it may be a question whether, in accepting and administering the patronage, your father has not accepted also the other duties assigned. It is doubtful, however; but even if they hit that nail,—and they are far off from that yet,—the point is so nice, as Sir Abraham says, that you would force them into fifteen thousand pounds' cost before they could bring it to an issue! and where's that sum of money to come from?"

The archdeacon rubbed his hands with delight; he had never doubted the justice of his case, but he had begun to have some dread of unjust success on the part of his enemies. It was delightful to him thus to hear that their cause was surrounded with such rocks and shoals; such causes of shipwreck unseen by the landsman's eye, but visible enough to the keen eyes of practical law mariners. How wrong his wife was to wish that Bold should marry Eleanor! Bold! why, if he should be ass enough to persevere, he would be a beggar before he knew whom he was at law with!

"That's excellent, Chadwick;—that's excellent! I told you Sir Abraham was the man for us;" and he put down on the table the copy of the opinion, and patted it fondly.

"Don't you let that be seen, though, archdeacon."

"Who?—I!—not for worlds," said the doctor.

"People will talk, you know, archdeacon."

"Of course, of course," said the doctor.

"Because, if that gets abroad, it would teach them how to fight their own battle."

"Quite true," said the doctor.

"No one here in Barchester ought to see that but you and I, archdeacon."

"No, no, certainly no one else," said the archdeacon, pleased with the closeness of the confidence; "no one else shall."

"Mrs Grantly is very interested in the matter, I know," said Mr Chadwick.

Did the archdeacon wink, or did he not? I am inclined to think he did not quite wink; but that without such, perhaps, unseemly gesture he communicated to Mr Chadwick, with the corner of his eye, intimation that, deep as was Mrs Grantly's interest in the matter, it should not procure for her a perusal of that document; and at the same time he partly opened the small drawer, above spoken of, deposited the paper on the volume of Rabelais, and showed to Mr Chadwick the nature of the key which guarded these hidden treasures.

The careful steward then expressed himself contented. Ah! vain man! he could fasten up his Rabelais, and other things secret, with all the skill of Bramah or of Chubb; but where could he fasten up the key which solved these mechanical mysteries? It is probable to us that the contents of no drawer in that house were unknown to its mistress, and we think, moreover, that she was entitled to all such knowledge.

"But," said Mr Chadwick, "we must, of course, tell your father and Mr Harding so much of Sir Abraham's opinion as will satisfy them that the matter is doing well."

"Oh, certainly,—yes, of course," said the doctor.

"You had better let them know that Sir Abraham is of opinion that there is no case at any rate against Mr Harding; and that as the action is worded at present, it must fall to the ground; they must be nonsuited, if they carry it on; you had better tell Mr Harding, that Sir Abraham is clearly of opinion that he is only a servant, and as such not liable;—or if you like it, I'll see Mr Harding myself."

"Oh, I must see him to-morrow, and my father too, and I'll explain to them exactly so much;—you won't go before lunch, Mr Chadwick: well, if you will, you must, for I know your time is precious;" and he shook hands with the diocesan steward, and bowed him out.

The archdeacon had again recourse to his drawer, and twice read through the essence of Sir Abraham Haphazard's law-enlightened and law-bewildered brains. It was very clear that to Sir Abraham, the justice of the old men's claim or the justice of Mr Harding's defence were ideas that had never presented themselves. A legal victory over an opposing party was the service for which Sir Abraham was, as he imagined, to be paid; and that he, according to his lights, had diligently laboured to achieve, and with probable hope of success. Of the intense desire which Mr Harding felt to be assured on fit authority that he was wronging no man, that he was entitled in true equity to his income, that he might sleep at night without pangs of conscience, that he was no robber, no spoiler of the poor; that he and all the world might be openly convinced that he was not the man which *The Jupiter* had described him to be; of such longings on the part of Mr Harding, Sir Abraham was entirely ignorant; nor, indeed, could it be looked on as part of his business to gratify such desires. Such was not the system on which his battles were fought, and victories gained. Success was his object, and he was generally successful. He conquered his enemies by their weakness rather than by his own strength, and it had been found almost impossible to make up a case in which Sir Abraham, as an antagonist, would not find a flaw.

The archdeacon was delighted with the closeness of the reasoning. To do him justice, it was not a selfish triumph that he desired; he would personally lose nothing by defeat, or at least what he might lose did not actuate him; but neither was it love of justice which made him so anxious, nor even mainly solicitude for his father-in-law. He was fighting a part of a never-ending battle against a never-conquered foe—that of the church against its enemies.

He knew Mr Harding could not pay all the expense of these doings: for these long opinions of Sir Abraham's, these causes to be pleaded, these speeches to be made, these various courts through which the case was, he presumed, to be dragged. He knew that he and his father must at least bear the heavier portion of this tremendous cost; but to do the archdeacon justice, he did not recoil from this. He was a man fond of obtaining money, greedy of a large income, but open-handed enough in expending it, and it was a triumph to him to foresee the success of this measure, although he might be called on to pay so dearly for it himself.

Chapter IX

THE CONFERENCE

On the following morning the archdeacon was with his father betimes, and a note was sent down to the warden begging his attendance at the palace. Dr Grantly, as he cogitated on the matter, leaning back in his brougham as he journeyed into Barchester, felt that it would be difficult to communicate his own satisfaction either to his father or his father-in-law. He wanted success on his own side and discomfiture on that of his enemies. The bishop wanted peace on the subject; a settled peace if possible, but peace at any rate till the short remainder of his own days had spun itself out. Mr Harding required not only success and peace, but he also demanded that he might stand justified before the world.

The bishop, however, was comparatively easy to deal with; and before the arrival of the other, the dutiful son had persuaded his father that all was going on well, and then the warden arrived.

It was Mr Harding's wont, whenever he spent a morning at the palace, to seat himself immediately at the bishop's elbow, the bishop occupying a huge arm-chair fitted up with candle-sticks, a reading table, a drawer, and other paraphernalia, the position of which chair was never moved, summer or winter; and when, as was usual, the archdeacon was there also, he confronted the two elders, who thus were enabled to fight the battle against him together;—and together submit to defeat, for such was their constant fate.

Our warden now took his accustomed place, having greeted his son-in-law as he entered, and then affectionately inquired after his friend's health. There was a gentleness about the bishop to which the soft womanly affection of Mr Harding particularly endeared itself, and it was quaint to see how the two mild old priests pressed each other's hand, and smiled and made little signs of love.

"Sir Abraham's opinion has come at last," began the archdeacon. Mr Harding had heard so much, and was most anxious to know the result.

"It is quite favourable," said the bishop, pressing his friend's arm. "I am so glad."

Mr Harding looked at the mighty bearer of the important news for confirmation of these glad tidings.

"Yes," said the archdeacon; "Sir Abraham has given most minute attention to the case; indeed, I knew he would;—most minute attention; and his opinion is,—and as to his opinion on such a subject being correct, no one who knows Sir Abraham's character can doubt,—his opinion is, that they hav'n't got a leg to stand on."

"But as how, archdeacon?"

"Why, in the first place:—but you're no lawyer, warden, and I doubt you won't understand it; the gist of the matter is this:—under Hiram's will two paid guardians have been selected for the hospital; the law will say two paid servants, and you and I won't quarrel with the name."

"At any rate I will not if I am one of the servants," said Mr Harding. "A rose, you know—"

"Yes, yes," said the archdeacon, impatient of poetry at such a time. "Well, two paid servants, we'll say; one to look after the men, and the other to look after the money. You and Chadwick are these two servants, and whether either of you be paid too much, or too little, more or less in fact than the founder willed, it's as clear as daylight that no one can fall foul of either of you for receiving an allotted stipend."

"That does seem clear," said the bishop, who had winced visibly at the words servants and stipend, which, however, appeared to have caused no uneasiness to the archdeacon.

"Quite clear," said he, "and very satisfactory. In point of fact, it being necessary to select such servants for the use of the hospital, the pay to be given to them must depend on the rate of pay for such services, according to their market value at the period in question; and those who manage the hospital must be the only judges of this."

"And who does manage the hospital?" asked the warden. "Oh, let them find that out; that's another question: the action is brought against you and Chadwick; that's your defence, and a perfect and full defence it is. Now that I think very satisfactory."

"Well," said the bishop, looking inquiringly up into his friend's face, who sat silent awhile, and apparently not so well satisfied.

"And conclusive," continued the archdeacon; "if they press it to a jury, which they won't do, no twelve men in England will take five minutes to decide against them."

"But according to that" said Mr Harding, "I might as well have sixteen hundred a year as eight, if the managers choose to allot it to me; and as I am one of the managers, if not the chief manager, myself, that can hardly be a just arrangement."

"Oh, well; all that's nothing to the question. The question is, whether this intruding fellow, and a lot of cheating attorneys and pestilent dissenters, are to interfere with an arrangement which everyone knows is essentially just and serviceable to the church. Pray don't let us be splitting hairs, and that amongst ourselves, or there'll never be an end of the cause or the cost."

Mr Harding again sat silent for a while, during which the bishop once and again pressed his arm, and looked in his face to see if he could catch a gleam of a contented and eased mind; but there was no such gleam, and the poor warden continued playing sad dirges on invisible stringed instruments in all manner of positions; he was ruminating in his mind on this opinion of Sir Abraham, looking to it wearily and earnestly for satisfaction, but finding none. At last he said, "Did you see the opinion, archdeacon?"

The archdeacon said he had not,—that was to say, he had,—that was, he had not seen the opinion itself; he had seen what had been called a copy, but he could not say whether of a whole or part; nor could he say that what he had seen were the *ipsissima verba* of the great man himself; but what he had seen contained exactly the decision which he had announced, and which he again declared to be to his mind extremely satisfactory.

"I should like to see the opinion," said the warden; "that is, a copy of it."

"Well, I suppose you can if you make a point of it; but I don't see the use myself; of course it is essential that the purport of it should not be known, and it is therefore unadvisable to multiply copies."

"Why should it not be known?" asked the warden.

"What a question for a man to ask!" said the archdeacon, throwing up his hands in token of his surprise; "but it is like you:—a child is not more innocent than you are in matters of business. Can't you see that if we tell them that no action will lie against you, but that one may possibly lie against some other person or persons, that we shall be putting weapons into their hands, and be teaching them how to cut our own throats?"

The warden again sat silent, and the bishop again looked at him wistfully. "The only thing we have now to do," continued the archdeacon, "is to remain quiet, hold our peace, and let them play their own game as they please."

"We are not to make known then," said the warden, "that we have consulted the attorney-general, and that we are advised by him that the founder's will is fully and fairly carried out."

"God bless my soul!" said the archdeacon, "how odd it is that you will not see that all we are to do is to do nothing: why should we say anything about the founder's will? We are in possession; and we know that they are not in a position to put us out; surely that is enough for the present."

Mr Harding rose from his seat and paced thoughtfully up and down the library, the bishop the while watching him painfully at every turn, and the archdeacon continuing to pour forth his convictions that the affair was in a state to satisfy any prudent mind.

"And *The Jupiter*?" said the warden, stopping suddenly.

"Oh! *The Jupiter*," answered the other. "*The Jupiter* can break no bones. You must bear with that; there is much, of course, which it is our bounden duty to bear; it cannot be all roses for us here," and the archdeacon looked exceedingly moral; "besides, the matter is too trivial, of too little general interest to be mentioned again in *The Jupiter*, unless we stir up the subject." And the archdeacon again looked exceedingly knowing and worldly wise.

The warden continued his walk; the hard and stinging words of that newspaper article, each one of which had thrust a thorn as it were into his inmost soul, were fresh in his memory; he had read it more than once, word by word, and what was worse, he fancied it was as well known to everyone as to himself. Was he to be looked on as the unjust griping priest he had been there described? Was he to be pointed at as the consumer of the bread of the poor, and to be allowed no means of refuting such charges, of clearing his begrimed name, of standing innocent in the world, as hitherto he had stood? Was he to bear all this, to receive as usual his now hated income, and be known as one of those greedy priests who by their rapacity have brought disgrace on their church? And why? Why should he bear all this? Why should he die, for he felt that he could not live, under such a weight of obloquy? As he paced up and down the room he resolved in his misery and enthusiasm that he could with pleasure, if he were allowed, give up his place, abandon his pleasant home, leave the hospital, and live poorly, happily, and with an unsullied name, on the small remainder of his means.

He was a man somewhat shy of speaking of himself, even before those who knew him best, and whom he loved the most; but at last it burst forth from him, and with a somewhat jerking eloquence he declared that he could not, would not, bear this misery any longer.

"If it can be proved," said he at last, "that I have a just and honest right to this, as God well knows I always deemed I had; if this salary or stipend be really my due, I am not less anxious than another to retain it. I have the well-being of my child to look to. I am too old to miss without some pain the comforts to which I have been used; and I am, as others are, anxious to prove to the world that I have been right, and to uphold the place I have held; but I cannot do it at such a cost as this. I cannot bear this. Could you tell me to do so?" And he appealed, almost in tears, to the bishop, who had left his chair, and was now leaning on the warden's arm as he stood on the further side of the table facing the archdeacon. "Could you tell me to sit there at ease, indifferent, and satisfied, while such things as these are said loudly of me in the world?"

The bishop could feel for him and sympathise with him, but he could not advise him; he could only say, "No, no, you shall be asked to do nothing that is painful; you shall do just what your heart tells you to be right; you shall do whatever you think best yourself. Theophilus, don't advise him, pray don't advise the warden to do anything which is painful."

But the archdeacon, though he could not sympathise, could advise; and he saw that the time had come when it behoved him to do so in a somewhat peremptory manner.

"Why, my lord," he said, speaking to his father;—and when he called his father "my lord," the good old bishop shook in his shoes, for he knew that an evil time was coming. "Why, my lord, there are two ways of giving advice: there is advice that may be good for the present day; and there is advice that may be good for days to come: now I cannot bring myself to give the former, if it be incompatible with the other."

"No, no, no, I suppose not," said the bishop, re-seating himself, and shading his face with his hands. Mr Harding sat down with his back to the further wall, playing to himself some air fitted for so calamitous an occasion, and the archdeacon said out his say standing, with his back to the empty fire-place.

"It is not to be supposed but that much pain will spring out of this unnecessarily raised question. We must all have foreseen that, and the matter has in no wise gone on worse than we expected; but it will be weak, yes, and wicked also, to abandon the cause and own ourselves wrong, because the inquiry is painful. It is not only ourselves we have to look to; to a certain extent the interest of the church is in our keeping. Should it be found that one after another of those who hold preferment abandoned it whenever it might be attacked, is it not plain that such attacks would be renewed till nothing was left us? and, that if so deserted, the Church of England must fall to the ground altogether? If this be true of many, it is true of one. Were you, accused as you now are, to throw up the wardenship, and to relinquish the preferment which is your property, with the vain object of proving yourself disinterested, you would fail in that object, you would inflict a desperate blow on your brother clergymen, you would encourage every cantankerous dissenter in England to make a similar charge against some source of clerical revenue, and you would do your best to dishearten those who are most anxious to defend you and uphold your position. I can fancy nothing more weak, or more wrong. It is not that you think that there is any justice in these charges, or that you doubt your own right to the wardenship: you are convinced of your own honesty, and yet would yield to them through cowardice."

"Cowardice!" said the bishop, expostulating. Mr Harding sat unmoved, gazing on his son-in-law.

"Well; would it not be cowardice? Would he not do so because he is afraid to endure the evil things which will be falsely spoken of him? Would that not be cowardice? And now let us see the extent of the evil which you dread. *The Jupiter* publishes an article which a great many, no doubt, will read; but of those who understand the subject how many will believe *The Jupiter*? Everyone knows what its object is: it has taken up the case against Lord Guildford and against the Dean of Rochester, and that against half a dozen bishops; and does not everyone know that it would take up any case of the kind, right or wrong, false or true, with known justice or known injustice, if by doing so it could further its own views? Does not all the world know this of *The Jupiter*? Who that really knows you will think the worse of you for what *The Jupiter* says? And why care for those who do not know you? I will say nothing of your own comfort, but I do say that you could not be justified in throwing up, in a fit of passion, for such it would be, the only maintenance that Eleanor has; and if you did so, if you really did vacate the wardenship, and submit to ruin, what would that profit you? If you have no future right to the income,

52

you have had no past right to it; and the very fact of your abandoning your position would create a demand for repayment of that which you have already received and spent."

The poor warden groaned as he sat perfectly still, looking up at the hard-hearted orator who thus tormented him, and the bishop echoed the sound faintly from behind his hands; but the archdeacon cared little for such signs of weakness, and completed his exhortation.

"But let us suppose the office to be left vacant, and that your own troubles concerning it were over; would that satisfy you? Are your only aspirations in the matter confined to yourself and family? I know they are not. I know you are as anxious as any of us for the church to which we belong; and what a grievous blow would such an act of apostasy give her! You owe it to the church of which you are a member and a minister, to bear with this affliction, however severe it may be: you owe it to my father, who instituted you, to support his rights: you owe it to those who preceded you to assert the legality of their position; you owe it to those who are to come after you, to maintain uninjured for them that which you received uninjured from others; and you owe to us all the unflinching assistance of perfect brotherhood in this matter, so that upholding one another we may support our great cause without blushing and without disgrace."

And so the archdeacon ceased, and stood self-satisfied, watching the effect of his spoken wisdom.

The warden felt himself, to a certain extent, stifled; he would have given the world to get himself out into the open air without speaking to, or noticing those who were in the room with him; but this was impossible. He could not leave without saying something, and he felt himself confounded by the archdeacon's eloquence. There was a heavy, unfeeling, unanswerable truth in what he had said; there was so much practical, but odious common sense in it, that he neither knew how to assent or to differ. If it were necessary for him to suffer, he felt that he could endure without complaint and without cowardice, providing that he was self-satisfied of the justice of his own cause. What he could not endure was, that he should be accused by others, and not acquitted by himself. Doubting, as he had begun to doubt, the justice of his own position in the hospital, he knew that his own self-confidence would not be restored because Mr Bold had been in error as to some legal form; nor could he be satisfied to escape, because, through some legal fiction, he who received the greatest benefit from the hospital might be considered only as one of its servants.

The archdeacon's speech had silenced him,—stupefied him,—annihilated him; anything but satisfied him. With the bishop it fared not much better. He did not discern clearly how things were, but he saw enough to know that a battle was to be prepared for; a battle that would destroy his few remaining comforts, and bring him with sorrow to the grave.

The warden still sat, and still looked at the archdeacon, till his thoughts fixed themselves wholly on the means of escape from his present position, and he felt like a bird fascinated by gazing on a snake.

"I hope you agree with me," said the archdeacon at last, breaking the dread silence; "my lord, I hope you agree with me."

Oh, what a sigh the bishop gave! "My lord, I hope you agree with me," again repeated the merciless tyrant.

"Yes, I suppose so," groaned the poor old man, slowly.

"And you, warden?"

Mr Harding was now stirred to action;—he must speak and move, so he got up and took one turn before he answered.

"Do not press me for an answer just at present; I will do nothing lightly in the matter, and of whatever I do I will give you and the bishop notice." And so without another word he took his leave, escaping quickly through the palace hall, and down the lofty steps; nor did he breathe freely till he found himself alone under the huge elms of the silent close. Here he walked long and slowly, thinking on his case with a troubled air, and trying in vain to confute the archdeacon's argument. He then went home, resolved to bear it all,— ignominy, suspense, disgrace, self-doubt, and heart-burning,—and to do as those would have him, who he still believed were most fit and most able to counsel him aright.

Chapter X

TRIBULATION

Mr Harding was a sadder man than he had ever yet been when he returned to his own house. He had been wretched enough on that well-remembered morning when he was forced to expose before his son-in-law the publisher's account for ushering into the world his dear book of sacred music: when after making such payments as he could do unassisted, he found that he was a debtor of more than three hundred pounds; but his sufferings then were as nothing to his present misery;—then he had done wrong, and he knew it, and was able to resolve that he would not sin in like manner again; but now he could make no resolution, and comfort himself by no promises of firmness. He had been forced to think that his lot had placed him in a false position, and he was about to maintain that position against the opinion of the world and against his own convictions.

He had read with pity, amounting almost to horror, the strictures which had appeared from time to time against the Earl of Guildford as master of St Cross, and the invectives that had been heaped on rich diocesan dignitaries and overgrown sinecure pluralists. In judging of them, he judged leniently; the whole bias of his profession had taught him to think that they were more sinned against than sinning, and that the animosity with which they had been pursued was venomous and unjust; but he had not the less regarded their plight as most miserable. His hair had stood on end and his flesh had crept as he read the things which had been written; he had wondered how men could live under such a load of disgrace; how they could face their fellow-creatures while their names were bandied about so injuriously and so publicly;—and now this lot was to be his,—he, that shy, retiring man, who had so comforted himself in the hidden obscurity of his lot, who had so enjoyed the unassuming warmth of his own little corner,—he was now dragged forth into the glaring day, and gibbeted before ferocious multitudes. He entered his own house a crestfallen, humiliated man, without a hope of overcoming the wretchedness which affected him.

He wandered into the drawing-room where was his daughter; but he could not speak to her now, so he left it, and went into the book-room. He was not quick enough to escape Eleanor's glance, or to prevent her from seeing that he was disturbed; and in a little while she followed him. She found him seated in his accustomed chair with no book open before him, no pen ready in his hand, no ill-shapen notes of blotted music lying before him as was usual, none of those hospital accounts with which he was so precise and yet so unmethodical: he was doing nothing, thinking of nothing, looking at nothing; he was merely suffering.

"Leave me, Eleanor, my dear," he said; "leave me, my darling, for a few minutes, for I am busy."

Eleanor saw well how it was, but she did leave him, and glided silently back to her drawing-room. When he had sat a while, thus alone and unoccupied, he got up to walk again;—he could make more of his thoughts walking than sitting, and was creeping out into his garden, when he met Bunce on the threshold.

"Well, Bunce," said he, in a tone that for him was sharp, "what is it? do you want me?"

"I was only coming to ask after your reverence," said the old bedesman, touching his hat; "and to inquire about the news from London," he added after a pause.

The warden winced, and put his hand to his forehead and felt bewildered.

"Attorney Finney has been there this morning," continued Bunce, "and by his looks I guess he is not so well pleased as he once was, and it has got abroad somehow that the archdeacon has had down great news from London, and Handy and Moody are both as black as devils. And I hope," said the man, trying to assume a cheery tone, "that things are looking up, and that there'll be an end soon to all this stuff which bothers your reverence so sorely."

"Well, I wish there may be, Bunce."

"But about the news, your reverence?" said the old man, almost whispering.

Mr Harding walked on, and shook his head impatiently. Poor Bunce little knew how he was tormenting his patron.

"If there was anything to cheer you, I should be so glad to know it," said he, with a tone of affection which the warden in all his misery could not resist.

He stopped, and took both the old man's hands in his. "My friend," said he, "my dear old friend, there is nothing; there is no news to cheer me;—God's will be done": and two small hot tears broke away from his eyes and stole down his furrowed cheeks.

"Then God's will be done," said the other solemnly; "but they told me that there was good news from London, and I came to wish your reverence joy; but God's will be done;" and so the warden again walked on, and the bedesman, looking wistfully after him and receiving no encouragement to follow, returned sadly to his own abode.

For a couple of hours the warden remained thus in the garden, now walking, now standing motionless on the turf, and then, as his legs got weary, sitting unconsciously on the garden seats, and then walking again. And Eleanor, hidden behind the muslin curtains of the window, watched him through the trees as he now came in sight, and then again was concealed by the turnings of the walk; and thus the time passed away till five, when the warden crept back to the house and prepared for dinner.

It was but a sorry meal. The demure parlour-maid, as she handed the dishes and changed the plates, saw that all was not right, and was more demure than ever: neither father nor daughter could eat, and the hateful food was soon cleared away, and the bottle of port placed upon the table.

"Would you like Bunce to come in, papa?" said Eleanor, thinking that the company of the old man might lighten his sorrow.

"No, my dear, thank you, not to-day; but are not you going out, Eleanor, this lovely afternoon? don't stay in for me, my dear."

"I thought you seemed so sad, papa."

"Sad," said he, irritated; "well, people must all have their share of sadness here; I am not more exempt than another: but kiss me, dearest, and go now; I will, if possible, be more sociable when you return."

And Eleanor was again banished from her father's sorrow. Ah! her desire now was not to find him happy, but to be allowed to share his sorrows; not to force him to be sociable, but to persuade him to be trustful.

She put on her bonnet as desired, and went up to Mary Bold; this was now her daily haunt, for John Bold was up in London among lawyers and church reformers, diving deep into other questions than that of the wardenship of Barchester; supplying information to one member of Parliament, and dining with another; subscribing to funds for the abolition of clerical incomes, and seconding at that great national meeting at the Crown and Anchor a resolution to the effect, that no clergyman of the Church of England, be he who he might, should have more than a thousand a year, and none less than two hundred and fifty. His speech on this occasion was short, for fifteen had to speak, and the room was hired for two hours only, at the expiration of which the Quakers and Mr Cobden were to make use of it for an appeal to the public in aid of the Emperor of Russia; but it was sharp and effective; at least he was told so by a companion with whom he now lived much, and on whom he greatly depended,—one Tom Towers, a very leading genius, and supposed to have high employment on the staff of *The Jupiter*.

So Eleanor, as was now her wont, went up to Mary Bold, and Mary listened kindly, while the daughter spoke much of her father, and, perhaps kinder still, found a listener in Eleanor, while she spoke about her brother. In the meantime the warden sat alone, leaning on the arm of his chair; he had poured out a glass of wine, but had done so merely from habit, for he left it untouched; there he sat gazing at the open window, and thinking, if he can be said to have thought, of the happiness of his past life. All manner of past delights came before his mind, which at the time he had enjoyed without considering them; his easy days, his absence of all kind of hard work, his pleasant shady home, those twelve old neighbours whose welfare till now had been the source of so much pleasant care, the excellence of his children, the friendship of the dear old bishop, the solemn grandeur of those vaulted aisles, through which he loved to hear his own voice pealing; and then that friend of friends, that choice ally that had never deserted him, that eloquent companion that would always, when asked, discourse such pleasant music, that violoncello of his;— ah, how happy he had been! but it was over now; his easy days and absence of work had been the crime which brought on him his tribulation; his shady home was pleasant no longer; maybe it was no longer his; the old neighbours, whose welfare had been so desired by him, were his enemies; his daughter was as wretched as himself; and even the bishop was made miserable by his position. He could never again lift up his voice boldly as he had hitherto done among his brethren, for he felt that he was disgraced; and he feared even to touch his bow, for he knew how grievous a sound of wailing, how piteous a lamentation, it would produce.

He was still sitting in the same chair and the same posture, having hardly moved a limb for two hours, when Eleanor came back to tea, and succeeded in bringing him with her into the drawing-room.

The tea seemed as comfortless as the dinner, though the warden, who had hitherto eaten nothing all day, devoured the plateful of bread and butter, unconscious of what he was doing.

Eleanor had made up her mind to force him to talk to her, but she hardly knew how to commence: she must wait till the urn was gone, till the servant would no longer be coming in and out.

At last everything was gone, and the drawing-room door was permanently closed; then Eleanor, getting up and going round to her father, put her arm round his neck, and said, "Papa, won't you tell me what it is?"

"What what is, my dear?"

"This new sorrow that torments you; I know you are unhappy, papa."

"New sorrow! it's no new sorrow, my dear; we have all our cares sometimes;" and he tried to smile, but it was a ghastly failure; "but I shouldn't be so dull a companion; come, we'll have some music."

"No, papa, not tonight,—it would only trouble you tonight;" and she sat upon his knee, as she sometimes would in their gayest moods, and with her arm round his neck, she said: "Papa, I will not leave you till you talk to me; oh, if you only knew how much good it would do to you, to tell me of it all."

The father kissed his daughter, and pressed her to his heart; but still he said nothing: it was so hard to him to speak of his own sorrows; he was so shy a man even with his own child!

"Oh, papa, do tell me what it is; I know it is about the hospital, and what they are doing up in London, and what that cruel newspaper has said; but if there be such cause for sorrow, let us be sorrowful together; we are all in all to each other now: dear, dear papa, do speak to me."

Mr Harding could not well speak now, for the warm tears were running down his cheeks like rain in May, but he held his child close to his heart, and squeezed her hand as a lover might, and she kissed his forehead and his wet cheeks, and lay upon his bosom, and comforted him as a woman only can do.

"My own child," he said, as soon as his tears would let him speak, "my own, own child, why should you too be unhappy before it is necessary? It may come to that, that we must leave this place, but till that time comes, why should your young days be clouded?"

"And is that all, papa? If that be all, let us leave it, and have light hearts elsewhere: if that be all, let us go. Oh, papa, you and I could be happy if we had only bread to eat, so long as our hearts were light."

And Eleanor's face was lighted up with enthusiasm as she told her father how he might banish all his care; and a gleam of joy shot across his brow as this idea of escape again presented itself, and he again fancied for a moment that he could spurn away from him the income which the world envied him; that he could give the lie to that wielder of the tomahawk who had dared to write such things of him in *The Jupiter*; that he could leave Sir Abraham, and the archdeacon, and Bold, and the rest of them with their lawsuit among them, and wipe his hands altogether of so sorrow-stirring a concern. Ah, what happiness might there be in the distance, with Eleanor and him in some small cottage, and nothing left of their former grandeur but their music! Yes, they would walk forth with their music books, and their instruments, and shaking the dust from off their feet as they went, leave the ungrateful place. Never did a poor clergyman sigh for a warm benefice more anxiously than our warden did now to be rid of his.

"Give it up, papa," she said again, jumping from his knees and standing on her feet before him, looking boldly into his face; "give it up, papa."

Oh, it was sad to see how that momentary gleam of joy passed away; how the look of hope was dispersed from that sorrowful face, as the remembrance of the archdeacon came back upon our poor warden, and he reflected that he could not stir from his now hated post. He was as a man bound with iron, fettered with adamant: he was in no respect a free agent; he had no choice. "Give it up!" Oh if he only could: what an easy way that were out of all his troubles!

"Papa, don't doubt about it," she continued, thinking that his hesitation arose from his unwillingness to abandon so comfortable a home; "is it on my account that you would stay here? Do you think that I cannot be happy without a pony-carriage and a fine drawing-room? Papa, I never can be happy here, as long as there is a question as to your honour in staying here; but I could be gay as the day is long in the smallest tiny little cottage, if I could see you come in and go out with a light heart. Oh! papa, your face tells so much;

though you won't speak to me with your voice, I know how it is with you every time I look at you."

How he pressed her to his heart again with almost a spasmodic pressure! How he kissed her as the tears fell like rain from his old eyes! How he blessed her, and called her by a hundred soft sweet names which now came new to his lips! How he chid himself for ever having been unhappy with such a treasure in his house, such a jewel on his bosom, with so sweet a flower in the choice garden of his heart! And then the floodgates of his tongue were loosed, and, at length, with unsparing detail of circumstances, he told her all that he wished, and all that he could not do. He repeated those arguments of the archdeacon, not agreeing in their truth, but explaining his inability to escape from them;—how it had been declared to him that he was bound to remain where he was by the interests of his order, by gratitude to the bishop, by the wishes of his friends, by a sense of duty, which, though he could not understand it, he was fain to acknowledge. He told her how he had been accused of cowardice, and though he was not a man to make much of such a charge before the world, now in the full candour of his heart he explained to her that such an accusation was grievous to him; that he did think it would be unmanly to desert his post, merely to escape his present sufferings, and that, therefore, he must bear as best he might the misery which was prepared for him.

And did she find these details tedious? Oh, no; she encouraged him to dilate on every feeling he expressed, till he laid bare the inmost corners of his heart to her. They spoke together of the archdeacon, as two children might of a stern, unpopular, but still respected schoolmaster, and of the bishop as a parent kind as kind could be, but powerless against an omnipotent pedagogue.

And then when they had discussed all this, when the father had told all to the child, she could not be less confiding than he had been; and as John Bold's name was mentioned between them, she owned how well she had learned to love him,—"had loved him once," she said, "but she would not, could not do so now—no, even had her troth been plighted to him, she would have taken it back again;—had she sworn to love him as his wife, she would have discarded him, and not felt herself forsworn, when he proved himself the enemy of her father."

But the warden declared that Bold was no enemy of his, and encouraged her love; and gently rebuked, as he kissed her, the stern resolve she had made to cast him off; and then he spoke to her of happier days when their trials would all be over; and declared that her young heart should not be torn asunder to please either priest or prelate, dean or archdeacon. No, not if all Oxford were to convocate together, and agree as to the necessity of the sacrifice.

And so they greatly comforted each other;—and in what sorrow will not such mutual confidence give consolation!—and with a last expression of tender love they parted, and went comparatively happy to their rooms.

Chapter XI

IPHIGENIA

When Eleanor laid her head on her pillow that night, her mind was anxiously intent on some plan by which she might extricate her father from his misery; and, in her warm-hearted enthusiasm, self-sacrifice was decided on as the means to be adopted. Was not so good an Agamemnon worthy of an Iphigenia? She would herself personally implore John Bold to desist from his undertaking; she would explain to him her father's sorrows, the cruel misery of his position; she would tell him how her father would die if he were thus dragged before the public and exposed to such unmerited ignominy; she would appeal to his old friendship, to his generosity, to his manliness, to his mercy; if need were, she would kneel to him for the favour she would ask; but before she did this the idea of love must be banished. There must be no bargain in the matter. To his mercy, to his generosity, she could appeal; but as a pure maiden, hitherto even unsolicited, she could not appeal to his love, nor under such circumstances could she allow him to do so. Of course, when so provoked he would declare his passion; that was to be expected; there had been enough between them to make such a fact sure; but it was equally certain that he must be rejected. She could not be understood as saying, Make my father free and I am the reward. There would be no sacrifice in that;—not so had Jephthah's daughter saved her father;—not so could she show to that kindest, dearest of parents how much she was able to bear for his good. No; to one resolve must her whole soul be bound; and so resolving, she felt that she could make her great request to Bold with as much self-assured confidence as she could have done to his grandfather.

And now I own I have fears for my heroine; not as to the upshot of her mission,—not in the least as to that; as to the full success of her generous scheme, and the ultimate result of such a project, no one conversant with human nature and novels can have a doubt; but as to the amount of sympathy she may receive from those of her own sex. Girls below twenty and old ladies above sixty will do her justice; for in the female heart the soft springs of sweet romance reopen after many years, and again gush out with waters pure as in earlier days, and greatly refresh the path that leads downwards to the grave. But I fear that the majority of those between these two eras will not approve of Eleanor's plan. I fear that unmarried ladies of thirty-five will declare that there can be no probability of so absurd a project being carried through; that young women on their knees before their lovers are sure to get kissed, and that they would not put themselves in such a position did they not expect it; that Eleanor is going to Bold only because circumstances prevent Bold from coming to her; that she is certainly a little fool, or a little schemer, but that in all probability she is thinking a good deal more about herself than her father.

Dear ladies, you are right as to your appreciation of the circumstances, but very wrong as to Miss Harding's character. Miss Harding was much younger than you are, and could not, therefore, know, as you may do, to what dangers such an encounter might expose her. She may get kissed; I think it very probable that she will; but I give my solemn word and positive assurance, that the remotest idea of such a catastrophe never occurred to her as she made the great resolve now alluded to.

And then she slept; and then she rose refreshed; and met her father with her kindest embrace and most loving smiles; and on the whole their breakfast was by no means so triste as had been their dinner the day before; and then, making some excuse to her father for so soon leaving him, she started on the commencement of her operations.

She knew that John Bold was in London, and that, therefore, the scene itself could not be enacted to-day; but she also knew that he was soon to be home, probably on the next day, and it was necessary that some little plan for meeting him should be concerted with his sister Mary. When she got up to the house, she went, as usual, into the morning sitting-room, and was startled by perceiving, by a stick, a greatcoat, and sundry parcels which were lying about, that Bold must already have returned.

"John has come back so suddenly," said Mary, coming into the room; "he has been travelling all night."

"Then I'll come up again some other time," said Eleanor, about to beat a retreat in her sudden dismay.

"He's out now, and will be for the next two hours," said the other; "he's with that horrid Finney; he only came to see him, and he returns by the mail train tonight."

Returns by the mail train tonight, thought Eleanor to herself, as she strove to screw up her courage;—away again tonight;—then it must be now or never; and she again sat down, having risen to go.

She wished the ordeal could have been postponed: she had fully made up her mind to do the deed, but she had not made up her mind to do it this very day; and now she felt ill at ease, astray, and in difficulty.

"Mary," she began, "I must see your brother before he goes back."

"Oh yes, of course," said the other; "I know he'll be delighted to see you;" and she tried to treat it as a matter of course, but she was not the less surprised; for Mary and Eleanor had daily talked over John Bold and his conduct, and his love, and Mary would insist on calling Eleanor her sister, and would scold her for not calling Bold by his Christian name; and Eleanor would half confess her love, but like a modest maiden would protest against such familiarities even with the name of her lover; and so they talked hour after hour, and Mary Bold, who was much the elder, looked forward with happy confidence to the day when Eleanor would not be ashamed to call her her sister. She was, however, fully sure that just at present Eleanor would be much more likely to avoid her brother than to seek him.

"Mary, I must see your brother, now, to-day, and beg from him a great favour;" and she spoke with a solemn air, not at all usual to her; and then she went on, and opened to her friend all her plan, her well-weighed scheme for saving her father from a sorrow which would, she said, if it lasted, bring him to his grave. "But, Mary," she continued, "you must now, you know, cease any joking about me and Mr Bold; you must now say no more about that; I am not ashamed to beg this favour from your brother, but when I have done so, there can never be anything further between us;" and this she said with a staid and solemn air, quite worthy of Jephthah's daughter or of Iphigenia either.

It was quite clear that Mary Bold did not follow the argument. That Eleanor Harding should appeal, on behalf of her father, to Bold's better feelings seemed to Mary quite natural; it seemed quite natural that he should relent, overcome by such filial tears, and by so much beauty; but, to her thinking, it was at any rate equally natural, that having relented, John should put his arm round his mistress's waist, and say: "Now having settled that, let us be man and wife, and all will end happily!" Why his good nature should not be rewarded, when such reward would operate to the disadvantage of none, Mary, who had more sense than romance, could not understand; and she said as much.

Eleanor, however, was firm, and made quite an eloquent speech to support her own view of the question: she could not condescend, she said, to ask such a favour on any other terms than those proposed. Mary might, perhaps, think her high-flown, but she had her own ideas, and she could not submit to sacrifice her self-respect.

"But I am sure you love him;—don't you?" pleaded Mary; "and I am sure he loves you better than anything in the world."

Eleanor was going to make another speech, but a tear came to each eye, and she could not; so she pretended to blow her nose, and walked to the window, and made a little inward call on her own courage, and finding herself somewhat sustained, said sententiously: "Mary, this is nonsense."

"But you do love him," said Mary, who had followed her friend to the window, and now spoke with her arms close wound round the other's waist. "You do love him with all your heart,—you know you do; I defy you to deny it."

"I—" commenced Eleanor, turning sharply round to refute the charge; but the intended falsehood stuck in her throat, and never came to utterance. She could not deny her love, so she took plentifully to tears, and leant upon her friend's bosom and sobbed there, and protested that, love or no love, it would make no difference in her resolve, and called Mary, a thousand times, the most cruel of girls, and swore her to secrecy by a hundred oaths, and ended by declaring that the girl who could betray her friend's love, even to a brother, would be as black a traitor as a soldier in a garrison who should open the city gates to the enemy. While they were yet discussing the matter, Bold returned, and Eleanor was forced into sudden action: she had either to accomplish or abandon her plan; and having slipped into her friend's bedroom, as the gentleman closed the hall door, she washed the marks of tears from her eyes, and resolved within herself to go through with it. "Tell him I am here," said she, "and coming in; and mind, whatever you do, don't leave us." So Mary informed her brother, with a somewhat sombre air, that Miss Harding was in the next room, and was coming to speak to him.

Eleanor was certainly thinking more of her father than herself, as she arranged her hair before the glass, and removed the traces of sorrow from her face; and yet I should be untrue if I said that she was not anxious to appear well before her lover: why else was she so sedulous with that stubborn curl that would rebel against her hand, and smooth so eagerly her ruffled ribands? why else did she damp her eyes to dispel the redness, and bite her pretty lips to bring back the colour? Of course she was anxious to look her best, for she was but a mortal angel after all. But had she been immortal, had she flitted back to the sitting-room on a cherub's wings, she could not have had a more faithful heart, or a truer wish to save her father at any cost to herself.

John Bold had not met her since the day when she left him in dudgeon in the cathedral close. Since then his whole time had been occupied in promoting the cause against her father, and not unsuccessfully. He had often thought of her, and turned over in his mind a hundred schemes for showing her how disinterested was his love. He would write to her and beseech her not to allow the performance of a public duty to injure him in her estimation; he would write to Mr Harding, explain all his views, and boldly claim the warden's daughter, urging that the untoward circumstances between them need be no bar to their ancient friendship, or to a closer tie; he would throw himself on his knees before his mistress; he would wait and marry the daughter when the father has lost his home and his income; he would give up the lawsuit and go to Australia, with her of course, leaving *The Jupiter* and Mr Finney to complete the case between them. Sometimes as he woke in the morning fevered and impatient, he would blow out his brains and have done with all his cares;—but this idea was generally consequent on an imprudent supper enjoyed in company with Tom Towers.

How beautiful Eleanor appeared to him as she slowly walked into the room! Not for nothing had all those little cares been taken. Though her sister, the archdeacon's wife, had spoken slightingly of her charms, Eleanor was very beautiful when seen aright. Hers was not of those impassive faces, which have the beauty of a marble bust; finely chiselled features, perfect in every line, true to the rules of symmetry, as lovely to a stranger as to a friend, unvarying unless in sickness, or as age affects them. She had no startling brilliancy of beauty, no pearly whiteness, no radiant carnation. She had not the majestic contour that rivets attention, demands instant wonder, and then disappoints by the coldness of its charms. You might pass Eleanor Harding in the street without notice, but you could hardly pass an evening with her and not lose your heart.

She had never appeared more lovely to her lover than she now did. Her face was animated though it was serious, and her full dark lustrous eyes shone with anxious energy; her hand trembled as she took his, and she could hardly pronounce his name, when she addressed him. Bold wished with all his heart that the Australian scheme was in the act of realisation, and that he and Eleanor were away together, never to hear further of the lawsuit.

He began to talk, asked after her health,—said something about London being very stupid, and more about Barchester being very pleasant; declared the weather to be very hot, and then inquired after Mr Harding.

"My father is not very well," said Eleanor.

John Bold was very sorry,—so sorry: he hoped it was nothing serious, and put on the unmeaningly solemn face which people usually use on such occasions.

"I especially want to speak to you about my father, Mr Bold; indeed, I am now here on purpose to do so. Papa is very unhappy, very unhappy indeed, about this affair of the hospital: you would pity him, Mr Bold, if you could see how wretched it has made him."

"Oh, Miss Harding!"

"Indeed you would;—anyone would pity him; but a friend, an old friend as you are,—indeed you would. He is an altered man; his cheerfulness has all gone, and his sweet temper, and his kind happy tone of voice; you would hardly know him if you saw him, Mr Bold, he is so much altered; and—and—if this goes on, he will die." Here Eleanor had recourse to her handkerchief, and so also had her auditors; but she plucked up her courage, and went on with her tale. "He will break his heart, and die. I am sure, Mr Bold, it was not you who wrote those cruel things in the newspaper—"

John Bold eagerly protested that it was not, but his heart smote him as to his intimate alliance with Tom Towers.

"No, I am sure it was not; and papa has not for a moment thought so; you would not be so cruel;—but it has nearly killed him. Papa cannot bear to think that people should so speak of him, and that everybody should hear him so spoken of:—they have called him avaricious, and dishonest, and they say he is robbing the old men, and taking the money of the hospital for nothing."

"I have never said so, Miss Harding. I—"

"No," continued Eleanor, interrupting him, for she was now in the full flood-tide of her eloquence; "no, I am sure you have not; but others have said so; and if this goes on, if such things are written again, it will kill papa. Oh! Mr Bold, if you only knew the state he is in! Now papa does not care much about money."

Both her auditors, brother and sister, assented to this, and declared on their own knowledge that no man lived less addicted to filthy lucre than the warden.

"Oh! it's so kind of you to say so, Mary, and of you too, Mr Bold. I couldn't bear that people should think unjustly of papa. Do you know he would give up the hospital altogether, only he cannot. The archdeacon says it would be cowardly, and that he would be deserting his order, and injuring the church. Whatever may happen, papa will not do that: he would leave the place to-morrow willingly, and give up his house, and the income and all, if the archdeacon—"

Eleanor was going to say "would let him," but she stopped herself before she had compromised her father's dignity; and giving a long sigh, she added—"Oh, I do so wish he would."

"No one who knows Mr Harding personally accuses him for a moment," said Bold.

"It is he that has to bear the punishment; it is he that suffers," said Eleanor; "and what for? what has he done wrong? how has he deserved this persecution? he that never had an unkind thought in his life, he that never said an unkind word!" and here she broke down, and the violence of her sobs stopped her utterance.

Bold, for the fifth or sixth time, declared that neither he nor any of his friends imputed any blame personally to Mr Harding.

"Then why should he be persecuted?" ejaculated Eleanor through her tears, forgetting in her eagerness that her intention had been to humble herself as a suppliant before John Bold;—"why should he be singled out for scorn and disgrace? why should he be made so wretched? Oh! Mr Bold,"—and she turned towards him as though the kneeling scene were about to be commenced,—"oh! Mr Bold, why did you begin all this? You, whom we all so—so—valued!"

To speak the truth, the reformer's punishment was certainly come upon him, for his present plight was not enviable; he had nothing for it but to excuse himself by platitudes about public duty, which it is by no means worth while to repeat, and to reiterate his eulogy on Mr Harding's character. His position was certainly a cruel one: had any gentleman called upon him on behalf of Mr Harding he could of course have declined to enter upon the subject; but how could he do so with a beautiful girl, with the daughter of the man whom he had injured, with his own love?

In the meantime Eleanor recollected herself, and again summoned up her energies. "Mr Bold," said she, "I have come here to implore you to abandon this proceeding." He stood up from his seat, and looked beyond measure distressed. "To implore you to abandon it, to implore you to spare my father, to spare either his life or his reason, for one or the other will pay the forfeit if this goes on. I know how much I am asking, and how little right I have to ask anything; but I think you will listen to me as it is for my father. Oh, Mr Bold, pray, pray do this for us;—pray do not drive to distraction a man who has loved you so well."

She did not absolutely kneel to him, but she followed him as he moved from his chair, and laid her soft hands imploringly upon his arm. Ah! at any other time how exquisitely valuable would have been that touch! but now he was distraught, dumbfounded, and unmanned. What could he say to that sweet suppliant; how explain to her that the matter now was probably beyond his control; how tell her that he could not quell the storm which he had raised?

"Surely, surely, John, you cannot refuse her," said his sister.

"I would give her my soul," said he, "if it would serve her."

"Oh, Mr Bold," said Eleanor, "do not speak so; I ask nothing for myself; and what I ask for my father, it cannot harm you to grant."

"I would give her my soul, if it would serve her," said Bold, still addressing his sister; "everything I have is hers, if she will accept it; my house, my heart, my all; every hope of my breast is centred in her; her smiles are sweeter to me than the sun, and when I see her in sorrow as she now is, every nerve in my body suffers. No man can love better than I love her."

"No, no, no," ejaculated Eleanor; "there can be no talk of love between us. Will you protect my father from the evil you have brought upon him?"

"Oh, Eleanor, I will do anything; let me tell you how I love you!"

"No, no, no!" she almost screamed. "This is unmanly of you, Mr Bold. Will you, will you, will you leave my father to die in peace in his quiet home?" and seizing him by his arm and hand, she followed him across the room towards the door. "I will not leave you till you promise me; I'll cling to you in the street; I'll kneel to you before all the people. You shall promise me this, you shall promise me this, you shall—" And she clung to him with fixed tenacity, and reiterated her resolve with hysterical passion.

"Speak to her, John; answer her," said Mary, bewildered by the unexpected vehemence of Eleanor's manner; "you cannot have the cruelty to refuse her."

"Promise me, promise me," said Eleanor; "say that my father is safe;—one word will do. I know how true you are; say one word, and I will let you go."

She still held him, and looked eagerly into his face, with her hair dishevelled and her eyes all bloodshot. She had no thought now of herself, no care now for her appearance; and yet he thought he had never seen her half so lovely; he was amazed at the intensity of her beauty, and could hardly believe that it was she whom he had dared to love. "Promise me," said she; "I will not leave you till you have promised me."

"I will," said he at length; "I do—all I can do, I will do."

"Then may God Almighty bless you for ever and ever!" said Eleanor; and falling on her knees with her face in Mary's lap, she wept and sobbed like a child: her strength had carried her through her allotted task, but now it was well nigh exhausted.

In a while she was partly recovered, and got up to go, and would have gone, had not Bold made her understand that it was necessary for him to explain to her how far it was in his power to put an end to the proceedings which had been taken against Mr Harding. Had he spoken on any other subject, she would have vanished, but on that she was bound to hear him; and now the danger of her position commenced. While she had an active part to play, while she clung to him as a suppliant, it was easy enough for her to reject his proffered love, and cast from her his caressing words; but now—now that he had yielded, and was talking to her calmly and kindly as to her father's welfare, it was hard enough for her to do so. Then Mary Bold assisted her; but now she was quite on her brother's side. Mary said but little, but every word she did say gave some direct and deadly blow. The first thing she did was to make room for her brother between herself and Eleanor on the sofa: as the sofa was full large for three, Eleanor could not resent this, nor could she show suspicion by taking another seat; but she felt it to be a most unkind proceeding. And then Mary would talk as though they three were joined in some close peculiar bond together; as though they were in future always to wish together, contrive together, and act together; and Eleanor could not gainsay this; she could not make another speech, and say, "Mr Bold and I are strangers, Mary, and are always to remain so!"

He explained to her that, though undoubtedly the proceeding against the hospital had commenced solely with himself, many others were now interested in the matter, some of whom were much more influential than himself; that it was to him alone, however, that the lawyers looked for instruction as to their doings, and, more important still, for the payment of their bills; and he promised that he would at once give them notice that it was his intention to abandon the cause. He thought, he said, that it was not probable that any active steps would be taken after he had seceded from the matter, though it was possible that some passing allusion might still be made to the hospital in the daily *Jupiter*. He promised, however, that he would use his best influence to prevent any further personal allusion being made to Mr Harding. He then suggested that he would on that afternoon ride over himself to Dr Grantly, and inform him of his altered intentions on the subject, and with this view, he postponed his immediate return to London.

This was all very pleasant, and Eleanor did enjoy a sort of triumph in the feeling that she had attained the object for which she had sought this interview; but still the part of Iphigenia was to be played out. The gods had heard her prayer, granted her request, and were they not to have their promised sacrifice? Eleanor was not a girl to defraud them wilfully; so, as soon as she decently could, she got up for her bonnet.

"Are you going so soon?" said Bold, who half an hour since would have given a hundred pounds that he was in London, and she still at Barchester.

"Oh yes!" said she. "I am so much obliged to you; papa will feel this to be so kind." She did not quite appreciate all her father's feelings. "Of course I must tell him, and I will say that you will see the archdeacon."

"But may I not say one word for myself?" said Bold.

"I'll fetch you your bonnet, Eleanor," said Mary, in the act of leaving the room.

"Mary, Mary," said she, getting up and catching her by her dress; "don't go, I'll get my bonnet myself." But Mary, the traitress, stood fast by the door, and permitted no such retreat. Poor Iphigenia!

And with a volley of impassioned love, John Bold poured forth the feelings of his heart, swearing, as men do, some truths and many falsehoods; and Eleanor repeated with every shade of vehemence the "No, no, no," which had had a short time since so much effect; but now, alas! its strength was gone. Let her be never so vehement, her vehemence was not respected; all her "No, no, no's" were met with counter-asseverations, and at last were overpowered. The ground was cut from under her on every side. She was pressed to say whether her father would object; whether she herself had any aversion (aversion! God help her, poor girl! the word nearly made her jump into his arms); any other preference (this she loudly disclaimed); whether it was impossible that she should love him (Eleanor could not say that it was impossible): and so at last all her defences demolished, all her maiden barriers swept away, she capitulated, or rather marched out with the honours of war, vanquished evidently, palpably vanquished, but still not reduced to the necessity of confessing it.

And so the altar on the shore of the modern Aulis reeked with no sacrifice.

Chapter XII

MR BOLD'S VISIT TO PLUMSTEAD

Whether or no the ill-natured prediction made by certain ladies in the beginning of the last chapter was or was not carried out to the letter, I am not in a position to state. Eleanor, however, certainly did feel herself to have been baffled as she returned home with all her news to her father. Certainly she had been victorious, certainly she had achieved her object, certainly she was not unhappy, and yet she did not feel herself triumphant. Everything would run smooth now. Eleanor was not at all addicted to the Lydian school of romance; she by no means objected to her lover because he came in at the door under the name of Absolute, instead of pulling her out of a window under the name of Beverley; and yet she felt that she had been imposed upon, and could hardly think of Mary Bold with sisterly charity. "I did think I could have trusted Mary," she said to herself over and over again. "Oh that she should have dared to keep me in the room when I tried to get out!" Eleanor, however, felt that the game was up, and that she had now nothing further to do but to add to the budget of news which was prepared for her father, that John Bold was her accepted lover.

We will, however, now leave her on her way, and go with John Bold to Plumstead Episcopi, merely premising that Eleanor on reaching home will not find things so smooth as she fondly expected; two messengers had come, one to her father and the other to the archdeacon, and each of them much opposed to her quiet mode of solving all their difficulties; the one in the shape of a number of *The Jupiter*, and the other in that of a further opinion from Sir Abraham Haphazard.

John Bold got on his horse and rode off to Plumstead Episcopi; not briskly and with eager spur, as men do ride when self-satisfied with their own intentions; but slowly, modestly, thoughtfully, and somewhat in dread of the coming interview. Now and again he would recur to the scene which was just over, support himself by the remembrance of the silence that gives consent, and exult as a happy lover. But even this feeling was not without a shade of remorse. Had he not shown himself childishly weak thus to yield up the resolve of many hours of thought to the tears of a pretty girl? How was he to meet his lawyer? How was he to back out of a matter in which his name was already so publicly concerned? What, oh what! was he to say to Tom Towers? While meditating these painful things he reached the lodge leading up to the archdeacon's glebe, and for the first time in his life found himself within the sacred precincts.

All the doctor's children were together on the slope of the lawn, close to the road, as Bold rode up to the hall door. They were there holding high debate on matters evidently of deep interest at Plumstead Episcopi, and the voices of the boys had been heard before the lodge gate was closed.

Florinda and Grizzel, frightened at the sight of so well-known an enemy to the family, fled on the first appearance of the horseman, and ran in terror to their mother's arms; not for them was it, tender branches, to resent injuries, or as members of a church militant to put on armour against its enemies. But the boys stood their ground like heroes, and boldly demanded the business of the intruder.

"Do you want to see anybody here, sir?" said Henry, with a defiant eye and a hostile tone, which plainly said that at any rate no one there wanted to see the person so addressed; and as he spoke he brandished aloft his garden water-pot, holding it by the spout, ready for the braining of anyone.

"Henry," said Charles James slowly, and with a certain dignity of diction, "Mr Bold of course would not have come without wanting to see someone; if Mr Bold has a proper ground for wanting to see some person here, of course he has a right to come."

But Samuel stepped lightly up to the horse's head, and offered his services. "Oh, Mr Bold," said he, "papa, I'm sure, will be glad to see you; I suppose you want to see papa. Shall I hold your horse for you? Oh what a very pretty horse!" and he turned his head and winked funnily at his brothers. "Papa has heard such good news about the old hospital to-day. We know you'll be glad to hear it, because you're such a friend of grandpapa Harding, and so much in love with Aunt Nelly!"

"How d'ye do, lads?" said Bold, dismounting. "I want to see your father if he's at home."

"Lads!" said Henry, turning on his heel and addressing himself to his brother, but loud enough to be heard by Bold; "lads, indeed! if we're lads, what does he call himself?"

Charles James condescended to say nothing further, but cocked his hat with much precision, and left the visitor to the care of his youngest brother.

Samuel stayed till the servant came, chatting and patting the horse; but as soon as Bold had disappeared through the front door, he stuck a switch under the animal's tail to make him kick if possible.

The church reformer soon found himself *tête-à-tête* with the archdeacon in that same room, in that sanctum sanctorum of the rectory, to which we have already been introduced. As he entered he heard the click of a certain patent lock, but it struck him with no surprise; the worthy clergyman was no doubt hiding from eyes profane his last much-studied sermon; for the archdeacon, though he preached but seldom, was famous for his sermons. No room, Bold thought, could have been more becoming for a dignitary of the church; each wall was loaded with theology; over each separate bookcase was printed in small gold letters the names of those great divines whose works were ranged beneath: beginning from the early fathers in due chronological order, there were to be found the precious labours of the chosen servants of the church down to the last pamphlet written in opposition to the consecration of Dr Hampden; and raised above this were to be seen the busts of the greatest among the great: Chrysostom, St Augustine, Thomas à Becket, Cardinal Wolsey, Archbishop Laud, and Dr Philpotts.

Every appliance that could make study pleasant and give ease to the overtoiled brain was there; chairs made to relieve each limb and muscle; reading-desks and writing-desks to suit every attitude; lamps and candles mechanically contrived to throw their light on any favoured spot, as the student might desire; a shoal of newspapers to amuse the few leisure moments which might be stolen from the labours of the day; and then from the window a view right through a bosky vista along which ran a broad green path from the rectory to the church,—at the end of which the tawny-tinted fine old tower was seen with all its variegated pinnacles and parapets. Few parish churches in England are in better repair, or better worth keeping so, than that at Plumstead Episcopi; and yet it is built in a faulty style: the body of the church is low,—so low, that the nearly flat leaden roof would be visible from the churchyard, were it not for the carved parapet with which it is surrounded. It is cruciform, though the transepts are irregular, one being larger than the other; and the tower is much too high in proportion to the church. But the colour of the building is perfect; it is that rich yellow gray which one finds nowhere but in the south and west of England, and which is so strong a characteristic of most of our old houses of Tudor architecture. The stone work also is beautiful; the mullions of the windows and the thick tracery of the Gothic workmanship is as rich as fancy can desire; and though in gazing on such a structure one knows by rule that the old priests who built it, built it wrong, one cannot bring oneself to wish that they should have made it other than it is.

When Bold was ushered into the book-room, he found its owner standing with his back to the empty fire-place ready to receive him, and he could not but perceive that that expansive brow was elated with triumph, and that those full heavy lips bore more prominently than usual an appearance of arrogant success.

"Well, Mr Bold," said he;—"well, what can I do for you? Very happy, I can assure you, to do anything for such a friend of my father-in-law."

"I hope you'll excuse my calling, Dr Grantly."

"Certainly, certainly," said the archdeacon; "I can assure you, no apology is necessary from Mr Bold;—only let me know what I can do for him."

Dr Grantly was standing himself, and he did not ask Bold to sit, and therefore he had to tell his tale standing, leaning on the table, with his hat in his hand. He did, however, manage to tell it; and as the archdeacon never once interrupted him, or even encouraged him by a single word, he was not long in coming to the end of it.

"And so, Mr Bold, I'm to understand, I believe, that you are desirous of abandoning this attack upon Mr Harding."

"Oh, Dr Grantly, there has been no attack, I can assure you—"

"Well, well, we won't quarrel about words; I should call it an attack;—most men would so call an endeavour to take away from a man every shilling of income that he has to live upon; but it sha'n't be an attack, if you don't like it; you wish to abandon this—this little game of backgammon you've begun to play."

"I intend to put an end to the legal proceedings which I have commenced."

"I understand," said the archdeacon. "You've already had enough of it; well, I can't say that I am surprised; carrying on a losing lawsuit where one has nothing to gain, but everything to pay, is not pleasant."

Bold turned very red in the face. "You misinterpret my motives," said he; "but, however, that is of little consequence. I did not come to trouble you with my motives, but to tell you a matter of fact. Good-morning, Dr Grantly."

"One moment,—one moment," said the other. "I don't exactly appreciate the taste which induced you to make any personal communication to me on the subject; but I dare say I'm wrong, I dare say your judgment is the better of the two; but as you have done me the honour,—as you have, as it were, forced me into a certain amount of conversation on a subject which had better, perhaps, have been left to our lawyers, you will excuse me if I ask you to hear my reply to your communication."

"I am in no hurry, Dr Grantly."

"Well, I am, Mr Bold; my time is not exactly leisure time, and, therefore, if you please, we'll go to the point at once:—you're going to abandon this lawsuit?"—and he paused for a reply.

"Yes, Dr Grantly, I am."

"Having exposed a gentleman who was one of your father's warmest friends to all the ignominy and insolence which the press could heap upon his name, having somewhat ostentatiously declared that it was your duty as a man of high public virtue to protect those poor old fools whom you have humbugged there at the hospital, you now find that the game costs more than it's worth, and so you make up your mind to have done with it. A prudent resolution, Mr Bold; but it is a pity you should have been so long coming to it. Has it struck you that we may not now choose to give over? that we may find it necessary to punish the injury you have done to us? Are you aware, sir, that we have gone to enormous expense to resist this iniquitous attempt of yours?"

Bold's face was now furiously red, and he nearly crushed his hat between his hands; but he said nothing.

"We have found it necessary to employ the best advice that money could procure. Are you aware, sir, what may be the probable cost of securing the services of the attorney-general?"

"Not in the least, Dr Grantly."

"I dare say not, sir. When you recklessly put this affair into the hands of your friend Mr Finney, whose six-and-eightpences and thirteen-and-fourpences may, probably, not amount to a large sum, you were indifferent as to the cost and suffering which such a proceeding might entail on others; but are you aware, sir, that these crushing costs must now come out of your own pocket?"

"Any demand of such a nature which Mr Harding's lawyer may have to make will doubtless be made to my lawyer."

"'Mr Harding's lawyer and my lawyer!' Did you come here merely to refer me to the lawyers? Upon my word I think the honour of your visit might have been spared! And now, sir, I'll tell you what my opinion is:—my opinion is, that we shall not allow you to withdraw this matter from the courts."

"You can do as you please, Dr Grantly; good-morning."

"Hear me out, sir," said the archdeacon; "I have here in my hands the last opinion given in this matter by Sir Abraham Haphazard. I dare say you have already heard of this;—I dare say it has had something to do with your visit here to-day."

"I know nothing whatever of Sir Abraham Haphazard or his opinion."

"Be that as it may, here it is; he declares most explicitly that under no phasis of the affair whatever have you a leg to stand upon; that Mr Harding is as safe in his hospital as I am here in my rectory; that a more futile attempt to destroy a man was never made, than this which you have made to ruin Mr Harding. Here," and he slapped the paper on the table, "I have this opinion from the very first lawyer in the land; and under these circumstances you expect me to make you a low bow for your kind offer to release Mr Harding from the toils of your net! Sir, your net is not strong enough to hold him; sir, your net has fallen to pieces, and you knew that well enough before I told you;—and now, sir, I'll wish you good-morning, for I'm busy."

Bold was now choking with passion. He had let the archdeacon run on because he knew not with what words to interrupt him; but now that he had been so defied and insulted, he could not leave the room without some reply.

"Dr Grantly," he commenced.

"I have nothing further to say or to hear," said the archdeacon. "I'll do myself the honour to order your horse." And he rang the bell.

"I came here, Dr Grantly, with the warmest, kindest feelings—"

"Oh, of course you did; nobody doubts it."

"With the kindest feelings;—and they have been most grossly outraged by your treatment."

"Of course they have;—I have not chosen to see my father-in-law ruined; what an outrage that has been to your feelings!"

"The time will come, Dr Grantly, when you will understand why I called upon you to-day."

"No doubt, no doubt. Is Mr Bold's horse there? That's right; open the front door. Good-morning, Mr Bold;" and the doctor stalked into his own drawing-room, closing the door behind him, and making it quite impossible that John Bold should speak another word.

As he got on his horse, which he was fain to do feeling like a dog turned out of a kitchen, he was again greeted by little Sammy.

"Good-bye, Mr Bold; I hope we may have the pleasure of seeing you again before long; I am sure papa will always be glad to see you."

That was certainly the bitterest moment in John Bold's life. Not even the remembrance of his successful love could comfort him; nay, when he thought of Eleanor he felt that it was that very love which had brought him to such a pass. That he should have been so insulted, and be unable to reply! That he should have given up so much to the request of a girl, and then have had his motives so misunderstood! That he should have made so gross a mistake as this visit of his to the archdeacon's! He bit the top of his whip, till he penetrated the horn of which it was made: he struck the poor animal in his anger, and then was doubly angry with himself at his futile passion. He had been so completely checkmated, so palpably overcome! and what was he to do? He could not continue his action after pledging himself to abandon it; nor was there any revenge in that;—it was the very step to which his enemy had endeavoured to goad him!

He threw the reins to the servant who came to take his horse, and rushed upstairs into his drawing-room, where his sister Mary was sitting.

"If there be a devil," said he, "a real devil here on earth, it is Dr Grantly." He vouchsafed her no further intelligence, but again seizing his hat, he rushed out, and took his departure for London without another word to anyone.

Chapter XIII

THE WARDEN'S DECISION

The meeting between Eleanor and her father was not so stormy as that described in the last chapter, but it was hardly more successful. On her return from Bold's house she found her father in a strange state. He was not sorrowful and silent as he had been on that memorable day when his son-in-law lectured him as to all that he owed to his order; nor was he in his usual quiet mood. When Eleanor reached the hospital, he was walking to and fro upon the lawn, and she soon saw that he was much excited.

"I am going to London, my dear," he said as soon as he saw her.

"London, papa!"

"Yes, my dear, to London; I will have this matter settled some way; there are some things, Eleanor, which I cannot bear."

"Oh, papa, what is it?" said she, leading him by the arm into the house. "I had such good news for you, and now you make me fear I am too late." And then, before he could let her know what had caused this sudden resolve, or could point to the fatal paper which lay on the table, she told him that the lawsuit was over, that Bold had commissioned her to assure her father in his name that it would be abandoned,—that there was no further cause for misery, that the whole matter might be looked on as though it had never been discussed. She did not tell him with what determined vehemence she had obtained this concession in his favour, nor did she mention the price she was to pay for it.

The warden did not express himself peculiarly gratified at this intelligence, and Eleanor, though she had not worked for thanks, and was by no means disposed to magnify her own good offices, felt hurt at the manner in which her news was received. "Mr Bold can act as he thinks proper, my love," said he; "if Mr Bold thinks he has been wrong, of course he will discontinue what he is doing; but that cannot change my purpose."

"Oh, papa!" she exclaimed, all but crying with vexation; "I thought you would have been so happy;—I thought all would have been right now."

"Mr Bold," continued he, "has set great people to work,—so great that I doubt they are now beyond his control. Read that, my dear." The warden, doubling up a number of *The Jupiter*, pointed to the peculiar article which she was to read. It was to the last of the three leaders, which are generally furnished daily for the support of the nation, that Mr Harding directed her attention. It dealt some heavy blows on various clerical delinquents; on families who received their tens of thousands yearly for doing nothing; on men who, as the article stated, rolled in wealth which they had neither earned nor inherited, and which was in fact stolen from the poorer clergy. It named some sons of bishops, and grandsons of archbishops; men great in their way, who had redeemed their disgrace in the eyes of many by the enormity of their plunder; and then, having disposed of these leviathans, it descended to Mr Harding.

We alluded some weeks since to an instance of similar injustice, though in a more humble scale, in which the warden of an almshouse at Barchester has become possessed of the income of the greater part of the whole institution. Why an almshouse should have a warden we cannot pretend to explain, nor can we say what special need twelve old men can have for the services of a separate clergyman, seeing that they have twelve reserved seats for themselves in Barchester Cathedral. But be this as it may, let the gentleman call himself warden or precentor, or what he will, let him be never so scrupulous in exacting religious duties from his twelve dependents, or never so negligent as regards the services of the cathedral, it appears palpably clear that he can be entitled to no portion of the revenue of the hospital, excepting that which the founder set apart for him; and it is equally clear that the founder did not intend that three-fifths of his charity should be so consumed.

The case is certainly a paltry one after the tens of thousands with which we have been dealing, for the warden's income is after all but a poor eight hundred a year: eight hundred a year is not magnificent preferment of itself, and the warden may, for anything we know, be worth much more to the church; but if so, let the church pay him out of funds justly at its own disposal.

We allude to the question of the Barchester almshouse at the present moment, because we understand that a plea has been set up which will be peculiarly revolting to the minds of English churchmen. An action has been taken against Mr Warden Harding, on behalf of the almsmen, by a gentleman acting solely on public grounds, and it is to be argued that Mr Harding takes nothing but what he received as a servant of the hospital, and that he is not himself responsible for the amount of stipend given to him for his work. Such a plea would doubtless be fair, if anyone questioned the daily wages of a bricklayer employed on the building, or the fee of the charwoman who cleans it; but we cannot envy the feeling of a clergyman of the Church of England who could allow such an argument to be put in his mouth.

If this plea be put forward we trust Mr Harding will be forced as a witness to state the nature of his employment; the amount of work that he does; the income which he receives; and the source from whence he obtained his appointment. We do not think he will receive much public sympathy to atone for the annoyance of such an examination.

As Eleanor read the article her face flushed with indignation, and when she had finished it, she almost feared to look up at her father.

"Well, my dear," said he, "what do you think of that;—is it worth while to be a warden at that price?"

"Oh, papa;—dear papa!"

"Mr Bold can't un-write that, my dear;—Mr Bold can't say that that sha'n't be read by every clergyman at Oxford; nay, by every gentleman in the land;" and then he walked up and down the room, while Eleanor in mute despair followed him with her eyes. "And I'll tell you what, my dear," he continued, speaking now very calmly, and in a forced manner very unlike himself; "Mr Bold can't dispute the truth of every word in that article you have just read—nor can I." Eleanor stared at him, as though she scarcely understood the words he was speaking. "Nor can I, Eleanor: that's the worst of all, or would be so if there were no remedy. I have thought much of all this since we were together last night;" and he came and sat beside her, and put his arm round her waist as he had done then. "I have thought much of what the archdeacon has said, and of what this paper says; and I do believe I have no right to be here."

"No right to be warden of the hospital, papa?"

"No right to be warden with eight hundred a year; no right to be warden with such a house as this; no right to spend in luxury money that was intended for charity. Mr Bold may do as he pleases about his suit, but I hope he will not abandon it for my sake."

Poor Eleanor! this was hard upon her. Was it for this she had made her great resolve! For this that she had laid aside her quiet demeanour, and taken upon her the rants of a tragedy heroine! One may work and not for thanks, but yet feel hurt at not receiving them; and so it was with Eleanor: one may be disinterested in one's good actions, and yet feel discontented that they are not recognised. Charity may be given with the left hand so privily that the right hand does not know it, and yet the left hand may regret to feel that it has no immediate reward. Eleanor had had no wish to burden her father with a weight of obligation, and yet she had looked forward to much delight from the knowledge that she had freed him from his sorrows: now such hopes were entirely over: all that she had done was of no avail; she had humbled herself to Bold in vain; the evil was utterly beyond her power to cure!

She had thought also how gently she would whisper to her father all that her lover had said to her about herself, and how impossible she had found it to reject him: and then she had anticipated her father's kindly kiss and close embrace as he gave his sanction to her love. Alas! she could say nothing of this now. In speaking of Mr Bold, her father put him aside as one whose thoughts and sayings and acts could be of no moment. Gentle reader, did you ever feel yourself snubbed? Did you ever, when thinking much of your own importance, find yourself suddenly reduced to a nonentity? Such was Eleanor's feeling now.

"They shall not put forward this plea on my behalf," continued the warden. "Whatever may be the truth of the matter, that at any rate is not true; and the man who wrote that article is right in saying that such a plea is revolting to an honest mind. I will go up to London, my dear, and see these lawyers myself, and if no better excuse can be made for me than that, I and the hospital will part."

"But the archdeacon, papa?"

"I can't help it, my dear; there are some things which a man cannot bear:—I cannot bear that;" and he put his hand upon the newspaper.

"But will the archdeacon go with you?"

To tell the truth, Mr Harding had made up his mind to steal a march upon the archdeacon. He was aware that he could take no steps without informing his dread son-in-law, but he had resolved that he would send out a note to Plumstead Episcopi detailing his plans, but that the messenger should not leave Barchester till he himself had started for London; so that he might be a day before the doctor, who, he had no doubt, would follow him. In that day, if he had luck, he might arrange it all; he might explain to Sir Abraham that he, as warden, would have nothing further to do with the defence about to be set up; he might send in his official resignation to his friend the bishop, and so make public the whole transaction, that even the doctor would not be able to undo what he had done. He knew too well the doctor's strength and his own weakness to suppose he could do this, if they both reached London together; indeed, he would never be able to get to London, if the doctor knew of his intended journey in time to prevent it.

"No, I think not," said he. "I think I shall start before the archdeacon could be ready;—I shall go early to-morrow morning."

"That will be best, papa," said Eleanor, showing that her father's ruse was appreciated.

"Why yes, my love. The fact is, I wish to do all this before the archdeacon can—can interfere. There is a great deal of truth in all he says;—he argues very well, and I can't always answer him; but there is an old saying, Nelly: 'Everyone knows where his own shoe pinches!' He'll say that I want moral courage, and strength of character, and power of endurance, and it's all true; but I'm sure I ought not to remain here, if I have nothing better to put forward than a quibble: so, Nelly, we shall have to leave this pretty place."

Eleanor's face brightened up, as she assured her father how cordially she agreed with him.

"True, my love," said he, now again quite happy and at ease in his manner. "What good to us is this place or all the money, if we are to be ill-spoken of?"

"Oh, papa, I am so glad!"

"My darling child! It did cost me a pang at first, Nelly, to think that you should lose your pretty drawing-room, and your ponies, and your garden: the garden will be the worst of all;—but there is a garden at Crabtree, a very pretty garden."

Crabtree Parva was the name of the small living which Mr Harding had held as a minor canon, and which still belonged to him. It was only worth some eighty pounds a year, and a small house and glebe, all of which were now handed over to Mr Harding's curate; but it was to Crabtree glebe that Mr Harding thought of retiring. This parish must not be mistaken for that other living, Crabtree Canonicorum, as it is called. Crabtree Canonicorum is a very nice thing; there are only two hundred parishioners; there are four hundred acres of glebe; and the great and small tithes, which both go to the rector, are worth four hundred pounds a year more. Crabtree Canonicorum is in the gift of the dean and chapter, and is at this time possessed by the Honourable and Reverend Dr Vesey Stanhope, who also fills the prebendal stall of Goosegorge in Barchester Chapter, and holds the united rectory of Eiderdown and Stogpingum, or Stoke Pinquium, as it should be written. This is the same Dr Vesey Stanhope whose hospitable villa on the Lake of Como is so well known to the *élite* of English travellers, and whose collection of Lombard butterflies is supposed to be unique.

"Yes," said the warden, musing, "there is a very pretty garden at Crabtree;—but I shall be sorry to disturb poor Smith." Smith was the curate of Crabtree, a gentleman who was maintaining a wife and half a dozen children on the income arising from his profession.

Eleanor assured her father that, as far as she was concerned, she could leave her house and her ponies without a single regret. She was only so happy that he was going—going where he would escape all this dreadful turmoil.

"But we will take the music, my dear."

And so they went on planning their future happiness, and plotting how they would arrange it all without the interposition of the archdeacon, and at last they again became confidential, and then the warden did thank her for what she had done, and Eleanor, lying on her father's shoulder, did find an opportunity to tell her secret: and the father gave his blessing to his child, and said that the man whom she loved was honest, good, and kind-hearted, and right-thinking in the main,—one who wanted only a good wife to put him quite upright,—"a man, my love," he ended by saying, "to whom I firmly believe that I can trust my treasure with safety."

"But what will Dr Grantly say?"

"Well, my dear, it can't be helped;—we shall be out at Crabtree then."

And Eleanor ran upstairs to prepare her father's clothes for his journey; and the warden returned to his garden to make his last adieux to every tree, and shrub, and shady nook that he knew so well.

Chapter XIV

MOUNT OLYMPUS

Wretched in spirit, groaning under the feeling of insult, self-condemning, and ill-satisfied in every way, Bold returned to his London lodgings. Ill as he had fared in his interview with the archdeacon, he was not the less under the necessity of carrying out his pledge to Eleanor; and he went about his ungracious task with a heavy heart.

The attorneys whom he had employed in London received his instructions with surprise and evident misgiving; however, they could only obey, and mutter something of their sorrow that such heavy costs should only fall upon their own employer,—especially as nothing was wanting but perseverance to throw them on the opposite party. Bold left the office which he had latterly so much frequented, shaking the dust from off his feet; and before he was down the stairs, an edict had already gone forth for the preparation of the bill.

He next thought of the newspapers. The case had been taken up by more than one; and he was well aware that the keynote had been sounded by *The Jupiter*. He had been very intimate with Tom Towers, and had often discussed with him the affairs of the hospital. Bold could not say that the articles in that paper had been written at his own instigation. He did not even know, as a fact, that they had been written by his friend. Tom Towers had never said that such a view of the case, or such a side in the dispute, would be taken by the paper with which he was connected. Very discreet in such matters was Tom Towers, and altogether indisposed to talk loosely of the concerns of that mighty engine of which it was his high privilege to move in secret some portion. Nevertheless Bold believed that to him were owing those dreadful words which had caused such panic at Barchester,—and he conceived himself bound to prevent their repetition. With this view he betook himself from the attorneys' office to that laboratory where, with amazing chemistry, Tom Towers compounded thunderbolts for the destruction of all that is evil, and for the furtherance of all that is good, in this and other hemispheres.

Who has not heard of Mount Olympus,—that high abode of all the powers of type, that favoured seat of the great goddess Pica, that wondrous habitation of gods and devils, from whence, with ceaseless hum of steam and never-ending flow of Castalian ink, issue forth fifty thousand nightly edicts for the governance of a subject nation?

Velvet and gilding do not make a throne, nor gold and jewels a sceptre. It is a throne because the most exalted one sits there,—and a sceptre because the most mighty one wields it. So it is with Mount Olympus. Should a stranger make his way thither at dull noonday, or during the sleepy hours of the silent afternoon, he would find no acknowledged temple of power and beauty, no fitting fane for the great Thunderer, no proud fa-çades and pillared roofs to support the dignity of this greatest of earthly potentates. To the outward and uninitiated eye, Mount Olympus is a somewhat humble spot,—undistinguished, unadorned,—nay, almost mean. It stands alone, as it were, in a mighty city, close to the densest throng of men, but partaking neither of the noise nor the crowd; a small secluded, dreary spot, tenanted, one would say, by quite unambitious people at the easiest rents. "Is this Mount Olympus?" asks the unbelieving stranger. "Is it from these small, dark, dingy buildings that those infallible laws proceed which cabinets are called upon to obey; by which bishops are to be guided, lords and commons controlled, judges instructed in law, generals in strategy, admirals in naval tactics, and orange-women in the management of their barrows?" "Yes, my friend—from these walls. From here issue the only known infallible bulls for the guidance of British souls and bodies. This little court is the Vatican of England. Here reigns a pope, self-nominated, self-consecrated,—ay, and much stranger too,—self-believing!—a pope whom, if you cannot obey him, I would ad-vise you to disobey as silently as possible; a pope hitherto afraid of no Luther; a pope who manages his own inquisition, who punishes unbelievers as no most skilful inquisitor of Spain ever dreamt of doing;—one who can excommunicate thoroughly, fearfully, radical-ly; put you beyond the pale of men's charity; make you odious to your dearest friends, and turn you into a monster to be pointed at by the finger!" Oh heavens! and this is Mount Olympus!

It is a fact amazing to ordinary mortals that *The Jupiter* is never wrong. With what endless care, with what unsparing labour, do we not strive to get together for our great national council the men most fitting to compose it. And how we fail! Parliament is al-ways wrong: look at *The Jupiter*, and see how futile are their meetings, how vain their council, how needless all their trouble! With what pride do we regard our chief ministers, the great servants of state, the oligarchs of the nation on whose wisdom we lean, to whom we look for guidance in our difficulties! But what are they to the writers of *The Jupiter*? They hold council together and with anxious thought painfully elaborate their country's good; but when all is done, *The Jupiter* declares that all is naught. Why should we look to Lord John Russell;—why should we regard Palmerston and Gladstone, when Tom Towers without a struggle can put us right? Look at our generals, what faults they make; at our admirals, how inactive they are. What money, honesty, and science can do, is done; and yet how badly are our troops brought together, fed, conveyed, clothed, armed, and man-aged. The most excellent of our good men do their best to man our ships, with the assistance of all possible external appliances; but in vain. All, all is wrong—alas! alas! Tom Towers, and he alone, knows all about it. Why, oh why, ye earthly ministers, why have ye not followed more closely this heaven-sent messenger that is among us?

Were it not well for us in our ignorance that we confided all things to *The Jupiter*? Would it not be wise in us to abandon useless talking, idle thinking, and profitless labour? Away with majorities in the House of Commons, with verdicts from judicial bench given after much delay, with doubtful laws, and the fallible attempts of humanity! Does not *The Jupiter*, coming forth daily with fifty thousand impressions full of unerring decision on every mortal subject, set all matters sufficiently at rest? Is not Tom Towers here, able to guide us and willing?

Yes indeed, able and willing to guide all men in all things, so long as he is obeyed as autocrat should be obeyed,—with undoubting submission: only let not ungrateful minis-ters seek other colleagues than those whom Tom Towers may approve; let church and state, law and physic, commerce and agriculture, the arts of war, and the arts of peace, all listen and obey, and all will be made perfect. Has not Tom Towers an all-seeing eye? From the diggings of Australia to those of California, right round the habitable globe, does he not know, watch, and chronicle the doings of everyone? From a bishopric in New Zealand to an unfortunate director of a North-west passage, is he not the only fit judge of capability? From the sewers of London to the Central Railway of India,—from the palaces of St Petersburg to the cabins of Connaught, nothing can escape him. Britons have but to read, to obey, and be blessed. None but the fools doubt the wisdom of *The Jupiter*; none but the mad dispute its facts.

No established religion has ever been without its unbelievers, even in the country where it is the most firmly fixed; no creed has been without scoffers; no church has so prospered as to free itself entirely from dissent. There are those who doubt *The Jupiter*! They live and breathe the upper air, walking here unscathed, though scorned,—men, born of British mothers and nursed on English milk, who scruple not to say that Mount Olympus has its price, that Tom Towers can be bought for gold!

Such is Mount Olympus, the mouthpiece of all the wisdom of this great country. It may probably be said that no place in this 19th century is more worthy of notice. No treasury mandate armed with the signatures of all the government has half the power of one of those broad sheets, which fly forth from hence so abundantly, armed with no signature at all.

Some great man, some mighty peer,—we'll say a noble duke,—retires to rest feared and honoured by all his countrymen,—fearless himself; if not a good man, at any rate a mighty man,—too mighty to care much what men may say about his want of virtue. He rises in the morning degraded, mean, and miserable; an object of men's scorn, anxious only to retire as quickly as may be to some German obscurity, some unseen Italian privacy, or indeed, anywhere out of sight. What has made this awful change? what has so afflicted him? An article has appeared in *The Jupiter*; some fifty lines of a narrow column have destroyed all his grace's equanimity, and banished him for ever from the world. No man knows who wrote the bitter words; the clubs talk confusedly of the matter, whispering to each other this and that name; while Tom Towers walks quietly along Pall Mall, with his coat buttoned close against the east wind, as though he were a mortal man, and not a god dispensing thunderbolts from Mount Olympus.

It was not to Mount Olympus that our friend Bold betook himself. He had before now wandered round that lonely spot, thinking how grand a thing it was to write articles for *The Jupiter*; considering within himself whether by any stretch of the powers within him he could ever come to such distinction; wondering how Tom Towers would take any little humble offering of his talents; calculating that Tom Towers himself must have once had a beginning, have once doubted as to his own success. Towers could not have been born a writer in *The Jupiter*. With such ideas, half ambitious and half awe-struck, had Bold regarded the silent-looking workshop of the gods; but he had never yet by word or sign attempted to influence the slightest word of his unerring friend. On such a course was he now intent; and not without much inward palpitation did he betake himself to the quiet abode of wisdom, where Tom Towers was to be found o' mornings inhaling ambrosia and sipping nectar in the shape of toast and tea.

Not far removed from Mount Olympus, but somewhat nearer to the blessed regions of the West, is the most favoured abode of Themis. Washed by the rich tide which now passes from the towers of Cæsar to Barry's halls of eloquence; and again back, with new offerings of a city's tribute, from the palaces of peers to the mart of merchants, stand those quiet walls which Law has delighted to honour by its presence. What a world within a world is the Temple! how quiet are its "entangled walks," as someone lately has called them, and yet how close to the densest concourse of humanity! how gravely respectable its sober alleys, though removed but by a single step from the profanity of the Strand and the low iniquity of Fleet Street! Old St Dunstan, with its bell-smiting bludgeoners, has been removed; the ancient shops with their faces full of pleasant history are passing away one by one; the bar itself is to go—its doom has been pronounced by *The Jupiter*; rumour tells us of some huge building that is to appear in these latitudes dedicated to law, subversive of the courts of Westminster, and antagonistic to the Rolls and Lincoln's Inn; but nothing yet threatens the silent beauty of the Temple: it is the mediæval court of the metropolis.

Here, on the choicest spot of this choice ground, stands a lofty row of chambers, looking obliquely upon the sullied Thames; before the windows, the lawn of the Temple Gardens stretches with that dim yet delicious verdure so refreshing to the eyes of Londoners. If doomed to live within the thickest of London smoke you would surely say that that would be your chosen spot. Yes, you, you whom I now address, my dear, middle-aged bachelor friend, can nowhere be so well domiciled as here. No one here will ask whether you are out or at home; alone or with friends; here no Sabbatarian will investigate your Sundays, no censorious landlady will scrutinise your empty bottle, no valetudinarian neighbour will complain of late hours. If you love books, to what place are books so suitable? The whole spot is redolent of typography. Would you worship the Paphian goddess, the groves of Cyprus are not more taciturn than those of the Temple. Wit and wine are always here, and always together; the revels of the Temple are as those of polished Greece, where the wildest worshipper of Bacchus never forgot the dignity of the god whom he adored. Where can retirement be so complete as here? where can you be so sure of all the pleasures of society?

It was here that Tom Towers lived, and cultivated with eminent success the tenth Muse who now governs the periodical press. But let it not be supposed that his chambers were such, or so comfortless, as are frequently the gaunt abodes of legal aspirants. Four chairs, a half-filled deal book-case with hangings of dingy green baize, an old office table covered with dusty papers, which are not moved once in six months, and an older Pembroke brother with rickety legs, for all daily uses; a despatcher for the preparation of lobsters and coffee, and an apparatus for the cooking of toast and mutton chops; such utensils and luxuries as these did not suffice for the well-being of Tom Towers. He indulged in four rooms on the first floor, each of which was furnished, if not with the splendour, with probably more than the comfort of Stafford House. Every addition that science and art have lately made to the luxuries of modern life was to be found there. The room in which he usually sat was surrounded by book-shelves carefully filled; nor was there a volume there which was not entitled to its place in such a collection, both by its intrinsic worth and exterior splendour: a pretty portable set of steps in one corner of the room showed that those even on the higher shelves were intended for use. The chamber contained but two works of art:—the one, an admirable bust of Sir Robert Peel, by Power, declared the individual politics of our friend; and the other, a singularly long figure of a female devotee, by Millais, told equally plainly the school of art to which he was addicted. This picture was not hung, as pictures usually are, against the wall; there was no inch of wall vacant for such a purpose: it had a stand or desk erected for its own accommodation; and there on her pedestal, framed and glazed, stood the devotional lady looking intently at a lily as no lady ever looked before.

Our modern artists, whom we style Pre-Raphaelites, have delighted to go back, not only to the finish and peculiar manner, but also to the subjects of the early painters. It is impossible to give them too much praise for the elaborate perseverance with which they have equalled the minute perfections of the masters from whom they take their inspiration: nothing probably can exceed the painting of some of these latter-day pictures. It is, however, singular into what faults they fall as regards their subjects: they are not quite content to take the old stock groups,—a Sebastian with his arrows, a Lucia with her eyes in a dish, a Lorenzo with a gridiron, or the Virgin with two children. But they are anything but happy in their change. As a rule, no figure should be drawn in a position which it is impossible to suppose any figure should maintain. The patient endurance of St Sebastian, the wild ecstasy of St John in the Wilderness, the maternal love of the Virgin, are feelings naturally portrayed by a fixed posture; but the lady with the stiff back and bent neck, who looks at her flower, and is still looking from hour to hour, gives us an idea of pain without grace, and abstraction without a cause.

It was easy, from his rooms, to see that Tom Towers was a Sybarite, though by no means an idle one. He was lingering over his last cup of tea, surrounded by an ocean of newspapers, through which he had been swimming, when John Bold's card was brought in by his tiger. This tiger never knew that his master was at home, though he often knew that he was not, and thus Tom Towers was never invaded but by his own consent. On this occasion, after twisting the card twice in his fingers, he signified to his attendant imp that he was visible; and the inner door was unbolted, and our friend announced.

I have before said that he of *The Jupiter* and John Bold were intimate. There was no very great difference in their ages, for Towers was still considerably under forty; and when Bold had been attending the London hospitals, Towers, who was not then the great man that he had since become, had been much with him. Then they had often discussed together the objects of their ambition and future prospects; then Tom Towers was struggling hard to maintain himself, as a briefless barrister, by shorthand reporting for any of the papers that would engage him; then he had not dared to dream of writing leaders for *The Jupiter*, or canvassing the conduct of Cabinet ministers. Things had altered since that time: the briefless barrister was still briefless, but he now despised briefs: could he have been sure of a judge's seat, he would hardly have left his present career. It is true he wore no ermine, bore no outward marks of a world's respect; but with what a load of inward importance was he charged! It is true his name appeared in no large capitals; on no wall was chalked up "Tom Towers for ever;"—"Freedom of the Press and Tom Towers;" but what member of Parliament had half his power? It is true that in far-off provinces men did not talk daily of Tom Towers but they read *The Jupiter*, and acknowledged that without *The Jupiter* life was not worth having. This kind of hidden but still conscious glory suited the nature of the man. He loved to sit silent in a corner of his club and listen to the loud chattering of politicians, and to think how they all were in his power;—how he could smite the loudest of them, were it worth his while to raise his pen for such a purpose. He loved to watch the great men of whom he daily wrote, and flatter himself that he was greater than any of them. Each of them was responsible to his country, each of them must answer if inquired into, each of them must endure abuse with good humour, and insolence without anger. But to whom was he, Tom Towers, responsible? No one could insult him; no one could inquire into him. He could speak out withering words, and no one could answer him: ministers courted him, though perhaps they knew not his name; bishops feared him; judges doubted their own verdicts unless he confirmed them; and generals, in their councils of war, did not consider more deeply what the enemy would do, than what *The Jupiter* would say. Tom Towers never boasted of *The Jupiter*; he scarcely ever named the paper even to the most intimate of his friends; he did not even wish to be spoken of as connected with it; but he did not the less value his privileges, or think the less of his own importance. It is probable that Tom Towers considered himself the most powerful man in Europe; and so he walked on from day to day, studiously striving to look a man, but knowing within his breast that he was a god.

Chapter XV

TOM TOWERS, DR ANTICANT, AND MR SENTIMENT

"Ah, Bold! how are you? You haven't breakfasted?"

"Oh yes, hours ago. And how are you?"

When one Esquimau meets another, do the two, as an invariable rule, ask after each other's health? is it inherent in all human nature to make this obliging inquiry? Did any reader of this tale ever meet any friend or acquaintance without asking some such question, and did anyone ever listen to the reply? Sometimes a studiously courteous questioner will show so much thought in the matter as to answer it himself, by declaring that had he looked at you he needn't have asked; meaning thereby to signify that you are an absolute personification of health: but such persons are only those who premeditate small effects.

"I suppose you're busy?" inquired Bold.

"Why, yes, rather;—or I should say rather not. If I have a leisure hour in the day, this is it."

"I want to ask you if you can oblige me in a certain matter."

Towers understood in a moment, from the tone of his friend's voice, that the certain matter referred to the newspaper. He smiled, and nodded his head, but made no promise.

"You know this lawsuit that I've been engaged in," said Bold.

Tom Towers intimated that he was aware of the action which was pending about the hospital.

"Well, I've abandoned it."

Tom Towers merely raised his eyebrows, thrust his hands into his trowsers pockets, and waited for his friend to proceed.

"Yes, I've given it up. I needn't trouble you with all the history; but the fact is that the conduct of Mr Harding—Mr Harding is the—"

"Oh yes, the master of the place; the man who takes all the money and does nothing," said Tom Towers, interrupting him.

"Well, I don't know about that; but his conduct in the matter has been so excellent, so little selfish, so open, that I cannot proceed in the matter to his detriment." Bold's heart misgave him as to Eleanor as he said this; and yet he felt that what he said was not untrue. "I think nothing should now be done till the wardenship be vacant."

"And be again filled," said Towers, "as it certainly would, before anyone heard of the vacancy; and the same objection would again exist. It's an old story, that of the vested rights of the incumbent; but suppose the incumbent has only a vested wrong, and that the poor of the town have a vested right, if they only knew how to get at it: is not that something the case here?"

Bold couldn't deny it, but thought it was one of those cases which required a good deal of management before any real good could be done. It was a pity that he had not considered this before he crept into the lion's mouth, in the shape of an attorney's office.

"It will cost you a good deal, I fear," said Towers.

"A few hundreds," said Bold—"perhaps three hundred; I can't help that, and am prepared for it."

"That's philosophical. It's quite refreshing to hear a man talking of his hundreds in so purely indifferent a manner. But I'm sorry you are giving the matter up. It injures a man to commence a thing of this kind, and not carry it through. Have you seen that?" and he threw a small pamphlet across the table, which was all but damp from the press.

Bold had not seen it nor heard of it; but he was well acquainted with the author of it,— a gentleman whose pamphlets, condemnatory of all things in these modern days, had been a good deal talked about of late.

Dr Pessimist Anticant was a Scotchman, who had passed a great portion of his early days in Germany; he had studied there with much effect, and had learnt to look with German subtilty into the root of things, and to examine for himself their intrinsic worth and worthlessness. No man ever resolved more bravely than he to accept as good nothing that was evil; to banish from him as evil nothing that was good. 'Tis a pity that he should not have recognised the fact, that in this world no good is unalloyed, and that there is but little evil that has not in it some seed of what is goodly.

Returning from Germany, he had astonished the reading public by the vigour of his thoughts, put forth in the quaintest language. He cannot write English, said the critics. No matter, said the public; we can read what he does write, and that without yawning. And so Dr Pessimist Anticant became popular. Popularity spoilt him for all further real use, as it has done many another. While, with some diffidence, he confined his objurgations to the occasional follies or shortcomings of mankind; while he ridiculed the energy of the squire devoted to the slaughter of partridges, or the mistake of some noble patron who turned a poet into a gauger of beer-barrels, it was all well; we were glad to be told our faults and to look forward to the coming millennium, when all men, having sufficiently studied the works of Dr Anticant, would become truthful and energetic. But the doctor mistook the signs of the times and the minds of men, instituted himself censor of things in general, and began the great task of reprobating everything and everybody, without further promise of any millennium at all. This was not so well; and, to tell the truth, our author did not succeed in his undertaking. His theories were all beautiful, and the code of morals that he taught us certainly an improvement on the practices of the age. We all of us could, and many of us did, learn much from the doctor while he chose to remain vague, mysterious, and cloudy: but when he became practical, the charm was gone.

His allusion to the poet and the partridges was received very well. "Oh, my poor brother," said he, "slaughtered partridges a score of brace to each gun, and poets gauging ale-barrels, with sixty pounds a year, at Dumfries, are not the signs of a great era!— perhaps of the smallest possible era yet written of. Whatever economies we pursue, political or other, let us see at once that this is the maddest of the uneconomic: partridges killed by our land magnates at, shall we say, a guinea a head, to be retailed in Leadenhall at one shilling and ninepence, with one poacher in limbo for every fifty birds! our poet, maker, creator, gauging ale, and that badly, with no leisure for making or creating, only a little leisure for drinking, and such like beer-barrel avocations! Truly, a cutting of blocks with fine razors while we scrape our chins so uncomfortably with rusty knives! Oh, my political economist, master of supply and demand, division of labour and high pressure,—oh, my loud-speaking friend, tell me, if so much be in you, what is the demand for poets in these kingdoms of Queen Victoria, and what the vouchsafed supply?"

This was all very well: this gave us some hope. We might do better with our next poet, when we got one; and though the partridges might not be abandoned, something could perhaps be done as to the poachers. We were unwilling, however, to take lessons in politics from so misty a professor; and when he came to tell us that the heroes of Westminster were naught, we began to think that he had written enough. His attack upon despatch boxes was not thought to have much in it; but as it is short, the doctor shall again be allowed to speak his sentiments.

> Could utmost ingenuity in the management of red tape avail anything to men lying gasping,—we may say, all but dead; could despatch boxes with never-so-much velvet lining and Chubb's patent be of comfort to a people *in extremis*, I also, with so many others, would, with parched tongue, call on the name of Lord John Russell; or, my brother, at your advice, on Lord Aberdeen; or, my cousin, on Lord Derby, at yours; being, with my parched tongue, indifferent to such matters. 'Tis all one. Oh, Derby! Oh, Gladstone! Oh, Palmerston! Oh, Lord John! Each comes running with serene face and despatch box. Vain physicians! though there were hosts of such, no despatch box will cure this disorder! What! are there other doctors' new names, disciples who have not burdened their souls with tape? Well, let us call again. Oh, Disraeli, great oppositionist, man of the bitter brow! or, Oh, Molesworth, great reformer, thou who promisest Utopia. They come; each with that serene face, and each,—alas, me! alas, my country!—each with a despatch box!
>
> Oh, the serenity of Downing Street!
>
> My brothers, when hope was over on the battle-field, when no dimmest chance of victory remained, the ancient Roman could hide his face within his toga, and die gracefully. Can you and I do so now? If so, 'twere best for us; if not, oh my brothers, we must die disgracefully, for hope of life and victory I see none left to us in this world below. I for one cannot trust much to serene face and despatch box!

There might be truth in this, there might be depth of reasoning; but Englishmen did not see enough in the argument to induce them to withdraw their confidence from the present arrangements of the government, and Dr Anticant's monthly pamphlet on the decay of the world did not receive so much attention as his earlier works. He did not confine himself to politics in these publications, but roamed at large over all matters of public interest, and found everything bad. According to him nobody was true, and not only nobody, but nothing; a man could not take off his hat to a lady without telling a lie;—the lady would lie again in smiling. The ruffles of the gentleman's shirt would be fraught with deceit, and the lady's flounces full of falsehood. Was ever anything more severe than that attack of his on chip bonnets, or the anathemas with which he endeavoured to dust the powder out of the bishops' wigs?

The pamphlet which Tom Towers now pushed across the table was entitled "Modern Charity," and was written with the view of proving how much in the way of charity was done by our predecessors,—how little by the present age; and it ended by a comparison between ancient and modern times, very little to the credit of the latter.

"Look at this," said Towers, getting up and turning over the pages of the pamphlet, and pointing to a passage near the end. "Your friend the warden, who is so little selfish, won't like that, I fear." Bold read as follows—

Heavens, what a sight! Let us with eyes wide open see the godly man of four centuries since, the man of the dark ages; let us see how he does his godlike work, and, again, how the godly man of these latter days does his.

Shall we say that the former is one walking painfully through the world, regarding, as a prudent man, his worldly work, prospering in it as a diligent man will prosper, but always with an eye to that better treasure to which thieves do not creep in? Is there not much nobility in that old man, as, leaning on his oaken staff, he walks down the High Street of his native town, and receives from all courteous salutation and acknowledgment of his worth? A noble old man, my august inhabitants of Belgrave Square and such like vicinity,—a very noble old man, though employed no better than in the wholesale carding of wool.

This carding of wool, however, did in those days bring with it much profit, so that our ancient friend, when dying, was declared, in whatever slang then prevailed, to cut up exceeding well. For sons and daughters there was ample sustenance with assistance of due industry; for friends and relatives some relief for grief at this great loss; for aged dependents comfort in declining years. This was much for one old man to get done in that dark fifteenth century. But this was not all: coming generations of poor woolcarders should bless the name of this rich one; and a hospital should be founded and endowed with his wealth for the feeding of such of the trade as could not, by diligent carding, any longer duly feed themselves.

'Twas thus that an old man in the fifteenth century did his godlike work to the best of his power, and not ignobly, as appears to me.

We will now take our godly man of latter days. He shall no longer be a wool-carder, for such are not now men of mark. We will suppose him to be one of the best of the good, one who has lacked no opportunities. Our old friend was, after all, but illiterate; our modern friend shall be a man educated in all seemly knowledge; he shall, in short, be that blessed being,—a clergyman of the Church of England!

And now, in what perfectest manner does he in this lower world get his godlike work done and put out of hand? Heavens! in the strangest of manners. Oh, my brother! in a manner not at all to be believed, but by the most minute testimony of eyesight. He does it by the magnitude of his appetite,—by the power of his gorge; his only occupation is to swallow the bread prepared with so much anxious care for these impoverished carders of wool,—that, and to sing indifferently through his nose once in the week some psalm more or less long,—the shorter the better, we should be inclined to say.

Oh, my civilised friends!—great Britons that never will be slaves, men advanced to infinite state of freedom and knowledge of good and evil;—tell me, will you, what becoming monument you will erect to an highly-educated clergyman of the Church of England?

Bold certainly thought that his friend would not like that: he could not conceive anything that he would like less than this. To what a world of toil and trouble had he, Bold, given rise by his indiscreet attack upon the hospital!

"You see," said Towers, "that this affair has been much talked of, and the public are with you. I am sorry you should give the matter up. Have you seen the first number of 'The Almshouse'?"

No; Bold had not seen "The Almshouse." He had seen advertisements of Mr Popular Sentiment's new novel of that name, but had in no way connected it with Barchester Hospital, and had never thought a moment on the subject.

"It's a direct attack on the whole system," said Towers. "It'll go a long way to put down Rochester, and Barchester, and Dulwich, and St Cross, and all such hotbeds of peculation. It's very clear that Sentiment has been down to Barchester, and got up the whole story there; indeed, I thought he must have had it all from you; it's very well done, as you'll see: his first numbers always are."

Bold declared that Mr Sentiment had got nothing from him, and that he was deeply grieved to find that the case had become so notorious.

"The fire has gone too far to be quenched," said Towers; "the building must go now; and as the timbers are all rotten, why, I should be inclined to say, the sooner the better. I expected to see you get some *éclat* in the matter."

This was all wormwood to Bold. He had done enough to make his friend the warden miserable for life, and had then backed out just when the success of his project was sufficient to make the question one of real interest. How weakly he had managed his business! he had already done the harm, and then stayed his hand when the good which he had in view was to be commenced. How delightful would it have been to have employed all his energy in such a cause,—to have been backed by *The Jupiter*, and written up to by two of the most popular authors of the day! The idea opened a view into the very world in which he wished to live. To what might it not have given rise? what delightful intimacies,—what public praise,—to what Athenian banquets and rich flavour of Attic salt?

This, however, was now past hope. He had pledged himself to abandon the cause; and could he have forgotten the pledge, he had gone too far to retreat. He was now, this moment, sitting in Tom Towers' room with the object of deprecating any further articles in *The Jupiter*, and, greatly as he disliked the job, his petition to that effect must be made.

"I couldn't continue it," said he, "because I found I was in the wrong."

Tom Towers shrugged his shoulders. How could a successful man be in the wrong! "In that case," said he, "of course you must abandon it."

"And I called this morning to ask you also to abandon it," said Bold.

"To ask me," said Tom Towers, with the most placid of smiles, and a consummate look of gentle surprise, as though Tom Towers was well aware that he of all men was the last to meddle in such matters.

"Yes," said Bold, almost trembling with hesitation. "*The Jupiter*, you know, has taken the matter up very strongly. Mr Harding has felt what it has said deeply; and I thought that if I could explain to you that he personally has not been to blame, these articles might be discontinued."

How calmly impassive was Tom Towers' face, as this innocent little proposition was made! Had Bold addressed himself to the doorposts in Mount Olympus, they would have shown as much outward sign of assent or dissent. His quiescence was quite admirable; his discretion certainly more than human.

"My dear fellow," said he, when Bold had quite done speaking, "I really cannot answer for *The Jupiter*."

"But if you saw that these articles were unjust, I think that You would endeavour to put a stop to them. Of course nobody doubts that you could, if you chose."

"Nobody and everybody are always very kind, but unfortunately are generally very wrong."

"Come, come, Towers," said Bold, plucking up his courage, and remembering that for Eleanor's sake he was bound to make his best exertion; "I have no doubt in my own mind but that you wrote the articles yourself, and very well written they were: it will be a great favour if you will in future abstain from any personal allusion to poor Harding."

"My dear Bold," said Tom Towers, "I have a sincere regard for you. I have known you for many years, and value your friendship; I hope you will let me explain to you, without offence, that none who are connected with the public press can with propriety listen to interference."

"Interference!" said Bold, "I don't want to interfere."

"Ah, but, my dear fellow, you do; what else is it? You think that I am able to keep certain remarks out of a newspaper. Your information is probably incorrect, as most public gossip on such subjects is; but, at any rate, you think I have such power, and you ask me to use it: now that is interference."

"Well, if you choose to call it so."

"And now suppose for a moment that I had this power, and used it as you wish: isn't it clear that it would be a great abuse? Certain men are employed in writing for the public press; and if they are induced either to write or to abstain from writing by private motives, surely the public press would soon be of little value. Look at the recognised worth of different newspapers, and see if it does not mainly depend on the assurance which the public feel that such a paper is, or is not, independent. You alluded to *The Jupiter*: surely you cannot but see that the weight of *The Jupiter* is too great to be moved by any private request, even though it should be made to a much more influential person than myself: you've only to think of this, and you'll see that I am right."

The discretion of Tom Towers was boundless: there was no contradicting what he said, no arguing against such propositions. He took such high ground that there was no getting on to it. "The public is defrauded," said he, "whenever private considerations are allowed to have weight." Quite true, thou greatest oracle of the middle of the nineteenth century, thou sententious proclaimer of the purity of the press;—the public is defrauded when it is purposely misled. Poor public! how often is it misled! against what a world of fraud has it to contend!

Bold took his leave, and got out of the room as quickly as he could, inwardly denouncing his friend Tom Towers as a prig and a humbug. "I know he wrote those articles," said Bold to himself. "I know he got his information from me. He was ready enough to take my word for gospel when it suited his own views, and to set Mr Harding up before the public as an impostor on no other testimony than my chance conversation; but when I offer him real evidence opposed to his own views, he tells me that private motives are detrimental to public justice! Confound his arrogance! What is any public question but a conglomeration of private interests? What is any newspaper article but an expression of the views taken by one side? Truth! it takes an age to ascertain the truth of any question! The idea of Tom Towers talking of public motives and purity of purpose! Why, it wouldn't give him a moment's uneasiness to change his politics to-morrow, if the paper required it."

Such were John Bold's inward exclamations as he made his way out of the quiet labyrinth of the Temple; and yet there was no position of worldly power so coveted in Bold's ambition as that held by the man of whom he was thinking. It was the impregnability of the place which made Bold so angry with the possessor of it, and it was the same quality which made it appear so desirable.

Passing into the Strand, he saw in a bookseller's window an announcement of the first number of "The Almshouse;" so he purchased a copy, and hurrying back to his lodgings, proceeded to ascertain what Mr Popular Sentiment had to say to the public on the subject which had lately occupied so much of his own attention.

In former times great objects were attained by great work. When evils were to be reformed, reformers set about their heavy task with grave decorum and laborious argument. An age was occupied in proving a grievance, and philosophical researches were printed in folio pages, which it took a life to write, and an eternity to read. We get on now with a lighter step, and quicker: ridicule is found to be more convincing than argument, imaginary agonies touch more than true sorrows, and monthly novels convince, when learned quartos fail to do so. If the world is to be set right, the work will be done by shilling numbers.

Of all such reformers Mr Sentiment is the most powerful. It is incredible the number of evil practices he has put down: it is to be feared he will soon lack subjects, and that when he has made the working classes comfortable, and got bitter beer put into proper-sized pint bottles, there will be nothing further for him left to do. Mr Sentiment is certainly a very powerful man, and perhaps not the less so that his good poor people are so very good; his hard rich people so very hard; and the genuinely honest so very honest. Namby-pamby in these days is not thrown away if it be introduced in the proper quarters. Divine peeresses are no longer interesting, though possessed of every virtue; but a pattern peasant or an immaculate manufacturing hero may talk as much twaddle as one of Mrs Ratcliffe's heroines, and still be listened to. Perhaps, however, Mr Sentiment's great attraction is in his second-rate characters. If his heroes and heroines walk upon stilts, as heroes and heroines, I fear, ever must, their attendant satellites are as natural as though one met them in the street: they walk and talk like men and women, and live among our friends a rattling, lively life; yes, live, and will live till the names of their calling shall be forgotten in their own, and Buckett and Mrs Gamp will be the only words left to us to signify a detective police officer or a monthly nurse.

"The Almshouse" opened with a scene in a clergyman's house. Every luxury to be purchased by wealth was described as being there: all the appearances of household indulgence generally found amongst the most self-indulgent of the rich were crowded into this abode. Here the reader was introduced to the demon of the book, the Mephistopheles of the drama. What story was ever written without a demon? What novel, what history, what work of any sort, what world, would be perfect without existing principles both of good and evil? The demon of "The Almshouse" was the clerical owner of this comfortable abode. He was a man well stricken in years, but still strong to do evil: he was one who looked cruelly out of a hot, passionate, bloodshot eye; who had a huge red nose with a carbuncle, thick lips, and a great double, flabby chin, which swelled out into solid substance, like a turkey-cock's comb, when sudden anger inspired him: he had a hot, furrowed, low brow, from which a few grizzled hairs were not yet rubbed off by the friction of his handkerchief: he wore a loose unstarched white handkerchief, black loose ill-made clothes, and huge loose shoes, adapted to many corns and various bunions: his husky voice told tales of much daily port wine, and his language was not so decorous as became a clergyman. Such was the master of Mr Sentiment's "Almshouse." He was a widower, but at present accompanied by two daughters, and a thin and somewhat insipid curate. One of the young ladies was devoted to her father and the fashionable world, and she of course was the favourite; the other was equally addicted to Puseyism and the curate.

The second chapter of course introduced the reader to the more especial inmates of the hospital. Here were discovered eight old men; and it was given to be understood that four vacancies remained unfilled, through the perverse ill-nature of the clerical gentleman with the double chin. The state of these eight paupers was touchingly dreadful: sixpence-farthing a day had been sufficient for their diet when the almshouse was founded; and on sixpence-farthing a day were they still doomed to starve, though food was four times as dear, and money four times as plentiful. It was shocking to find how the conversation of these eight starved old men in their dormitory shamed that of the clergyman's family in his rich drawing-room. The absolute words they uttered were not perhaps spoken in the purest English, and it might be difficult to distinguish from their dialect to what part of the country they belonged; the beauty of the sentiment, however, amply atoned for the imperfection of the language; and it was really a pity that these eight old men could not be sent through the country as moral missionaries, instead of being immured and starved in that wretched almshouse.

Bold finished the number; and as he threw it aside, he thought that that at least had no direct appliance to Mr Harding, and that the absurdly strong colouring of the picture would disenable the work from doing either good or harm. He was wrong. The artist who paints for the million must use glaring colours, as no one knew better than Mr Sentiment when he described the inhabitants of his almshouse; and the radical reform which has now swept over such establishments has owed more to the twenty numbers of Mr Sentiment's novel, than to all the true complaints which have escaped from the public for the last half century.

Chapter XVI

A LONG DAY IN LONDON

The warden had to make use of all his very moderate powers of intrigue to give his son-in-law the slip, and get out of Barchester without being stopped on his road. No schoolboy ever ran away from school with more precaution and more dread of detection; no convict, slipping down from a prison wall, ever feared to see the gaoler more entirely than Mr Harding did to see his son-in-law as he drove up in the pony carriage to the railway station, on the morning of his escape to London.

The evening before he went he wrote a note to the archdeacon, explaining that he should start on the morrow on his journey; that it was his intention to see the attorney-general if possible, and to decide on his future plans in accordance with what he heard from that gentleman; he excused himself for giving Dr Grantly no earlier notice, by stating that his resolve was very sudden; and having entrusted this note to Eleanor, with the perfect, though not expressed, understanding that it was to be sent over to Plumstead Episcopi without haste, he took his departure.

He also prepared and carried with him a note for Sir Abraham Haphazard, in which he stated his name, explaining that he was the defendant in the case of "The Queen on behalf of the Wool-carders of Barchester *v*. Trustees under the will of the late John Hiram," for so was the suit denominated, and begged the illustrious and learned gentleman to vouch-safe to him ten minutes' audience at any hour on the next day. Mr Harding calculated that for that one day he was safe; his son-in-law, he had no doubt, would arrive in town by an early train, but not early enough to reach the truant till he should have escaped from his hotel after breakfast; and could he thus manage to see the lawyer on that very day, the deed might be done before the archdeacon could interfere.

On his arrival in town the warden drove, as was his wont, to the Chapter Hotel and Coffee House, near St Paul's. His visits to London of late had not been frequent; but in those happy days when "Harding's Church Music" was going through the press, he had been often there; and as the publisher's house was in Paternoster Row, and the printer's press in Fleet Street, the Chapter Hotel and Coffee House had been convenient. It was a quiet, sombre, clerical house, beseeming such a man as the warden, and thus he afterwards frequented it. Had he dared, he would on this occasion have gone elsewhere to throw the archdeacon further off the scent; but he did not know what violent steps his son-in-law might take for his recovery if he were not found at his usual haunt, and he deemed it not prudent to make himself the object of a hunt through London.

Arrived at his inn, he ordered dinner, and went forth to the attorney-general's chambers. There he learnt that Sir Abraham was in Court, and would not probably return that day. He would go direct from Court to the House; all appointments were, as a rule, made at the chambers; the clerk could by no means promise an interview for the next day; was able, on the other hand, to say that such interview was, he thought, impossible; but that Sir Abraham would certainly be at the House in the course of the night, where an answer from himself might possibly be elicited.

To the House Mr Harding went, and left his note, not finding Sir Abraham there. He added a most piteous entreaty that he might be favoured with an answer that evening, for which he would return. He then journeyed back sadly to the Chapter Coffee House, digesting his great thoughts, as best he might, in a clattering omnibus, wedged in between a wet old lady and a journeyman glazier returning from his work with his tools in his lap. In melancholy solitude he discussed his mutton chop and pint of port. What is there in this world more melancholy than such a dinner? A dinner, though eaten alone, in a country hotel may be worthy of some energy; the waiter, if you are known, will make much of you; the landlord will make you a bow and perhaps put the fish on the table; if you ring you are attended to, and there is some life about it. A dinner at a London eating-house is also lively enough, if it have no other attraction. There is plenty of noise and stir about it, and the rapid whirl of voices and rattle of dishes disperses sadness. But a solitary dinner in an old, respectable, sombre, solid London inn, where nothing makes any noise but the old waiter's creaking shoes; where one plate slowly goes and another slowly comes without a sound; where the two or three guests would as soon think of knocking each other down as of speaking; where the servants whisper, and the whole household is disturbed if an order be given above the voice,—what can be more melancholy than a mutton chop and a pint of port in such a place?

Having gone through this Mr Harding got into another omnibus, and again returned to the House. Yes, Sir Abraham was there, and was that moment on his legs, fighting eagerly for the hundred and seventh clause of the Convent Custody Bill. Mr Harding's note had been delivered to him; and if Mr Harding would wait some two or three hours, Sir Abraham could be asked whether there was any answer. The House was not full, and perhaps Mr Harding might get admittance into the Strangers' Gallery, which admission, with the help of five shillings, Mr Harding was able to effect.

This bill of Sir Abraham's had been read a second time and passed into committee. A hundred and six clauses had already been discussed and had occupied only four mornings and five evening sittings; nine of the hundred and six clauses were passed, fifty-five were withdrawn by consent, fourteen had been altered so as to mean the reverse of the original proposition, eleven had been postponed for further consideration, and seventeen had been directly negatived. The hundred and seventh ordered the bodily searching of nuns for jesuitical symbols by aged clergymen, and was considered to be the real mainstay of the whole bill. No intention had ever existed to pass such a law as that proposed, but the government did not intend to abandon it till their object was fully attained by the discussion of this clause. It was known that it would be insisted on with terrible vehemence by Protestant Irish members, and as vehemently denounced by the Roman Catholic; and it was justly considered that no further union between the parties would be possible after such a battle. The innocent Irish fell into the trap as they always do, and whiskey and poplins became a drug in the market.

A florid-faced gentleman with a nice head of hair, from the south of Ireland, had succeeded in catching the speaker's eye by the time that Mr Harding had got into the gallery, and was denouncing the proposed sacrilege, his whole face glowing with a fine theatrical frenzy.

"And this is a Christian country?" said he. (Loud cheers; counter cheers from the ministerial benches. "Some doubt as to that," from a voice below the gangway.) "No, it can be no Christian country, in which the head of the bar, the lagal adviser (loud laughter and cheers)—yes, I say the lagal adviser of the crown (great cheers and laughter)—can stand up in his seat in this house (prolonged cheers and laughter), and attempt to lagalise indacent assaults on the bodies of religious ladies." (Deafening cheers and laughter, which were prolonged till the honourable member resumed his seat.)

When Mr Harding had listened to this and much more of the same kind for about three hours, he returned to the door of the House, and received back from the messenger his own note, with the following words scrawled in pencil on the back of it: "To-morrow, 10 P.M.—my chambers.—A. H."

He was so far successful;—but 10 P.M.: what an hour Sir Abraham had named for a legal interview! Mr Harding felt perfectly sure that long before that Dr Grantly would be in London. Dr Grantly could not, however, know that this interview had been arranged, nor could he learn it unless he managed to get hold of Sir Abraham before that hour; and as this was very improbable, Mr Harding determined to start from his hotel early, merely leaving word that he should dine out, and unless luck were much against him, he might still escape the archdeacon till his return from the attorney-general's chambers.

He was at breakfast at nine, and for the twentieth time consulted his Bradshaw, to see at what earliest hour Dr Grantly could arrive from Barchester. As he examined the columns, he was nearly petrified by the reflection that perhaps the archdeacon might come up by the night-mail train! His heart sank within him at the horrid idea, and for a moment he felt himself dragged back to Barchester without accomplishing any portion of his object. Then he remembered that had Dr Grantly done so, he would have been in the hotel, looking for him long since.

"Waiter," said he, timidly.

The waiter approached, creaking in his shoes, but voiceless.

"Did any gentleman,—a clergyman, arrive here by the night-mail train?"

"No, sir, not one," whispered the waiter, putting his mouth nearly close to the warden's ear.

Mr Harding was reassured.

"Waiter," said he again, and the waiter again creaked up. "If anyone calls for me, I am going to dine out, and shall return about eleven o'clock."

The waiter nodded, but did not this time vouchsafe any reply; and Mr Harding, taking up his hat, proceeded out to pass a long day in the best way he could, somewhere out of sight of the archdeacon.

Bradshaw had told him twenty times that Dr Grantly could not be at Paddington station till 2 P.M., and our poor friend might therefore have trusted to the shelter of the hotel for some hours longer with perfect safety; but he was nervous. There was no knowing what steps the archdeacon might take for his apprehension: a message by electric telegraph might desire the landlord of the hotel to set a watch upon him; some letter might come which he might find himself unable to disobey; at any rate, he could not feel himself secure in any place at which the archdeacon could expect to find him; and at 10 A.M. he started forth to spend twelve hours in London.

Mr Harding had friends in town had he chosen to seek them; but he felt that he was in no humour for ordinary calls, and he did not now wish to consult with anyone as to the great step which he had determined to take. As he had said to his daughter, no one knows where the shoe pinches but the wearer. There are some points on which no man can be contented to follow the advice of another,—some subjects on which a man can consult his own conscience only. Our warden had made up his mind that it was good for him at any cost to get rid of this grievance; his daughter was the only person whose concurrence appeared necessary to him, and she did concur with him most heartily. Under such circum-circumstances he would not, if he could help it, consult anyone further, till advice would be useless. Should the archdeacon catch him, indeed, there would be much advice, and much consultation of a kind not to be avoided; but he hoped better things; and as he felt that he could not now converse on indifferent subjects, he resolved to see no one till after his interview with the attorney-general.

He determined to take sanctuary in Westminster Abbey, so he again went thither in an omnibus, and finding that the doors were not open for morning service, he paid his two-pence, and went in as a sightseer. It occurred to him that he had no definite place of rest for the day, and that he should be absolutely worn out before his interview if he attempted to walk about from 10 A.M. to 10 P.M., so he sat himself down on a stone step, and gazed up at the figure of William Pitt, who looks as though he had just entered the church for the first time in his life and was anything but pleased at finding himself there.

He had been sitting unmolested about twenty minutes when the verger asked him whether he wouldn't like to walk round. Mr Harding didn't want to walk anywhere, and declined, merely observing that he was waiting for the morning service. The verger, see-ing that he was a clergyman, told him that the doors of the choir were now open, and showed him into a seat. This was a great point gained; the archdeacon would certainly not come to morning service at Westminster Abbey, even though he were in London; and here the warden could rest quietly, and, when the time came, duly say his prayers.

He longed to get up from his seat, and examine the music-books of the choristers, and the copy of the litany from which the service was chanted, to see how far the little details at Westminster corresponded with those at Barchester, and whether he thought his own voice would fill the church well from the Westminster precentor's seat. There would, however, be impropriety in such meddling, and he sat perfectly still, looking up at the noble roof, and guarding against the coming fatigues of the day.

By degrees two or three people entered; the very same damp old woman who had nearly obliterated him in the omnibus, or some other just like her; a couple of young la-dies with their veils down, and gilt crosses conspicuous on their prayer-books; an old man on crutches; a party who were seeing the abbey, and thought they might as well hear the service for their twopence, as opportunity served; and a young woman with her prayer-book done up in her handkerchief, who rushed in late, and, in her hurried entry, tumbled over one of the forms, and made such a noise that everyone, even the officiating minor canon, was startled, and she herself was so frightened by the echo of her own catastrophe that she was nearly thrown into fits by the panic.

Mr Harding was not much edified by the manner of the service. The minor canon in question hurried in, somewhat late, in a surplice not in the neatest order, and was followed by a dozen choristers, who were also not as trim as they might have been: they all jostled into their places with a quick hurried step, and the service was soon commenced. Soon commenced and soon over,—for there was no music, and time was not unnecessarily lost in the chanting. On the whole Mr Harding was of opinion that things were managed bet-ter at Barchester, though even there he knew that there was room for improvement.

It appears to us a question whether any clergyman can go through our church service with decorum, morning after morning, in an immense building, surrounded by not more than a dozen listeners. The best actors cannot act well before empty benches, and though there is, of course, a higher motive in one case than the other, still even the best of cler-gymen cannot but be influenced by their audience; and to expect that a duty should be well done under such circumstances, would be to require from human nature more than human power.

When the two ladies with the gilt crosses, the old man with his crutch, and the still palpitating housemaid were going, Mr Harding found himself obliged to go too. The verger stood in his way, and looked at him and looked at the door, and so he went. But he returned again in a few minutes, and re-entered with another twopence. There was no other sanctuary so good for him.

As he walked slowly down the nave, and then up one aisle, and then again down the nave and up the other aisle, he tried to think gravely of the step he was about to take. He was going to give up eight hundred a year voluntarily; and doom himself to live for the rest of his life on about a hundred and fifty. He knew that he had hitherto failed to realise this fact as he ought to do. Could he maintain his own independence and support his daughter on a hundred and fifty pounds a year without being a burden on anyone? His son-in-law was rich, but nothing could induce him to lean on his son-in-law after acting, as he intended to do, in direct opposition to his son-in-law's counsel. The bishop was rich, but he was about to throw away the bishop's best gift, and that in a manner to injure materially the patronage of the giver: he could neither expect nor accept anything further from the bishop. There would be not only no merit, but positive disgrace, in giving up his wardenship, if he were not prepared to meet the world without it. Yes, he must from this time forward bound all his human wishes for himself and his daughter to the poor extent of so limited an income. He knew he had not thought sufficiently of this, that he had been carried away by enthusiasm, and had hitherto not brought home to himself the full reality of his position.

He thought most about his daughter, naturally. It was true that she was engaged, and he knew enough of his proposed son-in-law to be sure that his own altered circumstances would make no obstacle to such a marriage; nay, he was sure that the very fact of his poverty would induce Bold more anxiously to press the matter; but he disliked counting on Bold in this emergency, brought on, as it had been, by his doing. He did not like saying to himself, Bold has turned me out of my house and income, and, therefore, he must relieve me of my daughter; he preferred reckoning on Eleanor as the companion of his poverty and exile,—as the sharer of his small income.

Some modest provision for his daughter had been long since made. His life was insured for three thousand pounds, and this sum was to go to Eleanor. The archdeacon, for some years past, had paid the premium, and had secured himself by the immediate possession of a small property which was to have gone to Mrs Grantly after her father's death. This matter, therefore, had been taken out of the warden's hands long since, as, indeed, had all the business transactions of his family, and his anxiety was, therefore, confined to his own life income.

Yes. A hundred and fifty per annum was very small, but still it might suffice; but how was he to chant the litany at the cathedral on Sunday mornings, and get the service done at Crabtree Parva? True, Crabtree Church was not quite a mile and a half from the cathedral; but he could not be in two places at once. Crabtree was a small village, and afternoon service might suffice, but still this went against his conscience; it was not right that his parishioners should be robbed of any of their privileges on account of his poverty. He might, to be sure, make some arrangements for doing week-day service at the cathedral; but he had chanted the litany at Barchester so long, and had a conscious feeling that he did it so well, that he was unwilling to give up the duty.

Thinking of such things, turning over in his own mind together small desires and grave duties, but never hesitating for a moment as to the necessity of leaving the hospital, Mr Harding walked up and down the abbey, or sat still meditating on the same stone step, hour after hour. One verger went and another came, but they did not disturb him; every now and then they crept up and looked at him, but they did so with a reverential stare, and, on the whole, Mr Harding found his retreat well chosen. About four o'clock his comfort was disturbed by an enemy in the shape of hunger. It was necessary that he should dine, and it was clear that he could not dine in the abbey: so he left his sanctuary not willingly, and betook himself to the neighbourhood of the Strand to look for food.

His eyes had become so accustomed to the gloom of the church, that they were dazed when he got out into the full light of day, and he felt confused and ashamed of himself, as though people were staring at him. He hurried along, still in dread of the archdeacon, till he came to Charing Cross, and then remembered that in one of his passages through the Strand he had seen the words "Chops and Steaks" on a placard in a shop window. He remembered the shop distinctly; it was next door to a trunk-seller's, and there was a cigar shop on the other side. He couldn't go to his hotel for dinner, which to him hitherto was the only known mode of dining in London at his own expense; and, therefore, he would get a steak at the shop in the Strand. Archdeacon Grantly would certainly not come to such a place for his dinner.

He found the house easily,—just as he had observed it, between the trunks and the cigars. He was rather daunted by the huge quantity of fish which he saw in the window. There were barrels of oysters, hecatombs of lobsters, a few tremendous-looking crabs, and a tub full of pickled salmon; not, however, being aware of any connection between shellfish and iniquity, he entered, and modestly asked a slatternly woman, who was picking oysters out of a great watery reservoir, whether he could have a mutton chop and a potato.

The woman looked somewhat surprised, but answered in the affirmative, and a slipshod girl ushered him into a long back room, filled with boxes for the accommodation of parties, in one of which he took his seat. In a more miserably forlorn place he could not have found himself: the room smelt of fish, and sawdust, and stale tobacco smoke, with a slight taint of escaped gas; everything was rough and dirty, and disreputable; the cloth which they put before him was abominable; the knives and forks were bruised, and hacked, and filthy; and everything was impregnated with fish. He had one comfort, however: he was quite alone; there was no one there to look on his dismay; nor was it probable that anyone would come to do so. It was a London supper-house. About one o'clock at night the place would be lively enough, but at the present time his seclusion was as deep as it had been in the abbey.

In about half an hour the untidy girl, not yet dressed for her evening labours, brought him his chop and potatoes, and Mr Harding begged for a pint of sherry. He was impressed with an idea, which was generally prevalent a few years since, and is not yet wholly removed from the minds of men, that to order a dinner at any kind of inn, without also ordering a pint of wine for the benefit of the landlord, was a kind of fraud,—not punishable, indeed, by law, but not the less abominable on that account. Mr Harding remembered his coming poverty, and would willingly have saved his half-crown, but he thought he had no alternative; and he was soon put in possession of some horrid mixture procured from the neighbouring public-house.

His chop and potatoes, however, were eatable, and having got over as best he might the disgust created by the knives and forks, he contrived to swallow his dinner. He was not much disturbed: one young man, with pale face and watery fishlike eyes, wearing his hat ominously on one side, did come in and stare at him, and ask the girl, audibly enough, "Who that old cock was;" but the annoyance went no further, and the warden was left seated on his wooden bench in peace, endeavouring to distinguish the different scents arising from lobsters, oysters, and salmon.

Unknowing as Mr Harding was in the ways of London, he felt that he had somehow selected an ineligible dining-house, and that he had better leave it. It was hardly five o'clock;—how was he to pass the time till ten? Five miserable hours! He was already tired, and it was impossible that he should continue walking so long. He thought of getting into an omnibus, and going out to Fulham for the sake of coming back in another: this, however, would be weary work, and as he paid his bill to the woman in the shop, he asked her if there were any place near where he could get a cup of coffee. Though she did keep a shellfish supper-house, she was very civil, and directed him to the cigar divan on the other side of the street.

Mr Harding had not a much correcter notion of a cigar divan than he had of a London dinner-house, but he was desperately in want of rest, and went as he was directed. He thought he must have made some mistake when he found himself in a cigar shop, but the man behind the counter saw immediately that he was a stranger, and understood what he wanted. "One shilling, sir,—thank ye, sir,—cigar, sir?—ticket for coffee, sir;—you'll only have to call the waiter. Up those stairs, if you please, sir. Better take the cigar, sir,—you can always give it to a friend, you know. Well, sir, thank ye, sir;—as you are so good, I'll smoke it myself." And so Mr Harding ascended to the divan, with his ticket for coffee, but minus the cigar.

The place seemed much more suitable to his requirements than the room in which he had dined: there was, to be sure, a strong smell of tobacco, to which he was not accustomed; but after the shell-fish, the tobacco did not seem disagreeable. There were quantities of books, and long rows of sofas. What on earth could be more luxurious than a sofa, a book, and a cup of coffee? An old waiter came up to him, with a couple of magazines and an evening paper. Was ever anything so civil? Would he have a cup of coffee, or would he prefer sherbet? Sherbet! Was he absolutely in an Eastern divan, with the slight addition of all the London periodicals? He had, however, an idea that sherbet should be drunk sitting cross-legged, and as he was not quite up to this, he ordered the coffee.

The coffee came, and was unexceptionable. Why, this divan was a paradise! The civil old waiter suggested to him a game of chess: though a chess player he was not equal to this, so he declined, and, putting up his weary legs on the sofa, leisurely sipped his coffee, and turned over the pages of his Blackwood. He might have been so engaged for about an hour, for the old waiter enticed him to a second cup of coffee, when a musical clock began to play. Mr Harding then closed his magazine, keeping his place with his finger, and lay, listening with closed eyes to the clock. Soon the clock seemed to turn into a violoncello, with piano accompaniments, and Mr Harding began to fancy the old waiter was the Bishop of Barchester; he was inexpressibly shocked that the bishop should have brought him his coffee with his own hands; then Dr Grantly came in, with a basket full of lobsters, which he would not be induced to leave downstairs in the kitchen; and then the warden couldn't quite understand why so many people would smoke in the bishop's drawing-room; and so he fell fast asleep, and his dreams wandered away to his accustomed stall in Barchester Cathedral, and the twelve old men he was so soon about to leave for ever.

He was fatigued, and slept soundly for some time. Some sudden stop in the musical clock woke him at length, and he jumped up with a start, surprised to find the room quite full: it had been nearly empty when his nap began. With nervous anxiety he pulled out his watch, and found that it was half-past nine. He seized his hat, and, hurrying downstairs, started at a rapid pace for Lincoln's Inn.

It still wanted twenty minutes to ten when the warden found himself at the bottom of Sir Abraham's stairs, so he walked leisurely up and down the quiet inn to cool himself. It was a beautiful evening at the end of August. He had recovered from his fatigue; his sleep and the coffee had refreshed him, and he was surprised to find that he was absolutely enjoying himself, when the inn clock struck ten. The sound was hardly over before he knocked at Sir Abraham's door, and was informed by the clerk who received him that the great man would be with him immediately.

Chapter XVII

SIR ABRAHAM HAPHAZARD

Mr Harding was shown into a comfortable inner sitting-room, looking more like a gentleman's book-room than a lawyer's chambers, and there waited for Sir Abraham. Nor was he kept waiting long: in ten or fifteen minutes he heard a clatter of voices speaking quickly in the passage, and then the attorney-general entered.

"Very sorry to keep you waiting, Mr Warden," said Sir Abraham, shaking hands with him; "and sorry, too, to name so disagreeable an hour; but your notice was short, and as you said to-day, I named the very earliest hour that was not disposed of."

Mr Harding assured him that he was aware that it was he that should apologise.

Sir Abraham was a tall thin man, with hair prematurely gray, but bearing no other sign of age; he had a slight stoop, in his neck rather than his back, acquired by his constant habit of leaning forward as he addressed his various audiences. He might be fifty years old, and would have looked young for his age, had not constant work hardened his features, and given him the appearance of a machine with a mind. His face was full of intellect, but devoid of natural expression. You would say he was a man to use, and then have done with; a man to be sought for on great emergencies, but ill-adapted for ordinary services; a man whom you would ask to defend your property, but to whom you would be sorry to confide your love. He was bright as a diamond, and as cutting, and also as unimpressionable. He knew everyone whom to know was an honour, but he was without a friend; he wanted none, however, and knew not the meaning of the word in other than its parliamentary sense. A friend! Had he not always been sufficient to himself, and now, at fifty, was it likely that he should trust another? He was married, indeed, and had children, but what time had he for the soft idleness of conjugal felicity? His working days or term times were occupied from his time of rising to the late hour at which he went to rest, and even his vacations were more full of labour than the busiest days of other men. He never quarrelled with his wife, but he never talked to her;—he never had time to talk, he was so taken up with speaking. She, poor lady, was not unhappy; she had all that money could give her, she would probably live to be a peeress, and she really thought Sir Abraham the best of husbands.

Sir Abraham was a man of wit, and sparkled among the brightest at the dinner-tables of political grandees: indeed, he always sparkled; whether in society, in the House of Commons, or the courts of law, coruscations flew from him; glittering sparkles, as from hot steel, but no heat; no cold heart was ever cheered by warmth from him, no unhappy soul ever dropped a portion of its burden at his door.

With him success alone was praiseworthy, and he knew none so successful as himself. No one had thrust him forward; no powerful friends had pushed him along on his road to power. No; he was attorney-general, and would, in all human probability, be lord chancellor by sheer dint of his own industry and his own talent. Who else in all the world rose so high with so little help? A premier, indeed! Who had ever been premier without mighty friends? An archbishop! Yes, the son or grandson of a great noble, or else, probably, his tutor. But he, Sir Abraham, had had no mighty lord at his back; his father had been a country apothecary, his mother a farmer's daughter. Why should he respect any but himself? And so he glitters along through the world, the brightest among the bright; and when his glitter is gone, and he is gathered to his fathers, no eye will be dim with a tear, no heart will mourn for its lost friend.

"And so, Mr Warden," said Sir Abraham, "all our trouble about this lawsuit is at an end."

Mr Harding said he hoped so, but he didn't at all understand what Sir Abraham meant. Sir Abraham, with all his sharpness, could not have looked into his heart and read his intentions.

"All over. You need trouble yourself no further about it; of course they must pay the costs, and the absolute expense to you and Dr Grantly will be trifling,—that is, compared with what it might have been if it had been continued."

"I fear I don't quite understand you, Sir Abraham."

"Don't you know that their attorneys have noticed us that they have withdrawn the suit?"

Mr Harding explained to the lawyer that he knew nothing of this, although he had heard in a roundabout way that such an intention had been talked of; and he also at length succeeded in making Sir Abraham understand that even this did not satisfy him. The attorney-general stood up, put his hands into his breeches' pockets, and raised his eyebrows, as Mr Harding proceeded to detail the grievance from which he now wished to rid himself.

"I know I have no right to trouble you personally with this matter, but as it is of most vital importance to me, as all my happiness is concerned in it, I thought I might venture to seek your advice."

Sir Abraham bowed, and declared his clients were entitled to the best advice he could give them; particularly a client so respectable in every way as the Warden of Barchester Hospital.

"A spoken word, Sir Abraham, is often of more value than volumes of written advice. The truth is, I am ill-satisfied with this matter as it stands at present. I do see—I cannot help seeing, that the affairs of the hospital are not arranged according to the will of the founder."

"None of such institutions are, Mr Harding, nor can they be; the altered circumstances in which we live do not admit of it."

"Quite true—that is quite true; but I can't see that those altered circumstances give me a right to eight hundred a year. I don't know whether I ever read John Hiram's will, but were I to read it now I could not understand it. What I want you, Sir Abraham, to tell me, is this:—am I, as warden, legally and distinctly entitled to the proceeds of the property, after the due maintenance of the twelve bedesmen?"

Sir Abraham declared that he couldn't exactly say in so many words that Mr Harding was legally entitled to, &c., &c., &c., and ended in expressing a strong opinion that it would be madness to raise any further question on the matter, as the suit was to be,—nay, was, abandoned.

Mr Harding, seated in his chair, began to play a slow tune on an imaginary violoncello.

"Nay, my dear sir," continued the attorney-general, "there is no further ground for any question; I don't see that you have the power of raising it."

"I can resign," said Mr Harding, slowly playing away with his right hand, as though the bow were beneath the chair in which he was sitting.

"What! throw it up altogether?" said the attorney-general, gazing with utter astonishment at his client.

"Did you see those articles in *The Jupiter*?" said Mr Harding, piteously, appealing to the sympathy of the lawyer.

Sir Abraham said he had seen them. This poor little clergyman, cowed into such an act of extreme weakness by a newspaper article, was to Sir Abraham so contemptible an object, that he hardly knew how to talk to him as to a rational being.

"Hadn't you better wait," said he, "till Dr Grantly is in town with you? Wouldn't it be better to postpone any serious step till you can consult with him?"

Mr Harding declared vehemently that he could not wait, and Sir Abraham began seriously to doubt his sanity.

"Of course," said the latter, "if you have private means sufficient for your wants, and if this—"

"I haven't a sixpence, Sir Abraham," said the warden.

"God bless me! Why, Mr Harding, how do you mean to live?"

Mr Harding proceeded to explain to the man of law that he meant to keep his precentorship,—that was eighty pounds a year; and, also, that he meant to fall back upon his own little living of Crabtree, which was another eighty pounds. That, to be sure, the duties of the two were hardly compatible; but perhaps he might effect an exchange. And then, recollecting that the attorney-general would hardly care to hear how the service of a cathedral church is divided among the minor canons, stopped short in his explanations.

Sir Abraham listened in pitying wonder. "I really think, Mr Harding, you had better wait for the archdeacon. This is a most serious step,—one for which, in my opinion, there is not the slightest necessity; and, as you have done me the honour of asking my advice, I must implore you to do nothing without the approval of your friends. A man is never the best judge of his own position."

"A man is the best judge of what he feels himself. I'd sooner beg my bread till my death than read such another article as those two that have appeared, and feel, as I do, that the writer has truth on his side."

"Have you not a daughter, Mr Harding,—an unmarried daughter?"

"I have," said he, now standing also, but still playing away on his fiddle with his hand behind his back. "I have, Sir Abraham; and she and I are completely agreed on this subject."

"Pray excuse me, Mr Harding, if what I say seems impertinent; but surely it is you that should be prudent on her behalf. She is young, and does not know the meaning of living on an income of a hundred and sixty pounds a year. On her account give up this idea. Believe me, it is sheer Quixotism."

The warden walked away to the window, and then back to his chair; and then, irresolute what to say, took another turn to the window. The attorney-general was really extremely patient, but he was beginning to think that the interview had been long enough.

"But if this income be not justly mine, what if she and I have both to beg?" said the warden at last, sharply, and in a voice so different from that he had hitherto used, that Sir Abraham was startled. "If so, it would be better to beg."

"My dear sir, nobody now questions its justness."

"Yes, Sir Abraham, one does question it,—the most important of all witnesses against me;—I question it myself. My God knows whether or no I love my daughter; but I would sooner that she and I should both beg, than that she should live in comfort on money which is truly the property of the poor. It may seem strange to you, Sir Abraham, it is strange to myself, that I should have been ten years in that happy home, and not have thought of these things till they were so roughly dinned into my ears. I cannot boast of my conscience, when it required the violence of a public newspaper to awaken it; but, now that it is awake, I must obey it. When I came here, I did not know that the suit was withdrawn by Mr Bold, and my object was to beg you to abandon my defence. As there is no action, there can be no defence; but it is, at any rate, as well that you should know that from to-morrow I shall cease to be the warden of the hospital. My friends and I differ on this subject, Sir Abraham, and that adds much to my sorrow; but it cannot be helped." And, as he finished what he had to say, he played up such a tune as never before had graced the chambers of any attorney-general. He was standing up, gallantly fronting Sir Abraham, and his right arm passed with bold and rapid sweeps before him, as though he were embracing some huge instrument, which allowed him to stand thus erect; and with the fingers of his left hand he stopped, with preternatural velocity, a multitude of strings, which ranged from the top of his collar to the bottom of the lappet of his coat. Sir Abraham listened and looked in wonder. As he had never before seen Mr Harding, the meaning of these wild gesticulations was lost upon him; but he perceived that the gentleman who had a few minutes since been so subdued as to be unable to speak without hesitation, was now impassioned,—nay, almost violent.

"You'll sleep on this, Mr Harding, and to-morrow—"

"I have done more than sleep upon it," said the warden; "I have lain awake upon it, and that night after night. I found I could not sleep upon it: now I hope to do so."

The attorney-general had no answer to make to this; so he expressed a quiet hope that whatever settlement was finally made would be satisfactory; and Mr Harding withdrew, thanking the great man for his kind attention.

Mr Harding was sufficiently satisfied with the interview to feel a glow of comfort as he descended into the small old square of Lincoln's Inn. It was a calm, bright, beautiful night, and by the light of the moon, even the chapel of Lincoln's Inn, and the sombre row of chambers, which surround the quadrangle, looked well. He stood still a moment to collect his thoughts, and reflect on what he had done, and was about to do. He knew that the attorney-general regarded him as little better than a fool, but that he did not mind; he and the attorney-general had not much in common between them; he knew also that others, whom he did care about, would think so too; but Eleanor, he was sure, would exult in what he had done, and the bishop, he trusted, would sympathise with him.

In the meantime he had to meet the archdeacon, and so he walked slowly down Chancery Lane and along Fleet Street, feeling sure that his work for the night was not yet over. When he reached the hotel he rang the bell quietly, and with a palpitating heart; he almost longed to escape round the corner, and delay the coming storm by a further walk round St Paul's Churchyard, but he heard the slow creaking shoes of the old waiter approaching, and he stood his ground manfully.

Chapter XVIII

THE WARDEN IS VERY OBSTINATE

"Dr Grantly is here, sir," greeted his ears before the door was well open, "and Mrs Grantly. They have a sitting-room above, and are waiting up for you."

There was something in the tone of the man's voice which seemed to indicate that even he looked upon the warden as a runaway schoolboy, just recaptured by his guardian, and that he pitied the culprit, though he could not but be horrified at the crime.

The warden endeavoured to appear unconcerned, as he said, "Oh, indeed! I'll go up-stairs at once;" but he failed signally. There was, perhaps, a ray of comfort in the presence of his married daughter; that is to say, of comparative comfort, seeing that his son-in-law was there; but how much would he have preferred that they should both have been safe at Plumstead Episcopi! However, upstairs he went, the waiter slowly preceding him; and on the door being opened the archdeacon was discovered standing in the middle of the room, erect, indeed, as usual, but oh! how sorrowful! and on the dingy sofa behind him reclined his patient wife.

"Papa, I thought you were never coming back," said the lady; "it's twelve o'clock."

"Yes, my dear," said the warden. "The attorney-general named ten for my meeting; to be sure ten is late, but what could I do, you know? Great men will have their own way."

And he gave his daughter a kiss, and shook hands with the doctor, and again tried to look unconcerned.

"And you have absolutely been with the attorney-general?" asked the archdeacon.

Mr Harding signified that he had.

"Good heavens, how unfortunate!" And the archdeacon raised his huge hands in the manner in which his friends are so accustomed to see him express disapprobation and astonishment. "What will Sir Abraham think of it? Did you not know that it is not cus-tomary for clients to go direct to their counsel?"

"Isn't it?" asked the warden, innocently. "Well, at any rate, I've done it now. Sir Abraham didn't seem to think it so very strange."

The archdeacon gave a sigh that would have moved a man-of-war.

"But, papa, what did you say to Sir Abraham?" asked the lady.

"I asked him, my dear, to explain John Hiram's will to me. He couldn't explain it in the only way which would have satisfied me, and so I resigned the wardenship."

"Resigned it!" said the archdeacon, in a solemn voice, sad and low, but yet sufficiently audible,—a sort of whisper that Macready would have envied, and the galleries have applauded with a couple of rounds. "Resigned it! Good heavens!" And the dignitary of the church sank back horrified into a horsehair arm-chair.

"At least I told Sir Abraham that I would resign; and of course I must now do so."

"Not at all," said the archdeacon, catching a ray of hope. "Nothing that you say in such a way to your own counsel can be in any way binding on you; of course you were there to ask his advice. I'm sure Sir Abraham did not advise any such step."

Mr Harding could not say that he had.

"I am sure he disadvised you from it," continued the reverend cross-examiner.

Mr Harding could not deny this.

"I'm sure Sir Abraham must have advised you to consult your friends."

To this proposition also Mr Harding was obliged to assent.

"Then your threat of resignation amounts to nothing, and we are just where we were before."

Mr Harding was now standing on the rug, moving uneasily from one foot to the other. He made no distinct answer to the archdeacon's last proposition, for his mind was chiefly engaged on thinking how he could escape to bed. That his resignation was a thing finally fixed on, a fact all but completed, was not in his mind a matter of any doubt; he knew his own weakness; he knew how prone he was to be led; but he was not weak enough to give way now, to go back from the position to which his conscience had driven him, after having purposely come to London to declare his determination: he did not in the least doubt his resolution, but he greatly doubted his power of defending it against his son-in-law.

"You must be very tired, Susan," said he: "wouldn't you like to go to bed?"

But Susan didn't want to go till her husband went. She had an idea that her papa might be bullied if she were away: she wasn't tired at all, or at least she said so.

The archdeacon was pacing the room, expressing, by certain nods of his head, his opinion of the utter fatuity of his father-in-law.

"Why," at last he said,—and angels might have blushed at the rebuke expressed in his tone and emphasis,—"Why did you go off from Barchester so suddenly? Why did you take such a step without giving us notice, after what had passed at the palace?"

The warden hung his head, and made no reply: he could not condescend to say that he had not intended to give his son-in-law the slip; and as he had not the courage to avow it, he said nothing.

"Papa has been too much for you," said the lady.

The archdeacon took another turn, and again ejaculated, "Good heavens!" this time in a very low whisper, but still audible.

"I think I'll go to bed," said the warden, taking up a side candle.

"At any rate, you'll promise me to take no further step without consultation," said the archdeacon. Mr Harding made no answer, but slowly proceeded to light his candle.

"Of course," continued the other, "such a declaration as that you made to Sir Abraham means nothing. Come, warden, promise me this. The whole affair, you see, is already settled, and that with very little trouble or expense. Bold has been compelled to abandon his action, and all you have to do is to remain quiet at the hospital." Mr Harding still made no reply, but looked meekly into his son-in-law's face. The archdeacon thought he knew his father-in-law, but he was mistaken; he thought that he had already talked over a vacillating man to resign his promise. "Come," said he, "promise Susan to give up this idea of resigning the wardenship."

The warden looked at his daughter, thinking probably at the moment that if Eleanor were contented with him, he need not so much regard his other child, and said, "I am sure Susan will not ask me to break my word, or to do what I know to be wrong."

"Papa," said she, "it would be madness in you to throw up your preferment. What are you to live on?"

"God, that feeds the young ravens, will take care of me also," said Mr Harding, with a smile, as though afraid of giving offence by making his reference to scripture too solemn.

"Pish!" said the archdeacon, turning away rapidly. "If the ravens persisted in refusing the food prepared for them, they wouldn't be fed." A clergyman generally dislikes to be met in argument by any scriptural quotation; he feels as affronted as a doctor does, when recommended by an old woman to take some favourite dose, or as a lawyer when an unprofessional man attempts to put him down by a quibble.

"I shall have the living of Crabtree," modestly suggested the warden.

"Eighty pounds a year!" sneered the archdeacon.

"And the precentorship," said the father-in-law.

"It goes with the wardenship," said the son-in-law. Mr Harding was prepared to argue this point, and began to do so, but Dr Grantly stopped him. "My dear warden," said he, "this is all nonsense. Eighty pounds or a hundred and sixty makes very little difference. You can't live on it,—you can't ruin Eleanor's prospects for ever. In point of fact, you can't resign; the bishop wouldn't accept it; the whole thing is settled. What I now want to do is to prevent any inconvenient tittle-tattle,—any more newspaper articles."

"That's what I want, too," said the warden.

"And to prevent that," continued the other, "we mustn't let any talk of resignation get abroad."

"But I shall resign," said the warden, very, very meekly.

"Good heavens! Susan, my dear, what can I say to him?"

"But, papa," said Mrs Grantly, getting up, and putting her arm through that of her father, "what is Eleanor to do if you throw away your income?"

A hot tear stood in each of the warden's eyes as he looked round upon his married daughter. Why should one sister who was so rich predict poverty for another? Some such idea as this was on his mind, but he gave no utterance to it. Then he thought of the pelican feeding its young with blood from its own breast, but he gave no utterance to that either; and then of Eleanor waiting for him at home, waiting to congratulate him on the end of all his trouble.

"Think of Eleanor, papa," said Mrs Grantly.

"I do think of her," said her father.

"And you will not do this rash thing?" The lady was really moved beyond her usual calm composure.

"It can never be rash to do right," said he. "I shall certainly resign this wardenship."

"Then, Mr Harding, there is nothing before you but ruin," said the archdeacon, now moved beyond all endurance. "Ruin both for you and Eleanor. How do you mean to pay the monstrous expenses of this action?"

Mrs Grantly suggested that, as the action was abandoned, the costs would not be heavy.

"Indeed they will, my dear," continued he. "One cannot have the attorney-general up at twelve o'clock at night for nothing;—but of course your father has not thought of this."

"I will sell my furniture," said the warden.

"Furniture!" ejaculated the other, with a most powerful sneer.

"Come, archdeacon," said the lady, "we needn't mind that at present. You know you never expected papa to pay the costs."

"Such absurdity is enough to provoke Job," said the archdeacon, marching quickly up and down the room. "Your father is like a child. Eight hundred pounds a year!—eight hundred and eighty with the house,—with nothing to do. The very place for him. And to throw that up because some scoundrel writes an article in a newspaper! Well;—I have done my duty. If he chooses to ruin his child I cannot help it;" and he stood still at the fire-place, and looked at himself in a dingy mirror which stood on the chimney-piece.

There was a pause for about a minute, and then the warden, finding that nothing else was coming, lighted his candle, and quietly said, "Good-night."

"Good-night, papa," said the lady.

And so the warden retired; but, as he closed the door behind him, he heard the well-known ejaculation,—slower, lower, more solemn, more ponderous than ever,—"Good heavens!"

Chapter XIX

THE WARDEN RESIGNS

The party met the next morning at breakfast; and a very sombre affair it was,—very unlike the breakfasts at Plumstead Episcopi.

There were three thin, small, dry bits of bacon, each an inch long, served up under a huge old plated cover; there were four three-cornered bits of dry toast, and four square bits of buttered toast; there was a loaf of bread, and some oily-looking butter; and on the sideboard there were the remains of a cold shoulder of mutton. The archdeacon, however, had not come up from his rectory to St Paul's Churchyard to enjoy himself, and therefore nothing was said of the scanty fare.

The guests were as sorry as the viands;—hardly anything was said over the breakfast-table. The archdeacon munched his toast in ominous silence, turning over bitter thoughts in his deep mind. The warden tried to talk to his daughter, and she tried to answer him; but they both failed. There were no feelings at present in common between them. The warden was thinking only of getting back to Barchester, and calculating whether the archdeacon would expect him to wait for him; and Mrs Grantly was preparing herself for a grand attack which she was to make on her father, as agreed upon between herself and her husband during their curtain confabulation of that morning.

When the waiter had creaked out of the room with the last of the teacups, the archdeacon got up and went to the window as though to admire the view. The room looked out on a narrow passage which runs from St Paul's Churchyard to Paternoster Row; and Dr Grantly patiently perused the names of the three shopkeepers whose doors were in view. The warden still kept his seat at the table, and examined the pattern of the tablecloth; and Mrs Grantly, seating herself on the sofa, began to knit.

After a while the warden pulled his Bradshaw out of his pocket, and began laboriously to consult it. There was a train for Barchester at 10 A.M. That was out of the question, for it was nearly ten already. Another at 3 P.M.; another, the night-mail train, at 9 P.M. The three o'clock train would take him home to tea, and would suit very well.

"My dear," said he, "I think I shall go back home at three o'clock to-day. I shall get home at half-past eight. I don't think there's anything to keep me in London."

"The archdeacon and I return by the early train to-morrow, papa; won't you wait and go back with us?"

"Why, Eleanor will expect me tonight; and I've so much to do; and—"

"Much to do!" said the archdeacon sotto voce; but the warden heard him.

"You'd better wait for us, papa."

"Thank ye, my dear! I think I'll go this afternoon." The tamest animal will turn when driven too hard, and even Mr Harding was beginning to fight for his own way.

"I suppose you won't be back before three?" said the lady, addressing her husband.

"I must leave this at two," said the warden.

"Quite out of the question," said the archdeacon, answering his wife, and still reading the shopkeepers' names; "I don't suppose I shall be back till five."

There was another long pause, during which Mr Harding continued to study his Bradshaw.

"I must go to Cox and Cummins," said the archdeacon at last.

"Oh, to Cox and Cummins," said the warden. It was quite a matter of indifference to him where his son-in-law went. The names of Cox and Cummins had now no interest in his ears. What had he to do with Cox and Cummins further, having already had his suit finally adjudicated upon in a court of conscience, a judgment without power of appeal fully registered, and the matter settled so that all the lawyers in London could not disturb it. The archdeacon could go to Cox and Cummins, could remain there all day in anxious discussion; but what might be said there was no longer matter of interest to him, who was so soon to lay aside the name of warden of Barchester Hospital.

The archdeacon took up his shining new clerical hat, and put on his black new clerical gloves, and looked heavy, respectable, decorous, and opulent, a decided clergyman of the Church of England, every inch of him. "I suppose I shall see you at Barchester the day after to-morrow," said he.

The warden supposed he would.

"I must once more beseech you to take no further steps till you see my father; if you owe me nothing," and the archdeacon looked as though he thought a great deal were due to him, "at least you owe so much to my father;" and, without waiting for a reply, Dr Grantly wended his way to Cox and Cummins.

Mrs Grantly waited till the last fall of her husband's foot was heard, as he turned out of the court into St Paul's Churchyard, and then commenced her task of talking her father over.

"Papa," she began, "this is a most serious business."

"Indeed it is," said the warden, ringing the bell.

"I greatly feel the distress of mind you must have endured."

"I am sure you do, my dear;"—and he ordered the waiter to bring him pen, ink, and paper.

"Are you going to write, papa?"

"Yes, my dear;—I am going to write my resignation to the bishop."

"Pray, pray, papa, put it off till our return;—pray put it off till you have seen the bishop;—dear papa! for my sake, for Eleanor's!—"

"It is for your sake and Eleanor's that I do this. I hope, at least, that my children may never have to be ashamed of their father."

"How can you talk about shame, papa?" and she stopped while the waiter creaked in with the paper, and then slowly creaked out again; "how can you talk about shame? you know what all your friends think about this question."

The warden spread his paper on the table, placing it on the meagre blotting-book which the hotel afforded, and sat himself down to write.

"You won't refuse me one request, papa?" continued his daughter; "you won't refuse to delay your letter for two short days? Two days can make no possible difference."

"My dear," said he naïvely, "if I waited till I got to Barchester, I might, perhaps, be prevented."

"But surely you would not wish to offend the bishop?" said she.

"God forbid! The bishop is not apt to take offence, and knows me too well to take in bad part anything that I may be called on to do."

"But, papa—"

"Susan," said he, "my mind on this subject is made up; it is not without much repugnance that I act in opposition to the advice of such men as Sir Abraham Haphazard and the archdeacon; but in this matter I can take no advice, I cannot alter the resolution to which I have come."

"But two days, papa—"

"No;—nor can I delay it. You may add to my present unhappiness by pressing me, but you cannot change my purpose; it will be a comfort to me if you will let the matter rest": and, dipping his pen into the inkstand, he fixed his eyes intently on the paper.

There was something in his manner which taught his daughter to perceive that he was in earnest; she had at one time ruled supreme in her father's house, but she knew that there were moments when, mild and meek as he was, he would have his way, and the present was an occasion of the sort. She returned, therefore, to her knitting, and very shortly after left the room.

The warden was now at liberty to compose his letter, and, as it was characteristic of the man, it shall be given at full length. The official letter, which, when written, seemed to him to be too formally cold to be sent alone to so dear a friend, was accompanied by a private note; and both are here inserted.

The letter of resignation ran as follows:—

CHAPTER HOTEL, ST. PAUL'S,
LONDON,
August, 18—

My LORD BISHOP, It is with the greatest pain that I feel myself constrained to resign into your Lordship's hands the wardenship of the hospital at Barchester, which you so kindly conferred upon me, now nearly twelve years since.

> I need not explain the circumstances which have made this step appear necessary to me. You are aware that a question has arisen as to the right of the warden to the income which has been allotted to the wardenship; it has seemed to me that this right is not well made out, and I hesitate to incur the risk of taking an income to which my legal claim appears doubtful.
>
> The office of precentor of the cathedral is, as your Lordship is aware, joined to that of the warden; that is to say, the precentor has for many years been the warden of the hospital; there is, however, nothing to make the junction of the two offices necessary, and, unless you or the dean and chapter object to such an arrangement, I would wish to keep the precentorship. The income of this office will now be necessary to me; indeed, I do not know why I should be ashamed to say that I should have difficulty in supporting myself without it.
>
> Your Lordship, and such others as you may please to consult on the matter, will at once see that my resignation of the wardenship need offer not the slightest bar to its occupation by another person. I am thought in the wrong by all those whom I have consulted in the matter; I have very little but an inward and an unguided conviction of my own to bring me to this step, and I shall, indeed, be hurt to find that any slur is thrown on the preferment which your kindness bestowed on me, by my resignation of it. I, at any rate for one, shall look on any successor whom you may appoint as enjoying a cleri-

cal situation of the highest respectability, and one to which your Lordship's nomination gives an indefeasible right.

I cannot finish this official letter without again thanking your Lordship for all your great kindness, and I beg to subscribe myself—

Your Lordship's most obedient servant,
SEPTIMUS HARDING,
Warden of Barchester Hospital,
and Precentor of the Cathedral

He then wrote the following private note:—

My dear Bishop, I cannot send you the accompanying official letter without a warmer expression of thanks for all your kindness than would befit a document which may to a certain degree be made public. You, I know, will understand the feeling, and, perhaps, pity the weakness which makes me resign the hospital. I am not made of calibre strong enough to withstand public attack. Were I convinced that I stood on ground perfectly firm, that I was certainly justified in taking eight hundred a year under Hiram's will, I should feel bound by duty to retain the position, however unendurable might be the nature of the assault; but, as I do not feel this conviction, I cannot believe that you will think me wrong in what I am doing.

I had at one time an idea of keeping only some moderate portion of the income; perhaps three hundred a year, and of remitting the remainder to the trustees; but it occurred to me, and I think with reason, that by so doing I should place my successors in an invidious position, and greatly damage your patronage.

My dear friend, let me have a line from you to say that you do not blame me for what I am doing, and that the officiating vicar of Crabtree Parva will be the same to you as the warden of the hospital.

I am very anxious about the precentorship: the archdeacon thinks it must go with the wardenship; I think not, and, that, having it, I cannot be ousted. I will, however, be guided by you and the dean. No other duty will suit me so well, or come so much within my power of adequate performance.

I thank you from my heart for the preferment which I am now giving up, and for all your kindness, and am, dear bishop, now as always—

Yours most sincerely,
SEPTIMUS HARDING

London,—August, 18—

Having written these letters and made a copy of the former one for the benefit of the archdeacon, Mr Harding, whom we must now cease to call the warden, he having designated himself so for the last time, found that it was nearly two o'clock, and that he must prepare for his journey. Yes, from this time he never again admitted the name by which he had been so familiarly known, and in which, to tell the truth, he had rejoiced. The love of titles is common to all men, and a vicar or fellow is as pleased at becoming Mr Archdeacon or Mr Provost, as a lieutenant at getting his captaincy, or a city tallow-chandler in becoming Sir John on the occasion of a Queen's visit to a new bridge. But warden he was no longer, and the name of precentor, though the office was to him so dear, confers in itself no sufficient distinction; our friend, therefore, again became Mr Harding.

Mrs Grantly had gone out; he had, therefore, no one to delay him by further entreaties to postpone his journey; he had soon arranged his bag, and paid his bill, and, leaving a note for his daughter, in which he put the copy of his official letter, he got into a cab and drove away to the station with something of triumph in his heart.

Had he not cause for triumph? Had he not been supremely successful? Had he not for the first time in his life held his own purpose against that of his son-in-law, and manfully combated against great odds,—against the archdeacon's wife as well as the archdeacon? Had he not gained a great victory, and was it not fit that he should step into his cab with triumph?

He had not told Eleanor when he would return, but she was on the look-out for him by every train by which he could arrive, and the pony-carriage was at the Barchester station when the train drew up at the platform.

"My dear," said he, sitting beside her, as she steered her little vessel to one side of the road to make room for the clattering omnibus as they passed from the station into the town, "I hope you'll be able to feel a proper degree of respect for the vicar of Crabtree."

"Dear papa," said she, "I am so glad."

There was great comfort in returning home to that pleasant house, though he was to leave it so soon, and in discussing with his daughter all that he had done, and all that he had to do. It must take some time to get out of one house into another; the curate at Crabtree could not be abolished under six months, that is, unless other provision could be made for him; and then the furniture:—the most of that must be sold to pay Sir Abraham Haphazard for sitting up till twelve at night. Mr Harding was strangely ignorant as to lawyers' bills; he had no idea, from twenty pounds to two thousand, as to the sum in which he was indebted for legal assistance. True, he had called in no lawyer himself; true, he had been no consenting party to the employment of either Cox and Cummins, or Sir Abraham; he had never been consulted on such matters;—the archdeacon had managed all this himself, never for a moment suspecting that Mr Harding would take upon him to end the matter in a way of his own. Had the lawyers' bills been ten thousand pounds, Mr Harding could not have helped it; but he was not on that account disposed to dispute his own liability. The question never occurred to him; but it did occur to him that he had very little money at his banker's, that he could receive nothing further from the hospital, and that the sale of the furniture was his only resource.

"Not all, papa," said Eleanor pleadingly.

"Not quite all, my dear," said he; "that is, if we can help it. We must have a little at Crabtree,—but it can only be a little; we must put a bold front on it, Nelly; it isn't easy to come down from affluence to poverty."

And so they planned their future mode of life; the father taking comfort from the reflection that his daughter would soon be freed from it, and she resolving that her father would soon have in her own house a ready means of escape from the solitude of the Crabtree vicarage.

When the archdeacon left his wife and father-in-law at the Chapter Coffee House to go to Messrs Cox and Cummins, he had no very defined idea of what he had to do when he got there. Gentlemen when at law, or in any way engaged in matters requiring legal assistance, are very apt to go to their lawyers without much absolute necessity;—gentlemen when doing so, are apt to describe such attendance as quite compulsory, and very disagreeable. The lawyers, on the other hand, do not at all see the necessity, though they quite agree as to the disagreeable nature of the visit;—gentlemen when so engaged are usually somewhat gravelled at finding nothing to say to their learned friends; they generally talk a little politics, a little weather, ask some few foolish questions about their suit, and then withdraw, having passed half an hour in a small dingy waiting-room, in company with some junior assistant-clerk, and ten minutes with the members of the firm; the business is then over for which the gentleman has come up to London, probably a distance of a hundred and fifty miles. To be sure he goes to the play, and dines at his friend's club, and has

a bachelor's liberty and bachelor's recreation for three or four days; and he could not probably plead the desire of such gratifications as a reason to his wife for a trip to London.

Married ladies, when your husbands find they are positively obliged to attend their legal advisers, the nature of the duty to be performed is generally of this description.

The archdeacon would not have dreamt of leaving London without going to Cox and
Cummins; and yet he had nothing to say to them. The game was up; he plainly saw that
Mr Harding in this matter was not to be moved; his only remaining business on this head
was to pay the bill and have done with it; and I think it may be taken for granted, that
whatever the cause may be that takes a gentleman to a lawyer's chambers, he never goes
there to pay his bill.

Dr Grantly, however, in the eyes of Messrs Cox and Cummins, represented the spiritualities of the diocese of Barchester, as Mr Chadwick did the temporalities, and was,
therefore, too great a man to undergo the half-hour in the clerk's room. It will not be necessary that we should listen to the notes of sorrow in which the archdeacon bewailed to
Mr Cox the weakness of his father-in-law, and the end of all their hopes of triumph; nor
need we repeat the various exclamations of surprise with which the mournful intelligence
was received. No tragedy occurred, though Mr Cox, a short and somewhat bull-necked
man, was very near a fit of apoplexy when he first attempted to ejaculate that fatal word—
resign!

Over and over again did Mr Cox attempt to enforce on the archdeacon the propriety of
urging on Mr Warden the madness of the deed he was about to do.

"Eight hundred a year!" said Mr Cox.

"And nothing whatever to do!" said Mr Cummins, who had joined the conference.

"No private fortune, I believe," said Mr Cox.

"Not a shilling," said Mr Cummins, in a very low voice, shaking his head.

"I never heard of such a case in all my experience," said Mr Cox.

"Eight hundred a year, and as nice a house as any gentleman could wish to hang up his
hat in," said Mr Cummins.

"And an unmarried daughter, I believe," said Mr Cox, with much moral seriousness in
his tone. The archdeacon only sighed as each separate wail was uttered, and shook his
head, signifying that the fatuity of some people was past belief.

"I'll tell you what he might do," said Mr Cummins, brightening up. "I'll tell you how
you might save it:—let him exchange."

"Exchange where?" said the archdeacon.

"Exchange for a living. There's Quiverful, of Puddingdale;—he has twelve children,
and would be delighted to get the hospital. To be sure Puddingdale is only four hundred,
but that would be saving something out of the fire: Mr Harding would have a curate, and
still keep three hundred or three hundred and fifty."

The archdeacon opened his ears and listened; he really thought the scheme might do.

"The newspapers," continued Mr Cummins, "might hammer away at Quiverful every
day for the next six months without his minding them."

The archdeacon took up his hat, and returned to his hotel, thinking the matter over
deeply. At any rate he would sound Quiverful. A man with twelve children would do
much to double his income.

Chapter XX

FAREWELL

On the morning after Mr Harding's return home he received a note from the bishop full of affection, condolence, and praise. "Pray come to me at once," wrote the bishop, "that we may see what had better be done; as to the hospital, I will not say a word to dissuade you; but I don't like your going to Crabtree: at any rate, come to me at once."

Mr Harding did go to him at once; and long and confidential was the consultation between the two old friends. There they sat together the whole long day, plotting to get the better of the archdeacon, and to carry out little schemes of their own, which they knew would be opposed by the whole weight of his authority.

The bishop's first idea was, that Mr Harding, if left to himself, would certainly starve,—not in the figurative sense in which so many of our ladies and gentlemen do starve on incomes from one to five hundred a year; not that he would be starved as regarded dress coats, port wine, and pocket-money; but that he would positively perish of inanition for want of bread.

"How is a man to live, when he gives up all his income?" said the bishop to himself. And then the good-natured little man began to consider how his friend might be best rescued from a death so horrid and painful.

His first proposition to Mr Harding was, that they should live together at the palace. He, the bishop, positively assured Mr Harding that he wanted another resident chaplain,— not a young working chaplain, but a steady, middle-aged chaplain; one who would dine and drink a glass of wine with him, talk about the archdeacon, and poke the fire. The bishop did not positively name all these duties, but he gave Mr Harding to understand that such would be the nature of the service required.

It was not without much difficulty that Mr Harding made his friend see that this would not suit him; that he could not throw up the bishop's preferment, and then come and hang on at the bishop's table; that he could not allow people to say of him that it was an easy matter to abandon his own income, as he was able to sponge on that of another person. He succeeded, however, in explaining that the plan would not do, and then the bishop brought forward another which he had in his sleeve. He, the bishop, had in his will left certain moneys to Mr Harding's two daughters, imagining that Mr Harding would himself want no such assistance during his own lifetime. This legacy amounted to three thousand pounds each, duty free; and he now pressed it as a gift on his friend.

"The girls, you know," said he, "will have it just the same when you're gone,—and they won't want it sooner;—and as for the interest during my lifetime, it isn't worth talking about. I have more than enough."

With much difficulty and heartfelt sorrow, Mr Harding refused also this offer. No; his wish was to support himself, however poorly,—not to be supported on the charity of any-one. It was hard to make the bishop understand this; it was hard to make him comprehend that the only real favour he could confer was the continuation of his independent friend-ship; but at last even this was done. At any rate, thought the bishop, he will come and dine with me from time to time, and if he be absolutely starving I shall see it.

Touching the precentorship, the bishop was clearly of opinion that it could be held without the other situation,—an opinion from which no one differed; and it was therefore soon settled among all the parties concerned, that Mr Harding should still be the precentor of the cathedral.

On the day following Mr Harding's return, the archdeacon reached Plumstead full of Mr Cummins's scheme regarding Puddingdale and Mr Quiverful. On the very next morn-ing he drove over to Puddingdale, and obtained the full consent of the wretched clerical Priam, who was endeavouring to feed his poor Hecuba and a dozen of Hectors on the small proceeds of his ecclesiastical kingdom. Mr Quiverful had no doubts as to the legal rights of the warden; his conscience would be quite clear as to accepting the income; and as to *The Jupiter*, he begged to assure the archdeacon that he was quite indifferent to any emanations from the profane portion of the periodical press.

Having so far succeeded, he next sounded the bishop; but here he was astonished by most unexpected resistance. The bishop did not think it would do. "Not do, why not?" and seeing that his father was not shaken, he repeated the question in a severer form: "Why not do, my lord?"

His lordship looked very unhappy, and shuffled about in his chair, but still didn't give way; he thought Puddingdale wouldn't do for Mr Harding; it was too far from Barchester.

"Oh! of course he'll have a curate."

The bishop also thought that Mr Quiverful wouldn't do for the hospital; such an ex-change wouldn't look well at such a time; and, when pressed harder, he declared he didn't think Mr Harding would accept of Puddingdale under any circumstances.

"How is he to live?" demanded the archdeacon.

The bishop, with tears in his eyes, declared that he had not the slightest conception how life was to be sustained within him at all.

The archdeacon then left his father, and went down to the hospital; but Mr Harding wouldn't listen at all to the Puddingdale scheme. To his eyes it had no attraction; it sa-voured of simony, and was likely to bring down upon him harder and more deserved strictures than any he had yet received: he positively declined to become vicar of Pud-dingdale under any circumstances.

The archdeacon waxed wroth, talked big, and looked bigger; he said something about dependence and beggary, spoke of the duty every man was under to earn his bread, made passing allusions to the follies of youth and waywardness of age, as though Mr Harding were afflicted by both, and ended by declaring that he had done. He felt that he had left no stone unturned to arrange matters on the best and easiest footing; that he had, in fact, so arranged them, that he had so managed that there was no further need of any anxiety in the matter. And how had he been paid? His advice had been systematically rejected; he had been not only slighted, but distrusted and avoided; he and his measures had been ut-terly thrown over, as had been Sir Abraham, who, he had reason to know, was much pained at what had occurred. He now found it was useless to interfere any further, and he should retire. If any further assistance were required from him, he would probably be called on, and should be again happy to come forward. And so he left the hospital, and has not since entered it from that day to this.

And here we must take leave of Archdeacon Grantly. We fear that he is represented in these pages as being worse than he is; but we have had to do with his foibles, and not with his virtues. We have seen only the weak side of the man, and have lacked the opportunity of bringing him forward on his strong ground. That he is a man somewhat too fond of his own way, and not sufficiently scrupulous in his manner of achieving it, his best friends cannot deny. That he is bigoted in favour, not so much of his doctrines as of his cloth, is also true: and it is true that the possession of a large income is a desire that sits near his heart. Nevertheless, the archdeacon is a gentleman and a man of conscience; he spends his money liberally, and does the work he has to do with the best of his ability; he improves the tone of society of those among whom he lives. His aspirations are of a healthy, if not of the highest, kind. Though never an austere man, he upholds propriety of conduct both by example and precept. He is generous to the poor, and hospitable to the rich; in matters of religion he is sincere, and yet no Pharisee; he is in earnest, and yet no fanatic. On the whole, the Archdeacon of Barchester is a man doing more good than harm,—a man to be furthered and supported, though perhaps also to be controlled; and it is matter of regret to us that the course of our narrative has required that we should see more of his weakness than his strength.

Mr Harding allowed himself no rest till everything was prepared for his departure from the hospital. It may be as well to mention that he was not driven to the stern necessity of selling all his furniture: he had been quite in earnest in his intention to do so, but it was soon made known to him that the claims of Messrs Cox and Cummins made no such step obligatory. The archdeacon had thought it wise to make use of the threat of the lawyer's bill, to frighten his father-in-law into compliance; but he had no intention to saddle Mr Harding with costs, which had been incurred by no means exclusively for his benefit. The amount of the bill was added to the diocesan account, and was, in fact, paid out of the bishop's pocket, without any consciousness on the part of his lordship. A great part of his furniture he did resolve to sell, having no other means to dispose of it; and the ponies and carriage were transferred, by private contract, to the use of an old maiden lady in the city.

For his present use Mr Harding took a lodging in Barchester, and thither were conveyed such articles as he wanted for daily use:—his music, books, and instruments, his own arm-chair, and Eleanor's pet sofa; her teapoy and his cellaret, and also the slender but still sufficient contents of his wine-cellar. Mrs Grantly had much wished that her sister would reside at Plumstead, till her father's house at Crabtree should be ready for her; but Eleanor herself strongly resisted this proposal. It was in vain urged upon her, that a lady in lodgings cost more than a gentleman; and that, under her father's present circumstances, such an expense should be avoided. Eleanor had not pressed her father to give up the hospital in order that she might live at Plumstead Rectory and he alone in his Barchester lodgings; nor did Eleanor think that she would be treating a certain gentleman very fairly, if she betook herself to the house which he would be the least desirous of entering of any in the county. So she got a little bedroom for herself behind the sitting-room, and just over the little back parlour of the chemist, with whom they were to lodge. There was somewhat of a savour of senna softened by peppermint about the place; but, on the whole, the lodgings were clean and comfortable.

The day had been fixed for the migration of the ex-warden, and all Barchester were in a state of excitement on the subject. Opinion was much divided as to the propriety of Mr Harding's conduct. The mercantile part of the community, the mayor and corporation, and council, also most of the ladies, were loud in his praise. Nothing could be more noble, nothing more generous, nothing more upright. But the gentry were of a different way of thinking,—especially the lawyers and the clergymen. They said such conduct was very weak and undignified; that Mr Harding evinced a lamentable want of *esprit de corps*, as well as courage; and that such an abdication must do much harm, and could do but little good.

On the evening before he left, he summoned all the bedesmen into his parlour to wish them good-bye. With Bunce he had been in frequent communication since his return from London, and had been at much pains to explain to the old man the cause of his resignation, without in any way prejudicing the position of his successor. The others, also, he had seen more or less frequently; and had heard from most of them separately some expression of regret at his departure; but he had postponed his farewell till the last evening.

He now bade the maid put wine and glasses on the table; and had the chairs arranged around the room; and sent Bunce to each of the men to request they would come and say farewell to their late warden. Soon the noise of aged scuffling feet was heard upon the gravel and in the little hall, and the eleven men who were enabled to leave their rooms were assembled.

"Come in, my friends, come in," said the warden;—he was still warden then. "Come in, and sit down;" and he took the hand of Abel Handy, who was the nearest to him, and led the limping grumbler to a chair. The others followed slowly and bashfully; the infirm, the lame, and the blind: poor wretches! who had been so happy, had they but known it! Now their aged faces were covered with shame, and every kind word from their master was a coal of fire burning on their heads.

When first the news had reached them that Mr Harding was going to leave the hospital, it had been received with a kind of triumph;—his departure was, as it were, a prelude to success. He had admitted his want of right to the money about which they were disputing; and as it did not belong to him, of course, it did to them. The one hundred a year to each of them was actually becoming a reality; and Abel Handy was a hero, and Bunce a faint-hearted sycophant, worthy neither honour nor fellowship. But other tidings soon made their way into the old men's rooms. It was first notified to them that the income abandoned by Mr Harding would not come to them; and these accounts were confirmed by attorney Finney. They were then informed that Mr Harding's place would be at once filled by another. That the new warden could not be a kinder man they all knew; that he would be a less friendly one most suspected; and then came the bitter information that, from the moment of Mr Harding's departure, the twopence a day, his own peculiar gift, must of necessity be withdrawn.

And this was to be the end of all their mighty struggle,—of their fight for their rights,—of their petition, and their debates, and their hopes! They were to change the best of masters for a possible bad one, and to lose twopence a day each man! No; unfortunate as this was, it was not the worst, or nearly the worst, as will just now be seen.

"Sit down, sit down, my friends," said the warden; "I want to say a word to you and to drink your healths, before I leave you. Come up here, Moody, here is a chair for you; come, Jonathan Crumple;"—and by degrees he got the men to be seated. It was not surprising that they should hang back with faint hearts, having returned so much kindness with such deep ingratitude. Last of all of them came Bunce, and with sorrowful mien and slow step got into his accustomed seat near the fire-place.

When they were all in their places, Mr Harding rose to address them; and then finding himself not quite at home on his legs, he sat down again. "My dear old friends," said he, "you all know that I am going to leave you."

There was a sort of murmur ran round the room, intended, perhaps, to express regret at his departure; but it was but a murmur, and might have meant that or anything else.

"There has been lately some misunderstanding between us. You have thought, I believe, that you did not get all that you were entitled to, and that the funds of the hospital have not been properly disposed of. As for me, I cannot say what should be the disposition of these moneys, or how they should be managed, and I have therefore thought it best to go."

"We never wanted to drive your reverence out of it," said Handy.

"No, indeed, your reverence," said Skulpit. "We never thought it would come to this. When I signed the petition,—that is, I didn't sign it, because—"

"Let his reverence speak, can't you?" said Moody.

"No," continued Mr Harding; "I am sure you did not wish to turn me out; but I thought it best to leave you. I am not a very good hand at a lawsuit, as you may all guess; and when it seemed necessary that our ordinary quiet mode of living should be disturbed, I thought it better to go. I am neither angry nor offended with any man in the hospital."

Here Bunce uttered a kind of groan, very clearly expressive of disagreement.

"I am neither angry nor displeased with any man in the hospital," repeated Mr Harding, emphatically. "If any man has been wrong,—and I don't say any man has,—he has erred through wrong advice. In this country all are entitled to look for their own rights, and you have done no more. As long as your interests and my interests were at variance, I could give you no counsel on this subject; but the connection between us has ceased; my income can no longer depend on your doings, and therefore, as I leave you, I venture to offer to you my advice."

The men all declared that they would from henceforth be entirely guided by Mr Harding's opinion in their affairs.

"Some gentleman will probably take my place here very soon, and I strongly advise you to be prepared to receive him in a kindly spirit and to raise no further question among yourselves as to the amount of his income. Were you to succeed in lessening what he has to receive, you would not increase your own allowance. The surplus would not go to you; your wants are adequately provided for, and your position could hardly be improved."

"God bless your reverence, we knows it," said Spriggs.

"It's all true, your reverence," said Skulpit. "We sees it all now."

"Yes, Mr Harding," said Bunce, opening his mouth for the first time; "I believe they do understand it now, now that they've driven from under the same roof with them such a master as not one of them will ever know again,—now that they're like to be in sore want of a friend."

"Come, come, Bunce," said Mr Harding, blowing his nose and manœuvring to wipe his eyes at the same time.

"Oh, as to that," said Handy, "we none of us never wanted to do Mr Harding no harm; if he's going now, it's not along of us; and I don't see for what Mr Bunce speaks up agen us that way."

"You've ruined yourselves, and you've ruined me too, and that's why," said Bunce.

"Nonsense, Bunce," said Mr Harding; "there's nobody ruined at all. I hope you'll let me leave you all friends; I hope you'll all drink a glass of wine in friendly feeling with me and with one another. You'll have a good friend, I don't doubt, in your new warden; and if ever you want any other, why after all I'm not going so far off but that I shall sometimes see you;" and then, having finished his speech, Mr Harding filled all the glasses, and himself handed each a glass to the men round him, and raising his own said:—

"God bless you all! you have my heartfelt wishes for your welfare. I hope you may live contented, and die trusting in the Lord Jesus Christ, and thankful to Almighty God For the good things he has given you. God bless you, my friends!" and Mr Harding drank his wine.

Another murmur, somewhat more articulate than the first, passed round the circle, and this time it was intended to imply a blessing on Mr Harding. It had, however, but little cordiality in it. Poor old men! how could they be cordial with their sore consciences and shamed faces? how could they bid God bless him with hearty voices and a true benison, knowing, as they did, that their vile cabal had driven him from his happy home, and sent him in his old age to seek shelter under a strange roof-tree? They did their best, however; they drank their wine, and withdrew.

As they left the hall-door, Mr Harding shook hands with each of the men, and spoke a kind word to them about their individual cases and ailments; and so they departed, answering his questions in the fewest words, and retreated to their dens, a sorrowful repentant crew.

All but Bunce, who still remained to make his own farewell. "There's poor old Bell," said Mr Harding; "I mustn't go without saying a word to him; come through with me, Bunce, and bring the wine with you;" and so they went through to the men's cottages, and found the old man propped up as usual in his bed.

"I've come to say good-bye to you, Bell," said Mr Harding, speaking loud, for the old man was deaf.

"And are you going away, then, really?" asked Bell.

"Indeed I am, and I've brought you a glass of wine; so that we may part friends, as we lived, you know."

The old man took the proffered glass in his shaking hands, and drank it eagerly. "God bless you, Bell!" said Mr Harding; "good-bye, my old friend."

"And so you're really going?" the man again asked.

"Indeed I am, Bell."

The poor old bed-ridden creature still kept Mr Harding's hand in his own, and the warden thought that he had met with something like warmth of feeling in the one of all his subjects from whom it was the least likely to be expected; for poor old Bell had nearly outlived all human feelings. "And your reverence," said he, and then he paused, while his old palsied head shook horribly, and his shrivelled cheeks sank lower within his jaws, and his glazy eye gleamed with a momentary light; "and your reverence, shall we get the hundred a year, then?"

How gently did Mr Harding try to extinguish the false hope of money which had been so wretchedly raised to disturb the quiet of the dying man! One other week and his mortal coil would be shuffled off; in one short week would God resume his soul, and set it apart for its irrevocable doom; seven more tedious days and nights of senseless inactivity, and all would be over for poor Bell in this world; and yet, with his last audible words, he was demanding his moneyed rights, and asserting himself to be the proper heir of John Hiram's bounty! Not on him, poor sinner as he was, be the load of such sin!

Mr Harding returned to his parlour, meditating with a sick heart on what he had seen, and Bunce with him. We will not describe the parting of these two good men, for good men they were. It was in vain that the late warden endeavoured to comfort the heart of the old bedesman; poor old Bunce felt that his days of comfort were gone. The hospital had to him been a happy home, but it could be so no longer. He had had honour there, and friendship; he had recognised his master, and been recognised; all his wants, both of soul and body, had been supplied, and he had been a happy man. He wept grievously as he parted from his friend, and the tears of an old man are bitter. "It is all over for me in this world," said he, as he gave the last squeeze to Mr Harding's hand; "I have now to forgive those who have injured me;—and to die."

And so the old man went out, and then Mr Harding gave way to his grief and he too wept aloud.

Chapter XXI

CONCLUSION

Our tale is now done, and it only remains to us to collect the scattered threads of our little story, and to tie them into a seemly knot. This will not be a work of labour, either to the author or to his readers; we have not to deal with many personages, or with stirring events, and were it not for the custom of the thing, we might leave it to the imagination of all concerned to conceive how affairs at Barchester arranged themselves.

On the morning after the day last alluded to, Mr Harding, at an early hour, walked out of the hospital, with his daughter under his arm, and sat down quietly to breakfast at his lodgings over the chemist's shop. There was no parade about his departure; no one, not even Bunce, was there to witness it; had he walked to the apothecary's thus early to get a piece of court plaster, or a box of lozenges, he could not have done it with less appearance of an important movement. There was a tear in Eleanor's eye as she passed through the big gateway and over the bridge; but Mr Harding walked with an elastic step, and entered his new abode with a pleasant face.

"Now, my dear," said he, "you have everything ready, and you can make tea here just as nicely as in the parlour at the hospital." So Eleanor took off her bonnet and made the tea. After this manner did the late Warden of Barchester Hospital accomplish his flitting, and change his residence.

It was not long before the archdeacon brought his father to discuss the subject of a new warden. Of course he looked upon the nomination as his own, and he had in his eye three or four fitting candidates, seeing that Mr Cummins's plan as to the living of Puddingdale could not be brought to bear. How can I describe the astonishment which confounded him, when his father declared that he would appoint no successor to Mr Harding? "If we can get the matter set to rights, Mr Harding will return," said the bishop; "and if we cannot, it will be wrong to put any other gentleman into so cruel a position."

It was in vain that the archdeacon argued and lectured, and even threatened; in vain he my-lorded his poor father in his sternest manner; in vain his "good heavens!" were ejaculated in a tone that might have moved a whole synod, let alone one weak and aged bishop. Nothing could induce his father to fill up the vacancy caused by Mr Harding's retirement.

Even John Bold would have pitied the feelings with which the archdeacon returned to Plumstead: the church was falling, nay, already in ruins; its dignitaries were yielding without a struggle before the blows of its antagonists; and one of its most respected bishops, his own father,—the man considered by all the world as being in such matters under his, Dr Grantly's, control,—had positively resolved to capitulate, and own himself vanquished!

And how fared the hospital under this resolve of its visitor? Badly indeed. It is now some years since Mr Harding left it, and the warden's house is still tenantless. Old Bell has died, and Billy Gazy; the one-eyed Spriggs has drunk himself to death, and three others of the twelve have been gathered into the churchyard mould. Six have gone, and the six vacancies remain unfilled! Yes, six have died, with no kind friend to solace their last moments, with no wealthy neighbour to administer comforts and ease the stings of death. Mr Harding, indeed, did not desert them; from him they had such consolation as a dying man may receive from his Christian pastor; but it was the occasional kindness of a stranger which ministered to them, and not the constant presence of a master, a neighbour, and a friend.

Nor were those who remained better off than those who died. Dissensions rose among them, and contests for pre-eminence; and then they began to understand that soon one among them would be the last,—some one wretched being would be alone there in that now comfortless hospital,—the miserable relic of what had once been so good and so comfortable.

The building of the hospital itself has not been allowed to go to ruins. Mr Chadwick, who still holds his stewardship, and pays the accruing rents into an account opened at a bank for the purpose, sees to that; but the whole place has become disordered and ugly. The warden's garden is a wretched wilderness, the drive and paths are covered with weeds, the flower-beds are bare, and the unshorn lawn is now a mass of long damp grass and unwholesome moss. The beauty of the place is gone; its attractions have withered. Alas! a very few years since it was the prettiest spot in Barchester, and now it is a disgrace to the city.

Mr Harding did not go out to Crabtree Parva. An arrangement was made which respected the homestead of Mr Smith and his happy family, and put Mr Harding into possession of a small living within the walls of the city. It is the smallest possible parish, containing a part of the Cathedral Close and a few old houses adjoining. The church is a singular little Gothic building, perched over a gateway, through which the Close is entered, and is approached by a flight of stone steps which leads down under the archway of the gate. It is no bigger than an ordinary room,—perhaps twenty-seven feet long by eighteen wide,—but still it is a perfect church. It contains an old carved pulpit and reading-desk, a tiny altar under a window filled with dark old-coloured glass, a font, some half-dozen pews, and perhaps a dozen seats for the poor; and also a vestry. The roof is high pitched, and of black old oak, and the three large beams which support it run down to the side walls, and terminate in grotesquely carved faces,—two devils and an angel on one side, two angels and a devil on the other. Such is the church of St Cuthbert at Barchester, of which Mr Harding became rector, with a clear income of seventy-five pounds a year.

Here he performs afternoon service every Sunday, and administers the Sacrament once in every three months. His audience is not large; and, had they been so, he could not have accommodated them: but enough come to fill his six pews, and on the front seat of those devoted to the poor is always to be seen our old friend Mr Bunce, decently arrayed in his bedesman's gown.

Mr Harding is still precentor of Barchester; and it is very rarely the case that those who attend the Sunday morning service miss the gratification of hearing him chant the Litany, as no other man in England can do it. He is neither a discontented nor an unhappy man; he still inhabits the lodgings to which he went on leaving the hospital, but he now has them to himself. Three months after that time Eleanor became Mrs Bold, and of course removed to her husband's house.

There were some difficulties to be got over on the occasion of the marriage. The archdeacon, who could not so soon overcome his grief, would not be persuaded to grace the ceremony with his presence, but he allowed his wife and children to be there. The marriage took place in the cathedral, and the bishop himself officiated. It was the last occasion on which he ever did so; and, though he still lives, it is not probable that he will ever do so again.

Not long after the marriage, perhaps six months, when Eleanor's bridal-honours were fading, and persons were beginning to call her Mrs Bold without twittering, the archdeacon consented to meet John Bold at a dinner-party, and since that time they have become almost friends. The archdeacon firmly believes that his brother-in-law was, as a bachelor, an infidel, an unbeliever in the great truths of our religion; but that matrimony has opened his eyes, as it has those of others. And Bold is equally inclined to think that time has softened the asperities of the archdeacon's character. Friends though they are, they do not often revert to the feud of the hospital.

Mr Harding, we say, is not an unhappy man: he keeps his lodgings, but they are of little use to him, except as being the one spot on earth which he calls his own. His time is spent chiefly at his daughter's or at the palace; he is never left alone, even should he wish to be so; and within a twelvemonth of Eleanor's marriage his determination to live at his own lodging had been so far broken through and abandoned, that he consented to have his violoncello permanently removed to his daughter's house.

Every other day a message is brought to him from the bishop. "The bishop's compliments, and his lordship is not very well to-day, and he hopes Mr Harding will dine with him." This bulletin as to the old man's health is a myth; for though he is over eighty he is never ill, and will probably die some day, as a spark goes out, gradually and without a struggle. Mr Harding does dine with him very often, which means going to the palace at three and remaining till ten; and whenever he does not the bishop whines, and says that the port wine is corked, and complains that nobody attends to him, and frets himself off to bed an hour before his time.

It was long before the people of Barchester forgot to call Mr Harding by his long well-known name of Warden. It had become so customary to say Mr Warden, that it was not easily dropped. "No, no," he always says when so addressed, "not warden now, only precentor."

BARCHESTER TOWERS

CHAPTER I

WHO WILL BE THE NEW BISHOP?

In the latter days of July in the year 185—, a most important question was for ten days hourly asked in the cathedral city of Barchester, and answered every hour in various ways—Who was to be the new bishop?

The death of old Dr. Grantly, who had for many years filled that chair with meek authority, took place exactly as the ministry of Lord —— was going to give place to that of Lord ——. The illness of the good old man was long and lingering, and it became at last a matter of intense interest to those concerned whether the new appointment should be made by a conservative or liberal government.

It was pretty well understood that the outgoing premier had made his selection and that if the question rested with him, the mitre would descend on the head of Archdeacon Grantly, the old bishop's son. The archdeacon had long managed the affairs of the diocese, and for some months previous to the demise of his father rumour had confidently assigned to him the reversion of his father's honours.

Bishop Grantly died as he had lived, peaceably, slowly, without pain and without excitement. The breath ebbed from him almost imperceptibly, and for a month before his death it was a question whether he were alive or dead.

A trying time was this for the archdeacon, for whom was designed the reversion of his father's see by those who then had the giving away of episcopal thrones. I would not be understood to say that the prime minister had in so many words promised the bishopric to Dr. Grantly. He was too discreet a man for that. There is a proverb with reference to the killing of cats, and those who know anything either of high or low government places will be well aware that a promise may be made without positive words and that an expectant may be put into the highest state of encouragement, though the great man on whose breath he hangs may have done no more than whisper that "Mr. So-and-So is certainly a rising man."

Such a whisper had been made, and was known by those who heard it to signify that the cures of the diocese of Barchester should not be taken out of the hands of the archdeacon. The then prime minister was all in all at Oxford, and had lately passed a night at the house of the Master of Lazarus. Now the Master of Lazarus—which is, by the by, in many respects the most comfortable as well as the richest college at Oxford—was the archdeacon's most intimate friend and most trusted counsellor. On the occasion of the prime minister's visit, Dr. Grantly was of course present, and the meeting was very gracious. On the following morning Dr. Gwynne, the master, told the archdeacon that in his opinion the thing was settled.

At this time the bishop was quite on his last legs; but the ministry also were tottering. Dr. Grantly returned from Oxford, happy and elated, to resume his place in the palace and to continue to perform for the father the last duties of a son, which, to give him his due, he performed with more tender care than was to be expected from his usual somewhat worldly manners.

A month since, the physicians had named four weeks as the outside period during which breath could be supported within the body of the dying man. At the end of the month the physicians wondered, and named another fortnight. The old man lived on wine alone, but at the end of the fortnight he still lived, and the tidings of the fall of the ministry became more frequent. Sir Lamda Mewnew and Sir Omicron Pie, the two great London doctors, now came down for the fifth time and declared, shaking their learned heads, that another week of life was impossible; and as they sat down to lunch in the episcopal dining-room, whispered to the archdeacon their own private knowledge that the ministry must fall within five days. The son returned to his father's room and, after administering with his own hands the sustaining modicum of madeira, sat down by the bedside to calculate his chances.

The ministry were to be out within five days: his father was to be dead within—no, he rejected that view of the subject. The ministry were to be out, and the diocese might probably be vacant at the same period. There was much doubt as to the names of the men who were to succeed to power, and a week must elapse before a cabinet was formed. Would not vacancies be filled by the outgoing men during this week? Dr. Grantly had a kind of idea that such would be the case but did not know, and then he wondered at his own ignorance on such a question.

He tried to keep his mind away from the subject, but he could not. The race was so very close, and the stakes were so very high. He then looked at the dying man's impassive, placid face. There was no sign there of death or disease; it was something thinner than of yore, somewhat grayer, and the deep lines of age more marked; but, as far as he could judge, life might yet hang there for weeks to come. Sir Lamda Mewnew and Sir Omicron Pie had thrice been wrong, and might yet be wrong thrice again. The old bishop slept during twenty of the twenty-four hours, but during the short periods of his waking moments, he knew both his son and his dear old friend, Mr. Harding, the archdeacon's father-in-law, and would thank them tenderly for their care and love. Now he lay sleeping like a baby, resting easily on his back, his mouth just open, and his few gray hairs straggling from beneath his cap; his breath was perfectly noiseless, and his thin, wan hand, which lay above the coverlid, never moved. Nothing could be easier than the old man's passage from this world to the next.

But by no means easy were the emotions of him who sat there watching. He knew it must be now or never. He was already over fifty, and there was little chance that his friends who were now leaving office would soon return to it. No probable British prime minister but he who was now in, he who was so soon to be out, would think of making a bishop of Dr. Grantly. Thus he thought long and sadly, in deep silence, and then gazed at that still living face, and then at last dared to ask himself whether he really longed for his father's death.

The effort was a salutary one, and the question was answered in a moment. The proud, wishful, worldly man sank on his knees by the bedside and, taking the bishop's hand within his own, prayed eagerly that his sins might be forgiven him.

His face was still buried in the clothes when the door of the bedroom opened noiselessly and Mr. Harding entered with a velvet step. Mr. Harding's attendance at that bedside had been nearly as constant as that of the archdeacon, and his ingress and egress was as much a matter of course as that of his son-in-law. He was standing close beside the archdeacon before he was perceived, and would also have knelt in prayer had he not feared that his doing so might have caused some sudden start and have disturbed the dying man. Dr. Grantly, however, instantly perceived him and rose from his knees. As he did so Mr. Harding took both his hands and pressed them warmly. There was more fellowship between them at that moment than there had ever been before, and it so happened that after circumstances greatly preserved the feeling. As they stood there pressing each other's hands, the tears rolled freely down their cheeks.

"God bless you, my dears," said the bishop with feeble voice as he woke. "God bless you—may God bless you both, my dear children." And so he died.

There was no loud rattle in the throat, no dreadful struggle, no palpable sign of death, but the lower jaw fell a little from its place, and the eyes which had been so constantly closed in sleep now remained fixed and open. Neither Mr. Harding nor Dr. Grantly knew that life was gone, though both suspected it.

"I believe it's all over," said Mr. Harding, still pressing the other's hands. "I think—nay, I hope it is."

"I will ring the bell," said the other, speaking all but in a whisper. "Mrs. Phillips should be here."

Mrs. Phillips, the nurse, was soon in the room, and immediately, with practised hand, closed those staring eyes.

"It's all over, Mrs. Phillips?" asked Mr. Harding.

"My lord's no more," said Mrs. Phillips, turning round and curtseying low with solemn face; "his lordship's gone more like a sleeping babby than any that I ever saw."

"It's a great relief, Archdeacon," said Mr. Harding, "a great relief—dear, good, excellent old man. Oh that our last moments may be as innocent and as peaceful as his!"

"Surely," said Mrs. Phillips. "The Lord be praised for all his mercies; but, for a meek, mild, gentle-spoken Christian, his lordship was—" and Mrs. Phillips, with unaffected but easy grief, put up her white apron to her flowing eyes.

"You cannot but rejoice that it is over," said Mr. Harding, still consoling his friend. The archdeacon's mind, however, had already travelled from the death chamber to the closet of the prime minister. He had brought himself to pray for his father's life, but now that that life was done, minutes were too precious to be lost. It was now useless to dally with the fact of the bishop's death—useless to lose perhaps everything for the pretence of a foolish sentiment.

But how was he to act while his father-in-law stood there holding his hand? How, without appearing unfeeling, was he to forget his father in the bishop—to overlook what he had lost, and think only of what he might possibly gain?

"No, I suppose not," said he, at last, in answer to Mr. Harding. "We have all expected it so long."

Mr. Harding took him by the arm and led him from the room. "We will see him again to-morrow morning," said he; "we had better leave the room now to the women." And so they went downstairs.

It was already evening and nearly dark. It was most important that the prime minister should know that night that the diocese was vacant. Everything might depend on it; and so, in answer to Mr. Harding's further consolation, the archdeacon suggested that a telegraph message should be immediately sent off to London. Mr. Harding, who had really been somewhat surprised to find Dr. Grantly, as he thought, so much affected, was rather taken aback, but he made no objection. He knew that the archdeacon had some hope of succeeding to his father's place, though he by no means knew how highly raised that hope had been.

"Yes," said Dr. Grantly, collecting himself and shaking off his weakness, "we must send a message at once; we don't know what might be the consequence of delay. Will you do it?'

"I! Oh, yes; certainly. I'll do anything, only I don't know exactly what it is you want."

Dr. Grantly sat down before a writing-table and, taking pen and ink, wrote on a slip of paper as follows:—

> By Electric Telegraph.
> For the Earl of ——, Downing Street, or elsewhere.
> The Bishop of Barchester is dead.
> Message sent by the Rev. Septimus Harding.

"There," said he. "Just take that to the telegraph office at the railway station and give it in as it is; they'll probably make you copy it on to one of their own slips; that's all you'll have to do; then you'll have to pay them half a crown." And the archdeacon put his hand in his pocket and pulled out the necessary sum.

Mr. Harding felt very much like an errand-boy, and also felt that he was called on to perform his duties as such at rather an unseemly time, but he said nothing, and took the slip of paper and the proffered coin.

"But you've put my name into it, Archdeacon."

"Yes," said the other, "there should be the name of some clergyman, you know, and what name so proper as that of so old a friend as yourself? The earl won't look at the name, you may be sure of that; but my dear Mr. Harding, pray don't lose any time."

Mr. Harding got as far as the library door on his way to the station, when he suddenly remembered the news with which he was fraught when he entered the poor bishop's bed-room. He had found the moment so inopportune for any mundane tidings, that he had repressed the words which were on his tongue, and immediately afterwards all recollection of the circumstance was for the time banished by the scene which had occurred.

"But, Archdeacon," said he, turning back, "I forgot to tell you—the ministry are out."

"Out!" ejaculated the archdeacon, in a tone which too plainly showed his anxiety and dismay, although under the circumstances of the moment he endeavoured to control himself. "Out! Who told you so?"

Mr. Harding explained that news to this effect had come down by electric telegraph, and that the tidings had been left at the palace door by Mr. Chadwick.

The archdeacon sat silent for awhile meditating, and Mr. Harding stood looking at him. "Never mind," said the archdeacon at last; "send the message all the same. The news must be sent to someone, and there is at present no one else in a position to receive it. Do it at once, my dear friend; you know I would not trouble you, were I in a state to do it myself. A few minutes' time is of the greatest importance."

Mr. Harding went out and sent the message, and it may be as well that we should follow it to its destination. Within thirty minutes of its leaving Barchester it reached the Earl of —— in his inner library. What elaborate letters, what eloquent appeals, what indignant remonstrances he might there have to frame, at such a moment, may be conceived but not described! How he was preparing his thunder for successful rivals, standing like a British peer with his back to the sea-coal fire, and his hands in his breeches pockets—how his fine eye was lit up with anger, and his forehead gleamed with patriotism—how he stamped his foot as he thought of his heavy associates—how he all but swore as he remembered how much too clever one of them had been—my creative readers may imagine. But was he so engaged? No: history and truth compel me to deny it. He was sitting easily in a lounging chair, conning over a Newmarket list, and by his elbow on the table was lying open an uncut French novel on which he was engaged.

He opened the cover in which the message was enclosed and, having read it, he took his pen and wrote on the back of it—

For the Earl of ——,

With the Earl of ——'s compliments

and sent it off again on its journey. Thus terminated our unfortunate friend's chances of possessing the glories of a bishopric.

The names of many divines were given in the papers as that of the bishop-elect. "The British Grandmother" declared that Dr. Gwynne was to be the man, in compliment to the late ministry. This was a heavy blow to Dr. Grantly, but he was not doomed to see himself superseded by his friend. "The Anglican Devotee" put forward confidently the claims of a great London preacher of austere doctrines; and "The Eastern Hemisphere," an evening paper supposed to possess much official knowledge, declared in favour of an eminent naturalist, a gentleman most completely versed in the knowledge of rocks and minerals, but supposed by many to hold on religious subjects no special doctrines whatever. "The Jupiter," that daily paper which, as we all know, is the only true source of infallibly correct information on all subjects, for awhile was silent, but at last spoke out. The merits of all these candidates were discussed and somewhat irreverently disposed of, and then "The Jupiter" declared that Dr. Proudie was to be the man.

Dr. Proudie was the man. Just a month after the demise of the late bishop, Dr. Proudie kissed the Queen's hand as his successor-elect.

We must beg to be allowed to draw a curtain over the sorrows of the archdeacon as he sat, sombre and sad at heart, in the study of his parsonage at Plumstead Episcopi. On the day subsequent to the dispatch of the message he heard that the Earl of —— had consented to undertake the formation of a ministry, and from that moment he knew that his chance was over. Many will think that he was wicked to grieve for the loss of episcopal power, wicked to have coveted it, nay, wicked even to have thought about it, in the way and at the moments he had done so.

With such censures I cannot profess that I completely agree. The *nolo episcopari*, though still in use, is so directly at variance with the tendency of all human wishes, that it cannot be thought to express the true aspirations of rising priests in the Church of England. A lawyer does not sin in seeking to be a judge, or in compassing his wishes by all honest means. A young diplomat entertains a fair ambition when he looks forward to be the lord of a first-rate embassy; and a poor novelist, when he attempts to rival Dickens or rise above Fitzjeames, commits no fault, though he may be foolish. Sydney Smith truly said that in these recreant days we cannot expect to find the majesty of St. Paul beneath the cassock of a curate. If we look to our clergymen to be more than men, we shall probably teach ourselves to think that they are less, and can hardly hope to raise the character of the pastor by denying to him the right to entertain the aspirations of a man.

Our archdeacon was worldly—who among us is not so? He was ambitious—who among us is ashamed to own that "last infirmity of noble minds!" He was avaricious, my readers will say. No;—it was for no love of lucre that he wished to be Bishop of Barchester. He was his father's only child, and his father had left him great wealth. His preferment brought him in nearly three thousand a year. The bishopric, as cut down by the Ecclesiastical Commission, was only five. He would be a richer man as archdeacon than he could be as bishop. But he certainly did desire to play first fiddle; he did desire to sit in full lawn sleeves among the peers of the realm; and he did desire, if the truth must out, to be called "My lord" by his reverend brethren.

His hopes, however, were they innocent or sinful, were not fated to be realized, and Dr. Proudie was consecrated Bishop of Barchester.

CHAPTER II

HIRAM'S HOSPITAL ACCORDING TO ACT OF PARLIAMENT

It is hardly necessary that I should here give to the public any lengthened biography of Mr. Harding up to the period of the commencement of this tale. The public cannot have forgotten how ill that sensitive gentleman bore the attack that was made on him in the columns of "The Jupiter," with reference to the income which he received as warden of Hiram's Hospital, in the city of Barchester. Nor can it yet be forgotten that a lawsuit was instituted against him on the matter of that charity by Mr. John Bold, who afterwards married his, Mr. Harding's, younger and then only unmarried daughter. Under pressure of these attacks, Mr. Harding had resigned his wardenship, though strongly recommended to abstain from doing so both by his friends and by his lawyers. He did, however, resign it, and betook himself manfully to the duties of the small parish of St. Cuthbert's, in the city, of which he was vicar, continuing also to perform those of precentor of the cathedral, a situation of small emolument which had hitherto been supposed to be joined, as a matter of course, to the wardenship of the hospital above spoken of.

When he left the hospital from which he had been so ruthlessly driven, and settled himself down in his own modest manner in the High Street of Barchester, he had not expected that others would make more fuss about it than he was inclined to do himself; and the extent of his hope was, that the movement might have been made in time to prevent any further paragraphs in "The Jupiter." His affairs, however, were not allowed to subside thus quietly, and people were quite as much inclined to talk about the disinterested sacrifice he had made, as they had before been to upbraid him for his cupidity.

The most remarkable thing that occurred was the receipt of an autographed letter from the Archbishop of Canterbury, in which the primate very warmly praised his conduct, and begged to know what his intentions were for the future. Mr. Harding replied that he intended to be rector of St. Cuthbert's, in Barchester, and so that matter dropped. Then the newspapers took up his case, "The Jupiter" among the rest, and wafted his name in eulogistic strains through every reading-room in the nation. It was discovered also that he was the author of that great musical work, *Harding's Church Music*,—and a new edition was spoken of, though, I believe, never printed. It is, however, certain that the work was introduced into the Royal Chapel at St. James's, and that a long criticism appeared in the "Musical Scrutator," declaring that in no previous work of the kind had so much research been joined with such exalted musical ability, and asserting that the name of Harding would henceforward be known wherever the arts were cultivated, or religion valued.

This was high praise, and I will not deny that Mr. Harding was gratified by such flattery; for if Mr. Harding was vain on any subject, it was on that of music. But here the matter rested. The second edition, if printed, was never purchased; the copies which had been introduced into the Royal Chapel disappeared again, and were laid by in peace, with a load of similar literature. Mr. Towers of "The Jupiter" and his brethren occupied themselves with other names, and the undying fame promised to our friend was clearly intended to be posthumous.

Mr. Harding had spent much of his time with his friend the bishop; much with his daughter Mrs. Bold, now, alas, a widow; and had almost daily visited the wretched remnant of his former subjects, the few surviving bedesmen now left at Hiram's Hospital. Six of them were still living. The number, according to old Hiram's will, should always have been twelve. But after the abdication of their warden, the bishop had appointed no successor to him, no new occupants of the charity had been nominated, and it appeared as though the hospital at Barchester would fall into abeyance, unless the powers that be should take some steps towards putting it once more into working order.

During the past five years, the powers that be had not overlooked Barchester Hospital, and sundry political doctors had taken the matter in hand. Shortly after Mr. Harding's resignation, "The Jupiter" had very clearly shown what ought to be done. In about half a column it had distributed the income, rebuilt the buildings, put an end to all bickerings, regenerated kindly feeling, provided for Mr. Harding, and placed the whole thing on a footing which could not but be satisfactory to the city and Bishop of Barchester, and to the nation at large. The wisdom of this scheme was testified by the number of letters which "Common Sense," "Veritas," and "One that loves fair play" sent to "The Jupiter," all expressing admiration and amplifying on the details given. It is singular enough that no adverse letter appeared at all, and, therefore, none of course was written.

But Cassandra was not believed, and even the wisdom of "The Jupiter" sometimes falls on deaf ears. Though other plans did not put themselves forward in the columns of "The Jupiter," reformers of church charities were not slack to make known in various places their different nostrums for setting Hiram's Hospital on its feet again. A learned bishop took occasion, in the Upper House, to allude to the matter, intimating that he had communicated on the subject with his right reverend brother of Barchester. The radical member for Staleybridge had suggested that the funds should be alienated for the education of the agricultural poor of the country, and he amused the house by some anecdotes touching the superstition and habits of the agriculturists in question. A political pamphleteer had produced a few dozen pages, which he called "Who are John Hiram's heirs?" intending to give an infallible rule for the governance of all such establishments; and, at last, a member of the government promised that in the next session a short bill should be introduced for regulating the affairs of Barchester and other kindred concerns.

The next session came, and, contrary to custom, the bill came also. Men's minds were then intent on other things. The first threatenings of a huge war hung heavily over the nation, and the question as to Hiram's heirs did not appear to interest very many people either in or out of the house. The bill, however, was read and re-read, and in some undistinguished manner passed through its eleven stages without appeal or dissent. What would John Hiram have said in the matter, could he have predicted that some forty-five gentlemen would take on themselves to make a law altering the whole purport of his will, without in the least knowing at the moment of their making it, what it was that they were doing? It is however to be hoped that the under-secretary for the Home Office knew, for to him had the matter been confided.

The bill, however, did pass, and at the time at which this history is supposed to commence, it had been ordained that there should be, as heretofore, twelve old men in

Barchester Hospital, each with 1s. 4d. a day; that there should also be twelve old women to be located in a house to be built, each with 1s. 2d. a day; that there should be a matron, with a house and £70 a year; a steward with £150 a year; and latterly, a warden with £450 a year, who should have the spiritual guidance of both establishments, and the temporal guidance of that appertaining to the male sex. The bishop, dean, and warden were, as formerly, to appoint in turn the recipients of the charity, and the bishop was to appoint the officers. There was nothing said as to the wardenship being held by the precentor of the cathedral, nor a word as to Mr. Harding's right to the situation.

It was not, however, till some months after the death of the old bishop, and almost immediately consequent on the installation of his successor, that notice was given that the reform was about to be carried out. The new law and the new bishop were among the earliest works of a new ministry, or rather of a ministry who, having for awhile given place to their opponents, had then returned to power; and the death of Dr. Grantly occurred, as we have seen, exactly at the period of the change.

Poor Eleanor Bold! How well does that widow's cap become her, and the solemn gravity with which she devotes herself to her new duties. Poor Eleanor!

Poor Eleanor! I cannot say that with me John Bold was ever a favourite. I never thought him worthy of the wife he had won. But in her estimation he was most worthy. Hers was one of those feminine hearts which cling to a husband, not with idolatry, for worship can admit of no defect in its idol, but with the perfect tenacity of ivy. As the parasite plant will follow even the defects of the trunk which it embraces, so did Eleanor cling to and love the very faults of her husband. She had once declared that whatever her father did should in her eyes be right. She then transferred her allegiance, and became ever ready to defend the worst failings of her lord and master.

And John Bold was a man to be loved by a woman; he was himself affectionate; he was confiding and manly; and that arrogance of thought, unsustained by first-rate abilities, that attempt at being better than his neighbours which jarred so painfully on the feelings of his acquaintance, did not injure him in the estimation of his wife.

Could she even have admitted that he had a fault, his early death would have blotted out the memory of it. She wept as for the loss of the most perfect treasure with which mortal woman had ever been endowed; for weeks after he was gone the idea of future happiness in this world was hateful to her; consolation, as it is called, was insupportable, and tears and sleep were her only relief.

But God tempers the wind to the shorn lamb. She knew that she had within her the living source of other cares. She knew that there was to be created for her another subject of weal or woe, of unutterable joy or despairing sorrow, as God in his mercy might vouchsafe to her. At first this did but augment her grief! To be the mother of a poor infant, orphaned before it was born, brought forth to the sorrows of an ever desolate hearth, nurtured amidst tears and wailing, and then turned adrift into the world without the aid of a father's care! There was at first no joy in this.

By degrees, however, her heart became anxious for another object, and, before its birth, the stranger was expected with all the eagerness of a longing mother. Just eight months after the father's death a second John Bold was born, and if the worship of one creature can be innocent in another, let us hope that the adoration offered over the cradle of the fatherless infant may not be imputed as a sin.

It will not be worth our while to define the character of the child, or to point out in how far the faults of the father were redeemed within that little breast by the virtues of the mother. The baby, as a baby, was all that was delightful, and I cannot foresee that it will be necessary for us to inquire into the facts of his after-life. Our present business at Barchester will not occupy us above a year or two at the furthest, and I will leave it to some other pen to produce, if necessary, the biography of John Bold the Younger.

But, as a baby, this baby was all that could be desired. This fact no one attempted to deny. "Is he not delightful?" she would say to her father, looking up into his face from her knees, her lustrous eyes overflowing with soft tears, her young face encircled by her close widow's cap, and her hands on each side of the cradle in which her treasure was sleeping. The grandfather would gladly admit that the treasure was delightful, and the uncle arch-deacon himself would agree, and Mrs. Grantly, Eleanor's sister, would re-echo the word with true sisterly energy; and Mary Bold—but Mary Bold was a second worshipper at the same shrine.

The baby was really delightful; he took his food with a will, struck out his toes merrily whenever his legs were uncovered, and did not have fits. These are supposed to be the strongest points of baby perfection, and in all these our baby excelled.

And thus the widow's deep grief was softened, and a sweet balm was poured into the wound which she had thought nothing but death could heal. How much kinder is God to us than we are willing to be to ourselves! At the loss of every dear face, at the last going of every well-beloved one, we all doom ourselves to an eternity of sorrow, and look to waste ourselves away in an ever-running fountain of tears. How seldom does such grief endure! How blessed is the goodness which forbids it to do so! "Let me ever remember my living friends, but forget them as soon as dead," was the prayer of a wise man who understood the mercy of God. Few perhaps would have the courage to express such a wish, and yet to do so would only be to ask for that release from sorrow which a kind Cre-ator almost always extends to us.

I would not, however, have it imagined that Mrs. Bold forgot her husband. She daily thought of him with all conjugal love, and enshrined his memory in the innermost centre of her heart. But yet she was happy in her baby. It was so sweet to press the living toy to her breast, and feel that a human being existed who did owe, and was to owe, everything to her; whose daily food was drawn from herself; whose little wants could all be satisfied by her; whose little heart would first love her and her only; whose infant tongue would make its first effort in calling her by the sweetest name a woman can hear. And so Elea-nor's bosom became tranquil, and she set about her new duties eagerly and gratefully.

As regards the concerns of the world, John Bold had left his widow in prosperous cir-cumstances. He had bequeathed to her all that he possessed, and that comprised an income much exceeding what she or her friends thought necessary for her. It amounted to nearly a thousand a year; when she reflected on its extent, her dearest hope was to hand it over, not only unimpaired but increased, to her husband's son, to her own darling, to the little man who now lay sleeping on her knee, happily ignorant of the cares which were to be accu-mulated in his behalf.

When John Bold died, she earnestly implored her father to come and live with her, but this Mr. Harding declined, though for some weeks he remained with her as a visitor. He could not be prevailed upon to forego the possession of some small home of his own, and so remained in the lodgings he had first selected over a chemist's shop in the High Street of Barchester.

CHAPTER III

DR. AND MRS. PROUDIE

This narrative is supposed to commence immediately after the installation of Dr. Proudie. I will not describe the ceremony, as I do not precisely understand its nature. I am ignorant whether a bishop be chaired like a member of Parliament, or carried in a gilt coach like a lord mayor, or sworn like a justice of peace, or introduced like a peer to the upper house, or led between two brethren like a knight of the garter; but I do know that everything was properly done, and that nothing fit or becoming to a young bishop was omitted on the occasion.

Dr. Proudie was not the man to allow anything to be omitted that might be becoming to his new dignity. He understood well the value of forms, and knew that the due observance of rank could not be maintained unless the exterior trappings belonging to it were held in proper esteem. He was a man born to move in high circles; at least so he thought himself, and circumstances had certainly sustained him in this view. He was the nephew of an Irish baron by his mother's side, and his wife was the niece of a Scotch earl. He had for years held some clerical office appertaining to courtly matters, which had enabled him to live in London, and to entrust his parish to his curate. He had been preacher to the royal beefeaters, curator of theological manuscripts in the Ecclesiastical Courts, chaplain to the Queen's yeomanry guard, and almoner to his Royal Highness the Prince of Rappe-Blankenberg.

His residence in the metropolis, rendered necessary by duties thus entrusted to him, his high connexions, and the peculiar talents and nature of the man, recommended him to persons in power, and Dr. Proudie became known as a useful and rising clergyman.

Some few years since, even within the memory of many who are not yet willing to call themselves old, a liberal clergyman was a person not frequently to be met. Sydney Smith was such and was looked on as little better than an infidel; a few others also might be named, but they were *rarae aves* and were regarded with doubt and distrust by their brethren. No man was so surely a Tory as a country rector—nowhere were the powers that be so cherished as at Oxford.

When, however, Dr. Whately was made an archbishop, and Dr. Hampden some years afterwards regius professor, many wise divines saw that a change was taking place in men's minds, and that more liberal ideas would henceforward be suitable to the priests as well as to the laity. Clergymen began to be heard of who had ceased to anathematize papists on the one hand, or vilify dissenters on the other. It appeared clear that High Church principles, as they are called, were no longer to be surest claims to promotion with at any rate one section of statesmen, and Dr. Proudie was one among those who early in life adapted himself to the views held by the Whigs on most theological and religious subjects. He bore with the idolatry of Rome, tolerated even the infidelity of Socinianism, and was hand and glove with the Presbyterian Synods of Scotland and Ulster.

Such a man at such a time was found to be useful, and Dr. Proudie's name began to appear in the newspapers. He was made one of a commission who went over to Ireland to arrange matters preparative to the working of the national board; he became honorary secretary to another commission nominated to inquire into the revenues of cathedral chapters; he had had something to do with both the *regium donum* and the Maynooth grant.

It must not on this account be taken as proved that Dr. Proudie was a man of great mental powers, or even of much capacity for business, for such qualities had not been required in him. In the arrangement of those church reforms with which he was connected, the ideas and original conception of the work to be done were generally furnished by the liberal statesmen of the day, and the labour of the details was borne by officials of a lower rank. It was, however, thought expedient that the name of some clergyman should appear in such matters, and as Dr. Proudie had become known as a tolerating divine, great use of this sort was made of his name. If he did not do much active good, he never did any harm; he was amenable to those who were really in authority and, at the sittings of the various boards to which he belonged, maintained a kind of dignity which had its value.

He was certainly possessed of sufficient tact to answer the purpose for which he was required without making himself troublesome; but it must not therefore be surmised that he doubted his own power, or failed to believe that he could himself take a high part in high affairs when his own turn came. He was biding his time, and patiently looking forward to the days when he himself would sit authoritative at some board, and talk and direct, and rule the roost, while lesser stars sat round and obeyed, as he had so well accustomed himself to do.

His reward and his time had now come. He was selected for the vacant bishopric and, on the next vacancy which might occur in any diocese, would take his place in the House of Lords, prepared to give not a silent vote in all matters concerning the weal of the church establishment. Toleration was to be the basis on which he was to fight his battles, and in the honest courage of his heart he thought no evil would come to him in encountering even such foes as his brethren of Exeter and Oxford.

Dr. Proudie was an ambitious man, and before he was well consecrated Bishop of Barchester, he had begun to look up to archiepiscopal splendour, and the glories of Lambeth, or at any rate of Bishopsthorpe. He was comparatively young, and had, as he fondly flattered himself, been selected as possessing such gifts, natural and acquired, as must be sure to recommend him to a yet higher notice, now that a higher sphere was opened to him. Dr. Proudie was, therefore, quite prepared to take a conspicuous part in all theological affairs appertaining to these realms; and having such views, by no means intended to bury himself at Barchester as his predecessor had done. No! London should still be his ground: a comfortable mansion in a provincial city might be well enough for the dead months of the year. Indeed, Dr. Proudie had always felt it necessary to his position to retire from London when other great and fashionable people did so; but London should still be his fixed residence, and it was in London that he resolved to exercise that hospitality so peculiarly recommended to all bishops by St. Paul. How otherwise could he keep himself before the world? How else give to the government, in matters theological, the full benefit of his weight and talents?

This resolution was no doubt a salutary one as regarded the world at large, but was not likely to make him popular either with the clergy or people of Barchester. Dr. Grantly had always lived there—in truth, it was hard for a bishop to be popular after Dr. Grantly. His income had averaged £9,000 a year; his successor was to be rigidly limited to £5,000. He had but one child on whom to spend his money; Dr. Proudie had seven or eight. He had been a man of few personal expenses, and they had been confined to the tastes of a moderate gentleman; but Dr. Proudie had to maintain a position in fashionable society, and had that to do with comparatively small means. Dr. Grantly had certainly kept his carriage as became a bishop, but his carriage, horses, and coachman, though they did very well for Barchester, would have been almost ridiculous at Westminster. Mrs. Proudie determined that her husband's equipage should not shame her, and things on which Mrs. Proudie resolved were generally accomplished.

From all this it was likely to result that Dr. Proudie would not spend much money at Barchester, whereas his predecessor had dealt with the tradesmen of the city in a manner very much to their satisfaction. The Grantlys, father and son, had spent their money like gentlemen, but it soon became whispered in Barchester that Dr. Proudie was not unacquainted with those prudent devices by which the utmost show of wealth is produced from limited means.

In person Dr. Proudie is a good-looking man; spruce and dapper, and very tidy. He is somewhat below middle height, being about five feet four; but he makes up for the inches which he wants by the dignity with which he carries those which he has. It is no fault of his own if he has not a commanding eye, for he studies hard to assume it. His features are well formed, though perhaps the sharpness of his nose may give to his face in the eyes of some people an air of insignificance. If so, it is greatly redeemed by his mouth and chin, of which he is justly proud.

Dr. Proudie may well be said to have been a fortunate man, for he was not born to wealth, and he is now Bishop of Barchester; nevertheless, he has his cares. He has a large family, of whom the three eldest are daughters, now all grown up and fit for fashionable life;—and he has a wife. It is not my intention to breathe a word against the character of Mrs. Proudie, but still I cannot think that with all her virtues she adds much to her husband's happiness. The truth is that in matters domestic she rules supreme over her titular lord, and rules with a rod of iron. Nor is this all. Things domestic Dr. Proudie might have abandoned to her, if not voluntarily, yet willingly. But Mrs. Proudie is not satisfied with such home dominion, and stretches her power over all his movements, and will not even abstain from things spiritual. In fact, the bishop is hen-pecked.

The archdeacon's wife, in her happy home at Plumstead, knows how to assume the full privileges of her rank and express her own mind in becoming tone and place. But Mrs. Grantly's sway, if sway she has, is easy and beneficent. She never shames her husband; before the world she is a pattern of obedience; her voice is never loud, nor her looks sharp: doubtless she values power, and has not unsuccessfully striven to acquire it; but she knows what should be the limits of a woman's rule.

Not so Mrs. Proudie. This lady is habitually authoritative to all, but to her poor husband she is despotic. Successful as has been his career in the eyes of the world, it would seem that in the eyes of his wife he is never right. All hope of defending himself has long passed from him; indeed he rarely even attempts self-justification, and is aware that submission produces the nearest approach to peace which his own house can ever attain.

Mrs. Proudie has not been able to sit at the boards and committees to which her husband has been called by the State, nor, as he often reflects, can she make her voice heard in the House of Lords. It may be that she will refuse to him permission to attend to this branch of a bishop's duties; it may be that she will insist on his close attendance to his own closet. He has never whispered a word on the subject to living ears, but he has already made his fixed resolve. Should such attempt be made he will rebel. Dogs have turned against their masters, and even Neapolitans against their rulers, when oppression has been too severe. And Dr. Proudie feels within himself that if the cord be drawn too tight, he also can muster courage and resist.

The state of vassalage in which our bishop has been kept by his wife has not tended to exalt his character in the eyes of his daughters, who assume in addressing their father too much of that authority which is not properly belonging, at any rate, to them. They are, on the whole, fine engaging young ladies. They are tall and robust like their mother, whose high cheek-bones, and—we may say auburn hair they all inherit. They think somewhat too much of their grand-uncles, who have not hitherto returned the compliment by thinking much of them. But now that their father is a bishop, it is probable that family ties will be drawn closer. Considering their connexion with the church, they entertain but few prejudices against the pleasures of the world, and have certainly not distressed their parents, as too many English girls have lately done, by any enthusiastic wish to devote themselves to the seclusion of a Protestant nunnery. Dr. Proudie's sons are still at school.

One other marked peculiarity in the character of the bishop's wife must be mentioned. Though not averse to the society and manners of the world, she is in her own way a religious woman; and the form in which this tendency shows itself in her is by a strict observance of Sabbatarian rule. Dissipation and low dresses during the week are, under her control, atoned for by three services, an evening sermon read by herself, and a perfect abstinence from any cheering employment on the Sunday. Unfortunately for those under her roof to whom the dissipation and low dresses are not extended, her servants namely and her husband, the compensating strictness of the Sabbath includes all. Woe betide the recreant housemaid who is found to have been listening to the honey of a sweetheart in the Regent's park instead of the soul-stirring evening discourse of Mr. Slope. Not only is she sent adrift, but she is so sent with a character which leaves her little hope of a decent place. Woe betide the six-foot hero who escorts Mrs. Proudie to her pew in red plush breeches, if he slips away to the neighbouring beer-shop, instead of falling into the back seat appropriated to his use. Mrs. Proudie has the eyes of Argus for such offenders. Occasional drunkenness in the week may be overlooked, for six feet on low wages are hardly to be procured if the morals are always kept at a high pitch, but not even for grandeur or economy will Mrs. Proudie forgive a desecration of the Sabbath.

In such matters Mrs. Proudie allows herself to be often guided by that eloquent preacher, the Rev. Mr. Slope, and as Dr. Proudie is guided by his wife, it necessarily follows that the eminent man we have named has obtained a good deal of control over Dr. Proudie in matters concerning religion. Mr. Slope's only preferment has hitherto been that of reader and preacher in a London district church; and on the consecration of his friend the new bishop, he readily gave this up to undertake the onerous but congenial duties of domestic chaplain to his lordship.

Mr. Slope, however, on his first introduction must not be brought before the public at the tail of a chapter.

CHAPTER IV

THE BISHOP'S CHAPLAIN

Of the Rev. Mr. Slope's parentage I am not able to say much. I have heard it asserted that he is lineally descended from that eminent physician who assisted at the birth of Mr. T. Shandy, and that in early years he added an "e" to his name, for the sake of euphony, as other great men have done before him. If this be so, I presume he was christened Obadiah, for that is his name, in commemoration of the conflict in which his ancestor so distinguished himself. All my researches on the subject have, however, failed in enabling me to fix the date on which the family changed its religion.

He had been a sizar at Cambridge, and had there conducted himself at any rate successfully, for in due process of time he was an M.A., having university pupils under his care. From thence he was transferred to London, and became preacher at a new district church built on the confines of Baker Street. He was in this position when congenial ideas on religious subjects recommended him to Mrs. Proudie, and the intercourse had become close and confidential.

Having been thus familiarly thrown among the Misses Proudie, it was no more than natural that some softer feeling than friendship should be engendered. There have been some passages of love between him and the eldest hope, Olivia, but they have hitherto resulted in no favourable arrangement. In truth, Mr. Slope, having made a declaration of affection, afterwards withdrew it on finding that the doctor had no immediate worldly funds with which to endow his child, and it may easily be conceived that Miss Proudie, after such an announcement on his part, was not readily disposed to receive any further show of affection. On the appointment of Dr. Proudie to the bishopric of Barchester, Mr. Slope's views were in truth somewhat altered. Bishops, even though they be poor, can provide for clerical children, and Mr. Slope began to regret that he had not been more disinterested. He no sooner heard the tidings of the doctor's elevation than he recommenced his siege, not violently, indeed, but respectfully, and at a distance. Olivia Proudie, however, was a girl of spirit: she had the blood of two peers in her veins, and better still she had another lover on her books, so Mr. Slope sighed in vain, and the pair soon found it convenient to establish a mutual bond of inveterate hatred.

It may be thought singular that Mrs. Proudie's friendship for the young clergyman should remain firm after such an affair, but, to tell the truth, she had known nothing of it. Though very fond of Mr. Slope herself, she had never conceived the idea that either of her daughters would become so, and remembering their high birth and social advantages, expected for them matches of a different sort. Neither the gentleman nor the lady found it necessary to enlighten her. Olivia's two sisters had each known of the affair, as had all the servants, as had all the people living in the adjoining houses on either side, but Mrs. Proudie had been kept in the dark.

Mr. Slope soon comforted himself with the reflexion that, as he had been selected as chaplain to the bishop, it would probably be in his power to get the good things in the bishop's gift without troubling himself with the bishop's daughter, and he found himself able to endure the pangs of rejected love. As he sat himself down in the railway carriage, confronting the bishop and Mrs. Proudie as they started on their first journey to Barchester, he began to form in his own mind a plan of his future life. He knew well his patron's strong points, but he knew the weak ones as well. He understood correctly enough to what attempts the new bishop's high spirit would soar, and he rightly guessed that public life would better suit the great man's taste than the small details of diocesan duty.

He, therefore,—he, Mr. Slope,—would in effect be Bishop of Barchester. Such was his resolve, and to give Mr. Slope his due, he had both courage and spirit to bear him out in his resolution. He knew that he should have a hard battle to fight, for the power and patronage of the see would be equally coveted by another great mind—Mrs. Proudie would also choose to be Bishop of Barchester. Mr. Slope, however, flattered himself that he could outmanoeuvre the lady. She must live much in London, while he would always be on the spot. She would necessarily remain ignorant of much, while he would know everything belonging to the diocese. At first, doubtless, he must flatter and cajole, perhaps yield in some things, but he did not doubt of ultimate triumph. If all other means failed, he could join the bishop against his wife, inspire courage into the unhappy man, lay an axe to the root of the woman's power, and emancipate the husband.

Such were his thoughts as he sat looking at the sleeping pair in the railway carriage, and Mr. Slope is not the man to trouble himself with such thoughts for nothing. He is possessed of more than average abilities, and is of good courage. Though he can stoop to fawn, and stoop low indeed, if need be, he has still within him the power to assume the tyrant;—and with the power he has certainly the wish. His acquirements are not of the highest order, but such as they are, they are completely under control, and he knows the use of them. He is gifted with a certain kind of pulpit eloquence, not likely indeed to be persuasive with men, but powerful with the softer sex. In his sermons he deals greatly in denunciations, excites the minds of his weaker hearers with a not unpleasant terror, and leaves an impression on their minds that all mankind are in a perilous state, and all womankind, too, except those who attend regularly to the evening lectures in Baker Street. His looks and tones are extremely severe, so much so that one cannot but fancy that he regards the greater part of the world as being infinitely too bad for his care. As he walks through the streets his very face denotes his horror of the world's wickedness, and there is always an anathema lurking in the corner of his eye.

In doctrine he, like his patron, is tolerant of dissent, if so strict a mind can be called tolerant of anything. With Wesleyan-Methodists he has something in common, but his soul trembles in agony at the iniquities of the Puseyites. His aversion is carried to things outward as well as inward. His gall rises at a new church with a high-pitched roof; a full-breasted black silk waistcoat is with him a symbol of Satan; and a profane jest-book would not, in his view, more foully desecrate the church seat of a Christian than a book of prayer printed with red letters and ornamented with a cross on the back. Most active clergymen have their hobby, and Sunday observances are his. Sunday, however, is a word which never pollutes his mouth—it is always "the Sabbath." The "desecration of the Sabbath," as he delights to call it, is to him meat and drink: he thrives upon that as policemen do on the general evil habits of the community. It is the loved subject of all his evening discourses, the source of all his eloquence, the secret of all his power over the female heart. To him the revelation of God appears only in that one law given for Jewish observance. To him the mercies of our Saviour speak in vain, to him in vain has been preached that sermon which fell from divine lips on the mountain—"Blessed are the meek, for they shall inherit the earth"—"Blessed are the merciful, for they shall obtain mercy." To him the New Testament is comparatively of little moment, for from it can he draw no fresh authority for that dominion which he loves to exercise over at least a seventh part of man's allotted time here below.

Mr. Slope is tall, and not ill-made. His feet and hands are large, as has ever been the case with all his family, but he has a broad chest and wide shoulders to carry off these excrescences, and on the whole his figure is good. His countenance, however, is not specially prepossessing. His hair is lank and of a dull pale reddish hue. It is always formed into three straight, lumpy masses, each brushed with admirable precision and cemented with much grease; two of them adhere closely to the sides of his face, and the other lies at right angles above them. He wears no whiskers, and is always punctiliously shaven. His face is nearly of the same colour as his hair, though perhaps a little redder: it is not unlike beef—beef, however, one would say, of a bad quality. His forehead is capacious and high, but square and heavy and unpleasantly shining. His mouth is large, though his lips are thin and bloodless; and his big, prominent, pale-brown eyes inspire anything but confidence. His nose, however, is his redeeming feature: it is pronounced, straight and well-formed; though I myself should have liked it better did it not possess a somewhat spongy, porous appearance, as though it had been cleverly formed out of a red-coloured cork.

I never could endure to shake hands with Mr. Slope. A cold, clammy perspiration always exudes from him, the small drops are ever to be seen standing on his brow, and his friendly grasp is unpleasant.

Such is Mr. Slope—such is the man who has suddenly fallen into the midst of Barchester Close, and is destined there to assume the station which has heretofore been filled by the son of the late bishop. Think, oh, my meditative reader, what an associate we have here for those comfortable prebendaries, those gentlemanlike clerical doctors, those happy, well-used, well-fed minor canons who have grown into existence at Barchester under the kindly wings of Bishop Grantly!

But not as a mere associate for these does Mr. Slope travel down to Barchester with the bishop and his wife. He intends to be, if not their master, at least the chief among them. He intends to lead and to have followers; he intends to hold the purse-strings of the diocese and draw round him an obedient herd of his poor and hungry brethren.

And here we can hardly fail to draw a comparison between the archdeacon and our new private chaplain, and despite the manifold faults of the former, one can hardly fail to make it much to his advantage.

Both men are eager, much too eager, to support and increase the power of their order. Both are anxious that the world should be priest-governed, though they have probably never confessed so much, even to themselves. Both begrudge any other kind of dominion held by man over man. Dr. Grantly, if he admits the Queen's supremacy in things spiritual, only admits it as being due to the quasi-priesthood conveyed in the consecrating qualities of her coronation, and he regards things temporal as being by their nature subject to those which are spiritual. Mr. Slope's ideas of sacerdotal rule are of quite a different class. He cares nothing, one way or the other, for the Queen's supremacy; these to his ears are empty words, meaning nothing. Forms he regards but little, and such titular expressions as supremacy, consecration, ordination, and the like convey of themselves no significance to him. Let him be supreme who can. The temporal king, judge, or gaoler can work but on the body. The spiritual master, if he have the necessary gifts and can duly use them, has a wider field of empire. He works upon the soul. If he can make himself be believed, he can be all powerful over those who listen. If he be careful to meddle with none who are too strong in intellect, or too weak in flesh, he may indeed be supreme. And such was the ambition of Mr. Slope.

Dr. Grantly interfered very little with the worldly doings of those who were in any way subject to him. I do not mean to say that he omitted to notice misconduct among his clergy, immorality in his parish, or omissions in his family, but he was not anxious to do so where the necessity could be avoided. He was not troubled with a propensity to be curious, and as long as those around him were tainted with no heretical leaning towards dissent, as long as they fully and freely admitted the efficacy of Mother Church, he was willing that that mother should be merciful and affectionate, prone to indulgence, and unwilling to chastise. He himself enjoyed the good things of this world and liked to let it be known that he did so. He cordially despised any brother rector who thought harm of dinner-parties, or dreaded the dangers of a moderate claret-jug; consequently, dinner-parties and claret-jugs were common in the diocese. He liked to give laws and to be obeyed in them implicitly, but he endeavoured that his ordinances should be within the compass of the man and not unpalatable to the gentleman. He had ruled among his clerical neighbours now for sundry years, and as he had maintained his power without becoming unpopular, it may be presumed that he had exercised some wisdom.

Of Mr. Slope's conduct much cannot be said, as his grand career is yet to commence, but it may be premised that his tastes will be very different from those of the archdeacon. He conceives it to be his duty to know all the private doings and desires of the flock entrusted to his care. From the poorer classes he exacts an unconditional obedience to set rules of conduct, and if disobeyed he has recourse, like his great ancestor, to the fulminations of an Ernulfus: "Thou shalt be damned in thy going in and in thy coming out—in thy eating and thy drinking," &c. &c. &c. With the rich, experience has already taught him that a different line of action is necessary. Men in the upper walks of life do not mind being cursed, and the women, presuming that it be done in delicate phrase, rather like it. But he has not, therefore, given up so important a portion of believing Christians. With the men, indeed, he is generally at variance; they are hardened sinners, on whom the voice of the priestly charmer too often falls in vain; but with the ladies, old and young, firm and frail, devout and dissipated, he is, as he conceives, all powerful. He can reprove faults with so much flattery and utter censure in so caressing a manner that the female heart, if it glow with a spark of Low Church susceptibility, cannot withstand him. In many houses he is thus an admired guest: the husbands, for their wives' sake, are fain to admit him; and when once admitted it is not easy to shake him off. He has, however, a pawing, greasy way with him, which does not endear him to those who do not value him for their souls' sake, and he is not a man to make himself at once popular in a large circle such as is now likely to surround him at Barchester.

CHAPTER V

A MORNING VISIT

It was known that Dr. Proudie would immediately have to reappoint to the wardenship of the hospital under the act of Parliament to which allusion has been made; no one imagined that any choice was left to him—no one for a moment thought that he could appoint any other than Mr. Harding. Mr. Harding himself, when he heard how the matter had been settled, without troubling himself much on the subject, considered it as certain that he would go back to his pleasant house and garden. And though there would be much that was melancholy, nay, almost heartrending, in such a return, he still was glad that it was to be so. His daughter might probably be persuaded to return there with him. She had, indeed, all but promised to do so, though she still entertained an idea that that greatest of mortals, that important atom of humanity, that little god upon earth, Johnny Bold her baby, ought to have a house of his own over his head.

Such being the state of Mr. Harding's mind in the matter, he did not feel any peculiar personal interest in the appointment of Dr. Proudie to the bishopric. He, as well as others at Barchester, regretted that a man should be sent among them who, they were aware, was not of their way of thinking; but Mr. Harding himself was not a bigoted man on points of church doctrine, and he was quite prepared to welcome Dr. Proudie to Barchester in a graceful and becoming manner. He had nothing to seek and nothing to fear; he felt that it behoved him to be on good terms with his bishop, and he did not anticipate any obstacle that would prevent it.

In such a frame of mind he proceeded to pay his respects at the palace the second day after the arrival of the bishop and his chaplain. But he did not go alone. Dr. Grantly proposed to accompany him, and Mr. Harding was not sorry to have a companion, who would remove from his shoulders the burden of the conversation in such an interview. In the affair of the consecration Dr. Grantly had been introduced to the bishop, and Mr. Harding had also been there. He had, however, kept himself in the background, and he was now to be presented to the great man for the first time.

The archdeacon's feelings were of a much stronger nature. He was not exactly the man to overlook his own slighted claims, or to forgive the preference shown to another. Dr. Proudie was playing Venus to his Juno, and he was prepared to wage an internecine war against the owner of the wished-for apple, and all his satellites, private chaplains, and others.

Nevertheless, it behoved him also to conduct himself towards the intruder as an old archdeacon should conduct himself to an incoming bishop; and though he was well aware of all Dr. Proudie's abominable opinions as regarded dissenters, church reform, the hebdomadal council, and such like; though he disliked the man, and hated the doctrines, still he was prepared to show respect to the station of the bishop. So he and Mr. Harding called together at the palace.

His lordship was at home, and the two visitors were shown through the accustomed hall into the well-known room where the good old bishop used to sit. The furniture had been bought at a valuation, and every chair and table, every bookshelf against the wall, and every square in the carpet was as well known to each of them as their own bedrooms. Nevertheless they at once felt that they were strangers there. The furniture was for the most part the same, yet the place had been metamorphosed. A new sofa had been introduced, a horrid chintz affair, most unprelatical and almost irreligious; such a sofa as never yet stood in the study of any decent High Church clergyman of the Church of England. The old curtains had also given way. They had, to be sure, become dingy, and that which had been originally a rich and goodly ruby had degenerated into a reddish brown. Mr. Harding, however, thought the old reddish-brown much preferable to the gaudy buff-coloured trumpery moreen which Mrs. Proudie had deemed good enough for her husband's own room in the provincial city of Barchester.

Our friends found Dr. Proudie sitting on the old bishop's chair, looking very nice in his new apron; they found, too, Mr. Slope standing on the hearth-rug, persuasive and eager, just as the archdeacon used to stand; but on the sofa they also found Mrs. Proudie, an innovation for which a precedent might in vain be sought in all the annals of the Barchester bishopric!

There she was, however, and they could only make the best of her. The introductions were gone through in much form. The archdeacon shook hands with the bishop, and named Mr. Harding, who received such an amount of greeting as was due from a bishop to a precentor. His lordship then presented them to his lady wife; the archdeacon first, with archidiaconal honours, and then the precentor with diminished parade. After this Mr. Slope presented himself. The bishop, it is true, did mention his name, and so did Mrs. Proudie too, in a louder tone, but Mr. Slope took upon himself the chief burden of his own introduction. He had great pleasure in making himself acquainted with Dr. Grantly; he had heard much of the archdeacon's good works in that part of the diocese in which his duties as archdeacon had been exercised (thus purposely ignoring the archdeacon's hitherto unlimited dominion over the diocese at large). He was aware that his lordship depended greatly on the assistance which Dr. Grantly would be able to give him in that portion of his diocese. He then thrust out his hand and, grasping that of his new foe, bedewed it unmercifully. Dr. Grantly in return bowed, looked stiff, contracted his eyebrows, and wiped his hand with his pocket-handkerchief. Nothing abashed, Mr. Slope then noticed the precentor and descended to the grade of the lower clergy. He gave him a squeeze of the hand, damp indeed, but affectionate, and was very glad to make the acquaintance of Mr.—oh yes, Mr. Harding; he had not exactly caught the name. "Precentor in the cathedral," surmised Mr. Slope. Mr. Harding confessed that such was the humble sphere of his work. "Some parish duty as well," suggested Mr. Slope. Mr. Harding acknowledged the diminutive incumbency of St. Cuthbert's. Mr. Slope then left him alone, having condescended sufficiently, and joined the conversation among the higher powers.

There were four persons there, each of whom considered himself the most important personage in the diocese—himself, indeed, or herself, as Mrs. Proudie was one of them—and with such a difference of opinion it was not probable that they would get on pleasantly together. The bishop himself actually wore the visible apron, and trusted mainly to that—to that and his title, both being facts which could not be overlooked. The archdeacon knew his subject and really understood the business of bishoping, which the others did not, and this was his strong ground. Mrs. Proudie had her sex to back her, and her habit of command, and was nothing daunted by the high tone of Dr. Grantly's face and figure. Mr. Slope had only himself and his own courage and tact to depend on, but he nevertheless was perfectly self-assured, and did not doubt but that he should soon get the better of weak men who trusted so much to externals, as both bishop and archdeacon appeared to do.

"Do you reside in Barchester, Dr. Grantly?" asked the lady with her sweetest smile.

Dr. Grantly explained that he lived in his own parish of Plumstead Episcopi, a few miles out of the city. Whereupon the lady hoped that the distance was not too great for country visiting, as she would be so glad to make the acquaintance of Mrs. Grantly. She would take the earliest opportunity, after the arrival of her horses at Barchester; their horses were at present in London; their horses were not immediately coming down, as the bishop would be obliged, in a few days, to return to town. Dr. Grantly was no doubt aware that the bishop was at present much called upon by the "University Improvement Committee:" indeed, the committee could not well proceed without him, as their final report had now to be drawn up. The bishop had also to prepare a scheme for the "Manufacturing Towns Morning and Evening Sunday School Society," of which he was a patron, or president, or director, and therefore the horses would not come down to Barchester at present; but whenever the horses did come down, she would take the earliest opportunity of calling at Plumstead Episcopi, providing the distance was not too great for country visiting.

The archdeacon made his fifth bow—he had made one at each mention of the horses— and promised that Mrs. Grantly would do herself the honour of calling at the palace on an early day. Mrs. Proudie declared that she would be delighted: she hadn't liked to ask, not being quite sure whether Mrs. Grantly had horses; besides, the distance might have been, &c. &c.

Dr. Grantly again bowed but said nothing. He could have bought every individual possession of the whole family of the Proudies and have restored them as a gift, without much feeling the loss; and had kept a separate pair of horses for the exclusive use of his wife since the day of his marriage, whereas Mrs. Proudie had been hitherto jobbed about the streets of London at so much a month, during the season, and at other times had managed to walk, or hire a smart fly from the livery stables.

"Are the arrangements with reference to the Sabbath-day schools generally pretty good in your archdeaconry?" asked Mr. Slope.

"Sabbath-day schools!" repeated the archdeacon with an affectation of surprise. "Upon my word, I can't tell; it depends mainly on the parson's wife and daughters. There is none at Plumstead."

This was almost a fib on the part of the archdeacon, for Mrs. Grantly has a very nice school. To be sure it is not a Sunday-school exclusively, and is not so designated, but that exemplary lady always attends there for an hour before church, and hears the children say their catechism, and sees that they are clean and tidy for church, with their hands washed and their shoes tied; and Grisel and Florinda, her daughters, carry thither a basket of large buns, baked on the Saturday afternoon, and distribute them to all the children not especially under disgrace, which buns are carried home after church with considerable content, and eaten hot at tea, being then split and toasted. The children of Plumstead would indeed open their eyes if they heard their venerated pastor declare that there was no Sunday-school in his parish.

Mr. Slope merely opened his wide eyes wider and slightly shrugged his shoulders. He was not, however, prepared to give up his darling project.

"I fear there is a great deal of Sabbath travelling here," said he. "On looking at the 'Bradshaw,' I see that there are three trains in and three out every Sabbath. Could nothing be done to induce the company to withdraw them? Don't you think, Dr. Grantly, that a little energy might diminish the evil?"

"Not being a director, I really can't say. But if you can withdraw the passengers, the company I dare say will withdraw the trains," said the doctor. "It's merely a question of dividends."

"But surely, Dr. Grantly," said the lady; "surely we should look at it differently. You and I, for instance, in our position: surely we should do all that we can to control so grievous a sin. Don't you think so, Mr. Harding?" and she turned to the precentor, who was sitting mute and unhappy.

Mr. Harding thought that all porters and stokers, guards, brakesmen, and pointsmen ought to have an opportunity of going to church, and he hoped that they all had.

"But surely, surely," continued Mrs. Proudie, "surely that is not enough. Surely that will not secure such an observance of the Sabbath as we are taught to conceive is not only expedient but indispensable; surely—"

Come what come might, Dr. Grantly was not to be forced into a dissertation on a point of doctrine with Mrs. Proudie, nor yet with Mr. Slope, so without much ceremony he turned his back upon the sofa and began to hope that Dr. Proudie had found that the palace repairs had been such as to meet his wishes.

"Yes, yes," said his lordship; upon the whole he thought so—upon the whole, he didn't know that there was much ground for complaint; the architect, perhaps, might have—but his double, Mr. Slope, who had sidled over to the bishop's chair, would not allow his lordship to finish his ambiguous speech.

"There is one point I would like to mention, Mr. Archdeacon. His lordship asked me to step through the premises, and I see that the stalls in the second stable are not perfect."

"Why—there's standing there for a dozen horses," said the archdeacon.

"Perhaps so," said the other; "indeed, I've no doubt of it; but visitors, you know, often require so much accommodation. There are so many of the bishop's relatives who always bring their own horses."

Dr. Grantly promised that due provision for the relatives' horses should be made, as far at least as the extent of the original stable building would allow. He would himself communicate with the architect.

"And the coach-house, Dr. Grantly," continued Mr. Slope; "there is really hardly room for a second carriage in the large coach-house, and the smaller one, of course, holds only one."

"And the gas," chimed in the lady; "there is no gas through the house, none whatever, but in the kitchen and passages. Surely the palace should have been fitted through with pipes for gas, and hot water too. There is no hot water laid on anywhere above the ground-floor; surely there should be the means of getting hot water in the bedrooms without having it brought in jugs from the kitchen."

The bishop had a decided opinion that there should be pipes for hot water. Hot water was very essential for the comfort of the palace. It was, indeed, a requisite in any decent gentleman's house.

Mr. Slope had remarked that the coping on the garden wall was in many places imperfect.

Mrs. Proudie had discovered a large hole, evidently the work of rats, in the servants' hall.

The bishop expressed an utter detestation of rats. There was nothing, he believed, in this world that he so much hated as a rat.

Mr. Slope had, moreover, observed that the locks of the outhouses were very imperfect: he might specify the coal-cellar and the woodhouse.

Mrs. Proudie had also seen that those on the doors of the servants' bedrooms were in an-equally bad condition; indeed, the locks all through the house were old-fashioned and unserviceable.

The bishop thought that a great deal depended on a good lock and quite as much on the key. He had observed that the fault very often lay with the key, especially if the wards were in any way twisted.

Mr. Slope was going on with his catalogue of grievances, when he was somewhat loudly interrupted by the archdeacon, who succeeded in explaining that the diocesan architect, or rather his foreman, was the person to be addressed on such subjects, and that he, Dr. Grantly, had inquired as to the comfort of the palace merely as a point of compliment. He was sorry, however, that so many things had been found amiss: and then he rose from his chair to escape.

Mrs. Proudie, though she had contrived to lend her assistance in recapitulating the palatial dilapidations, had not on that account given up her hold of Mr. Harding, nor ceased from her cross-examinations as to the iniquity of Sabbatical amusements. Over and over again had she thrown out her "Surely, surely," at Mr. Harding's devoted head, and ill had that gentleman been able to parry the attack.

He had never before found himself subjected to such a nuisance. Ladies hitherto, when they had consulted him on religious subjects, had listened to what he might choose to say with some deference, and had differed, if they differed, in silence. But Mrs. Proudie interrogated him and then lectured. "Neither thou, nor thy son, nor thy daughter, thy manservant, nor thy maidservant," said she impressively, and more than once, as though Mr. Harding had forgotten the words. She shook her finger at him as she quoted the favourite law, as though menacing him with punishment, and then called upon him categorically to state whether he did not think that travelling on the Sabbath was an abomination and a desecration.

Mr. Harding had never been so hard pressed in his life. He felt that he ought to rebuke the lady for presuming so to talk to a gentleman and a clergyman many years her senior, but he recoiled from the idea of scolding the bishop's wife, in the bishop's presence, on his first visit to the palace; moreover, to tell the truth, he was somewhat afraid of her. She, seeing him sit silent and absorbed, by no means refrained from the attack.

"I hope, Mr. Harding," said she, shaking her head slowly and solemnly, "I hope you will not leave me to think that you approve of Sabbath travelling," and she looked a look of unutterable meaning into his eyes.

There was no standing this, for Mr. Slope was now looking at him, and so was the bishop, and so was the archdeacon, who had completed his adieux on that side of the room. Mr. Harding therefore got up also and, putting out his hand to Mrs. Proudie, said: "If you will come to St. Cuthbert's some Sunday, I will preach you a sermon on that subject."

And so the archdeacon and the precentor took their departure, bowing low to the lady, shaking hands with the lord, and escaping from Mr. Slope in the best manner each could. Mr. Harding was again maltreated, but Dr. Grantly swore deeply in the bottom of his heart, that no earthly consideration should ever again induce him to touch the paw of that impure and filthy animal.

And now, had I the pen of a mighty poet, would I sing in epic verse the noble wrath of the archdeacon. The palace steps descend to a broad gravel sweep, from whence a small gate opens out into the street, very near the covered gateway leading into the close. The road from the palace door turns to the left, through the spacious gardens, and terminates on the London road, half a mile from the cathedral.

Till they had both passed this small gate and entered the close, neither of them spoke a word, but the precentor clearly saw from his companion's face that a tornado was to be expected, nor was he himself inclined to stop it. Though by nature far less irritable than the archdeacon, even he was angry: he even—that mild and courteous man—was inclined to express himself in anything but courteous terms.

CHAPTER VI

WAR

"Good heavens!" exclaimed the archdeacon, as he placed his foot on the gravel walk of the close, and raising his hat with one hand, passed the other somewhat violently over his now grizzled locks; smoke issued forth from the uplifted beaver as it were a cloud of wrath, and the safety valve of his anger opened, and emitted a visible steam, preventing positive explosion and probable apoplexy. "Good heavens!"—and the archdeacon looked up to the gray pinnacles of the cathedral tower, making a mute appeal to that still living witness which had looked down on the doings of so many bishops of Barchester.

"I don't think I shall ever like that Mr. Slope," said Mr. Harding.

"Like him!" roared the archdeacon, standing still for a moment to give more force to his voice; "like him!" All the ravens of the close cawed their assent. The old bells of the tower, in chiming the hour, echoed the words, and the swallows flying out from their nests mutely expressed a similar opinion. Like Mr. Slope! Why no, it was not very probable that any Barchester-bred living thing should like Mr. Slope!

"Nor Mrs. Proudie either," said Mr. Harding.

The archdeacon hereupon forgot himself. I will not follow his example, nor shock my readers by transcribing the term in which he expressed his feeling as to the lady who had been named. The ravens and the last lingering notes of the clock bells were less scrupulous and repeated in correspondent echoes the very improper exclamation. The archdeacon again raised his hat, and another salutary escape of steam was effected.

There was a pause, during which the precentor tried to realize the fact that the wife of a Bishop of Barchester had been thus designated, in the close of the cathedral, by the lips of its own archdeacon; but he could not do it.

"The bishop seems to be a quiet man enough," suggested Mr. Harding, having acknowledged to himself his own failure.

"Idiot!" exclaimed the doctor, who for the nonce was not capable of more than such spasmodic attempts at utterance.

"Well, he did not seem very bright," said Mr. Harding, "and yet he has always had the reputation of a clever man. I suppose he's cautious and not inclined to express himself very freely."

The new Bishop of Barchester was already so contemptible a creature in Dr. Grantly's eyes that he could not condescend to discuss his character. He was a puppet to be played by others; a mere wax doll, done up in an apron and a shovel hat, to be stuck on a throne or elsewhere, and pulled about by wires as others chose. Dr. Grantly did not choose to let himself down low enough to talk about Dr. Proudie, but he saw that he would have to talk about the other members of his household, the coadjutor bishops, who had brought his lordship down, as it were, in a box, and were about to handle the wires as they willed. This in itself was a terrible vexation to the archdeacon. Could he have ignored the chaplain and have fought the bishop, there would have been, at any rate, nothing degrading in such a contest. Let the Queen make whom she would Bishop of Barchester; a man, or even an ape, when once a bishop, would be a respectable adversary, if he would but fight, himself. But what was such a person as Dr. Grantly to do when such another person as Mr. Slope was put forward as his antagonist?

If he, our archdeacon, refused the combat, Mr. Slope would walk triumphant over the field, and have the diocese of Barchester under his heel.

If, on the other hand, the archdeacon accepted as his enemy the man whom the new puppet bishop put before him as such, he would have to talk about Mr. Slope, and write about Mr. Slope, and in all matters treat with Mr. Slope, as a being standing, in some degree, on ground similar to his own. He would have to meet Mr. Slope, to—Bah! the idea was sickening. He could not bring himself to have to do with Mr. Slope.

"He is the most thoroughly bestial creature that ever I set my eyes upon," said the archdeacon.

"Who—the bishop?" asked the other innocently.

"Bishop! no—I'm not talking about the bishop. How on earth such a creature got ordained!—they'll ordain anybody now, I know, but he's been in the church these ten years, and they used to be a little careful ten years ago."

"Oh! You mean Mr. Slope."

"Did you ever see any animal less like a gentleman?" asked Dr. Grantly.

"I can't say I felt myself much disposed to like him."

"Like him!" again shouted the doctor, and the assenting ravens again cawed an echo; "of course, you don't like him: it's not a question of liking. But what are we to do with him?"

"Do with him?" asked Mr. Harding.

"Yes—what are we to do with him? How are we to treat him? There he is, and there he'll stay. He has put his foot in that palace, and he'll never take it out again till he's driven. How are we to get rid of him?"

"I don't suppose he can do us much harm."

"Not do harm!—Well, I think you'll find yourself of a different opinion before a month is gone. What would you say now, if he got himself put into the hospital? Would that be harm?"

Mr. Harding mused awhile and then said he didn't think the new bishop would put Mr. Slope into the hospital.

"If he doesn't put him there, he'll put him somewhere else where he'll be as bad. I tell you that that man, to all intents and purposes, will be Bishop of Barchester!" And again Dr. Grantly raised his hat and rubbed his hand thoughtfully and sadly over his head.

"Impudent scoundrel!" he continued after a while. "To dare to cross-examine me about the Sunday-schools in the diocese, and Sunday travelling too: I never in my life met his equal for sheer impudence. Why, he must have thought we were two candidates for ordination!"

"I declare I thought Mrs. Proudie was the worst of the two," said Mr. Harding.

"When a woman is impertinent, one must only put up with it, and keep out of her way in future, but I am not inclined to put up with Mr. Slope. 'Sabbath travelling!'" and the doctor attempted to imitate the peculiar drawl of the man he so much disliked: "'Sabbath travelling!' Those are the sort of men who will ruin the Church of England and make the profession of a clergyman disreputable. It is not the dissenters or the papists that we should fear, but the set of canting, low-bred hypocrites who are wriggling their way in among us; men who have no fixed principle, no standard ideas of religion or doctrine, but who take up some popular cry, as this fellow has done about 'Sabbath travelling.'"

Dr. Grantly did not again repeat the question aloud, but he did so constantly to himself: "What were they to do with Mr. Slope?" How was he openly, before the world, to show that he utterly disapproved of and abhorred such a man?

Hitherto Barchester had escaped the taint of any extreme rigour of church doctrine. The clergymen of the city and neighbourhood, though very well inclined to promote High Church principles, privileges, and prerogatives, had never committed themselves to tendencies which are somewhat too loosely called Puseyite practices. They all preached in their black gowns, as their fathers had done before them; they wore ordinary black cloth waistcoats; they had no candles on their altars, either lighted or unlighted; they made no private genuflexions, and were contented to confine themselves to such ceremonial observances as had been in vogue for the last hundred years. The services were decently and demurely read in their parish churches, chanting was confined to the cathedral, and the science of intoning was unknown. One young man who had come direct from Oxford as a curate to Plumstead had, after the lapse of two or three Sundays, made a faint attempt, much to the bewilderment of the poorer part of the congregation. Dr. Grantly had not been present on the occasion, but Mrs. Grantly, who had her own opinion on the subject, immediately after the service expressed a hope that the young gentleman had not been taken ill, and offered to send him all kinds of condiments supposed to be good for a sore throat. After that there had been no more intoning at Plumstead Episcopi.

But now the archdeacon began to meditate on some strong measures of absolute opposition. Dr. Proudie and his crew were of the lowest possible order of Church of England clergymen, and therefore it behoved him, Dr. Grantly, to be of the very highest. Dr. Proudie would abolish all forms and ceremonies, and therefore Dr. Grantly felt the sudden necessity of multiplying them. Dr. Proudie would consent to deprive the church of all collective authority and rule, and therefore Dr. Grantly would stand up for the full power of convocation and the renewal of all its ancient privileges.

It was true that he could not himself intone the service, but he could procure the co-operation of any number of gentlemanlike curates well trained in the mystery of doing so. He would not willingly alter his own fashion of dress, but he could people Barchester with young clergymen dressed in the longest frocks and in the highest-breasted silk waistcoats. He certainly was not prepared to cross himself, or to advocate the real presence, but without going this length there were various observances, by adopting which he could plainly show his antipathy to such men as Dr. Proudie and Mr. Slope.

All these things passed through his mind as he paced up and down the close with Mr. Harding. War, war, internecine war was in his heart. He felt that, as regarded himself and Mr. Slope, one of the two must be annihilated as far as the city of Barchester was concerned, and he did not intend to give way until there was not left to him an inch of ground on which he could stand. He still flattered himself that he could make Barchester too hot to hold Mr. Slope, and he had no weakness of spirit to prevent his bringing about such a consummation if it were in his power.

"I suppose Susan must call at the palace," said Mr. Harding.

"Yes, she shall call there, but it shall be once and once only. I dare say 'the horses' won't find it convenient to come out to Plumstead very soon, and when that once is done the matter may drop."

"I don't suppose Eleanor need call. I don't think Eleanor would get on at all well with Mrs. Proudie."

"Not the least necessity in life," replied the archdeacon, not without the reflexion that a ceremony which was necessary for his wife might not be at all binding on the widow of John Bold. "Not the slightest reason on earth why she should do so, if she doesn't like it. For myself, I don't think that any decent young woman should be subjected to the nuisance of being in the same room with that man."

And so the two clergymen parted, Mr. Harding going to his daughter's house, and the archdeacon seeking the seclusion of his brougham.

The new inhabitants of the palace did not express any higher opinion of their visitors than their visitors had expressed of them. Though they did not use quite such strong language as Dr. Grantly had done, they felt as much personal aversion, and were quite as well aware as he was that there would be a battle to be fought, and that there was hardly room for Proudieism in Barchester as long as Grantlyism was predominant.

Indeed, it may be doubted whether Mr. Slope had not already within his breast a better prepared system of strategy, a more accurately defined line of hostile conduct than the archdeacon. Dr. Grantly was going to fight because he found that he hated the man. Mr. Slope had predetermined to hate the man because he foresaw the necessity of fighting him. When he had first reviewed the *carte du pays* previous to his entry into Barchester, the idea had occurred to him of conciliating the archdeacon, of cajoling and flattering him into submission, and of obtaining the upper hand by cunning instead of courage. A little inquiry, however, sufficed to convince him that all his cunning would fail to win over such a man as Dr. Grantly to such a mode of action as that to be adopted by Mr. Slope, and then he determined to fall back upon his courage. He at once saw that open battle against Dr. Grantly and all Dr. Grantly's adherents was a necessity of his position, and he deliberately planned the most expedient methods of giving offence.

Soon after his arrival the bishop had intimated to the dean that, with the permission of the canon then in residence, his chaplain would preach in the cathedral on the next Sunday. The canon in residence happened to be the Hon. and Rev. Dr. Vesey Stanhope, who at this time was very busy on the shores of the Lake of Como, adding to that unique collection of butterflies for which he is so famous. Or rather, he would have been in residence but for the butterflies and other such summer-day considerations; and the vicar-choral, who was to take his place in the pulpit, by no means objected to having his work done for him by Mr. Slope.

Mr. Slope accordingly preached, and if a preacher can have satisfaction in being listened to, Mr. Slope ought to have been gratified. I have reason to think that he was gratified, and that he left the pulpit with the conviction that he had done what he intended to do when he entered it.

On this occasion the new bishop took his seat for the first time in the throne alloted to him. New scarlet cushions and drapery had been prepared, with new gilt binding and new fringe. The old carved oak-wood of the throne, ascending with its numerous grotesque pinnacles half-way up to the roof of the choir, had been washed, and dusted, and rubbed, and it all looked very smart. Ah! how often sitting there, in happy early days, on those lowly benches in front of the altar, have I whiled away the tedium of a sermon in considering how best I might thread my way up amidst those wooden towers and climb safely to the topmost pinnacle!

All Barchester went to hear Mr. Slope; either for that or to gaze at the new bishop. All the best bonnets of the city were there, and moreover all the best glossy clerical hats. Not a stall but had its fitting occupant, for though some of the prebendaries might be away in Italy or elsewhere, their places were filled by brethren who flocked into Barchester on the occasion. The dean was there, a heavy old man, now too old, indeed, to attend frequently in his place, and so was the archdeacon. So also were the chancellor, the treasurer, the precentor, sundry canons and minor canons, and every lay member of the choir, prepared to sing the new bishop in with due melody and harmonious expression of sacred welcome.

The service was certainly very well performed. Such was always the case at Barchester, as the musical education of the choir had been good, and the voices had been carefully selected. The psalms were beautifully chanted; the Te Deum was magnificently sung; and the litany was given in a manner which is still to be found at Barchester, but, if my taste be correct, is to be found nowhere else. The litany in Barchester cathedral has long been the special task to which Mr. Harding's skill and voice have been devoted. Crowded audiences generally make good performers, and though Mr. Harding was not aware of any extraordinary exertion on his part, yet probably he rather exceeded his usual mark. Others were doing their best, and it was natural that he should emulate his brethren. So the service went on, and at last Mr. Slope got into the pulpit.

He chose for his text a verse from the precepts addressed by St. Paul to Timothy, as to the conduct necessary in a spiritual pastor and guide, and it was immediately evident that the good clergy of Barchester were to have a lesson.

"Study to show thyself approved unto God, a workman that needeth not to be ashamed, rightly dividing the word of truth." These were the words of his text, and with such a subject in such a place, it may be supposed that such a preacher would be listened to by such an audience. He was listened to with breathless attention and not without considerable surprise. Whatever opinion of Mr. Slope might have been held in Barchester before he commenced his discourse, none of his hearers, when it was over, could mistake him either for a fool or a coward.

It would not be becoming were I to travesty a sermon, or even to repeat the language of it in the pages of a novel. In endeavouring to depict the characters of the persons of whom I write, I am to a certain extent forced to speak of sacred things. I trust, however, that I shall not be thought to scoff at the pulpit, though some may imagine that I do not feel all the reverence that is due to the cloth. I may question the infallibility of the teachers, but I hope that I shall not therefore be accused of doubt as to the thing to be taught.

Mr. Slope, in commencing his sermon, showed no slight tact in his ambiguous manner of hinting that, humble as he was himself, he stood there as the mouth-piece of the illustrious divine who sat opposite to him; and having premised so much, he gave forth a very accurate definition of the conduct which that prelate would rejoice to see in the clergymen now brought under his jurisdiction. It is only necessary to say that the peculiar points insisted upon were exactly those which were most distasteful to the clergy of the diocese, and most averse to their practice and opinions, and that all those peculiar habits and privileges which have always been dear to High Church priests, to that party which is now scandalously called the "high and dry church," were ridiculed, abused, and anathematized. Now, the clergymen of the diocese of Barchester are all of the high and dry church.

Having thus, according to his own opinion, explained how a clergyman should show himself approved unto God, as a workman that needeth not to be ashamed, he went on to explain how the word of truth should be divided; and here he took a rather narrow view of the question and fetched his arguments from afar. His object was to express his abomination of all ceremonious modes of utterance, to cry down any religious feeling which might be excited, not by the sense, but by the sound of words, and in fact to insult cathedral practices. Had St. Paul spoken of rightly pronouncing, instead of rightly dividing the word of truth, this part of his sermon would have been more to the purpose, but the preacher's immediate object was to preach Mr. Slope's doctrine, and not St. Paul's, and he contrived to give the necessary twist to the text with some skill.

He could not exactly say, preaching from a cathedral pulpit, that chanting should be abandoned in cathedral services. By such an assertion he would have overshot his mark and rendered himself absurd, to the delight of his hearers. He could, however, and did, allude with heavy denunciations to the practice of intoning in parish churches, although the practice was all but unknown in the diocese; and from thence he came round to the undue preponderance which, he asserted, music had over meaning in the beautiful service which they had just heard. He was aware, he said, that the practices of our ancestors could not be abandoned at a moment's notice; the feelings of the aged would be outraged, and the minds of respectable men would be shocked. There were many, he was aware, of not sufficient calibre of thought to perceive, of not sufficient education to know, that a mode of service which was effective when outward ceremonies were of more moment than inward feelings, had become all but barbarous at a time when inward conviction was everything, when each word of the minister's lips should fall intelligibly into the listener's heart. Formerly the religion of the multitude had been an affair of the imagination: now, in these latter days, it had become necessary that a Christian should have a reason for his faith—should not only believe, but digest—not only hear, but understand. The words of our morning service, how beautiful, how apposite, how intelligible they were, when read with simple and distinct decorum! But how much of the meaning of the words was lost when they were produced with all the meretricious charms of melody! &c. &c.

Here was a sermon to be preached before Mr. Archdeacon Grantly, Mr. Precentor Harding, and the rest of them! Before a whole dean and chapter assembled in their own cathedral! Before men who had grown old in the exercise of their peculiar services, with a full conviction of their excellence for all intended purposes! This too from such a man, a clerical *parvenu*, a man without a cure, a mere chaplain, an intruder among them; a fellow raked up, so said Dr. Grantly, from the gutters of Marylebone! They had to sit through it! None of them, not even Dr. Grantly, could close his ears, nor leave the house of God during the hours of service. They were under an obligation of listening, and that too without any immediate power of reply.

There is, perhaps, no greater hardship at present inflicted on mankind in civilized and free countries than the necessity of listening to sermons. No one but a preaching clergyman has, in these realms, the power of compelling an audience to sit silent and be tormented. No one but a preaching clergyman can revel in platitudes, truisms, and untruisms, and yet receive, as his undisputed privilege, the same respectful demeanour as though words of impassioned eloquence, or persuasive logic, fell from his lips. Let a professor of law or physics find his place in a lecture-room, and there pour forth jejune words and useless empty phrases, and he will pour them forth to empty benches. Let a barrister attempt to talk without talking well, and he will talk but seldom. A judge's charge need be listened to perforce by none but the jury, prisoner, and gaoler. A member of Parliament can be coughed down or counted out. Town-councillors can be tabooed. But no one can rid himself of the preaching clergyman. He is the bore of the age, the old man whom we Sindbads cannot shake off, the nightmare that disturbs our Sunday's rest, the incubus that overloads our religion and makes God's service distasteful. We are not forced into church! No: but we desire more than that. We desire not to be forced to stay away. We desire, nay, we are resolute, to enjoy the comfort of public worship, but we desire also that we may do so without an amount of tedium which ordinary human nature cannot endure with patience; that we may be able to leave the house of God without that anxious longing for escape which is the common consequence of common sermons.

With what complacency will a young parson deduce false conclusions from misunderstood texts, and then threaten us with all the penalties of Hades if we neglect to comply with the injunctions he has given us! Yes, my too self-confident juvenile friend, I do believe in those mysteries which are so common in your mouth; I do believe in the unadulterated word which you hold there in your hand; but you must pardon me if, in some things, I doubt your interpretation. The Bible is good, the prayer-book is good, nay, you yourself would be acceptable, if you would read to me some portion of those time-honoured discourses which our great divines have elaborated in the full maturity of their powers. But you must excuse me, my insufficient young lecturer, if I yawn over your imperfect sentences, your repeated phrases, your false pathos, your drawlings and denouncings, your humming and hawing, your oh-ing and ah-ing, your black gloves and your white handkerchief. To me, it all means nothing; and hours are too precious to be so wasted—if one could only avoid it.

And here I must make a protest against the pretence, so often put forward by the working clergy, that they are overburdened by the multitude of sermons to be preached. We are all too fond of our own voices, and a preacher is encouraged in the vanity of making his heard by the privilege of a compelled audience. His sermon is the pleasant morsel of his life, his delicious moment of self-exaltation. "I have preached nine sermons this week," said a young friend to me the other day, with hand languidly raised to his brow, the picture of an overburdened martyr. "Nine this week, seven last week, four the week before. I have preached twenty-three sermons this month. It is really too much."

"Too much, indeed," said I, shuddering; "too much for the strength of any one."

"Yes," he answered meekly, "indeed it is; I am beginning to feel it painfully."

"Would," said I, "you could feel it—would that you could be made to feel it." But he never guessed that my heart was wrung for the poor listeners.

There was, at any rate, no tedium felt in listening to Mr. Slope on the occasion in question. His subject came too home to his audience to be dull, and, to tell the truth, Mr. Slope had the gift of using words forcibly. He was heard through his thirty minutes of eloquence with mute attention and open ears, but with angry eyes, which glared round from one enraged parson to another, with wide-spread nostrils from which already burst forth fumes of indignation, and with many shufflings of the feet and uneasy motions of the body, which betokened minds disturbed, and hearts not at peace with all the world.

At last the bishop, who, of all the congregation, had been most surprised, and whose hair almost stood on end with terror, gave the blessing in a manner not at all equal to that in which he had long been practising it in his own study, and the congregation was free to go their way.

CHAPTER VII

THE DEAN AND CHAPTER TAKE COUNSEL

All Barchester was in a tumult. Dr. Grantly could hardly get himself out of the cathedral porch before he exploded in his wrath. The old dean betook himself silently to his deanery, afraid to speak, and there sat, half-stupefied, pondering many things in vain. Mr. Harding crept forth solitary and unhappy; and, slowly passing beneath the elms of the close, could scarcely bring himself to believe that the words which he had heard had proceeded from the pulpit of Barchester cathedral. Was he again to be disturbed? Was his whole life to be shown up as a useless sham a second time? Would he have to abdicate his precentorship, as he had his wardenship, and to give up chanting, as he had given up his twelve old bedesmen? And what if he did! Some other Jupiter, some other Mr. Slope, would come and turn him out of St. Cuthbert's. Surely he could not have been wrong all his life in chanting the litany as he had done! He began, however, to have his doubts. Doubting himself was Mr. Harding's weakness. It is not, however, the usual fault of his order.

Yes! All Barchester was in a tumult. It was not only the clergy who were affected. The laity also had listened to Mr. Slope's new doctrine, all with surprise, some with indignation, and some with a mixed feeling, in which dislike of the preacher was not so strongly blended. The old bishop and his chaplains, the dean and his canons and minor canons, the old choir, and especially Mr. Harding who was at the head of it, had all been popular in Barchester. They had spent their money and done good; the poor had not been ground down; the clergy in society had neither been overbearing nor austere; and the whole repute of the city was due to its ecclesiastical importance. Yet there were those who had heard Mr. Slope with satisfaction.

It is so pleasant to receive a fillip of excitement when suffering from the dull routine of everyday life! The anthems and Te Deums were in themselves delightful, but they had been heard so often! Mr. Slope was certainly not delightful, but he was new, and, moreover, clever. They had long thought it slow, so said now many of the Barchesterians, to go on as they had done in their old humdrum way, giving ear to none of the religious changes which were moving the world without. People in advance of the age now had new ideas, and it was quite time that Barchester should go in advance. Mr. Slope might be right. Sunday had certainly not been strictly kept in Barchester, except as regarded the cathedral services. Indeed the two hours between services had long been appropriated to morning calls and hot luncheons. Then, Sunday-schools! Really more ought to have been done as to Sunday-schools—Sabbath-day schools Mr. Slope had called them. The late bishop had really not thought of Sunday-schools as he should have done. (These people probably did not reflect that catechisms and collects are quite as hard work to the young mind as bookkeeping is to the elderly, and that quite as little feeling of worship enters into the one task as the other.) And then, as regarded that great question of musical services, there might be much to be said on Mr. Slope's side of the question. It certainly was the fact that people went to the cathedral to hear the music, &c. &c.

And so a party absolutely formed itself in Barchester on Mr. Slope's side of the question! This consisted, among the upper classes, chiefly of ladies. No man—that is, no gentleman—could possibly be attracted by Mr. Slope, or consent to sit at the feet of so abhorrent a Gamaliel. Ladies are sometimes less nice in their appreciation of physical disqualification; provided that a man speak to them well, they will listen, though he speak from a mouth never so deformed and hideous. Wilkes was most fortunate as a lover, and the damp, sandy-haired, saucer-eyed, red-fisted Mr. Slope was powerful only over the female breast.

There were, however, one or two of the neighbouring clergy who thought it not quite safe to neglect the baskets in which for the nonce were stored the loaves and fishes of the diocese of Barchester. They, and they only, came to call on Mr. Slope after his performance in the cathedral pulpit. Among these Mr. Quiverful, the rector of Puddingdale, whose wife still continued to present him from year to year with fresh pledges of her love, and so to increase his cares and, it is to be hoped, his happiness equally. Who can wonder that a gentleman with fourteen living children and a bare income of £400 a year should look after the loaves and fishes, even when they are under the thumb of a Mr. Slope?

Very soon after the Sunday on which the sermon was preached, the leading clergy of the neighbourhood held high debate together as to how Mr. Slope should be put down. In the first place, he should never again preach from the pulpit of Barchester cathedral. This was Dr. Grantly's earliest dictum, and they all agreed, providing only that they had the power to exclude him. Dr. Grantly declared that the power rested with the dean and chapter, observing that no clergyman out of the chapter had a claim to preach there, saving only the bishop himself. To this the dean assented, but alleged that contests on such a subject would be unseemly; to which rejoined a meagre little doctor, one of the cathedral prebendaries, that the contest must be all on the side of Mr. Slope if every prebendary were always there ready to take his own place in the pulpit. Cunning little meagre doctor, whom it suits well to live in his own cosy house within Barchester close, and who is well content to have his little fling at Dr. Vesey Stanhope and other absentees, whose Italian villas, or enticing London homes, are more tempting than cathedral stalls and residences!

To this answered the burly chancellor, a man rather silent indeed, but very sensible, that absent prebendaries had their vicars, and that in such case the vicar's right to the pulpit was the same as that of the higher order. To which the dean assented, groaning deeply at these truths. Thereupon, however, the meagre doctor remarked that they would be in the hands of their minor canons, one of whom might at any hour betray his trust. Whereon was heard from the burly chancellor an ejaculation sounding somewhat like "Pooh, pooh, pooh!" but it might be that the worthy man was but blowing out the heavy breath from his windpipe. Why silence him at all? suggested Mr. Harding. Let them not be ashamed to hear what any man might have to preach to them, unless he preached false doctrine; in which case, let the bishop silence him. So spoke our friend; vainly; for human ends must be attained by human means. But the dean saw a ray of hope out of those purblind old eyes of his. Yes, let them tell the bishop how distasteful to them was this Mr. Slope: a new bishop just come to his seat could not wish to insult his clergy while the gloss was yet fresh on his first apron.

Then up rose Dr. Grantly and, having thus collected the scattered wisdom of his associates, spoke forth with words of deep authority. When I say up rose the archdeacon, I speak of the inner man, which then sprang up to more immediate action, for the doctor had bodily been standing all along with his back to the dean's empty fire-grate, and the tails of his frock coat supported over his two arms. His hands were in his breeches pockets.

"It is quite clear that this man must not be allowed to preach again in this cathedral. We all see that, except our dear friend here, the milk of whose nature runs so softly that he would not have the heart to refuse the Pope the loan of his pulpit, if the Pope would come and ask it. We must not, however, allow the man to preach again here. It is not because his opinion on church matters may be different from ours—with that one would not quarrel. It is because he has purposely insulted us. When he went up into that pulpit last Sunday, his studied object was to give offence to men who had grown old in reverence of those things of which he dared to speak so slightingly. What! To come here a stranger, a young, unknown, and unfriended stranger, and tell us, in the name of the bishop his master, that we are ignorant of our duties, old-fashioned, and useless! I don't know whether most to admire his courage or his impudence! And one thing I will tell you: that sermon originated solely with the man himself. The bishop was no more a party to it than was the dean here. You all know how grieved I am to see a bishop in this diocese holding the latitudinarian ideas by which Dr. Proudie has made himself conspicuous. You all know how greatly I should distrust the opinion of such a man. But in this matter I hold him to be blameless. I believe Dr. Proudie has lived too long among gentlemen to be guilty, or to instigate another to be guilty, of so gross an outrage. No! That man uttered what was untrue when he hinted that he was speaking as the mouthpiece of the bishop. It suited his ambitious views at once to throw down the gauntlet to us—at once to defy us here in the quiet of our own religious duties—here within the walls of our own loved cathedral—here where we have for so many years exercised our ministry without schism and with good repute. Such an attack upon us, coming from such a quarter, is abominable."

"Abominable," groaned the dean. "Abominable," muttered the meagre doctor. "Abominable," re-echoed the chancellor, uttering the sound from the bottom of his deep chest. "I really think it was," said Mr. Harding.

"Most abominable and most unjustifiable," continued the archdeacon. "But, Mr. Dean, thank God, that pulpit is still our own: your own, I should say. That pulpit belongs solely to the dean and chapter of Barchester Cathedral, and as yet Mr. Slope is no part of that chapter. You, Mr. Dean, have suggested that we should appeal to the bishop to abstain from forcing this man on us; but what if the bishop allow himself to be ruled by his chaplain? In my opinion the matter is in our own hands. Mr. Slope cannot preach there without permission asked and obtained, and let that permission be invariably refused. Let all participation in the ministry of the cathedral service be refused to him. Then, if the bishop choose to interfere, we shall know what answer to make to the bishop. My friend here has suggested that this man may again find his way into the pulpit by undertaking the duty of some of your minor canons, but I am sure that we may fully trust to these gentlemen to support us, when it is known that the dean objects to any such transfer."

"Of course you may," said the chancellor.

There was much more discussion among the learned conclave, all of which, of course, ended in obedience to the archdeacon's commands. They had too long been accustomed to his rule to shake it off so soon, and in this particular case they had none of them a wish to abet the man whom he was so anxious to put down.

Such a meeting as that we have just recorded is not held in such a city as Barchester unknown and untold of. Not only was the fact of the meeting talked of in every respectable house, including the palace, but the very speeches of the dean, the archdeacon, and chancellor were repeated; not without many additions and imaginary circumstances, according to the tastes and opinions of the relaters.

All, however, agreed in saying that Mr. Slope was to be debarred from opening his mouth in the cathedral of Barchester; many believed that the vergers were to be ordered to refuse him even the accommodation of a seat; and some of the most far-going advocates for strong measures declared that his sermon was looked upon as an indictable offence, and that proceedings were to be taken against him for brawling.

The party who were inclined to defend him—the enthusiastically religious young ladies and the middle-aged spinsters desirous of a move—of course took up his defence the more warmly on account of this attack. If they could not hear Mr. Slope in the cathedral, they would hear him elsewhere; they would leave the dull dean, the dull old prebendaries, and the scarcely less dull young minor canons to preach to each other; they would work slippers and cushions and hem bands for Mr. Slope, make him a happy martyr, and stick him up in some new Sion or Bethesda, and put the cathedral quite out of fashion.

Dr. and Mrs. Proudie at once returned to London. They thought it expedient not to have to encounter any personal application from the dean and chapter respecting the sermon till the violence of the storm had expended itself; but they left Mr. Slope behind them nothing daunted, and he went about his work zealously, flattering such as would listen to his flattery, whispering religious twaddle into the ears of foolish women, ingratiating himself with the few clergy who would receive him, visiting the houses of the poor, inquiring into all people, prying into everything, and searching with his minutest eye into all palatial dilapidations. He did not, however, make any immediate attempt to preach again in the cathedral.

And so all Barchester was by the ears.

CHAPTER VIII

THE EX-WARDEN REJOICES IN HIS PROBABLE RETURN TO THE HOSPITAL

Among the ladies in Barchester who have hitherto acknowledged Mr. Slope as their spiritual director must not be reckoned either the Widow Bold or her sister-in-law. On the first outbreak of the wrath of the denizens of the close, none had been more animated against the intruder than these two ladies. And this was natural. Who could be so proud of the musical distinction of their own cathedral as the favourite daughter of the precentor? Who would be so likely to resent an insult offered to the old choir? And in such matters Miss Bold and her sister-in-law had but one opinion.

This wrath, however, has in some degree been mitigated, and I regret to say that these ladies allowed Mr. Slope to be his own apologist. About a fortnight after the sermon had been preached, they were both of them not a little surprised by hearing Mr. Slope announced, as the page in buttons opened Mrs. Bold's drawing-room door. Indeed, what living man could, by a mere morning visit, have surprised them more? Here was the great enemy of all that was good in Barchester coming into their own drawing-room, and they had no strong arm, no ready tongue, near at hand for their protection. The widow snatched her baby out of its cradle into her lap, and Mary Bold stood up ready to die manfully in that baby's behalf, should, under any circumstances, such a sacrifice become necessary.

In this manner was Mr. Slope received. But when he left, he was allowed by each lady to take her hand and to make his adieux as gentlemen do who have been graciously entertained! Yes, he shook hands with them, and was curtseyed out courteously, the buttoned page opening the door as he would have done for the best canon of them all. He had touched the baby's little hand and blessed him with a fervid blessing; he had spoken to the widow of her early sorrows, and Eleanor's silent tears had not rebuked him; he had told Mary Bold that her devotion would be rewarded, and Mary Bold had heard the praise without disgust. And how had he done all this? How had he so quickly turned aversion into, at any rate, acquaintance? How had he over-come the enmity with which these ladies had been ready to receive him, and made his peace with them so easily?

My readers will guess from what I have written that I myself do not like Mr. Slope, but I am constrained to admit that he is a man of parts. He knows how to say a soft word in the proper place; he knows how to adapt his flattery to the ears of his hearers; he knows the wiles of the serpent, and he uses them. Could Mr. Slope have adapted his manners to men as well as to women, could he ever have learnt the ways of a gentleman, he might have risen to great things.

He commenced his acquaintance with Eleanor by praising her father. He had, he said, become aware that he had unfortunately offended the feelings of a man of whom he could not speak too highly; he would not now allude to a subject which was probably too serious for drawing-room conversation, but he would say that it had been very far from him to utter a word in disparagement of a man of whom all the world, at least the clerical world, spoke so highly as it did of Mr. Harding. And so he went on, unsaying a great deal of his sermon, expressing his highest admiration for the precentor's musical talents, eulogizing the father and the daughter and the sister-in-law, speaking in that low silky whisper which he always had specially prepared for feminine ears, and, ultimately, gaining his object. When he left, he expressed a hope that he might again be allowed to call; and though Eleanor gave no verbal assent to this, she did not express dissent: and so Mr. Slope's right to visit at the widow's house was established.

The day after this visit Eleanor told her father of it and expressed an opinion that Mr. Slope was not quite so black as he had been painted. Mr. Harding opened his eyes rather wider than usual when he heard what had occurred, but he said little; he could not agree in any praise of Mr. Slope, and it was not his practice to say much evil of anyone. He did not, however, like the visit, and simple-minded as he was, he felt sure that Mr. Slope had some deeper motive than the mere pleasure of making soft speeches to two ladies.

Mr. Harding, however, had come to see his daughter with other purpose than that of speaking either good or evil of Mr. Slope. He had come to tell her that the place of warden in Hiram's Hospital was again to be filled up, and that in all probability he would once more return to his old home and his twelve bedesmen.

"But," said he, laughing, "I shall be greatly shorn of my ancient glory."

"Why so, Papa?"

"This new act of Parliament that is to put us all on our feet again," continued he, "settles my income at four hundred and fifty pounds per annum."

"Four hundred and fifty," said she, "instead of eight hundred! Well, that is rather shabby. But still, Papa, you'll have the dear old house and the garden?"

"My dear," said he, "it's worth twice the money;" and as he spoke he showed a jaunty kind of satisfaction in his tone and manner and in the quick, pleasant way in which he paced Eleanor's drawing-room. "It's worth twice the money. I shall have the house and the garden and a larger income than I can possibly want."

"At any rate, you'll have no extravagant daughter to provide for;" and as she spoke, the young widow put her arm within his, and made him sit on the sofa beside her; "at any rate, you'll not have that expense."

"No, my dear, and I shall be rather lonely without her; but we won't think of that now. As regards income, I shall have plenty for all I want. I shall have my old house, and I don't mind owning now that I have felt sometimes the inconvenience of living in a lodging. Lodgings are very nice for young men, but at my time of life there is a want of—I hardly know what to call it, perhaps not respectability—"

"Oh, Papa! I'm sure there's been nothing like that. Nobody has thought it; nobody in all Barchester has been more respected than you have been since you took those rooms in High Street. Nobody! Not the dean in his deanery, or the archdeacon out at Plumstead."

"The archdeacon would not be much obliged to you if he heard you," said he, smiling somewhat at the exclusive manner in which his daughter confined her illustration to the church dignitaries of the chapter of Barchester; "but at any rate I shall be glad to get back to the old house. Since I heard that it was all settled, I have begun to fancy that I can't be comfortable without my two sitting-rooms."

"Come and stay with me, Papa, till it is settled—there's a dear Papa."

"Thank ye, Nelly. But no, I won't do that. It would make two movings. I shall be very glad to get back to my old men again. Alas! alas! There have six of them gone in these few last years. Six out of twelve! And the others I fear have had but a sorry life of it there. Poor Bunce, poor old Bunce!"

Bunce was one of the surviving recipients of Hiram's charity, an old man, now over ninety, who had long been a favourite of Mr. Harding's.

"How happy old Bunce will be," said Mrs. Bold, clapping her soft hands softly. "How happy they all will be to have you back again. You may be sure there will soon be friendship among them again when you are there."

"But," said he, half-laughing, "I am to have new troubles, which will be terrible to me. There are to be twelve old women, and a matron. How shall I manage twelve women and a matron!"

"The matron will manage the women, of course."

"And who'll manage the matron?" said he.

"She won't want to be managed. She'll be a great lady herself, I suppose. But, Papa, where will the matron live? She is not to live in the warden's house with you, is she?"

"Well, I hope not, my dear."

"Oh, Papa, I tell you fairly, I won't have a matron for a new stepmother."

"You shan't, my dear; that is, if I can help it. But they are going to build another house for the matron and the women, and I believe they haven't even fixed yet on the site of the building."

"And have they appointed the matron?" said Eleanor.

"They haven't appointed the warden yet," replied he.

"But there's no doubt about that, I suppose," said his daughter.

Mr. Harding explained that he thought there was no doubt; that the archdeacon had declared as much, saying that the bishop and his chaplain between them had not the power to appoint anyone else, even if they had the will to do so, and sufficient impudence to carry out such a will. The archdeacon was of opinion that, though Mr. Harding had resigned his wardenship, and had done so unconditionally, he had done so under circumstances which left the bishop no choice as to his reappointment, now that the affair of the hospital had been settled on a new basis by act of Parliament. Such was the archdeacon's opinion, and his father-in-law received it without a shadow of doubt.

Dr. Grantly had always been strongly opposed to Mr. Harding's resignation of the place. He had done all in his power to dissuade him from it. He had considered that Mr. Harding was bound to withstand the popular clamour with which he was attacked for receiving so large an income as eight hundred a year from such a charity, and was not even yet satisfied that his father-in-law's conduct had not been pusillanimous and undignified. He looked also on this reduction of the warden's income as a shabby, paltry scheme on the part of government for escaping from a difficulty into which it had been brought by the public press. Dr. Grantly observed that the government had no more right to dispose of a sum of four hundred and fifty pounds a year out of the income of Hiram's legacy than of nine hundred; whereas, as he said, the bishop, dean, and chapter clearly had a right to settle what sum should be paid. He also declared that the government had no more right to saddle the charity with twelve old women than with twelve hundred; and he was, therefore, very indignant on the matter. He probably forgot when so talking that government had done nothing of the kind, and had never assumed any such might or any such right. He made the common mistake of attributing to the government, which in such matters is powerless, the doings of Parliament, which in such matters is omnipotent.

But though he felt that the glory and honour of the situation of warden of Barchester Hospital were indeed curtailed by the new arrangement; that the whole establishment had to a certain degree been made vile by the touch of Whig commissioners; that the place, with its lessened income, its old women, and other innovations, was very different from the hospital of former days; still the archdeacon was too practical a man of the world to wish that his father-in-law, who had at present little more than £200 per annum for all his wants, should refuse the situation, defiled, undignified, and commission-ridden as it was.

Mr. Harding had, accordingly, made up his mind that he would return to his old home at the hospital, and, to tell the truth, had experienced almost a childish pleasure in the idea of doing so. The diminished income was to him not even the source of momentary regret. The matron and the old women did rather go against the grain, but he was able to console himself with the reflection that, after all, such an arrangement might be of real service to the poor of the city. The thought that he must receive his reappointment as the gift of the new bishop, and probably through the hands of Mr. Slope, annoyed him a little, but his mind was set at rest by the assurance of the archdeacon that there would be no favour in such a presentation. The reappointment of the old warden would be regarded by all the world as a matter of course. Mr. Harding, therefore, felt no hesitation in telling his daughter that they might look upon his return to his old quarters as a settled matter.

"And you won't have to ask for it, Papa?"

"Certainly not, my dear. There is no ground on which I could ask for any favour from the bishop, whom, indeed, I hardly know. Nor would I ask a favour, the granting of which might possibly be made a question to be settled by Mr. Slope. No," said he, moved for a moment by a spirit very unlike his own, "I certainly shall be very glad to go back to the hospital; but I should never go there if it were necessary that my doing so should be the subject of a request to Mr. Slope."

This little outbreak of her father's anger jarred on the present tone of Eleanor's mind. She had not learnt to like Mr. Slope, but she had learnt to think that he had much respect for her father; and she would, therefore, willingly use her efforts to induce something like good feeling between them.

"Papa," said she, "I think you somewhat mistake Mr. Slope's character."

"Do I?" said he placidly.

"I think you do, Papa. I think he intended no personal disrespect to you when he preached the sermon which made the archdeacon and the dean so angry!"

"I never supposed he did, my dear. I hope I never inquired within myself whether he did or no. Such a matter would be unworthy of any inquiry, and very unworthy of the consideration of the chapter. But I fear he intended disrespect to the ministration of God's services, as conducted in conformity with the rules of the Church of England."

"But might it not be that he thought it his duty to express his dissent from that which you, and the dean, and all of us here so much approve?"

"It can hardly be the duty of a young man rudely to assail the religious convictions of his elders in the church. Courtesy should have kept him silent, even if neither charity nor modesty could do so."

"But Mr. Slope would say that on such a subject the commands of his heavenly Master do not admit of his being silent."

"Nor of his being courteous, Eleanor?"

"He did not say that, Papa."

"Believe me, my child, that Christian ministers are never called on by God's word to insult the convictions, or even the prejudices of their brethren, and that religion is at any rate not less susceptible of urbane and courteous conduct among men than any other study which men may take up. I am sorry to say that I cannot defend Mr. Slope's sermon in the cathedral. But come, my dear, put on your bonnet and let us walk round the dear old gardens at the hospital. I have never yet had the heart to go beyond the courtyard since we left the place. Now I think I can venture to enter."

Eleanor rang the bell and gave a variety of imperative charges as to the welfare of the precious baby, whom, all but unwillingly, she was about to leave for an hour or so, and then sauntered forth with her father to revisit the old hospital. It had been forbidden ground to her as well as to him since the day on which they had walked forth together from its walls.

CHAPTER IX

THE STANHOPE FAMILY

It is now three months since Dr. Proudie began his reign, and changes have already been effected in the diocese which show at least the energy of an active mind. Among other things absentee clergymen have been favoured with hints much too strong to be overlooked. Poor dear old Bishop Grantly had on this matter been too lenient, and the archdeacon had never been inclined to be severe with those who were absent on reputable pretences, and who provided for their duties in a liberal way.

Among the greatest of the diocesan sinners in this respect was Dr. Vesey Stanhope. Years had now passed since he had done a day's duty, and yet there was no reason against his doing duty except a want of inclination on his own part. He held a prebendal stall in the diocese, one of the best residences in the close, and the two large rectories of Crabtree Canonicorum and Stogpingum. Indeed, he had the cure of three parishes, for that of Ei-derdown was joined to Stogpingum. He had resided in Italy for twelve years. His first going there had been attributed to a sore throat, and that sore throat, though never repeated in any violent manner, had stood him in such stead that it had enabled him to live in easy idleness ever since.

He had now been summoned home—not, indeed, with rough violence, or by any peremptory command, but by a mandate which he found himself unable to disregard. Mr. Slope had written to him by the bishop's desire. In the first place, the bishop much wanted the valuable co-operation of Dr. Vesey Stanhope in the diocese; in the next, the bishop thought it his imperative duty to become personally acquainted with the most conspicuous of his diocesan clergy; then the bishop thought it essentially necessary for Dr. Stanhope's own interests that Dr. Stanhope should, at any rate for a time, return to Barchester; and lastly, it was said that so strong a feeling was at the present moment evinced by the hierarchs of the church with reference to the absence of its clerical members, that it behoved Dr. Vesey Stanhope not to allow his name to stand among those which would probably in a few months be submitted to the councils of the nation.

There was something so ambiguously frightful in this last threat that Dr. Stanhope determined to spend two or three summer months at his residence in Barchester. His rectories were inhabited by his curates, and he felt himself from disuse to be unfit for parochial duty; but his prebendal home was kept empty for him, and he thought it probable that he might be able now and again to preach a prebendal sermon. He arrived, therefore, with all his family at Barchester, and he and they must be introduced to my readers.

The great family characteristic of the Stanhopes might probably be said to be heart-lessness, but this want of feeling was, in most of them, accompanied by so great an amount of good nature as to make itself but little noticeable to the world. They were so prone to oblige their neighbours that their neighbours failed to perceive how indifferent to them was the happiness and well-being of those around them. The Stanhopes would visit you in your sickness (provided it were not contagious), would bring you oranges, French novels, and the last new bit of scandal, and then hear of your death or your recovery with an equally indifferent composure. Their conduct to each other was the same as to the world; they bore and forbore; and there was sometimes, as will be seen, much necessity for forbearing; but their love among themselves rarely reached above this. It is astonishing how much each of the family was able to do, and how much each did, to prevent the well-being of the other four.

For there were five in all; the doctor, namely, and Mrs. Stanhope, two daughters, and one son. The doctor, perhaps, was the least singular and most estimable of them all, and yet such good qualities as he possessed were all negative. He was a good-looking rather plethoric gentleman of about sixty years of age. His hair was snow-white, very plentiful, and somewhat like wool of the finest description. His whiskers were very large and very white, and gave to his face the appearance of a benevolent, sleepy old lion. His dress was always unexceptionable. Although he had lived so many years in Italy it was invariably of a decent clerical hue, but it never was hyperclerical. He was a man not given to much talk-ing, but what little he did say was generally well said. His reading seldom went beyond romances and poetry of the lightest and not always most moral description. He was thor-oughly a *bon vivant*; an accomplished judge of wine, though he never drank to excess; and a most inexorable critic in all affairs touching the kitchen. He had had much to forgive in his own family, since a family had grown up around him, and had forgiven everything— except inattention to his dinner. His weakness in that respect was now fully understood, and his temper but seldom tried. As Dr. Stanhope was a clergyman, it may be supposed that his religious convictions made up a considerable part of his character, but this was not so. That he had religious convictions must be believed, but he rarely obtruded them, even on his children. This abstinence on his part was not systematic, but very characteristic of the man. It was not that he had predetermined never to influence their thoughts, but he was so habitually idle that his time for doing so had never come till the opportunity for doing so was gone forever. Whatever conviction the father may have had, the children were at any rate but indifferent members of the church from which he drew his income.

Such was Dr. Stanhope. The features of Mrs. Stanhope's character were even less plainly marked than those of her lord. The *far niente* of her Italian life had entered into her very soul, and brought her to regard a state of inactivity as the only earthly good. In man-ner and appearance she was exceedingly prepossessing. She had been a beauty, and even now, at fifty-five, she was a handsome woman. Her dress was always perfect: she never dressed but once in the day, and never appeared till between three and four; but when she did appear, she appeared at her best. Whether the toil rested partly with her, or wholly with her handmaid, it is not for such a one as the author even to imagine. The structure of her attire was always elaborate and yet never over-laboured. She was rich in apparel but not bedizened with finery; her ornaments were costly, rare, and such as could not fail to attract notice, but they did not look as though worn with that purpose. She well knew the great architectural secret of decorating her constructions, and never descended to construct a decoration. But when we have said that Mrs. Stanhope knew how to dress and used her knowledge daily, we have said all. Other purpose in life she had none. It was something, indeed, that she did not interfere with the purposes of others. In early life she had under-gone great trials with reference to the doctor's dinners, but for the last ten or twelve years her elder daughter Charlotte had taken that labour off her hands, and she had had little to trouble her—little, that is, till the edict for this terrible English journey had gone forth: since then, indeed, her life had been laborious enough. For such a one, the toil of being carried from the shores of Como to the city of Barchester is more than labour enough, let the care of the carriers be ever so vigilant. Mrs. Stanhope had been obliged to have every one of her dresses taken in from the effects of the journey.

Charlotte Stanhope was at this time about thirty-five years old, and whatever may have been her faults, she had none of those which belong particularly to old young ladies. She neither dressed young, nor talked young, nor indeed looked young. She appeared to be perfectly content with her time of life, and in no way affected the graces of youth. She was a fine young woman, and had she been a man, would have been a very fine young man. All that was done in the house, and that was not done by servants, was done by her. She gave the orders, paid the bills, hired and dismissed the domestics, made the tea, carved the meat, and managed everything in the Stanhope household. She, and she alone, could ever induce her father to look into the state of his worldly concerns. She, and she alone, could in any degree control the absurdities of her sister. She, and she alone, prevented the whole family from falling into utter disrepute and beggary. It was by her advice that they now found themselves very unpleasantly situated in Barchester.

So far, the character of Charlotte Stanhope is not unprepossessing. But it remains to be said that the influence which she had in her family, though it had been used to a certain extent for their worldly well-being, had not been used to their real benefit, as it might have been. She had aided her father in his indifference to his professional duties, counselling him that his livings were as much his individual property as the estates of his elder brother were the property of that worthy peer. She had for years past stifled every little rising wish for a return to England which the doctor had from time to time expressed. She had encouraged her mother in her idleness, in order that she herself might be mistress and manager of the Stanhope household. She had encouraged and fostered the follies of her sister, though she was always willing, and often able, to protect her from their probable result. She had done her best, and had thoroughly succeeded in spoiling her brother, and turning him loose upon the world an idle man without a profession and without a shilling that he could call his own.

Miss Stanhope was a clever woman, able to talk on most subjects, and quite indifferent as to what the subject was. She prided herself on her freedom from English prejudice, and, she might have added, from feminine delicacy. On religion she was a pure free-thinker, and with much want of true affection, delighted to throw out her own views before the troubled mind of her father. To have shaken what remained of his Church of England faith would have gratified her much, but the idea of his abandoning his preferment in the church had never once presented itself to her mind. How could he indeed, when he had no income from any other source?

But the two most prominent members of the family still remain to be described. The second child had been christened Madeline and had been a great beauty. We need not say had been, for she was never more beautiful than at the time of which we write, though her person for many years had been disfigured by an accident. It is unnecessary that we should give in detail the early history of Madeline Stanhope. She had gone to Italy when about seventeen years of age, and had been allowed to make the most of her surpassing beauty in the salons of Milan and among the crowded villas along the shores of the Lake of Como. She had become famous for adventures in which her character was just not lost, and had destroyed the hearts of a dozen cavaliers without once being touched in her own. Blood had flowed in quarrels about her charms, and she had heard of these encounters with pleasurable excitement. It had been told of her that on one occasion she had stood by in the disguise of a page and had seen her lover fall.

As is so often the case, she had married the very worst of those who sought her hand. Why she had chosen Paulo Neroni, a man of no birth and no property, a mere captain in the Pope's guard, one who had come up to Milan either simply as an adventurer or else as a spy, a man of harsh temper and oily manners, mean in figure, swarthy in face, and so false in words as to be hourly detected, need not now be told. When the moment for doing so came, she had probably no alternative. He, at any rate, had become her husband, and after a prolonged honeymoon among the lakes, they had gone together to Rome, the papal captain having vainly endeavoured to induce his wife to remain behind him.

Six months afterwards she arrived at her father's house a cripple, and a mother. She had arrived without even notice, with hardly clothes to cover her, and without one of those many ornaments which had graced her bridal trousseau. Her baby was in the arms of a poor girl from Milan, whom she had taken in exchange for the Roman maid who had ac-companied her thus far, and who had then, as her mistress said, become homesick and had returned. It was clear that the lady had determined that there should be no witness to tell stories of her life in Rome.

She had fallen, she said, in ascending a ruin, and had fatally injured the sinews of her knee; so fatally that when she stood, she lost eight inches of her accustomed height; so fatally that when she essayed to move, she could only drag herself painfully along, with protruded hip and extended foot, in a manner less graceful than that of a hunchback. She had consequently made up her mind, once and forever, that she would never stand and never attempt to move herself.

Stories were not slow to follow her, averring that she had been cruelly ill-used by Neroni, and that to his violence had she owed her accident. Be that as it may, little had been said about her husband, but that little had made it clearly intelligible to the family that Signor Neroni was to be seen and heard of no more. There was no question as to re-admitting the poor, ill-used beauty to her old family rights, no question as to adopting her infant daughter beneath the Stanhope roof-tree. Though heartless, the Stanhopes were not selfish. The two were taken in, petted, made much of, for a time all but adored, and then felt by the two parents to be great nuisances in the house. But in the house the lady was, and there she remained, having her own way, though that way was not very conformable with the customary usages of an English clergyman.

Madame Neroni, though forced to give up all motion in the world, had no intention whatever of giving up the world itself. The beauty of her face was uninjured, and that beauty was of a peculiar kind. Her copious rich brown hair was worn in Grecian bandeaux round her head, displaying as much as possible of her forehead and cheeks. Her forehead, though rather low, was very beautiful from its perfect contour and pearly whiteness. Her eyes were long and large, and marvellously bright; might I venture to say bright as Lu-cifer's, I should perhaps best express the depth of their brilliancy. They were dreadful eyes to look at, such as would absolutely deter any man of quiet mind and easy spirit from at-tempting a passage of arms with such foes. There was talent in them, and the fire of passion and the play of wit, but there was no love. Cruelty was there instead, and courage, a desire of masterhood, cunning, and a wish for mischief. And yet, as eyes, they were very beautiful. The eyelashes were long and perfect, and the long, steady, unabashed gaze with which she would look into the face of her admirer fascinated while it frightened him. She was a basilisk from whom an ardent lover of beauty could make no escape. Her nose and mouth and teeth and chin and neck and bust were perfect, much more so at twenty-eight than they had been at eighteen. What wonder that with such charms still glowing in her face, and with such deformity destroying her figure, she should resolve to be seen, but only to be seen reclining on a sofa.

Her resolve had not been carried out without difficulty. She had still frequented the opera at Milan; she had still been seen occasionally in the salons of the noblesse; she had caused herself to be carried in and out from her carriage, and that in such a manner as in no wise to disturb her charms, disarrange her dress, or expose her deformities. Her sister always accompanied her and a maid, a manservant also, and on state occasions, two. It was impossible that her purpose could have been achieved with less; and yet, poor as she was, she had achieved her purpose. And then again the more dissolute Italian youths of Milan frequented the Stanhope villa and surrounded her couch, not greatly to her father's satisfaction. Sometimes his spirit would rise, a dark spot would show itself on his cheek, and he would rebel, but Charlotte would assuage him with some peculiar triumph of her culinary art and all again would be smooth for awhile.

Madeline affected all manner of rich and quaint devices in the garniture of her room, her person, and her feminine belongings. In nothing was this more apparent than in the visiting card which she had prepared for her use. For such an article one would say that she, in her present state, could have but small need, seeing how improbable it was that she should make a morning call: but not such was her own opinion. Her card was surrounded by a deep border of gilding; on this she had imprinted, in three lines

La Signora Madeline
Vesey Neroni.
—Nata Stanhope.

And over the name she had a bright gilt coronet, which certainly looked very magnificent. How she had come to concoct such a name for herself it would be difficult to explain. Her father had been christened Vesey as another man is christened Thomas, and she had no more right to assume it than would have the daughter of a Mr. Josiah Jones to call herself Mrs. Josiah Smith, on marrying a man of the latter name. The gold coronet was equally out of place, and perhaps inserted with even less excuse. Paulo Neroni had had not the faintest title to call himself a scion of even Italian nobility. Had the pair met in England Neroni would probably have been a count, but they had met in Italy, and any such pretence on his part would have been simply ridiculous. A coronet, however, was a pretty ornament, and if it could solace a poor cripple to have such on her card, who would begrudge it to her? Of her husband, or of his individual family, she never spoke, but with her admirers she would often allude in a mysterious way to her married life and isolated state, and, pointing to her daughter, would call her the last of the blood of the emperors, thus referring Neroni's extraction to the old Roman family from which the worst of the Caesars sprang.

The "signora" was not without talent and not without a certain sort of industry; she was an indomitable letter-writer, and her letters were worth the postage: they were full of wit, mischief, satire, love, latitudinarian philosophy, free religion, and, sometimes, alas, loose ribaldry. The subject, however, depended entirely on the recipient, and she was prepared to correspond with anyone but moral young ladies or stiff old women. She wrote also a kind of poetry, generally in Italian, and short romances, generally in French. She read much of a desultory sort of literature, and as a modern linguist had really made great proficiency. Such was the lady who had now come to wound the hearts of the men of Barchester.

Ethelbert Stanhope was in some respects like his younger sister, but he was less inestimable as a man than she as a woman. His great fault was an entire absence of that principle which should have induced him, as the son of a man without fortune, to earn his own bread. Many attempts had been made to get him to do so, but these had all been frustrated, not so much by idleness on his part as by a disinclination to exert himself in any way not to his taste. He had been educated at Eton and had been intended for the Church, but he had left Cambridge in disgust after a single term, and notified to his father his intention to study for the bar. Preparatory to that, he thought it well that he should attend a German university, and consequently went to Leipzig. There he remained two years and brought away a knowledge of German and a taste for the fine arts. He still, however, intended himself for the bar, took chambers, engaged himself to sit at the feet of a learned pundit, and spent a season in London. He there found that all his aptitudes inclined him to the life of an artist, and he determined to live by painting. With this object he returned to Milan, and had himself rigged out for Rome. As a painter he might have earned his bread, for he wanted only diligence to excel, but when at Rome his mind was carried away by other things: he soon wrote home for money, saying that he had been converted to the Mother Church, that he was already an acolyte of the Jesuits, and that he was about to start with others to Palestine on a mission for converting Jews. He did go to Judea, but being unable to convert the Jews, was converted by them. He again wrote home, to say that Moses was the only giver of perfect laws to the world, that the coming of the true Messiah was at hand, that great things were doing in Palestine, and that he had met one of the family of Sidonia, a most remarkable man, who was now on his way to western Europe, and whom he had induced to deviate from his route with the object of calling at the Stanhope villa. Ethelbert then expressed his hope that his mother and sisters would listen to this wonderful prophet. His father he knew could not do so from pecuniary considerations. This Sidonia, however, did not take so strong a fancy to him as another of that family once did to a young English nobleman. At least he provided him with no heaps of gold as large as lions, so that the Judaized Ethelbert was again obliged to draw on the revenues of the Christian Church.

It is needless to tell how the father swore that he would send no more money and receive no Jew, nor how Charlotte declared that Ethelbert could not be left penniless in Jerusalem, and how "La Signora Neroni" resolved to have Sidonia at her feet. The money was sent, and the Jew did come. The Jew did come, but he was not at all to the taste of "La Signora." He was a dirty little old man, and though he had provided no golden lions, he had, it seems, relieved young Stanhope's necessities. He positively refused to leave the villa till he had got a bill from the doctor on his London bankers.

Ethelbert did not long remain a Jew. He soon reappeared at the villa without prejudices on the subject of his religion, and with a firm resolve to achieve fame and fortune as a sculptor. He brought with him some models which he had originated at Rome and which really gave such fair promise that his father was induced to go to further expense in furthering these views. Ethelbert opened an establishment, or rather took lodgings and a workshop, at Carrara, and there spoilt much marble and made some few pretty images. Since that period, now four years ago, he had alternated between Carrara and the villa, but his sojourns at the workshop became shorter and shorter and those at the villa longer and longer. 'Twas no wonder, for Carrara is not a spot in which an Englishman would like to dwell.

When the family started for England, he had resolved not to be left behind, and, with the assistance of his elder sister, had carried his point against his father's wishes. It was necessary, he said, that he should come to England for orders. How otherwise was he to bring his profession to account?

In personal appearance Ethelbert Stanhope was the most singular of beings. He was certainly very handsome. He had his sister Madeline's eyes, without their stare and without their hard, cunning, cruel firmness. They were also very much lighter, and of so light and clear a blue as to make his face remarkable, if nothing else did so. On entering a room with him, Ethelbert's blue eyes would be the first thing you would see, and on leaving it almost the last you would forget. His light hair was very long and silky, coming down over his coat. His beard had been prepared in holy land, and was patriarchal. He never shaved and rarely trimmed it. It was glossy, soft, clean, and altogether not unprepossessing. It was such that ladies might desire to reel it off and work it into their patterns in lieu of floss silk. His complexion was fair and almost pink; he was small in height and slender in limb, but well-made; and his voice was of peculiar sweetness.

In manner and dress he was equally remarkable. He had none of the *mauvaise honte* of an Englishman. He required no introduction to make himself agreeable to any person. He habitually addressed strangers, ladies as well as men, without any such formality, and in doing so never seemed to meet with rebuke. His costume cannot be described because it was so various, but it was always totally opposed in every principle of colour and construction to the dress of those with whom he for the time consorted.

He was habitually addicted to making love to ladies, and did so without any scruples of conscience, or any idea that such a practice was amiss. He had no heart to touch himself, and was literally unaware that humanity was subject to such an infliction. He had not thought much about it, but, had he been asked, would have said that ill-treating a lady's heart meant injuring her promotion in the world. His principles therefore forbade him to pay attention to a girl if he thought any man was present whom it might suit her to marry. In this manner his good nature frequently interfered with his amusement, but he had no other motive in abstaining from the fullest declarations of love to every girl that pleased his eye.

Bertie Stanhope, as he was generally called, was, however, popular with both sexes—and with Italians as well as English. His circle of acquaintance was very large and embraced people of all sorts. He had no respect for rank, and no aversion to those below him. He had lived on familiar terms with English peers, German shopkeepers, and Roman priests. All people were nearly alike to him. He was above, or rather below, all prejudices. No virtue could charm him, no vice shock him. He had about him a natural good manner, which seemed to qualify him for the highest circles, and yet he was never out of place in the lowest. He had no principle, no regard for others, no self-respect, no desire to be other than a drone in the hive, if only he could, as a drone, get what honey was sufficient for him. Of honey, in his latter days, it may probably be presaged, that he will have but short allowance.

Such was the family of the Stanhopes, who, at this period, suddenly joined themselves to the ecclesiastical circle of Barchester close. Any stranger union it would be impossible perhaps to conceive. And it was not as though they all fell down into the cathedral precincts hitherto unknown and untalked of. In such case, no amalgamation would have been at all probable between the new-comers and either the Proudie set or the Grantly set. But such was far from being the case. The Stanhopes were all known by name in Barchester, and Barchester was prepared to receive them with open arms. The doctor was one of her prebendaries, one of her rectors, one of her pillars of strength; and was, moreover, counted on as a sure ally both by Proudies and Grantlys.

He himself was the brother of one peer, and his wife was the sister of another—and both these peers were lords of Whiggish tendency, with whom the new bishop had some sort of alliance. This was sufficient to give to Mr. Slope high hope that he might enlist Dr. Stanhope on his side, before his enemies could outmanoeuvre him. On the other hand, the old dean had many many years ago, in the days of the doctor's clerical energies, been instrumental in assisting him in his views as to preferment; and many many years ago also, the two doctors, Stanhope and Grantly, had, as young parsons, been joyous together in the common-rooms of Oxford. Dr. Grantly, consequently, did not doubt but that the newcomer would range himself under his banners.

Little did any of them dream of what ingredients the Stanhope family was now composed.

CHAPTER X

MRS. PROUDIE'S RECEPTION—COMMENCED

The bishop and his wife had spent only three or four days in Barchester on the occasion of their first visit. His lordship had, as we have seen, taken his seat on his throne, but his demeanour there, into which it had been his intention to infuse much hierarchal dignity, had been a good deal disarranged by the audacity of his chaplain's sermon. He had hardly dared to look his clergy in the face, and to declare by the severity of his countenance that in truth he meant all that his factotum was saying on his behalf; nor yet did he dare to throw Mr. Slope over, and show to those around him that he was no party to the sermon, and would resent it.

He had accordingly blessed his people in a shambling manner, not at all to his own satisfaction, and had walked back to his palace with his mind very doubtful as to what he would say to his chaplain on the subject. He did not remain long in doubt. He had hardly doffed his lawn when the partner of all his toils entered his study and exclaimed even before she had seated herself:

"Bishop, did you ever hear a more sublime, more spirit-moving, more appropriate discourse than that?"

"Well, my love; ha—hum—he!" The bishop did not know what to say.

"I hope, my lord, you don't mean to say you disapprove?"

There was a look about the lady's eye which did not admit of my lord's disapproving at that moment. He felt that if he intended to disapprove, it must be now or never; but he also felt that it could not be now. It was not in him to say to the wife of his bosom that Mr. Slope's sermon was ill-timed, impertinent, and vexatious.

"No, no," replied the bishop. "No, I can't say I disapprove—a very clever sermon and very well intended, and I dare say will do a great deal of good." This last praise was added, seeing that what he had already said by no means satisfied Mrs. Proudie.

"I hope it will," said she. "And I am sure it was well deserved. Did you ever in your life, bishop, hear anything so like play-acting as the way in which Mr. Harding sings the litany? I shall beg Mr. Slope to continue a course of sermons on the subject till all that is altered. We will have at any rate, in our cathedral, a decent, godly, modest morning service. There must be no more play-acting here now;" and so the lady rang for lunch.

The bishop knew more about cathedrals and deans and precentors and church services than his wife did, and also more of a bishop's powers. But he thought it better at present to let the subject drop.

"My dear," said he, "I think we must go back to London on Tuesday. I find my staying here will be very inconvenient to the Government."

The bishop knew that to this proposal his wife would not object, and he also felt that by thus retreating from the ground of battle the heat of the fight might be got over in his absence.

"Mr. Slope will remain here, of course?" said the lady.

"Oh, of course," said the bishop.

Thus, after less than a week's sojourn in his palace, did the bishop fly from Barchester; nor did he return to it for two months, the London season being then over. During that time Mr. Slope was not idle, but he did not again essay to preach in the cathedral. In answer to Mrs. Proudie's letters advising a course of sermons, he had pleaded that he would at any rate wish to put off such an undertaking till she was there to hear them.

He had employed his time in consolidating a Proudie and Slope party—or rather a Slope and Proudie party, and he had not employed his time in vain. He did not meddle with the dean and chapter, except by giving them little teasing intimations of the bishop's wishes about this and the bishop's feelings about that, in a manner which was to them sufficiently annoying, but which they could not resent. He preached once or twice in a distant church in the suburbs of the city, but made no allusion to the cathedral service. He commenced the establishment of two "Bishop's Barchester Sabbath-day schools," gave notice of a proposed "Bishop's Barchester Young Men's Sabbath Evening Lecture Room," and wrote three or four letters to the manager of the Barchester branch railway, informing him how anxious the bishop was that the Sunday trains should be discontinued.

At the end of two months, however, the bishop and the lady reappeared, and as a happy harbinger of their return, heralded their advent by the promise of an evening party on the largest scale. The tickets of invitation were sent out from London—they were dated from Bruton Street, and were dispatched by the odious Sabbath-breaking railway, in a huge brown paper parcel to Mr. Slope. Everybody calling himself a gentleman, or herself a lady, within the city of Barchester, and a circle of two miles round it, was included. Tickets were sent to all the diocesan clergy, and also to many other persons of priestly note, of whose absence the bishop, or at least the bishop's wife, felt tolerably confident. It was intended, however, to be a thronged and noticeable affair, and preparations were made for receiving some hundreds.

And now there arose considerable agitation among the Grantlyites whether or no they would attend the episcopal bidding. The first feeling with them all was to send the briefest excuses both for themselves and their wives and daughters. But by degrees policy prevailed over passion. The archdeacon perceived that he would be making a false step if he allowed the cathedral clergy to give the bishop just ground of umbrage. They all met in conclave and agreed to go. They would show that they were willing to respect the office, much as they might dislike the man. They agreed to go. The old dean would crawl in, if it were but for half an hour. The chancellor, treasurer, archdeacon, prebendaries, and minor canons would all go, and would all take their wives. Mr. Harding was especially bidden to do so, resolving in his heart to keep himself far removed from Mrs. Proudie. And Mrs. Bold was determined to go, though assured by her father that there was no necessity for such a sacrifice on her part. When all Barchester was to be there, neither Eleanor nor Mary Bold understood why they should stay away. Had they not been invited separately? And had not a separate little note from the chaplain, couched in the most respectful language, been enclosed with the huge episcopal card?

And the Stanhopes would be there, one and all. Even the lethargic mother would so far bestir herself on such an occasion. They had only just arrived. The card was at the residence waiting for them. No one in Barchester had seen them. What better opportunity could they have of showing themselves to the Barchester world? Some few old friends, such as the archdeacon and his wife, had called and had found the doctor and his eldest daughter, but the *élite* of the family were not yet known.

The doctor indeed wished in his heart to prevent the signora from accepting the bishop's invitation, but she herself had fully determined that she would accept it. If her father was ashamed of having his daughter carried into a bishop's palace, she had no such feeling.

"Indeed, I shall," she had said to her sister who had gently endeavoured to dissuade her, by saying that the company would consist wholly of parsons and parsons' wives. "Parsons, I suppose, are much the same as other men, if you strip them of their black coats; and as to their wives, I dare say they won't trouble me. You may tell Papa I don't at all mean to be left at home."

Papa was told, and felt that he could do nothing but yield. He also felt that it was useless for him now to be ashamed of his children. Such as they were, they had become such under his auspices; as he had made his bed, so he must lie upon it; as he had sown his seed, so must he reap his corn. He did not indeed utter such reflexions in such language, but such was the gist of his thought. It was not because Madeline was a cripple that he shrank from seeing her made one of the bishop's guests, but because he knew that she would practise her accustomed lures, and behave herself in a way that could not fail of being distasteful to the propriety of Englishwomen. These things had annoyed but not shocked him in Italy. There they had shocked no one; but here in Barchester, here among his fellow parsons, he was ashamed that they should be seen. Such had been his feelings, but he repressed them. What if his brother clergymen were shocked! They could not take from him his preferment because the manners of his married daughter were too free.

La Signora Neroni had, at any rate, no fear that she would shock anybody. Her ambition was to create a sensation, to have parsons at her feet, seeing that the manhood of Barchester consisted mainly of parsons, and to send, if possible, every parson's wife home with a green fit of jealousy. None could be too old for her, and hardly any too young. None too sanctified, and none too worldly. She was quite prepared to entrap the bishop himself, and then to turn up her nose at the bishop's wife. She did not doubt of success, for she had always succeeded; but one thing was absolutely necessary; she must secure the entire use of a sofa.

The card sent to Dr. and Mrs. Stanhope and family had been so sent in an envelope having on the cover Mr. Slope's name. The signora soon learnt that Mrs. Proudie was not yet at the palace and that the chaplain was managing everything. It was much more in her line to apply to him than to the lady, and she accordingly wrote him the prettiest little billet in the world. In five lines she explained everything, declared how impossible it was for her not to be desirous to make the acquaintance of such persons as the Bishop of Barchester and his wife, and she might add also of Mr. Slope, depicted her own grievous state, and concluded by being assured that Mrs. Proudie would forgive her extreme hardihood in petitioning to be allowed to be carried to a sofa. She then enclosed one of her beautiful cards. In return she received as polite an answer from Mr. Slope—a sofa should be kept in the large drawing-room, immediately at the top of the grand stairs, especially for her use.

And now the day of the party had arrived. The bishop and his wife came down from town only on the morning of the eventful day, as behoved such great people to do, but Mr. Slope had toiled day and night to see that everything should be in right order. There had been much to do. No company had been seen in the palace since heaven knows when. New furniture had been required, new pots and pans, new cups and saucers, new dishes and plates. Mrs. Proudie had at first declared that she would condescend to nothing so vulgar as eating and drinking, but Mr. Slope had talked, or rather written her out of economy. Bishops should be given to hospitality, and hospitality meant eating and drinking. So the supper was conceded; the guests, however, were to stand as they consumed it.

There were four rooms opening into each other on the first floor of the house, which were denominated the drawing-rooms, the reception-room, and Mrs. Proudie's boudoir. In olden days one of these had been Bishop Grantly's bedroom, and another his common sitting-room and study. The present bishop, however, had been moved down into a back parlour and had been given to understand that he could very well receive his clergy in the dining-room, should they arrive in too large a flock to be admitted into his small sanctum. He had been unwilling to yield, but after a short debate had yielded.

Mrs. Proudie's heart beat high as she inspected her suite of rooms. They were really very magnificent, or at least would be so by candlelight, and they had nevertheless been got up with commendable economy. Large rooms when full of people and full of light look well, because they are large, and are full, and are light. Small rooms are those which require costly fittings and rich furniture. Mrs. Proudie knew this, and made the most of it; she had therefore a huge gas lamp with a dozen burners hanging from each of the ceilings.

People were to arrive at ten, supper was to last from twelve till one, and at half-past one everybody was to be gone. Carriages were to come in at the gate in the town and depart at the gate outside. They were desired to take up at a quarter before one. It was managed excellently, and Mr. Slope was invaluable.

At half-past nine the bishop and his wife and their three daughters entered the great reception-room, and very grand and very solemn they were. Mr. Slope was downstairs giving the last orders about the wine. He well understood that curates and country vicars with their belongings did not require so generous an article as the dignitaries of the close. There is a useful gradation in such things, and Marsala at 20s. a dozen did very well for the exterior supplementary tables in the corner.

"Bishop," said the lady, as his lordship sat himself down, "don't sit on that sofa, if you please; it is to be kept separate for a lady."

The bishop jumped up and seated himself on a cane-bottomed chair. "A lady?" he inquired meekly; "do you mean one particular lady, my dear?"

"Yes, Bishop, one particular lady," said his wife, disdaining to explain.

"She has got no legs, Papa," said the youngest daughter, tittering.

"No legs!" said the bishop, opening his eyes.

"Nonsense, Netta, what stuff you talk," said Olivia. "She has got legs, but she can't use them. She has always to be kept lying down, and three or four men carry her about everywhere."

"Laws, how odd!" said Augusta. "Always carried about by four men! I'm sure I shouldn't like it. Am I right behind, Mamma? I feel as if I was open;" and she turned her back to her anxious parent.

"Open! To be sure you are," said she, "and a yard of petticoat strings hanging out. I don't know why I pay such high wages to Mrs. Richards if she can't take the trouble to see whether or no you are fit to be looked at," and Mrs. Proudie poked the strings here, and twitched the dress there, and gave her daughter a shove and a shake, and then pronounced it all right.

"But," rejoined the bishop, who was dying with curiosity about the mysterious lady and her legs, "who is it that is to have the sofa? What's her name, Netta?"

A thundering rap at the front door interrupted the conversation. Mrs. Proudie stood up and shook herself gently, and touched her cap on each side as she looked in the mirror. Each of the girls stood on tiptoe and rearranged the bows on their bosoms, and Mr. Slope rushed upstairs three steps at a time.

"But who is it, Netta?" whispered the bishop to his youngest daughter.

"La Signora Madeline Vesey Neroni," whispered back the daughter; "and mind you don't let anyone sit upon the sofa."

"La Signora Madeline Vicinironi!" muttered to himself the bewildered prelate. Had he been told that the Begum of Oude was to be there, or Queen Pomara of the Western Isles, he could not have been more astonished. La Signora Madeline Vicinironi, who, having no legs to stand on, had bespoken a sofa in his drawing-room! Who could she be? He however could now make no further inquiry, as Dr. and Mrs. Stanhope were announced. They had been sent on out of the way a little before the time, in order that the signora might have plenty of time to get herself conveniently packed into the carriage.

The bishop was all smiles for the prebendary's wife, and the bishop's wife was all smiles for the prebendary. Mr. Slope was presented and was delighted to make the acquaintance of one of whom he had heard so much. The doctor bowed very low, and then looked as though he could not return the compliment as regarded Mr. Slope, of whom, indeed, he had heard nothing. The doctor, in spite of his long absence, knew an English gentleman when he saw him.

And then the guests came in shoals: Mr. and Mrs. Quiverful and their three grown daughters. Mr. and Mrs. Chadwick and their three daughters. The burly chancellor and his wife and clerical son from Oxford. The meagre little doctor without incumbrance. Mr. Harding with Eleanor and Miss Bold. The dean leaning on a gaunt spinster, his only child now living with him, a lady very learned in stones, ferns, plants, and vermin, and who had written a book about petals. A wonderful woman in her way was Miss Trefoil. Mr. Finnie, the attorney, with his wife, was to be seen, much to the dismay of many who had never met him in a drawing-room before. The five Barchester doctors were all there, and old Scalpen, the retired apothecary and tooth-drawer, who was first taught to consider himself as belonging to the higher orders by the receipt of the bishop's card. Then came the archdeacon and his wife with their elder daughter Griselda, a slim, pale, retiring girl of seventeen who kept close to her mother, and looked out on the world with quiet watchful eyes, one who gave promise of much beauty when time should have ripened it.

And so the rooms became full, and knots were formed, and every newcomer paid his respects to my lord and passed on, not presuming to occupy too much of the great man's attention. The archdeacon shook hands very heartily with Dr. Stanhope, and Mrs. Grantly seated herself by the doctor's wife. And Mrs. Proudie moved about with well-regulated grace, measuring out the quantity of her favours to the quality of her guests, just as Mr. Slope had been doing with the wine. But the sofa was still empty, and five-and-twenty ladies and five gentlemen had been courteously warned off it by the mindful chaplain.

"Why doesn't she come?" said the bishop to himself. His mind was so preoccupied with the signora that he hardly remembered how to behave himself *en bishop*.

At last a carriage dashed up to the hall steps with a very different manner of approach from that of any other vehicle that had been there that evening. A perfect commotion took place. The doctor, who heard it as he was standing in the drawing-room, knew that his daughter was coming, and retired into the furthest corner, where he might not see her entrance. Mrs. Proudie perked herself up, feeling that some important piece of business was in hand. The bishop was instinctively aware that La Signora Vicinironi was come at last, and Mr. Slope hurried into the hall to give his assistance.

He was, however, nearly knocked down and trampled on by the cortège that he encountered on the hall steps. He got himself picked up, as well as he could, and followed the cortège upstairs. The signora was carried head foremost, her head being the care of her brother and an Italian manservant who was accustomed to the work; her feet were in the care of the lady's maid and the lady's Italian page; and Charlotte Stanhope followed to see that all was done with due grace and decorum. In this manner they climbed easily into the drawing-room, and a broad way through the crowd having been opened, the signora rested safely on her couch. She had sent a servant beforehand to learn whether it was a right- or a left-hand sofa, for it required that she should dress accordingly, particularly as regarded her bracelets.

And very becoming her dress was. It was white velvet, without any other garniture than rich white lace worked with pearls across her bosom, and the same round the armlets of her dress. Across her brow she wore a band of red velvet, on the centre of which shone a magnificent Cupid in mosaic, the tints of whose wings were of the most lovely azure, and the colour of his chubby cheeks the clearest pink. On the one arm which her position required her to expose she wore three magnificent bracelets, each of different stones. Beneath her on the sofa, and over the cushion and head of it, was spread a crimson silk mantle or shawl, which went under her whole body and concealed her feet. Dressed as she was and looking as she did, so beautiful and yet so motionless, with the pure brilliancy of her white dress brought out and strengthened by the colour beneath it, with that lovely head, and those large, bold, bright, staring eyes, it was impossible that either man or woman should do other than look at her.

Neither man nor woman for some minutes did do other.

Her bearers too were worthy of note. The three servants were Italian, and though perhaps not peculiar in their own country, were very much so in the palace at Barchester. The man especially attracted notice and created a doubt in the mind of some whether he were a friend or a domestic. The same doubt was felt as to Ethelbert. The man was attired in a loose-fitting, common, black-cloth morning-coat. He had a jaunty, fat, well-pleased, clean face on which no atom of beard appeared, and he wore round his neck a loose, black silk neck-handkerchief. The bishop essayed to make him a bow, but the man, who was well trained, took no notice of him and walked out of the room quite at his ease, followed by the woman and the boy.

Ethelbert Stanhope was dressed in light blue from head to foot. He had on the loosest possible blue coat, cut square like a shooting coat, and very short. It was lined with silk of azure blue. He had on a blue satin waistcoat, a blue neck-handkerchief which was fastened beneath his throat with a coral ring, and very loose blue trousers which almost concealed his feet. His soft, glossy beard was softer and more glossy than ever.

The bishop, who had made one mistake, thought that he also was a servant and therefore tried to make way for him to pass. But Ethelbert soon corrected the error.

CHAPTER XI

MRS. PROUDIE'S RECEPTION—CONCLUDED

"Bishop of Barchester, I presume?" said Bertie Stanhope, putting out his hand frankly; "I am delighted to make your acquaintance. We are in rather close quarters here, a'nt we?"

In truth they were. They had been crowded up behind the head of the sofa—the bishop in waiting to receive his guest, and the other in carrying her—and they now had hardly room to move themselves.

The bishop gave his hand quickly, made his little studied bow, and was delighted to make—He couldn't go on, for he did not know whether his friend was a signor, or a count or a prince.

"My sister really puts you all to great trouble," said Bertie.

"Not at all!" The bishop was delighted to have the opportunity of welcoming La Signora Vicinironi—so at least he said—and attempted to force his way round to the front of the sofa. He had, at any rate, learnt that his strange guests were brother and sister. The man, he presumed, must be Signor Vicinironi—or count, or prince, as it might be. It was wonderful what good English he spoke. There was just a twang of foreign accent, and no more.

"Do you like Barchester, on the whole?" asked Bertie.

The bishop, looking dignified, said that he did like Barchester.

"You've not been here very long, I believe," said Bertie.

"No—not long," said the bishop and tried again to make his way between the back of the sofa and a heavy rector, who was staring over it at the grimaces of the signora.

"You weren't a bishop before, were you?"

Dr. Proudie explained that this was the first diocese he had held.

"Ah—I thought so," said Bertie, "but you are changed about sometimes, a'nt you?"

"Translations are occasionally made," said Dr. Proudie, "but not so frequently as in former days."

"They've cut them all down to pretty nearly the same figure, haven't they?" said Bertie.

To this the bishop could not bring himself to make any answer, but again attempted to move the rector.

"But the work, I suppose, is different?" continued Bertie. "Is there much to do here, at Barchester?" This was said exactly in the tone that a young Admiralty clerk might use in asking the same question of a brother acolyte at the Treasury.

"The work of a bishop of the Church of England," said Dr. Proudie with considerable dignity, "is not easy. The responsibility which he has to bear is very great indeed."

"Is it?" said Bertie, opening wide his wonderful blue eyes. "Well, I never was afraid of responsibility. I once had thoughts of being a bishop, myself."

"Had thoughts of being a bishop!" said Dr. Proudie, much amazed.

"That is, a parson—a parson first, you know, and a bishop afterwards. If I had once begun, I'd have stuck to it. But, on the whole, I like the Church of Rome the best."

The bishop could not discuss the point, so he remained silent.

"Now, there's my father," continued Bertie; "he hasn't stuck to it. I fancy he didn't like saying the same thing over so often. By the by, Bishop, have you seen my father?"

The bishop was more amazed than ever. Had he seen his father? "No," he replied; he had not yet had the pleasure: he hoped he might; and, as he said so, he resolved to bear heavy on that fat, immovable rector, if ever he had the power of doing so.

"He's in the room somewhere," said Bertie, "and he'll turn up soon. By the by, do you know much about the Jews?"

At last the bishop saw a way out. "I beg your pardon," said he, "but I'm forced to go round the room."

"Well—I believe I'll follow in your wake," said Bertie. "Terribly hot—isn't it?" This he addressed to the fat rector with whom he had brought himself into the closest contact. "They've got this sofa into the worst possible part of the room; suppose we move it. Take care, Madeline."

The sofa had certainly been so placed that those who were behind it found great difficulty in getting out; there was but a narrow gangway, which one person could stop. This was a bad arrangement, and one which Bertie thought it might be well to improve.

"Take care, Madeline," said he, and turning to the fat rector, added, "Just help me with a slight push."

The rector's weight was resting on the sofa and unwittingly lent all its impetus to accelerate and increase the motion which Bertie intentionally originated. The sofa rushed from its moorings and ran half-way into the middle of the room. Mrs. Proudie was standing with Mr. Slope in front of the signora, and had been trying to be condescending and sociable; but she was not in the very best of tempers, for she found that, whenever she spoke to the lady, the lady replied by speaking to Mr. Slope. Mr. Slope was a favourite, no doubt, but Mrs. Proudie had no idea of being less thought of than the chaplain. She was beginning to be stately, stiff, and offended, when unfortunately the castor of the sofa caught itself in her lace train, and carried away there is no saying how much of her garniture. Gathers were heard to go, stitches to crack, plaits to fly open, flounces were seen to fall, and breadths to expose themselves; a long ruin of rent lace disfigured the carpet, and still clung to the vile wheel on which the sofa moved.

So, when a granite battery is raised, excellent to the eyes of warfaring men, is its strength and symmetry admired. It is the work of years. Its neat embrasures, its finished parapets, its casemated stories show all the skill of modern science. But, anon, a small spark is applied to the treacherous fusee—a cloud of dust arises to the heavens—and then nothing is to be seen but dirt and dust and ugly fragments.

We know what was the wrath of Juno when her beauty was despised. We know to what storms of passion even celestial minds can yield. As Juno may have looked at Paris on Mount Ida, so did Mrs. Proudie look on Ethelbert Stanhope when he pushed the leg of the sofa into her lace train.

"Oh, you idiot, Bertie!" said the signora, seeing what had been done, and what were to be the consequences.

"Idiot!" re-echoed Mrs. Proudie, as though the word were not half strong enough to express the required meaning; "I'll let him know—" and then looking round to learn, at a glance, the worst, she saw that at present it behoved her to collect the scattered *débris* of her dress.

Bertie, when he saw what he had done, rushed over the sofa and threw himself on one knee before the offended lady. His object, doubtless, was to liberate the torn lace from the castor, but he looked as though he were imploring pardon from a goddess.

"Unhand it, sir!" said Mrs. Proudie. From what scrap of dramatic poetry she had extracted the word cannot be said, but it must have rested on her memory, and now seemed opportunely dignified for the occasion.

"I'll fly to the looms of the fairies to repair the damage, if you'll only forgive me," said Ethelbert, still on his knees.

"Unhand it, sir!" said Mrs. Proudie with redoubled emphasis, and all but furious wrath. This allusion to the fairies was a direct mockery and intended to turn her into ridicule. So at least it seemed to her. "Unhand it, sir!" she almost screamed.

"It's not me; it's the cursed sofa," said Bertie, looking imploringly in her face and holding up both his hands to show that he was not touching her belongings, but still remaining on his knees.

Hereupon the Signora laughed; not loud, indeed, but yet audibly. And as the tigress bereft of her young will turn with equal anger on any within reach, so did Mrs. Proudie turn upon her female guest.

"Madam!" she said—and it is beyond the power of prose to tell of the fire which flashed from her eyes.

The signora stared her full in the face for a moment, and then turning to her brother said playfully, "Bertie, you idiot, get up."

By this time the bishop, and Mr. Slope, and her three daughters were around her, and had collected together the wide ruins of her magnificence. The girls fell into circular rank behind their mother, and thus following her and carrying out the fragments, they left the reception-rooms in a manner not altogether devoid of dignity. Mrs. Proudie had to retire and re-array herself.

As soon as the constellation had swept by, Ethelbert rose from his knees and, turning with mock anger to the fat rector, said: "After all it was your doing, sir—not mine. But perhaps you are waiting for preferment, and so I bore it."

Whereupon there was a laugh against the fat rector, in which both the bishop and the chaplain joined, and thus things got themselves again into order.

"Oh! my lord, I am so sorry for this accident," said the signora, putting out her hand so as to force the bishop to take it. "My brother is so thoughtless. Pray sit down, and let me have the pleasure of making your acquaintance. Though I am so poor a creature as to want a sofa, I am not so selfish as to require it all." Madeline could always dispose herself so as to make room for a gentleman, though, as she declared, the crinoline of her lady friends was much too bulky to be so accommodated.

"It was solely for the pleasure of meeting you that I have had myself dragged here," she continued. "Of course, with your occupation, one cannot even hope that you should have time to come to us, that is, in the way of calling. And at your English dinner-parties all is so dull and so stately. Do you know, my lord, that in coming to England my only consolation has been the thought that I should know you;" and she looked at him with the look of a she-devil.

The bishop, however, thought that she looked very like an angel and, accepting the proffered seat, sat down beside her. He uttered some platitude as to his deep obligation for the trouble she had taken, and wondered more and more who she was.

"Of course you know my sad story?" she continued.

The bishop didn't know a word of it. He knew, however, or thought he knew, that she couldn't walk into a room like other people, and so made the most of that. He put on a look of ineffable distress and said that he was aware how God had afflicted her.

The signora just touched the corner of her eyes with the most lovely of pocket-handkerchiefs. Yes, she said—she had been sorely tried—tried, she thought, beyond the common endurance of humanity; but while her child was left to her, everything was left. "Oh! my lord," she exclaimed, "you must see that infant—the last bud of a wondrous tree: you must let a mother hope that you will lay your holy hands on her innocent head and consecrate her for female virtues. May I hope it?" said she, looking into the bishop's eye and touching the bishop's arm with her hand.

The bishop was but a man and said she might. After all, what was it but a request that he would confirm her daughter?—a request, indeed, very unnecessary to make, as he should do so as a matter of course if the young lady came forward in the usual way.

"The blood of Tiberius," said the signora in all but a whisper; "the blood of Tiberius flows in her veins. She is the last of the Neros!"

The bishop had heard of the last of the Visigoths, and had floating in his brain some indistinct idea of the last of the Mohicans, but to have the last of the Neros thus brought before him for a blessing was very staggering. Still he liked the lady: she had a proper way of thinking and talked with more propriety than her brother. But who were they? It was now quite clear that that blue madman with the silky beard was not a Prince Vicini-roni. The lady was married and was of course one of the Vicinironi's by right of the husband. So the bishop went on learning.

"When will you see her? said the signora with a start.

"See whom?" said the bishop.

"My child," said the mother.

"What is the young lady's age?" asked the bishop.

"She is just seven," said the signora.

"Oh," said the bishop, shaking his head; "she is much too young—very much too young."

"But in sunny Italy, you know, we do not count by years," and the signora gave the bishop one of her very sweetest smiles.

"But indeed, she is a great deal too young," persisted the bishop; "we never confirm before—"

"But you might speak to her; you might let her hear from your consecrated lips that she is not a castaway because she is a Roman; that she may be a Nero and yet a Christian; that she may owe her black locks and dark cheeks to the blood of the pagan Caesars, and yet herself be a child of grace; you will tell her this, won't you, my friend?"

The friend said he would, and asked if the child could say her catechism.

"No," said the signora, "I would not allow her to learn lessons such as those in a land ridden over by priests and polluted by the idolatry of Rome. It is here, here in Barchester, that she must first be taught to lisp those holy words. Oh, that you could be her instruc-tor!"

Now, Dr. Proudie certainly liked the lady, but, seeing that he was a bishop, it was not probable that he was going to instruct a little girl in the first rudiments of her catechism; so he said he'd send a teacher.

"But you'll see her yourself, my lord?"

The bishop said he would, but where should he call.

"At Papa's house," said the Signora with an air of some little surprise at the question.

The bishop actually wanted the courage to ask her who was her papa, so he was forced at last to leave her without fathoming the mystery. Mrs. Proudie, in her second best, had now returned to the rooms, and her husband thought it as well that he should not remain in too close conversation with the lady whom his wife appeared to hold in such slight esteem. Presently he came across his youngest daughter.

"Netta," said he, "do you know who is the father of that Signora Vicinironi?"

"It isn't Vicinironi, Papa," said Netta; "but Vesey Neroni, and she's Doctor Stanhope's daughter. But I must go and do the civil to Griselda Grantly; I declare nobody has spoken a word to the poor girl this evening."

Dr. Stanhope! Dr. Vesey Stanhope! Dr. Vesey Stanhope's daughter, of whose marriage with a dissolute Italian scamp he now remembered to have heard something! And that impertinent blue cub who had examined him as to his episcopal bearings was old Stanhope's son, and the lady who had entreated him to come and teach her child the catechism was old Stanhope's daughter! The daughter of one of his own prebendaries! As these things flashed across his mind, he was nearly as angry as his wife had been. Nevertheless, he could not but own that the mother of the last of the Neros was an agreeable woman.

Dr. Proudie tripped out into the adjoining room, in which were congregated a crowd of Grantlyite clergymen, among whom the archdeacon was standing pre-eminent, while the old dean was sitting nearly buried in a huge arm chair by the fire-place. The bishop was very anxious to be gracious, and, if possible, to diminish the bitterness which his chaplain had occasioned. Let Mr. Slope do the *fortiter in re*, he himself would pour in the *suaviter in modo*.

"Pray don't stir, Mr. Dean, pray don't stir," he said as the old man essayed to get up; "I take it as a great kindness, your coming to such an *omnium gatherum* as this. But we have hardly got settled yet, and Mrs. Proudie has not been able to see her friends as she would wish to do. Well, Mr. Archdeacon, after all, we have not been so hard upon you at Oxford."

"No," said the archdeacon, "you've only drawn our teeth and cut out our tongues; you've allowed us still to breathe and swallow."

"Ha, ha, ha!" laughed the bishop; "it's not quite so easy to cut out the tongue of an Oxford magnate—and as for teeth—ha, ha, ha! Why, in the way we've left the matter, it's very odd if the heads of colleges don't have their own way quite as fully as when the hebdomadal board was in all its glory; what do you say, Mr. Dean?"

"An old man, my lord, never likes changes," said the dean.

"You must have been sad bunglers if it is so," said the archdeacon; "and indeed, to tell the truth, I think you have bungled it. At any rate, you must own this; you have not done the half what you boasted you would do."

"Now, as regards your system of professors—" began the chancellor slowly. He was never destined to get beyond such beginning.

"Talking of professors," said a soft clear voice, close behind the chancellor's elbow; "how much you Englishmen might learn from Germany; only you are all too proud."

The bishop, looking round, perceived that that abominable young Stanhope had pursued him. The dean stared at him as though he were some unearthly apparition; so also did two or three prebendaries and minor canons. The archdeacon laughed.

"The German professors are men of learning," said Mr. Harding, "but—"

"German professors!" groaned out the chancellor, as though his nervous system had received a shock which nothing but a week of Oxford air could cure.

"Yes," continued Ethelbert, not at all understanding why a German professor should be contemptible in the eyes of an Oxford don. "Not but what the name is best earned at Oxford. In Germany the professors do teach; at Oxford, I believe, they only profess to do so, and sometimes not even that. You'll have those universities of yours about your ears soon, if you don't consent to take a lesson from Germany."

181

There was no answering this. Dignified clergymen of sixty years of age could not condescend to discuss such a matter with a young man with such clothes and such a beard.

"Have you got good water out at Plumstead, Mr. Archdeacon?" said the bishop by way of changing the conversation.

"Pretty good," said Dr. Grantly.

"But by no means so good as his wine, my lord," said a witty minor canon.

"Nor so generally used," said another; "that is, for inward application."

"Ha, ha, ha!" laughed the bishop, "a good cellar of wine is a very comfortable thing in a house."

"Your German professors, Sir, prefer beer, I believe," said the sarcastic little meagre prebendary.

"They don't think much of either," said Ethelbert, "and that perhaps accounts for their superiority. Now the Jewish professor—"

The insult was becoming too deep for the spirit of Oxford to endure, so the archdeacon walked off one way and the chancellor another, followed by their disciples, and the bishop and the young reformer were left together on the hearth-rug.

"I was a Jew once myself," began Bertie.

The bishop was determined not to stand another examination, or be led on any terms into Palestine, so he again remembered that he had to do something very particular, and left young Stanhope with the dean. The dean did not get the worst of it for Ethelbert gave him a true account of his remarkable doings in the Holy Land.

"Oh, Mr. Harding," said the bishop, overtaking the *ci-devant* warden; "I wanted to say one word about the hospital. You know, of course, that it is to be filled up."

Mr. Harding's heart beat a little, and he said that he had heard so.

"Of course," continued the bishop; "there can be only one man whom I could wish to see in that situation. I don't know what your own views may be, Mr. Harding—"

"They are very simply told, my lord," said the other; "to take the place if it be offered me, and to put up with the want of it should another man get it."

The bishop professed himself delighted to hear it; Mr. Harding might be quite sure that no other man would get it. There were some few circumstances which would in a slight degree change the nature of the duties. Mr. Harding was probably aware of this, and would, perhaps, not object to discuss the matter with Mr. Slope. It was a subject to which Mr. Slope had given a good deal of attention.

Mr. Harding felt, he knew not why, oppressed and annoyed. What could Mr. Slope do to him? He knew that there were to be changes. The nature of them must be communicated to the warden through somebody, and through whom so naturally as the bishop's chaplain? 'Twas thus he tried to argue himself back to an easy mind, but in vain.

Mr. Slope in the meantime had taken the seat which the bishop had vacated on the signora's sofa, and remained with that lady till it was time to marshal the folk to supper. Not with contented eyes had Mrs. Proudie seen this. Had not this woman laughed at her distress, and had not Mr. Slope heard it? Was she not an intriguing Italian woman, half wife and half not, full of affectation, airs, and impudence? Was she not horribly bedizened with velvet and pearls, with velvet and pearls, too, which had not been torn off her back? Above all, did she not pretend to be more beautiful than her neighbours? To say that Mrs. Proudie was jealous would give a wrong idea of her feelings. She had not the slightest desire that Mr. Slope should be in love with herself. But she desired the incense of Mr. Slope's spiritual and temporal services, and did not choose that they should be turned out of their course to such an object as Signora Neroni. She considered also that Mr. Slope ought in duty to hate the signora, and it appeared from his manner that he was very far from hating her.

"Come, Mr. Slope," she said, sweeping by and looking all that she felt, "can't you make yourself useful? Do pray take Mrs. Grantly down to supper."

Mrs. Grantly heard and escaped. The words were hardly out of Mrs. Proudie's mouth before the intended victim had stuck her hand through the arm of one of her husband's curates and saved herself. What would the archdeacon have said had he seen her walking downstairs with Mr. Slope?

Mr. Slope heard also, but was by no means so obedient as was expected. Indeed, the period of Mr. Slope's obedience to Mrs. Proudie was drawing to a close. He did not wish yet to break with her, nor to break with her at all, if it could be avoided. But he intended to be master in that palace, and as she had made the same resolution it was not improbable that they might come to blows.

Before leaving the signora he arranged a little table before her and begged to know what he should bring her. She was quite indifferent, she said—nothing—anything. It was now she felt the misery of her position, now that she must be left alone. Well, a little chicken, some ham, and a glass of champagne.

Mr. Slope had to explain, not without blushing for his patron, that there was no champagne.

Sherry would do just as well. And then Mr. Slope descended with the learned Miss Trefoil on his arm. Could she tell him, he asked, whether the ferns of Barsetshire were equal to those of Cumberland? His strongest worldly passion was for ferns—and before she could answer him he left her wedged between the door and the sideboard. It was fifty minutes before she escaped, and even then unfed.

"You are not leaving us, Mr. Slope," said the watchful lady of the house, seeing her slave escaping towards the door, with stores of provisions held high above the heads of the guests.

Mr. Slope explained that the Signora Neroni was in want of her supper.

"Pray, Mr. Slope, let her brother take it to her," said Mrs. Proudie, quite out loud. "It is out of the question that you should be so employed. Pray, Mr. Slope, oblige me; I am sure Mr. Stanhope will wait upon his sister."

Ethelbert was most agreeably occupied in the furthest corner of the room, making himself both useful and agreeable to Mrs. Proudie's youngest daughter.

"I couldn't get out, madam, if Madeline were starving for her supper," said he; "I'm physically fixed, unless I could fly."

The lady's anger was increased by seeing that her daughter also had gone over to the enemy, and when she saw, that in spite of her remonstrances, in the teeth of her positive orders, Mr. Slope went off to the drawing-room, the cup of her indignation ran over, and she could not restrain herself. "Such manners I never saw," she said, muttering. "I cannot and will not permit it;" and then, after fussing and fuming for a few minutes, she pushed her way through the crowd and followed Mr. Slope.

When she reached the room above, she found it absolutely deserted, except by the guilty pair. The signora was sitting very comfortably up to her supper, and Mr. Slope was leaning over her and administering to her wants. They had been discussing the merits of Sabbath-day schools, and the lady had suggested that as she could not possibly go to the children, she might be indulged in the wish of her heart by having the children brought to her.

"And when shall it be, Mr. Slope?" said she.

Mr. Slope was saved the necessity of committing himself to a promise by the entry of Mrs. Proudie. She swept close up to the sofa so as to confront the guilty pair, stared full at them for a moment, and then said, as she passed on to the next room, "Mr. Slope, his lordship is especially desirous of your attendance below; you will greatly oblige me if you will join him." And so she stalked on.

Mr. Slope muttered something in reply, and prepared to go downstairs. As for the bishop's wanting him, he knew his lady patroness well enough to take that assertion at what it was worth; but he did not wish to make himself the hero of a scene, or to become conspicuous for more gallantry than the occasion required.

"Is she always like this?" said the signora.

"Yes—always—madam," said Mrs. Proudie, returning; "always the same—always equally adverse to impropriety of conduct of every description;" and she stalked back through the room again, following Mr. Slope out of the door.

The signora couldn't follow her, or she certainly would have done so. But she laughed loud, and sent the sound of it ringing through the lobby and down the stairs after Mrs. Proudie's feet. Had she been as active as Grimaldi, she could probably have taken no better revenge.

"Mr. Slope," said Mrs. Proudie, catching the delinquent at the door, "I am surprised you should leave my company to attend on such a painted Jezebel as that."

"But she's lame, Mrs. Proudie, and cannot move. Somebody must have waited upon her."

"Lame," said Mrs. Proudie; "I'd lame her if she belonged to me. What business had she here at all?—such impertinence—such affectation."

In the hall and adjacent rooms all manner of cloaking and shawling was going on, and the Barchester folk were getting themselves gone. Mrs. Proudie did her best to smirk at each and every one as they made their adieus, but she was hardly successful. Her temper had been tried fearfully. By slow degrees the guests went.

"Send back the carriage quick," said Ethelbert, as Dr. and Mrs. Stanhope took their departure.

The younger Stanhopes were left to the very last, and an uncomfortable party they made with the bishop's family. They all went into the dining-room, and then the bishop observing that "the lady" was alone in the drawing-room, they followed him up. Mrs. Proudie kept Mr. Slope and her daughters in close conversation, resolving that he should not be indulged, nor they polluted. The bishop, in mortal dread of Bertie and the Jews, tried to converse with Charlotte Stanhope about the climate of Italy. Bertie and the signora had no resource but in each other.

"Did you get your supper at last, Madeline?" said the impudent or else mischievous young man.

"Oh, yes," said Madeline; "Mr. Slope was so very kind as to bring it me. I fear, however, he put himself to more inconvenience than I wished."

Mrs. Proudie looked at her but said nothing. The meaning of her look might have been thus translated; "If ever you find yourself within these walls again, I'll give you leave to be as impudent and affected and as mischievous as you please."

At last the carriage returned with the three Italian servants, and La Signora Madeline Vesey Neroni was carried out, as she had been carried in.

The lady of the palace retired to her chamber by no means contented with the result of her first grand party at Barchester.

CHAPTER XII

SLOPE VERSUS HARDING

Two or three days after the party, Mr. Harding received a note begging him to call on Mr. Slope, at the palace, at an early hour on the following morning. There was nothing uncivil in the communication, and yet the tone of it was thoroughly displeasing. It was as follows:

MY DEAR MR. HARDING, Will you favour me by calling on me at the palace to-morrow morning at 9:30 A.M. The bishop wishes me to speak to you touching the hospital. I hope you will excuse my naming so early an hour. I do so as my time is greatly occupied. If, however, it is positively inconvenient to you, I will change it to 10. You will, perhaps, be kind enough to let me have a note in reply.

> Believe me to be,
> My dear Mr. Harding,
> Your assured friend,
> OBH. SLOPE

The Palace, Monday morning,
20th August, 185—

Mr. Harding neither could nor would believe anything of the sort, and he thought, moreover, that Mr. Slope was rather impertinent to call himself by such a name. His assured friend, indeed! How many assured friends generally fall to the lot of a man in this world? And by what process are they made? And how much of such process had taken place as yet between Mr. Harding and Mr. Slope? Mr. Harding could not help asking himself these questions as he read and re-read the note before him. He answered it, however, as follows:

DEAR SIR, I will call at the palace to-morrow at 9:30 A.M. as you desire.

> Truly yours,
> S. HARDING

High Street, Barchester, Monday

And on the following morning, punctually at half-past nine, he knocked at the palace door and asked for Mr. Slope. The bishop had one small room allotted to him on the ground-floor, and Mr. Slope had another. Into this latter Mr. Harding was shown and asked to sit down. Mr. Slope was not yet there. The ex-warden stood up at the window looking into the garden, and could not help thinking how very short a time had passed since the whole of that house had been open to him, as though he had been a child of the family, born and bred in it. He remembered how the old servants used to smile as they opened the door to him; how the familiar butler would say, when he had been absent a few hours longer than usual, "A sight of you, Mr. Harding, is good for sore eyes;" how the fussy housekeeper would swear that he couldn't have dined, or couldn't have breakfasted, or couldn't have lunched. And then, above all, he remembered the pleasant gleam of inward satisfaction which always spread itself over the old bishop's face whenever his friend entered his room.

A tear came into each eye as he reflected that all this was gone. What use would the hospital be to him now? He was alone in the world, and getting old; he would soon, very soon have to go and leave it all, as his dear old friend had gone; go, and leave the hospital, and his accustomed place in the cathedral, and his haunts and pleasures, to younger and perhaps wiser men. That chanting of his! Perhaps, in truth, the time for it was gone by. He felt as though the world were sinking from his feet; as though this, this was the time for him to turn with confidence to those hopes which he had preached with confidence to others. "What," said he to himself, "can a man's religion be worth if it does not support him against the natural melancholy of declining years?" And as he looked out through his dimmed eyes into the bright parterres of the bishop's garden, he felt that he had the support which he wanted.

Nevertheless, he did not like to be thus kept waiting. If Mr. Slope did not really wish to see him at half-past nine o'clock, why force him to come away from his lodgings with his breakfast in his throat? To tell the truth, it was policy on the part of Mr. Slope. Mr. Slope had made up his mind that Mr. Harding should either accept the hospital with abject submission, or else refuse it altogether, and had calculated that he would probably be more quick to do the latter, if he could be got to enter upon the subject in an ill-humour. Perhaps Mr. Slope was not altogether wrong in his calculation.

It was nearly ten when Mr. Slope hurried into the room and, muttering something about the bishop and diocesan duties, shook Mr. Harding's hand ruthlessly and begged him to be seated.

Now the air of superiority which this man assumed did go against the grain with Mr. Harding, and yet he did not know how to resent it. The whole tendency of his mind and disposition was opposed to any contra-assumption of grandeur on his own part, and he hadn't the worldly spirit or quickness necessary to put down insolent pretensions by downright and open rebuke, as the archdeacon would have done. There was nothing for Mr. Harding but to submit, and he accordingly did so.

"About the hospital, Mr. Harding?" began Mr. Slope, speaking of it as the head of a college at Cambridge might speak of some sizarship which had to be disposed of.

Mr. Harding crossed one leg over another, and then one hand over the other on the top of them, and looked Mr. Slope in the face; but he said nothing.

"It's to be filled up again," said Mr. Slope. Mr. Harding said that he had understood so.

"Of course, you know, the income will be very much reduced," continued Mr. Slope. "The bishop wished to be liberal, and he therefore told the government that he thought it ought to be put at not less than £450. I think on the whole the bishop was right, for though the services required will not be of a very onerous nature, they will be more so than they were before. And it is, perhaps, well that the clergy immediately attached to the cathedral town should be made as comfortable as the extent of the ecclesiastical means at our disposal will allow. Those are the bishop's ideas, and I must say mine also."

Mr. Harding sat rubbing one hand on the other, but said not a word.

"So much for the income, Mr. Harding. The house will, of course, remain to the warden, as before. It should, however, I think, be stipulated that he should paint inside every seven years, and outside every three years, and be subject to dilapidations, in the event of vacating, either by death or otherwise. But this is a matter on which the bishop must yet be consulted."

Mr. Harding still rubbed his hands and still sat silent, gazing up into Mr. Slope's unprepossessing face.

"Then, as to the duties," continued he, "I believe, if I am rightly informed, there can hardly be said to have been any duties hitherto," and he gave a sort of half-laugh, as though to pass off the accusation in the guise of a pleasantry.

Mr. Harding thought of the happy, easy years he had passed in his old home; of the worn-out, aged men whom he had succoured; of his good intentions; and of his work, which had certainly been of the lightest. He thought of these things, doubting for a moment whether he did or did not deserve the sarcasm. He gave his enemy the benefit of the doubt, and did not rebuke him. He merely observed, very tranquilly, and perhaps with too much humility, that the duties of the situation, such as they were, had, he believed, been done to the satisfaction of the late bishop.

Mr. Slope again smiled, and this time the smile was intended to operate against the memory of the late bishop rather than against the energy of the ex-warden; so it was understood by Mr. Harding. The colour rose to his cheeks, and he began to feel very angry.

"You must be aware, Mr. Harding, that things are a good deal changed in Barchester," said Mr. Slope.

Mr. Harding said that he was aware of it. "And not only in Barchester, Mr. Harding, but in the world at large. It is not only in Barchester that a new man is carrying out new measures and casting away the useless rubbish of past centuries. The same thing is going on throughout the country. Work is now required from every man who receives wages, and they who have to superintend the doing of work, and the paying of wages, are bound to see that this rule is carried out. New men, Mr. Harding, are now needed and are now forthcoming in the church, as well as in other professions."

All this was wormwood to our old friend. He had never rated very high his own abilities or activity, but all the feelings of his heart were with the old clergy, and any antipathies of which his heart was susceptible were directed against those new, busy, uncharitable, self-lauding men, of whom Mr. Slope was so good an example.

"Perhaps," said he, "the bishop will prefer a new man at the hospital?"

"By no means," said Mr. Slope. "The bishop is very anxious that you should accept the appointment, but he wishes you should understand beforehand what will be the required duties. In the first place, a Sabbath-day school will be attached to the hospital."

"What! For the old men?" asked Mr. Harding.

"No, Mr. Harding, not for the old men, but for the benefit of the children of such of the poor of Barchester as it may suit. The bishop will expect that you shall attend this school, and that the teachers shall be under your inspection and care."

Mr. Harding slipped his topmost hand off the other and began to rub the calf of the leg which was supported.

"As to the old men," continued Mr. Slope, "and the old women who are to form a part of the hospital, the bishop is desirous that you shall have morning and evening service on the premises every Sabbath, and one weekday service; that you shall preach to them once at least on Sundays; and that the whole hospital be always collected for morning and evening prayer. The bishop thinks that this will render it unnecessary that any separate seats in the cathedral should be reserved for the hospital inmates."

Mr. Slope paused, but Mr. Harding still said nothing.

"Indeed, it would be difficult to find seats for the women; on the whole, Mr. Harding, I may as well say at once, that for people of that class the cathedral service does not appear to me the most useful—even if it be so for any class of people."

"We will not discuss that, if you please," said Mr. Harding.

"I am not desirous of doing so; at least, not at the present moment. I hope, however, you fully understand the bishop's wishes about the new establishment of the hospital; and if, as I do not doubt, I shall receive from you an assurance that you accord with his lordship's views, it will give me very great pleasure to be the bearer from his lordship to you of the presentation to the appointment."

"But if I disagree with his lordship's views?" asked Mr. Harding.

"But I hope you do not," said Mr. Slope.

"But if I do?" again asked the other.

"If such unfortunately should be the case, which I can hardly conceive, I presume your own feelings will dictate to you the propriety of declining the appointment."

"But if I accept the appointment and yet disagree with the bishop, what then?"

This question rather bothered Mr. Slope. It was true that he had talked the matter over with the bishop and had received a sort of authority for suggesting to Mr. Harding the propriety of a Sunday school and certain hospital services, but he had no authority for saying that these propositions were to be made peremptory conditions attached to the appointment. The bishop's idea had been that Mr. Harding would of course consent and that the school would become, like the rest of those new establishments in the city, under the control of his wife and his chaplain. Mr. Slope's idea had been more correct. He intended that Mr. Harding should refuse the situation, and that an ally of his own should get it, but he had not conceived the possibility of Mr. Harding openly accepting the appointment and as openly rejecting the conditions.

"It is not, I presume, probable," said he, "that you will accept from the hands of the bishop a piece of preferment with a fixed predetermination to disacknowledge the duties attached to it."

"If I become warden," said Mr. Harding, "and neglect my duty, the bishop has means by which he can remedy the grievance."

"I hardly expected such an argument from you, or I may say the suggestion of such a line of conduct," said Mr. Slope with a great look of injured virtue.

"Nor did I expect such a proposition."

"I shall be glad at any rate to know what answer I am to make to his lordship," said Mr. Slope.

"I will take an early opportunity of seeing his lordship myself," said Mr. Harding.

"Such an arrangement," said Mr. Slope, "will hardly give his lordship satisfaction. Indeed, it is impossible that the bishop should himself see every clergyman in the diocese on every subject of patronage that may arise. The bishop, I believe, did see you on the matter, and I really cannot see why he should be troubled to do so again."

"Do you know, Mr. Slope, how long I have been officiating as a clergyman in this city?" Mr. Slope's wish was now nearly fulfilled. Mr. Harding had become angry, and it was probable that he might commit himself.

"I really do not see what that has to do with the question. You cannot think the bishop would be justified in allowing you to regard as a sinecure a situation that requires an active man, merely because you have been employed for many years in the cathedral."

"But it might induce the bishop to see me, if I asked him to do so. I shall consult my friends in this matter, Mr. Slope; but I mean to be guilty of no subterfuge—you may tell the bishop that as I altogether disagree with his views about the hospital, I shall decline the situation if I find that any such conditions are attached to it as those you have suggested;" and so saying, Mr. Harding took his hat and went his way.

Mr. Slope was contented. He considered himself at liberty to accept Mr. Harding's last speech as an absolute refusal of the appointment. At least, he so represented it to the bishop and to Mrs. Proudie.

"That is very surprising," said the bishop.

"Not at all," said Mrs. Proudie; "you little know how determined the whole set of them are to withstand your authority."

"But Mr. Harding was so anxious for it," said the bishop.

"Yes," said Mr. Slope, "if he can hold it without the slightest acknowledgement of your lordship's jurisdiction."

"That is out of the question," said the bishop.

"I should imagine it to be quite so," said the chaplain.

"Indeed, I should think so," said the lady.

"I really am sorry for it," said the bishop.

"I don't know that there is much cause for sorrow," said the lady. "Mr. Quiverful is a much more deserving man, more in need of it, and one who will make himself much more useful in the close neighbourhood of the palace."

"I suppose I had better see Quiverful?" said the chaplain.

"I suppose you had," said the bishop.

CHAPTER XIII

THE RUBBISH CART

Mr. Harding was not a happy man as he walked down the palace pathway and stepped out into the close. His preferment and pleasant house were a second time gone from him, but that he could endure. He had been schooled and insulted by a man young enough to be his son, but that he could put up with. He could even draw from the very injuries which had been inflicted on him some of that consolation which we may believe martyrs always receive from the injustice of their own sufferings, and which is generally proportioned in its strength to the extent of cruelty with which martyrs are treated. He had admitted to his daughter that he wanted the comfort of his old home, and yet he could have returned to his lodgings in the High Street, if not with exaltation, at least with satisfaction, had that been all. But the venom of the chaplain's harangue had worked into his blood, and sapped the life of his sweet contentment.

"New men are carrying out new measures and are carting away the useless rubbish of past centuries!" What cruel words these had been; and how often are they now used with all the heartless cruelty of a Slope! A man is sufficiently condemned if it can only be shown that either in politics or religion he does not belong to some new school established within the last score of years. He may then regard himself as rubbish and expect to be carted away. A man is nothing now unless he has within him a full appreciation of the new era, an era in which it would seem that neither honesty nor truth is very desirable, but in which success is the only touchstone of merit. We must laugh at everything that is established. Let the joke be ever so bad, ever so untrue to the real principles of joking; nevertheless we must laugh—or else beware the cart. We must talk, think, and live up to the spirit of the times, and write up to it too, if that cacoethes be upon us, or else we are nought. New men and new measures, long credit and few scruples, great success or wonderful ruin, such are now the tastes of Englishmen who know how to live. Alas, alas! Under such circumstances Mr. Harding could not but feel that he was an Englishman who did not know how to live. This new doctrine of Mr. Slope and the rubbish cart, new at least at Barchester, sadly disturbed his equanimity.

"The same thing is going on throughout the whole country! Work is now required from every man who receives wages!" And had he been living all his life receiving wages and doing no work? Had he in truth so lived as to be now in his old age justly reckoned as rubbish fit only to be hidden away in some huge dust-hole? The school of men to whom he professes to belong, the Grantlys, the Gwynnes, and the old high set of Oxford divines, are afflicted with no such self-accusations as these which troubled Mr. Harding. They, as a rule, are as satisfied with the wisdom and propriety of their own conduct as can be any Mr. Slope, or any Dr. Proudie, with his own. But unfortunately for himself Mr. Harding had little of this self-reliance. When he heard himself designated as rubbish by the Slopes of the world, he had no other resource than to make inquiry within his own bosom as to the truth of the designation. Alas, alas! The evidence seemed generally to go against him.

He had professed to himself in the bishop's parlour that in these coming sources of the sorrow of age, in these fits of sad regret from which the latter years of few reflecting men can be free, religion would suffice to comfort him. Yes, religion could console him for the loss of any worldly good, but was his religion of that active sort which would enable him so to repent of misspent years as to pass those that were left to him in a spirit of hope for the future? And such repentance itself, is it not a work of agony and of tears? It is very easy to talk of repentance, but a man has to walk over hot ploughshares before he can complete it; to be skinned alive as was St. Bartholomew; to be stuck full of arrows as was St. Sebastian; to lie broiling on a gridiron like St. Lorenzo! How if his past life required such repentance as this? Had he the energy to go through with it?

Mr. Harding, after leaving the palace, walked slowly for an hour or so beneath the shady elms of the close and then betook himself to his daughter's house. He had at any rate made up his mind that he would go out to Plumstead to consult Dr. Grantly, and that he would in the first instance tell Eleanor what had occurred.

And now he was doomed to undergo another misery. Mr. Slope had forestalled him at the widow's house. He had called there on the preceding afternoon. He could not, he had said, deny himself the pleasure of telling Mrs. Bold that her father was about to return to the pretty house at Hiram's Hospital. He had been instructed by the bishop to inform Mr. Harding that the appointment would now be made at once. The bishop was of course only too happy to be able to be the means of restoring to Mr. Harding the preferment which he had so long adorned. And then by degrees Mr. Slope had introduced the subject of the pretty school which he hoped before long to see attached to the hospital. He had quite fascinated Mrs. Bold by his description of this picturesque, useful, and charitable append-age, and she had gone so far as to say that she had no doubt her father would approve, and that she herself would gladly undertake a class.

Anyone who had heard the entirely different tone and seen the entirely different man-ner in which Mr. Slope had spoken of this projected institution to the daughter and to the father could not have failed to own that Mr. Slope was a man of genius. He said nothing to Mrs. Bold about the hospital sermons and services, nothing about the exclusion of the old men from the cathedral, nothing about dilapidation and painting, nothing about carting away the rubbish. Eleanor had said to herself that certainly she did not like Mr. Slope per-sonally, but that he was a very active, zealous clergyman and would no doubt be useful in Barchester. All this paved the way for much additional misery to Mr. Harding.

Eleanor put on her happiest face as she heard her father on the stairs, for she thought she had only to congratulate him; but directly she saw his face she knew that there was but little matter for congratulation. She had seen him with the same weary look of sorrow on one or two occasions before, and remembered it well. She had seen him when he first read that attack upon himself in "The Jupiter" which had ultimately caused him to resign the hospital, and she had seen him also when the archdeacon had persuaded him to remain there against his own sense of propriety and honour. She knew at a glance that his spirit was in deep trouble.

"Oh, Papa, what is it?" said she, putting down her boy to crawl upon the floor.

"I came to tell you, my dear," said he, "that I am going out to Plumstead: you won't come with me, I suppose?"

"To Plumstead, Papa? Shall you stay there?"

"I suppose I shall, to-night: I must consult the archdeacon about this weary hospital. Ah me! I wish I had never thought of it again."

"Why, Papa, what is the matter?"

"I've been with Mr. Slope, my dear, and he isn't the pleasantest companion in the world, at least not to me." Eleanor gave a sort of half-blush, but she was wrong if she imagined that her father in any way alluded to her acquaintance with Mr. Slope.

"Well, Papa."

"He wants to turn the hospital into a Sunday-school and a preaching-house, and I suppose he will have his way. I do not feel myself adapted for such an establishment, and therefore, I suppose, I must refuse the appointment."

"What would be the harm of the school, Papa?"

"The want of a proper schoolmaster, my dear."

"But that would of course be supplied."

"Mr. Slope wishes to supply it by making me his schoolmaster. But as I am hardly fit for such work, I intend to decline."

"Oh, Papa! Mr. Slope doesn't intend that. He was here yesterday, and what he intends—"

"He was here yesterday, was he?" asked Mr. Harding.

"Yes, Papa."

"And talking about the hospital?"

"He was saying how glad he would be, and the bishop too, to see you back there again. And then he spoke about the Sunday-school; and to tell the truth I agreed with him; and I thought you would have done so too. Mr. Slope spoke of a school, not inside the hospital, but just connected with it, of which you would be the patron and visitor; and I thought you would have liked such a school as that; and I promised to look after it and to take a class—and it all seemed so very—. But, oh, Papa! I shall be so miserable if I find I have done wrong."

"Nothing wrong at all, my dear," said he gently, very gently rejecting his daughter's caress. "There can be nothing wrong in your wishing to make yourself useful; indeed, you ought to do so by all means. Everyone must now exert himself who would not choose to go to the wall." Poor Mr. Harding thus attempted in his misery to preach the new doctrine to his child. "Himself or herself, it's all the same," he continued; "you will be quite right, my dear, to do something of this sort; but—"

"Well, Papa."

"I am not quite sure that if I were you I would select Mr. Slope for my guide."

"But I never have done so and never shall."

"It would be very wicked of me to speak evil of him, for to tell the truth I know no evil of him; but I am not quite sure that he is honest. That he is not gentlemanlike in his manners, of that I am quite sure."

"I never thought of taking him for my guide, Papa."

"As for myself, my dear," continued he, "we know the old proverb—'It's bad teaching an old dog tricks.' I must decline the Sunday-school, and shall therefore probably decline the hospital also. But I will first see your brother-in-law." So he took up his hat, kissed the baby, and withdrew, leaving Eleanor in as low spirits as himself.

All this was a great aggravation to his misery. He had so few with whom to sympathize that he could not afford to be cut off from the one whose sympathy was of the most value to him. And yet it seemed probable that this would be the case. He did not own to himself that he wished his daughter to hate Mr. Slope, yet had she expressed such a feeling there would have been very little bitterness in the rebuke he would have given her for so uncharitable a state of mind. The fact, however, was that she was on friendly terms with Mr. Slope, that she coincided with his views, adhered at once to his plans, and listened with delight to his teaching. Mr. Harding hardly wished his daughter to hate the man, but he would have preferred that to her loving him.

He walked away to the inn to order a fly, went home to put up his carpet-bag, and then started for Plumstead. There was, at any rate, no danger that the archdeacon would fraternize with Mr. Slope; but then he would recommend internecine war, public appeals, loud reproaches, and all the paraphernalia of open battle. Now that alternative was hardly more to Mr. Harding's taste than the other.

When Mr. Harding reached the parsonage, he found that the archdeacon was out, and would not be home till dinnertime, so he began his complaint to his elder daughter. Mrs. Grantly entertained quite as strong an antagonism to Mr. Slope as did her husband; she was also quite as alive to the necessity of combating the Proudie faction, of supporting the old church interest of the close, of keeping in her own set such of the loaves and fishes as duly belonged to it; and was quite as well prepared as her lord to carry on the battle without giving or taking quarter. Not that she was a woman prone to quarrelling, or ill-inclined to live at peace with her clerical neighbours; but she felt, as did the archdeacon, that the presence of Mr. Slope in Barchester was an insult to everyone connected with the late bishop, and that his assumed dominion in the diocese was a spiritual injury to her husband. Hitherto people had little guessed how bitter Mrs. Grantly could be. She lived on the best of terms with all the rectors' wives around her. She had been popular with all the ladies connected with the close. Though much the wealthiest of the ecclesiastical matrons of the county, she had so managed her affairs that her carriage and horses had given umbrage to none. She had never thrown herself among the county grandees so as to excite the envy of other clergymen's wives. She never talked too loudly of earls and countesses, or boasted that she gave her governess sixty pounds a year, or her cook seventy. Mrs. Grantly had lived the life of a wise, discreet, peace-making woman, and the people of Barchester were surprised at the amount of military vigour she displayed as general of the feminine Grantlyite forces.

Mrs. Grantly soon learned that her sister Eleanor had promised to assist Mr. Slope in the affairs of the hospital school, and it was on this point that her attention first fixed itself.

"How can Eleanor endure him?" said she.

"He is a very crafty man," said her father, "and his craft has been successful in making Eleanor think that he is a meek, charitable, good clergyman. God forgive me, if I wrong him, but such is not his true character in my opinion."

"His true character, indeed!" said she, with something approaching scorn for her father's moderation. "I only hope he won't have craft enough to make Eleanor forget herself and her position."

"Do you mean marry him?" said he, startled out of his usual demeanour by the abruptness and horror of so dreadful a proposition.

"What is there so improbable in it? Of course that would be his own object if he thought he had any chance of success. Eleanor has a thousand a year entirely at her own disposal, and what better fortune could fall to Mr. Slope's lot than the transferring of the disposal of such a fortune to himself?"

"But you can't think she likes him, Susan?"

"Why not?" said Susan. "Why shouldn't she like him? He's just the sort of man to get on with a woman left, as she is, with no one to look after her."

"Look after her!" said the unhappy father; "don't we look after her?"

"Ah, Papa, how innocent you are! Of course it was to be expected that Eleanor should marry again. I should be the last to advise her against it, if she would only wait the proper time, and then marry at least a gentleman."

"But you don't really mean to say that you suppose Eleanor has ever thought of marrying Mr. Slope? Why, Mr. Bold has only been dead a year."

"Eighteen months," said his daughter. "But I don't suppose Eleanor has ever thought about it. It is very probable, though, that he has; and that he will try and make her do so; and that he will succeed too, if we don't take care what we are about."

This was quite a new phase of the affair to poor Mr. Harding. To have thrust upon him as his son-in-law, as the husband of his favourite child, the only man in the world whom he really positively disliked, would be a misfortune which he felt he would not know how to endure patiently. But then, could there be any ground for so dreadful a surmise? In all worldly matters he was apt to look upon the opinion of his eldest daughter as one generally sound and trustworthy. In her appreciation of character, of motives, and the probable conduct both of men and women, she was usually not far wrong. She had early foreseen the marriage of Eleanor and John Bold; she had at a glance deciphered the character of the new bishop and his chaplain; could it possibly be that her present surmise should ever come forth as true?

"But you don't think that she likes him?" said Mr. Harding again.

"Well, Papa, I can't say that I think she dislikes him as she ought to do. Why is he visiting there as a confidential friend, when he never ought to have been admitted inside the house? Why is it that she speaks to him about your welfare and your position, as she clearly has done? At the bishop's party the other night I saw her talking to him for half an hour at the stretch."

"I thought Mr. Slope seemed to talk to nobody there but that daughter of Stanhope's," said Mr. Harding, wishing to defend his child.

"Oh, Mr. Slope is a cleverer man than you think of, Papa, and keeps more than one iron in the fire."

To give Eleanor her due, any suspicion as to the slightest inclination on her part towards Mr. Slope was a wrong to her. She had no more idea of marrying Mr. Slope than she had of marrying the bishop, and the idea that Mr. Slope would present himself as a suitor had never occurred to her. Indeed, to give her her due again, she had never thought about suitors since her husband's death. But nevertheless it was true that she had overcome all that repugnance to the man which was so strongly felt for him by the rest of the Grantly faction. She had forgiven him his sermon. She had forgiven him his Low Church tendencies, his Sabbath-schools, and puritanical observances. She had forgiven his pharisaical arrogance, and even his greasy face and oily, vulgar manners. Having agreed to overlook such offences as these, why should she not in time be taught to regard Mr. Slope as a suitor?

And as to him, it must also be affirmed that he was hitherto equally innocent of the crime imputed to him. How it had come to pass that a man whose eyes were generally so widely open to everything around him had not perceived that this young widow was rich as well as beautiful, cannot probably now be explained. But such was the fact. Mr. Slope had ingratiated himself with Mrs. Bold, merely as he had done with other ladies, in order to strengthen his party in the city. He subsequently amended his error, but it was not till after the interview between him and Mr. Harding.

CHAPTER XIV

THE NEW CHAMPION

The archdeacon did not return to the parsonage till close upon the hour of dinner, and there was therefore no time to discuss matters before that important ceremony. He seemed to be in an especial good humour, and welcomed his father-in-law with a sort of jovial earnestness that was usual with him when things on which he was intent were going on as he would have them.

"It's all settled, my dear," said he to his wife as he washed his hands in his dressing-room, while she, according to her wont, sat listening in the bedroom; "Arabin has agreed to accept the living. He'll be here next week." And the archdeacon scrubbed his hands and rubbed his face with a violent alacrity, which showed that Arabin's coming was a great point gained.

"Will he come here to Plumstead?" said the wife.

"He has promised to stay a month with us," said the archdeacon, "so that he may see what his parish is like. You'll like Arabin very much. He's a gentleman in every respect, and full of humour."

"He's very queer, isn't he?" asked the lady.

"Well—he is a little odd in some of his fancies, but there's nothing about him you won't like. He is as staunch a churchman as there is at Oxford. I really don't know what we should do without Arabin. It's a great thing for me to have him so near me, and if anything can put Slope down, Arabin will do it."

The Reverend Francis Arabin was a fellow of Lazarus, the favoured disciple of the great Dr. Gwynne, a High Churchman at all points—so high, indeed, that at one period of his career he had all but toppled over into the cesspool of Rome—a poet and also a polemical writer, a great pet in the common-rooms at Oxford, an eloquent clergyman, a droll, odd, humorous, energetic, conscientious man, and, as the archdeacon had boasted of him, a thorough gentleman. As he will hereafter be brought more closely to our notice, it is now only necessary to add that he had just been presented to the vicarage of St. Ewold by Dr. Grantly, in whose gift as archdeacon the living lay. St. Ewold is a parish lying just without the city of Barchester. The suburbs of the new town, indeed, are partly within its precincts, and the pretty church and parsonage are not much above a mile distant from the city gate.

St. Ewold is not a rich piece of preferment—it is worth some three or four hundred a year at most, and has generally been held by a clergyman attached to the cathedral choir. The archdeacon, however, felt, when the living on this occasion became vacant, that it imperatively behoved him to aid the force of his party with some tower of strength, if any such tower could be got to occupy St. Ewold's. He had discussed the matter with his brethren in Barchester, not in any weak spirit as the holder of patronage to be used for his own or his family's benefit, but as one to whom was committed a trust on the due administration of which much of the church's welfare might depend. He had submitted to them the name of Mr. Arabin, as though the choice had rested with them all in conclave, and they had unanimously admitted that, if Mr. Arabin would accept St. Ewold's, no better choice could possibly be made.

If Mr. Arabin would accept St. Ewold's! There lay the difficulty. Mr. Arabin was a man standing somewhat prominently before the world, that is, before the Church of England world. He was not a rich man, it is true, for he held no preferment but his fellowship; but he was a man not over-anxious for riches, not married of course, and one whose time was greatly taken up in discussing, both in print and on platforms, the privileges and practices of the church to which he belonged. As the archdeacon had done battle for its temporalities, so did Mr. Arabin do battle for its spiritualities, and both had done so conscientiously; that is, not so much each for his own benefit as for that of others.

Holding such a position as Mr. Arabin did, there was much reason to doubt whether he would consent to become the parson of St. Ewold's, and Dr. Grantly had taken the trouble to go himself to Oxford on the matter. Dr. Gwynne and Dr. Grantly together had succeeded in persuading this eminent divine that duty required him to go to Barchester. There were wheels within wheels in this affair. For some time past Mr. Arabin had been engaged in a tremendous controversy with no less a person than Mr. Slope, respecting the apostolic succession. These two gentlemen had never seen each other, but they had been extremely bitter in print. Mr. Slope had endeavoured to strengthen his cause by calling Mr. Arabin an owl, and Mr. Arabin had retaliated by hinting that Mr. Slope was an infidel. This battle had been commenced in the columns of "The Jupiter," a powerful newspaper, the manager of which was very friendly to Mr. Slope's view of the case. The matter, however, had become too tedious for the readers of "The Jupiter," and a little note had therefore been appended to one of Mr. Slope's most telling rejoinders, in which it had been stated that no further letters from the reverend gentlemen could be inserted except as advertisements.

Other methods of publication were, however, found, less expensive than advertisements in "The Jupiter," and the war went on merrily. Mr. Slope declared that the main part of the consecration of a clergyman was the self-devotion of the inner man to the duties of the ministry. Mr. Arabin contended that a man was not consecrated at all, had, indeed, no single attribute of a clergyman, unless he became so through the imposition of some bishop's hands, who had become a bishop through the imposition of other hands, and so on in a direct line to one of the apostles. Each had repeatedly hung the other on the horns of a dilemma, but neither seemed to be a whit the worse for the hanging; and so the war went on merrily.

Whether or no the near neighbourhood of the foe may have acted in any way as an inducement to Mr. Arabin to accept the living of St. Ewold, we will not pretend to say; but it had at any rate been settled in Dr. Gwynne's library, at Lazarus, that he would accept it, and that he would lend his assistance towards driving the enemy out of Barchester, or, at any rate, silencing him while he remained there. Mr. Arabin intended to keep his rooms at Oxford and to have the assistance of a curate at St. Ewold, but he promised to give as much time as possible to the neighbourhood of Barchester, and from so great a man Dr. Grantly was quite satisfied with such a promise. It was no small part of the satisfaction derivable from such an arrangement that Bishop Proudie would be forced to institute into a living immediately under his own nose the enemy of his favourite chaplain.

All through dinner the archdeacon's good humour shone brightly in his face. He ate of the good things heartily, he drank wine with his wife and daughter, he talked pleasantly of his doings at Oxford, told his father-in-law that he ought to visit Dr. Gwynne at Lazarus, and launched out again in praise of Mr. Arabin.

"Is Mr. Arabin married, Papa?" asked Griselda.

"No, my dear, the fellow of a college is never married."

"Is he a young man, Papa?"

"About forty, I believe," said the archdeacon.

"Oh!" said Griselda. Had her father said eighty, Mr. Arabin would not have appeared to her to be very much older.

When the two gentlemen were left alone over their wine, Mr. Harding told his tale of woe. But even this, sad as it was, did not much diminish the archdeacon's good humour, though it greatly added to his pugnacity.

"He can't do it," said Dr. Grantly over and over again, as his father-in-law explained to him the terms on which the new warden of the hospital was to be appointed; "he can't do it. What he says is not worth the trouble of listening to. He can't alter the duties of the place."

"Who can't?" asked the ex-warden.

"Neither the bishop nor the chaplain, nor yet the bishop's wife, who, I take it, has really more to say to such matters than either of the other two. The whole body corporate of the palace together have no power to turn the warden of the hospital into a Sunday-schoolmaster."

"But the bishop has the power to appoint whom he pleases, and—"

"I don't know that; I rather think he'll find he has no such power. Let him try it, and see what the press will say. For once we shall have the popular cry on our side. But Proudie, ass as he is, knows the world too well to get such a hornet's nest about his ears."

Mr. Harding winced at the idea of the press. He had had enough of that sort of publicity, and was unwilling to be shown up a second time either as a monster or as a martyr. He gently remarked that he hoped the newspapers would not get hold of his name again, and then suggested that perhaps it would be better that he should abandon his object. "I am getting old," said he, "and after all I doubt whether I am fit to undertake new duties."

"New duties?" said the archdeacon; "don't I tell you there shall be no new duties?"

"Or perhaps old duties either," said Mr. Harding; "I think I will remain content as I am." The picture of Mr. Slope carting away the rubbish was still present to his mind.

The archdeacon drank off his glass of claret and prepared himself to be energetic. "I do hope," said he, "that you are not going to be so weak as to allow such a man as Mr. Slope to deter you from doing what you know it is your duty to do. You know it is your duty to resume your place at the hospital now that parliament has so settled the stipend as to remove those difficulties which induced you to resign it. You cannot deny this, and should your timidity now prevent you from doing so, your conscience will hereafter never forgive you," and as he finished this clause of his speech, he pushed over the bottle to his companion.

"Your conscience will never forgive you," he continued. "You resigned the place from conscientious scruples, scruples which I greatly respected, though I did not share them. All your friends respected them, and you left your old house as rich in reputation as you were ruined in fortune. It is now expected that you will return. Dr. Gwynne was saying only the other day—"

"Dr. Gwynne does not reflect how much older a man I am now than when he last saw me."

"Old—nonsense," said the archdeacon; "you never thought yourself old till you listened to the impudent trash of that coxcomb at the palace."

"I shall be sixty-five if I live till November," said Mr. Harding.

"And seventy-five, if you live till November ten years," said the archdeacon. "And you bid fair to be as efficient then as you were ten years ago. But for heaven's sake let us have no pretence in this matter. Your plea of old age is a pretence. But you're not drinking your wine. It is only a pretence. The fact is, you are half-afraid of this Slope, and would rather subject yourself to comparative poverty and discomfort than come to blows with a man who will trample on you, if you let him."

"I certainly don't like coming to blows, if I can help it."

"Nor I neither—but sometimes we can't help it. This man's object is to induce you to refuse the hospital, that he may put some creature of his own into it; that he may show his power and insult us all by insulting you, whose cause and character are so intimately bound up with that of the chapter. You owe it to us all to resist him in this, even if you have no solicitude for yourself. But surely, for your own sake, you will not be so lily-livered as to fall into this trap which he has baited for you and let him take the very bread out of your mouth without a struggle."

Mr. Harding did not like being called lily-livered, and was rather inclined to resent it. "I doubt there is any true courage," said he, "in squabbling for money."

"If honest men did not squabble for money, in this wicked world of ours, the dishonest men would get it all, and I do not see that the cause of virtue would be much improved. No—we must use the means which we have. If we were to carry your argument home, we might give away every shilling of revenue which the church has, and I presume you are not prepared to say that the church would be strengthened by such a sacrifice." The archdeacon filled his glass and then emptied it, drinking with much reverence a silent toast to the well-being and permanent security of those temporalities which were so dear to his soul.

"I think all quarrels between a clergyman and his bishop should be avoided," said Mr. Harding.

"I think so too, but it is quite as much the duty of the bishop to look to that as of his inferior. I tell you what, my friend; I'll see the bishop in this matter—that is, if you will allow me—and you may be sure I will not compromise you. My opinion is that all this trash about the Sunday-schools and the sermons has originated wholly with Slope and Mrs. Proudie, and that the bishop knows nothing about it. The bishop can't very well refuse to see me, and I'll come upon him when he has neither his wife nor his chaplain by him. I think you'll find that it will end in his sending you the appointment without any condition whatever. And as to the seats in the cathedral, we may safely leave that to Mr. Dean. I believe the fool positively thinks that the bishop could walk away with the cathedral if he pleased."

And so the matter was arranged between them. Mr. Harding had come expressly for advice, and therefore felt himself bound to take the advice given him. He had known, moreover, beforehand that the archdeacon would not hear of his giving the matter up, and accordingly, though he had in perfect good faith put forward his own views, he was prepared to yield.

They therefore went into the drawing-room in good humour with each other, and the evening passed pleasantly in prophetic discussions on the future wars of Arabin and Slope. The frogs and the mice would be nothing to them, nor the angers of Agamemnon and Achilles. How the archdeacon rubbed his hands and plumed himself on the success of his last move. He could not himself descend into the arena with Slope, but Arabin would have no such scruples. Arabin was exactly the man for such work, and the only man whom he knew that was fit for it.

The archdeacon's good humour and high buoyancy continued till, when reclining on his pillow, Mrs. Grantly commenced to give him her view of the state of affairs at Barchester. And then certainly he was startled. The last words he said that night were as follows:—

"If she does, by heaven I'll never speak to her again. She dragged me into the mire once, but I'll not pollute myself with such filth as that—" And the archdeacon gave a shudder which shook the whole room, so violently was he convulsed with the thought which then agitated his mind.

Now in this matter the widow Bold was scandalously ill-treated by her relatives. She had spoken to the man three or four times, and had expressed her willingness to teach in a Sunday-school. Such was the full extent of her sins in the matter of Mr. Slope. Poor Eleanor! But time will show.

The next morning Mr. Harding returned to Barchester, no further word having been spoken in his hearing respecting Mr. Slope's acquaintance with his younger daughter. But he observed that the archdeacon at breakfast was less cordial than he had been on the preceding evening.

CHAPTER XV

THE WIDOW'S SUITORS

Mr. Slope lost no time in availing himself of the bishop's permission to see Mr. Quiverful, and it was in his interview with this worthy pastor that he first learned that Mrs. Bold was worth the wooing. He rode out to Puddingdale to communicate to the embryo warden the goodwill of the bishop in his favour, and during the discussion on the matter it was not unnatural that the pecuniary resources of Mr. Harding and his family should become the subject of remark.

Mr. Quiverful, with his fourteen children and his four hundred a year, was a very poor man, and the prospect of this new preferment, which was to be held together with his living, was very grateful to him. To what clergyman so circumstanced would not such a prospect be very grateful? But Mr. Quiverful had long been acquainted with Mr. Harding, and had received kindness at his hands, so that his heart misgave him as he thought of supplanting a friend at the hospital. Nevertheless, he was extremely civil, cringingly civil, to Mr. Slope; treated him quite as the great man; entreated this great man to do him the honour to drink a glass of sherry, at which, as it was very poor Marsala, the now pampered Slope turned up his nose; and ended by declaring his extreme obligation to the bishop and Mr. Slope and his great desire to accept the hospital, if—if it were certainly the case that Mr. Harding had refused it.

What man as needy as Mr. Quiverful would have been more disinterested?

"Mr. Harding did positively refuse it," said Mr. Slope with a certain air of offended dignity, "when he heard of the conditions to which the appointment is now subjected. Of course you understand, Mr. Quiverful, that the same conditions will be imposed on yourself."

Mr. Quiverful cared nothing for the conditions. He would have undertaken to preach any number of sermons Mr. Slope might have chosen to dictate, and to pass every remaining hour of his Sundays within the walls of a Sunday-school. What sacrifices, or at any rate, what promises would have been too much to make for such an addition to his income, and for such a house! But his mind still recurred to Mr. Harding.

"To be sure," said he; "Mr. Harding's daughter is very rich, and why should he trouble himself with the hospital?"

"You mean Mrs. Grantly," said Slope.

"I meant his widowed daughter," said the other. "Mrs. Bold has twelve hundred a year of her own, and I suppose Mr. Harding means to live with her."

"Twelve hundred a year of her own!" said Slope, and very shortly afterwards took his leave, avoiding, as far as it was possible for him to do, any further allusion to the hospital. "Twelve hundred a year!" said he to himself as he rode slowly home. If it were the fact that Mrs. Bold had twelve hundred a year of her own, what a fool would he be to oppose her father's return to his old place. The train of Mr. Slope's ideas will probably be plain to all my readers. Why should he not make the twelve hundred a year his own? And if he did so, would it not be well for him to have a father-in-law comfortably provided with the good things of this world? Would it not, moreover, be much more easy for him to gain the daughter if he did all in his power to forward the father's views?

These questions presented themselves to him in a very forcible way, and yet there were many points of doubt. If he resolved to restore to Mr. Harding his former place, he must take the necessary steps for doing so at once; he must immediately talk over the bishop, quarrel on the matter with Mrs. Proudie, whom he knew he could not talk over, and let Mr. Quiverful know that he had been a little too precipitate as to Mr. Harding's positive refusal. That he could effect all this he did not doubt, but he did not wish to effect it for nothing. He did not wish to give way to Mr. Harding and then be rejected by the daughter. He did not wish to lose one influential friend before he had gained another.

And thus he rode home, meditating many things in his mind. It occurred to him that Mrs. Bold was sister-in-law to the archdeacon, and that not even for twelve hundred a year would he submit to that imperious man. A rich wife was a great desideratum to him, but success in his profession was still greater; there were, moreover, other rich women who might be willing to become wives; and after all, this twelve hundred a year might, when inquired into, melt away into some small sum utterly beneath his notice. Then also he remembered that Mrs. Bold had a son.

Another circumstance also much influenced him, though it was one which may almost be said to have influenced him against his will. The vision of the Signora Neroni was perpetually before his eyes. It would be too much to say that Mr. Slope was lost in love, but yet he thought, and kept continually thinking, that he had never seen so beautiful a woman. He was a man whose nature was open to such impulses, and the wiles of the Italianized charmer had been thoroughly successful in imposing upon his thoughts. We will not talk about his heart: not that he had no heart, but because his heart had little to do with his present feelings. His taste had been pleased, his eyes charmed, and his vanity gratified. He had been dazzled by a sort of loveliness which he had never before seen, and had been caught by an easy, free, voluptuous manner which was perfectly new to him. He had never been so tempted before, and the temptation was now irresistible. He had not owned to himself that he cared for this woman more than for others around him, but yet he thought often of the time when he might see her next, and made, almost unconsciously, little cunning plans for seeing her frequently.

He had called at Dr. Stanhope's house the day after the bishop's party, and then the warmth of his admiration had been fed with fresh fuel. If the signora had been kind in her manner and flattering in her speech when lying upon the bishop's sofa, with the eyes of so many on her, she had been much more so in her mother's drawing-room, with no one present but her sister to repress either her nature or her art. Mr. Slope had thus left her quite bewildered, and could not willingly admit into his brain any scheme a part of which would be the necessity of his abandoning all further special friendship with this lady.

And so he slowly rode along, very meditative.

And here the author must beg it to be remembered that Mr. Slope was not in all things a bad man. His motives, like those of most men, were mixed, and though his conduct was generally very different from that which we would wish to praise, it was actuated perhaps as often as that of the majority of the world by a desire to do his duty. He believed in the religion which he taught, harsh, unpalatable, uncharitable as that religion was. He believed those whom he wished to get under his hoof, the Grantlys and Gwynnes of the church, to be the enemies of that religion. He believed himself to be a pillar of strength, destined to do great things, and with that subtle, selfish, ambiguous sophistry to which the minds of all men are so subject, he had taught himself to think that in doing much for the promotion of his own interests, he was doing much also for the promotion of religion. But Mr. Slope had never been an immoral man. Indeed, he had resisted temptations to immorality with a strength of purpose that was creditable to him. He had early in life devoted himself to works which were not compatible with the ordinary pleasures of youth, and he had abandoned such pleasures not without a struggle. It must therefore be conceived that he did not admit to himself that he warmly admired the beauty of a married woman without heart-felt stings of conscience; and to pacify that conscience he had to teach himself that the nature of his admiration was innocent.

And thus he rode along meditative and ill at ease. His conscience had not a word to say against his choosing the widow and her fortune. That he looked upon as a godly work rather than otherwise; as a deed which, if carried through, would redound to his credit as a Christian. On that side lay no future remorse, no conduct which he might probably have to forget, no inward stings. If it should turn out to be really the fact that Mrs. Bold had twelve hundred a year at her own disposal, Mr. Slope would rather look upon it as a duty which he owed his religion to make himself the master of the wife and the money; as a duty too, in which some amount of self-sacrifice would be necessary. He would have to give up his friendship with the signora, his resistance to Mr. Harding, his antipathy—no, he found on mature self-examination that he could not bring himself to give up his antipathy to Dr. Grantly. He would marry the lady as the enemy of her brother-in-law if such an arrangement suited her; if not, she must look elsewhere for a husband.

It was with such resolve as this that he reached Barchester. He would at once ascertain what the truth might be as to the lady's wealth, and having done this he would be ruled by circumstances in his conduct respecting the hospital. If he found that he could turn round and secure the place for Mr. Harding without much self-sacrifice, he would do so; but if not, he would woo the daughter in opposition to the father. But in no case would he succumb to the archdeacon.

He saw his horse taken round to the stable, and immediately went forth to commence his inquiries. To give Mr. Slope his due, he was not a man who ever let much grass grow under his feet.

Poor Eleanor! She was doomed to be the intended victim of more schemes than one.

About the time that Mr. Slope was visiting the vicar of Puddingdale, a discussion took place respecting her charms and wealth at Dr. Stanhope's house in the close. There had been morning callers there, and people had told some truth and also some falsehood respecting the property which John Bold had left behind him. By degrees the visitors went, and as the doctor went with them, and as the doctor's wife had not made her appearance, Charlotte Stanhope and her brother were left together. He was sitting idly at the table, scrawling caricatures of Barchester notables, then yawning, then turning over a book or two, and evidently at a loss how to kill his time without much labour.

"You haven't done much, Bertie, about getting any orders," said his sister.

"Orders!" said he; "who on earth is there at Barchester to give one orders? Who among the people here could possibly think it worth his while to have his head done into marble?"

"Then you mean to give up your profession," said she.

"No, I don't," said he, going on with some absurd portrait of the bishop. "Look at that, Lotte; isn't it the little man all over, apron and all? I'd go on with my profession at once, as you call it, if the governor would set me up with a studio in London; but as to sculpture at Barchester—I suppose half the people here don't know what a torso means."

"The governor will not give you a shilling to start you in London," said Lotte. "Indeed, he can't give you what would be sufficient, for he has not got it. But you might start yourself very well, if you pleased."

"How the deuce am I to do it?" said he.

"To tell you the truth, Bertie, you'll never make a penny by any profession."

"That's what I often think myself," said he, not in the least offended. "Some men have a great gift of making money, but they can't spend it. Others can't put two shillings together, but they have a great talent for all sorts of outlay. I begin to think that my genius is wholly in the latter line."

"How do you mean to live then?" asked the sister.

"I suppose I must regard myself as a young raven and look for heavenly manna; besides, we have all got something when the governor goes."

"Yes—you'll have enough to supply yourself with gloves and boots; that is, if the Jews have not got the possession of it all. I believe they have the most of it already. I wonder, Bertie, at your indifference; that you, with your talents and personal advantages, should never try to settle yourself in life. I look forward with dread to the time when the governor must go. Mother, and Madeline, and I—we shall be poor enough, but you will have absolutely nothing."

"Sufficient for the day is the evil thereof," said Bertie.

"Will you take my advice?" said his sister.

"*Cela dépend*," said the brother.

"Will you marry a wife with money?"

"At any rate," said he, "I won't marry one without; wives with money a'nt so easy to get now-a-days; the parsons pick them all up."

"And a parson will pick up the wife I mean for you, if you do not look quickly about it; the wife I mean is Mrs. Bold."

"Whew-w-w-w!" whistled Bertie, "a widow!"

"She is very beautiful," said Charlotte.

"With a son and heir all ready to my hand," said Bertie.

"A baby that will very likely die," said Charlotte.

"I don't see that," said Bertie. "But however, he may live for me—I don't wish to kill him; only, it must be owned that a ready-made family is a drawback."

"There is only one after all," pleaded Charlotte.

"And that a very little one, as the maidservant said," rejoined Bertie.

"Beggars mustn't be choosers, Bertie; you can't have everything."

"God knows I am not unreasonable," said he, "nor yet opinionated, and if you'll arrange it all for me, Lotte, I'll marry the lady. Only mark this: the money must be sure, and the income at my own disposal, at any rate for the lady's life."

Charlotte was explaining to her brother that he must make love for himself if he meant to carry on the matter, and was encouraging him to do so by warm eulogiums on Eleanor's beauty, when the signora was brought into the drawing-room. When at home, and subject to the gaze of none but her own family, she allowed herself to be dragged about by two persons, and her two bearers now deposited her on her sofa. She was not quite so grand in her apparel as she had been at the bishop's party, but yet she was dressed with much care, and though there was a look of care and pain about her eyes, she was, even by daylight, extremely beautiful.

"Well, Madeline, so I'm going to be married," Bertie began as soon as the servants had withdrawn.

"There's no other foolish thing left that you haven't done," said Madeline, "and therefore you are quite right to try that."

"Oh, you think it's a foolish thing, do you?" said he. "There's Lotte advising me to marry by all means. But on such a subject your opinion ought to be the best; you have experience to guide you."

"Yes, I have," said Madeline with a sort of harsh sadness in her tone, which seemed to say—"What is it to you if I am sad? I have never asked your sympathy."

Bertie was sorry when he saw that she was hurt by what he said, and he came and squatted on the floor close before her face to make his peace with her.

"Come, Mad, I was only joking; you know that. But in sober earnest, Lotte is advising me to marry. She wants me to marry this Mrs. Bold. She's a widow with lots of tin, a fine baby, a beautiful complexion, and the George and Dragon hotel up in the High Street. By Jove, Lotte, if I marry her, I'll keep the public-house myself—it's just the life to suit me."

"What," said Madeline, "that vapid, swarthy creature in the widow's cap, who looked as though her clothes had been stuck on her back with a pitchfork!" The signora never allowed any woman to be beautiful.

"Instead of being vapid," said Lotte, "I call her a very lovely woman. She was by far the loveliest woman in the rooms the other night; that is, excepting you, Madeline."

Even the compliment did not soften the asperity of the maimed beauty. "Every woman is charming according to Lotte," she said; "I never knew an eye with so little true appreciation. In the first place, what woman on earth could look well in such a thing as that she had on her head."

"Of course she wears a widow's cap, but she'll put that off when Bertie marries her."

"I don't see any of course in it," said Madeline. "The death of twenty husbands should not make me undergo such a penance. It is as much a relic of paganism as the sacrifice of a Hindu woman at the burning of her husband's body. If not so bloody, it is quite as barbarous, and quite as useless."

"But you don't blame her for that," said Bertie. "She does it because it's the custom of the country. People would think ill of her if she didn't do it."

"Exactly," said Madeline. "She is just one of those English nonentities who would tie her head up in a bag for three months every summer, if her mother and her grandmother had tied up their heads before her. It would never occur to her to think whether there was any use in submitting to such a nuisance."

"It's very hard in a country like England, for a young woman to set herself in opposition to prejudices of that sort," said the prudent Charlotte.

"What you mean is that it's very hard for a fool not to be a fool," said Madeline.

Bertie Stanhope had been so much knocked about the world from his earliest years that he had not retained much respect for the gravity of English customs; but even to his mind an idea presented itself that, perhaps in a wife, true British prejudice would not in the long run be less agreeable than Anglo-Italian freedom from restraint. He did not exactly say so, but he expressed the idea in another way.

"I fancy," said he, "that if I were to die, and then walk, I should think that my widow looked better in one of those caps than any other kind of head-dress."

"Yes—and you'd fancy also that she could do nothing better than shut herself up and cry for you, or else burn herself. But she would think differently. She'd probably wear one of those horrid she-helmets, because she'd want the courage not to do so; but she'd wear it with a heart longing for the time when she might be allowed to throw it off. I hate such shallow false pretences. For my part I would let the world say what it pleased, and show no grief if I felt none—and perhaps not, if I did."

"But wearing a widow's cap won't lessen her fortune," said Charlotte.

"Or increase it," said Madeline. "Then why on earth does she do it?"

"But Lotte's object is to make her put it off," said Bertie.

"If it be true that she has got twelve hundred a year quite at her own disposal, and she be not utterly vulgar in her manners, I would advise you to marry her. I dare say she's to be had for the asking: and as you are not going to marry her for love, it doesn't much matter whether she is good-looking or not. As to your really marrying a woman for love, I don't believe you are fool enough for that."

"Oh, Madeline!" exclaimed her sister.

"And oh, Charlotte!" said the other.

"You don't mean to say that no man can love a woman unless he be a fool?"

"I mean very much the same thing—that any man who is willing to sacrifice his interest to get possession of a pretty face is a fool. Pretty faces are to be had cheaper than that. I hate your mawkish sentimentality, Lotte. You know as well as I do in what way husbands and wives generally live together; you know how far the warmth of conjugal affection can withstand the trial of a bad dinner, of a rainy day, or of the least privation which poverty brings with it; you know what freedom a man claims for himself, what slavery he would exact from his wife if he could! And you know also how wives generally obey. Marriage means tyranny on one side and deceit on the other. I say that a man is a fool to sacrifice his interests for such a bargain. A woman, too generally, has no other way of living."

"But Bertie has no other way of living," said Charlotte.

"Then, in God's name, let him marry Mrs. Bold," said Madeline. And so it was settled between them.

But let the gentle-hearted reader be under no apprehension whatsoever. It is not destined that Eleanor shall marry Mr. Slope or Bertie Stanhope. And here perhaps it may be allowed to the novelist to explain his views on a very important point in the art of telling tales. He ventures to reprobate that system which goes so far to violate all proper confidence between the author and his readers by maintaining nearly to the end of the third volume a mystery as to the fate of their favourite personage. Nay, more, and worse than this, is too frequently done. Have not often the profoundest efforts of genius been used to baffle the aspirations of the reader, to raise false hopes and false fears, and to give rise to expectations which are never to be realized? Are not promises all but made of delightful horrors, in lieu of which the writer produces nothing but most commonplace realities in his final chapter? And is there not a species of deceit in this to which the honesty of the present age should lend no countenance?

And what can be the worth of that solicitude which a peep into the third volume can utterly dissipate? What the value of those literary charms which are absolutely destroyed by their enjoyment? When we have once learnt what was that picture before which was hung Mrs. Ratcliffe's solemn curtain, we feel no further interest about either the frame or the veil. They are to us merely a receptacle for old bones, an inappropriate coffin, which we would wish to have decently buried out of our sight.

And then how grievous a thing it is to have the pleasure of your novel destroyed by the ill-considered triumph of a previous reader. "Oh, you needn't be alarmed for Augusta; of course she accepts Gustavus in the end." "How very ill-natured you are, Susan," says Kitty with tears in her eyes: "I don't care a bit about it now." Dear Kitty, if you will read my book, you may defy the ill-nature of your sister. There shall be no secret that she can tell you. Nay, take the third volume if you please—learn from the last pages all the results of our troubled story, and the story shall have lost none of its interest, if indeed there be any interest in it to lose.

Our doctrine is that the author and the reader should move along together in full confidence with each other. Let the personages of the drama undergo ever so complete a comedy of errors among themselves, but let the spectator never mistake the Syracusan for the Ephesian; otherwise he is one of the dupes, and the part of a dupe is never dignified.

I would not for the value of this chapter have it believed by a single reader that my Eleanor could bring herself to marry Mr. Slope, or that she should be sacrificed to a Bertie Stanhope. But among the good folk of Barchester many believed both the one and the other.

CHAPTER XVI

BABY WORSHIP

"Diddle, diddle, diddle, diddle, dum, dum, dum," said or sung Eleanor Bold.

"Diddle, diddle, diddle, diddle, dum, dum, dum," continued Mary Bold, taking up the second part in this concerted piece.

The only audience at the concert was the baby, who however gave such vociferous applause that the performers, presuming it to amount to an encore, commenced again.

"Diddle, diddle, diddle, diddle, dum, dum, dum: hasn't he got lovely legs?" said the rapturous mother.

"H'm 'm 'm 'm 'm," simmered Mary, burying her lips in the little fellow's fat neck, by way of kissing him.

"H'm 'm 'm 'm 'm," simmered the mamma, burying her lips also in his fat, round, short legs. "He's a dawty little bold darling, so he is; and he has the nicest little pink legs in all the world, so he has;" and the simmering and the kissing went on over again, as though the ladies were very hungry and determined to eat him.

"Well, then, he's his own mother's own darling: well, he shall—oh, oh—Mary, Mary—did you ever see? What am I to do? My naughty, naughty, naughty, naughty little Johnny." All these energetic exclamations were elicited by the delight of the mother in finding that her son was strong enough and mischievous enough to pull all her hair out from under her cap. "He's been and pulled down all Mamma's hair, and he's the naughtiest, naughtiest, naughtiest little man that ever, ever, ever, ever, ever—"

A regular service of baby worship was going on. Mary Bold was sitting on a low easy chair, with the boy in her lap, and Eleanor was kneeling before the object of her idolatry. As she tried to cover up the little fellow's face with her long, glossy, dark brown locks, and permitted him to pull them hither and thither as he would, she looked very beautiful in spite of the widow's cap which she still wore. There was a quiet, enduring, grateful sweetness about her face which grew so strongly upon those who knew her, as to make the great praise of her beauty which came from her old friends appear marvellously exaggerated to those who were only slightly acquainted with her. Her loveliness was like that of many landscapes, which require to be often seen to be fully enjoyed. There was a depth of dark clear brightness in her eyes which was lost upon a quick observer, a character about her mouth which only showed itself to those with whom she familiarly conversed, a glorious form of head the perfect symmetry of which required the eye of an artist for its appreciation. She had none of that dazzling brilliancy, of that voluptuous Rubens beauty, of that pearly whiteness, and those vermilion tints which immediately entranced with the power of a basilisk men who came within reach of Madeline Neroni. It was all but impossible to resist the signora, but no one was called upon for any resistance towards Eleanor. You might begin to talk to her as though she were your sister, and it would not be till your head was on your pillow that the truth and intensity of her beauty would flash upon you, that the sweetness of her voice would come upon your ear. A sudden half-hour with the Neroni was like falling into a pit, an evening spent with Eleanor like an unexpected ramble in some quiet fields of asphodel.

"We'll cover him up till there shan't be a morsel of his little 'ittle 'ittle 'ittle nose to be seen," said the mother, stretching her streaming locks over the infant's face. The child screamed with delight, and kicked till Mary Bold was hardly able to hold him.

At this moment the door opened, and Mr. Slope was announced. Up jumped Eleanor and, with a sudden quick motion of her hands, pushed back her hair over her shoulders. It would have been perhaps better for her that she had not, for she thus showed more of her confusion than she would have done had she remained as she was. Mr. Slope, however, immediately recognized her loveliness and thought to himself that, irrespective of her fortune, she would be an inmate that a man might well desire for his house, a partner for his bosom's care very well qualified to make care lie easy. Eleanor hurried out of the room to readjust her cap, muttering some unnecessary apology about her baby. And while she is gone, we will briefly go back and state what had been hitherto the results of Mr. Slope's meditations on his scheme of matrimony.

His inquiries as to the widow's income had at any rate been so far successful as to induce him to determine to go on with the speculation. As regarded Mr. Harding, he had also resolved to do what he could without injury to himself. To Mrs. Proudie he determined not to speak on the matter, at least not at present. His object was to instigate a little rebellion on the part of the bishop. He thought that such a state of things would be advisable, not only in respect to Messrs. Harding and Quiverful, but also in the affairs of the diocese generally. Mr. Slope was by no means of opinion that Dr. Proudie was fit to rule, but he conscientiously thought it wrong that his brother clergy should be subjected to petticoat government. He therefore made up his mind to infuse a little of his spirit into the bishop, sufficient to induce him to oppose his wife, though not enough to make him altogether insubordinate.

He had therefore taken an opportunity of again speaking to his lordship about the hospital, and had endeavoured to make it appear that after all it would be unwise to exclude Mr. Harding from the appointment. Mr. Slope, however, had a harder task than he had imagined. Mrs. Proudie, anxious to assume to herself as much as possible of the merit of patronage, had written to Mrs. Quiverful, requesting her to call at the palace, and had then explained to that matron, with much mystery, condescension, and dignity, the good that was in store for her and her progeny. Indeed, Mrs. Proudie had been so engaged at the very time that Mr. Slope had been doing the same with the husband at Puddingdale Vicarage, and had thus in a measure committed herself. The thanks, the humility, the gratitude, the surprise of Mrs. Quiverful had been very overpowering; she had all but embraced the knees of her patroness, and had promised that the prayers of fourteen unprovided babes (so Mrs. Quiverful had described her own family, the eldest of which was a stout young woman of three-and-twenty) should be put up to heaven morning and evening for the munificent friend whom God had sent to them. Such incense as this was not unpleasing to Mrs. Proudie, and she made the most of it. She offered her general assistance to the fourteen unprovided babes, if, as she had no doubt, she should find them worthy; expressed a hope that the eldest of them would be fit to undertake tuition in her Sabbath-schools; and altogether made herself a very great lady in the estimation of Mrs. Quiverful.

Having done this, she thought it prudent to drop a few words before the bishop, letting him know that she had acquainted the Puddingdale family with their good fortune; so that he might perceive that he stood committed to the appointment. The husband well understood the ruse of his wife, but he did not resent it. He knew that she was taking the patronage out of his hands; he was resolved to put an end to her interference and reassume his powers. But then he thought this was not the best time to do it. He put off the evil hour, as many a man in similar circumstances has done before him.

Such having been the case, Mr. Slope naturally encountered a difficulty in talking over the bishop, a difficulty indeed which he found could not be overcome except at the cost of a general outbreak at the palace. A general outbreak at the present moment might be good policy, but it also might not. It was at any rate not a step to be lightly taken. He began by whispering to the bishop that he feared that public opinion would be against him if Mr. Harding did not reappear at the hospital. The bishop answered with some warmth that Mr. Quiverful had been promised the appointment on Mr. Slope's advice. "Not promised?" said Mr. Slope. "Yes, promised," replied the bishop, "and Mrs. Proudie has seen Mrs. Quiverful on the subject." This was quite unexpected on the part of Mr. Slope, but his presence of mind did not fail him, and he turned the statement to his own account.

"Ah, my lord," said he, "we shall all be in scrapes if the ladies interfere."

This was too much in unison with my lord's feelings to be altogether unpalatable, and yet such an allusion to interference demanded a rebuke. My lord was somewhat astounded also, though not altogether made miserable, by finding that there was a point of difference between his wife and his chaplain.

"I don't know what you mean by interference," said the bishop mildly. "When Mrs. Proudie heard that Mr. Quiverful was to be appointed, it was not unnatural that she should wish to see Mrs. Quiverful about the schools. I really cannot say that I see any interference."

"I only speak, my lord, for your own comfort," said Slope; "for your own comfort and dignity in the diocese. I can have no other motive. As far as personal feelings go, Mrs. Proudie is the best friend I have. I must always remember that. But still, in my present position, my first duty is to your lordship."

"I'm sure of that, Mr. Slope; I am quite sure of that;" said the bishop, mollified: "and you really think that Mr. Harding should have the hospital?"

"Upon my word, I'm inclined to think so. I am quite prepared to take upon myself the blame of first suggesting Mr. Quiverful's name. But since doing so, I have found that there is so strong a feeling in the diocese in favour of Mr. Harding that I think your lordship should give way. I hear also that Mr. Harding has modified the objections he first felt to your lordship's propositions. And as to what has passed between Mrs. Proudie and Mrs. Quiverful, the circumstance may be a little inconvenient, but I really do not think that that should weigh in a matter of so much moment."

And thus the poor bishop was left in a dreadfully undecided step as to what he should do. His mind, however, slightly inclined itself to the appointment of Mr. Harding, seeing that by such a step he should have the assistance of Mr. Slope in opposing Mrs. Proudie.

Such was the state of affairs at the palace, when Mr. Slope called at Mrs. Bold's house and found her playing with her baby. When she ran out of the room, Mr. Slope began praising the weather to Mary Bold, then he praised the baby and kissed him, and then he praised the mother, and then he praised Miss Bold herself. Mrs. Bold, however, was not long before she came back.

"I have to apologize for calling at so very early an hour," began Mr. Slope, "but I was really so anxious to speak to you that I hope you and Miss Bold will excuse me."

Eleanor muttered something in which the words "certainly," and "of course," and "not early at all," were just audible, and then apologized for her own appearance, declaring, with a smile, that her baby was becoming such a big boy that he was quite unmanageable.

"He's a great big naughty boy," said she to the child, "and we must send him away to a great big rough romping school, where they have great big rods and do terrible things to naughty boys who don't do what their own mammas tell them;" and she then commenced another course of kissing, being actuated thereto by the terrible idea of sending her child away which her own imagination had depicted.

"And where the masters don't have such beautiful long hair to be dishevelled," said Mr. Slope, taking up the joke and paying a compliment at the same time.

Eleanor thought he might as well have left the compliment alone, but she said nothing and looked nothing, being occupied as she was with the baby.

"Let me take him," said Mary. "His clothes are nearly off his back with his romping," and so saying she left the room with the child. Miss Bold had heard Mr. Slope say he had something pressing to say to Eleanor, and thinking that she might be *de trop*, took this opportunity of getting herself out of the room.

"Don't be long, Mary," said Eleanor as Miss Bold shut the door.

"I am glad, Mrs. Bold, to have the opportunity of having ten minutes' conversation with you alone," began Mr. Slope. "Will you let me openly ask you a plain question?"

"Certainly," said she.

"And I am sure you will give me a plain and open answer."

"Either that, or none at all," said she, laughing.

"My question is this, Mrs. Bold: is your father really anxious to go back to the hospital?"

"Why do you ask me?" said she. "Why don't you ask himself?"

"My dear Mrs. Bold, I'll tell you why. There are wheels within wheels, all of which I would explain to you, only I fear that there is not time. It is essentially necessary that I should have an answer to this question, otherwise I cannot know how to advance your father's wishes; and it is quite impossible that I should ask himself. No one can esteem your father more than I do, but I doubt if this feeling is reciprocal." It certainly was not. "I must be candid with you as the only means of avoiding ultimate consequences, which may be most injurious to Mr. Harding. I fear there is a feeling—I will not even call it a prejudice—with regard to myself in Barchester, which is not in my favour. You remember that sermon—"

"Oh, Mr. Slope, we need not go back to that," said Eleanor.

"For one moment, Mrs. Bold. It is not that I may talk of myself, but because it is so essential that you should understand how matters stand. That sermon may have been ill-judged—it was certainly misunderstood; but I will say nothing about that now; only this, that it did give rise to a feeling against myself which your father shares with others. It may be that he has proper cause, but the result is that he is not inclined to meet me on friendly terms. I put it to yourself whether you do not know this to be the case."

Eleanor made no answer, and Mr. Slope, in the eagerness of his address, edged his chair a little nearer to the widow's seat, unperceived by her.

"Such being so," continued Mr. Slope, "I cannot ask him this question as I can ask it of you. In spite of my delinquencies since I came to Barchester you have allowed me to regard you as a friend." Eleanor made a little motion with her head which was hardly confirmatory, but Mr. Slope if he noticed it, did not appear to do so. "To you I can speak openly and explain the feelings of my heart. This your father would not allow. Unfortunately, the bishop has thought it right that this matter of the hospital should pass through my hands. There have been some details to get up with which he would not trouble himself, and thus it has come to pass that I was forced to have an interview with your father on the matter."

"I am aware of that," said Eleanor.

"Of course," said he. "In that interview Mr. Harding left the impression on my mind that he did not wish to return to the hospital."

"How could that be?" said Eleanor, at last stirred up to forget the cold propriety of demeanour which she had determined to maintain.

"My dear Mrs. Bold, I give you my word that such was the case," said he, again getting a little nearer to her. "And what is more than that, before my interview with Mr. Harding, certain persons at the palace—I do not mean the bishop—had told me that such was the fact. I own, I hardly believed it; I own, I thought that your father would wish on every account, for conscience' sake, for the sake of those old men, for old association and the memory of dear days long gone by, on every account I thought that he would wish to resume his duties. But I was told that such was not his wish, and he certainly left me with the impression that I had been told the truth."

"Well!" said Eleanor, now sufficiently roused on the matter.

"I hear Miss Bold's step," said Mr. Slope; "would it be asking too great a favour to beg you to—I know you can manage anything with Miss Bold."

Eleanor did not like the word manage, but still she went out and asked Mary to leave them alone for another quarter of an hour.

"Thank you, Mrs. Bold—I am so very grateful for this confidence. Well, I left your father with this impression. Indeed, I may say that he made me understand that he declined the appointment."

"Not the appointment," said Eleanor. "I am sure he did not decline the appointment. But he said that he would not agree—that is, that he did not like the scheme about the schools and the services and all that. I am quite sure he never said that he wished to refuse the place."

"Oh, Mrs. Bold!" said Mr. Slope in a manner almost impassioned. "I would not for the world say to so good a daughter a word against so good a father. But you must, for his sake, let me show you exactly how the matter stands at present. Mr. Harding was a little flurried when I told him of the bishop's wishes about the school. I did so perhaps with the less caution because you yourself had so perfectly agreed with me on the same subject. He was a little put out and spoke warmly. 'Tell the bishop,' said he, 'that I quite disagree with him—and shall not return to the hospital as such conditions are attached to it.' What he said was to that effect; indeed, his words were, if anything, stronger than those. I had no alternative but to repeat them to his lordship, who said that he could look on them in no other light than a refusal. He also had heard the report that your father did not wish for the appointment, and putting all these things together, he thought he had no choice but to look for someone else. He has consequently offered the place to Mr. Quiverful."

"Offered the place to Mr. Quiverful!" repeated Eleanor, her eyes suffused with tears. "Then, Mr. Slope, there is an end of it."

"No, my friend—not so," said he. "It is to prevent such being the end of it that I am now here. I may at any rate presume that I have got an answer to my question, and that Mr. Harding is desirous of returning."

"Desirous of returning—of course he is," said Eleanor; "of course he wishes to have back his house and his income and his place in the world; to have back what he gave up with such self-denying honesty, if he can have them without restraints on his conduct to which at his age it would be impossible that he should submit. How can the bishop ask a man of his age to turn schoolmaster to a pack of children?"

"Out of the question," said Mr. Slope, laughing slightly; "of course no such demand shall be made on your father. I can at any rate promise you that I will not be the medium of any so absurd a requisition. We wished your father to preach in the hospital, as the inmates may naturally be too old to leave it, but even that shall not be insisted on. We wished also to attach a Sabbath-day school to the hospital, thinking that such an establishment could not but be useful under the surveillance of so good a clergyman as Mr. Harding, and also under your own. But, dear Mrs. Bold, we won't talk of these things now. One thing is clear: we must do what we can to annul this rash offer the bishop has made to Mr. Quiverful. Your father wouldn't see Quiverful, would he? Quiverful is an honourable man, and would not for a moment stand in your father's way."

"What?" said Eleanor. "Ask a man with fourteen children to give up his preferment! I am quite sure he will do no such thing."

"I suppose not," said Slope, and he again drew near to Mrs. Bold, so that now they were very close to each other. Eleanor did not think much about it but instinctively moved away a little. How greatly would she have increased the distance could she have guessed what had been said about her at Plumstead! "I suppose not. But it is out of the question that Quiverful should supersede your father—quite out of the question. The bishop has been too rash. An idea occurs to me which may perhaps, with God's blessing, put us right. My dear Mrs. Bold, would you object to seeing the bishop yourself?"

"Why should not my father see him?" said Eleanor. She had once before in her life interfered in her father's affairs, and then not to much advantage. She was older now and felt that she should take no step in a matter so vital to him without his consent.

"Why, to tell the truth," said Mr. Slope with a look of sorrow, as though he greatly bewailed the want of charity in his patron, "the bishop fancies that he has cause of anger against your father. I fear an interview would lead to further ill-will."

"Why," said Eleanor, "my father is the mildest, the gentlest man living."

"I only know," said Slope, "that he has the best of daughters. So you would not see the bishop? As to getting an interview, I could manage that for you without the slightest annoyance to yourself."

"I could do nothing, Mr. Slope, without consulting my father."

"Ah!" said he, "that would be useless; you would then only be your father's messenger. Does anything occur to yourself? Something must be done. Your father shall not be ruined by so ridiculous a misunderstanding."

Eleanor said that nothing occurred to her, but that it was very hard; the tears came to her eyes and rolled down her cheeks. Mr. Slope would have given much to have had the privilege of drying them, but he had tact enough to know that he had still a great deal to do before he could even hope for any privilege with Mrs. Bold.

"It cuts me to the heart to see you so grieved," said he. "But pray let me assure you that your father's interests shall not be sacrificed if it be possible for me to protect them. I will tell the bishop openly what are the facts. I will explain to him that he has hardly the right to appoint any other than your father, and will show him that if he does so he will be guilty of great injustice—and you, Mrs. Bold, you will have the charity at any rate to believe this of me, that I am truly anxious for your father's welfare—for his and for your own."

The widow hardly knew what answer to make. She was quite aware that her father would not be at all thankful to Mr. Slope; she had a strong wish to share her father's feelings; and yet she could not but acknowledge that Mr. Slope was very kind. Her father, who was generally so charitable to all men, who seldom spoke ill of anyone, had warned her against Mr. Slope, and yet she did not know how to abstain from thanking him. What interest could he have in the matter but that which he professed? Nevertheless there was that in his manner which even she distrusted. She felt, she did not know why, that there was something about him which ought to put her on her guard.

Mr. Slope read all this in her hesitating manner just as plainly as though she had opened her heart to him. It was the talent of the man that he could so read the inward feelings of women with whom he conversed. He knew that Eleanor was doubting him, and that, if she thanked him, she would only do so because she could not help it, but yet this did not make him angry or even annoy him. Rome was not built in a day.

"I did not come for thanks," continued he, seeing her hesitation, "and do not want them—at any rate before they are merited. But this I do want, Mrs. Bold, that I may make to myself friends in this fold to which it has pleased God to call me as one of the humblest of his shepherds. If I cannot do so, my task here must indeed be a sad one. I will at any rate endeavour to deserve them."

"I'm sure," said she, "you will soon make plenty of friends." She felt herself obliged to say something.

"That will be nothing unless they are such as will sympathize with my feelings; unless they are such as I can reverence and admire—and love. If the best and purest turn away from me, I cannot bring myself to be satisfied with the friendship of the less estimable. In such case I must live alone."

"Oh, I'm sure you will not do that, Mr. Slope." Eleanor meant nothing, but it suited him to appear to think some special allusion had been intended.

"Indeed, Mrs. Bold, I shall live alone, quite alone as far as the heart is concerned, if those with whom I yearn to ally myself turn away from me. But enough of this; I have called you my friend, and I hope you will not contradict me. I trust the time may come when I may also call your father so. May God bless you, Mrs. Bold, you and your darling boy. And tell your father from me that what can be done for his interest shall be done."

And so he took his leave, pressing the widow's hand rather more closely than usual. Circumstances, however, seemed just then to make this intelligible, and the lady did not feel called on to resent it.

"I cannot understand him," said Eleanor to Mary Bold a few minutes afterwards. "I do not know whether he is a good man or a bad man—whether he is true or false."

"Then give him the benefit of the doubt," said Mary, "and believe the best."

"On the whole, I think I do," said Eleanor. "I think I do believe that he means well—and if so, it is a shame that we should revile him and make him miserable while he is among us. But, oh, Mary, I fear Papa will be disappointed in the hospital."

CHAPTER XVII

WHO SHALL BE COCK OF THE WALK?

All this time things were going somewhat uneasily at the palace. The hint or two which Mr. Slope had given was by no means thrown away upon the bishop. He had a feeling that if he ever meant to oppose the now almost unendurable despotism of his wife, he must lose no further time in doing so; that if he ever meant to be himself master in his own diocese, let alone his own house, he should begin at once. It would have been easier to have done so from the day of his consecration than now, but easier now than when Mrs. Proudie should have succeeded in thoroughly mastering the diocesan details. Then the proffered assistance of Mr. Slope was a great thing for him, a most unexpected and invaluable aid. Hitherto he had looked on the two as allied forces and had considered that, as allies, they were impregnable. He had begun to believe that his only chance of escape would be by the advancement of Mr. Slope to some distant and rich preferment. But now it seemed that one of his enemies, certainly the least potent of them, but nevertheless one very important, was willing to desert his own camp. Assisted by Mr. Slope what might he not do? He walked up and down his little study, almost thinking that the time might come when he would be able to appropriate to his own use the big room upstairs in which his predecessor had always sat.

As he revolved these things in his mind a note was brought to him from Archdeacon Grantly, in which that divine begged his lordship to do him the honour of seeing him on the morrow—would his lordship have the kindness to name an hour? Dr. Grantly's proposed visit would have reference to the reappointment of Mr. Harding to the wardenship of Barchester Hospital. The bishop having read his note was informed that the archdeacon's servant was waiting for an answer.

Here at once a great opportunity offered itself to the bishop of acting on his own responsibility. He bethought himself however of his new ally and rang the bell for Mr. Slope. It turned out that Mr. Slope was not in the house, and then, greatly daring, the bishop with his own unassisted spirit wrote a note to the archdeacon saying that he would see him, and naming an hour for doing so. Having watched from his study-window that the messenger got safely off from the premises with this dispatch, he began to turn over in his mind what step he should next take.

To-morrow he would have to declare to the archdeacon either that Mr. Harding should have the appointment, or that he should not have it. The bishop felt that he could not honestly throw over the Quiverfuls without informing Mrs. Proudie, and he resolved at last to brave the lioness in her den and tell her that circumstances were such that it behoved him to reappoint Mr. Harding. He did not feel that he should at all derogate from his new courage by promising Mrs. Proudie that the very first piece of available preferment at his disposal should be given to Quiverful to atone for the injury done to him. If he could mollify the lioness with such a sop, how happy would he think his first efforts to have been!

Not without many misgivings did he find himself in Mrs. Proudie's boudoir. He had at first thought of sending for her. But it was not at all impossible that she might choose to take such a message amiss, and then also it might be some protection to him to have his daughters present at the interview. He found her sitting with her account-books before her, nibbling the end of her pencil, evidently immersed in pecuniary difficulties, and harassed in mind by the multiplicity of palatial expenses and the heavy cost of episcopal grandeur. Her daughters were around her. Olivia was reading a novel, Augusta was crossing a note to her bosom friend in Baker Street, and Netta was working diminutive coach wheels for the bottom of a petticoat. If the bishop could get the better of his wife in her present mood, he would be a man indeed. He might then consider the victory his own forever. After all, in such cases the matter between husband and wife stands much the same as it does between two boys at the same school, two cocks in the same yard, or two armies on the same continent. The conqueror once is generally the conqueror forever after. The prestige of victory is everything.

"Ahem—my dear," began the bishop, "if you are disengaged, I wished to speak to you." Mrs. Proudie put her pencil down carefully at the point to which she had totted her figures, marked down in her memory the sum she had arrived at, and then looked up, sourly enough, into her helpmate's face. "If you are busy, another time will do as well," continued the bishop, whose courage, like Bob Acres', had oozed out now that he found himself on the ground of battle.

"What is it about, Bishop?" asked the lady.

"Well—it was about those Quiverfuls—but I see you are engaged. Another time will do just as well for me."

"What about the Quiverfuls? It is quite understood, I believe, that they are to come to the hospital. There is to be no doubt about that, is there?" and as she spoke she kept her pencil sternly and vigorously fixed on the column of figures before her.

"Why, my dear, there is a difficulty," said the bishop.

"A difficulty!" said Mrs. Proudie, "what difficulty? The place has been promised to Mr. Quiverful, and of course he must have it. He has made all his arrangements. He has written for a curate for Puddingdale, he has spoken to the auctioneer about selling his farm, horses, and cows, and in all respects considers the place as his own. Of course he must have it."

Now, Bishop, look well to thyself and call up all the manhood that is in thee. Think how much is at stake. If now thou art not true to thy guns, no Slope can hereafter aid thee. How can he who deserts his own colours at the first smell of gunpowder expect faith in any ally? Thou thyself hast sought the battle-field: fight out the battle manfully now thou art there. Courage, Bishop, courage! Frowns cannot kill, nor can sharp words break any bones. After all, the apron is thine own. She can appoint no wardens, give away no benefices, nominate no chaplains, an' thou art but true to thyself. Up, man, and at her with a constant heart.

Some little monitor within the bishop's breast so addressed him. But then there was another monitor there which advised him differently, and as follows. Remember, Bishop, she is a woman, and such a woman too as thou well knowest: a battle of words with such a woman is the very mischief. Were it not better for thee to carry on this war, if it must be waged, from behind thine own table in thine own study? Does not every cock fight best on his own dunghill? Thy daughters also are here, the pledges of thy love, the fruits of thy

215

loins: is it well that they should see thee in the hour of thy victory over their mother? Nay, is it well that they should see thee in the possible hour of thy defeat? Besides, hast thou not chosen thy opportunity with wonderful little skill, indeed with no touch of that sagacity for which thou art famous? Will it not turn out that thou art wrong in this matter and thine enemy right; that thou hast actually pledged thyself in this matter of the hospital, and that now thou wouldest turn upon thy wife because she requires from thee but the fulfilment of thy promise? Art thou not a Christian bishop, and is not thy word to be held sacred whatever be the result? Return, Bishop, to thy sanctum on the lower floor and postpone thy combative propensities for some occasion in which at least thou mayest fight the battle against odds less tremendously against thee.

All this passed within the bishop's bosom while Mrs. Proudie still sat with her fixed pencil, and the figures of her sum still enduring on the tablets of her memory. "£4 17s. 7d." she said to herself. "Of course Mr. Quiverful must have the hospital," she said out loud to her lord.

"Well, my dear, I merely wanted to suggest to you that Mr. Slope seems to think that if Mr. Harding be not appointed, public feeling in the matter would be against us, and that the press might perhaps take it up."

"Mr. Slope seems to think!" said Mrs. Proudie in a tone of voice which plainly showed the bishop that he was right in looking for a breach in that quarter. "And what has Mr. Slope to do with it? I hope, my lord, you are not going to allow yourself to be governed by a chaplain." And now in her eagerness the lady lost her place in her account.

"Certainly not, my dear. Nothing I can assure you is less probable. But still, Mr. Slope may be useful in finding how the wind blows, and I really thought that if we could give something else as good to the Quiverfuls—"

"Nonsense," said Mrs. Proudie; "it would be years before you could give them anything else that could suit them half as well, and as for the press and the public and all that, remember there are two ways of telling a story. If Mr. Harding is fool enough to tell his tale, we can also tell ours. The place was offered to him, and he refused it. It has now been given to someone else, and there's an end of it. At least I should think so."

"Well, my dear, I rather believe you are right," said the bishop, and sneaking out of the room, he went downstairs, troubled in his mind as to how he should receive the archdeacon on the morrow. He felt himself not very well just at present, and began to consider that he might, not improbably, be detained in his room the next morning by an attack of bile. He was, unfortunately, very subject to bilious annoyances.

"Mr. Slope, indeed! I'll Slope him," said the indignant matron to her listening progeny. "I don't know what has come to Mr. Slope. I believe he thinks he is to be Bishop of Barchester himself, because I've taken him by the hand and got your father to make him his domestic chaplain."

"He was always full of impudence," said Olivia; "I told you so once before, Mamma." Olivia, however, had not thought him too impudent when once before he had proposed to make her Mrs. Slope.

"Well, Olivia, I always thought you liked him," said Augusta, who at that moment had some grudge against her sister. "I always disliked the man, because I think him thoroughly vulgar."

"There you're wrong," said Mrs. Proudie; "he's not vulgar at all; and what is more, he is a soul-stirring, eloquent preacher; but he must be taught to know his place if he is to remain in this house."

"He has the horridest eyes I ever saw in a man's head," said Netta; "and I tell you what, he's terribly greedy; did you see all the currant pie he ate yesterday?"

When Mr. Slope got home he soon learnt from the bishop, as much from his manner as his words, that Mrs. Proudie's behests in the matter of the hospital were to be obeyed. Dr. Proudie let fall something as to "this occasion only" and "keeping all affairs about patronage exclusively in his own hands." But he was quite decided about Mr. Harding; and as Mr. Slope did not wish to have both the prelate and the prelatess against him, he did not at present see that he could do anything but yield.

He merely remarked that he would of course carry out the bishop's views and that he was quite sure that if the bishop trusted to his own judgement things in the diocese would certainly be well ordered. Mr. Slope knew that if you hit a nail on the head often enough, it will penetrate at last.

He was sitting alone in his room on the same evening when a light knock was made on his door, and before he could answer it the door was opened, and his patroness appeared. He was all smiles in a moment, but so was not she also. She took, however, the chair that was offered to her, and thus began her expostulation:

"Mr. Slope, I did not at all approve your conduct the other night with that Italian woman. Anyone would have thought that you were her lover."

"Good gracious, my dear madam," said Mr. Slope with a look of horror. "Why, she is a married woman."

"That's more than I know," said Mrs. Proudie; "however she chooses to pass for such. But married or not married, such attention as you paid to her was improper. I cannot believe that you would wish to give offence in my drawing-room, Mr. Slope, but I owe it to myself and my daughters to tell you that I disapprove of your conduct."

Mr. Slope opened wide his huge protruding eyes and stared out of them with a look of well-feigned surprise. "Why, Mrs. Proudie," said he, "I did but fetch her something to eat when she said she was hungry."

"And you have called on her since," continued she, looking at the culprit with the stern look of a detective policeman in the act of declaring himself.

Mr. Slope turned over in his mind whether it would be well for him to tell this termagant at once that he should call on whom he liked and do what he liked, but he remembered that his footing in Barchester was not yet sufficiently firm, and that it would be better for him to pacify her.

"I certainly called since at Dr. Stanhope's house, and certainly saw Madame Neroni."

"Yes, and you saw her alone," said the episcopal Argus.

"Undoubtedly, I did," said Mr. Slope, "but that was because nobody else happened to be in the room. Surely it was no fault of mine if the rest of the family were out."

"Perhaps not, but I assure you, Mr. Slope, you will fall greatly in my estimation if I find that you allow yourself to be caught by the lures of that woman. I know women better than you do, Mr. Slope, and you may believe me that that signora, as she calls herself, is not a fitting companion for a strict evangelical unmarried young clergyman."

How Mr. Slope would have liked to laugh at her, had he dared! But he did not dare. So he merely said, "I can assure you, Mrs. Proudie, the lady in question is nothing to me."

"Well, I hope not, Mr. Slope. But I have considered it my duty to give you this caution. And now there is another thing I feel myself called on to speak about: it is your conduct to the bishop, Mr. Slope."

"My conduct to the bishop," said he, now truly surprised and ignorant what the lady alluded to.

"Yes, Mr. Slope, your conduct to the bishop. It is by no means what I would wish to see it."

"Has the bishop said anything, Mrs. Proudie?"

"No, the bishop has said nothing. He probably thinks that any remarks on the matter will come better from me, who first introduced you to his lordship's notice. The fact is, Mr. Slope, you are a little inclined to take too much upon yourself."

An angry spot showed itself on Mr. Slope's cheeks, and it was with difficulty that he controlled himself. But he did do so, and sat quite silent while the lady went on.

"It is the fault of many young men in your position, and therefore the bishop is not inclined at present to resent it. You will, no doubt, soon learn what is required from you and what is not. If you will take my advice, however, you will be careful not to obtrude advice upon the bishop in any matter touching patronage. If his lordship wants advice, he knows where to look for it." And then having added to her counsel a string of platitudes as to what was desirable and what not desirable in the conduct of a strictly evangelical unmarried young clergyman, Mrs. Proudie retreated, leaving the chaplain to his thoughts.

The upshot of his thoughts was this, that there certainly was not room in the diocese for the energies of both himself and Mrs. Proudie, and that it behoved him quickly to ascertain whether his energies or hers were to prevail.

CHAPTER XVIII

THE WIDOW'S PERSECUTION

Early on the following morning Mr. Slope was summoned to the bishop's dressing-room, and went there fully expecting that he should find his lordship very indignant and spirited up by his wife to repeat the rebuke which she had administered on the previous day. Mr. Slope had resolved that at any rate from him he would not stand it, and entered the dressing-room in rather a combative disposition; but he found the bishop in the most placid and gentlest of humours. His lordship complained of being rather unwell, had a slight headache, and was not quite the thing in his stomach; but there was nothing the matter with his temper.

"Oh, Slope," said he, taking the chaplain's proffered hand, "Archdeacon Grantly is to call on me this morning, and I really am not fit to see him. I fear I must trouble you to see him for me;" and then Dr. Proudie proceeded to explain what it was that must be said to Dr. Grantly. He was to be told in fact, in the civilest words in which the tidings could be conveyed, that Mr. Harding having refused the wardenship, the appointment had been offered to Mr. Quiverful and accepted by him.

Mr. Slope again pointed out to his patron that he thought he was perhaps not quite wise in his decision, and this he did *sotto voce*. But even with this precaution it was not safe to say much, and during the little that he did say, the bishop made a very slight, but still a very ominous gesture with his thumb towards the door which opened from his dressing-room to some inner sanctuary. Mr. Slope at once took the hint and said no more, but he perceived that there was to be confidence between him and his patron, that the league desired by him was to be made, and that this appointment of Mr. Quiverful was to be the last sacrifice offered on the altar of conjugal obedience. All this Mr. Slope read in the slight motion of the bishop's thumb, and he read it correctly. There was no need of parchments and seals, of attestations, explanations, and professions. The bargain was understood between them, and Mr. Slope gave the bishop his hand upon it. The bishop understood the little extra squeeze, and an intelligible gleam of assent twinkled in his eye.

"Pray be civil to the archdeacon, Mr. Slope," said he out loud, "but make him quite understand that in this matter Mr. Harding has put it out of my power to oblige him."

It would be a calumny on Mrs. Proudie to suggest that she was sitting in her bedroom with her ear at the keyhole during this interview. She had within her a spirit of decorum which prevented her from descending to such baseness. To put her ear to a keyhole, or to listen at a chink, was a trick for a housemaid. Mrs. Proudie knew this, and therefore did not do it; but she stationed herself as near to the door as she well could, that she might, if possible, get the advantage which the housemaid would have had, without descending to the housemaid's artifice.

It was little, however, that she heard, and that little was only sufficient to deceive her. She saw nothing of that friendly pressure, perceived nothing of that concluded bargain; she did not even dream of the treacherous resolves which those two false men had made together to upset her in the pride of her station, to dash the cup from her lip before she had drunk of it, to sweep away all her power before she had tasted its sweets! Traitors that they were, the husband of her bosom and the outcast whom she had fostered and brought to the warmth of the world's brightest fireside! But neither of them had the magnanimity of this woman. Though two men have thus leagued themselves together against her, even yet the battle is not lost.

Mr. Slope felt pretty sure that Dr. Grantly would decline the honour of seeing him, and such turned out to be the case. The archdeacon, when the palace door was opened to him, was greeted by a note. Mr. Slope presented his compliments, &c. &c. The bishop was ill in his room and very greatly regretted, &c. &c. Mr. Slope had been charged with the bishop's views, and if agreeable to the archdeacon, would do himself the honour, &c. &c. The archdeacon, however, was not agreeable, and having read his note in the hall, crumpled it up in his hand, and muttering something about sorrow for his lordship's illness, took his leave, without sending as much as a verbal message in answer to Mr. Slope's note.

"Ill!" said the archdeacon to himself as he flung himself into his brougham. "The man is absolutely a coward. He is afraid to see me. Ill, indeed!" The archdeacon was never ill himself, and did not therefore understand that anyone else could in truth be prevented by illness from keeping an appointment. He regarded all such excuses as subterfuges, and in the present instance he was not far wrong.

Dr. Grantly desired to be driven to his father-in-law's lodgings in the High Street, and hearing from the servant that Mr. Harding was at his daughter's, followed him to Mrs. Bold's house, and there found him. The archdeacon was fuming with rage when he got into the drawing-room, and had by this time nearly forgotten the pusillanimity of the bishop in the villainy of the chaplain.

"Look at that," said he, throwing Mr. Slope's crumpled note to Mr. Harding. "I am to be told that if I choose I may have the honour of seeing Mr. Slope, and that too after a positive engagement with the bishop."

"But he says the bishop is ill," said Mr. Harding.

"Pshaw! You don't mean to say that you are deceived by such an excuse as that. He was well enough yesterday. Now I tell you what, I will see the bishop, and I will tell him also very plainly what I think of his conduct. I will see him, or else Barchester will soon be too hot to hold him."

Eleanor was sitting in the room, but Dr. Grantly had hardly noticed her in his anger. Eleanor now said to him with the greatest innocence, "I wish you had seen Mr. Slope, Dr. Grantly, because I think perhaps it might have done good."

The archdeacon turned on her with almost brutal wrath. Had she at once owned that she had accepted Mr. Slope for her second husband, he could hardly have felt more convinced of her belonging body and soul to the Slope and Proudie party than he now did on hearing her express such a wish as this. Poor Eleanor!

"See him!" said the archdeacon glaring at her. "And why am I to be called on to lower myself in the world's esteem and my own by coming in contact with such a man as that? I have hitherto lived among gentlemen, and do not mean to be dragged into other company by anybody."

Poor Mr. Harding well knew what the archdeacon meant, but Eleanor was as innocent as her own baby. She could not understand how the archdeacon could consider himself to be dragged into bad company by condescending to speak to Mr. Slope for a few minutes when the interests of her father might be served by his doing so.

"I was talking for a full hour yesterday to Mr. Slope," said she with some little assumption of dignity, "and I did not find myself lowered by it."

"Perhaps not," said he. "But if you'll be good enough to allow me, I shall judge for myself in such matters. And I tell you what, Eleanor; it will be much better for you if you will allow yourself to be guided also by the advice of those who are your friends. If you do not, you will be apt to find that you have no friends left who can advise you."

Eleanor blushed up to the roots of her hair. But even now she had not the slightest idea of what was passing in the archdeacon's mind. No thought of love-making or love-receiving had yet found its way to her heart since the death of poor John Bold, and if it were possible that such a thought should spring there, the man must be far different from Mr. Slope that could give it birth.

Nevertheless Eleanor blushed deeply, for she felt she was charged with improper conduct, and she did so with the more inward pain because her father did not instantly rally to her side—that father for whose sake and love she had submitted to be the receptacle of Mr. Slope's confidence. She had given a detailed account of all that had passed to her father, and though he had not absolutely agreed with her about Mr. Slope's views touching the hospital, yet he had said nothing to make her think that she had been wrong in talking to him.

She was far too angry to humble herself before her brother-in-law. Indeed, she had never accustomed herself to be very abject before him, and they had never been confidential allies. "I do not the least understand what you mean, Dr. Grantly," said she. "I do not know that I can accuse myself of doing anything that my friends should disapprove. Mr. Slope called here expressly to ask what Papa's wishes were about the hospital, and as I believe he called with friendly intentions, I told him."

"Friendly intentions!" sneered the archdeacon.

"I believe you greatly wrong Mr. Slope," continued Eleanor, "but I have explained this to Papa already; and as you do not seem to approve of what I say, Dr. Grantly, I will with your permission leave you and Papa together;" so saying, she walked slowly out of the room.

All this made Mr. Harding very unhappy. It was quite clear that the archdeacon and his wife had made up their minds that Eleanor was going to marry Mr. Slope. Mr. Harding could not really bring himself to think that she would do so, but yet he could not deny that circumstances made it appear that the man's company was not disagreeable to her. She was now constantly seeing him, and yet she received visits from no other unmarried gentleman. She always took his part when his conduct was canvassed, although she was aware how personally objectionable he was to her friends. Then, again, Mr. Harding felt that if she should choose to become Mrs. Slope, he had nothing that he could justly urge against her doing so. She had full right to please herself, and he, as a father, could not say that she would disgrace herself by marrying a clergyman who stood so well before the world as Mr. Slope did. As for quarrelling with his daughter on account of such a marriage, and separating himself from her as the archdeacon had threatened to do, that, with Mr. Harding, would be out of the question. If she should determine to marry this man, he must get over his aversion as best he could. His Eleanor, his own old companion in their old happy home, must still be the friend of his bosom, the child of his heart. Let who would cast her off, he would not. If it were fated that he should have to sit in his old age at the same table with that man whom of all men he disliked the most, he would meet his fate as best he might. Anything to him would be preferable to the loss of his daughter.

Such being his feelings, he hardly knew how to take part with Eleanor against the archdeacon, or with the archdeacon against Eleanor. It will be said that he should never have suspected her.—Alas! he never should have done so. But Mr. Harding was by no means a perfect character. In his indecision, his weakness, his proneness to be led by others, his want of self-confidence, he was very far from being perfect. And then it must be remembered that such a marriage as that which the archdeacon contemplated with disgust, which we who know Mr. Slope so well would regard with equal disgust, did not appear so monstrous to Mr. Harding because in his charity he did not hate the chaplain as the archdeacon did, and as we do.

He was, however, very unhappy when his daughter left the room, and he had recourse to an old trick of his that was customary to him in his times of sadness. He began playing some slow tune upon an imaginary violoncello, drawing one hand slowly backwards and forwards as though he held a bow in it, and modulating the unreal chords with the other.

"She'll marry that man as sure as two and two make four," said the practical archdeacon.

"I hope not, I hope not," said the father. "But if she does, what can I say to her? I have no right to object to him."

"No right!" exclaimed Dr. Grantly.

"No right as her father. He is in my own profession and, for aught we know, a good man."

To this the archdeacon would by no means assent. It was not well, however, to argue the case against Eleanor in her own drawing-room, and so they both walked forth and discussed the matter in all its bearings under the elm-trees of the close. Mr. Harding also explained to his son-in-law what had been the purport, at any rate the alleged purport, of Mr. Slope's last visit to the widow. He, however, stated that he could not bring himself to believe that Mr. Slope had any real anxiety such as that he had pretended. "I cannot forget his demeanour to myself," said Mr. Harding, "and it is not possible that his ideas should have changed so soon."

"I see it all," said the archdeacon. "The sly *tartuffe*! He thinks to buy the daughter by providing for the father. He means to show how powerful he is, how good he is, and how much he is willing to do for her *beaux yeux*; yes, I see it all now. But we'll be too many for him yet, Mr. Harding;" he said, turning to his companion with some gravity and pressing his hand upon the other's arm. "It would, perhaps, be better for you to lose the hospital than get it on such terms."

"Lose it!" said Mr. Harding; "why I've lost it already. I don't want it. I've made up my mind to do without it. I'll withdraw altogether. I'll just go and write a line to the bishop and tell him that I withdraw my claim altogether."

Nothing would have pleased him better than to be allowed to escape from the trouble and difficulty in such a manner. But he was now going too fast for the archdeacon.

"No—no—no! We'll do no such thing," said Dr. Grantly. "We'll still have the hospital. I hardly doubt but that we'll have it. But not by Mr. Slope's assistance. If that be necessary, we'll lose it; but we'll have it, spite of his teeth, if we can. Arabin will be at Plumstead to-morrow; you must come over and talk to him."

The two now turned into the cathedral library, which was used by the clergymen of the close as a sort of ecclesiastical club-room, for writing sermons and sometimes letters; also for reading theological works and sometimes magazines and newspapers. The theological works were not disturbed, perhaps, quite as often as from the appearance of the building the outside public might have been led to expect. Here the two allies settled on their course of action. The archdeacon wrote a letter to the bishop, strongly worded, but still respectful, in which he put forward his father-in-law's claim to the appointment and expressed his own regret that he had not been able to see his lordship when he called. Of Mr. Slope he made no mention whatsoever. It was then settled that Mr. Harding should go out to Plumstead on the following day, and after considerable discussion on the matter the archdeacon proposed to ask Eleanor there also, so as to withdraw her, if possible, from Mr. Slope's attentions. "A week or two," said he, "may teach her what he is, and while she is there she will be out of harm's way. Mr. Slope won't come there after her."

Eleanor was not a little surprised when her brother-in-law came back and very civilly pressed her to go out to Plumstead with her father. She instantly perceived that her father had been fighting her battles for her behind her back. She felt thankful to him, and for his sake she would not show her resentment to the archdeacon by refusing his invitation. But she could not, she said, go on the morrow; she had an invitation to drink tea at the Stanhopes, which she had promised to accept. She would, she added, go with her father on the next day, if he would wait; or she would follow him.

"The Stanhopes!" said Dr. Grantly. "I did not know you were so intimate with them."

"I did not know it myself," said she, "till Miss Stanhope called yesterday. However, I like her very much, and I have promised to go and play chess with some of them."

"Have they a party there?" said the archdeacon, still fearful of Mr. Slope.

"Oh, no," said Eleanor; "Miss Stanhope said there was to be nobody at all. But she had heard that Mary had left me for a few weeks, and she had learnt from someone that I play chess, and so she came over on purpose to ask me to go in."

"Well, that's very friendly," said the ex-warden. "They certainly do look more like foreigners than English people, but I dare say they are none the worse for that."

The archdeacon was inclined to look upon the Stanhopes with favourable eyes, and had nothing to object on the matter. It was therefore arranged that Mr. Harding should postpone his visit to Plumstead for one day and then take with him Eleanor, the baby, and the nurse.

Mr. Slope is certainly becoming of some importance in Barchester.

CHAPTER XIX

BARCHESTER BY MOONLIGHT

There was much cause for grief and occasional perturbation of spirits in the Stanhope family, but yet they rarely seemed to be grieved or to be disturbed. It was the peculiar gift of each of them that each was able to bear his or her own burden without complaint, and perhaps without sympathy. They habitually looked on the sunny side of the wall, if there was a gleam on either side for them to look at; if there was none, they endured the shade with an indifference which, if not stoical, answered the end at which the Stoics aimed. Old Stanhope could not but feel that he had ill-performed his duties as a father and a clergyman, and could hardly look forward to his own death without grief at the position in which he would leave his family. His income for many years had been as high as £3,000 a year, and yet they had among them no other provision than their mother's fortune of £10,000. He had not only spent his income, but was in debt. Yet with all this he seldom showed much outward sign of trouble.

It was the same with the mother. If she added little to the pleasures of her children, she detracted still less: she neither grumbled at her lot, nor spoke much of her past or future sufferings; as long as she had a maid to adjust her dress, and had those dresses well made, nature with her was satisfied. It was the same with the children. Charlotte never rebuked her father with the prospect of their future poverty, nor did it seem to grieve her that she was becoming an old maid so quickly; her temper was rarely ruffled, and, if we might judge by her appearance, she was always happy. The signora was not so sweet-tempered, but she possessed much enduring courage; she seldom complained—never, indeed, to her family. Though she had a cause for affliction which would have utterly broken down the heart of most women as beautiful as she and as devoid of all religious support, yet she bore her suffering in silence, or alluded to it only to elicit the sympathy and stimulate the admiration of the men with whom she flirted. As to Bertie, one would have imagined from the sound of his voice and the gleam of his eye that he had not a sorrow nor a care in the world. Nor had he. He was incapable of anticipating to-morrow's griefs. The prospect of future want no more disturbed his appetite than does that of the butcher's knife disturb the appetite of the sheep.

Such was the usual tenor of their way; but there were rare exceptions. Occasionally the father would allow an angry glance to fall from his eye, and the lion would send forth a low dangerous roar as though he meditated some deed of blood. Occasionally also Madame Neroni would become bitter against mankind, more than usually antagonistic to the world's decencies, and would seem as though she was about to break from her moorings and allow herself to be carried forth by the tide of her feelings to utter ruin and shipwreck. She, however, like the rest of them, had no real feelings, could feel no true passion. In that was her security. Before she resolved on any contemplated escapade she would make a small calculation, and generally summed up that the Stanhope villa or even Barchester close was better than the world at large.

They were most irregular in their hours. The father was generally the earliest in the breakfast-parlour, and Charlotte would soon follow and give him his coffee, but the others breakfasted anywhere, anyhow, and at any time. On the morning after the archdeacon's futile visit to the palace, Dr. Stanhope came downstairs with an ominously dark look about his eyebrows; his white locks were rougher than usual, and he breathed thickly and loudly as he took his seat in his armchair. He had open letters in his hand, and when Charlotte came into the room, he was still reading them. She went up and kissed him as was her wont, but he hardly noticed her as she did so, and she knew at once that something was the matter.

"What's the meaning of that?" said he, throwing over the table a letter with a Milan postmark. Charlotte was a little frightened as she took it up, but her mind was relieved when she saw that it was merely the bill of their Italian milliner. The sum total was certainly large, but not so large as to create an important row.

"It's for our clothes, Papa, for six months before we came here. The three of us can't dress for nothing, you know."

"Nothing, indeed!" said he, looking at the figures which, in Milanese denominations, were certainly monstrous.

"The man should have sent it to me," said Charlotte.

"I wish he had with all my heart—if you would have paid it. I see enough in it to know that three quarters of it are for Madeline."

"She has little else to amuse her, sir," said Charlotte with true good nature.

"And I suppose he has nothing else to amuse him," said the doctor, throwing over another letter to his daughter. It was from some member of the family of Sidonia, and politely requested the father to pay a small trifle of £700, being the amount of a bill discounted in favour of Mr. Ethelbert Stanhope and now overdue for a period of nine months.

Charlotte read the letter, slowly folded it up, and put it under the edge of the tea-tray.

"I suppose he has nothing to amuse him but discounting bills with Jews. Does he think I'll pay that?"

"I am sure he thinks no such thing," said she.

"And who does he think will pay it?"

"As far as honesty goes I suppose it won't much matter if it is never paid," said she. "I dare say he got very little of it."

"I suppose it won't much matter either," said the father, "if he goes to prison and rots there. It seems to me that that's the other alternative."

Dr. Stanhope spoke of the custom of his youth. But his daughter, though she had lived so long abroad, was much more completely versed in the ways of the English world. "If the man arrests him," said she, "he must go through the court."

It is thus, thou great family of Sidonia—it is thus that we Gentiles treat thee, when, in our extremest need, thou and thine have aided us with mountains of gold as big as lions—and occasionally with wine-warrants and orders for dozens of dressing-cases.

"What, and become an insolvent?" said the doctor.

"He's that already," said Charlotte, wishing always to get over a difficulty.

"What a condition," said the doctor, "for the son of a clergyman of the Church of England."

"I don't see why clergymen's sons should pay their debts more than other young men," said Charlotte.

"He's had as much from me since he left school as is held sufficient for the eldest son of many a nobleman," said the angry father.

"Well, sir," said Charlotte, "give him another chance."

"What!" said the doctor, "do you mean that I am to pay that Jew?"

"Oh, no! I wouldn't pay him, he must take his chance; and if the worst comes to the worst, Bertie must go abroad. But I want you to be civil to Bertie and let him remain here as long as we stop. He has a plan in his head that may put him on his feet after all."

"Has he any plan for following up his profession?"

"Oh, he'll do that too; but that must follow. He's thinking of getting married."

Just at that moment the door opened, and Bertie came in whistling. The doctor immediately devoted himself to his egg and allowed Bertie to whistle himself round to his sister's side without noticing him.

Charlotte gave a sign to him with her eye, first glancing at her father, and then at the letter, the corner of which peeped out from under the tea-tray. Bertie saw and understood, and with the quiet motion of a cat he abstracted the letter and made himself acquainted with its contents. The doctor, however, had seen him, deep as he appeared to be mersed in his egg-shell, and said in his harshest voice, "Well, sir, do you know that gentleman?"

"Yes, sir," said Bertie. "I have a sort of acquaintance with him, but none that can justify him in troubling you. If you will allow me, sir, I will answer this."

"At any rate I shan't," said the father, and then he added, after a pause, "Is it true, sir, that you owe the man £700?"

"Well," said Bertie, "I think I should be inclined to dispute the amount, if I were in a condition to pay him such of it as I really do owe him."

"Has he your bill for £700?" said the father, speaking very loudly and very angrily.

"Well, I believe he has," said Bertie, "but all the money I ever got from him was £150."

"And what became of the £550?"

"Why, sir, the commission was £100 or so, and I took the remainder in paving-stones and rocking-horses."

"Paving-stones and rocking-horses!" said the doctor. "Where are they?"

"Oh, sir, I suppose they are in London somewhere—but I'll inquire if you wish for them."

"He's an idiot," said the doctor, "and it's sheer folly to waste more money on him. Nothing can save him from ruin," and so saying, the unhappy father walked out of the room.

"Would the governor like to have the paving-stones?" said Bertie to his sister.

"I'll tell you what," said she. "If you don't take care, you will find yourself loose upon the world without even a house over your head; you don't know him as well as I do. He's very angry."

Bertie stroked his big beard, sipped his tea, chatted over his misfortunes in a half-comic, half-serious tone, and ended by promising his sister that he would do his very best to make himself agreeable to the Widow Bold. Then Charlotte followed her father to his own room, softened down his wrath, and persuaded him to say nothing more about the Jew bill discounter, at any rate for a few weeks. He even went so far as to say he would pay the £700, or at any rate settle the bill, if he saw a certainty of his son's securing for himself anything like a decent provision in life. Nothing was said openly between them about poor Eleanor, but the father and the daughter understood each other.

They all met together in the drawing-room at nine o'clock, in perfect good humour with each other, and about that hour Mrs. Bold was announced. She had never been in the house before, though she had of course called, and now she felt it strange to find herself there in her usual evening dress, entering the drawing-room of these strangers in this friendly, unceremonious way, as though she had known them all her life. But in three minutes they made her at home. Charlotte tripped downstairs and took her bonnet from her, and Bertie came to relieve her from her shawl, and the signora smiled on her as she could smile when she chose to be gracious, and the old doctor shook hands with her in a kind benedictory manner that went to her heart at once and made her feel that he must be a good man.

She had not been seated for above five minutes when the door again opened and Mr. Slope was announced. She felt rather surprised, because she was told that nobody was to be there, and it was very evident from the manner of some of them that Mr. Slope was not unexpected. But still there was not much in it. In such invitations a bachelor or two more or less are always spoken of as nobodies, and there was no reason why Mr. Slope should not drink tea at Dr. Stanhope's as well as Eleanor herself. He, however, was very much surprised and not very much gratified at finding that his own embryo spouse made one of the party. He had come there to gratify himself by gazing on Madame Neroni's beauty and listening to and returning her flattery: and though he had not owned as much to himself, he still felt that if he spent the evening as he had intended to do, he might probably not thereby advance his suit with Mrs. Bold.

The signora, who had no idea of a rival, received Mr. Slope with her usual marks of distinction. As he took her hand, she made some confidential communication to him in a low voice, declaring that she had a plan to communicate to him after tea, and was evidently prepared to go on with her work of reducing the chaplain to a state of captivity. Poor Mr. Slope was rather beside himself. He thought that Eleanor could not but have learnt from his demeanour that he was an admirer of her own, and he had also flattered himself that the idea was not unacceptable to her. What would she think of him if he now devoted himself to a married woman!

But Eleanor was not inclined to be severe in her criticisms on him in this respect, and felt no annoyance of any kind, when she found herself seated between Bertie and Charlotte Stanhope. She had no suspicion of Mr. Slope's intentions; she had no suspicion even of the suspicion of other people; but still she felt well-pleased not to have Mr. Slope too near to her.

And she was not ill-pleased to have Bertie Stanhope near her. It was rarely indeed that he failed to make an agreeable impression on strangers. With a bishop indeed who thought much of his own dignity it was possible that he might fail, but hardly with a young and pretty woman. He possessed the tact of becoming instantly intimate with women without giving rise to any fear of impertinence. He had about him somewhat of the propensities of a tame cat. It seemed quite natural that he should be petted, caressed, and treated with familiar good nature, and that in return he should purr, and be sleek and graceful, and above all never show his claws. Like other tame cats, however, he had his claws, and sometimes made them dangerous.

When tea was over, Charlotte went to the open window and declared loudly that the full harvest moon was much too beautiful to be disregarded, and called them all to look at it. To tell the truth there was but one there who cared much about the moon's beauty, and that one was not Charlotte, but she knew how valuable an aid to her purpose the chaste goddess might become, and could easily create a little enthusiasm for the purpose of the moment. Eleanor and Bertie were soon with her. The doctor was now quiet in his arm-chair, and Mrs. Stanhope in hers, both prepared for slumber.

"Are you a Whewellite or a Brewsterite, or a t'othermanite, Mrs. Bold?" said Charlotte, who knew a little about everything, and had read about a third of each of the books to which she alluded.

"Oh!" said Eleanor; "I have not read any of the books, but I feel sure that there is one man in the moon at least, if not more."

"You don't believe in the pulpy gelatinous matter?" said Bertie.

"I heard about that," said Eleanor, "and I really think it's almost wicked to talk in such a manner. How can we argue about God's power in the other stars from the laws which he has given for our rule in this one?"

"How indeed!" said Bertie. "Why shouldn't there be a race of salamanders in Venus? And even if there be nothing but fish in Jupiter, why shouldn't the fish there be as wide awake as the men and women here?"

"That would be saying very little for them," said Charlotte. "I am for Dr. Whewell myself, for I do not think that men and women are worth being repeated in such countless worlds. There may be souls in other stars, but I doubt their having any bodies attached to them. But come, Mrs. Bold, let us put our bonnets on and walk round the close. If we are to discuss sidereal questions, we shall do so much better under the towers of the cathedral than stuck in this narrow window."

Mrs. Bold made no objection, and a party was made to walk out. Charlotte Stanhope well knew the rule as to three being no company, and she had therefore to induce her sister to allow Mr. Slope to accompany them.

"Come, Mr. Slope," she said, "I'm sure you'll join us. We shall be in again in a quarter of an hour, Madeline."

Madeline read in her eye all that she had to say, knew her object, and as she had to depend on her sister for so many of her amusements, she felt that she must yield. It was hard to be left alone while others of her own age walked out to feel the soft influence of the bright night, but it would be harder still to be without the sort of sanction which Charlotte gave to all her flirtations and intrigues. Charlotte's eye told her that she must give up just at present for the good of the family, and so Madeline obeyed.

But Charlotte's eyes said nothing of the sort to Mr. Slope. He had no objection at all to the *tête-à-tête* with the signora which the departure of the other three would allow him, and gently whispered to her, "I shall not leave you alone."

"Oh, yes," said she; "go—pray go, pray go, for my sake. Do not think that I am so selfish. It is understood that nobody is kept within for me. You will understand this too when you know me better. Pray join them, Mr. Slope, but when you come in speak to me for five minutes before you leave us."

Mr. Slope understood that he was to go, and he therefore joined the party in the hall. He would have had no objection at all to this arrangement, if he could have secured Mrs. Bold's arm; but this of course was out of the question. Indeed, his fate was very soon settled, for no sooner had he reached the hall-door than Miss Stanhope put her hand within his arm, and Bertie walked off with Eleanor just as naturally as though she were already his own property.

And so they sauntered forth: first they walked round the close, according to their avowed intent; then they went under the old arched gateway below St. Cuthbert's little church, and then they turned behind the grounds of the bishop's palace, and so on till they came to the bridge just at the edge of the town, from which passers-by can look down into the gardens of Hiram's Hospital; and here Charlotte and Mr. Slope, who were in advance, stopped till the other two came up to them. Mr. Slope knew that the gable-ends and old brick chimneys which stood up so prettily in the moonlight were those of Mr. Harding's late abode, and would not have stopped on such a spot, in such company, if he could have avoided it; but Miss Stanhope would not take the hint which he tried to give.

"This is a very pretty place, Mrs. Bold," said Charlotte; "by far the prettiest place near Barchester. I wonder your father gave it up."

It was a very pretty place, and now by the deceitful light of the moon looked twice larger, twice prettier, twice more antiquely picturesque than it would have done in truth-telling daylight. Who does not know the air of complex multiplicity and the mysterious interesting grace which the moon always lends to old gabled buildings half-surrounded, as was the hospital, by fine trees! As seen from the bridge on the night of which we are speaking, Mr. Harding's late abode did look very lovely, and though Eleanor did not grieve at her father's having left it, she felt at the moment an intense wish that he might be allowed to return.

"He is going to return to it almost immediately, is he not?" asked Bertie.

Eleanor made no immediate reply. Many such a question passes unanswered without the notice of the questioner, but such was not now the case. They all remained silent as though expecting her to reply, and after a moment or two, Charlotte said, "I believe it is settled that Mr. Harding returns to the hospital, is it not?"

"I don't think anything about it is settled yet," said Eleanor.

"But it must be a matter of course," said Bertie; "that is, if your father wishes it. Who else on earth could hold it after what has occurred?"

Eleanor quietly made her companion understand that the matter was one which she could not discuss in the present company, and then they passed on. Charlotte said she would go a short way up the hill out of the town so as to look back upon the towers of the cathedral, and as Eleanor leant upon Bertie's arm for assistance in the walk, she told him how the matter stood between her father and the bishop.

"And, he," said Bertie, pointing on to Mr. Slope, "what part does he take in it?"

Eleanor explained how Mr. Slope had at first endeavoured to tyrannize over her father, but how he had latterly come round and done all he could to talk the bishop over in Mr. Harding's favour. "But my father," she said, "is hardly inclined to trust him; they all say he is so arrogant to the old clergymen of the city."

"Take my word for it," said Bertie, "your father is right. If I am not very much mistaken, that man is both arrogant and false."

They strolled up to the top of the hill and then returned through the fields by a foot-path which leads by a small wooden bridge, or rather a plank with a rustic rail to it, over the river to the other side of the cathedral from that at which they had started. They had thus walked round the bishop's grounds, through which the river runs, and round the cathedral and adjacent fields, and it was past eleven before they reached the doctor's door.

"It is very late," said Eleanor; "it will be a shame to disturb your mother again at such an hour."

"Oh!" said Charlotte, laughing, "you won't disturb Mamma; I dare say she is in bed by this time, and Madeline would be furious if you did not come in and see her. Come, Bertie, take Mrs. Bold's bonnet from her."

They went upstairs and found the signora alone, reading. She looked somewhat sad and melancholy, but not more so perhaps than was sufficient to excite additional interest in the bosom of Mr. Slope; and she was soon deep in whispered intercourse with that happy gentleman, who was allowed to find a resting-place on her sofa. The signora had a way of whispering that was peculiarly her own, and was exactly the reverse of that which prevails among great tragedians. The great tragedian hisses out a positive whisper, made with bated breath, and produced by inarticulated tongue-formed sounds, but yet he is audible through the whole house. The signora, however, used no hisses and produced all her words in a clear, silver tone, but they could only be heard by the ear into which they were poured.

Charlotte hurried and scurried about the room hither and thither, doing, or pretending to do many things; then, saying something about seeing her mother, ran upstairs. Eleanor was thus left alone with Bertie, and she hardly felt an hour fly by her. To give Bertie his due credit, he could not have played his cards better. He did not make love to her, nor sigh, nor look languishing, but he was amusing and familiar, yet respectful; and when he left Eleanor at her own door at one o'clock, which he did by the by with the assistance of the now jealous Slope, she thought that he was one of the most agreeable men and the Stanhopes decidedly the most agreeable family that she had ever met.

CHAPTER XX

MR. ARABIN

The Rev. Francis Arabin, fellow of Lazarus, late professor of poetry at Oxford, and present vicar of St. Ewold, in the diocese of Barchester, must now be introduced personally to the reader. He is worthy of a new volume, and as he will fill a conspicuous place in it, it is desirable that he should be made to stand before the reader's eye by the aid of such portraiture as the author is able to produce.

It is to be regretted that no mental method of daguerreotype or photography has yet been discovered by which the characters of men can be reduced to writing and put into grammatical language with an unerring precision of truthful description. How often does the novelist feel, ay, and the historian also and the biographer, that he has conceived within his mind and accurately depicted on the tablet of his brain the full character and personage of a man, and that nevertheless, when he flies to pen and ink to perpetuate the portrait, his words forsake, elude, disappoint, and play the deuce with him, till at the end of a dozen pages the man described has no more resemblance to the man conceived than the sign-board at the corner of the street has to the Duke of Cambridge.

And yet such mechanical descriptive skill would hardly give more satisfaction to the reader than the skill of the photographer does to the anxious mother desirous to possess an absolute duplicate of her beloved child. The likeness is indeed true, but it is a dull, dead, unfeeling, inauspicious likeness. The face is indeed there, and those looking at it will know at once whose image it is, but the owner of the face will not be proud of the resemblance.

There is no royal road to learning, no short cut to the acquirement of any valuable art. Let photographers and daguerreotypers do what they will, and improve as they may with further skill on that which skill has already done, they will never achieve a portrait of the human face divine. Let biographers, novelists, and the rest of us groan as we may under the burdens which we so often feel too heavy for our shoulders; we must either bear them up like men, or own ourselves too weak for the work we have undertaken. There is no way of writing well and also of writing easily.

Labor omnia vincit improbus. Such should be the chosen motto of every labourer, and it may be that labour, if adequately enduring, may suffice at last to produce even some not untrue resemblance of the Rev. Francis Arabin.

Of his doings in the world, and of the sort of fame which he has achieved, enough has been already said. It has also been said that he is forty years of age, and still unmarried. He was the younger son of a country gentleman of small fortune in the north of England.

At an early age he went to Winchester, and was intended by his father for New College; but though studious as a boy, he was not studious within the prescribed limits, and at the age of eighteen he left school with a character for talent, but without a scholarship. All that he had obtained, over and above the advantage of his character, was a gold medal for English verse, and hence was derived a strong presumption on the part of his friends that he was destined to add another name to the imperishable list of English poets.

From Winchester he went to Oxford, and was entered as a commoner at Balliol. Here his special career very soon commenced. He utterly eschewed the society of fast men, gave no wine-parties, kept no horses, rowed no boats, joined no rows, and was the pride of his college tutor. Such at least was his career till he had taken his little go, and then he commenced a course of action which, though not less creditable to himself as a man, was hardly so much to the taste of the tutor. He became a member of a vigorous debating society, and rendered himself remarkable there for humorous energy. Though always in earnest, yet his earnestness was always droll. To be true in his ideas, unanswerable in his syllogisms, and just in his aspirations was not enough for him. He had failed, failed in his own opinion as well as that of others when others came to know him, if he could not reduce the arguments of his opponents to an absurdity and conquer both by wit and reason. To say that his object was ever to raise a laugh would be most untrue. He hated such common and unnecessary evidence of satisfaction on the part of his hearers. A joke that required to be laughed at was, with him, not worth uttering. He could appreciate by a keener sense than that of his ears the success of his wit, and would see in the eyes of his auditors whether or no he was understood and appreciated.

He had been a religious lad before he left school. That is, he had addicted himself to a party in religion, and having done so had received that benefit which most men do who become partisans in such a cause. We are much too apt to look at schism in our church as an unmitigated evil. Moderate schism, if there may be such a thing, at any rate calls attention to the subject, draws in supporters who would otherwise have been inattentive to the matter, and teaches men to think upon religion. How great an amount of good of this description has followed that movement in the Church of England which commenced with the publication of Froude's Remains!

As a boy young Arabin took up the cudgels on the side of the Tractarians, and at Oxford he sat for a while at the feet of the great Newman. To this cause he lent all his faculties. For it he concocted verses, for it he made speeches, for it he scintillated the brightest sparks of his quiet wit. For it he ate and drank and dressed and had his being. In due process of time he took his degree and wrote himself B.A., but he did not do so with any remarkable amount of academical éclat. He had occupied himself too much with High Church matters and the polemics, politics, and outward demonstrations usually concurrent with High Churchmanship to devote himself with sufficient vigour to the acquisition of a double first. He was not a double first, nor even a first class man, but he revenged himself on the university by putting firsts and double firsts out of fashion for the year and laughing down a species of pedantry which, at the age of twenty-three, leaves no room in a man's mind for graver subjects than conic sections or Greek accents.

Greek accents, however, and conic sections were esteemed necessaries at Balliol, and there was no admittance there for Mr. Arabin within the list of its fellows. Lazarus, however, the richest and most comfortable abode of Oxford dons, opened its bosom to the young champion of a church militant. Mr. Arabin was ordained, and became a fellow soon after taking his degree, and shortly after that was chosen professor of poetry.

And now came the moment of his great danger. After many mental struggles, and an agony of doubt which may be well surmised, the great prophet of the Tractarians confessed himself a Roman Catholic. Mr. Newman left the Church of England and with him carried many a waverer. He did not carry off Mr. Arabin, but the escape which that gentleman had was a very narrow one. He left Oxford for awhile that he might meditate in complete peace on the step which appeared to him to be all but unavoidable, and shut himself up in a little village on the sea-shore of one of our remotest counties, that he might learn by communing with his own soul whether or no he could with a safe conscience remain within the pale of his mother church.

Things would have gone badly with him there had he been left entirely to himself. Everything was against him: all his worldly interests required him to remain a Protestant, and he looked on his worldly interests as a legion of foes, to get the better of whom was a point of extremest honour. In his then state of ecstatic agony such a conquest would have cost him little; he could easily have thrown away all his livelihood; but it cost him much to get over the idea that by choosing the Church of England he should be open in his own mind to the charge that he had been led to such a choice by unworthy motives. Then his heart was against him: he loved with a strong and eager love the man who had hitherto been his guide, and yearned to follow his footsteps. His tastes were against him: the ceremonies and pomps of the Church of Rome, their august feasts and solemn fasts, invited his imagination and pleased his eye. His flesh was against him: how great an aid would it be to a poor, weak, wavering man to be constrained to high moral duties, self-denial, obedience, and chastity by laws which were certain in their enactments, and not to be broken without loud, palpable, unmistakable sin! Then his faith was against him: he required to believe so much; panted so eagerly to give signs of his belief; deemed it so insufficient to wash himself simply in the waters of Jordan; that some great deed, such as that of forsaking everything for a true Church, had for him allurements almost past withstanding.

Mr. Arabin was at this time a very young man, and when he left Oxford for his far retreat was much too confident in his powers of fence, and too apt to look down on the ordinary sense of ordinary people, to expect aid in the battle that he had to fight from any chance inhabitants of the spot which he had selected. But Providence was good to him; there, in that all but desolate place, on the storm-beat shore of that distant sea, he met one who gradually calmed his mind, quieted his imagination, and taught him something of a Christian's duty. When Mr. Arabin left Oxford, he was inclined to look upon the rural clergymen of most English parishes almost with contempt. It was his ambition, should he remain within the fold of their church, to do somewhat towards redeeming and rectifying their inferiority and to assist in infusing energy and faith into the hearts of Christian ministers, who were, as he thought, too often satisfied to go through life without much show of either.

And yet it was from such a one that Mr. Arabin in his extremest need received that aid which he so much required. It was from the poor curate of a small Cornish parish that he first learnt to know that the highest laws for the governance of a Christian's duty must act from within and not from without; that no man can become a serviceable servant solely by obedience to written edicts; and that the safety which he was about to seek within the gates of Rome was no other than the selfish freedom from personal danger which the bad soldier attempts to gain who counterfeits illness on the eve of battle.

Mr. Arabin returned to Oxford a humbler but a better and a happier man, and from that time forth he put his shoulder to the wheel as a clergyman of the Church for which he had been educated. The intercourse of those among whom he familiarly lived kept him staunch to the principles of that system of the Church to which he had always belonged. Since his severance from Mr. Newman, no one had had so strong an influence over him as the head of his college. During the time of his expected apostasy Dr. Gwynne had not felt much predisposition in favour of the young fellow. Though a High Churchman himself within moderate limits, Dr. Gwynne felt no sympathy with men who could not satisfy their faiths with the Thirty-nine Articles. He regarded the enthusiasm of such as Newman as a state of mind more nearly allied to madness than to religion, and when he saw it evinced by very young men, he was inclined to attribute a good deal of it to vanity. Dr. Gwynne himself, though a religious man, was also a thoroughly practical man of the world, and he regarded with no favourable eye the tenets of anyone who looked on the two things as incompatible. When he found that Mr. Arabin was a half Roman, he began to regret all he had done towards bestowing a fellowship on so unworthy a recipient; and when again he learnt that Mr. Arabin would probably complete his journey to Rome, he regarded with some satisfaction the fact that in such case the fellowship would be again vacant.

When, however, Mr. Arabin returned and professed himself a confirmed Protestant, the Master of Lazarus again opened his arms to him, and gradually he became the pet of the college. For some little time he was saturnine, silent, and unwilling to take any prominent part in university broils, but gradually his mind recovered, or rather made its tone, and he became known as a man always ready at a moment's notice to take up the cudgels in opposition to anything that savoured of an evangelical bearing. He was great in sermons, great on platforms, great at after-dinner conversations, and always pleasant as well as great. He took delight in elections, served on committees, opposed tooth and nail all projects of university reform, and talked jovially over his glass of port of the ruin to be anticipated by the Church and of the sacrilege daily committed by the Whigs. The ordeal through which he had gone in resisting the blandishments of the lady of Rome had certainly done much towards the strengthening of his character. Although in small and outward matters he was self-confident enough, nevertheless in things affecting the inner man he aimed at a humility of spirit which would never have been attractive to him but for that visit to the coast of Cornwall. This visit he now repeated every year.

Such is an interior view of Mr. Arabin at the time when he accepted the living of St. Ewold. Exteriorly, he was not a remarkable person. He was above the middle height, well-made, and very active. His hair, which had been jet black, was now tinged with gray, but his face bore no sign of years. It would perhaps be wrong to say that he was handsome, but his face was nevertheless pleasant to look upon. The cheek-bones were rather too high for beauty, and the formation of the forehead too massive and heavy: but the eyes, nose, and mouth were perfect. There was a continual play of lambent fire about his eyes, which gave promise of either pathos or humour whenever he essayed to speak, and that promise was rarely broken. There was a gentle play about his mouth which declared that his wit never descended to sarcasm, and that there was no ill-nature in his repartee.

Mr. Arabin was a popular man among women, but more so as a general than a special favourite. Living as a fellow at Oxford, marriage with him had been out of the question, and it may be doubted whether he had ever allowed his heart to be touched. Though belonging to a church in which celibacy is not the required lot of its ministers, he had come to regard himself as one of those clergymen to whom to be a bachelor is almost a necessity. He had never looked for parochial duty, and his career at Oxford was utterly incompatible with such domestic joys as a wife and nursery. He looked on women, therefore, in the same light that one sees them regarded by many Romish priests. He liked to have near him that which was pretty and amusing, but women generally were little more to him than children. He talked to them without putting out all his powers, and listened to them without any idea that what he should hear from them could either actuate his conduct or influence his opinion.

Such was Mr. Arabin, the new vicar of St. Ewold, who is going to stay with the Grantlys at Plumstead Episcopi.

Mr. Arabin reached Plumstead the day before Mr. Harding and Eleanor, and the Grantly family were thus enabled to make his acquaintance and discuss his qualifications before the arrival of the other guests. Griselda was surprised to find that he looked so young, but she told Florinda her younger sister, when they had retired for the night, that he did not talk at all like a young man: and she decided with the authority that seventeen has over sixteen that he was not at all nice, although his eyes were lovely. As usual, sixteen implicitly acceded to the dictum of seventeen in such a matter, and said that he certainly was not nice. They then branched off on the relative merits of other clerical bachelors in the vicinity, and both determined without any feeling of jealousy between them that a certain Rev. Augustus Green was by many degrees the most estimable of the lot. The gentleman in question had certainly much in his favour, as, having a comfortable allowance from his father, he could devote the whole proceeds of his curacy to violet gloves and unexceptionable neck ties. Having thus fixedly resolved that the new-comer had nothing about him to shake the pre-eminence of the exalted Green, the two girls went to sleep in each other's arms, contented with themselves and the world.

Mrs. Grantly at first sight came to much the same conclusion about her husband's favourite as her daughters had done, though, in seeking to measure his relative value, she did not compare him to Mr. Green; indeed, she made no comparison by name between him and anyone else; but she remarked to her husband that one person's swans were very often another person's geese, thereby clearly showing that Mr. Arabin had not yet proved his qualifications in swanhood to her satisfaction.

"Well, Susan," said he, rather offended at hearing his friend spoken of so disrespectfully, "if you take Mr. Arabin for a goose, I cannot say that I think very highly of your discrimination."

"A goose! No, of course, he's not a goose. I've no doubt he's a very clever man. But you're so matter-of-fact, Archdeacon, when it suits your purpose, that one can't trust oneself to any *façon de parler*. I've no doubt Mr. Arabin is a very valuable man—at Oxford—and that he'll be a good vicar at St. Ewold. All I mean is that, having passed one evening with him, I don't find him to be absolutely a paragon. In the first place, if I am not mistaken, he is a little inclined to be conceited."

"Of all the men that I know intimately," said the archdeacon, "Arabin is, in my opinion, the most free from any taint of self-conceit. His fault is that he's too diffident."

"Perhaps so," said the lady; "only I must own I did not find it out this evening."

Nothing further was said about him. Dr. Grantly thought that his wife was abusing Mr. Arabin merely because he had praised him, and Mrs. Grantly knew that it was useless arguing for or against any person in favour of or in opposition to whom the archdeacon had already pronounced a strong opinion.

In truth, they were both right. Mr. Arabin was a diffident man in social intercourse with those whom he did not intimately know; when placed in situations which it was his business to fill, and discussing matters with which it was his duty to be conversant, Mr. Arabin was from habit brazen-faced enough. When standing on a platform in Exeter Hall, no man would be less mazed than he by the eyes of the crowd before him, for such was the work which his profession had called on him to perform; but he shrank from a strong expression of opinion in general society, and his doing so not uncommonly made it appear that he considered the company not worth the trouble of his energy. He was averse to dictate when the place did not seem to him to justify dictation, and as those subjects on which people wished to hear him speak were such as he was accustomed to treat with decision, he generally shunned the traps there were laid to allure him into discussion, and, by doing so, not infrequently subjected himself to such charges as those brought against him by Mrs. Grantly.

Mr. Arabin, as he sat at his open window, enjoying the delicious moonlight and gazing at the gray towers of the church, which stood almost within the rectory grounds, little dreamed that he was the subject of so many friendly or unfriendly criticisms. Considering how much we are all given to discuss the characters of others, and discuss them often not in the strictest spirit of charity, it is singular how little we are inclined to think that others can speak ill-naturedly of us, and how angry and hurt we are when proof reaches us that they have done so. It is hardly too much to say that we all of us occasionally speak of our dearest friends in a manner in which those dearest friends would very little like to hear themselves mentioned, and that we nevertheless expect that our dearest friends shall invariably speak of us as though they were blind to all our faults, but keenly alive to every shade of our virtues.

It did not occur to Mr. Arabin that he was spoken of at all. It seemed to him, when he compared himself with his host, that he was a person of so little consequence to any, that he was worth no one's words or thoughts. He was utterly alone in the world as regarded domestic ties and those inner familiar relations which are hardly possible between others than husbands and wives, parents and children, or brothers and sisters. He had often discussed with himself the necessity of such bonds for a man's happiness in this world, and had generally satisfied himself with the answer that happiness in this world is not a necessity. Herein he deceived himself, or rather tried to do so. He, like others, yearned for the enjoyment of whatever he saw enjoyable, and though he attempted, with the modern stoicism of so many Christians, to make himself believe that joy and sorrow were matters which here should be held as perfectly indifferent, these things were not indifferent to him. He was tired of his Oxford rooms and his college life. He regarded the wife and children of his friend with something like envy; he all but coveted the pleasant drawing-room, with its pretty windows opening on to lawns and flower-beds, the apparel of the comfortable house, and—above all—the air of home which encompassed it all.

It will be said that no time can have been so fitted for such desires on his part as this, when he had just possessed himself of a country parish, of a living among fields and gardens, of a house which a wife would grace. It is true there was a difference between the opulence of Plumstead and the modest economy of St. Ewold, but surely Mr. Arabin was not a man to sigh after wealth! Of all men, his friends would have unanimously declared he was the last to do so. But how little our friends know us! In his period of stoical rejection of this world's happiness, he had cast from him as utter dross all anxiety as to fortune. He had, as it were, proclaimed himself to be indifferent to promotion, and those who chiefly admired his talents, and would mainly have exerted themselves to secure to them their deserved reward, had taken him at his word. And now, if the truth must out, he felt himself disappointed—disappointed not by them but by himself. The daydream of his youth was over, and at the age of forty he felt that he was not fit to work in the spirit of an apostle. He had mistaken himself, and learned his mistake when it was past remedy. He had professed himself indifferent to mitres and diaconal residences, to rich livings and pleasant glebes, and now he had to own to himself that he was sighing for the good things of other men on whom, in his pride, he had ventured to look down.

Not for wealth, in its vulgar sense, had he ever sighed; not for the enjoyment of rich things had he ever longed; but for the allotted share of worldly bliss which a wife, and children, and happy home could give him, for that usual amount of comfort which he had ventured to reject as unnecessary for him, he did now feel that he would have been wiser to have searched.

He knew that his talents, his position, and his friends would have won for him promotion, had he put himself in the way of winning it. Instead of doing so, he had allowed himself to be persuaded to accept a living which would give him an income of some £300 a year should he, by marrying, throw up his fellowship. Such, at the age of forty, was the worldly result of labour which the world had chosen to regard as successful. The world also thought that Mr. Arabin was, in his own estimation, sufficiently paid. Alas! Alas! The world was mistaken, and Mr. Arabin was beginning to ascertain that such was the case.

And here may I beg the reader not to be hard in his judgement upon this man. Is not the state at which he has arrived the natural result of efforts to reach that which is not the condition of humanity? Is not modern stoicism, built though it be on Christianity, as great an outrage on human nature as was the stoicism of the ancients? The philosophy of Zeno was built on true laws, but on true laws misunderstood and therefore misapplied. It is the same with our Stoics here, who would teach us that wealth and worldly comfort and happiness on earth are not worth the search. Alas, for a doctrine which can find no believing pupils and no true teachers!

The case of Mr. Arabin was the more singular, as he belonged to a branch of the Church of England well inclined to regard its temporalities with avowed favour, and had habitually lived with men who were accustomed to much worldly comfort. But such was his idiosyncrasy that these very facts had produced within him, in early life, a state of mind that was not natural to him. He was content to be a High Churchman, if he could be so on principles of his own and could strike out a course showing a marked difference from those with whom he consorted. He was ready to be a partisan as long as he was allowed to have a course of action and of thought unlike that of his party. His party had indulged him, and he began to feel that his party was right and himself wrong, just when such a conviction was too late to be of service to him. He discovered, when such discovery was no longer serviceable, that it would have been worth his while to have worked for the usual pay assigned to work in this world and have earned a wife and children, with a carriage for them to sit in; to have earned a pleasant dining-room, in which his friends could drink his wine, and the power of walking up the high street of his country town, with the knowledge that all its tradesmen would have gladly welcomed him within their doors. Other men arrived at those convictions in their start in life and so worked up to them. To him they had come when they were too late to be of use.

It has been said that Mr. Arabin was a man of pleasantry, and it may be thought that such a state of mind as that described would be antagonistic to humour. But surely such is not the case. Wit is the outward mental casing of the man, and has no more to do with the inner mind of thoughts and feelings than have the rich brocaded garments of the priest at the altar with the asceticism of the anchorite below them, whose skin is tormented with sackcloth and whose body is half-flayed with rods. Nay, will not such a one often rejoice more than any other in the rich show of his outer apparel? Will it not be food for his pride to feel that he groans inwardly while he shines outwardly? So it is with the mental efforts which men make. Those which they show forth daily to the world are often the opposites of the inner workings of the spirit.

In the archdeacon's drawing-room, Mr. Arabin had sparkled with his usual unaffected brilliancy, but when he retired to his bedroom, he sat there sad, at his open window, repining within himself that he also had no wife, no bairns, no soft sward of lawn duly mown for him to lie on, no herd of attendant curates, no bowings from the banker's clerks, no rich rectory. That apostleship that he had thought of had evaded his grasp, and he was now only vicar of St. Ewold's, with a taste for a mitre. Truly he had fallen between two stools.

CHAPTER XXI

ST. EWOLD'S PARSONAGE

When Mr. Harding and Mrs. Bold reached the rectory on the following morning, the archdeacon and his friend were at St. Ewold's. They had gone over that the new vicar might inspect his church and be introduced to the squire, and were not expected back before dinner. Mr. Harding rambled out by himself and strolled, as was his wont at Plumstead, about the lawn and round the church; and as he did so, the two sisters naturally fell into conversation about Barchester.

There was not much sisterly confidence between them. Mrs. Grantly was ten years older than Eleanor, and had been married while Eleanor was yet a child. They had never, therefore, poured into each other's ears their hopes and loves; and now that one was a wife and the other a widow, it was not probable that they would begin to do so. They lived too much asunder to be able to fall into that kind of intercourse which makes confidence between sisters almost a necessity; moreover, that which is so easy at eighteen is often very difficult at twenty-eight. Mrs. Grantly knew this, and did not, therefore, expect confidence from her sister; yet she longed to ask her whether in real truth Mr. Slope was agreeable to her.

It was by no means difficult to turn the conversation to Mr. Slope. That gentleman had become so famous at Barchester, had so much to do with all clergymen connected with the city, and was so specially concerned in the affairs of Mr. Harding, that it would have been odd if Mr. Harding's daughters had not talked about him. Mrs. Grantly was soon abusing him, which she did with her whole heart, and Mrs. Bold was nearly as eager to defend him. She positively disliked the man, would have been delighted to learn that he had taken himself off so that she should never see him again, had indeed almost a fear of him, and yet she constantly found herself taking his part. The abuse of other people, and abuse of a nature that she felt to be unjust, imposed this necessity on her, and at last made Mr. Slope's defence an habitual course of argument with her.

From Mr. Slope the conversation turned to the Stanhopes, and Mrs. Grantly was listening with some interest to Eleanor's account of the family, when it dropped out that Mr. Slope made one of the party.

"What!" said the lady of the rectory. "Was Mr. Slope there too?"

Eleanor merely replied that such had been the case.

"Why, Eleanor, he must be very fond of you, I think; he seems to follow you everywhere."

Even this did not open Eleanor's eyes. She merely laughed, and said that she imagined Mr. Slope found other attraction at Dr. Stanhope's. And so they parted. Mrs. Grantly felt quite convinced that the odious match would take place, and Mrs. Bold as convinced that that unfortunate chaplain, disagreeable as he must be allowed to be, was more sinned against than sinning.

The archdeacon of course heard before dinner that Eleanor had remained the day before in Barchester with the view of meeting Mr. Slope, and that she had so met him. He remembered how she had positively stated that there were to be no guests at the Stanhopes, and he did not hesitate to accuse her of deceit. Moreover, the fact, or rather presumed fact, of her being deceitful on such a matter spoke but too plainly in evidence against her as to her imputed crime of receiving Mr. Slope as a lover.

"I am afraid that anything we can do will be too late," said the archdeacon. "I own I am fairly surprised. I never liked your sister's taste with regard to men, but still I did not give her credit for—ugh!"

"And so soon, too," said Mrs. Grantly, who thought more, perhaps, of her sister's indecorum in having a lover before she had put off her weeds than her bad taste in having such a lover as Mr. Slope.

"Well, my dear, I shall be sorry to be harsh, or to do anything that can hurt your father; but, positively, neither that man nor his wife shall come within my doors."

Mrs. Grantly sighed, and then attempted to console herself and her lord by remarking that, after all, the thing was not accomplished yet. Now that Eleanor was at Plumstead, much might be done to wean her from her fatal passion. Poor Eleanor!

The evening passed off without anything to make it remarkable. Mr. Arabin discussed the parish of St. Ewold with the archdeacon, and Mrs. Grantly and Mr. Harding, who knew the personages of the parish, joined in. Eleanor also knew them, but she said little. Mr. Arabin did not apparently take much notice of her, and she was not in a humour to receive at that time with any special grace any special favourite of her brother-in-law. Her first idea on reaching her bedroom was that a much pleasanter family party might be met at Dr. Stanhope's than at the rectory. She began to think that she was getting tired of clergymen and their respectable, humdrum, wearisome mode of living, and that after all, people in the outer world, who had lived in Italy, London, or elsewhere, need not necessarily be regarded as atrocious and abominable. The Stanhopes, she had thought, were a giddy, thoughtless, extravagant set of people, but she had seen nothing wrong about them and had, on the other hand, found that they thoroughly knew how to make their house agreeable. It was a thousand pities, she thought, that the archdeacon should not have a little of the same *savoir vivre*. Mr. Arabin, as we have said, did not apparently take much notice of her, but yet he did not go to bed without feeling that he had been in company with a very pretty woman; and as is the case with most bachelors, and some married men, regarded the prospect of his month's visit at Plumstead in a pleasanter light when he learnt that a very pretty woman was to share it with him.

Before they all retired it was settled that the whole party should drive over on the following day to inspect the parsonage at St. Ewold. The three clergymen were to discuss dilapidations, and the two ladies were to lend their assistance in suggesting such changes as might be necessary for a bachelor's abode.

Accordingly, soon after breakfast the carriage was at the door. There was only room for four inside, and the archdeacon got upon the box. Eleanor found herself opposite to Mr. Arabin, and was, therefore, in a manner forced into conversation with him. They were soon on comfortable terms together, and had she thought about it, she would have thought that, in spite of his black cloth, Mr. Arabin would not have been a bad addition to the Stanhope family party.

Now that the archdeacon was away they could all trifle. Mr. Harding began by telling them in the most innocent manner imaginable an old legend about Mr. Arabin's new parish. There was, he said, in days of yore an illustrious priestess of St. Ewold, famed through the whole country for curing all manner of diseases. She had a well, as all priestesses have ever had, which well was extant to this day, and shared in the minds of many of the people the sanctity which belonged to the consecrated ground of the parish church. Mr. Arabin declared that he should look on such tenets on the part of his parishioners as anything but orthodox. And Mrs. Grantly replied that she so entirely disagreed with him as to think that no parish was in a proper state that had not its priestess as well as its priest. "The duties are never well done," said she, "unless they are so divided."

"I suppose, Papa," said Eleanor, "that in the olden times the priestess bore all the sway herself. Mr. Arabin, perhaps, thinks that such might be too much the case now if a sacred lady were admitted within the parish."

"I think, at any rate," said he, "that it is safer to run no such risk. No priestly pride has ever exceeded that of sacerdotal females. A very lowly curate I might, perhaps, essay to rule, but a curatess would be sure to get the better of me."

"There are certainly examples of such accidents happening," said Mrs. Grantly. "They do say that there is a priestess at Barchester who is very imperious in all things touching the altar. Perhaps the fear of such a fate as that is before your eyes."

When they were joined by the archdeacon on the gravel before the vicarage, they descended again to grave dullness. Not that Archdeacon Grantly was a dull man, but his frolic humours were of a cumbrous kind, and his wit, when he was witty, did not generally extend itself to his auditors. On the present occasion he was soon making speeches about wounded roofs and walls, which he declared to be in want of some surgeon's art. There was not a partition that he did not tap, nor a block of chimneys that he did not narrowly examine; all water-pipes, flues, cisterns, and sewers underwent an investigation; he even descended, in the care of his friend, so far as to bore sundry boards in the floors with a bradawl.

Mr. Arabin accompanied him through the rooms, trying to look wise in such domestic matters, and the other three also followed. Mrs. Grantly showed that she had not herself been priestess of a parish twenty years for nothing, and examined the bells and window-panes in a very knowing way.

"You will, at any rate, have a beautiful prospect out of your own window, if this is to be your private sanctum," said Eleanor. She was standing at the lattice of a little room upstairs, from which the view certainly was very lovely. It was from the back of the vicarage, and there was nothing to interrupt the eye between the house and the glorious gray pile of the cathedral. The intermediate ground, however, was beautifully studded with timber. In the immediate foreground ran the little river which afterwards skirted the city, and, just to the right of the cathedral, the pointed gables and chimneys of Hiram's Hospital peeped out of the elms which encompass it.

"Yes," said he, joining her. "I shall have a beautifully complete view of my adversaries. I shall sit down before the hostile town and fire away at them at a very pleasant distance. I shall just be able to lodge a shot in the hospital, should the enemy ever get possession of it, and as for the palace, I have it within full range."

"I never saw anything like you clergymen," said Eleanor; "You are always thinking of fighting each other."

"Either that," said he, "or else supporting each other. The pity is that we cannot do the one without the other. But are we not here to fight? Is not ours a church militant? What is all our work but fighting, and hard fighting, if it be well done?"

"But not with each other."

"That's as it may be. The same complaint which you make of me for battling with another clergyman of our own church, the Mohammedan would make against me for battling with the error of a priest of Rome. Yet, surely, you would not be inclined to say that I should be wrong to do battle with such as him. A pagan, too, with his multiplicity of gods, would think it equally odd that the Christian and the Mohammedan should disagree."

"Ah! But you wage your wars about trifles so bitterly."

"Wars about trifles," said he, "are always bitter, especially among neighbours. When the differences are great, and the parties comparative strangers, men quarrel with courtesy. What combatants are ever so eager as two brothers?"

"But do not such contentions bring scandal on the church?"

"More scandal would fall on the church if there were no such contentions. We have but one way to avoid them—by that of acknowledging a common head of our church, whose word on all points of doctrine shall be authoritative. Such a termination of our difficulties is alluring enough. It has charms which are irresistible to many, and all but irresistible, I own, to me."

"You speak now of the Church of Rome?" said Eleanor.

"No," said he, "not necessarily of the Church of Rome; but of a church with a head. Had it pleased God to vouchsafe to us such a church our path would have been easy. But easy paths have not been thought good for us." He paused and stood silent for awhile, thinking of the time when he had so nearly sacrificed all he had, his powers of mind, his free agency, the fresh running waters of his mind's fountain, his very inner self, for an easy path in which no fighting would be needed; and then he continued: "What you say is partly true: our contentions do bring on us some scandal. The outer world, though it constantly reviles us for our human infirmities and throws in our teeth the fact that being clergymen we are still no more than men, demands of us that we should do our work with godlike perfection. There is nothing god-like about us: we differ from each other with the acerbity common to man; we triumph over each other with human frailty; we allow differences on subjects of divine origin to produce among us antipathies and enmities which are anything but divine. This is all true. But what would you have in place of it? There is no infallible head for a church on earth. This dream of believing man has been tried, and we see in Italy and in Spain what has come of it. Grant that there are and have been no bickerings within the pale of the Pope's Church. Such an assumption would be utterly untrue, but let us grant it, and then let us say which church has incurred the heavier scandals."

There was a quiet earnestness about Mr. Arabin, as he half-acknowledged and half-defended himself from the charge brought against him, which surprised Eleanor. She had been used all her life to listen to clerical discussion, but the points at issue between the disputants had so seldom been of more than temporal significance as to have left on her mind no feeling of reverence for such subjects. There had always been a hard worldly leaven of the love either of income or of power in the strains she had heard; there had been no panting for the truth; no aspirations after religious purity. It had always been taken for granted by those around her that they were indubitably right; that there was no ground for doubt; that the hard uphill work of ascertaining what the duty of a clergyman should be had been already accomplished in full; and that what remained for an active militant parson to do was to hold his own against all comers. Her father, it is true, was an exception to this, but then he was so essentially anti-militant in all things that she classed him in her own mind apart from all others. She had never argued the matter within herself, or considered whether this common tone was or was not faulty; but she was sick of it without knowing that she was so. And now she found to her surprise, and not without a certain pleasurable excitement, that this new-comer among them spoke in a manner very different from that to which she was accustomed.

"It is so easy to condemn," said he, continuing the thread of his thoughts. "I know no life that must be so delicious as that of a writer for newspapers, or a leading member of the opposition—to thunder forth accusations against men in power; to show up the worst side of everything that is produced; to pick holes in every coat; to be indignant, sarcastic, jocose, moral, or supercilious; to damn with faint praise, or crush with open calumny! What can be so easy as this when the critic has to be responsible for nothing? You condemn what I do, but put yourself in my position and do the reverse, and then see if I cannot condemn you."

"Oh, Mr. Arabin, I do not condemn you."

"Pardon me, you do, Mrs. Bold—you as one of the world; you are now the opposition member; you are now composing your leading article, and well and bitterly you do it. 'Let dogs delight to bark and bite'—you fitly begin with an elegant quotation—'but if we are to have a church at all, in heaven's name let the pastors who preside over it keep their hands from each other's throats. Lawyers can live without befouling each other's names; doctors do not fight duels. Why is it that clergymen alone should indulge themselves in such unrestrained liberty of abuse against each other?' and so you go on reviling us for our ungodly quarrels, our sectarian propensities, and scandalous differences. It will, however, give you no trouble to write another article next week in which we, or some of us, shall be twitted with an unseemly apathy in matters of our vocation. It will not fall on you to reconcile the discrepancy; your readers will never ask you how the poor parson is to be urgent in season and out of season and yet never come in contact with men who think widely differently from him. You, when you condemn this foreign treaty, or that official arrangement, will have to incur no blame for the graver faults of any different measure. It is so easy to condemn—and so pleasant too, for eulogy charms no listeners as detraction does."

Eleanor only half-followed him in his raillery, but she caught his meaning. "I know I ought to apologize for presuming to criticize you," she said, "but I was thinking with sorrow of the ill-will that has lately come among us at Barchester, and I spoke more freely than I should have done."

"Peace on earth and goodwill among men, are, like heaven, promises for the future;" said he, following rather his own thoughts than hers. "When that prophecy is accomplished, there will no longer be any need for clergymen."

Here they were interrupted by the archdeacon, whose voice was heard from the cellar shouting to the vicar.

"Arabin, Arabin,"—and then, turning to his wife, who was apparently at his elbow—"where has he gone to? This cellar is perfectly abominable. It would be murder to put a bottle of wine into it till it has been roofed, walled, and floored. How on earth old Goodenough ever got on with it I cannot guess. But then Goodenough never had a glass of wine that any man could drink."

"What is it, Archdeacon?" said the vicar, running downstairs and leaving Eleanor above to her meditations.

"This cellar must be roofed, walled, and floored," repeated the archdeacon. "Now mind what I say, and don't let the architect persuade you that it will do; half of these fellows know nothing about wine. This place as it is now would be damp and cold in winter and hot and muggy in summer. I wouldn't give a straw for the best wine that ever was vinted, after it had lain here a couple of years."

Mr. Arabin assented and promised that the cellar should be reconstructed according to the archdeacon's receipt.

"And, Arabin, look here; was such an attempt at a kitchen grate ever seen?"

"The grate is really very bad," said Mrs. Grantly. "I am sure the priestess won't approve of it, when she is brought home to the scene of her future duties. Really, Mr. Arabin, no priestess accustomed to such an excellent well as that above could put up with such a grate as this."

"If there must be a priestess at St. Ewold's at all, Mrs. Grantly, I think we will leave her to her well and not call down her divine wrath on any of the imperfections rising from our human poverty. However, I own I am amenable to the attractions of a well-cooked dinner, and the grate shall certainly be changed."

By this time the archdeacon had again ascended, and was now in the dining-room. "Arabin," said he, speaking in his usual loud, clear voice and with that tone of dictation which was so common to him, "you must positively alter this dining-room—that is, re-model it altogether. Look here, it is just sixteen feet by fifteen; did any man ever hear of a dining-room of such proportions!" The archdeacon stepped the room long-ways and cross-ways with ponderous steps, as though a certain amount of ecclesiastical dignity could be imparted even to such an occupation as that by the manner of doing it. "Barely sixteen; you may call it a square."

"It would do very well for a round table," suggested the ex-warden.

Now there was something peculiarly unorthodox, in the archdeacon's estimation, in the idea of a round table. He had always been accustomed to a goodly board of decent length, comfortably elongating itself according to the number of the guests, nearly black with perpetual rubbing, and as bright as a mirror. Now round dinner-tables are generally of oak, or else of such new construction as not to have acquired the peculiar hue which was so pleasing to him. He connected them with what he called the nasty newfangled method of leaving a cloth on the table, as though to warn people that they were not to sit long. In his eyes there was something democratic and parvenu in a round table. He imagined that dissenters and calico-printers chiefly used them, and perhaps a few literary lions more conspicuous for their wit than their gentility. He was a little flurried at the idea of such an article being introduced into the diocese by a protégé of his own, and at the instigation of his father-in-law.

"A round dinner-table," said he with some heat, "is the most abominable article of furniture that ever was invented. I hope that Arabin has more taste than to allow such a thing in his house."

Poor Mr. Harding felt himself completely snubbed, and of course said nothing further; but Mr. Arabin, who had yielded submissively in the small matters of the cellar and kitchen grate, found himself obliged to oppose reforms which might be of a nature too expensive for his pocket.

"But it seems to me, Archdeacon, that I can't very well lengthen the room without pulling down the wall, and if I pull down the wall, I must build it up again; then if I throw out a bow on this side, I must do the same on the other, and if I do it for the ground floor, I must carry it up to the floor above. That will be putting a new front to the house and will cost, I suppose, a couple of hundred pounds. The ecclesiastical commissioners will hardly assist me when they hear that my grievance consists in having a dining-room only sixteen feet long."

The archdeacon proceeded to explain that nothing would be easier than adding six feet to the front of the dining-room without touching any other room in the house. Such irregularities of construction in small country-houses were, he said, rather graceful than otherwise, and he offered to pay for the whole thing out of his own pocket if it cost more than forty pounds. Mr. Arabin, however, was firm, and, although the archdeacon fussed and fumed about it, would not give way. Forty pounds, he said, was a matter of serious moment to him, and his friends, if under such circumstances they would be good-natured enough to come to him at all, must put up with the misery of a square room. He was willing to compromise matters by disclaiming any intention of having a round table.

"But," said Mrs. Grantly, "what if the priestess insists on having both the rooms enlarged?"

"The priestess in that case must do it for herself, Mrs. Grantly."

"I have no doubt she will be well able to do so," replied the lady; "to do that and many more wonderful things. I am quite sure that the priestess of St. Ewold, when she does come, won't come empty-handed."

Mr. Arabin, however, did not appear well inclined to enter into speculative expenses on such a chance as this, and therefore any material alterations in the house, the cost of which could not fairly be made to lie at the door either of the ecclesiastical commissioners or of the estate of the late incumbent, were tabooed. With this essential exception, the archdeacon ordered, suggested, and carried all points before him in a manner very much to his own satisfaction. A close observer, had there been one there, might have seen that his wife had been quite as useful in the matter as himself. No one knew better than Mrs. Grantly the appurtenances necessary to a comfortable house. She did not, however, think it necessary to lay claim to any of the glory which her lord and master was so ready to appropriate as his own.

Having gone through their work effectually and systematically, the party returned to Plumstead well satisfied with their expedition.

CHAPTER XXII

THE THORNES OF ULLATHORNE

On the following Sunday Mr. Arabin was to read himself in at his new church. It was agreed at the rectory that the archdeacon should go over with him and assist at the reading desk, and that Mr. Harding should take the archdeacon's duty at Plumstead Church. Mrs. Grantly had her school and her buns to attend to, and professed that she could not be spared, but Mrs. Bold was to accompany them. It was further agreed also that they would lunch at the squire's house and return home after the afternoon service.

Wilfred Thorne, Esq., of Ullathorne, was the squire of St. Ewold's—or, rather, the squire of Ullathorne, for the domain of the modern landlord was of wider notoriety than the fame of the ancient saint. He was a fair specimen of what that race has come to in our days which, a century ago, was, as we are told, fairly represented by Squire Western. If that representation be a true one, few classes of men can have made faster strides in improvement. Mr. Thorne, however, was a man possessed of quite a sufficient number of foibles to lay him open to much ridicule. He was still a bachelor, being about fifty, and was not a little proud of his person. When living at home at Ullathorne, there was not much room for such pride, and there therefore he always looked like a gentleman and like that which he certainly was, the first man in his parish. But during the month or six weeks which he annually spent in London, he tried so hard to look like a great man there also, which he certainly was not, that he was put down as a fool by many at his club. He was a man of considerable literary attainment in a certain way and on certain subjects. His favourite authors were Montaigne and Burton, and he knew more perhaps than any other man in his own county and the next to it of the English essayists of the two last centuries. He possessed complete sets of the Idler, the Spectator, the Tatler, the Guardian, and the Rambler, and would discourse by hours together on the superiority of such publications to anything which has since been produced in our Edinburghs and Quarterlies. He was proficient in all questions of genealogy, and knew enough of almost every gentleman's family in England to say of what blood and lineage were descended all those who had any claim to be considered as possessors of any such luxuries. For blood and lineage he himself had a most profound respect. He counted back his own ancestors to some period long antecedent to the Conquest, and could tell you, if you would listen to him, how it had come to pass that they, like Cedric the Saxon, had been permitted to hold their own among the Norman barons. It was not, according to his showing, on account of any weak complaisance on the part of his family towards their Norman neighbours. Some Ealfried of Ullathorne once fortified his own castle and held out, not only that, but the then existing cathedral of Barchester also, against one Geoffrey De Burgh, in the time of King John; and Mr. Thorne possessed the whole history of the siege written on vellum and illuminated in a most costly manner. It little signified that no one could read the writing, as, had that been possible, no one could have understood the language. Mr. Thorne could, however, give you all the particulars in good English, and had no objection to do so.

It would be unjust to say that he looked down on men whose families were of recent date. He did not do so. He frequently consorted with such, and had chosen many of his friends from among them. But he looked on them as great millionaires are apt to look on those who have small incomes; as men who have Sophocles at their fingers' ends regard those who know nothing of Greek. They might doubtless be good sort of people, entitled to much praise for virtue, very admirable for talent, highly respectable in every way, but they were without the one great good gift. Such was Mr. Thorne's way of thinking on this matter; nothing could atone for the loss of good blood; nothing could neutralize its good effects. Few indeed were now possessed of it, but the possession was on that account the more precious. It was very pleasant to hear Mr. Thorne descant on this matter. Were you in your ignorance to surmise that such a one was of a good family because the head of his family was a baronet of an old date, he would open his eyes with a delightful look of affected surprise, and modestly remind you that baronetcies only dated from James I. He would gently sigh if you spoke of the blood of the Fitzgeralds and De Burghs; would hardly allow the claims of the Howards and Lowthers; and has before now alluded to the Talbots as a family who had hardly yet achieved the full honours of a pedigree.

In speaking once of a wide-spread race whose name had received the honours of three coronets, scions from which sat for various constituencies, some one of whose members had been in almost every cabinet formed during the present century, a brilliant race such as there are few in England, Mr. Thorne had called them all "dirt." He had not intended any disrespect to these men. He admired them in many senses, and allowed them their privileges without envy. He had merely meant to express his feeling that the streams which ran through their veins were not yet purified by time to that perfection, had not become so genuine an ichor, as to be worthy of being called blood in the genealogical sense.

When Mr. Arabin was first introduced to him, Mr. Thorne had immediately suggested that he was one of the Arabins of Uphill Stanton. Mr. Arabin replied that he was a very distant relative of the family alluded to. To this Mr. Thorne surmised that the relationship could not be very distant. Mr. Arabin assured him that it was so distant that the families knew nothing of each other. Mr. Thorne laughed his gentle laugh at this and told Mr. Arabin that there was now existing no branch of his family separated from the parent stock at an earlier date than the reign of Elizabeth, and that therefore Mr. Arabin could not call himself distant. Mr. Arabin himself was quite clearly an Arabin of Uphill Stanton.

"But," said the vicar, "Uphill Stanton has been sold to the De Greys and has been in their hands for the last fifty years."

"And when it has been there one hundred and fifty, if it unluckily remain there so long," said Mr. Thorne, "your descendants will not be a whit the less entitled to describe themselves as being of the family of Uphill Stanton. Thank God no De Grey can buy that—and thank God no Arabin, and no Thorne, can sell it."

In politics Mr. Thorne was an unflinching conservative. He looked on those fifty-three Trojans who, as Mr. Dod tells us, censured free trade in November, 1852, as the only patriots left among the public men of England. When that terrible crisis of free trade had arrived, when the repeal of the Corn Laws was carried by those very men whom Mr. Thorne had hitherto regarded as the only possible saviours of his country, he was for a time paralysed. His country was lost; but that was comparatively a small thing. Other countries had flourished and fallen, and the human race still went on improving under

God's providence. But now all trust in human faith must forever be at an end. Not only must ruin come, but it must come through the apostasy of those who had been regarded as the truest of true believers. Politics in England, as a pursuit for gentlemen, must be at an end. Had Mr. Thorne been trodden under foot by a Whig, he could have borne it as a Tory and a martyr, but to be so utterly thrown over and deceived by those he had so earnestly supported, so thoroughly trusted, was more than he could endure and live. He therefore ceased to live as a politician, and refused to hold any converse with the world at large on the state of the country.

Such were Mr. Thorne's impressions for the first two or three years after Sir Robert Peel's apostasy, but by degrees his temper, as did that of others, cooled down. He began once more to move about, to frequent the bench and the market, and to be seen at dinners shoulder to shoulder with some of those who had so cruelly betrayed him. It was a necessity for him to live, and that plan of his for avoiding the world did not answer. He, however, and others around him who still maintained the same staunch principles of protection—men like himself who were too true to flinch at the cry of a mob—had their own way of consoling themselves. They were, and felt themselves to be, the only true depositaries left of certain Eleusinian mysteries, of certain deep and wondrous services of worship by which alone the gods could be rightly approached. To them and them only was it now given to know these things and to perpetuate them, if that might still be done, by the careful and secret education of their children.

We have read how private and peculiar forms of worship have been carried on from age to age in families which, to the outer world, have apparently adhered to the services of some ordinary church. And so by degrees it was with Mr. Thorne. He learnt at length to listen calmly while protection was talked of as a thing dead, although he knew within himself that it was still quick with a mystic life. Nor was he without a certain pleasure that such knowledge, though given to him, should be debarred from the multitude. He became accustomed to hear even among country gentlemen that free trade was after all not so bad, and to hear this without dispute, although conscious within himself that everything good in England had gone with his old palladium. He had within him something of the feeling of Cato, who gloried that he could kill himself because Romans were no longer worthy of their name. Mr. Thorne had no thought of killing himself, being a Christian and still possessing his £4000 a year, but the feeling was not on that account the less comfortable.

Mr. Thorne was a sportsman, and had been active though not outrageous in his sports. Previous to the great downfall of politics in his county, he had supported the hunt by every means in his power. He had preserved game till no goose or turkey could show a tail in the parish of St. Ewold's. He had planted gorse covers with more care than oaks and larches. He had been more anxious for the comfort of his foxes than of his ewes and lambs. No meet had been more popular than Ullathorne; no man's stables had been more liberally open to the horses of distant men than Mr. Thorne's; no man had said more, written more, or done more to keep the club up. The theory of protection could expand itself so thoroughly in the practices of a county hunt! But when the great ruin came; when the noble master of the Barsetshire hounds supported the recreant minister in the House of Lords and basely surrendered his truth, his manhood, his friends, and his honour for the hope of a garter, then Mr. Thorne gave up the hunt. He did not cut his covers, for that would not have been the act of a gentleman. He did not kill his foxes, for that according to his light would have been murder. He did not say that his covers should not be drawn, or his earths stopped, for that would have been illegal according to the by-laws prevailing among country gentlemen. But he absented himself from home on the occasion of every meet at Ullathorne, left the covers to their fate, and could not be persuaded to take his pink coat out of his press, or his hunters out of his stable. This lasted for two years, and then by degrees he came round. He first appeared at a neighbouring meet on a pony, dressed in his shooting-coat, as though he had trotted in by accident; then he walked up one morning on foot to see his favourite gorse drawn, and when his groom brought his mare out by chance, he did not refuse to mount her. He was next persuaded, by one of the immortal fifty-three, to bring his hunting materials over to the other side of the county and take a fortnight with the hounds there; and so gradually he returned to his old life. But in hunting as in other things he was only supported by an inward feeling of mystic superiority to those with whom he shared the common breath of outer life.

Mr. Thorne did not live in solitude at Ullathorne. He had a sister, who was ten years older than himself and who participated in his prejudices and feelings so strongly that she was a living caricature of all his foibles. She would not open a modern quarterly, did not choose to see a magazine in her drawing-room, and would not have polluted her fingers with a shred of the Times for any consideration. She spoke of Addison, Swift, and Steele as though they were still living, regarded Defoe as the best known novelist of his country, and thought of Fielding as a young but meritorious novice in the fields of romance. In poetry, she was familiar with names as late as Dryden, and had once been seduced into reading "The Rape of the Lock;" but she regarded Spenser as the purest type of her country's literature in this line. Genealogy was her favourite insanity. Those things which are the pride of most genealogists were to her contemptible. Arms and mottoes set her beside herself. Ealfried of Ullathorne had wanted no motto to assist him in cleaving to the brisket Geoffrey De Burgh, and Ealfried's great grandfather, the gigantic Ullafrid, had required no other arms than those which nature gave him to hurl from the top of his own castle a cousin of the base invading Norman. To her all modern English names were equally insignificant: Hengist, Horsa, and such like had for her ears the only true savour of nobility. She was not contented unless she could go beyond the Saxons, and would certainly have christened her children, had she had children, by the names of the ancient Britons. In some respects she was not unlike Scott's Ulrica, and had she been given to cursing, she would certainly have done so in the names of Mista, Skogula, and Zernebock. Not having submitted to the embraces of any polluting Norman, as poor Ulrica had done, and having assisted no parricide, the milk of human kindness was not curdled in her bosom. She never cursed therefore, but blessed rather. This, however, she did in a strange uncouth Saxon manner that would have been unintelligible to any peasants but her own.

As a politician, Miss Thorne had been so thoroughly disgusted with public life by base deeds long antecedent to the Corn Law question that that had but little moved her. In her estimation her brother had been a fast young man, hurried away by a too ardent temperament into democratic tendencies. Now happily he was brought to sounder views by seeing the iniquity of the world. She had not yet reconciled herself to the Reform Bill, and still groaned in spirit over the defalcations of the Duke as touching the Catholic Emancipation. If asked whom she thought the Queen should take as her counsellor, she would probably have named Lord Eldon, and when reminded that that venerable man was no longer present in the flesh to assist us, she would probably have answered with a sigh that none now could help us but the dead.

In religion Miss Thorne was a pure Druidess. We would not have it understood by that that she did actually in these latter days assist at any human sacrifices, or that she was in fact hostile to the Church of Christ. She had adopted the Christian religion as a milder form of the worship of her ancestors, and always appealed to her doing so as evidence that she had no prejudices against reform, when it could be shown that reform was salutary. This reform was the most modern of any to which she had as yet acceded, it being presumed that British ladies had given up their paint and taken to some sort of petticoats before the days of St. Augustine. That further feminine step in advance which combines paint and petticoats together had not found a votary in Miss Thorne.

But she was a Druidess in this, that she regretted she knew not what in the usages and practices of her Church. She sometimes talked and constantly thought of good things gone by, though she had but the faintest idea of what those good things had been. She imagined that a purity had existed which was now gone, that a piety had adorned our pastors and a simple docility our people, for which it may be feared history gave her but little true warrant. She was accustomed to speak of Cranmer as though he had been the firmest and most simple-minded of martyrs, and of Elizabeth as though the pure Protestant faith of her people had been the one anxiety of her life. It would have been cruel to undeceive her, had it been possible; but it would have been impossible to make her believe that the one was a time-serving priest, willing to go any length to keep his place, and that the other was in heart a papist, with this sole proviso, that she should be her own pope.

And so Miss Thorne went on sighing and regretting, looking back to the divine right of kings as the ruling axiom of a golden age, and cherishing, low down in the bottom of her heart of hearts, a dear unmentioned wish for the restoration of some exiled Stuart. Who would deny her the luxury of her sighs, or the sweetness of her soft regrets!

In her person and her dress she was perfect, and well she knew her own perfection. She was a small, elegantly made old woman, with a face from which the glow of her youth had not departed without leaving some streaks of a roseate hue. She was proud of her colour, proud of her grey hair which she wore in short crisp curls peering out all around her face from her dainty white lace cap. To think of all the money that she spent in lace used to break the heart of poor Mrs. Quiverful with her seven daughters. She was proud of her teeth, which were still white and numerous, proud of her bright cheery eye, proud of her short jaunty step; and very proud of the neat, precise, small feet with which those steps were taken. She was proud also, ay, very proud, of the rich brocaded silk in which it was her custom to ruffle through her drawing-room.

We know what was the custom of the lady of Branksome—

Nine-and-twenty knights of fame
Hung their shields in Branksome Hall.

The lady of Ullathorne was not so martial in her habits, but hardly less costly. She might have boasted that nine-and-twenty silken skirts might have been produced in her chamber, each fit to stand alone. The nine-and-twenty shields of the Scottish heroes were less independent and hardly more potent to withstand any attack that might be made on them. Miss Thorne when fully dressed might be said to have been armed cap-a-pie, and she was always fully dressed, as far as was ever known to mortal man. For all this rich attire Miss Thorne was not indebted to the generosity of her brother. She had a very comfortable independence of her own, which she divided among juvenile relatives, the milliners, and the poor, giving much the largest share to the latter. It may be imagined, therefore, that with all her little follies she was not unpopular. All her follies have, we believe, been told. Her virtues were too numerous to describe, and not sufficiently interesting to deserve description.

While we are on the subject of the Thornes, one word must be said of the house they lived in. It was not a large house, nor a fine house, nor perhaps to modern ideas a very commodious house, but by those who love the peculiar colour and peculiar ornaments of genuine Tudor architecture it was considered a perfect gem. We beg to own ourselves among the number, and therefore take this opportunity to express our surprise that so little is known by English men and women of the beauties of English architecture. The ruins of the Colosseum, the Campanile at Florence, St. Mark's, Cologne, the Bourse and Notre Dame are with our tourists as familiar as household words; but they know nothing of the glories of Wiltshire, Dorsetshire, and Somersetshire. Nay, we much question whether many noted travellers, men who have pitched their tents perhaps under Mount Sinai, are not still ignorant that there are glories in Wiltshire, Dorsetshire, and Somersetshire. We beg that they will go and see.

Mr. Thorne's house was called Ullathorne Court—and was properly so called, for the house itself formed two sides of a quadrangle, which was completed on the other two sides by a wall about twenty feet high. This wall was built of cut stone, rudely cut indeed, and now much worn, but of a beautiful, rich, tawny yellow colour, the effect of that stone-crop of minute growth which it had taken three centuries to produce. The top of this wall was ornamented by huge, round stone balls of the same colour as the wall itself. Entrance into the court was had through a pair of iron gates so massive that no one could comfortably open or close them—consequently, they were rarely disturbed. From the gateway two paths led obliquely across the court: that to the left reaching the hall-door, which was in the corner made by the angle of the house, and that to the right leading to the back entrance, which was at the further end of the longer portion of the building.

With those who are now adepts in contriving house accommodation, it will militate much against Ullathorne Court that no carriage could be brought to the hall-door. If you enter Ullathorne at all, you must do so, fair reader, on foot, or at least in a bath-chair. No vehicle drawn by horses ever comes within that iron gate. But this is nothing to the next horror that will encounter you. On entering the front door, which you do by no very grand portal, you find yourself immediately in the dining-room. What, no hall? exclaims my luxurious friend, accustomed to all the comfortable appurtenances of modern life. Yes, kind sir, a noble hall, if you will but observe it; a true old English hall of excellent dimensions for a country gentleman's family; but, if you please, no dining-parlour.

Both Mr. and Miss Thorne were proud of this peculiarity of their dwelling, though the brother was once all but tempted by his friends to alter it. They delighted in the knowledge that they, like Cedric, positively dined in their true hall, even though they so dined *tête-à-tête*. But though they had never owned, they had felt and endeavoured to remedy the discomfort of such an arrangement. A huge screen partitioned off the front door and a portion of the hall, and from the angle so screened off a second door led into a passage which ran along the larger side of the house next to the courtyard. Either my reader or I must be a bad hand at topography, if it be not clear that the great hall forms the ground-floor of the smaller portion of the mansion, that which was to your left as you entered the iron gate, and that it occupies the whole of this wing of the building. It must be equally clear that it looks out on a trim mown lawn, through three quadrangular windows with stone mullions, each window divided into a larger portion at the bottom, and a smaller portion at the top, and each portion again divided into five by perpendicular stone supporters. There may be windows which give a better light than such as these, and it may be, as my utilitarian friend observes, that the giving of light is the desired object of a window. I will not argue the point with him. Indeed I cannot. But I shall not the less die in the assured conviction that no sort or description of window is capable of imparting half so much happiness to mankind as that which had been adopted at Ullathorne Court. What, not an oriel? says Miss Diana de Midellage. No, Miss Diana, not even an oriel, beautiful as is an oriel window. It has not about it so perfect a feeling of quiet English homely comfort. Let oriel windows grace a college, or the half-public mansion of a potent peer, but for the sitting room of quiet country ladies, of ordinary homely folk, nothing can equal the square, mullioned windows of the Tudor architects.

The hall was hung round with family female insipidities by Lely and unprepossessing male Thornes in red coats by Kneller, each Thorne having been let into a panel in the wainscoting, in the proper manner. At the further end of the room was a huge fire-place, which afforded much ground of difference between the brother and sister. An antiquated grate that would hold about a hundredweight of coal, had been stuck on to the hearth by Mr. Thorne's father. This hearth had of course been intended for the consumption of wood faggots, and the iron dogs for the purpose were still standing, though half-buried in the masonry of the grate. Miss Thorne was very anxious to revert to the dogs. The dear good old creature was always glad to revert to anything, and had she been systematically indulged, would doubtless in time have reflected that fingers were made before forks and have reverted accordingly. But in the affairs of the fire-place Mr. Thorne would not revert. Country gentlemen around him all had comfortable grates in their dining-rooms. He was not exactly the man to have suggested a modern usage, but he was not so far prejudiced as to banish those which his father had prepared for his use. Mr. Thorne had indeed once suggested that with very little contrivance the front door might have been so altered as to open at least into the passage, but on hearing this, his sister Monica—such was Miss Thorne's name—had been taken ill and had remained so for a week. Before she came downstairs she received a pledge from her brother that the entrance should never be changed in her lifetime.

At the end of the hall opposite to the fire-place a door led into the drawing-room, which was of equal size, and lighted with precisely similar windows. But yet the aspect of the room was very different. It was papered, and the ceiling, which in the hall showed the old rafters, was whitened and finished with a modern cornice. Miss Thorne's drawing-room, or, as she always called it, withdrawing-room, was a beautiful apartment. The windows opened on to the full extent of the lovely trim garden; immediately before the windows were plots of flowers in stiff, stately, stubborn little beds, each bed surrounded by a stone coping of its own; beyond, there was a low parapet wall on which stood urns and images, fawns, nymphs, satyrs, and a whole tribe of Pan's followers; and then again, beyond that, a beautiful lawn sloped away to a sunk fence which divided the garden from the park. Mr. Thorne's study was at the end of the drawing-room, and beyond that were the kitchen and the offices. Doors opened into both Miss Thorne's withdrawing-room and Mr. Thorne's sanctum from the passage above alluded to, which, as it came to the latter room, widened itself so as to make space for the huge black oak stairs which led to the upper regions.

Such was the interior of Ullathorne Court. But having thus described it, perhaps somewhat too tediously, we beg to say that it is not the interior to which we wish to call the English tourist's attention, though we advise him to lose no legitimate opportunity of becoming acquainted with it in a friendly manner. It is the outside of Ullathorne that is so lovely. Let the tourist get admission at least into the garden and fling himself on that soft sward just opposite to the exterior angle of the house. He will there get the double frontage and enjoy that which is so lovely—the expanse of architectural beauty without the formal dullness of one long line.

It is the colour of Ullathorne that is so remarkable. It is of that delicious tawny hue which no stone can give, unless it has on it the vegetable richness of centuries. Strike the wall with your hand, and you will think that the stone has on it no covering, but rub it carefully, and you will find that the colour comes off upon your finger. No colourist that ever yet worked from a palette has been able to come up to this rich colouring of years crowding themselves on years.

Ullathorne is a high building for a country-house, for it possesses three stories, and in each story the windows are of the same sort as that described, though varying in size and varying also in their lines athwart the house. Those of the ground floor are all uniform in size and position. But those above are irregular both in size and place, and this irregularity gives a bizarre and not unpicturesque appearance to the building. Along the top, on every side, runs a low parapet, which nearly hides the roof, and at the corners are more figures of fawns and satyrs.

Such is Ullathorne House. But we must say one word of the approach to it, which shall include all the description which we mean to give of the church also. The picturesque old church of St. Ewold's stands immediately opposite to the iron gates which open into the court, and is all but surrounded by the branches of the lime-trees which form the avenue leading up to the house from both sides. This avenue is magnificent, but it would lose much of its value in the eyes of many proprietors by the fact that the road through it is not private property. It is a public lane between hedgerows, with a broad grass margin on each side of the road, from which the lime-trees spring. Ullathorne Court, therefore, does not stand absolutely surrounded by its own grounds, though Mr. Thorne is owner of all the adjacent land. This, however, is the source of very little annoyance to him. Men, when they are acquiring property, think much of such things, but they who live where their an-cestors have lived for years do not feel the misfortune. It never occurred either to Mr. or Miss Thorne that they were not sufficiently private because the world at large might, if it so wished, walk or drive by their iron gates. That part of the world which availed itself of the privilege was however very small.

Such a year or two since were the Thornes of Ullathorne. Such, we believe, are the in-habitants of many an English country-home. May it be long before their number diminishes.

CHAPTER XXIII

MR. ARABIN READS HIMSELF IN AT ST. EWOLD'S

On the Sunday morning the archdeacon with his sister-in-law and Mr. Arabin drove over to Ullathorne, as had been arranged. On their way thither the new vicar declared himself to be considerably disturbed in his mind at the idea of thus facing his parishioners for the first time. He had, he said, been always subject to *mauvaise honte* and an annoying degree of bashfulness, which often unfitted him for any work of a novel description; and now he felt this so strongly that he feared he should acquit himself badly in St. Ewold's reading-desk. He knew, he said, that those sharp little eyes of Miss Thorne would be on him, and that they would not approve. All this the archdeacon greatly ridiculed. He himself knew not, and had never known, what it was to be shy. He could not conceive that Miss Thorne, surrounded as she would be by the peasants of Ullathorne and a few of the poorer inhabitants of the suburbs of Barchester, could in any way affect the composure of a man well accustomed to address the learned congregation of St. Mary's at Oxford, and he laughed accordingly at the idea of Mr. Arabin's modesty.

Thereupon Mr. Arabin commenced to subtilize. The change, he said, from St. Mary's to St. Ewold's was quite as powerful on the spirits as would be that from St. Ewold's to St. Mary's. Would not a peer who, by chance of fortune, might suddenly be driven to herd among navvies be as afraid of the jeers of his companions as would any navvy suddenly exalted to a seat among the peers? Whereupon the archdeacon declared with a loud laugh that he would tell Miss Thorne that her new minister had likened her to a navvy. Eleanor, however, pronounced such a conclusion to be unfair; a comparison might be very just in its proportions which did not at all assimilate the things compared. But Mr. Arabin went on subtilizing, regarding neither the archdeacon's raillery nor Eleanor's defence. A young lady, he said, would execute with most perfect self-possession a difficult piece of music in a room crowded with strangers, who would not be able to express herself in intelligible language, even on any ordinary subject and among her most intimate friends, if she were required to do so standing on a box somewhat elevated among them. It was all an affair of education, and he at forty found it difficult to educate himself anew.

Eleanor dissented on the matter of the box, and averred she could speak very well about dresses, or babies, or legs of mutton from any box, provided it were big enough for her to stand upon without fear, even though all her friends were listening to her. The archdeacon was sure she would not be able to say a word, but this proved nothing in favour of Mr. Arabin. Mr. Arabin said that he would try the question out with Mrs. Bold, and get her on a box some day when the rectory might be full of visitors. To this Eleanor assented, making condition that the visitors should be of their own set, and the archdeacon cogitated in his mind whether by such a condition it was intended that Mr. Slope should be included, resolving also that, if so, the trial would certainly never take place in the rectory drawing-room at Plumstead.

And so arguing, they drove up to the iron gates of Ullathorne Court.

Mr. and Miss Thorne were standing ready dressed for church in the hall, and greeted their clerical visitors with cordiality. The archdeacon was an old favourite. He was a clergyman of the old school, and this recommended him to the lady. He had always been an opponent of free trade as long as free trade was an open question, and now that it was no longer so, he, being a clergyman, had not been obliged, like most of his lay Tory companions, to read his recantation. He could therefore be regarded as a supporter of the immaculate fifty-three, and was on this account a favourite with Mr. Thorne. The little bell was tinkling, and the rural population of the parish were standing about the lane, leaning on the church-stile and against the walls of the old court, anxious to get a look at their new minister as he passed from the house to the rectory. The archdeacon's servant had already preceded them thither with the vestments.

They all went forth together, and when the ladies passed into the church, the three gentlemen tarried a moment in the lane, that Mr. Thorne might name to the vicar with some kind of one-sided introduction the most leading among his parishioners.

"Here are our churchwardens, Mr. Arabin—Farmer Greenacre and Mr. Stiles. Mr. Stiles has the mill as you go into Barchester; and very good churchwardens they are."

"Not very severe, I hope," said Mr. Arabin. The two ecclesiastical officers touched their hats, and each made a leg in the approved rural fashion, assuring the vicar that they were very glad to have the honour of seeing him, and adding that the weather was very good for the harvest. Mr. Stiles, being a man somewhat versed in town life, had an impression of his own dignity, and did not quite like leaving his pastor under the erroneous idea that he being a churchwarden kept the children in order during church time. 'Twas thus he understood Mr. Arabin's allusion to his severity and hastened to put matters right by observing that "Sexton Clodheve looked to the younguns, and perhaps sometimes there may be a thought too much stick going on during sermon." Mr. Arabin's bright eye twinkled as he caught that of the archdeacon, and he smiled to himself as he observed how ignorant his officers were of the nature of their authority and of the surveillance which it was their duty to keep even over himself.

Mr. Arabin read the lessons and preached. It was enough to put a man a little out, let him have been ever so used to pulpit reading, to see the knowing way in which the farmers cocked their ears and set about a mental criticism as to whether their new minister did or did not fall short of the excellence of him who had lately departed from them. A mental and silent criticism it was for the existing moment, but soon to be made public among the elders of St. Ewold's over the green graves of their children and forefathers. The excellence, however, of poor old Mr. Goodenough had not been wonderful, and there were few there who did not deem that Mr. Arabin did his work sufficiently well, in spite of the slightly nervous affliction which at first impeded him, and which nearly drove the archdeacon beside himself.

But the sermon was the thing to try the man. It often surprises us that very young men can muster courage to preach for the first time to a strange congregation. Men who are as yet but little more than boys, who have but just left what indeed we may not call a school, but a seminary intended for their tuition as scholars, whose thoughts have been mostly of boating, cricketing, and wine-parties, ascend a rostrum high above the heads of the submissive crowd, not that they may read God's word to those below, but that they may preach their own word for the edification of their hearers. It seems strange to us that they are not stricken dumb by the new and awful solemnity of their position. "How am I, just turned twenty-three, who have never yet passed ten thoughtful days since the power of thought first came to me, how am I to instruct these greybeards who, with the weary thinking of so many years, have approached so near the grave? Can I teach them their duty? Can I explain to them that which I so imperfectly understand, that which years of study may have made so plain to them? Has my newly acquired privilege as one of God's ministers imparted to me as yet any fitness for the wonderful work of a preacher?"

It must be supposed that such ideas do occur to young clergymen, and yet they overcome, apparently with ease, this difficulty which to us appears to be all but insurmountable. We have never been subjected in the way of ordination to the power of a bishop's hands. It may be that there is in them something that sustains the spirit and banishes the natural modesty of youth. But for ourselves we must own that the deep affection which Dominie Sampson felt for his young pupils has not more endeared him to us than the bashful spirit which sent him mute and inglorious from the pulpit when he rose there with the futile attempt to preach God's gospel.

There is a rule in our church which forbids the younger order of our clergymen to perform a certain portion of the service. The absolution must be read by a minister in priest's orders. If there be no such minister present, the congregation can have the benefit of no absolution but that which each may succeed in administering to himself. The rule may be a good one, though the necessity for it hardly comes home to the general understanding. But this forbearance on the part of youth would be much more appreciated if it were extended likewise to sermons. The only danger would be that congregations would be too anxious to prevent their young clergymen from advancing themselves in the ranks of the ministry. Clergymen who could not preach would be such blessings that they would be bribed to adhere to their incompetence.

Mr. Arabin, however, had not the modesty of youth to impede him, and he succeeded with his sermon even better than with the lessons. He took for his text two verses out of the second epistle of St. John, "Whosoever transgresseth, and abideth not in the doctrine of Christ, hath not God. He that abideth in the doctrine of Christ, he hath both the Father and the Son. If there come any unto you, and bring not this doctrine, receive him not into your house, neither bid him God-speed." He told them that the house of theirs to which he alluded was this their church, in which he now addressed them for the first time; that their most welcome and proper manner of bidding him God-speed would be their patient obedience to his teaching of the gospel; but that he could put forward no claim to such conduct on their part unless he taught them the great Christian doctrine of works and faith combined. On this he enlarged, but not very amply, and after twenty minutes succeeded in sending his new friends home to their baked mutton and pudding well pleased with their new minister.

Then came the lunch at Ullathorne. As soon as they were in the hall Miss Thorne took Mr. Arabin's hand and assured him that she received him into her house, into the temple, she said, in which she worshipped, and bade him God-speed with all her heart. Mr. Arabin was touched and squeezed the spinster's hand without uttering a word in reply. Then Mr. Thorne expressed a hope that Mr. Arabin found the church well adapted for articulation, and Mr. Arabin having replied that he had no doubt he should as soon as he had learnt to pitch his voice to the building, they all sat down to the good things before them.

Miss Thorne took special care of Mrs. Bold. Eleanor still wore her widow's weeds, and therefore had about her that air of grave and sad maternity which is the lot of recent widows. This opened the soft heart of Miss Thorne, and made her look on her young guest as though too much could not be done for her. She heaped chicken and ham upon her plate and poured out for her a full bumper of port wine. When Eleanor, who was not sorry to get it, had drunk a little of it, Miss Thorne at once essayed to fill it again. To this Eleanor objected, but in vain. Miss Thorne winked and nodded and whispered, saying that it was the proper thing and must be done, and that she knew all about it; and so she desired Mrs. Bold to drink it up and not mind anybody.

"It is your duty, you know, to support yourself," she said into the ear of the young mother; "there's more than yourself depending on it;" and thus she coshered up Eleanor with cold fowl and port wine. How it is that poor men's wives, who have no cold fowl and port wine on which to be coshered up, nurse their children without difficulty, whereas the wives of rich men, who eat and drink everything that is good, cannot do so, we will for the present leave to the doctors and the mothers to settle between them.

And then Miss Thorne was great about teeth. Little Johnny Bold had been troubled for the last few days with his first incipient masticator, and with that freemasonry which exists among ladies, Miss Thorne became aware of the fact before Eleanor had half-finished her wing. The old lady prescribed at once a receipt which had been much in vogue in the young days of her grandmother, and warned Eleanor with solemn voice against the fallacies of modern medicine.

"Take his coral, my dear," said she, "and rub it well with carrot-juice; rub it till the juice dries on it, and then give it him to play with—"

"But he hasn't got a coral," said Eleanor.

"Not got a coral!" said Miss Thorne with almost angry vehemence. "Not got a coral— how can you expect that he should cut his teeth? Have you got Daffy's Elixir?"

Eleanor explained that she had not. It had not been ordered by Mr. Rerechild, the Barchester doctor whom she employed; and then the young mother mentioned some shockingly modern succedaneum which Mr. Rerechild's new lights had taught him to recommend.

Miss Thorne looked awfully severe. "Take care, my dear," said she, "that the man knows what he's about; take care he doesn't destroy your little boy. But"—and she softened into sorrow, as she said it, and spoke more in pity than in anger—"but I don't know who there is in Barchester now that you can trust. Poor dear old Doctor Bumpwell, indeed—"

"Why, Miss Thorne, he died when I was a little girl."

"Yes, my dear, he did, and an unfortunate day it was for Barchester. As to those young men that have come up since"—Mr. Rerechild, by the by, was quite as old as Miss Thorne herself—"one doesn't know where they came from or who they are, or whether they know anything about their business or not."

"I think there are very clever men in Barchester," said Eleanor.

"Perhaps there may be; only I don't know them: and it's admitted on all sides that medical men aren't now what they used to be. They used to be talented, observing, educated men. But now any whipper-snapper out of an apothecary's shop can call himself a doctor. I believe no kind of education is now thought necessary."

Eleanor was herself the widow of a medical man and felt a little inclined to resent all these hard sayings. But Miss Thorne was so essentially good-natured that it was impossible to resent anything she said. She therefore sipped her wine and finished her chicken.

"At any rate, my dear, don't forget the carrot-juice, and by all means get him a coral at once. My grandmother Thorne had the best teeth in the county and carried them to the grave with her at eighty. I have heard her say it was all the carrot-juice. She couldn't bear the Barchester doctors. Even poor old Dr. Bumpwell didn't please her." It clearly never occurred to Miss Thorne that some fifty years ago Dr. Bumpwell was only a rising man and therefore as much in need of character in the eyes of the then ladies of Ullathorne as the present doctors were in her own.

The archdeacon made a very good lunch, and talked to his host about turnip-drillers and new machines for reaping, while the host, thinking it only polite to attend to a stranger, and fearing that perhaps he might not care about turnip crops on a Sunday, mooted all manner of ecclesiastical subjects.

"I never saw a heavier lot of wheat, Thorne, than you've got there in that field beyond the copse. I suppose that's guano," said the archdeacon.

"Yes, guano. I get it from Bristol myself. You'll find you often have a tolerable congregation of Barchester people out here, Mr. Arabin. They are very fond of St. Ewold's, particularly of an afternoon when the weather is not too hot for the walk."

"I am under an obligation to them for staying away to-day, at any rate," said the vicar. "The congregation can never be too small for a maiden sermon."

"I got a ton and a half at Bradley's in High Street," said the archdeacon, "and it was a complete take in. I don't believe there was five hundredweight of guano in it."

"That Bradley never has anything good," said Miss Thorne, who had just caught the name during her whisperings with Eleanor. "And such a nice shop as there used to be in that very house before he came. Wilfred, don't you remember what good things old Ambleoff used to have?"

"There have been three men since Ambleoff's time," said the archdeacon, "and each as bad as the other. But who gets it for you at Bristol, Thorne?"

"I ran up myself this year and bought it out of the ship. I am afraid as the evenings get shorter, Mr. Arabin, you'll find the reading-desk too dark. I must send a fellow with an axe and make him lop off some of those branches."

Mr. Arabin declared that the morning light at any rate was perfect, and deprecated any interference with the lime-trees. And then they took a stroll out among the trim parterres, and Mr. Arabin explained to Mrs. Bold the difference between a naiad and a dryad, and dilated on vases and the shapes of urns. Miss Thorne busied herself among her pansies, and her brother, finding it quite impracticable to give anything of a peculiarly Sunday tone to the conversation, abandoned the attempt and had it out with the archdeacon about the Bristol guano.

At three o'clock they again went into church, and now Mr. Arabin read the service and the archdeacon preached. Nearly the same congregation was present, with some adventurous pedestrians from the city, who had not thought the heat of the midday August sun too great to deter them. The archdeacon took his text from the epistle to Philemon. "I beseech thee for my son Onesimus, whom I have begotten in my bonds." From such a text it may be imagined the kind of sermon which Dr. Grantly preached, and on the whole it was neither dull, nor bad, nor out of place.

He told them that it had become his duty to look about for a pastor for them, to supply the place of one who had been long among them, and that in this manner he regarded as a son him whom he had selected, as St. Paul had regarded the young disciple whom he sent forth. Then he took a little merit to himself for having studiously provided the best man he could without reference to patronage or favour; but he did not say that the best man according to his views was he who was best able to subdue Mr. Slope, and make that gentleman's situation in Barchester too hot to be comfortable. As to the bonds, they had consisted in the exceeding struggle which he had made to get a good clergyman for them. He deprecated any comparison between himself and St. Paul, but said that he was entitled to beseech them for their goodwill towards Mr. Arabin, in the same manner that the apostle had besought Philemon and his household with regard to Onesimus.

The archdeacon's sermon—text, blessing, and all—was concluded within the half-hour. Then they shook hands with their Ullathorne friends and returned to Plumstead. 'Twas thus that Mr. Arabin read himself in at St. Ewold's.

CHAPTER XXIV

MR. SLOPE MANAGES MATTERS VERY CLEVERLY AT PUDDINGDALE

The next two weeks passed pleasantly enough at Plumstead. The whole party there assembled seemed to get on well together. Eleanor made the house agreeable, and the archdeacon and Mr. Grantly seemed to have forgotten her iniquity as regarded Mr. Slope. Mr. Harding had his violoncello, and played to them while his daughters accompanied him. Johnny Bold, by the help either of Mr. Rerechild or else by that of his coral and carrot-juice, got through his teething troubles. There had been gaieties, too, of all sorts. They had dined at Ullathorne, and the Thornes had dined at the rectory. Eleanor had been duly put to stand on her box, and in that position had found herself quite unable to express her opinion on the merits of flounces, such having been the subject given to try her elocution. Mr. Arabin had of course been much in his own parish, looking to the doings at his vicarage, calling on his parishioners, and taking on himself the duties of his new calling. But still he had been every evening at Plumstead, and Mrs. Grantly was partly willing to agree with her husband that he was a pleasant inmate in a house.

They had also been at a dinner-party at Dr. Stanhope's, of which Mr. Arabin had made one. He also, mothlike, burnt his wings in the flames of the signora's candle. Mrs. Bold, too, had been there, and had felt somewhat displeased with the taste—want of taste she called it—shown by Mr. Arabin in paying so much attention to Madame Neroni. It was as infallible that Madeline should displease and irritate the women as that she should charm and captivate the men. The one result followed naturally on the other. It was quite true that Mr. Arabin had been charmed. He thought her a very clever and a very handsome woman; he thought also that her peculiar affliction entitled her to the sympathy of all. He had never, he said, met so much suffering joined to such perfect beauty and so clear a mind. 'Twas thus he spoke of the signora, coming home in the archdeacon's carriage, and Eleanor by no means liked to hear the praise. It was, however, exceedingly unjust of her to be angry with Mr. Arabin, as she had herself spent a very pleasant evening with Bertie Stanhope, who had taken her down to dinner and had not left her side for one moment after the gentlemen came out of the dining-room. It was unfair that she should amuse herself with Bertie and yet begrudge her new friend his license of amusing himself with Bertie's sister. And yet she did so. She was half-angry with him in the carriage, and said something about meretricious manners. Mr. Arabin did not understand the ways of women very well, or else he might have flattered himself that Eleanor was in love with him.

But Eleanor was not in love with him. How many shades there are between love and indifference, and how little the graduated scale is understood! She had now been nearly three weeks in the same house with Mr. Arabin, and had received much of his attention and listened daily to his conversation. He had usually devoted at least some portion of his evening to her exclusively. At Dr. Stanhope's he had devoted himself exclusively to another. It does not require that a woman should be in love to be irritated at this; it does not require that she should even acknowledge to herself that it is unpleasant to her. Eleanor had no such self-knowledge. She thought in her own heart that it was only on Mr. Arabin's account that she regretted that he could condescend to be amused by the signora. "I thought he had more mind," she said to herself as she sat watching her baby's cradle on her return from the party. "After all, I believe Mr. Stanhope is the pleasanter man of the two." Alas for the memory of poor John Bold! Eleanor was not in love with Bertie Stanhope, nor was she in love with Mr. Arabin. But her devotion to her late husband was fast fading when she could revolve in her mind, over the cradle of his infant, the faults and failings of other aspirants to her favour.

Will anyone blame my heroine for this? Let him or her rather thank God for all His goodness—for His mercy endureth forever.

Eleanor, in truth, was not in love; neither was Mr. Arabin. Neither indeed was Bertie Stanhope, though he had already found occasion to say nearly as much as that he was. The widow's cap had prevented him from making a positive declaration, when otherwise he would have considered himself entitled to do so on a third or fourth interview. It was, after all, but a small cap now, and had but little of the weeping willow left in its construction. It is singular how these emblems of grief fade away by unseen gradations. Each pretends to be the counterpart of the forerunner, and yet the last little bit of crimped white crape that sits so jauntily on the back of the head is as dissimilar to the first huge mountain of woe which disfigured the face of the weeper as the state of the Hindu is to the jointure of the English dowager.

But let it be clearly understood that Eleanor was in love with no one, and that no one was in love with Eleanor. Under these circumstances her anger against Mr. Arabin did not last long, and before two days were over they were both as good friends as ever. She could not but like him, for every hour spent in his company was spent pleasantly. And yet she could not quite like him, for there was always apparent in his conversation a certain feeling on his part that he hardly thought it worth his while to be in earnest. It was almost as though he were playing with a child. She knew well enough that he was in truth a sober, thoughtful man who, in some matters and on some occasions, could endure an agony of earnestness. And yet to her he was always gently playful. Could she have seen his brow once clouded, she might have learnt to love him.

So things went on at Plumstead, and on the whole not unpleasantly, till a huge storm darkened the horizon and came down upon the inhabitants of the rectory with all the fury of a water-spout. It was astonishing how in a few minutes the whole face of the heavens was changed. The party broke up from breakfast in perfect harmony, but fierce passions had arisen before the evening which did not admit of their sitting at the same board for dinner. To explain this it will be necessary to go back a little.

It will be remembered that the bishop expressed to Mr. Slope in his dressing-room his determination that Mr. Quiverful should be confirmed in his appointment to the hospital, and that his lordship requested Mr. Slope to communicate this decision to the archdeacon. It will also be remembered that the archdeacon had indignantly declined seeing Mr. Slope, and had instead written a strong letter to the bishop in which he all but demanded the situation of warden for Mr. Harding. To this letter the archdeacon received an immediate formal reply from Mr. Slope, in which it was stated that the bishop had received and would give his best consideration to the archdeacon's letter.

The archdeacon felt himself somewhat checkmated by this reply. What could he do with a man who would neither see him, nor argue with him by letter, and who had undoubtedly the power of appointing any clergyman he pleased? He had consulted with Mr. Arabin, who had suggested the propriety of calling in the aid of the Master of Lazarus. "If," said he, "you and Dr. Gwynne formally declare your intention of waiting upon the bishop, the bishop will not dare to refuse to see you; and if two such men as you are see him together, you will probably not leave him without carrying your point."

The archdeacon did not quite like admitting the necessity of his being backed by the Master of Lazarus before he could obtain admission into the episcopal palace of Barchester, but still he felt that the advice was good, and he resolved to take it. He wrote again to the bishop, expressing a hope that nothing further would be done in the matter of the hospital till the consideration promised by his lordship had been given, and then sent off a warm appeal to his friend the master, imploring him to come to Plumstead and assist in driving the bishop into compliance. The master had rejoined, raising some difficulty, but not declining, and the archdeacon had again pressed his point, insisting on the necessity for immediate action. Dr. Gwynne unfortunately had the gout, and could therefore name no immediate day, but still agreed to come, if it should be finally found necessary. So the matter stood, as regarded the party at Plumstead.

But Mr. Harding had another friend fighting his battle for him, quite as powerful as the Master of Lazarus, and this was Mr. Slope. Though the bishop had so pertinaciously insisted on giving way to his wife in the matter of the hospital, Mr. Slope did not think it necessary to abandon his object. He had, he thought, daily more and more reason to imagine that the widow would receive his overtures favourably, and he could not but feel that Mr. Harding at the hospital, and placed there by his means, would be more likely to receive him as a son-in-law than Mr. Harding growling in opposition and disappointment under the archdeacon's wing at Plumstead. Moreover, to give Mr. Slope due credit, he was actuated by greater motives even than these. He wanted a wife, and he wanted money, but he wanted power more than either. He had fully realized the fact that he must come to blows with Mrs. Proudie. He had no desire to remain in Barchester as her chaplain. Sooner than do so, he would risk the loss of his whole connexion with the diocese. What! Was he to feel within him the possession of no ordinary talents—was he to know himself to be courageous, firm, and, in matters where his conscience did not interfere, unscrupulous—and yet he contented to be the working factotum of a woman prelate? Mr. Slope had higher ideas of his own destiny. Either he or Mrs. Proudie must go to the wall, and now had come the time when he would try which it should be.

The bishop had declared that Mr. Quiverful should be the new warden. As Mr. Slope went downstairs, prepared to see the archdeacon, if necessary, but fully satisfied that no such necessity would arise, he declared to himself that Mr. Harding should be warden. With the object of carrying this point, he rode over to Puddingdale and had a further interview with the worthy expectant of clerical good things. Mr. Quiverful was on the whole a worthy man. The impossible task of bringing up as ladies and gentlemen fourteen children on an income which was insufficient to give them with decency the common necessaries of life, had had an effect upon him not beneficial either to his spirit or his keen sense of honour. Who can boast that he would have supported such a burden with a different result? Mr. Quiverful was an honest, painstaking, drudging man, anxious indeed for bread and meat, anxious for means to quiet his butcher and cover with returning smiles the now sour countenance of the baker's wife; but anxious also to be right with his own conscience. He was not careful, as another might be who sat on an easier worldly seat, to stand well with those around him, to shun a breath which might sully his name or a rumour which might affect his honour. He could not afford such niceties of conduct, such moral luxuries. It must suffice for him to be ordinarily honest according to the ordinary honesty of the world's ways, and to let men's tongues wag as they would.

He had felt that his brother clergymen, men whom he had known for the last twenty years, looked coldly on him from the first moment that he had shown himself willing to sit at the feet of Mr. Slope; he had seen that their looks grew colder still when it became bruited about that he was to be the bishop's new warden at Hiram's Hospital. This was painful enough, but it was the cross which he was doomed to bear. He thought of his wife, whose last new silk dress was six years in wear. He thought of all his young flock, whom he could hardly take to church with him on Sundays, for there were not decent shoes and stockings for them all to wear. He thought of the well-worn sleeves of his own black coat and of the stern face of the draper, from whom he would fain ask for cloth to make another, did he not know that the credit would be refused him. Then he thought of the comfortable house in Barchester, of the comfortable income, of his boys sent to school, of his girls with books in their hands instead of darning needles, of his wife's face again covered with smiles, and of his daily board again covered with plenty. He thought of these things; and do thou also, reader, think of them, and then wonder, if thou canst, that Mr. Slope had appeared to him to possess all those good gifts which could grace a bishop's chaplain. "How beautiful upon the mountains are the feet of him that bringeth good tidings."

Why, moreover, should the Barchester clergy have looked coldly on Mr. Quiverful? Had they not all shown that they regarded with complacency the loaves and fishes of their mother church? Had they not all, by some hook or crook, done better for themselves than he had done? They were not burdened as he was burdened. Dr. Grantly had five children and nearly as many thousands a year on which to feed them. It was very well for him to turn up his nose at a new bishop who could do nothing for him, and a chaplain who was beneath his notice; but it was cruel in a man so circumstanced to set the world against the father of fourteen children because he was anxious to obtain for them an honourable support! He, Mr. Quiverful, had not asked for the wardenship; he had not even accepted it till he had been assured that Mr. Harding had refused it. How hard then that he should be blamed for doing that which not to have done would have argued a most insane imprudence!

Thus in this matter of the hospital poor Mr. Quiverful had his trials, and he had also his consolations. On the whole the consolations were the more vivid of the two. The stern draper heard of the coming promotion, and the wealth of his warehouse was at Mr. Quiverful's disposal. Coming events cast their shadows before, and the coming event of Mr. Quiverful's transference to Barchester produced a delicious shadow in the shape of a new outfit for Mrs. Quiverful and her three elder daughters. Such consolations come home to the heart of a man, and quite home to the heart of a woman. Whatever the husband might feel, the wife cared nothing for frowns of dean, archdeacon, or prebendary. To her the outsides and insides of her husband and fourteen children were everything. In her bosom every other ambition had been swallowed up in that maternal ambition of seeing them and him and herself duly clad and properly fed. It had come to that with her that life had now no other purpose. She recked nothing of the imaginary rights of others. She had no patience with her husband when he declared to her that he could not accept the hospital unless he knew that Mr. Harding had refused it. Her husband had no right to be quixotic at the expense of fourteen children. The narrow escape of throwing away his good fortune which her lord had had, almost paralysed her. Now, indeed, they had received a full promise, not only from Mr. Slope, but also from Mrs. Proudie. Now, indeed, they might reckon with safety on their good fortune. But what if all had been lost? What if her fourteen bairns had been resteeped to the hips in poverty by the morbid sentimentality of their father? Mrs. Quiverful was just at present a happy woman, but yet it nearly took her breath away when she thought of the risk they had run.

"I don't know what your father means when he talks so much of what is due to Mr. Harding," she said to her eldest daughter. "Does he think that Mr. Harding would give him £450 a year out of fine feeling? And what signifies it whom he offends, as long as he gets the place? He does not expect anything better. It passes me to think how your father can be so soft, while everybody around him is so griping."

Thus, while the outer world was accusing Mr. Quiverful of rapacity for promotion and of disregard to his honour, the inner world of his own household was falling foul of him, with equal vehemence, for his willingness to sacrifice their interests to a false feeling of sentimental pride. It is astonishing how much difference the point of view makes in the aspect of all that we look at!

Such were the feelings of the different members of the family at Puddingdale on the occasion of Mr. Slope's second visit. Mrs. Quiverful, as soon as she saw his horse coming up the avenue from the vicarage gate, hastily packed up her huge basket of needlework and hurried herself and her daughter out of the room in which she was sitting with her husband. "It's Mr. Slope," she said. "He's come to settle with you about the hospital. I do hope we shall now be able to move at once." And she hastened to bid the maid of all work go to the door, so that the welcome great man might not be kept waiting.

Mr. Slope thus found Mr. Quiverful alone. Mrs. Quiverful went off to her kitchen and back settlements with anxious beating heart, almost dreading that there might be some slip between the cup of her happiness and the lip of her fruition, but yet comforting herself with the reflexion that after what had taken place, any such slip could hardly be possible.

Mr. Slope was all smiles as he shook his brother clergyman's hand and said that he had ridden over because he thought it right at once to put Mr. Quiverful in possession of the facts of the matter regarding the wardenship of the hospital. As he spoke, the poor expectant husband and father saw at a glance that his brilliant hopes were to be dashed to the ground, and that his visitor was now there for the purpose of unsaying what on his former visit he had said. There was something in the tone of the voice, something in the glance of the eye, which told the tale. Mr. Quiverful knew it all at once. He maintained his self-possession, however, smiled with a slight unmeaning smile, and merely said that he was obliged to Mr. Slope for the trouble he was taking.

"It has been a troublesome matter from first to last," said Mr. Slope, "and the bishop has hardly known how to act. Between ourselves—but mind this of course must go no further, Mr. Quiverful."

Mr. Quiverful said that of course it should not. "The truth is that poor Mr. Harding has hardly known his own mind. You remember our last conversation, no doubt."

Mr. Quiverful assured him that he remembered it very well indeed.

"You will remember that I told you that Mr. Harding had refused to return to the hospital."

Mr. Quiverful declared that nothing could be more distinct on his memory.

"And acting on this refusal, I suggested that you should take the hospital," continued Mr. Slope.

"I understood you to say that the bishop had authorised you to offer it to me."

"Did I? Did I go so far as that? Well, perhaps it may be that in my anxiety in your behalf I did commit myself further than I should have done. So far as my own memory serves me, I don't think I did go quite so far as that. But I own I was very anxious that you should get it, and I may have said more than was quite prudent."

"But," said Mr. Quiverful in his deep anxiety to prove his case, "my wife received as distinct a promise from Mrs. Proudie as one human being could give to another."

Mr. Slope smiled and gently shook his head. He meant the smile for a pleasant smile, but it was diabolical in the eyes of the man he was speaking to. "Mrs. Proudie!" he said. "If we are to go to what passes between the ladies in these matters, we shall really be in a nest of troubles from which we shall never extricate ourselves. Mrs. Proudie is a most excellent lady, kind-hearted, charitable, pious, and in every way estimable. But, my dear Mr. Quiverful, the patronage of the diocese is not in her hands."

Mr. Quiverful for a moment sat panic-stricken and silent. "Am I to understand, then, that I have received no promise?" he said as soon as he had sufficiently collected his thoughts.

"If you will allow me, I will tell you exactly how the matter rests. You certainly did receive a promise conditional on Mr. Harding's refusal. I am sure you will do me the justice to remember that you yourself declared that you could accept the appointment on no other condition than the knowledge that Mr. Harding had declined it."

"Yes," said Mr. Quiverful; "I did say that, certainly."

"Well, it now appears that he did not refuse it."

"But surely you told me, and repeated it more than once, that he had done so in your own hearing."

"So I understood him. But it seems I was in error. But don't for a moment, Mr. Quiverful, suppose that I mean to throw you over. No. Having held out my hand to a man in your position, with your large family and pressing claims, I am not now going to draw it back again. I only want you to act with me fairly and honestly."

"Whatever I do I shall endeavour at any rate to act fairly," said the poor man, feeling that he had to fall back for support on the spirit of martyrdom within him.

"I am sure you will," said the other. "I am sure you have no wish to obtain possession of an income which belongs by all right to another. No man knows better than you do Mr. Harding's history, or can better appreciate his character. Mr. Harding is very desirous of returning to his old position, and the bishop feels that he is at the present moment somewhat hampered, though of course he is not bound, by the conversation which took place on the matter between you and me."

"Well," said Mr. Quiverful, dreadfully doubtful as to what his conduct under such circumstances should be, and fruitlessly striving to harden his nerves with some of that instinct of self-preservation which made his wife so bold.

"The wardenship of this little hospital is not the only thing in the bishop's gift, Mr. Quiverful, nor is it by many degrees the best. And his lordship is not the man to forget anyone whom he has once marked with approval. If you would allow me to advise you as a friend—"

"Indeed, I shall be most grateful to you," said the poor vicar of Puddingdale.

"I should advise you to withdraw from any opposition to Mr. Harding's claims. If you persist in your demand, I do not think you will ultimately succeed. Mr. Harding has all but a positive right to the place. But if you will allow me to inform the bishop that you decline to stand in Mr. Harding's way, I think I may promise you—though, by the by, it must not be taken as a formal promise—that the bishop will not allow you to be a poorer man than you would have been had you become warden."

Mr. Quiverful sat in his armchair, silent, gazing at vacancy. What was he to say? All this that came from Mr. Slope was so true. Mr. Harding had a right to the hospital. The bishop had a great many good things to give away. Both the bishop and Mr. Slope would be excellent friends and terrible enemies to a man in his position. And then he had no proof of any promise; he could not force the bishop to appoint him.

"Well, Mr. Quiverful, what do you say about it?"

"Oh, of course, whatever you think fit, Mr. Slope. It's a great disappointment, a very great disappointment. I won't deny that I am a very poor man, Mr. Slope."

"In the end, Mr. Quiverful, you will find that it will have been better for you."

The interview ended in Mr. Slope receiving a full renunciation from Mr. Quiverful of any claim he might have to the appointment in question. It was only given verbally and without witnesses, but then the original promise was made in the same way.

Mr. Slope again assured him that he should not be forgotten, and then rode back to Barchester, satisfied that he would now be able to mould the bishop to his wishes.

CHAPTER XXV

FOURTEEN ARGUMENTS IN FAVOUR OF MR. QUIVERFUL'S CLAIMS

We have most of us heard of the terrible anger of a lioness when, surrounded by her cubs, she guards her prey. Few of us wish to disturb the mother of a litter of puppies when mouthing a bone in the midst of her young family. Medea and her children are familiar to us, and so is the grief of Constance. Mrs. Quiverful, when she first heard from her husband the news which he had to impart, felt within her bosom all the rage of the lioness, the rapacity of the hound, the fury of the tragic queen, and the deep despair of the bereaved mother.

Doubting, but yet hardly fearing, what might have been the tenor of Mr. Slope's discourse, she rushed back to her husband as soon as the front door was closed behind the visitor. It was well for Mr. Slope that he so escaped—the anger of such a woman, at such a moment, would have cowed even him. As a general rule, it is highly desirable that ladies should keep their temper: a woman when she storms always makes herself ugly, and usually ridiculous also. There is nothing so odious to man as a virago. Though Theseus loved an Amazon, he showed his love but roughly, and from the time of Theseus downward, no man ever wished to have his wife remarkable rather for forward prowess than retiring gentleness. A low voice "is an excellent thing in woman."

Such may be laid down as a very general rule; and few women should allow themselves to deviate from it, and then only on rare occasions. But if there be a time when a woman may let her hair to the winds, when she may loose her arms, and scream out trumpet-tongued to the ears of men, it is when nature calls out within her not for her own wants, but for the wants of those whom her womb has borne, whom her breasts have suckled, for those who look to her for their daily bread as naturally as man looks to his Creator.

There was nothing poetic in the nature of Mrs. Quiverful. She was neither a Medea nor a Constance. When angry, she spoke out her anger in plain words, and in a tone which might have been modulated with advantage; but she did so, at any rate, without affectation. Now, without knowing it, she rose to a tragic vein.

"Well, my dear, we are not to have it." Such were the words with which her ears were greeted when she entered the parlour, still hot from the kitchen fire. And the face of her husband spoke even more plainly than his words:—

E'en such a man, so faint, so spiritless,
So dull, so dead in look, so woe-begone,

Drew Priam's curtain in the dead of night.

"What!" said she—and Mrs. Siddons could not have put more passion into a single syllable—"What! Not have it? Who says so?" And she sat opposite to her husband, with her elbows on the table, her hands clasped together, and her coarse, solid, but once handsome face stretched over it towards him.

She sat as silent as death while he told his story, and very dreadful to him her silence was. He told it very lamely and badly but still in such a manner that she soon understood the whole of it.

"And so you have resigned it?" said she.

"I have had no opportunity of accepting it," he replied. "I had no witnesses to Mr. Slope's offer, even if that offer would bind the bishop. It was better for me, on the whole, to keep on good terms with such men than to fight for what I should never get!"

"Witnesses!" she screamed, rising quickly to her feet and walking up and down the room. "Do clergymen require witnesses to their words? He made the promise in the bishop's name, and if it is to be broken, I'll know the reason why. Did he not positively say that the bishop had sent him to offer you the place?"

"He did, my dear. But that is now nothing to the purpose."

"It is everything to the purpose, Mr. Quiverful. Witnesses indeed! And then to talk of your honour being questioned because you wish to provide for fourteen children. It is everything to the purpose; and so they shall know, if I scream it into their ears from the town cross of Barchester."

"You forget, Letitia, that the bishop has so many things in his gift. We must wait a little longer. That is all."

"Wait! Shall we feed the children by waiting? Will waiting put George, and Tom, and Sam out into the world? Will it enable my poor girls to give up some of their drudgery? Will waiting make Bessy and Jane fit even to be governesses? Will waiting pay for the things we got in Barchester last week?"

"It is all we can do, my dear. The disappointment is as much to me as to you; and yet, God knows, I feel it more for your sake than my own."

Mrs. Quiverful was looking full into her husband's face, and saw a small hot tear appear on each of those furrowed cheeks. This was too much for her woman's heart. He also had risen, and was standing with his back to the empty grate. She rushed towards him and, seizing him in her arms, sobbed aloud upon his bosom.

"You are too good, too soft, too yielding," she said at last. "These men, when they want you, they use you like a cat's paw; and when they want you no longer, they throw you aside like an old shoe. This is twice they have treated you so."

"In one way this will be all for the better," argued he. "It will make the bishop feel that he is bound to do something for me."

"At any rate he shall hear of it," said the lady, again reverting to her more angry mood. "At any rate he shall hear of it, and that loudly; and so shall she. She little knows Letitia Quiverful, if she thinks I will sit down quietly with the loss after all that passed between us at the palace. If there's any feeling within her, I'll make her ashamed of herself,"—and she paced the room again, stamping the floor as she went with her fat, heavy foot. "Good heavens! What a heart she must have within her to treat in such a way as this the father of fourteen unprovided children!"

Mr. Quiverful proceeded to explain that he didn't think that Mrs. Proudie had had anything to do with it.

"Don't tell me," said Mrs. Quiverful; "I know more about it than that. Doesn't all the world know that Mrs. Proudie is bishop of Barchester and that Mr. Slope is merely her creature? Wasn't it she that made me the promise, just as though the thing was in her own particular gift? I tell you, it was that woman who sent him over here to-day, because, for some reason of her own, she wants to go back from her word."

"My dear, you're wrong—"

"Now, Q., don't be so soft," she continued. "Take my word for it, the bishop knows no more about it than Jemima does." Jemima was the two-year-old. "And if you'll take my advice, you'll lose no time in going over and seeing him yourself."

Soft, however, as Mr. Quiverful might be, he would not allow himself to be talked out of his opinion on this occasion, and proceeded with much minuteness to explain to his wife the tone in which Mr. Slope had spoken of Mrs. Proudie's interference in diocesan matters. As he did so, a new idea gradually instilled itself into the matron's head, and a new course of conduct presented itself to her judgement. What if, after all, Mrs. Proudie knew nothing of this visit of Mr. Slope's? In that case, might it not be possible that that lady would still be staunch to her in this matter, still stand her friend, and, perhaps, possibly carry her through in opposition to Mr. Slope? Mrs. Quiverful said nothing as this vague hope occurred to her, but listened with more than ordinary patience to what her husband had to say. While he was still explaining that in all probability the world was wrong in its estimation of Mrs. Proudie's power and authority, she had fully made up her mind as to her course of action. She did not, however, proclaim her intention. She shook her head ominously as he continued his narration, and when he had completed, she rose to go, merely observing that it was cruel, cruel treatment. She then asked him if he would mind waiting for a late dinner instead of dining at their usual hour of three; and, having received from him a concession on this point, she proceeded to carry her purpose into execution.

She determined that she would at once go to the palace, that she would do so, if possible, before Mrs. Proudie could have had an interview with Mr. Slope, and that she would be either submissive, piteous, and pathetic, or else indignant, violent, and exacting, according to the manner in which she was received.

She was quite confident in her own power. Strengthened as she was by the pressing wants of fourteen children, she felt that she could make her way through legions of episcopal servants and force herself, if need be, into the presence of the lady who had so wronged her. She had no shame about it, no *mauvaise honte*, no dread of archdeacons. She would, as she declared to her husband, make her wail heard in the market-place if she did not get redress and justice. It might be very well for an unmarried young curate to be shamefaced in such matters; it might be all right that a snug rector, really in want of nothing, but still looking for better preferment, should carry on his affairs decently under the rose. But Mrs. Quiverful, with fourteen children, had given over being shamefaced and, in some things, had given over being decent. If it were intended that she should be ill-used in the manner proposed by Mr. Slope, it should not be done under the rose. All the world should know of it.

In her present mood, Mrs. Quiverful was not over-careful about her attire. She tied her bonnet under her chin, threw her shawl over her shoulders, armed herself with the old family cotton umbrella, and started for Barchester. A journey to the palace was not quite so easy a thing for Mrs. Quiverful as for our friend at Plumstead. Plumstead is nine miles from Barchester, and Puddingdale is but four. But the archdeacon could order round his brougham, and his high-trotting fast bay gelding would take him into the city within the hour. There was no brougham in the coach-house of Puddingdale Vicarage, no bay horse in the stables. There was no method of locomotion for its inhabitants but that which nature has assigned to man.

Mrs. Quiverful was a broad, heavy woman, not young, nor given to walking. In her kitchen, and in the family dormitories, she was active enough, but her pace and gait were not adapted for the road. A walk into Barchester and back in the middle of an August day would be to her a terrible task, if not altogether impracticable. There was living in the parish, about half a mile from the vicarage on the road to the city, a decent, kindly farmer, well to do as regards this world and so far mindful of the next that he attended his parish church with decent regularity. To him Mrs. Quiverful had before now appealed in some of her more pressing family troubles, and had not appealed in vain. At his door she now presented herself, and, having explained to his wife that most urgent business required her to go at once to Barchester, begged that Farmer Subsoil would take her thither in his tax-cart. The farmer did not reject her plan, and, as soon as Prince could be got into his collar, they started on their journey.

Mrs. Quiverful did not mention the purpose of her business, nor did the farmer alloy his kindness by any unseemly questions. She merely begged to be put down at the bridge going into the city and to be taken up again at the same place in the course of two hours. The farmer promised to be punctual to his appointment, and the lady, supported by her umbrella, took the short cut to the close and, in a few minutes, was at the bishop's door.

Hitherto she had felt no dread with regard to the coming interview. She had felt nothing but an indignant longing to pour forth her claims, and declare her wrongs, if those claims were not fully admitted. But now the difficulty of her situation touched her a little. She had been at the palace once before, but then she went to give grateful thanks. Those who have thanks to return for favours received find easy admittance to the halls of the great. Such is not always the case with men, or even with women, who have favours to beg. Still less easy is access for those who demand the fulfilment of promises already made.

Mrs. Quiverful had not been slow to learn the ways of the world. She knew all this, and she knew also that her cotton umbrella and all but ragged shawl would not command respect in the eyes of the palatial servants. If she were too humble, she knew well that she would never succeed. To overcome by imperious overbearing with such a shawl as hers upon her shoulders and such a bonnet on her head would have required a personal bearing very superior to that with which nature had endowed her. Of this also Mrs. Quiverful was aware. She must make it known that she was the wife of a gentleman and a clergyman, and must yet condescend to conciliate.

The poor lady knew but one way to overcome these difficulties at the very threshold of her enterprise, and to this she resorted. Low as were the domestic funds at Puddingdale, she still retained possession of half a crown, and this she sacrificed to the avarice of Mrs. Proudie's metropolitan sesquipedalian serving-man. She was, she said, Mrs. Quiverful of Puddingdale, the wife of the Rev. Mr. Quiverful. She wished to see Mrs. Proudie. It was indeed quite indispensable that she should see Mrs. Proudie. James Fitzplush looked worse than dubious, did not know whether his lady were out, or engaged, or in her bedroom; thought it most probable she was subject to one of these or to some other cause that would make her invisible; but Mrs. Quiverful could sit down in the waiting-room while inquiry was being made of Mrs. Proudie's maid.

"Look here, my man," said Mrs. Quiverful; "I must see her;" and she put her card and half-crown—think of it, my reader, think of it; her last half-crown—into the man's hand and sat herself down on a chair in the waiting-room.

Whether the bribe carried the day, or whether the bishop's wife really chose to see the vicar's wife, it boots not now to inquire. The man returned and, begging Mrs. Quiverful to follow him, ushered her into the presence of the mistress of the diocese.

Mrs. Quiverful at once saw that her patroness was in a smiling humour. Triumph sat throned upon her brow, and all the joys of dominion hovered about her curls. Her lord had that morning contested with her a great point. He had received an invitation to spend a couple of days with the archbishop. His soul longed for the gratification. Not a word, however, in his grace's note alluded to the fact of his being a married man; if he went at all, he must go alone. This necessity would have presented no insurmountable bar to the visit, or have militated much against the pleasure, had he been able to go without any reference to Mrs. Proudie. But this he could not do. He could not order his portmanteau to be packed and start with his own man, merely telling the lady of his heart that he would probably be back on Saturday. There are men—may we not rather say monsters?—who do such things, and there are wives—may we not rather say slaves?—who put up with such usage. But Dr. and Mrs. Proudie were not among the number.

The bishop, with some beating about the bush, made the lady understand that he very much wished to go. The lady, without any beating about the bush, made the bishop understand that she wouldn't hear of it. It would be useless here to repeat the arguments that were used on each side, and needless to record the result. Those who are married will understand very well how the battle was lost and won, and those who are single will never understand it till they learn the lesson which experience alone can give. When Mrs. Quiverful was shown into Mrs. Proudie's room, that lady had only returned a few minutes from her lord. But before she left him she had seen the answer to the archbishop's note written and sealed. No wonder that her face was wreathed with smiles as she received Mrs. Quiverful.

She instantly spoke of the subject which was so near the heart of her visitor. "Well, Mrs. Quiverful," said she, "is it decided yet when you are to move into Barchester?"

"That woman," as she had an hour or two since been called, became instantly re-endowed with all the graces that can adorn a bishop's wife. Mrs. Quiverful immediately saw that her business was to be piteous, and that nothing was to be gained by indignation—nothing, indeed, unless she could be indignant in company with her patroness.

"Oh, Mrs. Proudie," she began, "I fear we are not to move to Barchester at all."

"Why not?" said that lady sharply, dropping at a moment's notice her smiles and condescension, and turning with her sharp quick way to business which she saw at a glance was important.

And then Mrs. Quiverful told her tale. As she progressed in the history of her wrongs she perceived that the heavier she leant upon Mr. Slope the blacker became Mrs. Proudie's brow, but that such blackness was not injurious to her own case. When Mr. Slope was at Puddingdale Vicarage that morning she had regarded him as the creature of the lady-bishop; now she perceived that they were enemies. She admitted her mistake to herself without any pain or humiliation. She had but one feeling, and that was confined to her family. She cared little how she twisted and turned among these new-comers at the bishop's palace so long as she could twist her husband into the warden's house. She cared not which was her friend or which was her enemy, if only she could get this preferment which she so sorely wanted.

She told her tale, and Mrs. Proudie listened to it almost in silence. She told how Mr. Slope had cozened her husband into resigning his claim, and had declared that it was the bishop's will that none but Mr. Harding should be warden. Mrs. Proudie's brow became blacker and blacker. At last she started from her chair and, begging Mrs. Quiverful to sit and wait for her return, marched out of the room.

"Oh, Mrs. Proudie, it's for fourteen children—for fourteen children." Such was the burden that fell on her ear as she closed the door behind her.

CHAPTER XXVI

MRS. PROUDIE WRESTLES AND GETS A FALL

It was hardly an hour since Mrs. Proudie had left her husband's apartment victorious, and yet so indomitable was her courage that she now returned thither panting for another combat. She was greatly angry with what she thought was his duplicity. He had so clearly given her a promise on this matter of the hospital. He had been already so absolutely vanquished on that point. Mrs. Proudie began to feel that if every affair was to be thus discussed and battled about twice and even thrice, the work of the diocese would be too much even for her.

Without knocking at the door, she walked quickly into her husband's room and found him seated at his office table, with Mr. Slope opposite to him. Between his fingers was the very note which he had written to the archbishop in her presence—and it was open! Yes, he had absolutely violated the seal which had been made sacred by her approval. They were sitting in deep conclave, and it was too clear that the purport of the archbishop's invitation had been absolutely canvassed again, after it had been already debated and decided on in obedience to her behests! Mr. Slope rose from his chair and bowed slightly. The two opposing spirits looked each other fully in the face, and they knew that they were looking each at an enemy.

"What is this, Bishop, about Mr. Quiverful?" said she, coming to the end of the table and standing there.

Mr. Slope did not allow the bishop to answer but replied himself. "I have been out to Puddingdale this morning, ma'am, and have seen Mr. Quiverful. Mr. Quiverful has abandoned his claim to the hospital because he is now aware that Mr. Harding is desirous to fill his old place. Under these circumstances I have strongly advised his lordship to nominate Mr. Harding."

"Mr. Quiverful has not abandoned anything," said the lady, with a very imperious voice. "His lordship's word has been pledged to him, and it must be respected."

The bishop still remained silent. He was anxiously desirous of making his old enemy bite the dust beneath his feet. His new ally had told him that nothing was more easy for him than to do so. The ally was there now at his elbow to help him, and yet his courage failed him. It is so hard to conquer when the prestige of former victories is all against one. It is so hard for the cock who has once been beaten out of his yard to resume his courage and again take a proud place upon a dunghill.

"Perhaps I ought not to interfere," said Mr. Slope, "but yet—"

"Certainly you ought not," said the infuriated dame.

"But yet," continued Mr. Slope, not regarding the interruption, "I have thought it my imperative duty to recommend the bishop not to slight Mr. Harding's claims."

"Mr. Harding should have known his own mind," said the lady.

"If Mr. Harding be not replaced at the hospital, his lordship will have to encounter much ill-will, not only in the diocese, but in the world at large. Besides, taking a higher ground, his lordship, as I understand, feels it to be his duty to gratify, in this matter, so very worthy a man and so good a clergyman as Mr. Harding."

"And what is to become of the Sabbath-day school and of the Sunday services in the hospital?" said Mrs. Proudie, with something very nearly approaching to a sneer on her face.

"I understand that Mr. Harding makes no objection to the Sabbath-day school," said Mr. Slope. "And as to the hospital services, that matter will be best discussed after his appointment. If he has any permanent objection, then, I fear, the matter must rest."

"You have a very easy conscience in such matters, Mr. Slope," said she.

"I should not have an easy conscience," he rejoined, "but a conscience very far from being easy, if anything said or done by me should lead the bishop to act unadvisedly in this matter. It is clear that in the interview I had with Mr. Harding I misunderstood him—"

"And it is equally clear that you have misunderstood Mr. Quiverful," said she, now at the top of her wrath. "What business have you at all with these interviews? Who desired you to go to Mr. Quiverful this morning? Who commissioned you to manage this affair? Will you answer me, sir? Who sent you to Mr. Quiverful this morning?"

There was a dead pause in the room. Mr. Slope had risen from his chair, and was standing with his hand on the back of it, looking at first very solemn and now very black. Mrs. Proudie was standing as she had at first placed herself, at the end of the table, and as she interrogated her foe she struck her hand upon it with almost more than feminine vigour. The bishop was sitting in his easy chair twiddling his thumbs, turning his eyes now to his wife, and now to his chaplain, as each took up the cudgels. How comfortable it would be if they could fight it out between them without the necessity of any interference on his part; fight it out so that one should kill the other utterly, as far as diocesan life was concerned, so that he, the bishop, might know clearly by whom it behoved him to be led. There would be the comfort of quiet in either case; but if the bishop had a wish as to which might prove the victor, that wish was certainly not antagonistic to Mr. Slope.

"Better the d—— you know than the d—— you don't know," is an old saying, and perhaps a true one; but the bishop had not yet realized the truth of it.

"Will you answer me, sir?" she repeated. "Who instructed you to call on Mr. Quiverful this morning?" There was another pause. "Do you intend to answer me, sir?"

"I think, Mrs. Proudie, that under all the circumstances it will be better for me not to answer such a question," said Mr. Slope. Mr. Slope had many tones in his voice, all duly under his command; among them was a sanctified low tone and a sanctified loud tone—he now used the former.

"Did anyone send you, sir?"

"Mrs. Proudie," said Mr. Slope, "I am quite aware how much I owe to your kindness. I am aware also what is due by courtesy from a gentleman to a lady. But there are higher considerations than either of those, and I hope I shall be forgiven if I now allow myself to be actuated solely by them. My duty in this matter is to his lordship, and I can admit of no questioning but from him. He has approved of what I have done, and you must excuse me if I say that, having that approval and my own, I want none other."

What horrid words were these which greeted the ear of Mrs. Proudie? The matter was indeed too clear. There was premeditated mutiny in the camp. Not only had ill-conditioned minds become insubordinate by the fruition of a little power, but sedition had been overtly taught and preached. The bishop had not yet been twelve months in his chair, and rebellion had already reared her hideous head within the palace. Anarchy and misrule would quickly follow unless she took immediate and strong measures to put down the conspiracy which she had detected.

"Mr. Slope," she said with slow and dignified voice, differing much from that which she had hitherto used, "Mr. Slope, I will trouble you, if you please, to leave the apartment. I wish to speak to my lord alone."

Mr. Slope also felt that everything depended on the present interview. Should the bishop now be re-petticoated, his thraldom would be complete and forever. The present moment was peculiarly propitious for rebellion. The bishop had clearly committed himself by breaking the seal of the answer to the archbishop; he had therefore fear to influence him. Mr. Slope had told him that no consideration ought to induce him to refuse the archbishop's invitation; he had therefore hope to influence him. He had accepted Mr. Quiverful's resignation and therefore dreaded having to renew that matter with his wife. He had been screwed up to the pitch of asserting a will of his own, and might possibly be carried on till by an absolute success he should have been taught how possible it was to succeed. Now was the moment for victory or rout. It was now that Mr. Slope must make himself master of the diocese, or else resign his place and begin his search for fortune again. He saw all this plainly. After what had taken place any compromise between him and the lady was impossible. Let him once leave the room at her bidding and leave the bishop in her hands, and he might at once pack up his portmanteau and bid adieu to episcopal honours, Mrs. Bold, and the Signora Neroni.

And yet it was not so easy to keep his ground when he was bidden by a lady to go, or to continue to make a third in a party between a husband and wife when the wife expressed a wish for a *tête-à-tête* with her husband.

"Mr. Slope," she repeated, "I wish to be alone with my lord."

"His lordship has summoned me on most important diocesan business," said Mr. Slope, glancing with uneasy eye at Dr. Proudie. He felt that he must trust something to the bishop, and yet that that trust was so woefully ill-placed. "My leaving him at the present moment is, I fear, impossible."

"Do you bandy words with me, you ungrateful man?" said she. "My lord, will you do me the favour to beg Mr. Slope to leave the room?"

My lord scratched his head, but for the moment said nothing. This was as much as Mr. Slope expected from him, and was on the whole, for him, an active exercise of marital rights.

"My lord," said the lady, "is Mr. Slope to leave this room, or am I?"

Here Mrs. Proudie made a false step. She should not have alluded to the possibility of retreat on her part. She should not have expressed the idea that her order for Mr. Slope's expulsion could be treated otherwise than by immediate obedience. In answer to such a question the bishop naturally said in his own mind that, as it was necessary that one should leave the room, perhaps it might be as well that Mrs. Proudie did so. He did say so in his own mind, but externally he again scratched his head and again twiddled his thumbs.

Mrs. Proudie was boiling over with wrath. Alas, alas! Could she but have kept her temper as her enemy did, she would have conquered as she had ever conquered. But divine anger got the better of her, as it has done of other heroines, and she fell.

"My lord," said she, "am I to be vouchsafed an answer or am I not?"

At last he broke his deep silence and proclaimed himself a Slopeite. "Why, my dear," said he, "Mr. Slope and I are very busy."

That was all. There was nothing more necessary. He had gone to the battlefield, stood the dust and heat of the day, encountered the fury of the foe, and won the victory. How easy is success to those who will only be true to themselves!

Mr. Slope saw at once the full amount of his gain, and turned on the vanquished lady a look of triumph which she never forgot and never forgave. Here he was wrong. He should have looked humbly at her and, with meek entreating eye, have deprecated her anger. He should have said by his glance that he asked pardon for his success, and that he hoped forgiveness for the stand which he had been forced to make in the cause of duty. So might he perchance have somewhat mollified that imperious bosom and prepared the way for future terms. But Mr. Slope meant to rule without terms. Ah, forgetful, inexperienced man! Can you cause that little trembling victim to be divorced from the woman that possesses him? Can you provide that they shall be separated at bed and board? Is he not flesh of her flesh and bone of her bone, and must he not so continue? It is very well now for you to stand your ground and triumph as she is driven ignominiously from the room, but can you be present when those curtains are drawn, when that awful helmet of proof has been tied beneath the chin, when the small remnants of the bishop's prowess shall be cowed by the tassel above his head? Can you then intrude yourself when the wife wishes "to speak to my lord alone?"

But for the moment Mr. Slope's triumph was complete, for Mrs. Proudie without further parley left the room and did not forget to shut the door after her. Then followed a close conference between the new allies, in which was said much which it astonished Mr. Slope to say and the bishop to hear. And yet the one said it and the other heard it without ill-will. There was no mincing of matters now. The chaplain plainly told the bishop that the world gave him credit for being under the governance of his wife; that his credit and character in the diocese were suffering; that he would surely get himself in hot water if he allowed Mrs. Proudie to interfere in matters which were not suitable for a woman's powers; and in fact that he would become contemptible if he did not throw off the yoke under which he groaned. The bishop at first hummed and hawed and affected to deny the truth of what was said. But his denial was not stout and quickly broke down. He soon admitted by silence his state of vassalage and pledged himself, with Mr. Slope's assistance, to change his courses. Mr. Slope also did not make out a bad case for himself. He explained how it grieved him to run counter to a lady who had always been his patroness, who had befriended him in so many ways, who had, in fact, recommended him to the bishop's notice; but, as he stated, his duty was now imperative; he held a situation of peculiar confidence, and was immediately and especially attached to the bishop's person. In such a situation his conscience required that he should regard solely the bishop's interests, and therefore he had ventured to speak out.

The bishop took this for what it was worth, and Mr. Slope only intended that he should do so. It gilded the pill which Mr. Slope had to administer, and which the bishop thought would be less bitter than that other pill which he had so long been taking.

"My lord," had his immediate reward, like a good child. He was instructed to write and at once did write another note to the archbishop accepting his grace's invitation. This note Mr. Slope, more prudent than the lady, himself took away and posted with his own hands. Thus he made sure that this act of self-jurisdiction should be as nearly as possible a *fait accompli*. He begged, and coaxed, and threatened the bishop with a view of making him also write at once to Mr. Harding, but the bishop, though temporally emancipated from his wife, was not yet enthralled to Mr. Slope. He said, and probably said truly, that such an offer must be made in some official form; that he was not yet prepared to sign the form; and that he should prefer seeing Mr. Harding before he did so. Mr. Slope might, however, beg Mr. Harding to call upon him. Not disappointed with his achievement Mr. Slope went his way. He first posted the precious note which he had in his pocket, and then pursued other enterprises in which we must follow him in other chapters.

Mrs. Proudie, having received such satisfaction as was to be derived from slamming her husband's door, did not at once betake herself to Mrs. Quiverful. Indeed, for the first few moments after her repulse she felt that she could not again see that lady. She would have to own that she had been beaten, to confess that the diadem had passed from her brow, and the sceptre from her hand! No, she would send a message to her with a promise of a letter on the next day or the day after. Thus resolving, she betook herself to her bed-room, but here she again changed her mind. The air of that sacred enclosure somewhat restored her courage and gave her more heart. As Achilles warmed at the sight of his armour, as Don Quixote's heart grew strong when he grasped his lance, so did Mrs. Proudie look forward to fresh laurels, as her eye fell on her husband's pillow. She would not despair. Having so resolved, she descended with dignified mien and refreshed countenance to Mrs. Quiverful.

This scene in the bishop's study took longer in the acting than in the telling. We have not, perhaps, had the whole of the conversation. At any rate Mrs. Quiverful was beginning to be very impatient, and was thinking that Farmer Subsoil would be tired of waiting for her, when Mrs. Proudie returned. Oh, who can tell the palpitations of that maternal heart, as the suppliant looked into the face of the great lady to see written there either a promise of house, income, comfort and future competence, or else the doom of continued and ever-increasing poverty! Poor mother! Poor wife! There was little there to comfort you!

"Mrs. Quiverful," thus spoke the lady with considerable austerity, and without sitting down herself, "I find that your husband has behaved in this matter in a very weak and foolish manner."

Mrs. Quiverful immediately rose upon her feet, thinking it disrespectful to remain sitting while the wife of the bishop stood. But she was desired to sit down again, and made to do so, so that Mrs. Proudie might stand and preach over her. It is generally considered an offensive thing for a gentleman to keep his seat while another is kept standing before him, and we presume the same law holds with regard to ladies. It often is so felt, but we are inclined to say that it never produces half the discomfort or half the feeling of implied inferiority that is shown by a great man who desires his visitor to be seated while he himself speaks from his legs. Such a solecism in good breeding, when construed into English, means this: "The accepted rules of courtesy in the world require that I should offer you a seat; if I did not do so, you would bring a charge against me in the world of being arrogant and ill-mannered; I will obey the world, but, nevertheless, I will not put myself on an equality with you. You may sit down, but I won't sit with you. Sit, therefore, at my bidding, and I'll stand and talk at you!"

This was just what Mrs. Proudie meant to say, and Mrs. Quiverful, though she was too anxious and too flurried thus to translate the full meaning of the manoeuvre, did not fail to feel its effect. She was cowed and uncomfortable, and a second time essayed to rise from her chair.

"Pray be seated, Mrs. Quiverful, pray keep your seat. Your husband, I say, has been most weak and most foolish. It is impossible, Mrs. Quiverful, to help people who will not help themselves. I much fear that I can now do nothing for you in this matter."

"Oh, Mrs. Proudie, don't say so," said the poor woman, again jumping up.

"*Pray* be seated, Mrs. Quiverful. I must fear that I can do nothing further for you in this matter. Your husband has, in a most unaccountable manner, taken upon himself to resign that which I was empowered to offer him. As a matter of course, the bishop expects that his clergy shall know their own minds. What he may ultimately do—what we may finally decide on doing—I cannot now say. Knowing the extent of your family—"

"Fourteen children, Mrs. Proudie, fourteen of them! And barely bread—barely bread? It's hard for the children of a clergyman, it's hard for one who has always done his duty respectably!" Not a word fell from her about herself, but the tears came streaming down her big, coarse cheeks, on which the dust of the August road had left its traces.

Mrs. Proudie has not been portrayed in these pages as an agreeable or an amiable lady. There has been no intention to impress the reader much in her favour. It is ordained that all novels should have a male and a female angel and a male and a female devil. If it be considered that this rule is obeyed in these pages, the latter character must be supposed to have fallen to the lot of Mrs. Proudie. But she was not all devil. There was a heart inside that stiff-ribbed bodice, though not, perhaps, of large dimensions, and certainly not easily accessible. Mrs. Quiverful, however, did gain access, and Mrs. Proudie proved herself a woman. Whether it was the fourteen children with their probable bare bread and their possible bare backs, or the respectability of the father's work, or the mingled dust and tears on the mother's face, we will not pretend to say. But Mrs. Proudie was touched.

She did not show it as other women might have done. She did not give Mrs. Quiverful eau-de-Cologne, or order her a glass of wine. She did not take her to her toilet table and offer her the use of brushes and combs, towels and water. She did not say soft little speeches and coax her kindly back to equanimity. Mrs. Quiverful, despite her rough appearance, would have been as amenable to such little tender cares as any lady in the land. But none such were forthcoming. Instead of this, Mrs. Proudie slapped one hand upon the other and declared—not with an oath, for, as a lady and a Sabbatarian and a she-bishop, she could not swear, but with an adjuration—that she "wouldn't have it done."

The meaning of this was that she wouldn't have Mr. Quiverful's promised appointment cozened away by the treachery of Mr. Slope and the weakness of her husband. This meaning she very soon explained to Mrs. Quiverful.

"Why was your husband such a fool," said she, now dismounted from her high horse and sitting confidentially down close to her visitor, "as to take the bait which that man threw to him? If he had not been so utterly foolish, nothing could have prevented your going to the hospital."

Poor Mrs. Quiverful was ready enough with her own tongue in accusing her husband to his face of being soft, and perhaps did not always speak of him to her children quite so respectfully as she might have done. But she did not at all like to hear him abused by others, and began to vindicate him and to explain that of course he had taken Mr. Slope to be an emissary from Mrs. Proudie herself; that Mr. Slope was thought to be peculiarly her friend; and that, therefore, Mr. Quiverful would have been failing in respect to her had he assumed to doubt what Mr. Slope had said.

Thus mollified, Mrs. Proudie again declared that she "would not have it done," and at last sent Mrs. Quiverful home with an assurance that, to the furthest stretch of her power and influence in the palace, the appointment of Mr. Quiverful should be insisted on. As she repeated the word "insisted," she thought of the bishop in his night-cap and, with compressed lips, slightly shook her head. Oh, my aspiring pastors, divines to whose ears *nolo episcopari* are the sweetest of words, which of you would be a bishop on such terms as these?

Mrs. Quiverful got home in the farmer's cart, not indeed with a light heart, but satisfied that she had done right in making her visit.

CHAPTER XXVII

A LOVE SCENE

Mr. Slope, as we have said, left the palace with a feeling of considerable triumph. Not that he thought that his difficulties were all over—he did not so deceive himself—but he felt that he had played his first move well, as well as the pieces on the board would allow, and that he had nothing with which to reproach himself. He first of all posted the letter to the archbishop and, having made that sure, proceeded to push the advantage which he had gained. Had Mrs. Bold been at home, he would have called on her, but he knew that she was at Plumstead, so he wrote the following note. It was the beginning of what, he trusted, might be a long and tender series of epistles.

MY DEAR MRS. BOLD, You will understand perfectly that I cannot at present correspond with your father. I heartily wish that I could, and hope the day may be not long distant when mists shall have been cleared away, and we may know each other. But I cannot preclude myself from the pleasure of sending you these few lines to say that Mr. Q. has to-day, in my presence, resigned any title that he ever had to the wardenship of the hospital, and that the bishop has assured me that it is his intention to offer it to your esteemed father.

Will you, with my respectful compliments, ask him, who I believe is now a fellow-visitor with you, to call on the bishop either on Wednesday or Thursday, between ten and one. *This is by the bishop's desire.* If you will so far oblige me as to let me have a line naming either day, and the hour which will suit Mr. Harding, I will take care that the servants shall have orders to show him in without delay. Perhaps I should say no more—but still I wish you could make your father understand that no subject will be mooted between his lordship and him which will refer at all to the method in which he may choose to perform his duty. I for one am persuaded that no clergyman could perform it more satisfactorily than he did, or than he will do again.

On a former occasion I was indiscreet and much too impatient, considering your father's age and my own. I hope he will not now refuse my apology. I still hope also that with your aid and sweet pious labours we may live to attach such a Sabbath-school to the old endowment as may, by God's grace and furtherance, be a blessing to the poor of this city.

You will see at once that this letter is confidential. The subject, of course, makes it so. But, equally, of course, it is for your parent's eye as well as for your own, should you think proper to show it to him.

I hope my darling little friend Johnny is as strong as ever—dear little fellow. Does he still continue his rude assaults on those beautiful long silken tresses?

I can assure you your friends miss you from Barchester sorely, but it would be cruel to begrudge you your sojourn among flowers and fields during this truly sultry weather.

Pray believe me, my dear Mrs. Bold,

Yours most sincerely,

OBADIAH SLOPE

Barchester, Friday.

Now this letter, taken as a whole, and with the consideration that Mr. Slope wished to assume a great degree of intimacy with Eleanor, would not have been bad but for the allusion to the tresses. Gentlemen do not write to ladies about their tresses unless they are on very intimate terms indeed. But Mr. Slope could not be expected to be aware of this. He longed to put a little affection into his epistle, and yet he thought it injudicious, as the letter would, he knew, be shown to Mr. Harding. He would have insisted that the letter should be strictly private and seen by no eyes but Eleanor's own, had he not felt that such an injunction would have been disobeyed. He therefore restrained his passion, did not sign himself "yours affectionately," and contented himself instead with the compliment to the tresses.

Having finished his letter, he took it to Mrs. Bold's house and, learning there, from the servant, that things were to be sent out to Plumstead that afternoon, left it, with many injunctions, in her hands.

We will now follow Mr. Slope so as to complete the day with him and then return to his letter and its momentous fate in the next chapter.

There is an old song which gives us some very good advice about courting:—

It's gude to be off with the auld luve

Before ye be on wi' the new.

Of the wisdom of this maxim Mr. Slope was ignorant, and accordingly, having written his letter to Mrs. Bold, he proceeded to call upon the Signora Neroni. Indeed, it was hard to say which was the old love and which the new, Mr. Slope having been smitten with both so nearly at the same time. Perhaps he thought it not amiss to have two strings to his bow. But two strings to Cupid's bow are always dangerous to him on whose behalf they are to be used. A man should remember that between two stools he may fall to the ground. But in sooth Mr. Slope was pursuing Mrs. Bold in obedience to his better instincts, and the signora in obedience to his worser. Had he won the widow and worn her, no one could have blamed him. You, O reader, and I, and Eleanor's other friends would have received the story of such a winning with much disgust and disappointment, but we should have been angry with Eleanor, not with Mr. Slope. Bishop, male and female, dean and chapter and diocesan clergy in full congress could have found nothing to disapprove of in such an alliance. Convocation itself, that mysterious and mighty synod, could in no wise have fallen foul of it. The possession of £1000 a year and a beautiful wife would not at all have hurt the voice of the pulpit charmer, or lessened the grace and piety of the exemplary clergyman.

But not of such a nature were likely to be his dealings with the Signora Neroni. In the first place he knew that her husband was living, and therefore he could not woo her honestly. Then again she had nothing to recommend her to his honest wooing, had such been possible. She was not only portionless, but also from misfortune unfitted to be chosen as the wife of any man who wanted a useful mate. Mr. Slope was aware that she was a helpless, hopeless cripple.

But Mr. Slope could not help himself. He knew that he was wrong in devoting his time to the back drawing-room in Dr. Stanhope's house. He knew that what took place there would, if divulged, utterly ruin him with Mrs. Bold. He knew that scandal would soon come upon his heels and spread abroad among the black coats of Barchester some tidings, exaggerated tidings, of the sighs which he poured into the lady's ears. He knew that he was acting against the recognized principles of his life, against those laws of conduct by which he hoped to achieve much higher success. But, as we have said, he could not help himself. Passion, for the first time in his life, passion was too strong for him.

As for the signora, no such plea can be put forward for her, for in truth she cared no more for Mr. Slope than she did for twenty others who had been at her feet before him. She willingly, nay greedily, accepted his homage. He was the finest fly that Barchester had hitherto afforded to her web, and the signora was a powerful spider that made wondrous webs, and could in no way live without catching flies. Her taste in this respect was abominable, for she had no use for the victims when caught. She could not eat them matrimonially, as young lady flies do whose webs are most frequently of their mothers' weaving. Nor could she devour them by any escapade of a less legitimate description. Her unfortunate affliction precluded her from all hope of levanting with a lover. It would be impossible to run away with a lady who required three servants to move her from a sofa.

The signora was subdued by no passion. Her time for love was gone. She had lived out her heart, such heart as she had ever had, in her early years, at an age when Mr. Slope was thinking of the second book of Euclid and his unpaid bill at the buttery hatch. In age the lady was younger than the gentleman, but in feelings, in knowledge of the affairs of love, in intrigue, he was immeasurably her junior. It was necessary to her to have some man at her feet. It was the one customary excitement of her life. She delighted in the exercise of power which this gave her; it was now nearly the only food for her ambition; she would boast to her sister that she could make a fool of any man, and the sister, as little imbued with feminine delicacy as herself, good-naturedly thought it but fair that such amusement should be afforded to a poor invalid who was debarred from the ordinary pleasures of life.

Mr. Slope was madly in love but hardly knew it. The Signora spitted him, as a boy does a cockchafer on a cork, that she might enjoy the energetic agony of his gyrations. And she knew very well what she was doing.

Mr. Slope having added to his person all such adornments as are possible to a clergyman making a morning visit—such as a clean necktie, clean handkerchief, new gloves, and a *soupçon* of not unnecessary scent—called about three o'clock at the doctor's door. At about this hour the signora was almost always alone in the back drawing-room. The mother had not come down. The doctor was out or in his own room. Bertie was out, and Charlotte at any rate left the room if anyone called whose object was specially with her sister. Such was her idea of being charitable and sisterly.

Mr. Slope, as was his custom, asked for Mr. Stanhope, and was told, as was the servant's custom, that the signora was in the drawing-room. Upstairs he accordingly went. He found her, as he always did, lying on her sofa with a French volume before her and a beautiful little inlaid writing-case open on her table. At the moment of his entrance she was in the act of writing.

"Ah, my friend," said she, putting out her left hand to him across her desk, "I did not expect you to-day and was this very instant writing to you—"

Mr. Slope, taking the soft, fair, delicate hand in his—and very soft and fair and delicate it was—bowed over it his huge red head and kissed it. It was a sight to see, a deed to record if the author could fitly do it, a picture to put on canvas. Mr. Slope was big, awkward, cumbrous, and, having his heart in his pursuit, was ill at ease. The lady was fair, as we have said, and delicate; everything about her was fine and refined; her hand in his looked like a rose lying among carrots, and when he kissed it, he looked as a cow might do on finding such a flower among her food. She was graceful as a couchant goddess and, moreover, as self-possessed as Venus must have been when courting Adonis.

Oh, that such grace and such beauty should have condescended to waste itself on such a pursuit!

"I was in the act of writing to you," said she, "but now my scrawl may go into the basket;" and she raised the sheet of gilded note-paper from off her desk as though tear it.

"Indeed it shall not," said he, laying the embargo of half a stone weight of human flesh and blood upon the devoted paper. "Nothing that you write for my eyes, signora, shall be so desecrated," and he took up the letter, put that also among the carrots and fed on it, and then proceeded to read it.

"Gracious me! Mr. Slope," said she, "I hope you don't mean to say you keep all the trash I write to you. Half my time I don't know what I write, and when I do, I know it is only fit for the back of the fire. I hope you have not that ugly trick of keeping letters."

"At any rate, I don't throw them into a waste-paper basket. If destruction is their doomed lot, they perish worthily, and are burnt on a pyre, as Dido was of old."

"With a steel pen stuck through them, of course," said she, "to make the simile more complete. Of all the ladies of my acquaintance I think Lady Dido was the most absurd. Why did she not do as Cleopatra did? Why did she not take out her ships and insist on going with him? She could not bear to lose the land she had got by a swindle, and then she could not bear the loss of her lover. So she fell between two stools. Mr. Slope, whatever you do, never mingle love and business."

Mr. Slope blushed up to his eyes and over his mottled forehead to the very roots of his hair. He felt sure that the signora knew all about his intentions with reference to Mrs Bold. His conscience told him that he was detected. His doom was to be spoken; he was to be punished for his duplicity, and rejected by the beautiful creature before him. Poor man. He little dreamt that had all his intentions with reference to Mrs. Bold been known to the signora, it would only have added zest to that lady's amusement. It was all very well to have Mr. Slope at her feet, to show her power by making an utter fool of a clergyman, to gratify her own infidelity by thus proving the little strength which religion had in controlling the passions even of a religious man; but it would be an increased gratification if she could be made to understand that she was at the same time alluring her victim away from another, whose love if secured would be in every way beneficent and salutary.

The Signora had indeed discovered, with the keen instinct of such a woman, that Mr. Slope was bent on matrimony with Mrs. Bold, but in alluding to Dido she had not thought of it. She instantly perceived, however, from her lover's blushes, what was on his mind and was not slow in taking advantage of it.

She looked him full in the face, not angrily, nor yet with a smile, but with an intense and overpowering gaze; then, holding up her forefinger and slightly shaking her head, she said:—

"Whatever you do, my friend, do not mingle love and business. Either stick to your treasure and your city of wealth, or else follow your love like a true man. But never attempt both. If you do, you'll have to die with a broken heart as did poor Dido. Which is it to be with you, Mr. Slope, love or money?"

Mr. Slope was not so ready with a pathetic answer as he usually was with touching episodes in his extempore sermons. He felt that he ought to say something pretty, something also that should remove the impression on the mind of his lady-love. But he was rather put about how to do it.

"Love," said he, "true overpowering love, must be the strongest passion a man can feel; it must control every other wish, and put aside every other pursuit. But with me love will never act in that way unless it be returned;" and he threw upon the signora a look of tenderness which was intended to make up for all the deficiencies of his speech.

"Take my advice," said she. "Never mind love. After all, what is it? The dream of a few weeks. That is all its joy. The disappointment of a life is its Nemesis. Who was ever successful in true love? Success in love argues that the love is false. True love is always despondent or tragical. Juliet loved, Haidee loved, Dido loved, and what came of it? Troilus loved and ceased to be a man."

"Troilus loved and was fooled," said the more manly chaplain. "A man may love and yet not be a Troilus. All women are not Cressidas."

"No, all women are not Cressidas. The falsehood is not always on the woman's side. Imogen was true, but how was she rewarded? Her lord believed her to be the paramour of the first he who came near her in his absence. Desdemona was true and was smothered. Ophelia was true and went mad. There is no happiness in love, except at the end of an English novel. But in wealth, money, houses, lands, goods, and chattels, in the good things of this world, yes, in them there is something tangible, something that can be retained and enjoyed."

"Oh, no," said Mr. Slope, feeling himself bound to enter some protest against so very unorthodox a doctrine, "this world's wealth will make no one happy."

"And what will make you happy—you—you?" said she, raising herself up and speaking to him with energy across the table. "From what source do you look for happiness? Do not say that you look for none. I shall not believe you. It is a search in which every human being spends an existence."

"And the search is always in vain," said Mr. Slope. "We look for happiness on earth, while we ought to be content to hope for it in heaven."

"Pshaw! You preach a doctrine which you know you don't believe. It is the way with you all. If you know that there is no earthly happiness, why do you long to be a bishop or a dean? Why do you want lands and income?"

"I have the natural ambition of a man," said he.

"Of course you have, and the natural passions; and therefore I say that you don't believe the doctrine you preach. St. Paul was an enthusiast. He believed so that his ambition and passions did not war against his creed. So does the Eastern fanatic who passes half his life erect upon a pillar. As for me, I will believe in no belief that does not make itself manifest by outward signs. I will think no preaching sincere that is not recommended by the practice of the preacher."

Mr. Slope was startled and horrified, but he felt that he could not answer. How could he stand up and preach the lessons of his Master, being there, as he was, on the devil's business? He was a true believer, otherwise this would have been nothing to him. He had audacity for most things, but he had not audacity to make a plaything of the Lord's word. All this the signora understood, and felt much interest as she saw her cockchafer whirl round upon her pin.

"Your wit delights in such arguments," said he, "but your heart and your reason do not go along with them."

"My heart!" said she; "you quite mistake the principles of my composition if you imagine that there is such a thing about me." After all, there was very little that was false in anything that the signora said. If Mr. Slope allowed himself to be deceived, it was his own fault. Nothing could have been more open than her declarations about herself.

The little writing-table with her desk was still standing before her, a barrier, as it were, against the enemy. She was sitting as nearly upright as she ever did, and he had brought a chair close to the sofa, so that there was only the corner of the table between him and her.

It so happened that as she spoke her hand lay upon the table, and as Mr. Slope answered her he put his hand upon hers.

"No heart!" said he. "That is a heavy charge which you bring against yourself, and one of which I cannot find you guilty—"

She withdrew her hand, not quickly and angrily, as though insulted by his touch, but gently and slowly.

"You are in no condition to give a verdict on the matter," said she, "as you have not tried me. No, don't say that you intend doing so, for you know you have no intention of the kind; nor indeed have I, either. As for you, you will take your vows where they will result in something more substantial than the pursuit of such a ghostlike, ghastly love as mine—"

"Your love should be sufficient to satisfy the dream of a monarch," said Mr. Slope, not quite clear as to the meaning of his words.

"Say an archbishop, Mr. Slope," said she. Poor fellow! She was very cruel to him. He went round again upon his cork on this allusion to his profession. He tried, however, to smile and gently accused her of joking on a matter, which was, he said, to him of such vital moment.

"Why—what gulls do you men make of us," she replied. "How you fool us to the top of our bent; and of all men you clergymen are the most fluent of your honeyed, caressing words. Now look me in the face, Mr. Slope, boldly and openly."

Mr. Slope did look at her with a languishing loving eye, and as he did so he again put forth his hand to get hold of hers.

"I told you to look at me boldly, Mr. Slope, but confine your boldness to your eyes."

"Oh, Madeline!" he sighed.

"Well, my name is Madeline," said she, "but none except my own family usually call me so. Now look me in the face, Mr. Slope. Am I to understand that you say you love me?"

Mr. Slope never had said so. If he had come there with any formed plan at all, his intention was to make love to the lady without uttering any such declaration. It was, however, quite impossible that he should now deny his love. He had, therefore, nothing for it but to go down on his knees distractedly against the sofa and swear that he did love her with a love passing the love of man.

The signora received the assurance with very little palpitation or appearance of surprise. "And now answer me another question," said she. "When are you to be married to my dear friend Eleanor Bold?"

Poor Mr. Slope went round and round in mortal agony. In such a condition as his it was really very hard for him to know what answer to give. And yet no answer would be his surest condemnation. He might as well at once plead guilty to the charge brought against him.

"And why do you accuse me of such dissimulation?" said he.

"Dissimulation! I said nothing of dissimulation. I made no charge against you, and make none. Pray don't defend yourself to me. You swear that you are devoted to my beauty, and yet you are on the eve of matrimony with another. I feel this to be rather a compliment. It is to Mrs. Bold that you must defend yourself. That you may find difficult; unless, indeed, you can keep her in the dark. You clergymen are cleverer than other men."

"Signora, I have told you that I loved you, and now you rail at me."

"Rail at you. God bless the man; what would he have? Come, answer me this at your leisure—not without thinking now, but leisurely and with consideration—are you not going to be married to Mrs. Bold?"

"I am not," said he. And as he said it he almost hated, with an exquisite hatred, the woman whom he could not help loving with an exquisite love.

"But surely you are a worshipper of hers?"

"I am not," said Mr. Slope, to whom the word worshipper was peculiarly distasteful. The signora had conceived that it would be so.

"I wonder at that," said she. "Do you not admire her? To my eye she is the perfection of English beauty. And then she is rich, too. I should have thought she was just the person to attract you. Come, Mr. Slope, let me give you advice on this matter. Marry the charming widow; she will be a good mother to your children and an excellent mistress of a clergyman's household."

"Oh, signora, how can you be so cruel?"

"Cruel," said she, changing the voice of banter which she had been using for one which was expressively earnest in its tone; "is that cruelty?"

"How can I love another while my heart is entirely your own?"

"If that were cruelty, Mr. Slope, what might you say of me if I were to declare that I returned your passion? What would you think if I bound you even by a lover's oath to do daily penance at this couch of mine? What can I give in return for a man's love? Ah, dear friend, you have not realized the conditions of my fate."

Mr. Slope was not on his knees all this time. After his declaration of love, he had risen from them as quickly as he thought consistent with the new position which he now filled, and as he stood was leaning on the back of his chair. This outburst of tenderness on the signora's part quite overcame him and made him feel for the moment that he could sacrifice everything to be assured of the love of the beautiful creature before him, maimed, lame, and already married as she was.

"And can I not sympathize with your lot?" said he, now seating himself on her sofa and pushing away the table with his foot.

"Sympathy is so near to pity!" said she. "If you pity me, cripple as I am, I shall spurn you from me."

"Oh, Madeline, I will only love you," and again he caught her hand and devoured it with kisses. Now she did not draw it from him, but sat there as he kissed it, looking at him with her great eyes, just as a great spider would look at a great fly that was quite securely caught.

"Suppose Signor Neroni were to come to Barchester," said she. "Would you make his acquaintance?"

"Signor Neroni!" said he.

"Would you introduce him to the bishop, and Mrs. Proudie, and the young ladies?" said she, again having recourse to that horrid quizzing voice which Mr. Slope so particularly hated.

"Why do you ask such a question?" said he.

"Because it is necessary that you should know that there is a Signor Neroni. I think you had forgotten it."

"If I thought that you retained for that wretch one particle of the love of which he was never worthy, I would die before I would distract you by telling you what I feel. No! Were your husband the master of your heart, I might perhaps love you, but you should never know it."

"My heart again! How you talk. And you consider then that if a husband be not master of his wife's heart, he has no right to her fealty; if a wife ceases to love, she may cease to be true. Is that your doctrine on this matter, as a minister of the Church of England?"

Mr. Slope tried hard within himself to cast off the pollution with which he felt that he was defiling his soul. He strove to tear himself away from the noxious siren that had bewitched him. But he could not do it. He could not be again heart free. He had looked for rapturous joy in loving this lovely creature, and he already found that he met with little but disappointment and self-rebuke. He had come across the fruit of the Dead Sea, so sweet and delicious to the eye, so bitter and nauseous to the taste. He had put the apple to his mouth, and it had turned to ashes between his teeth. Yet he could not tear himself away. He knew, he could not but know, that she jeered at him, ridiculed his love, and insulted the weakness of his religion. But she half-permitted his adoration, and that half-permission added such fuel to his fire that all the fountain of his piety could not quench it. He began to feel savage, irritated, and revengeful. He meditated some severity of speech, some taunt that should cut her, as her taunts cut him. He reflected as he stood there for a moment, silent before her, that if he desired to quell her proud spirit, he should do so by being prouder even than herself; that if he wished to have her at his feet suppliant for his love, it behoved him to conquer her by indifference. All this passed through his mind. As far as dead knowledge went, he knew, or thought he knew, how a woman should be tamed. But when he essayed to bring his tactics to bear, he failed like a child. What chance has dead knowledge with experience in any of the transactions between man and man? What possible chance between man and woman? Mr. Slope loved furiously, insanely and truly, but he had never played the game of love. The signora did not love at all, but she was up to every move of the board. It was Philidor pitted against a schoolboy.

And so she continued to insult him, and he continued to bear it.

"Sacrifice the world for love!" she said in answer to some renewed vapid declaration of his passion. "How often has the same thing been said, and how invariably with the same falsehood!"

"Falsehood," said he. "Do you say that I am false to you? Do you say that my love is not real?"

"False? Of course it is false, false as the father of falsehood—if indeed falsehoods need a sire and are not self-begotten since the world began. You are ready to sacrifice the world for love? Come let us see what you will sacrifice. I care nothing for nuptial vows. The wretch, I think you were kind enough to call him so, whom I swore to love and obey is so base that he can only be thought of with repulsive disgust. In the council chamber of my heart I have divorced him. To me that is as good as though aged lords had gloated for months over the details of his licentious life. I care nothing for what the world can say. Will you be as frank? Will you take me to your home as your wife? Will you call me Mrs. Slope before bishop, dean, and prebendaries?" The poor tortured wretch stood silent, not knowing what to say. "What! You won't do that. Tell me, then, what part of the world is it that you will sacrifice for my charms?"

"Were you free to marry, I would take you to my house to-morrow and wish no higher privilege."

"I am free," said she, almost starting up in her energy. For though there was no truth in her pretended regard for her clerical admirer, there was a mixture of real feeling in the scorn and satire with which she spoke of love and marriage generally. "I am free—free as the winds. Come, will you take me as I am? Have your wish; sacrifice the world, and prove yourself a true man."

Mr. Slope should have taken her at her word. She would have drawn back, and he would have had the full advantage of the offer. But he did not. Instead of doing so, he stood wrapt in astonishment, passing his fingers through his lank red hair and thinking, as he stared upon her animated countenance, that her wondrous beauty grew more wonderful as he gazed on it. "Ha! ha! ha!" she laughed out loud. "Come, Mr. Slope, don't talk of sacrificing the world again. People beyond one-and-twenty should never dream of such a thing. You and I, if we have the dregs of any love left in us, if we have the remnants of a passion remaining in our hearts, should husband our resources better. We are not in our première jeunesse. The world is a very nice place. Your world, at any rate, is so. You have all manner of fat rectories to get and possible bishoprics to enjoy. Come, confess; on second thoughts you would not sacrifice such things for the smiles of a lame lady?"

It was impossible for him to answer this. In order to be in any way dignified, he felt that he must be silent.

"Come," said she, "don't boody with me: don't be angry because I speak out some home truths. Alas, the world, as I have found it, has taught me bitter truths. Come, tell me that I am forgiven. Are we not to be friends?" and she again put out her hand to him.

He sat himself down in the chair beside her, took her proffered hand, and leant over her.

"There," said she with her sweetest, softest smile—a smile to withstand which a man should be cased in triple steel, "there; seal your forgiveness on it," and she raised it towards his face. He kissed it again and again, and stretched over her as though desirous of extending the charity of his pardon beyond the hand that was offered to him. She managed, however, to check his ardour. For one so easily allured as this poor chaplain, her hand was surely enough.

"Oh, Madeline!" said he, "tell me that you love me—do you—do you love me?"

"Hush," said she. "There is my mother's step. Our tête-à-tête has been of monstrous length. Now you had better go. But we shall see you soon again, shall we not?"

Mr. Slope promised that he would call again on the following day.

"And, Mr. Slope," she continued, "pray answer my note. You have it in your hand, though I declare during these two hours you have not been gracious enough to read it. It is about the Sabbath-school and the children. You know how anxious I am to have them here. I have been learning the catechism myself, on purpose. You must manage it for me next week. I will teach them, at any rate, to submit themselves to their spiritual pastors and masters."

Mr. Slope said but little on the subject of Sabbath-schools, but he made his adieu, and betook himself home with a sad heart, troubled mind, and uneasy conscience.

CHAPTER XXVIII

MRS. BOLD IS ENTERTAINED BY DR. AND MRS. GRANTLY AT PLUMSTEAD

It will be remembered that Mr. Slope, when leaving his *billet-doux* at the house of Mrs. Bold, had been informed that it would be sent out to her at Plumstead that afternoon. The archdeacon and Mr. Harding had in fact come into town together in the brougham, and it had been arranged that they should call for Eleanor's parcels as they left on their way home. Accordingly they did so call, and the maid, as she handed to the coachman a small basket and large bundle carefully and neatly packed, gave in at the carriage window Mr. Slope's epistle. The archdeacon, who was sitting next to the window, took it and immediately recognized the hand-writing of his enemy.

"Who left this?" said he.

"Mr. Slope called with it himself, your Reverence," said the girl, "and was very anxious that Missus should have it to-day."

So the brougham drove off, and the letter was left in the archdeacon's hand. He looked at it as though he held a basket of adders. He could not have thought worse of the document had he read it and discovered it to be licentious and atheistical. He did, moreover, what so many wise people are accustomed to do in similar circumstances; he immediately condemned the person to whom the letter was written, as though she were necessarily a *participes criminis*.

Poor Mr. Harding, though by no means inclined to forward Mr. Slope's intimacy with his daughter, would have given anything to have kept the letter from his son-in-law. But that was now impossible. There it was in his hand, and he looked as thoroughly disgusted as though he were quite sure that it contained all the rhapsodies of a favoured lover.

"It's very hard on me," said he after awhile, "that this should go on under my roof."

Now here the archdeacon was certainly most unreasonable. Having invited his sister-in-law to his house, it was a natural consequence that she should receive her letters there. And if Mr. Slope chose to write to her, his letter would, as a matter of course, be sent after her. Moreover, the very fact of an invitation to one's house implies confidence on the part of the inviter. He had shown that he thought Mrs. Bold to be a fit person to stay with him by his asking her to do so, and it was most cruel to her that he should complain of her violating the sanctity of his roof-tree, when the laches committed were none of her committing.

Mr. Harding felt this, and felt also that when the archdeacon talked thus about his roof, what he said was most offensive to himself as Eleanor's father. If Eleanor did receive a letter from Mr. Slope, what was there in that to pollute the purity of Dr. Grantly's household? He was indignant that his daughter should be so judged and so spoken of, and he made up his mind that even as Mrs. Slope she must be dearer to him than any other creature on God's earth. He almost broke out and said as much, but for the moment he restrained himself.

"Here," said the archdeacon, handing the offensive missile to his father-in-law, "I am not going to be the bearer of his love-letters. You are her father and may do as you think fit with it."

By doing as he thought fit with it, the archdeacon certainly meant that Mr. Harding would be justified in opening and reading the letter, and taking any steps which might in consequence be necessary. To tell the truth, Dr. Grantly did feel rather a stronger curiosity than was justified by his outraged virtue to see the contents of the letter. Of course he could not open it himself, but he wished to make Mr. Harding understand that he, as Eleanor's father, would be fully justified in doing so. The idea of such a proceeding never occurred to Mr. Harding. His authority over Eleanor ceased when she became the wife of John Bold. He had not the slightest wish to pry into her correspondence. He consequently put the letter into his pocket, and only wished that he had been able to do so without the archdeacon's knowledge. They both sat silent during half the journey home, and then Dr. Grantly said, "Perhaps Susan had better give it to her. She can explain to her sister better than either you or I can do how deep is the disgrace of such an acquaintance."

"I think you are very hard upon Eleanor," replied Mr. Harding. "I will not allow that she has disgraced herself, nor do I think it likely that she will do so. She has a right to correspond with whom she pleases, and I shall not take upon myself to blame her because she gets a letter from Mr. Slope."

"I suppose," said Dr. Grantly, "you don't wish her to marry the man. I suppose you'll admit that she would disgrace herself if she did do so."

"I do not wish her to marry him," said the perplexed father. "I do not like him, and do not think he would make a good husband. But if Eleanor chooses to do so, I shall certainly not think that she disgraces herself."

"Good heavens!" exclaimed Dr. Grantly and threw himself back into the corner of his brougham. Mr. Harding said nothing more, but commenced playing a dirge with an imaginary fiddle bow upon an imaginary violoncello, for which there did not appear to be quite room enough in the carriage; he continued the tune, with sundry variations, till he arrived at the rectory door.

The archdeacon had been meditating sad things in his mind. Hitherto he had always looked on his father-in-law as a true partisan, though he knew him to be a man devoid of all the combative qualifications for that character. He had felt no fear that Mr. Harding would go over to the enemy, though he had never counted much on the ex-warden's prowess in breaking the hostile ranks. Now, however, it seemed that Eleanor, with her wiles, had completely trepanned and bewildered her father, cheated him out of his judgement, robbed him of the predilections and tastes of his life, and caused him to be tolerant of a man whose arrogance and vulgarity would, a few years since, have been unendurable to him. That the whole thing was as good as arranged between Eleanor and Mr. Slope there was no longer any room to doubt. That Mr. Harding knew that such was the case, even this could hardly be doubted. It was too manifest that he at any rate suspected it and was prepared to sanction it.

And to tell the truth, such was the case. Mr. Harding disliked Mr. Slope as much as it was in his nature to dislike any man. Had his daughter wished to do her worst to displease him by a second marriage, she could hardly have succeeded better than by marrying Mr. Slope. But, as he said to himself now very often, what right had he to condemn her if she did nothing that was really wrong? If she liked Mr. Slope, it was her affair. It was indeed miraculous to him that a woman with such a mind, so educated, so refined, so nice in her tastes, should like such a man. Then he asked himself whether it was possible that she did so.

Ah, thou weak man; most charitable, most Christian, but weakest of men! Why couldn't thou not have asked herself? Was she not the daughter of thy loins, the child of thy heart, the best beloved to thee of all humanity? Had she not proved to thee, by years of closest affection, her truth and goodness and filial obedience? And yet, knowing and feeling all this, thou couldst endure to go groping in darkness, hearing her named in strains which wounded thy loving heart, and being unable to defend her as thou shouldst have done!

Mr. Harding had not believed, did not believe, that his daughter meant to marry this man, but he feared to commit himself to such an opinion. If she did do it there would be then no means of retreat. The wishes of his heart were: first, that there should be no truth in the archdeacon's surmises; and in this wish he would have fain trusted entirely, had he dared so to do; secondly, that the match might be prevented, if unfortunately, it had been contemplated by Eleanor; thirdly, that should she be so infatuated as to marry this man, he might justify his conduct and declare that no cause existed for his separating himself from her.

He wanted to believe her incapable of such a marriage; he wanted to show that he so believed of her; but he wanted also to be able to say hereafter that she had done nothing amiss, if she should unfortunately prove herself to be different from what he thought her to be.

Nothing but affection could justify such fickleness, but affection did justify it. There was but little of the Roman about Mr. Harding. He could not sacrifice his Lucretia even though she should be polluted by the accepted addresses of the clerical Tarquin at the palace. If Tarquin could be prevented, well and good, but if not, the father would still open his heart to his daughter and accept her as she presented herself, Tarquin and all.

Dr. Grantly's mind was of a stronger calibre, and he was by no means deficient in heart. He loved with an honest genuine love his wife and children and friends. He loved his father-in-law, and was quite prepared to love Eleanor too, if she would be one of his party, if she would be on his side, if she would regard the Slopes and the Proudies as the enemies of mankind and acknowledge and feel the comfortable merits of the Gwynnes and Arabins. He wished to be what he called "safe" with all those whom he had admitted to the penetralia of his house and heart. He could luxuriate in no society that was deficient in a certain feeling of faithful, staunch High Churchism, which to him was tantamount to freemasonry. He was not strict in his lines of definition. He endured without impatience many different shades of Anglo-church conservatism; but with the Slopes and Proudies he could not go on all fours.

He was wanting in, moreover, or perhaps it would be more correct to say, he was not troubled by that womanly tenderness which was so peculiar to Mr. Harding. His feelings towards his friends were that while they stuck to him, he would stick to them; that he would work with them shoulder and shoulder; that he would be faithful to the faithful. He knew nothing of that beautiful love which can be true to a false friend.

And thus these two men, each miserable enough in his own way, returned to Plumstead.

It was getting late when they arrived there, and the ladies had already gone up to dress. Nothing more was said as the two parted in the hall. As Mr. Harding passed to his own room he knocked at Eleanor's door and handed in the letter. The archdeacon hurried to his own territory, there to unburden his heart to his faithful partner.

What colloquy took place between the marital chamber and the adjoining dressing-room shall not be detailed. The reader, now intimate with the persons concerned, can well imagine it. The whole tenor of it also might be read in Mrs. Grantly's brow as she came down to dinner.

Eleanor, when she received the letter from her father's hand, had no idea from whom it came. She had never seen Mr. Slope's handwriting, or if so had forgotten it, and did not think of him as she twisted the letter as people do twist letters when they do not immediately recognize their correspondents either by the writing or the seal. She was sitting at her glass, brushing her hair and rising every other minute to play with her boy, who was sprawling on the bed and who engaged pretty nearly the whole attention of the maid as well as of his mother.

At last, sitting before her toilet-table, she broke the seal and, turning over the leaf, saw Mr. Slope's name. She first felt surprised, and then annoyed, and then anxious. As she read it she became interested. She was so delighted to find that all obstacles to her father's return to the hospital were apparently removed that she did not observe the fulsome language in which the tidings were conveyed. She merely perceived that she was commissioned to tell her father that such was the case, and she did not realize the fact that such a communication should not have been made, in the first instance, to her by an unmarried young clergyman. She felt, on the whole, grateful to Mr. Slope and anxious to get on her dress that she might run with the news to her father. Then she came to the allusion to her own pious labours, and she said in her heart that Mr. Slope was an affected ass. Then she went on again and was offended by her boy being called Mr. Slope's darling—he was nobody's darling but her own, or at any rate not the darling of a disagreeable stranger like Mr. Slope. Lastly she arrived at the tresses and felt a qualm of disgust. She looked up in the glass, and there they were before her, long and silken, certainly, and very beautiful. I will not say but that she knew them to be so, but she felt angry with them and brushed them roughly and carelessly. She crumpled the letter up with angry violence, and resolved, almost without thinking of it, that she would not show it to her father. She would merely tell him the contents of it. She then comforted herself again with her boy, had her dress fastened, and went down to dinner.

As she tripped down the stairs she began to ascertain that there was some difficulty in her situation. She could not keep from her father the news about the hospital, nor could she comfortably confess the letter from Mr. Slope before the Grantlys. Her father had already gone down. She had heard his step upon the lobby. She resolved therefore to take him aside and tell him her little bit of news. Poor girl! She had no idea how severely the unfortunate letter had already been discussed.

When she entered the drawing-room, the whole party were there, including Mr. Arabin, and the whole party looked glum and sour. The two girls sat silent and apart as though they were aware that something was wrong. Even Mr. Arabin was solemn and silent. Eleanor had not seen him since breakfast. He had been the whole day at St. Ewold's, and such having been the case, it was natural that he should tell how matters were going on there. He did nothing of the kind, however, but remained solemn and silent. They were all solemn and silent. Eleanor knew in her heart that they had been talking about her, and her heart misgave her as she thought of Mr. Slope and his letter. At any rate she felt it to be quite impossible to speak to her father alone while matters were in this state.

Dinner was soon announced, and Dr. Grantly, as was his wont, gave Eleanor his arm. But he did so as though the doing it were an outrage on his feelings rendered necessary by sternest necessity. With quick sympathy Eleanor felt this, and hardly put her fingers on his coat-sleeve. It may be guessed in what way the dinner-hour was passed. Dr. Grantly said a few words to Mr. Arabin, Mr. Arabin said a few words to Mrs. Grantly, she said a few words to her father, and he tried to say a few words to Eleanor. She felt that she had been tried and found guilty of something, though she knew not what. She longed to say out to them all, "Well, what is it that I have done; out with it, and let me know my crime; for heaven's sake let me hear the worst of it;" but she could not. She could say nothing, but sat there silent, half-feeling that she was guilty, and trying in vain to pretend even to eat her dinner.

At last the cloth was drawn, and the ladies were not long following it. When they were gone, the gentlemen were somewhat more sociable but not much so. They could not of course talk over Eleanor's sins. The archdeacon had indeed so far betrayed his sister-in-law as to whisper into Mr. Arabin's ear in the study, as they met there before dinner, a hint of what he feared. He did so with the gravest and saddest of fears, and Mr. Arabin became grave and apparently sad enough as he heard it. He opened his eyes, and his mouth and said in a sort of whisper "Mr. Slope!" in the same way as he might have said "The Cholera!" had his friend told him that that horrid disease was in his nursery. "I fear so, I fear so," said the archdeacon, and then together they left the room.

We will not accurately analyse Mr. Arabin's feelings on receipt of such astounding tidings. It will suffice to say that he was surprised, vexed, sorrowful, and ill at ease. He had not perhaps thought very much about Eleanor, but he had appreciated her influence, and had felt that close intimacy with her in a country-house was pleasant to him, and also beneficial. He had spoken highly of her intelligence to the archdeacon, and had walked about the shrubberies with her, carrying her boy on his back. When Mr. Arabin had called Johnny his darling, Eleanor was not angry.

Thus the three men sat over their wine, all thinking of the same subject, but unable to speak of it to each other. So we will leave them and follow the ladies into the drawing-room.

Mrs. Grantly had received a commission from her husband, and had undertaken it with some unwillingness. He had desired her to speak gravely to Eleanor and to tell her that, if she persisted in her adherence to Mr. Slope, she could no longer look for the countenance of her present friends. Mrs. Grantly probably knew her sister better than the doctor did, and assured him that it would be in vain to talk to her. The only course likely to be of any service in her opinion was to keep Eleanor away from Barchester. Perhaps she might have added, for she had a very keen eye in such things, that there might also be ground for hope in keeping Eleanor near Mr. Arabin. Of this, however, she said nothing. But the archdeacon would not be talked over; he spoke much of his conscience, and declared that, if Mrs. Grantly would not do it, he would. So instigated, the lady undertook the task, stating, however, her full conviction that her interference would be worse than useless. And so it proved.

As soon as they were in the drawing-room Mrs. Grantly found some excuse for sending her girls away, and then began her task. She knew well that she could exercise but very slight authority over her sister. Their various modes of life, and the distance between their residences, had prevented any very close confidence. They had hardly lived together since Eleanor was a child. Eleanor had, moreover, especially in latter years, resented in a quiet sort of way the dictatorial authority which the archdeacon seemed to exercise over her father, and on this account had been unwilling to allow the archdeacon's wife to exercise authority over herself.

"You got a note just before dinner, I believe," began the eldest sister.

Eleanor acknowledged that she had done so, and felt that she turned red as she acknowledged it. She would have given anything to have kept her colour, but the more she tried to do so the more signally she failed.

"Was it not from Mr. Slope?"

Eleanor said that the letter was from Mr. Slope.

"Is he a regular correspondent of yours, Eleanor?"

"Not exactly," said she, already beginning to feel angry at the cross-examination. She determined, and why it would be difficult to say, that nothing should induce her to tell her sister Susan what was the subject of the letter. Mrs. Grantly, she knew, was instigated by the archdeacon, and she would not plead to any arraignment made against her by him.

"But, Eleanor dear, why do you get letters from Mr. Slope at all, knowing, as you do, he is a person so distasteful to Papa, and to the archdeacon, and indeed to all your friends?"

"In the first place, Susan, I don't get letters from him; and in the next place, as Mr. Slope wrote the one letter which I have got, and as I only received it, which I could not very well help doing, as Papa handed it to me, I think you had better ask Mr. Slope instead of me."

"What was his letter about, Eleanor?"

"I cannot tell you," said she, "because it was confidential. It was on business respecting a third person."

"It was in no way personal to yourself then?"

"I won't exactly say that, Susan," said she, getting more and more angry at her sister's questions.

"Well, I must say it's rather singular," said Mrs. Grantly, affecting to laugh, "that a young lady in your position should receive a letter from an unmarried gentleman of which she will not tell the contents and which she is ashamed to show to her sister."

"I am not ashamed," said Eleanor, blazing up. "I am not ashamed of anything in the matter; only I do not choose to be cross-examined as to my letters by anyone."

"Well, dear," said the other, "I cannot but tell you that I do not think Mr. Slope a proper correspondent for you."

"If he be ever so improper, how can I help his having written to me? But you are all prejudiced against him to such an extent that that which would be kind and generous in another man is odious and impudent in him. I hate a religion that teaches one to be so one-sided in one's charity."

"I am sorry, Eleanor, that you hate the religion you find here, but surely you should remember that in such matters the archdeacon must know more of the world than you do. I don't ask you to respect or comply with me, although I am, unfortunately, so many years your senior; but surely, in such a matter as this, you might consent to be guided by the archdeacon. He is most anxious to be your friend, if you will let him."

"In such a matter as what?" said Eleanor very testily. "Upon my word I don't know what this is all about."

"We all want you to drop Mr. Slope."

"You all want me to be as illiberal as yourselves. That I shall never be. I see no harm in Mr. Slope's acquaintance, and I shall not insult the man by telling him that I do. He has thought it necessary to write to me, and I do not want the archdeacon's advice about the letter. If I did, I would ask it."

"Then, Eleanor, it is my duty to tell you," and now she spoke with a tremendous gravity, "that the archdeacon thinks that such a correspondence is disgraceful, and that he cannot allow it to go on in his house."

Eleanor's eyes flashed fire as she answered her sister, jumping up from her seat as she did so. "You may tell the archdeacon that wherever I am I shall receive what letters I please and from whom I please. And as for the word 'disgraceful,' if Dr. Grantly has used it of me, he has been unmanly and inhospitable," and she walked off to the door. "When

Papa comes from the dining-room I will thank you to ask him to step up to my bedroom. I will show him Mr. Slope's letter, but I will show it to no one else." And so saying, she retreated to her baby.

She had no conception of the crime with which she was charged. The idea that she could be thought by her friends to regard Mr. Slope as a lover had never flashed upon her. She conceived that they were all prejudiced and illiberal in their persecution of him, and therefore she would not join in the persecution, even though she greatly disliked the man.

Eleanor was very angry as she seated herself in a low chair by her open window at the foot of her child's bed. "To dare to say I have disgraced myself," she repeated to herself more than once. "How Papa can put up with that man's arrogance! I will certainly not sit down to dinner in his house again unless he begs my pardon for that word." And then a thought struck her that Mr. Arabin might perchance hear of her "disgraceful" correspondence with Mr. Slope, and she turned crimson with pure vexation. Oh, if she had known the truth! If she could have conceived that Mr. Arabin had been informed as a fact that she was going to marry Mr. Slope!

She had not been long in her room before her father joined her. As he left the drawing-room Mrs. Grantly took her husband into the recess of the window and told him how signally she had failed.

"I will speak to her myself before I go to bed," said the archdeacon.

"Pray do no such thing," said she; "you can do no good and will only make an unseemly quarrel in the house. You have no idea how headstrong she can be."

The archdeacon declared that as to that he was quite indifferent. He knew his duty and would do it. Mr. Harding was weak in the extreme in such matters. He would not have it hereafter on his conscience that he had not done all that in him lay to prevent so disgraceful an alliance. It was in vain that Mrs. Grantly assured him that speaking to Eleanor angrily would only hasten such a crisis and render it certain, if at present there were any doubt. He was angry, self-willed, and sore. The fact that a lady of his household had received a letter from Mr. Slope had wounded his pride in the sorest place, and nothing could control him.

Mr. Harding looked worn and woe-begone as he entered his daughter's room. These sorrows worried him sadly. He felt that if they were continued, he must go to the wall in the manner so kindly prophesied to him by the chaplain. He knocked gently at his daughter's door, waited till he was distinctly bade to enter, and then appeared as though he and not she were the suspected criminal.

Eleanor's arm was soon within his, and she had soon kissed his forehead and caressed him, not with joyous but with eager love. "Oh, Papa," she said, "I do so want to speak to you. They have been talking about me downstairs to-night—don't you know they have, Papa?"

Mr. Harding confessed with a sort of murmur that the archdeacon had been speaking of her.

"I shall hate Dr. Grantly soon—"

"Oh, my dear!"

"Well, I shall. I cannot help it. He is so uncharitable, so unkind, so suspicious of everyone that does not worship himself: and then he is so monstrously arrogant to other people who have a right to their opinions as well as he has to his own."

"He is an earnest, eager man, my dear, but he never means to be unkind."

"He is unkind, Papa, most unkind. There, I got that letter from Mr. Slope before dinner. It was you yourself who gave it to me. There, pray read it. It is all for you. It should have been addressed to you. You know how they have been talking about it downstairs. You know how they behaved to me at dinner. And since dinner Susan has been preaching to me, till I could not remain in the room with her. Read it, Papa, and then say whether that is a letter that need make Dr. Grantly so outrageous."

Mr. Harding took his arm from his daughter's waist and slowly read the letter. She expected to see his countenance lit with joy as he learnt that his path back to the hospital was made so smooth; but she was doomed to disappointment, as had once been the case before on a somewhat similar occasion. His first feeling was one of unmitigated disgust that Mr. Slope should have chosen to interfere in his behalf. He had been anxious to get back to the hospital, but he would have infinitely sooner resigned all pretensions to the place than have owed it in any manner to Mr. Slope's influence in his favour. Then he thoroughly disliked the tone of Mr. Slope's letter; it was unctuous, false, and unwholesome, like the man. He saw, which Eleanor had failed to see, that much more had been intended than was expressed. The appeal to Eleanor's pious labours as separate from his own grated sadly against his feelings as a father. And then, when he came to the "darling boy" and the "silken tresses," he slowly closed and folded the letter in despair. It was impossible that Mr. Slope should so write unless he had been encouraged. It was impossible Eleanor should have received such a letter, and have received it without annoyance, unless she were willing to encourage him. So at least Mr. Harding argued to himself.

How hard it is to judge accurately of the feelings of others. Mr. Harding, as he came to the close of the letter, in his heart condemned his daughter for indelicacy, and it made him miserable to do so. She was not responsible for what Mr. Slope might write. True. But then she expressed no disgust at it. She had rather expressed approval of the letter as a whole. She had given it to him to read, as a vindication for herself and also for him. The father's spirits sank within him as he felt that he could not acquit her.

And yet it was the true feminine delicacy of Eleanor's mind which brought on her this condemnation. Listen to me, ladies, and I beseech you to acquit her. She thought of this man, this lover of whom she was so unconscious, exactly as her father did, exactly as the Grantlys did. At least she esteemed him personally as they did. But she believed him to be in the main an honest man, and one truly inclined to assist her father. She felt herself bound, after what had passed, to show this letter to Mr. Harding. She thought it necessary that he should know what Mr. Slope had to say. But she did not think it necessary to apologize for, or condemn, or even allude to the vulgarity of the man's tone, which arose, as does all vulgarity, from ignorance. It was nauseous to her to have a man like Mr. Slope commenting on her personal attractions, and she did not think it necessary to dilate with her father upon what was nauseous. She never supposed they could disagree on such a subject. It would have been painful for her to point it out, painful for her to speak strongly against a man of whom, on the whole, she was anxious to think and speak well. In encountering such a man she had encountered what was disagreeable, as she might do in walking the streets. But in such encounters she never thought it necessary to dwell on what disgusted her.

And he, foolish, weak, loving man, would not say one word, though one word would have cleared up everything. There would have been a deluge of tears, and in ten minutes everyone in the house would have understood how matters really were. The father would have been delighted. The sister would have kissed her sister and begged a thousand pardons. The archdeacon would have apologized and wondered, and raised his eyebrows, and gone to bed a happy man. And Mr. Arabin—Mr. Arabin would have dreamt of Eleanor, have awoke in the morning with ideas of love, and retired to rest the next evening with schemes of marriage. But, alas, all this was not to be.

Mr. Harding slowly folded the letter, handed it back to her, kissed her forehead, and bade God bless her. He then crept slowly away to his own room.

As soon as he had left the passage, another knock was given at Eleanor's door, and Mrs. Grantly's very demure own maid, entering on tiptoe, wanted to know would Mrs. Bold be so kind as to speak to the archdeacon for two minutes in the archdeacon's study, if not disagreeable. The archdeacon's compliments, and he wouldn't detain her two minutes.

Eleanor thought it was very disagreeable; she was tired and fagged and sick at heart; her present feelings towards Dr. Grantly were anything but those of affection. She was, however, no coward, and therefore promised to be in the study in five minutes. So she arranged her hair, tied on her cap, and went down with a palpitating heart.

CHAPTER XXIX

A SERIOUS INTERVIEW

There are people who delight in serious interviews, especially when to them appertains the part of offering advice or administering rebuke, and perhaps the archdeacon was one of these. Yet on this occasion he did not prepare himself for the coming conversation with much anticipation of pleasure. Whatever might be his faults he was not an inhospitable man, and he almost felt that he was sinning against hospitality in upbraiding Eleanor in his own house. Then, also, he was not quite sure that he would get the best of it. His wife had told him that he decidedly would not, and he usually gave credit to what his wife said. He was, however, so convinced of what he considered to be the impropriety of Eleanor's conduct, and so assured also of his own duty in trying to check it, that his conscience would not allow him to take his wife's advice and go to bed quietly.

Eleanor's face as she entered the room was not such as to reassure him. As a rule she was always mild in manner and gentle in conduct; but there was that in her eye which made it not an easy task to scold her. In truth she had been little used to scolding. No one since her childhood had tried it but the archdeacon, and he had generally failed when he did try it. He had never done so since her marriage; and now, when he saw her quiet, easy step as she entered his room, he almost wished that he had taken his wife's advice.

He began by apologizing for the trouble he was giving her. She begged him not to mention it, assured him that walking downstairs was no trouble to her at all, and then took a seat and waited patiently for him to begin his attack.

"My dear Eleanor," he said, "I hope you believe me when I assure you that you have no sincerer friend than I am." To this Eleanor answered nothing, and therefore he proceeded. "If you had a brother of your own, I should not probably trouble you with what I am going to say. But as it is I cannot but think that it must be a comfort to you to know that you have near you one who is as anxious for your welfare as any brother of your own could be."

"I never had a brother," said she.

"I know you never had, and it is therefore that I speak to you."

"I never had a brother," she repeated, "but I have hardly felt the want. Papa has been to me both father and brother."

"Your father is the fondest and most affectionate of men. But—"

"He is—the fondest and most affectionate of men, and the best of counsellors. While he lives I can never want advice."

This rather put the archdeacon out. He could not exactly contradict what his sister-in-law said about her father, and yet he did not at all agree with her. He wanted her to understand that he tendered his assistance because her father was a soft, good-natured gentleman not sufficiently knowing in the ways of the world; but he could not say this to her. So he had to rush into the subject-matter of his proffered counsel without any acknowledgement on her part that she could need it, or would be grateful for it.

"Susan tells me that you received a letter this evening from Mr. Slope."

"Yes; Papa brought it in the brougham. Did he not tell you?"

"And Susan says that you objected to let her know what it was about."

"I don't think she asked me. But had she done so, I should not have told her. I don't think it nice to be asked about one's letters. If one wishes to show them, one does so without being asked."

"True. Quite so. What you say is quite true. But is not the fact of your receiving letters from Mr. Slope, which you do not wish to show to your friends, a circumstance which must excite some—some surprise—some suspicion—"

"Suspicion!" said she, not speaking above her usual voice, speaking still in a soft, womanly tone but yet with indignation. "Suspicion! And who suspects me, and of what?" And then there was a pause, for the archdeacon was not quite ready to explain the ground of his suspicion. "No, Dr. Grantly, I did not choose to show Mr. Slope's letter to Susan. I could not show it to anyone till Papa had seen it. If you have any wish to read it now, you can do so," and she handed the letter to him over the table.

This was an amount of compliance which he had not at all expected, and which rather upset him in his tactics. However, he took the letter, perused it carefully, and then refolding it, kept it on the table under his hand. To him it appeared to be in almost every respect the letter of a declared lover; it seemed to corroborate his worst suspicions; and the fact of Eleanor's showing it to him was all but tantamount to a declaration on her part that it was her pleasure to receive love-letters from Mr. Slope. He almost entirely overlooked the real subject-matter of the epistle, so intent was he on the forthcoming courtship and marriage.

"I'll thank you to give it me back, if you please, Dr. Grantly."

He took it in his hand and held it up, but made no immediate overture to return it. "And Mr. Harding has seen this?" said he.

"Of course he has," said she; "it was written that he might see it. It refers solely to his business—of course I showed it to him."

"And, Eleanor, do you think that that is a proper letter for you—for a person in your condition—to receive from Mr. Slope?"

"Quite a proper letter," said she, speaking, perhaps, a little out of obstinacy, probably forgetting at the moment the objectionable mention of her silken curls.

"Then, Eleanor, it is my duty to tell you that I wholly differ from you."

"So I suppose," said she, instigated now by sheer opposition and determination not to succumb. "You think Mr. Slope is a messenger direct from Satan. I think he is an industrious, well-meaning clergyman. It's a pity that we differ as we do. But, as we do differ, we had probably better not talk about it."

Here Eleanor undoubtedly put herself in the wrong. She might probably have refused to talk to Dr. Grantly on the matter in dispute without any impropriety, but, having consented to listen to him, she had no business to tell him that he regarded Mr. Slope as an emissary from the evil one; nor was she justified in praising Mr. Slope, seeing that in her heart of hearts she did not think well of him. She was, however, wounded in spirit, and angry, and bitter. She had been subjected to contumely and cross-questioning and ill-usage through the whole evening. No one, not even Mr. Arabin, not even her father, had been kind to her. All this she attributed to the prejudice and conceit of the archdeacon, and therefore she resolved to set no bounds to her antagonism to him. She would neither give nor take quarter. He had greatly presumed in daring to question her about her correspondence, and she was determined to show that she thought so.

"Eleanor, you are forgetting yourself," said he, looking very sternly at her. "Otherwise you would never tell me that I conceive any man to be a messenger from Satan."

"But you do," said she. "Nothing is too bad for him. Give me that letter, if you please;" and she stretched out her hand and took it from him. "He has been doing his best to serve Papa, doing more than any of Papa's friends could do; and yet, because he is the chaplain of a bishop whom you don't like, you speak of him as though he had no right to the usage of a gentleman."

"He has done nothing for your father."

"I believe that he has done a great deal; and, as far as I am concerned, I am grateful to him. Nothing that you can say can prevent my being so. I judge people by their acts, and his, as far as I can see them, are good." She then paused for a moment. "If you have nothing further to say, I shall be obliged by being permitted to say good night—I am very tired."

Dr. Grantly had, as he thought, done his best to be gracious to his sister-in-law. He had endeavoured not to be harsh to her, and had striven to pluck the sting from his rebuke. But he did not intend that she should leave him without hearing him.

"I have something to say, Eleanor, and I fear I must trouble you to hear it. You profess that it is quite proper that you should receive from Mr. Slope such letters as that you have in your hand. Susan and I think very differently. You are, of course, your own mistress, and much as we both must grieve should anything separate you from us, we have no power to prevent you from taking steps which may lead to such a separation. If you are so wilful as to reject the counsel of your friends, you must be allowed to cater for yourself. But, Eleanor, I may at any rate ask you this. Is it worth your while to break away from all those you have loved—from all who love you—for the sake of Mr. Slope?"

"I don't know what you mean, Dr. Grantly; I don't know what you're talking about. I don't want to break away from anybody."

"But you will do so if you connect yourself with Mr. Slope. Eleanor, I must speak out to you. You must choose between your sister and myself and our friends, and Mr. Slope and his friends. I say nothing of your father, as you may probably understand his feelings better than I do."

"What do you mean, Dr. Grantly? What am I to understand? I never heard such wicked prejudice in my life."

"It is no prejudice, Eleanor. I have known the world longer than you have done. Mr. Slope is altogether beneath you. You ought to know and feel that he is so. Pray—pray think of this before it is too late."

"Too late!"

"Or if you will not believe me, ask Susan; you cannot think she is prejudiced against you. Or even consult your father—he is not prejudiced against you. Ask Mr. Arabin—"

"You haven't spoken to Mr. Arabin about this!" said she, jumping up and standing before him.

"Eleanor, all the world in and about Barchester will be speaking of it soon."

"But have you spoken to Mr. Arabin about me and Mr. Slope?"

"Certainly I have, and he quite agrees with me."

"Agrees with what?" said she. "I think you are trying to drive me mad."

"He agrees with me and Susan that it is quite impossible you should be received at Plumstead as Mrs. Slope."

Not being favourites with the tragic muse, we do not dare to attempt any description of Eleanor's face when she first heard the name of Mrs. Slope pronounced as that which would or should or might at some time appertain to herself. The look, such as it was, Dr. Grantly did not soon forget. For a moment or two she could find no words to express her deep anger and deep disgust; indeed, at this conjuncture, words did not come to her very freely.

"How dare you be so impertinent?" at last she said, and then she hurried out of the room without giving the archdeacon the opportunity of uttering another word. It was with difficulty she contained herself till she reached her own room; and then, locking the door, she threw herself on her bed and sobbed as though her heart would break.

But even yet she had no conception of the truth. She had no idea that her father and her sister had for days past conceived in sober earnest the idea that she was going to marry this man. She did not even then believe that the archdeacon thought that she would do so. By some manoeuvre of her brain she attributed the origin of the accusation to Mr. Arabin, and as she did so her anger against him was excessive, and the vexation of her spirit almost unendurable. She could not bring herself to think that the charge was made seriously. It appeared to her most probable that the archdeacon and Mr. Arabin had talked over her objectionable acquaintance with Mr. Slope; that Mr. Arabin in his jeering, sarcastic way had suggested the odious match as being the severest way of treating with contumely her acquaintance with his enemy; and that the archdeacon, taking the idea from him, thought proper to punish her by the allusion. The whole night she lay awake thinking of what had been said, and this appeared to be the most probable solution.

But the reflexion that Mr. Arabin should have in any way mentioned her name in connexion with that of Mr. Slope was overpowering; and the spiteful ill-nature of the archdeacon in repeating the charge to her made her wish to leave his house almost before the day had broken. One thing was certain: nothing should make her stay there beyond the following morning, and nothing should make her sit down to breakfast in company with Dr. Grantly. When she thought of the man whose name had been linked with her own, she cried from sheer disgust. It was only because she would be thus disgusted, thus pained and shocked and cut to the quick, that the archdeacon had spoken the horrid word. He wanted to make her quarrel with Mr. Slope, and therefore he had outraged her by his abominable vulgarity. She determined that at any rate he should know that she appreciated it.

Nor was the archdeacon a bit better satisfied with the result of his serious interview than was Eleanor. He gathered from it, as indeed he could hardly fail to do, that she was very angry with him, but he thought that she was thus angry, not because she was suspected of an intention to marry Mr. Slope, but because such an intention was imputed to her as a crime. Dr. Grantly regarded this supposed union with disgust, but it never occurred to him that Eleanor was outraged because she looked at it exactly in the same light.

He returned to his wife, vexed and somewhat disconsolate, but nevertheless confirmed in his wrath against his sister-in-law. "Her whole behaviour," said he, "has been most objectionable. She handed me his love-letter to read as though she were proud of it. And she is proud of it. She is proud of having this slavering, greedy man at her feet. She will throw herself and John Bold's money into his lap; she will ruin her boy, disgrace her father and you, and be a wretched miserable woman."

His spouse, who was sitting at her toilet-table, continued her avocations, making no answer to all this. She had known that the archdeacon would gain nothing by interfering, but she was too charitable to provoke him by saying so while he was in such deep sorrow.

"This comes of a man making such a will as that of Bold's," he continued. "Eleanor is no more fitted to be trusted with such an amount of money in her own hands than is a charity-school girl." Still Mrs. Grantly made no reply. "But I have done my duty; I can do

nothing further. I have told her plainly that she cannot be allowed to form a link of connexion between me and that man. From henceforward it will not be in my power to make
her welcome at Plumstead. I cannot have Mr. Slope's love-letters coming here. Susan, I
think you had better let her understand that, as her mind on this subject seems to be irrevocably fixed, it will be better for all parties that she should return to Barchester."

Now Mrs. Grantly was angry with Eleanor—nearly as angry as her husband—but she
had no idea of turning her sister out of the house. She therefore at length spoke out and
explained to the archdeacon in her own mild, seducing way that he was fuming and fussing and fretting himself very unnecessarily. She declared that things, if left alone, would
arrange themselves much better than he could arrange them, and at last succeeded in inducing him to go to bed in a somewhat less inhospitable state of mind.

On the following morning Eleanor's maid was commissioned to send word into the
dining-room that her mistress was not well enough to attend prayers and that she would
breakfast in her own room. Here she was visited by her father, and declared to him her
intention of returning immediately to Barchester. He was hardly surprised by the announcement. All the household seemed to be aware that something had gone wrong.
Everyone walked about with subdued feet, and people's shoes seemed to creak more than
usual. There was a look of conscious intelligence on the faces of the women, and the men
attempted, but in vain, to converse as though nothing were the matter. All this had
weighed heavily on the heart of Mr. Harding, and when Eleanor told him that her immediate return to Barchester was a necessity, he merely sighed piteously and said that he would
be ready to accompany her.

But here she objected strenuously. She had a great wish, she said, to go alone; a great
desire that it might be seen that her father was not implicated in her quarrel with Dr.
Grantly. To this at last he gave way; but not a word passed between them about Mr.
Slope—not a word was said, not a question asked as to the serious interview on the preceding evening. There was, indeed, very little confidence between them, though neither of
them knew why it should be so. Eleanor once asked him whether he would not call upon
the bishop, but he answered rather tartly that he did not know—he did not think he should,
but he could not say just at present. And so they parted. Each was miserably anxious for
some show of affection, for some return of confidence, for some sign of the feeling that
usually bound them together. But none was given. The father could not bring himself to
question his daughter about her supposed lover, and the daughter would not sully her
mouth by repeating the odious word with which Dr. Grantly had roused her wrath. And so
they parted.

There was some trouble in arranging the method of Eleanor's return. She begged her
father to send for a post-chaise, but when Mrs. Grantly heard of this, she objected strongly. If Eleanor would go away in dudgeon with the archdeacon, why should she let all the
servants and all the neighbourhood know that she had done so? So at last Eleanor consented to make use of the Plumstead carriage, and as the archdeacon had gone out
immediately after breakfast and was not to return till dinner-time, she also consented to
postpone her journey till after lunch, and to join the family at that time. As to the subject
of the quarrel not a word was said by anyone. The affair of the carriage was arranged by
Mr. Harding, who acted as Mercury between the two ladies; they, when they met, kissed
each other very lovingly and then sat down each to her crochet work as though nothing
was amiss in all the world.

CHAPTER XXX

ANOTHER LOVE SCENE

But there was another visitor at the rectory whose feelings in this unfortunate matter must be somewhat strictly analysed. Mr. Arabin had heard from his friend of the probability of Eleanor's marriage with Mr. Slope with amazement, but not with incredulity. It has been said that he was not in love with Eleanor, and up to this period this certainly had been true. But as soon as he heard that she loved someone else, he began to be very fond of her himself. He did not make up his mind that he wished to have her for his wife; he had never thought of her, and did not now think of her, in connexion with himself; but he experienced an inward, indefinable feeling of deep regret, a gnawing sorrow, an unconquerable depression of spirits, and also a species of self-abasement that he—he, Mr. Arabin—had not done something to prevent that other he, that vile he whom he so thoroughly despised, from carrying off this sweet prize.

Whatever man may have reached the age of forty unmarried without knowing something of such feelings must have been very successful or else very cold-hearted.

Mr. Arabin had never thought of trimming the sails of his bark so that he might sail as convoy to this rich argosy. He had seen that Mrs. Bold was beautiful, but he had not dreamt of making her beauty his own. He knew that Mrs. Bold was rich, but he had had no more idea of appropriating her wealth than that of Dr. Grantly. He had discovered that Mrs. Bold was intelligent, warm-hearted, agreeable, sensible, all in fact that a man could wish his wife to be; but the higher were her attractions, the greater her claims to consideration, the less had he imagined that he might possibly become the possessor of them. Such had been his instinct rather than his thoughts, so humble and so diffident. Now his diffidence was to be rewarded by his seeing this woman, whose beauty was to his eyes perfect, whose wealth was such as to have deterred him from thinking of her, whose widowhood would have silenced him had he not been so deterred, by his seeing her become the prey of—Obadiah Slope!

On the morning of Mrs. Bold's departure he got on his horse to ride over to St. Ewold's. As he rode he kept muttering to himself a line from Van Artevelde,
How little flattering is woman's love.
And then he strove to recall his mind and to think of other affairs—his parish, his college, his creed—but his thoughts would revert to Mr. Slope and the Flemish chieftain.

When we think upon it,
How little flattering is woman's love,
Given commonly to whosoe'er is nearest

And propped with most advantage.

It was not that Mrs. Bold should marry anyone but him—he had not put himself forward as a suitor—but that she should marry Mr. Slope; and so he repeated over again—

> Outward grace
> Nor inward light is needful—day by day
> Men wanting both are mated with the best
> And loftiest of God's feminine creation,
> Whose love takes no distinction but of gender,
> And ridicules the very name of choice.

And so he went on, troubled much in his mind. He had but an uneasy ride of it that morning, and little good did he do at St. Ewold's.

The necessary alterations in his house were being fast completed, and he walked through the rooms, and went up and down the stairs, and rambled through the garden, but he could not wake himself to much interest about them. He stood still at every window to look out and think upon Mr. Slope. At almost every window he had before stood and chatted with Eleanor. She and Mrs. Grantly had been there continually; and while Mrs. Grantly had been giving orders, and seeing that orders had been complied with, he and Eleanor had conversed on all things appertaining to a clergyman's profession. He thought how often he had laid down the law to her and how sweetly she had borne with his somewhat dictatorial decrees. He remembered her listening intelligence, her gentle but quick replies, her interest in all that concerned the church, in all that concerned him; and then he struck his riding-whip against the window-sill and declared to himself that it was impossible that Eleanor Bold should marry Mr. Slope.

And yet he did not really believe, as he should have done, that it was impossible. He should have known her well enough to feel that it was truly impossible. He should have been aware that Eleanor had that within her which would surely protect her from such degradation. But he, like so many others, was deficient in confidence in woman. He said to himself over and over again that it was impossible that Eleanor Bold should become Mrs. Slope, and yet he believed that she would do so. And so he rambled about, and could do and think of nothing. He was thoroughly uncomfortable, thoroughly ill at ease, cross with himself and everybody else, and feeding in his heart on animosity towards Mr. Slope. This was not as it should be, as he knew and felt, but he could not help himself. In truth Mr. Arabin was now in love with Mrs. Bold, though ignorant of the fact himself. He was in love and, though forty years old, was in love without being aware of it. He fumed and fretted and did not know what was the matter, as a youth might do at one-and-twenty. And so having done no good at St. Ewold's, he rode back much earlier than was usual with him, instigated by some inward, unacknowledged hope that he might see Mrs. Bold before she left.

Eleanor had not passed a pleasant morning. She was irritated with everyone, and not least with herself. She felt that she had been hardly used, but she felt also that she had not played her own cards well. She should have held herself so far above suspicion as to have received her sister's innuendoes and the archdeacon's lecture with indifference. She had not done this, but had shown herself angry and sore, and was now ashamed of her own petulance, yet unable to discontinue it.

The greater part of the morning she had spent alone, but after awhile her father joined her. He had fully made up his mind that, come what come might, nothing should separate him from his younger daughter. It was a hard task for him to reconcile himself to the idea of seeing her at the head of Mr. Slope's table, but he got through it. Mr. Slope, as he argued to himself, was a respectable man and a clergyman, and he, as Eleanor's father, had no right even to endeavour to prevent her from marrying such a one. He longed to tell her how he had determined to prefer her to all the world, how he was prepared to admit that she was not wrong, how thoroughly he differed from Dr. Grantly; but he could not bring himself to mention Mr. Slope's name. There was yet a chance that they were all wrong in their surmise, and being thus in doubt, he could not bring himself to speak openly to her on the subject.

He was sitting with her in the drawing-room, with his arm round her waist, saying every now and then some little soft words of affection and working hard with his imaginary fiddle-bow, when Mr. Arabin entered the room. He immediately got up, and the two made some trite remarks to each other, neither thinking of what he was saying, while Eleanor kept her seat on the sofa, mute and moody. Mr. Arabin was included in the list of those against whom her anger was excited. He, too, had dared to talk about her acquaintance with Mr. Slope; he, too, had dared to blame her for not making an enemy of his enemy. She had not intended to see him before her departure, and was now but little inclined to be gracious.

There was a feeling through the whole house that something was wrong. Mr. Arabin, when he saw Eleanor, could not succeed in looking or in speaking as though he knew nothing of all this. He could not be cheerful and positive and contradictory with her, as was his wont. He had not been two minutes in the room before he felt that he had done wrong to return; and the moment he heard her voice, he thoroughly wished himself back at St. Ewold's. Why, indeed, should he have wished to have aught further to say to the future wife of Mr. Slope?

"I am sorry to hear that you are to leave us so soon," said he, striving in vain to use his ordinary voice. In answer to this she muttered something about the necessity of her being in Barchester, and betook herself most industriously to her crochet work.

Then there was a little more trite conversation between Mr. Arabin and Mr. Harding— trite, and hard, and vapid, and senseless. Neither of them had anything to say to the other, and yet neither at such a moment liked to remain silent. At last Mr. Harding, taking advantage of a pause, escaped out of the room, and Eleanor and Mr. Arabin were left together.

"Your going will be a great break-up to our party," said he.

She again muttered something which was all but inaudible, but kept her eyes fixed upon her work.

"We have had a very pleasant month here," said he; "at least I have; and I am sorry it should be so soon over."

"I have already been from home longer than I intended," said she, "and it is time that I should return."

"Well, pleasant hours and pleasant days must come to an end. It is a pity that so few of them are pleasant; or perhaps, rather—"

"It is a pity, certainly, that men and women do so much to destroy the pleasantness of their days," said she, interrupting him. "It is a pity that there should be so little charity abroad."

"Charity should begin at home," said he, and he was proceeding to explain that he as a clergyman could not be what she would call charitable at the expense of those principles which he considered it his duty to teach, when he remembered that it would be worse than vain to argue on such a matter with the future wife of Mr. Slope. "But you are just leaving us," he continued, "and I will not weary your last hour with another lecture. As it is, I fear I have given you too many."

"You should practise as well as preach, Mr. Arabin."

"Undoubtedly I should. So should we all. All of us who presume to teach are bound to do our utmost towards fulfilling our own lessons. I thoroughly allow my deficiency in doing so, but I do not quite know now to what you allude. Have you any special reason for telling me now that I should practise as well as preach?"

Eleanor made no answer. She longed to let him know the cause of her anger, to upbraid him for speaking of her disrespectfully, and then at last to forgive him, and so part friends. She felt that she would be unhappy to leave him in her present frame of mind, but yet she could hardly bring herself to speak to him of Mr. Slope. And how could she allude to the innuendo thrown out by the archdeacon, and thrown out, as she believed, at the instigation of Mr. Arabin? She wanted to make him know that he was wrong, to make him aware that he had ill-treated her, in order that the sweetness of her forgiveness might be enhanced. She felt that she liked him too well to be contented to part with him in displeasure, yet she could not get over her deep displeasure without some explanation, some acknowledgement on his part, some assurance that he would never again so sin against her.

"Why do you tell me that I should practise what I preach?" continued he.

"All men should do so."

"Certainly. That is as it were understood and acknowledged. But you do not say so to all men, or to all clergymen. The advice, good as it is, is not given except in allusion to some special deficiency. If you will tell me my special deficiency, I will endeavour to profit by the advice."

She paused for awhile and then, looking full in his face, she said, "You are not bold enough, Mr. Arabin, to speak out to me openly and plainly, and yet you expect me, a woman, to speak openly to you. Why did you speak calumny of me to Dr. Grantly behind my back?"

"Calumny!" said he, and his whole face became suffused with blood. "What calumny? If I have spoken calumny of you, I will beg your pardon, and his to whom I spoke it, and God's pardon also. But what calumny have I spoken of you to Dr. Grantly?"

She also blushed deeply. She could not bring herself to ask him whether he had not spoken of her as another man's wife. "You know that best yourself," said she. "But I ask you as a man of honour, if you have not spoken of me as you would not have spoken of your own sister—or rather I will not ask you," she continued, finding that he did not immediately answer her. "I will not put you to the necessity of answering such a question. Dr. Grantly has told me what you said."

"Dr. Grantly certainly asked me for my advice, and I gave it. He asked me—"

"I know he did, Mr. Arabin. He asked you whether he would be doing right to receive me at Plumstead if I continued my acquaintance with a gentleman who happens to be personally disagreeable to yourself and to him."

"You are mistaken, Mrs. Bold. I have no personal knowledge of Mr. Slope; I never met him in my life."

"You are not the less individually hostile to him. It is not for me to question the propriety of your enmity, but I had a right to expect that my name should not have been mixed up in your hostilities. This has been done, and been done by you in a manner the most injurious and the most distressing to me as a woman. I must confess, Mr. Arabin, that from you I expected a different sort of usage."

As she spoke she with difficulty restrained her tears—but she did restrain them. Had she given way and sobbed aloud, as in such cases a woman should do, he would have melted at once, implored her pardon, perhaps knelt at her feet and declared his love. Everything would have been explained, and Eleanor would have gone back to Barchester with a contented mind. How easily would she have forgiven and forgotten the archdeacon's suspicions had she but heard the whole truth from Mr. Arabin. But then where would have been my novel? She did not cry, and Mr. Arabin did not melt.

"You do me an injustice," said he. "My advice was asked by Dr. Grantly, and I was obliged to give it."

"Dr. Grantly has been most officious, most impertinent. I have as complete a right to form my acquaintance as he has to form his. What would you have said had I consulted you as to the propriety of my banishing Dr. Grantly from my house because he knows Lord Tattenham Corner? I am sure Lord Tattenham is quite as objectionable an acquaintance for a clergyman as Mr. Slope is for a clergyman's daughter."

"I do not know Lord Tattenham Corner."

"No, but Dr. Grantly does. It is nothing to me if he knows all the young lords on every race-course in England. I shall not interfere with him, nor shall he with me."

"I am sorry to differ with you, Mrs. Bold, but as you have spoken to me on this matter, and especially as you blame me for what little I said on the subject, I must tell you that I do differ from you. Dr. Grantly's position as a man in the world gives him a right to choose his own acquaintances, subject to certain influences. If he chooses them badly, those influences will be used. If he consorts with persons unsuitable to him, his bishop will interfere. What the bishop is to Dr. Grantly, Dr. Grantly is to you."

"I deny it. I utterly deny it," said Eleanor, jumping from her seat and literally flashing before Mr. Arabin, as she stood on the drawing-room floor. He had never seen her so excited, he had never seen her look half so beautiful.

"I utterly deny it," said she. "Dr. Grantly has no sort of jurisdiction over me whatsoever. Do you and he forget that I am not altogether alone in the world? Do you forget that I have a father? Dr. Grantly, I believe, always has forgotten it.

"From you, Mr. Arabin," she continued, "I would have listened to advice because I should have expected it to have been given as one friend may advise another—not as a schoolmaster gives an order to a pupil. I might have differed from you—on this matter I should have done so—but had you spoken to me in your usual manner and with your usual freedom, I should not have been angry. But now—was it manly of you, Mr. Arabin, to speak of me in this way—so disrespectful—so—? I cannot bring myself to repeat what you said. You must understand what I feel. Was it just of you to speak of me in such a way and to advise my sister's husband to turn me out of my sister's house because I chose to know a man of whose doctrine you disapprove?"

"I have no alternative left to me, Mrs. Bold," said he, standing with his back to the fire-place, looking down intently at the carpet pattern, and speaking with a slow, measured voice, "but to tell you plainly what did take place between me and Dr. Grantly."

"Well," said she, finding that he paused for a moment.

"I am afraid that what I may say may pain you."

"It cannot well do so more than what you have already done," said she.

"Dr. Grantly asked me whether I thought it would be prudent for him to receive you in his house as the wife of Mr. Slope, and I told him that I thought it would be imprudent. Believing it to be utterly impossible that Mr. Slope and—"

"Thank you, Mr. Arabin, that is sufficient. I do not want to know your reasons," said she, speaking with a terribly calm voice. "I have shown to this gentleman the commonplace civility of a neighbour; and because I have done so, because I have not indulged against him in all the rancour and hatred which you and Dr. Grantly consider due to all clergymen who do not agree with yourselves, you conclude that I am to marry him; or rather you do not conclude so—no rational man could really come to such an outrageous conclusion without better ground; you have not thought so, but, as I am in a position in which such an accusation must be peculiarly painful, it is made in order that I may be terrified into hostility against this enemy of yours."

As she finished speaking, she walked to the drawing-room window and stepped out into the garden. Mr. Arabin was left in the room, still occupied in counting the pattern on the carpet. He had, however, distinctly heard and accurately marked every word that she had spoken. Was it not clear from what she had said that the archdeacon had been wrong in imputing to her any attachment to Mr. Slope? Was it not clear that Eleanor was still free to make another choice? It may seem strange that he should for a moment have had a doubt, and yet he did doubt. She had not absolutely denied the charge; she had not expressly said that it was untrue. Mr. Arabin understood little of the nature of a woman's feelings, or he would have known how improbable it was that she should make any clearer declaration than she had done. Few men do understand the nature of a woman's heart, till years have robbed such understanding of its value. And it is well that it should be so, or men would triumph too easily.

Mr. Arabin stood counting the carpet, unhappy, wretchedly unhappy, at the hard words that had been spoken to him, and yet happy, exquisitely happy, as he thought that after all the woman whom he so regarded was not to become the wife of the man whom he so much disliked. As he stood there he began to be aware that he was himself in love. Forty years had passed over his head, and as yet woman's beauty had never given him an uneasy hour. His present hour was very uneasy.

Not that he remained there for half or a quarter of that time. In spite of what Eleanor had said, Mr. Arabin was, in truth, a manly man. Having ascertained that he loved this woman, and having now reason to believe that she was free to receive his love, at least if she pleased to do so, he followed her into the garden to make such wooing as he could.

He was not long in finding her. She was walking to and fro beneath the avenue of elms that stood in the archdeacon's grounds, skirting the churchyard. What had passed between her and Mr. Arabin had not, alas, tended to lessen the acerbity of her spirit. She was very angry—more angry with him than with anyone. How could he have so misunderstood her? She had been so intimate with him, had allowed him such latitude in what he had chosen to say to her, had complied with his ideas, cherished his views, fostered his precepts, cared for his comforts, made much of him in every way in which a pretty woman can make much of an unmarried man without committing herself or her feelings! She had been doing this, and while she had been doing it he had regarded her as the affianced wife of another man.

As she passed along the avenue, every now and then an unbidden tear would force itself on her cheek, and as she raised her hand to brush it away, she stamped with her little foot upon the sward with very spite to think that she had been so treated.

Mr. Arabin was very near to her when she first saw him, and she turned short round and retraced her steps down the avenue, trying to rid her cheeks of all trace of the tell-tale tears. It was a needless endeavour, for Mr. Arabin was in a state of mind that hardly allowed him to observe such trifles. He followed her down the walk and overtook her just as she reached the end of it.

He had not considered how he would address her; he had not thought what he would say. He had only felt that it was wretchedness to him to quarrel with her, and that it would be happiness to be allowed to love her. And yet he could not lower himself by asking her pardon. He had done her no wrong. He had not calumniated her, not injured her, as she had accused him of doing. He could not confess sins of which he had not been guilty. He could only let the past be past and ask her as to her and his hopes for the future.

"I hope we are not to part as enemies?" said he.

"There shall be no enmity on my part," said Eleanor; "I endeavour to avoid all enmities. It would be a hollow pretence were I to say that there can be true friendship between us, after what has just passed. People cannot make their friends of those whom they despise."

"And am I despised?"

"I must have been so before you could have spoken of me as you did. And I was deceived, cruelly deceived. I believed that you thought well of me; I believed that you esteemed me."

"Thought well of you and esteemed you!" said he. "In justifying myself before you, I must use stronger words than those." He paused for a moment, and Eleanor's heart beat with painful violence within her bosom as she waited for him to go on. "I have esteemed, do esteem you, as I never yet esteemed any woman. Think well of you! I never thought to think so well, so much of any human creature. Speak calumny of you! Insult you! Wilfully injure you! I wish it were my privilege to shield you from calumny, insult, and injury. Calumny! Ah me! 'Twere almost better that it were so. Better than to worship with a sinful worship; sinful and vain also." And then he walked along beside her, with his hands clasped behind his back, looking down on the grass beneath his feet and utterly at a loss how to express his meaning. And Eleanor walked beside him determined at least to give him no assistance.

"Ah me!" he uttered at last, speaking rather to himself than to her. "Ah me! These Plumstead walks were pleasant enough, if one could have but heart's ease, but without that the dull, dead stones of Oxford were far preferable—and St. Ewold's, too. Mrs. Bold, I am beginning to think that I mistook myself when I came hither. A Romish priest now would have escaped all this. Oh, Father of heaven, how good for us would it be if thou couldest vouchsafe to us a certain rule."

"And have we not a certain rule, Mr. Arabin?"

"Yes—yes, surely; 'Lead us not into temptation but deliver us from evil.' But what is temptation? What is evil? Is this evil—is this temptation?"

Poor Mr. Arabin! It would not come out of him, that deep, true love of his. He could not bring himself to utter it in plain language that would require and demand an answer. He knew not how to say to the woman by his side, "Since the fact is that you do not love that other man, that you are not to be his wife, can you love me, will you be my wife?" These were the words which were in his heart, but with all his sighs he could not draw them to his lips. He would have given anything, everything for power to ask this simple question, but glib as was his tongue in pulpits and on platforms, now he could not find a word wherewith to express the plain wish of his heart.

And yet Eleanor understood him as thoroughly as though he had declared his passion with all the elegant fluency of a practised Lothario. With a woman's instinct, she followed every bend of his mind as he spoke of the pleasantness of Plumstead and the stones of Oxford, as he alluded to the safety of the Romish priest and the hidden perils of temptation. She knew that it all meant love. She knew that this man at her side, this accomplished scholar, this practised orator, this great polemical combatant, was striving and striving in vain to tell her that his heart was no longer his own.

She knew this, and felt a sort of joy in knowing it; yet she would not come to his aid. He had offended her deeply, had treated her unworthily, the more unworthily seeing that he had learnt to love her, and Eleanor could not bring herself to abandon her revenge. She did not ask herself whether or no she would ultimately accept his love. She did not even acknowledge to herself that she now perceived it with pleasure. At the present moment it did not touch her heart; it merely appeased her pride and flattered her vanity. Mr. Arabin had dared to associate her name with that of Mr. Slope, and now her spirit was soothed by finding that he would fain associate it with his own. And so she walked on beside him, inhaling incense but giving out no sweetness in return.

"Answer me this," said Mr. Arabin, stopping suddenly in his walk and stepping forward so that he faced his companion. "Answer me this one question. You do not love Mr. Slope? You do not intend to be his wife?"

Mr. Arabin certainly did not go the right way to win such a woman as Eleanor Bold. Just as her wrath was evaporating, as it was disappearing before the true warmth of his untold love, he rekindled it by a most useless repetition of his original sin. Had he known what he was about, he should never have mentioned Mr. Slope's name before Eleanor Bold, till he had made her all his own. Then, and not till then, he might have talked of Mr. Slope with as much triumph as he chose.

"I shall answer no such question," said she; "and what is more, I must tell you that nothing can justify your asking it. Good morning!"

And so saying, she stepped proudly across the lawn and, passing through the drawing-room window, joined her father and sister at lunch in the dining-room. Half an hour afterwards she was in the carriage, and so she left Plumstead without again seeing Mr. Arabin.

His walk was long and sad among the sombre trees that overshadowed the churchyard. He left the archdeacon's grounds that he might escape attention, and sauntered among the green hillocks under which lay at rest so many of the once loving swains and forgotten beauties of Plumstead. To his ears Eleanor's last words sounded like a knell never to be reversed. He could not comprehend that she might be angry with him, indignant with him, remorseless with him, and yet love him. He could not make up his mind whether or no Mr. Slope was in truth a favoured rival. If not, why should she not have answered his question?

Poor Mr. Arabin—untaught, illiterate, boorish, ignorant man! That at forty years of age you should know so little of the workings of a woman's heart!

CHAPTER XXXI

THE BISHOP'S LIBRARY

And thus the pleasant party at Plumstead was broken up. It had been a very pleasant party as long as they had all remained in good humour with one another. Mrs. Grantly had felt her house to be gayer and brighter than it had been for many a long day, and the archdeacon had been aware that the month had passed pleasantly without attributing the pleasure to any other special merits than those of his own hospitality. Within three or four days of Eleanor's departure, Mr. Harding had also returned, and Mr. Arabin had gone to Oxford to spend one week there previous to his settling at the vicarage of St. Ewold's. He had gone laden with many messages to Dr. Gwynne touching the iniquity of the doings in Barchester palace and the peril in which it was believed the hospital still stood in spite of the assurances contained in Mr. Slope's inauspicious letter.

During Eleanor's drive into Barchester she had not much opportunity of reflecting on Mr. Arabin. She had been constrained to divert her mind both from his sins and his love by the necessity of conversing with her sister and maintaining the appearance of parting with her on good terms. When the carriage reached her own door, and while she was in the act of giving her last kiss to her sister and nieces, Mary Bold ran out and exclaimed:

"Oh, Eleanor, have you heard? Oh, Mrs. Grantly, have you heard what has happened? The poor dean!"

"Good heavens!" said Mrs. Grantly. "What—what has happened?"

"This morning at nine he had a fit of apoplexy, and he has not spoken since. I very much fear that by this time he is no more."

Mrs. Grantly had been very intimate with the dean, and was therefore much shocked. Eleanor had not known him so well; nevertheless, she was sufficiently acquainted with his person and manners to feel startled and grieved also at the tidings she now received. "I will go at once to the deanery," said Mrs. Grantly; "the archdeacon, I am sure, will be there. If there is any news to send you, I will let Thomas call before he leaves town." And so the carriage drove off, leaving Eleanor and her baby with Mary Bold.

Mrs. Grantly had been quite right. The archdeacon was at the deanery. He had come into Barchester that morning by himself, not caring to intrude himself upon Eleanor, and he also immediately on his arrival had heard of the dean's fit. There was, as we have before said, a library or reading-room connecting the cathedral with the dean's house. This was generally called the bishop's library, because a certain bishop of Barchester was supposed to have added it to the cathedral. It was built immediately over a portion of the cloisters, and a flight of stairs descended from it into the room in which the cathedral clergymen put their surplices on and off. As it also opened directly into the dean's house, it was the passage through which that dignitary usually went to his public devotions. Who had or had not the right of entry into it, it might be difficult to say; but the people of Barchester believed that it belonged to the dean, and the clergymen of Barchester believed that it belonged to the chapter.

On the morning in question most of the resident clergymen who constituted the chapter, and some few others, were here assembled, and among them as usual the archdeacon towered with high authority. He had heard of the dean's fit before he was over the bridge which led into the town, and had at once come to the well-known clerical trysting place. He had been there by eleven o'clock, and had remained ever since. From time to time the medical men who had been called in came through from the deanery into the library, uttered little bulletins, and then returned. There was, it appears, very little hope of the old man's rallying, indeed no hope of anything like a final recovery. The only question was whether he must die at once speechless, unconscious, stricken to death by his first heavy fit, or whether by due aid of medical skill he might not be so far brought back to this world as to become conscious of his state and enabled to address one prayer to his Maker before he was called to meet Him face to face at the judgement seat.

Sir Omicron Pie had been sent for from London. That great man had shown himself a wonderful adept at keeping life still moving within an old man's heart in the case of good old Bishop Grantly, and it might be reasonably expected that he would be equally successful with a dean. In the meantime Dr. Fillgrave and Mr. Rerechild were doing their best, and poor Miss Trefoil sat at the head of her father's bed, longing, as in such cases daughters do long, to be allowed to do something to show her love—if it were only to chafe his feet with her hands, or wait in menial offices on those autocratic doctors—anything so that now in the time of need she might be of use.

The archdeacon alone of the attendant clergy had been admitted for a moment into the sick man's chamber. He had crept in with creaking shoes, had said with smothered voice a word of consolation to the sorrowing daughter, had looked on the distorted face of his old friend with solemn but yet eager scrutinising eye, as though he said in his heart "and so some day it will probably be with me," and then, having whispered an unmeaning word or two to the doctors, had creaked his way back again into the library.

"He'll never speak again, I fear," said the archdeacon as he noiselessly closed the door, as though the unconscious dying man, from whom all sense had fled, would have heard in his distant chamber the spring of the lock which was now so carefully handled.

"Indeed! Indeed! Is he so bad?" said the meagre little prebendary, turning over in his own mind all the probable candidates for the deanery and wondering whether the archdeacon would think it worth his while to accept it. "The fit must have been very violent."

"When a man over seventy has a stroke of apoplexy, it seldom comes very lightly," said the burly chancellor.

"He was an excellent, sweet-tempered man," said one of the vicars choral. "Heaven knows how we shall repair his loss."

"He was indeed," said a minor canon, "and a great blessing to all those privileged to take a share in the services of our cathedral. I suppose the government will appoint, Mr. Archdeacon. I trust we may have no stranger."

"We will not talk about his successor," said the archdeacon, "while there is yet hope."

"Oh, no, of course not," said the minor canon. "It would be exceedingly indecorous; but—"

"I know of no man," said the meagre little prebendary, "who has better interest with the present government than Mr. Slope."

"Mr. Slope," said two or three at once almost sotto voce. "Mr. Slope Dean of Barchester!"

"Pooh!" exclaimed the burly chancellor.

"The bishop would do anything for him," said the little prebendary.

"And so would Mrs. Proudie," said the vicar choral.

"Pooh!" said the chancellor.

The archdeacon had almost turned pale at the idea. What if Mr. Slope should become Dean of Barchester? To be sure there was no adequate ground, indeed no ground at all, for presuming that such a desecration could even be contemplated. But nevertheless it was on the cards. Dr. Proudie had interest with the government, and the man carried as it were Dr. Proudie in his pocket. How should they all conduct themselves if Mr. Slope were to become Dean of Barchester? The bare idea for a moment struck even Dr. Grantly dumb.

"It would certainly not be very pleasant for us to have Mr. Slope at the deanery," said the little prebendary, chuckling inwardly at the evident consternation which his surmise had created.

"About as pleasant and as probable as having you in the palace," said the chancellor.

"I should think such an appointment highly improbable," said the minor canon, "and, moreover, extremely injudicious. Should not you, Mr. Archdeacon?"

"I should presume such a thing to be quite out of the question," said the archdeacon, "but at the present moment I am thinking rather of our poor friend who is lying so near us than of Mr. Slope."

"Of course, of course," said the vicar choral with a very solemn air; "of course you are. So are we all. Poor Dr. Trefoil; the best of men, but—"

"It's the most comfortable dean's residence in England," said a second prebendary. "Fifteen acres in the grounds. It is better than many of the bishops' palaces."

"And full two thousand a year," said the meagre doctor.

"It is cut down to £1,200," said the chancellor.

"No," said the second prebendary. "It is to be fifteen. A special case was made."

"No such thing," said the chancellor.

"You'll find I'm right," said the prebendary.

"I'm sure I read it in the report," said the minor canon.

"Nonsense," said the chancellor. "They couldn't do it. There were to be no exceptions but London and Durham."

"And Canterbury and York," said the vicar choral modestly.

"What do you say, Grantly?" said the meagre little doctor.

"Say about what?" said the archdeacon, who had been looking as though he were thinking about his friend the dean, but who had in reality been thinking about Mr. Slope.

"What is the next dean to have, twelve or fifteen?"

"Twelve," said the archdeacon authoritatively, thereby putting an end at once to all doubt and dispute among his subordinates as far as that subject was concerned.

"Well, I certainly thought it was fifteen," said the minor canon.

"Pooh!" said the burly chancellor. At this moment the door opened and in came Dr. Fillgrave.

"How is he?" "Is he conscious?" "Can he speak?" "I hope not dead?" "No worse news, Doctor, I trust?" "I hope, I trust, something better, Doctor?" said half a dozen voices all at once, each in a tone of extremest anxiety. It was pleasant to see how popular the good old dean was among his clergy.

"No change, gentlemen; not the slightest change. But a telegraphic message has arrived—Sir Omicron Pie will be here by the 9.15 P.M. train. If any man can do anything, Sir Omicron Pie will do it. But all that skill can do has been done."

"We are sure of that, Dr. Fillgrave," said the archdeacon; "we are quite sure of that. But yet you know—"

"Oh, quite right," said the doctor, "quite right—I should have done just the same—I advised it at once. I said to Rerechild at once that with such a life and such a man, Sir Omicron should be summoned—of course I knew expense was nothing—so distinguished, you know, and so popular. Nevertheless, all that human skill can do has been done."

Just at this period Mrs. Grantly's carriage drove into the close, and the archdeacon went down to confirm the news which she had heard before.

By the 9.15 P.M. train Sir Omicron Pie did arrive. And in the course of the night a sort of consciousness returned to the poor old dean. Whether this was due to Sir Omicron Pie is a question on which it may be well not to offer an opinion. Dr. Fillgrave was very clear in his own mind, but Sir Omicron himself is thought to have differed from that learned doctor. At any rate Sir Omicron expressed an opinion that the dean had yet some days to live.

For the eight or ten next days, accordingly, the poor dean remained in the same state, half-conscious and half-comatose; and the attendant clergy began to think that no new appointment would be necessary for some few months to come.

CHAPTER XXXII

A NEW CANDIDATE FOR ECCLESIASTICAL HONOURS

The dean's illness occasioned much mental turmoil in other places besides the deanery and adjoining library, and the idea which occurred to the meagre little prebendary about Mr. Slope did not occur to him alone.

The bishop was sitting listlessly in his study when the news reached him of the dean's illness. It was brought to him by Mr. Slope, who of course was not the last person in Barchester to hear it. It was also not slow in finding its way to Mrs. Proudie's ears. It may be presumed that there was not just then much friendly intercourse between these two rival claimants for his lordship's obedience. Indeed, though living in the same house, they had not met since the stormy interview between them in the bishop's study on the preceding day.

On that occasion Mrs. Proudie had been defeated. That the prestige of continual victory should have been torn from her standards was a subject of great sorrow to that militant lady; but, though defeated, she was not overcome. She felt that she might yet recover her lost ground, that she might yet hurl Mr. Slope down to the dust from which she had picked him, and force her sinning lord to sue for pardon in sackcloth and ashes.

On that memorable day, memorable for his mutiny and rebellion against her high behests, he had carried his way with a high hand, and had really begun to think it possible that the days of his slavery were counted. He had begun to hope that he was now about to enter into a free land, a land delicious with milk which he himself might quaff and honey which would not tantalize him by being only honey to the eye. When Mrs. Proudie banged the door as she left his room, he felt himself every inch a bishop. To be sure, his spirit had been a little cowed by his chaplain's subsequent lecture, but on the whole he was highly pleased with himself, and he flattered himself that the worst was over. "*Ce n'est que le premier pas qui coûte*," he reflected, and now that the first step had been so magnanimously taken, all the rest would follow easily.

He met his wife as a matter of course at dinner, where little or nothing was said that could ruffle the bishop's happiness. His daughters and the servants were present and protected him.

He made one or two trifling remarks on the subject of his projected visit to the archbishop, in order to show to all concerned that he intended to have his own way; the very servants, perceiving the change, transferred a little of their reverence from their mistress to their master. All which the master perceived, and so also did the mistress. But Mrs. Proudie bided her time.

After dinner he returned to his study, where Mr. Slope soon found him, and there they had tea together and planned many things. For some few minutes the bishop was really happy; but as the clock on the chimney-piece warned him that the stilly hours of night were drawing on, as he looked at his chamber candlestick and knew that he must use it, his heart sank within him again. He was as a ghost, all whose power of wandering free through these upper regions ceases at cock-crow; or, rather, he was the opposite of the ghost, for till cock-crow he must again be a serf. And would that be all? Could he trust himself to come down to breakfast a free man in the morning?

He was nearly an hour later than usual when he betook himself to his rest. Rest! What rest? However, he took a couple of glasses of sherry and mounted the stairs. Far be it from us to follow him thither. There are some things which no novelist, no historian, should attempt; some few scenes in life's drama which even no poet should dare to paint. Let that which passed between Dr. Proudie and his wife on this night be understood to be among them.

He came down the following morning a sad and thoughtful man. He was attenuated in appearance—one might almost say emaciated. I doubt whether his now grizzled locks had not palpably become more grey than on the preceding evening. At any rate he had aged materially. Years do not make a man old gradually and at an even pace. Look through the world and see if this is not so always, except in those rare cases in which the human being lives and dies without joys and without sorrows, like a vegetable. A man shall be possessed of florid, youthful blooming health till, it matters not what age—thirty; forty; fifty—then comes some nipping frost, some period of agony, that robs the fibres of the body of their succulence, and the hale and hearty man is counted among the old.

He came down and breakfasted alone; Mrs. Proudie, being indisposed, took her coffee in her bedroom, and her daughters waited upon her there. He ate his breakfast alone, and then, hardly knowing what he did, he betook himself to his usual seat in his study. He tried to solace himself with his coming visit to the archbishop. That effort of his own free will at any rate remained to him as an enduring triumph. But somehow, now that he had achieved it, he did not seem to care so much about it. It was his ambition that had prompted him to take his place at the archiepiscopal table, and his ambition was now quite dead within him.

He was thus seated when Mr. Slope made his appearance, with breathless impatience.

"My lord, the dean is dead."

"Good heavens!" exclaimed the bishop, startled out of his apathy by an announcement so sad and so sudden.

"He is either dead or now dying. He has had an apoplectic fit, and I am told that there is not the slightest hope; indeed, I do not doubt that by this time he is no more."

Bells were rung, and servants were immediately sent to inquire. In the course of the morning the bishop, leaning on his chaplain's arm, himself called at the deanery door. Mrs. Proudie sent to Miss Trefoil all manner of offers of assistance. The Misses Proudie sent also, and there was immense sympathy between the palace and the deanery. The answer to all inquiries was unvaried. The dean was just the same, and Sir Omicron Pie was expected down by the 9.15 P.M. train.

And then Mr. Slope began to meditate, as others also had done, as to who might possibly be the new dean, and it occurred to him, as it had also occurred to others, that it might be possible that he should be the new dean himself. And then the question as to the twelve hundred, or fifteen hundred, or two thousand ran in his mind, as it had run through those of the other clergymen in the cathedral library.

Whether it might be two thousand, or fifteen, or twelve hundred, it would in any case undoubtedly be a great thing for him, if he could get it. The gratification to his ambition would be greater even than that of his covetousness. How glorious to out-top the archdeacon in his own cathedral city; to sit above prebendaries and canons and have the cathedral pulpit and all the cathedral services altogether at his own disposal!

But it might be easier to wish for this than to obtain it. Mr. Slope, however, was not without some means of forwarding his views, and he at any rate did not let the grass grow under his feet. In the first place, he thought—and not vainly—that he could count upon what assistance the bishop could give him. He immediately changed his views with regard to his patron; he made up his mind that if he became dean, he would hand his lordship back again to his wife's vassalage; and he thought it possible that his lordship might not be sorry to rid himself of one of his mentors. Mr. Slope had also taken some steps towards making his name known to other men in power. There was a certain chief-commissioner of national schools, who at the present moment was presumed to stand especially high in the good graces of the government bigwigs, and with him Mr. Slope had contrived to establish a sort of epistolary intimacy. He thought that he might safely apply to Sir Nicholas Fitzwhiggin, and he felt sure that if Sir Nicholas chose to exert himself, the promise of such a piece of preferment would be had for the asking.

Then he also had the press at his bidding, or flattered himself that he had so. "The Daily Jupiter" had taken his part in a very thorough manner in those polemical contests of his with Mr. Arabin; he had on more than one occasion absolutely had an interview with a gentleman on the staff of that paper who, if not the editor, was as good as the editor; and he had long been in the habit of writing telling letters on all manner of ecclesiastical abuses, which he signed with his initials, and sent to his editorial friend with private notes signed in his own name. Indeed, he and Mr. Towers—such was the name of the powerful gentleman of the press with whom he was connected—were generally very amiable with each other. Mr. Slope's little productions were always printed and occasionally commented upon; and thus, in a small sort of way, he had become a literary celebrity. This public life had great charms for him, though it certainly also had its drawbacks. On one occasion, when speaking in the presence of reporters, he had failed to uphold and praise and swear by that special line of conduct which had been upheld and praised and sworn by in "The Jupiter," and then he had been much surprised and at the moment not a little irritated to find himself lacerated most unmercifully by his old ally. He was quizzed and bespattered and made a fool of, just as though, or rather worse than if, he had been a constant enemy instead of a constant friend. He had hitherto not learnt that a man who aspires to be on the staff of "The Jupiter" must surrender all individuality. But ultimately this little castigation had broken no bones between him and his friend Mr. Towers. Mr. Slope was one of those who understood the world too well to show himself angry with such a potentate as "The Jupiter." He had kissed the rod that scourged him, and now thought that he might fairly look for his reward. He determined that he would at once let Mr. Towers know that he was a candidate for the place which was about to become vacant. More than one piece of preferment had lately been given away much in accordance with advice tendered to the government in the columns of "The Jupiter."

But it was incumbent on Mr. Slope first to secure the bishop. He specially felt that it behoved him to do this before the visit to the archbishop was made. It was really quite providential that the dean should have fallen ill just at the very nick of time. If Dr. Proudie could be instigated to take the matter up warmly, he might manage a good deal while staying at the archbishop's palace. Feeling this very strongly, Mr. Slope determined to sound the bishop that very afternoon. He was to start on the following morning to London, and therefore not a moment could be lost with safety.

He went into the bishop's study about five o'clock and found him still sitting alone. It might have been supposed that he had hardly moved since the little excitement occasioned by his walk to the dean's door. He still wore on his face that dull, dead look of half-unconscious suffering. He was doing nothing, reading nothing, thinking of nothing, but simply gazing on vacancy when Mr. Slope for the second time that day entered his room.

"Well, Slope," said he somewhat impatiently, for, to tell the truth, he was not anxious just at present to have much conversation with Mr. Slope.

"Your lordship will be sorry to hear that as yet the poor dean has shown no sign of amendment."

"Oh—ah—hasn't he? Poor man! I'm sure I'm very sorry. I suppose Sir Omicron has not arrived yet?"

"No, not till the 9.15 P.M. train."

"I wonder they didn't have a special. They say Dr. Trefoil is very rich."

"Very rich, I believe," said Mr. Slope. "But the truth is, all the doctors in London can do no good—no other good than to show that every possible care has been taken. Poor Dr. Trefoil is not long for this world, my lord."

"I suppose not—I suppose not."

"Oh, no; indeed, his best friends could not wish that he should outlive such a shock, for his intellects cannot possibly survive it."

"Poor man! Poor man!" said the bishop.

"It will naturally be a matter of much moment to your lordship who is to succeed him," said Mr. Slope. "It would be a great thing if you could secure the appointment for some person of your own way of thinking on important points. The party hostile to us are very strong here in Barchester—much too strong."

"Yes, yes. If poor Dr. Trefoil is to go, it will be a great thing to get a good man in his place."

"It will be everything to your lordship to get a man on whose co-operation you can reckon. Only think what trouble we might have if Dr. Grantly, or Dr. Hyandry, or any of that way of thinking were to get it."

"It is not very probable that Lord —— will give it to any of that school; why should he?"

"No. Not probable; certainly not; but it's possible. Great interest will probably be made. If I might venture to advise your lordship, I would suggest that you should discuss the matter with his grace next week. I have no doubt that your wishes, if made known and backed by his grace, would be paramount with Lord ——."

"Well, I don't know that; Lord —— has always been very kind to me, very kind. But I am unwilling to interfere in such matters unless asked. And indeed if asked, I don't know whom, at this moment, I should recommend."

Mr. Slope, even Mr. Slope, felt at the present rather abashed. He hardly knew how to frame his little request in language sufficiently modest. He had recognized and acknowledged to himself the necessity of shocking the bishop in the first instance by the temerity of his application, and his difficulty was how best to remedy that by his adroitness and eloquence. "I doubted myself," said he, "whether your lordship would have anyone immediately in your eye, and it is on this account that I venture to submit to you an idea that I have been turning over in my own mind. If poor Dr. Trefoil must go, I really do not see why, with your lordship's assistance, I should not hold the preferment myself."

"You!" exclaimed the bishop in a manner that Mr. Slope could hardly have considered complimentary.

The ice was now broken, and Mr. Slope became fluent enough. "I have been thinking of looking for it. If your lordship will press the matter on the archbishop, I do not doubt but I shall succeed. You see I shall be the first to move, which is a great matter. Then I can count upon assistance from the public press: my name is known, I may say, somewhat favourably known, to that portion of the press which is now most influential with the government; and I have friends also in the government. But nevertheless it is to you, my lord, that I look for assistance. It is from your hands that I would most willingly receive the benefit. And, which should ever be the chief consideration in such matters, you must know better than any other person whatsoever what qualifications I possess."

The bishop sat for awhile dumbfounded. Mr. Slope Dean of Barchester! The idea of such a transformation of character would never have occurred to his own unaided intellect. At first he went on thinking why, for what reasons, on what account, Mr. Slope should be Dean of Barchester. But by degrees the direction of his thoughts changed, and he began to think why, for what reasons, on what account, Mr. Slope should not be Dean of Barchester. As far as he himself, the bishop, was concerned, he could well spare the services of his chaplain. That little idea of using Mr. Slope as a counterpoise to his wife had well nigh evaporated. He had all but acknowledged the futility of the scheme. If indeed he could have slept in his chaplain's bedroom instead of his wife's, there might have been something in it. But——. And thus as Mr. Slope was speaking, the bishop began to recognize the idea that that gentleman might become Dean of Barchester without impropriety—not moved, indeed, by Mr. Slope's eloquence, for he did not follow the tenor of his speech, but led thereto by his own cogitations.

"I need not say," continued Mr. Slope, "that it would be my chief desire to act in all matters connected with the cathedral as far as possible in accordance with your views. I know your lordship so well (and I hope you know me well enough to have the same feelings) that I am satisfied that my being in that position would add materially to your own comfort, and enable you to extend the sphere of your useful influence. As I said before, it is most desirable that there should be but one opinion among the dignitaries of the same diocese. I doubt much whether I would accept such an appointment in any diocese in which I should be constrained to differ much from the bishop. In this case there would be a delightful uniformity of opinion."

Mr. Slope perfectly well perceived that the bishop did not follow a word that he said, but nevertheless he went on talking. He knew it was necessary that Dr. Proudie should recover from his surprise, and he knew also that he must give him the opportunity of appearing to have been persuaded by argument. So he went on and produced a multitude of fitting reasons all tending to show that no one on earth could make so good a Dean of Barchester as himself, that the government and the public would assuredly coincide in desiring that he, Mr. Slope, should be Dean of Barchester, but that for high considerations of ecclesiastical polity it would be especially desirable that this piece of preferment should be so bestowed through the instrumentality of the bishop of the diocese.

"But I really don't know what I could do in the matter," said the bishop.

"If you would mention it to the archbishop; if you could tell his grace that you consider such an appointment very desirable, that you have it much at heart with a view to putting an end to schism in the diocese; if you did this with your usual energy, you would probably find no difficulty in inducing his grace to promise that he would mention it to Lord ——. Of course you would let the archbishop know that I am not looking for the preferment solely through his intervention; that you do not exactly require him to ask it as a favour; that you expect that I shall get it through other sources, as is indeed the case; but that you are very anxious that his grace should express his approval of such an arrangement to Lord ——."

It ended in the bishop promising to do as he was bid. Not that he so promised without a stipulation. "About that hospital," he said in the middle of the conference. "I was never so troubled in my life"—which was about the truth. "You haven't spoken to Mr. Harding since I saw you?"

Mr. Slope assured his patron that he had not.

"Ah well, then—I think upon the whole it will be better to let Quiverful have it. It has been half-promised to him, and he has a large family and is very poor. I think on the whole it will be better to make out the nomination for Mr. Quiverful."

"But, my lord," said Mr. Slope, still thinking that he was bound to make a fight for his own view on this matter, and remembering that it still behoved him to maintain his lately acquired supremacy over Mrs. Proudie, lest he should fail in his views regarding the deanery, "but, my lord, I am really much afraid—"

"Remember, Mr. Slope," said the bishop, "I can hold out no sort of hope to you in this matter of succeeding poor Dr. Trefoil. I will certainly speak to the archbishop, as you wish it, but I cannot think—"

"Well, my lord," said Mr. Slope, fully understanding the bishop and in his turn interrupting him, "perhaps your lordship is right about Mr. Quiverful. I have no doubt I can easily arrange matters with Mr. Harding, and I will make out the nomination for your signature as you direct."

"Yes, Slope, I think that will be best; and you may be sure that any little that I can do to forward your views shall be done."

And so they parted.

Mr. Slope had now much business on his hands. He had to make his daily visit to the signora. This common prudence should have now induced him to omit, but he was infatuated, and could not bring himself to be commonly prudent. He determined therefore that he would drink tea at the Stanhopes', and he determined also, or thought that he determined, that having done so he would go thither no more. He had also to arrange his matters with Mrs. Bold. He was of opinion that Eleanor would grace the deanery as perfectly as she would the chaplain's cottage, and he thought, moreover, that Eleanor's fortune would excellently repair any dilapidations and curtailments in the dean's stipend which might have been made by that ruthless ecclesiastical commission.

Touching Mrs. Bold his hopes now soared high. Mr. Slope was one of that numerous multitude of swains who think that all is fair in love, and he had accordingly not refrained from using the services of Mrs. Bold's own maid. From her he had learnt much of what had taken place at Plumstead—not exactly with truth, for "the own maid" had not been able to divine the exact truth, but with some sort of similitude to it. He had been told that the archdeacon and Mrs. Grantly and Mr. Harding and Mr. Arabin had all quarrelled with "missus" for having received a letter from Mr. Slope; that "missus" had positively refused to give the letter up; that she had received from the archdeacon the option of giving up either Mr. Slope and his letter, or else the society of Plumstead Rectory; and that "missus" had declared, with much indignation, that "she didn't care a straw for the society of Plumstead Rectory," and that she wouldn't give up Mr. Slope for any of them.

Considering the source from whence this came, it was not quite so untrue as might have been expected. It showed pretty plainly what had been the nature of the conversation in the servants' hall; and, coupled as it was with the certainty of Eleanor's sudden return, it appeared to Mr. Slope to be so far worthy of credit as to justify him in thinking that the fair widow would in all human probability accept his offer.

All this work was therefore to be done. It was desirable, he thought, that he should make his offer before it was known that Mr. Quiverful was finally appointed to the hospital. In his letter to Eleanor he had plainly declared that Mr. Harding was to have the appointment. It would be very difficult to explain this away, and were he to write another letter to Eleanor, telling the truth and throwing the blame on the bishop, it would naturally injure him in her estimation. He determined therefore to let that matter disclose itself as it would, and to lose no time in throwing himself at her feet.

Then he had to solicit the assistance of Sir Nicholas Fitzwhiggin and Mr. Towers, and he went directly from the bishop's presence to compose his letters to those gentlemen. As Mr. Slope was esteemed an adept at letter writing, they shall be given in full.

(Private)   Palace, Barchester, Sept. 185—

My dear Sir Nicholas,

I hope that the intercourse which has been between us will preclude you from regarding my present application as an intrusion. You cannot, I imagine, have yet heard that poor old Dr. Trefoil has been seized with apoplexy. It is a subject of profound grief to everyone in Barchester, for he has always been an excellent man—excellent as a man and as a clergyman. He is, however, full of years, and his life could not under any circumstances have been much longer spared. You may probably have known him.

> There is, it appears, no probable chance of his recovery. Sir Omicron Pie is, I believe, at present with him. At any rate the medical men here have declared that one or two days more must limit the tether of his mortal coil. I sincerely trust that his soul may wing its flight to that haven where it may forever be at rest and forever be happy.
>
> The bishop has been speaking to me about the preferment, and he is anxious that it should be conferred on me. I confess that I can hardly venture, at my age, to look for such advancement, but I am so far encouraged by his lordship that I believe I shall be induced to do so. His lordship goes to —— to-morrow and is intent on mentioning the subject to the archbishop.
>
> I know well how deservedly great is your weight with the present government. In any matter touching church preferment you would of course be listened to. Now that the matter has been put into my head, I am of course anxious to be successful. If you can assist me by your good word, you will confer on me one additional favour.
>
> I had better add, that Lord —— cannot as yet know of this piece of preferment having fallen in, or rather of its certainty of falling (for poor dear Dr. Trefoil is past hope). Should Lord —— first hear it from you, that might probably be thought to give you a fair claim to express your opinion.
>
> Of course our grand object is that we should all be of one opinion in church matters. This is most desirable at Barchester; it is this that makes our good bishop so anxious about it. You may probably think it expedient to point this out to Lord —— if it shall be in your power to oblige me by mentioning the subject to his lordship.
>
> Believe me,
>   My dear Sir Nicholas,
>   Your most faithful servant,   OBADIAH SLOPE

His letter to Mr. Towers was written in quite a different strain. Mr. Slope conceived that he completely understood the difference in character and position of the two men whom he addressed. He knew that for such a man as Sir Nicholas Fitzwhiggin a little flummery was necessary, and that it might be of the easy, everyday description. Accordingly his letter to Sir Nicholas was written, *currente calamo*, with very little trouble. But to such a man as Mr. Towers it was not so easy to write a letter that should be effective and yet not offensive, that should carry its point without undue interference. It was not difficult to flatter Dr. Proudie or Sir Nicholas Fitzwhiggin, but very difficult to flatter Mr. Towers without letting the flattery declare itself. This, however, had to be done. Moreover, this letter must, in appearance at least, be written without effort, and be fluent, uncon-strained, and demonstrative of no doubt or fear on the part of the writer. Therefore the epistle to Mr. Towers was studied, and re-copied, and elaborated at the cost of so many minutes that Mr. Slope had hardly time to dress himself and reach Dr. Stanhope's that evening.

When dispatched, it ran as follows:—

(Private)   Barchester, Sept. 185—

(He purposely omitted any allusion to the "palace," thinking that Mr. Towers might not like it. A great man, he remembered, had been once much condemned for dating a letter from Windsor Castle.)

MY DEAR SIR, We were all a good deal shocked here this morning by hearing that poor old Dean Trefoil had been stricken with apoplexy. The fit took him about 9 A.M. I am writing now to save the post, and he is still alive, but past all hope or possibility, I believe, of living. Sir Omicron Pie is here, or will be very shortly, but all that even Sir Omicron can do is to ratify the sentence of his less distinguished brethren that nothing can be done. Poor Dr. Trefoil's race on this side the grave is run. I do not know whether you knew him. He was a good, quiet, charitable man, of the old school, of course, as any clergyman over seventy years of age must necessarily be.

But I do not write merely with the object of sending you such news as this: doubtless someone of your Mercuries will have seen and heard and re-ported so much; I write, as you usually do yourself, rather with a view to the future than to the past.

Rumour is already rife here as to Dr. Trefoil's successor, and among those named as possible future deans your humble servant is, I believe, not the least frequently spoken of; in short, I am looking for the preferment. You may probably know that since Bishop Proudie came to the diocese I have exerted myself here a good deal and, I may certainly say, not without some success. He and I are nearly always of the same opinion on points of doctrine as well as church discipline, and therefore I have had, as his confi-dential chaplain, very much in my own hands; but I confess to you that I have a higher ambition than to remain the chaplain of any bishop.

There are no positions in which more energy is now needed than those of our deans. The whole of our enormous cathedral establishments have been allowed to go to sleep—nay, they are all but dead and ready for the sepulchre! And yet of what prodigious moment they might be made if, as was intended, they were so managed as to lead the way and show an exam-ple for all our parochial clergy!

The bishop here is most anxious for my success; indeed, he goes to-morrow to press the matter on the archbishop. I believe also I may count on the support of at least one most effective member of the government. But I confess that the support of "The Jupiter," if I be thought worthy of it, would be more gratifying to me than any other; more gratifying if by it I should be successful, and more gratifying also if, although so supported, I should be unsuccessful.

The time has, in fact, come in which no government can venture to fill up the high places of the Church in defiance of the public press. The age of honourable bishops and noble deans has gone by, and any clergyman how-ever humbly born can now hope for success if his industry, talent, and character be sufficient to call forth the manifest opinion of the public in his favour.

319

At the present moment we all feel that any counsel given in such matters by "The Jupiter" has the greatest weight—is, indeed, generally followed; and we feel also—I am speaking of clergymen of my own age and standing—that it should be so. There can be no patron less interested than "The Jupiter," and none that more thoroughly understands the wants of the people.

I am sure you will not suspect me of asking from you any support which the paper with which you are connected cannot conscientiously give me. My object in writing is to let you know that I am a candidate for the appointment. It is for you to judge whether or no you can assist my views. I should not, of course, have written to you on such a matter had I not believed (and I have had good reason so to believe) that "The Jupiter" approves of my views on ecclesiastical polity.

The bishop expresses a fear that I may be considered too young for such a station, my age being thirty-six. I cannot think that at the present day any hesitation need be felt on such a point. The public has lost its love for antiquated servants. If a man will ever be fit to do good work, he will be fit at thirty-six years of age.

Believe me very faithfully yours,

OBADIAH SLOPE

T. Towers, Esq.,

—— Court,

Middle Temple.

Having thus exerted himself, Mr. Slope posted his letters and passed the remainder of the evening at the feet of his mistress.

Mr. Slope will be accused of deceit in his mode of canvassing. It will be said that he lied in the application he made to each of his three patrons. I believe it must be owned that he did so. He could not hesitate on account of his youth and yet be quite assured that he was not too young. He could not count chiefly on the bishop's support and chiefly also on that of the newspaper. He did not think that the bishop was going to —— to press the matter on the archbishop. It must be owned that in his canvassing Mr. Slope was as false as he well could be.

Let it, however, be asked of those who are conversant with such matters, whether he was more false than men usually are on such occasions. We English gentlemen hate the name of a lie, but how often do we find public men who believe each other's words?

CHAPTER XXXIII

MRS. PROUDIE VICTRIX

The next week passed over at Barchester with much apparent tranquillity. The hearts, however, of some of the inhabitants were not so tranquil as the streets of the city. The poor old dean still continued to live, just as Sir Omicron Pie had prophesied that he would do, much to the amazement, and some thought disgust, of Dr. Fillgrave. The bishop still remained away. He had stayed a day or two in town and had also remained longer at the archbishop's than he had intended. Mr. Slope had as yet received no line in answer to either of his letters, but he had learnt the cause of this. Sir Nicholas was stalking a deer, or attending the Queen, in the Highlands, and even the indefatigable Mr. Towers had stolen an autumn holiday, and had made one of the yearly tribe who now ascend Mont Blanc. Mr. Slope learnt that he was not expected back till the last day of September.

Mrs. Bold was thrown much with the Stanhopes, of whom she became fonder and fonder. If asked, she would have said that Charlotte Stanhope was her especial friend, and so she would have thought. But, to tell the truth, she liked Bertie nearly as well; she had no more idea of regarding him as a lover than she would have had of looking at a big tame dog in such a light. Bertie had become very intimate with her, and made little speeches to her, and said little things of a sort very different from the speeches and sayings of other men. But then this was almost always done before his sisters; and he, with his long silken beard, his light blue eyes, and strange dress, was so unlike other men. She admitted him to a kind of familiarity which she had never known with anyone else, and of which she by no means understood the danger. She blushed once at finding that she had called him Bertie and, on the same day, only barely remembered her position in time to check herself from playing upon him some personal practical joke to which she was instigated by Charlotte.

In all this Eleanor was perfectly innocent, and Bertie Stanhope could hardly be called guilty. But every familiarity into which Eleanor was entrapped was deliberately planned by his sister. She knew well how to play her game, and played it without mercy; she knew, none so well, what was her brother's character, and she would have handed over to him the young widow, and the young widow's money, and the money of the widow's child, without remorse. With her pretended friendship and warm cordiality, she strove to connect Eleanor so closely with her brother as to make it impossible that she should go back even if she wished it. But Charlotte Stanhope knew really nothing of Eleanor's character, did not even understand that there were such characters. She did not comprehend that a young and pretty woman could be playful and familiar with a man such as Bertie Stanhope and yet have no idea in her head, no feeling in her heart, that she would have been ashamed to own to all the world. Charlotte Stanhope did not in the least conceive that her new friend was a woman whom nothing could entrap into an inconsiderate marriage, whose mind would have revolted from the slightest impropriety had she been aware that any impropriety existed.

Miss Stanhope, however, had tact enough to make herself and her father's house very agreeable to Mrs. Bold. There was with them all an absence of stiffness and formality which was peculiarly agreeable to Eleanor after the great dose of clerical arrogance which she had lately been constrained to take. She played chess with them, walked with them, and drank tea with them; studied or pretended to study astronomy; assisted them in writing stories in rhyme, in turning prose tragedy into comic verse, or comic stories into would-be tragic poetry. She had no idea before that she had any such talents. She had not conceived the possibility of her doing such things as she now did. She found with the Stanhopes new amusements and employments, new pursuits, which in themselves could not be wrong, and which were exceedingly alluring.

Is it not a pity that people who are bright and clever should so often be exceedingly improper, and that those who are never improper should so often be dull and heavy? Now Charlotte Stanhope was always bright and never heavy, but then her propriety was doubtful.

But during all this time Eleanor by no means forgot Mr. Arabin, nor did she forget Mr. Slope. She had parted from Mr. Arabin in her anger. She was still angry at what she regarded as his impertinent interference, but nevertheless she looked forward to meeting him again, and also looked forward to forgiving him. The words that Mr. Arabin had uttered still sounded in her ears. She knew that if not intended for a declaration of love, they did signify that he loved her, and she felt also that if he ever did make such a declaration, it might be that she should not receive it unkindly. She was still angry with him, very angry with him; so angry that she would bite her lip and stamp her foot as she thought of what he had said and done. Nevertheless, she yearned to let him know that he was forgiven; all that she required was that he should own that he had sinned.

She was to meet him at Ullathorne on the last day of the present month. Miss Thorne had invited all the country round to a breakfast on the lawn. There were to be tents, and archery, and dancing for the ladies on the lawn and for the swains and girls in the paddock. There were to be fiddlers and fifers, races for the boys, poles to be climbed, ditches full of water to be jumped over, horse-collars to be grinned through (this latter amusement was an addition of the stewards, and not arranged by Miss Thorne in the original programme), and every game to be played which, in a long course of reading, Miss Thorne could ascertain to have been played in the good days of Queen Elizabeth. Everything of more modern growth was to be tabooed, if possible. On one subject Miss Thorne was very unhappy. She had been turning in her mind the matter of a bull-ring, but could not succeed in making anything of it. She would not for the world have done, or allowed to be done, anything that was cruel; as to the promoting the torture of a bull for the amusement of her young neighbours, it need hardly be said that Miss Thorne would be the last to think of it. And yet there was something so charming in the name. A bull-ring, however, without a bull would only be a memento of the decadence of the times, and she felt herself constrained to abandon the idea. Quintains, however, she was determined to have, and had poles and swivels and bags of flour prepared accordingly. She would no doubt have been anxious for something small in the way of a tournament, but, as she said to her brother, that had been tried, and the age had proved itself too decidedly inferior to its forerunners to admit of such a pastime. Mr. Thorne did not seem to participate much in her regret, feeling perhaps that a full suit of chain-armour would have added but little to his own personal comfort.

This party at Ullathorne had been planned in the first place as a sort of welcoming to Mr. Arabin on his entrance into St. Ewold's parsonage; an intended harvest-home gala for the labourers and their wives and children had subsequently been amalgamated with it, and thus it had grown to its present dimensions. All the Plumstead party had of course been asked, and at the time of the invitation Eleanor had intended to have gone with her sister. Now her plans were altered, and she was going with the Stanhopes. The Proudies were also to be there, and, as Mr. Slope had not been included in the invitation to the palace, the signora, whose impudence never deserted her, asked permission of Miss Thorne to bring him.

This permission Miss Thorne gave, having no other alternative; but she did so with a trembling heart, fearing Mr. Arabin would be offended. Immediately on his return she apologized, almost with tears, so dire an enmity was presumed to rage between the two gentlemen. But Mr. Arabin comforted her by an assurance that he should meet Mr. Slope with the greatest pleasure imaginable and made her promise that she would introduce them to each other.

But this triumph of Mr. Slope's was not so agreeable to Eleanor, who since her return to Barchester had done her best to avoid him. She would not give way to the Plumstead folk when they so ungenerously accused her of being in love with this odious man; but, nevertheless, knowing that she was so accused, she was fully alive to the expediency of keeping out of his way and dropping him by degrees. She had seen very little of him since her return. Her servant had been instructed to say to all visitors that she was out. She could not bring herself to specify Mr. Slope particularly, and in order to avoid him she had thus debarred herself from all her friends. She had excepted Charlotte Stanhope and, by degrees, a few others also. Once she had met him at the Stanhopes', but as a rule, Mr. Slope's visits there were made in the morning and hers in the evening. On that one occasion Charlotte had managed to preserve her from any annoyance. This was very good-natured on the part of Charlotte, as Eleanor thought, and also very sharp-witted, as Eleanor had told her friend nothing of her reasons for wishing to avoid that gentleman. The fact, however, was that Charlotte had learnt from her sister that Mr. Slope would probably put himself forward as a suitor for the widow's hand, and she was consequently sufficiently alive to the expediency of guarding Bertie's future wife from any danger in that quarter.

Nevertheless the Stanhopes were pledged to take Mr. Slope with them to Ullathorne. An arrangement was therefore necessarily made, which was very disagreeable to Eleanor. Dr. Stanhope, with herself, Charlotte, and Mr. Slope, were to go together, and Bertie was to follow with his sister Madeline. It was clearly visible by Eleanor's face that this assortment was very disagreeable to her, and Charlotte, who was much encouraged thereby in her own little plan, made a thousand apologies.

"I see you don't like it, my dear," said she, "but we could not manage otherwise. Bertie would give his eyes to go with you, but Madeline cannot possibly go without him. Nor could we possibly put Mr. Slope and Madeline in the same carriage without anyone else. They'd both be ruined forever, you know, and not admitted inside Ullathorne gates, I should imagine, after such an impropriety."

"Of course that wouldn't do," said Eleanor, "but couldn't I go in the carriage with the signora and your brother?"

"Impossible!" said Charlotte. "When she is there, there is only room for two." The Signora, in truth, did not care to do her travelling in the presence of strangers.

"Well, then," said Eleanor, "you are all so kind, Charlotte, and so good to me that I am sure you won't be offended, but I think I'll not go at all."

"Not go at all!—what nonsense!—indeed you shall." It had been absolutely determined in family counsel that Bertie should propose on that very occasion.

"Or I can take a fly," said Eleanor. "You know I am not embarrassed by so many diffi-culties as you young ladies; I can go alone."

"Nonsense, my dear! Don't think of such a thing; after all, it is only for an hour or so; and, to tell the truth, I don't know what it is you dislike so. I thought you and Mr. Slope were great friends. What is it you dislike?"

"Oh, nothing particular," said Eleanor; "only I thought it would be a family party."

"Of course it would be much nicer, much more snug, if Bertie could go with us. It is he that is badly treated. I can assure you he is much more afraid of Mr. Slope than you are. But you see Madeline cannot go out without him—and she, poor creature, goes out so seldom! I am sure you don't begrudge her this, though her vagary does knock about our own party a little."

Of course Eleanor made a thousand protestations and uttered a thousand hopes that Madeline would enjoy herself. And of course she had to give way and undertake to go in the carriage with Mr. Slope. In fact, she was driven either to do this or to explain why she would not do so. Now she could not bring herself to explain to Charlotte Stanhope all that had passed at Plumstead.

But it was to her a sore necessity. She thought of a thousand little schemes for avoid-ing it; she would plead illness and not go at all; she would persuade Mary Bold to go, although not asked, and then make a necessity of having a carriage of her own to take her sister-in-law; anything, in fact, she could do, rather than be seen by Mr. Arabin getting out of the same carriage with Mr. Slope. However, when the momentous morning came, she had no scheme matured, and then Mr. Slope handed her into Dr. Stanhope's carriage and, following her steps, sat opposite to her.

The bishop returned on the eve of the Ullathorne party, and was received at home with radiant smiles by the partner of all his cares. On his arrival he crept up to his dressing-room with somewhat of a palpitating heart; he had overstayed his alloted time by three days, and was not without much fear of penalties. Nothing, however, could be more affec-tionately cordial than the greeting he received; the girls came out and kissed him in a manner that was quite soothing to his spirit; and Mrs. Proudie, "albeit, unused to the melt-ing mood," squeezed him in her arms and almost in words called him her dear, darling, good, pet, little bishop. All this was a very pleasant surprise.

Mrs. Proudie had somewhat changed her tactics; not that she had seen any cause to disapprove of her former line of conduct, but she had now brought matters to such a point that she calculated that she might safely do so. She had got the better of Mr. Slope, and she now thought well to show her husband that when allowed to get the better of every-body, when obeyed by him and permitted to rule over others, she would take care that he should have his reward. Mr. Slope had not a chance against her; not only could she stun the poor bishop by her midnight anger, but she could assuage and soothe him, if she so willed, by daily indulgences. She could furnish his room for him, turn him out as smart a bishop as any on the bench, give him good dinners, warm fires, and an easy life—all this she would do if he would but be quietly obedient. But, if not,—! To speak sooth, however, his sufferings on that dreadful night had been so poignant as to leave him little spirit for further rebellion.

As soon as he had dressed himself, she returned to his room. "I hope you enjoyed yourself at ——," said she, seating herself on one side of the fire while he remained in his armchair on the other, stroking the calves of his legs. It was the first time he had had a fire in his room since the summer, and it pleased him, for the good bishop loved to be warm and cosy. Yes, he said, he had enjoyed himself very much. Nothing could be more polite than the archbishop, and Mrs. Archbishop had been equally charming.

Mrs. Proudie was delighted to hear it; nothing, she declared, pleased her so much as to think

Her bairn respectit like the lave.

She did not put it precisely in these words, but what she said came to the same thing; and then, having petted and fondled her little man sufficiently, she proceeded to business. "The poor dean is still alive," said she.

"So I hear, so I hear," said the bishop. "I'll go to the deanery directly after breakfast to-morrow."

"We are going to this party at Ullathorne to-morrow morning, my dear; we must be there early, you know—by twelve o'clock I suppose."

"Oh—ah!" said the bishop; "then I'll certainly call the next day."

"Was much said about it at ——?" asked Mrs. Proudie.

"About what?" said the bishop.

"Filling up the dean's place," said Mrs. Proudie. As she spoke, a spark of the wonted fire returned to her eye, and the bishop felt himself to be a little less comfortable than before.

"Filling up the dean's place; that is, if the dean dies? Very little, my dear. It was mentioned, just mentioned."

"And what did you say about it, Bishop?"

"Why, I said that I thought that if, that is, should—should the dean die, that is, I said I thought—" As he went on stammering and floundering, he saw that his wife's eye was fixed sternly on him. Why should he encounter such evil for a man whom he loved so slightly as Mr. Slope? Why should he give up his enjoyments and his ease and such dignity as might be allowed to him to fight a losing battle for a chaplain? The chaplain, after all, if successful, would be as great a tyrant as his wife. Why fight at all? Why contend? Why be uneasy? From that moment he determined to fling Mr. Slope to the winds and take the goods the gods provided.

"I am told," said Mrs. Proudie, speaking very slowly, "that Mr. Slope is looking to be the new dean."

"Yes—certainly, I believe he is," said the bishop.

"And what does the archbishop say about that?" asked Mrs. Proudie.

"Well, my dear, to tell the truth, I promised Mr. Slope to speak to the archbishop. Mr. Slope spoke to me about it. It is very arrogant of him, I must say—but that is nothing to me."

"Arrogant!" said Mrs. Proudie; "it is the most impudent piece of pretension I ever heard of in my life. Mr. Slope Dean of Barchester, indeed! And what did you do in the matter, Bishop?"

"Why, my dear, I did speak to the archbishop."

"You don't mean to tell me," said Mrs. Proudie, "that you are going to make yourself ridiculous by lending your name to such a preposterous attempt as this? Mr. Slope Dean of Barchester, indeed!" And she tossed her head and put her arms akimbo with an air of confident defiance that made her husband quite sure that Mr. Slope never would be Dean of Barchester. In truth, Mrs. Proudie was all but invincible; had she married Petruchio, it may be doubted whether that arch wife-tamer would have been able to keep her legs out of those garments which are presumed by men to be peculiarly unfitted for feminine use.

"It is preposterous, my dear."

"Then why have you endeavoured to assist him?"

"Why—my dear, I haven't assisted him—much."

"But why have you done it at all? Why have you mixed your name up in anything so ridiculous? What was it you did say to the archbishop?"

325

"Why, I just did mention it; I just did say that—that in the event of the poor dean's death, Mr. Slope would—would—"

"Would what?"

"I forget how I put it—would take it if he could get it; something of that sort. I didn't say much more than that."

"You shouldn't have said anything at all. And what did the archbishop say?"

"He didn't say anything; he just bowed and rubbed his hands. Somebody else came up at the moment, and as we were discussing the new parochial universal school committee, the matter of the new dean dropped; after that I didn't think it wise to renew it."

"Renew it! I am very sorry you ever mentioned it. What will the archbishop think of you?"

"You may be sure, my dear, the archbishop thought very little about it."

"But why did you think about it, Bishop? How could you think of making such a creature as that Dean of Barchester? Dean of Barchester! I suppose he'll be looking for a bishopric some of these days—a man that hardly knows who his own father was; a man that I found without bread to his mouth or a coat to his back. Dean of Barchester, indeed! I'll dean him."

Mrs. Proudie considered herself to be in politics a pure Whig; all her family belonged to the Whig party. Now, among all ranks of Englishmen and Englishwomen (Mrs. Proudie should, I think, be ranked among the former on the score of her great strength of mind), no one is so hostile to lowly born pretenders to high station as the pure Whig.

The bishop thought it necessary to exculpate himself. "Why, my dear," said he, "it appeared to me that you and Mr. Slope did not get on quite so well as you used to do!"

"Get on!" said Mrs. Proudie, moving her foot uneasily on the hearth-rug and compressing her lips in a manner that betokened much danger to the subject of their discourse.

"I began to find that he was objectionable to you"—Mrs. Proudie's foot worked on the hearth-rug with great rapidity—"and that you would be more comfortable if he was out of the palace"—Mrs. Proudie smiled, as a hyena may probably smile before he begins his laugh—"and therefore I thought that if he got this place, and so ceased to be my chaplain, you might be pleased at such an arrangement."

And then the hyena laughed out. Pleased at such an arrangement! Pleased at having her enemy converted into a dean with twelve hundred a year! Medea, when she describes the customs of her native country (I am quoting from Robson's edition), assures her astonished auditor that in her land captives, when taken, are eaten.

"You pardon them?" says Medea.

"We do indeed," says the mild Grecian.

"We eat them!" says she of Colchis, with terrific energy.

Mrs. Proudie was the Medea of Barchester; she had no idea of not eating Mr. Slope. Pardon him! Merely get rid of him! Make a dean of him! It was not so they did with their captives in her country, among people of her sort! Mr. Slope had no such mercy to expect; she would pick him to the very last bone.

"Oh, yes, my dear, of course he'll cease to be your chaplain," said she. "After what has passed, that must be a matter of course. I couldn't for a moment think of living in the same house with such a man. Besides, he has shown himself quite unfit for such a situation; making broils and quarrels among the clergy; getting you, my dear, into scrapes; and taking upon himself as though he were as good as bishop himself. Of course he'll go. But because he leaves the palace, that is no reason why he should get into the deanery."

"Oh, of course not!" said the bishop; "but to save appearances, you know, my dear—"

"I don't want to save appearances; I want Mr. Slope to appear just what he is—a false, designing, mean, intriguing man. I have my eye on him; he little knows what I see. He is misconducting himself in the most disgraceful way with that lame Italian woman. That family is a disgrace to Barchester, and Mr. Slope is a disgrace to Barchester. If he doesn't look well to it, he'll have his gown stripped off his back instead of having a dean's hat on his head. Dean, indeed! The man has gone mad with arrogance."

The bishop said nothing further to excuse either himself or his chaplain, and having shown himself passive and docile, was again taken into favour. They soon went to dinner, and he spent the pleasantest evening he had had in his own house for a long time. His daughter played and sang to him as he sipped his coffee and read his newspaper, and Mrs. Proudie asked good-natured little questions about the archbishop; and then he went happily to bed and slept as quietly as though Mrs. Proudie had been Griselda herself. While shaving himself in the morning and preparing for the festivities of Ullathorne, he fully resolved to run no more tilts against a warrior so fully armed at all points as was Mrs. Proudie.

CHAPTER XXXIV

OXFORD—THE MASTER AND TUTOR OF LAZARUS

Mr. Arabin, as we have said, had but a sad walk of it under the trees of Plumstead churchyard. He did not appear to any of the family till dinner-time, and then he seemed, as far as their judgement went, to be quite himself. He had, as was his wont, asked himself a great many questions and given himself a great many answers; and the upshot of this was that he had sent himself down for an ass. He had determined that he was much too old and much too rusty to commence the manoeuvres of love-making; that he had let the time slip through his hands which should have been used for such purposes; and that now he must lie on his bed as he had made it. Then he asked himself whether in truth he did love this woman; and he answered himself, not without a long struggle, but at last honestly, that he certainly did love her. He then asked himself whether he did not also love her money, and he again answered himself that he did so. But here he did not answer honestly. It was and ever had been his weakness to look for impure motives for his own conduct. No doubt, circumstanced as he was, with a small living and a fellowship, accustomed as he had been to collegiate luxuries and expensive comforts, he might have hesitated to marry a penni-less woman had he felt ever so strong a predilection for the woman herself; no doubt Eleanor's fortune put all such difficulties out of the question; but it was equally without doubt that his love for her had crept upon him without the slightest idea on his part that he could ever benefit his own condition by sharing her wealth.

When he had stood on the hearth-rug, counting the pattern and counting also the future chances of his own life, the remembrances of Mrs. Bold's comfortable income had certain-ly not damped his first assured feeling of love for her. And why should it have done so? Need it have done so with the purest of men? Be that as it may, Mr. Arabin decided against himself; he decided that it had done so in his case, and that he was not the purest of men.

He also decided, which was more to his purpose, that Eleanor did not care a straw for him, and that very probably she did care a straw for his rival. Then he made up his mind not to think of her any more, and went on thinking of her till he was almost in a state to drown himself in the little brook which ran at the bottom of the archdeacon's grounds.

And ever and again his mind would revert to the Signora Neroni, and he would make comparisons between her and Eleanor Bold, not always in favour of the latter. The signora had listened to him, and flattered him, and believed in him; at least she had told him so. Mrs. Bold had also listened to him, but had never flattered him; had not always believed in him; and now had broken from him in violent rage. The signora, too, was the more lovely woman of the two, and had also the additional attraction of her affliction—for to him it was an attraction.

But he never could have loved the Signora Neroni as he felt that he now loved Eleanor; and so he flung stones into the brook, instead of flinging in himself, and sat down on its margin as sad a gentleman as you shall meet in a summer's day.

He heard the dinner-bell ring from the churchyard, and he knew that it was time to recover his self-possession. He felt that he was disgracing himself in his own eyes, that he had been idling his time and neglecting the high duties which he had taken upon himself to perform. He should have spent this afternoon among the poor at St. Ewold's, instead of wandering about at Plumstead, an ancient, love-lorn swain, dejected and sighing, full of imaginary sorrows and Wertherian grief. He was thoroughly ashamed of himself, and determined to lose no time in retrieving his character, so damaged in his own eyes.

Thus when he appeared at dinner he was as animated as ever and was the author of most of the conversation which graced the archdeacon's board on that evening. Mr. Harding was ill at ease and sick at heart, and did not care to appear more comfortable than he really was; what little he did say was said to his daughter. He thought that the archdeacon and Mr. Arabin had leagued together against Eleanor's comfort, and his wish now was to break away from the pair and undergo in his Barchester lodgings whatever Fate had in store for him. He hated the name of the hospital; his attempt to regain his lost inheritance there had brought upon him so much suffering. As far as he was concerned, Mr. Quiverful was now welcome to the place.

And the archdeacon was not very lively. The poor dean's illness was of course discussed in the first place. Dr. Grantly did not mention Mr. Slope's name in connexion with the expected event of Dr. Trefoil's death; he did not wish to say anything about Mr. Slope just at present, nor did he wish to make known his sad surmises; but the idea that his enemy might possibly become Dean of Barchester made him very gloomy. Should such an event take place, such a dire catastrophe come about, there would be an end to his life as far as his life was connected with the city of Barchester. He must give up all his old haunts, all his old habits, and live quietly as a retired rector at Plumstead. It had been a severe trial for him to have Dr. Proudie in the palace, but with Mr. Slope also in the deanery he felt that he should be unable to draw his breath in Barchester close.

Thus it came to pass that in spite of the sorrow at his heart, Mr. Arabin was apparently the gayest of the party. Both Mr. Harding and Mrs. Grantly were in a slight degree angry with him on account of his want of gloom. To the one it appeared as though he were triumphing at Eleanor's banishment, and to the other that he was not affected as he should have been by all the sad circumstances of the day—Eleanor's obstinacy, Mr. Slope's success, and the poor dean's apoplexy. And so they were all at cross-purposes.

Mr. Harding left the room almost together with the ladies, and then the archdeacon opened his heart to Mr. Arabin. He still harped upon the hospital. "What did that fellow mean," said he, "by saying in his letter to Mrs. Bold that if Mr. Harding would call on the bishop, it would be all right? Of course I would not be guided by anything he might say, but still it may be well that Mr. Harding should see the bishop. It would be foolish to let the thing slip through our fingers because Mrs. Bold is determined to make a fool of herself."

Mr. Arabin hinted that he was not quite so sure that Mrs. Bold would make a fool of herself. He said that he was not convinced that she did regard Mr. Slope so warmly as she was supposed to do. The archdeacon questioned and cross-questioned him about this, but elicited nothing, and at last remained firm in his own conviction that he was destined, *malgré lui*, to be the brother-in-law of Mr. Slope. Mr. Arabin strongly advised that Mr.

Harding should take no step regarding the hospital in connexion with, or in consequence of, Mr. Slope's letter. "If the bishop really means to confer the appointment on Mr. Harding," argued Mr. Arabin, "he will take care to let him have some other intimation than a message conveyed through a letter to a lady. Were Mr. Harding to present himself at the palace, he might merely be playing Mr. Slope's game;" and thus it was settled that nothing should be done till the great Dr. Gwynne's arrival, or at any rate without that potentate's sanction.

It was droll to observe how these men talked of Mr. Harding as though he were a puppet, and planned their intrigues and small ecclesiastical manoeuvres in reference to Mr. Harding's future position without dreaming of taking him into their confidence. There was a comfortable house and income in question, and it was very desirable, and certainly very just, that Mr. Harding should have them; but that at present was not the main point; it was expedient to beat the bishop and, if possible, to smash Mr. Slope. Mr. Slope had set up, or was supposed to have set up, a rival candidate. Of all things the most desirable would have been to have had Mr. Quiverful's appointment published to the public and then annulled by the clamour of an indignant world, loud in the defence of Mr. Harding's rights. But of such an event the chance was small; a slight fraction only of the world would be indignant, and that fraction would be one not accustomed to loud speaking. And then the preferment had, in a sort of way, been offered to Mr. Harding and had, in a sort of way, been refused by him.

Mr. Slope's wicked, cunning hand had been peculiarly conspicuous in the way in which this had been brought to pass, and it was the success of Mr. Slope's cunning which was so painfully grating to the feelings of the archdeacon. That which of all things he most dreaded was that he should be outgeneralled by Mr. Slope; and just at present it appeared probable that Mr. Slope would turn his flank, steal a march on him, cut off his provisions, carry his strong town by a *coup de main*, and at last beat him thoroughly in a regular pitched battle. The archdeacon felt that his flank had been turned when desired to wait on Mr. Slope instead of the bishop, that a march had been stolen when Mr. Harding was induced to refuse the bishop's offer, that his provisions would be cut off when Mr. Quiverful got the hospital, that Eleanor was the strong town doomed to be taken, and that Mr. Slope, as Dean of Barchester, would be regarded by all the world as conqueror in the final conflict.

Dr. Gwynne was the *Deus ex machina* who was to come down upon the Barchester stage and bring about deliverance from these terrible evils. But how can melodramatic *dénouements* be properly brought about, how can vice and Mr. Slope be punished, and virtue and the archdeacon be rewarded, while the avenging god is laid up with the gout? In the mean time evil may be triumphant, and poor innocence, transfixed to the earth by an arrow from Dr. Proudie's quiver, may lie dead upon the ground, not to be resuscitated even by Dr. Gwynne.

Two or three days after Eleanor's departure, Mr. Arabin went to Oxford and soon found himself closeted with the august head of his college. It was quite clear that Dr. Gwynne was not very sanguine as to the effects of his journey to Barchester, and not over-anxious to interfere with the bishop. He had had the gout, but was very nearly convalescent, and Mr. Arabin at once saw that had the mission been one of which the master thoroughly approved, he would before this have been at Plumstead.

As it was, Dr. Gwynne was resolved on visiting his friend, and willingly promised to return to Barchester with Mr. Arabin. He could not bring himself to believe that there was any probability that Mr. Slope would be made Dean of Barchester. Rumour, he said, had reached even his ears, not at all favourable to that gentleman's character, and he expressed himself strongly of opinion that any such appointment was quite out of the question. At this stage of the proceedings, the master's right-hand man, Tom Staple, was called in to assist at the conference. Tom Staple was the Tutor of Lazarus and, moreover, a great man at Oxford. Though universally known by a species of nomenclature so very undignified, Tom Staple was one who maintained a high dignity in the university. He was, as it were, the leader of the Oxford tutors, a body of men who consider themselves collectively as being by very little, if at all, second in importance to the heads themselves. It is not always the case that the master, or warden, or provost, or principal can hit it off exactly with his tutor. A tutor is by no means indisposed to have a will of his own. But at Lazarus they were great friends and firm allies at the time of which we are writing.

Tom Staple was a hale, strong man of about forty-five, short in stature, swarthy in face, with strong, sturdy black hair and crisp black beard of which very little was allowed to show itself in shape of whiskers. He always wore a white neckcloth, clean indeed, but not tied with that scrupulous care which now distinguishes some of our younger clergy. He was, of course, always clothed in a seemly suit of solemn black. Mr. Staple was a decent cleanly liver, not over-addicted to any sensuality; but nevertheless a somewhat warmish hue was beginning to adorn his nose, the peculiar effect, as his friends averred, of a certain pipe of port introduced into the cellars of Lazarus the very same year in which the tutor entered it as a freshman. There was also, perhaps, a little redolence of port wine, as it were the slightest possible twang, in Mr. Staple's voice.

In these latter days Tom Staple was not a happy man; university reform had long been his bugbear, and now was his bane. It was not with him, as with most others, an affair of politics, respecting which, when the need existed, he could, for parties' sake or on behalf of principle, maintain a certain amount of necessary zeal; it was not with him a subject for dilettante warfare and courteous, commonplace opposition. To him it was life and death. The *status quo* of the university was his only idea of life, and any reformation was as bad to him as death. He would willingly have been a martyr in the cause, had the cause admitted of martyrdom.

At the present day, unfortunately, public affairs will allow of no martyrs, and therefore it is that there is such a deficiency of zeal. Could gentlemen of £10,000 a year have died on their own door-steps in defence of protection, no doubt some half-dozen glorious old baronets would have so fallen, and the school of protection would at this day have been crowded with scholars. Who can fight strenuously in any combat in which there is no danger? Tom Staple would have willingly been impaled before a Committee of the House, could he by such self-sacrifice have infused his own spirit into the component members of the hebdomadal board.

Tom Staple was one of those who in his heart approved of the credit system which had of old been in vogue between the students and tradesmen of the university. He knew and acknowledged to himself that it was useless in these degenerate days publicly to contend with "The Jupiter" on such a subject. "The Jupiter" had undertaken to rule the university, and Tom Staple was well aware that "The Jupiter" was too powerful for him. But in secret, and among his safe companions, he would argue that the system of credit was an ordeal good for young men to undergo.

The bad men, said he, the weak and worthless, blunder into danger and burn their feet; but the good men, they who have any character, they who have that within them which can reflect credit on their alma mater, they come through scatheless. What merit will there be to a young man to get through safely, if he be guarded and protected and restrained like a schoolboy? By so doing, the period of the ordeal is only postponed, and the manhood of the man will be deferred from the age of twenty to that of twenty-four. If you bind him with leading-strings at college, he will break loose while eating for the bar in London; bind him there, and he will break loose afterwards, when he is a married man. The wild oats must be sown somewhere. 'Twas thus that Tom Staple would argue of young men, not, indeed, with much consistency, but still with some practical knowledge of the subject gathered from long experience.

And now Tom Staple proffered such wisdom as he had for the assistance of Dr. Gwynne and Mr. Arabin.

"Quite out of the question," said he, arguing that Mr. Slope could not possibly be made the new Dean of Barchester.

"So I think," said the master. "He has no standing, and, if all I hear be true, very little character."

"As to character," said Tom Staple, "I don't think much of that. They rather like loose parsons for deans; a little fast living, or a dash of infidelity, is no bad recommendation to a cathedral close. But they couldn't make Mr. Slope; the last two deans have been Cambridge men; you'll not show me an instance of their making three men running from the same university. We don't get our share and never shall, I suppose, but we must at least have one out of three."

"Those sort of rules are all gone by now," said Mr. Arabin.

"Everything has gone by, I believe," said Tom Staple. "The cigar has been smoked out, and we are the ashes."

"Speak for yourself, Staple," said the master.

"I speak for all," said the tutor stoutly. "It is coming to that, that there will be no life left anywhere in the country. No one is any longer fit to rule himself, or those belonging to him. The Government is to find us all in everything, and the press is to find the Government. Nevertheless, Mr. Slope won't be Dean of Barchester."

"And who will be warden of the hospital?" said Mr. Arabin.

"I hear that Mr. Quiverful is already appointed," said Tom Staple.

"I think not," said the master. "And I think, moreover, that Dr. Proudie will not be so short-sighted as to run against such a rock: Mr. Slope should himself have sense enough to prevent it."

"But perhaps Mr. Slope may have no objection to see his patron on a rock," said the suspicious tutor.

"What could he get by that?" asked Mr. Arabin.

"It is impossible to see the doubles of such a man," said Mr. Staple. "It seems quite clear that Bishop Proudie is altogether in his hands, and it is equally clear that he has been moving heaven and earth to get this Mr. Quiverful into the hospital, although he must know that such an appointment would be most damaging to the bishop. It is impossible to understand such a man, and dreadful to think," added Tom Staple, sighing deeply, "that the welfare and fortunes of good men may depend on his intrigues."

Dr. Gwynne or Mr. Staple were not in the least aware, nor even was Mr. Arabin, that this Mr. Slope, of whom they were talking, had been using his utmost efforts to put their own candidate into the hospital, and that in lieu of being permanent in the palace, his own expulsion therefrom had been already decided on by the high powers of the diocese.

"I'll tell you what," said the tutor, "if this Quiverful is thrust into the hospital and Dr. Trefoil does die, I should not wonder if the Government were to make Mr. Harding Dean of Barchester. They would feel bound to do something for him after all that was said when he resigned."

Dr. Gwynne at the moment made no reply to this suggestion, but it did not the less impress itself on his mind. If Mr. Harding could not be warden of the hospital, why should he not be Dean of Barchester?

And so the conference ended without any very fixed resolution, and Dr. Gwynne and Mr. Arabin prepared for their journey to Plumstead on the morrow.

CHAPTER XXXV

MISS THORNE'S FÊTE CHAMPÊTRE

The day of the Ullathorne party arrived, and all the world were there—or at least so much of the world as had been included in Miss Thorne's invitation. As we have said, the bishop returned home on the previous evening, and on the same evening and by the same train came Dr. Gwynne and Mr. Arabin from Oxford. The archdeacon with his brougham was in waiting for the Master of Lazarus, so that there was a goodly show of church dignitaries on the platform of the railway.

The Stanhope party was finally arranged in the odious manner already described, and Eleanor got into the doctor's carriage full of apprehension and presentiment of further misfortune, whereas Mr. Slope entered the vehicle elate with triumph.

He had received that morning a very civil note from Sir Nicholas Fitzwhiggin, not promising much, indeed, but then Mr. Slope knew, or fancied that he knew, that it was not etiquette for government officers to make promises. Though Sir Nicholas promised nothing he implied a good deal, declared his conviction that Mr. Slope would make an excellent dean, and wished him every kind of success. To be sure he added that, not being in the cabinet, he was never consulted on such matters, and that even if he spoke on the subject, his voice would go for nothing. But all this Mr. Slope took for the prudent reserve of official life. To complete his anticipated triumphs, another letter was brought to him just as he was about to start to Ullathorne.

Mr. Slope also enjoyed the idea of handing Mrs. Bold out of Dr. Stanhope's carriage before the multitude at Ullathorne gate as much as Eleanor dreaded the same ceremony. He had fully made up his mind to throw himself and his fortune at the widow's feet, and had almost determined to select the present propitious morning for doing so. The signora had of late been less than civil to him. She had indeed admitted his visits and listened, at any rate without anger, to his love, but she had tortured him and reviled him, jeered at him and ridiculed him, while she allowed him to call her the most beautiful of living women, to kiss her hand, and to proclaim himself with reiterated oaths her adorer, her slave and worshipper.

Miss Thorne was in great perturbation, yet in great glory, on the morning of the gala day. Mr. Thorne also, though the party was none of his giving, had much heavy work on his hands. But perhaps the most overtasked, the most anxious, and the most effective of all the Ullathorne household was Mr. Plomacy, the steward. This last personage had, in the time of Mr. Thorne's father, when the Directory held dominion in France, gone over to Paris with letters in his boot-heel for some of the royal party, and such had been his good luck that he had returned safe. He had then been very young and was now very old, but the exploit gave him a character for political enterprise and secret discretion which still availed him as thoroughly as it had done in its freshest gloss. Mr. Plomacy had been steward of Ullathorne for more than fifty years, and a very easy life he had had of it. Who could require much absolute work from a man who had carried safely at his heel that which, if discovered, would have cost him his head? Consequently Mr. Plomacy had never worked hard, and of latter years had never worked at all. He had a taste for timber, and therefore he marked the trees that were to be cut down; he had a taste for gardening, and would therefore allow no shrub to be planted or bed to be made without his express sanction. In these matters he was sometimes driven to run counter to his mistress, but he rarely allowed his mistress to carry the point against him.

But on occasions such as the present Mr. Plomacy came out strong. He had the honour of the family at heart; he thoroughly appreciated the duties of hospitality; and therefore, when gala doings were going on, he always took the management into his own hands and reigned supreme over master and mistress.

To give Mr. Plomacy his due, old as he was, he thoroughly understood such work as he had in hand, and did it well.

The order of the day was to be as follows. The quality, as the upper classes in rural districts are designated by the lower with so much true discrimination, were to eat a breakfast, and the non-quality were to eat a dinner. Two marquees had been erected for these two banquets: that for the quality on the esoteric or garden side of a certain deep ha-ha; and that for the non-quality on the exoteric or paddock side of the same. Both were of huge dimensions—that on the outer side was, one may say, on an egregious scale—but Mr. Plomacy declared that neither would be sufficient. To remedy this, an auxiliary banquet was prepared in the dining-room, and a subsidiary board was to be spread *sub dio* for the accommodation of the lower class of yokels on the Ullathorne property.

No one who has not had a hand in the preparation of such an affair can understand the manifold difficulties which Miss Thorne encountered in her project. Had she not been made throughout of the very finest whalebone, riveted with the best Yorkshire steel, she must have sunk under them. Had not Mr. Plomacy felt how much was justly expected from a man who at one time carried the destinies of Europe in his boot, he would have given way, and his mistress, so deserted, must have perished among her poles and canvas.

In the first place there was a dreadful line to be drawn. Who were to dispose themselves within the ha-ha, and who without? To this the unthinking will give an off-hand answer, as they will to every ponderous question. Oh, the bishop and such-like within the ha-ha, and Farmer Greenacre and such-like without. True, my unthinking friend, but who shall define these such-likes? It is in such definitions that the whole difficulty of society consists. To seat the bishop on an arm-chair on the lawn and place Farmer Greenacre at the end of a long table in the paddock is easy enough, but where will you put Mrs. Lookaloft, whose husband, though a tenant on the estate, hunts in a red coat, whose daughters go to a fashionable seminary in Barchester, who calls her farm-house Rosebank, and who has a pianoforte in her drawing-room? The Misses Lookaloft, as they call themselves, won't sit contented among the bumpkins. Mrs. Lookaloft won't squeeze her fine clothes on a bench and talk familiarly about cream and ducklings to good Mrs. Greenacre. And yet Mrs. Lookaloft is no fit companion and never has been the associate of the Thornes and the Grantlys. And if Mrs. Lookaloft be admitted within the sanctum of fashionable life, if she be allowed with her three daughters to leap the ha-ha, why not the wives and daughters of other families also? Mrs. Greenacre is at present well contented with the paddock, but she might cease to be so if she saw Mrs. Lookaloft on the lawn. And thus poor Miss Thorne had a hard time of it.

And how was she to divide her guests between the marquee and the parlour? She had a countess coming, an Honourable John and an Honourable George, and a whole bevy of Ladies Amelia, Rosina, Margaretta, &c; she had a leash of baronets with their baronettes; and, as we all know, she had a bishop. If she put them on the lawn, no one would go into the parlour; if she put them into the parlour, no one would go into the tent. She thought of keeping the old people in the house and leaving the lawn to the lovers. She might as well have seated herself at once in a hornet's nest. Mr. Plomacy knew better than this. "Bless your soul, ma'am," said he, "there won't be no old ladies—not one, barring yourself and old Mrs. Clantantram."

Personally Miss Thorne accepted this distinction in her favour as a compliment to her good sense, but nevertheless she had no desire to be closeted on the coming occasion with Mrs. Clantantram. She gave up all idea of any arbitrary division of her guests and determined if possible to put the bishop on the lawn and the countess in the house, to sprinkle the baronets, and thus divide the attractions. What to do with the Lookalofts even Mr. Plomacy could not decide. They must take their chance. They had been specially told in the invitation that all the tenants had been invited, and they might probably have the good sense to stay away if they objected to mix with the rest of the tenantry.

Then Mr. Plomacy declared his apprehension that the Honourable Johns and Honourable Georges would come in a sort of amphibious costume, half-morning, half-evening, satin neck-handkerchiefs, frock-coats, primrose gloves, and polished boots; and that, being so dressed, they would decline riding at the quintain, or taking part in any of the athletic games which Miss Thorne had prepared with so much fond care. If the Lord Johns and Lord Georges didn't ride at the quintain, Miss Thorne might be sure that nobody else would.

"But," said she in dolorous voice, all but overcome by her cares, "it was specially signified that there were to be sports."

"And so there will be, of course," said Mr. Plomacy. "They'll all be sporting with the young ladies in the laurel walks. Them's the sports they care most about now-a-days. If you gets the young men at the quintain, you'll have all the young women in the pouts."

"Can't they look on as their great grandmothers did before them?" said Miss Thorne.

"It seems to me that the ladies ain't contented with looking now-a-days. Whatever the men do they'll do. If you'll have side-saddles on the nags; and let them go at the quintain too, it'll answer capital, no doubt."

Miss Thorne made no reply. She felt that she had no good ground on which to defend her sex of the present generation from the sarcasm of Mr. Plomacy. She had once declared, in one of her warmer moments, "that now-a-days the gentlemen were all women, and the ladies all men." She could not alter the debased character of the age. But, such being the case, why should she take on herself to cater for the amusement of people of such degraded tastes? This question she asked herself more than once, and she could only answer herself with a sigh. There was her own brother Wilfred, on whose shoulders rested all the ancient honours of Ullathorne house; it was very doubtful whether even he would consent to "go at the quintain," as Mr. Plomacy not injudiciously expressed it.

And now the morning arrived. The Ullathorne household was early on the move. Cooks were cooking in the kitchen long before daylight, and men were dragging out tables and hammering red baize on to benches at the earliest dawn. With what dread eagerness did Miss Thorne look out at the weather as soon as the parting veil of night permitted her to look at all! In this respect, at any rate, there was nothing to grieve her. The glass had been rising for the last three days, and the morning broke with that dull, chill, steady, grey haze which in autumn generally presages a clear and dry day. By seven she was dressed and down. Miss Thorne knew nothing of the modern luxury of *désha-*

billes. She would as soon have thought of appearing before her brother without her stockings as without her stays—and Miss Thorne's stays were no trifle.

And yet there was nothing for her to do when down. She fidgeted out to the lawn and then back into the kitchen. She put on her high-heeled clogs and fidgeted out into the paddock. Then she went into the small home park where the quintain was erected. The pole and cross-bar and the swivel and the target and the bag of flour were all complete. She got up on a carpenter's bench and touched the target with her hand; it went round with beautiful ease; the swivel had been oiled to perfection. She almost wished to take old Plomacy at his word, to get on a side-saddle and have a tilt at it herself. What must a young man be, thought she, who could prefer maundering among laurel trees with a wishy-washy schoolgirl to such fun as this? "Well," said she aloud to herself, "one man can take a horse to water, but a thousand can't make him drink. There it is. If they haven't the spirit to enjoy it, the fault shan't be mine;" and so she returned to the house.

At a little after eight her brother came down, and they had a sort of scrap breakfast in his study. The tea was made without the customary urn, and they dispensed with the usual rolls and toast. Eggs also were missing, for every egg in the parish had been whipped into custards, baked into pies, or boiled into lobster salad. The allowance of fresh butter was short, and Mr. Thorne was obliged to eat the leg of a fowl without having it devilled in the manner he loved.

"I have been looking at the quintain, Wilfred," said she, "and it appears to be quite right."

"Oh—ah, yes," said he. "It seemed to be so yesterday when I saw it." Mr. Thorne was beginning to be rather bored by his sister's love of sports, and had especially no affection for this quintain post.

"I wish you'd just try it after breakfast," said she. "You could have the saddle put on Mark Antony, and the pole is there all handy. You can take the flour bag off, you know, if you think Mark Antony won't be quick enough," added Miss Thorne, seeing that her brother's countenance was not indicative of complete accordance with her little proposition.

Now Mark Antony was a valuable old hunter, excellently suited to Mr. Thorne's usual requirements, steady indeed at his fences, but extremely sure, very good in deep ground, and safe on the roads. But he had never yet been ridden at a quintain, and Mr. Thorne was not inclined to put him to the trial, either with or without the bag of flour. He hummed and hawed and finally declared that he was afraid Mark Antony would shy.

"Then try the cob," said the indefatigable Miss Thorne.

"He's in physic," said Wilfred.

"There's the Beelzebub colt," said his sister. "I know he's in the stable because I saw Peter exercising him just now."

"My dear Monica, he's so wild that it's as much as I can do to manage him at all. He'd destroy himself and me, too, if I attempted to ride him at such a rattletrap as that."

A rattletrap! The quintain that she had put up with so much anxious care; the game that she had prepared for the amusement of the stalwart yeomen of the country; the sport that had been honoured by the affection of so many of their ancestors! It cut her to the heart to hear it so denominated by her own brother. There were but the two of them left together in the world, and it had ever been one of the rules by which Miss Thorne had regulated her conduct through life to say nothing that could provoke her brother. She had often had to suffer from his indifference to time-honoured British customs, but she had always suffered in silence. It was part of her creed that the head of the family should never be upbraided in his own house, and Miss Thorne had lived up to her creed. Now, however, she was greatly tried. The colour mounted to her ancient cheek, and the fire blazed in her still bright eyes; but yet she said nothing. She resolved that, at any rate, to him nothing more should be said about the quintain that day.

She sipped her tea in silent sorrow and thought with painful regret of the glorious days when her great ancestor Ealfried had successfully held Ullathorne against a Norman invader. There was no such spirit now left in her family except that small useless spark which burnt in her own bosom. And she herself, was not she at this moment intent on entertaining a descendant of those very Normans, a vain proud countess with a Frenchified name who would only think that she graced Ullathorne too highly by entering its portals? Was it likely that an Honourable John, the son of an Earl De Courcy, should ride at a quintain in company with Saxon yeomen? And why should she expect her brother to do that which her brother's guests would decline to do?

Some dim faint idea of the impracticability of her own views flitted across her brain. Perhaps it was necessary that races doomed to live on the same soil should give way to each other and adopt each other's pursuits. Perhaps it was impossible that after more than five centuries of close intercourse, Normans should remain Normans, and Saxons, Saxons. Perhaps, after all, her neighbours were wiser than herself. Such ideas did occasionally present themselves to Miss Thorne's mind and make her sad enough. But it never occurred to her that her favourite quintain was but a modern copy of a Norman knight's amusement, an adaptation of the noble tourney to the tastes and habits of the Saxon yeomen. Of this she was ignorant, and it would have been cruelty to instruct her.

When Mr. Thorne saw the tear in her eye, he repented himself of his contemptuous expression. By him also it was recognized as a binding law that every whim of his sister was to be respected. He was not perhaps so firm in his observances to her as she was in hers to him. But his intentions were equally good, and whenever he found that he had forgotten them, it was matter of grief to him.

"My dear Monica," said he, "I beg your pardon. I don't in the least mean to speak ill of the game. When I called it a rattletrap, I merely meant that it was so for a man of my age. You know you always forget that I an't a young man."

"I am quite sure you are not an old man, Wilfred," said she, accepting the apology in her heart and smiling at him with the tear still on her cheek.

"If I was five-and-twenty, or thirty," continued he, "I should like nothing better than riding at the quintain all day."

"But you are not too old to hunt or to shoot," said she. "If you can jump over a ditch and hedge, I am sure you could turn the quintain round."

"But when I ride over the hedges, my dear—and it isn't very often I do that—but when I do ride over the hedges, there isn't any bag of flour coming after me. Think how I'd look taking the countess out to breakfast with the back of my head all covered with meal."

Miss, Thorne said nothing further. She didn't like the allusion to the countess. She couldn't be satisfied with the reflection that the sports at Ullathorne should be interfered with by the personal attentions necessary for a Lady De Courcy. But she saw that it was useless for her to push the matter further. It was conceded that Mr. Thorne was to be spared the quintain, and Miss Thorne determined to trust wholly to a youthful knight of hers, an immense favourite, who, as she often declared, was a pattern to the young men of the age and an excellent sample of an English yeoman.

This was Farmer Greenacre's eldest son, who, to tell the truth, had from his earliest years taken the exact measure of Miss Thorne's foot. In his boyhood he had never failed to obtain from her apples, pocket-money, and forgiveness for his numerous trespasses; and now in his early manhood he got privileges and immunities which were equally valuable. He was allowed a day or two's shooting in September; he schooled the squire's horses; got slips of trees out of the orchard and roots of flowers out of the garden; and had the fishing of the little river altogether in his own hands. He had undertaken to come mounted on a nag of his father's and show the way at the quintain post. Whatever young Greenacre did the others would do after him. The juvenile Lookalofts might stand aloof, but the rest of the youth of Ullathorne would be sure to venture if Harry Greenacre showed the way. And so Miss Thorne made up her mind to dispense with the noble Johns and Georges and trust, as her ancestors had done before her, to the thews and sinews of native Ullathorne growth.

At about nine the lower orders began to congregate in the paddock and park, under the surveillance of Mr. Plomacy and the head gardener and head groom, who were sworn in as his deputies and were to assist him in keeping the peace and promoting the sports. Many of the younger inhabitants of the neighbourhood, thinking that they could not have too much of a good thing, had come at a very early hour, and the road between the house and the church had been thronged for some time before the gates were thrown open.

And then another difficulty of huge dimensions arose, a difficulty which Mr. Plomacy had indeed foreseen and for which he was in some sort provided. Some of those who wished to share Miss Thorne's hospitality were not so particular as they should have been as to the preliminary ceremony of an invitation. They doubtless conceived that they had been overlooked by accident, and instead of taking this in dudgeon, as their betters would have done, they good-naturedly put up with the slight, and showed that they did so by presenting themselves at the gate in their Sunday best.

Mr. Plomacy, however, well-knew who were welcome and who were not. To some, even though uninvited, he allowed ingress. "Don't be too particular, Plomacy," his mistress had said, "especially with the children. If they live anywhere near, let them in."

Acting on this hint, Mr. Plomacy did let in many an eager urchin and a few tidily dressed girls with their swains who in no way belonged to the property. But to the denizens of the city he was inexorable. Many a Barchester apprentice made his appearance there that day and urged with piteous supplication that he had been working all the week in making saddles and boots for the use of Ullathorne, in compounding doses for the horses, or cutting up carcasses for the kitchen. No such claim was allowed. Mr. Plomacy knew nothing about the city apprentices; he was to admit the tenants and labourers on the estate; Miss Thorne wasn't going to take in the whole city of Barchester; and so on.

Nevertheless, before the day was half over, all this was found to be useless. Almost anybody who chose to come made his way into the park, and the care of the guardians was transferred to the tables on which the banquet was spread. Even here there was many an unauthorised claimant for a place, of whom it was impossible to get quit without more commotion than the place and food were worth.

CHAPTER XXXVI

ULLATHORNE SPORTS—ACT I

The trouble in civilized life of entertaining company, as it is called too generally without much regard to strict veracity, is so great that it cannot but be matter of wonder that people are so fond of attempting it. It is difficult to ascertain what is the *quid pro quo*. If they who give such laborious parties, and who endure such toil and turmoil in the vain hope of giving them successfully, really enjoyed the parties given by others, the matter could be understood. A sense of justice would induce men and women to undergo, in behalf of others, those miseries which others had undergone in their behalf. But they all profess that going out is as great a bore as receiving, and to look at them when they are out, one cannot but believe them.

Entertain! Who shall have sufficient self-assurance, who shall feel sufficient confidence in his own powers to dare to boast that he can entertain his company? A clown can sometimes do so, and sometimes a dancer in short petticoats and stuffed pink legs; occasionally, perhaps, a singer. But beyond these, success in this art of entertaining is not often achieved. Young men and girls linking themselves kind with kind, pairing like birds in spring because nature wills it, they, after a simple fashion, do entertain each other. Few others even try.

Ladies, when they open their houses, modestly confessing, it may be presumed, their own incapacity, mainly trust to wax candles and upholstery. Gentlemen seem to rely on their white waistcoats. To these are added, for the delight of the more sensual, champagne and such good things of the table as fashion allows to be still considered as comestible. Even in this respect the world is deteriorating. All the good soups are now tabooed, and at the houses of one's accustomed friends—small barristers, doctors, government clerks, and such-like (for we cannot all of us always live as grandees, surrounded by an elysium of livery servants)—one gets a cold potato handed to one as a sort of finale to one's slice of mutton. Alas for those happy days when one could say to one's neighbour, "Jones, shall I give you some mashed turnip? May I trouble you for a little cabbage?" And then the pleasure of drinking wine with Mrs. Jones and Miss Smith—with all the Joneses and all the Smiths! These latter-day habits are certainly more economical.

Miss Thorne, however, boldly attempted to leave the modern, beaten track, and made a positive effort to entertain her guests. Alas! She did so with but moderate success. They had all their own way of going, and would not go her way. She piped to them, but they would not dance. She offered to them good, honest household cake made of currants and flour and eggs and sweetmeat, but they would feed themselves on trashy wafers from the shop of the Barchester pastry-cook, on chalk and gum and adulterated sugar. Poor Miss Thorne! Yours is not the first honest soul that has vainly striven to recall the glories of happy days gone by! If fashion suggests to a Lady De Courcy that, when invited to a *déjeuner* at twelve she ought to come at three, no eloquence of thine will teach her the advantage of a nearer approach to punctuality.

She had fondly thought that when she called on her friends to come at twelve, and specially begged them to believe that she meant it, she would be able to see them comfortably seated in their tents at two. Vain woman—or rather ignorant woman—ignorant of the advances of that civilization which the world had witnessed while she was growing old. At twelve she found herself alone, dressed in all the glory of the newest of her many suits of raiment—with strong shoes however, and a serviceable bonnet on her head, and a warm, rich shawl on her shoulders. Thus clad, she peered out into the tent, went to the ha-ha, and satisfied herself that at any rate the youngsters were amusing themselves, spoke a word to Mrs. Greenacre over the ditch, and took one look at the quintain. Three or four young farmers were turning the machine round and round and poking at the bag of flour in a manner not at all intended by the inventor of the game; but no mounted sportsmen were there. Miss Thorne looked at her watch. It was only fifteen minutes past twelve, and it was understood that Harry Greenacre was not to begin till the half-hour.

Miss Thorne returned to her drawing-room rather quicker than was her wont, fearing that the countess might come and find none to welcome her. She need not have hurried, for no one was there. At half-past twelve she peeped into the kitchen; at a quarter to one she was joined by her brother; and just then the first fashionable arrival took place. Mrs. Clantantram was announced.

No announcement was necessary, indeed, for the good lady's voice was heard as she walked across the courtyard to the house, scolding the unfortunate postilion who had driven her from Barchester. At the moment Miss Thorne could not but be thankful that the other guests were more fashionable and were thus spared the fury of Mrs. Clantantram's indignation.

"Oh, Miss Thorne, look here!" said she as soon as she found herself in the drawing-room; "do look at my roque-laure. It's clean spoilt, and forever. I wouldn't but wear it because I knew you wished us all to be grand to-day, and yet I had my misgivings. Oh dear, oh dear! It was five-and-twenty shillings a yard."

The Barchester post-horses had misbehaved in some unfortunate manner just as Mrs. Clantantram was getting out of the chaise and had nearly thrown her under the wheel.

Mrs. Clantantram belonged to other days, and therefore, though she had but little else to recommend her, Miss Thorne was to a certain extent fond of her. She sent the roque-laure away to be cleaned, and lent her one of her best shawls out of her own wardrobe.

The next comer was Mr. Arabin, who was immediately informed of Mrs. Clantantram's misfortune and of her determination to pay neither master nor post-boy, although, as she remarked, she intended to get her lift home before she made known her mind upon that matter. Then a good deal of rustling was heard in the sort of lobby that was used for the ladies' outside cloaks, and the door having been thrown wide open, the servant announced, not in the most confident of voices, Mrs. Lookaloft, and the Miss Lookalofts, and Mr. Augustus Lookaloft.

Poor man!—we mean the footman. He knew, none better, that Mrs. Lookaloft had no business there, that she was not wanted there, and would not be welcome. But he had not the courage to tell a stout lady with a low dress, short sleeves, and satin at eight shillings a yard that she had come to the wrong tent; he had not dared to hint to young ladies with white dancing shoes and long gloves that there was a place ready for them in the paddock. And thus Mrs. Lookaloft carried her point, broke through the guards, and made her way

into the citadel. That she would have to pass an uncomfortable time there she had surmised before. But nothing now could rob her of the power of boasting that she had con-
consorted on the lawn with the squire and Miss Thorne, with a countess, a bishop, and the
county grandees, while Mrs. Greenacre and such-like were walking about with the
ploughboys in the park. It was a great point gained by Mrs. Lookaloft, and it might be
fairly expected that from this time forward the tradesmen of Barchester would, with undoubting pens, address her husband as T. Lookaloft, Esquire.

Mrs. Lookaloft's pluck carried her through everything, and she walked triumphant into
the Ullathorne drawing-room; but her children did feel a little abashed at the sort of reception they met with. It was not in Miss Thorne's heart to insult her own guests, but neither
was it in her disposition to overlook such effrontery.

"Oh, Mrs. Lookaloft, is this you?" said she. "And your daughters and son? Well, we're
very glad to see you, but I'm sorry you've come in such low dresses, as we are all going
out of doors. Could we lend you anything?"

"Oh dear, no thank ye, Miss Thorne," said the mother; "the girls and myself are quite
used to low dresses, when we're out."

"Are you, indeed?" said Miss Thorne shuddering—but the shudder was lost on Mrs.
Lookaloft.

"And where's Lookaloft?" said the master of the house, coming up to welcome his tenant's wife. Let the faults of the family be what they would, he could not but remember that
their rent was well paid; he was therefore not willing to give them a cold shoulder.

"Such a headache, Mr. Thorne!" said Mrs. Lookaloft. "In fact he couldn't stir, or you
may be certain on such a day he would not have absented hisself."

"Dear me," said Miss Thorne. "If he is so ill, I'm sure you'd wish to be with him."

"Not at all!" said Mrs. Lookaloft. "Not at all, Miss Thorne. It is only bilious you know,
and when he's that way, he can bear nobody nigh him."

The fact, however, was that Mr. Lookaloft, having either more sense or less courage
than his wife, had not chosen to intrude on Miss Thorne's drawing-room, and as he could
not very well have gone among the plebeians while his wife was with the patricians, he
thought it most expedient to remain at Rosebank.

Mrs. Lookaloft soon found herself on a sofa, and the Miss Lookalofts on two chairs,
while Mr. Augustus stood near the door; and here they remained till in due time they were
seated, all four together, at the bottom of the dining-room table.

Then the Grantlys came—the archdeacon and Mrs. Grantly and the two girls, and Dr.
Gwynne and Mr. Harding. As ill-luck would have it, they were closely followed by Dr.
Stanhope's carriage. As Eleanor looked out of the carriage window, she saw her brother-
in-law helping the ladies out and threw herself back into her seat, dreading to be discovered. She had had an odious journey. Mr. Slope's civility had been more than ordinarily
greasy; and now, though he had not in fact said anything which she could notice, she had
for the first time entertained a suspicion that he was intending to make love to her. Was it
after all true that she had been conducting herself in a way that justified the world in
thinking that she liked the man? After all, could it be possible that the archdeacon and Mr.
Arabin were right, and that she was wrong? Charlotte Stanhope had also been watching
Mr. Slope and had come to the conclusion that it behoved her brother to lose no further
time, if he meant to gain the widow. She almost regretted that it had not been contrived
that Bertie should be at Ullathorne before them.

Dr. Grantly did not see his sister-in-law in company with Mr. Slope, but Mr. Arabin
did. Mr. Arabin came out with Mr. Thorne to the front door to welcome Mrs. Grantly, and
he remained in the courtyard till all their party had passed on. Eleanor hung back in the
carriage as long as she well could, but she was nearest to the door, and when Mr. Slope,

having alighted, offered her his hand, she had no alternative but to take it. Mr. Arabin, standing at the open door while Mrs. Grantly was shaking hands with someone within, saw a clergyman alight from the carriage whom he at once knew to be Mr. Slope, and then he saw this clergyman hand out Mrs. Bold. Having seen so much, Mr. Arabin, rather sick at heart, followed Mrs. Grantly into the house.

Eleanor was, however, spared any further immediate degradation, for Dr. Stanhope gave her his arm across the courtyard, and Mr. Slope was fain to throw away his attention upon Charlotte.

They had hardly passed into the house, and from the house to the lawn, when, with a loud rattle and such noise as great men and great women are entitled to make in their passage through the world, the Proudies drove up. It was soon apparent that no everyday comer was at the door. One servant whispered to another that it was the bishop, and the word soon ran through all the hangers-on and strange grooms and coachmen about the place. There was quite a little cortège to see the bishop and his "lady" walk across the courtyard, and the good man was pleased to see that the church was held in such respect in the parish of St. Ewold's.

And now the guests came fast and thick, and the lawn began to be crowded, and the room to be full. Voices buzzed, silk rustled against silk, and muslin crumpled against muslin. Miss Thorne became more happy than she had been, and again bethought her of her sports. There were targets and bows and arrows prepared at the further end of the lawn. Here the gardens of the place encroached with a somewhat wide sweep upon the paddock and gave ample room for the doings of the toxophilites. Miss Thorne got together such daughters of Diana as could bend a bow and marshalled them to the targets. There were the Grantly girls and the Proudie girls and the Chadwick girls, and the two daughters of the burly chancellor, and Miss Knowle; and with them went Frederick and Augustus Chadwick, and young Knowle of Knowle Park, and Frank Foster of the Elms, and Mr. Vellem Deeds, the dashing attorney of the High Street, and the Rev. Mr. Green, and the Rev. Mr. Brown, and the Rev. Mr. White, all of whom, as in duty bound, attended the steps of the three Miss Proudies.

"Did you ever ride at the quintain, Mr. Foster?" said Miss Thorne as she walked with her party across the lawn.

"The quintain?" said young Foster, who considered himself a dab at horsemanship. "Is it a sort of gate, Miss Thorne?"

Miss Thorne had to explain the noble game she spoke of, and Frank Foster had to own that he never had ridden at the quintain.

"Would you like to come and see?" said Miss Thorne. "There'll be plenty here you know without you, if you like it."

"Well, I don't mind," said Frank. "I suppose the ladies can come too."

"Oh, yes," said Miss Thorne; "those who like it. I have no doubt they'll go to see your prowess, if you'll ride, Mr. Foster."

Mr. Foster looked down at a most unexceptionable pair of pantaloons, which had arrived from London only the day before. They were the very things, at least he thought so, for a picnic or fête champêtre, but he was not prepared to ride in them. Nor was he more encouraged than had been Mr. Thorne by the idea of being attacked from behind by the bag of flour, which Miss Thorne had graphically described to him.

"Well, I don't know about riding, Miss Thorne," said he; "I fear I'm not quite prepared."

Miss Thorne sighed but said nothing further. She left the toxophilites to their bows and arrows and returned towards the house. But as she passed by the entrance to the small park, she thought that she might at any rate encourage the yeomen by her presence, as she could not induce her more fashionable guests to mix with them in their manly amusements. Accordingly she once more betook herself to the quintain post.

Here to her great delight she found Harry Greenacre ready mounted, with his pole in his hand, and a lot of comrades standing round him, encouraging him to the assault. She stood at a little distance and nodded to him in token of her good pleasure.

"Shall I begin, ma'am?" said Harry, fingering his long staff in a rather awkward way, while his horse moved uneasily beneath him, not accustomed to a rider armed with such a weapon.

"Yes, yes," said Miss Thorne, standing triumphant as the queen of beauty on an inverted tub which some chance had brought thither from the farmyard.

"Here goes then," said Harry as he wheeled his horse round to get the necessary momentum of a sharp gallop. The quintain post stood right before him, and the square board at which he was to tilt was fairly in his way. If he hit that duly in the middle, and maintained his pace as he did so, it was calculated that he would be carried out of reach of the flour bag, which, suspended at the other end of the cross-bar on the post, would swing round when the board was struck. It was also calculated that if the rider did not maintain his pace, he would get a blow from the flour bag just at the back of his head, and bear about him the signs of his awkwardness to the great amusement of the lookers-on.

Harry Greenacre did not object to being powdered with flour in the service of his mistress and therefore gallantly touched his steed with his spur, having laid his lance in rest to the best of his ability. But his ability in this respect was not great, and his appurtenances probably not very good; consequently, he struck his horse with his pole unintentionally on the side of the head as he started. The animal swerved and shied and galloped off wide of the quintain. Harry, well-accustomed to manage a horse, but not to do so with a twelve-foot rod on his arm, lowered his right hand to the bridle, and thus the end of the lance came to the ground and got between the legs of the steed. Down came rider and steed and staff. Young Greenacre was thrown some six feet over the horse's head, and poor Miss Thorne almost fell off her tub in a swoon.

"Oh, gracious, he's killed," shrieked a woman who was near him when he fell.

"The Lord be good to him! His poor mother, his poor mother!" said another.

"Well, drat them dangerous plays all the world over," said an old crone.

"He has broke his neck sure enough, if ever man did," said a fourth.

Poor Miss Thorne. She heard all this and yet did not quite swoon. She made her way through the crowd as best she could, sick herself almost to death. Oh, his mother—his poor mother! How could she ever forgive herself. The agony of that moment was terrific. She could hardly get to the place where the poor lad was lying, as three or four men in front were about the horse, which had risen with some difficulty, but at last she found herself close to the young farmer.

"Has he marked himself? For heaven's sake tell me that: has he marked his knees?" said Harry, slowly rising and rubbing his left shoulder with his right hand and thinking only of his horse's legs. Miss Thorne soon found that he had not broken his neck, nor any of his bones, nor been injured in any essential way. But from that time forth she never instigated anyone to ride at a quintain.

Eleanor left Dr. Stanhope as soon as she could do so civilly and went in quest of her father, whom she found on the lawn in company with Mr. Arabin. She was not sorry to find them together. She was anxious to disabuse at any rate her father's mind as to this report which had got abroad respecting her, and would have been well pleased to have been able to do the same with regard to Mr. Arabin. She put her own through her father's arm, coming up behind his back, and then tendered her hand also to the vicar of St. Ewold's.

"And how did you come?" said Mr. Harding, when the first greeting was over.

"The Stanhopes brought me," said she; "their carriage was obliged to come twice, and has now gone back for the signora." As she spoke she caught Mr. Arabin's eye and saw that he was looking pointedly at her with a severe expression. She understood at once the accusation contained in his glance. It said as plainly as an eye could speak, "Yes, you came with the Stanhopes, but you did so in order that you might be in company with Mr. Slope."

"Our party," said she, still addressing her father, "consisted of the doctor and Charlotte Stanhope, myself, and Mr. Slope." As she mentioned the last name she felt her father's arm quiver slightly beneath her touch. At the same moment Mr. Arabin turned away from them and, joining his hands behind his back, strolled slowly away by one of the paths.

"Papa," said she, "it was impossible to help coming in the same carriage with Mr. Slope; it was quite impossible. I had promised to come with them before I dreamt of his coming, and afterwards I could not get out of it without explaining and giving rise to talk. You weren't at home, you know. I couldn't possibly help it." She said all this so quickly that by the time her apology was spoken she was quite out of breath.

"I don't know why you should have wished to help it, my dear," said her father.

"Yes, Papa, you do. You must know, you do know all the things they said at Plumstead. I am sure you do. You know all the archdeacon said. How unjust he was; and Mr. Arabin too. He's a horrid man, a horrid odious man, but—"

"Who is an odious man, my dear? Mr. Arabin?"

"No; but Mr. Slope. You know I mean Mr. Slope. He's the most odious man I ever met in my life, and it was most unfortunate my having to come here in the same carriage with him. But how could I help it?"

A great weight began to move itself off Mr. Harding's mind. So, after all, the archdeacon with all his wisdom, and Mrs. Grantly with all her tact, and Mr. Arabin with all his talent, were in the wrong. His own child, his Eleanor, the daughter of whom he was so proud, was not to become the wife of a Mr. Slope. He had been about to give his sanction to the marriage, so certified had he been of the fact, and now he learnt that this imputed lover of Eleanor's was at any rate as much disliked by her as by any one of the family. Mr. Harding, however, was by no means sufficiently a man of the world to conceal the blunder he had made. He could not pretend that he had entertained no suspicion; he could not make believe that he had never joined the archdeacon in his surmises. He was greatly surprised, and gratified beyond measure, and he could not help showing that such was the case.

"My darling girl," said he, "I am so delighted, so overjoyed. My own child; you have taken such a weight off my mind."

"But surely, Papa, *you* didn't think—"

"I didn't know what to think, my dear. The archdeacon told me that—"

"The archdeacon!" said Eleanor, her face lighting up with passion. "A man like the archdeacon might, one would think, be better employed than in traducing his sister-in-law and creating bitterness between a father and his daughter!"

"He didn't mean to do that, Eleanor."

"What did he mean then? Why did he interfere with me and fill your mind with such falsehood?"

"Never mind it now, my child; never mind it now. We shall all know you better now."

"Oh, Papa, that you should have thought it! That you should have suspected me!"

"I don't know what you mean by suspicion, Eleanor. There would be nothing disgraceful, you know, nothing wrong in such a marriage. Nothing that could have justified my interfering as your father." And Mr. Harding would have proceeded in his own defence to make out that Mr. Slope after all was a very good sort of man and a very fitting second husband for a young widow, had he not been interrupted by Eleanor's greater energy.

"It would be disgraceful," said she; "it would be wrong; it would be abominable. Could I do such a horrid thing, I should expect no one to speak to me. Ugh—" and she shuddered as she thought of the matrimonial torch which her friends had been so ready to light on her behalf. "I don't wonder at Dr. Grantly; I don't wonder at Susan; but, oh, Papa, I do wonder at you. How could you, how could you believe it?" Poor Eleanor, as she thought of her father's defalcation, could resist her tears no longer, and was forced to cover her face with her handkerchief.

The place was not very opportune for her grief. They were walking through the shrubberies, and there were many people near them. Poor Mr. Harding stammered out his excuse as best he could, and Eleanor with an effort controlled her tears and returned her handkerchief to her pocket. She did not find it difficult to forgive her father, nor could she altogether refuse to join him in the returning gaiety of spirit to which her present avowal gave rise. It was such a load off his heart to think that he should not be called on to welcome Mr. Slope as his son-in-law. It was such a relief to him to find that his daughter's feelings and his own were now, as they ever had been, in unison. He had been so unhappy for the last six weeks about this wretched Mr. Slope! He was so indifferent as to the loss of the hospital, so thankful for the recovery of his daughter, that, strong as was the ground for Eleanor's anger, she could not find it in her heart to be long angry with him.

"Dear Papa," she said, hanging closely to his arm, "never suspect me again: promise me that you never will. Whatever I do you may be sure I shall tell you first; you may be sure I shall consult you."

And Mr. Harding did promise, and owned his sin, and promised again. And so, while he promised amendment and she uttered forgiveness, they returned together to the drawing-room windows.

And what had Eleanor meant when she declared that *whatever she did*, she would tell her father first? What was she thinking of doing?

So ended the first act of the melodrama which Eleanor was called on to perform this day at Ullathorne.

CHAPTER XXXVII

THE SIGNORA NERONI, THE COUNTESS DE COURCY, AND MRS. PROUDIE MEET EACH OTHER AT ULLATHORNE

And now there were new arrivals. Just as Eleanor reached the drawing-room the signora was being wheeled into it. She had been brought out of the carriage into the dining-room and there placed on a sofa, and was now in the act of entering the other room, by the joint aid of her brother and sister, Mr. Arabin, and two servants in livery. She was all in her glory, and looked so pathetically happy, so full of affliction and grace, was so beautiful, so pitiable, and so charming that it was almost impossible not to be glad she was there.

Miss Thorne was unaffectedly glad to welcome her. In fact, the signora was a sort of lion; and though there was no drop of the Leohunter blood in Miss Thorne's veins, she nevertheless did like to see attractive people at her house. The signora was attractive, and on her first settlement in the dining-room she had whispered two or three soft feminine words into Miss Thorne's ear which, at the moment, had quite touched that lady's heart.

"Oh, Miss Thorne; where is Miss Thorne?" she said as soon as her attendants had placed her in her position just before one of the windows, from whence she could see all that was going on upon the lawn. "How am I to thank you for permitting a creature like me to be here? But if you knew the pleasure you give me, I am sure you would excuse the trouble I bring with me." And as she spoke she squeezed the spinster's little hand between her own.

"We are delighted to see you here," said Miss Thorne; "you give us no trouble at all, and we think it a great favour conferred by you to come and see us—don't we, Wilfred?"

"A very great favour indeed," said Mr. Thorne with a gallant bow but of a somewhat less cordial welcome than that conceded by his sister. Mr. Thorne had heard perhaps more of the antecedents of his guest than his sister had done, and had not as yet undergone the power of the signora's charms.

But while the mother of the last of the Neros was thus in her full splendour, with crowds of people gazing at her and the élite of the company standing round her couch, her glory was paled by the arrival of the Countess De Courcy. Miss Thorne had now been waiting three hours for the countess, and could not therefore but show very evident gratification when the arrival at last took place. She and her brother of course went off to welcome the titled grandees, and with them, alas, went many of the signora's admirers.

"Oh, Mr. Thorne," said the countess, while in the act of being disrobed of her fur cloaks and rerobed in her gauze shawls, "what dreadful roads you have; perfectly frightful."

It happened that Mr. Thorne was waywarden for the district and, not liking the attack, began to excuse his roads.

"Oh, yes, indeed they are," said the countess not minding him in the least; "perfectly dreadful—are they not, Margaretta? Why, my dear Miss Thorne, we left Courcy Castle just at eleven; it was only just past eleven, was it not, George? And—"

"Just past one I think you mean," said the Honourable George, turning from the group and eyeing the signora through his glass. The signora gave him back his own, as the saying is, and more with it, so that the young nobleman was forced to avert his glance and drop his glass.

"I say, Thorne," whispered he, "who the deuce is that on the sofa?"

"Dr. Stanhope's daughter," whispered back Mr. Thorne. "Signora Neroni, she calls herself."

"Whew—ew—ew!" whistled the Honourable George. "The devil she is. I have heard no end of stories about that filly. You must positively introduce me, Thorne; you positively must."

Mr. Thorne, who was respectability itself, did not quite like having a guest about whom the Honourable George De Courcy had heard no end of stories, but he couldn't help himself. He merely resolved that before he went to bed he would let his sister know somewhat of the history of the lady she was so willing to welcome. The innocence of Miss Thorne at her time of life was perfectly charming, but even innocence may be dangerous.

"George may say what he likes," continued the countess, urging her excuses to Miss Thorne; "I am sure we were past the castle gate before twelve—weren't we, Margaretta?"

"Upon my word I don't know," said the Lady Margaretta, "for I was half-asleep. But I do know that I was called some time in the middle of the night and was dressing myself before daylight."

Wise people, when they are in the wrong, always put themselves right by finding fault with the people against whom they have sinned. Lady De Courcy was a wise woman, and therefore, having treated Miss Thorne very badly by staying away till three o'clock, she assumed the offensive and attacked Mr. Thorne's roads. Her daughter, not less wise, attacked Miss Thorne's early hours. The art of doing this is among the most precious of those usually cultivated by persons who know how to live. There is no withstanding it. Who can go systematically to work and, having done battle with the primary accusation and settled that, then bring forward a countercharge and support that also? Life is not long enough for such labours. A man in the right relies easily on his rectitude and therefore goes about unarmed. His very strength is his weakness. A man in the wrong knows that he must look to his weapons; his very weakness is his strength. The one is never prepared for combat, the other is always ready. Therefore it is that in this world the man that is in the wrong almost invariably conquers the man that is in the right, and invariably despises him.

A man must be an idiot or else an angel who, after the age of forty, shall attempt to be just to his neighbours. Many like the Lady Margaretta have learnt their lesson at a much earlier age. But this of course depends on the school in which they have been taught.

Poor Miss Thorne was altogether overcome. She knew very well that she had been ill-treated, and yet she found herself making apologies to Lady De Courcy. To do her ladyship justice, she received them very graciously, and allowed herself, with her train of daughters, to be led towards the lawn.

There were two windows in the drawing-room wide open for the countess to pass through, but she saw that there was a woman on a sofa, at the third window, and that that woman had, as it were, a following attached to her. Her ladyship therefore determined to investigate the woman. The De Courcy's were hereditarily shortsighted, and had been so for thirty centuries at least. So Lady De Courcy, who when she entered the family had adopted the family habits, did as her son had done before her and, taking her glass to investigate the Signora Neroni, pressed in among the gentlemen who surrounded the couch, and bowed slightly to those whom she chose to honour by her acquaintance.

In order to get to the window she had to pass close to the front of the couch, and as she did so she stared hard at the occupant. The occupant, in return, stared hard at the countess. The countess, who, since her countess-ship commenced, had been accustomed to see all eyes not royal, ducal, or marquesal fall before her own, paused as she went on, raised her eyebrows, and stared even harder than before. But she had now to do with one who cared little for countesses. It was, one may say, impossible for mortal man or woman to abash Madeline Neroni. She opened her large, bright, lustrous eyes wider and wider, till she seemed to be all eyes. She gazed up into the lady's face, not as though she did it with an effort, but as if she delighted in doing it. She used no glass to assist her effrontery, and needed none. The faintest possible smile of derision played round her mouth, and her nostrils were slightly dilated, as if in sure anticipation of her triumph. And it was sure. The Countess De Courcy, in spite of her thirty centuries and De Courcy Castle, and the fact that Lord De Courcy was grand master of the ponies to the Prince of Wales, had not a chance with her. At first the little circlet of gold wavered in the countess's hand, then the hand shook, then the circlet fell, the countess's head tossed itself into the air, and the countess's feet shambled out to the lawn. She did not, however, go so fast but what she heard the signora's voice, asking:

"Who on earth is that woman, Mr. Slope?"

"That is Lady De Courcy."

"Oh, ah. I might have supposed so. Ha, ha, ha. Well, that's as good as a play."

It was as good as a play to any there who had eyes to observe it and wit to comment on what they observed.

But the Lady De Courcy soon found a congenial spirit on the lawn. There she encountered Mrs. Proudie, and as Mrs. Proudie was not only the wife of a bishop but was also the cousin of an earl, Lady De Courcy considered her to be the fittest companion she was likely to meet in that assemblage. They were accordingly delighted to see each other. Mrs. Proudie by no means despised a countess, and as this countess lived in the county and within a sort of extensive visiting distance of Barchester, she was glad to have this opportunity of ingratiating herself.

"My dear Lady De Courcy, I am so delighted," said she, looking as little grim as it was in her nature to do. "I hardly expected to see you here. It is such a distance, and then, you know, such a crowd."

"And such roads, Mrs. Proudie! I really wonder how the people ever get about. But I don't suppose they ever do."

"Well, I really don't know, but I suppose not. The Thornes don't, I know," said Mrs. Proudie. "Very nice person, Miss Thorne, isn't she?"

"Oh, delightful, and so queer; I've known her these twenty years. A great pet of mine is dear Miss Thorne. She is so very strange, you know. She always makes me think of the Eskimos and the Indians. Isn't her dress quite delightful?"

"Delightful," said Mrs. Proudie. "I wonder now whether she paints. Did you ever see such colour?"

"Oh, of course," said Lady De Courcy; "that is, I have no doubt she does. But, Mrs. Proudie, who is that woman on the sofa by the window? Just step this way and you'll see her, there—" and the countess led her to a spot where she could plainly see the signora's well-remembered face and figure.

She did not however do so without being equally well seen by the signora. "Look, look," said that lady to Mr. Slope, who was still standing near to her; "see the high spiritualities and temporalities of the land in league together, and all against poor me. I'll wager my bracelet, Mr. Slope, against your next sermon that they've taken up their position there on purpose to pull me to pieces. Well, I can't rush to the combat, but I know how to protect myself if the enemy come near me."

But the enemy knew better. They could gain nothing by contact with the Signora Neroni, and they could abuse her as they pleased at a distance from her on the lawn.

"She's that horrid Italian woman, Lady De Courcy; you must have heard of her."

"What Italian woman?" said her ladyship, quite alive to the coming story. "I don't think I've heard of any Italian woman coming into the country. She doesn't look Italian, either."

"Oh, you must have heard of her," said Mrs. Proudie. "No, she's not absolutely Italian. She is Dr. Stanhope's daughter—Dr. Stanhope the prebendary—and she calls herself the Signora Neroni."

"Oh-h-h-h!" exclaimed the countess.

"I was sure you had heard of her," continued Mrs. Proudie. "I don't know anything about her husband. They do say that some man named Neroni is still alive. I believe she did marry such a man abroad, but I do not at all know who or what he was."

"Oh-h-h-h!" exclaimed the countess, shaking her head with much intelligence, as every additional "h" fell from her lips. "I know all about it now. I have heard George mention her. George knows all about her. George heard about her in Rome."

"She's an abominable woman, at any rate," said Mrs. Proudie.

"Insufferable," said the countess.

"She made her way into the palace once, before I knew anything about her, and I cannot tell you how dreadfully indecent her conduct was."

"Was it?" said the delighted countess.

"Insufferable," said the prelatess.

"But why does she lie on a sofa?" asked Lady De Courcy.

"She has only one leg," replied Mrs. Proudie.

"Only one leg!" said Lady De Courcy, who felt to a certain degree dissatisfied that the signora was thus incapacitated. "Was she born so?"

"Oh, no," said Mrs. Proudie—and her ladyship felt some what recomforted by the assurance—"she had two. But that Signor Neroni beat her, I believe, till she was obliged to have one amputated. At any rate, she entirely lost the use of it."

"Unfortunate creature!" said the countess, who herself knew something of matrimonial trials.

"Yes," said Mrs. Proudie, "one would pity her in spite of her past bad conduct, if she now knew how to behave herself. But she does not. She is the most insolent creature I ever put my eyes on."

"Indeed she is," said Lady De Courcy.

"And her conduct with men is so abominable that she is not fit to be admitted into any lady's drawing-room."

"Dear me!" said the countess, becoming again excited, happy and merciless.

"You saw that man standing near her—the clergyman with the red hair?"

"Yes, yes."

"She has absolutely ruined that man. The bishop—or I should rather take the blame on myself, for it was I—I brought him down from London to Barchester. He is a tolerable preacher, an active young man, and I therefore introduced him to the bishop. That woman, Lady De Courcy, has got hold of him and has so disgraced him that I am forced to require that he shall leave the palace; and I doubt very much whether he won't lose his gown!"

"Why, what an idiot the man must be!" said the countess.

"You don't know the intriguing villainy of that woman," said Mrs. Proudie, remembering her torn flounces.

"But you say she has only got one leg!"

"She is as full of mischief as tho' she had ten. Look at her eyes, Lady De Courcy. Did you ever see such eyes in a decent woman's head?"

"Indeed, I never did, Mrs. Proudie."

"And her effrontery, and her voice! I quite pity her poor father, who is really a good sort of man."

"Dr. Stanhope, isn't he?"

"Yes, Dr. Stanhope. He is one of our prebendaries—a good, quiet sort of man himself. But I am surprised that he should let his daughter conduct herself as she does."

"I suppose he can't help it," said the countess.

"But a clergyman, you know, Lady De Courcy! He should at any rate prevent her from exhibiting in public, if he cannot induce her to behave at home. But he is to be pitied. I believe he has a desperate life of it with the lot of them. That apish-looking man there, with the long beard and the loose trousers—he is the woman's brother. He is nearly as bad as she is. They are both of them infidels."

"Infidels!" said Lady De Courcy, "and their father a prebendary!"

"Yes, and likely to be the new dean, too," said Mrs. Proudie.

"Oh, yes, poor dear Dr. Trefoil!" said the countess, who had once in her life spoken to that gentleman. "I was so distressed to hear it, Mrs. Proudie. And so Dr. Stanhope is to be the new dean! He comes of an excellent family, and I wish him success in spite of his daughter. Perhaps, Mrs. Proudie, when he is dean, they'll be better able to see the error of their ways."

To this Mrs. Proudie said nothing. Her dislike of the Signora Neroni was too deep to admit of her even hoping that that lady should see the error of her ways. Mrs. Proudie looked on the signora as one of the lost—one of those beyond the reach of Christian charity—and was therefore able to enjoy the luxury of hating her without the drawback of wishing her eventually well out of her sins.

Any further conversation between these congenial souls was prevented by the advent of Mr. Thorne, who came to lead the countess to the tent. Indeed, he had been desired to do so some ten minutes since, but he had been delayed in the drawing-room by the signora. She had contrived to detain him, to get him near to her sofa, and at last to make him seat himself on a chair close to her beautiful arm. The fish took the bait, was hooked, and caught, and landed. Within that ten minutes he had heard the whole of the signora's history in such strains as she chose to use in telling it. He learnt from the lady's own lips the whole of that mysterious tale to which the Honourable George had merely alluded. He discovered that the beautiful creature lying before him had been more sinned against than sinning. She had owned to him that she had been weak, confiding, and indifferent to the world's opinion, and that she had therefore been ill-used, deceived, and evil spoken of. She had spoken to him of her mutilated limb, her youth destroyed in fullest bloom, her beauty robbed of its every charm, her life blighted, her hopes withered, and as she did so a tear dropped from her eye to her cheek. She had told him of these things and asked for his sympathy.

What could a good-natured, genial, Anglo-Saxon Squire Thorne do but promise to sympathize with her? Mr. Thorne did promise to sympathize; promised also to come and see the last of the Neros, to hear more of those fearful Roman days, of those light and innocent but dangerous hours which flitted by so fast on the shores of Como, and to make himself the confidant of the signora's sorrows.

We need hardly say that he dropped all idea of warning his sister against the dangerous lady. He had been mistaken—never so much mistaken in his life. He had always regarded that Honourable George as a coarse, brutal-minded young man; now he was more convinced than ever that he was so. It was by such men as the Honourable George that the reputations of such women as Madeline Neroni were imperilled and damaged. He would go and see the lady in her own house; he was fully sure in his own mind of the soundness of his own judgement; if he found her, as he believed he should do, an injured, well-disposed, warm-hearted woman, he would get his sister Monica to invite her out to Ullathorne.

"No," said she, as at her instance he got up to leave her and declared that he himself would attend upon her wants; "no, no, my friend; I positively put a veto upon your doing so. What, in your own house, with an assemblage round you such as there is here! Do you wish to make every woman hate me and every man stare at me? I lay a positive order on you not to come near me again to-day. Come and see me at home. It is only at home that I can talk, it is only at home that I really can live and enjoy myself. My days of going out, days such as these, are rare indeed. Come and see me at home, Mr. Thorne, and then I will not bid you to leave me."

It is, we believe, common with young men of five-and-twenty to look on their seniors—on men of, say, double their own age—as so many stocks and stones—stocks and stones, that is, in regard to feminine beauty. There never was a greater mistake. Women, indeed, generally know better, but on this subject men of one age are thoroughly ignorant of what is the very nature of mankind of other ages. No experience of what goes on in the world, no reading of history, no observation of life, has any effect in teaching the truth. Men of fifty don't dance mazurkas, being generally too fat and wheezy; nor do they sit for the hour together on river-banks at their mistresses' feet, being somewhat afraid of rheumatism. But for real true love—love at first sight, love to devotion, love that robs a man of his sleep, love that "will gaze an eagle blind," love that "will hear the lowest sound when the suspicious tread of theft is stopped," love that is "like a Hercules, still climbing trees in the Hesperides"—we believe the best age is from forty-five to seventy; up to that, men are generally given to mere flirting.

At the present moment Mr. Thorne, *ætat.* fifty, was over head and ears in love at first sight with the Signora Madeline Vesey Neroni, nata Stanhope.

Nevertheless, he was sufficiently master of himself to offer his arm with all propriety to Lady De Courcy, and the countess graciously permitted herself to be led to the tent. Such had been Miss Thorne's orders, as she had succeeded in inducing the bishop to lead old Lady Knowle to the top of the dining-room. One of the baronets was sent off in quest of Mrs. Proudie and found that lady on the lawn not in the best of humours. Mr. Thorne and the countess had left her too abruptly; she had in vain looked about for an attendant chaplain, or even a stray curate; they were all drawing long bows with the young ladies at the bottom of the lawn, or finding places for their graceful co-toxophilites in some snug corner of the tent. In such position Mrs. Proudie had been wont in earlier days to fall back upon Mr. Slope, but now she could never fall back upon him again. She gave her head one shake as she thought of her lone position, and that shake was as good as a week deducted from Mr. Slope's longer sojourn in Barchester. Sir Harkaway Gorse, however, relieved her present misery, though his doing so by no means mitigated the sinning chaplain's doom.

And now the eating and drinking began in earnest. Dr. Grantly, to his great horror, found himself leagued to Mrs. Clantantram. Mrs. Clantantram had a great regard for the archdeacon, which was not cordially returned, and when she, coming up to him, whispered in his ear, "Come, Archdeacon, I'm sure you won't begrudge an old friend the favour of your arm," and then proceeded to tell him the whole history of her roquelaure, he resolved that he would shake her off before he was fifteen minutes older. But latterly the archdeacon had not been successful in his resolutions, and on the present occasion Mrs. Clantantram stuck to him till the banquet was over.

Dr. Gwynne got a baronet's wife, and Mrs. Grantly fell to the lot of a baronet. Charlotte Stanhope attached herself to Mr. Harding in order to make room for Bertie, who succeeded in sitting down in the dining-room next to Mrs. Bold. To speak sooth, now that he had love in earnest to make, his heart almost failed him.

Eleanor had been right glad to avail herself of his arm, seeing that Mr. Slope was hovering nigh her. In striving to avoid that terrible Charybdis of a Slope she was in great danger of falling into an unseen Scylla on the other hand, that Scylla being Bertie Stanhope. Nothing could be more gracious than she was to Bertie. She almost jumped at his proffered arm. Charlotte perceived this from a distance and triumphed in her heart; Bertie felt it and was encouraged; Mr. Slope saw it and glowered with jealousy. Eleanor and Bertie sat down to table in the dining-room, and as she took her seat at his right hand she found that Mr. Slope was already in possession of the chair at her own.

As these things were going on in the dining-room, Mr. Arabin was hanging enraptured and alone over the signora's sofa, and Eleanor from her seat could look through the open door and see that he was doing so.

CHAPTER XXXVIII

THE BISHOP SITS DOWN TO BREAKFAST, AND THE DEAN DIES

The Bishop of Barchester said grace over the well-spread board in the Ullathorne dining-room; while he did so, the last breath was flying from the Dean of Barchester as he lay in his sick room in the deanery. When the Bishop of Barchester raised his first glass of champagne to his lips, the deanship of Barchester was a good thing in the gift of the prime minister. Before the Bishop of Barchester had left the table, the minister of the day was made aware of the fact at his country-seat in Hampshire, and had already turned over in his mind the names of five very respectable aspirants for the preferment. It is at present only necessary to say that Mr. Slope's name was not among the five.

"'Twas merry in the hall when the beards wagged all," and the clerical beards wagged merrily in the hall of Ullathorne that day. It was not till after the last cork had been drawn, the last speech made, the last nut cracked, that tidings reached and were whispered about that the poor dean was no more. It was well for the happiness of the clerical beards that this little delay took place, as otherwise decency would have forbidden them to wag at all.

But there was one sad man among them that day. Mr. Arabin's beard did not wag as it should have done. He had come there hoping the best, striving to think the best, about Eleanor; turning over in his mind all the words he remembered to have fallen from her about Mr. Slope, and trying to gather from them a conviction unfavourable to his rival. He had not exactly resolved to come that day to some decisive proof as to the widow's intention, but he had meant, if possible, to recultivate his friendship with Eleanor, and in his present frame of mind any such recultivation must have ended in a declaration of love.

He had passed the previous night alone at his new parsonage, and it was the first night that he had so passed. It had been dull and sombre enough. Mrs. Grantly had been right in saying that a priestess would be wanting at St. Ewold's. He had sat there alone with his glass before him, and then with his tea-pot, thinking about Eleanor Bold. As is usual in such meditations, he did little but blame her; blame her for liking Mr. Slope, and blame her for not liking him; blame her for her cordiality to himself, and blame her for her want of cordiality; blame her for being stubborn, headstrong, and passionate; and yet the more he thought of her the higher she rose in his affection. If only it should turn out, if only it could be made to turn out, that she had defended Mr. Slope, not from love, but on principle, all would be right. Such principle in itself would be admirable, lovable, womanly; he felt that he could be pleased to allow Mr. Slope just so much favour as that. But if—And then Mr. Arabin poked his fire most unnecessarily, spoke crossly to his new parlour-maid who came in for the tea-things, and threw himself back in his chair determined to go to sleep. Why had she been so stiff-necked when asked a plain question? She could not but have known in what light he regarded her. Why had she not answered a plain question and so put an end to his misery? Then, instead of going to sleep in his armchair, Mr. Arabin walked about the room as though he had been possessed.

On the following morning, when he attended Miss Thorne's behests, he was still in a somewhat confused state. His first duty had been to converse with Mrs. Clantantram, and that lady had found it impossible to elicit the slightest sympathy from him on the subject of her roquelaure. Miss Thorne had asked him whether Mrs. Bold was coming with the Grantlys, and the two names of Bold and Grantly together had nearly made him jump from his seat.

He was in this state of confused uncertainty, hope, and doubt, when he saw Mr. Slope, with his most polished smile, handing Eleanor out of her carriage. He thought of nothing more. He never considered whether the carriage belonged to her or to Mr. Slope, or to anyone else to whom they might both be mutually obliged without any concert between themselves. This sight in his present state of mind was quite enough to upset him and his resolves. It was clear as noon-day. Had he seen her handed into a carriage by Mr. Slope at a church door with a white veil over her head, the truth could not be more manifest. He went into the house and, as we have seen, soon found himself walking with Mr. Harding. Shortly afterwards Eleanor came up, and then he had to leave his companion and either go about alone or find another. While in this state he was encountered by the archdeacon.

"I wonder," said Dr. Grantly, "if it be true that Mr. Slope and Mrs. Bold came here together. Susan says she is almost sure she saw their faces in the same carriage as she got out of her own."

Mr. Arabin had nothing for it but to bear his testimony to the correctness of Mrs. Grantly's eyesight.

"It is perfectly shameful," said the archdeacon; "or, I should rather say, shameless. She was asked here as my guest, and if she be determined to disgrace herself, she should have feeling enough not to do so before my immediate friends. I wonder how that man got himself invited. I wonder whether she had the face to bring him."

To this Mr. Arabin could answer nothing, nor did he wish to answer anything. Though he abused Eleanor to himself, he did not choose to abuse her to anyone else, nor was he well-pleased to hear anyone else speak ill of her. Dr. Grantly, however, was very angry and did not spare his sister-in-law. Mr. Arabin therefore left him as soon as he could and wandered back into the house.

He had not been there long when the signora was brought in. For some time he kept himself out of temptation, and merely hovered round her at a distance; but as soon as Mr. Thorne had left her, he yielded himself up to the basilisk and allowed himself to be made prey of.

It is impossible to say how the knowledge had been acquired, but the signora had a sort of instinctive knowledge that Mr. Arabin was an admirer of Mrs. Bold. Men hunt foxes by the aid of dogs, and are aware that they do so by the strong organ of smell with which the dog is endowed. They do not, however, in the least comprehend how such a sense can work with such acuteness. The organ by which women instinctively, as it were, know and feel how other women are regarded by men, and how also men are regarded by other women, is equally strong, and equally incomprehensible. A glance, a word, a motion, suffices: by some such acute exercise of her feminine senses the signora was aware that Mr. Arabin loved Eleanor Bold; therefore, by a further exercise of her peculiar feminine propensities, it was quite natural for her to entrap Mr. Arabin into her net.

The work was half-done before she came to Ullathorne, and when could she have a better opportunity of completing it? She had had almost enough of Mr. Slope, though she could not quite resist the fun of driving a very sanctimonious clergyman to madness by a desperate and ruinous passion. Mr. Thorne had fallen too easily to give much pleasure in the chase. His position as a man of wealth might make his alliance of value, but as a lover he was very second-rate. We may say that she regarded him somewhat as a sportsman does a pheasant. The bird is so easily shot that he would not be worth the shooting were it not for the very respectable appearance that he makes in a larder. The signora would not waste much time in shooting Mr. Thorne, but still he was worth bagging for family uses.

But Mr. Arabin was game of another sort. The signora was herself possessed of quite sufficient intelligence to know that Mr. Arabin was a man more than usually intellectual. She knew also that, as a clergyman, he was of a much higher stamp than Mr. Slope and that, as a gentleman, he was better educated than Mr. Thorne. She would never have attempted to drive Mr. Arabin into ridiculous misery as she did Mr. Slope, nor would she think it possible to dispose of him in ten minutes as she had done with Mr. Thorne.

Such were her reflexions about Mr. Arabin. As to Mr. Arabin, it cannot be said that he reflected at all about the signora. He knew that she was beautiful, and he felt that she was able to charm him. He required charming in his present misery, and therefore he went and stood at the head of her couch. She knew all about it. Such were her peculiar gifts. It was her nature to see that he required charming, and it was her province to charm him. As the Eastern idler swallows his dose of opium, as the London reprobate swallows his dose of gin, so with similar desires and for similar reasons did Mr. Arabin prepare to swallow the charms of the Signora Neroni.

"Why an't you shooting with bows and arrows, Mr. Arabin?" said she, when they were nearly alone together in the drawing-room, "or talking with young ladies in shady bowers, or turning your talents to account in some way? What was a bachelor like you asked here for? Don't you mean to earn your cold chicken and champagne? Were I you, I should be ashamed to be so idle."

Mr. Arabin murmured some sort of answer. Though he wished to be charmed, he was hardly yet in a mood to be playful in return.

"Why what ails you, Mr. Arabin?" said she. "Here you are in your own parish—Miss Thorne tells me that her party is given expressly in your honour—and yet you are the only dull man at it. Your friend Mr. Slope was with me a few minutes since, full of life and spirits; why don't you rival him?"

It was not difficult for so acute an observer as Madeline Neroni to see that she had hit the nail on the head and driven the bolt home. Mr. Arabin winced visibly before her attack, and she knew at once that he was jealous of Mr. Slope.

"But I look on you and Mr. Slope as the very antipodes of men," said she. "There is nothing in which you are not each the reverse of the other, except in belonging to the same profession—and even in that you are so unlike as perfectly to maintain the rule. He is gregarious; you are given to solitude. He is active; you are passive. He works; you think. He likes women; you despise them. He is fond of position and power; and so are you, but for directly different reasons. He loves to be praised; you very foolishly abhor it. He will gain his rewards, which will be an insipid, useful wife, a comfortable income, and a reputation for sanctimony; you will also gain yours."

"Well, and what will they be?" said Mr. Arabin, who knew that he was being flattered and yet suffered himself to put up with it. "What will be my rewards?"

"The heart of some woman whom you will be too austere to own that you love, and the respect of some few friends which you will be too proud to own that you value."

"Rich rewards," said he; "but of little worth, if they are to be so treated."

"Oh, you are not to look for such success as awaits Mr. Slope. He is born to be a successful man. He suggests to himself an object and then starts for it with eager intention. Nothing will deter him from his pursuit. He will have no scruples, no fears, no hesitation. His desire is to be a bishop with a rising family—the wife will come first, and in due time the apron. You will see all this, and then—"

"Well, and what then?"

"Then you will begin to wish that you had done the same."

Mr. Arabin looked placidly out at the lawn and, resting his shoulder on the head of the sofa, rubbed his chin with his hand. It was a trick he had when he was thinking deeply, and what the signora said made him think. Was it not all true? Would he not hereafter look back, if not at Mr. Slope, at some others, perhaps not equally gifted with himself, who had risen in the world while he had lagged behind, and then wish that he had done the same?

"Is not such the doom of all speculative men of talent?" said she. "Do they not all sit wrapt as you now are, cutting imaginary silken cords with their fine edges, while those not so highly tempered sever the everyday Gordian knots of the world's struggle and win wealth and renown? Steel too highly polished, edges too sharp, do not do for this world's work, Mr. Arabin."

Who was this woman that thus read the secrets of his heart and re-uttered to him the unwelcome bodings of his own soul? He looked full into her face when she had done speaking and said, "Am I one of those foolish blades, too sharp and too fine to do a useful day's work?"

"Why do you let the Slopes of the world outdistance you?" said she. "Is not the blood in your veins as warm as his? Does not your pulse beat as fast? Has not God made you a man and intended you to do a man's work here, ay, and to take a man's wages also?"

Mr. Arabin sat ruminating, rubbing his face, and wondering why these things were said to him, but he replied nothing. The signora went on:

"The greatest mistake any man ever made is to suppose that the good things of the world are not worth the winning. And it is a mistake so opposed to the religion which you preach! Why does God permit his bishops one after another to have their five thousands and ten thousands a year if such wealth be bad and not worth having? Why are beautiful things given to us, and luxuries and pleasant enjoyments, if they be not intended to be used? They must be meant for someone, and what is good for a layman surely cannot be bad for a clerk. You try to despise these good things, but you only try—you don't succeed."

"Don't I?" said Mr. Arabin, still musing, not knowing what he said.

"I ask you the question: do you succeed?"

Mr. Arabin looked at her piteously. It seemed to him as though he were being interrogated by some inner spirit of his own, to whom he could not refuse an answer, and to whom he did not dare to give a false reply.

"Come, Mr. Arabin, confess; do you succeed? Is money so contemptible? Is worldly power so worthless? Is feminine beauty a trifle to be so slightly regarded by a wise man?"

"Feminine beauty!" said he, gazing into her face, as though all the feminine beauty in the world were concentrated there. "Why do you say I do not regard it?"

"If you look at me like that, Mr. Arabin, I shall alter my opinion—or should do so, were I not of course aware that I have no beauty of my own worth regarding."

The gentleman blushed crimson, but the lady did not blush at all. A slightly increased colour animated her face, just so much so as to give her an air of special interest. She expected a compliment from her admirer, but she was rather gratified than otherwise by finding that he did not pay it to her. Messrs. Slope and Thorne, Messrs. Brown, Jones, and

Robinson, they all paid her compliments. She was rather in hopes that she would ultimately succeed in inducing Mr. Arabin to abuse her.

"But your gaze," said she, "is one of wonder, not of admiration. You wonder at my audacity in asking you such questions about yourself."

"Well, I do rather," said he.

"Nevertheless, I expect an answer, Mr. Arabin. Why were women made beautiful if men are not to regard them?"

"But men do regard them," he replied.

"And why not you?"

"You are begging the question, Madame Neroni."

"I am sure I shall beg nothing, Mr. Arabin, which you will not grant, and I do beg for an answer. Do you not as a rule think women below your notice as companions? Let us see. There is the Widow Bold looking round at you from her chair this minute. What would you say to her as a companion for life?"

Mr. Arabin, rising from his position, leaned over the sofa and looked through the drawing-room door to the place where Eleanor was seated between Bertie Stanhope and Mr. Slope. She at once caught his glance and averted her own. She was not pleasantly placed in her present position. Mr. Slope was doing his best to attract her attention, and she was striving to prevent his doing so by talking to Mr. Stanhope, while her mind was intently fixed on Mr. Arabin and Madame Neroni. Bertie Stanhope endeavoured to take advantage of her favours, but he was thinking more of the manner in which he would by and by throw himself at her feet than of amusing her at the present moment.

"There," said the signora. "She was stretching her beautiful neck to look at you, and now you have disturbed her. Well, I declare I believe I am wrong about you; I believe that you do think Mrs. Bold a charming woman. Your looks seem to say so, and by her looks I should say that she is jealous of me. Come, Mr. Arabin, confide in me, and if it is so, I'll do all in my power to make up the match."

It is needless to say that the signora was not very sincere in her offer. She was never sincere on such subjects. She never expected others to be so, nor did she expect others to think her so. Such matters were her playthings, her billiard table, her hounds and hunters, her waltzes and polkas, her picnics and summer-day excursions. She had little else to amuse her, and therefore played at love-making in all its forms. She was now playing at it with Mr. Arabin, and did not at all expect the earnestness and truth of his answer.

"All in your power would be nothing," said he, "for Mrs. Bold is, I imagine, already engaged to another."

"Then you own the impeachment yourself."

"You cross-question me rather unfairly," he replied, "and I do not know why I answer you at all. Mrs. Bold is a very beautiful woman, and as intelligent as beautiful. It is impossible to know her without admiring her."

"So you think the widow a very beautiful woman?"

"Indeed I do."

"And one that would grace the parsonage of St. Ewold's."

"One that would well grace any man's house."

"And you really have the effrontery to tell me this," said she; "to tell me, who, as you very well know, set up to be a beauty myself, and who am at this very moment taking such an interest in your affairs, you really have the effrontery to tell me that Mrs. Bold is the most beautiful woman you know."

"I did not say so," said Mr. Arabin; "you are more beautiful—"

"Ah, come now, that is something like. I thought you could not be so unfeeling."

"You are more beautiful, perhaps more clever."

"Thank you, thank you, Mr. Arabin. I knew that you and I should be friends."

"But—"

"Not a word further. I will not hear a word further. If you talk till midnight you cannot improve what you have said."

"But Madame Neroni, Mrs. Bold—"

"I will not hear a word about Mrs. Bold. Dread thoughts of strychnine did pass across my brain, but she is welcome to the second place."

"Her place—"

"I won't hear anything about her or her place. I am satisfied, and that is enough. But Mr. Arabin, I am dying with hunger; beautiful and clever as I am, you know I cannot go to my food, and yet you do not bring it to me."

This at any rate was so true as to make it necessary that Mr. Arabin should act upon it, and he accordingly went into the dining-room and supplied the signora's wants.

"And yourself?" said she.

"Oh," said he, "I am not hungry. I never eat at this hour."

"Come, come, Mr. Arabin, don't let love interfere with your appetite. It never does with mine. Give me half a glass more champagne and then go to the table. Mrs. Bold will do me an injury if you stay talking to me any longer."

Mr. Arabin did as he was bid. He took her plate and glass from her and, going into the dining-room, helped himself to a sandwich from the crowded table and began munching it in a corner.

As he was doing so Miss Thorne, who had hardly sat down for a moment, came into the room and, seeing him standing, was greatly distressed.

"Oh, my dear Mr. Arabin," said she, "have you never sat down yet? I am so distressed. You of all men, too."

Mr. Arabin assured her that he had only just come into the room.

"That is the very reason why you should lose no more time. Come, I'll make room for you. Thank'ee, my dear," she said, seeing that Mrs. Bold was making an attempt to move from her chair, "but I would not for worlds see you stir, for all the ladies would think it necessary to follow. But, perhaps, if Mr. Stanhope has done—just for a minute, Mr. Stanhope, till I can get another chair."

And so Bertie had to rise to make way for his rival. This he did, as he did everything, with an air of good-humoured pleasantry which made it impossible for Mr. Arabin to refuse the proffered seat.

"His bishopric let another take," said Bertie, the quotation being certainly not very appropriate either for the occasion or the person spoken to. "I have eaten and am satisfied; Mr. Arabin, pray take my chair. I wish for your sake that it really was a bishop's seat."

Mr. Arabin did sit down, and as he did so Mrs. Bold got up as though to follow her neighbour.

"Pray, pray don't move," said Miss Thorne, almost forcing Eleanor back into her chair. "Mr. Stanhope is not going to leave us. He will stand behind you like a true knight as he is. And now I think of it, Mr. Arabin, let me introduce you to Mr. Slope. Mr. Slope, Mr. Arabin." And the two gentlemen bowed stiffly to each other across the lady whom they both intended to marry, while the other gentleman who also intended to marry her stood behind, watching them.

The two had never met each other before, and the present was certainly not a good opportunity for much cordial conversation, even if cordial conversation between them had been possible. As it was, the whole four who formed the party seemed as though their tongues were tied. Mr. Slope, who was wide awake to what he hoped was his coming opportunity, was not much concerned in the interest of the moment. His wish was to see

Eleanor move, that he might pursue her. Bertie was not exactly in the same frame of mind; the evil day was near enough; there was no reason why he should precipitate it. He had made up his mind to marry Eleanor Bold if he could, and was resolved to-day to take the first preliminary step towards doing so. But there was time enough before him. He was not going to make an offer of marriage over the table-cloth. Having thus good-naturedly made way for Mr. Arabin, he was willing also to let him talk to the future Mrs. Stanhope as long as they remained in their present position.

Mr. Arabin, having bowed to Mr. Slope, began eating his food without saying a word further. He was full of thought, and though he ate he did so unconsciously.

But poor Eleanor was the most to be pitied. The only friend on whom she thought she could rely was Bertie Stanhope, and he, it seemed, was determined to desert her. Mr. Arabin did not attempt to address her. She said a few words in reply to some remarks from Mr. Slope and then, feeling the situation too much for her, started from her chair in spite of Miss Thorne and hurried from the room. Mr. Slope followed her, and young Stanhope lost the occasion.

Madeline Neroni, when she was left alone, could not help pondering much on the singular interview she had had with this singular man. Not a word that she had spoken to him had been intended by her to be received as true, and yet he had answered her in the very spirit of truth. He had done so, and she had been aware that he had so done. She had wormed from him his secret, and he, debarred as it would seem from man's usual privilege of lying, had innocently laid bare his whole soul to her. He loved Eleanor Bold, but Eleanor was not in his eye so beautiful as herself. He would fain have Eleanor for his wife, but yet he had acknowledged that she was the less gifted of the two. The man had literally been unable to falsify his thoughts when questioned, and had been compelled to be true *malgré lui*, even when truth must have been so disagreeable to him.

This teacher of men, this Oxford pundit, this double-distilled quintessence of university perfection, this writer of religious treatises, this speaker of ecclesiastical speeches, had been like a little child in her hands; she had turned him inside out and read his very heart as she might have done that of a young girl. She could not but despise him for his facile openness, and yet she liked him for it, too. It was a novelty to her, a new trait in a man's character. She felt also that she could never so completely make a fool of him as she did of the Slopes and Thornes. She felt that she never could induce Mr. Arabin to make protestations to her that were not true, or to listen to nonsense that was mere nonsense.

It was quite clear that Mr. Arabin was heartily in love with Mrs. Bold; and the signora, with very unwonted good nature, began to turn it over in her mind whether she could not do him a good turn. Of course Bertie was to have the first chance. It was an understood family arrangement that her brother was, if possible, to marry the Widow Bold. Madeline knew too well his necessities and what was due to her sister to interfere with so excellent a plan, as long as it might be feasible. But she had strong suspicion that it was not feasible. She did not think it likely that Mrs. Bold would accept a man in her brother's position, and she had frequently said so to Charlotte. She was inclined to believe that Mr. Slope had more chance of success, and with her it would be a labour of love to rob Mr. Slope of his wife.

And so the signora resolved, should Bertie fail, to do a good-natured act for once in her life and give up Mr. Arabin to the woman whom he loved.

CHAPTER XXXIX

THE LOOKALOFTS AND THE GREENACRES

On the whole, Miss Thorne's provision for the amusement and feeding of the outer classes in the exoteric paddock was not unsuccessful.

Two little drawbacks to the general happiness did take place, but they were of a temporary nature, and apparent rather than real. The first was the downfall of young Harry Greenacre, and the other the uprise of Mrs. Lookaloft and her family.

As to the quintain, it became more popular among the boys on foot than it would ever have been among the men on horseback, even had young Greenacre been more successful. It was twirled round and round till it was nearly twirled out of the ground, and the bag of flour was used with great gusto in powdering the backs and heads of all who could be coaxed within its vicinity.

Of course it was reported all through the assemblage that Harry was dead, and there was a pathetic scene between him and his mother when it was found that he had escaped scatheless from the fall. A good deal of beer was drunk on the occasion, and the quintain was "dratted" and "bothered," and very generally anathematized by all the mothers who had young sons likely to be placed in similar jeopardy. But the affair of Mrs. Lookaloft was of a more serious nature.

"I do tell 'ee plainly—face to face—she be there in madam's drawing-room; herself and Gussy, and them two walloping gals, dressed up to their very eyeses." This was said by a very positive, very indignant, and very fat farmer's wife, who was sitting on the end of a bench leaning on the handle of a huge, cotton umbrella.

"But: you didn't zee her, Dame Guffern?" said Mrs. Greenacre, whom this information, joined to the recent peril undergone by her son, almost overpowered. Mr. Greenacre held just as much land as Mr. Lookaloft, paid his rent quite as punctually, and his opinion in the vestry room was reckoned to be every whit as good. Mrs. Lookaloft's rise in the world had been wormwood to Mrs. Greenacre. She had no taste herself for the sort of finery which had converted Barleystubb farm into Rosebank and which had occasionally graced Mr. Lookaloft's letters with the dignity of esquirehood. She had no wish to convert her own homestead into Violet Villa, or to see her goodman go about with a new-fangled handle to his name. But it was a mortal injury to her that Mrs. Lookaloft should be successful in her hunt after such honours. She had abused and ridiculed Mrs. Lookaloft to the extent of her little power. She had pushed against her going out of church, and had excused herself with all the easiness of equality. "Ah, dame, I axes pardon, but you be grown so mortal stout these times." She had inquired with apparent cordiality of Mr.

Lookaloft after "the woman that owned him," and had, as she thought, been on the whole able to hold her own pretty well against her aspiring neighbour. Now, however, she found herself distinctly put into a separate and inferior class. Mrs. Lookaloft was asked into the Ullathorne drawing-room merely because she called her house Rosebank and had talked over her husband into buying pianos and silk dresses instead of putting his money by to stock farms for his sons.

Mrs. Greenacre, much as she reverenced Miss Thorne, and highly as she respected her husband's landlord, could not but look on this as an act of injustice done to her and hers. Hitherto the Lookalofts had never been recognized as being of a different class from the Greenacres. Their pretensions were all self-pretensions, their finery was all paid for by themselves and not granted to them by others. The local sovereigns of the vicinity, the district fountains of honour, had hitherto conferred on them the stamp of no rank. Hitherto their crinoline petticoats, late hours, and mincing gait had been a fair subject of Mrs. Greenacre's raillery, and this raillery had been a safety-valve for her envy. Now, however, and from henceforward, the case would be very different. Now the Lookalofts would boast that their aspirations had been sanctioned by the gentry of the country; now they would declare with some show of truth that their claims to peculiar consideration had been recognized. They had sat as equal guests in the presence of bishops and baronets; they had been curtseyed to by Miss Thorne on her own drawing-room carpet; they were about to sit down to table in company with a live countess! Bab Lookaloft, as she had always been called by the young Greenacres in the days of their juvenile equality, might possibly sit next to the Honourable George, and that wretched Gussy might be permitted to hand a custard to the Lady Margaretta De Courcy.

The fruition of those honours, or such of them as fell to the lot of the envied family, was not such as should have caused much envy. The attention paid to the Lookalofts by the De Courcys was very limited, and the amount of entertainment which they received from the bishop's society was hardly in itself a recompense for the dull monotony of their day. But of what they endured Mrs. Greenacre took no account; she thought only of what she considered they must enjoy, and of the dreadfully exalted tone of living which would be manifested by the Rosebank family, as the consequence of their present distinction.

"But did 'ee zee 'em there, dame, did 'ee zee 'em there with your own eyes?" asked poor Mrs. Greenacre, still hoping that there might be some ground for doubt.

"And how could I do that, unless so be I was there myself?" asked Mrs. Guffern. "I didn't zet eyes on none of them this blessed morning, but I zee'd them as did. You know our John; well, he will be for keeping company with Betsey Rusk, madam's own maid, you know. And Betsey isn't none of your common kitchen wenches. So Betsey, she come out to our John, you know, and she's always vastly polite to me, is Betsey Rusk, I must say. So before she took so much as one turn with John she told me every ha'porth that was going on up in the house."

"Did she now?" said Mrs. Greenacre.

"Indeed she did," said Mrs. Guffern.

"And she told you them people was up there in the drawing-room?"

"She told me she zee'd 'em come in—that they was dressed finer by half nor any of the family, with all their neckses and buzoms stark naked as a born babby."

"The minxes!" exclaimed Mrs. Greenacre, who felt herself more put about by this than any other mark of aristocratic distinction which her enemies had assumed.

"Yes, indeed," continued Mrs. Guffern, "as naked as you please, while all the quality was dressed just as you and I be, Mrs. Greenacre."

"Drat their impudence," said Mrs. Greenacre, from whose well-covered bosom all milk of human kindness was receding, as far as the family of the Lookalofts were concerned.

"So says I," said Mrs. Guffern; "and so says my goodman, Thomas Guffern, when he hear'd it. 'Molly,' says he to me, 'if ever you takes to going about o' mornings with yourself all naked in them ways, I begs you won't come back no more to the old house.' So says I, 'Thomas, no more I wull.' 'But,' says he, 'drat it, how the deuce does she manage with her rheumatiz, and she not a rag on her;'" and Mrs. Guffern laughed loudly as she thought of Mrs. Lookaloft's probable sufferings from rheumatic attacks.

"But to liken herself that way to folk that ha' blood in their veins," said Mrs. Greena-cre.

"Well, but that warn't all neither that Betsey told. There they all swelled into madam's drawing-room, like so many turkey cocks, as much as to say, 'and who dare say no to us?' and Gregory was thinking of telling of 'em to come down here, only his heart failed him 'cause of the grand way they was dressed. So in they went, but madam looked at them as glum as death."

"Well, now," said Mrs. Greenacre, greatly relieved, "so they wasn't axed different from us at all then?"

"Betsey says that Gregory says that madam wasn't a bit too well pleased to see them where they was, and that to his believing they was expected to come here just like the rest of us."

There was great consolation in this. Not that Mrs. Greenacre was altogether satisfied. She felt that justice to herself demanded that Mrs. Lookaloft should not only not be en-couraged, but that she should also be absolutely punished. What had been done at that scriptural banquet, of which Mrs. Greenacre so often read the account to her family? Why had not Miss Thorne boldly gone to the intruder and said, "Friend, thou hast come up hither to high places not fitted to thee. Go down lower, and thou wilt find thy mates." Let the Lookalofts be treated at the present moment with ever so cold a shoulder, they would still be enabled to boast hereafter of their position, their aspirations, and their honour.

"Well, with all her grandeur, I do wonder that she be so mean," continued Mrs. Greenacre, unable to dismiss the subject. "Did you hear, goodman?" she went on, about to repeat the whole story to her husband who then came up. "There's Dame Lookaloft and Bab and Gussy and the lot of 'em all sitting as grand as fivepence in madam's drawing-room, and they not axed no more nor you nor me. Did you ever hear tell the like o' that?"

"Well, and what for shouldn't they?" said Farmer Greenacre.

"Likening theyselves to the quality, as though they was estated folk, or the like o' that!" said Mrs. Guffern.

"Well, if they likes it, and madam likes it, they's welcome for me," said the farmer. "Now I likes this place better, 'cause I be more at home-like, and don't have to pay for them fine clothes for the missus. Everyone to his taste, Mrs. Guffern, and if neighbour Lookaloft thinks that he has the best of it, he's welcome."

Mrs. Greenacre sat down by her husband's side to begin the heavy work of the ban-quet, and she did so in some measure with restored tranquillity, but nevertheless she shook her head at her gossip to show that in this instance she did not quite approve of her hus-band's doctrine.

"And I'll tell 'ee what, dames," continued he; "if so be that we cannot enjoy the dinner that madam gives us because Mother Lookaloft is sitting up there on a grand sofa, I think we ought all to go home. If we greet at that, what'll we do when true sorrow comes across us? How would you be now, Dame, if the boy there had broke his neck when he got the tumble?"

Mrs. Greenacre was humbled and said nothing further on the matter. But let prudent men such as Mr. Greenacre preach as they will, the family of the Lookalofts certainly does occasion a good deal of heart-burning in the world at large.

It was pleasant to see Mr. Plomacy as, leaning on his stout stick, he went about among the rural guests, acting as a sort of head constable as well as master of the revels. "Now, young'un, if you can't manage to get along without that screeching, you'd better go to the other side of the twelve-acre field and take your dinner with you. Come, girls, what do you stand there for, twirling of your thumbs? Come out, and let the lads see you; you've no need to be so ashamed of your faces. Hollo there, who are you? How did you make your way in here?"

This last disagreeable question was put to a young man of about twenty-four who did not, in Mr. Plomacy's eye, bear sufficient vestiges of a rural education and residence.

"If you please, your Worship, Master Barrell the coachman let me in at the church wicket, 'cause I do be working mostly al'ays for the family."

"Then Master Barrell the coachman may let you out again," said Mr. Plomacy, not even conciliated by the magisterial dignity which had been conceded to him. "What's your name? And what trade are you? And who do you work for?"

"I'm Stubbs, your worship, Bob Stubbs; and—and—and—"

"And what's your trade, Stubbs?"

"Plasterer, please your worship."

"I'll plaster you, and Barrell too; you'll just walk out of this 'ere field as quick as you walked in. We don't want no plasterers; when we do, we'll send for 'em. Come my buck, walk."

Stubbs the plasterer was much downcast at this dreadful edict. He was a sprightly fellow, and had contrived since his ingress into the Ullathorne elysium to attract to himself a forest nymph, to whom he was whispering a plasterer's usual soft nothings, when he was encountered by the great Mr. Plomacy. It was dreadful to be thus dissevered from his dryad and sent howling back to a Barchester pandemonium just as the nectar and ambrosia were about to descend on the fields of asphodel. He began to try what prayers would do, but city prayers were vain against the great rural potentate. Not only did Mr. Plomacy order his exit but, raising his stick to show the way which led to the gate that had been left in the custody of that false Cerberus Barrell, proceeded himself to see the edict of banishment carried out.

The goddess Mercy, however, the sweetest goddess that ever sat upon a cloud, and the dearest to poor, frail, erring man, appeared on the field in the person of Mr. Greenacre. Never was interceding goddess more welcome.

"Come, man," said Mr. Greenacre, "never stick at trifles such a day as this. I know the lad well. Let him bide at my axing. Madam won't miss what he can eat and drink, I know."

Now Mr. Plomacy and Mr. Greenacre were sworn friends. Mr. Plomacy had at his own disposal as comfortable a room as there was in Ullathorne House, but he was a bachelor, and alone there, and, moreover, smoking in the house was not allowed even to Mr. Plomacy. His moments of truest happiness were spent in a huge armchair in the warmest corner of Mrs. Greenacre's beautifully clean front kitchen. 'Twas there that the inner man dissolved itself and poured itself out in streams of pleasant chat; 'twas there that he was respected and yet at his ease; 'twas there, and perhaps there only, that he could unburden himself from the ceremonies of life without offending the dignity of those above him, or incurring the familiarity of those below. 'Twas there that his long pipe was always to be found on the accustomed chimney-board, not only permitted but encouraged.

Such being the state of the case, it was not to be supposed that Mr. Plomacy could refuse such a favour to Mr. Greenacre; but nevertheless he did not grant it without some further show of austere authority.

"Eat and drink, Mr. Greenacre! No. It's not what he eats and drinks, but the example such a chap shows, coming in where he's not invited—a chap of his age, too. He too that never did a day's work about Ullathorne since he was born. Plasterer! I'll plaster him!"

"He worked long enough for me, then, Mr. Plomacy. And a good hand he is at setting tiles as any in Barchester," said the other, not sticking quite to veracity, as indeed mercy never should. "Come, come, let him alone to-day and quarrel with him to-morrow. You wouldn't shame him before his lass there?"

"It goes against the grain with me, then," said Mr. Plomacy. "And take care, you Stubbs, and behave yourself. If I hear a row, I shall know where it comes from. I'm up to you Barchester journeymen; I know what stuff you're made of."

And so Stubbs went off happy, pulling at the forelock of his shock head of hair in honour of the steward's clemency and giving another double pull at it in honour of the farmer's kindness. And as he went he swore within his grateful heart that if ever Farmer Greenacre wanted a day's work done for nothing, he was the lad to do it for him. Which promise it was not probable that he would ever be called on to perform.

But Mr. Plomacy was not quite happy in his mind, for he thought of the unjust steward and began to reflect whether he had not made for himself friends of the mammon of un-righteousness. This, however, did not interfere with the manner in which he performed his duties at the bottom of the long board; nor did Mr. Greenacre perform his the worse at the top on account of the good wishes of Stubbs the plasterer. Moreover the guests did not think it anything amiss when Mr. Plomacy, rising to say grace, prayed that God would make them all truly thankful for the good things which Madame Thorne in her great liber-ality had set before them!

All this time the quality in the tent on the lawn were getting on swimmingly—that is, if champagne without restriction can enable quality folk to swim. Sir Harkaway Gorse proposed the health of Miss Thorne, and likened her to a blood race-horse, always in con-dition and not to be tired down by any amount of work. Mr. Thorne returned thanks, saying he hoped his sister would always be found able to run when called upon, and then gave the health and prosperity of the De Courcy family. His sister was very much hon-oured by seeing so many of them at her poor board. They were all aware that important avocations made the absence of the earl necessary. As his duty to his prince had called him from his family hearth, he, Mr. Thorne, could not venture to regret that he did not see him at Ullathorne; but nevertheless he would venture to say—that was, to express a wish—an opinion, he meant to say—And so Mr. Thorne became somewhat gravelled, as country gentlemen in similar circumstances usually do; but he ultimately sat down, declar-ing that he had much satisfaction in drinking the noble earl's health, together with that of the countess, and all the family of De Courcy Castle.

And then the Honourable George returned thanks. We will not follow him through the different periods of his somewhat irregular eloquence. Those immediately in his neigh-bourhood found it at first rather difficult to get him on his legs, but much greater difficulty was soon experienced in inducing him to resume his seat. One of two arrangements should certainly be made in these days: either let all speech-making on festive occasions be utterly tabooed and made as it were impossible; or else let those who are to exercise the privilege be first subjected to a competing examination before the civil-service examining commissioners. As it is now, the Honourable Georges do but little honour to our exertions in favour of British education.

In the dining-room the bishop went through the honours of the day with much more neatness and propriety. He also drank Miss Thorne's health, and did it in a manner becom-ing the bench which he adorned. The party there was perhaps a little more dull, a shade less lively than that in the tent. But what was lost in mirth was fully made up in decorum.

And so the banquets passed off at the various tables with great éclat and universal delight.

CHAPTER XL

ULLATHORNE SPORTS—ACT II

"That which has made them drunk has made me bold." 'Twas thus that Mr. Slope encouraged himself, as he left the dining-room in pursuit of Eleanor. He had not indeed seen in that room any person really intoxicated, but there had been a good deal of wine drunk, and Mr. Slope had not hesitated to take his share, in order to screw himself up to the undertaking which he had in hand. He is not the first man who has thought it expedient to call in the assistance of Bacchus on such an occasion.

Eleanor was out through the window and on the grass before she perceived that she was followed. Just at that moment the guests were nearly all occupied at the tables. Here and there were to be seen a constant couple or two, who preferred their own sweet discourse to the jingle of glasses or the charms of rhetoric which fell from the mouths of the Honourable George and the Bishop of Barchester; but the grounds were as nearly vacant as Mr. Slope could wish them to be.

Eleanor saw that she was pursued, and as a deer, when escape is no longer possible, will turn to bay and attack the hounds, so did she turn upon Mr. Slope.

"Pray don't let me take you from the room," said she, speaking with all the stiffness which she knew how to use. "I have come out to look for a friend. I must beg of you, Mr. Slope, to go back."

But Mr. Slope would not be thus entreated. He had observed all day that Mrs. Bold was not cordial to him, and this had to a certain extent oppressed him. But he did not deduce from this any assurance that his aspirations were in vain. He saw that she was angry with him. Might she not be so because he had so long tampered with her feelings—might it not arise from his having, as he knew was the case, caused her name to be bruited about in conjunction with his own without having given her the opportunity of confessing to the world that henceforth their names were to be one and the same? Poor lady. He had within him a certain Christian conscience-stricken feeling of remorse on this head. It might be that he had wronged her by his tardiness. He had, however, at the present moment imbibed too much of Mr. Thorne's champagne to have any inward misgivings. He was right in repeating the boast of Lady Macbeth: he was not drunk, but he was bold enough for anything. It was a pity that in such a state he could not have encountered Mrs. Proudie.

"You must permit me to attend you," said he; "I could not think of allowing you to go alone."

"Indeed you must, Mr. Slope," said Eleanor still very stiffly, "for it is my special wish to be alone."

The time for letting the great secret escape him had already come. Mr. Slope saw that it must be now or never, and he was determined that it should be now. This was not his first attempt at winning a fair lady. He had been on his knees, looked unutterable things with his eyes, and whispered honeyed words before this. Indeed, he was somewhat an adept at these things, and had only to adapt to the perhaps different taste of Mrs. Bold the well-remembered rhapsodies which had once so much gratified Olivia Proudie.

"Do not ask me to leave you, Mrs. Bold," said he with an impassioned look, impassioned and sanctified as well, with that sort of look which is not uncommon with gentlemen of Mr. Slope's school and which may perhaps be called the tender-pious. "Do not ask me to leave you till I have spoken a few words with which my heart is full—which I have come hither purposely to say."

Eleanor saw how it was now. She knew directly what it was she was about to go through, and very miserable the knowledge made her. Of course she could refuse Mr. Slope, and there would be an end of that, one might say. But there would not be an end of it, as far as Eleanor was concerned. The very fact of Mr. Slope's making an offer to her would be a triumph to the archdeacon and, in a great measure, a vindication of Mr. Arabin's conduct. The widow could not bring herself to endure with patience the idea that she had been in the wrong. She had defended Mr. Slope, she had declared herself quite justified in admitting him among her acquaintance, had ridiculed the idea of his considering himself as more than an acquaintance, and had resented the archdeacon's caution in her behalf: now it was about to be proved to her in a manner sufficiently disagreeable that the archdeacon had been right, and she herself had been entirely wrong.

"I don't know what you can have to say to me, Mr. Slope, that you could not have said when we were sitting at table just now;" and she closed her lips, and steadied her eyeballs, and looked at him in a manner that ought to have frozen him.

But gentlemen are not easily frozen when they are full of champagne, and it would not at any time have been easy to freeze Mr. Slope.

"There are things, Mrs. Bold, which a man cannot well say before a crowd; which perhaps he cannot well say at any time; which indeed he may most fervently desire to get spoken, and which he may yet find it almost impossible to utter. It is such things as these that I now wish to say to you;" and then the tender-pious look was repeated, with a little more emphasis even than before.

Eleanor had not found it practicable to stand stock still before the dining-room window, there receive his offer in full view of Miss Thorne's guests. She had therefore in self-defence walked on, and thus Mr. Slope had gained his object of walking with her. He now offered her his arm.

"Thank you, Mr. Slope, I am much obliged to you; but for the very short time that I shall remain with you I shall prefer walking alone."

"And must it be so short?" said he. "Must it be—"

"Yes," said Eleanor, interrupting him, "as short as possible, if you please, sir."

"I had hoped, Mrs. Bold—I had hoped—"

"Pray hope nothing, Mr. Slope, as far as I am concerned; pray do not; I do not know and need not know what hope you mean. Our acquaintance is very slight, and will probably remain so. Pray, pray let that be enough; there is at any rate no necessity for us to quarrel."

Mrs. Bold was certainly treating Mr. Slope rather cavalierly, and he felt it so. She was rejecting him before he had offered himself, and informing him at the same time that he was taking a great deal too much on himself to be so familiar. She did not even make an attempt

From such a sharp and waspish word as "no"
To pluck the sting.

He was still determined to be very tender and very pious, seeing that, in spite of all Mrs. Bold had said to him, he had not yet abandoned hope; but he was inclined also to be somewhat angry. The widow was bearing herself, as he thought, with too high a hand, was speaking of herself in much too imperious a tone. She had clearly no idea that an honour was being conferred on her. Mr. Slope would be tender as long as he could, but he began to think if that failed it would not be amiss if he also mounted himself for awhile on his high horse. Mr. Slope could undoubtedly be very tender, but he could be very savage also, and he knew his own abilities.

"That is cruel," said he, "and unchristian, too. The worst of us are still bidden to hope. What have I done that you should pass on me so severe a sentence?" And then he paused a moment, during which the widow walked steadily on with measured steps, saying nothing further.

"Beautiful woman," at last he burst forth, "beautiful woman, you cannot pretend to be ignorant that I adore you. Yes, Eleanor, yes, I love you. I love you with the truest affection which man can bear to woman. Next to my hopes of heaven are my hopes of possessing you." (Mr. Slope's memory here played him false, or he would not have omitted the deanery.) "How sweet to walk to heaven with you by my side, with you for my guide, mutual guides. Say, Eleanor, dearest Eleanor, shall we walk that sweet path together?"

Eleanor had no intention of ever walking together with Mr. Slope on any other path than that special one of Miss Thorne's which they now occupied, but as she had been unable to prevent the expression of Mr. Slope's wishes and aspirations, she resolved to hear him out to the end before she answered him.

"Ah, Eleanor," he continued, and it seemed to be his idea that as he had once found courage to pronounce her Christian name, he could not utter it often enough. "Ah, Eleanor, will it not be sweet, with the Lord's assistance, to travel hand in hand through this mortal valley which His mercies will make pleasant to us, till hereafter we shall dwell together at the foot of His throne?" And then a more tenderly pious glance than ever beamed from the lover's eyes. "Ah, Eleanor—"

"My name, Mr. Slope, is Mrs. Bold," said Eleanor, who, though determined to hear out the tale of his love, was too much disgusted by his blasphemy to be able to bear much more of it.

"Sweetest angel, be not so cold," said he, and as he said it the champagne broke forth, and he contrived to pass his arm round her waist. He did this with considerable cleverness, for up to this point Eleanor had contrived with tolerable success to keep her distance from him. They had got into a walk nearly enveloped by shrubs, and Mr. Slope therefore no doubt considered that as they were now alone it was fitting that he should give her some outward demonstration of that affection of which he talked so much. It may perhaps be presumed that the same stamp of measures had been found to succeed with Olivia Proudie. Be this as it may, it was not successful with Eleanor Bold.

She sprang from him as she would have jumped from an adder, but she did not spring far—not, indeed, beyond arm's length—and then, quick as thought, she raised her little hand and dealt him a box on the ear with such right goodwill that it sounded among the trees like a miniature thunderclap.

And now it is to be feared that every well-bred reader of these pages will lay down the book with disgust, feeling that, after all, the heroine is unworthy of sympathy. She is a hoyden, one will say. At any rate she is not a lady, another will exclaim. I have suspected her all through, a third will declare; she has no idea of the dignity of a matron, or of the peculiar propriety which her position demands. At one moment she is romping with young

Stanhope; then she is making eyes at Mr. Arabin; anon she comes to fisticuffs with a third lover—and all before she is yet a widow of two years' standing.

She cannot altogether be defended, and yet it may be averred that she is not a hoyden, not given to romping nor prone to boxing. It were to be wished devoutly that she had not struck Mr. Slope in the face. In doing so she derogated from her dignity and committed herself. Had she been educated in Belgravia, had she been brought up by any sterner mentor than that fond father, had she lived longer under the rule of a husband, she might, perhaps, have saved herself from this great fault. As it was, the provocation was too much for her, the temptation to instant resentment of the insult too strong. She was too keen in the feeling of independence, a feeling dangerous for a young woman, but one in which her position peculiarly tempted her to indulge. And then Mr. Slope's face, tinted with a deeper dye than usual by the wine he had drunk, simpering and puckering itself with pseudo-pity and tender grimaces, seemed specially to call for such punishment. She had, too, a true instinct as to the man; he was capable of rebuke in this way and in no other. To him the blow from her little hand was as much an insult as a blow from a man would have been to another. It went directly to his pride. He conceived himself lowered in his dignity and personally outraged. He could almost have struck at her again in his rage. Even the pain was a great annoyance to him, and the feeling that his clerical character had been wholly disregarded sorely vexed him.

There are such men: men who can endure no taint on their personal self-respect, even from a woman; men whose bodies are to themselves such sacred temples that a joke against them is desecration, and a rough touch downright sacrilege. Mr. Slope was such a man, and therefore the slap on the face that he got from Eleanor was, as far as he was concerned, the fittest rebuke which could have been administered to him.

But nevertheless, she should not have raised her hand against the man. Ladies' hands, so soft, so sweet, so delicious to the touch, so graceful to the eye, so gracious in their gentle doings, were not made to belabour men's faces. The moment the deed was done Eleanor felt that she had sinned against all propriety, and would have given little worlds to recall the blow. In her first agony of sorrow she all but begged the man's pardon. Her next impulse, however, and the one which she obeyed, was to run away.

"I never, never will speak another word to you," she said, gasping with emotion and the loss of breath which her exertion and violent feelings occasioned her, and so saying she put foot to the ground and ran quickly back along the path to the house.

But how shall I sing the divine wrath of Mr. Slope, or how invoke the tragic muse to describe the rage which swelled the celestial bosom of the bishop's chaplain? Such an undertaking by no means befits the low-heeled buskin of modern fiction. The painter put a veil over Agamemnon's face when called on to depict the father's grief at the early doom of his devoted daughter. The god, when he resolved to punish the rebellious winds, abstained from mouthing empty threats. We will not attempt to tell with what mighty surgings of the inner heart Mr. Slope swore to revenge himself on the woman who had disgraced him, nor will we vainly strive to depict his deep agony of soul.

There he is, however, alone in the garden walk, and we must contrive to bring him out of it. He was not willing to come forth quite at once. His cheek was stinging with the weight of Eleanor's fingers, and he fancied that everyone who looked at him would be able to see on his face the traces of what he had endured. He stood awhile, becoming redder and redder with rage. He stood motionless, undecided, glaring with his eyes, thinking of the pains and penalties of Hades, and meditating how he might best devote his enemy to the infernal gods with all the passion of his accustomed eloquence. He longed in his heart to be preaching at her. 'Twas thus that he was ordinarily avenged of sinning mortal men and women. Could he at once have ascended his Sunday rostrum and fulminated at her such denunciations as his spirit delighted in, his bosom would have been greatly eased.

But how preach to Mr. Thorne's laurels, or how preach indeed at all in such a vanity fair as this now going on at Ullathorne? And then he began to feel a righteous disgust at the wickedness of the doings around him. He had been justly chastised for lending, by his presence, a sanction to such worldly lures. The gaiety of society, the mirth of banquets, the laughter of the young, and the eating and drinking of the elders were, for awhile, without excuse in his sight. What had he now brought down upon himself by sojourning thus in the tents of the heathen? He had consorted with idolaters round the altars of Baal, and therefore a sore punishment had come upon him. He then thought of the Signora Neroni, and his soul within him was full of sorrow. He had an inkling—a true inkling—that he was a wicked, sinful man, but it led him in no right direction; he could admit no charity in his heart. He felt debasement coming on him, and he longed to shake it off, to rise up in his stirrup, to mount to high places and great power, that he might get up into a mighty pulpit and preach to the world a loud sermon against Mrs. Bold.

There he stood fixed to the gravel for about ten minutes. Fortune favoured him so far that no prying eyes came to look upon him in his misery. Then a shudder passed over his whole frame; he collected himself and slowly wound his way round to the lawn, advancing along the path and not returning in the direction which Eleanor had taken. When he reached the tent, he found the bishop standing there in conversation with the Master of Lazarus. His lordship had come out to air himself after the exertion of his speech.

"This is very pleasant—very pleasant, my lord, is it not?" said Mr. Slope with his most gracious smile, pointing to the tent; "very pleasant. It is delightful to see so many persons enjoying themselves so thoroughly."

Mr. Slope thought he might force the bishop to introduce him to Dr. Gwynne. A very great example had declared and practised the wisdom of being everything to everybody, and Mr. Slope was desirous of following it. His maxim was never to lose a chance. The bishop, however, at the present moment was not very anxious to increase Mr. Slope's circle of acquaintance among his clerical brethren. He had his own reasons for dropping any marked allusion to his domestic chaplain, and he therefore made his shoulder rather cold for the occasion.

"Very, very," said he without turning round, or even deigning to look at Mr. Slope. "And therefore, Dr. Gwynne, I really think that you will find that the hebdomadal board will exercise as wide and as general an authority as at the present moment. I, for one, Dr. Gwynne—"

"Dr. Gwynne," said Mr. Slope, raising his hat and resolving not to be outwitted by such an insignificant little goose as the Bishop of Barchester.

The Master of Lazarus also raised his hat and bowed very politely to Mr. Slope. There is not a more courteous gentleman in the queen's dominions than the Master of Lazarus.

"My lord," said Mr. Slope, "pray do me the honour of introducing me to Dr. Gwynne. The opportunity is too much in my favour to be lost."

The bishop had no help for it. "My chaplain, Dr. Gwynne," said he, "my present chaplain, Mr. Slope." He certainly made the introduction as unsatisfactory to the chaplain as possible, and by the use of the word "present" seemed to indicate that Mr. Slope might probably not long enjoy the honour which he now held. But Mr. Slope cared nothing for this. He understood the innuendo, and disregarded it. It might probably come to pass that he would be in a situation to resign his chaplaincy before the bishop was in a situation to dismiss him from it. What need the future Dean of Barchester care for the bishop, or for the bishop's wife? Had not Mr. Slope, just as he was entering Dr. Stanhope's carriage, received an all-important note from Tom Towers of "The Jupiter"? Had he not that note this moment in his pocket?

So disregarding the bishop, he began to open out a conversation with the Master of Lazarus.

But suddenly an interruption came, not altogether unwelcome to Mr. Slope. One of the bishop's servants came up to his master's shoulder with a long, grave face and whispered into the bishop's ear.

"What is it, John?" said the bishop.

"The dean, my lord; he is dead."

Mr. Slope had no further desire to converse with the Master of Lazarus, and was very soon on his road back to Barchester.

Eleanor, as we have said, having declared her intention of never holding further communication with Mr. Slope, ran hurriedly back towards the house. The thought, however, of what she had done grieved her greatly, and she could not abstain from bursting into tears. 'Twas thus she played the second act in that day's melodrama.

CHAPTER XLI

MRS. BOLD CONFIDES HER SORROW TO HER FRIEND MISS STANHOPE

When Mrs. Bold came to the end of the walk and faced the lawn, she began to bethink herself what she should do. Was she to wait there till Mr. Slope caught her, or was she to go in among the crowd with tears in her eyes and passion in her face? She might in truth have stood there long enough without any reasonable fear of further immediate persecution from Mr. Slope, but we are all inclined to magnify the bugbears which frighten us. In her present state of dread she did not know of what atrocity he might venture to be guilty. Had anyone told her a week ago that he would have put his arm round her waist at this party of Miss Thorne's, she would have been utterly incredulous. Had she been informed that he would be seen on the following Sunday walking down the High Street in a scarlet coat and top boots, she would not have thought such a phenomenon more improbable.

But this improbable iniquity he had committed, and now there was nothing she could not believe of him. In the first place it was quite manifest that he was tipsy; in the next place it was to be taken as proved that all his religion was sheer hypocrisy; and finally the man was utterly shameless. She therefore stood watching for the sound of his footfall, not without some fear that he might creep out at her suddenly from among the bushes.

As she thus stood she saw Charlotte Stanhope at a little distance from her, walking quickly across the grass. Eleanor's handkerchief was in her hand, and putting it to her face so as to conceal her tears, she ran across the lawn and joined her friend.

"Oh, Charlotte," she said, almost too much out of breath to speak very plainly; "I am so glad I have found you."

"Glad you have found me!" said Charlotte, laughing; "that's a good joke. Why Bertie and I have been looking for you everywhere. He swears that you have gone off with Mr. Slope, and is now on the point of hanging himself."

"Oh, Charlotte, don't," said Mrs. Bold.

"Why, my child, what on earth is the matter with you?" said Miss Stanhope, perceiving that Eleanor's hand trembled on her own arm, and finding also that her companion was still half-choked by tears. "Goodness heaven! Something has distressed you. What is it? What can I do for you?"

Eleanor answered her only by a sort of spasmodic gurgle in her throat. She was a good deal upset, as people say, and could not at the moment collect herself.

"Come here, this way, Mrs. Bold; come this way, and we shall not be seen. What has happened to vex you so? What can I do for you? Can Bertie do anything?"

"Oh, no, no, no, no," said Eleanor. "There is nothing to be done. Only that horrid man—"

"What horrid man?" asked Charlotte.

There are some moments in life in which both men and women feel themselves imperatively called on to make a confidence, in which not to do so requires a disagreeable resolution and also a disagreeable suspicion. There are people of both sexes who never make confidences, who are never tempted by momentary circumstances to disclose their secrets, but such are generally dull, close, unimpassioned spirits, "gloomy gnomes, who live in cold dark mines." There was nothing of the gnome about Eleanor, and she therefore resolved to tell Charlotte Stanhope the whole story about Mr. Slope.

"That horrid man; that Mr. Slope," said she. "Did you not see that he followed me out of the dining-room?"

"Of course I did, and was sorry enough, but I could not help it. I knew you would be annoyed. But you and Bertie managed it badly between you."

"It was not his fault nor mine either. You know how I disliked the idea of coming in the carriage with that man."

"I am sure I am very sorry if that has led to it."

"I don't know what has led to it," said Eleanor, almost crying again. "But it has not been my fault."

"But what has he done, my dear?"

"He's an abominable, horrid, hypocritical man, and it would serve him right to tell the bishop all about it."

"Believe me, if you want to do him an injury, you had far better tell Mrs. Proudie. But what did he do, Mrs. Bold?"

"Ugh!" exclaimed Eleanor.

"Well, I must confess he's not very nice," said Charlotte Stanhope.

"Nice!" said Eleanor. "He is the most fulsome, fawning, abominable man I ever saw. What business had he to come to me?—I that never gave him the slightest tittle of encouragement—I that always hated him, though I did take his part when others ran him down."

"That's just where it is, my dear. He has heard that and therefore fancied that of course you were in love with him."

This was wormwood to Eleanor. It was in fact the very thing which all her friends had been saying for the last month past—and which experience now proved to be true. Eleanor resolved within herself that she would never again take any man's part. The world, with all its villany and all its ill-nature, might wag as it liked: she would not again attempt to set crooked things straight.

"But what did he do, my dear?" said Charlotte, who was really rather interested in the subject.

"He—he—he—"

"Well—come, it can't have been anything so very horrid, for the man was not tipsy."

"Oh, I am sure he was" said Eleanor. "I am sure he must have been tipsy."

"Well, I declare I didn't observe it. But what was it, my love?"

"Why, I believe I can hardly tell you. He talked such horrid stuff that you never heard the like: about religion, and heaven, and love. Oh, dear—he is such a nasty man."

"I can easily imagine the sort of stuff he would talk. Well—and then—?"

"And then—he took hold of me."

"Took hold of you?"

"Yes—he somehow got close to me and took hold of me—"

"By the waist?"

"Yes," said Eleanor shuddering.

"And then—"

"Then I jumped away from him, and gave him a slap on the face, and ran away along the path till I saw you."

"Ha, ha, ha!" Charlotte Stanhope laughed heartily at the finale to the tragedy. It was delightful to her to think that Mr. Slope had had his ears boxed. She did not quite appreciate the feeling which made her friend so unhappy at the result of the interview. To her thinking the matter had ended happily enough as regarded the widow, who indeed was entitled to some sort of triumph among her friends. Whereas to Mr. Slope would be due all those gibes and jeers which would naturally follow such an affair. His friends would ask him whether his ears tingled whenever he saw a widow, and he would be cautioned that beautiful things were made to be looked at and not to be touched.

Such were Charlotte Stanhope's views on such matters, but she did not at the present moment clearly explain them to Mrs. Bold. Her object was to endear herself to her friend, and therefore, having had her laugh, she was ready enough to offer sympathy. Could Bertie do anything? Should Bertie speak to the man and warn him that in future he must behave with more decorum? Bertie indeed, she declared, would be more angry than anyone else when he heard to what insult Mrs. Bold had been subjected.

"But you won't tell him?" said Mrs. Bold with a look of horror.

"Not if you don't like it," said Charlotte; "but considering everything, I would strongly advise it. If you had a brother, you know, it would be unnecessary. But it is very right that Mr. Slope should know that you have somebody by you that will and can protect you."

"But my father is here."

"Yes, but it is so disagreeable for clergymen to have to quarrel with each other; and circumstanced as your father is just at this moment, it would be very inexpedient that there should be anything unpleasant between him and Mr. Slope. Surely you and Bertie are intimate enough for you to permit him to take your part."

Charlotte Stanhope was very anxious that her brother should at once on that very day settle matters with his future wife. Things had now come to that point between him and his father, and between him and his creditors, that he must either do so, or leave Barchester; either do that, or go back to his unwashed associates, dirty lodgings, and poor living at Carrara. Unless he could provide himself with an income, he must go to Carrara, or to ——
—. His father the prebendary had not said this in so many words, but had he done so, he could not have signified it more plainly.

Such being the state of the case it was very necessary that no more time should be lost. Charlotte had seen her brother's apathy, when he neglected to follow Mrs. Bold out of the room, with anger which she could hardly suppress. It was grievous to think that Mr. Slope should have so distanced him. Charlotte felt that she had played her part with sufficient skill. She had brought them together and induced such a degree of intimacy that her brother was really relieved from all trouble and labour in the matter. And moreover it was quite plain that Mrs. Bold was very fond of Bertie. And now it was plain enough also that he had nothing to fear from his rival, Mr. Slope.

There was certainly an awkwardness in subjecting Mrs. Bold to a second offer on the same day. It would have been well perhaps to have put the matter off for a week, could a week have been spared. But circumstances are frequently too peremptory to be arranged as we would wish to arrange them, and such was the case now. This being so, could not this affair of Mr. Slope's be turned to advantage? Could it not be made the excuse for bringing Bertie and Mrs. Bold into still closer connexion—into such close connexion that they could not fail to throw themselves into each other's arms? Such was the game which Miss Stanhope now at a moment's notice resolved to play.

And very well she played it. In the first place it was arranged that Mr. Slope should not return in the Stanhopes' carriage to Barchester. It so happened that Mr. Slope was already gone, but of that of course they knew nothing. The signora should be induced to go first, with only the servants and her sister, and Bertie should take Mr. Slope's place in the second journey. Bertie was to be told in confidence of the whole affair, and when the carriage was gone off with its first load, Eleanor was to be left under Bertie's special protection, so as to insure her from any further aggression from Mr. Slope. While the carriage was getting ready, Bertie was to seek out that gentleman and make him understand that he must provide himself with another conveyance back to Barchester. Their immediate object should be to walk about together in search of Bertie. Bertie in short was to be the Pegasus on whose wings they were to ride out of their present dilemma.

There was a warmth of friendship and cordial kindliness in all this that was very soothing to the widow; but yet, though she gave way to it, she was hardly reconciled to doing so. It never occurred to her that, now that she had killed one dragon, another was about to spring up in her path; she had no remote idea that she would have to encounter another suitor in her proposed protector, but she hardly liked the thought of putting herself so much into the hands of young Stanhope. She felt that if she wanted protection, she should go to her father. She felt that she should ask him to provide a carriage for her back to Barchester. Mrs. Clantantram she knew would give her a seat. She knew that she should not throw herself entirely upon friends whose friendship dated, as it were, but from yesterday. But yet she could not say no to one who was so sisterly in her kindness, so eager in her good nature, so comfortably sympathetic as Charlotte Stanhope. And thus she gave way to all the propositions made to her.

They first went into the dining-room, looking for their champion, and from thence to the drawing-room. Here they found Mr. Arabin, still hanging over the signora's sofa; or rather they found him sitting near her head, as a physician might have sat had the lady been his patient. There was no other person in the room. The guests were some in the tent, some few still in the dining room, some at the bows and arrows, but most of them walking with Miss Thorne through the park and looking at the games that were going on.

All that had passed, and was passing between Mr. Arabin and the lady, it is unnecessary to give in detail. She was doing with him as she did with all others. It was her mission to make fools of men, and she was pursuing her mission with Mr. Arabin. She had almost got him to own his love for Mrs. Bold and had subsequently almost induced him to acknowledge a passion for herself. He, poor man, was hardly aware what he was doing or saying, hardly conscious whether was in heaven or in hell. So little had he known of female attractions of that peculiar class which the signora owned, that he became affected with a kind of temporary delirium when first subjected to its power. He lost his head rather than this heart, and toppled about mentally, reeling in his ideas as a drunken man does on his legs. She had whispered to him words that really meant nothing but which, coming from such beautiful lips and accompanied by such lustrous glances, seemed to have a mysterious significance, which he felt though he could not understand.

In being thus besirened, Mr. Arabin behaved himself very differently from Mr. Slope. The signora had said truly that the two men were the contrasts of each other—that the one was all for action, the other all for thought. Mr. Slope, when this lady laid upon his senses the overpowering breath of her charms, immediately attempted to obtain some fruition, to achieve some mighty triumph. He began by catching at her hand and progressed by kissing it. He made vows of love and asked for vows in return. He promised everlasting devotion, knelt before her, and swore that had she been on Mount Ida, Juno would have had no cause to hate the offspring of Venus. But Mr. Arabin uttered no oaths, kept his hand mostly in his trousers pocket, and had no more thought of kissing Madame Neroni than of kissing the Countess De Courcy.

As soon as Mr. Arabin saw Mrs. Bold enter the room he blushed and rose from his chair; then he sat down again, and then again got up. The signora saw the blush at once and smiled at the poor victim, but Eleanor was too much confused to see anything.

"Oh, Madeline," said Charlotte, "I want to speak to you particularly; we must arrange about the carriage, you know," and she stooped down to whisper to her sister. Mr. Arabin immediately withdrew to a little distance, and as Charlotte had in fact much to explain before she could make the new carriage arrangement intelligible, he had nothing to do but to talk to Mrs. Bold.

"We have had a very pleasant party," said he, using the tone he would have used had he declared that the sun was shining very brightly, or the rain falling very fast.

"Very," said Eleanor, who never in her life had passed a more unpleasant day.

"I hope Mr. Harding has enjoyed himself."

"Oh, yes, very much," said Eleanor, who had not seen her father since she parted from him soon after her arrival.

"He returns to Barchester to-night, I suppose."

"Yes, I believe so—that is, I think he is staying at Plumstead."

"Oh, staying at Plumstead," said Mr. Arabin.

"He came from there this morning. I believe he is going back, he didn't exactly say, however."

"I hope Mrs. Grantly is quite well."

"She seemed to be quite well. She is here; that is, unless she has gone away."

"Oh, yes, to be sure. I was talking to her. Looking very well indeed." Then there was a considerable pause; for Charlotte could not at once make Madeline understand why she was to be sent home in a hurry without her brother.

"Are you returning to Plumstead, Mrs. Bold?" Mr. Arabin merely asked this by way of making conversation, but he immediately perceived that he was approaching dangerous ground.

"No," said Mrs. Bold very quietly; "I am going home to Barchester."

"Oh, ah, yes. I had forgotten that you had returned." And then Mr. Arabin, finding it impossible to say anything further, stood silent till Charlotte had completed her plans, and Mrs. Bold stood equally silent, intently occupied as it appeared in the arrangement of her rings.

And yet these two people were thoroughly in love with each other; and though one was a middle-aged clergyman, and the other a lady at any rate past the wishy-washy bread-and-butter period of life, they were as unable to tell their own minds to each other as any Damon and Phillis, whose united ages would not make up that to which Mr. Arabin had already attained.

Madeline Neroni consented to her sister's proposal, and then the two ladies again went off in quest of Bertie Stanhope.

CHAPTER XLII

ULLATHORNE SPORTS—ACT III

And now Miss Thorne's guests were beginning to take their departure, and the amusement of those who remained was becoming slack. It was getting dark, and ladies in morning costumes were thinking that, if they were to appear by candlelight, they ought to readjust themselves. Some young gentlemen had been heard to talk so loud that prudent mammas determined to retire judiciously, and the more discreet of the male sex, whose libations had been moderate, felt that there was not much more left for them to do.

Morning parties, as a rule, are failures. People never know how to get away from them gracefully. A picnic on an island or a mountain or in a wood may perhaps be permitted. There is no master of the mountain bound by courtesy to bid you stay while in his heart he is longing for your departure. But in a private house or in private grounds a morning party is a bore. One is called on to eat and drink at unnatural hours. One is obliged to give up the day, which is useful, and is then left without resource for the evening, which is useless. One gets home fagged and *désoeuvré*, and yet at an hour too early for bed. There is no comfortable resource left. Cards in these genteel days are among the things tabooed, and a rubber of whist is impracticable.

All this began now to be felt. Some young people had come with some amount of hope that they might get up a dance in the evening, and were unwilling to leave till all such hope was at an end. Others, fearful of staying longer than was expected, had ordered their carriages early, and were doing their best to go, solicitous for their servants and horses. The countess and her noble brood were among the first to leave, and as regarded the Hon. George, it was certainly time that he did so. Her ladyship was in a great fret and fume. Those horrid roads would, she was sure, be the death of her if unhappily she were caught in them by the dark night. The lamps she was assured were good, but no lamp could withstand the jolting of the roads of East Barsetshire. The De Courcy property lay in the western division of the county.

Mrs. Proudie could not stay when the countess was gone. So the bishop was searched for by the Revs. Messrs. Grey and Green and found in one corner of the tent enjoying himself thoroughly in a disquisition on the hebdomadal board. He obeyed, however, the behests of his lady without finishing the sentence in which he was promising to Dr. Gwynne that his authority at Oxford should remain unimpaired, and the episcopal horses turned their noses towards the palatial stables. Then the Grantlys went. Before they did so, Mr. Harding managed to whisper a word into his daughter's ear. Of course, he said, he would undeceive the Grantlys as to that foolish rumour about Mr. Slope.

"No, no, no," said Eleanor; "pray do not—pray wait till I see you. You will be home in a day or two, and then I will explain to you everything."

"I shall be home to-morrow," said he.

"I am so glad," said Eleanor. "You will come and dine with me, and then we shall be so comfortable."

Mr. Harding promised. He did not exactly know what there was to be explained, or why Dr. Grantly's mind should not be disabused of the mistake into which he had fallen, but nevertheless he promised. He owed some reparation to his daughter, and he thought that he might best make it by obedience.

And thus the people were thinning off by degrees as Charlotte and Eleanor walked about in quest of Bertie. Their search might have been long had they not happened to hear his voice. He was comfortably ensconced in the ha-ha, with his back to the sloping side, smoking a cigar, and eagerly engaged in conversation with some youngster from the further side of the county, whom he had never met before, who was also smoking under Bertie's pupilage and listening with open ears to an account given by his companion of some of the pastimes of Eastern clime.

"Bertie, I am seeking you everywhere," said Charlotte. "Come up here at once."

Bertie looked up out of the ha-ha and saw the two ladies before him. As there was nothing for him but to obey, he got up and threw away his cigar. From the first moment of his acquaintance with her he had liked Eleanor Bold. Had he been left to his own devices, had she been penniless, and had it then been quite out of the question that he should marry her, he would most probably have fallen violently in love with her. But now he could not help regarding her somewhat as he did the marble workshops at Carrara, as he had done his easel and palette, as he had done the lawyer's chambers in London—in fact, as he had invariably regarded everything by which it had been proposed to him to obtain the means of living. Eleanor Bold appeared before him, no longer as a beautiful woman, but as a new profession called matrimony. It was a profession indeed requiring but little labour, and one in which an income was insured to him. But nevertheless he had been as it were goaded on to it; his sister had talked to him of Eleanor, just as she had talked of busts and portraits. Bertie did not dislike money, but he hated the very thought of earning it. He was now called away from his pleasant cigar to earn it, by offering himself as a husband to Mrs. Bold. The work indeed was made easy enough, for in lieu of his having to seek the widow, the widow had apparently come to seek him.

He made some sudden absurd excuse to his auditor and then, throwing away his cigar, climbed up the wall of the ha-ha and joined the ladies on the lawn.

"Come and give Mrs. Bold an arm," said Charlotte, "while I set you on a piece of duty which, as a *preux chevalier*, you must immediately perform. Your personal danger will, I fear, be insignificant, as your antagonist is a clergyman."

Bertie immediately gave his arm to Eleanor, walking between her and his sister. He had lived too long abroad to fall into the Englishman's habit of offering each an arm to two ladies at the same time—a habit, by the by, which foreigners regard as an approach to bigamy, or a sort of incipient Mormonism.

The little history of Mr. Slope's misconduct was then told to Bertie by his sister, Eleanor's ears tingling the while. And well they might tingle. If it were necessary to speak of the outrage at all, why should it be spoken of to such a person as Mr. Stanhope, and why in her own hearing? She knew she was wrong, and was unhappy and dispirited, yet she could think of no way to extricate herself, no way to set herself right. Charlotte spared her as much as she possibly could, spoke of the whole thing as though Mr. Slope had taken a glass of wine too much, said that of course there would be nothing more about it, but that steps must be taken to exclude Mr. Slope from the carriage.

"Mrs. Bold need be under no alarm about that," said Bertie, "for Mr. Slope has gone this hour past. He told me that business made it necessary that he should start at once for Barchester."

"He is not so tipsy, at any rate, but what he knows his fault," said Charlotte. "Well, my dear, that is one difficulty over. Now I'll leave you with your true knight and get Madeline off as quickly as I can. The carriage is here, I suppose, Bertie?"

"It has been here for the last hour."

"That's well. Good-bye, my dear. Of course you'll come in to tea. I shall trust to you to bring her, Bertie, even by force if necessary." And so saying, Charlotte ran off across the lawn, leaving her brother alone with the widow.

As Miss Stanhope went off, Eleanor bethought herself that, as Mr. Slope had taken his departure, there no longer existed any necessity for separating Mr. Stanhope from his sister Madeline, who so much needed his aid. It had been arranged that he should remain so as to preoccupy Mr. Slope's place in the carriage, and act as a social policeman to effect the exclusion of that disagreeable gentleman. But Mr. Slope had effected his own exclusion, and there was no possible reason now why Bertie should not go with his sister—at least Eleanor saw none, and she said as much.

"Oh, let Charlotte have her own way," said he. "She has arranged it, and there will be no end of confusion if we make another change. Charlotte always arranges everything in our house and rules us like a despot."

"But the signora?" said Eleanor.

"Oh, the signora can do very well without me. Indeed, she will have to do without me," he added, thinking rather of his studies in Carrara than of his Barchester hymeneals.

"Why, you are not going to leave us?" asked Eleanor.

It has been said that Bertie Stanhope was a man without principle. He certainly was so. He had no power of using active mental exertion to keep himself from doing evil. Evil had no ugliness in his eyes; virtue no beauty. He was void of any of these feelings which actuate men to do good. But he was perhaps equally void of those which actuate men to do evil. He got into debt with utter recklessness, thinking nothing as to whether the tradesmen would ever be paid or not. But he did not invent active schemes of deceit for the sake of extracting the goods of others. If a man gave him credit, that was the man's look-out; Bertie Stanhope troubled himself nothing further. In borrowing money he did the same; he gave people references to "his governor;" told them that the "old chap" had a good income; and agreed to pay sixty per cent for the accommodation. All this he did without a scruple of conscience; but then he never contrived active villainy.

In this affair of his marriage it had been represented to him as a matter of duty that he ought to put himself in possession of Mrs. Bold's hand and fortune, and at first he had so regarded it. About her he had thought but little. It was the customary thing for men situated as he was to marry for money, and there was no reason why he should not do what others around him did. And so he consented. But now he began to see the matter in another light. He was setting himself down to catch this woman, as a cat sits to catch a mouse. He was to catch her, and swallow her up, her and her child, and her houses and land, in order that he might live on her instead of on his father. There was a cold, calculating, cautious cunning about this quite at variance with Bertie's character. The prudence of the measure was quite as antagonistic to his feelings as the iniquity.

And then, should he be successful, what would be the reward? Having satisfied his creditors with half of the widow's fortune, he would be allowed to sit down quietly at Barchester, keeping economical house with the remainder. His duty would be to rock the cradle of the late Mr. Bold's child, and his highest excitement a demure party at Plumstead

Rectory, should it ultimately turn out that the archdeacon would be sufficiently reconciled to receive him.

There was very little in the programme to allure such a man as Bertie Stanhope. Would not the Carrara workshop, or whatever worldly career fortune might have in store for him, would not almost anything be better than this? The lady herself was undoubtedly all that was desirable, but the most desirable lady becomes nauseous when she has to be taken as a pill. He was pledged to his sister, however, and let him quarrel with whom he would, it behoved him not to quarrel with her. If she were lost to him, all would be lost that he could ever hope to derive henceforward from the paternal roof-tree. His mother was apparently indifferent to his weal or woe, to his wants or his warfare. His father's brow got blacker and blacker from day to day, as the old man looked at his hopeless son. And as for Madeline—poor Madeline, whom of all of them he liked the best—she had enough to do to shift for herself. No; come what might, he must cling to his sister and obey her behests, let them be ever so stern—or at the very least seem to obey them. Could not some happy deceit bring him through in this matter, so that he might save appearances with his sister and yet not betray the widow to her ruin? What if he made a confederate of Eleanor? 'Twas in this spirit that Bertie Stanhope set about his wooing.

"But you are not going to leave Barchester?" asked Eleanor.

"I do not know," he replied; "I hardly know yet what I am going to do. But it is at any rate certain that I must do something."

"You mean about your profession?" said she.

"Yes, about my profession, if you can call it one."

"And is it not one?" said Eleanor. "Were I a man, I know none I should prefer to it, except painting. And I believe the one is as much in your power as the other."

"Yes, just about equally so," said Bertie with a little touch of inward satire directed at himself. He knew in his heart that he would never make a penny by either.

"I have often wondered, Mr. Stanhope, why you do not exert yourself more," said Eleanor, who felt a friendly fondness for the man with whom she was walking. "But I know it is very impertinent in me to say so."

"Impertinent!" said he. "Not so, but much too kind. It is much too kind in you to take any interest in so idle a scamp."

"But you are not a scamp, though you are perhaps idle. And I do take an interest in you, a very great interest," she added in a voice which almost made him resolve to change his mind. "And when I call you idle, I know you are only so for the present moment. Why can't you settle steadily to work here in Barchester?"

"And make busts of the bishop, dean, and chapter? Or perhaps, if I achieve a great success, obtain a commission to put up an elaborate tombstone over a prebendary's widow, a dead lady with a Grecian nose, a bandeau, and an intricate lace veil; lying of course on a marble sofa from among the legs of which death will be creeping out and poking at his victim with a small toasting-fork."

Eleanor laughed, but yet she thought that if the surviving prebendary paid the bill, the object of the artist as a professional man would in a great measure be obtained.

"I don't know about the dean and chapter and the prebendary's widow," said Eleanor. "Of course you must take them as they come. But the fact of your having a great cathedral in which such ornaments are required could not but be in your favour."

"No real artist could descend to the ornamentation of a cathedral," said Bertie, who had his ideas of the high ecstatic ambition of art, as indeed all artists have who are not in receipt of a good income. "Buildings should be fitted to grace the sculpture, not the sculpture to grace the building."

"Yes, when the work of art is good enough to merit it. Do you, Mr. Stanhope, do something sufficiently excellent and we ladies of Barchester will erect for it a fitting receptacle. Come, what shall the subject be?"

"I'll put you in your pony chair, Mrs. Bold, as Dannecker put Ariadne on her lion. Only you must promise to sit for me."

"My ponies are too tame, I fear, and my broad-brimmed straw hat will not look so well in marble as the lace veil of the prebendary's wife."

"If you will not consent to that, Mrs. Bold, I will consent to try no other subject in Barchester."

"You are determined then to push your fortune in other lands?"

"I am determined," said Bertie slowly and significantly, as he tried to bring up his mind to a great resolve; "I am determined in this matter to be guided wholly by you."

"Wholly by me?" said Eleanor, astonished at, and not quite liking, his altered manner.

"Wholly by you," said Bertie, dropping his companion's arm and standing before her on the path. In their walk they had come exactly to the spot in which Eleanor had been provoked into slapping Mr. Slope's face. Could it be possible that this place was peculiarly unpropitious to her comfort? Could it be possible that she should here have to encounter yet another amorous swain?

"If you will be guided by me, Mr. Stanhope, you will set yourself down to steady and persevering work, and you will be ruled by your father as to the place in which it will be most advisable for you to do so."

"Nothing could be more prudent, if only it were practicable. But now, if you will let me, I will tell you how it is that I will be guided by you, and why. Will you let me tell you?"

"I really do not know what you can have to tell."

"No, you cannot know. It is impossible that you should. But we have been very good friends, Mrs. Bold, have we not?"

"Yes, I think we have," said she, observing in his demeanour an earnestness very unusual with him.

"You were kind enough to say just now that you took an interest in me, and I was perhaps vain enough to believe you."

"There is no vanity in that; I do so as your sister's brother—and as my own friend also."

"Well, I don't deserve that you should feel so kindly towards me," said Bertie, "but upon my word I am very grateful for it," and he paused awhile, hardly knowing how to introduce the subject that he had in hand.

And it was no wonder that he found it difficult. He had to make known to his companion the scheme that had been prepared to rob her of her wealth, he had to tell her that he had intended to marry her without loving her, or else that he loved her without intending to marry her; and he had also to bespeak from her not only his own pardon, but also that of his sister, and induce Mrs. Bold to protest in her future communion with Charlotte that an offer had been duly made to her and duly rejected.

Bertie Stanhope was not prone to be very diffident of his own conversational powers, but it did seem to him that he was about to tax them almost too far. He hardly knew where to begin, and he hardly knew where he should end.

By this time Eleanor was again walking on slowly by his side, not taking his arm as she had heretofore done but listening very intently for whatever Bertie might have to say to her.

"I wish to be guided by you," said he; "indeed, in this matter there is no one else who can set me right."

"Oh, that must be nonsense," said she.

"Well, listen to me now, Mrs. Bold, and if you can help it, pray don't be angry with me."

"Angry!" said she.

"Oh, indeed you will have cause to be so. You know how very much attached to you my sister Charlotte is."

Eleanor acknowledged that she did.

"Indeed she is; I never knew her to love anyone so warmly on so short an acquaintance. You know also how well she loves me?"

Eleanor now made no answer, but she felt the blood tingle in her cheek as she gathered from what he said the probable result of this double-barrelled love on the part of Miss Stanhope.

"I am her only brother, Mrs. Bold, and it is not to be wondered at that she should love me. But you do not yet know Charlotte—you do not know how entirely the well-being of our family hangs on her. Without her to manage for us, I do not know how we should get on from day to day. You cannot yet have observed all this."

Eleanor had indeed observed a good deal of this; she did not, however, now say so, but allowed him to proceed with his story.

"You cannot therefore be surprised that Charlotte should be most anxious to do the best for us all."

Eleanor said that she was not at all surprised.

"And she has had a very difficult game to play, Mrs. Bold—a very difficult game. Poor Madeline's unfortunate marriage and terrible accident, my mother's ill-health, my father's absence from England, and last, and worse perhaps, my own roving, idle spirit have almost been too much for her. You cannot wonder if among all her cares one of the foremost is to see me settled in the world."

Eleanor on this occasion expressed no acquiescence. She certainly supposed that a formal offer was to be made and could not but think that so singular an exordium was never before made by a gentleman in a similar position. Mr. Slope had annoyed her by the excess of his ardour. It was quite clear that no such danger was to be feared from Mr. Stanhope. Prudential motives alone actuated him. Not only was he about to make love because his sister told him, but he also took the precaution of explaining all this before he began. 'Twas thus, we may presume, that the matter presented itself to Mrs. Bold.

When he had got so far, Bertie began poking the gravel with a little cane which he carried. He still kept moving on, but very slowly, and his companion moved slowly by his side, not inclined to assist him in the task the performance of which appeared to be difficult to him.

"Knowing how fond she is of yourself, Mrs. Bold, cannot you imagine what scheme should have occurred to her?"

"I can imagine no better scheme, Mr. Stanhope, than the one I proposed to you just now."

"No," said he somewhat lackadaisically; "I suppose that would be the best, but Charlotte thinks another plan might be joined with it. She wants me to marry you."

A thousand remembrances flashed across Eleanor's mind all in a moment—how Charlotte had talked about and praised her brother, how she had continually contrived to throw the two of them together, how she had encouraged all manner of little intimacies, how she had with singular cordiality persisted in treating Eleanor as one of the family. All this had been done to secure her comfortable income for the benefit of one of the family!

Such a feeling as this is very bitter when it first impresses itself on a young mind. To the old, such plots and plans, such matured schemes for obtaining the goods of this world without the trouble of earning them, such long-headed attempts to convert "tuum" into "meum" are the ways of life to which they are accustomed. 'Tis thus that many live, and it therefore behoves all those who are well-to-do in the world to be on their guard against those who are not. With them it is the success that disgusts, not the attempt. But Eleanor had not yet learnt to look on her money as a source of danger; she had not begun to regard herself as fair game to be hunted down by hungry gentlemen. She had enjoyed the society of the Stanhopes, she had greatly liked the cordiality of Charlotte, and had been happy in her new friends. Now she saw the cause of all this kindness, and her mind was opened to a new phase of human life.

"Miss Stanhope," said she haughtily, "has been contriving for me a great deal of honour, but she might have saved herself the trouble. I am not sufficiently ambitious."

"Pray don't be angry with her, Mrs. Bold," said he, "or with me either."

"Certainly not with you, Mr. Stanhope," said she with considerable sarcasm in her tone. "Certainly not with you."

"No—nor with her," said he imploringly.

"And why, may I ask you, Mr. Stanhope, have you told me this singular story? For I may presume I may judge by your manner of telling it that—that—that you and your sister are not exactly of one mind on the subject."

"No, we are not."

"And if so," said Mrs. Bold, who was now really angry with the unnecessary insult which she thought had been offered to her. "And if so, why has it been worth your while to tell me all this?"

"I did once think, Mrs. Bold—that you—that you—"

The widow now again became entirely impassive, and would not lend the slightest assistance to her companion.

"I did once think that you perhaps might—might have been taught to regard me as more than a friend."

"Never!" said Mrs. Bold, "never. If I have ever allowed myself to do anything to encourage such an idea, I have been very much to blame—very much to blame indeed."

"You never have," said Bertie, who really had a good-natured anxiety to make what he said as little unpleasant as possible. "You never have, and I have seen for some time that I had no chance—but my sister's hopes ran higher. I have not mistaken you, Mrs. Bold, though perhaps she has."

"Then why have you said all this to me?"

"Because I must not anger her."

"And will not this anger her? Upon my word, Mr. Stanhope, I do not understand the policy of your family. Oh, how I wish I was at home!" And as she expressed the wish she could restrain herself no longer and burst out into a flood of tears.

Poor Bertie was greatly moved. "You shall have the carriage to yourself going home," said he; "at least you and my father. As for me, I can walk, or for the matter of that it does not much signify what I do." He perfectly understood that part of Eleanor's grief arose from the apparent necessity of her going back to Barchester in the carriage with her second suitor.

This somewhat mollified her. "Oh, Mr. Stanhope," said she, "why should you have made me so miserable? What will you have gained by telling me all this?"

He had not even yet explained to her the most difficult part of his proposition; he had not told her that she was to be a party to the little deception which he intended to play off upon his sister. This suggestion had still to be made, and as it was absolutely necessary, he proceeded to make it.

We need not follow him through the whole of his statement. At last, and not without considerable difficulty, he made Eleanor understand why he had let her into his confidence, seeing that he no longer intended her the honour of a formal offer. At last he made her comprehend the part which she was destined to play in this little family comedy.

But when she did understand it, she was only more angry with him than ever; more angry, not only with him, but with Charlotte also. Her fair name was to be bandied about between them in different senses, and each sense false. She was to be played off by the sister against the father, and then by the brother against the sister. Her dear friend Charlotte, with all her agreeable sympathy and affection, was striving to sacrifice her for the Stanhope family welfare; and Bertie, who, as he now proclaimed himself, was over head and ears in debt, completed the compliment of owning that he did not care to have his debts paid at so great a sacrifice of himself. Then she was asked to conspire together with this unwilling suitor for the sake of making the family believe that he had in obedience to their commands done his best to throw himself thus away!

She lifted up her face when he had finished, and looking at him with much dignity, even through her tears, she said:

"I regret to say it, Mr. Stanhope, but after what has passed I believe that all intercourse between your family and myself had better cease."

"Well, perhaps it had," said Bertie naïvely; "perhaps that will be better at any rate for a time; and then Charlotte will think you are offended at what I have done."

"And now I will go back to the house, if you please," said Eleanor. "I can find my way by myself, Mr. Stanhope: after what has passed," she added, "I would rather go alone."

"But I must find the carriage for you, Mrs. Bold; and I must tell my father that you will return with him alone; and I must make some excuse to him for not going with you; and I must bid the servant put you down at your own house, for I suppose you will not now choose to see them again in the close."

There was a truth about this, and a perspicuity in making arrangements for lessening her immediate embarrassment, which had some effect in softening Eleanor's anger. So she suffered herself to walk by his side over the now deserted lawn, till they came to the drawing-room window. There was something about Bertie Stanhope which gave him, in the estimation of everyone, a different standing from that which any other man would occupy under similar circumstances. Angry as Eleanor was, and great as was her cause for anger, she was not half as angry with him as she would have been with anyone else. He was apparently so simple, so good-natured, so unaffected and easy to talk to, that she had already half-forgiven him before he was at the drawing-room window.

When they arrived there, Dr. Stanhope was sitting nearly alone with Mr. and Miss Thorne; one or two other unfortunates were there, who from one cause or another were still delayed in getting away, but they were every moment getting fewer in number.

As soon as he had handed Eleanor over to his father, Bertie started off to the front gate in search of the carriage, and there he waited leaning patiently against the front wall, comfortably smoking a cigar, till it came up. When he returned to the room, Dr. Stanhope and Eleanor were alone with their hosts.

"At last, Miss Thorne," said he cheerily, "I have come to relieve you. Mrs. Bold and my father are the last roses of the very delightful summer you have given us, and desirable as Mrs. Bold's society always is, now at least you must be glad to see the last flowers plucked from the tree."

Miss Thorne declared that she was delighted to have Mrs. Bold and Dr. Stanhope still with her, and Mr. Thorne would have said the same, had he not been checked by a yawn, which he could not suppress.

"Father, will you give your arm to Mrs. Bold?" said Bertie: and so the last adieux were made, and the prebendary led out Mrs. Bold, followed by his son.

"I shall be home soon after you," said he as the two got into the carriage.

"Are you not coming in the carriage?" said the father.

"No, no; I have someone to see on the road, and shall walk. John, mind you drive to Mrs. Bold's house first."

Eleanor, looking out of the window, saw him with his hat in his hand, bowing to her with his usual gay smile, as though nothing had happened to mar the tranquillity of the day. It was many a long year before she saw him again. Dr. Stanhope hardly spoke to her on her way home, and she was safely deposited by John at her own hall-door before the carriage drove into the close.

And thus our heroine played the last act of that day's melodrama.

CHAPTER XLIII

MR. AND MRS. QUIVERFUL ARE MADE HAPPY. MR. SLOPE IS ENCOURAGED BY THE PRESS

Before she started for Ullathorne, Mrs. Proudie, careful soul, caused two letters to be written, one by herself and one by her lord, to the inhabitants of Puddingdale vicarage, which made happy the hearth of those within it.

As soon as the departure of the horses left the bishop's stable-groom free for other services, that humble denizen of the diocese started on the bishop's own pony with the two dispatches. We have had so many letters lately that we will spare ourselves these. That from the bishop was simply a request that Mr. Quiverful would wait upon his lordship the next morning at 11 A.M.; that from the lady was as simply a request that Mrs. Quiverful would do the same by her, though it was couched in somewhat longer and more grandiloquent phraseology.

It had become a point of conscience with Mrs. Proudie to urge the settlement of this great hospital question. She was resolved that Mr. Quiverful should have it. She was resolved that there should be no more doubt or delay, no more refusals and resignations, no more secret negotiations carried on by Mr. Slope on his own account in opposition to her behests.

"Bishop," she said immediately after breakfast on the morning of that eventful day, "have you signed the appointment yet?"

"No, my dear, not yet; it is not exactly signed as yet."

"Then do it," said the lady.

The bishop did it, and a very pleasant day indeed he spent at Ullathorne. And when he got home, he had a glass of hot negus in his wife's sitting-room, and read the last number of the Little Dorrit of the day with great inward satisfaction. Oh, husbands, oh, my marital friends, what great comfort is there to be derived from a wife well obeyed!

Much perturbation and flutter, high expectation and renewed hopes, were occasioned at Puddingdale, by the receipt of these episcopal dispatches. Mrs. Quiverful, whose careful ear caught the sound of the pony's feet as he trotted up to the vicarage kitchen door, brought them in hurriedly to her husband. She was at the moment concocting the Irish stew destined to satisfy the noonday wants of fourteen young birds, let alone the parent couple. She had taken the letters from the man's hands between the folds of her capacious apron so as to save them from the contamination of the stew, and in this guise she brought them to her husband's desk.

They at once divided the spoil, each taking that addressed to the other. "Quiverful," said she with impressive voice, "you are to be at the palace at eleven to-morrow."

"And so are you, my dear," said he, almost gasping with the importance of the tidings—and then they exchanged letters.

"She'd never have sent for me again," said the lady, "if it wasn't all right."

"Oh, my dear, don't be too certain," said the gentleman, "Only think if it should be wrong."

"She'd never have sent for me, Q., if it wasn't all right," again argued the lady. "She's stiff and hard and proud as piecrust, but I think she's right at bottom." Such was Mrs. Quiverful's verdict about Mrs. Proudie, to which in after times she always adhered. People when they get their income doubled usually think that those through whose instrumentality this little ceremony is performed are right at bottom.

"Oh, Letty!" said Mr. Quiverful, rising from his well-worn seat.

"Oh, Q.!" said Mrs. Quiverful, and then the two, unmindful of the kitchen apron, the greasy fingers, and the adherent Irish stew, threw themselves warmly into each other's arms.

"For heaven's sake, don't let anyone cajole you out of it again," said the wife.

"Let me alone for that," said the husband with a look of almost fierce determination, pressing his fist as he spoke rigidly on his desk, as though he had Mr. Slope's head below his knuckles and meant to keep it there.

"I wonder how soon it will be?" said she.

"I wonder whether it will be at all?" said he, still doubtful.

"Well, I won't say too much," said the lady. "The cup has slipped twice before, and it may fall altogether this time, but I'll not believe it. He'll give you the appointment to-morrow. You'll find he will."

"Heaven send he may," said Mr. Quiverful solemnly. And who that considers the weight of the burden on this man's back will say that the prayer was an improper one? There were fourteen of them—fourteen of them living—as Mrs. Quiverful had so powerfully urged in the presence of the bishop's wife. As long as promotion cometh from any human source, whether north or south, east or west, will not such a claim as this hold good, in spite of all our examination tests, *detur digniori's*, and optimist tendencies? It is fervently to be hoped that it may. Till we can become divine, we must be content to be human, lest in our hurry for a change we sink to something lower.

And then the pair, sitting down lovingly together, talked over all their difficulties, as they so often did, and all their hopes, as they so seldom were enabled to do.

"You had better call on that man, Q., as you come away from the palace," said Mrs. Quiverful, pointing to an angry call for money from the Barchester draper, which the postman had left at the vicarage that morning. Cormorant that he was, unjust, hungry cormorant! When rumour first got abroad that the Quiverfuls were to go to the hospital, this fellow with fawning eagerness had pressed his goods upon the wants of the poor clergyman. He had done so, feeling that he should be paid from the hospital funds, and flattering himself that a man with fourteen children, and money wherewithal to clothe them, could not but be an excellent customer. As soon as the second rumour reached him, he applied for his money angrily.

And "the fourteen"—or such of them as were old enough to hope and discuss their hopes—talked over their golden future. The tall grown girls whispered to each other of possible Barchester parties, of possible allowances for dress, of a possible piano—the one they had in the vicarage was so weather-beaten with the storms of years and children as to be no longer worthy of the name—of the pretty garden, and the pretty house. 'Twas of such things it most behoved them to whisper.

And the younger fry, they did not content themselves with whispers, but shouted to each other of their new playground beneath our dear ex-warden's well-loved elms, of their future own gardens, of marbles to be procured in the wished-for city, and of the rumour which had reached them of a Barchester school.

'Twas in vain that their cautious mother tried to instil into their breasts the very feeling she had striven to banish from that of their father; 'twas in vain that she repeated to the girls that "there's many a slip 'twixt the cup and the lip;" 'twas in vain she attempted to make the children believe that they were to live at Puddingdale all their lives. Hopes mounted high, and would not have themselves quelled. The neighbouring farmers heard the news and came in to congratulate them. 'Twas Mrs. Quiverful herself who had kindled the fire, and in the first outbreak of her renewed expectations she did it so thoroughly that it was quite past her power to put it out again.

Poor matron! Good, honest matron, doing thy duty in the state to which thou hast been called, heartily if not contentedly; let the fire burn on; on this occasion the flames will not scorch; they shall warm thee and thine. 'Tis ordained that that husband of thine, that Q. of thy bosom, shall reign supreme for years to come over the bedesmen of Hiram's Hospital.

And the last in all Barchester to mar their hopes, had he heard and seen all that passed at Puddingdale that day, would have been Mr. Harding. What wants had he to set in opposition to those of such a regiment of young ravens? There are fourteen of them living! With him, at any rate, let us say that that argument would have been sufficient for the appointment of Mr. Quiverful.

In the morning Q. and his wife kept their appointments with that punctuality which bespeaks an expectant mind. The friendly farmer's gig was borrowed, and in that they went, discussing many things by the way. They had instructed the household to expect them back by one, and injunctions were given to the eldest pledge to have ready by that accustomed hour the remainder of the huge stew which the provident mother had prepared on the previous day. The hands of the kitchen clock came round to two, three, four, before the farmer's gig wheels were again heard at the vicarage gate. With what palpitating hearts were the returning wanderers greeted!

"I suppose, children, you all thought we were never coming back any more?" said the mother as she slowly let down her solid foot till it rested on the step of the gig. "Well, such a day as we've had!" and then leaning heavily on a big boy's shoulder, she stepped once more on terra firma.

There was no need for more than the tone of her voice to tell them that all was right. The Irish stew might burn itself to cinders now.

Then there was such kissing and hugging, such crying and laughing. Mr. Quiverful could not sit still at all, but kept walking from room to room, then out into the garden, then down the avenue into the road, and then back again to his wife. She, however, lost no time so idly.

"We must go to work at once, girls, and that in earnest. Mrs. Proudie expects us to be in the hospital house on the 15th of October."

Had Mrs. Proudie expressed a wish that they should all be there on the next morning, the girls would have had nothing to say against it.

"And when will the pay begin?" asked the eldest boy.

"To-day, my dear," said the gratified mother.

"Oh, that is jolly," said the boy.

"Mrs. Proudie insisted on our going down to the house," continued the mother, "and when there, I thought I might save a journey by measuring some of the rooms and windows; so I got a knot of tape from Bobbins. Bobbins is as civil as you please, now."

"I wouldn't thank him," said Letty the younger.

"Oh, it's the way of the world, my dear. They all do just the same. You might just as well be angry with the turkey cock for gobbling at you. It's the bird's nature." And as she enunciated to her bairns the upshot of her practical experience, she pulled from her pocket the portions of tape which showed the length and breadth of the various rooms at the hospital house.

And so we will leave her happy in her toils.

The Quiverfuls had hardly left the palace, and Mrs. Proudie was still holding forth on the matter to her husband, when another visitor was announced in the person of Dr. Gwynne. The Master of Lazarus had asked for the bishop and not for Mrs. Proudie, and therefore when he was shown into the study, he was surprised rather than rejoiced to find the lady there.

But we must go back a little, and it shall be but a little, for a difficulty begins to make itself manifest in the necessity of disposing of all our friends in the small remainder of this one volume. Oh, that Mr. Longman would allow me a fourth! It should transcend the other three as the seventh heaven transcends all the lower stages of celestial bliss.

Going home in the carriage that evening from Ullathorne, Dr. Gwynne had not without difficulty brought round his friend the archdeacon to a line of tactics much less bellicose than that which his own taste would have preferred. "It will be unseemly in us to show ourselves in a bad humour; moreover, we have no power in this matter, and it will therefore be bad policy to act as though we had." 'Twas thus the Master of Lazarus argued. "If," he continued, "the bishop be determined to appoint another to the hospital, threats will not prevent him, and threats should not be lightly used by an archdeacon to his bishop. If he will place a stranger in the hospital, we can only leave him to the indignation of others. It is probable that such a step may not eventually injure your father-in-law. I will see the bishop, if you will allow me—alone." At this the archdeacon winced visibly. "Yes, alone; for so I shall be calmer; and then I shall at any rate learn what he does mean to do in the matter."

The archdeacon puffed and blew, put up the carriage window and then put it down again, argued the matter up to his own gate, and at last gave way. Everybody was against him, his own wife, Mr. Harding, and Dr. Gwynne.

"Pray keep him out of hot water, Dr. Gwynne," Mrs. Grantly had said to her guest.

"My dearest madam, I'll do my best," the courteous master had replied. 'Twas thus he did it and earned for himself the gratitude of Mrs. Grantly.

And now we may return to the bishop's study.

Dr. Gwynne had certainly not foreseen the difficulty which here presented itself. He— together with all the clerical world of England—had heard it rumoured about that Mrs. Proudie did not confine herself to her wardrobes, still-rooms, and laundries; but yet it had never occurred to him that if he called on a bishop at one o'clock in the day, he could by any possibility find him closeted with his wife; or that if he did so, the wife would remain longer than necessary to make her curtsey. It appeared, however, as though in the present case Mrs. Proudie had no idea of retreating.

The bishop had been very much pleased with Dr. Gwynne on the preceding day, and of course thought that Dr. Gwynne had been as much pleased with him. He attributed the visit solely to compliment, and thought it an extremely gracious and proper thing for the Master of Lazarus to drive over from Plumstead specially to call at the palace so soon after his arrival in the country. The fact that they were not on the same side either in politics or doctrines made the compliment the greater. The bishop, therefore, was all smiles. And Mrs. Proudie, who liked people with good handles to their names, was also very well disposed to welcome the Master of Lazarus.

"We had a charming party at Ullathorne, Master, had we not?" said she. "I hope Mrs. Grantly got home without fatigue."

Dr. Gwynne said that they had all been a little tired, but were none the worse this morning.

"An excellent person, Miss Thorne," suggested the bishop.

"And an exemplary Christian, I am told," said Mrs. Proudie.

Dr. Gwynne declared that he was very glad to hear it.

"I have not seen her Sabbath-day schools yet," continued the lady, "but I shall make a point of doing so before long."

Dr. Gwynne merely bowed at this intimation. He had heard something of Mrs. Proudie and her Sunday-schools, both from Dr. Grantly and Mr. Harding.

"By the by, Master," continued the lady, "I wonder whether Mrs. Grantly would like me to drive over and inspect her Sabbath-day school. I hear that it is most excellently kept."

Dr. Gwynne really could not say. He had no doubt Mrs. Grantly would be most happy to see Mrs. Proudie any day Mrs. Proudie would do her the honour of calling: that was, of course, if Mrs. Grantly should happen to be at home.

A slight cloud darkened the lady's brow. She saw that her offer was not taken in good part. This generation of unregenerated vipers was still perverse, stiff-necked, and hardened in their iniquity. "The archdeacon, I know," said she, "sets his face against these institutions."

At this Dr. Gwynne laughed slightly. It was but a smile. Had he given his cap for it he could not have helped it.

Mrs. Proudie frowned again. "'Suffer little children, and forbid them not,'" she said. "Are we not to remember that, Dr. Gwynne? 'Take heed that ye despise not one of these little ones.' Are we not to remember that, Dr. Gwynne?" And at each of these questions she raised at him her menacing forefinger.

"Certainly, madam, certainly," said the master, "and so does the archdeacon, I am sure, on weekdays as well as on Sundays."

"On weekdays you can't take heed not to despise them," said Mrs. Proudie, "because then they are out in the fields. On weekdays they belong to their parents, but on Sundays they ought to belong to the clergyman." And the finger was again raised.

The master began to understand and to share the intense disgust which the archdeacon always expressed when Mrs. Proudie's name was mentioned. What was he to do with such a woman as this? To take his hat and go would have been his natural resource, but then he did not wish to be foiled in his object.

"My lord," said he, "I wanted to ask you a question on business, if you could spare me one moment's leisure. I know I must apologize for so disturbing you, but in truth I will not detain you five minutes."

"Certainly, Master, certainly," said the bishop; "my time is quite yours—pray make no apology, pray make no apology."

"You have a great deal to do just at the present moment, Bishop. Do not forget how extremely busy you are at present," said Mrs. Proudie, whose spirit was now up, for she was angry with her visitor.

"I will not delay his lordship much above a minute," said the Master of Lazarus, rising from his chair and expecting that Mrs. Proudie would now go, or else that the bishop would lead the way into another room.

But neither event seemed likely to occur, and Dr. Gwynne stood for a moment silent in the middle of the room.

"Perhaps it's about Hiram's Hospital?" suggested Mrs. Proudie.

Dr. Gwynne, lost in astonishment, and not knowing what else on earth to do, confessed that his business with the bishop was connected with Hiram's Hospital.

"His lordship has finally conferred the appointment on Mr. Quiverful this morning," said the lady.

Dr. Gwynne made a simple reference to the bishop, and finding that the lady's statement was formally confirmed, he took his leave. "That comes of the reform bill," he said to himself as he walked down the bishop's avenue. "Well, at any rate the Greek play bishops were not so bad as that."

It has been said that Mr. Slope, as he started for Ullathorne, received a dispatch from his friend Mr. Towers, which had the effect of putting him in that high good humour which subsequent events somewhat untowardly damped. It ran as follows. Its shortness will be its sufficient apology.

MY DEAR SIR, I wish you every success. I don't know that I can help you, but if I can, I will.

> Yours ever,
> T. T.
> 30/9/185—

There was more in this than in all Sir Nicholas Fitzwhiggin's flummery; more than in all the bishop's promises, even had they been ever so sincere; more than in any archbishop's good word, even had it been possible to obtain it. Tom Towers would do for him what he could.

Mr. Slope had from his youth upwards been a firm believer in the public press. He had dabbled in it himself ever since he had taken his degree, and he regarded it as the great arranger and distributor of all future British terrestrial affairs whatever. He had not yet arrived at the age, an age which sooner or later comes to most of us, which dissipates the golden dreams of youth. He delighted in the idea of wresting power from the hands of his country's magnates and placing it in a custody which was at any rate nearer to his own reach. Sixty thousand broadsheets dispersing themselves daily among his reading fellow citizens formed in his eyes a better depot for supremacy than a throne at Windsor, a cabinet in Downing Street, or even an assembly at Westminster. And on this subject we must not quarrel with Mr. Slope, for the feeling is too general to be met with disrespect.

Tom Towers was as good, if not better, than his promise. On the following morning "The Jupiter," spouting forth public opinion with sixty thousand loud clarions, did proclaim to the world that Mr. Slope was the fitting man for the vacant post. It was pleasant for Mr. Slope to read the following lines in the Barchester news-room, which he did within thirty minutes after the morning train from London had reached the city.

> It is just now five years since we called the attention of our readers to the quiet city of Barchester. From that day to this, we have in no way meddled with the affairs of that happy ecclesiastical community. Since then, an old bishop has died there, and a young bishop has been installed; but we believe we did not do more than give some customary record of the interesting event. Nor are we now about to meddle very deeply in the affairs of the diocese. If any of the chapter feel a qualm of conscience on reading thus far, let it be quieted. Above all, let the mind of the new bishop be at rest. We are now not armed for war, but approach the reverend towers of the old cathedral with an olive branch in our hands.

It will be remembered that at the time alluded to, now five years past, we had occasion to remark on the state of a charity in Barchester called Hiram's Hospital. We thought that it was maladministered, and that the very estimable and reverend gentleman who held the office of warden was somewhat too highly paid for duties which were somewhat too easily performed. This gentleman—and we say it in all sincerity and with no touch of sarcasm—had never looked on the matter in this light before. We do not wish to take praise to ourselves whether praise be due to us or not. But the consequence of our remark was that the warden did look into the matter, and finding on so doing that he himself could come to no other opinion than that expressed by us, he very creditably threw up the appointment. The then bishop as creditably declined to fill the vacancy till the affair was put on a better footing. Parliament then took it up, and we have now the satisfaction of informing our readers that Hiram's Hospital will be immediately reopened under new auspices. Heretofore, provision was made for the maintenance of twelve old men. This will now be extended to the fair sex, and twelve elderly women, if any such can be found in Barchester, will be added to the establishment. There will be a matron; there will, it is hoped, be schools attached for the poorest of the children of the poor, and there will be a steward. The warden, for there will still be a warden, will receive an income more in keeping with the extent of the charity than that heretofore paid. The stipend we believe will be £450. We may add that the excellent house which the former warden inhabited will still be attached to the situation.

Barchester Hospital cannot perhaps boast a world-wide reputation, but as we adverted to its state of decadence, we think it right also to advert to its renaissance. May it go on and prosper. Whether the salutary reform which has been introduced within its walls has been carried as far as could have been desired may be doubtful. The important question of the school appears to be somewhat left to the discretion of the new warden. This might have been made the most important part of the establishment, and the new warden, whom we trust we shall not offend by the freedom of our remarks, might have been selected with some view to his fitness as schoolmaster. But we will not now look a gift-horse in the mouth. May the hospital go on and prosper! The situation of warden has of course been offered to the gentleman who so honourably vacated it five years since, but we are given to understand that he has declined it. Whether the ladies who have been introduced be in his estimation too much for his powers of control, whether it be that the diminished income does not offer to him sufficient temptation to resume his old place, or that he has in the meantime assumed other clerical duties, we do not know. We are, however, informed that he has refused the offer and that the situation has been accepted by Mr. Quiverful, the vicar of Puddingdale.

So much we think is due to Hiram redivivus. But while we are on the subject of Barchester, we will venture with all respectful humility to express our opinion on another matter connected with the ecclesiastical polity of that ancient city. Dr. Trefoil, the dean, died yesterday. A short record of his death, giving his age and the various pieces of preferment which he has at different times held, will be found in another column of this paper. The only fault we knew in him was his age, and as that is a crime of which we all hope to be guilty, we will not bear heavily on it. May he rest in peace! But though the great age of an expiring dean cannot be made matter of reproach, we are not inclined to look on such a fault as at all pardonable in a dean just brought to the birth. We do hope that the days of sexagenarian appointments are past. If we want deans, we must want them for some purpose. That purpose will necessarily be better fulfilled by a man of forty than by a man of sixty. If we are to pay deans at all, we are to pay them for some sort of work. That work, be it what it may, will be best performed by a workman in the prime of life. Dr. Trefoil, we see, was eighty when he died. As we have as yet completed no plan for pensioning superannuated clergymen, we do not wish to get rid of any existing deans of that age. But we prefer having as few such as possible. If a man of seventy be now appointed, we beg to point out to Lord —— that he will be past all use in a year or two, if indeed he be not so at the present moment. His lordship will allow us to remind him that all men are not evergreens like himself.

We hear that Mr. Slope's name has been mentioned for this preferment. Mr. Slope is at present chaplain to the bishop. A better man could hardly be selected. He is a man of talent, young, active, and conversant with the affairs of the cathedral; he is moreover, we conscientiously believe, a truly pious clergyman. We know that his services in the city of Barchester have been highly appreciated. He is an eloquent preacher and a ripe scholar. Such a selection as this would go far to raise the confidence of the public in the present administration of church patronage and would teach men to believe that from henceforth the establishment of our church will not afford easy couches to worn-out clerical voluptuaries.

Standing at a reading-desk in the Barchester news-room, Mr. Slope digested this article with considerable satisfaction. What was therein said as to the hospital was now comparatively a matter of indifference to him. He was certainly glad that he had not succeeded in restoring to the place the father of that virago who had so audaciously outraged all decency in his person, and was so far satisfied. But Mrs. Proudie's nominee was appointed, and he was so far dissatisfied. His mind, however, was now soaring above Mrs. Bold or Mrs. Proudie. He was sufficiently conversant with the tactics of "The Jupiter" to know that the pith of the article would lie in the last paragraph. The place of honour was given to him, and it was indeed as honourable as even he could have wished. He was very grateful to his friend Mr. Towers, and with full heart looked forward to the day when he might entertain him in princely style at his own full-spread board in the deanery dining-room.

It had been well for Mr. Slope that Dr. Trefoil had died in the autumn. Those caterers for our morning repast, the staff of "The Jupiter," had been sorely put to it for the last month to find a sufficiency of proper pabulum. Just then there was no talk of a new American president. No wonderful tragedies had occurred on railway trains in Georgia, or elsewhere. There was a dearth of broken banks, and a dead dean with the necessity for a live one was a godsend. Had Dr. Trefoil died in June, Mr. Towers would probably not have known so much about the piety of Mr. Slope.

And here we will leave Mr. Slope for awhile in his triumph, explaining, however, that his feelings were not altogether of a triumphant nature. His rejection by the widow, or rather the method of his rejection, galled him terribly. For days to come he positively felt the sting upon his cheek whenever he thought of what had been done to him. He could not refrain from calling her by harsh names, speaking to himself as he walked through the streets of Barchester. When he said his prayers, he could not bring himself to forgive her. When he strove to do so, his mind recoiled from the attempt, and in lieu of forgiving ran off in a double spirit of vindictiveness, dwelling on the extent of the injury he had received. And so his prayers dropped senseless from his lips.

And then the signora—what would he not have given to be able to hate her also? As it was, he worshipped the very sofa on which she was ever lying.

And thus it was not all rose colour with Mr. Slope, although his hopes ran high.

CHAPTER XLIV

MRS. BOLD AT HOME

Poor Mrs. Bold, when she got home from Ullathorne on the evening of Miss Thorne's party, was very unhappy and, moreover, very tired. Nothing fatigues the body so much as weariness of spirit, and Eleanor's spirit was indeed weary.

Dr. Stanhope had civilly but not very cordially asked her in to tea, and her manner of refusal convinced the worthy doctor that he need not repeat the invitation. He had not exactly made himself a party to the intrigue which was to convert the late Mr. Bold's patrimony into an income for his hopeful son, but he had been well aware what was going on. And he was well aware also, when he perceived that Bertie declined accompanying them home in the carriage, that the affair had gone off.

Eleanor was very much afraid that Charlotte would have darted out upon her, as the prebendary got out at his own door, but Bertie had thoughtfully saved her from this by causing the carriage to go round by her own house. This also Dr. Stanhope understood and allowed to pass by without remark.

When she got home, she found Mary Bold in the drawing-room with the child in her lap. She rushed forward and, throwing herself on her knees, kissed the little fellow till she almost frightened him.

"Oh, Mary, I am so glad you did not go. It was an odious party."

Now the question of Mary's going had been one greatly mooted between them. Mrs. Bold, when invited, had been the guest of the Grantlys, and Miss Thorne, who had chiefly known Eleanor at the hospital or at Plumstead Rectory, had forgotten all about Mary Bold. Her sister-in-law had implored her to go under her wing and had offered to write to Miss Thorne, or to call on her. But Miss Bold had declined. In fact, Mr. Bold had not been very popular with such people as the Thornes, and his sister would not go among them unless she were specially asked to do so.

"Well, then," said Mary cheerfully, "I have the less to regret."

"You have nothing to regret; but oh! Mary, I have—so much—so much;" and then she began kissing her boy, whom her caresses had roused from his slumbers. When she raised her head, Mary saw that the tears were running down her cheeks.

"Good heavens, Eleanor, what is the matter? What has happened to you—Eleanor—dearest Eleanor—what is the matter?" and Mary got up with the boy still in her arms.

"Give him to me—give him to me," said the young mother. "Give him to me, Mary," and she almost tore the child out of her sister's arms. The poor little fellow murmured somewhat at the disturbance but nevertheless nestled himself close into his mother's bosom.

"Here, Mary, take the cloak from me. My own own darling, darling, darling jewel. You are not false to me. Everybody else is false; everybody else is cruel. Mamma will care for nobody, nobody, nobody, but her own, own, own little man;" and she again kissed and pressed the baby and cried till the tears ran down over the child's face.

"Who has been cruel to you, Eleanor?" said Mary. "I hope I have not."

Now in this matter Eleanor had great cause for mental uneasiness. She could not certainly accuse her loving sister-in-law of cruelty; but she had to do that which was more galling: she had to accuse herself of imprudence against which her sister-in-law had warned her. Miss Bold had never encouraged Eleanor's acquaintance with Mr. Slope, and she had positively discouraged the friendship of the Stanhopes, as far as her usual gentle mode of speaking had permitted. Eleanor had only laughed at her, however, when she said that she disapproved of married women who lived apart from their husbands and suggested that Charlotte Stanhope never went to church. Now, however, Eleanor must either hold her tongue, which was quite impossible, or confess herself to have been utterly wrong, which was nearly equally so. So she staved off the evil day by more tears, and consoled herself by inducing little Johnny to rouse himself sufficiently to return her caresses.

"He is a darling—as true as gold. What would mamma do without him? Mamma would lie down and die if she had not her own Johnny Bold to give her comfort." This and much more she said of the same kind, and for a time made no other answer to Mary's inquiries.

This kind of consolation from the world's deceit is very common. Mothers obtain it from their children, and men from their dogs. Some men even do so from their walking-sticks, which is just as rational. How is it that we can take joy to ourselves in that we are not deceived by those who have not attained the art to deceive us? In a true man, if such can be found, or a true woman, much consolation may indeed be taken.

In the caresses of her child, however, Eleanor did receive consolation, and may ill befall the man who would begrudge it to her. The evil day, however, was only postponed. She had to tell her disagreeable tale to Mary, and she had also to tell it to her father. Must it not, indeed, be told to the whole circle of her acquaintance before she could be made to stand all right with them? At the present moment there was no one to whom she could turn for comfort. She hated Mr. Slope; that was a matter of course; in that feeling she revelled. She hated and despised the Stanhopes; but that feeling distressed her greatly. She had, as it were, separated herself from her old friends to throw herself into the arms of this family; and then how had they intended to use her? She could hardly reconcile herself to her own father, who had believed ill of her. Mary Bold had turned Mentor. That she could have forgiven had the Mentor turned out to be in the wrong, but Mentors in the right are not to be pardoned. She could not but hate the archdeacon, and now she hated him worse than ever, for she must in some sort humble herself before him. She hated her sister, for she was part and parcel of the archdeacon. And she would have hated Mr. Arabin if she could. He had pretended to regard her, and yet before her face he had hung over that Italian woman as though there had been no beauty in the world but hers—no other woman worth a moment's attention. And Mr. Arabin would have to learn all this about Mr. Slope! She told herself that she hated him, and she knew that she was lying to herself as she did so. She had no consolation but her baby, and of that she made the most. Mary, though she could not surmise what it was that had so violently affected her sister-in-law, saw at once that her grief was too great to be kept under control and waited patiently till the child should be in his cradle.

"You'll have some tea, Eleanor," she said.

"Oh, I don't care," said she, though in fact she must have been very hungry, for she had eaten nothing at Ullathorne.

Mary quietly made the tea, and buttered the bread, laid aside the cloak, and made things look comfortable.

"He's fast asleep," said she; "you're very tired; let me take him up to bed."

But Eleanor would not let her sister touch him. She looked wistfully at her baby's eyes, saw that they were lost in the deepest slumber, and then made a sort of couch for him on the sofa. She was determined that nothing should prevail upon her to let him out of her sight that night.

"Come, Nelly," said Mary, "don't be cross with me. I at least have done nothing to offend you."

"I an't cross," said Eleanor.

"Are you angry then? Surely you can't be angry with me."

"No, I an't angry—at least not with you."

"If you are not, drink the tea I have made for you. I am sure you must want it."

Eleanor did drink it, and allowed herself to be persuaded. She ate and drank, and as the inner woman was recruited she felt a little more charitable towards the world at large. At last she found words to begin her story, and before she went to bed she had made a clean breast of it and told everything—everything, that is, as to the lovers she had rejected; of Mr. Arabin she said not a word.

"I know I was wrong," said she, speaking of the blow she had given to Mr. Slope; "but I didn't know what he might do, and I had to protect myself."

"He richly deserved it," said Mary.

"Deserved it!" said Eleanor, whose mind as regarded Mr. Slope was almost bloodthirsty. "Had I stabbed him with a dagger, he would have deserved it. But what will they say about it at Plumstead?"

"I don't think I should tell them," said Mary. Eleanor began to think that she would not.

There could have been no kinder comforter than Mary Bold. There was not the slightest dash of triumph about her when she heard of the Stanhope scheme, nor did she allude to her former opinion when Eleanor called her late friend Charlotte a base, designing woman. She re-echoed all the abuse that was heaped on Mr. Slope's head and never hinted that she had said as much before. "I told you so, I told you so!" is the croak of a true Job's comforter. But Mary, when she found her friend lying in her sorrow and scraping herself with potsherds, forbore to argue and to exult. Eleanor acknowledged the merit of the forbearance, and at length allowed herself to be tranquilised.

On the next day she did not go out of the house. Barchester she thought would be crowded with Stanhopes and Slopes; perhaps also with Arabins and Grantlys. Indeed, there was hardly anyone among her friends whom she could have met without some cause of uneasiness.

In the course of the afternoon she heard that the dean was dead, and she also heard that Mr. Quiverful had been finally appointed to the hospital.

In the evening her father came to her, and then the story, or as much of it as she could bring herself to tell him, had to be repeated. He was not in truth much surprised at Mr. Slope's effrontery, but he was obliged to act as though he had been to save his daughter's feelings. He was, however, anything but skilful in his deceit, and she saw through it.

"I see," said she, "that you think it only in the common course of things that Mr. Slope should have treated me in this way." She had said nothing to him about the embrace, nor yet of the way in which it had been met.

"I do not think it at all strange," said he, "that anyone should admire my Eleanor."

"It is strange to me," said she, "that any man should have so much audacity, without ever having received the slightest encouragement."

To this Mr. Harding answered nothing. With the archdeacon it would have been the text for a rejoinder which would not have disgraced Bildad the Shuhite.

"But you'll tell the archdeacon?" asked Mr. Harding.

"Tell him what?" said she sharply.

"Or Susan?" continued Mr. Harding. "You'll tell Susan; you'll let them know that they wronged you in supposing that this man's addresses would be agreeable to you."

"They may find that out their own way," said she; "I shall not ever willingly mention Mr. Slope's name to either of them."

"But I may."

"I have no right to hinder you from doing anything that may be necessary to your own comfort, but pray do not do it for my sake. Dr. Grantly never thought well of me, and never will. I don't know now that I am even anxious that he should do so."

And then they went to the affair of the hospital. "But is it true, Papa?"

"What, my dear?" said he. "About the dean? Yes, I fear quite true. Indeed I know there is no doubt about it."

"Poor Miss Trefoil, I am so sorry for her. But I did not mean that," said Eleanor. "But about the hospital, Papa?"

"Yes, my dear. I believe it is true that Mr. Quiverful is to have it."

"Oh, what a shame."

"No, my dear, not at all, not at all a shame: I am sure I hope it will suit him."

"But, Papa, you know it is a shame. After all your hopes, all your expectations to get back to your old house, to see it given away in this way to a perfect stranger!"

"My dear, the bishop had a right to give it to whom he pleased."

"I deny that, Papa. He had no such right. It is not as though you were a candidate for a new piece of preferment. If the bishop has a grain of justice—"

"The bishop offered it to me on his terms, and as I did not like the terms, I refused it. After that, I cannot complain."

"Terms! He had no right to make terms."

"I don't know about that; but it seems he had the power. But to tell you the truth, Nelly, I am as well satisfied as it is. When the affair became the subject of angry discussion, I thoroughly wished to be rid of it altogether."

"But you did want to go back to the old house, Papa. You told me so yourself."

"Yes, my dear, I did. For a short time I did wish it. And I was foolish in doing so. I am getting old now, and my chief worldly wish is for peace and rest. Had I gone back to the hospital, I should have had endless contentions with the bishop, contentions with his chaplain, and contentions with the archdeacon. I am not up to this now; I am not able to meet such troubles; and therefore I am not ill-pleased to find myself left to the little church of St. Cuthbert's. I shall never starve," added he, laughing, "as long as you are here."

"But will you come and live with me, Papa?" she said earnestly, taking him by both his hands. "If you will do that, if you will promise that, I will own that you are right."

"I will dine with you to-day at any rate."

"No, but live here altogether. Give up that close, odious little room in High Street."

"My dear, it's a very nice little room, and you are really quite uncivil."

"Oh, Papa, don't joke. It's not a nice place for you. You say you are growing old, though I am sure you are not."

"Am not I, my dear?"

"No, Papa, not old—not to say old. But you are quite old enough to feel the want of a decent room to sit in. You know how lonely Mary and I are here. You know nobody ever sleeps in the big front bedroom. It is really unkind of you to remain up there alone, when you are so much wanted here."

"Thank you, Nelly—thank you. But, my dear—"

"If you had been living here, Papa, with us, as I really think you ought to have done, considering how lonely we are, there would have been none of all this dreadful affair about Mr. Slope."

Mr. Harding, however, did not allow himself to be talked over into giving up his own and only little *pied à terre* in the High Street. He promised to come and dine with his daughter, and stay with her, and visit her, and do everything but absolutely live with her. It did not suit the peculiar feelings of the man to tell his daughter that though she had rejected Mr. Slope, and been ready to reject Mr. Stanhope, some other more favoured suitor would probably soon appear, and that on the appearance of such a suitor the big front bedroom might perhaps be more frequently in requisition than at present. But doubtless such an idea crossed his mind, and added its weight to the other reasons which made him decide on still keeping the close, odious little room in High Street.

The evening passed over quietly and in comfort. Eleanor was always happier with her father than with anyone else. He had not, perhaps, any natural taste for baby-worship, but he was always ready to sacrifice himself, and therefore made an excellent third in a trio with his daughter and Mary Bold in singing the praises of the wonderful child.

They were standing together over their music in the evening, the baby having again been put to bed upon the sofa, when the servant brought in a very small note in a beautiful pink envelope. It quite filled the room with perfume as it lay upon the small salver. Mary Bold and Mrs. Bold were both at the piano, and Mr. Harding was sitting close to them, with the violoncello between his legs, so that the elegancy of the epistle was visible to them all.

"Please ma'am, Dr. Stanhope's coachman says he is to wait for an answer," said the servant.

Eleanor got very red in the face as she took the note in her hand. She had never seen the writing before. Charlotte's epistles, to which she was well accustomed, were of a very different style and kind. She generally wrote on large note-paper; she twisted up her letters into the shape and sometimes into the size of cocked hats; she addressed them in a sprawling, manly hand, and not unusually added a blot or a smudge, as though such were her own peculiar sign-manual. The address of this note was written in a beautiful female hand, and the gummed wafer bore on it an impress of a gilt coronet. Though Eleanor had never seen such a one before, she guessed that it came from the signora. Such epistles were very numerously sent out from any house in which the signora might happen to be dwelling, but they were rarely addressed to ladies. When the coachman was told by the lady's maid to take the letter to Mrs. Bold, he openly expressed his opinion that there was some mistake about it. Whereupon the lady's maid boxed the coachman's ears. Had Mr. Slope seen in how meek a spirit the coachman took the rebuke, he might have learnt a useful lesson, both in philosophy and religion.

The note was as follows. It may be taken as a faithful promise that no further letter whatever shall be transcribed at length in these pages.

MY DEAR MRS. BOLD, May I ask you, as a great favour, to call on me to-morrow. You can say what hour will best suit you, but quite early, if you can. I need hardly say that if I could call upon you, I should not take this liberty with you.

> I partly know what occurred the other day, and I promise you that you
> shall meet with no annoyance if you will come to me. My brother leaves us
> for London to-day; from thence he goes to Italy.

It will probably occur to you that I should not thus intrude on you, unless I had that to say to you which may be of considerable moment. Pray therefore excuse me, even if you do not grant my request.

And believe me,
Very sincerely yours,   M. VESEY NERONI.
Thursday Evening

The three of them sat in consultation on this epistle for some ten or fifteen minutes, and then decided that Eleanor should write a line saying that she would see the signora the next morning at twelve o'clock.

CHAPTER XLV

THE STANHOPES AT HOME

We must now return to the Stanhopes and see how they behaved themselves on their return from Ullathorne.

Charlotte, who came back in the first homeward journey with her sister, waited in palpitating expectation till the carriage drove up to the door a second time. She did not run down, or stand at the window, or show in any outward manner that she looked for anything wonderful to occur; but when she heard the carriage wheels, she stood up with erect ears, listening for Eleanor's footfall on the pavement, or the cheery sound of Bertie's voice welcoming her in. Had she heard either, she would have felt that all was right; but neither sound was there for her to hear. She heard only her father's slow step as he ponderously let himself down from the carriage and slowly walked along the hall, till he got into his own private room on the ground floor. "Send Miss Stanhope to me," he said to the servant.

"There's something wrong now," said Madeline, who was lying on her sofa in the back drawing-room.

"It's all up with Bertie," replied Charlotte. "I know, I know," she said to the servant as he brought up the message. "Tell my father I will be with him immediately."

"Bertie's wooing has gone astray," said Madeline. "I knew it would."

"It has been his own fault then. She was ready enough, I am quite sure," said Charlotte with that sort of ill-nature which is not uncommon when one woman speaks of another.

"What will you say to him now?" By "him," the signora meant their father.

"That will be as I find him. He was ready to pay two hundred pounds for Bertie to stave off the worst of his creditors, if this marriage had gone on. Bertie must now have the money instead and go and take his chance."

"Where is he now?"

"Heaven knows! Smoking in the bottom of Mr. Thorne's ha-ha, or philandering with some of those Miss Chadwicks. Nothing will ever make an impression on him. But he'll be furious if I don't go down."

"No, nothing ever will. But don't be long, Charlotte, for I want my tea."

And so Charlotte went down to her father. There was a very black cloud on the old man's brow—blacker than his daughter could ever yet remember to have seen there. He was sitting in his own armchair, not comfortably over the fire, but in the middle of the room, waiting till she should come and listen to him.

"What has become of your brother?" he said as soon as the door was shut.

"I should rather ask you," said Charlotte. "I left you both at Ullathorne when I came away. What have you done with Mrs. Bold?"

"Mrs. Bold! Nonsense. The woman has gone home as she ought to do. And heartily glad I am that she should not be sacrificed to so heartless a reprobate."

"Oh, Papa!"

"A heartless reprobate! Tell me now where he is and what he is going to do. I have allowed myself to be fooled between you. Marriage, indeed! Who on earth that has money, or credit, or respect in the world to lose would marry him?"

"It is no use your scolding me, Papa. I have done the best I could for him and you."

"And Madeline is nearly as bad," said the prebendary, who was in truth very, very angry.

"Oh, I suppose we are all bad," replied Charlotte.

The old man emitted a huge, leonine sigh. If they were all bad, who had made them so? If they were unprincipled, selfish, and disreputable, who was to be blamed for the education which had had so injurious an effect?

"I know you'll ruin me among you," said he.

"Why, Papa, what nonsense that is. You are living within your income this minute, and if there are any new debts, I don't know of them. I am sure there ought to be none, for we are dull enough here."

"Are those bills of Madeline's paid?"

"No, they are not. Who was to pay them?"

"Her husband may pay them."

"Her husband! Would you wish me to tell her you say so? Do you wish to turn her out of your house?"

"I wish she would know how to behave herself."

"Why, what on earth has she done now? Poor Madeline! To-day is only the second time she has gone out since we came to this vile town."

He then sat silent for a time, thinking in what shape he would declare his resolve. "Well, Papa," said Charlotte, "shall I stay here, or may I go upstairs and give Mamma her tea?"

"You are in your brother's confidence. Tell me what he is going to do."

"Nothing, that I am aware of."

"Nothing—nothing! Nothing but eat and drink and spend every shilling of my money he can lay his hands upon. I have made up my mind, Charlotte. He shall eat and drink no more in this house."

"Very well. Then I suppose he must go back to Italy."

"He may go where he pleases."

"That's easily said, Papa, but what does it mean? You can't let him—"

"It means this?" said the doctor, speaking more loudly than was his wont and with wrath flashing from his eyes; "that as sure as God rules in heaven I will not maintain him any longer in idleness."

"Oh, ruling in heaven!" said Charlotte. "It is no use talking about that. You must rule him here on earth; and the question is, how can you do it. You can't turn him out of the house penniless, to beg about the street."

"He may beg where he likes."

"He must go back to Carrara. That is the cheapest place he can live at, and nobody there will give him credit for above two or three hundred pauls. But you must let him have the means of going."

"As sure as—"

"Oh, Papa, don't swear. You know you must do it. You were ready to pay two hundred pounds for him if this marriage came off. Half that will start him to Carrara."

"What? Give him a hundred pounds?"

"You know we are all in the dark, Papa," said she, thinking it expedient to change the conversation. "For anything we know he may be at this moment engaged to Mrs. Bold."

"Fiddlestick," said the father, who had seen the way in which Mrs. Bold had got into the carriage while his son stood apart without even offering her his hand.

"Well, then, he must go to Carrara," said Charlotte.

Just at this moment the lock of the front door was heard, and Charlotte's quick ears detected her brother's catlike step in the hall. She said nothing, feeling that for the present Bertie had better keep out of her father's way. But Dr. Stanhope also heard the sound of the lock.

"Who's that?" he demanded. Charlotte made no reply, and he asked again, "Who is that that has just come in? Open the door. Who is it?"

"I suppose it is Bertie."

"Bid him come here," said the father. But Bertie, who was close to the door and heard the call, required no further bidding, but walked in with a perfectly unconcerned and cheerful air. It was this peculiar *insouciance* which angered Dr. Stanhope, even more than his son's extravagance.

"Well, sir?" said the doctor.

"And how did you get home, sir, with your fair companion?" said Bertie. "I suppose she is not upstairs, Charlotte?"

"Bertie," said Charlotte, "Papa is in no humour for joking. He is very angry with you."

"Angry!" said Bertie, raising his eyebrows as though he had never yet given his parent cause for a single moment's uneasiness.

"Sit down, if you please, sir," said Dr. Stanhope very sternly but not now very loudly. "And I'll trouble you to sit down, too, Charlotte. Your mother can wait for her tea a few minutes."

Charlotte sat down on the chair nearest to the door in somewhat of a perverse sort of manner, as much as though she would say—"Well, here I am; you shan't say I don't do what I am bid; but I'll be whipped if I give way to you." And she was determined not to give way. She too was angry with Bertie, but she was not the less ready on that account to defend him from his father. Bertie also sat down. He drew his chair close to the library-table, upon which he put his elbow, and then resting his face comfortably on one hand, he began drawing little pictures on a sheet of paper with the other. Before the scene was over he had completed admirable figures of Miss Thorne, Mrs. Proudie, and Lady De Courcy, and begun a family piece to comprise the whole set of the Lookalofts.

"Would it suit you, sir," said the father, "to give me some idea as to what your present intentions are? What way of living you propose to yourself?"

"I'll do anything you can suggest, sir," replied Bertie.

"No, I shall suggest nothing further. My time for suggesting has gone by. I have only one order to give, and that is that you leave my house."

"To-night?" said Bertie, and the simple tone of the question left the doctor without any adequately dignified method of reply.

"Papa does not quite mean to-night," said Charlotte; "at least I suppose not."

"To-morrow, perhaps," suggested Bertie.

"Yes, sir, to-morrow," said the doctor. "You shall leave this to-morrow."

"Very well, sir. Will the 4.30 P.M. train be soon enough?" and Bertie, as he asked, put the finishing touch to Miss Thorne's high-heeled boots.

"You may go how and when and where you please, so that you leave my house to-morrow. You have disgraced me, sir; you have disgraced yourself, and me, and your sisters."

"I am glad at least, sir, that I have not disgraced my mother," said Bertie.

Charlotte could hardly keep her countenance, but the doctor's brow grew still blacker than ever. Bertie was executing his *chef d'oeuvre* in the delineation of Mrs. Proudie's nose and mouth.

"You are a heartless reprobate, sir; a heartless, thankless, good-for-nothing reprobate. I have done with you. You are my son—that I cannot help—but you shall have no more part or parcel in me as my child, nor I in you as your father."

"Oh, Papa, Papa! You must not, shall not say so," said Charlotte.

"I will say so, and do say so," said the father, rising from his chair. "And now leave the room, sir."

"Stop, stop," said Charlotte. "Why don't you speak, Bertie? Why don't you look up and speak? It is your manner that makes Papa so angry."

"He is perfectly indifferent to all decency, to all propriety," said the doctor; then he shouted out, "Leave the room, sir! Do you hear what I say?"

"Papa, Papa, I will not let you part so. I know you will be sorry for it." And then she added, getting up and whispering into his ear, "Is he only to blame? Think of that. We have made our own bed, and, such as it is, we must lie on it. It is no use for us to quarrel among ourselves," and as she finished her whisper, Bertie finished off the countess's bustle, which was so well done that it absolutely seemed to be swaying to and fro on the paper with its usual lateral motion.

"My father is angry at the present time," said Bertie, looking up for a moment from his sketches, "because I am not going to marry Mrs. Bold. What can I say on the matter? It is true that I am not going to marry her. In the first place—"

"That is not true, sir," said Dr. Stanhope, "but I will not argue with you."

"You were angry just this moment because I would not speak," said Bertie, going on with a young Lookaloft.

"Give over drawing," said Charlotte, going up to him and taking the paper from under his hand. The caricatures, however, she preserved and showed them afterwards to the friends of the Thornes, the Proudies, and De Courcys. Bertie, deprived of his occupation, threw himself back in his chair and waited further orders.

"I think it will certainly be for the best that Bertie should leave this at once; perhaps to-morrow," said Charlotte; "but pray, Papa, let us arrange some scheme together."

"If he will leave this to-morrow, I will give him £10, and he shall be paid £5 a month by the banker at Carrara as long as he stays permanently in that place."

"Well, sir, it won't be long," said Bertie, "for I shall be starved to death in about three months."

"He must have marble to work with," said Charlotte.

"I have plenty there in the studio to last me three months," said Bertie. "It will be no use attempting anything large in so limited a time—unless I do my own tombstone."

Terms, however, were ultimately come to somewhat more liberal than those proposed, and the doctor was induced to shake hands with his son and bid him good night. Dr. Stanhope would not go up to tea, but had it brought to him in his study by his daughter.

But Bertie went upstairs and spent a pleasant evening. He finished the Lookalofts, greatly to the delight of his sisters, though the manner of portraying their *décolleté* dresses was not the most refined. Finding how matters were going, he by degrees allowed it to escape from him that he had not pressed his suit upon the widow in a very urgent way.

"I suppose, in point of fact, you never proposed at all?" said Charlotte.

"Oh, she understood that she might have me if she wished," said he.

"And she didn't wish," said the Signora.

"You have thrown me over in the most shameful manner," said Charlotte. "I suppose you told her all about my little plan?"

"Well, it came out somehow—at least the most of it."

"There's an end of that alliance," said Charlotte, "but it doesn't matter much. I suppose we shall all be back at Como soon."

"I am sure I hope so," said the signora. "I'm sick of the sight of black coats. If that Mr. Slope comes here any more, he'll be the death of me."

"You've been the ruin of him, I think," said Charlotte.

"And as for a second black-coated lover of mine, I am going to make a present of him to another lady with most singular disinterestedness."

The next day, true to his promise, Bertie packed up and went off by the 4.30 P.M. train, with £20 in his pocket, bound for the marble quarries of Carrara. And so he disappears from our scene.

At twelve o'clock on the day following that on which Bertie went, Mrs. Bold, true also to her word, knocked at Dr. Stanhope's door with a timid hand and palpitating heart. She was at once shown up to the back drawing-room, the folding doors of which were closed, so that in visiting the signora Eleanor was not necessarily thrown into any communion with those in the front room. As she went up the stairs, she saw none of the family and was so far saved much of the annoyance which she had dreaded.

"This is very kind of you, Mrs. Bold; very kind, after what has happened," said the lady on the sofa with her sweetest smile.

"You wrote in such a strain that I could not but come to you."

"I did, I did; I wanted to force you to see me."

"Well, signora, I am here."

"How cold you are to me. But I suppose I must put up with that. I know you think you have reason to be displeased with us all. Poor Bertie; if you knew all, you would not be angry with him."

"I am not angry with your brother—not in the least. But I hope you did not send for me here to talk about him."

"If you are angry with Charlotte, that is worse, for you have no warmer friend in all Barchester. But I did not send for you to talk about this—pray bring your chair nearer, Mrs. Bold, so that I may look at you. It is so unnatural to see you keeping so far off from me."

Eleanor did as she was bid and brought her chair close to the sofa.

"And now, Mrs. Bold, I am going to tell you something which you may perhaps think indelicate, but yet I know that I am right in doing so."

Hereupon Mrs. Bold said nothing but felt inclined to shake in her chair. The signora, she knew, was not very particular, and that which to her appeared to be indelicate might to Mrs. Bold appear to be extremely indecent.

"I believe you know Mr. Arabin?"

Mrs. Bold would have given the world not to blush, but her blood was not at her own command. She did blush up to her forehead, and the signora, who had made her sit in a special light in order that she might watch her, saw that she did so.

"Yes, I am acquainted with him. That is, slightly. He is an intimate friend of Dr. Grantly, and Dr. Grantly is my brother-in-law."

"Well, if you know Mr. Arabin, I am sure you must like him. I know and like him much. Everybody that knows him must like him."

Mrs. Bold felt it quite impossible to say anything in reply to this. Her blood was rushing about her body she knew not how or why. She felt as though she were swinging in her chair, and she knew that she was not only red in the face but also almost suffocated with heat. However, she sat still and said nothing.

"How stiff you are with me, Mrs. Bold," said the signora; "and I the while am doing for you all that one woman can do to serve another."

A kind of thought came over the widow's mind that perhaps the signora's friendship was real, and that at any rate it could not hurt her; and another kind of thought, a glimmering of a thought, came to her also—that Mr. Arabin was too precious to be lost. She despised the signora, but might she not stoop to conquer? It should be but the smallest fraction of a stoop!

"I don't want to be stiff," she said, "but your questions are so very singular."

"Well, then, I will ask you one more singular still," said Madeline Neroni, raising herself on her elbow and turning her own face full upon her companion's. "Do you love him, love him with all your heart and soul, with all the love your bosom can feel? For I can tell you that he loves you, adores you, worships you, thinks of you and nothing else, is now thinking of you as he attempts to write his sermon for next Sunday's preaching. What would I not give to be loved in such a way by such a man, that is, if I were an object fit for any man to love!"

Mrs. Bold got up from her seat and stood speechless before the woman who was now addressing her in this impassioned way. When the signora thus alluded to herself, the widow's heart was softened, and she put her own hand, as though caressingly, on that of her companion, which was resting on the table. The signora grasped it and went on speaking.

"What I tell you is God's own truth; and it is for you to use it as may be best for your own happiness. But you must not betray me. He knows nothing of this. He knows nothing of my knowing his inmost heart. He is simple as a child in these matters. He told me his secret in a thousand ways because he could not dissemble, but he does not dream that he has told it. You know it now, and I advise you to use it."

Eleanor returned the pressure of the other's hand with an infinitesimal *soupçon* of a squeeze.

"And remember," continued the signora, "he is not like other men. You must not expect him to come to you with vows and oaths and pretty presents, to kneel at your feet, and kiss your shoe-strings. If you want that, there are plenty to do it, but he won't be one of them." Eleanor's bosom nearly burst with a sigh, but Madeline, not heeding her, went on. "With him, yea will stand for yea, and nay for nay. Though his heart should break for it, the woman who shall reject him once will have rejected him once and for all. Remember that. And now, Mrs. Bold, I will not keep you, for you are fluttered. I partly guess what use you will make of what I have said to you. If ever you are a happy wife in that man's house, we shall be far away, but I shall expect you to write me one line to say that you have forgiven the sins of the family."

Eleanor half-whispered that she would, and then, without uttering another word, crept out of the room and down the stairs, opened the front door for herself without hearing or seeing anyone, and found herself in the close.

It would be difficult to analyse Eleanor's feelings as she walked home. She was nearly stupefied by the things that had been said to her. She felt sore that her heart should have been so searched and riddled by a comparative stranger, by a woman whom she had never liked and never could like. She was mortified that the man whom she owned to herself that she loved should have concealed his love from her and shown it to another. There was much to vex her proud spirit. But there was, nevertheless, an under stratum of joy in all this which buoyed her up wondrously. She tried if she could disbelieve what Madame Neroni had said to her, but she found that she could not. It was true; it must be true. She could not, would not, did not doubt it.

On one point she fully resolved to follow the advice given her. If it should ever please Mr. Arabin to put such a question to her as that suggested, her "yea" should be "yea." Would not all her miseries be at an end if she could talk of them to him openly, with her head resting on his shoulder?

CHAPTER XLVI

MR. SLOPE'S PARTING INTERVIEW WITH THE SIGNORA

On the following day the signora was in her pride. She was dressed in her brightest of morning dresses, and had quite a levée round her couch. It was a beautifully bright October afternoon; all the gentlemen of the neighbourhood were in Barchester, and those who had the entry of Dr. Stanhope's house were in the signora's back drawing-room. Charlotte and Mrs. Stanhope were in the front room, and such of the lady's squires as could not for the moment get near the centre of attraction had to waste their fragrance on the mother and sister.

The first who came and the last to leave was Mr. Arabin. This was the second visit he had paid to Madame Neroni since he had met her at Ullathorne. He came, he knew not why, to talk about, he knew not what. But, in truth, the feelings which now troubled him were new to him, and he could not analyse them. It may seem strange that he should thus come dangling about Madame Neroni because he was in love with Mrs. Bold; but it was nevertheless the fact; and though he could not understand why he did so, Madame Neroni understood it well enough.

She had been gentle and kind to him and had encouraged his staying. Therefore he stayed on. She pressed his hand when he first greeted her; she made him remain near her and whispered to him little nothings. And then her eye, brilliant and bright, now mirthful, now melancholy, and invincible in either way! What man with warm feelings, blood un-chilled, and a heart not guarded by a triple steel of experience could have withstood those eyes! The lady, it is true, intended to do him no mortal injury; she merely chose to inhale a slight breath of incense before she handed the casket over to another. Whether Mrs. Bold would willingly have spared even so much is another question.

And then came Mr. Slope. All the world now knew that Mr. Slope was a candidate for the deanery and that he was generally considered to be the favourite. Mr. Slope, therefore, walked rather largely upon the earth. He gave to himself a portly air, such as might become a dean, spoke but little to other clergymen, and shunned the bishop as much as possible. How the meagre little prebendary, and the burly chancellor, and all the minor canons and vicars choral, ay, and all the choristers, too, cowered and shook and walked about with long faces when they read or heard of that article in "The Jupiter." Now were coming the days when nothing would avail to keep the impure spirit from the cathedral pulpit. That pulpit would indeed be his own. Precentors, vicars, and choristers might hang up their harps on the willows. Ichabod! Ichabod! The glory of their house was departing from them.

Mr. Slope, great as he was with embryo grandeur, still came to see the signora. Indeed, he could not keep himself away. He dreamed of that soft hand which he had kissed so often, and of that imperial brow which his lips had once pressed; and he then dreamed also of further favours.

And Mr. Thorne was there also. It was the first visit he had ever paid to the signora, and he made it not without due preparation. Mr. Thorne was a gentleman usually precise in his dress and prone to make the most of himself in an unpretending way. The grey hairs in his whiskers were eliminated perhaps once a month; those on his head were softened by a mixture which we will not call a dye—it was only a wash. His tailor lived in St. James's Street, and his bootmaker at the corner of that street and Piccadilly. He was particular in the article of gloves, and the getting up of his shirts was a matter not lightly thought of in the Ullathorne laundry. On the occasion of the present visit he had rather overdone his usual efforts, and caused some little uneasiness to his sister, who had not hitherto received very cordially the proposition for a lengthened visit from the signora at Ullathorne.

There were others also there—young men about the city who had not much to do and who were induced by the lady's charms to neglect that little—but all gave way to Mr. Thorne, who was somewhat of a grand signor, as a country gentleman always is in a provincial city.

"Oh, Mr. Thorne, this is so kind of you!" said the signora. "You promised to come, but I really did not expect it. I thought you country gentlemen never kept your pledges."

"Oh, yes, sometimes," said Mr. Thorne, looking rather sheepish and making his salutations a little too much in the style of the last century.

"You deceive none but your consti—stit—stit—what do you call the people that carry you about in chairs and pelt you with eggs and apples when they make you a member of Parliament?"

"One another also, sometimes, signora," said Mr. Slope, with a very deanish sort of smirk on his face. "Country gentlemen do deceive one another sometimes, don't they, Mr. Thorne?"

Mr. Thorne gave him a look which undeaned him completely for the moment, but he soon remembered his high hopes and, recovering himself quickly, sustained his probable coming dignity by a laugh at Mr. Thorne's expense.

"I never deceive a lady, at any rate," said Mr. Thorne, "especially when the gratification of my own wishes is so strong an inducement to keep me true, as it now is."

Mr. Thorne went on thus awhile with antediluvian grimaces and compliments which he had picked up from Sir Charles Grandison, and the signora at every grimace and at every bow smiled a little smile and bowed a little bow. Mr. Thorne, however, was kept standing at the foot of the couch, for the new dean sat in the seat of honour near the table. Mr. Arabin the while was standing with his back to the fire, his coat-tails under his arms, gazing at her with all his eyes—not quite in vain, for every now and again a glance came up at him, bright as a meteor out of heaven.

"Oh, Mr. Thorne, you promised to let me introduce my little girl to you. Can you spare a moment—will you see her now?"

Mr. Thorne assured her that he could and would see the young lady with the greatest pleasure in life. "Mr. Slope, might I trouble you to ring the bell?" said she, and when Mr. Slope got up, she looked at Mr. Thorne and pointed to the chair. Mr. Thorne, however, was much too slow to understand her, and Mr. Slope would have recovered his seat had not the signora, who never chose to be unsuccessful, somewhat summarily ordered him out of it.

"Oh, Mr. Slope, I must ask you to let Mr. Thorne sit here just for a moment or two. I am sure you will pardon me. We can take a liberty with you this week. Next week, you know, when you move into the dean's house, we shall all be afraid of you."

Mr. Slope, with an air of much indifference, rose from his seat and, walking into the next room, became greatly interested in Mrs. Stanhope's worsted work.

And then the child was brought in. She was a little girl, about eight years of age, like her mother, only that her enormous eyes were black, and her hair quite jet. Her complexion, too, was very dark and bespoke her foreign blood. She was dressed in the most outlandish and extravagant way in which clothes could be put on a child's back. She had great bracelets on her naked little arms, a crimson fillet braided with gold round her head, and scarlet shoes with high heels. Her dress was all flounces and stuck out from her as though the object were to make it lie off horizontally from her little hips. It did not nearly cover her knees, but this was atoned for by a loose pair of drawers, which seemed made throughout of lace; then she had on pink silk stockings. It was thus that the last of the Neros was habitually dressed at the hour when visitors were wont to call.

"Julia, my love," said the mother—Julia was ever a favourite name with the ladies of that family. "Julia, my love, come here. I was telling you about the beautiful party poor Mamma went to. This is Mr. Thorne; will you give him a kiss, dearest?"

Julia put up her face to be kissed, as she did to all her mother's visitors, and then Mr. Thorne found that he had got her and, what was much more terrific to him, all her finery, into his arms. The lace and starch crumpled against his waistcoat and trousers, the greasy black curls hung upon his cheek, and one of the bracelet clasps scratched his ear. He did not at all know how to hold so magnificent a lady, nor holding her what to do with her. However, he had on other occasions been compelled to fondle little nieces and nephews, and now set about the task in the mode he always had used.

"Diddle, diddle, diddle, diddle," said he, putting the child on one knee and working away with it as though he were turning a knife-grinder's wheel with his foot.

"Mamma, Mamma," said Julia crossly, "I don't want to be diddle diddled. Let me go, you naughty old man, you."

Poor Mr. Thorne put the child down quietly on the ground and drew back his chair; Mr. Slope, who had returned to the pole star that attracted him, laughed aloud; Mr. Arabin winced and shut his eyes; and the signora pretended not to hear her daughter.

"Go to Aunt Charlotte, lovey," said the mamma, "and ask her if it is not time for you to go out."

But little Miss Julia, though she had not exactly liked the nature of Mr. Thorne's attention, was accustomed to be played with by gentlemen, and did not relish the idea of being sent so soon to her aunt.

"Julia, go when I tell you, my dear." But Julia still went pouting about the room. "Charlotte, do come and take her," said the signora. "She must go out, and the days get so short now." And thus ended the much-talked-of interview between Mr. Thorne and the last of the Neros.

Mr. Thorne recovered from the child's crossness sooner than from Mr. Slope's laughter. He could put up with being called an old man by an infant, but he did not like to be laughed at by the bishop's chaplain, even though that chaplain was about to become a dean. He said nothing, but he showed plainly enough that he was angry.

The signora was ready enough to avenge him. "Mr. Slope," said she, "I hear that you are triumphing on all sides."

"How so?" said he, smiling. He did not dislike being talked to about the deanery, though, of course, he strongly denied the imputation.

"You carry the day both in love and war." Mr. Slope hereupon did not look quite so satisfied as he had done.

"Mr. Arabin," continued the signora, "don't you think Mr. Slope is a very lucky man?"

"Not more so than he deserves, I am sure," said Mr. Arabin.

"Only think, Mr. Thorne, he is to be our new dean; of course we all know that."

"Indeed, signora," said Mr. Slope, "we all know nothing about it. I can assure you I myself—"

"He is to be the new dean—there is no manner of doubt of it, Mr. Thorne."

"Hum!" said Mr. Thorne.

"Passing over the heads of old men like my father and Archdeacon Grantly—"

"Oh—oh!" said Mr. Slope.

"The archdeacon would not accept it," said Mr. Arabin, whereupon Mr. Slope smiled abominably and said, as plainly as a look could speak, that the grapes were sour.

"Going over all our heads," continued the signora, "for of course I consider myself one of the chapter."

"If I am ever dean," said Mr. Slope, "that is, were I ever to become so, I should glory in such a canoness."

"Oh, Mr. Slope, stop; I haven't half done. There is another canoness for you to glory in. Mr. Slope is not only to have the deanery but a wife to put in it."

Mr. Slope again looked disconcerted.

"A wife with a large fortune, too. It never rains but it pours, does it, Mr. Thorne?"

"No, never," said Mr. Thorne, who did not quite relish talking about Mr. Slope and his affairs.

"When will it be, Mr. Slope?"

"When will what be?" said he.

"Oh, we know when the affair of the dean will be: a week will settle that. The new hat, I have no doubt, has been already ordered. But when will the marriage come off?"

"Do you mean mine or Mr. Arabin's?" said he, striving to be facetious.

"Well, just then I meant yours, though, perhaps, after all, Mr. Arabin's may be first. But we know nothing of him. He is too close for any of us. Now all is open and above board with you—which, by the by, Mr. Arabin, I beg to tell you I like much the best. He who runs can read that Mr. Slope is a favoured lover. Come, Mr. Slope, when is the widow to be made Mrs. Dean?"

To Mr. Arabin this badinage was peculiarly painful, and yet he could not tear himself away and leave it. He believed, still believed with that sort of belief which the fear of a thing engenders, that Mrs. Bold would probably become the wife of Mr. Slope. Of Mr. Slope's little adventure in the garden he knew nothing. For aught he knew, Mr. Slope might have had an adventure of quite a different character. He might have thrown himself at the widow's feet, been accepted, and then returned to town a jolly, thriving wooer. The signora's jokes were bitter enough to Mr. Slope, but they were quite as bitter to Mr. Arabin. He still stood leaning against the fire-place, fumbling with his hands in his trousers pockets.

"Come, come, Mr. Slope, don't be so bashful," continued the signora. "We all know that you proposed to the lady the other day at Ullathorne. Tell us with what words she accepted you. Was it with a simple 'yes,' or with the two 'no no's' which make an affirmative? Or did silence give consent? Or did she speak out with that spirit which so well becomes a widow and say openly, 'By my troth, sir, you shall make me Mrs. Slope as soon as it is your pleasure to do so.'"

Mr. Slope had seldom in his life felt himself less at his ease. There sat Mr. Thorne, laughing silently. There stood his old antagonist, Mr. Arabin, gazing at him with all his eyes. There round the door between the two rooms were clustered a little group of people, including Miss Stanhope and the Revs. Messrs. Grey and Green, all listening to his discomfiture. He knew that it depended solely on his own wit whether or no he could throw the joke back upon the lady. He knew that it stood him to do so if he possibly could, but he had not a word. "'Tis conscience that makes cowards of us all." He felt on his cheek the sharp points of Eleanor's fingers, and did not know who might have seen the blow, who might have told the tale to this pestilent woman who took such delight in jeering him. He stood there, therefore, red as a carbuncle and mute as a fish; grinning sufficiently to show his teeth; an object of pity.

But the signora had no pity; she knew nothing of mercy. Her present object was to put Mr. Slope down, and she was determined to do it thoroughly, now that she had him in her power.

"What, Mr. Slope, no answer? Why it can't possibly be that the woman has been fool enough to refuse you? She can't surely be looking out after a bishop. But I see how it is, Mr. Slope. Widows are proverbially cautious. You should have let her alone till the new hat was on your head, till you could show her the key of the deanery."

"Signora," said he at last, trying to speak in a tone of dignified reproach, "you really permit yourself to talk on solemn subjects in a very improper way."

"Solemn subjects—what solemn subject? Surely a dean's hat is not such a solemn subject."

"I have no aspirations such as those you impute to me. Perhaps you will drop the subject."

"Oh, certainly, Mr. Slope; but one word first. Go to her again with the prime minister's letter in your pocket. I'll wager my shawl to your shovel she does not refuse you then."

"I must say, signora, that I think you are speaking of the lady in a very unjustifiable manner."

"And one other piece of advice, Mr. Slope; I'll only offer you one other;" and then she commenced singing—
"It's gude to be merry and wise, Mr. Slope;
   It's gude to be honest and true;
 It's gude to be off with the old love—Mr. Slope,
   Before you are on with the new.
   "Ha, ha, ha!"

And the signora, throwing herself back on her sofa, laughed merrily. She little recked how those who heard her would, in their own imaginations, fill up the little history of Mr. Slope's first love. She little cared that some among them might attribute to her the honour of his earlier admiration. She was tired of Mr. Slope and wanted to get rid of him; she had ground for anger with him, and she chose to be revenged.

How Mr. Slope got out of that room he never himself knew. He did succeed ultimately, and probably with some assistance, in getting his hat and escaping into the air. At last his love for the signora was cured. Whenever he again thought of her in his dreams, it was not as of an angel with azure wings. He connected her rather with fire and brimstone, and though he could still believe her to be a spirit, he banished her entirely out of heaven and found a place for her among the infernal gods. When he weighed in the balance, as he not seldom did, the two women to whom he had attached himself in Barchester, the pre-eminent place in his soul's hatred was usually allotted to the signora.

CHAPTER XLVII

THE DEAN ELECT

During the entire next week Barchester was ignorant who was to be its new dean. On Sunday morning Mr. Slope was decidedly the favourite, but he did not show himself in the cathedral, and then he sank a point or two in the betting. On Monday he got a scolding from the bishop in the hearing of the servants, and down he went till nobody would have him at any price; but on Tuesday he received a letter, in an official cover, marked private, by which he fully recovered his place in the public favour. On Wednesday he was said to be ill, and that did not look well; but on Thursday morning he went down to the railway station with a very jaunty air; and when it was ascertained that he had taken a first-class ticket for London, there was no longer any room for doubt on the matter.

While matters were in this state of ferment at Barchester, there was not much mental comfort at Plumstead. Our friend the archdeacon had many grounds for inward grief. He was much displeased at the result of Dr. Gwynne's diplomatic mission to the palace, and did not even scruple to say to his wife that had he gone himself, he would have managed the affair much better. His wife did not agree with him, but that did not mend the matter.

Mr. Quiverful's appointment to the hospital was, however, a *fait accompli*, and Mr. Harding's acquiescence in that appointment was not less so. Nothing would induce Mr. Harding to make a public appeal against the bishop, and the Master of Lazarus quite approved of his not doing so.

"I don't know what has come to the master," said the archdeacon over and over again. "He used to be ready enough to stand up for his order."

"My dear Archdeacon," Mrs. Grantly would say in reply, "what is the use of always fighting? I really think the master is right." The master, however, had taken steps of his own of which neither the archdeacon nor his wife knew anything.

Then Mr. Slope's successes were henbane to Dr. Grantly, and Mrs. Bold's improprieties were as bad. What would be all the world to Archdeacon Grantly if Mr. Slope should become Dean of Barchester and marry his wife's sister! He talked of it and talked of it till he was nearly ill. Mrs. Grantly almost wished that the marriage were done and over, so that she might hear no more about it.

And there was yet another ground of misery which cut him to the quick nearly as closely as either of the others. That paragon of a clergyman whom he had bestowed upon St. Ewold's, that college friend of whom he had boasted so loudly, that ecclesiastical knight before whose lance Mr. Slope was to fall and bite the dust, that worthy bulwark of the church as it should be, that honoured representative of Oxford's best spirit, was—so at least his wife had told him half a dozen times—misconducting himself!

Nothing had been seen of Mr. Arabin at Plumstead for the last week, but a good deal had, unfortunately, been heard of him. As soon as Mrs. Grantly had found herself alone with the archdeacon, on the evening of the Ullathorne party, she had expressed herself very forcibly as to Mr. Arabin's conduct on that occasion. He had, she declared, looked and acted and talked very unlike a decent parish clergyman. At first the archdeacon had laughed at this, and assured her that she need not trouble herself—that Mr. Arabin would be found to be quite safe. But by degrees he began to find that his wife's eyes had been sharper than his own. Other people coupled the signora's name with that of Mr. Arabin. The meagre little prebendary who lived in the close told him to a nicety how often Mr. Arabin had visited at Dr. Stanhope's, and how long he had remained on the occasion of each visit. He had asked after Mr. Arabin at the cathedral library, and an officious little vicar choral had offered to go and see whether he could be found at Dr. Stanhope's. Rumour, when she has contrived to sound the first note on her trumpet, soon makes a loud peal audible enough. It was too clear that Mr. Arabin had succumbed to the Italian woman, and that the archdeacon's credit would suffer fearfully if something were not done to rescue the brand from the burning. Besides, to give the archdeacon his due, he was really attached to Mr. Arabin, and grieved greatly at his backsliding.

They were sitting, talking over their sorrows, in the drawing-room before dinner on the day after Mr. Slope's departure for London, and on this occasion Mrs. Grantly spoke out her mind freely. She had opinions of her own about parish clergymen, and now thought it right to give vent to them.

"If you would have been led by me, Archdeacon, you would never have put a bachelor into St. Ewold's."

"But my dear, you don't meant to say that all bachelor clergymen misbehave themselves."

"I don't know that clergymen are so much better than other men," said Mrs. Grantly. "It's all very well with a curate, whom you have under your own eye and whom you can get rid of if he persists in improprieties."

"But Mr. Arabin was a fellow, and couldn't have had a wife."

"Then I would have found someone who could."

"But, my dear, are fellows never to get livings?"

"Yes, to be sure they are, when they get engaged. I never would put a young man into a living unless he were married, or engaged to be married. Now, here is Mr. Arabin. The whole responsibility lies upon you."

"There is not at this moment a clergyman in all Oxford more respected for morals and conduct than Arabin."

"Oh, Oxford!" said the lady, with a sneer. "What men choose to do at Oxford nobody ever hears of. A man may do very well at Oxford who would bring disgrace on a parish; and to tell you the truth, it seems to me that Mr. Arabin is just such a man."

The archdeacon groaned deeply, but he had no further answer to make.

"You really must speak to him, Archdeacon. Only think what the Thornes will say if they hear that their parish clergyman spends his whole time philandering with this woman."

The archdeacon groaned again. He was a courageous man, and knew well enough how to rebuke the younger clergymen of the diocese, when necessary. But there was that about Mr. Arabin which made the doctor feel that it would be very difficult to rebuke him with good effect.

"You can advise him to find a wife for himself, and he will understand well enough what that means," said Mrs. Grantly.

The archdeacon had nothing for it but groaning. There was Mr. Slope: he was going to be made dean; he was going to take a wife; he was about to achieve respectability and wealth, an excellent family mansion, and a family carriage; he would soon be among the comfortable *élite* of the ecclesiastical world of Barchester; whereas his own *protégé*, the true scion of the true church, by whom he had sworn, would be still but a poor vicar, and that with a very indifferent character for moral conduct! It might be all very well recommending Mr. Arabin to marry, but how would Mr. Arabin, when married, support a wife?

Things were ordering themselves thus in Plumstead drawing-room when Dr. and Mrs. Grantly were disturbed in their sweet discourse by the quick rattle of a carriage and pair of horses on the gravel sweep. The sound was not that of visitors, whose private carriages are generally brought up to country-house doors with demure propriety, but betokened rather the advent of some person or persons who were in a hurry to reach the house, and had no intention of immediately leaving it. Guests invited to stay a week, and who were conscious of arriving after the first dinner-bell, would probably approach in such a manner. So might arrive an attorney with the news of a granduncle's death, or a son from college with all the fresh honours of a double first. No one would have had himself driven up to the door of a country-house in such a manner who had the slightest doubt of his own right to force an entry.

"Who is it?" said Mrs. Grantly, looking at her husband.

"Who on earth can it be?" said the archdeacon to his wife. He then quietly got up and stood with the drawing-room door open in his hand. "Why, it's your father!"

It was indeed Mr. Harding, and Mr. Harding alone. He had come by himself in a post-chaise with a couple of horses from Barchester, arriving almost after dark, and evidently full of news. His visits had usually been made in the quietest manner; he had rarely presumed to come without notice, and had always been driven up in a modest old green fly, with one horse, that hardly made itself heard as it crawled up to the hall-door.

"Good gracious, Warden, is it you?" said the archdeacon, forgetting in his surprise the events of the last few years. "But come in; nothing the matter, I hope."

"We are very glad you are come, Papa," said his daughter. "I'll go and get your room ready at once."

"I an't warden, Archdeacon," said Mr. Harding; "Mr. Quiverful is warden."

"Oh, I know, I know," said the archdeacon petulantly. "I forgot all about it at the moment. Is anything the matter?"

"Don't go this moment, Susan," said Mr. Harding. "I have something to tell you."

"The dinner-bell will ring in five minutes," said she.

"Will it?" said Mr. Harding. "Then perhaps I had better wait." He was big with news which he had come to tell, but which he knew could not be told without much discussion. He had hurried away to Plumstead as fast as two horses could bring him, and now, finding himself there, he was willing to accept the reprieve which dinner would give him.

"If you have anything of moment to tell us," said the archdeacon, "pray let us hear it at once. Has Eleanor gone off?"

"No, she has not," said Mr. Harding with a look of great displeasure.

"Has Slope been made dean?"

"No, he has not, but—"

"But what?" said the archdeacon, who was becoming very impatient.

"They have—"

"They have what?" said the archdeacon.

"They have offered it to me," said Mr. Harding, with a modesty which almost prevented his speaking.

"Good heavens!" said the archdeacon, and sunk back exhausted in an easy chair.

"My dear, dear father," said Mrs. Grantly, and threw her arms round her father's neck.

"So I thought I had better come out and consult with you at once," said Mr. Harding.

"Consult!" shouted the archdeacon. "But, my dear Harding, I congratulate you with my whole heart—with my whole heart; I do indeed. I never heard anything in my life that gave me so much pleasure;" and he got hold of both his father-in-law's hands, and shook them as though he were going to shake them off, and walked round and round the room, twirling a copy of "The Jupiter" over his head to show his extreme exultation.

"But—" began Mr. Harding.

"But me no buts," said the archdeacon. "I never was so happy in my life. It was just the proper thing to do. Upon my honour I'll never say another word against Lord —— the longest day I have to live."

"That's Dr. Gwynne's doing, you may be sure," said Mrs. Grantly, who greatly liked the Master of Lazarus, he being an orderly married man with a large family.

"I suppose it is," said the archdeacon.

"Oh, Papa, I am so truly delighted!" said Mrs. Grantly, getting up and kissing her father.

"But, my dear," said Mr. Harding. It was all in vain that he strove to speak; nobody would listen to him.

"Well, Mr. Dean," said the archdeacon, triumphing, "the deanery gardens will be some consolation for the hospital elms. Well, poor Quiverful! I won't begrudge him his good fortune any longer."

"No, indeed," said Mrs. Grantly. "Poor woman, she has fourteen children. I am sure I am very glad they have got it."

"So am I," said Mr. Harding.

"I would give twenty pounds," said the archdeacon, "to see how Mr. Slope will look when he hears it." The idea of Mr. Slope's discomfiture formed no small part of the archdeacon's pleasure.

At last Mr. Harding was allowed to go upstairs and wash his hands, having, in fact, said very little of all that he had come out to Plumstead on purpose to say. Nor could anything more be said till the servants were gone after dinner. The joy of Dr. Grantly was so uncontrollable that he could not refrain from calling his father-in-law Mr. Dean before the men, and therefore it was soon matter of discussion in the lower regions how Mr. Harding, instead of his daughter's future husband, was to be the new dean, and various were the opinions on the matter. The cook and butler, who were advanced in years, thought that it was just as it should be; but the footman and lady's maid, who were younger, thought it was a great shame that Mr. Slope should lose his chance.

"He's a mean chap all the same," said the footman, "and it an't along of him that I says so. But I always did admire the missus's sister; and she'd well become the situation."

While these were the ideas downstairs, a very great difference of opinion existed above. As soon as the cloth was drawn and the wine on the table, Mr. Harding made for himself an opportunity of speaking. It was, however, with much inward troubling that he said:

"It's very kind of Lord ——, very kind, and I feel it deeply, most deeply. I am, I must confess, gratified by the offer—"

"I should think so," said the archdeacon.

"But all the same I am afraid that I can't accept it."

The decanter almost fell from the archdeacon's hand upon the table, and the start he made was so great as to make his wife jump up from her chair. Not accept the deanship! If it really ended in this, there would be no longer any doubt that his father-in-law was demented. The question now was whether a clergyman with low rank and preferment amounting to less than £200 a year should accept high rank, £1,200 a year, and one of the most desirable positions which his profession had to afford!

"What!" said the archdeacon, gasping for breath and staring at his guest as though the violence of his emotion had almost thrown him into a fit. "What!"

"I do not find myself fit for new duties," urged Mr. Harding.

"New duties! What duties?" said the archdeacon with unintended sarcasm.

"Oh, Papa," said Mrs. Grantly, "nothing can be easier than what a dean has to do. Surely you are more active than Dr. Trefoil."

"He won't have half as much to do as he has at present," said Dr. Grantly.

"Did you see what 'The Jupiter' said the other day about young men?"

"Yes, and I saw that 'The Jupiter' said all that it could to induce the appointment of Mr. Slope. Perhaps you would wish to see Mr. Slope made dean."

Mr. Harding made no reply to this rebuke, though he felt it strongly. He had not come over to Plumstead to have further contention with his son-in-law about Mr. Slope, so he allowed it to pass by.

"I know I cannot make you understand my feeling," he said, "for we have been cast in different moulds. I may wish that I had your spirit and energy and power of combatting; but I have not. Every day that is added to my life increases my wish for peace and rest."

"And where on earth can a man have peace and rest if not in a deanery!" said the archdeacon.

"People will say that I am too old for it."

"Good heavens! People! What people? What need you care for any people?"

"But I think myself I am too old for any new place."

"Dear Papa," said Mrs. Grantly, "men ten years older than you are appointed to new situations day after day."

"My dear," said he, "it is impossible that I should make you understand my feelings, nor do I pretend to any great virtue in the matter. The truth is, I want the force of character which might enable me to stand against the spirit of the times. The call on all sides now is for young men, and I have not the nerve to put myself in opposition to the demand. Were 'The Jupiter,' when it hears of my appointment, to write article after article setting forth my incompetency, I am sure it would cost me my reason. I ought to be able to bear with such things, you will say. Well, my dear, I own that I ought. But I feel my weakness, and I know that I can't. And to tell you the truth, I know no more than a child what the dean has to do."

"Pshaw!" exclaimed the archdeacon.

"Don't be angry with me, Archdeacon: don't let us quarrel about it, Susan. If you knew how keenly I feel the necessity of having to disoblige you in this matter, you would not be angry with me."

This was a dreadful blow to Dr. Grantly. Nothing could possibly have suited him better than having Mr. Harding in the deanery. Though he had never looked down on Mr. Harding on account of his recent poverty, he did fully recognize the satisfaction of having those belonging to him in comfortable positions. It would be much more suitable that Mr. Harding should be Dean of Barchester than vicar of St. Cuthbert's and precentor to boot. And then the great discomfiture of that arch-enemy of all that was respectable in Barchester, of that new Low Church clerical parvenu that had fallen amongst them, that alone would be worth more, almost, than the situation itself. It was frightful to think that such unhoped-for good fortune should be marred by the absurd crotchets and unwholesome hallucinations by which Mr. Harding allowed himself to be led astray. To have the cup so near his lips and then to lose the drinking of it was more than Dr. Grantly could endure.

And yet it appeared as though he would have to endure it. In vain he threatened and in vain he coaxed. Mr. Harding did not indeed speak with perfect decision of refusing the proffered glory, but he would not speak with anything like decision of accepting it. When pressed again and again, he would again and again allege that he was wholly unfitted to new duties. It was in vain that the archdeacon tried to insinuate, though he could not plainly declare, that there were no new duties to perform. It was in vain he hinted that in all cases of difficulty he, he the archdeacon, was willing and able to guide a weak-minded dean. Mr. Harding seemed to have a foolish idea, not only that there were new duties to do, but that no one should accept the place who was not himself prepared to do them.

The conference ended in an understanding that Mr. Harding should at once acknowledge the letter he had received from the minister's private secretary, and should beg that he might be allowed two days to make up his mind; and that during those two days the matter should be considered.

On the following morning the archdeacon was to drive Mr. Harding back to Barchester.

CHAPTER XLVIII

MISS THORNE SHOWS HER TALENT AT MATCH-MAKING

On Mr. Harding's return to Barchester from Plumstead, which was effected by him in due course in company with the archdeacon, more tidings of a surprising nature met him. He was, during the journey, subjected to such a weight of unanswerable argument, all of which went to prove that it was his bounden duty not to interfere with the paternal Government that was so anxious to make him a dean, that when he arrived at the chemist's door in High Street, he hardly knew which way to turn himself in the matter. But, perplexed as he was, he was doomed to further perplexity. He found a note there from his daughter begging him most urgently to come to her immediately. But we must again go back a little in our story.

Miss Thorne had not been slow to hear the rumours respecting Mr. Arabin which had so much disturbed the happiness of Mrs. Grantly. And she, also, was unhappy to think that her parish clergyman should be accused of worshipping a strange goddess. She, also, was of opinion that rectors and vicars should all be married, and with that good-natured energy which was characteristic of her, she put her wits to work to find a fitting match for Mr. Arabin. Mrs. Grantly, in this difficulty, could think of no better remedy than a lecture from the archdeacon. Miss Thorne thought that a young lady, marriageable and with a dowry, might be of more efficacy. In looking through the catalogue of her unmarried friends who might possibly be in want of a husband, and might also be fit for such promotion as a country parsonage affords, she could think of no one more eligible than Mrs. Bold; consequently, losing no time, she went into Barchester on the day of Mr. Slope's discomfiture, the same day that her brother had had his interesting interview with the last of the Neros, and invited Mrs. Bold to bring her nurse and baby to Ullathorne and make them a protracted visit.

Miss Thorne suggested a month or two, intending to use her influence afterwards in prolonging it so as to last out the winter, in order that Mr. Arabin might have an opportunity of becoming fairly intimate with his intended bride. "We'll have Mr. Arabin, too," said Miss Thorne to herself; "and before the spring they'll know each other; and in twelve or eighteen months' time, if all goes well, Mrs. Bold will be domiciled at St. Ewold's;" and then the kind-hearted lady gave herself some not undeserved praise for her match-making genius.

Eleanor was taken a little by surprise, but the matter ended in her promising to go to Ullathorne for at any rate a week or two; on the day previous to that on which her father drove out to Plumstead, she had had herself driven out to Ullathorne.

Miss Thorne would not perplex her with her embryo lord on that same evening, thinking that she would allow her a few hours to make herself at home; but on the following morning Mr. Arabin arrived. "And now," said Miss Thorne to herself, "I must contrive to throw them in each other's way." That same day, after dinner, Eleanor, with an assumed air of dignity which she could not maintain, with tears which she could not suppress, with a flutter which she could not conquer, and a joy which she could not hide, told Miss Thorne that she was engaged to marry Mr. Arabin and that it behoved her to get back home to Barchester as quick as she could.

To say simply that Miss Thorne was rejoiced at the success of the scheme would give a very faint idea of her feelings on the occasion. My readers may probably have dreamt before now that they have had before them some terribly long walk to accomplish, some journey of twenty or thirty miles, an amount of labour frightful to anticipate, and that immediately on starting they have ingeniously found some accommodating short cut which has brought them without fatigue to their work's end in five minutes. Miss Thorne's waking feelings were somewhat of the same nature. My readers may perhaps have had to do with children, and may on some occasion have promised to their young charges some great gratification intended to come off, perhaps at the end of the winter, or at the beginning of summer. The impatient juveniles, however, will not wait, and clamorously demand their treat before they go to bed. Miss Thorne had a sort of feeling that her children were equally unreasonable. She was like an inexperienced gunner, who has ill-calculated the length of the train that he has laid. The gun-powder exploded much too soon, and poor Miss Thorne felt that she was blown up by the strength of her own petard.

Miss Thorne had had lovers of her own, but they had been gentlemen of old-fashioned and deliberate habits. Miss Thorne's heart also had not always been hard, though she was still a virgin spinster; but it had never yielded in this way at the first assault. She had intended to bring together a middle-aged, studious clergyman and a discreet matron who might possibly be induced to marry again, and in doing so she had thrown fire among tinder. Well, it was all as it should be, but she did feel perhaps a little put out by the precipitancy of her own success, and perhaps a little vexed at the readiness of Mrs. Bold to be wooed.

She said, however, nothing about it to anyone, and ascribed it all to the altered manners of the new age. Their mothers and grandmothers were perhaps a little more deliberate, but it was admitted on all sides that things were conducted very differently now than in former times. For aught Miss Thorne knew of the matter, a couple of hours might be quite sufficient under the new régime to complete that for which she in her ignorance had allotted twelve months.

But we must not pass over the wooing so cavalierly. It has been told, with perhaps tedious accuracy, how Eleanor disposed of two of her lovers at Ullathorne; and it must also be told with equal accuracy, and if possible with less tedium, how she encountered Mr. Arabin.

It cannot be denied that when Eleanor accepted Miss Thorne's invitation she remembered that Ullathorne was in the parish of St. Ewold's. Since her interview with the signora she had done little else than think about Mr. Arabin and the appeal that had been made to her. She could not bring herself to believe, or try to bring herself to believe, that what she had been told was untrue. Think of it how she would, she could not but accept it as a fact that Mr. Arabin was fond of her; and then when she went further and asked herself the question, she could not but accept it as a fact also that she was fond of him. If it were destined for her to be the partner of his hopes and sorrows, to whom could she look for friendship so properly as to Miss Thorne? This invitation was like an ordained step towards the fulfilment of her destiny, and when she also heard that Mr. Arabin was expected to be at Ullathorne on the following day, it seemed as though all the world were conspiring in her favour. Well, did she not deserve it? In that affair of Mr. Slope had not all the world conspired against her?

She could not, however, make herself easy and at home. When, in the evening after dinner, Miss Thorne expatiated on the excellence of Mr. Arabin's qualities, and hinted that any little rumour which might be ill-naturedly spread abroad concerning him really meant nothing, Mrs. Bold found herself unable to answer. When Miss Thorne went a little further and declared that she did not know a prettier vicarage-house in the county than St. Ewold's, Mrs. Bold, remembering the projected bow-window and the projected priestess, still held her tongue, though her ears tingled with the conviction that all the world knew that she was in love with Mr. Arabin. Well, what would that matter if they could only meet and tell each other what each now longed to tell?

And they did meet. Mr. Arabin came early in the day and found the two ladies together at work in the drawing-room. Miss Thorne, who, had she known all the truth, would have vanished into air at once, had no conception that her immediate absence would be a blessing, and remained chatting with them till luncheon-time. Mr. Arabin could talk about nothing but the Signora Neroni's beauty, would discuss no people but the Stanhopes. This was very distressing to Eleanor and not very satisfactory to Miss Thorne. But yet there was evidence of innocence in his open avowal of admiration.

And then they had lunch, and then Mr. Arabin went out on parish duty, and Eleanor and Miss Thorne were left to take a walk together.

"Do you think the Signora Neroni is so lovely as people say?" Eleanor asked as they were coming home.

"She is very beautiful, certainly, very beautiful," Miss Thorne answered; "but I do not know that anyone considers her lovely. She is a woman all men would like to look at, but few, I imagine, would be glad to take her to their hearths, even were she unmarried and not afflicted as she is."

There was some little comfort in this. Eleanor made the most of it till she got back to the house. She was then left alone in the drawing-room, and just as it was getting dark Mr. Arabin came in.

It was a beautiful afternoon in the beginning of October, and Eleanor was sitting in the window to get the advantage of the last daylight for her novel. There was a fire in the comfortable room, but the weather was not cold enough to make it attractive; and as she could see the sun set from where she sat, she was not very attentive to her book.

Mr. Arabin, when he entered, stood awhile with his back to the fire in his usual way, merely uttering a few commonplace remarks about the beauty of the weather, while he plucked up courage for more interesting converse. It cannot probably be said that he had resolved then and there to make an offer to Eleanor. Men, we believe, seldom make such resolves. Mr. Slope and Mr. Stanhope had done so, it is true, but gentlemen generally propose without any absolutely defined determination as to their doing so. Such was now the case with Mr. Arabin.

"It is a lovely sunset," said Eleanor, answering him on the dreadfully trite subject which he had chosen.

Mr. Arabin could not see the sunset from the hearth-rug, so he had to go close to her.

"Very lovely," said he, standing modestly so far away from her as to avoid touching the flounces of her dress. Then it appeared that he had nothing further to say; so, after gazing for a moment in silence at the brightness of the setting sun, he returned to the fire.

Eleanor found that it was quite impossible for herself to commence a conversation. In the first place she could find nothing to say; words, which were generally plenty enough with her, would not come to her relief. And moreover, do what she would, she could hardly prevent herself from crying.

"Do you like Ullathorne?" said Mr. Arabin, speaking from the safely distant position which he had assumed on the hearth-rug.

"Yes, indeed, very much!"

"I don't mean Mr. and Miss Thorne—I know you like them—but the style of the house. There is something about old-fashioned mansions, built as this is, and old-fashioned gardens, that to me is especially delightful."

"I like everything old-fashioned," said Eleanor; "old-fashioned things are so much the honestest."

"I don't know about that," said Mr. Arabin, gently laughing. "That is an opinion on which very much may be said on either side. It is strange how widely the world is divided on a subject which so nearly concerns us all, and which is so close beneath our eyes. Some think that we are quickly progressing towards perfection, while others imagine that virtue is disappearing from the earth."

"And you, Mr. Arabin, what do you think?" said Eleanor. She felt somewhat surprised at the tone which his conversation was taking, and yet she was relieved at his saying something which enabled herself to speak without showing her own emotion.

"What do I think, Mrs. Bold?" and then he rumbled his money with his hands in his trousers pockets, and looked and spoke very little like a thriving lover. "It is the bane of my life that on important subjects I acquire no fixed opinion. I think, and think, and go on thinking, and yet my thoughts are running ever in different directions. I hardly know whether or no we do lean more confidently than our fathers did on those high hopes to which we profess to aspire."

"I think the world grows more worldly every day," said Eleanor.

"That is because you see more of it than when you were younger. But we should hardly judge by what we see—we see so very, very little." There was then a pause for awhile, during which Mr. Arabin continued to turn over his shillings and half-crowns. "If we believe in Scripture, we can hardly think that mankind in general will now be allowed to retrograde."

Eleanor, whose mind was certainly engaged otherwise than on the general state of mankind, made no answer to this. She felt thoroughly dissatisfied with herself. She could not force her thoughts away from the topic on which the signora had spoken to her in so strange a way, and yet she knew that she could not converse with Mr. Arabin in an unrestrained, natural tone till she did so. She was most anxious not to show to him any special emotion, and yet she felt that if he looked at her, he would at once see that she was not at ease.

But he did not look at her. Instead of doing so, he left the fire-place and began walking up and down the room. Eleanor took up her book resolutely, but she could not read, for there was a tear in her eye, and do what she would, it fell on her cheek. When Mr. Arabin's back was turned to her, she wiped it away; but another was soon coursing down her face in its place. They would come—not a deluge of tears that would have betrayed her at once, but one by one, single monitors. Mr. Arabin did not observe her closely, and they passed unseen.

Mr. Arabin, thus pacing up and down the room, took four or five turns before he spoke another word, and Eleanor sat equally silent with her face bent over her book. She was afraid that her tears would get the better of her, and was preparing for an escape from the room, when Mr. Arabin in his walk stood opposite to her. He did not come close up but stood exactly on the spot to which his course brought him, and then, with his hands under his coat-tails, thus made his confession.

"Mrs. Bold," said he, "I owe you retribution for a great offence of which I have been guilty towards you." Eleanor's heart beat so that she could not trust herself to say that he had never been guilty of any offence. So Mr. Arabin thus went on.

"I have thought much of it since, and I am now aware that I was wholly unwarranted in putting to you a question which I once asked you. It was indelicate on my part, and perhaps unmanly. No intimacy which may exist between myself and your connexion, Dr. Grantly, could justify it. Nor could the acquaintance which existed between ourselves." This word acquaintance struck cold on Eleanor's heart. Was this to be her doom after all? "I therefore think it right to beg your pardon in a humble spirit, and I now do so."

What was Eleanor to say to him? She could not say much because she was crying, and yet she must say something. She was most anxious to say that something graciously, kindly, and yet not in such a manner as to betray herself. She had never felt herself so much at a loss for words.

"Indeed, I took no offence, Mr. Arabin."

"Oh, but you did! And had you not done so, you would not have been yourself. You were as right to be offended as I was wrong so to offend you. I have not forgiven myself, but I hope to hear that you forgive me."

She was now past speaking calmly, though she still continued to hide her tears; and Mr. Arabin, after pausing a moment in vain for her reply, was walking off towards the door. She felt that she could not allow him to go unanswered without grievously sinning against all charity; so, rising from her seat, she gently touched his arm and said, "Oh, Mr. Arabin, do not go till I speak to you! I do forgive you. You know that I forgive you."

He took the hand that had so gently touched his arm and then gazed into her face as if he would peruse there, as though written in a book, the whole future destiny of his life; as he did so, there was a sober, sad seriousness in his own countenance which Eleanor found herself unable to sustain. She could only look down upon the carpet, let her tears trickle as they would, and leave her hand within his.

It was but for a minute that they stood so, but the duration of that minute was sufficient to make it ever memorable to them both. Eleanor was sure now that she was loved. No words, be their eloquence what it might, could be more impressive than that eager, melancholy gaze.

Why did he look so into her eyes? Why did he not speak to her? Could it be that he looked for her to make the first sign?

And he, though he knew but little of women, even he knew that he was loved. He had only to ask, and it would be all his own, that inexpressible loveliness, those ever-speaking but yet now mute eyes, that feminine brightness and eager, loving spirit which had so attracted him since first he had encountered it at St. Ewold's. It might, must, all be his own now. On no other supposition was it possible that she should allow her hand to remain thus clasped within his own. He had only to ask. Ah, but that was the difficulty. Did a minute suffice for all this? Nay, perhaps it might be more than a minute.

"Mrs. Bold—" at last he said and then stopped himself.

If he could not speak, how was she to do so? He had called her by her name, the same name that any merest stranger would have used! She withdrew her hand from his and moved as though to return to her seat. "Eleanor!" he then said in his softest tone, as though the courage of a lover were as yet but half-assumed, as though he were still afraid of giving offence by the freedom which he took. She looked slowly, gently, almost piteously up into his face. There was at any rate no anger there to deter him.

"Eleanor!" he again exclaimed, and in a moment he had her clasped to his bosom. How this was done, whether the doing was with him or her, whether she had flown thither conquered by the tenderness of his voice, or he with a violence not likely to give offence had drawn her to his breast, neither of them knew; nor can I declare. There was now that sympathy between them which hardly admitted of individual motion. They were one and the same—one flesh—one spirit—one life.

"Eleanor, my own Eleanor, my own, my wife!" She ventured to look up at him through her tears, and he, bowing his face down over hers, pressed his lips upon her brow—his virgin lips, which, since a beard first grew upon his chin, had never yet tasted the luxury of a woman's cheek.

She had been told that her yea must be yea, or her nay, nay, but she was called on for neither the one nor the other. She told Miss Thorne that she was engaged to Mr. Arabin, but no such words had passed between them, no promises had been asked or given.

"Oh, let me go," said she, "let me go now. I am too happy to remain—let me go, that I may be alone." He did not try to hinder her; he did not repeat the kiss; he did not press another on her lips. He might have done so, had he been so minded. She was now all his own. He took his arm from round her waist, his arm that was trembling with a new delight, and let her go. She fled like a roe to her own chamber, and then, having turned the bolt, she enjoyed the full luxury of her love. She idolised, almost worshipped this man who had so meekly begged her pardon. And he was now her own. Oh, how she wept and cried and laughed as the hopes and fears and miseries of the last few weeks passed in remembrance through her mind.

Mr. Slope! That anyone should have dared to think that she who had been chosen by him could possibly have mated herself with Mr. Slope! That they should have dared to tell him, also, and subject her bright happiness to such needless risk! And then she smiled with joy as she thought of all the comforts that she could give him—not that he cared for comforts, but that it would be so delicious for her to give.

She got up and rang for her maid that she might tell her little boy of his new father, and in her own way she did tell him. She desired her maid to leave her, in order that she might be alone with her child; and then, while he lay sprawling on the bed, she poured forth the praises, all unmeaning to him, of the man she had selected to guard his infancy.

She could not be happy, however, till she had made Mr. Arabin take the child to himself and thus, as it were, adopt him as his own. The moment the idea struck her she took the baby up in her arms and, opening her door, ran quickly down to the drawing-room. She at once found, by his step still pacing on the floor, that he was there, and a glance within the room told her that he was alone. She hesitated a moment and then hurried in with her precious charge.

Mr. Arabin met her in the middle of the room. "There," said she, breathless with her haste; "there, take him—take him, and love him."

Mr. Arabin took the little fellow from her and, kissing him again and again, prayed God to bless him. "He shall be all as my own—all as my own," said he. Eleanor, as she stooped to take back her child, kissed the hand that held him and then rushed back with her treasure to her chamber.

It was thus that Mr. Harding's younger daughter was won for the second time. At dinner neither she nor Mr. Arabin were very bright, but their silence occasioned no remark. In the drawing-room, as we have before said, she told Miss Thorne what had occurred. The next morning she returned to Barchester, and Mr. Arabin went over with his budget of news to the archdeacon. As Doctor Grantly was not there, he could only satisfy himself by telling Mrs. Grantly how that he intended himself the honour of becoming her brother-in-law. In the ecstasy of her joy at hearing such tidings Mrs. Grantly vouchsafed him a warmer welcome than any he had yet received from Eleanor.

"Good heavens!" she exclaimed—it was the general exclamation of the rectory. "Poor Eleanor! Dear Eleanor! What a monstrous injustice has been done her! Well, it shall all be made up now." And then she thought of the signora. "What lies people tell," she said to herself.

But people in this matter had told no lies at all.

CHAPTER XLIX

THE BEELZEBUB COLT

When Miss Thorne left the dining-room, Eleanor had formed no intention of revealing to her what had occurred, but when she was seated beside her hostess on the sofa, the secret dropped from her almost unawares. Eleanor was but a bad hypocrite, and she found herself quite unable to continue talking about Mr. Arabin as though he were a stranger while her heart was full of him. When Miss Thorne, pursuing her own scheme with discreet zeal, asked the young widow whether, in her opinion, it would not be a good thing for Mr. Arabin to get married, she had nothing for it but to confess the truth. "I suppose it would," said Eleanor rather sheepishly. Whereupon Miss Thorne amplified on the idea. "Oh, Miss Thorne," said Eleanor, "he is going to be married: I am engaged to him."

Now Miss Thorne knew very well that there had been no such engagement when she had been walking with Mrs. Bold in the morning. She had also heard enough to be tolerably sure that there had been no preliminaries to such an engagement. She was, therefore, as we have before described, taken a little by surprise. But nevertheless, she embraced her guest and cordially congratulated her.

Eleanor had no opportunity of speaking another word to Mr. Arabin that evening, except such words as all the world might hear; and these, as may be supposed, were few enough. Miss Thorne did her best to leave them in privacy, but Mr. Thorne, who knew nothing of what had occurred, and another guest, a friend of his, entirely interfered with her good intentions. So poor Eleanor had to go to bed without one sign of affection. Her state, nevertheless, was not to be pitied.

The next morning she was up early. It was probable, she thought, that by going down a little before the usual hour of breakfast she might find Mr. Arabin alone in the dining-room. Might it not be that he also would calculate that an interview would thus be possible? Thus thinking, Eleanor was dressed a full hour before the time fixed in the Ullathorne household for morning prayers. She did not at once go down. She was afraid to seem to be too anxious to meet her lover, though heaven knows her anxiety was intense enough. She therefore sat herself down at her window, and repeatedly looking at her watch, nursed her child till she thought she might venture forth.

When she found herself at the dining-room door, she stood a moment, hesitating to turn the handle; but when she heard Mr. Thorne's voice inside she hesitated no longer. Her object was defeated, and she might now go in as soon as she liked without the slightest imputation on her delicacy. Mr. Thorne and Mr. Arabin were standing on the hearth-rug, discussing the merits of the Beelzebub colt; or rather, Mr. Thorne was discussing, and Mr.

Arabin was listening. That interesting animal had rubbed the stump of his tail against the wall of his stable and occasioned much uneasiness to the Ullathorne master of the horse. Had Eleanor but waited another minute, Mr. Thorne would have been in the stables.

Mr. Thorne, when he saw his lady guest, repressed his anxiety. The Beelzebub colt must do without him. And so the three stood, saying little or nothing to each other, till at last the master of the house, finding that he could no longer bear his present state of suspense respecting his favourite young steed, made an elaborate apology to Mrs. Bold and escaped. As he shut the door behind him Eleanor almost wished that he had remained. It was not that she was afraid of Mr. Arabin, but she hardly yet knew how to address him.

He, however, soon relieved her from her embarrassment. He came up to her, and taking both her hands in his, he said, "So, Eleanor, you and I are to be man and wife. Is it so?"

She looked up into his face, and her lips formed themselves into a single syllable. She uttered no sound, but he could read the affirmative plainly in her face.

"It is a great trust," said he, "a very great trust."

"It is—it is," said Eleanor, not exactly taking what he had said in the sense that he had meant. "It is a very, very great trust, and I will do my utmost to deserve it."

"And I also will do my utmost to deserve it," said Mr. Arabin very solemnly. And then, winding his arm round her waist, he stood there gazing at the fire, and she, with her head leaning on his shoulder, stood by him, well satisfied with her position. They neither of them spoke, or found any want of speaking. All that was needful for them to say had been said. The yea, yea, had been spoken by Eleanor in her own way—and that way had been perfectly satisfactory to Mr. Arabin.

And now it remained to them each to enjoy the assurance of the other's love. And how great that luxury is! How far it surpasses any other pleasure which God has allowed to his creatures! And to a woman's heart how doubly delightful!

When the ivy has found its tower, when the delicate creeper has found its strong wall, we know how the parasite plants grow and prosper. They were not created to stretch forth their branches alone, and endure without protection the summer's sun and the winter's storm. Alone they but spread themselves on the ground and cower unseen in the dingy shade. But when they have found their firm supporters, how wonderful is their beauty; how all-pervading and victorious! What is the turret without its ivy, or the high garden wall without the jasmine which gives it its beauty and fragrance? The hedge without the honeysuckle is but a hedge.

There is a feeling still half-existing, but now half-conquered by the force of human nature, that a woman should be ashamed of her love till the husband's right to her compels her to acknowledge it. We would fain preach a different doctrine. A woman should glory in her love, but on that account let her take the more care that it be such as to justify her glory.

Eleanor did glory in hers, and she felt, and had cause to feel, that it deserved to be held as glorious. She could have stood there for hours with his arm round her, had fate and Mr. Thorne permitted it. Each moment she crept nearer to his bosom and felt more and more certain that there was her home. What now to her was the archdeacon's arrogance, her sister's coldness, or her dear father's weakness? What need she care for the duplicity of such friends as Charlotte Stanhope? She had found the strong shield that should guard her from all wrongs, the trusty pilot that should henceforward guide her through the shoals and rocks. She would give up the heavy burden of her independence, and once more assume the position of a woman and the duties of a trusting and loving wife.

And he, too, stood there fully satisfied with his place. They were both looking intently on the fire, as though they could read there their future fate, till at last Eleanor turned her face towards his. "How sad you are," she said, smiling; and indeed his face was, if not sad, at least serious. "How sad you are, love!"

"Sad," said he, looking down at her; "no, certainly not sad." Her sweet, loving eyes were turned towards him, and she smiled softly as he answered her. The temptation was too strong even for the demure propriety of Mr. Arabin, and bending over her, he pressed his lips to hers.

Immediately after this Mr. Thorne appeared, and they were both delighted to hear that the tail of the Beelzebub colt was not materially injured.

It had been Mr. Harding's intention to hurry over to Ullathorne as soon as possible after his return to Barchester, in order to secure the support of his daughter in his meditated revolt against the archdeacon as touching the deanery; but he was spared the additional journey by hearing that Mrs. Bold had returned unexpectedly home. As soon as he had read her note he started off, and found her waiting for him in her own house.

How much each of them had to tell the other, and how certain each was that the story which he or she had to tell would astonish the other!

"My dear, I am so anxious to see you," said Mr. Harding, kissing his daughter.

"Oh, Papa, I have so much to tell you!" said the daughter, returning the embrace.

"My dear, they have offered me the deanery!" said Mr. Harding, anticipating by the suddenness of the revelation the tidings which Eleanor had to give him.

"Oh, Papa," said she, forgetting her own love and happiness in her joy at the surprising news. "Oh, Papa, can it be possible? Dear Papa, how thoroughly, thoroughly happy that makes me!"

"But, my dear, I think it best to refuse it."

"Oh, Papa!"

"I am sure you will agree with me, Eleanor, when I explain it to you. You know, my dear, how old I am. If I live I—"

"But, Papa, I must tell you about myself."

"Well, my dear."

"I do so wonder how you'll take it."

"Take what?"

"If you don't rejoice at it, if it doesn't make you happy, if you don't encourage me, I shall break my heart."

"If that be the case, Nelly, I certainly will encourage you."

"But I fear you won't. I do so fear you won't. And yet you can't but think I am the most fortunate woman living on God's earth."

"Are you, dearest? Then I certainly will rejoice with you. Come, Nelly, come to me and tell me what it is."

"I am going—"

He led her to the sofa and, seating himself beside her, took both her hands in his. "You are going to be married, Nelly. Is not that it?"

"Yes," she said faintly. "That is, if you will approve;" and then she blushed as she remembered the promise which she had so lately volunteered to him and which she had so utterly forgotten in making her engagement with Mr. Arabin.

Mr. Harding thought for a moment who the man could be whom he was to be called upon to welcome as his son-in-law. A week since he would have had no doubt whom to name. In that case he would have been prepared to give his sanction, although he would have done so with a heavy heart. Now he knew that at any rate it would not be Mr. Slope, though he was perfectly at a loss to guess who could possibly have filled the place. For a moment he thought that the man might be Bertie Stanhope, and his very soul sank within him.

"Well, Nelly?"

"Oh, Papa, promise to me that, for my sake, you will love him."

"Come, Nelly, come; tell me who it is."

"But will you love him, Papa?"

"Dearest, I must love anyone that you love." Then she turned her face to his and whispered into his ear the name of Mr. Arabin.

No man that she could have named could have more surprised or more delighted him. Had he looked round the world for a son-in-law to his taste, he could have selected no one whom he would have preferred to Mr. Arabin. He was a clergyman; he held a living in the neighbourhood; he was of a set to which all Mr. Harding's own partialities most closely adhered; he was the great friend of Dr. Grantly; and he was, moreover, a man of whom Mr. Harding knew nothing but what he approved. Nevertheless, his surprise was so great as to prevent the immediate expression of his joy. He had never thought of Mr. Arabin in connexion with his daughter; he had never imagined that they had any feeling in common. He had feared that his daughter had been made hostile to clergymen of Mr. Arabin's stamp by her intolerance of the archdeacon's pretensions. Had he been put to wish, he might have wished for Mr. Arabin for a son-in-law; but had he been put to guess, the name would never have occurred to him.

"Mr. Arabin!" he exclaimed; "impossible!"

"Oh, Papa, for heaven's sake don't say anything against him! If you love me, don't say anything against him. Oh, Papa, it's done and mustn't be undone—oh, Papa!"

Fickle Eleanor! Where was the promise that she would make no choice for herself without her father's approval? She had chosen, and now demanded his acquiescence. "Oh, Papa, isn't he good? Isn't he noble? Isn't he religious, high-minded, everything that a good man possibly can be?" She clung to her father, beseeching him for his consent.

"My Nelly, my child, my own daughter! He is; he is noble and good and high-minded; he is all that a woman can love and a man admire. He shall be my son, my own son. He shall be as close to my heart as you are. My Nelly, my child, my happy, happy child!"

We need not pursue the interview any further. By degrees they returned to the subject of the new promotion. Eleanor tried to prove to him, as the Grantlys had done, that his age could be no bar to his being a very excellent dean, but those arguments had now even less weight on him than before. He said little or nothing but sat, meditative. Every now and then he would kiss his daughter and say "yes," or "no," or "very true," or "well, my dear, I can't quite agree with you there," but he could not be got to enter sharply into the question of "to be, or not to be" Dean of Barchester. Of her and her happiness, of Mr. Arabin and his virtues, he would talk as much as Eleanor desired—and to tell the truth, that was not a little—but about the deanery he would now say nothing further. He had got a new idea into his head—why should not Mr. Arabin be the new dean?

CHAPTER L

THE ARCHDEACON IS SATISFIED WITH THE STATE OF AFFAIRS

The archdeacon, in his journey into Barchester, had been assured by Mr. Harding that all their prognostications about Mr. Slope and Eleanor were groundless. Mr. Harding, however, had found it very difficult to shake his son-in-law's faith in his own acuteness. The matter had, to Dr. Grantly, been so plainly corroborated by such patent evidence, borne out by such endless circumstances, that he at first refused to take as true the positive statement which Mr. Harding made to him of Eleanor's own disavowal of the impeachment. But at last he yielded in a qualified way. He brought himself to admit that he would at the present regard his past convictions as a mistake, but in doing this he so guarded himself that if, at any future time, Eleanor should come forth to the world as Mrs. Slope, he might still be able to say: "There, I told you so. Remember what you said and what I said; and remember also for coming years, that I was right in this matter—as in all others."

He carried, however, his concession so far as to bring himself to undertake to call at Eleanor's house, and he did call accordingly, while the father and daughter were yet in the middle of their conference. Mr. Harding had had so much to hear and to say that he had forgotten to advise Eleanor of the honour that awaited her, and she heard her brother-in-law's voice in the hall while she was quite unprepared to see him.

"There's the archdeacon," she said, springing up.

"Yes, my dear. He told me to tell you that he would come and see you; but to tell the truth I had forgotten all about it."

Eleanor fled away, regardless of all her father's entreaties. She could not now, in the first hours of her joy, bring herself to bear all the archdeacon's retractions, apologies, and congratulations. He would have so much to say, and would be so tedious in saying it; consequently, the archdeacon, when he was shown into the drawing-room, found no one there but Mr. Harding.

"You must excuse Eleanor," said Mr. Harding.

"Is anything the matter?" asked the doctor, who at once anticipated that the whole truth about Mr. Slope had at last come out.

"Well, something is the matter. I wonder now whether you will be much surprised."

The archdeacon saw by his father-in-law's manner that after all he had nothing to tell him about Mr. Slope. "No," said he, "certainly not—nothing will ever surprise me again." Very many men now-a-days besides the archdeacon adopt or affect to adopt the *nil admi-*

rari doctrine; but nevertheless, to judge from their appearance, they are just as subject to sudden emotions as their grandfathers and grandmothers were before them.

"What do you think Mr. Arabin has done?"

"Mr. Arabin! It's nothing about that daughter of Stanhope's, I hope?"

"No, not that woman," said Mr. Harding, enjoying his joke in his sleeve.

"Not that woman! Is he going to do anything about any woman? Why can't you speak out, if you have anything to say? There is nothing I hate so much as these sort of mysteries."

"There shall be no mystery with you, Archdeacon, though of course it must go no further at present."

"Well."

"Except Susan. You must promise me you'll tell no one else."

"Nonsense!" exclaimed the archdeacon, who was becoming angry in his suspense. "You can't have any secret about Mr. Arabin."

"Only this—that he and Eleanor are engaged."

It was quite clear to see, by the archdeacon's face, that he did not believe a word of it. "Mr. Arabin! It's impossible!"

"Eleanor, at any rate, has just now told me so."

"It's impossible," repeated the archdeacon.

"Well, I can't say I think it impossible. It certainly took me by surprise, but that does not make it impossible."

"She must be mistaken."

Mr. Harding assured him that there was no mistake; that he would find, on returning home, that Mr. Arabin had been at Plumstead with the express object of making the same declaration; that even Miss Thorne knew all about it; and that, in fact, the thing was as clearly settled as any such arrangement between a lady and a gentleman could well be.

"Good heavens!" said the archdeacon, walking up and down Eleanor's drawing-room. "Good heavens! Good heavens!"

Now these exclamations certainly betokened faith. Mr. Harding properly gathered from it that, at last, Dr. Grantly did believe the fact. The first utterance clearly evinced a certain amount of distaste at the information he had received; the second simply indicated surprise; in the tone of the third Mr. Harding fancied that he could catch a certain gleam of satisfaction.

The archdeacon had truly expressed the workings of his mind. He could not but be disgusted to find how utterly astray he had been in all his anticipations. Had he only been lucky enough to have suggested this marriage himself when he first brought Mr. Arabin into the country, his character for judgement and wisdom would have received an addition which would have classed him at any rate next to Solomon. And why had he not done so? Might he not have foreseen that Mr. Arabin would want a wife in his parsonage? He had foreseen that Eleanor would want a husband, but should he not also have perceived that Mr. Arabin was a man much more likely to attract her than Mr. Slope? The archdeacon found that he had been at fault and, of course, could not immediately get over his discomfiture.

Then his surprise was intense. How sly this pair of young turtle-doves had been with him. How egregiously they had hoaxed him. He had preached to Eleanor against her fancied attachment to Mr. Slope at the very time that she was in love with his own protégé, Mr. Arabin, and had absolutely taken that same Mr. Arabin into his confidence with reference to his dread of Mr. Slope's alliance. It was very natural that the archdeacon should feel surprise.

But there was also great ground for satisfaction. Looking at the match by itself, it was the very thing to help the doctor out of his difficulties. In the first place, the assurance that he should never have Mr. Slope for his brother-in-law was in itself a great comfort. Then Mr. Arabin was, of all men, the one with whom it would best suit him to be so intimately connected. But the crowning comfort was the blow which this marriage would give to Mr. Slope. He had now certainly lost his wife; rumour was beginning to whisper that he might possibly lose his position in the palace; and if Mr. Harding would only be true, the great danger of all would be surmounted. In such case it might be expected that Mr. Slope would own himself vanquished, and take himself altogether away from Barchester. And so the archdeacon would again be able to breathe pure air.

"Well, well," said he. "Good heavens! Good heavens!" and the tone of the fifth exclamation made Mr. Harding fully aware that content was reigning in the archdeacon's bosom.

And then slowly, gradually, and craftily Mr. Harding propounded his own new scheme. Why should not Mr. Arabin be the new dean?

Slowly, gradually, and thoughtfully Dr. Grantly fell into his father-in-law's views. Much as he liked Mr. Arabin, sincere as was his admiration for that gentleman's ecclesiastical abilities, he would not have sanctioned a measure which would rob his father-in-law of his fairly earned promotion, were it at all practicable to induce his father-in-law to accept the promotion which he had earned. But the archdeacon had, on a former occasion, received proof of the obstinacy with which Mr. Harding could adhere to his own views in opposition to the advice of all his friends. He knew tolerably well that nothing would induce the meek, mild man before him to take the high place offered to him, if he thought it wrong to do so. Knowing this, he also said to himself more than once: "Why should not Mr. Arabin be Dean of Barchester?" It was at last arranged between them that they would together start to London by the earliest train on the following morning, making a little detour to Oxford on their journey. Dr. Gwynne's counsels, they imagined, might perhaps be of assistance to them.

These matters settled, the archdeacon hurried off, that he might return to Plumstead and prepare for his journey. The day was extremely fine, and he came into the city in an open gig. As he was driving up the High Street he encountered Mr. Slope at a crossing. Had he not pulled up rather sharply, he would have run over him. The two had never spoken to each other since they had met on a memorable occasion in the bishop's study. They did not speak now, but they looked each other full in the face, and Mr. Slope's countenance was as impudent, as triumphant, as defiant as ever. Had Dr. Grantly not known to the contrary, he would have imagined that his enemy had won the deanship, the wife, and all the rich honours for which he had been striving. As it was, he had lost everything that he had in the world, and had just received his *congé* from the bishop.

In leaving the town the archdeacon drove by the well-remembered entrance of Hiram's Hospital. There, at the gate, was a large, untidy farmer's wagon, laden with untidy-looking furniture; and there, inspecting the arrival, was good Mrs. Quiverful—not dressed in her Sunday best, not very clean in her apparel, not graceful as to her bonnet and shawl, or, indeed, with many feminine charms as to her whole appearance. She was busy at domestic work in her new house, and had just ventured out, expecting to see no one on the arrival of the family chattels. The archdeacon was down upon her before she knew where she was.

Her acquaintance with Dr. Grantly or his family was very slight indeed. The archdeacon, as a matter of course, knew every clergyman in the archdeaconry—it may almost be said in the diocese—and had some acquaintance, more or less intimate, with their wives and families. With Mr. Quiverful he had been concerned on various matters of business, but of Mrs. Q. he had seen very little. Now, however, he was in too gracious a mood to pass her by unnoticed. The Quiverfuls, one and all, had looked for the bitterest hostility from Dr. Grantly; they knew his anxiety that Mr. Harding should return to his old home at the hospital, and they did not know that a new home had been offered to him at the deanery. Mrs. Quiverful was therefore not a little surprised, and not a little rejoiced also, at the tone in which she was addressed.

"How do you do, Mrs. Quiverful, how do you do?" said he, stretching his left hand out of the gig as he spoke to her. "I am very glad to see you employed in so pleasant and useful a manner; very glad indeed."

Mrs. Quiverful thanked him, and shook hands with him, and looked into his face suspiciously. She was not sure whether the congratulations and kindness were or were not ironical.

"Pray tell Mr. Quiverful from me," he continued, "that I am rejoiced at his appointment. It's a comfortable place, Mrs. Quiverful, and a comfortable house, and I am very glad to see you in it. Good-bye—good-bye." And he drove on, leaving the lady well pleased and astonished at his good nature. On the whole things were going well with the archdeacon, and he could afford to be charitable to Mrs. Quiverful. He looked forth from his gig smilingly on all the world, and forgave everyone in Barchester their sins, excepting only Mrs. Proudie and Mr. Slope. Had he seen the bishop, he would have felt inclined to pat even him kindly on the head.

He determined to go home by St. Ewold's. This would take him some three miles out of his way, but he felt that he could not leave Plumstead comfortably without saying one word of good-fellowship to Mr. Arabin. When he reached the parsonage, the vicar was still out, but from what he had heard, he did not doubt but that he would meet him on the road between their two houses. He was right in this, for about half-way home, at a narrow turn, he came upon Mr. Arabin, who was on horseback.

"Well, well, well, well," said the archdeacon loudly, joyously, and with supreme good humour; "well, well, well, well; so, after all, we have no further cause to fear Mr. Slope."

"I hear from Mrs. Grantly that they have offered the deanery to Mr. Harding," said the other.

"Mr. Slope has lost more than the deanery I find," and then the archdeacon laughed jocosely. "Come, come, Arabin, you have kept your secret well enough. I know all about it now."

"I have had no secret, Archdeacon," said the other with a quiet smile. "None at all—not for a day. It was only yesterday that I knew my own good fortune, and to-day I went over to Plumstead to ask your approval. From what Mrs. Grantly has said to me, I am led to hope that I shall have it."

"With all my heart, with all my heart," said the archdeacon cordially, holding his friend fast by the hand. "It's just as I would have it. She is an excellent young woman; she will not come to you empty-handed; and I think she will make you a good wife. If she does her duty by you as her sister does by me, you'll be a happy man; that's all I can say." And as he finished speaking a tear might have been observed in each of the doctor's eyes.

Mr. Arabin warmly returned the archdeacon's grasp, but he said little. His heart was too full for speaking, and he could not express the gratitude which he felt. Dr. Grantly understood him as well as though he had spoken for an hour.

"And mind, Arabin," said he, "no one but myself shall tie the knot. We'll get Eleanor out to Plumstead, and it shall come off there. I'll make Susan stir herself, and we'll do it in style. I must be off to London to-morrow on special business. Harding goes with me. But I'll be back before your bride has got her wedding-dress ready." And so they parted.

On his journey home the archdeacon occupied his mind with preparations for the marriage festivities. He made a great resolve that he would atone to Eleanor for all the injury he had done her by the munificence of his future treatment. He would show her what was the difference in his eyes between a Slope and an Arabin. On one other thing also he decided with a firm mind: if the affair of the dean should not be settled in Mr. Arabin's favour, nothing should prevent him putting a new front and bow-window to the dining-room at St. Ewold's parsonage.

"So we're sold after all, Sue," said he to his wife, accosting her with a kiss as soon as he entered his house. He did not call his wife Sue above twice or thrice in a year, and these occasions were great high days.

"Eleanor has had more sense than we gave her credit for," said Mrs. Grantly.

And there was great content in Plumstead Rectory that evening. Mrs. Grantly promised her husband that she would now open her heart and take Mr. Arabin into it. Hitherto she had declined to do so.

CHAPTER LI

MR. SLOPE BIDS FAREWELL TO THE PALACE
AND ITS INHABITANTS

We must now take leave of Mr. Slope, and of the bishop also, and of Mrs. Proudie. These leave-takings in novels are as disagreeable as they are in real life; not so sad, indeed, for they want the reality of sadness; but quite as perplexing, and generally less satisfactory. What novelist, what Fielding, what Scott, what George Sand, or Sue, or Dumas, can impart an interest to the last chapter of his fictitious history? Promises of two children and superhuman happiness are of no avail, nor assurance of extreme respectability carried to an age far exceeding that usually allotted to mortals. The sorrows of our heroes and heroines, they are your delight, oh public!—their sorrows, or their sins, or their absurdities; not their virtues, good sense, and consequent rewards. When we begin to tint our final pages with *couleur de rose*, as in accordance with fixed rule we must do, we altogether extinguish our own powers of pleasing. When we become dull, we offend your intellect; and we must become dull or we should offend your taste. A late writer, wishing to sustain his interest to the last page, hung his hero at the end of the third volume. The consequence was that no one would read his novel. And who can apportion out and dovetail his incidents, dialogues, characters, and descriptive morsels so as to fit them all exactly into 930 pages, without either compressing them unnaturally, or extending them artificially at the end of his labour? Do I not myself know that I am at this moment in want of a dozen pages, and that I am sick with cudgelling my brains to find them? And then, when everything is done, the kindest-hearted critic of them all invariably twits us with the incompetency and lameness of our conclusion. We have either become idle and neglected it, or tedious and overlaboured it. It is insipid or unnatural, overstrained or imbecile. It means nothing, or attempts too much. The last scene of all, as all last scenes we fear must be,

Is second childishness, and mere oblivion,
Sans teeth, sans eyes, sans taste, sans everything.

I can only say that if some critic who thoroughly knows his work, and has laboured on it till experience has made him perfect, will write the last fifty pages of a novel in the way they should be written, I, for one, will in future do my best to copy the example. Guided by my own lights only, I confess that I despair of success.

For the last week or ten days Mr. Slope had seen nothing of Mrs. Proudie, and very little of the bishop. He still lived in the palace, and still went through his usual routine work; but the confidential doings of the diocese had passed into other hands. He had seen this clearly and marked it well, but it had not much disturbed him. He had indulged in other hopes till the bishop's affairs had become dull to him, and he was moreover aware that, as regarded the diocese, Mrs. Proudie had checkmated him. It has been explained, in the beginning of these pages, how three or four were contending together as to who, in fact, should be Bishop of Barchester. Each of these had now admitted to himself (or boasted to herself) that Mrs. Proudie was victorious in the struggle. They had gone through a competitive examination of considerable severity, and she had come forth the winner, *facile princeps*. Mr. Slope had for a moment run her hard, but it was only for a moment. It had become, as it were, acknowledged that Hiram's Hospital should be the testing-point between them, and now Mr. Quiverful was already in the hospital, the proof of Mrs. Proudie's skill and courage.

All this did not break down Mr. Slope's spirit, because he had other hopes. But, alas, at last there came to him a note from his friend Sir Nicholas, informing him that the deanship was disposed of. Let us give Mr. Slope his due. He did not lie prostrate under this blow, or give himself up to vain lamentations; he did not henceforward despair of life and call upon gods above and gods below to carry him off. He sat himself down in his chair, counted out what monies he had in hand for present purposes and what others were coming in to him, bethought himself as to the best sphere for his future exertions, and at once wrote off a letter to a rich sugar-refiner's wife in Baker Street, who, as he well knew, was much given to the entertainment and encouragement of serious young evangelical clergymen. He was again, he said, "upon the world, having found the air of a cathedral town, and the very nature of cathedral services, uncongenial to his spirit;" and then he sat awhile, making firm resolves as to his manner of parting from the bishop, and also as to his future conduct.

At last he rose, and twitched his mantle blue (black),
To-morrow to fresh woods and pastures new.

Having received a formal command to wait upon the bishop, he rose and proceeded to obey it. He rang the bell and desired the servant to inform his master that, if it suited his lordship, he, Mr. Slope, was ready to wait upon him. The servant, who well understood that Mr. Slope was no longer in the ascendant, brought back a message saying that "his lordship desired that Mr. Slope would attend him immediately in his study." Mr. Slope waited about ten minutes more to prove his independence, and then he went into the bishop's room. There, as he had expected, he found Mrs. Proudie, together with her husband.

"Hum, ha—Mr. Slope, pray take a chair," said the gentleman bishop.

"Pray be seated, Mr. Slope," said the lady bishop.

"Thank ye, thank ye," said Mr. Slope, and walking round to the fire, he threw himself into one of the armchairs that graced the hearth-rug.

"Mr. Slope," said the bishop, "it has become necessary that I should speak to you definitively on a matter that has for some time been pressing itself on my attention."

"May I ask whether the subject is in any way connected with myself?" said Mr. Slope.

"It is so—certainly—yes, it certainly is connected with yourself, Mr. Slope."

"Then, my lord, if I may be allowed to express a wish, I would prefer that no discussion on the subject should take place between us in the presence of a third person."

"Don't alarm yourself, Mr. Slope," said Mrs. Proudie, "no discussion is at all necessary. The bishop merely intends to express his own wishes."

"I merely intend, Mr. Slope, to express my own wishes—no discussion will be at all necessary," said the bishop, reiterating his wife's words.

"That is more, my lord, than we any of us can be sure of," said Mr. Slope; "I cannot, however, force Mrs. Proudie to leave the room; nor can I refuse to remain here if it be your lordship's wish that I should do so."

"It is his lordship's wish, certainly," said Mrs. Proudie.

"Mr. Slope," began the bishop in a solemn, serious voice, "it grieves me to have to find fault. It grieves me much to have to find fault with a clergyman—but especially so with a clergyman in your position."

"Why, what have I done amiss, my lord?" demanded Mr. Slope boldly.

"What have you done amiss, Mr. Slope?" said Mrs. Proudie, standing erect before the culprit and raising that terrible forefinger. "Do you dare to ask the bishop what you have done amiss? Does not your conscience—"

"Mrs. Proudie, pray let it be understood, once for all, that I will have no words with you."

"Ah, sir, but you will have words," said she; "you must have words. Why have you had so many words with that Signora Neroni? Why have you disgraced yourself, you a clergyman, too, by constantly consorting with such a woman as that—with a married woman—with one altogether unfit for a clergyman's society?"

"At any rate I was introduced to her in your drawing-room," retorted Mr. Slope.

"And shamefully you behaved there," said Mrs. Proudie; "most shamefully. I was wrong to allow you to remain in the house a day after what I then saw. I should have insisted on your instant dismissal."

"I have yet to learn, Mrs. Proudie, that you have the power to insist either on my going from hence or on my staying here."

"What!" said the lady. "I am not to have the privilege of saying who shall and who shall not frequent my own drawing-room! I am not to save my servants and dependants from having their morals corrupted by improper conduct! I am not to save my own daughters from impurity! I will let you see, Mr. Slope, whether I have the power or whether I have not. You will have the goodness to understand that you no longer fill any situation about the bishop, and as your room will be immediately wanted in the palace for another chaplain, I must ask you to provide yourself with apartments as soon as may be convenient to you."

"My lord," said Mr. Slope, appealing to the bishop, and so turning his back completely on the lady, "will you permit me to ask that I may have from your own lips any decision that you may have come to on this matter?"

"Certainly, Mr. Slope, certainly," said the bishop; "that is but reasonable. Well, my decision is that you had better look for some other preferment. For the situation which you have lately held I do not think that you are well suited."

"And what, my lord, has been my fault?"

"That Signora Neroni is one fault," said Mrs. Proudie; "and a very abominable fault she is; very abominable and very disgraceful. Fie, Mr. Slope, fie! You an evangelical clergyman indeed!"

"My lord, I desire to know for what fault I am turned out of your lordship's house."

"You hear what Mrs. Proudie says," said the bishop.

"When I publish the history of this transaction, my lord, as I decidedly shall do in my own vindication, I presume you will not wish me to state that you have discarded me at your wife's bidding—because she has objected to my being acquainted with another lady, the daughter of one of the prebendaries of the chapter?"

"You may publish what you please, sir," said Mrs. Proudie. "But you will not be insane enough to publish any of your doings in Barchester. Do you think I have not heard of your kneelings at that creature's feet—that is, if she has any feet—and of your constant slobbering over her hand? I advise you to beware, Mr. Slope, of what you do and say. Clergymen have been unfrocked for less than what you have been guilty of."

"My lord, if this goes on I shall be obliged to indict this woman—Mrs. Proudie I mean—for defamation of character."

"I think, Mr. Slope, you had better now retire," said the bishop. "I will enclose to you a cheque for any balance that may be due to you; under the present circumstances, it will of course be better for all parties that you should leave the palace at the earliest possible moment. I will allow you for your journey back to London and for your maintenance in Barchester for a week from this date."

"If, however, you wish to remain in this neighbourhood;" said Mrs. Proudie, "and will solemnly pledge yourself never again to see that woman, and will promise also to be more circumspect in your conduct, the bishop will mention your name to Mr. Quiverful, who now wants a curate at Puddingdale. The house is, I imagine, quite sufficient for your requirements, and there will moreover be a stipend of fifty pounds a year."

"May God forgive you, madam, for the manner in which you have treated me," said Mr. Slope, looking at her with a very heavenly look; "and remember this, madam, that you yourself may still have a fall;" and he looked at her with a very worldly look. "As to the bishop, I pity him!" And so saying, Mr. Slope left the room. Thus ended the intimacy of the Bishop of Barchester with his first confidential chaplain.

Mrs. Proudie was right in this; namely, that Mr. Slope was not insane enough to publish to the world any of his doings in Barchester. He did not trouble his friend Mr. Towers with any written statement of the iniquity of Mrs. Proudie, or the imbecility of her husband. He was aware that it would be wise in him to drop for the future all allusion to his doings in the cathedral city. Soon after the interview just recorded he left Barchester, shaking the dust off his feet as he entered the railway carriage; and he gave no longing, lingering look after the cathedral towers as the train hurried him quickly out of their sight.

It is well known that the family of the Slopes never starve: they always fall on their feet, like cats; and let them fall where they will, they live on the fat of the land. Our Mr. Slope did so. On his return to town he found that the sugar-refiner had died and that his widow was inconsolable—in other words, in want of consolation. Mr. Slope consoled her, and soon found himself settled with much comfort in the house in Baker Street. He possessed himself, also, before long, of a church in the vicinity of the Red Road, and became known to fame as one of the most eloquent preachers and pious clergymen in that part of the metropolis. There let us leave him.

Of the bishop and his wife very little further need be said. From that time forth nothing material occurred to interrupt the even course of their domestic harmony. Very speedily, a further vacancy on the bench of bishops gave to Dr. Proudie the seat in the House of Lords, which he at first so anxiously longed for. But by this time he had become a wiser man. He did certainly take his seat, and occasionally registered a vote in favour of Government views on ecclesiastical matters. But he had thoroughly learnt that his proper sphere of action lay in close contiguity with Mrs. Proudie's wardrobe. He never again aspired to disobey, or seemed even to wish for autocratic diocesan authority. If ever he thought of freedom, he did so as men think of the millennium, as of a good time which may be coming, but which nobody expects to come in their day. Mrs. Proudie might be said still to bloom, and was, at any rate, strong, and the bishop had no reason to apprehend that he would be speedily visited with the sorrows of a widower's life.

He is still Bishop of Barchester. He has so graced that throne that the Government has been averse to translate him, even to higher dignities. There may he remain, under safe pupilage, till the newfangled manners of the age have discovered him to be superannuated and bestowed on him a pension. As for Mrs. Proudie, our prayers for her are that she may live forever.

CHAPTER LII

THE NEW DEAN TAKES POSSESSION OF THE DEANERY, AND THE NEW WARDEN OF THE HOSPITAL

Mr. Harding and the archdeacon together made their way to Oxford, and there, by dint of cunning argument, they induced the Master of Lazarus also to ask himself this momentous question: "Why should not Mr. Arabin be Dean of Barchester?" He, of course, for awhile tried his hand at persuading Mr. Harding that he was foolish, overscrupulous, self-willed, and weak-minded; but he tried in vain. If Mr. Harding would not give way to Dr. Grantly, it was not likely that he would give way to Dr. Gwynne, more especially now that so admirable a scheme as that of inducting Mr. Arabin into the deanery had been set on foot. When the master found that his eloquence was vain, and heard also that Mr. Arabin was about to become Mr. Harding's son-in-law, he confessed that he also would, under such circumstances, be glad to see his old friend and protégé, the fellow of his college, placed in the comfortable position that was going a-begging.

"It might be the means you know, Master, of keeping Mr. Slope out," said the archdeacon with grave caution.

"He has no more chance of it," said the master, "than our college chaplain. I know more about it than that."

Mrs. Grantly had been right in her surmise. It was the Master of Lazarus who had been instrumental in representing in high places the claims which Mr. Harding had upon the Government, and he now consented to use his best endeavours towards getting the offer transferred to Mr. Arabin. The three of them went on to London together, and there they remained a week, to the great disgust of Mrs. Grantly, and most probably also of Mrs. Gwynne. The minister was out of town in one direction, and his private secretary in another. The clerks who remained could do nothing in such a matter as this, and all was difficulty and confusion. The two doctors seemed to have plenty to do; they bustled here and they bustled there, and complained at their club in the evenings that they had been driven off their legs; but Mr. Harding had no occupation. Once or twice he suggested that he might perhaps return to Barchester. His request, however, was peremptorily refused, and he had nothing for it but to while away his time in Westminster Abbey.

At length an answer from the great man came. The Master of Lazarus had made his proposition through the Bishop of Belgravia. Now this bishop, though but newly gifted with his diocesan honours, was a man of much weight in the clerico-political world. He was, if not as pious, at any rate as wise as St. Paul, and had been with so much effect all things to all men that, though he was great among the dons of Oxford, he had been selected for the most favourite seat on the bench by a Whig prime minister. To him Dr. Gwynne had made known his wishes and his arguments, and the bishop had made them known to the Marquis of Kensington-Gore. The marquis, who was Lord High Steward of the Pantry Board, and who by most men was supposed to hold the highest office out of the cabinet, trafficked much in affairs of this kind. He not only suggested the arrangement to the minister over a cup of coffee, standing on a drawing-room rug in Windsor Castle, but he also favourably mentioned Mr. Arabin's name in the ear of a distinguished person.

And so the matter was arranged. The answer of the great man came, and Mr. Arabin was made Dean of Barchester. The three clergymen who had come up to town on this important mission dined together with great glee on the day on which the news reached them. In a silent, decent, clerical manner they toasted Mr. Arabin with full bumpers of claret. The satisfaction of all of them was supreme. The Master of Lazarus had been successful in his attempt, and success is dear to us all. The archdeacon had trampled upon Mr. Slope, and had lifted to high honours the young clergyman whom he had induced to quit the retirement and comfort of the university. So at least the archdeacon thought; though, to speak sooth, not he, but circumstances, had trampled on Mr. Slope. But the satisfaction of Mr. Harding was, of all, perhaps, the most complete. He laid aside his usual melancholy manner and brought forth little quiet jokes from the inmost mirth of his heart; he poked his fun at the archdeacon about Mr. Slope's marriage, and quizzed him for his improper love for Mrs. Proudie. On the following day they all returned to Barchester.

It was arranged that Mr. Arabin should know nothing of what had been done till he received the minister's letter from the hands of his embryo father-in-law. In order that no time might be lost, a message had been sent to him by the preceding night's post, begging him to be at the deanery at the hour that the train from London arrived. There was nothing in this which surprised Mr. Arabin. It had somehow got about through all Barchester that Mr. Harding was the new dean, and all Barchester was prepared to welcome him with pealing bells and full hearts. Mr. Slope had certainly had a party; there had certainly been those in Barchester who were prepared to congratulate him on his promotion with assumed sincerity, but even his own party was not broken-hearted by his failure. The inhabitants of the city, even the high-souled, ecstatic young ladies of thirty-five, had begun to comprehend that their welfare, and the welfare of the place, was connected in some mysterious manner with daily chants and bi-weekly anthems. The expenditure of the palace had not added much to the popularity of the bishop's side of the question; and, on the whole, there was a strong reaction. When it became known to all the world that Mr. Harding was to be the new dean, all the world rejoiced heartily.

Mr. Arabin, we have said, was not surprised at the summons which called him to the deanery. He had not as yet seen Mr. Harding since Eleanor had accepted him, nor had he seen him since he had learnt his future father-in-law's preferment. There was nothing more natural, more necessary, than that they should meet each other at the earliest possible moment. Mr. Arabin was waiting in the deanery parlour when Mr. Harding and Dr. Grantly were driven up from the station.

There was some excitement in the bosoms of them all, as they met and shook hands; by far too much to enable either of them to begin his story and tell it in a proper equable style of narrative. Mr. Harding was some minutes quite dumbfounded, and Mr. Arabin could only talk in short, spasmodic sentences about his love and good fortune. He slipped in, as best he could, some sort of congratulation about the deanship, and then went on with his hopes and fears—hopes that he might be received as a son, and fears that he hardly deserved such good fortune. Then he went back to the dean; it was the most thoroughly satisfactory appointment, he said, of which he had ever heard.

"But! But! But—" said Mr. Harding, and then, failing to get any further, he looked imploringly at the archdeacon.

"The truth is, Arabin," said the doctor, "that, after all you are not destined to be son-in-law to a dean. Nor am I either: more's the pity."

Mr. Arabin looked at him for explanation. "Is not Mr. Harding to be the new dean?"

"It appears not," said the archdeacon. Mr. Arabin's face fell a little, and he looked from one to the other. It was plainly to be seen from them both that there was no cause of unhappiness in the matter, at least not of unhappiness to them; but there was as yet no elucidation of the mystery.

"Think how old I am," said Mr. Harding imploringly.

"Fiddlestick!" said the archdeacon.

"That's all very well, but it won't make a young man of me," said Mr. Harding.

"And who is to be dean?" asked Mr. Arabin.

"Yes, that's the question," said the archdeacon. "Come, Mr. Precentor, since you obstinately refuse to be anything else, let us know who is to be the man. He has got the nomination in his pocket."

With eyes brim full of tears, Mr. Harding pulled out the letter and handed it to his future son-in-law. He tried to make a little speech but failed altogether. Having given up the document, he turned round to the wall, feigning to blow his nose, and then sat himself down on the old dean's dingy horsehair sofa. And here we find it necessary to bring our account of the interview to an end.

Nor can we pretend to describe the rapture with which Mr. Harding was received by his daughter. She wept with grief and wept with joy—with grief that her father should, in his old age, still be without that rank and worldly position which, according to her ideas, he had so well earned; and with joy in that he, her darling father, should have bestowed on that other dear one the good things of which he himself would not open his hand to take possession. And here Mr. Harding again showed his weakness. In the *mêlée* of this exposal of their loves and reciprocal affection, he found himself unable to resist the entreaties of all parties that the lodgings in the High Street should be given up. Eleanor would not live in the deanery, she said, unless her father lived there also. Mr. Arabin would not be dean, unless Mr. Harding would be co-dean with him. The archdeacon declared that his father-in-law should not have his own way in everything, and Mrs. Grantly carried him off to Plumstead, that he might remain there till Mr. and Mrs. Arabin were in a state to receive him in their own mansion.

Pressed by such arguments as these, what could a weak old man do but yield?

But there was yet another task which it behoved Mr. Harding to do before he could allow himself to be at rest. Little has been said in these pages of the state of those remaining old men who had lived under his sway at the hospital. But not on this account must it be presumed that he had forgotten them, or that in their state of anarchy and in their want of due government he had omitted to visit them. He visited them constantly, and had latterly given them to understand that they would soon be required to subscribe their adherence to a new master. There were now but five of them, one of them having been but quite lately carried to his rest—but five of the full number, which had hitherto been twelve, and which was now to be raised to twenty-four, including women. Of these, old Bunce, who for many years had been the favourite of the late warden, was one; and Abel Handy, who had been the humble means of driving that warden from his home, was another.

Mr. Harding now resolved that he himself would introduce the new warden to the hospital. He felt that many circumstances might conspire to make the men receive Mr.

Quiverful with aversion and disrespect; he felt also that Mr. Quiverful might himself feel some qualms of conscience if he entered the hospital with an idea that he did so in hostility to his predecessor. Mr. Harding therefore determined to walk in, arm in arm with Mr. Quiverful, and to ask from these men their respectful obedience to their new master.

On returning to Barchester, he found that Mr. Quiverful had not yet slept in the hospital house, or entered on his new duties. He accordingly made known to that gentleman his wishes, and his proposition was not rejected.

It was a bright, clear morning, though in November, that Mr. Harding and Mr. Quiverful, arm in arm, walked through the hospital gate. It was one trait in our old friend's character that he did nothing with parade. He omitted, even in the more important doings of his life, that sort of parade by which most of us deem it necessary to grace our important doings. We have house-warmings, christenings, and gala days; we keep, if not our own birthdays, those of our children; we are apt to fuss ourselves if called upon to change our residences and have, almost all of us, our little state occasions. Mr. Harding had no state occasions. When he left his old house, he went forth from it with the same quiet composure as though he were merely taking his daily walk; now that he re-entered it with another warden under his wing, he did so with the same quiet step and calm demeanour. He was a little less upright than he had been five years, nay, it was now nearly six years ago; he walked perhaps a little slower; his footfall was perhaps a thought less firm; otherwise one might have said that he was merely returning with a friend under his arm.

This friendliness was everything to Mr. Quiverful. To him, even in his poverty, the thought that he was supplanting a brother clergyman so kind and courteous as Mr. Harding had been very bitter. Under his circumstances it had been impossible for him to refuse the proffered boon; he could not reject the bread that was offered to his children, or refuse to ease the heavy burden that had so long oppressed that poor wife of his; nevertheless, it had been very grievous to him to think that in going to the hospital he might encounter the ill-will of his brethren in the diocese. All this Mr. Harding had fully comprehended. It was for such feelings as these, for the nice comprehension of such motives, that his heart and intellect were peculiarly fitted. In most matters of worldly import the archdeacon set down his father-in-law as little better than a fool. And perhaps he was right. But in some other matters, equally important if they be rightly judged, Mr. Harding, had he been so minded, might with as much propriety have set down his son-in-law for a fool. Few men, however, are constituted as was Mr. Harding. He had that nice appreciation of the feelings of others which belongs of right exclusively to women.

Arm in arm they walked into the inner quadrangle of the building, and there the five old men met them. Mr. Harding shook hands with them all, and then Mr. Quiverful did the same. With Bunce Mr. Harding shook hands twice, and Mr. Quiverful was about to repeat the same ceremony, but the old man gave him no encouragement.

"I am very glad to know that at last you have a new warden," said Mr. Harding in a very cheery voice.

"We be very old for any change," said one of them, "but we do suppose it be all for the best."

"Certainly—certainly it is for the best," said Mr. Harding. "You will again have a clergyman of your own church under the same roof with you, and a very excellent clergyman you will have. It is a great satisfaction to me to know that so good a man is coming to take care of you, and that it is no stranger, but a friend of my own who will allow me from time to time to come in and see you."

"We be very thankful to your Reverence," said another of them.

442

"I need not tell you, my good friends," said Mr. Quiverful, "how extremely grateful I am to Mr. Harding for his kindness to me—I must say his uncalled-for, unexpected kindness."

"He be always very kind," said a third.

"What I can do to fill the void which he left here I will do. For your sake and my own I will do so, and especially for his sake. But to you who have known him, I can never be the same well-loved friend and father that he has been."

"No, sir, no," said old Bunce, who hitherto had held his peace; "no one can be that. Not if the new bishop sent a hangel to us out of heaven. We doesn't doubt you'll do your best, sir, but you'll not be like the old master—not to us old ones."

"Fie, Bunce, fie; how dare you talk in that way?" said Mr. Harding; but as he scolded the old man he still held him by his arm and pressed it with warm affection.

There was no getting up any enthusiasm in the matter. How could five old men tottering away to their final resting place be enthusiastic on the reception of a stranger? What could Mr. Quiverful be to them, or they to Mr. Quiverful? Had Mr. Harding indeed come back to them, some last flicker of joyous light might have shone forth on their aged cheeks; but it was in vain to bid them rejoice because Mr. Quiverful was about to move his fourteen children from Puddingdale into the hospital house. In reality they did no doubt receive advantage, spiritual as well as corporal, but this they could neither anticipate nor acknowledge.

It was a dull affair enough, this introduction of Mr. Quiverful, but still it had its effect. The good which Mr. Harding intended did not fall to the ground. All the Barchester world, including the five old bedesmen, treated Mr. Quiverful with the more respect because Mr. Harding had thus walked in, arm in arm with him, on his first entrance to his duties.

And here in their new abode we will leave Mr. and Mrs. Quiverful and their fourteen children. May they enjoy the good things which Providence has at length given to them!

CHAPTER LIII

CONCLUSION

The end of a novel, like the end of a children's dinner party, must be made up of sweetmeats and sugar-plums. There is now nothing else to be told but the gala doings of Mr. Arabin's marriage, nothing more to be described than the wedding-dresses, no further dialogue to be recorded than that which took place between the archdeacon, who married them, and Mr. Arabin and Eleanor, who were married.

"Wilt thou have this woman to thy wedded wife," and "wilt thou have this man to thy wedded husband, to live together according to God's ordinance?"

Mr. Arabin and Eleanor each answered, "I will."

We have no doubt that they will keep their promises, the more especially as the Signora Neroni had left Barchester before the ceremony was performed.

Mrs. Bold had been somewhat more than two years a widow before she was married to her second husband, and little Johnny was then able with due assistance to walk on his own legs into the drawing-room to receive the salutations of the assembled guests. Mr. Harding gave away the bride, the archdeacon performed the service, and the two Miss Grantlys, who were joined in their labours by other young ladies of the neighbourhood, performed the duties of bridesmaids with equal diligence and grace. Mrs. Grantly superintended the breakfast and bouquets, and Mary Bold distributed the cards and cake. The archdeacon's three sons had also come home for the occasion. The elder was great with learning, being regarded by all who knew him as a certain future double first. The second, however, bore the palm on this occasion, being resplendent in a new uniform. The third was just entering the university, and was probably the proudest of the three.

But the most remarkable feature in the whole occasion was the excessive liberality of the archdeacon. He literally made presents to everybody. As Mr. Arabin had already moved out of the parsonage of St. Ewold's, that scheme of elongating the dining-room was of course abandoned; but he would have refurnished the whole deanery had he been allowed. He sent down a magnificent piano by Erard, gave Mr. Arabin a cob which any dean in the land might have been proud to bestride, and made a special present to Eleanor of a new pony chair that had gained a prize in the Exhibition. Nor did he even stay his hand here; he bought a set of cameos for his wife and a sapphire bracelet for Miss Bold; showered pearls and work-boxes on his daughters; and to each of his sons he presented a check for £20. On Mr. Harding he bestowed a magnificent violoncello with all the new-fashioned arrangements and expensive additions, which on account of these novelties that gentleman could never use with satisfaction to his audience or pleasure to himself.

Those who knew the archdeacon well perfectly understood the causes of his extravagance. 'Twas thus that he sang his song of triumph over Mr. Slope. This was his pæan, his hymn of thanksgiving, his loud oration. He had girded himself with his sword and gone forth to the war; now he was returning from the field laden with the spoils of the foe. The cob and the cameos, the violoncello and the pianoforte, were all as it were trophies reft from the tent of his now-conquered enemy.

The Arabins after their marriage went abroad for a couple of months, according to the custom in such matters now duly established, and then commenced their deanery life under good auspices. And nothing can be more pleasant than the present arrangement of ecclesiastical affairs in Barchester. The titular bishop never interfered, and Mrs. Proudie not often. Her sphere is more extended, more noble, and more suited to her ambition than that of a cathedral city. As long as she can do what she pleases with the diocese, she is willing to leave the dean and chapter to themselves. Mr. Slope tried his hand at subverting the old-established customs of the close, and from his failure she had learnt experience. The burly chancellor and the meagre little prebendary are not teased by any application respecting Sabbath-day schools, the dean is left to his own dominions, and the intercourse between Mrs. Proudie and Mrs. Arabin is confined to a yearly dinner given by each to the other. At these dinners Dr. Grantly will not take a part, but he never fails to ask for and receive a full account of all that Mrs. Proudie either does or says.

His ecclesiastical authority has been greatly shorn since the palmy days in which he reigned supreme as mayor of the palace to his father, but nevertheless such authority as is now left to him he can enjoy without interference. He can walk down the High Street of Barchester without feeling that those who see him are comparing his claims with those of Mr. Slope. The intercourse between Plumstead and the deanery is of the most constant and familiar description. Since Eleanor has been married to a clergyman, and especially to a dignitary of the church, Mrs. Grantly has found many more points of sympathy with her sister; and on a coming occasion, which is much looked forward to by all parties, she intends to spend a month or two at the deanery. She never thought of spending a month in Barchester when little Johnny Bold was born!

The two sisters do not quite agree on matters of church doctrine, though their differences are of the most amicable description. Mrs. Arabin's church is two degrees higher than that of Mrs. Grantly. This may seem strange to those who will remember that Eleanor was once accused of partiality to Mr. Slope, but it is no less the fact. She likes her husband's silken vest, she likes his adherence to the rubric, she specially likes the eloquent philosophy of his sermons, and she likes the red letters in her own prayer-book. It must not be presumed that she has a taste for candles, or that she is at all astray about the real presence, but she has an inkling that way. She sent a handsome subscription towards certain very heavy ecclesiastical legal expenses which have lately been incurred in Bath, her name of course not appearing; she assumes a smile of gentle ridicule when the Archbishop of Canterbury is named; and she has put up a memorial window in the cathedral.

Mrs. Grantly, who belongs to the high and dry church, the High Church as it was some fifty years since, before tracts were written and young clergymen took upon themselves the highly meritorious duty of cleaning churches, rather laughs at her sister. She shrugs her shoulders and tells Miss Thorne that she supposes Eleanor will have an oratory in the deanery before she has done. But she is not on that account a whit displeased. A few High Church vagaries do not, she thinks, sit amiss on the shoulders of a young dean's wife. It shows at any rate that her heart is in the subject, and it shows moreover that she is removed, wide as the poles asunder, from that cesspool of abomination in which it was once suspected that she would wallow and grovel. Anathema maranatha! Let anything else be held as blessed, so that that be well cursed. Welcome kneelings and bowings, welcome matins and complines, welcome bell, book, and candle, so that Mr. Slope's dirty surplices and ceremonial Sabbaths be held in due execration!

If it be essentially and absolutely necessary to choose between the two, we are inclined to agree with Mrs. Grantly that the bell, book, and candle are the lesser evil of the two. Let it however be understood that no such necessity is admitted in these pages.

Dr. Arabin (we suppose he must have become a doctor when he became a dean) is more moderate and less outspoken on doctrinal points than his wife, as indeed in his station it behoves him to be. He is a studious, thoughtful, hard-working man. He lives constantly at the deanery and preaches nearly every Sunday. His time is spent in sifting and editing old ecclesiastical literature and in producing the same articles new. At Oxford he is generally regarded as the most promising clerical ornament of the age. He and his wife live together in perfect mutual confidence. There is but one secret in her bosom which he has not shared. He has never yet learned how Mr. Slope had his ears boxed.

The Stanhopes soon found that Mr. Slope's power need no longer operate to keep them from the delight of their Italian villa. Before Eleanor's marriage they had all migrated back to the shores of Como. They had not been resettled long before the signora received from Mrs. Arabin a very pretty though very short epistle, in which she was informed of the fate of the writer. This letter was answered by another—bright, charming, and witty, as the signora's letters always were—and so ended the friendship between Eleanor and the Stanhopes.

One word of Mr. Harding, and we have done. He is still precentor of Barchester and still pastor of the little church of St. Cuthbert's. In spite of what he has so often said himself, he is not even yet an old man. He does such duties as fall to his lot well and conscientiously, and is thankful that he has never been tempted to assume others for which he might be less fitted.

The author now leaves him in the hands of his readers: not as a hero, not as a man to be admired and talked of, not as a man who should be toasted at public dinners and spoken of with conventional absurdity as a perfect divine, but as a good man, without guile, believing humbly in the religion which he has striven to teach, and guided by the precepts which he has striven to learn.

DOCTOR THORNE

CHAPTER I

THE GRESHAMS OF GRESHAMSBURY

Before the reader is introduced to the modest country medical practitioner who is to be the chief personage of the following tale, it will be well that he should be made acquainted with some particulars as to the locality in which, and the neighbours among whom, our doctor followed his profession.

There is a county in the west of England not so full of life, indeed, nor so widely spoken of as some of its manufacturing leviathan brethren in the north, but which is, nevertheless, very dear to those who know it well. Its green pastures, its waving wheat, its deep and shady and—let us add—dirty lanes, its paths and stiles, its tawny-coloured, well-built rural churches, its avenues of beeches, and frequent Tudor mansions, its constant county hunt, its social graces, and the general air of clanship which pervades it, has made it to its own inhabitants a favoured land of Goshen. It is purely agricultural; agricultural in its produce, agricultural in its poor, and agricultural in its pleasures. There are towns in it, of course; dépôts from whence are brought seeds and groceries, ribbons and fire-shovels; in which markets are held and county balls are carried on; which return members to Parliament, generally—in spite of Reform Bills, past, present, and coming—in accordance with the dictates of some neighbouring land magnate: from whence emanate the country postmen, and where is located the supply of post-horses necessary for county visitings. But these towns add nothing to the importance of the county; they consist, with the exception of the assize town, of dull, all but death-like single streets. Each possesses two pumps, three hotels, ten shops, fifteen beer-houses, a beadle, and a market-place.

Indeed, the town population of the county reckons for nothing when the importance of the county is discussed, with the exception, as before said, of the assize town, which is also a cathedral city. Herein is a clerical aristocracy, which is certainly not without its due weight. A resident bishop, a resident dean, an archdeacon, three or four resident prebendaries, and all their numerous chaplains, vicars, and ecclesiastical satellites, do make up a society sufficiently powerful to be counted as something by the county squirearchy. In other respects the greatness of Barsetshire depends wholly on the landed powers.

Barsetshire, however, is not now so essentially one whole as it was before the Reform Bill divided it. There is in these days an East Barsetshire, and there is a West Barsetshire; and people conversant with Barsetshire doings declare that they can already decipher some difference of feeling, some division of interests. The eastern moiety of the county is more purely Conservative than the western; there is, or was, a taint of Peelism in the latter; and then, too, the residence of two such great Whig magnates as the Duke of Omnium and the Earl de Courcy in that locality in some degree overshadows and renders less influential the gentlemen who live near them.

It is to East Barsetshire that we are called. When the division above spoken of was first contemplated, in those stormy days in which gallant men were still combatting reform ministers, if not with hope, still with spirit, the battle was fought by none more bravely than by John Newbold Gresham of Greshamsbury, the member for Barsetshire. Fate, however, and the Duke of Wellington were adverse, and in the following Parliament John Newbold Gresham was only member for East Barsetshire.

Whether or not it was true, as stated at the time, that the aspect of the men with whom he was called on to associate at St Stephen's broke his heart, it is not for us now to inquire. It is certainly true that he did not live to see the first year of the reformed Parliament brought to a close. The then Mr Gresham was not an old man at the time of his death, and his eldest son, Francis Newbold Gresham, was a very young man; but, notwithstanding his youth, and notwithstanding other grounds of objection which stood in the way of such preferment, and which must be explained, he was chosen in his father's place. The father's services had been too recent, too well appreciated, too thoroughly in unison with the feelings of those around him to allow of any other choice; and in this way young Frank Gresham found himself member for East Barsetshire, although the very men who elected him knew that they had but slender ground for trusting him with their suffrages.

Frank Gresham, though then only twenty-four years of age, was a married man, and a father. He had already chosen a wife, and by his choice had given much ground of distrust to the men of East Barsetshire. He had married no other than Lady Arabella de Courcy, the sister of the great Whig earl who lived at Courcy Castle in the west; that earl who not only voted for the Reform Bill, but had been infamously active in bringing over other young peers so to vote, and whose name therefore stank in the nostrils of the staunch Tory squires of the county.

Not only had Frank Gresham so wedded, but having thus improperly and unpatriotically chosen a wife, he had added to his sins by becoming recklessly intimate with his wife's relations. It is true that he still called himself a Tory, belonged to the club of which his father had been one of the most honoured members, and in the days of the great battle got his head broken in a row, on the right side; but, nevertheless, it was felt by the good men, true and blue, of East Barsetshire, that a constant sojourner at Courcy Castle could not be regarded as a consistent Tory. When, however, his father died, that broken head served him in good stead: his sufferings in the cause were made the most of; these, in unison with his father's merits, turned the scale, and it was accordingly decided, at a meeting held at the George and Dragon, at Barchester, that Frank Gresham should fill his father's shoes.

But Frank Gresham could not fill his father's shoes; they were too big for him. He did become member for East Barsetshire, but he was such a member—so lukewarm, so indifferent, so prone to associate with the enemies of the good cause, so little willing to fight the good fight, that he soon disgusted those who most dearly loved the memory of the old squire.

De Courcy Castle in those days had great allurements for a young man, and all those allurements were made the most of to win over young Gresham. His wife, who was a year or two older than himself, was a fashionable woman, with thorough Whig tastes and aspirations, such as became the daughter of a great Whig earl; she cared for politics, or thought that she cared for them, more than her husband did; for a month or two previous to her engagement she had been attached to the Court, and had been made to believe that much of the policy of England's rulers depended on the political intrigues of England's women. She was one who would fain be doing something if she only knew how, and the first important attempt she made was to turn her respectable young Tory husband into a second-rate Whig bantling. As this lady's character will, it is hoped, show itself in the following pages, we need not now describe it more closely.

It is not a bad thing to be son-in-law to a potent earl, member of Parliament for a county, and a possessor of a fine old English seat, and a fine old English fortune. As a very young man, Frank Gresham found the life to which he was thus introduced agreeable enough. He consoled himself as best he might for the blue looks with which he was greeted by his own party, and took his revenge by consorting more thoroughly than ever with his political adversaries. Foolishly, like a foolish moth, he flew to the bright light, and, like the moths, of course he burnt his wings. Early in 1833 he had become a member of Parliament, and in the autumn of 1834 the dissolution came. Young members of three or four-and-twenty do not think much of dissolutions, forget the fancies of their constituents, and are too proud of the present to calculate much as to the future. So it was with Mr Gresham. His father had been member for Barsetshire all his life, and he looked forward to similar prosperity as though it were part of his inheritance; but he failed to take any of the steps which had secured his father's seat.

In the autumn of 1834 the dissolution came, and Frank Gresham, with his honourable lady wife and all the de Courcys at his back, found that he had mortally offended the county. To his great disgust another candidate was brought forward as a fellow to his late colleague, and though he manfully fought the battle, and spent ten thousand pounds in the contest, he could not recover his position. A high Tory, with a great Whig interest to back him, is never a popular person in England. No one can trust him, though there may be those who are willing to place him, untrusted, in high positions. Such was the case with Mr Gresham. There were many who were willing, for family considerations, to keep him in Parliament; but no one thought that he was fit to be there. The consequences were, that a bitter and expensive contest ensued. Frank Gresham, when twitted with being a Whig, foreswore the de Courcy family; and then, when ridiculed as having been thrown over by the Tories, foreswore his father's old friends. So between the two stools he fell to the ground, and, as a politician, he never again rose to his feet.

He never again rose to his feet; but twice again he made violent efforts to do so. Elections in East Barsetshire, from various causes, came quick upon each other in those days, and before he was eight-and-twenty years of age Mr Gresham had three times contested the county and been three times beaten. To speak the truth of him, his own spirit would have been satisfied with the loss of the first ten thousand pounds; but Lady Arabella was made of higher mettle. She had married a man with a fine place and a fine fortune; but she had nevertheless married a commoner and had in so far derogated from her high birth. She felt that her husband should be by rights a member of the House of Lords; but, if not, that it was at least essential that he should have a seat in the lower chamber. She would by degrees sink into nothing if she allowed herself to sit down, the mere wife of a mere country squire.

Thus instigated, Mr Gresham repeated the useless contest three times, and repeated it each time at a serious cost. He lost his money, Lady Arabella lost her temper, and things at Greshamsbury went on by no means as prosperously as they had done in the days of the old squire.

In the first twelve years of their marriage, children came fast into the nursery at Greshamsbury. The first that was born was a boy; and in those happy halcyon days, when the old squire was still alive, great was the joy at the birth of an heir to Greshamsbury; bonfires gleamed through the country-side, oxen were roasted whole, and the customary paraphernalia of joy, usual to rich Britons on such occasions were gone through with wondrous éclat. But when the tenth baby, and the ninth little girl, was brought into the world, the outward show of joy was not so great.

Then other troubles came on. Some of these little girls were sickly, some very sickly. Lady Arabella had her faults, and they were such as were extremely detrimental to her husband's happiness and her own; but that of being an indifferent mother was not among them. She had worried her husband daily for years because he was not in Parliament, she had worried him because he would not furnish the house in Portman Square, she had worried him because he objected to have more people every winter at Greshamsbury Park than the house would hold; but now she changed her tune and worried him because Selina coughed, because Helena was hectic, because poor Sophy's spine was weak, and Matilda's appetite was gone.

Worrying from such causes was pardonable it will be said. So it was; but the manner was hardly pardonable. Selina's cough was certainly not fairly attributable to the old-fashioned furniture in Portman Square; nor would Sophy's spine have been materially benefited by her father having a seat in Parliament; and yet, to have heard Lady Arabella discussing those matters in family conclave, one would have thought that she would have expected such results.

As it was, her poor weak darlings were carried about from London to Brighton, from Brighton to some German baths, from the German baths back to Torquay, and thence—as regarded the four we have named—to that bourne from whence no further journey could be made under the Lady Arabella's directions.

The one son and heir to Greshamsbury was named as his father, Francis Newbold Gresham. He would have been the hero of our tale had not that place been pre-occupied by the village doctor. As it is, those who please may so regard him. It is he who is to be our favourite young man, to do the love scenes, to have his trials and his difficulties, and to win through them or not, as the case may be. I am too old now to be a hard-hearted author, and so it is probable that he may not die of a broken heart. Those who don't approve of a middle-aged bachelor country doctor as a hero, may take the heir to Greshamsbury in his stead, and call the book, if it so please them, "The Loves and Adventures of Francis Newbold Gresham the Younger."

And Master Frank Gresham was not ill adapted for playing the part of a hero of this sort. He did not share his sisters' ill-health, and though the only boy of the family, he excelled all his sisters in personal appearance. The Greshams from time immemorial had been handsome. They were broad browed, blue eyed, fair haired, born with dimples in their chins, and that pleasant, aristocratic dangerous curl of the upper lip which can equally express good humour or scorn. Young Frank was every inch a Gresham, and was the darling of his father's heart.

The de Courcys had never been plain. There was too much hauteur, too much pride, we may perhaps even fairly say, too much nobility in their gait and manners, and even in their faces, to allow of their being considered plain; but they were not a race nurtured by Venus or Apollo. They were tall and thin, with high cheek-bones, high foreheads, and large, dignified, cold eyes. The de Courcy girls had all good hair; and, as they also possessed easy manners and powers of talking, they managed to pass in the world for beauties till they were absorbed in the matrimonial market, and the world at large cared no longer whether they were beauties or not. The Misses Gresham were made in the de Courcy mould, and were not on this account the less dear to their mother.

The two eldest, Augusta and Beatrice, lived, and were apparently likely to live. The four next faded and died one after another—all in the same sad year—and were laid in the neat, new cemetery at Torquay. Then came a pair, born at one birth, weak, delicate, frail little flowers, with dark hair and dark eyes, and thin, long, pale faces, with long, bony hands, and long bony feet, whom men looked on as fated to follow their sisters with quick steps. Hitherto, however, they had not followed them, nor had they suffered as their sisters had suffered; and some people at Greshamsbury attributed this to the fact that a change had been made in the family medical practitioner.

Then came the youngest of the flock, she whose birth we have said was not heralded with loud joy; for when she came into the world, four others, with pale temples, wan, worn cheeks, and skeleton, white arms, were awaiting permission to leave it.

Such was the family when, in the year 1854, the eldest son came of age. He had been educated at Harrow, and was now still at Cambridge; but, of course, on such a day as this he was at home. That coming of age must be a delightful time to a young man born to inherit broad acres and wide wealth. Those full-mouthed congratulations; those warm prayers with which his manhood is welcomed by the grey-haired seniors of the county; the affectionate, all but motherly caresses of neighbouring mothers who have seen him grow up from his cradle, of mothers who have daughters, perhaps, fair enough, and good enough, and sweet enough even for him; the soft-spoken, half-bashful, but tender greetings of the girls, who now, perhaps for the first time, call him by his stern family name, instructed by instinct rather than precept that the time has come when the familiar Charles or familiar John must by them be laid aside; the "lucky dogs," and hints of silver spoons which are poured into his ears as each young compeer slaps his back and bids him live a thousand years and then never die; the shouting of the tenantry, the good wishes of the old farmers who come up to wring his hand, the kisses which he gets from the farmers' wives, and the kisses which he gives to the farmers' daughters; all these things must make the twenty-first birthday pleasant enough to a young heir. To a youth, however, who feels that he is now liable to arrest, and that he inherits no other privilege, the pleasure may very possibly not be quite so keen.

The case with young Frank Gresham may be supposed to much nearer the former than the latter; but yet the ceremony of his coming of age was by no means like that which fate had accorded to his father. Mr Gresham was now an embarrassed man, and though the world did not know it, or, at any rate, did not know that he was deeply embarrassed, he had not the heart to throw open his mansion and receive the county with a free hand as though all things were going well with him.

Nothing was going well with him. Lady Arabella would allow nothing near him or around him to be well. Everything with him now turned to vexation; he was no longer a joyous, happy man, and the people of East Barsetshire did not look for gala doings on a grand scale when young Gresham came of age.

Gala doings, to a certain extent, there were there. It was in July, and tables were spread under the oaks for the tenants. Tables were spread, and meat, and beer, and wine were there, and Frank, as he walked round and shook his guests by the hand, expressed a hope that their relations with each other might be long, close, and mutually advantageous.

We must say a few words now about the place itself. Greshamsbury Park was a fine old English gentleman's seat—was and is; but we can assert it more easily in past tense, as we are speaking of it with reference to a past time. We have spoken of Greshamsbury Park; there was a park so called, but the mansion itself was generally known as Greshamsbury House, and did not stand in the park. We may perhaps best describe it by saying that the village of Greshamsbury consisted of one long, straggling street, a mile in length, which in the centre turned sharp round, so that one half of the street lay directly at right angles to the other. In this angle stood Greshamsbury House, and the gardens and grounds around it filled up the space so made. There was an entrance with large gates at each end of the village, and each gate was guarded by the effigies of two huge pagans with clubs, such being the crest borne by the family; from each entrance a broad road, quite straight, running through to a majestic avenue of limes, led up to the house. This was built in the richest, perhaps we should rather say in the purest, style of Tudor architecture; so much so that, though Greshamsbury is less complete than Longleat, less magnificent than Hatfield, it may in some sense be said to be the finest specimen of Tudor architecture of which the country can boast.

It stands amid a multitude of trim gardens and stone-built terraces, divided one from another: these to our eyes are not so attractive as that broad expanse of lawn by which our country houses are generally surrounded; but the gardens of Greshamsbury have been celebrated for two centuries, and any Gresham who would have altered them would have been considered to have destroyed one of the well-known landmarks of the family.

Greshamsbury Park—properly so called—spread far away on the other side of the village. Opposite to the two great gates leading up to the mansion were two smaller gates, the one opening on to the stables, kennels, and farm-yard, and the other to the deer park. This latter was the principal entrance to the demesne, and a grand and picturesque entrance it was. The avenue of limes which on one side stretched up to the house, was on the other extended for a quarter of a mile, and then appeared to be terminated only by an abrupt rise in the ground. At the entrance there were four savages and four clubs, two to each portal, and what with the massive iron gates, surmounted by a stone wall, on which stood the family arms supported by two other club-bearers, the stone-built lodges, the Doric, ivy-covered columns which surrounded the circle, the four grim savages, and the extent of the space itself through which the high road ran, and which just abutted on the village, the spot was sufficiently significant of old family greatness.

Those who examined it more closely might see that under the arms was a scroll bearing the Gresham motto, and that the words were repeated in smaller letters under each of the savages. "Gardez Gresham," had been chosen in the days of motto-choosing probably by some herald-at-arms as an appropriate legend for signifying the peculiar attributes of the family. Now, however, unfortunately, men were not of one mind as to the exact idea signified. Some declared, with much heraldic warmth, that it was an address to the savages, calling on them to take care of their patron; while others, with whom I myself am inclined to agree, averred with equal certainty that it was an advice to the people at large, especially to those inclined to rebel against the aristocracy of the county, that they should "beware the Gresham." The latter signification would betoken strength—so said the holders of this doctrine; the former weakness. Now the Greshams were ever a strong people, and never addicted to a false humility.

We will not pretend to decide the question. Alas! either construction was now equally unsuited to the family fortunes. Such changes had taken place in England since the Greshams had founded themselves that no savage could any longer in any way protect them; they must protect themselves like common folk, or live unprotected. Nor now was it necessary that any neighbour should shake in his shoes when the Gresham frowned. It would have been to be wished that the present Gresham himself could have been as indifferent to the frowns of some of his neighbours.

But the old symbols remained, and may such symbols long remain among us; they are still lovely and fit to be loved. They tell us of the true and manly feelings of other times; and to him who can read aright, they explain more fully, more truly than any written history can do, how Englishmen have become what they are. England is not yet a commercial country in the sense in which that epithet is used for her; and let us still hope that she will not soon become so. She might surely as well be called feudal England, or chivalrous England. If in western civilised Europe there does exist a nation among whom there are high signors, and with whom the owners of the land are the true aristocracy, the aristocracy that is trusted as being best and fittest to rule, that nation is the English. Choose out the ten leading men of each great European people. Choose them in France, in Austria, Sardinia, Prussia, Russia, Sweden, Denmark, Spain (?), and then select the ten in England whose names are best known as those of leading statesmen; the result will show in which country there still exists the closest attachment to, the sincerest trust in, the old feudal and now so-called landed interests.

England a commercial country! Yes; as Venice was. She may excel other nations in commerce, but yet it is not that in which she most prides herself, in which she most excels. Merchants as such are not the first men among us; though it perhaps be open, barely open, to a merchant to become one of them. Buying and selling is good and necessary; it is very necessary, and may, possibly, be very good; but it cannot be the noblest work of man; and let us hope that it may not in our time be esteemed the noblest work of an Englishman.

Greshamsbury Park was very large; it lay on the outside of the angle formed by the village street, and stretched away on two sides without apparent limit or boundaries visible from the village road or house. Indeed, the ground on this side was so broken up into abrupt hills, and conical-shaped, oak-covered excrescences, which were seen peeping up through and over each other, that the true extent of the park was much magnified to the eye. It was very possible for a stranger to get into it and to find some difficulty in getting out again by any of its known gates; and such was the beauty of the landscape, that a lover of scenery would be tempted thus to lose himself.

I have said that on one side lay the kennels, and this will give me an opportunity of describing here one especial episode, a long episode, in the life of the existing squire. He had once represented his county in Parliament, and when he ceased to do so he still felt an ambition to be connected in some peculiar way with that county's greatness; he still desired that Gresham of Greshamsbury should be something more in East Barsetshire than Jackson of the Grange, or Baker of Mill Hill, or Bateson of Annesgrove. They were all his friends, and very respectable country gentlemen; but Mr Gresham of Greshamsbury should be more than this: even he had enough of ambition to be aware of such a longing. Therefore, when an opportunity occurred he took to hunting the county.

For this employment he was in every way well suited—unless it was in the matter of finance. Though he had in his very earliest manly years given such great offence by indifference to his family politics, and had in a certain degree fostered the ill-feeling by contesting the county in opposition to the wishes of his brother squires, nevertheless, he bore a loved and popular name. Men regretted that he should not have been what they wished him to be, that he should not have been such as was the old squire; but when they found that such was the case, that he could not be great among them as a politician, they were still willing that he should be great in any other way if there were county greatness for which he was suited. Now he was known as an excellent horseman, as a thorough sportsman, as one knowing in dogs, and tender-hearted as a sucking mother to a litter of young foxes; he had ridden in the county since he was fifteen, had a fine voice for a view-hallo, knew every hound by name, and could wind a horn with sufficient music for all hunting purposes; moreover, he had come to his property, as was well known through all Barsetshire, with a clear income of fourteen thousand a year.

Thus, when some old worn-out master of hounds was run to ground, about a year after Mr Gresham's last contest for the county, it seemed to all parties to be a pleasant and rational arrangement that the hounds should go to Greshamsbury. Pleasant, indeed, to all except the Lady Arabella; and rational, perhaps, to all except the squire himself.

All this time he was already considerably encumbered. He had spent much more than he should have done, and so indeed had his wife, in those two splendid years in which they had figured as great among the great ones of the earth. Fourteen thousand a year ought to have been enough to allow a member of Parliament with a young wife and two or three children to live in London and keep up their country family mansion; but then the de

Courcys were very great people, and Lady Arabella chose to live as she had been accustomed to do, and as her sister-in-law the countess lived: now Lord de Courcy had much more than fourteen thousand a year. Then came the three elections, with their vast attendant cost, and then those costly expedients to which gentlemen are forced to have recourse who have lived beyond their income, and find it impossible so to reduce their establishments as to live much below it. Thus when the hounds came to Greshamsbury, Mr Gresham was already a poor man.

Lady Arabella said much to oppose their coming; but Lady Arabella, though it could hardly be said of her that she was under her husband's rule, certainly was not entitled to boast that she had him under hers. She then made her first grand attack as to the furniture in Portman Square; and was then for the first time specially informed that the furniture there was not matter of much importance, as she would not in future be required to move her family to that residence during the London seasons. The sort of conversations which grew from such a commencement may be imagined. Had Lady Arabella worried her lord less, he might perhaps have considered with more coolness the folly of encountering so prodigious an increase to the expense of his establishment; had he not spent so much money in a pursuit which his wife did not enjoy, she might perhaps have been more sparing in her rebukes as to his indifference to her London pleasures. As it was, the hounds came to Greshamsbury, and Lady Arabella did go to London for some period in each year, and the family expenses were by no means lessened.

The kennels, however, were now again empty. Two years previous to the time at which our story begins, the hounds had been carried off to the seat of some richer sportsman. This was more felt by Mr Gresham than any other misfortune which he had yet incurred. He had been master of hounds for ten years, and that work he had at any rate done well. The popularity among his neighbours which he had lost as a politician he had regained as a sportsman, and he would fain have remained autocratic in the hunt, had it been possible. But he so remained much longer than he should have done, and at last they went away, not without signs and sounds of visible joy on the part of Lady Arabella.

But we have kept the Greshamsbury tenantry waiting under the oak-trees by far too long. Yes; when young Frank came of age there was still enough left at Greshamsbury, still means enough at the squire's disposal, to light one bonfire, to roast, whole in its skin, one bullock. Frank's virility came on him not quite unmarked, as that of the parson's son might do, or the son of the neighbouring attorney. It could still be reported in the Barsetshire Conservative *Standard* that "The beards wagged all" at Greshamsbury, now as they had done for many centuries on similar festivals. Yes; it was so reported. But this, like so many other such reports, had but a shadow of truth in it. "They poured the liquor in," certainly, those who were there; but the beards did not wag as they had been wont to wag in former years. Beards won't wag for the telling. The squire was at his wits' end for money, and the tenants one and all had so heard. Rents had been raised on them; timber had fallen fast; the lawyer on the estate was growing rich; tradesmen in Barchester, nay, in Greshamsbury itself, were beginning to mutter; and the squire himself would not be merry. Under such circumstances the throats of a tenantry will still swallow, but their beards will not wag.

"I minds well," said Farmer Oaklerath to his neighbour, "when the squoire hisself comed of age. Lord love 'ee! There was fun going that day. There was more yale drank then than's been brewed at the big house these two years. T'old squoire was a one'er."

"And I minds when squoire was borned; minds it well," said an old farmer sitting opposite. "Them was the days! It an't that long ago neither. Squoire a'nt come o' fifty yet; no, nor an't nigh it, though he looks it. Things be altered at Greemsbury"—such was the rural pronunciation—"altered sadly, neebor Oaklerath. Well, well; I'll soon be gone, I will, and so it an't no use talking; but arter paying one pound fifteen for them acres for more nor fifty year, I didn't think I'd ever be axed for forty shilling."

Such was the style of conversation which went on at the various tables. It had certainly been of a very different tone when the squire was born, when he came of age, and when, just two years subsequently, his son had been born. On each of these events similar rural fêtes had been given, and the squire himself had on these occasions been frequent among his guests. On the first, he had been carried round by his father, a whole train of ladies and nurses following. On the second, he had himself mixed in all the sports, the gayest of the gay, and each tenant had squeezed his way up to the lawn to get a sight of the Lady Arabella, who, as was already known, was to come from Courcy Castle to Greshamsbury to be their mistress. It was little they any of them cared now for the Lady Arabella. On the third, he himself had borne his child in his arms as his father had before borne him; he was then in the zenith of his pride, and though the tenantry whispered that he was somewhat less familiar with them than of yore, that he had put on somewhat too much of the de Courcy airs, still he was their squire, their master, the rich man in whose hand they lay. The old squire was then gone, and they were proud of the young member and his lady bride in spite of a little hauteur. None of them were proud of him now.

He walked once round among the guests, and spoke a few words of welcome at each table; and as he did so the tenants got up and bowed and wished health to the old squire, happiness to the young one, and prosperity to Greshamsbury; but, nevertheless, it was but a tame affair.

There were also other visitors, of the gentle sort, to do honour to the occasion; but not such swarms, not such a crowd at the mansion itself and at the houses of the neighbouring gentry as had always been collected on these former gala doings. Indeed, the party at Greshamsbury was not a large one, and consisted chiefly of Lady de Courcy and her suite. Lady Arabella still kept up, as far as she was able, her close connexion with Courcy Castle. She was there as much as possible, to which Mr Gresham never objected; and she took her daughters there whenever she could, though, as regarded the two elder girls, she was interfered with by Mr Gresham, and not unfrequently by the girls themselves. Lady Arabella had a pride in her son, though he was by no means her favourite child. He was, however, the heir of Greshamsbury, of which fact she was disposed to make the most, and he was also a fine gainly open-hearted young man, who could not but be dear to any mother. Lady Arabella did love him dearly, though she felt a sort of disappointment in regard to him, seeing that he was not so much like a de Courcy as he should have been. She did love him dearly; and, therefore, when he came of age she got her sister-in-law and all the Ladies Amelia, Rosina etc., to come to Greshamsbury; and she also, with some difficulty, persuaded the Honourable Georges and the Honourable Johns to be equally condescending. Lord de Courcy himself was in attendance at the Court—or said that he was—and Lord Porlock, the eldest son, simply told his aunt when he was invited that he never bored himself with those sort of things.

Then there were the Bakers, and the Batesons, and the Jacksons, who all lived near and returned home at night; there was the Reverend Caleb Oriel, the High-Church rector, with his beautiful sister, Patience Oriel; there was Mr Yates Umbleby, the attorney and agent; and there was Dr Thorne, and the doctor's modest, quiet-looking little niece, Miss Mary.

CHAPTER II

LONG, LONG AGO

As Dr Thorne is our hero—or I should rather say my hero, a privilege of selecting for themselves in this respect being left to all my readers—and as Miss Mary Thorne is to be our heroine, a point on which no choice whatsoever is left to any one, it is necessary that they shall be introduced and explained and described in a proper, formal manner. I quite feel that an apology is due for beginning a novel with two long dull chapters full of description. I am perfectly aware of the danger of such a course. In so doing I sin against the golden rule which requires us all to put our best foot foremost, the wisdom of which is fully recognised by novelists, myself among the number. It can hardly be expected that any one will consent to go through with a fiction that offers so little of allurement in its first pages; but twist it as I will I cannot do otherwise. I find that I cannot make poor Mr Gresham hem and haw and turn himself uneasily in his arm-chair in a natural manner till I have said why he is uneasy. I cannot bring in my doctor speaking his mind freely among the bigwigs till I have explained that it is in accordance with his usual character to do so. This is unartistic on my part, and shows want of imagination as well as want of skill. Whether or not I can atone for these faults by straightforward, simple, plain story-telling—that, indeed, is very doubtful.

Dr Thorne belonged to a family in one sense as good, and at any rate as old, as that of Mr Gresham; and much older, he was apt to boast, than that of the de Courcys. This trait in his character is mentioned first, as it was the weakness for which he was most conspicuous. He was second cousin to Mr Thorne of Ullathorne, a Barsetshire squire living in the neighbourhood of Barchester, and who boasted that his estate had remained in his family, descending from Thorne to Thorne, longer than had been the case with any other estate or any other family in the county.

But Dr Thorne was only a second cousin; and, therefore, though he was entitled to talk of the blood as belonging to some extent to himself, he had no right to lay claim to any position in the county other than such as he might win for himself if he chose to locate himself in it. This was a fact of which no one was more fully aware than our doctor himself. His father, who had been first cousin of a former Squire Thorne, had been a clerical dignitary in Barchester, but had been dead now many years. He had had two sons; one he had educated as a medical man, but the other, and the younger, whom he had intended for the Bar, had not betaken himself in any satisfactory way to any calling. This son had been first rusticated from Oxford, and then expelled; and thence returning to Barchester, had been the cause to his father and brother of much suffering.

Old Dr Thorne, the clergyman, died when the two brothers were yet young men, and left behind him nothing but some household and other property of the value of about two thousand pounds, which he bequeathed to Thomas, the elder son, much more than that having been spent in liquidating debts contracted by the younger. Up to that time there had been close harmony between the Ullathorne family and that of the clergyman; but a month or two before the doctor's death—the period of which we are speaking was about two-and-twenty years before the commencement of our story—the then Mr Thorne of Ullathorne had made it understood that he would no longer receive at his house his cousin Henry, whom he regarded as a disgrace to the family.

Fathers are apt to be more lenient to their sons than uncles to their nephews, or cousins to each other. Dr Thorne still hoped to reclaim his black sheep, and thought that the head of his family showed an unnecessary harshness in putting an obstacle in his way of doing so. And if the father was warm in support of his profligate son, the young medical aspirant was warmer in support of his profligate brother. Dr Thorne, junior, was no roué himself, but perhaps, as a young man, he had not sufficient abhorrence of his brother's vices. At any rate, he stuck to him manfully; and when it was signified in the Close that Henry's company was not considered desirable at Ullathorne, Dr Thomas Thorne sent word to the squire that under such circumstances his visits there would also cease.

This was not very prudent, as the young Galen had elected to establish himself in Barchester, very mainly in expectation of the help which his Ullathorne connexion would give him. This, however, in his anger he failed to consider; he was never known, either in early or in middle life, to consider in his anger those points which were probably best worth his consideration. This, perhaps, was of the less moment as his anger was of an unenduring kind, evaporating frequently with more celerity than he could get the angry words out of his mouth. With the Ullathorne people, however, he did establish a quarrel sufficiently permanent to be of vital injury to his medical prospects.

And then the father died, and the two brothers were left living together with very little means between them. At this time there were living, in Barchester, people of the name of Scatcherd. Of that family, as then existing, we have only to do with two, a brother and a sister. They were in a low rank of life, the one being a journeyman stone-mason, and the other an apprentice to a straw-bonnet maker; but they were, nevertheless, in some sort remarkable people. The sister was reputed in Barchester to be a model of female beauty of the strong and robuster cast, and had also a better reputation as being a girl of good character and honest, womanly conduct. Both of her beauty and of her reputation her brother was exceedingly proud, and he was the more so when he learnt that she had been asked in marriage by a decent master-tradesman in the city.

Roger Scatcherd had also a reputation, but not for beauty or propriety of conduct. He was known for the best stone-mason in the four counties, and as the man who could, on occasion, drink the most alcohol in a given time in the same localities. As a workman, indeed, he had higher reputate even than this: he was not only a good and very quick stone-mason, but he had also a capacity for turning other men into good stone-masons: he had a gift of knowing what a man could and should do; and, by degrees, he taught himself what five, and ten, and twenty—latterly, what a thousand and two thousand men might accomplish among them: this, also, he did with very little aid from pen and paper, with which he was not, and never became, very conversant. He had also other gifts and other propensities. He could talk in a manner dangerous to himself and others; he could persuade without knowing that he did so; and being himself an extreme demagogue, in those noisy times just prior to the Reform Bill, he created a hubbub in Barchester of which he himself had had no previous conception.

Henry Thorne among his other bad qualities had one which his friends regarded as worse than all the others, and which perhaps justified the Ullathorne people in their severity. He loved to consort with low people. He not only drank—that might have been forgiven—but he drank in tap-rooms with vulgar drinkers; so said his friends, and so said his enemies. He denied the charge as being made in the plural number, and declared that his only low co-reveller was Roger Scatcherd. With Roger Scatcherd, at any rate, he associated, and became as democratic as Roger was himself. Now the Thornes of Ullathorne were of the very highest order of Tory excellence.

Whether or not Mary Scatcherd at once accepted the offer of the respectable tradesman, I cannot say. After the occurrence of certain events which must here shortly be told, she declared that she never had done so. Her brother averred that she most positively had. The respectable tradesman himself refused to speak on the subject.

It is certain, however, that Scatcherd, who had hitherto been silent enough about his sister in those social hours which he passed with his gentleman friend, boasted of the engagement when it was, as he said, made; and then boasted also of the girl's beauty. Scatcherd, in spite of his occasional intemperance, looked up in the world, and the coming marriage of his sister was, he thought, suitable to his own ambition for his family.

Henry Thorne had already heard of, and already seen, Mary Scatcherd; but hitherto she had not fallen in the way of his wickedness. Now, however, when he heard that she was to be decently married, the devil tempted him to tempt her. It boots not to tell all the tale. It came out clearly enough when all was told, that he made her most distinct promises of marriage; he even gave her such in writing; and having in this way obtained from her her company during some of her little holidays—her Sundays or summer evenings—he seduced her. Scatcherd accused him openly of having intoxicated her with drugs; and Thomas Thorne, who took up the case, ultimately believed the charge. It became known in Barchester that she was with child, and that the seducer was Henry Thorne.

Roger Scatcherd, when the news first reached him, filled himself with drink, and then swore that he would kill them both. With manly wrath, however, he set forth, first against the man, and that with manly weapons. He took nothing with him but his fists and a big stick as he went in search of Henry Thorne.

The two brothers were then lodging together at a farm-house close abutting on the town. This was not an eligible abode for a medical practitioner; but the young doctor had not been able to settle himself eligibly since his father's death; and wishing to put what constraint he could upon his brother, had so located himself. To this farm-house came Roger Scatcherd one sultry summer evening, his anger gleaming from his bloodshot eyes, and his rage heightened to madness by the rapid pace at which he had run from the city, and by the ardent spirits which were fermenting within him.

At the very gate of the farm-yard, standing placidly with his cigar in his mouth, he encountered Henry Thorne. He had thought of searching for him through the whole premises, of demanding his victim with loud exclamations, and making his way to him through all obstacles. In lieu of that, there stood the man before him.

"Well, Roger, what's in the wind?" said Henry Thorne.

They were the last words he ever spoke. He was answered by a blow from the black-thorn. A contest ensued, which ended in Scatcherd keeping his word—at any rate, as regarded the worst offender. How the fatal blow on the temple was struck was never exactly determined: one medical man said it might have been done in a fight with a heavy-headed stick; another thought that a stone had been used; a third suggested a stone-mason's hammer. It seemed, however, to be proved subsequently that no hammer was taken out, and Scatcherd himself persisted in declaring that he had taken in his hand no weapon but the stick. Scatcherd, however, was drunk; and even though he intended to tell the truth, may have been mistaken. There were, however, the facts that Thorne was dead; that Scatcherd had sworn to kill him about an hour previously; and that he had without delay accomplished his threat. He was arrested and tried for murder; all the distressing circumstances of the case came out on the trial: he was found guilty of manslaughter, and sentenced to be imprisoned for six months. Our readers will probably think that the punishment was too severe.

Thomas Thorne and the farmer were on the spot soon after Henry Thorne had fallen. The brother was at first furious for vengeance against his brother's murderer; but, as the facts came out, as he learnt what had been the provocation given, what had been the feelings of Scatcherd when he left the city, determined to punish him who had ruined his sister, his heart was changed. Those were trying days for him. It behoved him to do what in him lay to cover his brother's memory from the obloquy which it deserved; it behoved him also to save, or to assist to save, from undue punishment the unfortunate man who had shed his brother's blood; and it behoved him also, at least so he thought, to look after that poor fallen one whose misfortunes were less merited than those either of his brother or of hers.

And he was not the man to get through these things lightly, or with as much ease as he perhaps might conscientiously have done. He would pay for the defence of the prisoner; he would pay for the defence of his brother's memory; and he would pay for the poor girl's comforts. He would do this, and he would allow no one to help him. He stood alone in the world, and insisted on so standing. Old Mr Thorne of Ullathorne offered again to open his arms to him; but he had conceived a foolish idea that his cousin's severity had driven his brother on to his bad career, and he would consequently accept no kindness from Ullathorne. Miss Thorne, the old squire's daughter—a cousin considerably older than himself, to whom he had at one time been much attached—sent him money; and he returned it to her under a blank cover. He had still enough for those unhappy purposes which he had in hand. As to what might happen afterwards, he was then mainly indifferent.

The affair made much noise in the county, and was inquired into closely by many of the county magistrates; by none more closely than by John Newbold Gresham, who was then alive. Mr Gresham was greatly taken with the energy and justice shown by Dr Thorne on the occasion; and when the trial was over, he invited him to Greshamsbury. The visit ended in the doctor establishing himself in that village.

We must return for a moment to Mary Scatcherd. She was saved from the necessity of encountering her brother's wrath, for that brother was under arrest for murder before he could get at her. Her immediate lot, however, was a cruel one. Deep as was her cause for anger against the man who had so inhumanly used her, still it was natural that she should turn to him with love rather than with aversion. To whom else could she in such plight look for love? When, therefore, she heard that he was slain, her heart sank within her; she turned her face to the wall, and laid herself down to die: to die a double death, for herself and the fatherless babe that was now quick within her.

But, in fact, life had still much to offer, both to her and to her child. For her it was still destined that she should, in a distant land, be the worthy wife of a good husband, and the happy mother of many children. For that embryo one it was destined—but that may not be so quickly told: to describe her destiny this volume has yet to be written.

Even in those bitterest days God tempered the wind to the shorn lamb. Dr Thorne was by her bedside soon after the bloody tidings had reached her, and did for her more than either her lover or her brother could have done. When the baby was born, Scatcherd was still in prison, and had still three months' more confinement to undergo. The story of her great wrongs and cruel usage was much talked of, and men said that one who had been so injured should be regarded as having in nowise sinned at all.

461

One man, at any rate, so thought. At twilight, one evening, Thorne was surprised by a visit from a demure Barchester hardware dealer, whom he did not remember ever to have addressed before. This was the former lover of poor Mary Scatcherd. He had a proposal to make, and it was this:—if Mary would consent to leave the country at once, to leave it without notice from her brother, or talk or éclat on the matter, he would sell all that he had, marry her, and emigrate. There was but one condition; she must leave her baby behind her. The hardware-man could find it in his heart to be generous, to be generous and true to his love; but he could not be generous enough to father the seducer's child.

"I could never abide it, sir, if I took it," said he; "and she,—why in course she would always love it the best."

In praising his generosity, who can mingle any censure for such manifest prudence? He would still make her the wife of his bosom, defiled in the eyes of the world as she had been; but she must be to him the mother of his own children, not the mother of another's child.

And now again our doctor had a hard task to win through. He saw at once that it was his duty to use his utmost authority to induce the poor girl to accept such an offer. She liked the man; and here was opened to her a course which would have been most desirable, even before her misfortune. But it is hard to persuade a mother to part with her first babe; harder, perhaps, when the babe had been so fathered and so born than when the world has shone brightly on its earliest hours. She at first refused stoutly: she sent a thousand loves, a thousand thanks, profusest acknowledgements for his generosity to the man who showed her that he loved her so well; but Nature, she said, would not let her leave her child.

"And what will you do for her here, Mary?" said the doctor. Poor Mary replied to him with a deluge of tears.

"She is my niece," said the doctor, taking up the tiny infant in his huge hands; "she is already the nearest thing, the only thing that I have in this world. I am her uncle, Mary. If you will go with this man I will be father to her and mother to her. Of what bread I eat, she shall eat; of what cup I drink, she shall drink. See, Mary, here is the Bible;" and he covered the book with his hand. "Leave her to me, and by this word she shall be my child."

The mother consented at last; left her baby with the doctor, married, and went to America. All this was consummated before Roger Scatcherd was liberated from jail. Some conditions the doctor made. The first was, that Scatcherd should not know his sister's child was thus disposed of. Dr Thorne, in undertaking to bring up the baby, did not choose to encounter any tie with persons who might hereafter claim to be the girl's relations on the other side. Relations she would undoubtedly have had none had she been left to live or die as a workhouse bastard; but should the doctor succeed in life, should he ultimately be able to make this girl the darling of his own house, and then the darling of some other house, should she live and win the heart of some man whom the doctor might delight to call his friend and nephew; then relations might spring up whose ties would not be advantageous.

No man plumed himself on good blood more than Dr Thorne; no man had greater pride in his genealogical tree, and his hundred and thirty clearly proved descents from MacAdam; no man had a stronger theory as to the advantage held by men who have grandfathers over those who have none, or have none worth talking about. Let it not be thought that our doctor was a perfect character. No, indeed; most far from perfect. He had within him an inner, stubborn, self-admiring pride, which made him believe himself to be better and higher than those around him, and this from some unknown cause which he could hardly explain to himself. He had a pride in being a poor man of a high family; he had a pride in repudiating the very family of which he was proud; and he had a special pride in keeping his pride silently to himself. His father had been a Thorne, and his mother a Thorold. There was no better blood to be had in England. It was in the possession of such properties as these that he condescended to rejoice; this man, with a man's heart, a man's courage, and a man's humanity! Other doctors round the county had ditch-water in their veins; he could boast of a pure ichor, to which that of the great Omnium family was but a muddy puddle. It was thus that he loved to excel his brother practitioners, he who might have indulged in the pride of excelling them both in talent and in energy! We speak now of his early days; but even in his maturer life, the man, though mellowed, was the same.

This was the man who now promised to take to his bosom as his own child a poor bastard whose father was already dead, and whose mother's family was such as the Scatcherds! It was necessary that the child's history should be known to none. Except to the mother's brother it was an object of interest to no one. The mother had for some short time been talked of; but now the nine-days' wonder was a wonder no longer. She went off to her far-away home; her husband's generosity was duly chronicled in the papers, and the babe was left untalked of and unknown.

It was easy to explain to Scatcherd that the child had not lived. There was a parting interview between the brother and sister in the jail, during which, with real tears and unaffected sorrow, the mother thus accounted for the offspring of her shame. Then she started, fortunate in her coming fortunes; and the doctor took with him his charge to the new country in which they were both to live. There he found for her a fitting home till she should be old enough to sit at his table and live in his bachelor house; and no one but old Mr Gresham knew who she was, or whence she had come.

Then Roger Scatcherd, having completed his six months' confinement, came out of prison.

Roger Scatcherd, though his hands were now red with blood, was to be pitied. A short time before the days of Henry Thorne's death he had married a young wife in his own class of life, and had made many resolves that henceforward his conduct should be such as might become a married man, and might not disgrace the respectable brother-in-law he was about to have given him. Such was his condition when he first heard of his sister's plight. As has been said, he filled himself with drink and started off on the scent of blood.

During his prison days his wife had to support herself as she might. The decent articles of furniture which they had put together were sold; she gave up their little house, and, bowed down by misery, she also was brought near to death. When he was liberated he at once got work; but those who have watched the lives of such people know how hard it is for them to recover lost ground. She became a mother immediately after his liberation, and when her child was born they were in direst want; for Scatcherd was again drinking, and his resolves were blown to the wind.

The doctor was then living at Greshamsbury. He had gone over there before the day on which he undertook the charge of poor Mary's baby, and soon found himself settled as the Greshamsbury doctor. This occurred very soon after the birth of the young heir. His predecessor in this career had "bettered" himself, or endeavoured to do so, by seeking the practice of some large town, and Lady Arabella, at a very critical time, was absolutely left with no other advice than that of a stranger, picked up, as she declared to Lady de Courcy, somewhere about Barchester jail, or Barchester court-house, she did not know which.

Of course Lady Arabella could not suckle the young heir herself. Ladies Arabella never can. They are gifted with the powers of being mothers, but not nursing-mothers. Nature gives them bosoms for show, but not for use. So Lady Arabella had a wet-nurse. At the end of six months the new doctor found Master Frank was not doing quite so well as he should do; and after a little trouble it was discovered that the very excellent young woman who had been sent express from Courcy Castle to Greshamsbury—a supply being kept up on the lord's demesne for the family use—was fond of brandy. She was at once sent back to the castle, of course; and, as Lady de Courcy was too much in dudgeon to send another, Dr Thorne was allowed to procure one. He thought of the misery of Roger Scatcherd's wife, thought also of her health, and strength, and active habits; and thus Mrs Scatcherd became the foster-mother to young Frank Gresham.

One other episode we must tell of past times. Previous to his father's death, Dr Thorne was in love. Nor had he altogether sighed and pleaded in vain; though it had not quite come to that, that the young lady's friends, or even the young lady herself, had actually accepted his suit. At that time his name stood well in Barchester. His father was a prebendary; his cousins and his best friends were the Thornes of Ullathorne, and the lady, who shall be nameless, was not thought to be injudicious in listening to the young doctor. But when Henry Thorne went so far astray, when the old doctor died, when the young doctor quarrelled with Ullathorne, when the brother was killed in a disgraceful quarrel, and it turned out that the physician had nothing but his profession and no settled locality in which to exercise it; then, indeed, the young lady's friends thought that she was injudicious, and the young lady herself had not spirit enough, or love enough, to be disobedient. In those stormy days of the trial she told Dr Thorne that perhaps it would be wise that they should not see each other any more.

Dr Thorne, so counselled, at such a moment,—so informed then, when he most required comfort from his love, at once swore loudly that he agreed with her. He rushed forth with a bursting heart, and said to himself that the world was bad, all bad. He saw the lady no more; and, if I am rightly informed, never again made matrimonial overtures to any one.

CHAPTER III

DR THORNE

And thus Dr Thorne became settled for life in the little village of Greshamsbury. As was then the wont with many country practitioners, and as should be the wont with them all if they consulted their own dignity a little less and the comforts of their customers somewhat more, he added the business of a dispensing apothecary to that of physician. In doing so, he was of course much reviled. Many people around him declared that he could not truly be a doctor, or, at any rate, a doctor to be so called; and his brethren in the art living around him, though they knew that his diplomas, degrees, and certificates were all *en règle*, rather countenanced the report. There was much about this new-comer which did not endear him to his own profession. In the first place he was a new-comer, and, as such, was of course to be regarded by other doctors as being *de trop*. Greshamsbury was only fifteen miles from Barchester, where there was a regular dépôt of medical skill, and but eight from Silverbridge, where a properly established physician had been in residence for the last forty years. Dr Thorne's predecessor at Greshamsbury had been a humble-minded general practitioner, gifted with a due respect for the physicians of the county; and he, though he had been allowed to physic the servants, and sometimes the children of Greshamsbury, had never had the presumption to put himself on a par with his betters.

Then, also, Dr Thorne, though a graduated physician, though entitled beyond all dispute to call himself a doctor, according to all the laws of all the colleges, made it known to the East Barsetshire world, very soon after he had seated himself at Greshamsbury, that his rate of pay was to be seven-and-sixpence a visit within a circuit of five miles, with a proportionally increased charge at proportionally increased distances. Now there was something low, mean, unprofessional, and democratic in this; so, at least, said the children of Æsculapius gathered together in conclave at Barchester. In the first place, it showed that this Thorne was always thinking of his money, like an apothecary, as he was; whereas, it would have behoved him, as a physician, had he had the feelings of a physician under his hat, to have regarded his own pursuits in a purely philosophical spirit, and to have taken any gain which might have accrued as an accidental adjunct to his station in life. A physician should take his fee without letting his left hand know what his right hand was doing; it should be taken without a thought, without a look, without a move of the facial muscles; the true physician should hardly be aware that the last friendly grasp of the hand had been made more precious by the touch of gold. Whereas, that fellow Thorne would lug out half a crown from his breeches pocket and give it in change for a ten shilling piece. And then it was clear that this man had no appreciation of the dignity of a learned profession. He might constantly be seen compounding medicines in the shop, at the left hand of his front door; not making experiments philosophically in materia medica for the benefit of coming ages—which, if he did, he should have done in the seclusion of his study, far from profane eyes—but positively putting together common powders for rural bowels, or spreading vulgar ointments for agricultural ailments.

A man of this sort was not fit society for Dr Fillgrave of Barchester. That must be admitted. And yet he had been found to be fit society for the old squire of Greshamsbury, whose shoe-ribbons Dr Fillgrave would not have objected to tie; so high did the old squire stand in the county just previous to his death. But the spirit of the Lady Arabella was known by the medical profession of Barsetshire, and when that good man died it was felt that Thorne's short tenure of Greshamsbury favour was already over. The Barsetshire regulars were, however, doomed to disappointment. Our doctor had already contrived to endear himself to the heir; and though there was not even then much personal love between him and the Lady Arabella, he kept his place at the great house unmoved, not only in the nursery and in the bedrooms, but also at the squire's dining-table.

Now there was in this, it must be admitted, quite enough to make him unpopular with his brethren; and this feeling was soon shown in a marked and dignified manner. Dr Fillgrave, who had certainly the most respectable professional connexion in the county, who had a reputation to maintain, and who was accustomed to meet, on almost equal terms, the great medical baronets from the metropolis at the houses of the nobility—Dr Fillgrave declined to meet Dr Thorne in consultation. He exceedingly regretted, he said, most exceedingly, the necessity which he felt of doing so: he had never before had to perform so painful a duty; but, as a duty which he owed to his profession, he must perform it. With every feeling of respect for Lady ——, a sick guest at Greshamsbury—and for Mr Gresham, he must decline to attend in conjunction with Dr Thorne. If his services could be made available under any other circumstances, he would go to Greshamsbury as fast as post-horses could carry him.

Then, indeed, there was war in Barsetshire. If there was on Dr Thorne's cranium one bump more developed than another, it was that of combativeness. Not that the doctor was a bully, or even pugnacious, in the usual sense of the word; he had no disposition to provoke a fight, no propense love of quarrelling; but there was that in him which would allow him to yield to no attack. Neither in argument nor in contest would he ever allow himself to be wrong; never at least to any one but to himself; and on behalf of his special hobbies, he was ready to meet the world at large.

It will therefore be understood, that when such a gauntlet was thus thrown in his very teeth by Dr Fillgrave, he was not slow to take it up. He addressed a letter to the Barsetshire Conservative *Standard*, in which he attacked Dr Fillgrave with some considerable acerbity. Dr Fillgrave responded in four lines, saying that on mature consideration he had made up his mind not to notice any remarks that might be made on him by Dr Thorne in the public press. The Greshamsbury doctor then wrote another letter, more witty and much more severe than the last; and as this was copied into the Bristol, Exeter, and Gloucester papers, Dr Fillgrave found it very difficult to maintain the magnanimity of his reticence. It is sometimes becoming enough for a man to wrap himself in the dignified toga of silence, and proclaim himself indifferent to public attacks; but it is a sort of dignity which it is very difficult to maintain. As well might a man, when stung to madness by wasps, endeavour to sit in his chair without moving a muscle, as endure with patience and without reply the courtesies of a newspaper opponent. Dr Thorne wrote a third letter, which was too much for medical flesh and blood to bear. Dr Fillgrave answered it, not, indeed, in his own name, but in that of a brother doctor; and then the war raged merrily. It is hardly too much to say that Dr Fillgrave never knew another happy hour. Had he dreamed of what materials was made that young compounder of doses at Greshamsbury he would have met him in consultation, morning, noon, and night, without objection; but having begun the war, he was constrained to go on with it: his brethren would allow him no alternative. Thus he was continually being brought up to the fight, as a prize-fighter may be seen to be, who is carried up round after round, without any hope on his own part, and who, in each round, drops to the ground before the very wind of his opponent's blows.

But Dr Fillgrave, though thus weak himself, was backed in practice and in countenance by nearly all his brethren in the county. The guinea fee, the principle of *giving* advice and of selling no medicine, the great resolve to keep a distinct barrier between the physician and the apothecary, and, above all, the hatred of the contamination of a bill, were strong in the medical mind of Barsetshire. Dr Thorne had the provincial medical world against him, and so he appealed to the metropolis. The *Lancet* took the matter up in his favour, but the *Journal of Medical Science* was against him; the *Weekly Chirurgeon*, noted for its medical democracy, upheld him as a medical prophet, but the *Scalping Knife*, a monthly periodical got up in dead opposition to the *Lancet*, showed him no mercy. So the war went on, and our doctor, to a certain extent, became a noted character.

He had, moreover, other difficulties to encounter in his professional career. It was something in his favour that he understood his business; something that he was willing to labour at it with energy; and resolved to labour at it conscientiously. He had also other gifts, such as conversational brilliancy, an aptitude for true good fellowship, firmness in friendship, and general honesty of disposition, which stood him in stead as he advanced in life. But, at his first starting, much that belonged to himself personally was against him. Let him enter what house he would, he entered it with a conviction, often expressed to himself, that he was equal as a man to the proprietor, equal as a human being to the proprietress. To age he would allow deference, and to special recognised talent—at least so he said; to rank also, he would pay that respect which was its clear and recognised prerogative; he would let a lord walk out of a room before him if he did not happen to forget it; in speaking to a duke he would address him as his Grace; and he would in no way assume a familiarity with bigger men than himself, allowing to the bigger man the privilege of making the first advances. But beyond this he would admit that no man should walk the earth with his head higher than his own.

He did not talk of these things much; he offended no rank by boasts of his own equality; he did not absolutely tell the Earl de Courcy in words, that the privilege of dining at Courcy Castle was to him no greater than the privilege of dining at Courcy Parsonage; but there was that in his manner that told it. The feeling in itself was perhaps good, and was certainly much justified by the manner in which he bore himself to those below him in rank; but there was folly in the resolution to run counter to the world's recognised rules on such matters; and much absurdity in his mode of doing so, seeing that at heart he was a thorough Conservative. It is hardly too much to say that he naturally hated a lord at first sight; but, nevertheless, he would have expended his means, his blood, and spirit, in fighting for the upper house of Parliament.

Such a disposition, until it was thoroughly understood, did not tend to ingratiate him with the wives of the country gentlemen among whom he had to look for practice. And then, also, there was not much in his individual manner to recommend him to the favour of ladies. He was brusque, authoritative, given to contradiction, rough though never dirty in his personal belongings, and inclined to indulge in a sort of quiet raillery, which sometimes was not thoroughly understood. People did not always know whether he was laughing at them or with them; and some people were, perhaps, inclined to think that a doctor should not laugh at all when called in to act doctorially.

When he was known, indeed, when the core of the fruit had been reached, when the huge proportions of that loving trusting heart had been learned, and understood, and appreciated, when that honesty had been recognised, that manly, and almost womanly ten-tenderness had been felt, then, indeed, the doctor was acknowledged to be adequate in his profession. To trifling ailments he was too often brusque. Seeing that he accepted money for the cure of such, he should, we may say, have cured them without an offensive man-ner. So far he is without defence. But to real suffering no one found him brusque; no patient lying painfully on a bed of sickness ever thought him rough.

Another misfortune was, that he was a bachelor. Ladies think, and I, for one, think that ladies are quite right in so thinking, that doctors should be married men. All the world feels that a man when married acquires some of the attributes of an old woman—he be-comes, to a certain extent, a motherly sort of being; he acquires a conversance with women's ways and women's wants, and loses the wilder and offensive sparks of his virili-ty. It must be easier to talk to such a one about Matilda's stomach, and the growing pains in Fanny's legs, than to a young bachelor. This impediment also stood much in Dr Thorne's way during his first years at Greshamsbury.

But his wants were not at first great; and though his ambition was perhaps high, it was not of an impatient nature. The world was his oyster; but, circumstanced as he was, he knew that it was not for him to open it with his lancet all at once. He had bread to earn, which he must earn wearily; he had a character to make, which must come slowly; it satis-fied his soul that, in addition to his immortal hopes, he had a possible future in this world to which he could look forward with clear eyes, and advance with a heart that would know no fainting.

On his first arrival at Greshamsbury he had been put by the squire into a house, which he still occupied when that squire's grandson came of age. There were two decent, com-modious, private houses in the village—always excepting the rectory, which stood grandly in its own grounds, and, therefore, was considered as ranking above the village residences—of these two Dr Thorne had the smaller. They stood exactly at the angle be-fore described, on the outer side of it, and at right angles to each other. They both possessed good stables and ample gardens; and it may be as well to specify, that Mr Um-bleby, the agent and lawyer to the estate, occupied the larger one.

Here Dr Thorne lived for eleven or twelve years, all alone; and then for ten or eleven more with his niece, Mary Thorne. Mary was thirteen when she came to take up perma-nent abode as mistress of the establishment—or, at any rate, to act as the only mistress which the establishment possessed. This advent greatly changed the tenor of the doctor's ways. He had been before pure bachelor; not a room in his house had been comfortably furnished; he at first commenced in a makeshift sort of way, because he had not at his command the means of commencing otherwise; and he had gone on in the same fashion, because the exact time had never come at which it was imperative in him to set his house in order. He had had no fixed hour for his meals, no fixed place for his books, no fixed wardrobe for his clothes. He had a few bottles of good wine in his cellar, and occasionally asked a brother bachelor to take a chop with him; but beyond this he had touched very little on the cares of housekeeping. A slop-bowl full of strong tea, together with bread, and butter, and eggs, was produced for him in the morning, and he expected that at whatever hour he might arrive in the evening, some food should be presented to him wherewith to satisfy the cravings of nature; if, in addition to this, he had another slop-bowl of tea in the evening, he got all that he ever required, or all, at least, that he ever demanded.

But when Mary came, or rather, when she was about to come, things were altogether changed at the doctor's. People had hitherto wondered—and especially Mrs Umbleby—how a gentleman like Dr Thorne could continue to live in so slovenly a manner; and how people again wondered, and again especially Mrs Umbleby, how the doctor could possibly think it necessary to put such a lot of furniture into a house because a little chit of a girl of twelve years of age was coming to live with him.

Mrs Umbleby had great scope for her wonder. The doctor made a thorough revolution in his household, and furnished his house from the ground to the roof completely. He painted—for the first time since the commencement of his tenancy—he papered, he carpeted, and curtained, and mirrored, and linened, and blanketed, as though a Mrs Thorne with a good fortune were coming home to-morrow; and all for a girl of twelve years old. "And how," said Mrs Umbleby, to her friend Miss Gushing, "how did he find out what to buy?" as though the doctor had been brought up like a wild beast, ignorant of the nature of tables and chairs, and with no more developed ideas of drawing-room drapery than an hippopotamus.

To the utter amazement of Mrs Umbleby and Miss Gushing, the doctor did it all very well. He said nothing about it to any one—he never did say much about such things—but he furnished his house well and discreetly; and when Mary Thorne came home from her school at Bath, to which she had been taken some six years previously, she found herself called upon to be the presiding genius of a perfect paradise.

It has been said that the doctor had managed to endear himself to the new squire before the old squire's death, and that, therefore, the change at Greshamsbury had had no professional ill effects upon him. Such was the case at the time; but, nevertheless, all did not go smoothly in the Greshamsbury medical department. There was six or seven years' difference in age between Mr Gresham and the doctor, and, moreover, Mr Gresham was young for his age, and the doctor old; but, nevertheless, there was a very close attachment between them early in life. This was never thoroughly sundered, and, backed by this, the doctor did maintain himself for some years before the fire of Lady Arabella's artillery. But drops falling, if they fall constantly, will bore through a stone.

Dr Thorne's pretensions, mixed with his subversive professional democratic tendencies, his seven-and-sixpenny visits, added to his utter disregard of Lady Arabella's airs, were too much for her spirit. He brought Frank through his first troubles, and that at first ingratiated her; he was equally successful with the early dietary of Augusta and Beatrice; but, as his success was obtained in direct opposition to the Courcy Castle nursery principles, this hardly did much in his favour. When the third daughter was born, he at once declared that she was a very weakly flower, and sternly forbade the mother to go to London. The mother, loving her babe, obeyed; but did not the less hate the doctor for the order, which she firmly believed was given at the instance and express dictation of Mr Gresham. Then another little girl came into the world, and the doctor was more imperative than ever as to the nursery rules and the excellence of country air. Quarrels were thus engendered, and Lady Arabella was taught to believe that this doctor of her husband's was after all no Solomon. In her husband's absence she sent for Dr Fillgrave, giving very express intimation that he would not have to wound either his eyes or dignity by encountering his enemy; and she found Dr Fillgrave a great comfort to her.

Then Dr Thorne gave Mr Gresham to understand that, under such circumstances, he could not visit professionally at Greshamsbury any longer. The poor squire saw there was no help for it, and though he still maintained his friendly connexion with his neighbour, the seven-and-sixpenny visits were at an end. Dr Fillgrave from Barchester, and the gentleman at Silverbridge, divided the responsibility between them, and the nursery principles of Courcy Castle were again in vogue at Greshamsbury.

So things went on for years, and those years were years of sorrow. We must not ascribe to our doctor's enemies the sufferings, and sickness, and deaths that occurred. The four frail little ones that died would probably have been taken had Lady Arabella been more tolerant of Dr Thorne. But the fact was, that they did die; and that the mother's heart then got the better of the woman's pride, and Lady Arabella humbled herself before Dr Thorne. She humbled herself, or would have done so, had the doctor permitted her. But he, with his eyes full of tears, stopped the utterance of her apology, took her two hands in his, pressed them warmly, and assured her that his joy in returning would be great, for the love that he bore to all that belonged to Greshamsbury. And so the seven-and-sixpenny visits were recommenced; and the great triumph of Dr Fillgrave came to an end.

Great was the joy in the Greshamsbury nursery when the second change took place. Among the doctor's attributes, not hitherto mentioned, was an aptitude for the society of children. He delighted to talk to children, and to play with them. He would carry them on his back, three or four at a time, roll with them on the ground, race with them in the garden, invent games for them, contrive amusements in circumstances which seemed quite adverse to all manner of delight; and, above all, his physic was not nearly so nasty as that which came from Silverbridge.

He had a great theory as to the happiness of children; and though he was not disposed altogether to throw over the precepts of Solomon—always bargaining that he should, under no circumstances, be himself the executioner—he argued that the principal duty which a parent owed to a child was to make him happy. Not only was the man to be made happy—the future man, if that might be possible—but the existing boy was to be treated with equal favour; and his happiness, so said the doctor, was of much easier attainment.

"Why struggle after future advantage at the expense of present pain, seeing that the results were so very doubtful?" Many an opponent of the doctor had thought to catch him on the hip when so singular a doctrine was broached; but they were not always successful. "What!" said his sensible enemies, "is Johnny not to be taught to read because he does not like it?" "Johnny must read by all means," would the doctor answer; "but is it necessary that he should not like it? If the preceptor have it in him, may not Johnny learn, not only to read, but to like to learn to read?"

"But," would say his enemies, "children must be controlled." "And so must men also," would say the doctor. "I must not steal your peaches, nor make love to your wife, nor libel your character. Much as I might wish through my natural depravity to indulge in such vices, I am debarred from them without pain, and I may almost say without unhappiness."

And so the argument went on, neither party convincing the other. But, in the meantime, the children of the neighbourhood became very fond of Dr Thorne.

Dr Thorne and the squire were still fast friends, but circumstances had occurred, spreading themselves now over a period of many years, which almost made the poor squire uneasy in the doctor's company. Mr Gresham owed a large sum of money, and he had, moreover, already sold a portion of his property. Unfortunately it had been the pride of the Greshams that their acres had descended from one to another without an entail, so that each possessor of Greshamsbury had had the full power to dispose of the property as he pleased. Any doubt as to its going to the male heir had never hitherto been felt. It had occasionally been encumbered by charges for younger children; but these charges had been liquidated, and the property had come down without any burden to the present squire. Now a portion of this had been sold, and it had been sold to a certain degree through the agency of Dr Thorne.

This made the squire an unhappy man. No man loved his family name and honour, his old family blazon and standing more thoroughly than he did; he was every whit a Gresham at heart; but his spirit had been weaker than that of his forefathers; and, in his days, for the first time, the Greshams were to go to the wall! Ten years before the beginning of our story it had been necessary to raise a large sum of money to meet and pay off pressing liabilities, and it was found that this could be done with more material advantage by selling a portion of the property than in any other way. A portion of it, about a third of the whole in value, was accordingly sold.

Boxall Hill lay half-way between Greshamsbury and Barchester, and was known as having the best partridge shooting in the county; as having on it also a celebrated fox cover, Boxall Gorse, held in very high repute by Barsetshire sportsmen. There was no residence on the immediate estate, and it was altogether divided from the remainder of the Greshamsbury property. This, with many inward and outward groans, Mr Gresham permitted to be sold.

It was sold, and sold well, by private contract to a native of Barchester, who, having risen from the world's ranks, had made for himself great wealth. Somewhat of this man's character must hereafter be told; it will suffice to say that he relied for advice in money matters upon Dr Thorne, and that at Dr Thorne's suggestion he had purchased Boxall Hill, partridge-shooting and gorse cover all included. He had not only bought Boxall Hill, but had subsequently lent the squire large sums of money on mortgage, in all which transactions the doctor had taken part. It had therefore come to pass that Mr Gresham was not unfrequently called upon to discuss his money affairs with Dr Thorne, and occasionally to submit to lectures and advice which might perhaps as well have been omitted.

So much for Dr Thorne. A few words must still be said about Miss Mary before we rush into our story; the crust will then have been broken, and the pie will be open to the guests. Little Miss Mary was kept at a farm-house till she was six; she was then sent to school at Bath, and transplanted to the doctor's newly furnished house a little more than six years after that. It must not be supposed that he had lost sight of his charge during her earlier years. He was much too well aware of the nature of the promise which he had made to the departing mother to do that. He had constantly visited his little niece, and long before the first twelve years of her life were over had lost all consciousness of his promise, and of his duty to the mother, in the stronger ties of downright personal love for the only creature that belonged to him.

When Mary came home the doctor was like a child in his glee. He prepared surprises for her with as much forethought and trouble as though he were contriving mines to blow up an enemy. He took her first into the shop, and then into the kitchen, thence to the dining-rooms, after that to his and her bedrooms, and so on till he came to the full glory of the new drawing-room, enhancing the pleasure by little jokes, and telling her that he should never dare to come into the last paradise without her permission, and not then till he had taken off his boots. Child as she was, she understood the joke, and carried it on like a little queen; and so they soon became the firmest of friends.

But though Mary was a queen, it was still necessary that she should be educated. Those were the earlier days in which Lady Arabella had humbled herself, and to show her humility she invited Mary to share the music-lessons of Augusta and Beatrice at the great house. A music-master from Barchester came over three times a week, and remained for three hours, and if the doctor chose to send his girl over, she could pick up what was going on without doing any harm. So said the Lady Arabella. The doctor with many thanks and with no hesitation, accepted the offer, merely adding, that he had perhaps better settle separately with Signor Cantabili, the music-master. He was very much obliged to Lady Arabella for giving his little girl permission to join her lessons to those of the Miss Greshams.

It need hardly be said that the Lady Arabella was on fire at once. Settle with Signor Cantabili! No, indeed; she would do that; there must be no expense whatever incurred in such an arrangement on Miss Thorne's account! But here, as in most things, the doctor carried his point. It being the time of the lady's humility, she could not make as good a fight as she would otherwise have done; and thus she found, to her great disgust, that

Mary Thorne was learning music in her schoolroom on equal terms, as regarded payment, with her own daughters. The arrangement having been made could not be broken, especially as the young lady in nowise made herself disagreeable; and more especially as the Miss Greshams themselves were very fond of her.

And so Mary Thorne learnt music at Greshamsbury, and with her music she learnt other things also; how to behave herself among girls of her own age; how to speak and talk as other young ladies do; how to dress herself, and how to move and walk. All which, she, being quick to learn, learnt without trouble at the great house. Something also she learnt of French, seeing that the Greshamsbury French governess was always in the room.

And then, some few years later, there came a rector, and a rector's sister; and with the latter Mary studied German, and French also. From the doctor himself she learnt much; the choice, namely, of English books for her own reading, and habits of thought somewhat akin to his own, though modified by the feminine softness of her individual mind.

And so Mary Thorne grew up and was educated. Of her personal appearance it certainly is my business as an author to say something. She is my heroine, and, as such, must necessarily be very beautiful; but, in truth, her mind and inner qualities are more clearly distinct to my brain than her outward form and features. I know that she was far from being tall, and far from being showy; that her feet and hands were small and delicate; that her eyes were bright when looked at, but not brilliant so as to make their brilliancy palpably visible to all around her; her hair was dark brown, and worn very plainly brushed from her forehead; her lips were thin, and her mouth, perhaps, in general inexpressive, but when she was eager in conversation it would show itself to be animated with curves of wondrous energy; and, quiet as she was in manner, sober and demure as was her usual settled appearance, she could talk, when the fit came on her, with an energy which in truth surprised those who did not know her; aye, and sometimes those who did. Energy! nay, it was occasionally a concentration of passion, which left her for the moment perfectly unconscious of all other cares but solicitude for that subject which she might then be advocating.

All her friends, including the doctor, had at times been made unhappy by this vehemence of character; but yet it was to that very vehemence that she owed it that all her friends so loved her. It had once nearly banished her in early years from the Greshamsbury schoolroom; and yet it ended in making her claim to remain there so strong, that Lady Arabella could no longer oppose it, even when she had the wish to do so.

A new French governess had lately come to Greshamsbury, and was, or was to be, a great pet with Lady Arabella, having all the great gifts with which a governess can be endowed, and being also a protégée from the castle. The castle, in Greshamsbury parlance, always meant that of Courcy. Soon after this a valued little locket belonging to Augusta Gresham was missing. The French governess had objected to its being worn in the schoolroom, and it had been sent up to the bedroom by a young servant-girl, the daughter of a small farmer on the estate. The locket was missing, and after a while, a considerable noise in the matter having been made, was found, by the diligence of the governess, somewhere among the belongings of the English servant. Great was the anger of Lady Arabella, loud were the protestations of the girl, mute the woe of her father, piteous the tears of her mother, inexorable the judgment of the Greshamsbury world. But something occurred, it matters now not what, to separate Mary Thorne in opinion from that world at large. Out she then spoke, and to her face accused the governess of the robbery. For two days Mary was in disgrace almost as deep as that of the farmer's daughter. But she was neither quiet nor dumb in her disgrace. When Lady Arabella would not hear her, she went to Mr Gresham. She forced her uncle to move in the matter. She gained over to her side, one by one, the potentates of the parish, and ended by bringing Mam'selle Larron down on her knees with a confession of the facts. From that time Mary Thorne was dear to the tenantry of Greshamsbury; and specially dear at one small household, where a rough-spoken father of a family was often heard to declare, that for Miss Mary Thorne he'd face man or magistrate, duke or devil.

And so Mary Thorne grew up under the doctor's eye, and at the beginning of our tale she was one of the guests assembled at Greshamsbury on the coming of age of the heir, she herself having then arrived at the same period of her life.

CHAPTER IV

LESSONS FROM COURCY CASTLE

It was the first of July, young Frank Gresham's birthday, and the London season was not yet over; nevertheless, Lady de Courcy had managed to get down into the country to grace the coming of age of the heir, bringing with her all the Ladies Amelia, Rosina, Margaretta, and Alexandrina, together with such of the Honourable Johns and Georges as could be collected for the occasion.

The Lady Arabella had contrived this year to spend ten weeks in town, which, by a little stretching, she made to pass for the season; and had managed, moreover, at last to refurnish, not ingloriously, the Portman Square drawing-room. She had gone up to London under the pretext, imperatively urged, of Augusta's teeth—young ladies' teeth are not unfrequently of value in this way;—and having received authority for a new carpet, which was really much wanted, had made such dexterous use of that sanction as to run up an upholsterer's bill of six or seven hundred pounds. She had of course had her carriage and horses; the girls of course had gone out; it had been positively necessary to have a few friends in Portman Square; and, altogether, the ten weeks had not been unpleasant, and not inexpensive.

For a few confidential minutes before dinner, Lady de Courcy and her sister-in-law sat together in the latter's dressing-room, discussing the unreasonableness of the squire, who had expressed himself with more than ordinary bitterness as to the folly—he had probably used some stronger word—of these London proceedings.

"Heavens!" said the countess, with much eager animation; "what can the man expect? What does he wish you to do?"

"He would like to sell the house in London, and bury us all here for ever. Mind, I was there only for ten weeks."

"Barely time for the girls to get their teeth properly looked at! But Arabella, what does he say?" Lady de Courcy was very anxious to learn the exact truth of the matter, and ascertain, if she could, whether Mr Gresham was really as poor as he pretended to be.

"Why, he said yesterday that he would have no more going to town at all; that he was barely able to pay the claims made on him, and keep up the house here, and that he would not—"

"Would not what?" asked the countess.

"Why, he said that he would not utterly ruin poor Frank."

"Ruin Frank!"

"That's what he said."

"But, surely, Arabella, it is not so bad as that? What possible reason can there be for him to be in debt?"

"He is always talking of those elections."

"But, my dear, Boxall Hill paid all that off. Of course Frank will not have such an income as there was when you married into the family; we all know that. And whom will he have to thank but his father? But Boxall Hill paid all those debts, and why should there be any difficulty now?"

"It was those nasty dogs, Rosina," said the Lady Arabella, almost in tears.

"Well, I for one never approved of the hounds coming to Greshamsbury. When a man has once involved his property he should not incur any expenses that are not absolutely necessary. That is a golden rule which Mr Gresham ought to have remembered. Indeed, I put it to him nearly in those very words; but Mr Gresham never did, and never will receive with common civility anything that comes from me."

"I know, Rosina, he never did; and yet where would he have been but for the de Courcys?" So exclaimed, in her gratitude, the Lady Arabella; to speak the truth, however, but for the de Courcys, Mr Gresham might have been at this moment on the top of Boxall Hill, monarch of all he surveyed.

"As I was saying," continued the countess, "I never approved of the hounds coming to Greshamsbury; but yet, my dear, the hounds can't have eaten up everything. A man with ten thousand a year ought to be able to keep hounds; particularly as he had a subscription."

"He says the subscription was little or nothing."

"That's nonsense, my dear. Now, Arabella, what does he do with his money? That's the question. Does he gamble?"

"Well," said Lady Arabella, very slowly, "I don't think he does." If the squire did gamble he must have done it very slyly, for he rarely went away from Greshamsbury, and certainly very few men looking like gamblers were in the habit of coming thither as guests. "I don't think he does gamble." Lady Arabella put her emphasis on the word gamble, as though her husband, if he might perhaps be charitably acquitted of that vice, was certainly guilty of every other known in the civilised world.

"I know he used," said Lady de Courcy, looking very wise, and rather suspicious. She certainly had sufficient domestic reasons for disliking the propensity; "I know he used; and when a man begins, he is hardly ever cured."

"Well, if he does, I don't know it," said the Lady Arabella.

"The money, my dear, must go somewhere. What excuse does he give when you tell him you want this and that—all the common necessaries of life, that you have always been used to?"

"He gives no excuse; sometimes he says the family is so large."

"Nonsense! Girls cost nothing; there's only Frank, and he can't have cost anything yet. Can he be saving money to buy back Boxall Hill?"

"Oh no!" said the Lady Arabella, quickly. "He is not saving anything; he never did, and never will save, though he is so stingy to me. He *is* hard pushed for money, I know that."

"Then where has it gone?" said the Countess de Courcy, with a look of stern decision.

"Heaven only knows! Now, Augusta is to be married. I must of course have a few hundred pounds. You should have heard how he groaned when I asked him for it. Heaven only knows where the money goes!" And the injured wife wiped a piteous tear from her eye with her fine dress cambric handkerchief. "I have all the sufferings and privations of a poor man's wife, but I have none of the consolations. He has no confidence in me; he never tells me anything; he never talks to me about his affairs. If he talks to any one it is to that horrid doctor."

"What, Dr Thorne?" Now the Countess de Courcy hated Dr Thorne with a holy hatred.

"Yes; Dr Thorne. I believe that he knows everything; and advises everything, too. Whatever difficulties poor Gresham may have, I do believe Dr Thorne has brought them about. I do believe it, Rosina."

"Well, that is surprising. Mr Gresham, with all his faults, is a gentleman; and how he can talk about his affairs with a low apothecary like that, I, for one, cannot imagine. Lord de Courcy has not always been to me all that he should have been; far from it." And Lady de Courcy thought over in her mind injuries of a much graver description than any that her sister-in-law had ever suffered; "but I have never known anything like that at Courcy Castle. Surely Umbleby knows all about it, doesn't he?"

"Not half so much as the doctor," said Lady Arabella.

The countess shook her head slowly; the idea of Mr Gresham, a country gentleman of good estate like him, making a confidant of a country doctor was too great a shock for her nerves; and for a while she was constrained to sit silent before she could recover herself.

"One thing at any rate is certain, Arabella," said the countess, as soon as she found herself again sufficiently composed to offer counsel in a properly dictatorial manner. "One thing at any rate is certain; if Mr Gresham be involved so deeply as you say, Frank has but one duty before him. He must marry money. The heir of fourteen thousand a year may indulge himself in looking for blood, as Mr Gresham did, my dear"—it must be understood that there was very little compliment in this, as the Lady Arabella had always conceived herself to be a beauty—"or for beauty, as some men do," continued the countess, thinking of the choice that the present Earl de Courcy had made; "but Frank must marry money. I hope he will understand this early; do make him understand this before he makes a fool of himself; when a man thoroughly understands this, when he knows what his circumstances require, why, the matter becomes easy to him. I hope that Frank understands that he has no alternative. In his position he must marry money."

But, alas! alas! Frank Gresham had already made a fool of himself.

"Well, my boy, I wish you joy with all my heart," said the Honourable John, slapping his cousin on the back, as he walked round to the stable-yard with him before dinner, to inspect a setter puppy of peculiarly fine breed which had been sent to Frank as a birthday present. "I wish I were an elder son; but we can't all have that luck."

"Who wouldn't sooner be the younger son of an earl than the eldest son of a plain squire?" said Frank, wishing to say something civil in return for his cousin's civility.

"I wouldn't for one," said the Honourable John. "What chance have I? There's Porlock as strong as a horse; and then George comes next. And the governor's good for these twenty years." And the young man sighed as he reflected what small hope there was that all those who were nearest and dearest to him should die out of his way, and leave him to the sweet enjoyment of an earl's coronet and fortune. "Now, you're sure of your game some day; and as you've no brothers, I suppose the squire'll let you do pretty well what you like. Besides, he's not so strong as my governor, though he's younger."

Frank had never looked at his fortune in this light before, and was so slow and green that he was not much delighted at the prospect now that it was offered to him. He had always, however, been taught to look to his cousins, the de Courcys, as men with whom it would be very expedient that he should be intimate; he therefore showed no offence, but changed the conversation.

"Shall you hunt with the Barsetshire this season, John? I hope you will; I shall."

"Well, I don't know. It's very slow. It's all tillage here, or else woodland. I rather fancy I shall go to Leicestershire when the partridge-shooting is over. What sort of a lot do you mean to come out with, Frank?"

Frank became a little red as he answered, "Oh, I shall have two," he said; "that is, the mare I have had these two years, and the horse my father gave me this morning."

"What! only those two? and the mare is nothing more than a pony."

"She is fifteen hands," said Frank, offended.

"Well, Frank, I certainly would not stand that," said the Honourable John. "What, go out before the county with one untrained horse and a pony; and you the heir to Greshamsbury!"

"I'll have him so trained before November," said Frank, "that nothing in Barsetshire shall stop him. Peter says"—Peter was the Greshamsbury stud-groom—"that he tucks up his hind legs beautifully."

"But who the deuce would think of going to work with one horse; or two either, if you insist on calling the old pony a huntress? I'll put you up to a trick, my lad: if you stand that you'll stand anything; and if you don't mean to go in leading-strings all your life, now is the time to show it. There's young Baker—Harry Baker, you know—he came of age last year, and he has as pretty a string of nags as any one would wish to set eyes on; four hunters and a hack. Now, if old Baker has four thousand a year it's every shilling he has got."

This was true, and Frank Gresham, who in the morning had been made so happy by his father's present of a horse, began to feel that hardly enough had been done for him. It was true that Mr Baker had only four thousand a year; but it was also true that he had no other child than Harry Baker; that he had no great establishment to keep up; that he owed a shilling to no one; and, also, that he was a great fool in encouraging a mere boy to ape all the caprices of a man of wealth. Nevertheless, for a moment, Frank Gresham did feel that, considering his position, he was being treated rather unworthily.

"Take the matter in your own hands, Frank," said the Honourable John, seeing the impression that he had made. "Of course the governor knows very well that you won't put up with such a stable as that. Lord bless you! I have heard that when he married my aunt, and that was when he was about your age, he had the best stud in the whole county; and then he was in Parliament before he was three-and-twenty."

"His father, you know, died when he was very young," said Frank.

"Yes; I know he had a stroke of luck that doesn't fall to everyone; but—"

Young Frank's face grew dark now instead of red. When his cousin submitted to him the necessity of having more than two horses for his own use he could listen to him; but when the same monitor talked of the chance of a father's death as a stroke of luck, Frank was too much disgusted to be able to pretend to pass it over with indifference. What! was he thus to think of his father, whose face was always lighted up with pleasure when his boy came near to him, and so rarely bright at any other time? Frank had watched his father closely enough to be aware of this; he knew how his father delighted in him; he had had cause to guess that his father had many troubles, and that he strove hard to banish the memory of them when his son was with him. He loved his father truly, purely, and thoroughly, liked to be with him, and would be proud to be his confidant. Could he then listen quietly while his cousin spoke of the chance of his father's death as a stroke of luck?

"I shouldn't think it a stroke of luck, John. I should think it the greatest misfortune in the world."

It is so difficult for a young man to enumerate sententiously a principle of morality, or even an expression of ordinary good feeling, without giving himself something of a ridiculous air, without assuming something of a mock grandeur!

"Oh, of course, my dear fellow," said the Honourable John, laughing; "that's a matter of course. We all understand that without saying it. Porlock, of course, would feel exactly the same about the governor; but if the governor were to walk, I think Porlock would console himself with the thirty thousand a year."

"I don't know what Porlock would do; he's always quarrelling with my uncle, I know. I only spoke of myself; I never quarrelled with my father, and I hope I never shall."

"All right, my lad of wax, all right. I dare say you won't be tried; but if you are, you'll find before six months are over, that it's a very nice thing to master of Greshamsbury."

"I'm sure I shouldn't find anything of the kind."

"Very well, so be it. You wouldn't do as young Hatherly did, at Hatherly Court, in Gloucestershire, when his father kicked the bucket. You know Hatherly, don't you?"

"No; I never saw him."

"He's Sir Frederick now, and has, or had, one of the finest fortunes in England, for a commoner; the most of it is gone now. Well, when he heard of his governor's death, he was in Paris, but he went off to Hatherly as fast as special train and post-horses would carry him, and got there just in time for the funeral. As he came back to Hatherly Court from the church, they were putting up the hatchment over the door, and Master Fred saw that the undertakers had put at the bottom 'Resurgam.' You know what that means?"

"Oh, yes," said Frank.

"'I'll come back again,'" said the Honourable John, construing the Latin for the benefit of his cousin. "'No,' said Fred Hatherly, looking up at the hatchment; 'I'm blessed if you do, old gentleman. That would be too much of a joke; I'll take care of that.' So he got up at night, and he got some fellows with him, and they climbed up and painted out 'Resurgam,' and they painted into its place, 'Requiescat in pace;' which means, you know, 'you'd a great deal better stay where you are.' Now I call that good. Fred Hatherly did that as sure as—as sure as—as sure as anything."

Frank could not help laughing at the story, especially at his cousin's mode of translating the undertaker's mottoes; and then they sauntered back from the stables into the house to dress for dinner.

Dr Thorne had come to the house somewhat before dinner-time, at Mr Gresham's request, and was now sitting with the squire in his own book-room—so called—while Mary was talking to some of the girls upstairs.

"I must have ten or twelve thousand pounds; ten at the very least," said the squire, who was sitting in his usual arm-chair, close to his littered table, with his head supported on his hand, looking very unlike the father of an heir of a noble property, who had that day come of age.

It was the first of July, and of course there was no fire in the grate; but, nevertheless, the doctor was standing with his back to the fireplace, with his coat-tails over his arms, as though he were engaged, now in summer as he so often was in winter, in talking, and roasting his hinder person at the same time.

"Twelve thousand pounds! It's a very large sum of money."

"I said ten," said the squire.

"Ten thousand pounds is a very large sum of money. There is no doubt he'll let you have it. Scatcherd will let you have it; but I know he'll expect to have the title deeds."

"What! for ten thousand pounds?" said the squire. "There is not a registered debt against the property but his own and Armstrong's."

"But his own is very large already."

"Armstrong's is nothing; about four-and-twenty thousand pounds."

"Yes; but he comes first, Mr Gresham."

"Well, what of that? To hear you talk, one would think that there was nothing left of Greshamsbury. What's four-and-twenty thousand pounds? Does Scatcherd know what rent-roll is?"

"Oh, yes, he knows it well enough: I wish he did not."

"Well, then, why does he make such a bother about a few thousand pounds? The title-deeds, indeed!"

"What he means is, that he must have ample security to cover what he has already advanced before he goes on. I wish to goodness you had no further need to borrow. I did think that things were settled last year."

"Oh if there's any difficulty, Umbleby will get it for me."

"Yes; and what will you have to pay for it?"

"I'd sooner pay double than be talked to in this way," said the squire, angrily, and, as he spoke, he got up hurriedly from his chair, thrust his hands into his trousers-pockets, walked quickly to the window, and immediately walking back again, threw himself once more into his chair.

"There are some things a man cannot bear, doctor," said he, beating the devil's tattoo on the floor with one of his feet, "though God knows I ought to be patient now, for I am made to bear a good many things. You had better tell Scatcherd that I am obliged to him for his offer, but that I will not trouble him."

The doctor during this little outburst had stood quite silent with his back to the fire-place and his coat-tails hanging over his arms; but though his voice said nothing, his face said much. He was very unhappy; he was greatly grieved to find that the squire was so soon again in want of money, and greatly grieved also to find that this want had made him so bitter and unjust. Mr Gresham had attacked him; but as he was determined not to quarrel with Mr Gresham, he refrained from answering.

The squire also remained silent for a few minutes; but he was not endowed with the gift of silence, and was soon, as it were, compelled to speak again.

"Poor Frank!" said he. "I could yet be easy about everything if it were not for the injury I have done him. Poor Frank!"

The doctor advanced a few paces from off the rug, and taking his hand out of his pocket, he laid it gently on the squire's shoulder. "Frank will do very well yet," said the he. "It is not absolutely necessary that a man should have fourteen thousand pounds a year to be happy."

"My father left me the property entire, and I should leave it entire to my son;—but you don't understand this."

The doctor did understand the feeling fully. The fact, on the other hand, was that, long as he had known him, the squire did not understand the doctor.

"I would you could, Mr Gresham," said the doctor, "so that your mind might be happier; but that cannot be, and, therefore, I say again, that Frank will do very well yet, although he will not inherit fourteen thousand pounds a year; and I would have you say the same thing to yourself."

"Ah! you don't understand it," persisted the squire. "You don't know how a man feels when he—Ah, well! it's no use my troubling you with what cannot be mended. I wonder whether Umbleby is about the place anywhere?"

The doctor was again standing with his back against the chimney-piece, and with his hands in his pockets.

"You did not see Umbleby as you came in?" again asked the squire.

"No, I did not; and if you will take my advice you will not see him now; at any rate with reference to this money."

"I tell you I must get it from someone; you say Scatcherd won't let me have it."

"No, Mr Gresham; I did not say that."

"Well, you said what was as bad. Augusta is to be married in September, and the money must be had. I have agreed to give Moffat six thousand pounds, and he is to have the money down in hard cash."

"Six thousand pounds," said the doctor. "Well, I suppose that is not more than your daughter should have. But then, five times six are thirty; thirty thousand pounds will be a large sum to make up."

The father thought to himself that his younger girls were but children, and that the trouble of arranging their marriage portions might well be postponed a while. Sufficient for the day is the evil thereof.

"That Moffat is a griping, hungry fellow," said the squire. "I suppose Augusta likes him; and, as regards money, it is a good match."

"If Miss Gresham loves him, that is everything. I am not in love with him myself; but then, I am not a young lady."

"The de Courcys are very fond of him. Lady de Courcy says that he is a perfect gentleman, and thought very much of in London."

"Oh! if Lady de Courcy says that, of course, it's all right," said the doctor, with a quiet sarcasm, that was altogether thrown away on the squire.

The squire did not like any of the de Courcys; especially, he did not like Lady de Courcy; but still he was accessible to a certain amount of gratification in the near connexion which he had with the earl and countess; and when he wanted to support his family greatness, would sometimes weakly fall back upon the grandeur of Courcy Castle. It was only when talking to his wife that he invariably snubbed the pretensions of his noble relatives.

The two men after this remained silent for a while; and then the doctor, renewing the subject for which he had been summoned into the book-room, remarked, that as Scatcherd was now in the country—he did not say, was now at Boxall Hill, as he did not wish to wound the squire's ears—perhaps he had better go and see him, and ascertain in what way this affair of the money might be arranged. There was no doubt, he said, that Scatcherd would supply the sum required at a lower rate of interest than that at which it could be procured through Umbleby's means.

"Very well," said the squire. "I'll leave it in your hands, then. I think ten thousand pounds will do. And now I'll dress for dinner." And then the doctor left him.

Perhaps the reader will suppose after this that the doctor had some pecuniary interest of his own in arranging the squire's loans; or, at any rate, he will think that the squire must have so thought. Not in the least; neither had he any such interest, nor did the squire think that he had any. What Dr Thorne did in this matter the squire well knew was done for love. But the squire of Greshamsbury was a great man at Greshamsbury; and it behoved him to maintain the greatness of his squirehood when discussing his affairs with the village doctor. So much he had at any rate learnt from his contact with the de Courcys.

And the doctor—proud, arrogant, contradictory, headstrong as he was—why did he bear to be thus snubbed? Because he knew that the squire of Greshamsbury, when struggling with debt and poverty, required an indulgence for his weakness. Had Mr Gresham been in easy circumstances, the doctor would by no means have stood so placidly with his hands in his pockets, and have had Mr Umbleby thus thrown in his teeth. The doctor loved the squire, loved him as his own oldest friend; but he loved him ten times better as being in adversity than he could ever have done had things gone well at Greshamsbury in his time.

While this was going on downstairs, Mary was sitting upstairs with Beatrice Gresham in the schoolroom. The old schoolroom, so called, was now a sitting-room, devoted to the use of the grown-up young ladies of the family, whereas one of the old nurseries was now the modern schoolroom. Mary well knew her way to the sanctum, and, without asking any questions, walked up to it when her uncle went to the squire. On entering the room she found that Augusta and the Lady Alexandrina were also there, and she hesitated for a moment at the door.

"Come in, Mary," said Beatrice, "you know my cousin Alexandrina." Mary came in, and having shaken hands with her two friends, was bowing to the lady, when the lady condescended, put out her noble hand, and touched Miss Thorne's fingers.

Beatrice was Mary's friend, and many heart-burnings and much mental solicitude did that young lady give to her mother by indulging in such a friendship. But Beatrice, with some faults, was true at heart, and she persisted in loving Mary Thorne in spite of the hints which her mother so frequently gave as to the impropriety of such an affection.

Nor had Augusta any objection to the society of Miss Thorne. Augusta was a strong-minded girl, with much of the de Courcy arrogance, but quite as well inclined to show it in opposition to her mother as in any other form. To her alone in the house did Lady Arabella show much deference. She was now going to make a suitable match with a man of large fortune, who had been procured for her as an eligible *parti* by her aunt, the countess. She did not pretend, had never pretended, that she loved Mr Moffat, but she knew, she said, that in the present state of her father's affairs such a match was expedient. Mr Moffat was a young man of very large fortune, in Parliament, inclined to business, and in every way recommendable. He was not a man of birth, to be sure; that was to be lamented;—in confessing that Mr Moffat was not a man of birth, Augusta did not go so far as to admit that he was the son of a tailor; such, however, was the rigid truth in this matter—he was not a man of birth, that was to be lamented; but in the present state of affairs at Greshamsbury, she understood well that it was her duty to postpone her own feelings in some respect. Mr Moffat would bring fortune; she would bring blood and connexion. And as she so said, her bosom glowed with strong pride to think that she would be able to contribute so much more towards the proposed future partnership than her husband would do.

'Twas thus that Miss Gresham spoke of her match to her dear friends, her cousins the de Courcys for instance, to Miss Oriel, her sister Beatrice, and even to Mary Thorne. She had no enthusiasm, she admitted, but she thought she had good judgment. She thought she had shown good judgment in accepting Mr Moffat's offer, though she did not pretend to any romance of affection. And, having so said, she went to work with considerable mental satisfaction, choosing furniture, carriages, and clothes, not extravagantly as her mother would have done, not in deference to sterner dictates of the latest fashion as her aunt would have done, with none of the girlish glee in new purchases which Beatrice would have felt, but with sound judgment. She bought things that were rich, for her husband was to be rich, and she meant to avail herself of his wealth; she bought things that were fashionable, for she meant to live in the fashionable world; but she bought what was good, and strong, and lasting, and worth its money.

Augusta Gresham had perceived early in life that she could not obtain success either as an heiress, or as a beauty, nor could she shine as a wit; she therefore fell back on such qualities as she had, and determined to win the world as a strong-minded, useful woman. That which she had of her own was blood; having that, she would in all ways do what in her lay to enhance its value. Had she not possessed it, it would to her mind have been the vainest of pretences.

When Mary came in, the wedding preparations were being discussed. The number and names of the bridesmaids were being settled, the dresses were on the tapis, the invitations to be given were talked over. Sensible as Augusta was, she was not above such feminine cares; she was, indeed, rather anxious that the wedding should go off well. She was a little ashamed of her tailor's son, and therefore anxious that things should be as brilliant as possible.

The bridesmaid's names had just been written on a card as Mary entered the room. There were the Ladies Amelia, Rosina, Margaretta, and Alexandrina of course at the head of it; then came Beatrice and the twins; then Miss Oriel, who, though only a parson's sister, was a person of note, birth, and fortune. After this there had been here a great discussion whether or not there should be any more. If there were to be one more there must be two. Now Miss Moffat had expressed a direct wish, and Augusta, though she would much rather have done without her, hardly knew how to refuse. Alexandrina—we hope we may be allowed to drop the "lady" for the sake of brevity, for the present scene only—was dead against such an unreasonable request. "We none of us know her, you know; and it would not be comfortable." Beatrice strongly advocated the future sister-in-law's acceptance into the bevy; she had her own reasons; she was pained that Mary Thorne should not be among the number, and if Miss Moffat were accepted, perhaps Mary might be brought in as her colleague.

"If you have Miss Moffat," said Alexandrina, "you must have dear Pussy too; and I really think that Pussy is too young; it will be troublesome." Pussy was the youngest Miss Gresham, who was now only eight years old, and whose real name was Nina.

"Augusta," said Beatrice, speaking with some slight hesitation, some soupçon of doubt, before the high authority of her noble cousin, "if you do have Miss Moffat would you mind asking Mary Thorne to join her? I think Mary would like it, because, you see, Patience Oriel is to be one; and we have known Mary much longer than we have known Patience."

Then out and spake the Lady Alexandrina.

"Beatrice, dear, if you think of what you are asking, I am sure you will see that it would not do; would not do at all. Miss Thorne is a very nice girl, I am sure; and, indeed, what little I have seen of her I highly approve. But, after all, who is she? Mamma, I know, thinks that Aunt Arabella has been wrong to let her be here so much, but—"

Beatrice became rather red in the face, and, in spite of the dignity of her cousin, was preparing to defend her friend.

"Mind, I am not saying a word against Miss Thorne."

"If I am married before her, she shall be one of my bridesmaids," said Beatrice.

"That will probably depend on circumstances," said the Lady Alexandrina; I find that I cannot bring my courteous pen to drop the title. "But Augusta is very peculiarly situated. Mr Moffat is, you see, not of the very highest birth; and, therefore, she should take care that on her side every one about her is well born."

"Then you cannot have Miss Moffat," said Beatrice.

"No; I would not if I could help it," said the cousin.

"But the Thornes are as good a family as the Greshams," said Beatrice. She had not quite the courage to say, as good as the de Courcys.

"I dare say they are; and if this was Miss Thorne of Ullathorne, Augusta probably would not object to her. But can you tell me who Miss Mary Thorne is?"

"She is Dr Thorne's niece."

"You mean that she is called so; but do you know who her father was, or who her mother was? I, for one, must own I do not. Mamma, I believe, does, but—"

At this moment the door opened gently and Mary Thorne entered the room.

It may easily be conceived, that while Mary was making her salutations the three other young ladies were a little cast aback. The Lady Alexandrina, however, quickly recovered herself, and, by her inimitable presence of mind and facile grace of manner, soon put the matter on a proper footing.

"We were discussing Miss Gresham's marriage," said she; "I am sure I may mention to an acquaintance of so long standing as Miss Thorne, that the first of September has been now fixed for the wedding."

Miss Gresham! Acquaintance of so long standing! Why, Mary and Augusta Gresham had for years, we will hardly say now for how many, passed their mornings together in the same schoolroom; had quarrelled, and squabbled, and caressed and kissed, and been all but as sisters to each other. Acquaintance indeed! Beatrice felt that her ears were tingling, and even Augusta was a little ashamed. Mary, however, knew that the cold words had come from a de Courcy, and not from a Gresham, and did not, therefore, resent them.

"So it's settled, Augusta, is it?" said she; "the first of September. I wish you joy with all my heart," and, coming round, she put her arm over Augusta's shoulder and kissed her. The Lady Alexandrina could not but think that the doctor's niece uttered her congratulations very much as though she were speaking to an equal; very much as though she had a father and mother of her own.

"You will have delicious weather," continued Mary. "September, and the beginning of October, is the nicest time of the year. If I were going honeymooning it is just the time of year I would choose."

"I wish you were, Mary," said Beatrice.

"So do not I, dear, till I have found some decent sort of a body to honeymoon along with me. I won't stir out of Greshamsbury till I have sent you off before me, at any rate. And where will you go, Augusta?"

"We have not settled that," said Augusta. "Mr Moffat talks of Paris."

"Who ever heard of going to Paris in September?" said the Lady Alexandrina.

"Or who ever heard of the gentleman having anything to say on the matter?" said the doctor's niece. "Of course Mr Moffat will go wherever you are pleased to take him."

The Lady Alexandrina was not pleased to find how completely the doctor's niece took upon herself to talk, and sit, and act at Greshamsbury as though she was on a par with the young ladies of the family. That Beatrice should have allowed this would not have surprised her; but it was to be expected that Augusta would have shown better judgment.

"These things require some tact in their management; some delicacy when high interests are at stake," said she; "I agree with Miss Thorne in thinking that, in ordinary circumstances, with ordinary people, perhaps, the lady should have her way. Rank, however, has its drawbacks, Miss Thorne, as well as its privileges."

"I should not object to the drawbacks," said the doctor's niece, "presuming them to be of some use; but I fear I might fail in getting on so well with the privileges."

The Lady Alexandrina looked at her as though not fully aware whether she intended to be pert. In truth, the Lady Alexandrina was rather in the dark on the subject. It was almost impossible, it was incredible, that a fatherless, motherless, doctor's niece should be pert to an earl's daughter at Greshamsbury, seeing that that earl's daughter was the cousin of the Miss Greshams. And yet the Lady Alexandrina hardly knew what other construction to put on the words she had just heard.

It was at any rate clear to her that it was not becoming that she should just then stay any longer in that room. Whether she intended to be pert or not, Miss Mary Thorne was, to say the least, very free. The de Courcy ladies knew what was due to them—no ladies better; and, therefore, the Lady Alexandrina made up her mind at once to go to her own bedroom.

"Augusta," she said, rising slowly from her chair with much stately composure, "it is nearly time to dress; will you come with me? We have a great deal to settle, you know."

So she swam out of the room, and Augusta, telling Mary that she would see her again at dinner, swam—no, tried to swim—after her. Miss Gresham had had great advantages;

but she had not been absolutely brought up at Courcy Castle, and could not as yet quite assume the Courcy style of swimming.

"There," said Mary, as the door closed behind the rustling muslins of the ladies. "There, I have made an enemy for ever, perhaps two; that's satisfactory."

"And why have you done it, Mary? When I am fighting your battles behind your back, why do you come and upset it all by making the whole family of the de Courcys dislike you? In such a matter as that, they'll all go together."

"I am sure they will," said Mary; "whether they would be equally unanimous in a case of love and charity, that, indeed, is another question."

"But why should you try to make my cousin angry; you that ought to have so much sense? Don't you remember what you were saying yourself the other day, of the absurdity of combatting pretences which the world sanctions?"

"I do, Trichy, I do; don't scold me now. It is so much easier to preach than to practise. I do so wish I was a clergyman."

"But you have done so much harm, Mary."

"Have I?" said Mary, kneeling down on the ground at her friend's feet. "If I humble myself very low; if I kneel through the whole evening in a corner; if I put my neck down and let all your cousins trample on it, and then your aunt, would not that make atonement? I would not object to wearing sackcloth, either; and I'd eat a little ashes—or, at any rate, I'd try."

"I know you're clever, Mary; but still I think you're a fool. I do, indeed."

"I am a fool, Trichy, I do confess it; and am not a bit clever; but don't scold me; you see how humble I am; not only humble but umble, which I look upon to be the comparative, or, indeed, superlative degree. Or perhaps there are four degrees; humble, umble, stumble, tumble; and then, when one is absolutely in the dirt at their feet, perhaps these big people won't wish one to stoop any further."

"Oh, Mary!"

"And, oh, Trichy! you don't mean to say I mayn't speak out before you. There, perhaps you'd like to put your foot on my neck." And then she put her head down to the footstool and kissed Beatrice's feet.

"I'd like, if I dared, to put my hand on your cheek and give you a good slap for being such a goose."

"Do; do, Trichy: you shall tread on me, or slap me, or kiss me; whichever you like."

"I can't tell you how vexed I am," said Beatrice; "I wanted to arrange something."

"Arrange something! What? arrange what? I love arranging. I fancy myself qualified to be an arranger-general in female matters. I mean pots and pans, and such like. Of course I don't allude to extraordinary people and extraordinary circumstances that require tact, and delicacy, and drawbacks, and that sort of thing."

"Very well, Mary."

"But it's not very well; it's very bad if you look like that. Well, my pet, there I won't. I won't allude to the noble blood of your noble relatives either in joke or in earnest. What is it you want to arrange, Trichy?"

"I want you to be one of Augusta's bridesmaids."

"Good heavens, Beatrice! Are you mad? What! Put me, even for a morning, into the same category of finery as the noble blood from Courcy Castle!"

"Patience is to be one."

"But that is no reason why Impatience should be another, and I should be very impatient under such honours. No, Trichy; joking apart, do not think of it. Even if Augusta wished it I should refuse. I should be obliged to refuse. I, too, suffer from pride; a pride quite as unpardonable as that of others: I could not stand with your four lady-cousins be-hind your sister at the altar. In such a galaxy they would be the stars and I—"

"Why, Mary, all the world knows that you are prettier than any of them!"

"I am all the world's very humble servant. But, Trichy, I should not object if I were as ugly as the veiled prophet and they all as beautiful as Zuleika. The glory of that galaxy will be held to depend not on its beauty, but on its birth. You know how they would look at me; how they would scorn me; and there, in church, at the altar, with all that is solemn round us, I could not return their scorn as I might do elsewhere. In a room I'm not a bit afraid of them all." And Mary was again allowing herself to be absorbed by that feeling of indomitable pride, of antagonism to the pride of others, which she herself in her cooler moments was the first to blame.

"You often say, Mary, that that sort of arrogance should be despised and passed over without notice."

"So it should, Trichy. I tell you that as a clergyman tells you to hate riches. But though the clergyman tells you so, he is not the less anxious to be rich himself."

"I particularly wish you to be one of Augusta's bridesmaids."

"And I particularly wish to decline the honour; which honour has not been, and will not be, offered to me. No, Trichy. I will not be Augusta's bridesmaid, but—but—but—"

"But what, dearest?"

"But, Trichy, when some one else is married, when the new wing has been built to a house that you know of—"

"Now, Mary, hold your tongue, or you know you'll make me angry."

"I do so like to see you angry. And when that time comes, when that wedding does take place, then I will be a bridesmaid, Trichy. Yes! even though I am not invited. Yes! though all the de Courcys in Barsetshire should tread upon me and obliterate me. Though I should be as dust among the stars, though I should creep up in calico among their satins and lace, I will nevertheless be there; close, close to the bride; to hold something for her, to touch her dress, to feel that I am near to her, to—to—to—" and she threw her arms round her companion, and kissed her over and over again. "No, Trichy; I won't be Augus-ta's bridesmaid; I'll bide my time for bridesmaiding."

What protestations Beatrice made against the probability of such an event as foreshad-owed in her friend's promise we will not repeat. The afternoon was advancing, and the ladies also had to dress for dinner, to do honour to the young heir.

CHAPTER V

FRANK GRESHAM'S FIRST SPEECH

We have said, that over and above those assembled in the house, there came to the Greshamsbury dinner on Frank's birthday the Jacksons of the Grange, consisting of Mr and Mrs Jackson; the Batesons from Annesgrove, viz., Mr and Mrs Bateson, and Miss Bateson, their daughter—an unmarried lady of about fifty; the Bakers of Mill Hill, father and son; and Mr Caleb Oriel, the rector, with his beautiful sister, Patience. Dr Thorne, and his niece Mary, we count among those already assembled at Greshamsbury.

There was nothing very magnificent in the number of the guests thus brought together to do honour to young Frank; but he, perhaps, was called on to take a more prominent part in the proceedings, to be made more of a hero than would have been the case had half the county been there. In that case the importance of the guests would have been so great that Frank would have got off with a half-muttered speech or two; but now he had to make a separate oration to every one, and very weary work he found it.

The Batesons, Bakers, and Jacksons were very civil; no doubt the more so from an unconscious feeling on their part, that as the squire was known to be a little out at elbows as regards money, any deficiency on their part might be considered as owing to the present state of affairs at Greshamsbury. Fourteen thousand a year will receive honour; in that case there is no doubt, and the man absolutely possessing it is not apt to be suspicious as to the treatment he may receive; but the ghost of fourteen thousand a year is not always so self-assured. Mr Baker, with his moderate income, was a very much richer man than the squire; and, therefore, he was peculiarly forward in congratulating Frank on the brilliancy of his prospects.

Poor Frank had hardly anticipated what there would be to do, and before dinner was announced he was very tired of it. He had no warmer feeling for any of the grand cousins than a very ordinary cousinly love; and he had resolved, forgetful of birth and blood, and all those gigantic considerations which, now that manhood had come upon him, he was bound always to bear in mind,—he had resolved to sneak out to dinner comfortably with Mary Thorne if possible; and if not with Mary, then with his other love, Patience Oriel.

Great, therefore, was his consternation at finding that, after being kept continually in the foreground for half an hour before dinner, he had to walk out to the dining-room with his aunt the countess, and take his father's place for the day at the bottom of the table.

"It will now depend altogether upon yourself, Frank, whether you maintain or lose that high position in the county which has been held by the Greshams for so many years," said the countess, as she walked through the spacious hall, resolving to lose no time in teaching to her nephew that great lesson which it was so imperative that he should learn.

Frank took this as an ordinary lecture, meant to inculcate general good conduct, such as old bores of aunts are apt to inflict on youthful victims in the shape of nephews and nieces.

"Yes," said Frank; "I suppose so; and I mean to go along all square, aunt, and no mistake. When I get back to Cambridge, I'll read like bricks."

His aunt did not care two straws about his reading. It was not by reading that the Greshams of Greshamsbury had held their heads up in the county, but by having high blood and plenty of money. The blood had come naturally to this young man; but it behoved him to look for the money in a great measure himself. She, Lady de Courcy, could doubtless help him; she might probably be able to fit him with a wife who would bring her money onto his birth. His reading was a matter in which she could in no way assist him; whether his taste might lead him to prefer books or pictures, or dogs and horses, or turnips in drills, or old Italian plates and dishes, was a matter which did not much signify; with which it was not at all necessary that his noble aunt should trouble herself.

"Oh! you are going to Cambridge again, are you? Well, if your father wishes it;—though very little is ever gained now by a university connexion."

"I am to take my degree in October, aunt; and I am determined, at any rate, that I won't be plucked."

"Plucked!"

"No; I won't be plucked. Baker was plucked last year, and all because he got into the wrong set at John's. He's an excellent fellow if you knew him. He got among a set of men who did nothing but smoke and drink beer. Malthusians, we call them."

"Malthusians!"

"'Malt,' you know, aunt, and 'use;' meaning that they drink beer. So poor Harry Baker got plucked. I don't know that a fellow's any the worse; however, I won't get plucked."

By this time the party had taken their place round the long board, Mr Gresham sitting at the top, in the place usually occupied by Lady Arabella. She, on the present occasion, sat next to her son on the one side, as the countess did on the other. If, therefore, Frank now went astray, it would not be from want of proper leading.

"Aunt, will you have some beef?" said he, as soon as the soup and fish had been disposed of, anxious to perform the rites of hospitality now for the first time committed to his charge.

"Do not be in a hurry, Frank," said his mother; "the servants will—"

"Oh! ah! I forgot; there are cutlets and those sort of things. My hand is not in yet for this work, aunt. Well, as I was saying about Cambridge—"

"Is Frank to go back to Cambridge, Arabella?" said the countess to her sister-in-law, speaking across her nephew.

"So his father seems to say."

"Is it not a waste of time?" asked the countess.

"You know I never interfere," said the Lady Arabella; "I never liked the idea of Cambridge myself at all. All the de Courcys were Christ Church men; but the Greshams, it seems, were always at Cambridge."

"Would it not be better to send him abroad at once?"

"Much better, I would think," said the Lady Arabella; "but you know, I never interfere: perhaps you would speak to Mr Gresham."

The countess smiled grimly, and shook her head with a decidedly negative shake. Had she said out loud to the young man, "Your father is such an obstinate, pig-headed, ignorant fool, that it is no use speaking to him; it would be wasting fragrance on the desert air," she could not have spoken more plainly. The effect on Frank was this: that he said to himself, speaking quite as plainly as Lady de Courcy had spoken by her shake of the face, "My mother and aunt are always down on the governor, always; but the more they are down on him the more I'll stick to him. I certainly will take my degree: I will read like bricks; and I'll begin to-morrow."

"Now will you take some beef, aunt?" This was said out loud.

The Countess de Courcy was very anxious to go on with her lesson without loss of time; but she could not, while surrounded by guests and servants, enunciate the great secret: "You must marry money, Frank; that is your one great duty; that is the matter to be borne steadfastly in your mind." She could not now, with sufficient weight and impress of emphasis, pour this wisdom into his ears; the more especially as he was standing up to his work of carving, and was deep to his elbows in horse-radish, fat, and gravy. So the countess sat silent while the banquet proceeded.

"Beef, Harry?" shouted the young heir to his friend Baker. "Oh! but I see it isn't your turn yet. I beg your pardon, Miss Bateson," and he sent to that lady a pound and a half of excellent meat, cut out with great energy in one slice, about half an inch thick.

And so the banquet went on.

Before dinner Frank had found himself obliged to make numerous small speeches in answer to the numerous individual congratulations of his friends; but these were as nothing to the one great accumulated onus of an oration which he had long known that he should have to sustain after the cloth was taken away. Someone of course would propose his health, and then there would be a clatter of voices, ladies and gentlemen, men and girls; and when that was done he would find himself standing on his legs, with the room about him, going round and round and round.

Having had a previous hint of this, he had sought advice from his cousin, the Honourable George, whom he regarded as a dab at speaking; at least, so he had heard the Honourable George say of himself.

"What the deuce is a fellow to say, George, when he stands up after the clatter is done?"

"Oh, it's the easiest thing in life," said the cousin. "Only remember this: you mustn't get astray; that is what they call presence of mind, you know. I'll tell you what I do, and I'm often called up, you know; at our agriculturals I always propose the farmers' daughters: well, what I do is this—I keep my eye steadfastly fixed on one of the bottles, and never move it."

"On one of the bottles!" said Frank; "wouldn't it be better if I made a mark of some old covey's head? I don't like looking at the table."

"The old covey'd move, and then you'd be done; besides there isn't the least use in the world in looking up. I've heard people say, who go to those sort of dinners every day of their lives, that whenever anything witty is said; the fellow who says it is sure to be looking at the mahogany."

"Oh, you know I shan't say anything witty; I'll be quite the other way."

"But there's no reason you shouldn't learn the manner. That's the way I succeeded. Fix your eye on one of the bottles; put your thumbs in your waist-coat pockets; stick out your elbows, bend your knees a little, and then go ahead."

"Oh, ah! go ahead; that's all very well; but you can't go ahead if you haven't got any steam."

"A very little does it. There can be nothing so easy as your speech. When one has to say something new every year about the farmers' daughters, why one has to use one's brains a bit. Let's see: how will you begin? Of course, you'll say that you are not accustomed to this sort of thing; that the honour conferred upon you is too much for your feelings; that the bright array of beauty and talent around you quite overpowers your tongue, and all that sort of thing. Then declare you're a Gresham to the backbone."

"Oh, they know that."

"Well, tell them again. Then of course you must say something about us; or you'll have the countess as black as old Nick."

"Abut my aunt, George? What on earth can I say about her when she's there herself before me?"

"Before you! of course; that's just the reason. Oh, say any lie you can think of; you must say something about us. You know we've come down from London on purpose."

Frank, in spite of the benefit he was receiving from his cousin's erudition, could not help wishing in his heart that they had all remained in London; but this he kept to himself. He thanked his cousin for his hints, and though he did not feel that the trouble of his mind was completely cured, he began to hope that he might go through the ordeal without disgracing himself.

Nevertheless, he felt rather sick at heart when Mr Baker got up to propose the toast as soon as the servants were gone. The servants, that is, were gone officially; but they were there in a body, men and women, nurses, cooks, and ladies' maids, coachmen, grooms, and footmen, standing in two doorways to hear what Master Frank would say. The old housekeeper headed the maids at one door, standing boldly inside the room; and the butler controlled the men at the other, marshalling them back with a drawn corkscrew.

Mr Baker did not say much; but what he did say, he said well. They had all seen Frank Gresham grow up from a child; and were now required to welcome as a man amongst them one who was well qualified to carry on the honour of that loved and respected family. His young friend, Frank, was every inch a Gresham. Mr Baker omitted to make mention of the infusion of de Courcy blood, and the countess, therefore, drew herself up on her chair and looked as though she were extremely bored. He then alluded tenderly to his own long friendship with the present squire, Francis Newbold Gresham the elder; and sat down, begging them to drink health, prosperity, long life, and an excellent wife to their dear young friend, Francis Newbold Gresham the younger.

There was a great jingling of glasses, of course; made the merrier and the louder by the fact that the ladies were still there as well as the gentlemen. Ladies don't drink toasts frequently; and, therefore, the occasion coming rarely was the more enjoyed. "God bless you, Frank!" "Your good health, Frank!" "And especially a good wife, Frank!" "Two or three of them, Frank!" "Good health and prosperity to you, Mr Gresham!" "More power to you, Frank, my boy!" "May God bless you and preserve you, my dear boy!" and then a merry, sweet, eager voice from the far end of the table, "Frank! Frank! Do look at me, pray do Frank; I am drinking your health in real wine; ain't I, papa?" Such were the addresses which greeted Mr Francis Newbold Gresham the younger as he essayed to rise up on his feet for the first time since he had come to man's estate.

When the clatter was at an end, and he was fairly on his legs, he cast a glance before him on the table, to look for a decanter. He had not much liked his cousin's theory of sticking to the bottle; nevertheless, in the difficulty of the moment, it was well to have any system to go by. But, as misfortune would have it, though the table was covered with bottles, his eye could not catch one. Indeed, his eye first could catch nothing, for the things swam before him, and the guests all seemed to dance in their chairs.

Up he got, however, and commenced his speech. As he could not follow his preceptor's advice as touching the bottle, he adopted his own crude plan of "making a mark on some old covey's head," and therefore looked dead at the doctor.

"Upon my word, I am very much obliged to you, gentlemen and ladies, ladies and gentlemen, I should say, for drinking my health, and doing me so much honour, and all that sort of thing. Upon my word I am. Especially to Mr Baker. I don't mean you, Harry, you're not Mr Baker."

"As much as you're Mr Gresham, Master Frank."

"But I am not Mr Gresham; and I don't mean to be for many a long year if I can help it; not at any rate till we have had another coming of age here."

"Bravo, Frank; and whose will that be?"

"That will be my son, and a very fine lad he will be; and I hope he'll make a better speech than his father. Mr Baker said I was every inch a Gresham. Well, I hope I am." Here the countess began to look cold and angry. "I hope the day will never come when my father won't own me for one."

"There's no fear, no fear," said the doctor, who was almost put out of countenance by the orator's intense gaze. The countess looked colder and more angry, and muttered something to herself about a bear-garden.

"Gardez Gresham; eh? Harry! mind that when you're sticking in a gap and I'm coming after you. Well, I am sure I am very obliged to you for the honour you have all done me, especially the ladies, who don't do this sort of thing on ordinary occasions. I wish they did; don't you, doctor? And talking of the ladies, my aunt and cousins have come all the way from London to hear me make this speech, which certainly is not worth the trouble; but, all the same I am very much obliged to them." And he looked round and made a little bow at the countess. "And so I am to Mr and Mrs Jackson, and Mr and Mrs and Miss Bateson, and Mr Baker—I'm not at all obliged to you, Harry—and to Mr Oriel and Miss Oriel, and to Mr Umbleby, and to Dr Thorne, and to Mary—I beg her pardon, I mean Miss Thorne." And then he sat down, amid the loud plaudits of the company, and a string of blessings which came from the servants behind him.

After this the ladies rose and departed. As she went, Lady Arabella, kissed her son's forehead, and then his sisters kissed him, and one or two of his lady-cousins; and then Miss Bateson shook him by the hand. "Oh, Miss Bateson," said he, "I thought the kissing was to go all round." So Miss Bateson laughed and went her way; and Patience Oriel nodded at him, but Mary Thorne, as she quietly left the room, almost hidden among the extensive draperies of the grander ladies, hardly allowed her eyes to meet his.

He got up to hold the door for them as they passed; and as they went, he managed to take Patience by the hand; he took her hand and pressed it for a moment, but dropped it quickly, in order that he might go through the same ceremony with Mary, but Mary was too quick for him.

"Frank," said Mr Gresham, as soon as the door was closed, "bring your glass here, my boy;" and the father made room for his son close beside himself. "The ceremony is now over, so you may have your place of dignity." Frank sat himself down where he was told, and Mr Gresham put his hand on his son's shoulder and half caressed him, while the tears stood in his eyes. "I think the doctor is right, Baker, I think he'll never make us ashamed of him."

"I am sure he never will," said Mr Baker.

"I don't think he ever will," said Dr Thorne.

The tones of the men's voices were very different. Mr Baker did not care a straw about it; why should he? He had an heir of his own as well as the squire; one also who was the apple of *his* eye. But the doctor,—he did care; he had a niece, to be sure, whom he loved, perhaps as well as these men loved their sons; but there was room in his heart also for young Frank Gresham.

After this small exposé of feeling they sat silent for a moment or two. But silence was not dear to the heart of the Honourable John, and so he took up the running.

"That's a niceish nag you gave Frank this morning," he said to his uncle. "I was looking at him before dinner. He is a Monsoon, isn't he?"

"Well I can't say I know how he was bred," said the squire. "He shows a good deal of breeding."

"He's a Monsoon, I'm sure," said the Honourable John. "They've all those ears, and that peculiar dip in the back. I suppose you gave a goodish figure for him?"

"Not so very much," said the squire.

"He's a trained hunter, I suppose?"

"If not, he soon will be," said the squire.

"Let Frank alone for that," said Harry Baker.

"He jumps beautifully, sir," said Frank. "I haven't tried him myself, but Peter made him go over the bar two or three times this morning."

The Honourable John was determined to give his cousin a helping hand, as he considered it. He thought that Frank was very ill-used in being put off with so incomplete a stud, and thinking also that the son had not spirit enough to attack his father himself on the subject, the Honourable John determined to do it for him.

"He's the making of a very nice horse, I don't doubt. I wish you had a string like him, Frank."

Frank felt the blood rush to his face. He would not for worlds have his father think that he was discontented, or otherwise than pleased with the present he had received that morning. He was heartily ashamed of himself in that he had listened with a certain degree of complacency to his cousin's tempting; but he had no idea that the subject would be repeated—and then repeated, too, before his father, in a manner to vex him on such a day as this, before such people as were assembled there. He was very angry with his cousin, and for a moment forgot all his hereditary respect for a de Courcy.

"I tell you what, John," said he, "do you choose your day, some day early in the season, and come out on the best thing you have, and I'll bring, not the black horse, but my old mare; and then do you try and keep near me. If I don't leave you at the back of Godspeed before long, I'll give you the mare and the horse too."

The Honourable John was not known in Barsetshire as one of the most forward of its riders. He was a man much addicted to hunting, as far as the get-up of the thing was concerned; he was great in boots and breeches; wondrously conversant with bits and bridles; he had quite a collection of saddles; and patronised every newest invention for carrying spare shoes, sandwiches, and flasks of sherry. He was prominent at the cover side;—some people, including the master of hounds, thought him perhaps a little too loudly prominent; he affected a familiarity with the dogs, and was on speaking acquaintance with every man's horse. But when the work was cut out, when the pace began to be sharp, when it behoved a man either to ride or visibly to decline to ride, then—so at least said they who had not the de Courcy interest quite closely at heart—then, in those heart-stirring moments, the Honourable John was too often found deficient.

There was, therefore, a considerable laugh at his expense when Frank, instigated to his innocent boast by a desire to save his father, challenged his cousin to a trial of prowess. The Honourable John was not, perhaps, as much accustomed to the ready use of his tongue as was his honourable brother, seeing that it was not his annual business to depict the glories of the farmers' daughters; at any rate, on this occasion he seemed to be at some loss for words; he shut up, as the slang phrase goes, and made no further allusion to the necessity of supplying young Gresham with a proper string of hunters.

But the old squire had understood it all; had understood the meaning of his nephew's attack; had thoroughly understood also the meaning of his son's defence, and the feeling which actuated it. He also had thought of the stableful of horses which had belonged to himself when he came of age; and of the much more humble position which his son would have to fill than that which *his* father had prepared for him. He thought of this, and was sad enough, though he had sufficient spirit to hide from his friends around him the fact, that the Honourable John's arrow had not been discharged in vain.

"He shall have Champion," said the father to himself. "It is time for me to give it up."

Now Champion was one of the two fine old hunters which the squire kept for his own use. And it might have been said of him now, at the period of which we are speaking, that the only really happy moments of his life were those which he spent in the field. So much as to its being time for him to give up.

CHAPTER VI

FRANK GRESHAM'S EARLY LOVES

It was, we have said, the first of July, and such being the time of the year, the ladies, after sitting in the drawing-room for half an hour or so, began to think that they might as well go through the drawing-room windows on to the lawn. First one slipped out a little way, and then another; and then they got on to the lawn; and then they talked of their hats; till, by degrees, the younger ones of the party, and at last of the elder also, found themselves dressed for walking.

The windows, both of the drawing-room and the dining-room, looked out on to the lawn; and it was only natural that the girls should walk from the former to the latter. It was only natural that they, being there, should tempt their swains to come to them by the sight of their broad-brimmed hats and evening dresses; and natural, also, that the temptation should not be resisted. The squire, therefore, and the elder male guests soon found themselves alone round their wine.

"Upon my word, we were enchanted by your eloquence, Mr Gresham, were we not?" said Miss Oriel, turning to one of the de Courcy girls who was with her.

Miss Oriel was a very pretty girl; a little older than Frank Gresham,—perhaps a year or so. She had dark hair, large round dark eyes, a nose a little too broad, a pretty mouth, a beautiful chin, and, as we have said before, a large fortune;—that is, moderately large— let us say twenty thousand pounds, there or thereabouts. She and her brother had been living at Greshamsbury for the last two years, the living having been purchased for him— such were Mr Gresham's necessities—during the lifetime of the last old incumbent. Miss Oriel was in every respect a nice neighbour; she was good-humoured, lady-like, lively, neither too clever nor too stupid, belonging to a good family, sufficiently fond of this world's good things, as became a pretty young lady so endowed, and sufficiently fond, also, of the other world's good things, as became the mistress of a clergyman's house.

"Indeed, yes," said the Lady Margaretta. "Frank is very eloquent. When he described our rapid journey from London, he nearly moved me to tears. But well as he talks, I think he carves better."

"I wish you'd had to do it, Margaretta; both the carving and talking."

"Thank you, Frank; you're very civil."

"But there's one comfort, Miss Oriel; it's over now, and done. A fellow can't be made to come of age twice."

"But you'll take your degree, Mr Gresham; and then, of course, there'll be another speech; and then you'll get married, and there will be two or three more."

"I'll speak at your wedding, Miss Oriel, long before I do at my own."

"I shall not have the slightest objection. It will be so kind of you to patronise my husband."

"But, by Jove, will he patronise me? I know you'll marry some awful bigwig, or some terribly clever fellow; won't she, Margaretta?"

"Miss Oriel was saying so much in praise of you before you came out," said Margaretta, "that I began to think that her mind was intent on remaining at Greshamsbury all her life."

Frank blushed, and Patience laughed. There was but a year's difference in their age; Frank, however, was still a boy, though Patience was fully a woman.

"I am ambitious, Lady Margaretta," said she. "I own it; but I am moderate in my ambition. I do love Greshamsbury, and if Mr Gresham had a younger brother, perhaps, you know—"

"Another just like myself, I suppose," said Frank.

"Oh, yes. I could not possibly wish for any change."

"Just as eloquent as you are, Frank," said the Lady Margaretta.

"And as good a carver," said Patience.

"Miss Bateson has lost her heart to him for ever, because of his carving," said the Lady Margaretta.

"But perfection never repeats itself," said Patience.

"Well, you see, I have not got any brothers," said Frank; "so all I can do is to sacrifice myself."

"Upon my word, Mr Gresham, I am under more than ordinary obligations to you; I am indeed," and Miss Oriel stood still in the path, and made a very graceful curtsy. "Dear me! only think, Lady Margaretta, that I should be honoured with an offer from the heir the very moment he is legally entitled to make one."

"And done with so much true gallantry, too," said the other; "expressing himself quite willing to postpone any views of his own or your advantage."

"Yes," said Patience; "that's what I value so much: had he loved me now, there would have been no merit on his part; but a sacrifice, you know—"

"Yes, ladies are so fond of such sacrifices, Frank, upon my word, I had no idea you were so very excellent at making speeches."

"Well," said Frank, "I shouldn't have said sacrifice, that was a slip; what I meant was—"

"Oh, dear me," said Patience, "wait a minute; now we are going to have a regular declaration. Lady Margaretta, you haven't got a scent-bottle, have you? And if I should faint, where's the garden-chair?"

"Oh, but I'm not going to make a declaration at all," said Frank.

"Are you not? Oh! Now, Lady Margaretta, I appeal to you; did you not understand him to say something very particular?"

"Certainly, I thought nothing could be plainer," said the Lady Margaretta.

"And so, Mr Gresham, I am to be told, that after all it means nothing," said Patience, putting her handkerchief up to her eyes.

"It means that you are an excellent hand at quizzing a fellow like me."

"Quizzing! No; but you are an excellent hand at deceiving a poor girl like me. Well, remember I have got a witness; here is Lady Margaretta, who heard it all. What a pity it is that my brother is a clergyman. You calculated on that, I know; or you would never had served me so."

She said so just as her brother joined them, or rather just as he had joined Lady Margaretta de Courcy; for her ladyship and Mr Oriel walked on in advance by themselves.

Lady Margaretta had found it rather dull work, making a third in Miss Oriel's flirtation with her cousin; the more so as she was quite accustomed to take a principal part herself in all such transactions. She therefore not unwillingly walked on with Mr Oriel. Mr Oriel, it must be conceived, was not a common, everyday parson, but had points about him which made him quite fit to associate with an earl's daughter. And as it was known that he was not a marrying man, having very exalted ideas on that point connected with his profession, the Lady Margaretta, of course, had the less objection to trust herself alone with him.

But directly she was gone, Miss Oriel's tone of banter ceased. It was very well making a fool of a lad of twenty-one when others were by; but there might be danger in it when they were alone together.

"I don't know any position on earth more enviable than yours, Mr Gresham," said she, quite soberly and earnestly; "how happy you ought to be."

"What, in being laughed at by you, Miss Oriel, for pretending to be a man, when you choose to make out that I am only a boy? I can bear to be laughed at pretty well generally, but I can't say that your laughing at me makes me feel so happy as you say I ought to be."

Frank was evidently of an opinion totally different from that of Miss Oriel. Miss Oriel, when she found herself *tête-à-tête* with him, thought it was time to give over flirting; Frank, however, imagined that it was just the moment for him to begin. So he spoke and looked very languishing, and put on him quite the airs of an Orlando.

"Oh, Mr Gresham, such good friends as you and I may laugh at each other, may we not?"

"You may do what you like, Miss Oriel: beautiful women I believe always may; but you remember what the spider said to the fly, 'That which is sport to you, may be death to me.'" Anyone looking at Frank's face as he said this, might well have imagined that he was breaking his very heart for love of Miss Oriel. Oh, Master Frank! Master Frank! if you act thus in the green leaf, what will you do in the dry?

While Frank Gresham was thus misbehaving himself, and going on as though to him belonged the privilege of falling in love with pretty faces, as it does to ploughboys and other ordinary people, his great interests were not forgotten by those guardian saints who were so anxious to shower down on his head all manner of temporal blessings.

Another conversation had taken place in the Greshamsbury gardens, in which nothing light had been allowed to present itself; nothing frivolous had been spoken. The countess, the Lady Arabella, and Miss Gresham had been talking over Greshamsbury affairs, and they had latterly been assisted by the Lady Amelia, than whom no de Courcy ever born was more wise, more solemn, more prudent, or more proud. The ponderosity of her qualifications for nobility was sometimes too much even for her mother, and her devotion to the peerage was such, that she would certainly have declined a seat in heaven if offered to her without the promise that it should be in the upper house.

The subject first discussed had been Augusta's prospects. Mr Moffat had been invited to Courcy Castle, and Augusta had been taken thither to meet him, with the express intention on the part of the countess, that they should be man and wife. The countess had been careful to make it intelligible to her sister-in-law and niece, that though Mr Moffat would do excellently well for a daughter of Greshamsbury, he could not be allowed to raise his eyes to a female scion of Courcy Castle.

"Not that we personally dislike him," said the Lady Amelia; "but rank has its drawbacks, Augusta." As the Lady Amelia was now somewhat nearer forty than thirty, and was still allowed to walk,

"In maiden meditation, fancy free,"

it may be presumed that in her case rank had been found to have serious drawbacks. To this Augusta said nothing in objection. Whether desirable by a de Courcy or not, the match was to be hers, and there was no doubt whatever as to the wealth of the man whose name she was to take; the offer had been made, not to her, but to her aunt; the acceptance had been expressed, not by her, but by her aunt. Had she thought of recapitulating in her memory all that had ever passed between Mr Moffat and herself, she would have found that it did not amount to more than the most ordinary conversation between chance partners in a ball-room. Nevertheless, she was to be Mrs Moffat. All that Mr Gresham knew of him was, that when he met the young man for the first and only time in his life, he found him extremely hard to deal with in the matter of money. He had insisted on having ten thousand pounds with his wife, and at last refused to go on with the match unless he got six thousand pounds. This latter sum the poor squire had undertaken to pay him.

Mr Moffat had been for a year or two M.P. for Barchester; having been assisted in his views on that ancient city by all the de Courcy interest. He was a Whig, of course. Not only had Barchester, departing from the light of other days, returned a Whig member of Parliament, but it was declared, that at the next election, now near at hand, a Radical would be sent up, a man pledged to the ballot, to economies of all sorts, one who would carry out Barchester politics in all their abrupt, obnoxious, pestilent virulence. This was one Scatcherd, a great railway contractor, a man who was a native of Barchester, who had bought property in the neighbourhood, and who had achieved a sort of popularity there and elsewhere by the violence of his democratic opposition to the aristocracy. According to this man's political tenets, the Conservatives should be laughed at as fools, but the Whigs should be hated as knaves.

Mr Moffat was now coming down to Courcy Castle to look after his electioneering interests, and Miss Gresham was to return with her aunt to meet him. The countess was very anxious that Frank should also accompany them. Her great doctrine, that he must marry money, had been laid down with authority, and received without doubt. She now pushed it further, and said that no time should be lost; that he should not only marry money, but do so very early in life; there was always danger in delay. The Greshams—of course she alluded only to the males of the family—were foolishly soft-hearted; no one could say what might happen. There was that Miss Thorne always at Greshamsbury.

This was more than the Lady Arabella could stand. She protested that there was at least no ground for supposing that Frank would absolutely disgrace his family.

Still the countess persisted: "Perhaps not," she said; "but when young people of perfectly different ranks were allowed to associate together, there was no saying what danger might arise. They all knew that old Mr Bateson—the present Mr Bateson's father—had gone off with the governess; and young Mr Everbeery, near Taunton, had only the other day married a cook-maid."

"But Mr Everbeery was always drunk, aunt," said Augusta, feeling called upon to say something for her brother.

"Never mind, my dear; these things do happen, and they are very dreadful."

"Horrible!" said the Lady Amelia; "diluting the best blood of the country, and paving the way for revolutions." This was very grand; but, nevertheless, Augusta could not but feel that she perhaps might be about to dilute the blood of her coming children in marrying the tailor's son. She consoled herself by trusting that, at any rate, she paved the way for no revolutions.

"When a thing is so necessary," said the countess, "it cannot be done too soon. Now, Arabella, I don't say that anything will come of it; but it may: Miss Dunstable is coming down to us next week. Now, we all know that when old Dunstable died last year, he left over two hundred thousand to his daughter."

"It is a great deal of money, certainly," said Lady Arabella.

"It would pay off everything, and a great deal more," said the countess.

"It was ointment, was it not, aunt?" said Augusta.

"I believe so, my dear; something called the ointment of Lebanon, or something of that sort: but there's no doubt about the money."

"But how old is she, Rosina?" asked the anxious mother.

"About thirty, I suppose; but I don't think that much signifies."

"Thirty," said Lady Arabella, rather dolefully. "And what is she like? I think that Frank already begins to like girls that are young and pretty."

"But surely, aunt," said the Lady Amelia, "now that he has come to man's discretion, he will not refuse to consider all that he owes to his family. A Mr Gresham of Greshamsbury has a position to support." The de Courcy scion spoke these last words in the sort of tone that a parish clergyman would use, in warning some young farmer's son that he should not put himself on an equal footing with the ploughboys.

It was at last decided that the countess should herself convey to Frank a special invitation to Courcy Castle, and that when she got him there, she should do all that lay in her power to prevent his return to Cambridge, and to further the Dunstable marriage.

"We did think of Miss Dunstable for Porlock, once," she said, naïvely; "but when we found that it wasn't much over two hundred thousand, why, that idea fell to the ground." The terms on which the de Courcy blood might be allowed to dilute itself were, it must be presumed, very high indeed.

Augusta was sent off to find her brother, and to send him to the countess in the small drawing-room. Here the countess was to have her tea, apart from the outer common world, and here, without interruption, she was to teach her great lesson to her nephew.

Augusta did find her brother, and found him in the worst of bad society—so at least the stern de Courcys would have thought. Old Mr Bateson and the governess, Mr Everbeery and his cook's diluted blood, and ways paved for revolutions, all presented themselves to Augusta's mind when she found her brother walking with no other company than Mary Thorne, and walking with her, too, in much too close proximity.

How he had contrived to be off with the old love and so soon on with the new, or rather, to be off with the new love and again on with the old, we will not stop to inquire. Had Lady Arabella, in truth, known all her son's doings in this way, could she have guessed how very nigh he had approached the iniquity of old Mr Bateson, and to the folly of young Mr Everbeery, she would in truth have been in a hurry to send him off to Courcy Castle and Miss Dunstable. Some days before the commencement of our story, young Frank had sworn in sober earnest—in what he intended for his most sober earnest, his most earnest sobriety—that he loved Mary Thorne with a love for which words could find no sufficient expression—with a love that could never die, never grow dim, never become less, which no opposition on the part of others could extinguish, which no opposition on her part could repel; that he might, could, would, and should have her for his wife, and that if she told him she didn't love him, he would—

"Oh, oh! Mary; do you love me? Don't you love me? Won't you love me? Say you will. Oh, Mary, dearest Mary, will you? won't you? do you? don't you? Come now, you have a right to give a fellow an answer."

With such eloquence had the heir of Greshamsbury, when not yet twenty-one years of age, attempted to possess himself of the affections of the doctor's niece. And yet three days afterwards he was quite ready to flirt with Miss Oriel.

If such things are done in the green wood, what will be done in the dry?

And what had Mary said when these fervent protestations of an undying love had been thrown at her feet? Mary, it must be remembered, was very nearly of the same age as

Frank; but, as I and others have so often said before, "Women grow on the sunny side of the wall." Though Frank was only a boy, it behoved Mary to be something more than a girl. Frank might be allowed, without laying himself open to much just reproach, to throw all of what he believed to be his heart into a protestation of what he believed to be love; but Mary was in duty bound to be more thoughtful, more reticent, more aware of the facts of their position, more careful of her own feelings, and more careful also of his.

And yet she could not put him down as another young lady might put down another young gentleman. It is very seldom that a young man, unless he be tipsy, assumes an unwelcome familiarity in his early acquaintance with any girl; but when acquaintance has been long and intimate, familiarity must follow as a matter of course. Frank and Mary had been so much together in his holidays, had so constantly consorted together as boys and girls, that, as regarded her, he had not that innate fear of a woman which represses a young man's tongue; and she was so used to his good-humour, his fun, and high jovial spirits, and was, withal, so fond of them and him, that it was very difficult for her to mark with accurate feeling, and stop with reserved brow, the shade of change from a boy's liking to a man's love.

And Beatrice, too, had done harm in this matter. With a spirit painfully unequal to that of her grand relatives, she had quizzed Mary and Frank about their early flirtations. This she had done; but had instinctively avoided doing so before her mother and sister, and had thus made a secret of it, as it were, between herself, Mary, and her brother;—had given currency, as it were, to the idea that there might be something serious between the two. Not that Beatrice had ever wished to promote a marriage between them, or had even thought of such a thing. She was girlish, thoughtless, imprudent, inartistic, and very unlike a de Courcy. Very unlike a de Courcy she was in all that; but, nevertheless, she had the de Courcy veneration for blood, and, more than that, she had the Gresham feeling joined to that of the de Courcys. The Lady Amelia would not for worlds have had the de Courcy blood defiled; but gold she thought could not defile. Now Beatrice was ashamed of her sister's marriage, and had often declared, within her own heart, that nothing could have made her marry a Mr Moffat.

She had said so also to Mary, and Mary had told her that she was right. Mary also was proud of blood, was proud of her uncle's blood, and the two girls talked together in all the warmth of girlish confidence, of the great glories of family traditions and family honours. Beatrice had talked in utter ignorance as to her friend's birth; and Mary, poor Mary, she had talked, being as ignorant; but not without a strong suspicion that, at some future time, a day of sorrow would tell her some fearful truth.

On one point Mary's mind was strongly made up. No wealth, no mere worldly advantage could make any one her superior. If she were born a gentlewoman, then was she fit to match with any gentleman. Let the most wealthy man in Europe pour all his wealth at her feet, she could, if so inclined, give him back at any rate more than that. That offered at her feet she knew she would never tempt her to yield up the fortress of her heart, the guardianship of her soul, the possession of her mind; not that alone, nor that, even, as any possible slightest fraction of a make-weight.

If she were born a gentlewoman! And then came to her mind those curious questions; what makes a gentleman? what makes a gentlewoman? What is the inner reality, the spiritualised quintessence of that privilege in the world which men call rank, which forces the thousands and hundreds of thousands to bow down before the few elect? What gives, or can give it, or should give it?

And she answered the question. Absolute, intrinsic, acknowledged, individual merit must give it to its possessor, let him be whom, and what, and whence he might. So far the spirit of democracy was strong with her. Beyond this it could be had but by inheritance, received as it were second-hand, or twenty-second-hand. And so far the spirit of aristocracy was strong within her. All this she had, as may be imagined, learnt in early years from her uncle; and all this she was at great pains to teach Beatrice Gresham, the chosen of her heart.

When Frank declared that Mary had a right to give him an answer, he meant that he had a right to expect one. Mary acknowledged this right, and gave it to him.

"Mr Gresham," she said.

"Oh, Mary; Mr Gresham!"

"Yes, Mr Gresham. It must be Mr Gresham after that. And, moreover, it must be Miss Thorne as well."

"I'll be shot if it shall, Mary."

"Well; I can't say that I shall be shot if it be not so; but if it be not so, if you do not agree that it shall be so, I shall be turned out of Greshamsbury."

"What! you mean my mother?" said Frank.

"Indeed, I mean no such thing," said Mary, with a flash from her eye that made Frank almost start. "I mean no such thing. I mean you, not your mother. I am not in the least afraid of Lady Arabella; but I am afraid of you."

"Afraid of me, Mary!"

"Miss Thorne; pray, pray, remember. It must be Miss Thorne. Do not turn me out of Greshamsbury. Do not separate me from Beatrice. It is you that will drive me out; no one else. I could stand my ground against your mother—I feel I could; but I cannot stand against you if you treat me otherwise than—than—"

"Otherwise than what? I want to treat you as the girl I have chosen from all the world as my wife."

"I am sorry you should so soon have found it necessary to make a choice. But, Mr Gresham, we must not joke about this at present. I am sure you would not willingly injure me; but if you speak to me, or of me, again in that way, you will injure me, injure me so much that I shall be forced to leave Greshamsbury in my own defence. I know you are too generous to drive me to that."

And so the interview had ended. Frank, of course, went upstairs to see if his new pocket-pistols were all ready, properly cleaned, loaded, and capped, should he find, after a few days' experience, that prolonged existence was unendurable.

However, he managed to live through the subsequent period; doubtless with a view of preventing any disappointment to his father's guests.

CHAPTER VII

THE DOCTOR'S GARDEN

Mary had contrived to quiet her lover with considerable propriety of demeanour. Then came on her the somewhat harder task of quieting herself. Young ladies, on the whole, are perhaps quite as susceptible of the softer feelings as young gentlemen are. Now Frank Gresham was handsome, amiable, by no means a fool in intellect, excellent in heart; and he was, moreover, a gentleman, being the son of Mr Gresham of Greshamsbury. Mary had been, as it were, brought up to love him. Had aught but good happened to him, she would have cried as for a brother. It must not therefore be supposed that when Frank Gresham told her that he loved her, she had heard it altogether unconcerned.

He had not, perhaps, made his declaration with that propriety of language in which such scenes are generally described as being carried on. Ladies may perhaps think that Mary should have been deterred, by the very boyishness of his manner, from thinking at all seriously on the subject. His "will you, won't you—do you, don't you?" does not sound like the poetic raptures of a highly inspired lover. But, nevertheless, there had been warmth, and a reality in it not in itself repulsive; and Mary's anger—anger? no, not anger—her objections to the declarations were probably not based on the absurdity of her lover's language.

We are inclined to think that these matters are not always discussed by mortal lovers in the poetically passionate phraseology which is generally thought to be appropriate for their description. A man cannot well describe that which he has never seen nor heard; but the absolute words and acts of one such scene did once come to the author's knowledge. The couple were by no means plebeian, or below the proper standard of high bearing and high breeding; they were a handsome pair, living among educated people, sufficiently given to mental pursuits, and in every way what a pair of polite lovers ought to be. The all-important conversation passed in this wise. The site of the passionate scene was the sea-shore, on which they were walking, in autumn.

Gentleman. "Well, Miss ——, the long and short of it is this: here I am; you can take me or leave me."

Lady—scratching a gutter on the sand with her parasol, so as to allow a little salt water to run out of one hole into another. "Of course, I know that's all nonsense."

Gentleman. "Nonsense! By Jove, it isn't nonsense at all: come, Jane; here I am: come, at any rate you can say something."

Lady. "Yes, I suppose I can say something."

Gentleman. "Well, which is it to be; take me or leave me?"

Lady—very slowly, and with a voice perhaps hardly articulate, carrying on, at the same time, her engineering works on a wider scale. "Well, I don't exactly want to leave you."

And so the matter was settled: settled with much propriety and satisfaction; and both the lady and gentleman would have thought, had they ever thought about the matter at all, that this, the sweetest moment of their lives, had been graced by all the poetry by which such moments ought to be hallowed.

When Mary had, as she thought, properly subdued young Frank, the offer of whose love she, at any rate, knew was, at such a period of his life, an utter absurdity, then she found it necessary to subdue herself. What happiness on earth could be greater than the possession of such a love, had the true possession been justly and honestly within her reach? What man could be more lovable than such a man as would grow from such a boy? And then, did she not love him,—love him already, without waiting for any change? Did she not feel that there was that about him, about him and about herself, too, which might so well fit them for each other? It would be so sweet to be the sister of Beatrice, the daughter of the squire, to belong to Greshamsbury as a part and parcel of itself.

But though she could not restrain these thoughts, it never for a moment occurred to her to take Frank's offer in earnest. Though she was a grown woman, he was still a boy. He would have to see the world before he settled in it, and would change his mind about woman half a score of times before he married. Then, too, though she did not like the Lady Arabella, she felt that she owed something, if not to her kindness, at least to her forbearance; and she knew, felt inwardly certain, that she would be doing wrong, that the world would say she was doing wrong, that her uncle would think her wrong, if she endeavoured to take advantage of what had passed.

She had not for an instant doubted; not for a moment had she contemplated it as possible that she should ever become Mrs Gresham because Frank had offered to make her so; but, nevertheless, she could not help thinking of what had occurred—of thinking of it, most probably much more than Frank did himself.

A day or two afterwards, on the evening before Frank's birthday, she was alone with her uncle, walking in the garden behind their house, and she then essayed to question him, with the object of learning if she were fitted by her birth to be the wife of such a one as Frank Gresham. They were in the habit of walking there together when he happened to be at home of a summer's evening. This was not often the case, for his hours of labour extended much beyond those usual to the upper working world, the hours, namely, between breakfast and dinner; but those minutes that they did thus pass together, the doctor regarded as perhaps the pleasantest of his life.

"Uncle," said she, after a while, "what do you think of this marriage of Miss Gresham's?"

"Well, Minnie"—such was his name of endearment for her—"I can't say I have thought much about it, and I don't suppose anybody else has either."

"She must think about it, of course; and so must he, I suppose."

"I'm not so sure of that. Some folks would never get married if they had to trouble themselves with thinking about it."

"I suppose that's why you never got married, uncle?"

"Either that, or thinking of it too much. One is as bad as the other."

Mary had not contrived to get at all near her point as yet; so she had to draw off, and after a while begin again.

"Well, I have been thinking about it, at any rate, uncle."

"That's very good of you; that will save me the trouble; and perhaps save Miss Gresham too. If you have thought it over thoroughly, that will do for all."

"I believe Mr Moffat is a man of no family."

"He'll mend in that point, no doubt, when he has got a wife."

"Uncle, you're a goose; and what is worse, a very provoking goose."

"Niece, you're a gander; and what is worse, a very silly gander. What is Mr Moffat's family to you and me? Mr Moffat has that which ranks above family honours. He is a very rich man."

"Yes," said Mary, "I know he is rich; and a rich man I suppose can buy anything— except a woman that is worth having."

"A rich man can buy anything," said the doctor; "not that I meant to say that Mr Moffat has bought Miss Gresham. I have no doubt that they will suit each other very well," he added with an air of decisive authority, as though he had finished the subject.

But his niece was determined not to let him pass so. "Now, uncle," said she, "you know you are pretending to a great deal of worldly wisdom, which, after all, is not wisdom at all in your eyes."

"Am I?"

"You know you are: and as for the impropriety of discussing Miss Gresham's marriage—"

"I did not say it was improper."

"Oh, yes, you did; of course such things must be discussed. How is one to have an opinion if one does not get it by looking at the things which happen around us?"

"Now I am going to be blown up," said Dr Thorne.

"Dear uncle, do be serious with me."

"Well, then, seriously, I hope Miss Gresham will be very happy as Mrs Moffat."

"Of course you do: so do I. I hope it as much as I can hope what I don't at all see ground for expecting."

"People constantly hope without any such ground."

"Well, then, I'll hope in this case. But, uncle—"

"Well, my dear?"

"I want your opinion, truly and really. If you were a girl—"

"I am perfectly unable to give any opinion founded on so strange an hypothesis."

"Well; but if you were a marrying man."

"The hypothesis is quite as much out of my way."

"But, uncle, I am a girl, and perhaps I may marry;—or at any rate think of marrying some day."

"The latter alternative is certainly possible enough."

"Therefore, in seeing a friend taking such a step, I cannot but speculate on the matter as though I were myself in her place. If I were Miss Gresham, should I be right?"

"But, Minnie, you are not Miss Gresham."

"No, I am Mary Thorne; it is a very different thing, I know. I suppose *I* might marry any one without degrading myself."

It was almost ill-natured of her to say this; but she had not meant to say it in the sense which the sounds seemed to bear. She had failed in being able to bring her uncle to the point she wished by the road she had planned, and in seeking another road, she had abruptly fallen into unpleasant places.

"I should be very sorry that my niece should think so," said he; "and am sorry, too, that she should say so. But, Mary, to tell the truth, I hardly know at what you are driving. You are, I think, not so clear minded—certainly, not so clear worded—as is usual with you."

"I will tell you, uncle;" and, instead of looking up into his face, she turned her eyes down on the green lawn beneath her feet.

"Well, Minnie, what is it?" and he took both her hands in his.

"I think that Miss Gresham should not marry Mr Moffat. I think so because her family is high and noble, and because he is low and ignoble. When one has an opinion on such matters, one cannot but apply it to things and people around one; and having applied my opinion to her, the next step naturally is to apply it to myself. Were I Miss Gresham, I would not marry Mr Moffat though he rolled in gold. I know where to rank Miss Gresham. What I want to know is, where I ought to rank myself?"

They had been standing when she commenced her last speech; but as she finished it, the doctor moved on again, and she moved with him. He walked on slowly without answering her; and she, out of her full mind, pursued aloud the tenor of her thoughts.

"If a woman feels that she would not lower herself by marrying in a rank beneath herself, she ought also to feel that she would not lower a man that she might love by allowing him to marry into a rank beneath his own—that is, to marry her."

"That does not follow," said the doctor quickly. "A man raises a woman to his own standard, but a woman must take that of the man she marries."

Again they were silent, and again they walked on, Mary holding her uncle's arm with both her hands. She was determined, however, to come to the point, and after considering for a while how best she might do it, she ceased to beat any longer about the bush, and asked him a plain question.

"The Thornes are as good a family as the Greshams, are they not?"

"In absolute genealogy they are, my dear. That is, when I choose to be an old fool and talk of such matters in a sense different from that in which they are spoken of by the world at large, I may say that the Thornes are as good, or perhaps better, than the Greshams, but I should be sorry to say so seriously to any one. The Greshams now stand much higher in the county than the Thornes do."

"But they are of the same class."

"Yes, yes; Wilfred Thorne of Ullathorne, and our friend the squire here, are of the same class."

"But, uncle, I and Augusta Gresham—are we of the same class?"

"Well, Minnie, you would hardly have me boast that I am the same class with the squire—I, a poor country doctor?"

"You are not answering me fairly, dear uncle; dearest uncle, do you not know that you are not answering me fairly? You know what I mean. Have I a right to call the Thornes of Ullathorne my cousins?"

"Mary, Mary, Mary!" said he after a minute's pause, still allowing his arm to hang loose, that she might hold it with both her hands. "Mary, Mary, Mary! I would that you had spared me this!"

"I could not have spared it to you for ever, uncle."

"I would that you could have done so; I would that you could!"

"It is over now, uncle: it is told now. I will grieve you no more. Dear, dear, dearest! I should love you more than ever now; I would, I would, I would if that were possible. What should I be but for you? What must I have been but for you?" And she threw herself on his breast, and clinging with her arms round his neck, kissed his forehead, cheeks, and lips.

There was nothing more said then on the subject between them. Mary asked no further question, nor did the doctor volunteer further information. She would have been most anxious to ask about her mother's history had she dared to do so; but she did not dare to ask; she could not bear to be told that her mother had been, perhaps was, a worthless woman. That she was truly a daughter of a brother of the doctor, that she did know. Little as she had heard of her relatives in her early youth, few as had been the words which had fallen from her uncle in her hearing as to her parentage, she did know this, that she was the daughter of Henry Thorne, a brother of the doctor, and a son of the old prebendary. Trifling little things that had occurred, accidents which could not be prevented, had told her this; but not a word had ever passed any one's lips as to her mother. The doctor, when speaking of his youth, had spoken of her father; but no one had spoken of her mother. She had long known that she was the child of a Thorne; now she knew also that she was no cousin of the Thornes of Ullathorne; no cousin, at least, in the world's ordinary language, no niece indeed of her uncle, unless by his special permission that she should be so.

When the interview was over, she went up alone to the drawing-room, and there she sat thinking. She had not been there long before her uncle came up to her. He did not sit down, or even take off the hat which he still wore; but coming close to her, and still standing, he spoke thus:—

"Mary, after what has passed I should be very unjust and very cruel to you not to tell you one thing more than you have now learned. Your mother was unfortunate in much, not in everything; but the world, which is very often stern in such matters, never judged her to have disgraced herself. I tell you this, my child, in order that you may respect her memory;" and so saying, he again left her without giving her time to speak a word.

What he then told her he had told in mercy. He felt what must be her feelings when she reflected that she had to blush for her mother; that not only could she not speak of her mother, but that she might hardly think of her with innocence; and to mitigate such sorrow as this, and also to do justice to the woman whom his brother had so wronged, he had forced himself to reveal so much as is stated above.

And then he walked slowly by himself, backwards and forwards through the garden, thinking of what he had done with reference to this girl, and doubting whether he had done wisely and well. He had resolved, when first the little infant was given over to his charge, that nothing should be known of her or by her as to her mother. He was willing to devote himself to this orphan child of his brother, this last seedling of his father's house; but he was not willing so to do this as to bring himself in any manner into familiar contact with the Scatcherds. He had boasted to himself that he, at any rate, was a gentleman; and that she, if she were to live in his house, sit at his table, and share his hearth, must be a lady. He would tell no lie about her; he would not to any one make her out to be aught other or aught better than she was; people would talk about her of course, only let them not talk to him; he conceived of himself—and the conception was not without due ground—that should any do so, he had that within him which would silence them. He would never claim for this little creature—thus brought into the world without a legitimate position in which to stand—he would never claim for her any station that would not properly be her own. He would make for her a station as best he could. As he might sink or swim, so should she.

So he had resolved; but things had arranged themselves, as they often do, rather than been arranged by him. During ten or twelve years no one had heard of Mary Thorne; the memory of Henry Thorne and his tragic death had passed away; the knowledge that an infant had been born whose birth was connected with that tragedy, a knowledge never widely spread, had faded down into utter ignorance. At the end of these twelve years, Dr Thorne had announced, that a young niece, a child of a brother long since dead, was coming to live with him. As he had contemplated, no one spoke to him; but some people did no doubt talk among themselves. Whether or not the exact truth was surmised by any, it matters not to say; with absolute exactness, probably not; with great approach to it, probably yes. By one person, at any rate, no guess whatever was made; no thought relative to Dr Thorne's niece ever troubled him; no idea that Mary Scatcherd had left a child in England ever occurred to him; and that person was Roger Scatcherd, Mary's brother.

To one friend, and only one, did the doctor tell the whole truth, and that was to the old squire. "I have told you," said the doctor, "partly that you may know that the child has no right to mix with your children if you think much of such things. Do you, however, see to this. I would rather that no one else should be told."

No one else had been told; and the squire had "seen to it," by accustoming himself to look at Mary Thorne running about the house with his own children as though she were of the same brood. Indeed, the squire had always been fond of Mary, had personally noticed her, and, in the affair of Mam'selle Larron, had declared that he would have her placed at once on the bench of magistrates;—much to the disgust of the Lady Arabella.

And so things had gone on and on, and had not been thought of with much downright thinking; till now, when she was one-and-twenty years of age, his niece came to him, asking as to her position, and inquiring in what rank of life she was to look for a husband.

And so the doctor walked backwards and forwards through the garden, slowly, thinking now with some earnestness what if, after all, he had been wrong about his niece? What if by endeavouring to place her in the position of a lady, he had falsely so placed her, and robbed her of all legitimate position? What if there was no rank of life to which she could now properly attach herself?

And then, how had it answered, that plan of his of keeping her all to himself? He, Dr Thorne, was still a poor man; the gift of saving money had not been his; he had ever had a comfortable house for her to live in, and, in spite of Doctors Fillgrave, Century, Rerechild, and others, had made from his profession an income sufficient for their joint wants; but he had not done as others do: he had no three or four thousand pounds in the Three per Cents. on which Mary might live in some comfort when he should die. Late in life he had insured his life for eight hundred pounds; and to that, and that only, had he to trust for Mary's future maintenance. How had it answered, then, this plan of letting her be unknown to, and undreamed of by, those who were as near to her on her mother's side as he was on the father's? On that side, though there had been utter poverty, there was now absolute wealth.

But when he took her to himself, had he not rescued her from the very depths of the lowest misery: from the degradation of the workhouse; from the scorn of honest-born charity-children; from the lowest of the world's low conditions? Was she not now the apple of his eye, his one great sovereign comfort—his pride, his happiness, his glory? Was he to make her over, to make any portion of her over to others, if, by doing so, she might be able to share the wealth, as well as the coarse manners and uncouth society of her at present unknown connexions? He, who had never worshipped wealth on his own behalf; he, who had scorned the idol of gold, and had ever been teaching her to scorn it; was he now to show that his philosophy had all been false as soon as the temptation to do so was put in his way?

But yet, what man would marry this bastard child, without a sixpence, and bring not only poverty, but ill blood also on his own children? It might be very well for him, Dr Thorne; for him whose career was made, whose name, at any rate, was his own; for him who had a fixed standing-ground in the world; it might be well for him to indulge in large views of a philosophy antagonistic to the world's practice; but had he a right to do it for his niece? What man would marry a girl so placed? For those among whom she might have legitimately found a level, education had now utterly unfitted her. And then, he well knew that she would never put out her hand in token of love to any one without telling all she knew and all she surmised as to her own birth.

And that question of this evening; had it not been instigated by some appeal to her heart? Was there not already within her breast some cause for disquietude which had made her so pertinacious? Why else had she told him then, for the first time, that she did not know where to rank herself? If such an appeal had been made to her, it must have come from young Frank Gresham. What, in such case, would it behove him to do? Should he pack up his all, his lancet-cases, pestle and mortar, and seek anew fresh ground in a new world, leaving behind a huge triumph to those learned enemies of his, Fillgrave, Century, and Rerechild? Better that than remain at Greshamsbury at the cost of his child's heart and pride.

And so he walked slowly backwards and forwards through his garden, meditating these things painfully enough.

CHAPTER VIII

MATRIMONIAL PROSPECTS

It will of course be remembered that Mary's interview with the other girls at Greshamsbury took place some two or three days subsequently to Frank's generous offer of his hand and heart. Mary had quite made up her mind that the whole thing was to be regarded as a folly, and that it was not to be spoken of to any one; but yet her heart was sore enough. She was full of pride, and yet she knew she must bow her neck to the pride of others. Being, as she was herself, nameless, she could not but feel a stern, unflinching antagonism, the antagonism of a democrat, to the pretensions of others who were blessed with that of which she had been deprived. She had this feeling; and yet, of all the things that she coveted, she most coveted that, for glorying in which, she was determined to heap scorn on others. She said to herself, proudly, that God's handiwork was the inner man, the inner woman, the naked creature animated by a living soul; that all other adjuncts were but man's clothing for the creature; all others, whether stitched by tailors or contrived by kings. Was it not within her capacity to do as nobly, to love as truly, to worship her God in heaven with as perfect a faith, and her god on earth with as leal a troth, as though blood had descended to her purely through scores of purely born progenitors? So to herself she spoke; and yet, as she said it, she knew that were she a man, such a man as the heir of Greshamsbury should be, nothing would tempt her to sully her children's blood by mating herself with any one that was base born. She felt that were she an Augusta Gresham, no Mr Moffat, let his wealth be what it might, should win her hand unless he too could tell of family honours and a line of ancestors.

And so, with a mind at war with itself, she came forth armed to do battle against the world's prejudices, those prejudices she herself loved so well.

And was she to give up her old affections, her feminine loves, because she found that she was a cousin to nobody? Was she no longer to pour out her heart to Beatrice Gresham with all the girlish volubility of an equal? Was she to be severed from Patience Oriel, and banished—or rather was she to banish herself—from the free place she had maintained in the various youthful female conclaves held within that parish of Greshamsbury?

Hitherto, what Mary Thorne would say, what Miss Thorne suggested in such or such a matter, was quite as frequently asked as any opinion from Augusta Gresham—quite as frequently, unless when it chanced that any of the de Courcy girls were at the house. Was this to be given up? These feelings had grown up among them since they were children, and had not hitherto been questioned among them. Now they were questioned by Mary

Thorne. Was she in fact to find that her position had been a false one, and must be changed?

Such had been her feelings when she protested that she would not be Augusta Gresham's bridesmaid, and offered to put her neck beneath Beatrice's foot; when she drove the Lady Margaretta out of the room, and gave her own opinion as to the proper grammatical construction of the word humble; such also had been her feelings when she kept her hand so rigidly to herself while Frank held the dining-room door open for her to pass through.

"Patience Oriel," said she to herself, "can talk to him of her father and mother: let Patience take his hand; let her talk to him;" and then, not long afterwards, she saw that Patience did talk to him; and seeing it, she walked along silent, among some of the old people, and with much effort did prevent a tear from falling down her cheek.

But why was the tear in her eye? Had she not proudly told Frank that his love-making was nothing but a boy's silly rhapsody? Had she not said so while she had yet reason to hope that her blood was as good as his own? Had she not seen at a glance that his love tirade was worthy of ridicule, and of no other notice? And yet there was a tear now in her eye because this boy, whom she had scolded from her, whose hand, offered in pure friendship, she had just refused, because he, so rebuffed by her, had carried his fun and gallantry to one who would be less cross to him!

She could hear as she was walking, that while Lady Margaretta was with them, their voices were loud and merry; and her sharp ear could also hear, when Lady Margaretta left them, that Frank's voice became low and tender. So she walked on, saying nothing, looking straight before her, and by degrees separating herself from all the others.

The Greshamsbury grounds were on one side somewhat too closely hemmed in by the village. On this side was a path running the length of one of the streets of the village; and far down the path, near to the extremity of the gardens, and near also to a wicket-gate which led out into the village, and which could be opened from the inside, was a seat, under a big yew-tree, from which, through a breach in the houses, might be seen the parish church, standing in the park on the other side. Hither Mary walked alone, and here she seated herself, determined to get rid of her tears and their traces before she again showed herself to the world.

"I shall never be happy here again," said she to herself; "never. I am no longer one of them, and I cannot live among them unless I am so." And then an idea came across her mind that she hated Patience Oriel; and then, instantly another idea followed it—quick as such thoughts are quick—that she did not hate Patience Oriel at all; that she liked her, nay, loved her; that Patience Oriel was a sweet girl; and that she hoped the time would come when she might see her the lady of Greshamsbury. And then the tear, which had been no whit controlled, which indeed had now made itself master of her, came to a head, and, bursting through the floodgates of the eye, came rolling down, and in its fall, wetted her hand as it lay on her lap. "What a fool! what an idiot! what an empty-headed cowardly fool I am!" said she, springing up from the bench on her feet.

As she did so, she heard voices close to her, at the little gate. They were those of her uncle and Frank Gresham.

"God bless you, Frank!" said the doctor, as he passed out of the grounds. "You will excuse a lecture, won't you, from so old a friend?—though you are a man now, and discreet, of course, by Act of Parliament."

"Indeed I will, doctor," said Frank. "I will excuse a longer lecture than that from you."

"At any rate it won't be to-night," said the doctor, as he disappeared. "And if you see Mary, tell her that I am obliged to go; and that I will send Janet down to fetch her."

Now Janet was the doctor's ancient maid-servant.

Mary could not move on without being perceived; she therefore stood still till she heard the click of the door, and then began walking rapidly back to the house by the path which had brought her thither. The moment, however, that she did so, she found that she was followed; and in a very few moments Frank was alongside of her.

"Oh, Mary!" said he, calling to her, but not loudly, before he quite overtook her, "how odd that I should come across you just when I have a message for you! and why are you all alone?"

Mary's first impulse was to reiterate her command to him to call her no more by her Christian name; but her second impulse told her that such an injunction at the present moment would not be prudent on her part. The traces of her tears were still there; and she well knew that a very little, the slightest show of tenderness on his part, the slightest effort on her own to appear indifferent, would bring down more than one other such intruder. It would, moreover, be better for her to drop all outward sign that she remembered what had taken place. So long, then, as he and she were at Greshamsbury together, he should call her Mary if he pleased. He would soon be gone; and while he remained, she would keep out of his way.

"Your uncle has been obliged to go away to see an old woman at Silverbridge."

"At Silverbridge! why, he won't be back all night. Why could not the old woman send for Dr Century?"

"I suppose she thought two old women could not get on well together."

Mary could not help smiling. She did not like her uncle going off so late on such a journey; but it was always felt as a triumph when he was invited into the strongholds of his enemies.

"And Janet is to come over for you. However, I told him it was quite unnecessary to disturb another old woman, for that I should of course see you home."

"Oh, no, Mr Gresham; indeed you'll not do that."

"Indeed, and indeed, I shall."

"What! on this great day, when every lady is looking for you, and talking of you. I suppose you want to set the countess against me for ever. Think, too, how angry Lady Arabella will be if you are absent on such an errand as this."

"To hear you talk, Mary, one would think that you were going to Silverbridge your-self."

"Perhaps I am."

"If I did not go with you, some of the other fellows would. John, or George—"

"Good gracious, Frank! Fancy either of the Mr de Courcys walking home with me!"

She had forgotten herself, and the strict propriety on which she had resolved, in the impossibility of forgoing her little joke against the de Courcy grandeur; she had forgotten herself, and had called him Frank in her old, former, eager, free tone of voice; and then, remembering she had done so, she drew herself up, but her lips, and determined to be doubly on her guard in the future.

"Well, it shall be either one of them or I," said Frank: "perhaps you would prefer my cousin George to me?"

"I should prefer Janet to either, seeing that with her I should not suffer the extreme nuisance of knowing that I was a bore."

"A bore! Mary, to me?"

"Yes, Mr Gresham, a bore to you. Having to walk home through the mud with village young ladies is boring. All gentlemen feel it to be so."

"There is no mud; if there were you would not be allowed to walk at all."

"Oh! village young ladies never care for such things, though fashionable gentlemen do."

"I would carry you home, Mary, if it would do you a service," said Frank, with considerable pathos in his voice.

"Oh, dear me! pray do not, Mr Gresham. I should not like it at all," said she: "a wheelbarrow would be preferable to that."

"Of course. Anything would be preferable to my arm, I know."

"Certainly; anything in the way of a conveyance. If I were to act baby; and you were to act nurse, it really would not be comfortable for either of us."

Frank Gresham felt disconcerted, though he hardly knew why. He was striving to say something tender to his lady-love; but every word that he spoke she turned into joke. Mary did not answer him coldly or unkindly; but, nevertheless, he was displeased. One does not like to have one's little offerings of sentimental service turned into burlesque when one is in love in earnest. Mary's jokes had appeared so easy too; they seemed to come from a heart so little troubled. This, also, was cause of vexation to Frank. If he could but have known all, he would, perhaps, have been better pleased.

He determined not to be absolutely laughed out of his tenderness. When, three days ago, he had been repulsed, he had gone away owning to himself that he had been beaten; owning so much, but owning it with great sorrow and much shame. Since that he had come of age; since that he had made speeches, and speeches had been made to him; since that he had gained courage by flirting with Patience Oriel. No faint heart ever won a fair lady, as he was well aware; he resolved, therefore, that his heart should not be faint, and that he would see whether the fair lady might not be won by becoming audacity.

"Mary," said he, stopping in the path—for they were now near the spot where it broke out upon the lawn, and they could already hear the voices of the guests—"Mary, you are unkind to me."

"I am not aware of it, Mr Gresham; but if I am, do not you retaliate. I am weaker than you, and in your power; do not you, therefore, be unkind to me."

"You refused my hand just now," continued he. "Of all the people here at Greshamsbury, you are the only one that has not wished me joy; the only one—"

"I do wish you joy; I will wish you joy; there is my hand," and she frankly put out her ungloved hand. "You are quite man enough to understand me: there is my hand; I trust you use it only as it is meant to be used."

He took it in his and pressed it cordially, as he might have done that of any other friend in such a case; and then—did not drop it as he should have done. He was not a St Anthony, and it was most imprudent in Miss Thorne to subject him to such a temptation.

"Mary," said he; "dear Mary! dearest Mary! if you did but know how I love you!"

As he said this, holding Miss Thorne's hand, he stood on the pathway with his back towards the lawn and house, and, therefore, did not at first see his sister Augusta, who had just at that moment come upon them. Mary blushed up to her straw hat, and, with a quick jerk, recovered her hand. Augusta saw the motion, and Mary saw that Augusta had seen it.

From my tedious way of telling it, the reader will be led to imagine that the hand-squeezing had been protracted to a duration quite incompatible with any objection to such an arrangement on the part of the lady; but the fault is mine: in no part hers. Were I possessed of a quick spasmodic style of narrative, I should have been able to include it all—Frank's misbehaviour, Mary's immediate anger, Augusta's arrival, and keen, Argus-eyed inspection, and then Mary's subsequent misery—in five words and half a dozen dashes and inverted commas. The thing should have been so told; for, to do Mary justice, she did not leave her hand in Frank's a moment longer than she could help herself.

Frank, feeling the hand withdrawn, and hearing, when it was too late, the step on the gravel, turned sharply round. "Oh, it's you, is it, Augusta? Well, what do you want?"

Augusta was not naturally very ill-natured, seeing that in her veins the high de Courcy blood was somewhat tempered by an admixture of the Gresham attributes; nor was she predisposed to make her brother her enemy by publishing to the world any of his little tender peccadilloes; but she could not but bethink herself of what her aunt had been saying as to the danger of any such encounters as that she just now had beheld; she could not but start at seeing her brother thus, on the very brink of the precipice of which the countess had specially forewarned her mother. She, Augusta, was, as she well knew, doing her duty by her family by marrying a tailor's son for whom she did not care a chip, seeing the tailor's son was possessed of untold wealth. Now when one member of a household is making a struggle for a family, it is painful to see the benefit of that struggle negatived by the folly of another member. The future Mrs Moffat did feel aggrieved by the fatuity of the young heir, and, consequently, took upon herself to look as much like her Aunt de Courcy as she could do.

"Well, what is it?" said Frank, looking rather disgusted. "What makes you stick your chin up and look in that way?" Frank had hitherto been rather a despot among his sisters, and forgot that the eldest of them was now passing altogether from under his sway to that of the tailor's son.

"Frank," said Augusta, in a tone of voice which did honour to the great lessons she had lately received. "Aunt de Courcy wants to see you immediately in the small drawing-room;" and, as she said so, she resolved to say a few words of advice to Miss Thorne as soon as her brother should have left them.

"In the small drawing-room, does she? Well, Mary, we may as well go together, for I suppose it is tea-time now."

"You had better go at once, Frank," said Augusta; "the countess will be angry if you keep her waiting. She has been expecting you these twenty minutes. Mary Thorne and I can return together."

There was something in the tone in which the words, "Mary Thorne," were uttered, which made Mary at once draw herself up. "I hope," said she, "that Mary Thorne will never be any hindrance to either of you."

Frank's ear had also perceived that there was something in the tone of his sister's voice not boding comfort to Mary; he perceived that the de Courcy blood in Augusta's veins was already rebelling against the doctor's niece on his part, though it had condescended to submit itself to the tailor's son on her own part.

"Well, I am going," said he; "but look here Augusta, if you say one word of Mary—"

Oh, Frank! Frank! you boy, you very boy! you goose, you silly goose! Is that the way you make love, desiring one girl not to tell of another, as though you were three children, tearing your frocks and trousers in getting through the same hedge together? Oh, Frank! Frank! you, the full-blown heir of Greshamsbury? You, a man already endowed with a man's discretion? You, the forward rider, that did but now threaten young Harry Baker and the Honourable John to eclipse them by prowess in the field? You, of age? Why, thou canst not as yet have left thy mother's apron-string!

"If you say one word of Mary—"

So far had he got in his injunction to his sister, but further than that, in such a case, was he never destined to proceed. Mary's indignation flashed upon him, striking him dumb long before the sound of her voice reached his ears; and yet she spoke as quick as the words would come to her call, and somewhat loudly too.

"Say one word of Mary, Mr Gresham! And why should she not say as many words of Mary as she may please? I must tell you all now, Augusta! and I must also beg you not to be silent for my sake. As far as I am concerned, tell it to whom you please. This was the second time your brother—"

"Mary, Mary," said Frank, deprecating her loquacity.

"I beg your pardon, Mr Gresham; you have made it necessary that I should tell your sister all. He has now twice thought it well to amuse himself by saying to me words which it was ill-natured in him to speak, and—"

"Ill-natured, Mary!"

"Ill-natured in him to speak," continued Mary, "and to which it would be absurd for me to listen. He probably does the same to others," she added, being unable in heart to forget that sharpest of her wounds, that flirtation of his with Patience Oriel; "but to me it is almost cruel. Another girl might laugh at him, or listen to him, as she would choose; but I can do neither. I shall now keep away from Greshamsbury, at any rate till he has left it; and, Augusta, I can only beg you to understand, that, as far as I am concerned, there is nothing which may not be told to all the world."

And, so saying, she walked on a little in advance of them, as proud as a queen. Had Lady de Courcy herself met her at this moment, she would almost have felt herself forced to shrink out of the pathway. "Not say a word of me!" she repeated to herself, but still out loud. "No word need be left unsaid on my account; none, none."

Augusta followed her, dumfounded at her indignation; and Frank also followed, but not in silence. When his first surprise at Mary's great anger was over, he felt himself called upon to say some word that might tend to exonerate his lady-love; and some word also of protestation as to his own purpose.

"There is nothing to be told, nothing, at least of Mary," he said, speaking to his sister; "but of me, you may tell this, if you choose to disoblige your brother—that I love Mary Thorne with all my heart; and that I will never love any one else."

By this time they had reached the lawn, and Mary was able to turn away from the path which led up to the house. As she left them she said in a voice, now low enough, "I cannot prevent him from talking nonsense, Augusta; but you will bear me witness, that I do not willingly hear it." And, so saying, she started off almost in a run towards the distant part of the gardens, in which she saw Beatrice.

Frank, as he walked up to the house with his sister, endeavoured to induce her to give him a promise that she would tell no tales as to what she had heard and seen.

"Of course, Frank, it must be all nonsense," she had said; "and you shouldn't amuse yourself in such a way."

"Well, but, Guss, come, we have always been friends; don't let us quarrel just when you are going to be married." But Augusta would make no promise.

Frank, when he reached the house, found the countess waiting for him, sitting in the little drawing-room by herself,—somewhat impatiently. As he entered he became aware that there was some peculiar gravity attached to the coming interview. Three persons, his mother, one of his younger sisters, and the Lady Amelia, each stopped him to let him know that the countess was waiting; and he perceived that a sort of guard was kept upon the door to save her ladyship from any undesirable intrusion.

The countess frowned at the moment of his entrance, but soon smoothed her brow, and invited him to take a chair ready prepared for him opposite to the elbow of the sofa on which she was leaning. She had a small table before her, on which was her teacup, so that she was able to preach at him nearly as well as though she had been ensconced in a pulpit.

"My dear Frank," said she, in a voice thoroughly suitable to the importance of the communication, "you have to-day come of age."

Frank remarked that he understood that such was the case, and added that "that was the reason for all the fuss."

"Yes; you have to-day come of age. Perhaps I should have been glad to see such an occasion noticed at Greshamsbury with some more suitable signs of rejoicing."

"Oh, aunt! I think we did it all very well."

"Greshamsbury, Frank, is, or at any rate ought to be, the seat of the first commoner in Barsetshire.

"Well; so it is. I am quite sure there isn't a better fellow than father anywhere in the county."

The countess sighed. Her opinion of the poor squire was very different from Frank's. "It is no use now," said she, "looking back to that which cannot be cured. The first commoner in Barsetshire should hold a position—I will not of course say equal to that of a peer."

"Oh dear no; of course not," said Frank; and a bystander might have thought that there was a touch of satire in his tone.

"No, not equal to that of a peer; but still of very paramount importance. Of course my first ambition is bound up in Porlock."

"Of course," said Frank, thinking how very weak was the staff on which his aunt's ambition rested; for Lord Porlock's youthful career had not been such as to give unmitigated satisfaction to his parents.

"Is bound up in Porlock:" and then the countess plumed herself; but the mother sighed. "And next to Porlock, Frank, my anxiety is about you."

"Upon my honour, aunt, I am very much obliged. I shall be all right, you'll see."

"Greshamsbury, my dear boy, is not now what it used to be."

"Isn't it?" asked Frank.

"No, Frank; by no means. I do not wish to say a word against your father. It may, perhaps have been his misfortune, rather than his fault—"

"She is always down on the governor; always," said Frank to himself; resolving to stick bravely to the side of the house to which he had elected to belong.

"But there is the fact, Frank, too plain to us all; Greshamsbury is not what it was. It is your duty to restore it to its former importance."

"My duty!" said Frank, rather puzzled.

"Yes, Frank, your duty. It all depends on you now. Of course you know that your father owes a great deal of money."

Frank muttered something. Tidings had in some shape reached his ear that his father was not comfortably circumstances as regarded money.

"And then, he has sold Boxall Hill. It cannot be expected that Boxall Hill shall be repurchased, as some horrid man, a railway-maker, I believe—"

"Yes; that's Scatcherd."

"Well, he has built a house there, I'm told; so I presume that it cannot be bought back: but it will be your duty, Frank, to pay all the debts that there are on the property, and to purchase what, at any rate, will be equal to Boxall Hill."

Frank opened his eyes wide and stared at his aunt, as though doubting much whether or no she were in her right mind. He pay off the family debts! He buy up property of four thousand pounds a year! He remained, however, quite quiet, waiting the elucidation of the mystery.

"Frank, of course you understand me."

Frank was obliged to declare, that just at the present moment he did not find his aunt so clear as usual.

"You have but one line of conduct left you, Frank: your position, as heir to Greshamsbury, is a good one; but your father has unfortunately so hampered you with regard to money, that unless you set the matter right yourself, you can never enjoy that position. Of course you must marry money."

"Marry money!" said he, considering for the first time that in all probability Mary Thorne's fortune would not be extensive. "Marry money!"

"Yes, Frank. I know no man whose position so imperatively demands it; and luckily for you, no man can have more facility for doing so. In the first place you are very handsome."

Frank blushed like a girl of sixteen.

"And then, as the matter is made plain to you at so early an age, you are not of course hampered by any indiscreet tie; by any absurd engagement."

Frank blushed again; and then saying to himself, "How much the old girl knows about it!" felt a little proud of his passion for Mary Thorne, and of the declaration he had made to her.

"And your connexion with Courcy Castle," continued the countess, now carrying up the list of Frank's advantages to its great climax, "will make the matter so easy for you, that really, you will hardly have any difficulty."

Frank could not but say how much obliged he felt to Courcy Castle and its inmates.

"Of course I would not wish to interfere with you in any underhand way, Frank; but I will tell you what has occurred to me. You have heard, probably, of Miss Dunstable?"

"The daughter of the ointment of Lebanon man?"

"And of course you know that her fortune is immense," continued the countess, not deigning to notice her nephew's allusion to the ointment. "Quite immense when compared with the wants and position of any commoner. Now she is coming to Courcy Castle, and I wish you to come and meet her."

"But, aunt, just at this moment I have to read for my degree like anything. I go up, you know, in October."

"Degree!" said the countess. "Why, Frank, I am talking to you of your prospects in life, of your future position, of that on which everything hangs, and you tell me of your degree!"

Frank, however, obstinately persisted that he must take his degree, and that he should commence reading hard at six A.M. to-morrow morning.

"You can read just as well at Courcy Castle. Miss Dunstable will not interfere with that," said his aunt, who knew the expediency of yielding occasionally; "but I must beg you will come over and meet her. You will find her a most charming young woman, remarkably well educated I am told, and—"

"How old is she?" asked Frank.

"I really cannot say exactly," said the countess; "but it is not, I imagine, matter of much moment."

"Is she thirty?" asked Frank, who looked upon an unmarried woman of that age as quite an old maid.

"I dare say she may be about that age," said the countess, who regarded the subject from a very different point of view.

"Thirty!" said Frank out loud, but speaking, nevertheless, as though to himself.

"It is a matter of no moment," said his aunt, almost angrily. "When the subject itself is of such vital importance, objections of no real weight should not be brought into view. If you wish to hold up your head in the country; if you wish to represent your county in Parliament, as has been done by your father, your grandfather, and your great-grandfathers; if you wish to keep a house over your head, and to leave Greshamsbury to your son after you, you must marry money. What does it signify whether Miss Dunstable be twenty-eight or thirty? She has got money; and if you marry her, you may then consider that your position in life is made."

Frank was astonished at his aunt's eloquence; but, in spite of that eloquence, he made up his mind that he would not marry Miss Dunstable. How could he, indeed, seeing that his troth was already plighted to Mary Thorne in the presence of his sister? This circumstance, however, he did not choose to plead to his aunt, so he recapitulated any other objections that presented themselves to his mind.

In the first place, he was so anxious about his degree that he could not think of marrying at present; then he suggested that it might be better to postpone the question till the season's hunting should be over; he declared that he could not visit Courcy Castle till he got a new suit of clothes home from the tailor; and ultimately remembered that he had a particular engagement to go fly-fishing with Mr Oriel on that day week.

None, however, of these valid reasons were sufficiently potent to turn the countess from her point.

"Nonsense, Frank," said she, "I wonder that you can talk of fly-fishing when the property of Greshamsbury is at stake. You will go with Augusta and myself to Courcy Castle to-morrow."

"To-morrow, aunt!" he said, in the tone in which a condemned criminal might make his ejaculation on hearing that a very near day had been named for his execution. "To-morrow!"

"Yes, we return to-morrow, and shall be happy to have your company. My friends, including Miss Dunstable, come on Thursday. I am quite sure you will like Miss Dunstable. I have settled all that with your mother, so we need say nothing further about it. And now, good-night, Frank."

Frank, finding that there was nothing more to be said, took his departure, and went out to look for Mary. But Mary had gone home with Janet half an hour since, so he betook himself to his sister Beatrice.

"Beatrice," said he, "I am to go to Courcy Castle to-morrow."

"So I heard mamma say."

"Well; I only came of age to-day, and I will not begin by running counter to them. But I tell you what, I won't stay above a week at Courcy Castle for all the de Courcys in Barsetshire. Tell me, Beatrice, did you ever hear of a Miss Dunstable?"

CHAPTER IX

SIR ROGER SCATCHERD

Enough has been said in this narrative to explain to the reader that Roger Scatcherd, who was whilom a drunken stone-mason in Barchester, and who had been so prompt to avenge the injury done to his sister, had become a great man in the world. He had become a contractor, first for little things, such as half a mile or so of a railway embankment, or three or four canal bridges, and then a contractor for great things, such as Government hospitals, locks, docks, and quays, and had latterly had in his hands the making of whole lines of railway.

He had been occasionally in partnership with one man for one thing, and then with another for another; but had, on the whole, kept his interests to himself, and now at the time of our story, he was a very rich man.

And he had acquired more than wealth. There had been a time when the Government wanted the immediate performance of some extraordinary piece of work, and Roger Scatcherd had been the man to do it. There had been some extremely necessary bit of a railway to be made in half the time that such work would properly demand, some speculation to be incurred requiring great means and courage as well, and Roger Scatcherd had been found to be the man for the time. He was then elevated for the moment to the dizzy pinnacle of a newspaper hero, and became one of those "whom the king delighteth to honour." He went up one day to kiss Her Majesty's hand, and come down to his new grand house at Boxall Hill, Sir Roger Scatcherd, Bart.

"And now, my lady," said he, when he explained to his wife the high state to which she had been called by his exertions and the Queen's prerogative, "let's have a bit of dinner, and a drop of som'at hot." Now the drop of som'at hot signified a dose of alcohol sufficient to send three ordinary men very drunk to bed.

While conquering the world Roger Scatcherd had not conquered his old bad habits. Indeed, he was the same man at all points that he had been when formerly seen about the streets of Barchester with his stone-mason's apron tucked up round his waist. The apron he had abandoned, but not the heavy prominent thoughtful brow, with the wildly flashing eye beneath it. He was still the same good companion, and still also the same hard-working hero. In this only had he changed, that now he would work, and some said equally well, whether he were drunk or sober. Those who were mostly inclined to make a miracle of him—and there was a school of worshippers ready to adore him as their idea of a divine, superhuman, miracle-moving, inspired prophet—declared that his wondrous work was best done, his calculations most quickly and most truly made, that he saw with most accurate eye into the far-distant balance of profit and loss, when he was under the influence of the rosy god. To these worshippers his breakings-out, as his periods of intemperance were called in his own set, were his moments of peculiar inspiration—his divine frenzies, in which he communicated most closely with those deities who preside over trade transactions; his Eleusinian mysteries, to approach him in which was permitted only to a few of the most favoured.

"Scatcherd has been drunk this week past," they would say one to another, when the moment came at which it was to be decided whose offer should be accepted for constructing a harbour to hold all the commerce of Lancashire, or to make a railway from Bombay to Canton. "Scatcherd has been drunk this week past; I am told that he has taken over three gallons of brandy." And then they felt sure that none but Scatcherd would be called upon to construct the dock or make the railway.

But be this as it may, be it true or false that Sir Roger was most efficacious when in his cups, there can be no doubt that he could not wallow for a week in brandy, six or seven times every year, without in a great measure injuring, and permanently injuring, the outward man. Whatever immediate effect such symposiums might have on the inner mind—symposiums indeed they were not; posiums I will call them, if I may be allowed; for in latter life, when he drank heavily, he drank alone—however little for evil, or however much for good the working of his brain might be affected, his body suffered greatly. It was not that he became feeble or emaciated, old-looking or inactive, that his hand shook, or that his eye was watery; but that in the moments of his intemperance his life was often not worth a day's purchase. The frame which God had given to him was powerful beyond the power of ordinary men; powerful to act in spite of these violent perturbations; powerful to repress and conquer the qualms and headaches and inward sicknesses to which the votaries of Bacchus are ordinarily subject; but this power was not without its limit. If encroached on too far, it would break and fall and come asunder, and then the strong man would at once become a corpse.

Scatcherd had but one friend in the world. And, indeed, this friend was no friend in the ordinary acceptance of the word. He neither ate with him nor drank with him, nor even frequently talked with him. Their pursuits in life were wide asunder. Their tastes were all different. The society in which each moved very seldom came together. Scatcherd had nothing in unison with this solitary friend; but he trusted him, and he trusted no other living creature on God's earth.

He trusted this man; but even him he did not trust thoroughly; not at least as one friend should trust another. He believed that this man would not rob him; would probably not lie to him; would not endeavour to make money of him; would not count him up or speculate on him, and make out a balance of profit and loss; and, therefore, he determined to use him. But he put no trust whatever in his friend's counsel, in his modes of thought; none in his theory, and none in his practice. He disliked his friend's counsel, and, in fact, disliked his society, for his friend was somewhat apt to speak to him in a manner approaching to severity. Now Roger Scatcherd had done many things in the world, and made much money; whereas his friend had done but few things, and made no money. It was not to be endured that the practical, efficient man should be taken to task by the man who proved himself to be neither practical nor efficient; not to be endured, certainly, by Roger Scatcherd, who looked on men of his own class as the men of the day, and on himself as by no means the least among them.

The friend was our friend Dr Thorne.

The doctor's first acquaintance with Scatcherd has been already explained. He was necessarily thrown into communication with the man at the time of the trial, and Scatcherd then had not only sufficient sense, but sufficient feeling also to know that the doctor behaved very well. This communication had in different ways been kept up between them. Soon after the trial Scatcherd had begun to rise, and his first savings had been entrusted to the doctor's care. This had been the beginning of a pecuniary connexion which had never wholly ceased, and which had led to the purchase of Boxall Hill, and to the loan of large sums of money to the squire.

In another way also there had been a close alliance between them, and one not always of a very pleasant description. The doctor was, and long had been, Sir Roger's medical attendant, and, in his unceasing attempts to rescue the drunkard from the fate which was so much to be dreaded, he not unfrequently was driven into a quarrel with his patient.

One thing further must be told of Sir Roger. In politics he was as violent a Radical as ever, and was very anxious to obtain a position in which he could bring his violence to bear. With this view he was about to contest his native borough of Barchester, in the hope of being returned in opposition to the de Courcy candidate; and with this object he had now come down to Boxall Hill.

Nor were his claims to sit for Barchester such as could be despised. If money were to be of avail, he had plenty of it, and was prepared to spend it; whereas, rumour said that Mr Moffat was equally determined to do nothing so foolish. Then again, Sir Roger had a sort of rough eloquence, and was able to address the men of Barchester in language that would come home to their hearts, in words that would endear him to one party while they made him offensively odious to the other; but Mr Moffat could make neither friends nor enemies by his eloquence. The Barchester roughs called him a dumb dog that could not bark, and sometimes sarcastically added that neither could he bite. The de Courcy interest, however, was at his back, and he had also the advantage of possession. Sir Roger, therefore, knew that the battle was not to be won without a struggle.

Dr Thorne got safely back from Silverbridge that evening, and found Mary waiting to give him his tea. He had been called there to a consultation with Dr Century, that amiable old gentleman having so far fallen away from the high Fillgrave tenets as to consent to the occasional endurance of such degradation.

The next morning he breakfasted early, and, having mounted his strong iron-grey cob, started for Boxall Hill. Not only had he there to negotiate the squire's further loan, but also to exercise his medical skill. Sir Roger having been declared contractor for cutting a canal from sea to sea, through the Isthmus of Panama, had been making a week of it; and the result was that Lady Scatcherd had written rather peremptorily to her husband's medical friend.

The doctor consequently trotted off to Boxall Hill on his iron-grey cob. Among his other merits was that of being a good horseman, and he did much of his work on horseback. The fact that he occasionally took a day with the East Barsetshires, and that when he did so he thoroughly enjoyed it, had probably not failed to add something to the strength of the squire's friendship.

"Well, my lady, how is he? Not much the matter, I hope?" said the doctor, as he shook hands with the titled mistress of Boxall Hill in a small breakfast-parlour in the rear of the house. The show-rooms of Boxall Hill were furnished most magnificently, but they were set apart for company; and as the company never came—seeing that they were never invited—the grand rooms and the grand furniture were not of much material use to Lady Scatcherd.

"Indeed then, doctor, he's just bad enough," said her ladyship, not in a very happy tone of voice; "just bad enough. There's been some'at at the back of his head, rapping, and rapping, and rapping; and if you don't do something, I'm thinking it will rap him too hard yet."

"Is he in bed?"

"Why, yes, he is in bed; for when he was first took he couldn't very well help hisself, so we put him to bed. And then, he don't seem to be quite right yet about the legs, so he hasn't got up; but he's got that Winterbones with him to write for him, and when Winterbones is there, Scatcherd might as well be up for any good that bed'll do him."

Mr Winterbones was confidential clerk to Sir Roger. That is to say, he was a writing-machine of which Sir Roger made use to do certain work which could not well be adjusted without some contrivance. He was a little, withered, dissipated, broken-down man, whom gin and poverty had nearly burnt to a cinder, and dried to an ash. Mind he had none left, nor care for earthly things, except the smallest modicum of substantial food, and the largest allowance of liquid sustenance. All that he had ever known he had forgotten, except how to count up figures and to write: the results of his counting and his writing never stayed with him from one hour to another; nay, not from one folio to another. Let him, however, be adequately screwed up with gin, and adequately screwed down by the presence of his master, and then no amount of counting and writing would be too much for him. This was Mr Winterbones, confidential clerk to the great Sir Roger Scatcherd.

"We must send Winterbones away, I take it," said the doctor.

"Indeed, doctor, I wish you would. I wish you'd send him to Bath, or anywhere else out of the way. There is Scatcherd, he takes brandy; and there is Winterbones, he takes gin; and it'd puzzle a woman to say which is worst, master or man."

It will seem from this, that Lady Scatcherd and the doctor were on very familiar terms as regarded her little domestic inconveniences.

"Tell Sir Roger I am here, will you?" said the doctor.

"You'll take a drop of sherry before you go up?" said the lady.

"Not a drop, thank you," said the doctor.

"Or, perhaps, a little cordial?"

"Not of drop of anything, thank you; I never do, you know."

"Just a thimbleful of this?" said the lady, producing from some recess under a sideboard a bottle of brandy; "just a thimbleful? It's what he takes himself."

When Lady Scatcherd found that even this argument failed, she led the way to the great man's bedroom.

"Well, doctor! well, doctor! well, doctor!" was the greeting with which our son of Galen was saluted some time before he entered the sick-room. His approaching step was heard, and thus the ci-devant Barchester stone-mason saluted his coming friend. The voice was loud and powerful, but not clear and sonorous. What voice that is nurtured on brandy can ever be clear? It had about it a peculiar huskiness, a dissipated guttural tone, which Thorne immediately recognised, and recognised as being more marked, more guttural, and more husky than heretofore.

"So you've smelt me out, have you, and come for your fee? Ha! ha! ha! Well, I have had a sharpish bout of it, as her ladyship there no doubt has told you. Let her alone to make the worst of it. But, you see, you're too late, man. I've bilked the old gentleman again without troubling you."

"Anyway, I'm glad you're something better, Scatcherd."

"Something! I don't know what you call something. I never was better in my life. Ask Winterbones there."

"Indeed, now, Scatcherd, you ain't; you're bad enough if you only knew it. And as for Winterbones, he has no business here up in your bedroom, which stinks of gin so, it does. Don't you believe him, doctor; he ain't well, nor yet nigh well."

Winterbones, when the above ill-natured allusion was made to the aroma coming from his libations, might be seen to deposit surreptitiously beneath the little table at which he sat, the cup with which he had performed them.

The doctor, in the meantime, had taken Sir Roger's hand on the pretext of feeling his pulse, but was drawing quite as much information from the touch of the sick man's skin, and the look of the sick man's eye.

"I think Mr Winterbones had better go back to the London office," said he. "Lady Scatcherd will be your best clerk for some time, Sir Roger."

"Then I'll be d—— if Mr Winterbones does anything of the kind," said he; "so there's an end of that."

"Very well," said the doctor. "A man can die but once. It is my duty to suggest measures for putting off the ceremony as long as possible. Perhaps, however, you may wish to hasten it."

"Well, I am not very anxious about it, one way or the other," said Scatcherd. And as he spoke there came a fierce gleam from his eye, which seemed to say—"If that's the bugbear with which you wish to frighten me, you will find that you are mistaken."

"Now, doctor, don't let him talk that way, don't," said Lady Scatcherd, with her handkerchief to her eyes.

"Now, my lady, do you cut it; cut at once," said Sir Roger, turning hastily round to his better-half; and his better-half, knowing that the province of a woman is to obey, did cut it. But as she went she gave the doctor a pull by the coat's sleeve, so that thereby his healing faculties might be sharpened to the very utmost.

"The best woman in the world, doctor; the very best," said he, as the door closed behind the wife of his bosom.

"I'm sure of it," said the doctor.

"Yes, till you find a better one," said Scatcherd. "Ha! ha! ha! but good or bad, there are some things which a woman can't understand, and some things which she ought not to be let to understand."

"It's natural she should be anxious about your health, you know."

"I don't know that," said the contractor. "She'll be very well off. All that whining won't keep a man alive, at any rate."

There was a pause, during which the doctor continued his medical examination. To this the patient submitted with a bad grace; but still he did submit.

"We must turn over a new leaf, Sir Roger; indeed we must."

"Bother," said Sir Roger.

"Well, Scatcherd; I must do my duty to you, whether you like it or not."

"That is to say, I am to pay you for trying to frighten me."

"No human nature can stand such shocks as these much longer."

"Winterbones," said the contractor, turning to his clerk, "go down, go down, I say; but don't be out of the way. If you go to the public-house, by G——, you may stay there for me. When I take a drop,—that is if I ever do, it does not stand in the way of work." So Mr Winterbones, picking up his cup again, and concealing it in some way beneath his coat flap, retreated out of the room, and the two friends were alone.

"Scatcherd," said the doctor, "you have been as near your God, as any man ever was who afterwards ate and drank in this world."

"Have I, now?" said the railway hero, apparently somewhat startled.

"Indeed you have; indeed you have."

"And now I'm all right again?"

"All right! How can you be all right, when you know that your limbs refuse to carry you? All right! why the blood is still beating round your brain with a violence that would destroy any other brain but yours."

"Ha! ha! ha!" laughed Scatcherd. He was very proud of thinking himself to be differently organised from other men. "Ha! ha! ha! Well, and what am I to do now?"

The whole of the doctor's prescription we will not give at length. To some of his ordinances Sir Roger promised obedience; to others he objected violently, and to one or two he flatly refused to listen. The great stumbling-block was this, that total abstinence from business for two weeks was enjoined; and that it was impossible, so Sir Roger said, that he should abstain for two days.

"If you work," said the doctor, "in your present state, you will certainly have recourse to the stimulus of drink; and if you drink, most assuredly you will die."

"Stimulus! Why do you think I can't work without Dutch courage?"

"Scatcherd, I know that there is brandy in the room at this moment, and that you have been taking it within these two hours."

"You smell that fellow's gin," said Scatcherd.

"I feel the alcohol working within your veins," said the doctor, who still had his hand on his patient's arm.

Sir Roger turned himself roughly in the bed so as to get away from his Mentor, and then he began to threaten in his turn.

"I'll tell you what it is, doctor; I've made up my mind, and I'll do it. I'll send for Fillgrave."

"Very well," said he of Greshamsbury, "send for Fillgrave. Your case is one in which even he can hardly go wrong."

"You think you can hector me, and do as you like because you had me under your thumb in other days. You're a very good fellow, Thorne, but I ain't sure that you are the best doctor in all England."

"You may be sure I am not; you may take me for the worst if you will. But while I am here as your medical adviser, I can only tell you the truth to the best of my thinking. Now the truth is this, that another bout of drinking will in all probability kill you; and any recourse to stimulus in your present condition may do so."

"I'll send for Fillgrave—"

"Well, send for Fillgrave, only do it at once. Believe me at any rate in this, that whatever you do, you should do at once. Oblige me in this; let Lady Scatcherd take away that brandy bottle till Dr Fillgrave comes."

"I'm d—— if I do. Do you think I can't have a bottle of brandy in my room without swigging?"

"I think you'll be less likely to swig it if you can't get at it."

Sir Roger made another angry turn in his bed as well as his half-paralysed limbs would let him; and then, after a few moments' peace, renewed his threats with increased violence.

"Yes; I'll have Fillgrave over here. If a man be ill, really ill, he should have the best advice he can get. I'll have Fillgrave, and I'll have that other fellow from Silverbridge to meet him. What's his name?—Century."

The doctor turned his head away; for though the occasion was serious, he could not help smiling at the malicious vengeance with which his friend proposed to gratify himself.

"I will; and Rerechild too. What's the expense? I suppose five or six pound apiece will do it; eh, Thorne?"

"Oh, yes; that will be liberal I should say. But, Sir Roger, will you allow me to suggest what you ought to do? I don't know how far you may be joking—"

"Joking!" shouted the baronet; "you tell a man he's dying and joking in the same breath. You'll find I'm not joking."

"Well I dare say not. But if you have not full confidence in me—"

"I have no confidence in you at all."

"Then why not send to London? Expense is no object to you."

"It is an object; a great object."

"Nonsense! Send to London for Sir Omicron Pie: send for some man whom you will really trust when you see him.

"There's not one of the lot I'd trust as soon as Fillgrave. I've known Fillgrave all my life, and I trust him. I'll send for Fillgrave and put my case in his hands. If any one can do anything for me, Fillgrave is the man."

"Then in God's name send for Fillgrave," said the doctor. "And now, good-bye, Scatcherd; and as you do send for him, give him a fair chance. Do not destroy yourself by more brandy before he comes."

"That's my affair, and his; not yours," said the patient.

"So be it; give me your hand, at any rate, before I go. I wish you well through it, and when you are well, I'll come and see you."

"Good-bye—good-bye; and look here, Thorne, you'll be talking to Lady Scatcherd downstairs I know; now, no nonsense. You understand me, eh? no nonsense, you know."

CHAPTER X

SIR ROGER'S WILL

Dr Thorne left the room and went downstairs, being fully aware that he could not leave the house without having some communication with Lady Scatcherd. He was not sooner within the passage than he heard the sick man's bell ring violently; and then the servant, passing him on the staircase, received orders to send a mounted messenger immediately to Barchester. Dr Fillgrave was to be summoned to come as quickly as possible to the sick man's room, and Mr Winterbones was to be sent up to write the note.

Sir Roger was quite right in supposing that there would be some words between the doctor and her ladyship. How, indeed, was the doctor to get out of the house without such, let him wish it ever so much? There were words; and these were protracted, while the doctor's cob was being ordered round, till very many were uttered which the contractor would probably have regarded as nonsense.

Lady Scatcherd was no fit associate for the wives of English baronets;—was no doubt by education and manners much better fitted to sit in their servants' halls; but not on that account was she a bad wife or a bad woman. She was painfully, fearfully, anxious for that husband of hers, whom she honoured and worshipped, as it behoved her to do, above all other men. She was fearfully anxious as to his life, and faithfully believed, that if any man could prolong it, it was that old and faithful friend whom she had known to be true to her lord since their early married troubles.

When, therefore, she found that he had been dismissed, and that a stranger was to be sent for in his place, her heart sank low within her.

"But, doctor," she said, with her apron up to her eyes, "you ain't going to leave him, are you?"

Dr Thorne did not find it easy to explain to her ladyship that medical etiquette would not permit him to remain in attendance on her husband after he had been dismissed and another physician called in his place.

"Etiquette!" said she, crying. "What's etiquette to do with it when a man is a-killing hisself with brandy?"

"Fillgrave will forbid that quite as strongly as I can do."

"Fillgrave!" said she. "Fiddlesticks! Fillgrave, indeed!"

Dr Thorne could almost have embraced her for the strong feeling of thorough confidence on the one side, and thorough distrust on the other, which she contrived to throw into those few words.

"I'll tell you what, doctor; I won't let the messenger go. I'll bear the brunt of it. He can't do much now he ain't up, you know. I'll stop the boy; we won't have no Fillgraves here."

This, however, was a step to which Dr Thorne would not assent. He endeavoured to explain to the anxious wife, that after what had passed he could not tender his medical services till they were again asked for.

"But you can slip in as a friend, you know; and then by degrees you can come round him, eh? can't you now, doctor? And as to the payment—"

All that Dr Thorne said on the subject may easily be imagined. And in this way, and in partaking of the lunch which was forced upon him, an hour had nearly passed between his leaving Sir Roger's bedroom and putting his foot in the stirrup. But no sooner had the cob begun to move on the gravel-sweep before the house, than one of the upper windows opened, and the doctor was summoned to another conference with the sick man.

"He says you are to come back, whether or no," said Mr Winterbones, screeching out of the window, and putting all his emphasis on the last words.

"Thorne! Thorne! Thorne!" shouted the sick man from his sick-bed, so loudly that the doctor heard him, seated as he was on horseback out before the house.

"You're to come back, whether or no," repeated Winterbones, with more emphasis, evidently conceiving that there was a strength of injunction in that "whether or no" which would be found quite invincible.

Whether actuated by these magic words, or by some internal process of thought, we will not say; but the doctor did slowly, and as though unwillingly, dismount again from his steed, and slowly retrace his steps into the house.

"It is no use," he said to himself, "for that messenger has already gone to Barchester."

"I have sent for Dr Fillgrave," were the first words which the contractor said to him when he again found himself by the bedside.

"Did you call me back to tell me that?" said Thorne, who now really felt angry at the impertinent petulance of the man before him: "you should consider, Scatcherd, that my time may be of value to others, if not to you."

"Now don't be angry, old fellow," said Scatcherd, turning to him, and looking at him with a countenance quite different from any that he had shown that day; a countenance in which there was a show of manhood,—some show also of affection. "You ain't angry now because I've sent for Fillgrave?"

"Not in the least," said the doctor very complacently. "Not in the least. Fillgrave will do as much good as I can do you."

"And that's none at all, I suppose; eh, Thorne?"

"That depends on yourself. He will do you good if you will tell him the truth, and will then be guided by him. Your wife, your servant, any one can be as good a doctor to you as either he or I; as good, that is, in the main point. But you have sent for Fillgrave now; and of course you must see him. I have much to do, and you must let me go."

Scatcherd, however, would not let him go, but held his hand fast. "Thorne," said he, "if you like it, I'll make them put Fillgrave under the pump directly he comes here. I will indeed, and pay all the damage myself."

This was another proposition to which the doctor could not consent; but he was utterly unable to refrain from laughing. There was an earnest look of entreaty about Sir Roger's face as he made the suggestion; and, joined to this, there was a gleam of comic satisfaction in his eye which seemed to promise, that if he received the least encouragement he would put his threat into execution. Now our doctor was not inclined to taking any steps towards subjecting his learned brother to pump discipline; but he could not but admit to himself that the idea was not a bad one.

"I'll have it done, I will, by heavens! if you'll only say the word," protested Sir Roger.

But the doctor did not say the word, and so the idea was passed off.

"You shouldn't be so testy with a man when he is ill," said Scatcherd, still holding the doctor's hand, of which he had again got possession; "specially not an old friend; and specially again when you're been a-blowing of him up."

It was not worth the doctor's while to aver that the testiness had all been on the other side, and that he had never lost his good-humour; so he merely smiled, and asked Sir Roger if he could do anything further for him.

"Indeed you can, doctor; and that's why I sent for you,—why I sent for you yesterday. Get out of the room, Winterbones," he then said, gruffly, as though he were dismissing from his chamber a dirty dog. Winterbones, not a whit offended, again hid his cup under his coat-tail and vanished.

"Sit down, Thorne, sit down," said the contractor, speaking quite in a different manner from any that he had yet assumed. "I know you're in a hurry, but you must give me half an hour. I may be dead before you can give me another; who knows?"

The doctor of course declared that he hoped to have many a half-hour's chat with him for many a year to come.

"Well, that's as may be. You must stop now, at any rate. You can make the cob pay for it, you know."

The doctor took a chair and sat down. Thus entreated to stop, he had hardly any alternative but to do so.

"It wasn't because I'm ill that I sent for you, or rather let her ladyship send for you. Lord bless you, Thorne; do you think I don't know what it is that makes me like this? When I see that poor wretch, Winterbones, killing himself with gin, do you think I don't know what's coming to myself as well as him?

"Why do you take it then? Why do you do it? Your life is not like his. Oh, Scatcherd! Scatcherd!" and the doctor prepared to pour out the flood of his eloquence in beseeching this singular man to abstain from his well-known poison.

"Is that all you know of human nature, doctor? Abstain. Can you abstain from breathing, and live like a fish does under water?"

"But Nature has not ordered you to drink, Scatcherd."

"Habit is second nature, man; and a stronger nature than the first. And why should I not drink? What else has the world given me for all that I have done for it? What other resource have I? What other gratification?"

"Oh, my God! Have you not unbounded wealth? Can you not do anything you wish? be anything you choose?"

"No," and the sick man shrieked with an energy that made him audible all through the house. "I can do nothing that I would choose to do; be nothing that I would wish to be! What can I do? What can I be? What gratification can I have except the brandy bottle? If I go among gentlemen, can I talk to them? If they have anything to say about a railway, they will ask me a question: if they speak to me beyond that, I must be dumb. If I go among my workmen, can they talk to me? No; I am their master, and a stern master. They bob their heads and shake in their shoes when they see me. Where are my friends? Here!" said he, and he dragged a bottle from under his very pillow. "Where are my amusements? Here!" and he brandished the bottle almost in the doctor's face. "Where is my one resource, my one gratification, my only comfort after all my toils. Here, doctor; here, here, here!" and, so saying, he replaced his treasure beneath his pillow.

There was something so horrifying in this, that Dr Thorne shrank back amazed, and was for a moment unable to speak.

"But, Scatcherd," he said at last; "surely you would not die for such a passion as that?"

"Die for it? Aye, would I. Live for it while I can live; and die for it when I can live no longer. Die for it! What is that for a man to do? Do not men die for a shilling a day? What is a man the worse for dying? What can I be the worse for dying? A man can die but once, you said just now. I'd die ten times for this."

"You are speaking now either in madness, or else in folly, to startle me."

"Folly enough, perhaps, and madness enough, also. Such a life as mine makes a man a fool, and makes him mad too. What have I about me that I should be afraid to die? I'm worth three hundred thousand pounds; and I'd give it all to be able to go to work to-morrow with a hod and mortar, and have a fellow clap his hand upon my shoulder, and say: 'Well, Roger, shall us have that 'ere other half-pint this morning?' I'll tell you what, Thorne, when a man has made three hundred thousand pounds, there's nothing left for him but to die. It's all he's good for then. When money's been made, the next thing is to spend it. Now the man who makes it has not the heart to do that."

The doctor, of course, in hearing all this, said something of a tendency to comfort and console the mind of his patient. Not that anything he could say would comfort or console the man; but that it was impossible to sit there and hear such fearful truths—for as regarded Scatcherd they were truths—without making some answer.

"This is as good as a play, isn't, doctor?" said the baronet. "You didn't know how I could come out like one of those actor fellows. Well, now, come; at last I'll tell you why I have sent for you. Before that last burst of mine I made my will."

"You had a will made before that."

"Yes, I had. That will is destroyed. I burnt it with my own hand, so that there should be no mistake about it. In that will I had named two executors, you and Jackson. I was then partner with Jackson in the York and Yeovil Grand Central. I thought a deal of Jackson then. He's not worth a shilling now."

"Well, I'm exactly in the same category."

"No, you're not. Jackson is nothing without money; but money'll never make you."

"No, nor I shan't make money," said the doctor.

"No, you never will. Nevertheless, there's my other will, there, under that desk there; and I've put you in as sole executor."

"You must alter that, Scatcherd; you must indeed; with three hundred thousand pounds to be disposed of, the trust is far too much for any one man: besides you must name a younger man; you and I are of the same age, and I may die the first."

"Now, doctor, doctor, no humbug; let's have no humbug from you. Remember this; if you're not true, you're nothing."

"Well, but, Scatcherd—"

"Well, but doctor, there's the will, it's already made. I don't want to consult you about that. You are named as executor, and if you have the heart to refuse to act when I'm dead, why, of course, you can do so."

The doctor was no lawyer, and hardly knew whether he had any means of extricating himself from this position in which his friend was determined to place him.

"You'll have to see that will carried out, Thorne. Now I'll tell you what I have done."

"You're not going to tell me how you have disposed of your property?"

"Not exactly; at least not all of it. One hundred thousand I've left in legacies, including, you know, what Lady Scatcherd will have."

"Have you not left the house to Lady Scatcherd?"

"No; what the devil would she do with a house like this? She doesn't know how to live in it now she has got it. I have provided for her; it matters not how. The house and the estate, and the remainder of my money, I have left to Louis Philippe."

"What! two hundred thousand pounds?" said the doctor.

"And why shouldn't I leave two hundred thousand pounds to my son, even to my eldest son if I had more than one? Does not Mr Gresham leave all his property to his heir? Why should not I make an eldest son as well as Lord de Courcy or the Duke of Omnium? I suppose a railway contractor ought not to be allowed an eldest son by Act of Parliament! Won't my son have a title to keep up? And that's more than the Greshams have among them."

The doctor explained away what he said as well as he could. He could not explain that what he had really meant was this, that Sir Roger Scatcherd's son was not a man fit to be trusted with the entire control of an enormous fortune.

Sir Roger Scatcherd had but one child; that child which had been born in the days of his early troubles, and had been dismissed from his mother's breast in order that the mother's milk might nourish the young heir of Greshamsbury. The boy had grown up, but had become strong neither in mind nor body. His father had determined to make a gentleman of him, and had sent to Eton and to Cambridge. But even this receipt, generally as it is recognised, will not make a gentleman. It is hard, indeed, to define what receipt will do so, though people do have in their own minds some certain undefined, but yet tolerably correct ideas on the subject. Be that as it may, two years at Eton, and three terms at Cambridge, did not make a gentleman of Louis Philippe Scatcherd.

Yes; he was christened Louis Philippe, after the King of the French. If one wishes to look out in the world for royal nomenclature, to find children who have been christened after kings and queens, or the uncles and aunts of kings and queens, the search should be made in the families of democrats. None have so servile a deference for the very nail-parings of royalty; none feel so wondering an awe at the exaltation of a crowned head; none are so anxious to secure themselves some shred or fragment that has been consecrated by the royal touch. It is the distance which they feel to exist between themselves and the throne which makes them covet the crumbs of majesty, the odds and ends and chance splinters of royalty.

There was nothing royal about Louis Philippe Scatcherd but his name. He had now come to man's estate, and his father, finding the Cambridge receipt to be inefficacious, had sent him abroad to travel with a tutor. The doctor had from time to time heard tidings of this youth; he knew that he had already shown symptoms of his father's vices, but no symptoms of his father's talents; he knew that he had begun life by being dissipated, without being generous; and that at the age of twenty-one he had already suffered from delirium tremens.

It was on this account that he had expressed disapprobation, rather than surprise, when he heard that his father intended to bequeath the bulk of his large fortune to the uncontrolled will of this unfortunate boy.

"I have toiled for my money hard, and I have a right to do as I like with it. What other satisfaction can it give me?"

The doctor assured him that he did not at all mean to dispute this.

"Louis Philippe will do well enough, you'll find," continued the baronet, understanding what was passing within his companion's breast. "Let a young fellow sow his wild oats while he is young, and he'll be steady enough when he grows old."

"But what if he never lives to get through the sowing?" thought the doctor to himself. "What if the wild-oats operation is carried on in so violent a manner as to leave no strength in the soil for the product of a more valuable crop?" It was of no use saying this, however, so he allowed Scatcherd to continue.

"If I'd had a free fling when I was a youngster, I shouldn't have been so fond of the brandy bottle now. But any way, my son shall be my heir. I've had the gumption to make the money, but I haven't the gumption to spend it. My son, however, shall be able to ruffle it with the best of them. I'll go bail he shall hold his head higher than ever young Gresham will be able to hold his. They are much of the same age, as well I have cause to remember;—and so has her ladyship there."

Now the fact was, that Sir Roger Scatcherd felt in his heart no special love for young Gresham; but with her ladyship it might almost be a question whether she did not love the youth whom she had nursed almost as well as that other one who was her own proper offspring.

"And will you not put any check on thoughtless expenditure? If you live ten or twenty years, as we hope you may, it will become unnecessary; but in making a will, a man should always remember he may go off suddenly."

"Especially if he goes to bed with a brandy bottle under his head; eh, doctor? But, mind, that's a medical secret, you know; not a word of that out of the bedroom."

Dr Thorne could but sigh. What could he say on such a subject to such a man as this?

"Yes, I have put a check on his expenditure. I will not let his daily bread depend on any man; I have therefore left him five hundred a year at his own disposal, from the day of my death. Let him make what ducks and drakes of that he can."

"Five hundred a year certainly is not much," said the doctor.

"No; nor do I want to keep him to that. Let him have whatever he wants if he sets about spending it properly. But the bulk of the property—this estate of Boxall Hill, and the Greshamsbury mortgage, and those other mortgages—I have tied up in this way: they shall be all his at twenty-five; and up to that age it shall be in your power to give him what he wants. If he shall die without children before he shall be twenty-five years of age, they are all to go to Mary's eldest child."

Now Mary was Sir Roger's sister, the mother, therefore, of Miss Thorne, and, consequently, the wife of the respectable ironmonger who went to America, and the mother of a family there.

"Mary's eldest child!" said the doctor, feeling that the perspiration had nearly broken out on his forehead, and that he could hardly control his feelings. "Mary's eldest child! Scatcherd, you should be more particular in your description, or you will leave your best legacy to the lawyers."

"I don't know, and never heard the name of one of them."

"But do you mean a boy or a girl?"

"They may be all girls for what I know, or all boys; besides, I don't care which it is. A girl would probably do best with it. Only you'd have to see that she married some decent fellow; you'd be her guardian."

"Pooh, nonsense," said the doctor. "Louis will be five-and-twenty in a year or two."

"In about four years."

"And for all that's come and gone yet, Scatcherd, you are not going to leave us yourself quite so soon as all that."

"Not if I can help it, doctor; but that's as may be."

"The chances are ten to one that such a clause in your will will never come to bear."

"Quite so, quite so. If I die, Louis Philippe won't; but I thought it right to put in something to prevent his squandering it all before he comes to his senses."

"Oh! quite right, quite right. I think I would have named a later age than twenty-five."

"So would not I. Louis Philippe will be all right by that time. That's my lookout. And now, doctor, you know my will; and if I die to-morrow, you will know what I want you to do for me."

"You have merely said the eldest child, Scatcherd?"

"That's all; give it here, and I'll read it to you."

"No, no; never mind. The eldest child! You should be more particular, Scatcherd; you should, indeed. Consider what an enormous interest may have to depend on those words."

"Why, what the devil could I say? I don't know their names; never even heard them. But the eldest is the eldest, all the world over. Perhaps I ought to say the youngest, seeing that I am only a railway contractor."

Scatcherd began to think that the doctor might now as well go away and leave him to the society of Winterbones and the brandy; but, much as our friend had before expressed himself in a hurry, he now seemed inclined to move very leisurely. He sat there by the bedside, resting his hands on his knees and gazing unconsciously at the counterpane. At last he gave a deep sigh, and then he said, "Scatcherd, you must be more particular in this. If I am to have anything to do with it, you must, indeed, be more explicit."

"Why, how the deuce can I be more explicit? Isn't her eldest living child plain enough, whether he be Jack, or she be Gill?"

"What did your lawyer say to this, Scatcherd?"

"Lawyer! You don't suppose I let my lawyer know what I was putting. No; I got the form and the paper, and all that from him, and had him here, in one room, while Winterbones and I did it in another. It's all right enough. Though Winterbones wrote it, he did it in such a way he did not know what he was writing."

The doctor sat a while longer, still looking at the counterpane, and then got up to depart. "I'll see you again soon," said he; "to-morrow, probably."

"To-morrow!" said Sir Roger, not at all understanding why Dr Thorne should talk of returning so soon. "To-morrow! why I ain't so bad as that, man, am I? If you come so often as that you'll ruin me."

"Oh, not as a medical man; not as that; but about this will, Scatcherd. I must think if over; I must, indeed."

"You need not give yourself the least trouble in the world about my will till I'm dead; not the least. And who knows—maybe, I may be settling your affairs yet; eh, doctor? looking after your niece when you're dead and gone, and getting a husband for her, eh? Ha! ha! ha!"

And then, without further speech, the doctor went his way.

CHAPTER XI

THE DOCTOR DRINKS HIS TEA

The doctor got on his cob and went his way, returning duly to Greshamsbury. But, in truth, as he went he hardly knew whither he was going, or what he was doing. Sir Roger had hinted that the cob would be compelled to make up for lost time by extra exertion on the road; but the cob had never been permitted to have his own way as to pace more satisfactorily than on the present occasion. The doctor, indeed, hardly knew that he was on horseback, so completely was he enveloped in the cloud of his own thoughts.

In the first place, that alternative which it had become him to put before the baronet as one unlikely to occur—that of the speedy death of both father and son—was one which he felt in his heart of hearts might very probably come to pass.

"The chances are ten to one that such a clause will never be brought to bear." This he had said partly to himself, so as to ease the thoughts which came crowding on his brain; partly, also, in pity for the patient and the father. But now that he thought the matter over, he felt that there were no such odds. Were not the odds the other way? Was it not almost probable that both these men might be gathered to their long account within the next four years? One, the elder, was a strong man, indeed; one who might yet live for years to come if he would but give himself fair play. But then, he himself protested, and protested with a truth too surely grounded, that fair play to himself was beyond his own power to give. The other, the younger, had everything against him. Not only was he a poor, puny creature, without physical strength, one of whose life a friend could never feel sure under any circumstances, but he also was already addicted to his father's vices; he also was already killing himself with alcohol.

And then, if these two men did die within the prescribed period, if this clause in Sir Roger's will were brought to bear, if it should become his, Dr Thorne's, duty to see that clause carried out, how would he be bound to act? That woman's eldest child was his own niece, his adopted bairn, his darling, the pride of his heart, the cynosure of his eye, his child also, his own Mary. Of all his duties on this earth, next to that one great duty to his God and conscience, was his duty to her. What, under these circumstances, did his duty to her require of him?

But then, that one great duty, that duty which she would be the first to expect from him; what did that demand of him? Had Scatcherd made his will without saying what its clauses were, it seemed to Thorne that Mary must have been the heiress, should that clause become necessarily operative. Whether she were so or not would at any rate be for lawyers to decide. But now the case was very different. This rich man had confided in him, and would it not be a breach of confidence, an act of absolute dishonesty—an act of dishonesty both to Scatcherd and to that far-distant American family, to that father, who, in former days, had behaved so nobly, and to that eldest child of his, would it not be gross dishonesty to them all if he allowed this man to leave a will by which his property might go to a person never intended to be his heir?

Long before he had arrived at Greshamsbury his mind on this point had been made up. Indeed, it had been made up while sitting there by Scatcherd's bedside. It had not been difficult to make up his mind to so much; but then, his way out of this dishonesty was not so easy for him to find. How should he set this matter right so as to inflict no injury on his niece, and no sorrow to himself—if that indeed could be avoided?

And then other thoughts crowded on his brain. He had always professed—professed at any rate to himself and to her—that of all the vile objects of a man's ambition, wealth, wealth merely for its own sake, was the vilest. They, in their joint school of inherent philosophy, had progressed to ideas which they might find it not easy to carry out, should they be called on by events to do so. And if this would have been difficult to either when acting on behalf of self alone, how much more difficult when one might have to act for the other! This difficulty had now come to the uncle. Should he, in this emergency, take upon himself to fling away the golden chance which might accrue to his niece if Scatcherd should be encouraged to make her partly his heir?

"He'd want her to go and live there—to live with him and his wife. All the money in the Bank of England would not pay her for such misery," said the doctor to himself, as he slowly rode into his own yard.

On one point, and one only, had he definitely made up his mind. On the following day he would go over again to Boxall Hill, and would tell Scatcherd the whole truth. Come what might, the truth must be the best. And so, with some gleam of comfort, he went into the house, and found his niece in the drawing-room with Patience Oriel.

"Mary and I have been quarrelling," said Patience. "She says the doctor is the greatest man in a village; and I say the parson is, of course."

"I only say that the doctor is the most looked after," said Mary. "There's another horrid message for you to go to Silverbridge, uncle. Why can't that Dr Century manage his own people?"

"She says," continued Miss Oriel, "that if a parson was away for a month, no one would miss him; but that a doctor is so precious that his very minutes are counted."

"I am sure uncle's are. They begrudge him his meals. Mr Oriel never gets called away to Silverbridge."

"No; we in the Church manage our parish arrangements better than you do. We don't let strange practitioners in among our flocks because the sheep may chance to fancy them. Our sheep have to put up with our spiritual doses whether they like them or not. In that respect we are much the best off. I advise you, Mary, to marry a clergyman, by all means."

"I will when you marry a doctor," said she.

"I am sure nothing on earth would give me greater pleasure," said Miss Oriel, getting up and curtseying very low to Dr Thorne; "but I am not quite prepared for the agitation of an offer this morning, so I'll run away."

And so she went; and the doctor, getting on his other horse, started again for Silverbridge, wearily enough. "She's happy now where she is," said he to himself, as he rode along. "They all treat her there as an equal at Greshamsbury. What though she be no cousin to the Thornes of Ullathorne. She has found her place there among them all, and keeps it on equal terms with the best of them. There is Miss Oriel; her family is high; she is rich, fashionable, a beauty, courted by every one; but yet she does not look down on Mary. They are equal friends together. But how would it be if she were taken to Boxall

Hill, even as a recognised niece of the rich man there? Would Patience Oriel and Beatrice Gresham go there after her? Could she be happy there as she is in my house here, poor though it be? It would kill her to pass a month with Lady Scatcherd and put up with that man's humours, to see his mode of life, to be dependent on him, to belong to him." And then the doctor, hurrying on to Silverbridge, again met Dr Century at the old lady's bed-side, and having made his endeavours to stave off the inexorable coming of the grim visitor, again returned to his own niece and his own drawing-room.

"You must be dead, uncle," said Mary, as she poured out his tea for him, and prepared the comforts of that most comfortable meal—tea, dinner, and supper, all in one. "I wish Silverbridge was fifty miles off."

"That would only make the journey worse; but I am not dead yet, and, what is more to the purpose, neither is my patient." And as he spoke he contrived to swallow a jorum of scalding tea, containing in measure somewhat near a pint. Mary, not a whit amazed at this feat, merely refilled the jorum without any observation; and the doctor went on stirring the mixture with his spoon, evidently oblivious that any ceremony had been performed by either of them since the first supply had been administered to him.

When the clatter of knives and forks was over, the doctor turned himself to the hearthrug, and putting one leg over the other, he began to nurse it as he looked with com-placency at his third cup of tea, which stood untasted beside him. The fragments of the solid banquet had been removed, but no sacrilegious hand had been laid on the teapot and the cream-jug.

"Mary," said he, "suppose you were to find out to-morrow morning that, by some ac-cident, you had become a great heiress, would you be able to suppress your exultation?"

"The first thing I'd do, would be to pronounce a positive edict that you should never go to Silverbridge again; at least without a day's notice."

"Well, and what next? what would you do next?"

"The next thing—the next thing would be to send to Paris for a French bonnet exactly like the one Patience Oriel had on. Did you see it?"

"Well I can't say I did; bonnets are invisible now; besides I never remark anybody's clothes, except yours."

"Oh! do look at Miss Oriel's bonnet the next time you see her. I cannot understand why it should be so, but I am sure of this—no English fingers could put together such a bonnet as that; and I am nearly sure that no French fingers could do it in England."

"But you don't care so much about bonnets, Mary!" This the doctor said as an asser-tion; but there was, nevertheless, somewhat of a question involved in it.

"Don't I, though?" said she. "I do care very much about bonnets; especially since I saw Patience this morning. I asked how much it cost—guess."

"Oh! I don't know—a pound?"

"A pound, uncle!"

"What! a great deal more? Ten pounds?"

"Oh, uncle."

"What! more than ten pounds? Then I don't think even Patience Oriel ought to give it."

"No, of course she would not; but, uncle, it really cost a hundred francs!"

"Oh! a hundred francs; that's four pounds, isn't it? Well, and how much did your last new bonnet cost?"

"Mine! oh, nothing—five and ninepence, perhaps; I trimmed it myself. If I were left a great fortune, I'd send to Paris to-morrow; no, I'd go myself to Paris to buy a bonnet, and I'd take you with me to choose it."

The doctor sat silent for a while meditating about this, during which he unconsciously absorbed the tea beside him; and Mary again replenished his cup.

"Come, Mary," said he at last, "I'm in a generous mood; and as I am rather more rich than usual, we'll send to Paris for a French bonnet. The going for it must wait a while longer I am afraid."

"You're joking."

"No, indeed. If you know the way to send—that I must confess would puzzle me; but if you'll manage the sending, I'll manage the paying; and you shall have a French bonnet."

"Uncle!" said she, looking up at him.

"Oh, I'm not joking; I owe you a present, and I'll give you that."

"And if you do, I'll tell you what I'll do with it. I'll cut it into fragments, and burn them before your face. Why, uncle, what do you take me for? You're not a bit nice to-night to make such an offer as that to me; not a bit, not a bit." And then she came over from her seat at the tea-tray and sat down on a foot-stool close at his knee. "Because I'd have a French bonnet if I had a large fortune, is that a reason why I should like one now? if you were to pay four pounds for a bonnet for me, it would scorch my head every time I put it on."

"I don't see that: four pounds would not ruin me. However, I don't think you'd look a bit better if you had it; and, certainly, I should not like to scorch these locks," and putting his hand upon her shoulders, he played with her hair.

"Patience has a pony-phaeton, and I'd have one if I were rich; and I'd have all my books bound as she does; and, perhaps, I'd give fifty guineas for a dressing-case."

"Fifty guineas!"

"Patience did not tell me; but so Beatrice says. Patience showed it to me once, and it is a darling. I think I'd have the dressing-case before the bonnet. But, uncle—"

"Well?"

"You don't suppose I want such things?"

"Not improperly. I am sure you do not."

"Not properly, or improperly; not much, or little. I covet many things; but nothing of that sort. You know, or should know, that I do not. Why did you talk of buying a French bonnet for me?"

Dr Thorne did not answer this question, but went on nursing his leg.

"After all," said he, "money is a fine thing."

"Very fine, when it is well come by," she answered; "that is, without detriment to the heart or soul."

"I should be a happier man if you were provided for as is Miss Oriel. Suppose, now, I could give you up to a rich man who would be able to insure you against all wants?"

"Insure me against all wants! Oh, that would be a man. That would be selling me, wouldn't it, uncle? Yes, selling me; and the price you would receive would be freedom from future apprehensions as regards me. It would be a cowardly sale for you to make; and then, as to me—me the victim. No, uncle; you must bear the misery of having to provide for me—bonnets and all. We are in the same boat, and you shan't turn me overboard."

"But if I were to die, what would you do then?"

"And if I were to die, what would you do? People must be bound together. They must depend on each other. Of course, misfortunes may come; but it is cowardly to be afraid of them beforehand. You and I are bound together, uncle; and though you say these things to tease me, I know you do not wish to get rid of me."

"Well, well; we shall win through, doubtless; if not in one way, then in another."

"Win through! Of course we shall; who doubts our winning? but, uncle—"

"But, Mary."

"Well?"

"You haven't got another cup of tea, have you?"

"Oh, uncle! you have had five."

"No, my dear! not five; only four—only four, I assure you; I have been very particular to count. I had one while I was—"

"Five uncle; indeed and indeed."

"Well, then, as I hate the prejudice which attaches luck to an odd number, I'll have a sixth to show that I am not superstitious."

While Mary was preparing the sixth jorum, there came a knock at the door. Those late summonses were hateful to Mary's ear, for they were usually the forerunners of a midnight ride through the dark lanes to some farmer's house. The doctor had been in the saddle all day, and, as Janet brought the note into the room, Mary stood up as though to defend her uncle from any further invasion on his rest.

"A note from the house, miss," said Janet: now "the house," in Greshamsbury parlance, always meant the squire's mansion.

"No one ill at the house, I hope," said the doctor, taking the note from Mary's hand. "Oh—ah—yes; it's from the squire—there's nobody ill: wait a minute, Janet, and I'll write a line. Mary, lend me your desk."

The squire, anxious as usual for money, had written to ask what success the doctor had had in negotiating the new loan with Sir Roger. The fact, however, was, that in his visit at Boxall Hill, the doctor had been altogether unable to bring on the carpet the matter of this loan. Subjects had crowded themselves in too quickly during that interview—those two interviews at Sir Roger's bedside; and he had been obliged to leave without even alluding to the question.

"I must at any rate go back now," said he to himself. So he wrote to the squire, saying that he was to be at Boxall Hill again on the following day, and that he would call at the house on his return.

"That's settled, at any rate," said he.

"What's settled?" said Mary.

"Why, I must go to Boxall Hill again to-morrow. I must go early, too, so we'd better both be off to bed. Tell Janet I must breakfast at half-past seven."

"You couldn't take me, could you? I should so like to see that Sir Roger."

"To see Sir Roger! Why, he's ill in bed."

"That's an objection, certainly; but some day, when he's well, could not you take me over? I have the greatest desire to see a man like that; a man who began with nothing and now has more than enough to buy the whole parish of Greshamsbury."

"I don't think you'd like him at all."

"Why not? I am sure I should; I am sure I should like him, and Lady Scatcherd, too. I've heard you say that she is an excellent woman."

"Yes, in her way; and he, too, is good in his way; but they are neither of them in your way: they are extremely vulgar—"

"Oh! I don't mind that; that would make them more amusing; one doesn't go to those sort of people for polished manners."

"I don't think you'd find the Scatcherds pleasant acquaintances at all," said the doctor, taking his bed-candle, and kissing his niece's forehead as he left the room.

CHAPTER XII

WHEN GREEK MEETS GREEK, THEN COMES THE TUG OF WAR

The doctor, that is our doctor, had thought nothing more of the message which had been sent to that other doctor, Dr Fillgrave; nor in truth did the baronet. Lady Scatcherd had thought of it, but her husband during the rest of the day was not in a humour which allowed her to remind him that he would soon have a new physician on his hands; so she left the difficulty to arrange itself, waiting in some little trepidation till Dr Fillgrave should show himself.

It was well that Sir Roger was not dying for want of his assistance, for when the message reached Barchester, Dr Fillgrave was some five or six miles out of town, at Plumstead; and as he did not get back till late in the evening, he felt himself necessitated to put off his visit to Boxall Hill till next morning. Had he chanced to have been made acquainted with that little conversation about the pump, he would probably have postponed it even yet a while longer.

He was, however, by no means sorry to be summoned to the bedside of Sir Roger Scatcherd. It was well known at Barchester, and very well known to Dr Fillgrave, that Sir Roger and Dr Thorne were old friends. It was very well known to him also, that Sir Roger, in all his bodily ailments, had hitherto been contented to entrust his safety to the skill of his old friend. Sir Roger was in his way a great man, and much talked of in Barchester, and rumour had already reached the ears of the Barchester Galen, that the great railway contractor was ill. When, therefore, he received a peremptory summons to go over to Boxall Hill, he could not but think that some pure light had broken in upon Sir Roger's darkness, and taught him at last where to look for true medical accomplishment.

And then, also, Sir Roger was the richest man in the county, and to county practitioners a new patient with large means is a godsend; how much greater a godsend when he be not only acquired, but taken also from some rival practitioner, need hardly be explained.

Dr Fillgrave, therefore, was somewhat elated when, after a very early breakfast, he stepped into the post-chaise which was to carry him to Boxall Hill. Dr Fillgrave's professional advancement had been sufficient to justify the establishment of a brougham, in which he paid his ordinary visits round Barchester; but this was a special occasion, requiring special speed, and about to produce no doubt a special guerdon, and therefore a pair of post-horses were put into request.

It was hardly yet nine when the post-boy somewhat loudly rang the bell at Sir Roger's door; and then Dr Fillgrave, for the first time, found himself in the new grand hall of Box-all Hill house.

"I'll tell my lady," said the servant, showing him into the grand dining-room; and there for some fifteen minutes or twenty minutes Dr Fillgrave walked up and down the length of the Turkey carpet all alone.

Dr Fillgrave was not a tall man, and was perhaps rather more inclined to corpulence than became his height. In his stocking-feet, according to the usually received style of measurement, he was five feet five; and he had a little round abdominal protuberance, which an inch and a half added to the heels of his boots hardly enabled him to carry off as well as he himself would have wished. Of this he was apparently conscious, and it gave to him an air of not being entirely at his ease. There was, however, a personal dignity in his demeanour, a propriety in his gait, and an air of authority in his gestures which should prohibit one from stigmatizing those efforts at altitude as a failure. No doubt he did achieve much; but, nevertheless, the effort would occasionally betray itself, and the story of the frog and the ox would irresistibly force itself into one's mind at those moments when it most behoved Dr Fillgrave to be magnificent.

But if the bulgy roundness of his person and the shortness of his legs in any way de-tracted from his personal importance, these trifling defects were, he was well aware, more than atoned for by the peculiar dignity of his countenance. If his legs were short, his face was not; if there was any undue preponderance below the waistcoat, all was in due sym-metry above the necktie. His hair was grey, not grizzled nor white, but properly grey; and stood up straight from off his temples on each side with an unbending determination of purpose. His whiskers, which were of an admirable shape, coming down and turning gracefully at the angle of his jaw, were grey also, but somewhat darker than his hair. His enemies in Barchester declared that their perfect shade was produced by a leaden comb. His eyes were not brilliant, but were very effective, and well under command. He was rather short-sighted, and a pair of eye-glasses was always on his nose, or in his hand. His nose was long, and well pronounced, and his chin, also, was sufficiently prominent; but the great feature of his face was his mouth. The amount of secret medical knowledge of which he could give assurance by the pressure of those lips was truly wonderful. By his lips, also, he could be most exquisitely courteous, or most sternly forbidding. And not only could he be either the one or the other; but he could at his will assume any shade of difference between the two, and produce any mixture of sentiment.

When Dr Fillgrave was first shown into Sir Roger's dining-room, he walked up and down the room for a while with easy, jaunty step, with his hands joined together behind his back, calculating the price of the furniture, and counting the heads which might be adequately entertained in a room of such noble proportions; but in seven or eight minutes an air of impatience might have been seen to suffuse his face. Why could he not be shown into the sick man's room? What necessity could there be for keeping him there, as though he were some apothecary with a box of leeches in his pocket? He then rang the bell, per-haps a little violently. "Does Sir Roger know that I am here?" he said to the servant. "I'll tell my lady," said the man, again vanishing.

For five minutes more he walked up and down, calculating no longer the value of the furniture, but rather that of his own importance. He was not wont to be kept waiting in this way; and though Sir Roger Scatcherd was at present a great and rich man, Dr Fillgrave had remembered him a very small and a very poor man. He now began to think of Sir Roger as the stone-mason, and to chafe somewhat more violently at being so kept by such a man.

When one is impatient, five minutes is as the duration of all time, and a quarter of an hour is eternity. At the end of twenty minutes the step of Dr Fillgrave up and down the room had become very quick, and he had just made up his mind that he would not stay there all day to the serious detriment, perhaps fatal injury, of his other expectant patients. His hand was again on the bell, and was about to be used with vigour, when the door opened and Lady Scatcherd entered.

The door opened and Lady Scatcherd entered; but she did so very slowly, as though she were afraid to come into her own dining-room. We must go back a little and see how she had been employed during those twenty minutes.

"Oh, laws!" Such had been her first exclamation on hearing that the doctor was in the dining-room. She was standing at the time with her housekeeper in a small room in which she kept her linen and jam, and in which, in company with the same housekeeper, she spent the happiest moments of her life.

"Oh laws! now, Hannah, what shall we do?"

"Send 'un up at once to master, my lady! let John take 'un up."

"There'll be such a row in the house, Hannah; I know there will."

"But surely didn't he send for 'un? Let the master have the row himself, then; that's what I'd do, my lady," added Hannah, seeing that her ladyship still stood trembling in doubt, biting her thumb-nail.

"You couldn't go up to the master yourself, could you now, Hannah?" said Lady Scatcherd in her most persuasive tone.

"Why no," said Hannah, after a little deliberation; "no, I'm afeard I couldn't."

"Then I must just face it myself." And up went the wife to tell her lord that the physician for whom he had sent had come to attend his bidding.

In the interview which then took place the baronet had not indeed been violent, but he had been very determined. Nothing on earth, he said, should induce him to see Dr Fillgrave and offend his dear old friend Dr Thorne.

"But Roger," said her ladyship, half crying, or rather pretending to cry in her vexation, "what shall I do with the man? How shall I get him out of the house?"

"Put him under the pump," said the baronet; and he laughed his peculiar low guttural laugh, which told so plainly of the havoc which brandy had made in his throat.

"That's nonsense, Roger; you know I can't put him under the pump. Now you are ill, and you'd better see him just for five minutes. I'll make it all right with Dr Thorne."

"I'll be d—— if I do, my lady." All the people about Boxall Hill called poor Lady Scatcherd "my lady" as if there was some excellent joke in it; and, so, indeed, there was.

"You know you needn't mind nothing he says, nor yet take nothing he sends: and I'll tell him not to come no more. Now do 'ee see him, Roger."

But there was no coaxing Roger over now, or indeed ever: he was a wilful, headstrong, masterful man; a tyrant always though never a cruel one; and accustomed to rule his wife and household as despotically as he did his gangs of workmen. Such men it is not easy to coax over.

"You go down and tell him I don't want him, and won't see him, and that's an end of it. If he chose to earn his money, why didn't he come yesterday when he was sent for? I'm well now, and don't want him; and what's more, I won't have him. Winterbones, lock the door."

So Winterbones, who during this interview had been at work at his little table, got up to lock the door, and Lady Scatcherd had no alternative but to pass through it before the last edict was obeyed.

Lady Scatcherd, with slow step, went downstairs and again sought counsel with Hannah, and the two, putting their heads together, agreed that the only cure for the present evil was to found in a good fee. So Lady Scatcherd, with a five-pound note in her hand, and trembling in every limb, went forth to encounter the august presence of Dr Fillgrave.

As the door opened, Dr Fillgrave dropped the bell-rope which was in his hand, and bowed low to the lady. Those who knew the doctor well, would have known from his bow that he was not well pleased; it was as much as though he said, "Lady Scatcherd, I am your most obedient humble servant; at any rate it appears that it is your pleasure to treat me as such."

Lady Scatcherd did not understand all this; but she perceived at once that the man was angry.

"I hope Sir Roger does not find himself worse," said the doctor. "The morning is getting on; shall I step up and see him?"

"Hem! ha! oh! Why, you see, Dr Fillgrave, Sir Roger finds hisself vastly better this morning, vastly so."

"I'm very glad to hear it; but as the morning is getting on, shall I step up to see Sir Roger?"

"Why, Dr Fillgrave, sir, you see, he finds hisself so much hisself this morning, that he a'most thinks it would be a shame to trouble you."

"A shame to trouble me!" This was the sort of shame which Dr Fillgrave did not at all comprehend. "A shame to trouble me! Why Lady Scatcherd—"

Lady Scatcherd saw that she had nothing for it but to make the whole matter intelligible. Moreover, seeing that she appreciated more thoroughly the smallness of Dr Fillgrave's person than she did the peculiar greatness of his demeanour, she began to be a shade less afraid of him than she had thought she should have been.

"Yes, Dr Fillgrave; you see, when a man like he gets well, he can't abide the idea of doctors: now, yesterday, he was all for sending for you; but to-day he comes to hisself, and don't seem to want no doctor at all."

Then did Dr Fillgrave seem to grow out of his boots, so suddenly did he take upon himself sundry modes of expansive attitude;—to grow out of his boots and to swell upwards, till his angry eyes almost looked down on Lady Scatcherd, and each erect hair bristled up towards the heavens.

"This is very singular, very singular, Lady Scatcherd; very singular, indeed; very singular; quite unusual. I have come here from Barchester, at some considerable inconvenience, at some very considerable inconvenience, I may say, to my regular patients; and—and—and—I don't know that anything so very singular ever occurred to me before." And then Dr Fillgrave, with a compression of his lips which almost made the poor woman sink into the ground, moved towards the door.

Then Lady Scatcherd bethought her of her great panacea. "It isn't about the money, you know, doctor," said she; "of course Sir Roger don't expect you to come here with post-horses for nothing." In this, by the by, Lady Scatcherd did not stick quite close to veracity, for Sir Roger, had he known it, would by no means have assented to any payment; and the note which her ladyship held in her hand was taken from her own private purse. "It ain't at all about the money, doctor;" and then she tendered the bank-note, which she thought would immediately make all things smooth.

Now Dr Fillgrave dearly loved a five-pound fee. What physician is so unnatural as not to love it? He dearly loved a five-pound fee; but he loved his dignity better. He was angry also; and like all angry men, he loved his grievance. He felt that he had been badly treated; but if he took the money he would throw away his right to indulge in any such feeling. At that moment his outraged dignity and his cherished anger were worth more than a five-pound note. He looked at it with wishful but still averted eyes, and then sternly refused the tender.

"No, madam," said he; "no, no;" and with his right hand raised with his eye-glasses in it, he motioned away the tempting paper. "No; I should have been happy to have given Sir Roger the benefit of any medical skill I may have, seeing that I was specially called in—"

"But, doctor; if the man's well, you know—"

"Oh, of course; if he's well, and does not choose to see me, there's an end of it. Should he have any relapse, as my time is valuable, he will perhaps oblige me by sending else-where. Madam, good morning. I will, if you will allow me, ring for my carriage—that is, post-chaise."

"But, doctor, you'll take the money; you must take the money; indeed you'll take the money," said Lady Scatcherd, who had now become really unhappy at the idea that her husband's unpardonable whim had brought this man with post-horses all the way from Barchester, and that he was to be paid nothing for his time nor costs.

"No, madam, no. I could not think of it. Sir Roger, I have no doubt, will know better another time. It is not a question of money; not at all."

"But it is a question of money, doctor; and you really shall, you must." And poor Lady Scatcherd, in her anxiety to acquit herself at any rate of any pecuniary debt to the doctor, came to personal close quarters with him, with the view of forcing the note into his hands.

"Quite impossible, quite impossible," said the doctor, still cherishing his grievance, and valiantly rejecting the root of all evil. "I shall not do anything of the kind, Lady Scatcherd."

"Now doctor, do 'ee; to oblige me."

"Quite out of the question." And so, with his hands and hat behind his back, in token of his utter refusal to accept any pecuniary accommodation of his injury, he made his way backwards to the door, her ladyship perseveringly pressing him in front. So eager had been the attack on him, that he had not waited to give his order about the post-chaise, but made his way at once towards the hall.

"Now, do 'ee take it, do 'ee," pressed Lady Scatcherd.

"Utterly out of the question," said Dr Fillgrave, with great deliberation, as he backed his way into the hall. As he did so, of course he turned round,—and he found himself al-most in the arms of Dr Thorne.

As Burley must have glared at Bothwell when they rushed together in the dread en-counter on the mountain side; as Achilles may have glared at Hector when at last they met, each resolved to test in fatal conflict the prowess of the other, so did Dr Fillgrave glare at his foe from Greshamsbury, when, on turning round on his exalted heel, he found his nose on a level with the top button of Dr Thorne's waistcoat.

And here, if it be not too tedious, let us pause a while to recapitulate and add up the undoubted grievances of the Barchester practitioner. He had made no effort to ingratiate himself into the sheepfold of that other shepherd-dog; it was not by his seeking that he was now at Boxall Hill; much as he hated Dr Thorne, full sure as he felt of that man's utter ignorance, of his incapacity to administer properly even a black dose, of his murdering propensities and his low, mean, unprofessional style of practice; nevertheless, he had done nothing to undermine him with these Scatcherds. Dr Thorne might have sent every moth-er's son at Boxall Hill to his long account, and Dr Fillgrave would not have interfered;—would not have interfered unless specially and duly called upon to do so.

But he had been specially and duly called on. Before such a step was taken some words must undoubtedly have passed on the subject between Thorne and the Scatcherds. Thorne must have known what was to be done. Having been so called, Dr Fillgrave had come—had come all the way in a post-chaise—had been refused admittance to the sick man's room, on the plea that the sick man was no longer sick; and just as he was about to retire fee-less—for the want of the fee was not the less a grievance from the fact of its having been tendered and refused—fee-less, dishonoured, and in dudgeon, he encountered this other doctor—this very rival whom he had been sent to supplant; he encountered him in the very act of going to the sick man's room.

What mad fanatic Burley, what god-succoured insolent Achilles, ever had such cause to swell with wrath as at that moment had Dr Fillgrave? Had I the pen of Moliere, I could fitly tell of such medical anger, but with no other pen can it be fitly told. He did swell, and when the huge bulk of his wrath was added to his natural proportions, he loomed gigantic before the eyes of the surrounding followers of Sir Roger.

Dr Thorne stepped back three steps and took his hat from his head, having, in the passage from the hall-door to the dining-room, hitherto omitted to do so. It must be borne in mind that he had no conception whatever that Sir Roger had declined to see the physician for whom he had sent; none whatever that the physician was now about to return, fee-less, to Barchester.

Dr Thorne and Dr Fillgrave were doubtless well-known enemies. All the world of Barchester, and all that portion of the world of London which is concerned with the lancet and the scalping-knife, were well aware of this: they were continually writing against each other; continually speaking against each other; but yet they had never hitherto come to that positive personal collision which is held to justify a cut direct. They very rarely saw each other; and when they did meet, it was in some casual way in the streets of Barchester or elsewhere, and on such occasions their habit had been to bow with very cold propriety.

On the present occasion, Dr Thorne of course felt that Dr Fillgrave had the whip-hand of him; and, with a sort of manly feeling on such a point, he conceived it to be most compatible with his own dignity to show, under such circumstances, more than his usual courtesy—something, perhaps, amounting almost to cordiality. He had been supplanted, *quoad* doctor, in the house of this rich, eccentric, railway baronet, and he would show that he bore no malice on that account.

So he smiled blandly as he took off his hat, and in a civil speech he expressed a hope that Dr Fillgrave had not found his patient to be in any very unfavourable state.

Here was an aggravation to the already lacerated feelings of the injured man. He had been brought thither to be scoffed at and scorned at, that he might be a laughing-stock to his enemies, and food for mirth to the vile-minded. He swelled with noble anger till he would have burst, had it not been for the opportune padding of his frock-coat.

"Sir," said he; "sir:" and he could hardly get his lips open to give vent to the tumult of his heart. Perhaps he was not wrong; for it may be that his lips were more eloquent than would have been his words.

"What's the matter?" said Dr Thorne, opening his eyes wide, and addressing Lady Scatcherd over the head and across the hairs of the irritated man below him. "What on earth is the matter? Is anything wrong with Sir Roger?"

"Oh, laws, doctor!" said her ladyship. "Oh, laws; I'm sure it ain't my fault. Here's Dr Fillgrave in a taking, and I'm quite ready to pay him,—quite. If a man gets paid, what more can he want?" And she again held out the five-pound note over Dr Fillgrave's head.

What more, indeed, Lady Scatcherd, can any of us want, if only we could keep our tempers and feelings a little in abeyance? Dr Fillgrave, however, could not so keep his; and, therefore, he did want something more, though at the present moment he could have hardly said what.

Lady Scatcherd's courage was somewhat resuscitated by the presence of her ancient trusty ally; and, moreover, she began to conceive that the little man before her was unreasonable beyond all conscience in his anger, seeing that that for which he was ready to work had been offered to him without any work at all.

"Madam," said he, again turning round at Lady Scatcherd, "I was never before treated in such a way in any house in Barchester—never—never."

"Good heavens, Dr Fillgrave!" said he of Greshamsbury, "what is the matter?"

"I'll let you know what is the matter, sir," said he, turning round again as quickly as before. "I'll let you know what is the matter. I'll publish this, sir, to the medical world;" and as he shrieked out the words of the threat, he stood on tiptoes and brandished his eye-glasses up almost into his enemy's face.

"Don't be angry with Dr Thorne," said Lady Scatcherd. "Any ways, you needn't be angry with him. If you must be angry with anybody—"

"I shall be angry with him, madam," ejaculated Dr Fillgrave, making another sudden demi-pirouette. "I am angry with him—or, rather, I despise him;" and completing the circle, Dr Fillgrave again brought himself round in full front of his foe.

Dr Thorne raised his eyebrows and looked inquiringly at Lady Scatcherd; but there was a quiet sarcastic motion round his mouth which by no means had the effect of throwing oil on the troubled waters.

"I'll publish the whole of this transaction to the medical world, Dr Thorne—the whole of it; and if that has not the effect of rescuing the people of Greshamsbury out of your hands, then—then—then, I don't know what will. Is my carriage—that is, post-chaise there?" and Dr Fillgrave, speaking very loudly, turned majestically to one of the servants.

"What have I done to you, Dr Fillgrave," said Dr Thorne, now absolutely laughing, "that you should determined to take my bread out of my mouth? I am not interfering with your patient. I have come here simply with reference to money matters appertaining to Sir Roger."

"Money matters! Very well—very well; money matters. That is your idea of medical practice! Very well—very well. Is my post-chaise at the door? I'll publish it all to the medical world—every word—every word of it, every word of it."

"Publish what, you unreasonable man?"

"Man! sir; whom do you call a man? I'll let you know whether I'm a man—post-chaise there!"

"Don't 'ee call him names now, doctor; don't 'ee, pray don't 'ee," said Lady Scatcherd.

By this time they had all got somewhere nearer the hall-door; but the Scatcherd retainers were too fond of the row to absent themselves willingly at Dr Fillgrave's bidding, and it did not appear that any one went in search of the post-chaise.

"Man! sir; I'll let you know what it is to speak to me in that style. I think, sir, you hardly know who I am."

"All that I know of you at present is, that you are my friend Sir Roger's physician, and I cannot conceive what has occurred to make you so angry." And as he spoke, Dr Thorne looked carefully at him to see whether that pump-discipline had in truth been applied. There were no signs whatever that cold water had been thrown upon Dr Fillgrave.

"My post-chaise—is my post-chaise there? The medical world shall know all; you may be sure, sir, the medical world shall know it all;" and thus, ordering his post-chaise, and threatening Dr Thorne with the medical world, Dr Fillgrave made his way to the door.

But the moment he put on his hat he returned. "No, madam," said he. "No; it is quite out of the question: such an affair is not to be arranged by such means. I'll publish it all to the medical world—post-chaise there!" and then, using all his force, he flung as far as he could into the hall a light bit of paper. It fell at Dr Thorne's feet, who, raising it, found that it was a five-pound note.

"I put it into his hat just while he was in his tantrum," said Lady Scatcherd. "And I thought that perhaps he would not find it till he got to Barchester. Well I wish he'd been paid, certainly, although Sir Roger wouldn't see him;" and in this manner Dr Thorne got some glimpse of understanding into the cause of the great offence.

"I wonder whether Sir Roger will see *me*," said he, laughing.

CHAPTER XIII

THE TWO UNCLES

"Ha! ha! ha! Ha! ha! ha!" laughed Sir Roger, lustily, as Dr Thorne entered the room. "Well, if that ain't rich, I don't know what is. Ha! ha! ha! But why did they not put him under the pump, doctor?"

The doctor, however, had too much tact, and too many things of importance to say, to allow of his giving up much time to the discussion of Dr Fillgrave's wrath. He had come determined to open the baronet's eyes as to what would be the real effect of his will, and he had also to negotiate a loan for Mr Gresham, if that might be possible. Dr Thorne therefore began about the loan, that being the easier subject, and found that Sir Roger was quite clear-headed as to his money concerns, in spite of his illness. Sir Roger was willing enough to lend Mr Gresham more money—six, eight, ten, twenty thousand; but then, in doing so, he should insist on obtaining possession of the title-deeds.

"What! the title-deeds of Greshamsbury for a few thousand pounds?" said the doctor.

"I don't know whether you call ninety thousand pounds a few thousands; but the debt will about amount to that."

"Ah! that's the old debt."

"Old and new together, of course; every shilling I lend more weakens my security for what I have lent before."

"But you have the first claim, Sir Roger."

"It ought to be first and last to cover such a debt as that. If he wants further accommodation, he must part with his deeds, doctor."

The point was argued backwards and forwards for some time without avail, and the doctor then thought it well to introduce the other subject.

"Well, Sir Roger, you're a hard man."

"No I ain't," said Sir Roger; "not a bit hard; that is, not a bit too hard. Money is always hard. I know I found it hard to come by; and there is no reason why Squire Gresham should expect to find me so very soft."

"Very well; there is an end of that. I thought you would have done as much to oblige me, that is all."

"What! take bad security to oblige you?"

"Well, there's an end of that."

"I'll tell you what; I'll do as much to oblige a friend as any one. I'll lend you five thousand pounds, you yourself, without security at all, if you want it."

"But you know I don't want it; or, at any rate, shan't take it."

"But to ask me to go on lending money to a third party, and he over head and ears in debt, by way of obliging you, why, it's a little too much."

"Well, there's and end of it. Now I've something to say to you about that will of yours."

"Oh! that's settled."

"No, Scatcherd; it isn't settled. It must be a great deal more settled before we have done with it, as you'll find when you hear what I have to tell you."

"What you have to tell me!" said Sir Roger, sitting up in bed; "and what have you to tell me?"

"Your will says you sister's eldest child."

"Yes; but that's only in the event of Louis Philippe dying before he is twenty-five."

"Exactly; and now I know something about your sister's eldest child, and, therefore, I have come to tell you."

"You know something about Mary's eldest child?"

"I do, Scatcherd; it is a strange story, and maybe it will make you angry. I cannot help it if it does so. I should not tell you this if I could avoid it; but as I do tell you, for your sake, as you will see, and not for my own, I must implore you not to tell my secret to others."

Sir Roger now looked at him with an altered countenance. There was something in his voice of the authoritative tone of other days, something in the doctor's look which had on the baronet the same effect which in former days it had sometimes had on the stone-mason.

"Can you give me a promise, Scatcherd, that what I am about to tell you shall not be repeated?"

"A promise! Well, I don't know what it's about, you know. I don't like promises in the dark."

"Then I must leave it to your honour; for what I have to say must be said. You remember my brother, Scatcherd?"

Remember his brother! thought the rich man to himself. The name of the doctor's brother had not been alluded to between them since the days of that trial; but still it was impossible but that Scatcherd should well remember him.

"Yes, yes; certainly. I remember your brother," said he. "I remember him well; there's no doubt about that."

"Well, Scatcherd," and, as he spoke, the doctor laid his hand with kindness on the other's arm. "Mary's eldest child was my brother's child as well.

"But there is no such child living," said Sir Roger; and, in his violence, as he spoke he threw from off him the bedclothes, and tried to stand upon the floor. He found, however, that he had no strength for such an effort, and was obliged to remain leaning on the bed and resting on the doctor's arm.

"There was no such child ever lived," said he. "What do you mean by this?"

Dr Thorne would say nothing further till he had got the man into bed again. This he at last effected, and then he went on with the story in his own way.

"Yes, Scatcherd, that child is alive; and for fear that you should unintentionally make her your heir, I have thought it right to tell you this."

"A girl, is it?"

"Yes, a girl."

"And why should you want to spite her? If she is Mary's child, she is your brother's child also. If she is my niece, she must be your niece too. Why should you want to spite her? Why should you try to do her such a terrible injury?"

"I do not want to spite her."

"Where is she? Who is she? What is she called? Where does she live?"

The doctor did not at once answer all these questions. He had made up his mind that he would tell Sir Roger that this child was living, but he had not as yet resolved to make known all the circumstances of her history. He was not even yet quite aware whether it would be necessary to say that this foundling orphan was the cherished darling of his own house.

"Such a child, is, at any rate, living," said he; "of that I give you my assurance; and under your will, as now worded, it might come to pass that that child should be your heir. I do not want to spite her, but I should be wrong to let you make your will without such knowledge, seeing that I am possessed of it myself."

"But where is the girl?"

"I do not know that that signifies."

"Signifies! Yes; it does signify a great deal. But, Thorne, Thorne, now that I remember it, now that I can think of things, it was—was it not you yourself who told me that the baby did not live?"

"Very possibly."

"And was it a lie that you told me?"

"If so, yes. But it is no lie that I tell you now."

"I believed you then, Thorne; then, when I was a poor, broken-down day-labourer, lying in jail, rotting there; but I tell you fairly, I do not believe you now. You have some scheme in this."

"Whatever scheme I may have, you can frustrate by making another will. What can I gain by telling you this? I only do so to induce you to be more explicit in naming your heir."

They both remained silent for a while, during which the baronet poured out from his hidden resource a glass of brandy and swallowed it.

"When a man is taken aback suddenly by such tidings as these, he must take a drop of something, eh, doctor?"

Dr Thorne did not see the necessity; but the present, he felt, was no time for arguing the point.

"Come, Thorne, where is the girl? You must tell me that. She is my niece, and I have a right to know. She shall come here, and I will do something for her. By the Lord! I would as soon she had the money as any one else, if she is anything of a good 'un;—some of it, that is. Is she a good 'un?"

"Good!" said the doctor, turning away his face. "Yes; she is good enough."

"She must be grown up by now. None of your light skirts, eh?"

"She is a good girl," said the doctor somewhat loudly and sternly. He could hardly trust himself to say much on this point.

"Mary was a good girl, a very good girl, till"—and Sir Roger raised himself up in his bed with his fist clenched, as though he were again about to strike that fatal blow at the farm-yard gate. "But come, it's no good thinking of that; you behaved well and manly, always. And so poor Mary's child is alive; at least, you say so."

"I say so, and you may believe it. Why should I deceive you?"

"No, no; I don't see why. But then why did you deceive me before?"

To this the doctor chose to make no answer, and again there was silence for a while.

"What do you call her, doctor?"

"Her name is Mary."

"The prettiest women's name going; there's no name like it," said the contractor, with an unusual tenderness in his voice. "Mary—yes; but Mary what? What other name does she go by?"

Here the doctor hesitated.

"Mary Scatcherd—eh?"

"No. Not Mary Scatcherd."

"Not Mary Scatcherd! Mary what, then? You, with your d—— pride, wouldn't let her be called Mary Thorne, I know."

This was too much for the doctor. He felt that there were tears in his eyes, so he walked away to the window to dry them, unseen. Had he had fifty names, each more sacred than the other, the most sacred of them all would hardly have been good enough for her.

"Mary what, doctor? Come, if the girl is to belong to me, if I am to provide for her, I must know what to call her, and where to look for her."

"Who talked of your providing for her?" said the doctor, turning round at the rival uncle. "Who said that she was to belong to you? She will be no burden to you; you are only told of this that you may not leave your money to her without knowing it. She is provided for—that is, she wants nothing; she will do well enough; you need not trouble yourself about her."

"But if she's Mary's child, Mary's child in real truth, I will trouble myself about her. Who else should do so? For the matter of that, I'd as soon say her as any of those others in America. What do I care about blood? I shan't mind her being a bastard. That is to say, of course, if she's decently good. Did she ever get any kind of teaching; book-learning, or anything of that sort?"

Dr Thorne at this moment hated his friend the baronet with almost a deadly hatred; that he, rough brute as he was—for he was a rough brute—that he should speak in such language of the angel who gave to that home in Greshamsbury so many of the joys of Paradise—that he should speak of her as in some degree his own, that he should inquire doubtingly as to her attributes and her virtues. And then the doctor thought of her Italian and French readings, of her music, of her nice books, and sweet lady ways, of her happy companionship with Patience Oriel, and her dear, bosom friendship with Beatrice Gresham. He thought of her grace, and winning manners, and soft, polished feminine beauty; and, as he did so, he hated Sir Roger Scatcherd, and regarded him with loathing, as he might have regarded a wallowing hog.

At last a light seemed to break in upon Sir Roger's mind. Dr Thorne, he perceived, did not answer his last question. He perceived, also, that the doctor was affected with some more than ordinary emotion. Why should it be that this subject of Mary Scatcherd's child moved him so deeply? Sir Roger had never been at the doctor's house at Greshamsbury, had never seen Mary Thorne, but he had heard that there lived with the doctor some young female relative; and thus a glimmering light seemed to come in upon Sir Roger's bed.

He had twitted the doctor with his pride; had said that it was impossible that the girl should be called Mary Thorne. What if she were so called? What if she were now warming herself at the doctor's hearth?

"Well, come, Thorne, what is it you call her? Tell it out, man. And, look you, if it's your name she bears, I shall think more of you, a deal more than ever I did yet. Come, Thorne, I'm her uncle too. I have a right to know. She is Mary Thorne, isn't she?"

The doctor had not the hardihood nor the resolution to deny it. "Yes," said he, "that is her name; she lives with me."

"Yes, and lives with all those grand folks at Greshamsbury too. I have heard of that."

"She lives with me, and belongs to me, and is as my daughter."

"She shall come over here. Lady Scatcherd shall have her to stay with her. She shall come to us. And as for my will, I'll make another. I'll—"

"Yes, make another will—or else alter that one. But as to Miss Thorne coming here—"

"What! Mary—"

"Well, Mary. As to Mary Thorne coming here, that I fear will not be possible. She cannot have two homes. She has cast her lot with one of her uncles, and she must remain with him now."

"Do you mean to say that she must never have any relation but one?"

"But one such as I am. She would not be happy over here. She does not like new faces. You have enough depending on you; I have but her."

"Enough! why, I have only Louis Philippe. I could provide for a dozen girls."

"Well, well, well, we will not talk about that."

"Ah! but, Thorne, you have told me of this girl now, and I cannot but talk of her. If you wished to keep the matter dark, you should have said nothing about it. She is my niece as much as yours. And, Thorne, I loved my sister Mary quite as well as you loved your brother; quite as well."

Any one who might now have heard and seen the contractor would have hardly thought him to be the same man who, a few hours before, was urging that the Barchester physician should be put under the pump.

"You have your son, Scatcherd. I have no one but that girl."

"I don't want to take her from you. I don't want to take her; but surely there can be no harm in her coming here to see us? I can provide for her, Thorne, remember that. I can provide for her without reference to Louis Philippe. What are ten or fifteen thousand pounds to me? Remember that, Thorne."

Dr Thorne did remember it. In that interview he remembered many things, and much passed through his mind on which he felt himself compelled to resolve somewhat too suddenly. Would he be justified in rejecting, on behalf of Mary, the offer of pecuniary provision which this rich relative seemed so well inclined to make? Or, if he accepted it, would he in truth be studying her interests? Scatcherd was a self-willed, obstinate man—now indeed touched by unwonted tenderness; but he was one to whose lasting tenderness Dr Thorne would be very unwilling to trust his darling. He did resolve, that on the whole he should best discharge his duty, even to her, by keeping her to himself, and rejecting, on her behalf, any participation in the baronet's wealth. As Mary herself had said, "some people must be bound together;" and their destiny, that of himself and his niece, seemed to have so bound them. She had found her place at Greshamsbury, her place in the world; and it would be better for her now to keep it, than to go forth and seek another that would be richer, but at the same time less suited to her.

"No, Scatcherd," he said at last, "she cannot come here; she would not be happy here, and, to tell the truth, I do not wish her to know that she has other relatives."

"Ah! she would be ashamed of her mother, you mean, and of her mother's brother too, eh? She's too fine a lady, I suppose, to take me by the hand and give me a kiss, and call me her uncle? I and Lady Scatcherd would not be grand enough for her, eh?"

"You may say what you please, Scatcherd: I of course cannot stop you."

"But I don't know how you'll reconcile what you are doing to your conscience. What right can you have to throw away the girl's chance, now that she has a chance? What fortune can you give her?"

"I have done what little I could," said Thorne, proudly.

"Well, well, well, well, I never heard such a thing in my life; never. Mary's child, my own Mary's child, and I'm not to see her! But, Thorne, I tell you what; I will see her. I'll go over to her, I'll go to Greshamsbury, and tell her who I am, and what I can do for her. I tell you fairly I will. You shall not keep her away from those who belong to her, and can do her a good turn. Mary's daughter; another Mary Scatcherd! I almost wish she were called Mary Scatcherd. Is she like her, Thorne? Come tell me that; is she like her mother."

"I do not remember her mother; at least not in health."

"Not remember her! ah, well. She was the handsomest girl in Barchester, anyhow. That was given up to her. Well, I didn't think to be talking of her again. Thorne, you cannot but expect that I shall go over and see Mary's child?"

"Now, Scatcherd, look here," and the doctor, coming away from the window, where he had been standing, sat himself down by the bedside, "you must not come over to Greshamsbury."

"Oh! but I shall."

"Listen to me, Scatcherd. I do not want to praise myself in any way; but when that girl was an infant, six months old, she was like to be a thorough obstacle to her mother's fortune in life. Tomlinson was willing to marry your sister, but he would not marry the child too. Then I took the baby, and I promised her mother that I would be to her as a father. I have kept my word as fairly as I have been able. She has sat at my hearth, and drunk of my cup, and been to me as my own child. After that, I have a right to judge what is best for her. Her life is not like your life, and her ways are not as your ways—"

"Ah, that is just it; we are too vulgar for her."

"You may take it as you will," said the doctor, who was too much in earnest to be in the least afraid of offending his companion. "I have not said so; but I do say that you and she are unlike in your way of living."

"She wouldn't like an uncle with a brandy bottle under his head, eh?"

"You could not see her without letting her know what is the connexion between you; of that I wish to keep her in ignorance."

"I never knew any one yet who was ashamed of a rich connexion. How do you mean to get a husband for her, eh?"

"I have told you of her existence," continued the doctor, not appearing to notice what the baronet had last said, "because I found it necessary that you should know the fact of your sister having left this child behind her; you would otherwise have made a will different from that intended, and there might have been a lawsuit, and mischief and misery when we are gone. You must perceive that I have done this in honesty to you; and you yourself are too honest to repay me by taking advantage of this knowledge to make me unhappy."

"Oh, very well, doctor. At any rate, you are a brick, I will say that. But I'll think of all this, I'll think of it; but it does startle me to find that poor Mary has a child living so near to me."

"And now, Scatcherd, I will say good-bye. We part as friends, don't we?"

"Oh, but doctor, you ain't going to leave me so. What am I to do? What doses shall I take? How much brandy may I drink? May I have a grill for dinner? D—— me, doctor, you have turned Fillgrave out of the house. You mustn't go and desert me."

Dr Thorne laughed, and then, sitting himself down to write medically, gave such prescriptions and ordinances as he found to be necessary. They amounted but to this: that the man was to drink, if possible, no brandy; and if that were not possible, then as little as might be.

This having been done, the doctor again proceeded to take his leave; but when he got to the door he was called back. "Thorne! Thorne! About that money for Mr Gresham; do what you like, do just what you like. Ten thousand, is it? Well, he shall have it. I'll make Winterbones write about it at once. Five per cent., isn't it? No, four and a half. Well, he shall have ten thousand more."

"Thank you, Scatcherd, thank you, I am really very much obliged to you, I am indeed. I wouldn't ask it if I was not sure your money is safe. Good-bye, old fellow, and get rid of that bedfellow of yours," and again he was at the door.

"Thorne," said Sir Roger once more. "Thorne, just come back for a minute. You wouldn't let me send a present would you,—fifty pounds or so,—just to buy a few flounces?"

The doctor contrived to escape without giving a definite answer to this question; and then, having paid his compliments to Lady Scatcherd, remounted his cob and rode back to Greshamsbury.

CHAPTER XIV

SENTENCE OF EXILE

Dr Thorne did not at once go home to his own house. When he reached the Greshamsbury gates, he sent his horse to its own stable by one of the people at the lodge, and then walked on to the mansion. He had to see the squire on the subject of the forthcoming loan, and he had also to see Lady Arabella.

The Lady Arabella, though she was not personally attached to the doctor with quite so much warmth as some others of her family, still had reasons of her own for not dispensing with his visits to the house. She was one of his patients, and a patient fearful of the disease with which she was threatened. Though she thought the doctor to be arrogant, deficient as to properly submissive demeanour towards herself, an instigator to marital parsimony in her lord, one altogether opposed to herself and her interest in Greshamsbury politics, nevertheless, she did feel trust in him as a medical man. She had no wish to be rescued out of his hands by any Dr Fillgrave, as regarded that complaint of hers, much as she may have desired, and did desire, to sever him from all Greshamsbury councils in all matters not touching the healing art.

Now the complaint of which the Lady Arabella was afraid, was cancer: and her only present confidant in this matter was Dr Thorne.

The first of the Greshamsbury circle whom he saw was Beatrice, and he met her in the garden.

"Oh, doctor," said she, "where has Mary been this age? She has not been up here since Frank's birthday."

"Well, that was only three days ago. Why don't you go down and ferret her out in the village?"

"So I have done. I was there just now, and found her out. She was out with Patience Oriel. Patience is all and all with her now. Patience is all very well, but if they throw me over—"

"My dear Miss Gresham, Patience is and always was a virtue."

"A poor, beggarly, sneaking virtue after all, doctor. They should have come up, seeing how deserted I am here. There's absolutely nobody left."

"Has Lady de Courcy gone?"

"Oh, yes! All the de Courcys have gone. I think, between ourselves, Mary stays away because she does not love them too well. They have all gone, and taken Augusta and Frank with them."

"Has Frank gone to Courcy Castle?"

"Oh, yes; did you not hear? There was rather a fight about it. Master Frank wanted to get off, and was as hard to catch as an eel, and then the countess was offended; and papa said he didn't see why Frank was to go if he didn't like it. Papa is very anxious about his degree, you know."

The doctor understood it all as well as though it had been described to him at full length. The countess had claimed her prey, in order that she might carry him off to Miss Dunstable's golden embrace. The prey, not yet old enough and wise enough to connect the worship of Plutus with that of Venus, had made sundry futile feints and dodges in the vain hope of escape. Then the anxious mother had enforced the de Courcy behests with all a mother's authority. But the father, whose ideas on the subject of Miss Dunstable's wealth had probably not been consulted, had, as a matter of course, taken exactly the other side of the question. The doctor did not require to be told all this in order to know how the battle had raged. He had not yet heard of the great Dunstable scheme; but he was sufficiently acquainted with Greshamsbury tactics to understand that the war had been carried on somewhat after this fashion.

As a rule, when the squire took a point warmly to heart, he was wont to carry his way against the de Courcy interest. He could be obstinate enough when it so pleased him, and had before now gone so far as to tell his wife, that her thrice-noble sister-in-law might remain at home at Courcy Castle—or, at any rate, not come to Greshamsbury—if she could not do so without striving to rule him and every one else when she got here. This had of course been repeated to the countess, who had merely replied to it by a sisterly whisper, in which she sorrowfully intimated that some men were born brutes, and always would remain so.

"I think they all are," the Lady Arabella had replied; wishing, perhaps, to remind her sister-in-law that the breed of brutes was as rampant in West Barsetshire as in the eastern division of the county.

The squire, however, had not fought on this occasion with all his vigour. There had, of course, been some passages between him and his son, and it had been agreed that Frank should go for a fortnight to Courcy Castle.

"We mustn't quarrel with them, you know, if we can help it," said the father; "and, therefore, you must go sooner or later."

"Well, I suppose so; but you don't know how dull it is, governor."

"Don't I!" said Gresham.

"There's a Miss Dunstable to be there; did you ever hear of her, sir?"

"No, never."

"She's a girl whose father used to make ointment, or something of that sort."

"Oh, yes, to be sure; the ointment of Lebanon. He used to cover all the walls in London. I haven't heard of him this year past."

"No; that's because he's dead. Well, she carries on the ointment now, I believe; at any rate, she has got all the money. I wonder what she's like."

"You'd better go and see," said the father, who now began to have some inkling of an idea why the two ladies were so anxious to carry his son off to Courcy Castle at this exact time. And so Frank had packed up his best clothes, given a last fond look at the new black horse, repeated his last special injunctions to Peter, and had then made one of the stately *cortège* which proceeded through the county from Greshamsbury to Courcy Castle.

"I am very glad of that, very," said the squire, when he heard that the money was to be forthcoming. "I shall get it on easier terms from him than elsewhere; and it kills me to have continual bother about such things." And Mr Gresham, feeling that that difficulty was tided over for a time, and that the immediate pressure of little debts would be abated, stretched himself on his easy chair as though he were quite comfortable;—one may say almost elated.

How frequent it is that men on their road to ruin feel elation such as this! A man signs away a moiety of his substance; nay, that were nothing; but a moiety of the substance of his children; he puts his pen to the paper that ruins him and them; but in doing so he frees himself from a score of immediate little pestering, stinging troubles: and, therefore, feels as though fortune has been almost kind to him.

The doctor felt angry with himself for what he had done when he saw how easily the squire adapted himself to this new loan. "It will make Scatcherd's claim upon you very heavy," said he.

Mr Gresham at once read all that was passing through the doctor's mind. "Well, what else can I do?" said he. "You wouldn't have me allow my daughter to lose this match for the sake of a few thousand pounds? It will be well at any rate to have one of them settled. Look at that letter from Moffat."

The doctor took the letter and read it. It was a long, wordy, ill-written rigmarole, in which that amorous gentleman spoke with much rapture of his love and devotion for Miss Gresham; but at the same time declared, and most positively swore, that the adverse cruelty of his circumstances was such, that it would not allow him to stand up like a man at the hymeneal altar until six thousand pounds hard cash had been paid down at his banker's.

"It may be all right," said the squire; "but in my time gentlemen were not used to write such letters as that to each other."

The doctor shrugged his shoulders. He did not know how far he would be justified in saying much, even to his friend the squire, in dispraise of his future son-in-law.

"I told him that he should have the money; and one would have thought that that would have been enough for him. Well: I suppose Augusta likes him. I suppose she wishes the match; otherwise, I would give him such an answer to that letter as would startle him a little."

"What settlement is he to make?" said Thorne.

"Oh, that's satisfactory enough; couldn't be more so; a thousand a year and the house at Wimbledon for her; that's all very well. But such a lie, you know, Thorne. He's rolling in money, and yet he talks of this beggarly sum as though he couldn't possibly stir without it."

"If I might venture to speak my mind," said Thorne.

"Well?" said the squire, looking at him earnestly.

"I should be inclined to say that Mr Moffat wants to cry off, himself."

"Oh, impossible; quite impossible. In the first place, he was so very anxious for the match. In the next place, it is such a great thing for him. And then, he would never dare; you see, he is dependent on the de Courcys for his seat."

"But suppose he loses his seat?"

"But there is not much fear of that, I think. Scatcherd may be a very fine fellow, but I think they'll hardly return him at Barchester."

"I don't understand much about it," said Thorne; "but such things do happen."

"And you believe that this man absolutely wants to get off the match; absolutely thinks of playing such a trick as that on my daughter;—on me?"

"I don't say he intends to do it; but it looks to me as though he were making a door for himself, or trying to make a door: if so, your having the money will stop him there."

"But, Thorne, don't you think he loves the girl? If I thought not—"

The doctor stood silent for a moment, and then he said, "I am not a love-making man myself, but I think that if I were much in love with a young lady I should not write such a letter as that to her father."

"By heavens! If I thought so," said the squire—"but, Thorne, we can't judge of those fellows as one does of gentlemen; they are so used to making money, and seeing money made, that they have an eye to business in everything."

"Perhaps so, perhaps so," muttered the doctor, showing evidently that he still doubted the warmth of Mr Moffat's affection.

"The match was none of my making, and I cannot interfere now to break it off: it will give her a good position in the world; for, after all, money goes a great way, and it is something to be in Parliament. I can only hope she likes him. I do truly hope she likes him;" and the squire also showed by the tone of his voice that, though he might hope that his daughter was in love with her intended husband, he hardly conceived it to be possible that she should be so.

And what was the truth of the matter? Miss Gresham was no more in love with Mr Moffat than you are—oh, sweet, young, blooming beauty! Not a whit more; not, at least, in your sense of the word, nor in mine. She had by no means resolved within her heart that of all the men whom she had ever seen, or ever could see, he was far away the nicest and best. That is what you will do when you are in love, if you be good for anything. She had no longing to sit near to him—the nearer the better; she had no thought of his taste and his choice when she bought her ribbons and bonnets; she had no indescribable desire that all her female friends should be ever talking to her about him. When she wrote to him, she did not copy her letters again and again, so that she might be, as it were, ever speaking to him; she took no special pride in herself because he had chosen her to be his life's partner. In point of fact, she did not care one straw about him.

And yet she thought she loved him; was, indeed, quite confident that she did so; told her mother that she was sure Gustavus would wish this, she knew Gustavus would like that, and so on; but as for Gustavus himself, she did not care a chip for him.

She was in love with her match just as farmers are in love with wheat at eighty shillings a quarter; or shareholders—innocent gudgeons—with seven and half per cent. interest on their paid-up capital. Eighty shillings a quarter, and seven and half per cent. interest, such were the returns which she had been taught to look for in exchange for her young heart; and, having obtained them, or being thus about to obtain them, why should not her young heart be satisfied? Had she not sat herself down obediently at the feet of her lady Gamaliel, and should she not be rewarded? Yes, indeed, she shall be rewarded.

And then the doctor went to the lady. On their medical secrets we will not intrude; but there were other matters bearing on the course of our narrative, as to which Lady Arabella found it necessary to say a word or so to the doctor; and it is essential that we should know what was the tenor of those few words so spoken.

How the aspirations, and instincts, and feelings of a household become changed as the young birds begin to flutter with feathered wings, and have half-formed thoughts of leaving the parental nest! A few months back, Frank had reigned almost autocratic over the lesser subjects of the kingdom of Greshamsbury. The servants, for instance, always obeyed him, and his sisters never dreamed of telling anything which he directed should not be told. All his mischief, all his troubles, and all his loves were confided to them, with the sure conviction that they would never be made to stand in evidence against him.

Trusting to this well-ascertained state of things, he had not hesitated to declare his love for Miss Thorne before his sister Augusta. But his sister Augusta had now, as it were, been received into the upper house; having duly received, and duly profited by the lessons of her great instructress, she was now admitted to sit in conclave with the higher powers: her sympathies, of course, became changed, and her confidence was removed from the young and giddy and given to the ancient and discreet. She was as a schoolboy, who, having finished his schooling, and being fairly forced by necessity into the stern bread-earning world, undertakes the new duties of tutoring. Yesterday he was taught, and fought, of course, against the schoolmaster; to-day he teaches, and fights as keenly for him. So it was with Augusta Gresham, when, with careful brow, she whispered to her mother that there was something wrong between Frank and Mary Thorne.

"Stop it at once, Arabella: stop it at once," the countess had said; "that, indeed, will be ruin. If he does not marry money, he is lost. Good heavens! the doctor's niece! A girl that nobody knows where she comes from!"

"He's going with you to-morrow, you know," said the anxious mother.

"Yes; and that is so far well: if he will be led by me, the evil may be remedied before he returns; but it is very, very hard to lead young men. Arabella, you must forbid that girl to come to Greshamsbury again on any pretext whatever. The evil must be stopped at once."

"But she is here so much as a matter of course."

"Then she must be here as a matter of course no more: there has been folly, very great folly, in having her here. Of course she would turn out to be a designing creature with such temptation before her; with such a prize within her reach, how could she help it?"

"I must say, aunt, she answered him very properly," said Augusta.

"Nonsense," said the countess; "before you, of course she did. Arabella, the matter must not be left to the girl's propriety. I never knew the propriety of a girl of that sort to be fit to be depended upon yet. If you wish to save the whole family from ruin, you must take steps to keep her away from Greshamsbury now at once. Now is the time; now that Frank is to be away. Where so much, so very much depends on a young man's marrying money, not one day ought to be lost."

Instigated in this manner, Lady Arabella resolved to open her mind to the doctor, and to make it intelligible to him that, under present circumstances, Mary's visits at Greshamsbury had better be discontinued. She would have given much, however, to have escaped this business. She had in her time tried one or two falls with the doctor, and she was conscious that she had never yet got the better of him: and then she was in a slight degree afraid of Mary herself. She had a presentiment that it would not be so easy to banish Mary from Greshamsbury: she was not sure that that young lady would not boldly assert her right to her place in the school-room; appeal loudly to the squire, and perhaps, declare her determination of marrying the heir, out before them all. The squire would be sure to uphold her in that, or in anything else.

And then, too, there would be the greatest difficulty in wording her request to the doctor; and Lady Arabella was sufficiently conscious of her own weakness to know that she was not always very good at words. But the doctor, when hard pressed, was never at fault: he could say the bitterest things in the quietest tone, and Lady Arabella had a great dread of these bitter things. What, also, if he should desert her himself; withdraw from her his skill and knowledge of her bodily wants and ailments now that he was so necessary to her? She had once before taken that measure of sending to Barchester for Dr Fillgrave, but it had answered with her hardly better than with Sir Roger and Lady Scatcherd.

When, therefore, Lady Arabella found herself alone with the doctor, and called upon to say out her say in what best language she could select for the occasion, she did not feel to very much at her ease. There was that about the man before her which cowed her, in spite of her being the wife of the squire, the sister of an earl, a person quite acknowledged to be of the great world, and the mother of the very important young man whose affections were now about to be called in question. Nevertheless, there was the task to be done, and with a mother's courage she essayed it.

"Dr Thorne," said she, as soon as their medical conference was at an end, "I am very glad you came over to-day, for I had something special which I wanted to say to you:" so

far she got, and then stopped; but, as the doctor did not seem inclined to give her any assistance, she was forced to flounder on as best she could.

"Something very particular indeed. You know what a respect and esteem, and I may
say affection, we all have for you,"—here the doctor made a low bow—"and I may say for
Mary also;" here the doctor bowed himself again. "We have done what little we could to
be pleasant neighbours, and I think you'll believe me when I say that I am a true friend to
you and dear Mary—"

The doctor knew that something very unpleasant was coming, but he could not at all
guess what might be its nature. He felt, however, that he must say something; so he expressed a hope that he was duly sensible of all the acts of kindness he had ever received
from the squire and the family at large.

"I hope, therefore, my dear doctor, you won't take amiss what I am going to say."

"Well, Lady Arabella, I'll endeavour not to do so."

"I am sure I would not give any pain if I could help it, much less to you. But there are
occasions, doctor, in which duty must be paramount; paramount to all other considerations, you know, and, certainly, this occasion is one of them."

"But what is the occasion, Lady Arabella?"

"I'll tell you, doctor. You know what Frank's position is?"

"Frank's position! as regards what?"

"Why, his position in life; an only son, you know."

"Oh, yes; I know his position in that respect; an only son, and his father's heir; and a
very fine fellow, he is. You have but one son, Lady Arabella, and you may well be proud
of him."

Lady Arabella sighed. She did not wish at the present moment to express herself as being in any way proud of Frank. She was desirous rather, on the other hand, of showing
that she was a good deal ashamed of him; only not quite so much ashamed of him as it
behoved the doctor to be of his niece.

"Well, perhaps so; yes," said Lady Arabella, "he is, I believe, a very good young man,
with an excellent disposition; but, doctor, his position is very precarious; and he is just at
that time of life when every caution is necessary."

To the doctor's ears, Lady Arabella was now talking of her son as a mother might of
her infant when whooping-cough was abroad or croup imminent. "There is nothing on
earth the matter with him, I should say," said the doctor. "He has every possible sign of
perfect health."

"Oh yes; his health! Yes, thank God, his health is good; that is a great blessing." And
Lady Arabella thought of her four flowerets that had already faded. "I am sure I am most
thankful to see him growing up so strong. But it is not that I mean, doctor."

"Then what is it, Lady Arabella?"

"Why, doctor, you know the squire's position with regard to money matters?"

Now the doctor undoubtedly did know the squire's position with regard to money matters,—knew it much better than did Lady Arabella; but he was by no means inclined to
talk on that subject to her ladyship. He remained quite silent, therefore, although Lady
Arabella's last speech had taken the form of a question. Lady Arabella was a little offended at this want of freedom on his part, and become somewhat sterner in her tone—a
thought less condescending in her manner.

"The squire has unfortunately embarrassed the property, and Frank must look forward
to inherit it with very heavy encumbrances; I fear very heavy indeed, though of what exact
nature I am kept in ignorance."

Looking at the doctor's face, she perceived that there was no probability whatever that
her ignorance would be enlightened by him.

"And, therefore, it is highly necessary that Frank should be very careful."

"As to his private expenditure, you mean?" said the doctor.

"No; not exactly that: though of course he must be careful as to that, too; that's of course. But that is not what I mean, doctor; his only hope of retrieving his circumstances is by marrying money."

"With every other conjugal blessing that a man can have, I hope he may have that also." So the doctor replied with imperturbable face; but not the less did he begin to have a shade of suspicion of what might be the coming subject of the conference. It would be untrue to say that he had ever thought it probable that the young heir should fall in love with his niece; that he had ever looked forward to such a chance, either with complacency or with fear; nevertheless, the idea had of late passed through his mind. Some word had fallen from Mary, some closely watched expression of her eye, or some quiver in her lip when Frank's name was mentioned, had of late made him involuntarily think that such might not be impossible; and then, when the chance of Mary becoming the heiress to so large a fortune had been forced upon his consideration, he had been unable to prevent himself from building happy castles in the air, as he rode slowly home from Boxall Hill. But not a whit the more on that account was he prepared to be untrue to the squire's interest or to encourage a feeling which must be distasteful to all the squire's friends.

"Yes, doctor; he must marry money."

"And worth, Lady Arabella; and a pure feminine heart; and youth and beauty. I hope he will marry them all."

Could it be possible, that in speaking of a pure feminine heart, and youth and beauty, and such like gewgaws, the doctor was thinking of his niece? Could it be that he had absolutely made up his mind to foster and encourage this odious match?

The bare idea made Lady Arabella wrathful, and her wrath gave her courage. "He must marry money, or he will be a ruined man. Now, doctor, I am informed that things—words that is—have passed between him and Mary which never ought to have been allowed."

And now also the doctor was wrathful. "What things? what words?" said he, appearing to Lady Arabella as though he rose in his anger nearly a foot in altitude before her eyes. "What has passed between them? and who says so?"

"Doctor, there have been love-makings, you may take my word for it; love-makings of a very, very, very advanced description."

This, the doctor could not stand. No, not for Greshamsbury and its heir; not for the squire and all his misfortunes; not for Lady Arabella and the blood of all the de Courcys could he stand quiet and hear Mary thus accused. He sprang up another foot in height, and expanded equally in width as he flung back the insinuation.

"Who says so? Whoever says so, whoever speaks of Miss Thorne in such language, says what is not true. I will pledge my word—"

"My dear doctor, my dear doctor, what took place was quite clearly heard; there was no mistake about it, indeed."

"What took place? What was heard?"

"Well, then, I don't want, you know, to make more of it than can be helped. The thing must be stopped, that is all."

"What thing? Speak out, Lady Arabella. I will not have Mary's conduct impugned by innuendoes. What is it that eavesdroppers have heard?"

"Dr Thorne, there have been no eavesdroppers."

"And no talebearers either? Will you ladyship oblige me by letting me know what is the accusation which you bring against my niece?"

"There has been most positively an offer made, Dr Thorne."

"And who made it?"

"Oh, of course I am not going to say but what Frank must have been very imprudent. Of course he has been to blame. There has been fault on both sides, no doubt."

"I utterly deny it. I positively deny it. I know nothing of the circumstances; have heard nothing about it—"

"Then of course you can't say," said Lady Arabella.

"I know nothing of the circumstance; have heard nothing about it," continued Dr Thorne; "but I do know my niece, and am ready to assert that there has not been fault on both sides. Whether there has been any fault on any side, that I do not yet know."

"I can assure you, Dr Thorne, that an offer was made by Frank; such an offer cannot be without its allurements to a young lady circumstanced like your niece."

"Allurements!" almost shouted the doctor, and, as he did so, Lady Arabella stepped back a pace or two, retreating from the fire which shot out of his eyes. "But the truth is, Lady Arabella, you do not know my niece. If you will have the goodness to let me understand what it is that you desire I will tell you whether I can comply with your wishes."

"Of course it will be very inexpedient that the young people should be thrown together again;—for the present, I mean."

"Well!"

"Frank has now gone to Courcy Castle; and he talks of going from thence to Cambridge. But he will doubtless be here, backwards and forwards; and perhaps it will be better for all parties—safer, that is, doctor—if Miss Thorne were to discontinue her visits to Greshamsbury for a while."

"Very well!" thundered out the doctor. "Her visits to Greshamsbury shall be discontinued."

"Of course, doctor, this won't change the intercourse between us; between you and the family."

"Not change it!" said he. "Do you think that I will break bread in a house from whence she has been ignominiously banished? Do you think that I can sit down in friendship with those who have spoken of her as you have now spoken? You have many daughters; what would you say if I accused one of them as you have accused her?"

"Accused, doctor! No, I don't accuse her. But prudence, you know, does sometimes require us—"

"Very well; prudence requires you to look after those who belong to you; and prudence requires me to look after my one lamb. Good morning, Lady Arabella."

"But, doctor, you are not going to quarrel with us? You will come when we want you; eh! won't you?"

Quarrel! quarrel with Greshamsbury! Angry as he was, the doctor felt that he could ill bear to quarrel with Greshamsbury. A man past fifty cannot easily throw over the ties that have taken twenty years to form, and wrench himself away from the various close ligatures with which, in such a period, he has become bound. He could not quarrel with the squire; he could ill bear to quarrel with Frank; though he now began to conceive that Frank had used him badly, he could not do so; he could not quarrel with the children, who had almost been born into his arms; nor even with the very walls, and trees, and grassy knolls with which he was so dearly intimate. He could not proclaim himself an enemy to Greshamsbury; and yet he felt that fealty to Mary required of him that, for the present, he should put on an enemy's guise.

"If you want me, Lady Arabella, and send for me, I will come to you; otherwise I will, if you please, share the sentence which has been passed on Mary. I will now wish you good morning." And then bowing low to her, he left the room and the house, and sauntered slowly away to his own home.

What was he to say to Mary? He walked very slowly down the Greshamsbury avenue, with his hands clasped behind his back, thinking over the whole matter; thinking of it, or rather trying to think of it. When a man's heart is warmly concerned in any matter, it is almost useless for him to endeavour to think of it. Instead of thinking, he gives play to his feelings, and feeds his passion by indulging it. "Allurements!" he said to himself, repeating Lady Arabella's words. "A girl circumstanced like my niece! How utterly incapable is such a woman as that to understand the mind, and heart, and soul of such a one as Mary Thorne!" And then his thoughts recurred to Frank. "It has been ill done of him; ill done of him: young as he is, he should have had feeling enough to have spared me this. A thoughtless word has been spoken which will now make her miserable!" And then, as he walked on, he could not divest his mind of the remembrance of what had passed between him and Sir Roger. What, if after all, Mary should become the heiress to all that money? What, if she should become, in fact, the owner of Greshamsbury? for, indeed it seemed too possible that Sir Roger's heir would be the owner of Greshamsbury.

The idea was one which he disliked to entertain, but it would recur to him again and again. It might be, that a marriage between his niece and the nominal heir to the estate might be of all the matches the best for young Gresham to make. How sweet would be the revenge, how glorious the retaliation on Lady Arabella, if, after what had now been said, it should come to pass that all the difficulties of Greshamsbury should be made smooth by Mary's love, and Mary's hand! It was a dangerous subject on which to ponder; and, as he sauntered down the road, the doctor did his best to banish it from his mind,—not altogether successfully.

But as he went he again encountered Beatrice. "Tell Mary I went to her to-day," said she, "and that I expect her up here to-morrow. If she does not come, I shall be savage."

"Do not be savage," said he, putting out his hand, "even though she should not come."

Beatrice immediately saw that his manner with her was not playful, and that his face was serious. "I was only in joke," said she; "of course I was only joking. But is anything the matter? Is Mary ill?"

"Oh, no; not ill at all; but she will not be here to-morrow, nor probably for some time. But, Miss Gresham, you must not be savage with her."

Beatrice tried to interrogate him, but he would not wait to answer her questions. While she was speaking he bowed to her in his usual old-fashioned courteous way, and passed on out of hearing. "She will not come up for some time," said Beatrice to herself. "Then mamma must have quarrelled with her." And at once in her heart she acquitted her friend of all blame in the matter, whatever it might be, and condemned her mother unheard.

The doctor, when he arrived at his own house, had in nowise made up his mind as to the manner in which he would break the matter to Mary; but by the time that he had reached the drawing-room, he had made up his mind to this, that he would put off the evil hour till the morrow. He would sleep on the matter—lie awake on it, more probably—and then at breakfast, as best he could, tell her what had been said of her.

Mary that evening was more than usually inclined to be playful. She had not been quite certain till the morning, whether Frank had absolutely left Greshamsbury, and had, therefore, preferred the company of Miss Oriel to going up to the house. There was a peculiar cheerfulness about her friend Patience, a feeling of satisfaction with the world and those in it, which Mary always shared with her; and now she had brought home to the doctor's fireside, in spite of her young troubles, a smiling face, if not a heart altogether happy.

"Uncle," she said at last, "what makes you so sombre? Shall I read to you?"

"No; not to-night, dearest."

"Why, uncle; what is the matter?"

"Nothing, nothing."

"Ah, but it is something, and you shall tell me;" getting up, she came over to his arm-chair, and leant over his shoulder.

He looked at her for a minute in silence, and then, getting up from his chair, passed his arm round her waist, and pressed her closely to his heart.

"My darling!" he said, almost convulsively. "My best own, truest darling!" and Mary, looking up into his face, saw that big tears were running down his cheeks.

But still he told her nothing that night.

CHAPTER XV

COURCY

When Frank Gresham expressed to his father an opinion that Courcy Castle was dull, the squire, as may be remembered, did not pretend to differ from him. To men such as the squire, and such as the squire's son, Courcy Castle was dull. To what class of men it would not be dull the author is not prepared to say; but it may be presumed that the de Courcys found it to their liking, or they would have made it other than it was.

The castle itself was a huge brick pile, built in the days of William III, which, though they were grand for days of the construction of the Constitution, were not very grand for architecture of a more material description. It had, no doubt, a perfect right to be called a castle, as it was entered by a castle-gate which led into a court, the porter's lodge for which was built as it were into the wall; there were attached to it also two round, stumpy adjuncts, which were, perhaps properly, called towers, though they did not do much in the way of towering; and, moreover, along one side of the house, over what would otherwise have been the cornice, there ran a castellated parapet, through the assistance of which, the imagination no doubt was intended to supply the muzzles of defiant artillery. But any artillery which would have so presented its muzzle must have been very small, and it may be doubted whether even a bowman could have obtained shelter there.

The grounds about the castle were not very inviting, nor, as grounds, very extensive; though, no doubt, the entire domain was such as suited the importance of so puissant a nobleman as Earl de Courcy. What, indeed, should have been the park was divided out into various large paddocks. The surface was flat and unbroken; and though there were magnificent elm-trees standing in straight lines, like hedgerows, the timber had not that beautiful, wild, scattered look which generally gives the great charm to English scenery.

The town of Courcy—for the place claimed to rank as a town—was in many particulars like the castle. It was built of dingy-red brick—almost more brown than red—and was solid, dull-looking, ugly and comfortable. It consisted of four streets, which were formed by two roads crossing each other, making at the point of junction a centre for the town. Here stood the Red Lion; had it been called the brown lion, the nomenclature would have been more strictly correct; and here, in the old days of coaching, some life had been wont to stir itself at those hours in the day and night when the Freetraders, Tallyhoes, and Royal Mails changed their horses. But now there was a railway station a mile and a half distant, and the moving life of the town of Courcy was confined to the Red Lion omnibus, which seemed to pass its entire time in going up and down between the town and the station, quite unembarrassed by any great weight of passengers.

There were, so said the Courcyites when away from Courcy, excellent shops in the place; but they were not the less accustomed, when at home among themselves, to complain to each other of the vile extortion with which they were treated by their neighbours. The ironmonger, therefore, though he loudly asserted that he could beat Bristol in the quality of his wares in one direction, and undersell Gloucester in another, bought his tea and sugar on the sly in one of those larger towns; and the grocer, on the other hand, equally distrusted the pots and pans of home production. Trade, therefore, at Courcy, had not thriven since the railway had opened: and, indeed, had any patient inquirer stood at the cross through one entire day, counting customers who entered the neighbouring shops, he might well have wondered that any shops in Courcy could be kept open.

And how changed has been the bustle of that once noisy inn to the present death-like silence of its green courtyard! There, a lame ostler crawls about with his hands thrust into the capacious pockets of his jacket, feeding on memory. That weary pair of omnibus jades, and three sorry posters, are all that now grace those stables where horses used to be stalled in close contiguity by the dozen; where twenty grains apiece, abstracted from every feed of oats consumed during the day, would have afforded a daily quart to the lucky pilferer.

Come, my friend, and discourse with me. Let us know what are thy ideas of the inestimable benefits which science has conferred on us in these, our latter days. How dost thou, among others, appreciate railways and the power of steam, telegraphs, telegrams, and our new expresses? But indifferently, you say. "Time was I've zeed vifteen pair o' 'osses go out of this 'ere yard in vour-and-twenty hour; and now there be'ant vifteen, no, not ten, in vour-and-twenty days! There was the duik—not this 'un; he be'ant no gude; but this 'un's vather—why, when he'd come down the road, the cattle did be a-going, vour days an eend. Here'd be the tooter and the young gen'lmen, and the governess and the young leddies, and then the servants—they'd be al'ays the grandest folk of all—and then the duik and the doochess—Lord love 'ee, zur; the money did fly in them days! But now—" and the feeling of scorn and contempt which the lame ostler was enabled by his native talent to throw into the word "now," was quite as eloquent against the power of steam as anything that has been spoken at dinners, or written in pamphlets by the keenest admirers of latter-day lights.

"Why, luke at this 'ere town," continued he of the sieve, "the grass be a-growing in the very streets;—that can't be no gude. Why, luke 'ee here, zur; I do be a-standing at this 'ere gateway, just this way, hour arter hour, and my heyes is hopen mostly;—I zees who's a-coming and who's a-going. Nobody's a-coming and nobody's a-going; that can't be no gude. Luke at that there homnibus; why, darn me—" and now, in his eloquence at this peculiar point, my friend became more loud and powerful than ever—"why, darn me, if maister harns enough with that there bus to put hiron on them 'osses' feet, I'll—be—blowed!" And as he uttered this hypothetical denunciation on himself he spoke very slowly, bringing out every word as it were separately, and lowering himself at his knees at every sound, moving at the same time his right hand up and down. When he had finished, he fixed his eyes upon the ground, pointing downwards, as if there was to be the site of his doom if the curse that he had called down upon himself should ever come to pass; and then, waiting no further converse, he hobbled away, melancholy, to his deserted stables.

Oh, my friend! my poor lame friend! it will avail nothing to tell thee of Liverpool and Manchester; of the glories of Glasgow, with her flourishing banks; of London, with its third millions of inhabitants; of the great things which commerce is doing for this nation of thine! What is commerce to thee, unless it be commerce in posting on that worn-out, all but useless great western turnpike-road? There is nothing left for thee but to be carted away as rubbish—for thee and for many of us in these now prosperous days; oh, my melancholy, care-ridden friend!

Courcy Castle was certainly a dull place to look at, and Frank, in his former visits, had found that the appearance did not belie the reality. He had been but little there when the earl had been at Courcy; and as he had always felt from his childhood a peculiar distaste to the governance of his aunt the countess, this perhaps may have added to his feeling of dislike. Now, however, the castle was to be fuller than he had ever before known it; the earl was to be at home; there was some talk of the Duke of Omnium coming for a day or two, though that seemed doubtful; there was some faint doubt of Lord Porlock; Mr Moffat, intent on the coming election—and also, let us hope, on his coming bliss—was to be one of the guests; and there was also to be the great Miss Dunstable.

Frank, however, found that those grandees were not expected quite immediately. "I might go back to Greshamsbury for three or four days as she is not to be here," he said naïvely to his aunt, expressing, with tolerable perspicuity, his feeling, that he regarded his visit to Courcy Castle quite as a matter of business. But the countess would hear of no such arrangement. Now that she had got him, she was not going to let him fall back into the perils of Miss Thorne's intrigues, or even of Miss Thorne's propriety. "It is quite essential," she said, "that you should be here a few days before her, so that she may see that you are at home." Frank did not understand the reasoning; but he felt himself unable to rebel, and he therefore, remained there, comforting himself, as best he might, with the eloquence of the Honourable George, and the sporting humours of the Honourable John.

Mr Moffat's was the earliest arrival of any importance. Frank had not hitherto made the acquaintance of his future brother-in-law, and there was, therefore, some little interest in the first interview. Mr Moffat was shown into the drawing-room before the ladies had gone up to dress, and it so happened that Frank was there also. As no one else was in the room but his sister and two of his cousins, he had expected to see the lovers rush into each other's arms. But Mr Moffat restrained his ardour, and Miss Gresham seemed contented that he should do so.

He was a nice, dapper man, rather above the middle height, and good-looking enough had he had a little more expression in his face. He had dark hair, very nicely brushed, small black whiskers, and a small black moustache. His boots were excellently well made, and his hands were very white. He simpered gently as he took hold of Augusta's fingers, and expressed a hope that she had been quite well since last he had the pleasure of seeing her. Then he touched the hands of the Lady Rosina and the Lady Margaretta.

"Mr Moffat, allow me to introduce you to my brother?"

"Most happy, I'm sure," said Mr Moffat, again putting out his hand, and allowing it to slip through Frank's grasp, as he spoke in a pretty, mincing voice: "Lady Arabella quite well?—and your father, and sisters? Very warm isn't it?—quite hot in town, I do assure you."

"I hope Augusta likes him," said Frank to himself, arguing on the subject exactly as his father had done; "but for an engaged lover he seems to me to have a very queer way with him." Frank, poor fellow! who was of a coarser mould, would, under such circumstances, have been all for kissing—sometimes, indeed, even under other circumstances.

Mr Moffat did not do much towards improving the conviviality of the castle. He was, of course, a good deal intent upon his coming election, and spent much of his time with Mr Nearthewinde, the celebrated parliamentary agent. It behoved him to be a good deal at Barchester, canvassing the electors and undermining, by Mr Nearthewinde's aid, the mines for blowing him out of his seat, which were daily being contrived by Mr Closerstil, on behalf of Sir Roger. The battle was to be fought on the internecine principle, no quarter being given or taken on either side; and of course this gave Mr Moffat as much as he knew how to do.

Mr Closerstil was well known to be the sharpest man at his business in all England, unless the palm should be given to his great rival Mr Nearthewinde; and in this instance he was to be assisted in the battle by a very clever young barrister, Mr Romer, who was an admirer of Sir Roger's career in life. Some people in Barchester, when they saw Sir Roger, Closerstil and Mr Romer saunter down the High Street, arm in arm, declared that it was all up with poor Moffat; but others, in whose head the bump of veneration was strongly pronounced, whispered to each other that great shibboleth—the name of the Duke of Omnium—and mildly asserted it to be impossible that the duke's nominee should be thrown out.

Our poor friend the squire did not take much interest in the matter, except in so far that he liked his son-in-law to be in Parliament. Both the candidates were in his eye equally wrong in their opinions. He had long since recanted those errors of his early youth, which had cost him his seat for the county, and had abjured the de Courcy politics. He was staunch enough as a Tory now that his being so would no longer be of the slightest use to him; but the Duke of Omnium, and Lord de Courcy, and Mr Moffat were all Whigs; Whigs, however, differing altogether in politics from Sir Roger, who belonged to the Manchester school, and whose pretensions, through some of those inscrutable twists in modern politics which are quite unintelligible to the minds of ordinary men outside the circle, were on this occasion secretly favoured by the high Conservative party.

How Mr Moffat, who had been brought into the political world by Lord de Courcy, obtained all the weight of the duke's interest I never could exactly learn. For the duke and the earl did not generally act as twin-brothers on such occasions.

There is a great difference in Whigs. Lord de Courcy was a Court Whig, following the fortunes, and enjoying, when he could get it, the sunshine of the throne. He was a sojourner at Windsor, and a visitor at Balmoral. He delighted in gold sticks, and was never so happy as when holding some cap of maintenance or spur of precedence with due dignity and acknowledged grace in the presence of all the Court. His means had been somewhat embarrassed by early extravagance; and, therefore, as it was to his taste to shine, it suited him to shine at the cost of the Court rather than at his own.

The Duke of Omnium was a Whig of a very different calibre. He rarely went near the presence of majesty, and when he did do so, he did it merely as a disagreeable duty incident to his position. He was very willing that the Queen should be queen so long as he was allowed to be Duke of Omnium. Nor had he begrudged Prince Albert any of his honours till he was called Prince Consort. Then, indeed, he had, to his own intimate friends, made some remark in three words, not flattering to the discretion of the Prime Minister. The Queen might be queen so long as he was Duke of Omnium. Their revenues were about the same, with the exception, that the duke's were his own, and he could do what he liked with them. This remembrance did not unfrequently present itself to the duke's mind. In person, he was a plain, thin man, tall, but undistinguished in appearance, except that there was a gleam of pride in his eye which seemed every moment to be saying, "I am the Duke of Omnium." He was unmarried, and, if report said true, a great debauchee; but if so he had always kept his debaucheries decently away from the eyes of the world, and was not, therefore, open to that loud condemnation which should fall like a hailstorm round the ears of some more open sinners.

Why these two mighty nobles put their heads together in order that the tailor's son should represent Barchester in Parliament, I cannot explain. Mr Moffat, was, as has been said, Lord de Courcy's friend; and it may be that Lord de Courcy was able to repay the duke for his kindness, as touching Barchester, with some little assistance in the county representation.

The next arrival was that of the Bishop of Barchester; a meek, good, worthy man, much attached to his wife, and somewhat addicted to his ease. She, apparently, was made in a different mould, and by her energy and diligence atoned for any want in those qualities which might be observed in the bishop himself. When asked his opinion, his lordship would generally reply by saying—"Mrs Proudie and I think so and so." But before that opinion was given, Mrs Proudie would take up the tale, and she, in her more concise manner, was not wont to quote the bishop as having at all assisted in the consideration of the subject. It was well known in Barsetshire that no married pair consorted more closely or more tenderly together; and the example of such conjugal affection among persons in the upper classes is worth mentioning, as it is believed by those below them, and too often with truth, that the sweet bliss of connubial reciprocity is not so common as it should be among the magnates of the earth.

But the arrival even of the bishop and his wife did not make the place cheerful to Frank Gresham, and he began to long for Miss Dunstable, in order that he might have something to do. He could not get on at all with Mr Moffat. He had expected that the man would at once have called him Frank, and that he would have called the man Gustavus; but they did not even get beyond Mr Moffat and Mr Gresham. "Very hot in Barchester to-day, very," was the nearest approach to conversation which Frank could attain with him; and as far as he, Frank, could see, Augusta never got much beyond it. There might be *tête-à-tête* meetings between them, but, if so, Frank could not detect when they took place; and so, opening his heart at last to the Honourable George, for the want of a better confidant, he expressed his opinion that his future brother-in-law was a muff.

"A muff—I believe you too. What do you think now? I have been with him and Nearthewinde in Barchester these three days past, looking up the electors' wives and daughters, and that kind of thing."

"I say, if there is any fun in it you might as well take me with you."

"Oh, there is not much fun; they are mostly so slobbered and dirty. A sharp fellow in Nearthewinde, and knows what he is about well."

"Does he look up the wives and daughters too?"

"Oh, he goes on every tack, just as it's wanted. But there was Moffat, yesterday, in a room behind the milliner's shop near Cuthbert's Gate; I was with him. The woman's husband is one of the choristers and an elector, you know, and Moffat went to look for his vote. Now, there was no one there when we got there but the three young women, the wife, that is, and her two girls—very pretty women they are too."

"I say, George, I'll go and get the chorister's vote for Moffat; I ought to do it as he's to be my brother-in-law."

"But what do you think Moffat said to the women?"

"Can't guess—he didn't kiss any of them, did he?"

"Kiss any of them? No; but he begged to give them his positive assurance as a gentleman, that if he was returned to Parliament he would vote for an extension of the franchise, and the admission of the Jews into Parliament."

"Well, he is a muff!" said Frank.

CHAPTER XVI

MISS DUNSTABLE

At last the great Miss Dunstable came. Frank, when he heard that the heiress had arrived, felt some slight palpitation at his heart. He had not the remotest idea in the world of marrying her; indeed, during the last week past, absence had so heightened his love for Mary Thorne that he was more than ever resolved that he would never marry any one but her. He knew that he had made her a formal offer for her hand, and that it behoved him to keep to it, let the charms of Miss Dunstable be what they might; but, nevertheless, he was prepared to go through a certain amount of courtship, in obedience to his aunt's behests, and he felt a little nervous at being brought up in that way, face to face, to do battle with two hundred thousand pounds.

"Miss Dunstable has arrived," said his aunt to him, with great complacency, on his return from an electioneering visit to the beauties of Barchester which he made with his cousin George on the day after the conversation which was repeated at the end of the last chapter. "She has arrived, and is looking remarkably well; she has quite a *distingué* air, and will grace any circle to which she may be introduced. I will introduce you before dinner, and you can take her out."

"I couldn't propose to her to-night, I suppose?" said Frank, maliciously.

"Don't talk nonsense, Frank," said the countess, angrily. "I am doing what I can for you, and taking on an infinity of trouble to endeavour to place you in an independent position; and now you talk nonsense to me."

Frank muttered some sort of apology, and then went to prepare himself for the encounter.

Miss Dunstable, though she had come by train, had brought with her her own carriage, her own horses, her own coachman and footman, and her own maid, of course. She had also brought with her half a score of trunks, full of wearing apparel; some of them nearly as rich as that wonderful box which was stolen a short time since from the top of a cab. But she brought all these things, not in the least because she wanted them herself, but because she had been instructed to do so.

Frank was a little more than ordinarily careful in dressing. He spoilt a couple of white neckties before he was satisfied, and was rather fastidious as the set of his hair. There was not much of the dandy about him in the ordinary meaning of the word; but he felt that it was incumbent on him to look his best, seeing what it was expected that he should now do. He certainly did not mean to marry Miss Dunstable; but as he was to have a flirtation with her, it was well that he should do so under the best possible auspices.

When he entered the drawing-room he perceived at once that the lady was there. She was seated between the countess and Mrs Proudie; and mammon, in her person, was receiving worship from the temporalities and spiritualities of the land. He tried to look unconcerned, and remained in the farther part of the room, talking with some of his cousins; but he could not keep his eye off the future possible Mrs Frank Gresham; and it seemed as though she was as much constrained to scrutinise him as he felt to scrutinise her.

Lady de Courcy had declared that she was looking extremely well, and had particularly alluded to her *distingué* appearance. Frank at once felt that he could not altogether go along with his aunt in this opinion. Miss Dunstable might be very well; but her style of beauty was one which did not quite meet with his warmest admiration.

In age she was about thirty; but Frank, who was no great judge in these matters, and who was accustomed to have very young girls round him, at once put her down as being ten years older. She had a very high colour, very red cheeks, a large mouth, big white teeth, a broad nose, and bright, small, black eyes. Her hair also was black and bright, but very crisp, and strong, and was combed close round her face in small crisp black ringlets. Since she had been brought out into the fashionable world some one of her instructors in fashion had given her to understand that curls were not the thing. "They'll always pass muster," Miss Dunstable had replied, "when they are done up with bank-notes." It may therefore be presumed that Miss Dunstable had a will of her own.

"Frank," said the countess, in the most natural and unpremeditated way, as soon as she caught her nephew's eye, "come here. I want to introduce you to Miss Dunstable." The introduction was then made. "Mrs Proudie, would you excuse me? I must positively go and say a few words to Mrs Barlow, or the poor woman will feel herself huffed;" and, so saying, she moved off, leaving the coast clear for Master Frank.

He of course slipped into his aunt's place, and expressed a hope that Miss Dunstable was not fatigued by her journey.

"Fatigued!" said she, in a voice rather loud, but very good-humoured, and not altogether unpleasing; "I am not to be fatigued by such a thing as that. Why, in May we came through all the way from Rome to Paris without sleeping—that is, without sleeping in a bed—and we were upset three times out of the sledges coming over the Simplon. It was such fun! Why, I wasn't to say tired even then."

"All the way from Rome to Paris!" said Mrs Proudie—in a tone of astonishment, meant to flatter the heiress—"and what made you in such a hurry?"

"Something about money matters," said Miss Dunstable, speaking rather louder than usual. "Something to do with the ointment. I was selling the business just then."

Mrs Proudie bowed, and immediately changed the conversation. "Idolatry is, I believe, more rampant than ever in Rome," said she; "and I fear there is no such thing at all as Sabbath observance."

"Oh, not in the least," said Miss Dunstable, with rather a joyous air; "Sundays and week-days are all the same there."

"How very frightful!" said Mrs Proudie.

"But it's a delicious place. I do like Rome, I must say. And as for the Pope, if he wasn't quite so fat he would be the nicest old fellow in the world. Have you been in Rome, Mrs Proudie?"

Mrs Proudie sighed as she replied in the negative, and declared her belief that danger was to be apprehended from such visits.

"Oh!—ah!—the malaria—of course—yes; if you go at the wrong time; but nobody is such a fool as that now."

"I was thinking of the soul, Miss Dunstable," said the lady-bishop, in her peculiar, grave tone. "A place where there are no Sabbath observances—"

"And have you been in Rome, Mr Gresham?" said the young lady, turning almost abruptly round to Frank, and giving a somewhat uncivilly cold shoulder to Mrs Proudie's exhortation. She, poor lady, was forced to finish her speech to the Honourable George, who was standing near to her. He having an idea that bishops and all their belongings, like other things appertaining to religion, should, if possible, be avoided; but if that were not possible, should be treated with much assumed gravity, immediately put on a long face, and remarked that—"it was a deuced shame: for his part he always liked to see people go quiet on Sundays. The parsons had only one day out of seven, and he thought they were fully entitled to that." Satisfied with which, or not satisfied, Mrs Proudie had to remain silent till dinner-time.

"No," said Frank; "I never was in Rome. I was in Paris once, and that's all." And then, feeling a not unnatural anxiety as to the present state of Miss Dunstable's worldly concerns, he took an opportunity of falling back on that part of the conversation which Mrs Proudie had exercised so much tact in avoiding.

"And was it sold?" said he.

"Sold! what sold?"

"You were saying about the business—that you came back without going to bed because of selling the business."

"Oh!—the ointment. No; it was not sold. After all, the affair did not come off, and I might have remained and had another roll in the snow. Wasn't it a pity?"

"So," said Frank to himself, "if I should do it, I should be owner of the ointment of Lebanon: how odd!" And then he gave her his arm and handed her down to dinner.

He certainly found that the dinner was less dull than any other he had sat down to at Courcy Castle. He did not fancy that he should ever fall in love with Miss Dunstable; but she certainly was an agreeable companion. She told him of her tour, and the fun she had in her journeys; how she took a physician with her for the benefit of her health, whom she generally was forced to nurse; of the trouble it was to her to look after and wait upon her numerous servants; of the tricks she played to bamboozle people who came to stare at her; and, lastly, she told him of a lover who followed her from country to country, and was now in hot pursuit of her, having arrived in London the evening before she left.

"A lover?" said Frank, somewhat startled by the suddenness of the confidence.

"A lover—yes—Mr Gresham; why should I not have a lover?"

"Oh!—no—of course not. I dare say you have a good many."

"Only three or four, upon my word; that is, only three or four that I favour. One is not bound to reckon the others, you know."

"No, they'd be too numerous. And so you have three whom you favour, Miss Dunstable;" and Frank sighed, as though he intended to say that the number was too many for his peace of mind.

"Is not that quite enough? But of course I change them sometimes;" and she smiled on him very good-naturedly. "It would be very dull if I were always to keep the same."

"Very dull indeed," said Frank, who did not quite know what to say.

"Do you think the countess would mind my having one or two of them here if I were to ask her?"

"I am quite sure she would," said Frank, very briskly. "She would not approve of it at all; nor should I."

"You—why, what have you to do with it?"

"A great deal—so much so that I positively forbid it; but, Miss Dunstable—"

"Well, Mr Gresham?"

"We will contrive to make up for the deficiency as well as possible, if you will permit us to do so. Now for myself—"

"Well, for yourself?"

At this moment the countess gleamed her accomplished eye round the table, and Miss Dunstable rose from her chair as Frank was preparing his attack, and accompanied the other ladies into the drawing-room.

His aunt, as she passed him, touched his arm lightly with her fan, so lightly that the action was perceived by no one else. But Frank well understood the meaning of the touch, and appreciated the approbation which it conveyed. He merely blushed, however, at his own dissimulation; for he felt more certain that ever that he would never marry Miss Dunstable, and he felt nearly equally sure that Miss Dunstable would never marry him.

Lord de Courcy was now at home; but his presence did not add much hilarity to the claret-cup. The young men, however, were very keen about the election, and Mr Nearthewinde, who was one of the party, was full of the most sanguine hopes.

"I have done one good at any rate," said Frank; "I have secured the chorister's vote."

"What! Bagley?" said Nearthewinde. "The fellow kept out of my way, and I couldn't see him."

"I haven't exactly seen him," said Frank; "but I've got his vote all the same."

"What! by a letter?" said Mr Moffat.

"No, not by letter," said Frank, speaking rather low as he looked at the bishop and the earl; "I got a promise from his wife: I think he's a little in the henpecked line."

"Ha—ha—ha!" laughed the good bishop, who, in spite of Frank's modulation of voice, had overheard what had passed. "Is that the way you manage electioneering matters in our cathedral city? Ha—ha—ha!" The idea of one of his choristers being in the henpecked line was very amusing to the bishop.

"Oh, I got a distinct promise," said Frank, in his pride; and then added incautiously, "but I had to order bonnets for the whole family."

"Hush-h-h-h!" said Mr Nearthewinde, absolutely flabbergasted by such imprudence on the part of one of his client's friends. "I am quite sure that your order had no effect, and was intended to have no effect on Mr Bagley's vote."

"Is that wrong?" said Frank; "upon my word I thought that it was quite legitimate."

"One should never admit anything in electioneering matters, should one?" said George, turning to Mr Nearthewinde.

"Very little, Mr de Courcy; very little indeed—the less the better. It's hard to say in these days what is wrong and what is not. Now, there's Reddypalm, the publican, the man who has the Brown Bear. Well, I was there, of course: he's a voter, and if any man in Barchester ought to feel himself bound to vote for a friend of the duke's, he ought. Now, I was so thirsty when I was in that man's house that I was dying for a glass of beer; but for the life of me I didn't dare order one."

"Why not?" said Frank, whose mind was only just beginning to be enlightened by the great doctrine of purity of election as practised in English provincial towns.

"Oh, Closerstil had some fellow looking at me; why, I can't walk down that town without having my very steps counted. I like sharp fighting myself, but I never go so sharp as that."

"Nevertheless I got Bagley's vote," said Frank, persisting in praise of his own electioneering prowess; "and you may be sure of this, Mr Nearthewinde, none of Closerstil's men were looking at me when I got it."

"Who'll pay for the bonnets, Frank?" said George.

"Oh, I'll pay for them if Moffat won't. I think I shall keep an account there; they seem to have good gloves and those sort of things."

"Very good, I have no doubt," said George.

"I suppose your lordship will be in town soon after the meeting of Parliament?" said the bishop, questioning the earl.

"Oh! yes; I suppose I must be there. I am never allowed to remain very long in quiet. It is a great nuisance; but it is too late to think of that now."

"Men in high places, my lord, never were, and never will be, allowed to consider themselves. They burn their torches not in their own behalf," said the bishop, thinking, perhaps, as much of himself as he did of his noble friend. "Rest and quiet are the comforts of those who have been content to remain in obscurity."

"Perhaps so," said the earl, finishing his glass of claret with an air of virtuous resignation. "Perhaps so." His own martyrdom, however, had not been severe, for the rest and quiet of home had never been peculiarly satisfactory to his tastes. Soon after this they all went to the ladies.

It was some little time before Frank could find an opportunity of recommencing his allotted task with Miss Dunstable. She got into conversation with the bishop and some other people, and, except that he took her teacup and nearly managed to squeeze one of her fingers as he did so, he made very little further progress till towards the close of the evening.

At last he found her so nearly alone as to admit of his speaking to her in his low confidential voice.

"Have you managed that matter with my aunt?"

"What matter?" said Miss Dunstable; and her voice was not low, nor particularly confidential.

"About those three or four gentlemen whom you wish to invite here?"

"Oh! my attendant knights! no, indeed; you gave me such very slight hope of success; besides, you said something about my not wanting them."

"Yes I did; I really think they'd be quite unnecessary. If you should want any one to defend you—"

"At these coming elections, for instance."

"Then, or at any other time, there are plenty here who will be ready to stand up for you."

"Plenty! I don't want plenty: one good lance in the olden days was always worth more than a score of ordinary men-at-arms."

"But you talked about three or four."

"Yes; but then you see, Mr Gresham, I have never yet found the one good lance—at least, not good enough to suit my ideas of true prowess."

What could Frank do but declare that he was ready to lay his own in rest, now and always in her behalf? His aunt had been quite angry with him, and had thought that he turned her into ridicule, when he spoke of making an offer to her guest that very evening; and yet here he was so placed that he had hardly an alternative. Let his inward resolution to abjure the heiress be ever so strong, he was now in a position which allowed him no choice in the matter. Even Mary Thorne could hardly have blamed him for saying, that so far as his own prowess went, it was quite at Miss Dunstable's service. Had Mary been looking on, she, perhaps, might have thought that he could have done so with less of that look of devotion which he threw into his eyes.

"Well, Mr Gresham, that's very civil—very civil indeed," said Miss Dunstable. "Upon my word, if a lady wanted a true knight she might do worse than trust to you. Only I fear that your courage is of so exalted a nature that you would be ever ready to do battle for any beauty who might be in distress—or, indeed, who might not. You could never confine your valour to the protection of one maiden."

"Oh, yes! but I would though if I liked her," said Frank. "There isn't a more constant fellow in the world than I am in that way—you try me, Miss Dunstable."

"When young ladies make such trials as that, they sometimes find it too late to go back if the trial doesn't succeed, Mr Gresham."

"Oh, of course there's always some risk. It's like hunting; there would be no fun if there was no danger."

"But if you get a tumble one day you can retrieve your honour the next; but a poor girl, if she once trusts a man who says that he loves her, has no such chance. For myself, I would never listen to a man unless I'd known him for seven years at least."

"Seven years!" said Frank, who could not help thinking that in seven years' time Miss Dunstable would be almost an old woman. "Seven days is enough to know any person."

"Or perhaps seven hours; eh, Mr Gresham?"

"Seven hours—well, perhaps seven hours, if they happen to be a good deal together during the time."

"There's nothing after all like love at first sight, is there, Mr Gresham?"

Frank knew well enough that she was quizzing him, and could not resist the temptation he felt to be revenged on her. "I am sure it's very pleasant," said he; "but as for myself, I have never experienced it."

"Ha, ha, ha!" laughed Miss Dunstable. "Upon my word, Mr Gresham, I like you amazingly. I didn't expect to meet anybody down here that I should like half so much. You must come and see me in London, and I'll introduce you to my three knights," and so saying, she moved away and fell into conversation with some of the higher powers.

Frank felt himself to be rather snubbed, in spite of the strong expression which Miss Dunstable had made in his favour. It was not quite clear to him that she did not take him for a boy. He was, to be sure, avenged on her for that by taking her for a middle-aged woman; but, nevertheless, he was hardly satisfied with himself; "I might give her a heartache yet," said he to himself, "and she might find afterwards that she was left in the lurch with all her money." And so he retired, solitary, into a far part of the room, and began to think of Mary Thorne. As he did so, and as his eyes fell upon Miss Dunstable's stiff curls, he almost shuddered.

And then the ladies retired. His aunt, with a good-natured smile on her face, come to him as she was leaving the room, the last of the bevy, and putting her hand on his arm, led him out into a small unoccupied chamber which opened from the grand saloon.

"Upon my word, Master Frank," said she, "you seem to be losing no time with the heiress. You have quite made an impression already."

"I don't know much about that, aunt," said he, looking rather sheepish.

"Oh, I declare you have; but, Frank, my dear boy, you should not precipitate these sort of things too much. It is well to take a little more time: it is more valued; and perhaps, you know, on the whole—"

Perhaps Frank might know; but it was clear that Lady de Courcy did not: at any rate, she did not know how to express herself. Had she said out her mind plainly, she would probably have spoken thus: "I want you to make love to Miss Dunstable, certainly; or at any rate to make an offer to her; but you need not make a show of yourself and of her, too, by doing it so openly as all that." The countess, however, did not want to reprimand her obedient nephew, and therefore did not speak out her thoughts.

"Well?" said Frank, looking up into her face.

"Take a *leetle* more time—that is all, my dear boy; slow and sure, you know;" so the countess again patted his arm and went away to bed.

"Old fool!" muttered Frank to himself, as he returned to the room where the men were still standing. He was right in this: she was an old fool, or she would have seen that there was no chance whatever that her nephew and Miss Dunstable should become man and wife.

"Well Frank," said the Honourable John; "so you're after the heiress already."

"He won't give any of us a chance," said the Honourable George. "If he goes on in that way she'll be Mrs Gresham before a month is over. But, Frank, what will she say of your manner of looking for Barchester votes?"

"Mr Gresham is certainly an excellent hand at canvassing," said Mr Nearthewinde; "only a little too open in his manner of proceeding."

"I got that chorister for you at any rate," said Frank. "And you would never have had him without me."

"I don't think half so much of the chorister's vote as that of Miss Dunstable," said the Honourable George: "that's the interest that is really worth looking after."

"But, surely," said Mr Moffat, "Miss Dunstable has no property in Barchester?" Poor man! his heart was so intent on his election that he had not a moment to devote to the claims of love.

CHAPTER XVII

THE ELECTION

And now the important day of the election had arrived, and some men's hearts beat quickly enough. To be or not to a member of the British Parliament is a question of very considerable moment in a man's mind. Much is often said of the great penalties which the ambitious pay for enjoying this honour; of the tremendous expenses of elections; of the long, tedious hours of unpaid labour: of the weary days passed in the House; but, nevertheless, the prize is one very well worth the price paid for it—well worth any price that can be paid for it short of wading through dirt and dishonour.

No other great European nation has anything like it to offer to the ambition of its citizens; for in no other great country of Europe, not even in those which are free, has the popular constitution obtained, as with us, true sovereignty and power of rule. Here it is so; and when a man lays himself out to be a member of Parliament, he plays the highest game and for the highest stakes which the country affords.

To some men, born silver-spooned, a seat in Parliament comes as a matter of course. From the time of their early manhood they hardly know what it is not to sit there; and the honour is hardly appreciated, being too much a matter of course. As a rule, they never know how great a thing it is to be in Parliament; though, when reverse comes, as reverses occasionally will come, they fully feel how dreadful it is to be left out.

But to men aspiring to be members, or to those who having been once fortunate have again to fight the battle without assurance of success, the coming election must be matter of dread concern. Oh, how delightful to hear that the long-talked-of rival has declined the contest, and that the course is clear! or to find by a short canvass that one's majority is safe, and the pleasures of crowing over an unlucky, friendless foe quite secured!

No such gratification as this filled the bosom of Mr Moffat on the morning of the Barchester election. To him had been brought no positive assurance of success by his indefatigable agent, Mr Nearthewinde. It was admitted on all sides that the contest would be a very close one; and Mr Nearthewinde would not do more than assert that they ought to win unless things went very wrong with them.

Mr Nearthewinde had other elections to attend to, and had not been remaining at Courcy Castle ever since the coming of Miss Dunstable: but he had been there, and at Barchester, as often as possible, and Mr Moffat was made greatly uneasy by reflecting how very high the bill would be.

The two parties had outdone each other in the loudness of their assertions, that each would on his side conduct the election in strict conformity to law. There was to be no bribery. Bribery! who, indeed, in these days would dare to bribe; to give absolute money for an absolute vote, and pay for such an article in downright palpable sovereigns? No. Purity was much too rampant for that, and the means of detection too well understood. But purity was to be carried much further than this. There should be no treating; no hiring of two hundred voters to act as messengers at twenty shillings a day in looking up some four hundred other voters; no bands were to be paid for; no carriages furnished; no ribbons supplied. British voters were to vote, if vote they would, for the love and respect they bore to their chosen candidate. If so actuated, they would not vote, they might stay away; no other inducement would be offered.

So much was said loudly—very loudly—by each party; but, nevertheless, Mr Moffat, early in these election days, began to have some misgivings about the bill. The proclaimed arrangement had been one exactly suitable to his taste; for Mr Moffat loved his money. He was a man in whose breast the ambition of being great in the world, and of joining himself to aristocratic people was continually at war with the great cost which such tastes occasioned. His last election had not been a cheap triumph. In one way or another money had been dragged from him for purposes which had been to his mind unintelligible; and when, about the middle of his first session, he had, with much grumbling, settled all demands, he had questioned with himself whether his whistle was worth its cost.

He was therefore a great stickler for purity of election; although, had he considered the matter, he should have known that with him money was his only passport into that Elysium in which he had now lived for two years. He probably did not consider it; for when, in those canvassing days immediately preceding the election, he had seen that all the beerhouses were open, and half the population was drunk, he had asked Mr Nearthewinde whether this violation of the treaty was taking place only on the part of his opponent, and whether, in such case, it would not be duly noticed with a view to a possible future petition.

Mr Nearthewinde assured him triumphantly that half at least of the wallowing swine were his own especial friends; and that somewhat more than half of the publicans of the town were eagerly engaged in fighting his, Mr Moffat's battle. Mr Moffat groaned, and would have expostulated had Mr Nearthewinde been willing to hear him. But that gentleman's services had been put into requisition by Lord de Courcy rather than by the candidate. For the candidate he cared but little. To pay the bill would be enough for him. He, Mr Nearthewinde, was doing his business as he well knew how to do it; and it was not likely that he should submit to be lectured by such as Mr Moffat on a trumpery score of expense.

It certainly did appear on the morning of the election as though some great change had been made in that resolution of the candidates to be very pure. From an early hour rough bands of music were to be heard in every part of the usually quiet town; carts and gigs, omnibuses and flys, all the old carriages from all the inn-yards, and every vehicle of any description which could be pressed into the service were in motion; if the horses and postboys were not to be paid for by the candidates, the voters themselves were certainly very liberal in their mode of bringing themselves to the poll. The election district of the city of Barchester extended for some miles on each side of the city, so that the omnibuses and flys had enough to do. Beer was to be had at the public-houses, almost without question, by all who chose to ask for it; and rum and brandy were dispensed to select circles within the bars with equal profusion. As for ribbons, the mercers' shops must have been emptied of that article, as far as scarlet and yellow were concerned. Scarlet was Sir Roger's colour, while the friends of Mr Moffat were decked with yellow. Seeing what he did see, Mr Moffat might well ask whether there had not been a violation of the treaty of purity!

At the time of this election there was some question whether England should go to war with all her energy; or whether it would not be better for her to save her breath to cool her porridge, and not meddle more than could be helped with foreign quarrels. The last view of the matter was advocated by Sir Roger, and his motto of course proclaimed the merits of domestic peace and quiet. "Peace abroad and a big loaf at home," was consequently displayed on four or five huge scarlet banners, and carried waving over the heads of the people. But Mr Moffat was a staunch supporter of the Government, who were already inclined to be belligerent, and "England's honour" was therefore the legend under which he selected to do battle. It may, however, be doubted whether there was in all Barchester one inhabitant—let alone one elector—so fatuous as to suppose that England's honour was in any special manner dear to Mr Moffat; or that he would be a whit more sure of a big loaf than he was now, should Sir Roger happily become a member of the legislature.

And then the fine arts were resorted to, seeing that language fell short in telling all that was found necessary to be told. Poor Sir Roger's failing as regards the bottle was too well known; and it was also known that, in acquiring his title, he had not quite laid aside the rough mode of speech which he had used in his early years. There was, consequently, a great daub painted up on sundry walls, on which a navvy, with a pimply, bloated face, was to be seen standing on a railway bank, leaning on a spade holding a bottle in one hand, while he invited a comrade to drink. "Come, Jack, shall us have a drop of some'at short?" were the words coming out of the navvy's mouth; and under this was painted in huge letters,

"THE LAST NEW BARONET."

But Mr Moffat hardly escaped on easier terms. The trade by which his father had made his money was as well known as that of the railway contractor; and every possible symbol of tailordom was displayed in graphic portraiture on the walls and hoardings of the city. He was drawn with his goose, with his scissors, with his needle, with his tapes; he might be seen measuring, cutting, stitching, pressing, carrying home his bundle, and presenting his little bill; and under each of these representations was repeated his own motto: "England's honour."

Such were the pleasant little amenities with which the people of Barchester greeted the two candidates who were desirous of the honour of serving them in Parliament.

The polling went on briskly and merrily. There were somewhat above nine hundred registered voters, of whom the greater portion recorded their votes early in the day. At two o'clock, according to Sir Roger's committee, the numbers were as follows:—

Scatcherd	275
Moffat	268

Whereas, by the light afforded by Mr Moffat's people, they stood in a slightly different ratio to each other, being written thus:—

Moffat	277
Scatcherd	269

This naturally heightened the excitement, and gave additional delight to the proceedings. At half-past two it was agreed by both sides that Mr Moffat was ahead; the Moffatites claiming a majority of twelve, and the Scatcherdites allowing a majority of one. But by three o'clock sundry good men and true, belonging to the railway interest, had made their way to the booth in spite of the efforts of a band of roughs from Courcy, and Sir Roger was again leading, by ten or a dozen, according to his own showing. One little transaction

574

which took place in the earlier part of the day deserves to be recorded. There was in Barchester an honest publican—honest as the world of publicans goes—who not only was possessed of a vote, but possessed also of a son who was a voter. He was one Reddypalm, and in former days, before he had learned to appreciate the full value of an Englishman's franchise, he had been a declared Liberal and an early friend of Roger Scatcherd's. In latter days he had governed his political feelings with more decorum, and had not allowed himself to be carried away by such foolish fervour as he had evinced in his youth. On this special occasion, however, his line of conduct was so mysterious as for a while to baffle even those who knew him best.

His house was apparently open in Sir Roger's interest. Beer, at any rate, was flowing there as elsewhere; and scarlet ribbons going in—not, perhaps, in a state of perfect steadiness—came out more unsteady than before. Still had Mr Reddypalm been deaf to the voice of that charmer, Closerstil, though he had charmed with all his wisdom. Mr Reddypalm had stated, first his unwillingness to vote at all:—he had, he said, given over politics, and was not inclined to trouble his mind again with the subject; then he had spoken of his great devotion to the Duke of Omnium, under whose grandfathers his grandfather had been bred: Mr Nearthewinde had, as he said, been with him, and proved to him beyond a shadow of a doubt that it would show the deepest ingratitude on his part to vote against the duke's candidate.

Mr Closerstil thought he understood all this, and sent more, and still more men to drink beer. He even caused—taking infinite trouble to secure secrecy in the matter—three gallons of British brandy to be ordered and paid for as the best French. But, nevertheless, Mr Reddypalm made no sign to show that he considered that the right thing had been done. On the evening before the election, he told one of Mr Closerstil's confidential men, that he had thought a good deal about it, and that he believed he should be constrained by his conscience to vote for Mr Moffat.

We have said that Mr Closerstil was accompanied by a learned friend of his, one Mr Romer, a barrister, who was greatly interested in Sir Roger, and who, being a strong Liberal, was assisting in the canvass with much energy. He, hearing how matters were likely to go with this conscientious publican, and feeling himself peculiarly capable of dealing with such delicate scruples, undertook to look into the case in hand. Early, therefore, on the morning of the election, he sauntered down the cross street in which hung out the sign of the Brown Bear, and, as he expected, found Mr Reddypalm near his own door.

Now it was quite an understood thing that there was to be no bribery. This was understood by no one better than by Mr Romer, who had, in truth, drawn up many of the published assurances to that effect. And, to give him his due, he was fully minded to act in accordance with these assurances. The object of all the parties was to make it worth the voters' while to give their votes; but to do so without bribery. Mr Romer had repeatedly declared that he would have nothing to do with any illegal practising; but he had also declared that, as long as all was done according to law, he was ready to lend his best efforts to assist Sir Roger. How he assisted Sir Roger, and adhered to the law, will now be seen.

Oh, Mr Romer! Mr Romer! is it not the case with thee that thou "wouldst not play false, and yet wouldst wrongly win?" Not in electioneering, Mr Romer, any more than in other pursuits, can a man touch pitch and not be defiled; as thou, innocent as thou art, wilt soon learn to thy terrible cost.

"Well, Reddypalm," said Mr Romer, shaking hands with him. Mr Romer had not been equally cautious as Nearthewinde, and had already drunk sundry glasses of ale at the Brown Bear, in the hope of softening the stern Bear-warden. "How is it to be to-day? Which is to be the man?"

"If any one knows that, Mr Romer, you must be the man. A poor numbskull like me knows nothing of them matters. How should I? All I looks to, Mr Romer, is selling a trifle of drink now and then—selling it, and getting paid for it, you know, Mr Romer."

"Yes, that's important, no doubt. But come, Reddypalm, such an old friend of Sir Roger as you are, a man he speaks of as one of his intimate friends, I wonder how you can hesitate about it? Now with another man, I should think that he wanted to be paid for voting—"

"Oh, Mr Romer!—fie—fie—fie!"

"I know it's not the case with you. It would be an insult to offer you money, even if money were going. I should not mention this, only as money is not going, neither on our side nor on the other, no harm can be done."

"Mr Romer, if you speak of such a thing, you'll hurt me. I know the value of an Englishman's franchise too well to wish to sell it. I would not demean myself so low; no, not though five-and-twenty pound a vote was going, as there was in the good old times—and that's not so long ago neither."

"I am sure you wouldn't, Reddypalm; I'm sure you wouldn't. But an honest man like you should stick to old friends. Now, tell me," and putting his arm through Reddypalm's, he walked with him into the passage of his own house; "Now, tell me—is there anything wrong? It's between friends, you know. Is there anything wrong?"

"I wouldn't sell my vote for untold gold," said Reddypalm, who was perhaps aware that untold gold would hardly be offered to him for it.

"I am sure you would not," said Mr Romer.

"But," said Reddypalm, "a man likes to be paid his little bill."

"Surely, surely," said the barrister.

"And I did say two years since, when your friend Mr Closerstil brought a friend of his down to stand here—it wasn't Sir Roger then—but when he brought a friend of his down, and when I drew two or three hogsheads of ale on their side, and when my bill was questioned and only half-settled, I did say that I wouldn't interfere with no election no more. And no more I will, Mr Romer—unless it be to give a quiet vote for the nobleman under whom I and mine always lived respectable."

"Oh!" said Mr Romer.

"A man do like to have his bill paid, you know, Mr Romer."

Mr Romer could not but acknowledge that this was a natural feeling on the part of an ordinary mortal publican.

"It goes agin the grain with a man not to have his little bill paid, and specially at election time," again urged Mr Reddypalm.

Mr Romer had not much time to think about it; but he knew well that matters were so nearly balanced, that the votes of Mr Reddypalm and his son were of inestimable value.

"If it's only about your bill," said Mr Romer, "I'll see to have that settled. I'll speak to Closerstil about that."

"All right!" said Reddypalm, seizing the young barrister's hand, and shaking it warmly; "all right!" And late in the afternoon when a vote or two became matter of intense interest, Mr Reddypalm and his son came up to the hustings and boldly tendered theirs for their old friend, Sir Roger.

There was a great deal of eloquence heard in Barchester on that day. Sir Roger had by this time so far recovered as to be able to go through the dreadfully hard work of canvassing and addressing the electors from eight in the morning till near sunset. A very perfect recovery, most men will say. Yes; a perfect recovery as regarded the temporary use of his faculties, both physical and mental; though it may be doubted whether there can be any permanent recovery from such disease as his. What amount of brandy he consumed to

576

enable him to perform this election work, and what lurking evil effect the excitement might have on him—of these matters no record was kept in the history of those proceedings.

Sir Roger's eloquence was of a rough kind; but not perhaps the less operative on those for whom it was intended. The aristocracy of Barchester consisted chiefly of clerical dignitaries, bishops, deans, prebendaries, and such like: on them and theirs it was not probable that anything said by Sir Roger would have much effect. Those men would either abstain from voting, or vote for the railway hero, with the view of keeping out the de Courcy candidate. Then came the shopkeepers, who might also be regarded as a stiff-necked generation, impervious to electioneering eloquence. They would, generally, support Mr Moffat. But there was an inferior class of voters, ten-pound freeholders, and such like, who, at this period, were somewhat given to have an opinion of their own, and over them it was supposed that Sir Roger did obtain some power by his gift of talking.

"Now, gentlemen, will you tell me this," said he, bawling at the top of his voice from off the portico which graced the door of the Dragon of Wantley, at which celebrated inn Sir Roger's committee sat:—"Who is Mr Moffat, and what has he done for us? There have been some picture-makers about the town this week past. The Lord knows who they are; I don't. These clever fellows do tell you who I am, and what I've done. I ain't very proud of the way they've painted me, though there's something about it I ain't ashamed of either. See here," and he held up on one side of him one of the great daubs of himself—"just hold it there till I can explain it," and he handed the paper to one of his friends. "That's me," said Sir Roger, putting up his stick, and pointing to the pimply-nosed representation of himself.

"Hurrah! Hur-r-rah! more power to you—we all know who you are, Roger. You're the boy! When did you get drunk last?" Such-like greetings, together with a dead cat which was flung at him from the crowd, and which he dexterously parried with his stick, were the answers which he received to this exordium.

"Yes," said he, quite undismayed by this little missile which had so nearly reached him: "that's me. And look here; this brown, dirty-looking broad streak here is intended for a railway; and that thing in my hand—not the right hand; I'll come to that presently—"

"How about the brandy, Roger?"

"I'll come to that presently. I'll tell you about the brandy in good time. But that thing in my left hand is a spade. Now, I never handled a spade, and never could; but, boys, I handled a chisel and mallet; and many a hundred block of stone has come out smooth from under that hand;" and Sir Roger lifted up his great broad palm wide open.

"So you did, Roger, and well we minds it."

"The meaning, however, of that spade is to show that I made the railway. Now I'm very much obliged to those gentlemen over at the White Horse for putting up this picture of me. It's a true picture, and it tells you who I am. I did make that railway. I have made thousands of miles of railway; I am making thousands of miles of railways—some in Europe, some in Asia, some in America. It's a true picture," and he poked his stick through it and held it up to the crowd. "A true picture: but for that spade and that railway, I shouldn't be now here asking your votes; and, when next February comes, I shouldn't be sitting in Westminster to represent you, as, by God's grace, I certainly will do. That tells you who I am. But now, will you tell me who Mr Moffat is?"

"How about the brandy, Roger?"

"Oh, yes, the brandy! I was forgetting that and the little speech that is coming out of my mouth—a deal shorter speech, and a better one than what I am making now. Here, in the right hand you see a brandy bottle. Well, boys, I'm not a bit ashamed of that; as long as a man does his work—and the spade shows that—it's only fair he should have something to comfort him. I'm always able to work, and few men work much harder. I'm always able to work, and no man has a right to expect more of me. I never expect more than that from those who work for me."

"No more you don't, Roger: a little drop's very good, ain't it, Roger? Keeps the cold from the stomach, eh, Roger?"

"Then as to this speech, 'Come, Jack, let's have a drop of some'at short.' Why, that's a good speech too. When I do drink I like to share with a friend; and I don't care how humble that friend is."

"Hurrah! more power. That's true too, Roger; may you never be without a drop to wet your whistle."

"They say I'm the last new baronet. Well, I ain't ashamed of that; not a bit. When will Mr Moffat get himself made a baronet? No man can truly say I'm too proud of it. I have never stuck myself up; no, nor stuck my wife up either: but I don't see much to be ashamed of because the bigwigs chose to make a baronet of me."

"Nor, no more thee h'ant, Roger. We'd all be barrownites if so be we knew the way."

"But now, having polished off this bit of picture, let me ask you who Mr Moffat is? There are pictures enough about him, too; though Heaven knows where they all come from. I think Sir Edwin Landseer must have done this one of the goose; it is so deadly natural. Look at it; there he is. Upon my word, whoever did that ought to make his fortune at some of these exhibitions. Here he is again, with a big pair of scissors. He calls himself 'England's honour;' what the deuce England's honour has to do with tailoring, I can't tell you: perhaps Mr Moffat can. But mind you, my friends, I don't say anything against tailoring: some of you are tailors, I dare say."

"Yes, we be," said a little squeaking voice from out of the crowd.

"And a good trade it is. When I first knew Barchester there were tailors here could lick any stone-mason in the trade; I say nothing against tailors. But it isn't enough for a man to be a tailor unless he's something else along with it. You're not so fond of tailors that you'll send one up to Parliament merely because he is a tailor."

"We won't have no tailors. No; nor yet no cabbaging. Take a go of brandy, Roger; you're blown."

"No, I'm not blown yet. I've a deal more to say about Mr Moffat before I shall be blown. What has he done to entitle him to come here before you and ask you to send him to Parliament? Why; he isn't even a tailor. I wish he were. There's always some good in a fellow who knows how to earn his own bread. But he isn't a tailor; he can't even put a stitch in towards mending England's honour. His father was a tailor; not a Barchester tailor, mind you, so as to give him any claim on your affections; but a London tailor. Now the question is, do you want to send the son of a London tailor up to Parliament to represent you?"

"No, we don't; nor yet we won't either."

"I rather think not. You've had him once, and what has he done for you? Has he said much for you in the House of Commons? Why, he's so dumb a dog that he can't bark even for a bone. I'm told it's quite painful to hear him fumbling and mumbling and trying to get up a speech there over at the White Horse. He doesn't belong to the city; he hasn't done anything for the city; and he hasn't the power to do anything for the city. Then, why on earth does he come here? I'll tell you. The Earl de Courcy brings him. He's going to marry the Earl de Courcy's niece; for they say he's very rich—this tailor's son—only they do say also that he doesn't much like to spend his money. He's going to marry Lord de Courcy's niece, and Lord de Courcy wishes that his nephew should be in Parliament. There, that's the claim which Mr Moffat has here on the people of Barchester. He's Lord de Courcy's nominee, and those who feel themselves bound hand and foot, heart and soul, to Lord de

Courcy, had better vote for him. Such men have my leave. If there are enough of such at Barchester to send him to Parliament, the city in which I was born must be very much altered since I was a young man."

And so finishing his speech, Sir Roger retired within, and recruited himself in the usual manner.

Such was the flood of eloquence at the Dragon of Wantly. At the White Horse, meanwhile, the friends of the de Courcy interest were treated perhaps to sounder political views; though not expressed in periods so intelligibly fluent as those of Sir Roger.

Mr Moffat was a young man, and there was no knowing to what proficiency in the Parliamentary gift of public talking he might yet attain; but hitherto his proficiency was not great. He had, however, endeavoured to make up by study for any want of readiness of speech, and had come to Barchester daily, for the last four days, fortified with a very pretty harangue, which he had prepared for himself in the solitude of his chamber. On the three previous days matters had been allowed to progress with tolerable smoothness, and he had been permitted to deliver himself of his elaborate eloquence with few other interruptions than those occasioned by his own want of practice. But on this, the day of days, the Barchesterian roughs were not so complaisant. It appeared to Mr Moffat, when he essayed to speak, that he was surrounded by enemies rather than friends; and in his heart he gave great blame to Mr Nearthewinde for not managing matters better for him.

"Men of Barchester," he began, in a voice which was every now and then preternaturally loud, but which, at each fourth or fifth word, gave way from want of power, and descended to its natural weak tone. "Men of Barchester—electors and non-electors—"

"We is hall electors; hall on us, my young kiddy."

"Electors and non-electors, I now ask your suffrages, not for the first time—"

"Oh! we've tried you. We know what you're made on. Go on, Snip; don't you let 'em put you down."

"I've had the honour of representing you in Parliament for the last two years and—"

"And a deuced deal you did for us, didn't you?"

"What could you expect from the ninth part of a man? Never mind, Snip—go on; don't you be out by any of them. Stick to your wax and thread like a man—like the ninth part of a man—go on a little faster, Snip."

"For the last two years—and—and—" Here Mr Moffat looked round to his friends for some little support, and the Honourable George, who stood close behind him, suggested that he had gone through it like a brick.

"And—and I went through it like a brick," said Mr Moffat, with the gravest possible face, taking up in his utter confusion the words that were put into his mouth.

"Hurray!—so you did—you're the real brick. Well done, Snip; go it again with the wax and thread!"

"I am a thorough-paced reformer," continued Mr Moffat, somewhat reassured by the effect of the opportune words which his friend had whispered into his ear. "A thorough-paced reformer—a thorough-paced reformer—"

"Go on, Snip. We all know what that means."

"A thorough-paced reformer—"

"Never mind your paces, man; but get on. Tell us something new. We're all reformers, we are."

Poor Mr Moffat was a little thrown back. It wasn't so easy to tell these gentlemen anything new, harnessed as he was at this moment; so he looked back at his honourable supporter for some further hint. "Say something about their daughters," whispered George, whose own flights of oratory were always on that subject. Had he counselled Mr

Moffat to say a word or two about the tides, his advice would not have been less to the purpose.

"Gentlemen," he began again—"you all know that I am a thorough-paced reformer—"

"Oh, drat your reform. He's a dumb dog. Go back to your goose, Snippy; you never were made for this work. Go to Courcy Castle and reform that."

Mr Moffat, grieved in his soul, was becoming inextricably bewildered by such facetiæ as these, when an egg,—and it may be feared not a fresh egg,—flung with unerring precision, struck him on the open part of his well-plaited shirt, and reduced him to speechless despair.

An egg is a means of delightful support when properly administered; but it is not calculated to add much spirit to a man's eloquence, or to ensure his powers of endurance, when supplied in the manner above described. Men there are, doubtless, whose tongues would not be stopped even by such an argument as this; but Mr Moffat was not one of them. As the insidious fluid trickled down beneath his waistcoat, he felt that all further powers of coaxing the electors out of their votes, by words flowing from his tongue sweeter than honey, was for that occasion denied to him. He could not be self-confident, energetic, witty, and good-humoured with a rotten egg drying through his clothes. He was forced, therefore, to give way, and with sadly disconcerted air retired from the open window at which he had been standing.

It was in vain that the Honourable George, Mr Nearthewinde, and Frank endeavoured again to bring him to the charge. He was like a beaten prize-fighter, whose pluck has been cowed out of him, and who, if he stands up, only stands up to fall. Mr Moffat got sulky also, and when he was pressed, said that Barchester and the people in it might be d——. "With all my heart," said Mr Nearthewinde. "That wouldn't have any effect on their votes."

But, in truth, it mattered very little whether Mr Moffat spoke, or whether he didn't speak. Four o'clock was the hour for closing the poll, and that was now fast coming. Tremendous exertions had been made about half-past three, by a safe emissary sent from Nearthewinde, to prove to Mr Reddypalm that all manner of contingent advantages would accrue to the Brown Bear if it should turn out that Mr Moffat should take his seat for Barchester. No bribe was, of course, offered or even hinted at. The purity of Barchester was not contaminated during the day by one such curse as this. But a man, and a publican, would be required to do some great deed in the public line; to open some colossal tap; to draw beer for the million; and no one would be so fit as Mr Reddypalm—if only it might turn out that Mr Moffat should, in the coming February, take his seat as member for Barchester.

But Mr Reddypalm was a man of humble desires, whose ambitions soared no higher than this—that his little bills should be duly settled. It is wonderful what love an innkeeper has for his bill in its entirety. An account, with a respectable total of five or six pounds, is brought to you, and you complain but of one article; that fire in the bedroom was never lighted; or that second glass of brandy and water was never called for. You desire to have the shilling expunged, and all your host's pleasure in the whole transaction is destroyed. Oh! my friends, pay for the brandy and water, though you never drank it; suffer the fire to pass, though it never warmed you. Why make a good man miserable for such a trifle?

It became notified to Reddypalm with sufficient clearness that his bill for the past election should be paid without further question; and, therefore, at five o'clock the Mayor of Barchester proclaimed the results of the contest in the following figures:—

Scatcherd	378
Moffat	376

Mr Reddypalm's two votes had decided the question. Mr Nearthewinde immediately went up to town; and the dinner party at Courcy Castle that evening was not a particularly pleasant meal.

This much, however, had been absolutely decided before the yellow committee concluded their labour at the White Horse: there should be a petition. Mr Nearthewinde had not been asleep, and already knew something of the manner in which Mr Reddypalm's mind had been quieted.

CHAPTER XVIII

THE RIVALS

The intimacy between Frank and Miss Dunstable grew and prospered. That is to say, it prospered as an intimacy, though perhaps hardly as a love affair. There was a continued succession of jokes between them, which no one else in the castle understood; but the very fact of there being such a good understanding between them rather stood in the way of, than assisted, that consummation which the countess desired. People, when they are in love with each other, or even when they pretend to be, do not generally show it by loud laughter. Nor is it frequently the case that a wife with two hundred thousand pounds can be won without some little preliminary despair. Now there was no despair at all about Frank Gresham.

Lady de Courcy, who thoroughly understood that portion of the world in which she herself lived, saw that things were not going quite as they should do, and gave much and repeated advice to Frank on the subject. She was the more eager in doing this, because she imagined Frank had done what he could to obey her first precepts. He had not turned up his nose at Miss Dunstable's curls, nor found fault with her loud voice: he had not objected to her as ugly, nor even shown any dislike to her age. A young man who had been so amenable to reason was worthy of further assistance; and so Lady de Courcy did what she could to assist him.

"Frank, my dear boy," she would say, "you are a little too noisy, I think. I don't mean for myself, you know; I don't mind it. But Miss Dunstable would like it better if you were a little more quiet with her."

"Would she, aunt?" said Frank, looking demurely up into the countess's face. "I rather think she likes fun and noise, and that sort of thing. You know she's not very quiet herself."

"Ah!—but Frank, there are times, you know, when that sort of thing should be laid aside. Fun, as you call it, is all very well in its place. Indeed, no one likes it better than I do. But that's not the way to show admiration. Young ladies like to be admired; and if you'll be a little more soft-mannered with Miss Dunstable, I'm sure you'll find it will answer better."

And so the old bird taught the young bird how to fly—very needlessly—for in this matter of flying, Nature gives her own lessons thoroughly; and the ducklings will take the water, even though the maternal hen warn them against the perfidious element never so loudly.

Soon after this, Lady de Courcy began to be not very well pleased in the matter. She took it into her head that Miss Dunstable was sometimes almost inclined to laugh at her; and on one or two occasions it almost seemed as though Frank was joining Miss Dunstable in doing so. The fact indeed was, that Miss Dunstable was fond of fun; and, endowed as she was with all the privileges which two hundred thousand pounds may be supposed to give to a young lady, did not very much care at whom she laughed. She was able to make a tolerably correct guess at Lady de Courcy's plan towards herself; but she did not for a moment think that Frank had any intention of furthering his aunt's views. She was, therefore, not at all ill-inclined to have her revenge on the countess.

"How very fond your aunt is of you!" she said to him one wet morning, as he was sauntering through the house; now laughing, and almost romping with her—then teasing his sister about Mr Moffat—and then bothering his lady-cousins out of all their propriety.

"Oh, very!" said Frank: "she is a dear, good woman, is my Aunt de Courcy."

"I declare she takes more notice of you and your doings than of any of your cousins. I wonder they ain't jealous."

"Oh! they're such good people. Bless me, they'd never be jealous."

"You are so much younger than they are, that I suppose she thinks you want more of her care."

"Yes; that's it. You see she's fond of having a baby to nurse."

"Tell me, Mr Gresham, what was it she was saying to you last night? I know we had been misbehaving ourselves dreadfully. It was all your fault; you would make me laugh so."

"That's just what I said to her."

"She was talking about me, then?"

"How on earth should she talk of any one else as long as you are here? Don't you know that all the world is talking about you?"

"Is it?—dear me, how kind! But I don't care a straw about any world just at present but Lady de Courcy's world. What did she say?"

"She said you were very beautiful—"

"Did she?—how good of her!"

"No; I forgot. It—it was I that said that; and she said—what was it she said? She said, that after all, beauty was but skin deep—and that she valued you for your virtues and prudence rather than your good looks."

"Virtues and prudence! She said I was prudent and virtuous?"

"Yes."

"And you talked of my beauty? That was so kind of you. You didn't either of you say anything about other matters?"

"What other matters?"

"Oh! I don't know. Only some people are sometimes valued rather for what they've got than for any good qualities belonging to themselves intrinsically."

"That can never be the case with Miss Dunstable; especially not at Courcy Castle," said Frank, bowing easily from the corner of the sofa over which he was leaning.

"Of course not," said Miss Dunstable; and Frank at once perceived that she spoke in a tone of voice differing much from that half-bantering, half-good-humoured manner that was customary with her. "Of course not: any such idea would be quite out of the question with Lady de Courcy." She paused for a moment, and then added in a tone different again, and unlike any that he had yet heard from her:—"It is, at any rate, out of the question with Mr Frank Gresham—of that I am quite sure."

Frank ought to have understood her, and have appreciated the good opinion which she intended to convey; but he did not entirely do so. He was hardly honest himself towards her; and he could not at first perceive that she intended to say that she thought him so. He knew very well that she was alluding to her own huge fortune, and was alluding also to the fact that people of fashion sought her because of it; but he did not know that she intended to express a true acquittal as regarded him of any such baseness.

And did he deserve to be acquitted? Yes, upon the whole he did;—to be acquitted of that special sin. His desire to make Miss Dunstable temporarily subject to his sway arose, not from a hankering after her fortune, but from an ambition to get the better of a contest in which other men around him seemed to be failing.

For it must not be imagined that, with such a prize to be struggled for, all others stood aloof and allowed him to have his own way with the heiress, undisputed. The chance of a wife with two hundred thousand pounds is a godsend which comes in a man's life too seldom to be neglected, let that chance be never so remote.

Frank was the heir to a large embarrassed property; and, therefore, the heads of families, putting their wisdoms together, had thought it most meet that this daughter of Plutus should, if possible, fall to his lot. But not so thought the Honourable George; and not so thought another gentleman who was at that time an inmate of Courcy Castle.

These suitors perhaps somewhat despised their young rival's efforts. It may be that they had sufficient worldly wisdom to know that so important a crisis of life is not settled among quips and jokes, and that Frank was too much in jest to be in earnest. But be that as it may, his love-making did not stand in the way of their love-making; nor his hopes, if he had any, in the way of their hopes.

The Honourable George had discussed the matter with the Honourable John in a properly fraternal manner. It may be that John had also an eye to the heiress; but, if so, he had ceded his views to his brother's superior claims; for it came about that they understood each other very well, and John favoured George with salutary advice on the occasion.

"If it is to be done at all, it should be done very sharp," said John.

"As sharp as you like," said George. "I'm not the fellow to be studying three months in what attitude I'll fall at a girl's feet."

"No: and when you are there you mustn't take three months more to study how you'll get up again. If you do it at all, you must do it sharp," repeated John, putting great stress on his advice.

"I have said a few soft words to her already, and she didn't seem to take them badly," said George.

"She's no chicken, you know," remarked John; "and with a woman like that, beating about the bush never does any good. The chances are she won't have you—that's of course; plums like that don't fall into a man's mouth merely for shaking the tree. But it's possible she may; and if she will, she's as likely to take you to-day as this day six months. If I were you I'd write her a letter."

"Write her a letter—eh?" said George, who did not altogether dislike the advice, for it seemed to take from his shoulders the burden of preparing a spoken address. Though he was so glib in speaking about the farmers' daughters, he felt that he should have some little difficulty in making known his passion to Miss Dunstable by word of mouth.

"Yes; write a letter. If she'll take you at all, she'll take you that way; half the matches going are made up by writing letters. Write her a letter and get it put on her dressing-table." George said that he would, and so he did.

George spoke quite truly when he hinted that he had said a few soft things to Miss Dunstable. Miss Dunstable, however, was accustomed to hear soft things. She had been carried much about in society among fashionable people since, on the settlement of her father's will, she had been pronounced heiress to all the ointment of Lebanon; and many men had made calculations respecting her similar to those which were now animating the brain of the Honourable George de Courcy. She was already quite accustomed to being the target at which spendthrifts and the needy rich might shoot their arrows: accustomed to being shot at, and tolerably accustomed to protect herself without making scenes in the world, or rejecting the advantageous establishments offered to her with any loud expressions of disdain. The Honourable George, therefore, had been permitted to say soft things very much as a matter of course.

And very little more outward fracas arose from the correspondence which followed than had arisen from the soft things so said. George wrote the letter, and had it duly conveyed to Miss Dunstable's bed-chamber. Miss Dunstable duly received it, and had her answer conveyed back discreetly to George's hands. The correspondence ran as follows:—

Courcy Castle, Aug. —, 185—.

MY DEAREST MISS DUNSTABLE, I cannot but flatter myself that you must have perceived from my manner that you are not indifferent to me. Indeed, indeed, you are not. I may truly say, and swear [these last strong words had been put in by the special counsel of the Honourable John], that if ever a man loved a woman truly, I truly love you. You may think it very odd that I should say this in a letter instead of speaking it out before your face; but your powers of raillery are so great ["touch her up about her wit" had been the advice of the Honourable John] that I am all but afraid to encounter them. Dearest, dearest Martha—oh do not blame me for so addressing you!—if you will trust your happiness to me you shall never find that you have been deceived. My ambition shall be to make you shine in that circle which you are so well qualified to adorn, and to see you firmly fixed in that sphere of fashion for which all your tastes adapt you.

I may safely assert—and I do assert it with my hand on my heart—that I am actuated by no mercenary motives. Far be it from me to marry any woman—no, not a princess—on account of her money. No marriage can be happy without mutual affection; and I do fully trust—no, not trust, but hope—that there may be such between you and me, dearest Miss Dunstable. Whatever settlements you might propose, I should accede to. It is you, your sweet person, that I love, not your money.

For myself, I need not remind you that I am the second son of my father; and that, as such, I hold no inconsiderable station in the world. My intention is to get into Parliament, and to make a name for myself, if I can, among those who shine in the House of Commons. My elder brother, Lord Porlock, is, you are aware, unmarried; and we all fear that the family honours are not likely to be perpetuated by him, as he has all manner of troublesome liaisons which will probably prevent his settling in life. There is nothing at all of that kind in my way. It will indeed be a delight to place a coronet on the head of my lovely Martha: a coronet which can give no fresh grace to her, but which will be so much adorned by her wearing it.

Dearest Miss Dunstable, I shall wait with the utmost impatience for your answer; and now, burning with hope that it may not be altogether unfavourable to my love, I beg permission to sign myself—
Your own most devoted,
GEORGE DE COURCY.

The ardent lover had not to wait long for an answer from his mistress. She found this letter on her toilet-table one night as she went to bed. The next morning she came down to breakfast and met her swain with the most unconcerned air in the world; so much so that he began to think, as he munched his toast with rather a shamefaced look, that the letter on which so much was to depend had not yet come safely to hand. But his suspense was not of a prolonged duration. After breakfast, as was his wont, he went out to the stables with his brother and Frank Gresham; and while there, Miss Dunstable's man, coming up to him, touched his hat, and put a letter into his hand.

Frank, who knew the man, glanced at the letter and looked at his cousin; but he said nothing. He was, however, a little jealous, and felt that an injury was done to him by any correspondence between Miss Dunstable and his cousin George.

Miss Dunstable's reply was as follows; and it may be remarked that it was written in a very clear and well-penned hand, and one which certainly did not betray much emotion of the heart:—

MY DEAR MR DE COURCY, I am sorry to say that I had not perceived from your manner that you entertained any peculiar feelings towards me; as, had I done so, I should at once have endeavoured to put an end to them. I am much flattered by the way in which you speak of me; but I am in too humble a position to return your affection; and can, therefore, only express a hope that you may be soon able to eradicate it from your bosom. A letter is a very good way of making an offer, and as such I do not think it at all odd; but I certainly did not expect such an honour last night. As to my raillery, I trust it has never yet hurt you. I can assure you it never shall. I hope you will soon have a worthier ambition than that to which you allude; for I am well aware that no attempt will ever make me shine anywhere.

> I am quite sure you have had no mercenary motives: such motives in marriage are very base, and quite below your name and lineage. Any little fortune that I may have must be a matter of indifference to one who looks forward, as you do, to put a coronet on his wife's brow. Nevertheless, for the sake of the family, I trust that Lord Porlock, in spite of his obstacles, may live to do the same for a wife of his own some of these days. I am glad to hear that there is nothing to interfere with your own prospects of domestic felicity.
>
> Sincerely hoping that you may be perfectly successful in your proud ambition to shine in Parliament, and regretting extremely that I cannot share that ambition with you, I beg to subscribe myself, with very great respect,—
> Your sincere well-wisher,
> MARTHA DUNSTABLE.

The Honourable George, with that modesty which so well became him, accepted Miss Dunstable's reply as a final answer to his little proposition, and troubled her with no further courtship. As he said to his brother John, no harm had been done, and he might have better luck next time. But there was an inmate of Courcy Castle who was somewhat more pertinacious in his search after love and wealth. This was no other than Mr Moffat: a gentleman whose ambition was not satisfied by the cares of his Barchester contest, or the possession of one affianced bride.

Mr Moffat was, as we have said, a man of wealth; but we all know, from the lessons of early youth, how the love of money increases and gains strength by its own success. Nor was he a man of so mean a spirit as to be satisfied with mere wealth. He desired also place and station, and gracious countenance among the great ones of the earth. Hence had come his adherence to the de Courcys; hence his seat in Parliament; and hence, also, his perhaps ill-considered match with Miss Gresham.

There is no doubt but that the privilege of matrimony offers opportunities to money-loving young men which ought not to be lightly abused. Too many young men marry without giving any consideration to the matter whatever. It is not that they are indifferent to money, but that they recklessly miscalculate their own value, and omit to look around and see how much is done by those who are more careful. A man can be young but once, and, except in cases of a special interposition of Providence, can marry but once. The chance once thrown away may be said to be irrevocable! How, in after-life, do men toil and turmoil through long years to attain some prospect of doubtful advancement! Half that trouble, half that care, a tithe of that circumspection would, in early youth, have probably secured to them the enduring comfort of a wife's wealth.

You will see men labouring night and day to become bank directors; and even a bank direction may only be the road to ruin. Others will spend years in degrading subserviency to obtain a niche in a will; and the niche, when at last obtained and enjoyed, is but a sorry payment for all that has been endured. Others, again, struggle harder still, and go through even deeper waters: they make wills for themselves, forge stock-shares, and fight with unremitting, painful labour to appear to be the thing that they are not. Now, in many of these cases, all this might have been spared had the men made adequate use of those opportunities which youth and youthful charms afford once—and once only. There is no road to wealth so easy and respectable as that of matrimony; that, is of course, provided that the aspirant declines the slow course of honest work. But then, we can so seldom put old heads on young shoulders!

In the case of Mr Moffat, we may perhaps say that a specimen was produced of this bird, so rare in the land. His shoulders were certainly young, seeing that he was not yet six-and-twenty; but his head had ever been old. From the moment when he was first put forth to go alone—at the age of twenty-one—his life had been one calculation how he could make the most of himself. He had allowed himself to be betrayed into no folly by an unguarded heart; no youthful indiscretion had marred his prospects. He had made the most of himself. Without wit, or depth, or any mental gift—without honesty of purpose or industry for good work—he had been for two years sitting member for Barchester; was the guest of Lord de Courcy; was engaged to the eldest daughter of one of the best commoners' families in England; and was, when he first began to think of Miss Dunstable, sanguine that his re-election to Parliament was secure.

When, however, at this period he began to calculate what his position in the world really was, it occurred to him that he was doing an ill-judged thing in marrying Miss Gresham. Why marry a penniless girl—for Augusta's trifle of a fortune was not a penny in his estimation—while there was Miss Dunstable in the world to be won? His own six or seven thousand a year, quite unembarrassed as it was, was certainly a great thing; but what might he not do if to that he could add the almost fabulous wealth of the great heiress? Was she not here, put absolutely in his path? Would it not be a wilful throwing away of a chance not to avail himself of it? He must, to be sure, lose the de Courcy friendship; but if he should then have secured his Barchester seat for the usual term of parliamentary session, he might be able to spare that. He would also, perhaps, encounter some Gresham enmity: this was a point on which he did think more than once: but what will not a man encounter for the sake of two hundred thousand pounds?

It was thus that Mr Moffat argued with himself, with much prudence, and brought himself to resolve that he would at any rate become a candidate for the great prize. He also, therefore, began to say soft things; and it must be admitted that he said them with more considerate propriety than had the Honourable George. Mr Moffat had an idea that Miss Dunstable was not a fool, and that in order to catch her he must do more than endeavour to lay salt on her tail, in the guise of flattery. It was evident to him that she was a bird of some cunning, not to be caught by an ordinary gin, such as those commonly in use with the Honourable Georges of Society.

It seemed to Mr Moffat, that though Miss Dunstable was so sprightly, so full of fun, and so ready to chatter on all subjects, she well knew the value of her own money, and of her position as dependent on it: he perceived that she never flattered the countess, and seemed to be no whit absorbed by the titled grandeur of her host's family. He gave her credit, therefore, for an independent spirit: and an independent spirit in his estimation was one that placed its sole dependence on a respectable balance at its banker's.

Working on these ideas, Mr Moffat commenced operations in such manner that his overtures to the heiress should not, if unsuccessful, interfere with the Greshamsbury engagement. He began by making common cause with Miss Dunstable: their positions in the world, he said to her, were closely similar. They had both risen from the lower class by the strength of honest industry: they were both now wealthy, and had both hitherto made such use of their wealth as to induce the highest aristocracy of England to admit them into their circles.

"Yes, Mr Moffat," had Miss Dunstable remarked; "and if all that I hear be true, to admit you into their very families."

At this Mr Moffat slightly demurred. He would not affect, he said, to misunderstand what Miss Dunstable meant. There had been something said on the probability of such an event; but he begged Miss Dunstable not to believe all that she heard on such subjects.

"I do not believe much," said she; "but I certainly did think that that might be credited."

Mr Moffat then went on to show how it behoved them both, in holding out their hands half-way to meet the aristocratic overtures that were made to them, not to allow themselves to be made use of. The aristocracy, according to Mr Moffat, were people of a very nice sort; the best acquaintance in the world; a portion of mankind to be noticed by whom should be one of the first objects in the life of the Dunstables and the Moffats. But the Dunstables and Moffats should be very careful to give little or nothing in return. Much, very much in return, would be looked for. The aristocracy, said Mr Moffat, were not a people to allow the light of their countenance to shine forth without looking for a *quid pro quo*, for some compensating value. In all their intercourse with the Dunstables and Moffats, they would expect a payment. It was for the Dunstables and Moffats to see that, at any rate, they did not pay more for the article they got than its market value.

The way in which she, Miss Dunstable, and he, Mr Moffat, would be required to pay would be by taking each of them some poor scion of the aristocracy in marriage; and thus expending their hard-earned wealth in procuring high-priced pleasures for some well-born pauper. Against this, peculiar caution was to be used. Of course, the further induction to be shown was this: that people so circumstanced should marry among themselves; the Dunstables and the Moffats each with the other, and not tumble into the pitfalls prepared for them.

Whether these great lessons had any lasting effect on Miss Dunstable's mind may be doubted. Perhaps she had already made up her mind on the subject which Mr Moffat so well discussed. She was older than Mr Moffat, and, in spite of his two years of parliamentary experience, had perhaps more knowledge of the world with which she had to deal. But she listened to what he said with complacency; understood his object as well as she had that of his aristocratic rival; was no whit offended; but groaned in her spirit as she thought of the wrongs of Augusta Gresham.

But all this good advice, however, would not win the money for Mr Moffat without some more decided step; and that step he soon decided on taking, feeling assured that what he had said would have its due weight with the heiress.

The party at Courcy Castle was now soon about to be broken up. The male de Courcys were going down to a Scotch mountain. The female de Courcys were to be shipped off to an Irish castle. Mr Moffat was to go up to town to prepare his petition. Miss Dunstable was again about to start on a foreign tour in behalf of her physician and attendants; and Frank Gresham was at last to be allowed to go to Cambridge; that is to say, unless his success with Miss Dunstable should render such a step on his part quite preposterous.

"I think you may speak now, Frank," said the countess. "I really think you may: you have known her now for a considerable time; and, as far as I can judge, she is very fond of you."

"Nonsense, aunt," said Frank; "she doesn't care a button for me."

"I think differently; and lookers-on, you know, always understand the game best. I suppose you are not afraid to ask her."

"Afraid!" said Frank, in a tone of considerable scorn. He almost made up his mind that he would ask her to show that he was not afraid. His only obstacle to doing so was, that he had not the slightest intention of marrying her.

There was to be but one other great event before the party broke up, and that was a dinner at the Duke of Omnium's. The duke had already declined to come to Courcy; but he had in a measure atoned for this by asking some of the guests to join a great dinner which he was about to give to his neighbours.

Mr Moffat was to leave Courcy Castle the day after the dinner-party, and he therefore determined to make his great attempt on the morning of that day. It was with some difficulty that he brought about an opportunity; but at last he did so, and found himself alone with Miss Dunstable in the walks of Courcy Park.

"It is a strange thing, is it not," said he, recurring to his old view of the same subject, "that I should be going to dine with the Duke of Omnium—the richest man, they say, among the whole English aristocracy?"

"Men of that kind entertain everybody, I believe, now and then," said Miss Dunstable, not very civilly.

"I believe they do; but I am not going as one of the everybodies. I am going from Lord de Courcy's house with some of his own family. I have no pride in that—not the least; I have more pride in my father's honest industry. But it shows what money does in this country of ours."

"Yes, indeed; money does a great deal many queer things." In saying this Miss Dunstable could not but think that money had done a very queer thing in inducing Miss Gresham to fall in love with Mr Moffat.

"Yes; wealth is very powerful: here we are, Miss Dunstable, the most honoured guests in the house."

"Oh! I don't know about that; you may be, for you are a member of Parliament, and all that—"

"No; not a member now, Miss Dunstable."

"Well, you will be, and that's all the same; but I have no such title to honour, thank God."

They walked on in silence for a little while, for Mr Moffat hardly knew how to manage the business he had in hand. "It is quite delightful to watch these people," he said at last; "now they accuse us of being tuft-hunters."

"Do they?" said Miss Dunstable. "Upon my word I didn't know that anybody ever so accused me."

"I didn't mean you and me personally."

"Oh! I'm glad of that."

"But that is what the world says of persons of our class. Now it seems to me that the toadying is all on the other side. The countess here does toady you, and so do the young ladies."

"Do they? if so, upon my word I didn't know it. But, to tell the truth, I don't think much of such things. I live mostly to myself, Mr Moffat."

"I see that you do, and I admire you for it; but, Miss Dunstable, you cannot always live so," and Mr Moffat looked at her in a manner which gave her the first intimation of his coming burst of tenderness.

"That's as may be, Mr Moffat," said she.

He went on beating about the bush for some time—giving her to understand how necessary it was that persons situated as they were should live either for themselves or for each other, and that, above all things, they should beware of falling into the mouths of voracious aristocratic lions who go about looking for prey—till they came to a turn in the grounds; at which Miss Dunstable declared her determination of going in. She had walked enough, she said. As by this time Mr Moffat's immediate intentions were becoming visible she thought it prudent to retire. "Don't let me take you in, Mr Moffat; but my boots are a little damp, and Dr Easyman will never forgive me if I do not hurry in as fast as I can."

"Your feet damp?—I hope not: I do hope not," said he, with a look of the greatest solicitude.

"Oh! it's nothing to signify; but it's well to be prudent, you know. Good morning, Mr Moffat."

"Miss Dunstable!"

"Eh—yes!" and Miss Dunstable stopped in the grand path. "I won't let you return with me, Mr Moffat, because I know you were not coming in so soon."

"Miss Dunstable; I shall be leaving this to-morrow."

"Yes; and I go myself the day after."

"I know it. I am going to town and you are going abroad. It may be long—very long—before we meet again."

"About Easter," said Miss Dunstable; "that is, if the doctor doesn't knock up on the road."

"And I had, had wished to say something before we part for so long a time. Miss Dunstable—"

"Stop!—Mr Moffat. Let me ask you one question. I'll hear anything that you have got to say, but on one condition: that is, that Miss Augusta Gresham shall be by while you say it. Will you consent to that?"

"Miss Augusta Gresham," said he, "has no right to listen to my private conversation."

"Has she not, Mr Moffat? then I think she should have. I, at any rate, will not so far interfere with what I look on as her undoubted privileges as to be a party to any secret in which she may not participate."

"But, Miss Dunstable—"

"And to tell you fairly, Mr Moffat, any secret that you do tell me, I shall most undoubtedly repeat to her before dinner. Good morning, Mr Moffat; my feet are certainly a little damp, and if I stay a moment longer, Dr Easyman will put off my foreign trip for at least a week." And so she left him standing alone in the middle of the gravel-walk.

For a moment or two, Mr Moffat consoled himself in his misfortune by thinking how he might best avenge himself on Miss Dunstable. Soon, however, such futile ideas left his brain. Why should he give over the chase because the rich galleon had escaped him on this, his first cruise in pursuit of her? Such prizes were not to be won so easily. Her present objection clearly consisted in his engagement to Miss Gresham, and in that only. Let that engagement be at an end, notoriously and publicly broken off, and this objection would fall to the ground. Yes; ships so richly freighted were not to be run down in one summer morning's plain sailing. Instead of looking for his revenge on Miss Dunstable, it would be more prudent in him—more in keeping with his character—to pursue his object, and overcome such difficulties as he might find in his way.

CHAPTER XIX

THE DUKE OF OMNIUM

The Duke of Omnium was, as we have said, a bachelor. Not the less on that account did he on certain rare gala days entertain the beauty of the county at his magnificent rural seat, or the female fashion of London in Belgrave Square; but on this occasion the dinner at Gatherum Castle—for such was the name of his mansion—was to be confined to the lords of the creation. It was to be one of those days on which he collected round his board all the notables of the county, in order that his popularity might not wane, or the established glory of his hospitable house become dim.

On such an occasion it was not probable that Lord de Courcy would be one of the guests. The party, indeed, who went from Courcy Castle was not large, and consisted of the Honourable George, Mr Moffat, and Frank Gresham. They went in a tax-cart, with a tandem horse, driven very knowingly by George de Courcy; and the fourth seat on the back of the vehicle was occupied by a servant, who was to look after the horses at Gatherum.

The Honourable George drove either well or luckily, for he reached the duke's house in safety; but he drove very fast. Poor Miss Dunstable! what would have been her lot had anything but good happened to that vehicle, so richly freighted with her three lovers! They did not quarrel as to the prize, and all reached Gatherum Castle in good humour with each other.

The castle was new building of white stone, lately erected at an enormous cost by one of the first architects of the day. It was an immense pile, and seemed to cover ground enough for a moderate-sized town. But, nevertheless, report said that when it was completed, the noble owner found that he had no rooms to live in; and that, on this account, when disposed to study his own comfort, he resided in a house of perhaps one-tenth the size, built by his grandfather in another county.

Gatherum Castle would probably be called Italian in its style of architecture; though it may, I think, be doubted whether any such edifice, or anything like it, was ever seen in any part of Italy. It was a vast edifice; irregular in height—or it appeared to be so—having long wings on each side too high to be passed over by the eye as mere adjuncts to the mansion, and a portico so large as to make the house behind it look like another building of a greater altitude. This portico was supported by Ionic columns, and was in itself doubtless a beautiful structure. It was approached by a flight of steps, very broad and very grand; but, as an approach by a flight of steps hardly suits an Englishman's house, to the immediate entrance of which it is necessary that his carriage should drive, there was another front door in one of the wings which was commonly used. A carriage, however, could on very stupendously grand occasions—the visits, for instance, of queens and kings, and royal dukes—be brought up under the portico; as the steps had been so constructed as to admit of a road, with a rather stiff ascent, being made close in front of the wing up into the very porch.

Opening from the porch was the grand hall, which extended up to the top of the house. It was magnificent, indeed; being decorated with many-coloured marbles, and hung round with various trophies of the house of Omnium; banners were there, and armour; the sculptured busts of many noble progenitors; full-length figures in marble of those who had been especially prominent; and every monument of glory that wealth, long years, and great achievements could bring together. If only a man could but live in his hall and be for ever happy there! But the Duke of Omnium could not live happily in his hall; and the fact was, that the architect, in contriving this magnificent entrance for his own honour and fame, had destroyed the duke's house as regards most of the ordinary purposes of residence.

Nevertheless, Gatherum Castle is a very noble pile; and, standing as it does on an eminence, has a very fine effect when seen from many a distant knoll and verdant-wooded hill.

At seven o'clock Mr de Courcy and his friends got down from their drag at the smaller door—for this was no day on which to mount up under the portico; nor was that any suitable vehicle to have been entitled to such honour. Frank felt some excitement a little stronger than that usual to him at such moments, for he had never yet been in company with the Duke of Omnium; and he rather puzzled himself to think on what points he would talk to the man who was the largest landowner in that county in which he himself had so great an interest. He, however, made up his mind that he would allow the duke to choose his own subjects; merely reserving to himself the right of pointing out how deficient in gorse covers was West Barsetshire—that being the duke's division.

They were soon divested of their coats and hats, and, without entering on the magnificence of the great hall, were conducted through rather a narrow passage into rather a small drawing-room—small, that is, in proportion to the number of gentlemen there assembled. There might be about thirty, and Frank was inclined to think that they were almost crowded. A man came forward to greet them when their names were announced; but our hero at once knew that he was not the duke; for this man was fat and short, whereas the duke was thin and tall.

There was a great hubbub going on; for everybody seemed to be talking to his neighbour; or, in default of a neighbour, to himself. It was clear that the exalted rank of their host had put very little constraint on his guests' tongues, for they chatted away with as much freedom as farmers at an ordinary.

"Which is the duke?" at last Frank contrived to whisper to his cousin.

"Oh;—he's not here," said George; "I suppose he'll be in presently. I believe he never shows till just before dinner."

Frank, of course, had nothing further to say; but he already began to feel himself a little snubbed: he thought that the duke, duke though he was, when he asked people to dinner should be there to tell them that he was glad to see them.

More people flashed into the room, and Frank found himself rather closely wedged in with a stout clergyman of his acquaintance. He was not badly off, for Mr Athill was a friend of his own, who had held a living near Greshamsbury. Lately, however, at the lamented decease of Dr Stanhope—who had died of apoplexy at his villa in Italy—Mr Athill had been presented with the better preferment of Eiderdown, and had, therefore, removed to another part of the county. He was somewhat of a bon-vivant, and a man who thoroughly understood dinner-parties; and with much good nature he took Frank under his special protection.

"You stick to me, Mr Gresham," he said, "when we go into the dining-room. I'm an old hand at the duke's dinners, and know how to make a friend comfortable as well as myself."

"But why doesn't the duke come in?" demanded Frank.

"He'll be here as soon as dinner is ready," said Mr Athill. "Or, rather, the dinner will be ready as soon as he is here. I don't care, therefore, how soon he comes."

Frank did not understand this, but he had nothing to do but to wait and see how things went.

He was beginning to be impatient, for the room was now nearly full, and it seemed evident that no other guests were coming; when suddenly a bell rang, and a gong was sounded, and at the same instant a door that had not yet been used flew open, and a very plainly dressed, plain, tall man entered the room. Frank at once knew that he was at last in the presence of the Duke of Omnium.

But his grace, late as he was in commencing the duties as host, seemed in no hurry to make up for lost time. He quietly stood on the rug, with his back to the empty grate, and spoke one or two words in a very low voice to one or two gentlemen who stood nearest to him. The crowd, in the meanwhile, became suddenly silent. Frank, when he found that the duke did not come and speak to him, felt that he ought to go and speak to the duke; but no one else did so, and when he whispered his surprise to Mr Athill, that gentleman told him that this was the duke's practice on all such occasions.

"Fothergill," said the duke—and it was the only word he had yet spoken out loud—"I believe we are ready for dinner." Now Mr Fothergill was the duke's land-agent, and he it was who had greeted Frank and his friends at their entrance.

Immediately the gong was again sounded, and another door leading out of the drawing-room into the dining-room was opened. The duke led the way, and then the guests followed. "Stick close to me, Mr Gresham," said Athill, "we'll get about the middle of the table, where we shall be cosy—and on the other side of the room, out of this dreadful draught—I know the place well, Mr Gresham; stick to me."

Mr Athill, who was a pleasant, chatty companion, had hardly seated himself, and was talking to Frank as quickly as he could, when Mr Fothergill, who sat at the bottom of the table, asked him to say grace. It seemed to be quite out of the question that the duke should take any trouble with his guests whatever. Mr Athill consequently dropped the word he was speaking, and uttered a prayer—if it was a prayer—that they might all have grateful hearts for that which God was about to give them.

If it was a prayer! As far as my own experience goes, such utterances are seldom prayers, seldom can be prayers. And if not prayers, what then? To me it is unintelligible that the full tide of glibbest chatter can be stopped at a moment in the midst of profuse good living, and the Giver thanked becomingly in words of heartfelt praise. Setting aside for the moment what one daily hears and sees, may not one declare that a change so sudden is not within the compass of the human mind? But then, to such reasoning one cannot but add what one does hear and see; one cannot but judge of the ceremony by the manner in which one sees it performed—uttered, that is—and listened to. Clergymen there are—one meets them now and then—who endeavour to give to the dinner-table grace some of the solemnity of a church ritual, and what is the effect? Much the same as though one were to be interrupted for a minute in the midst of one of our church liturgies to hear a drinking-song.

And it will be argued, that a man need be less thankful because, at the moment of receiving, he utters no thanksgiving? or will it be thought that a man is made thankful because what is called a grace is uttered after dinner? It can hardly be imagined that any one will so argue, or so think.

Dinner-graces are, probably, the last remaining relic of certain daily services[1] which the Church in olden days enjoined: nones, complines, and vespers were others. Of the nones and complines we have happily got quit; and it might be well if we could get rid of the dinner-graces also. Let any man ask himself whether, on his own part, they are acts of prayer and thanksgiving—and if not that, what then?

When the large party entered the dining-room one or two gentlemen might be seen to come in from some other door and set themselves at the table near to the duke's chair. These were guests of his own, who were staying in the house, his particular friends, the men with whom he lived: the others were strangers whom he fed, perhaps once a year, in order that his name might be known in the land as that of one who distributed food and wine hospitably through the county. The food and wine, the attendance also, and the view of the vast repository of plate he vouchsafed willingly to his county neighbours;—but it was beyond his good nature to talk to them. To judge by the present appearance of most of them, they were quite as well satisfied to be left alone.

Frank was altogether a stranger there, but Mr Athill knew every one at the table.

"That's Apjohn," said he: "don't you know, Mr Apjohn, the attorney from Barchester? he's always here; he does some of Fothergill's law business, and makes himself useful. If any fellow knows the value of a good dinner, he does. You'll see that the duke's hospitality will not be thrown away on him."

"It's very much thrown away upon me, I know," said Frank, who could not at all put up with the idea of sitting down to dinner without having been spoken to by his host.

"Oh, nonsense!" said his clerical friend; "you'll enjoy yourself amazingly by and by. There is not such champagne in any other house in Barsetshire; and then the claret—" And Mr Athill pressed his lips together, and gently shook his head, meaning to signify by the motion that the claret of Gatherum Castle was sufficient atonement for any penance which a man might have to go through in his mode of obtaining it.

"Who's that funny little man sitting there, next but one to Mr de Courcy? I never saw such a queer fellow in my life."

"Don't you know old Bolus? Well, I thought every one in Barsetshire knew Bolus; you especially should do so, as he is such a dear friend of Dr Thorne."

"A dear friend of Dr Thorne?"

"Yes; he was apothecary at Scarington in the old days, before Dr Fillgrave came into vogue. I remember when Bolus was thought to be a very good sort of doctor."

"Is he—is he—" whispered Frank, "is he by way of a gentleman?"

"Ha! ha! ha! Well, I suppose we must be charitable, and say that he is quite as good, at any rate, as many others there are here—" and Mr Athill, as he spoke, whispered into Frank's ear, "You see there's Finnie here, another Barchester attorney. Now, I really think where Finnie goes Bolus may go too."

"The more the merrier, I suppose," said Frank.

"Well, something a little like that. I wonder why Thorne is not here? I'm sure he was asked."

"Perhaps he did not particularly wish to meet Finnie and Bolus. Do you know, Mr Athill, I think he was quite right not to come. As for myself, I wish I was anywhere else."

---

[1] It is, I know, alleged that graces are said before dinner, because our Saviour uttered a blessing before his last supper. I cannot say that the idea of such analogy is pleasing to me.

"Ha! ha! ha! You don't know the duke's ways yet; and what's more, you're young, you happy fellow! But Thorne should have more sense; he ought to show himself here."

The gormandizing was now going on at a tremendous rate. Though the volubility of their tongues had been for a while stopped by the first shock of the duke's presence, the guests seemed to feel no such constraint upon their teeth. They fed, one may almost say, rabidly, and gave their orders to the servants in an eager manner; much more impressive than that usual at smaller parties. Mr Apjohn, who sat immediately opposite to Frank, had, by some well-planned manoeuvre, contrived to get before him the jowl of a salmon; but, unfortunately, he was not for a while equally successful in the article of sauce. A very limited portion—so at least thought Mr Apjohn—had been put on his plate; and a servant, with a huge sauce tureen, absolutely passed behind his back inattentive to his audible requests. Poor Mr Apjohn in his despair turned round to arrest the man by his coat-tails; but he was a moment too late, and all but fell backwards on the floor. As he righted himself he muttered an anathema, and looked with a face of anguish at his plate.

"Anything the matter, Apjohn?" said Mr Fothergill, kindly, seeing the utter despair written on the poor man's countenance; "can I get anything for you?"

"The sauce!" said Mr Apjohn, in a voice that would have melted a hermit; and as he looked at Mr Fothergill, he pointed at the now distant sinner, who was dispensing his melted ambrosia at least ten heads upwards, away from the unfortunate supplicant.

Mr Fothergill, however, knew where to look for balm for such wounds, and in a minute or two, Mr Apjohn was employed quite to his heart's content.

"Well," said Frank to his neighbour, "it may be very well once in a way; but I think that on the whole Dr Thorne is right."

"My dear Mr Gresham, see the world on all sides," said Mr Athill, who had also been somewhat intent on the gratification of his own appetite, though with an energy less evident than that of the gentleman opposite. "See the world on all sides if you have an opportunity; and, believe me, a good dinner now and then is a very good thing."

"Yes; but I don't like eating it with hogs."

"Whish-h! softly, softly, Mr Gresham, or you'll disturb Mr Apjohn's digestion. Upon my word, he'll want it all before he has done. Now, I like this kind of thing once in a way."

"Do you?" said Frank, in a tone that was almost savage.

"Yes; indeed I do. One sees so much character. And after all, what harm does it do?"

"My idea is that people should live with those whose society is pleasant to them."

"Live—yes, Mr Gresham—I agree with you there. It wouldn't do for me to live with the Duke of Omnium; I shouldn't understand, or probably approve, his ways. Nor should I, perhaps, much like the constant presence of Mr Apjohn. But now and then—once in a year or so—I do own I like to see them both. Here's the cup; now, whatever you do, Mr Gresham, don't pass the cup without tasting it."

And so the dinner passed on, slowly enough as Frank thought, but all too quickly for Mr Apjohn. It passed away, and the wine came circulating freely. The tongues again were loosed, the teeth being released from their labours, and under the influence of the claret the duke's presence was forgotten.

But very speedily the coffee was brought. "This will soon be over now," said Frank, to himself, thankfully; for, though he be no means despised good claret, he had lost his temper too completely to enjoy it at the present moment. But he was much mistaken; the farce as yet was only at its commencement. The duke took his cup of coffee, and so did the few friends who sat close to him; but the beverage did not seem to be in great request with the majority of the guests. When the duke had taken his modicum, he rose up and silently retired, saying no word and making no sign. And then the farce commenced.

"Now, gentlemen," said Mr Fothergill, cheerily, "we are all right. Apjohn, is there claret there? Mr Bolus, I know you stick to the Madeira; you are quite right, for there isn't much of it left, and my belief is there'll never be more like it."

And so the duke's hospitality went on, and the duke's guests drank merrily for the next two hours.

"Shan't we see any more of him?" asked Frank.

"Any more of whom?" said Mr Athill.

"Of the duke?"

"Oh, no; you'll see no more of him. He always goes when the coffee comes. It's brought in as an excuse. We've had enough of the light of his countenance to last till next year. The duke and I are excellent friends; and have been so these fifteen years; but I never see more of him than that."

"I shall go away," said Frank.

"Nonsense. Mr de Courcy and your other friend won't stir for this hour yet."

"I don't care. I shall walk on, and they may catch me. I may be wrong; but it seems to me that a man insults me when he asks me to dine with him and never speaks to me. I don't care if he be ten times Duke of Omnium; he can't be more than a gentleman, and as such I am his equal." And then, having thus given vent to his feelings in somewhat high-flown language, he walked forth and trudged away along the road towards Courcy.

Frank Gresham had been born and bred a Conservative, whereas the Duke of Omnium was well known as a consistent Whig. There is no one so devoutly resolved to admit of no superior as your Conservative, born and bred, no one so inclined to high domestic despotism as your thoroughgoing consistent old Whig.

When he had proceeded about six miles, Frank was picked up by his friends; but even then his anger had hardly cooled.

"Was the duke as civil as ever when you took your leave of him?" said he to his cousin George, as he took his seat on the drag.

"The juke was jeuced jude wine—lem me tell you that, old fella," hiccupped out the Honourable George, as he touched up the leader under the flank.

CHAPTER XX

THE PROPOSAL

And now the departures from Courcy Castle came rapidly one after another, and there remained but one more evening before Miss Dunstable's carriage was to be packed. The countess, in the early moments of Frank's courtship, had controlled his ardour and checked the rapidity of his amorous professions; but as days, and at last weeks, wore away, she found that it was necessary to stir the fire which she had before endeavoured to slacken.

"There will be nobody here to-night but our own circle," said she to him, "and I really think you should tell Miss Dunstable what your intentions are. She will have fair ground to complain of you if you do not."

Frank began to feel that he was in a dilemma. He had commenced making love to Miss Dunstable partly because he liked the amusement, and partly from a satirical propensity to quiz his aunt by appearing to fall into her scheme. But he had overshot the mark, and did not know what answer to give when he was thus called upon to make a downright proposal. And then, although he did not care two rushes about Miss Dunstable in the way of love, he nevertheless experienced a sort of jealousy when he found that she appeared to be indifferent to him, and that she corresponded the meanwhile with his cousin George. Though all their flirtations had been carried on on both sides palpably by way of fun, though Frank had told himself ten times a day that his heart was true to Mary Thorne, yet he had an undefined feeling that it behoved Miss Dunstable to be a little in love with him. He was not quite at ease in that she was not a little melancholy now that his departure was so nigh; and, above all, he was anxious to know what were the real facts about that letter. He had in his own breast threatened Miss Dunstable with a heartache; and now, when the time for their separation came, he found that his own heart was the more likely to ache of the two.

"I suppose I must say something to her, or my aunt will never be satisfied," said he to himself as he sauntered into the little drawing-room on that last evening. But at the very time he was ashamed of himself, for he knew he was going to ask badly.

His sister and one of his cousins were in the room, but his aunt, who was quite on the alert, soon got them out of it, and Frank and Miss Dunstable were alone.

"So all our fun and all our laughter is come to an end," said she, beginning the conversation. "I don't know how you feel, but for myself I really am a little melancholy at the idea of parting;" and she looked up at him with her laughing black eyes, as though she never had, and never could have a care in the world.

"Melancholy! oh, yes; you look so," said Frank, who really did feel somewhat lacka-daisically sentimental.

"But how thoroughly glad the countess must be that we are both going," continued she. "I declare we have treated her most infamously. Ever since we've been here we've had all the amusement to ourselves. I've sometimes thought she would turn me out of the house."

"I wish with all my heart she had."

"Oh, you cruel barbarian! why on earth should you wish that?"

"That I might have joined you in your exile. I hate Courcy Castle, and should have re-joiced to leave—and—and—"

"And what?"

"And I love Miss Dunstable, and should have doubly, trebly rejoiced to leave it with her."

Frank's voice quivered a little as he made this gallant profession; but still Miss Dun-stable only laughed the louder. "Upon my word, of all my knights you are by far the best behaved," said she, "and say much the prettiest things." Frank became rather red in the face, and felt that he did so. Miss Dunstable was treating him like a boy. While she pre-tended to be so fond of him she was only laughing at him, and corresponding the while with his cousin George. Now Frank Gresham already entertained a sort of contempt for his cousin, which increased the bitterness of his feelings. Could it really be possible that George had succeeded while he had utterly failed; that his stupid cousin had touched the heart of the heiress while she was playing with him as with a boy?

"Of all your knights! Is that the way you talk to me when we are going to part? When was it, Miss Dunstable, that George de Courcy became one of them?"

Miss Dunstable for a while looked serious enough. "What makes you ask that?" said she. "What makes you inquire about Mr de Courcy?"

"Oh, I have eyes, you know, and can't help seeing. Not that I see, or have seen any-thing that I could possibly help."

"And what have you seen, Mr Gresham?"

"Why, I know you have been writing to him."

"Did he tell you so?"

"No; he did not tell me; but I know it."

For a moment she sat silent, and then her face again resumed its usual happy smile. "Come, Mr Gresham, you are not going to quarrel with me, I hope, even if I did write a letter to your cousin. Why should I not write to him? I correspond with all manner of peo-ple. I'll write to you some of these days if you'll let me, and will promise to answer my letters."

Frank threw himself back on the sofa on which he was sitting, and, in doing so, brought himself somewhat nearer to his companion than he had been; he then drew his hand slowly across his forehead, pushing back his thick hair, and as he did so he sighed somewhat plaintively.

"I do not care," said he, "for the privilege of correspondence on such terms. If my cousin George is to be a correspondent of yours also, I will give up my claim."

And then he sighed again, so that it was piteous to hear him. He was certainly an arrant puppy, and an egregious ass into the bargain; but then, it must be remembered in his fa-vour that he was only twenty-one, and that much had been done to spoil him. Miss Dunstable did remember this, and therefore abstained from laughing at him.

"Why, Mr Gresham, what on earth do you mean? In all human probability I shall nev-er write another line to Mr de Courcy; but, if I did, what possible harm could it do you?"

"Oh, Miss Dunstable! you do not in the least understand what my feelings are."

"Don't I? Then I hope I never shall. I thought I did. I thought they were the feelings of a good, true-hearted friend; feelings that I could sometimes look back upon with pleasure as being honest when so much that one meets is false. I have become very fond of you, Mr Gresham, and I should be sorry to think that I did not understand your feelings."

This was almost worse and worse. Young ladies like Miss Dunstable—for she was still to be numbered in the category of young ladies—do not usually tell young gentlemen that they are very fond of them. To boys and girls they may make such a declaration. Now Frank Gresham regarded himself as one who had already fought his battles, and fought them not without glory; he could not therefore endure to be thus openly told by Miss Dunstable that she was very fond of him.

"Fond of me, Miss Dunstable! I wish you were."

"So I am—very."

"You little know how fond I am of you, Miss Dunstable," and he put out his hand to take hold of hers. She then lifted up her own, and slapped him lightly on the knuckles.

"And what can you have to say to Miss Dunstable that can make it necessary that you should pinch her hand? I tell you fairly, Mr Gresham, if you make a fool of yourself, I shall come to a conclusion that you are all fools, and that it is hopeless to look out for any one worth caring for."

Such advice as this, so kindly given, so wisely meant, so clearly intelligible, he should have taken and understood, young as he was. But even yet he did not do so.

"A fool of myself! Yes; I suppose I must be a fool if I have so much regard for Miss Dunstable as to make it painful for me to know that I am to see her no more: a fool: yes, of course I am a fool—a man is always a fool when he loves."

Miss Dunstable could not pretend to doubt his meaning any longer; and was determined to stop him, let it cost what it would. She now put out her hand, not over white, and, as Frank soon perceived, gifted with a very fair allowance of strength.

"Now, Mr Gresham," said she, "before you go any further you shall listen to me. Will you listen to me for a moment without interrupting me?"

Frank was of course obliged to promise that he would do so.

"You are going—or rather you were going, for I shall stop you—to make a profession of love."

"A profession!" said Frank making a slight unsuccessful effort to get his hand free.

"Yes; a profession—a false profession, Mr Gresham,—a false profession—a false profession. Look into your heart—into your heart of hearts. I know you at any rate have a heart; look into it closely. Mr Gresham, you know you do not love me; not as a man should love the woman whom he swears to love."

Frank was taken aback. So appealed to he found that he could not any longer say that he did love her. He could only look into her face with all his eyes, and sit there listening to her.

"How is it possible that you should love me? I am Heaven knows how many years your senior. I am neither young nor beautiful, nor have I been brought up as she should be whom you in time will really love and make your wife. I have nothing that should make you love me; but—but I am rich."

"It is not that," said Frank, stoutly, feeling himself imperatively called upon to utter something in his own defence.

"Ah, Mr Gresham, I fear it is that. For what other reason can you have laid your plans to talk in this way to such a woman as I am?"

"I have laid no plans," said Frank, now getting his hand to himself. "At any rate, you wrong me there, Miss Dunstable."

"I like you so well—nay, love you, if a woman may talk of love in the way of friendship—that if money, money alone would make you happy, you should have it heaped on
you. If you want it, Mr Gresham, you shall have it."

"I have never thought of your money," said Frank, surlily.

"But it grieves me," continued she, "it does grieve me, to think that you, you, you—so
young, so gay, so bright—that you should have looked for it in this way. From others I
have taken it just as the wind that whistles;" and now two big slow tears escaped from her
eyes, and would have rolled down her rosy cheeks were it not that she brushed them off
with the back of her hand.

"You have utterly mistaken me, Miss Dunstable," said Frank.

"If I have, I will humbly beg your pardon," said she. "But—but—but—"

"You have; indeed you have."

"How can I have mistaken you? Were you not about to say that you loved me; to talk
absolute nonsense; to make me an offer? If you were not, if I have mistaken you indeed, I
will beg your pardon."

Frank had nothing further to say in his own defence. He had not wanted Miss Dunstable's money—that was true; but he could not deny that he had been about to talk that
absolute nonsense of which she spoke with so much scorn.

"You would almost make me think that there are none honest in this fashionable world
of yours. I well know why Lady de Courcy has had me here: how could I help knowing it?
She has been so foolish in her plans that ten times a day she has told her own secret. But I
have said to myself twenty times, that if she were crafty, you were honest."

"And am I dishonest?"

"I have laughed in my sleeve to see how she played her game, and to hear others
around playing theirs; all of them thinking that they could get the money of the poor fool
who had come at their beck and call; but I was able to laugh at them as long as I thought
that I had one true friend to laugh with me. But one cannot laugh with all the world
against one."

"I am not against you, Miss Dunstable."

"Sell yourself for money! why, if I were a man I would not sell one jot of liberty for
mountains of gold. What! tie myself in the heyday of my youth to a person I could never
love, for a price! perjure myself, destroy myself—and not only myself, but her also, in
order that I might live idly! Oh, heavens! Mr Gresham! can it be that the words of such a
woman as your aunt have sunk so deeply in your heart; have blackened you so foully as to
make you think of such vile folly as this? Have you forgotten your soul, your spirit, your
man's energy, the treasure of your heart? And you, so young! For shame, Mr Gresham! for
shame—for shame."

Frank found the task before him by no means an easy one. He had to make Miss Dunstable understand that he had never had the slightest idea of marrying her, and that he had
made love to her merely with the object of keeping his hand in for the work as it were;
with that object, and the other equally laudable one of interfering with his cousin George.

And yet there was nothing for him but to get through this task as best he might. He
was goaded to it by the accusations which Miss Dunstable brought against him; and he
began to feel, that though her invective against him might be bitter when he had told the
truth, they could not be so bitter as those she now kept hinting at under her mistaken impression as to his views. He had never had any strong propensity for money-hunting; but
now that offence appeared in his eyes abominable, unmanly, and disgusting. Any imputation would be better than that.

"Miss Dunstable, I never for a moment thought of doing what you accuse me of; on my honour, I never did. I have been very foolish—very wrong—idiotic, I believe; but I have never intended that."

"Then, Mr Gresham, what did you intend?"

This was rather a difficult question to answer; and Frank was not very quick in attempting it. "I know you will not forgive me," he said at last; "and, indeed, I do not see how you can. I don't know how it came about; but this is certain, Miss Dunstable; I have never for a moment thought about your fortune; that is, thought about it in the way of coveting it."

"You never thought of making me your wife, then?"

"Never," said Frank, looking boldly into her face.

"You never intended really to propose to go with me to the altar, and then make yourself rich by one great perjury?"

"Never for a moment," said he.

"You have never gloated over me as the bird of prey gloats over the poor beast that is soon to become carrion beneath its claws? You have not counted me out as equal to so much land, and calculated on me as a balance at your banker's? Ah, Mr Gresham," she continued, seeing that he stared as though struck almost with awe by her strong language; "you little guess what a woman situated as I am has to suffer."

"I have behaved badly to you, Miss Dunstable, and I beg your pardon; but I have never thought of your money."

"Then we will be friends again, Mr Gresham, won't we? It is so nice to have a friend like you. There, I think I understand it now; you need not tell me."

"It was half by way of making a fool of my aunt," said Frank, in an apologetic tone.

"There is merit in that, at any rate," said Miss Dunstable. "I understand it all now; you thought to make a fool of me in real earnest. Well, I can forgive that; at any rate it is not mean."

It may be, that Miss Dunstable did not feel much acute anger at finding that this young man had addressed her with words of love in the course of an ordinary flirtation, although that flirtation had been unmeaning and silly. This was not the offence against which her heart and breast had found peculiar cause to arm itself; this was not the injury from which she had hitherto experienced suffering.

At any rate, she and Frank again became friends, and, before the evening was over, they perfectly understood each other. Twice during this long *tête-à-tête* Lady de Courcy came into the room to see how things were going on, and twice she went out almost unnoticed. It was quite clear to her that something uncommon had taken place, was taking place, or would take place; and that should this be for weal or for woe, no good could now come from her interference. On each occasion, therefore, she smiled sweetly on the pair of turtle-doves, and glided out of the room as quietly as she had glided into it.

But at last it became necessary to remove them; for the world had gone to bed. Frank, in the meantime, had told to Miss Dunstable all his love for Mary Thorne, and Miss Dunstable had enjoined him to be true to his vows. To her eyes there was something of heavenly beauty in young, true love—of beauty that was heavenly because it had been unknown to her.

"Mind you let me hear, Mr Gresham," said she. "Mind you do; and, Mr Gresham, never, never forget her for one moment; not for one moment, Mr Gresham."

Frank was about to swear that he never would—again, when the countess, for the third time, sailed into the room.

"Young people," said she, "do you know what o'clock it is?"

602

"Dear me, Lady de Courcy, I declare it is past twelve; I really am ashamed of myself. How glad you will be to get rid of me to-morrow!"

"No, no, indeed we shan't; shall we, Frank?" and so Miss Dunstable passed out.

Then once again the aunt tapped her nephew with her fan. It was the last time in her life that she did so. He looked up in her face, and his look was enough to tell her that the acres of Greshamsbury were not to be reclaimed by the ointment of Lebanon.

Nothing further on the subject was said. On the following morning Miss Dunstable took her departure, not much heeding the rather cold words of farewell which her hostess gave her; and on the following day Frank started for Greshamsbury.

CHAPTER XXI

MR MOFFAT FALLS INTO TROUBLE

We will now, with the reader's kind permission, skip over some months in our narrative. Frank returned from Courcy Castle to Greshamsbury, and having communicated to his mother—much in the same manner as he had to the countess—the fact that his mission had been unsuccessful, he went up after a day or two to Cambridge. During his short stay at Greshamsbury he did not even catch a glimpse of Mary. He asked for her, of course, and was told that it was not likely that she would be at the house just at present. He called at the doctor's, but she was denied to him there; "she was out," Janet said,—"probably with Miss Oriel." He went to the parsonage and found Miss Oriel at home; but Mary had not been seen that morning. He then returned to the house; and, having come to the conclusion that she had not thus vanished into air, otherwise than by preconcerted arrangement, he boldly taxed Beatrice on the subject.

Beatrice looked very demure; declared that no one in the house had quarrelled with Mary; confessed that it had been thought prudent that she should for a while stay away from Greshamsbury; and, of course, ended by telling her brother everything, including all the scenes that had passed between Mary and herself.

"It is out of the question your thinking of marrying her, Frank," said she. "You must know that nobody feels it more strongly than poor Mary herself;" and Beatrice looked the very personification of domestic prudence.

"I know nothing of the kind," said he, with the headlong imperative air that was usual with him in discussing matters with his sisters. "I know nothing of the kind. Of course I cannot say what Mary's feelings may be: a pretty life she must have had of it among you. But you may be sure of this, Beatrice, and so may my mother, that nothing on earth shall make me give her up—nothing." And Frank, as he made the protestation, strengthened his own resolution by thinking of all the counsel that Miss Dunstable had given him.

The brother and sister could hardly agree, as Beatrice was dead against the match. Not that she would not have liked Mary Thorne for a sister-in-law, but that she shared to a certain degree the feeling which was now common to all the Greshams—that Frank must marry money. It seemed, at any rate, to be imperative that he should either do that or not marry at all. Poor Beatrice was not very mercenary in her views: she had no wish to sacrifice her brother to any Miss Dunstable; but yet she felt, as they all felt—Mary Thorne included—that such a match as that, of the young heir with the doctor's niece, was not to be thought of;—not to be spoken of as a thing that was in any way possible. Therefore, Beatrice, though she was Mary's great friend, though she was her brother's favourite sister, could give Frank no encouragement. Poor Frank! circumstances had made but one bride possible to him: he must marry money.

His mother said nothing to him on the subject: when she learnt that the affair with Miss Dunstable was not to come off, she merely remarked that it would perhaps be best for him to return to Cambridge as soon as possible. Had she spoken her mind out, she would probably have also advised him to remain there as long as possible. The countess had not omitted to write to her when Frank left Courcy Castle; and the countess's letter certainly made the anxious mother think that her son's education had hardly yet been completed. With this secondary object, but with that of keeping him out of the way of Mary Thorne in the first place, Lady Arabella was now quite satisfied that her son should enjoy such advantages as an education completed at the university might give him.

With his father Frank had a long conversation; but, alas! the gist of his father's conversation was this, that it behoved him, Frank, to marry money. The father, however, did not put it to him in the cold, callous way in which his lady-aunt had done, and his lady-mother. He did not bid him go and sell himself to the first female he could find possessed of wealth. It was with inward self-reproaches, and true grief of spirit, that the father told the son that it was not possible for him to do as those may do who are born really rich, or really poor.

"If you marry a girl without a fortune, Frank, how are you to live?" the father asked, after having confessed how deep he himself had injured his own heir.

"I don't care about money, sir," said Frank. "I shall be just as happy as if Boxall Hill had never been sold. I don't care a straw about that sort of thing."

"Ah! my boy; but you will care: you will soon find that you do care."

"Let me go into some profession. Let me go to the Bar. I am sure I could earn my own living. Earn it! of course I could, why not I as well as others? I should like of all things to be a barrister."

There was much more of the same kind, in which Frank said all that he could think of to lessen his father's regrets. In their conversation not a word was spoken about Mary Thorne. Frank was not aware whether or no his father had been told of the great family danger which was dreaded in that quarter. That he had been told, we may surmise, as Lady Arabella was not wont to confine the family dangers to her own bosom. Moreover, Mary's presence had, of course, been missed. The truth was, that the squire had been told, with great bitterness, of what had come to pass, and all the evil had been laid at his door. He it had been who had encouraged Mary to be regarded almost as a daughter of the house of Greshamsbury; he it was who taught that odious doctor—odious in all but his aptitude for good doctoring—to think himself a fit match for the aristocracy of the county. It had been his fault, this great necessity that Frank should marry money; and now it was his fault that Frank was absolutely talking of marrying a pauper.

By no means in quiescence did the squire hear these charges brought against him. The Lady Arabella, in each attack, got quite as much as she gave, and, at last, was driven to retreat in a state of headache, which she declared to be chronic; and which, so she assured her daughter Augusta, must prevent her from having any more lengthened conversations with her lord—at any rate for the next three months. But though the squire may be said to have come off on the whole as victor in these combats, they did not perhaps have, on that account, the less effect upon him. He knew it was true that he had done much towards ruining his son; and he also could think of no other remedy than matrimony. It was Frank's doom, pronounced even by the voice of his father, that he must marry money.

And so, Frank went off again to Cambridge, feeling himself, as he went, to be a much lesser man in Greshamsbury estimation than he had been some two months earlier, when his birthday had been celebrated. Once during his short stay at Greshamsbury he had seen the doctor; but the meeting had been anything but pleasant. He had been afraid to ask after Mary; and the doctor had been too diffident of himself to speak of her. They had met casually on the road, and, though each in his heart loved the other, the meeting had been anything but pleasant.

And so Frank went back to Cambridge; and, as he did so, he stoutly resolved that nothing should make him untrue to Mary Thorne. "Beatrice," said he, on the morning he went away, when she came into his room to superintend his packing—"Beatrice, if she ever talks about me—"

"Oh, Frank, my darling Frank, don't think of it—it is madness; she knows it is madness."

"Never mind; if she ever talks about me, tell her that the last word I said was, that I would never forget her. She can do as she likes."

Beatrice made no promise, never hinted that she would give the message; but it may be taken for granted that she had not been long in company with Mary Thorne before she did give it.

And then there were other troubles at Greshamsbury. It had been decided that Augusta's marriage was to take place in September; but Mr Moffat had, unfortunately, been obliged to postpone the happy day. He himself had told Augusta—not, of course, without protestations as to his regret—and had written to this effect to Mr Gresham, "Electioneering matters, and other troubles had," he said, "made this peculiarly painful postponement absolutely necessary."

Augusta seemed to bear her misfortune with more equanimity than is, we believe, usual with young ladies under such circumstances. She spoke of it to her mother in a very matter-of-fact way, and seemed almost contented at the idea of remaining at Greshamsbury till February; which was the time now named for the marriage. But Lady Arabella was not equally well satisfied, nor was the squire.

"I half believe that fellow is not honest," he had once said out loud before Frank, and this set Frank a-thinking of what dishonesty in the matter it was probable that Mr Moffat might be guilty, and what would be the fitting punishment for such a crime. Nor did he think on the subject in vain; especially after a conference on the matter which he had with his friend Harry Baker. This conference took place during the Christmas vacation.

It should be mentioned, that the time spent by Frank at Courcy Castle had not done much to assist him in his views as to an early degree, and that it had at last been settled that he should stay up at Cambridge another year. When he came home at Christmas he found that the house was not peculiarly lively. Mary was absent on a visit with Miss Oriel. Both these young ladies were staying with Miss Oriel's aunt, in the neighbourhood of London; and Frank soon learnt that there was no chance that either of them would be home before his return. No message had been left for him by Mary—none at least had been left with Beatrice; and he began in his heart to accuse her of coldness and perfidy;—not, certainly, with much justice, seeing that she had never given him the slightest encouragement.

The absence of Patience Oriel added to the dullness of the place. It was certainly hard upon Frank that all the attraction of the village should be removed to make way and prepare for his return—harder, perhaps, on them; for, to tell the truth, Miss Oriel's visit had been entirely planned to enable her to give Mary a comfortable way of leaving Greshamsbury during the time that Frank should remain at home. Frank thought himself cruelly used. But what did Mr Oriel think when doomed to eat his Christmas pudding alone, because the young squire would be unreasonable in his love? What did the doctor think, as he sat solitary by his deserted hearth—the doctor, who no longer permitted himself to enjoy the comforts of the Greshamsbury dining-table? Frank hinted and grumbled; talked to

Beatrice of the determined constancy of his love, and occasionally consoled himself by a stray smile from some of the neighbouring belles. The black horse was made perfect; the old grey pony was by no means discarded; and much that was satisfactory was done in the sporting line. But still the house was dull, and Frank felt that he was the cause of its being so. Of the doctor he saw but little: he never came to Greshamsbury unless to see Lady Arabella as doctor, or to be closeted with the squire. There were no social evenings with him; no animated confabulations at the doctor's house; no discourses between them, as there had wont to be, about the merits of the different covers, and the capacities of the different hounds. These were dull days on the whole for Frank; and sad enough, we may say, for our friend the doctor.

In February, Frank again went back to college; having settled with Harry Baker certain affairs which weighed on his mind. He went back to Cambridge, promising to be home on the 20th of the month, so as to be present at his sister's wedding. A cold and chilling time had been named for these hymeneal joys, but one not altogether unsuited to the feelings of the happy pair. February is certainly not a warm month; but with the rich it is generally a cosy, comfortable time. Good fires, winter cheer, groaning tables, and warm blankets, make a fictitious summer, which, to some tastes, is more delightful than the long days and the hot sun. And some marriages are especially winter matches. They depend for their charm on the same substantial attractions: instead of heart beating to heart in sympathetic unison, purse chinks to purse. The rich new furniture of the new abode is looked to instead of the rapture of a pure embrace. The new carriage is depended on rather than the new heart's companion; and the first bright gloss, prepared by the upholsterer's hands, stands in lieu of the rosy tints which young love lends to his true votaries.

Mr Moffat had not spent his Christmas at Greshamsbury. That eternal election petition, those eternal lawyers, the eternal care of his well-managed wealth, forbade him the enjoyment of any such pleasures. He could not come to Greshamsbury for Christmas, nor yet for the festivities of the new year; but now and then he wrote prettily worded notes, sending occasionally a silver-gilt pencil-case, or a small brooch, and informed Lady Arabella that he looked forward to the 20th of February with great satisfaction. But, in the meanwhile, the squire became anxious, and at last went up to London; and Frank, who was at Cambridge, bought the heaviest cutting whip to be found in that town, and wrote a confidential letter to Harry Baker.

Poor Mr Moffat! It is well known that none but the brave deserve the fair; but thou, without much excuse for bravery, had secured for thyself one who, at any rate, was fair enough for thee. Would it not have been well hadst thou looked into thyself to see what real bravery might be in thee, before thou hadst prepared to desert this fair one thou hadst already won? That last achievement, one may say, did require some special courage.

Poor Mr Moffat! It is wonderful that as he sat in that gig, going to Gatherum Castle, planning how he would be off with Miss Gresham and afterwards on with Miss Dunstable, it is wonderful that he should not then have cast his eye behind him, and looked at that stalwart pair of shoulders which were so close to his own back. As he afterwards pondered on his scheme while sipping the duke's claret, it is odd that he should not have observed the fiery pride of purpose and power of wrath which was so plainly written on that young man's brow: or, when he matured, and finished, and carried out his purpose, that he did not think of that keen grasp which had already squeezed his own hand with somewhat too warm a vigour, even in the way of friendship.

Poor Mr Moffat! it is probable that he forgot to think of Frank at all as connected with his promised bride; it is probable that he looked forward only to the squire's violence and the enmity of the house of Courcy; and that he found from enquiry at his heart's pulses, that he was man enough to meet these. Could he have guessed what a whip Frank Gresham would have bought at Cambridge—could he have divined what a letter would have been written to Harry Baker—it is probable, nay, we think we may say certain, that Miss Gresham would have become Mrs Moffat.

Miss Gresham, however, never did become Mrs Moffat. About two days after Frank's departure for Cambridge—it is just possible that Mr Moffat was so prudent as to make himself aware of the fact—but just two days after Frank's departure, a very long, elaborate, and clearly explanatory letter was received at Greshamsbury. Mr Moffat was quite sure that Miss Gresham and her very excellent parents would do him the justice to believe that he was not actuated, &c., &c., &c. The long and the short of this was, that Mr Moffat signified his intention of breaking off the match without offering any intelligible reason.

Augusta again bore her disappointment well: not, indeed, without sorrow and heartache, and inward, hidden tears; but still well. She neither raved, nor fainted, nor walked about by moonlight alone. She wrote no poetry, and never once thought of suicide. When, indeed, she remembered the rosy-tinted lining, the unfathomable softness of that Longacre carriage, her spirit did for one moment give way; but, on the whole, she bore it as a strong-minded woman and a de Courcy should do.

But both Lady Arabella and the squire were greatly vexed. The former had made the match, and the latter, having consented to it, had incurred deeper responsibilities to enable him to bring it about. The money which was to have been given to Mr Moffat was still to the fore; but alas! how much, how much that he could ill spare, had been thrown away on bridal preparations! It is, moreover, an unpleasant thing for a gentleman to have his daughter jilted; perhaps peculiarly so to have her jilted by a tailor's son.

Lady Arabella's woe was really piteous. It seemed to her as though cruel fate were heaping misery after misery upon the wretched house of Greshamsbury. A few weeks since things were going so well with her! Frank then was all but the accepted husband of almost untold wealth—so, at least, she was informed by her sister-in-law—whereas, Augusta, was the accepted wife of wealth, not indeed untold, but of dimensions quite sufficiently respectable to cause much joy in the telling. Where now were her golden hopes? Where now the splendid future of her poor duped children? Augusta was left to pine alone; and Frank, in a still worse plight, insisted on maintaining his love for a bastard and a pauper.

For Frank's affair she had received some poor consolation by laying all the blame on the squire's shoulders. What she had then said was now repaid to her with interest; for not only had she been the maker of Augusta's match, but she had boasted of the deed with all a mother's pride.

It was from Beatrice that Frank had obtained his tidings. This last resolve on the part of Mr Moffat had not altogether been unsuspected by some of the Greshams, though altogether unsuspected by the Lady Arabella. Frank had spoken of it as a possibility to Beatrice, and was not quite unprepared when the information reached him. He consequently bought his big cutting whip, and wrote his confidential letter to Harry Baker.

On the following day Frank and Harry might have been seen, with their heads nearly close together, leaning over one of the tables in the large breakfast-room at the Tavistock Hotel in Covent Garden. The ominous whip, to the handle of which Frank had already made his hand well accustomed, was lying on the table between them; and ever and anon Harry Baker would take it up and feel its weight approvingly. Oh, Mr Moffat! poor Mr Moffat! go not out into the fashionable world to-day; above all, go not to that club of thine in Pall Mall; but, oh! especially go not there, as is thy wont to do, at three o'clock in the afternoon!

With much care did those two young generals lay their plans of attack. Let it not for a moment be thought that it was ever in the minds of either of them that two men should attack one. But it was thought that Mr Moffat might be rather coy in coming out from his seclusion to meet the proffered hand of his once intended brother-in-law when he should see that hand armed with a heavy whip. Baker, therefore, was content to act as a decoy duck, and remarked that he might no doubt make himself useful in restraining the public mercy, and, probably, in controlling the interference of policemen.

"It will be deuced hard if I can't get five or six shies at him," said Frank, again clutching his weapon almost spasmodically. Oh, Mr Moffat! five or six shies with such a whip, and such an arm! For myself, I would sooner join in a second Balaclava gallop than encounter it.

At ten minutes before four these two heroes might be seen walking up Pall Mall, towards the —— Club. Young Baker walked with an eager disengaged air. Mr Moffat did not know his appearance; he had, therefore, no anxiety to pass along unnoticed. But Frank had in some mysterious way drawn his hat very far over his forehead, and had buttoned his shooting-coat up round his chin. Harry had recommended to him a great-coat, in order that he might the better conceal his face; but Frank had found that the great-coat was an encumbrance to his arm. He put it on, and when thus clothed he had tried the whip, he found that he cut the air with much less potency than in the lighter garment. He contented himself, therefore, with looking down on the pavement as he walked along, letting the long point of the whip stick up from his pocket, and flattering himself that even Mr Moffat would not recognise him at the first glance. Poor Mr Moffat! If he had but had the chance!

And now, having arrived at the front of the club, the two friends for a moment separate: Frank remains standing on the pavement, under the shade of the high stone area-railing, while Harry jauntily skips up three steps at a time, and with a very civil word of inquiry of the hall porter, sends in his card to Mr Moffat—

MR HARRY BAKER

Mr Moffat, never having heard of such a gentleman in his life, unwittingly comes out into the hall, and Harry, with the sweetest smile, addresses him.

Now the plan of the campaign had been settled in this wise: Baker was to send into the club for Mr Moffat, and invite that gentleman down into the street. It was probable that the invitation might be declined; and it had been calculated in such case that the two gentlemen would retire for parley into the strangers' room, which was known to be immediately opposite the hall door. Frank was to keep his eye on the portals, and if he found that Mr Moffat did not appear as readily as might be desired, he also was to ascend the steps and hurry into the strangers' room. Then, whether he met Mr Moffat there or elsewhere, or wherever he might meet him, he was to greet him with all the friendly vigour in his power, while Harry disposed of the club porters.

But fortune, who ever favours the brave, specially favoured Frank Gresham on this occasion. Just as Harry Baker had put his card into the servant's hand, Mr Moffat, with his hat on, prepared for the street, appeared in the hall; Mr Baker addressed him with his sweetest smile, and begged the pleasure of saying a word or two as they descended into the street. Had not Mr Moffat been going thither it would have been very improbable that he should have done so at Harry's instance. But, as it was, he merely looked rather solemn at his visitor—it was his wont to look solemn—and continued the descent of the steps.

Frank, his heart leaping the while, saw his prey, and retreated two steps behind the area-railing, the dread weapon already well poised in his hand. Oh! Mr Moffat! Mr Moffat! if there be any goddess to interfere in thy favour, let her come forward now without delay; let her now bear thee off on a cloud if there be one to whom thou art sufficiently dear! But there is no such goddess.

Harry smiled blandly till they were well on the pavement, saying some nothing, and keeping the victim's face averted from the avenging angel; and then, when the raised hand was sufficiently nigh, he withdrew two steps towards the nearest lamp-post. Not for him was the honour of the interview;—unless, indeed, succouring policemen might give occasion for some gleam of glory.

But succouring policemen were no more to be come by than goddesses. Where were ye, men, when that savage whip fell about the ears of the poor ex-legislator? In Scotland Yard, sitting dozing on your benches, or talking soft nothings to the housemaids round the corner; for ye were not walking on your beats, nor standing at coign of vantage, to watch the tumults of the day. But had ye been there what could ye have done? Had Sir Richard himself been on the spot Frank Gresham would still, we may say, have had his five shies at that unfortunate one.

When Harry Baker quickly seceded from the way, Mr Moffat at once saw the fate before him. His hair doubtless stood on end, and his voice refused to give the loud screech with which he sought to invoke the club. An ashy paleness suffused his cheeks, and his tottering steps were unable to bear him away in flight. Once, and twice, the cutting whip came well down across his back. Had he been wise enough to stand still and take his thrashing in that attitude, it would have been well for him. But men so circumstanced have never such prudence. After two blows he made a dash at the steps, thinking to get back into the club; but Harry, who had by no means reclined in idleness against the lamp-post, here stopped him: "You had better go back into the street," said Harry; "indeed you had," giving him a shove from off the second step.

Then of course Frank could not do other than hit him anywhere. When a gentleman is dancing about with much energy it is hardly possible to strike him fairly on his back. The blows, therefore, came now on his legs and now on his head; and Frank unfortunately got more than his five or six shies before he was interrupted.

The interruption however came, all too soon for Frank's idea of justice. Though there be no policeman to take part in a London row, there are always others ready enough to do so; amateur policemen, who generally sympathise with the wrong side, and, in nine cases out of ten, expend their generous energy in protecting thieves and pickpockets. When it was seen with what tremendous ardour that dread weapon fell about the ears of the poor undefended gentleman, interference there was at last, in spite of Harry Baker's best endeavours, and loudest protestations.

"Do not interrupt them, sir," said he; "pray do not. It is a family affair, and they will neither of them like it."

In the teeth, however, of these assurances, rude people did interfere, and after some nine or ten shies Frank found himself encompassed by the arms, and encumbered by the weight of a very stout gentleman, who hung affectionately about his neck and shoulders; whereas, Mr Moffat was already receiving consolation from two motherly females, sitting in a state of syncope on the good-natured knees of a fishmonger's apprentice.

Frank was thoroughly out of breath: nothing came from his lips but half-muttered expletives and unintelligible denunciations of the iniquity of his foe. But still he struggled to be at him again. We all know how dangerous is the taste of blood; now cruelty will become a custom even with the most tender-hearted. Frank felt that he had hardly fleshed his virgin lash: he thought, almost with despair, that he had not yet at all succeeded as became a man and a brother; his memory told him of but one or two of the slightest touches that had gone well home to the offender. He made a desperate effort to throw off that incubus round his neck and rush again to the combat.

"Harry—Harry; don't let him go—don't let him go," he barely articulated.

"Do you want to murder the man, sir; to murder him?" said the stout gentleman over his shoulder, speaking solemnly into his very ear.

"I don't care," said Frank, struggling manfully but uselessly. "Let me out, I say; I don't care—don't let him go, Harry, whatever you do."

"He has got it prettily tidily," said Harry; "I think that will perhaps do for the present."

By this time there was a considerable concourse. The club steps were crowded with the members; among whom there were many of Mr Moffat's acquaintance. Policemen also now flocked up, and the question arose as to what should be done with the originators of the affray. Frank and Harry found that they were to consider themselves under a gentle arrest, and Mr Moffat, in a fainting state, was carried into the interior of the club.

Frank, in his innocence, had intended to have celebrated this little affair when it was over by a light repast and a bottle of claret with his friend, and then to have gone back to Cambridge by the mail train. He found, however, that his schemes in this respect were frustrated. He had to get bail to attend at Marlborough Street police-office should he be wanted within the next two or three days; and was given to understand that he would be under the eye of the police, at any rate until Mr Moffat should be out of danger.

"Out of danger!" said Frank to his friend with a startled look. "Why I hardly got at him." Nevertheless, they did have their slight repast, and also their bottle of claret.

On the second morning after this occurrence, Frank was again sitting in that public room at the Tavistock, and Harry was again sitting opposite to him. The whip was not now so conspicuously produced between them, having been carefully packed up and put away among Frank's other travelling properties. They were so sitting, rather glum, when the door swung open, and a heavy, quick step was heard advancing towards them. It was the squire; whose arrival there had been momentarily expected.

"Frank," said he—"Frank, what on earth is all this?" and as he spoke he stretched out both hands, the right to his son and the left to his friend.

"He has given a blackguard a licking, that is all," said Harry.

Frank felt that his hand was held with a peculiarly warm grasp; and he could not but think that his father's face, raised though his eyebrows were—though there was on it an intended expression of amazement and, perhaps, regret—nevertheless he could not but think that his father's face looked kindly at him.

"God bless my soul, my dear boy! what have you done to the man?"

"He's not a ha'porth the worse, sir," said Frank, still holding his father's hand.

"Oh, isn't he!" said Harry, shrugging his shoulders. "He must be made of some very tough article then."

"But my dear boys, I hope there's no danger. I hope there's no danger."

"Danger!" said Frank, who could not yet induce himself to believe that he had been allowed a fair chance with Mr Moffat.

"Oh, Frank! Frank! how could you be so rash? In the middle of Pall Mall, too. Well! well! well! All the women down at Greshamsbury will have it that you have killed him."

"I almost wish I had," said Frank.

"Oh, Frank! Frank! But now tell me—"

And then the father sat well pleased while he heard, chiefly from Harry Baker, the full story of his son's prowess. And then they did not separate without another slight repast and another bottle of claret.

Mr Moffat retired to the country for a while, and then went abroad; having doubtless learnt that the petition was not likely to give him a seat for the city of Barchester. And this was the end of the wooing with Miss Gresham.

CHAPTER XXII

SIR ROGER IS UNSEATED

After this, little occurred at Greshamsbury, or among Greshamsbury people, which it will be necessary for us to record. Some notice was, of course, taking of Frank's prolonged absence from his college; and tidings, perhaps exaggerated tidings, of what had happened in Pall Mall were not slow to reach the High Street of Cambridge. But that affair was gradually hushed up; and Frank went on with his studies.

He went back to his studies: it then being an understood arrangement between him and his father that he should not return to Greshamsbury till the summer vacation. On this occasion, the squire and Lady Arabella had, strange to say, been of the same mind. They both wished to keep their son away from Miss Thorne; and both calculated, that at his age and with his disposition, it was not probable that any passion would last out a six months' absence. "And when the summer comes it will be an excellent opportunity for us to go abroad," said Lady Arabella. "Poor Augusta will require some change to renovate her spirits."

To this last proposition the squire did not assent. It was, however, allowed to pass over; and this much was fixed, that Frank was not to return home till midsummer.

It will be remembered that Sir Roger Scatcherd had been elected as sitting member for the city of Barchester; but it will also be remembered that a petition against his return was threatened. Had that petition depended solely on Mr Moffat, Sir Roger's seat no doubt would have been saved by Frank Gresham's cutting whip. But such was not the case. Mr Moffat had been put forward by the de Courcy interest; and that noble family with its dependants was not to go to the wall because Mr Moffat had had a thrashing. No; the petition was to go on; and Mr Nearthewinde declared, that no petition in his hands had half so good a chance of success. "Chance, no, but certainty," said Mr Nearthewinde; for Mr Nearthewinde had learnt something with reference to that honest publican and the payment of his little bill.

The petition was presented and duly backed; the recognisances were signed, and all the proper formalities formally executed; and Sir Roger found that his seat was in jeopardy. His return had been a great triumph to him; and, unfortunately, he had celebrated that triumph as he had been in the habit of celebrating most of the very triumphant occasions of his life. Though he was than hardly yet recovered from the effects of his last attack, he indulged in another violent drinking bout; and, strange to say, did so without any immediate visible bad effects.

In February he took his seat amidst the warm congratulations of all men of his own class, and early in the month of April his case came on for trial. Every kind of electioneering sin known to the electioneering world was brought to his charge; he was accused of falseness, dishonesty, and bribery of every sort: he had, it was said in the paper of indictment, bought votes, obtained them by treating, carried them off by violence, conquered them by strong drink, polled them twice over, counted those of dead men, stolen them, forged them, and created them by every possible, fictitious contrivance: there was no description of wickedness appertaining to the task of procuring votes of which Sir Roger had not been guilty, either by himself or by his agents. He was quite horror-struck at the list of his own enormities. But he was somewhat comforted when Mr Closerstil told him that the meaning of it all was that Mr Romer, the barrister, had paid a former bill due to Mr Reddypalm, the publican.

"I fear he was indiscreet, Sir Roger; I really fear he was. Those young men always are. Being energetic, they work like horses; but what's the use of energy without discretion, Sir Roger?"

"But, Mr Closerstil, I knew nothing about it from first to last."

"The agency can be proved, Sir Roger," said Mr Closerstil, shaking his head. And then there was nothing further to be said on the matter.

In these days of snow-white purity all political delinquency is abominable in the eyes of British politicians; but no delinquency is so abominable as that of venality at elections. The sin of bribery is damnable. It is the one sin for which, in the House of Commons, there can be no forgiveness. When discovered, it should render the culprit liable to political death, without hope of pardon. It is treason against a higher throne than that on which the Queen sits. It is a heresy which requires an *auto-da-fé*. It is a pollution to the whole House, which can only be cleansed by a great sacrifice. Anathema maranatha! out with it from amongst us, even though the half of our heart's blood be poured forth in the conflict! out with it, and for ever!

Such is the language of patriotic members with regard to bribery; and doubtless, if sincere, they are in the right. It is a bad thing, certainly, that a rich man should buy votes; bad also that a poor man should sell them. By all means let us repudiate such a system with heartfelt disgust.

With heartfelt disgust, if we can do so, by all means; but not with disgust pretended only and not felt in the heart at all. The laws against bribery at elections are now so stringent that an unfortunate candidate may easily become guilty, even though actuated by the purest intentions. But not the less on that account does any gentleman, ambitious of the honour of serving his country in Parliament, think it necessary as a preliminary measure to provide a round sum of money at his banker's. A candidate must pay for no treating, no refreshments, no band of music; he must give neither ribbons to the girls nor ale to the men. If a huzza be uttered in his favour, it is at his peril; it may be necessary for him to prove before a committee that it was the spontaneous result of British feeling in his favour, and not the purchased result of British beer. He cannot safely ask any one to share his hotel dinner. Bribery hides itself now in the most impalpable shapes, and may be effected by the offer of a glass of sherry. But not the less on this account does a poor man find that he is quite unable to overcome the difficulties of a contested election.

We strain at our gnats with a vengeance, but we swallow our camels with ease. For what purpose is it that we employ those peculiarly safe men of business—Messrs Nearthewinde and Closerstil—when we wish to win our path through all obstacles into that sacred recess, if all be so open, all so easy, all so much above board? Alas! the money is still necessary, is still prepared, or at any rate expended. The poor candidate of course knows nothing of the matter till the attorney's bill is laid before him, when all danger of petitions has passed away. He little dreamed till then, not he, that there had been banqueting and junketings, secret doings and deep drinkings at his expense. Poor candidate! Poor member! Who was so ignorant as he! 'Tis true he has paid such bills before; but 'tis equally true that he specially begged his managing friend, Mr Nearthewinde, to be very careful that all was done according to law! He pays the bill, however, and on the next election will again employ Mr Nearthewinde.

Now and again, at rare intervals, some glimpse into the inner sanctuary does reach the eyes of ordinary mortal men without; some slight accidental peep into those mysteries from whence all corruption has been so thoroughly expelled; and then, how delightfully refreshing is the sight, when, perhaps, some ex-member, hurled from his paradise like a fallen peri, reveals the secret of that pure heaven, and, in the agony of his despair, tells us all that it cost him to sit for —— through those few halcyon years!

But Mr Nearthewinde is a safe man, and easy to be employed with but little danger. All these stringent bribery laws only enhance the value of such very safe men as Mr Nearthewinde. To him, stringent laws against bribery are the strongest assurance of valuable employment. Were these laws of a nature to be evaded with ease, any indifferent attorney might manage a candidate's affairs and enable him to take his seat with security.

It would have been well for Sir Roger if he had trusted solely to Mr Closerstil; well also for Mr Romer had he never fished in those troubled waters. In due process of time the hearing of the petition came on, and then who so happy, sitting at his ease at his London Inn, blowing his cloud from a long pipe, with measureless content, as Mr Reddypalm? Mr Reddypalm was the one great man of the contest. All depended on Mr Reddypalm; and well he did his duty.

The result of the petition was declared by the committee to be as follows:—that Sir Roger's election was null and void—that the election altogether was null and void—that Sir Roger had, by his agent, been guilty of bribery in obtaining a vote, by the payment of a bill alleged to have been previously refused payment—that Sir Roger himself knew nothing about it;—this is always a matter of course;—but that Sir Roger's agent, Mr Romer, had been wittingly guilty of bribery with reference to the transaction above described. Poor Sir Roger! Poor Mr Romer.

Poor Mr Romer indeed! His fate was perhaps as sad as well might be, and as foul a blot to the purism of these very pure times in which we live. Not long after those days, it so happening that some considerable amount of youthful energy and quidnunc ability were required to set litigation afloat at Hong-Kong, Mr Romer was sent thither as the fittest man for such work, with rich assurance of future guerdon. Who so happy then as Mr Romer! But even among the pure there is room for envy and detraction. Mr Romer had not yet ceased to wonder at new worlds, as he skimmed among the islands of that southern ocean, before the edict had gone forth for his return. There were men sitting in that huge court of Parliament on whose breasts it lay as an intolerable burden, that England should be represented among the antipodes by one who had tampered with the purity of the franchise. For them there was no rest till this great disgrace should be wiped out and atoned for. Men they were of that calibre, that the slightest reflection on them of such a stigma seemed to themselves to blacken their own character. They could not break bread with satisfaction till Mr Romer was recalled. He was recalled, and of course ruined—and the minds of those just men were then at peace.

To any honourable gentleman who really felt his brow suffused with a patriotic blush, as he thought of his country dishonoured by Mr Romer's presence at Hong-Kong—to any such gentleman, if any such there were, let all honour be given, even though the intensity of his purity may create amazement to our less finely organised souls. But if no such blush suffused the brow of any honourable gentleman; if Mr Romer was recalled from quite other feelings—what then in lieu of honour shall we allot to those honourable gentlemen who were most concerned?

Sir Roger, however, lost his seat, and, after three months of the joys of legislation, found himself reduced by a terrible blow to the low level of private life.

And the blow to him was very heavy. Men but seldom tell the truth of what is in them, even to their dearest friends; they are ashamed of having feelings, or rather of showing that they are troubled by any intensity of feeling. It is the practice of the time to treat all pursuits as though they were only half important to us, as though in what we desire we were only half in earnest. To be visibly eager seems childish, and is always bad policy; and men, therefore, nowadays, though they strive as hard as ever in the service of ambition—harder than ever in that of mammon—usually do so with a pleasant smile on, as though after all they were but amusing themselves with the little matter in hand.

Perhaps it had been so with Sir Roger in those electioneering days when he was looking for votes. At any rate, he had spoken of his seat in Parliament as but a doubtful good. "He was willing, indeed, to stand, having been asked; but the thing would interfere wonderfully with his business; and then, what did he know about Parliament? Nothing on earth: it was the maddest scheme, but nevertheless, he was not going to hang back when called upon—he had always been rough and ready when wanted,—and there he was now ready as ever, and rough enough too, God knows."

'Twas thus that he had spoken of his coming parliamentary honours; and men had generally taken him at his word. He had been returned, and this success had been hailed as a great thing for the cause and class to which he belonged. But men did not know that his inner heart was swelling with triumph, and that his bosom could hardly contain his pride as he reflected that the poor Barchester stone-mason was now the representative in Parliament of his native city. And so, when his seat was attacked, he still laughed and joked. "They were welcome to it for him," he said; "he could keep it or want it; and of the two, perhaps, the want of it would come most convenient to him. He did not exactly think that he had bribed any one; but if the bigwigs chose to say so, it was all one to him. He was rough and ready, now as ever," &c., &c.

But when the struggle came, it was to him a fearful one; not the less fearful because there was no one, no, not one friend in all the world, to whom he could open his mind and speak out honestly what was in his heart. To Dr Thorne he might perhaps have done so had his intercourse with the doctor been sufficiently frequent; but it was only now and again when he was ill, or when the squire wanted to borrow money, that he saw Dr Thorne. He had plenty of friends, heaps of friends in the parliamentary sense; friends who talked about him, and lauded him at public meetings; who shook hands with him on platforms, and drank his health at dinners; but he had no friend who could sit with him over his own hearth, in true friendship, and listen to, and sympathise with, and moderate the sighings of the inner man. For him there was no sympathy; no tenderness of love; no retreat, save into himself, from the loud brass band of the outer world.

The blow hit him terribly hard. It did not come altogether unexpectedly, and yet, when it did come, it was all but unendurable. He had made so much of the power of walking into that august chamber, and sitting shoulder to shoulder in legislative equality with the sons of dukes and the curled darlings of the nation. Money had given him nothing, nothing but the mere feeling of brute power: with his three hundred thousand pounds he had felt himself to be no more palpably near to the goal of his ambition than when he had chipped stones for three shillings and sixpence a day. But when he was led up and introduced at that table, when he shook the old premier's hand on the floor of the House of Commons, when he heard the honourable member for Barchester alluded to in grave debate as the greatest living authority on railway matters, then, indeed, he felt that he had achieved something.

And now this cup was ravished from his lips, almost before it was tasted. When he was first told as a certainty that the decision of the committee was against him, he bore up against the misfortune like a man. He laughed heartily, and declared himself well rid of a very profitless profession; cut some little joke about Mr Moffat and his thrashing, and left on those around him an impression that he was a man so constituted, so strong in his own resolves, so steadily pursuant of his own work, that no little contentions of this kind could affect him. Men admired his easy laughter, as, shuffling his half-crowns with both his hands in his trouser-pockets, he declared that Messrs Romer and Reddypalm were the best friends he had known for this many a day.

But not the less did he walk out from the room in which he was standing a broken-hearted man. Hope could not buoy him up as she may do other ex-members in similarly disagreeable circumstances. He could not afford to look forward to what further favours parliamentary future might have in store for him after a lapse of five or six years. Five or six years! Why, his life was not worth four years' purchase; of that he was perfectly aware: he could not now live without the stimulus of brandy; and yet, while he took it, he knew he was killing himself. Death he did not fear; but he would fain have wished, after his life of labour, to have lived, while yet he could live, in the blaze of that high world to which for a moment he had attained.

He laughed loud and cheerily as he left his parliamentary friends, and, putting himself into the train, went down to Boxall Hill. He laughed loud and cheerily; but he never laughed again. It had not been his habit to laugh much at Boxall Hill. It was there he kept his wife, and Mr Winterbones, and the brandy bottle behind his pillow. He had not often there found it necessary to assume that loud and cheery laugh.

On this occasion he was apparently well in health when he got home; but both Lady Scatcherd and Mr Winterbones found him more than ordinarily cross. He made an affectation at sitting very hard to business, and even talked of going abroad to look at some of his foreign contracts. But even Winterbones found that his patron did not work as he had been wont to do; and at last, with some misgivings, he told Lady Scatcherd that he feared that everything was not right.

"He's always at it, my lady, always," said Mr Winterbones.

"Is he?" said Lady Scatcherd, well understanding what Mr Winterbones's allusion meant.

"Always, my lady. I never saw nothing like it. Now, there's me—I can always go my half-hour when I've had my drop; but he, why, he don't go ten minutes, not now."

This was not cheerful to Lady Scatcherd; but what was the poor woman to do? When she spoke to him on any subject he only snarled at her; and now that the heavy fit was on him, she did not dare even to mention the subject of his drinking. She had never known him so savage in his humour as he was now, so bearish in his habits, so little inclined to humanity, so determined to rush headlong down, with his head between his legs, into the bottomless abyss.

She thought of sending for Dr Thorne; but she did not know under what guise to send for him,—whether as doctor or as friend: under neither would he now be welcome; and she well knew that Sir Roger was not the man to accept in good part either a doctor or a friend who might be unwelcome. She knew that this husband of hers, this man who, with all his faults, was the best of her friends, whom of all she loved best—she knew that he was killing himself, and yet she could do nothing. Sir Roger was his own master, and if kill himself he would, kill himself he must.

And kill himself he did. Not indeed by one sudden blow. He did not take one huge dose of his consuming poison and then fall dead upon the floor. It would perhaps have been better for himself, and better for those around him, had he done so. No; the doctors had time to congregate around his bed; Lady Scatcherd was allowed a period of nurse-tending; the sick man was able to say his last few words and bid adieu to his portion of the lower world with dying decency. As these last words will have some lasting effect upon the surviving personages of our story, the reader must be content to stand for a short while by the side of Sir Roger's sick-bed, and help us to bid him God-speed on the journey which lies before him.

CHAPTER XXIII

RETROSPECTIVE

It was declared in the early pages of this work that Dr Thorne was to be our hero; but it would appear very much as though he had latterly been forgotten. Since that evening when he retired to rest without letting Mary share the grievous weight which was on his mind, we have neither seen nor heard aught of him.

It was then full midsummer, and it is now early spring: and during the intervening months the doctor had not had a happy time of it. On that night, as we have before told, he took his niece to his heart; but he could not then bring himself to tell her that which it was so imperative that she should know. Like a coward, he would put off the evil hour till the next morning, and thus robbed himself of his night's sleep.

But when the morning came the duty could not be postponed. Lady Arabella had given him to understand that his niece would no longer be a guest at Greshamsbury; and it was quite out of the question that Mary, after this, should be allowed to put her foot within the gate of the domain without having learnt what Lady Arabella had said. So he told it her before breakfast, walking round their little garden, she with her hand in his.

He was perfectly thunderstruck by the collected—nay, cool way in which she received his tidings. She turned pale, indeed; he felt also that her hand somewhat trembled in his own, and he perceived that for a moment her voice shook; but no angry word escaped her lip, nor did she even deign to repudiate the charge, which was, as it were, conveyed in Lady Arabella's request. The doctor knew, or thought he knew—nay, he did know—that Mary was wholly blameless in the matter: that she had at least given no encouragement to any love on the part of the young heir; but, nevertheless, he had expected that she would avouch her own innocence. This, however, she by no means did.

"Lady Arabella is quite right," she said, "quite right; if she has any fear of that kind, she cannot be too careful."

"She is a selfish, proud woman," said the doctor; "quite indifferent to the feelings of others; quite careless how deeply she may hurt her neighbours, if, in doing so, she may possibly benefit herself."

"She will not hurt me, uncle, nor yet you. I can live without going to Greshamsbury."

"But it is not to be endured that she should dare to cast an imputation on my darling."

"On me, uncle? She casts no imputation on me. Frank has been foolish: I have said nothing of it, for it was not worth while to trouble you. But as Lady Arabella chooses to interfere, I have no right to blame her. He has said what he should not have said; he has been foolish. Uncle, you know I could not prevent it."

"Let her send him away then, not you; let her banish him."

"Uncle, he is her son. A mother can hardly send her son away so easily: could you send me away, uncle?"

He merely answered her by twining his arm round her waist and pressing her to his side. He was well sure that she was badly treated; and yet now that she so unaccountably took Lady Arabella's part, he hardly knew how to make this out plainly to be the case.

"Besides, uncle, Greshamsbury is in a manner his own; how can he be banished from his father's house? No, uncle; there is an end of my visits there. They shall find that I will not thrust myself in their way."

And then Mary, with a calm brow and steady gait, went in and made the tea.

And what might be the feelings of her heart when she so sententiously told her uncle that Frank had been foolish? She was of the same age with him; as impressionable, though more powerful in hiding such impressions,—as all women should be; her heart was as warm, her blood as full of life, her innate desire for the companionship of some much-loved object as strong as his. Frank had been foolish in avowing his passion. No such folly as that could be laid at her door. But had she been proof against the other folly? Had she been able to walk heart-whole by his side, while he chatted his commonplaces about love? Yes, they are commonplaces when we read of them in novels; common enough, too, to some of us when we write them; but they are by no means commonplace when first heard by a young girl in the rich, balmy fragrance of a July evening stroll.

Nor are they commonplaces when so uttered for the first or second time at least, or perhaps the third. 'Tis a pity that so heavenly a pleasure should pall upon the senses.

If it was so that Frank's folly had been listened to with a certain amount of pleasure, Mary did not even admit so much to herself. But why should it have been otherwise? Why should she have been less prone to love than he was? Had he not everything which girls do love? which girls should love? which God created noble, beautiful, all but godlike, in order that women, all but goddesslike, might love? To love thoroughly, truly, heartily, with her whole body, soul, heart, and strength; should not that be counted for a merit in a woman? And yet we are wont to make a disgrace of it. We do so most unnaturally, most unreasonably; for we expect our daughters to get themselves married off our hands. When the period of that step comes, then love is proper enough; but up to that—before that—as regards all those preliminary passages which must, we suppose, be necessary—in all those it becomes a young lady to be icy-hearted as a river-god in winter.

"O whistle and I'll come to you, my lad!
O whistle and I'll come to you, my lad!
Tho' father and mither and a' should go mad,
O whistle and I'll come to you, my lad!"

This is the kind of love which a girl should feel before she puts her hand proudly in that of her lover, and consents that they two shall be made one flesh.

Mary felt no such love as this. She, too, had some inner perception of that dread destiny by which it behoved Frank Gresham to be forewarned. She, too—though she had never heard so much said in words—had an almost instinctive knowledge that his fate required him to marry money. Thinking over this in her own way, she was not slow to convince herself that it was out of the question that she should allow herself to love Frank Gresham. However well her heart might be inclined to such a feeling, it was her duty to repress it. She resolved, therefore, to do so; and she sometimes flattered herself that she had kept her resolution.

These were bad times for the doctor, and bad times for Mary too. She had declared that she could live without going to Greshamsbury; but she did not find it so easy. She had been going to Greshamsbury all her life, and it was as customary with her to be there as at home. Such old customs are not broken without pain. Had she left the place it would have been far different; but, as it was, she daily passed the gates, daily saw and spoke to some of the servants, who knew her as well as they did the young ladies of the family—was in hourly contact, as it were, with Greshamsbury. It was not only that she did not go there, but that everyone knew that she had suddenly discontinued doing so. Yes, she could live without going to Greshamsbury; but for some time she had but a poor life of it. She felt, nay, almost heard, that every man and woman, boy and girl, in the village was telling his and her neighbour that Mary Thorne no longer went to the house because of Lady Arabella and the young squire.

But Beatrice, of course, came to her. What was she to say to Beatrice? The truth! Nay, but it is not always so easy to say the truth, even to one's dearest friends.

"But you'll come up now he has gone?" said Beatrice.

"No, indeed," said Mary; "that would hardly be pleasant to Lady Arabella, nor to me either. No, Trichy, dearest; my visits to dear old Greshamsbury are done, done, done: perhaps in some twenty years' time I may be walking down the lawn with your brother, and discussing our childish days—that is, always, if the then Mrs Gresham shall have invited me."

"How can Frank have been so wrong, so unkind, so cruel?" said Beatrice.

This, however, was a light in which Miss Thorne did not take any pleasure in discussing the matter. Her ideas of Frank's fault, and unkindness, and cruelty, were doubtless different from those of his sister. Such cruelty was not unnaturally excused in her eyes by many circumstances which Beatrice did not fully understand. Mary was quite ready to go hand in hand with Lady Arabella and the rest of the Greshamsbury fold in putting an end, if possible, to Frank's passion: she would give no one a right to accuse her of assisting to ruin the young heir; but she could hardly bring herself to admit that he was so very wrong—no, nor yet even so very cruel.

And then the squire came to see her, and this was a yet harder trial than the visit of Beatrice. It was so difficult for her to speak to him that she could not but wish him away; and yet, had he not come, had he altogether neglected her, she would have felt it to be unkind. She had ever been his pet, had always received kindness from him.

"I am sorry for all this, Mary; very sorry," said he, standing up, and holding both her hands in his.

"It can't be helped, sir," said she, smiling.

"I don't know," said he; "I don't know—it ought to be helped somehow—I am quite sure you have not been to blame."

"No," said she, very quietly, as though the position was one quite a matter of course. "I don't think I have been very much to blame. There will be misfortunes sometimes when nobody is to blame."

"I do not quite understand it all," said the squire; "but if Frank—"

"Oh! we will not talk about him," said she, still laughing gently.

"You can understand, Mary, how dear he must be to me; but if—"

"Mr Gresham, I would not for worlds be the cause of any unpleasantness between you and him."

"But I cannot bear to think that we have banished you, Mary."

"It cannot be helped. Things will all come right in time."

"But you will be so lonely here."

"Oh! I shall get over all that. Here, you know, Mr Gresham, 'I am monarch of all I survey;' and there is a great deal in that."

The squire did not quite catch her meaning, but a glimmering of it did reach him. It was competent to Lady Arabella to banish her from Greshamsbury; it was within the sphere of the squire's duties to prohibit his son from an imprudent match; it was for the Greshams to guard their Greshamsbury treasure as best they could within their own territories: but let them beware that they did not attack her on hers. In obedience to the first expression of their wishes, she had submitted herself to this public mark of their disapproval because she had seen at once, with her clear intellect, that they were only doing that which her conscience must approve. Without a murmur, therefore, she consented to be pointed at as the young lady who had been turned out of Greshamsbury because of the young squire. She had no help for it. But let them take care that they did not go beyond that. Outside those Greshamsbury gates she and Frank Gresham, she and Lady Arabella met on equal terms; let them each fight their own battle.

The squire kissed her forehead affectionately and took his leave, feeling, somehow, that he had been excused and pitied, and made much of; whereas he had called on his young neighbour with the intention of excusing, and pitying, and making much of her. He was not quite comfortable as he left the house; but, nevertheless, he was sufficiently honest-hearted to own to himself that Mary Thorne was a fine girl. Only that it was so absolutely necessary that Frank should marry money—and only, also, that poor Mary was such a birthless foundling in the world's esteem—only, but for these things, what a wife she would have made for that son of his!

To one person only did she talk freely on the subject, and that one was Patience Oriel; and even with her the freedom was rather of the mind than of the heart. She never said a word of her feeling with reference to Frank, but she said much of her position in the village, and of the necessity she was under to keep out of the way.

"It is very hard," said Patience, "that the offence should be all with him, and the punishment all with you."

"Oh! as for that," said Mary, laughing, "I will not confess to any offence, nor yet to any punishment; certainly not to any punishment."

"It comes to the same thing in the end."

"No, not so, Patience; there is always some little sting of disgrace in punishment: now I am not going to hold myself in the least disgraced."

"But, Mary, you must meet the Greshams sometimes."

"Meet them! I have not the slightest objection on earth to meet all, or any of them. They are not a whit dangerous to me, my dear. 'Tis I that am the wild beast, and 'tis they that must avoid me," and then she added, after a pause—slightly blushing—"I have not the slightest objection even to meet him if chance brings him in my way. Let them look to that. My undertaking goes no further than this, that I will not be seen within their gates."

But the girls so far understood each other that Patience undertook, rather than promised, to give Mary what assistance she could; and, despite Mary's bravado, she was in such a position that she much wanted the assistance of such a friend as Miss Oriel.

After an absence of some six weeks, Frank, as we have seen, returned home. Nothing was said to him, except by Beatrice, as to these new Greshamsbury arrangements; and he, when he found Mary was not at the place, went boldly to the doctor's house to seek her. But it has been seen, also, that she discreetly kept out of his way. This she had thought fit to do when the time came, although she had been so ready with her boast that she had no objection on earth to meet him.

After that there had been the Christmas vacation, and Mary had again found discretion to be the better part of valour. This was doubtless disagreeable enough. She had no particular wish to spend her Christmas with Miss Oriel's aunt instead of at her uncle's fireside. Indeed, her Christmas festivities had hitherto been kept at Greshamsbury, the doctor and herself having made a part of the family circle there assembled. This was out of the question now; and perhaps the absolute change to old Miss Oriel's house was better for her than the lesser change to her uncle's drawing-room. Besides, how could she have de-meaned herself when she met Frank in their parish church? All this had been fully under-understood by Patience, and, therefore, had this Christmas visit been planned.

And then this affair of Frank and Mary Thorne ceased for a while to be talked of at Greshamsbury, for that other affair of Mr Moffat and Augusta monopolised the rural at-tention. Augusta, as we have said, bore it well, and sustained the public gaze without much flinching. Her period of martyrdom, however, did not last long, for soon the news arrived of Frank's exploit in Pall Mall; and then the Greshamsburyites forgot to think much more of Augusta, being fully occupied in thinking of what Frank had done.

The tale, as it was first told, declared that Frank had followed Mr Moffat up into his club; had dragged him thence into the middle of Pall Mall, and had then slaughtered him on the spot. This was by degrees modified till a sobered fiction became generally preva-lent, that Mr Moffat was lying somewhere, still alive, but with all his bones in a general state of compound fracture. This adventure again brought Frank into the ascendant, and restored to Mary her former position as the Greshamsbury heroine.

"One cannot wonder at his being very angry," said Beatrice, discussing the matter with Mary—very imprudently.

"Wonder—no; the wonder would have been if he had not been angry. One might have been quite sure that he would have been angry enough."

"I suppose it was not absolutely right for him to beat Mr Moffat," said Beatrice, apolo-getically.

"Not right, Trichy? I think he was very right."

"Not to beat him so very much, Mary!"

"Oh, I suppose a man can't exactly stand measuring how much he does these things. I like your brother for what he has done, and I say so frankly—though I suppose I ought to eat my tongue out before I should say such a thing, eh, Trichy?"

"I don't know that there's any harm in that," said Beatrice, demurely. "If you both liked each other there would be no harm in that—if that were all."

"Wouldn't there?" said Mary, in a low tone of bantering satire; "that is so kind, Trichy, coming from you—from one of the family, you know."

"You are well aware, Mary, that if I could have my wishes—"

"Yes: I am well aware what a paragon of goodness you are. If you could have your way I should be admitted into heaven again; shouldn't I? Only with this proviso, that if a stray angel should ever whisper to me with bated breath, mistaking me, perchance, for one of his own class, I should be bound to close my ears to his whispering, and remind him humbly that I was only a poor mortal. You would trust me so far, wouldn't you, Trichy?"

"I would trust you in any way, Mary. But I think you are unkind in saying such things to me."

"Into whatever heaven I am admitted, I will go only on this understanding: that I am to be as good an angel as any of those around me."

"But, Mary dear, why do you say this to me?"

"Because—because—because—ah me! Why, indeed, but because I have no one else to say it to. Certainly not because you have deserved it."

"It seems as though you were finding fault with me."

"And so I am; how can I do other than find fault? How can I help being sore? Trichy, you hardly realise my position; you hardly see how I am treated; how I am forced to allow myself to be treated without a sign of complaint. You don't see it all. If you did, you would not wonder that I should be sore."

Beatrice did not quite see it all; but she saw enough of it to know that Mary was to be pitied; so, instead of scolding her friend for being cross, she threw her arms round her and kissed her affectionately.

But the doctor all this time suffered much more than his niece did. He could not complain out loudly; he could not aver that his pet lamb had been ill treated; he could not even have the pleasure of openly quarrelling with Lady Arabella; but not the less did he feel it to be most cruel that Mary should have to live before the world as an outcast, because it had pleased Frank Gresham to fall in love with her.

But his bitterness was not chiefly against Frank. That Frank had been very foolish he could not but acknowledge; but it was a kind of folly for which the doctor was able to find excuse. For Lady Arabella's cold propriety he could find no excuse.

With the squire he had spoken no word on the subject up to this period of which we are now writing. With her ladyship he had never spoken on it since that day when she had told him that Mary was to come no more to Greshamsbury. He never now dined or spent his evenings at Greshamsbury, and seldom was to be seen at the house, except when called in professionally. The squire, indeed, he frequently met; but he either did so in the village, or out on horseback, or at his own house.

When the doctor first heard that Sir Roger had lost his seat, and had returned to Boxall Hill, he resolved to go over and see him. But the visit was postponed from day to day, as visits are postponed which may be made any day, and he did not in fact go till he was summoned there somewhat peremptorily. A message was brought to him one evening to say that Sir Roger had been struck by paralysis, and that not a moment was to be lost.

"It always happens at night," said Mary, who had more sympathy for the living uncle whom she did know, than for the other dying uncle whom she did not know.

"What matters?—there—just give me my scarf. In all probability I may not be home to-night—perhaps not till late to-morrow. God bless you, Mary!" and away the doctor went on his cold bleak ride to Boxall Hill.

"Who will be his heir?" As the doctor rode along, he could not quite rid his mind of this question. The poor man now about to die had wealth enough to make many heirs. What if his heart should have softened towards his sister's child! What if Mary should be found in a few days to be possessed of such wealth that the Greshams should be again be happy to welcome her at Greshamsbury!

The doctor was not a lover of money—and he did his best to get rid of such pernicious thoughts. But his longings, perhaps, were not so much that Mary should be rich, as that she should have the power of heaping coals of fire upon the heads of those people who had so injured her.

CHAPTER XXIV

LOUIS SCATCHERD

When Dr Thorne reached Boxall Hill he found Mr Rerechild from Barchester there before him. Poor Lady Scatcherd, when her husband was stricken by the fit, hardly knew in her dismay what adequate steps to take. She had, as a matter of course, sent for Dr Thorne; but she had thought that in so grave a peril the medical skill of no one man could suffice. It was, she knew, quite out of the question for her to invoke the aid of Dr Fillgrave, whom no earthly persuasion would have brought to Boxall Hill; and as Mr Rerechild was supposed in the Barchester world to be second—though at a long interval—to that great man, she had applied for his assistance.

Now Mr Rerechild was a follower and humble friend of Dr Fillgrave; and was wont to regard anything that came from the Barchester doctor as sure light from the lamp of Æsculapius. He could not therefore be other than an enemy of Dr Thorne. But he was a prudent, discreet man, with a long family, averse to professional hostilities, as knowing that he could make more by medical friends than medical foes, and not at all inclined to take up any man's cudgel to his own detriment. He had, of course, heard of that dreadful affront which had been put upon his friend, as had all the "medical world"—all the medical world at least of Barsetshire; and he had often expressed his sympathy with Dr Fillgrave and his abhorrence of Dr Thorne's anti-professional practices. But now that he found himself about to be brought in contact with Dr Thorne, he reflected that the Galen of Greshamsbury was at any rate equal in reputation to him of Barchester; that the one was probably on the rise, whereas the other was already considered by some as rather antiquated; and he therefore wisely resolved that the present would be an excellent opportunity for him to make a friend of Dr Thorne.

Poor Lady Scatcherd had an inkling that Dr Fillgrave and Mr Rerechild were accustomed to row in the same boat, and she was not altogether free from fear that there might be an outbreak. She therefore took an opportunity before Dr Thorne's arrival to deprecate any wrathful tendency.

"Oh, Lady Scatcherd! I have the greatest respect for Dr Thorne," said he; "the greatest possible respect; a most skilful practitioner—something brusque certainly, and perhaps a little obstinate. But what then? we all have our faults, Lady Scatcherd."

"Oh—yes; we all have, Mr Rerechild; that's certain."

"There's my friend Fillgrave—Lady Scatcherd. He cannot bear anything of that sort. Now I think he's wrong; and so I tell him." Mr Rerechild was in error here; for he had never yet ventured to tell Dr Fillgrave that he was wrong in anything. "We must bear and forbear, you know. Dr Thorne is an excellent man—in his way very excellent, Lady Scatcherd."

This little conversation took place after Mr Rerechild's first visit to his patient: what steps were immediately taken for the relief of the sufferer we need not describe. They were doubtless well intended, and were, perhaps, as well adapted to stave off the coming evil day as any that Dr Fillgrave, or even the great Sir Omicron Pie might have used.

And then Dr Thorne arrived.

"Oh, doctor! doctor!" exclaimed Lady Scatcherd, almost hanging round his neck in the hall. "What are we to do? What are we to do? He's very bad."

"Has he spoken?"

"No; nothing like a word: he has made one or two muttered sounds; but, poor soul, you could make nothing of it—oh, doctor! doctor! he has never been like this before."

It was easy to see where Lady Scatcherd placed any such faith as she might still have in the healing art. "Mr Rerechild is here and has seen him," she continued. "I thought it best to send for two, for fear of accidents. He has done something—I don't know what. But, doctor, do tell the truth now; I look to you to tell me the truth."

Dr Thorne then went up and saw his patient; and had he literally complied with Lady Scatcherd's request, he might have told her at once that there was no hope. As, however, he had not the heart to do this, he mystified the case as doctors so well know how to do, and told her that "there was cause to fear, great cause for fear; he was sorry to say, very great cause for much fear."

Dr Thorne promised to stay the night there, and, if possible, the following night also; and then Lady Scatcherd became troubled in her mind as to what she should do with Mr Rerechild. He also declared, with much medical humanity, that, let the inconvenience be what it might, he too would stay the night. "The loss," he said, "of such a man as Sir Roger Scatcherd was of such paramount importance as to make other matters trivial. He would certainly not allow the whole weight to fall on the shoulders of his friend Dr Thorne: he also would stay at any rate that night by the sick man's bedside. By the following morning some change might be expected."

"I say, Dr Thorne," said her ladyship, calling the doctor into the housekeeping-room, in which she and Hannah spent any time that they were not required upstairs; "just come in, doctor: you couldn't tell him we don't want him any more, could you?"

"Tell whom?" said the doctor.

"Why—Mr Rerechild: mightn't he go away, do you think?"

Dr Thorne explained that Mr Rerechild certainly might go away if he pleased; but that it would by no means be proper for one doctor to tell another to leave the house. And so Mr Rerechild was allowed to share the glories of the night.

In the meantime the patient remained speechless; but it soon became evident that Nature was using all her efforts to make one final rally. From time to time he moaned and muttered as though he was conscious, and it seemed as though he strove to speak. He gradually became awake, at any rate to suffering, and Dr Thorne began to think that the last scene would be postponed for yet a while longer.

"Wonderful strong constitution—eh, Dr Thorne? wonderful!" said Mr Rerechild.

"Yes; he has been a strong man."

"Strong as a horse, Dr Thorne. Lord, what that man would have been if he had given himself a chance! You know his constitution of course."

"Yes; pretty well. I've attended him for many years."

"Always drinking, I suppose; always at it—eh?"

"He has not been a temperate man, certainly."

"The brain, you see, clean gone—and not a particle of coating left to the stomach; and yet what a struggle he makes—an interesting case, isn't it?"

"It's very sad to see such an intellect so destroyed."

"Very sad, very sad indeed. How Fillgrave would have liked to have seen this case. He is a clever man, is Fillgrave—in his way, you know."

"I'm sure he is," said Dr Thorne.

"Not that he'd make anything of a case like this now—he's not, you know, quite—quite—perhaps not quite up to the new time of day, if one may say so."

"He has had a very extensive provincial practice," said Dr Thorne.

"Oh, very—very; and made a tidy lot of money too, has Fillgrave. He's worth six thousand pounds, I suppose; now that's a good deal of money to put by in a little town like Barchester."

"Yes, indeed."

"What I say to Fillgrave is this—keep your eyes open; one should never be too old to learn—there's always something new worth picking up. But, no—he won't believe that. He can't believe that any new ideas can be worth anything. You know a man must go to the wall in that way—eh, doctor?"

And then again they were called to their patient. "He's doing finely, finely," said Mr Rerechild to Lady Scatcherd. "There's fair ground to hope he'll rally; fair ground, is there not, doctor?"

"Yes; he'll rally; but how long that may last, that we can hardly say."

"Oh, no, certainly not, certainly not—that is not with any certainty; but still he's doing finely, Lady Scatcherd, considering everything."

"How long will you give him, doctor?" said Mr Rerechild to his new friend, when they were again alone. "Ten days? I dare say ten days, or from that to a fortnight, not more; but I think he'll struggle on ten days."

"Perhaps so," said the doctor. "I should not like to say exactly to a day."

"No, certainly not. We cannot say exactly to a day; but I say ten days; as for anything like a recovery, that you know—"

"Is out of the question," said Dr Thorne, gravely.

"Quite so; quite so; coating of the stomach clean gone, you know; brain destroyed: did you observe the periporollida? I never saw them so swelled before: now when the periporollida are swollen like that—"

"Yes, very much; it's always the case when paralysis has been brought about by intemperance."

"Always, always; I have remarked that always; the periporollida in such cases are always extended; most interesting case, isn't it? I do wish Fillgrave could have seen it. But, I believe you and Fillgrave don't quite—eh?"

"No, not quite," said Dr Thorne; who, as he thought of his last interview with Dr Fillgrave, and of that gentleman's exceeding anger as he stood in the hall below, could not keep himself from smiling, sad as the occasion was.

Nothing would induce Lady Scatcherd to go to bed; but the two doctors agreed to lie down, each in a room on one side of the patient. How was it possible that anything but good should come to him, being so guarded? "He is going on finely, Lady Scatcherd, quite finely," were the last words Mr Rerechild said as he left the room.

And then Dr Thorne, taking Lady Scatcherd's hand and leading her out into another chamber, told her the truth.

"Lady Scatcherd," said he, in his tenderest voice—and his voice could be very tender when occasion required it—"Lady Scatcherd, do not hope; you must not hope; it would be cruel to bid you do so."

"Oh, doctor! oh, doctor!"

"My dear friend, there is no hope."

"Oh, Dr Thorne!" said the wife, looking wildly up into her companion's face, though she hardly yet realised the meaning of what he said, although her senses were half stunned by the blow.

"Dear Lady Scatcherd, is it not better that I should tell you the truth?"

"Oh, I suppose so; oh yes, oh yes; ah me! ah me! ah me!" And then she began rocking herself backwards and forwards on her chair, with her apron up to her eyes. "What shall I do? what shall I do?"

"Look to Him, Lady Scatcherd, who only can make such grief endurable."

"Yes, yes, yes; I suppose so. Ah me! ah me! But, Dr Thorne, there must be some chance—isn't there any chance? That man says he's going on so well."

"I fear there is no chance—as far as my knowledge goes there is no chance."

"Then why does that chattering magpie tell such lies to a woman? Ah me! ah me! ah me! oh, doctor! doctor! what shall I do? what shall I do?" and poor Lady Scatcherd, fairly overcome by her sorrow, burst out crying like a great school-girl.

And yet what had her husband done for her that she should thus weep for him? Would not her life be much more blessed when this cause of all her troubles should be removed from her? Would she not then be a free woman instead of a slave? Might she not then expect to begin to taste the comforts of life? What had that harsh tyrant of hers done that was good or serviceable for her? Why should she thus weep for him in paroxysms of truest grief?

We hear a good deal of jolly widows; and the slanderous raillery of the world tells much of conjugal disturbances as a cure for which women will look forward to a state of widowhood with not unwilling eyes. The raillery of the world is very slanderous. In our daily jests we attribute to each other vices of which neither we, nor our neighbours, nor our friends, nor even our enemies are ever guilty. It is our favourite parlance to talk of the family troubles of Mrs Green on our right, and to tell how Mrs Young on our left is strongly suspected of having raised her hand to her lord and master. What right have we to make these charges? What have we seen in our own personal walks through life to make us believe that women are devils? There may possibly have been a Xantippe here and there, but Imogenes are to be found under every bush. Lady Scatcherd, in spite of the life she had led, was one of them.

"You should send a message up to London for Louis," said the doctor.

"We did that, doctor; we did that to-day—we sent up a telegraph. Oh me! oh me! poor boy, what will he do? I shall never know what to do with him, never! never!" And with such sorrowful wailings she sat rocking herself through the long night, every now and then comforting herself by the performance of some menial service in the sick man's room.

Sir Roger passed the night much as he had passed the day, except that he appeared gradually to be growing nearer to a state of consciousness. On the following morning they succeeded at last in making Mr Rerechild understand that they were not desirous of keeping him longer from his Barchester practice; and at about twelve o'clock Dr Thorne also went, promising that he would return in the evening, and again pass the night at Boxall Hill.

In the course of the afternoon Sir Roger once more awoke to his senses, and when he did so his son was standing at his bedside. Louis Philippe Scatcherd—or as it may be more convenient to call him, Louis—was a young man just of the age of Frank Gresham. But there could hardly be two youths more different in their appearance. Louis, though his father and mother were both robust persons, was short and slight, and now of a sickly frame. Frank was a picture of health and strength; but, though manly in disposition, was by no means precocious either in appearance or manners. Louis Scatcherd looked as though he was four years the other's senior. He had been sent to Eton when he was fifteen, his father being under the impression that this was the most ready and best-recognised method of making him a gentleman. Here he did not altogether fail as regarded the coveted object of his becoming the companion of gentlemen. He had more pocket-money than any other lad in the school, and was possessed also of a certain effrontery which carried him ahead among boys of his own age. He gained, therefore, a degree of éclat, even among those who knew, and very frequently said to each other, that young Scatcherd was not fit to be their companion except on such open occasions as those of cricket-matches and boat-races. Boys, in this respect, are at least as exclusive as men, and understand as well the difference between an inner and an outer circle. Scatcherd had many companions at school who were glad enough to go up to Maidenhead with him in his boat; but there was not one among them who would have talked to him of his sister.

Sir Roger was vastly proud of his son's success, and did his best to stimulate it by lavish expenditure at the Christopher, whenever he could manage to run down to Eton. But this practice, though sufficiently unexceptionable to the boys, was not held in equal delight by the masters. To tell the truth, neither Sir Roger nor his son were favourites with these stern custodians. At last it was felt necessary to get rid of them both; and Louis was not long in giving them an opportunity, by getting tipsy twice in one week. On the second occasion he was sent away, and he and Sir Roger, though long talked of, were seen no more at Eton.

But the universities were still open to Louis Philippe, and before he was eighteen he was entered as a gentleman-commoner at Trinity. As he was, moreover, the eldest son of a baronet, and had almost unlimited command of money, here also he was enabled for a while to shine.

To shine! but very fitfully; and one may say almost with a ghastly glare. The very lads who had eaten his father's dinners at Eton, and shared his four-oar at Eton, knew much better than to associate with him at Cambridge now that they had put on the *toga virilis*. They were still as prone as ever to fun, frolic, and devilry—perhaps more so than ever, seeing that more was in their power; but they acquired an idea that it behoved them to be somewhat circumspect as to the men with whom their pranks were perpetrated. So, in those days, Louis Scatcherd was coldly looked on by his whilom Eton friends.

But young Scatcherd did not fail to find companions at Cambridge also. There are few places indeed in which a rich man cannot buy companionship. But the set with whom he lived at Cambridge were the worst of the place. They were fast, slang men, who were fast and slang, and nothing else—men who imitated grooms in more than their dress, and who looked on the customary heroes of race-courses as the highest lords of the ascendant upon earth. Among those at college young Scatcherd did shine as long as such lustre was permitted him. Here, indeed, his father, who had striven only to encourage him at Eton, did strive somewhat to control him. But that was not now easy. If he limited his son's allowance, he only drove him to do his debauchery on credit. There were plenty to lend money to the son of the great millionaire; and so, after eighteen months' trial of a university education, Sir Roger had no alternative but to withdraw his son from his *alma mater*.

What was he then to do with him? Unluckily it was considered quite unnecessary to take any steps towards enabling him to earn his bread. Now nothing on earth can be more difficult than bringing up well a young man who has not to earn his own bread, and who has no recognised station among other men similarly circumstanced. Juvenile dukes, and sprouting earls, find their duties and their places as easily as embryo clergymen and sucking barristers. Provision is made for their peculiar positions: and, though they may possibly go astray, they have a fair chance given to them of running within the posts. The same may be said of such youths as Frank Gresham. There are enough of them in the community to have made it necessary that their well-being should be a matter of care and forethought. But there are but few men turned out in the world in the position of Louis Scatcherd; and, of those few, but very few enter the real battle of life under good auspices.

Poor Sir Roger, though he had hardly time with all his multitudinous railways to look into this thoroughly, had a glimmering of it. When he saw his son's pale face, and paid his wine bills, and heard of his doings in horse-flesh, he did know that things were not going well; he did understand that the heir to a baronetcy and a fortune of some ten thousand a year might be doing better. But what was he to do? He could not watch over his boy himself; so he took a tutor for him and sent him abroad.

Louis and the tutor got as far as Berlin, with what mutual satisfaction to each other need not be specially described. But from Berlin Sir Roger received a letter in which the tutor declined to go any further in the task which he had undertaken. He found that he had no influence over his pupil, and he could not reconcile it to his conscience to be the spectator of such a life as that which Mr Scatcherd led. He had no power in inducing Mr Scatcherd to leave Berlin; but he would remain there himself till he should hear from Sir Roger. So Sir Roger had to leave the huge Government works which he was then erecting on the southern coast, and hurry off to Berlin to see what could be done with young Hopeful.

The young Hopeful was by no means a fool; and in some matters was more than a match for his father. Sir Roger, in his anger, threatened to cast him off without a shilling. Louis, with mixed penitence and effrontery, reminded him that he could not change the descent of the title; promised amendment; declared that he had done only as do other young men of fortune; and hinted that the tutor was a strait-laced ass. The father and the son returned together to Boxall Hill, and three months afterwards Mr Scatcherd set up for himself in London.

And now his life, if not more virtuous, was more crafty than it had been. He had no tutor to watch his doings and complain of them, and he had sufficient sense to keep himself from absolute pecuniary ruin. He lived, it is true, where sharpers and blacklegs had too often opportunities of plucking him; but, young as he was, he had been sufficiently long about the world to take care he was not openly robbed; and as he was not openly robbed, his father, in a certain sense, was proud of him.

Tidings, however, came—came at least in those last days—which cut Sir Roger to the quick; tidings of vice in the son which the father could not but attribute to his own example. Twice the mother was called up to the sick-bed of her only child, while he lay raving in that horrid madness by which the outraged mind avenges itself on the body! Twice he was found raging in delirium tremens, and twice the father was told that a continuance of such life must end in an early death.

It may easily be conceived that Sir Roger was not a happy man. Lying there with that brandy bottle beneath his pillow, reflecting in his moments of rest that that son of his had his brandy bottle beneath his pillow, he could hardly have been happy. But he was not a man to say much about his misery. Though he could restrain neither himself nor his heir, he could endure in silence; and in silence he did endure, till, opening his eyes to the consciousness of death, he at last spoke a few words to the only friend he knew.

Louis Scatcherd was not a fool, nor was he naturally, perhaps, of a depraved disposition; but he had to reap the fruits of the worst education which England was able to give him. There were moments in his life when he felt that a better, a higher, nay, a much happier career was open to him than that which he had prepared himself to lead. Now and then he would reflect what money and rank might have done for him; he would look with

629

wishful eyes to the proud doings of others of his age; would dream of quiet joys, of a sweet wife, of a house to which might be asked friends who were neither jockeys nor drunkards; he would dream of such things in his short intervals of constrained sobriety; but the dream would only serve to make him moody.

This was the best side of his character; the worst, probably, was that which was brought into play by the fact that he was not a fool. He would have a better chance of redemption in this world—perhaps also in another—had he been a fool. As it was, he was no fool: he was not to be done, not he; he knew, no one better, the value of a shilling; he knew, also, how to keep his shillings, and how to spend them. He consorted much with blacklegs and such-like, because blacklegs were to his taste. But he boasted daily, nay, hourly to himself, and frequently to those around him, that the leeches who were stuck round him could draw but little blood from him. He could spend his money freely; but he would so spend it that he himself might reap the gratification of the expenditure. He was acute, crafty, knowing, and up to every damnable dodge practised by men of the class with whom he lived. At one-and-twenty he was that most odious of all odious characters—a close-fisted reprobate.

He was a small man, not ill-made by Nature, but reduced to unnatural tenuity by dissipation—a corporeal attribute of which he was apt to boast, as it enabled him, as he said, to put himself up at 7 st. 7 lb. without any "d—— nonsense of not eating and drinking." The power, however, was one of which he did not often avail himself, as his nerves were seldom in a fit state for riding. His hair was dark red, and he wore red moustaches, and a great deal of red beard beneath his chin, cut in a manner to make him look like an American. His voice also had a Yankee twang, being a cross between that of an American trader and an English groom; and his eyes were keen and fixed, and cold and knowing.

Such was the son whom Sir Roger saw standing at his bedside when first he awoke to consciousness. It must not be supposed that Sir Roger looked at him with our eyes. To him he was an only child, the heir of his wealth, the future bearer of his title; the most heart-stirring remembrancer of those other days, when he had been so much a poorer, and so much a happier man. Let that boy be bad or good, he was all Sir Roger had; and the father was still able to hope, when others thought that all ground for hope was gone.

The mother also loved her son with a mother's natural love; but Louis had ever been ashamed of his mother, and had, as far as possible, estranged himself from her. Her heart, perhaps, fixed itself with almost a warmer love on Frank Gresham, her foster-son. Frank she saw but seldom, but when she did see him he never refused her embrace. There was, too, a joyous, genial lustre about Frank's face which always endeared him to women, and made his former nurse regard him as the pet creation of the age. Though she but seldom interfered with any monetary arrangement of her husband's, yet once or twice she had ventured to hint that a legacy left to the young squire would make her a happy woman. Sir Roger, however, on these occasions had not appeared very desirous of making his wife happy.

"Ah, Louis! is that you?" ejaculated Sir Roger, in tones hardly more than half-formed: afterwards, in a day or two that is, he fully recovered his voice; but just then he could hardly open his jaws, and spoke almost through his teeth. He managed, however, to put out his hand and lay it on the counterpane, so that his son could take it.

"Why, that's well, governor," said the son; "you'll be as right as a trivet in a day or two—eh, governor?"

The "governor" smiled with a ghastly smile. He already pretty well knew that he would never again be "right," as his son called it, on that side of the grave. It did not, moreover, suit him to say much just at that moment, so he contented himself with holding his son's hand. He lay still in this position for a moment, and then, turning round painfully on his side, endeavoured to put his hand to the place where his dire enemy usually was concealed. Sir Roger, however, was too weak now to be his own master; he was at length, though too late, a captive in the hands of nurses and doctors, and the bottle had now been removed.

Then Lady Scatcherd came in, and seeing that her husband was no longer unconscious, she could not but believe that Dr Thorne had been wrong; she could not but think that there must be some ground for hope. She threw herself on her knees at the bedside, bursting into tears as she did so, and taking Sir Roger's hand in hers covered it with kisses.

"Bother!" said Sir Roger.

She did not, however, long occupy herself with the indulgence of her feelings; but going speedily to work, produced such sustenance as the doctors had ordered to be given when the patient might awake. A breakfast-cup was brought to him, and a few drops were put into his mouth; but he soon made it manifest that he would take nothing more of a description so perfectly innocent.

"A drop of brandy—just a little drop," said he, half-ordering, and half-entreating.

"Ah, Roger!" said Lady Scatcherd.

"Just a little drop, Louis," said the sick man, appealing to his son.

"A little will be good for him; bring the bottle, mother," said the son.

After some altercation the brandy bottle was brought, and Louis, with what he thought a very sparing hand, proceeded to pour about half a wine-glassful into the cup. As he did so, Sir Roger, weak as he was, contrived to shake his son's arm, so as greatly to increase the dose.

"Ha! ha! ha!" laughed the sick man, and then greedily swallowed the dose.

CHAPTER XXV

SIR ROGER DIES

That night the doctor stayed at Boxall Hill, and the next night; so that it became a customary thing for him to sleep there during the latter part of Sir Roger's illness. He returned home daily to Greshamsbury; for he had his patients there, to whom he was as necessary as to Sir Roger, the foremost of whom was Lady Arabella. He had, therefore, no slight work on his hands, seeing that his nights were by no means wholly devoted to rest.

Mr Rerechild had not been much wrong as to the remaining space of life which he had allotted to the dying man. Once or twice Dr Thorne had thought that the great original strength of his patient would have enabled him to fight against death for a somewhat longer period; but Sir Roger would give himself no chance. Whenever he was strong enough to have a will of his own, he insisted on having his very medicine mixed with brandy; and in the hours of the doctor's absence, he was too often successful in his attempts.

"It does not much matter," Dr Thorne had said to Lady Scatcherd. "Do what you can to keep down the quantity, but do not irritate him by refusing to obey. It does not much signify now." So Lady Scatcherd still administered the alcohol, and he from day to day invented little schemes for increasing the amount, over which he chuckled with ghastly laughter.

Two or three times during these days Sir Roger essayed to speak seriously to his son; but Louis always frustrated him. He either got out of the room on some excuse, or made his mother interfere on the score that so much talking would be bad for his father. He already knew with tolerable accuracy what was the purport of his father's will, and by no means approved of it; but as he could not now hope to induce his father to alter it so as to make it more favourable to himself, he conceived that no conversation on matters of business could be of use to him.

"Louis," said Sir Roger, one afternoon to his son; "Louis, I have not done by you as I ought to have done—I know that now."

"Nonsense, governor; never mind about that now; I shall do well enough, I dare say. Besides, it isn't too late; you can make it twenty-three years instead of twenty-five, if you like it."

"I do not mean as to money, Louis. There are things besides money which a father ought to look to."

"Now, father, don't fret yourself—I'm all right; you may be sure of that."

"Louis, it's that accursed brandy—it's that that I'm afraid of: you see me here, my boy, how I'm lying here now."

"Don't you be annoying yourself, governor; I'm all right—quite right; and as for you, why, you'll be up and about yourself in another month or so."

"I shall never be off this bed, my boy, till I'm carried into my coffin, on those chairs there. But I'm not thinking of myself, Louis, but you; think what you may have before you if you can't avoid that accursed bottle."

"I'm all right, governor; right as a trivet. It's very little I take, except at an odd time or so."

"Oh, Louis! Louis!"

"Come, father, cheer up; this sort of thing isn't the thing for you at all. I wonder where mother is: she ought to be here with the broth; just let me go, and I'll see for her."

The father understood it all. He saw that it was now much beyond his faded powers to touch the heart or conscience of such a youth as his son had become. What now could he do for his boy except die? What else, what other benefit, did his son require of him but to die; to die so that his means of dissipation might be unbounded? He let go the unresisting hand which he held, and, as the young man crept out of the room, he turned his face to the wall. He turned his face to the wall and held bitter commune with his own heart. To what had he brought himself? To what had he brought his son? Oh, how happy would it have been for him could he have remained all his days a working stone-mason in Barchester! How happy could he have died as such, years ago! Such tears as those which wet that pillow are the bitterest which human eyes can shed.

But while they were dropping, the memoir of his life was in quick course of preparation. It was, indeed, nearly completed, with considerable detail. He had lingered on four days longer than might have been expected, and the author had thus had more than usual time for the work. In these days a man is nobody unless his biography is kept so far posted up that it may be ready for the national breakfast-table on the morning after his demise. When it chances that the dead hero is one who was taken in his prime of life, of whose departure from among us the most far-seeing biographical scribe can have no prophetic inkling, this must be difficult. Of great men, full of years, who are ripe for the sickle, who in the course of Nature must soon fall, it is of course comparatively easy for an active compiler to have his complete memoir ready in his desk. But in order that the idea of omnipresent and omniscient information may be kept up, the young must be chronicled as quickly as the old. In some cases this task must, one would say, be difficult. Nevertheless, it is done.

The memoir of Sir Roger Scatcherd was progressing favourably. In this it was told how fortunate had been his life; how, in his case, industry and genius combined had triumphed over the difficulties which humble birth and deficient education had thrown in his way; how he had made a name among England's great men; how the Queen had delighted to honour him, and nobles had been proud to have him for a guest at their mansions. Then followed a list of all the great works which he had achieved, of the railroads, canals, docks, harbours, jails, and hospitals which he had constructed. His name was held up as an example to the labouring classes of his countrymen, and he was pointed at as one who had lived and died happy—ever happy, said the biographer, because ever industrious. And so a great moral question was inculcated. A short paragraph was devoted to his appearance in Parliament; and unfortunate Mr Romer was again held up for disgrace, for the thirtieth time, as having been the means of depriving our legislative councils of the great assistance of Sir Roger's experience.

"Sir Roger," said the biographer in his concluding passage, "was possessed of an iron frame; but even iron will yield to the repeated blows of the hammer. In the latter years of his life he was known to overtask himself; and at length the body gave way, though the mind remained firm to the *last*. The subject of this memoir was only fifty-nine when he was taken from us."

And thus Sir Roger's life was written, while the tears were yet falling on his pillow at Boxall Hill. It was a pity that a proof-sheet could not have been sent to him. No man was vainer of his reputation, and it would have greatly gratified him to know that posterity was about to speak of him in such terms—to speak of him with a voice that would be audible for twenty-four hours.

Sir Roger made no further attempt to give counsel to his son. It was too evidently useless. The old dying lion felt that the lion's power had already passed from him, and that he was helpless in the hands of the young cub who was so soon to inherit the wealth of the forest. But Dr Thorne was more kind to him. He had something yet to say as to his worldly hopes and worldly cares; and his old friend did not turn a deaf ear to him.

It was during the night that Sir Roger was most anxious to talk, and most capable of talking. He would lie through the day in a state half-comatose; but towards evening he would rouse himself, and by midnight he would be full of fitful energy. One night, as he lay wakeful and full of thought, he thus poured forth his whole heart to Dr Thorne.

"Thorne," said he, "I told you about my will, you know."

"Yes," said the other; "and I have blamed myself greatly that I have not again urged you to alter it. Your illness came too suddenly, Scatcherd; and then I was averse to speak of it."

"Why should I alter it? It is a good will; as good as I can make. Not but that I have altered it since I spoke to you. I did it that day after you left me."

"Have you definitely named your heir in default of Louis?"

"No—that is—yes—I had done that before; I have said Mary's eldest child: I have not altered that."

"But, Scatcherd, you must alter it."

"Must! well then I won't; but I'll tell you what I have done. I have added a postscript—a codicil they call it—saying that you, and you only, know who is her eldest child. Winterbones and Jack Martin have witnessed that."

Dr Thorne was going to explain how very injudicious such an arrangement appeared to be; but Sir Roger would not listen to him. It was not about that that he wished to speak to him. To him it was matter of but minor interest who might inherit his money if his son should die early; his care was solely for his son's welfare. At twenty-five the heir might make his own will—might bequeath all this wealth according to his own fancy. Sir Roger would not bring himself to believe that his son could follow him to the grave in so short a time.

"Never mind that, doctor, now; but about Louis; you will be his guardian, you know."

"Not his guardian. He is more than of age."

"Ah! but doctor, you will be his guardian. The property will not be his till he be twenty-five. You will not desert him?"

"I will not desert him; but I doubt whether I can do much for him—what can I do, Scatcherd?"

"Use the power that a strong man has over a weak one. Use the power that my will will give you. Do for him as you would for a son of your own if you saw him going in bad courses. Do as a friend should do for a friend that is dead and gone. I would do so for you, doctor, if our places were changed."

"What I can do, that I will do," said Thorne, solemnly, taking as he spoke the contractor's hand in his own with a tight grasp.

"I know you will; I know you will. Oh! doctor, may you never feel as I do now! May you on your death-bed have no dread as I have, as to the fate of those you will leave behind you!"

Doctor Thorne felt that he could not say much in answer to this. The future fate of Louis Scatcherd was, he could not but own to himself, greatly to be dreaded. What good, what happiness, could be presaged for such a one as he was? What comfort could he offer to the father? And then he was called on to compare, as it were, the prospects of this unfortunate with those of his own darling; to contrast all that was murky, foul, and disheartening, with all that was perfect—for to him she was all but perfect; to liken Louis Scatcherd to the angel who brightened his own hearthstone. How could he answer to such an appeal?

He said nothing; but merely tightened his grasp of the other's hand, to signify that he would do, as best he could, all that was asked of him. Sir Roger looked up sadly into the doctor's face, as though expecting some word of consolation. There was no comfort, no consolation to come to him!

"For three or four years he must greatly depend upon you," continued Sir Roger.

"I will do what I can," said the doctor. "What I can do I will do. But he is not a child, Scatcherd: at his age he must stand or fall mainly by his own conduct. The best thing for him will be to marry."

"Exactly; that's just it, Thorne: I was coming to that. If he would marry, I think he would do well yet, for all that has come and gone. If he married, of course you would let him have the command of his own income."

"I will be governed entirely by your wishes: under any circumstances his income will, as I understand, be quite sufficient for him, married or single."

"Ah!—but, Thorne, I should like to think he should shine with the best of them. For what have I made the money if not for that? Now if he marries—decently, that is—some woman you know that can assist him in the world, let him have what he wants. It is not to save the money that I put it into your hands."

"No, Scatcherd; not to save the money, but to save him. I think that while you are yet with him you should advise him to marry."

"He does not care a straw for what I advise, not one straw. Why should he? How can I tell him to be sober when I have been a beast all my life myself? How can I advise him? That's where it is! It is that that now kills me. Advise! Why, when I speak to him he treats me like a child."

"He fears that you are too weak, you know: he thinks that you should not be allowed to talk."

"Nonsense! he knows better; you know better. Too weak! what signifies? Would I not give all that I have of strength at one blow if I could open his eyes to see as I see but for one minute?" And the sick man raised himself up in his bed as though he were actually going to expend all that remained to him of vigour in the energy of a moment.

"Gently, Scatcherd; gently. He will listen to you yet; but do not be so unruly."

"Thorne, you see that bottle there? Give me half a glass of brandy."

The doctor turned round in his chair; but he hesitated in doing as he was desired.

"Do as I ask you, doctor. It can do no harm now; you know that well enough. Why torture me now?"

"No, I will not torture you; but you will have water with it?"

"Water! No; the brandy by itself. I tell you I cannot speak without it. What's the use of canting now? You know it can make no difference."

Sir Roger was right. It could make no difference; and Dr Thorne gave him the half glass of brandy.

"Ah, well; you've a stingy hand, doctor; confounded stingy. You don't measure your medicines out in such light doses."

"You will be wanting more before morning, you know."

"Before morning! indeed I shall; a pint or so before that. I remember the time, doctor, when I have drunk to my own cheek above two quarts between dinner and breakfast! aye, and worked all the day after it!"

"You have been a wonderful man, Scatcherd, very wonderful."

"Aye, wonderful! well, never mind. It's over now. But what was I saying?—about Louis, doctor; you'll not desert him?"

"Certainly not."

"He's not strong; I know that. How should he be strong, living as he has done? Not that it seemed to hurt me when I was his age."

"You had the advantage of hard work."

"That's it. Sometimes I wish that Louis had not a shilling in the world; that he had to trudge about with an apron round his waist as I did. But it's too late now to think of that. If he would only marry, doctor."

Dr Thorne again expressed an opinion that no step would be so likely to reform the habits of the young heir as marriage; and repeated his advice to the father to implore his son to take a wife.

"I'll tell you what, Thorne," said he. And then, after a pause, he went on. "I have not half told you as yet what is on my mind; and I'm nearly afraid to tell it; though, indeed, I don't know why I should be."

"I never knew you afraid of anything yet," said the doctor, smiling gently.

"Well, then, I'll not end by turning coward. Now, doctor, tell the truth to me; what do you expect me to do for that girl of yours that we were talking of—Mary's child?"

There was a pause for a moment, for Thorne was slow to answer him.

"You would not let me see her, you know, though she is my niece as truly as she is yours."

"Nothing," at last said the doctor, slowly. "I expect nothing. I would not let you see her, and therefore, I expect nothing."

"She will have it all if poor Louis should die," said Sir Roger.

"If you intend it so you should put her name into the will," said the other. "Not that I ask you or wish you to do so. Mary, thank God, can do without wealth."

"Thorne, on one condition I will put her name into it. I will alter it all on one condition. Let the two cousins be man and wife—let Louis marry poor Mary's child."

The proposition for a moment took away the doctor's breath, and he was unable to answer. Not for all the wealth of India would he have given up his lamb to that young wolf, even though he had had the power to do so. But that lamb—lamb though she was—had, as he well knew, a will of her own on such a matter. What alliance could be more impossible, thought he to himself, than one between Mary Thorne and Louis Scatcherd?

"I will alter it all if you will give me your hand upon it that you will do your best to bring about this marriage. Everything shall be his on the day he marries her; and should he die unmarried, it shall all then be hers by name. Say the word, Thorne, and she shall come here at once. I shall yet have time to see her."

But Dr Thorne did not say the word; just at the moment he said nothing, but he slowly shook his head.

"Why not, Thorne?"

"My friend, it is impossible."

"Why impossible?"

"Her hand is not mine to dispose of, nor is her heart."

"Then let her come over herself."

"What! Scatcherd, that the son might make love to her while the father is so danger-ously ill! Bid her come to look for a rich husband! That would not be seemly, would it?"

"No; not for that: let her come merely that I may see her; that we may all know her. I will leave the matter then in your hands if you will promise me to do your best."

"But, my friend, in this matter I cannot do my best. I can do nothing. And, indeed, I may say at once, that it is altogether out of the question. I know—"

"What do you know?" said the baronet, turning on him almost angrily. "What can you know to make you say that it is impossible? Is she a pearl of such price that a man may not win her?"

"She is a pearl of great price."

"Believe me, doctor, money goes far in winning such pearls."

"Perhaps so; I know little about it. But this I do know, that money will not win her. Let us talk of something else; believe me it is useless for us to think of this."

"Yes; if you set your face against it obstinately. You must think very poorly of Louis if you suppose that no girl can fancy him."

"I have not said so, Scatcherd."

"To have the spending of ten thousand a year, and be a baronet's lady! Why, doctor, what is it you expect for this girl?"

"Not much, indeed; not much. A quiet heart and a quiet home; not much more."

"Thorne, if you will be ruled by me in this, she shall be the most topping woman in this county."

"My friend, my friend, why thus grieve me? Why should you thus harass yourself? I tell you it is impossible. They have never seen each other; they have nothing, and can have nothing in common; their tastes, and wishes, and pursuits are different. Besides, Scatcherd, marriages never answer that are so made; believe me, it is impossible."

The contractor threw himself back on his bed, and lay for some ten minutes perfectly quiet; so much so that the doctor began to think that he was sleeping. So thinking, and wearied by the watching, Dr Thorne was beginning to creep quietly from the room, when his companion again roused himself, almost with vehemence.

"You won't do this thing for me, then?" said he.

"Do it! It is not for you or me to do such things as that. Such things must be left to those concerned themselves."

"You will not even help me?"

"Not in this thing, Sir Roger."

"Then, by ——, she shall not under any circumstances ever have a shilling of mine. Give me some of that stuff there," and he again pointed to the brandy bottle which stood ever within his sight.

The doctor poured out and handed to him another small modicum of spirit.

"Nonsense, man; fill the glass. I'll stand no nonsense now. I'll be master in my own house to the last. Give it here, I tell you. Ten thousand devils are tearing me within. You—you could have comforted me; but you would not. Fill the glass I tell you."

"I should be killing you were I to do it."

"Killing me! killing me! you are always talking of killing me. Do you suppose that I am afraid to die? Do not I know how soon it is coming? Give me the brandy, I say, or I will be out across the room to fetch it."

"No, Scatcherd. I cannot give it to you; not while I am here. Do you remember how you were engaged this morning?"—he had that morning taken the sacrament from the parish clergyman—"you would not wish to make me guilty of murder, would you?"

"Nonsense! You are talking nonsense; habit is second nature. I tell you I shall sink without it. Why, you know I always get it directly your back is turned. Come, I will not be bullied in my own house; give me that bottle, I say!"—and Sir Roger essayed, vainly enough, to raise himself from the bed.

"Stop, Scatcherd; I will give it you—I will help you. It may be that habit is second nature." Sir Roger in his determined energy had swallowed, without thinking of it, the small quantity which the doctor had before poured out for him, and still held the empty glass within his hand. This the doctor now took and filled nearly to the brim.

"Come, Thorne, a bumper; a bumper for this once. 'Whatever the drink, it a bumper must be.' You stingy fellow! I would not treat you so. Well—well."

"It's as full as you can hold it, Scatcherd."

"Try me; try me! my hand is a rock; at least at holding liquor." And then he drained the contents of the glass, which were sufficient in quantity to have taken away the breath from any ordinary man.

"Ah, I'm better now. But, Thorne, I do love a full glass, ha! ha! ha!"

There was something frightful, almost sickening, in the peculiar hoarse guttural tone of his voice. The sounds came from him as though steeped in brandy, and told, all too plainly, the havoc which the alcohol had made. There was a fire too about his eyes which contrasted with his sunken cheeks: his hanging jaw, unshorn beard, and haggard face were terrible to look at. His hands and arms were hot and clammy, but so thin and wasted! Of his lower limbs the lost use had not returned to him, so that in all his efforts at vehemence he was controlled by his own want of vitality. When he supported himself, half-sitting against the pillows, he was in a continual tremor; and yet, as he boasted, he could still lift his glass steadily to his mouth. Such now was the hero of whom that ready compiler of memoirs had just finished his correct and succinct account.

After he had had his brandy, he sat glaring a while at vacancy, as though he was dead to all around him, and was thinking—thinking—thinking of things in the infinite distance of the past.

"Shall I go now," said the doctor, "and send Lady Scatcherd to you?"

"Wait a while, doctor; just one minute longer. So you will do nothing for Louis, then?"

"I will do everything for him that I can do."

"Ah, yes! everything but the one thing that will save him. Well, I will not ask you again. But remember, Thorne, I shall alter my will to-morrow."

"Do so by all means; you may well alter it for the better. If I may advise you, you will have down your own business attorney from London. If you will let me send he will be here before to-morrow night."

"Thank you for nothing, Thorne: I can manage that matter myself. Now leave me; but remember, you have ruined that girl's fortune."

The doctor did leave him, and went not altogether happy to his room. He could not but confess to himself that he had, despite himself as it were, fed himself with hope that Mary's future might be made more secure, aye, and brighter too, by some small unheeded fraction broken off from the huge mass of her uncle's wealth. Such hope, if it had amounted to hope, was now all gone. But this was not all, nor was this the worst of it. That he had done right in utterly repudiating all idea of a marriage between Mary and her cousin—of that he was certain enough; that no earthly consideration would have induced Mary to plight her troth to such a man—that, with him, was as certain as doom. But how far had he done right in keeping her from the sight of her uncle? How could he justify it to himself if he had thus robbed her of her inheritance, seeing that he had done so from a selfish fear lest she, who was now all his own, should be known to the world as belonging to others rather than to him? He had taken upon him on her behalf to reject wealth as valueless; and yet he had no sooner done so than he began to consume his hours with reflecting how great to her would be the value of wealth. And thus, when Sir Roger told him, as he left the room, that he had ruined Mary's fortune, he was hardly able to bear the taunt with equanimity.

On the next morning, after paying his professional visit to his patient, and satisfying himself that the end was now drawing near with steps terribly quickened, he went down to Greshamsbury.

"How long is this to last, uncle?" said his niece, with sad voice, as he again prepared to return to Boxall Hill.

"Not long, Mary; do not begrudge him a few more hours of life."

"No, I do not, uncle. I will say nothing more about it. Is his son with him?" And then, perversely enough, she persisted in asking numerous questions about Louis Scatcherd.

"Is he likely to marry, uncle?"

"I hope so, my dear."

"Will he be so very rich?"

"Yes; ultimately he will be very rich."

"He will be a baronet, will he not?"

"Yes, my dear."

"What is he like, uncle?"

"Like—I never know what a young man is like. He is like a man with red hair."

"Uncle, you are the worst hand in describing I ever knew. If I'd seen him for five minutes, I'd be bound to make a portrait of him; and you, if you were describing a dog, you'd only say what colour his hair was."

"Well, he's a little man."

"Exactly, just as I should say that Mrs Umbleby had a red-haired little dog. I wish I had known these Scatcherds, uncle. I do so admire people that can push themselves in the world. I wish I had known Sir Roger."

"You will never know him now, Mary."

"I suppose not. I am so sorry for him. Is Lady Scatcherd nice?"

"She is an excellent woman."

"I hope I may know her some day. You are so much there now, uncle; I wonder whether you ever mention me to them. If you do, tell her from me how much I grieve for her."

That same night Dr Thorne again found himself alone with Sir Roger. The sick man was much more tranquil, and apparently more at ease than he had been on the preceding night. He said nothing about his will, and not a word about Mary Thorne; but the doctor knew that Winterbones and a notary's clerk from Barchester had been in the bedroom a great part of the day; and, as he knew also that the great man of business was accustomed to do his most important work by the hands of such tools as these, he did not doubt but that the will had been altered and remodelled. Indeed, he thought it more than probable, that when it was opened it would be found to be wholly different in its provisions from that which Sir Roger had already described.

"Louis is clever enough," he said, "sharp enough, I mean. He won't squander the property."

"He has good natural abilities," said the doctor.

"Excellent, excellent," said the father. "He may do well, very well, if he can only be kept from this;" and Sir Roger held up the empty wine-glass which stood by his bedside. "What a life he may have before him!—and to throw it away for this!" and as he spoke he took the glass and tossed it across the room. "Oh, doctor! would that it were all to begin again!"

"We all wish that, I dare say, Scatcherd."

"No, you don't wish it. You ain't worth a shilling, and yet you regret nothing. I am worth half a million in one way or the other, and I regret everything—everything—everything!"

"You should not think in that way, Scatcherd; you need not think so. Yesterday you told Mr Clarke that you were comfortable in your mind." Mr Clarke was the clergyman who had visited him.

"Of course I did. What else could I say when he asked me? It wouldn't have been civil to have told him that his time and words were all thrown away. But, Thorne, believe me, when a man's heart is sad—sad—sad to the core, a few words from a parson at the last moment will never make it all right."

"May He have mercy on you, my friend!—if you will think of Him, and look to Him, He will have mercy on you."

"Well—I will try, doctor; but would that it were all to do again. You'll see to the old woman for my sake, won't you?"

"What, Lady Scatcherd?"

"Lady Devil! If anything angers me now it is that 'ladyship'—her to be my lady! Why, when I came out of jail that time, the poor creature had hardly a shoe to her foot. But it wasn't her fault, Thorne; it was none of her doing. She never asked for such nonsense."

"She has been an excellent wife, Scatcherd; and what is more, she is an excellent woman. She is, and ever will be, one of my dearest friends."

"Thank'ee, doctor, thank'ee. Yes; she has been a good wife—better for a poor man than a rich one; but then, that was what she was born to. You won't let her be knocked about by them, will you, Thorne?"

Dr Thorne again assured him, that as long as he lived Lady Scatcherd should never want one true friend; in making this promise, however, he managed to drop all allusion to the obnoxious title.

"You'll be with him as much as possible, won't you?" again asked the baronet, after lying quite silent for a quarter of an hour.

"With whom?" said the doctor, who was then all but asleep.

"With my poor boy; with Louis."

"If he will let me, I will," said the doctor.

"And, doctor, when you see a glass at his mouth, dash it down; thrust it down, though you thrust out the teeth with it. When you see that, Thorne, tell him of his father—tell him what his father might have been but for that; tell him how his father died like a beast, because he could not keep himself from drink."

These, reader, were the last words spoken by Sir Roger Scatcherd. As he uttered them he rose up in bed with the same vehemence which he had shown on the former evening. But in the very act of doing so he was again struck by paralysis, and before nine on the following morning all was over.

"Oh, my man—my own, own man!" exclaimed the widow, remembering in the paroxysm of her grief nothing but the loves of their early days; "the best, the brightest, the cleverest of them all!"

Some weeks after this Sir Roger was buried, with much pomp and ceremony, within the precincts of Barchester Cathedral; and a monument was put up to him soon after, in which he was portrayed as smoothing a block of granite with a mallet and chisel; while his eagle eye, disdaining such humble work, was fixed upon some intricate mathematical instrument above him. Could Sir Roger have seen it himself, he would probably have declared, that no workman was ever worth his salt who looked one way while he rowed another.

Immediately after the funeral the will was opened, and Dr Thorne discovered that the clauses of it were exactly identical with those which his friend had described to him some months back. Nothing had been altered; nor had the document been unfolded since that strange codicil was added, in which it was declared that Dr Thorne knew—and only Dr Thorne—who was the eldest child of the testator's only sister. At the same time, however, a joint executor with Dr Thorne had been named—one Mr Stock, a man of railway fame—and Dr Thorne himself was made a legatee to the humble extent of a thousand pounds. A life income of a thousand pounds a year was left to Lady Scatcherd.

CHAPTER XXVI

WAR

We need not follow Sir Roger to his grave, nor partake of the baked meats which were furnished for his funeral banquet. Such men as Sir Roger Scatcherd are always well buried, and we have already seen that his glories were duly told to posterity in the graphic diction of his sepulchral monument. In a few days the doctor had returned to his quiet home, and Sir Louis found himself reigning at Boxall Hill in his father's stead—with, however, a much diminished sway, and, as he thought it, but a poor exchequer. We must soon return to him and say something of his career as a baronet; but for the present, we may go back to our more pleasant friends at Greshamsbury.

But our friends at Greshamsbury had not been making themselves pleasant—not so pleasant to each other as circumstances would have admitted. In those days which the doctor had felt himself bound to pass, if not altogether at Boxall Hill, yet altogether away from his own home, so as to admit of his being as much as possible with his patient, Mary had been thrown more than ever with Patience Oriel, and, also, almost more than ever with Beatrice Gresham. As regarded Mary, she would doubtless have preferred the companionship of Patience, though she loved Beatrice far the best; but she had no choice. When she went to the parsonage Beatrice came there also, and when Patience came to the doctor's house Beatrice either accompanied or followed her. Mary could hardly have rejected their society, even had she felt it wise to do so. She would in such case have been all alone, and her severance from the Greshamsbury house and household, from the big family in which she had for so many years been almost at home, would have made such solitude almost unendurable.

And then these two girls both knew—not her secret: she had no secret—but the little history of her ill-treatment. They knew that though she had been blameless in this matter, yet she had been the one to bear the punishment; and, as girls and bosom friends, they could not but sympathise with her, and endow her with heroic attributes; make her, in fact, as we are doing, their little heroine for the nonce. This was, perhaps, not serviceable for Mary; but it was far from being disagreeable.

The tendency to finding matter for hero-worship in Mary's endurance was much stronger with Beatrice than with Miss Oriel. Miss Oriel was the elder, and naturally less afflicted with the sentimentalism of romance. She had thrown herself into Mary's arms because she had seen that it was essentially necessary for Mary's comfort that she should do so. She was anxious to make her friend smile, and to smile with her. Beatrice was quite as true in her sympathy; but she rather wished that she and Mary might weep in unison, shed mutual tears, and break their hearts together.

Patience had spoken of Frank's love as a misfortune, of his conduct as erroneous, and to be excused only by his youth, and had never appeared to surmise that Mary also might be in love as well as he. But to Beatrice the affair was a tragic difficulty, admitting of no solution; a Gordian knot, not to be cut; a misery now and for ever. She would always talk about Frank when she and Mary were alone; and, to speak the truth, Mary did not stop her as she perhaps should have done. As for a marriage between them, that was impossible; Beatrice was well sure of that: it was Frank's unfortunate destiny that he must marry money—money, and, as Beatrice sometimes thoughtlessly added, cutting Mary to the quick,—money and family also. Under such circumstances a marriage between them was quite impossible; but not the less did Beatrice declare, that she would have loved Mary as her sister-in-law had it been possible; and how worthy Frank was of a girl's love, had such love been permissible.

"It is so cruel," Beatrice would say; "so very, very, cruel. You would have suited him in every way."

"Nonsense, Trichy; I should have suited him in no possible way at all; nor he me."

"Oh, but you would—exactly. Papa loves you so well."

"And mamma; that would have been so nice."

"Yes; and mamma, too—that is, had you had a fortune," said the daughter, naïvely. "She always liked you personally, always."

"Did she?"

"Always. And we all love you so."

"Especially Lady Alexandrina."

"That would not have signified, for Frank cannot endure the de Courcys himself."

"My dear, it does not matter one straw whom your brother can endure or not endure just at present. His character is to be formed, and his tastes, and his heart also."

"Oh, Mary!—his heart."

"Yes, his heart; not the fact of his having a heart. I think he has a heart; but he himself does not yet understand it."

"Oh, Mary! you do not know him."

Such conversations were not without danger to poor Mary's comfort. It came soon to be the case that she looked rather for this sort of sympathy from Beatrice, than for Miss Oriel's pleasant but less piquant gaiety.

So the days of the doctor's absence were passed, and so also the first week after his return. During this week it was almost daily necessary that the squire should be with him. The doctor was now the legal holder of Sir Roger's property, and, as such, the holder also of all the mortgages on Mr Gresham's property; and it was natural that they should be much together. The doctor would not, however, go up to Greshamsbury on any other than medical business; and it therefore became necessary that the squire should be a good deal at the doctor's house.

Then the Lady Arabella became unhappy in her mind. Frank, it was true, was away at Cambridge, and had been successfully kept out of Mary's way since the suspicion of danger had fallen upon Lady Arabella's mind. Frank was away, and Mary was systematically banished, with due acknowledgement from all the powers in Greshamsbury. But this was not enough for Lady Arabella as long as her daughter still habitually consorted with the female culprit, and as long as her husband consorted with the male culprit. It seemed to Lady Arabella at this moment as though, in banishing Mary from the house, she had in effect banished herself from the most intimate of the Greshamsbury social circles. She magnified in her own mind the importance of the conferences between the girls, and was not without some fear that the doctor might be talking the squire over into very dangerous compliance.

She resolved, therefore, on another duel with the doctor. In the first she had been pre-eminently and unexpectedly successful. No young sucking dove could have been more mild than that terrible enemy whom she had for years regarded as being too puissant for attack. In ten minutes she had vanquished him, and succeeded in banishing both him and his niece from the house without losing the value of his services. As is always the case with us, she had begun to despise the enemy she had conquered, and to think that the foe, once beaten, could never rally.

Her object was to break off all confidential intercourse between Beatrice and Mary, and to interrupt, as far as she could do it, that between the doctor and the squire. This, it may be said, could be more easily done by skilful management within her own household. She had, however, tried that and failed. She had said much to Beatrice as to the impru-dence of her friendship with Mary, and she had done this purposely before the squire; injudiciously however,—for the squire had immediately taken Mary's part, and had de-clared that he had no wish to see a quarrel between his family and that of the doctor; that Mary Thorne was in every way a good girl, and an eligible friend for his own child; and had ended by declaring, that he would not have Mary persecuted for Frank's fault. This had not been the end, nor nearly the end of what had been said on the matter at Gresh-amsbury; but the end, when it came, came in this wise, that Lady Arabella determined to say a few words to the doctor as to the expediency of forbidding familiar intercourse be-tween Mary and any of the Greshamsbury people.

With this view Lady Arabella absolutely bearded the lion in his den, the doctor in his shop. She had heard that both Mary and Beatrice were to pass a certain afternoon at the parsonage, and took that opportunity of calling at the doctor's house. A period of many years had passed since she had last so honoured that abode. Mary, indeed, had been so much one of her own family that the ceremony of calling on her had never been thought necessary; and thus, unless Mary had been absolutely ill, there would have been nothing to bring her ladyship to the house. All this she knew would add to the importance of the occasion, and she judged it prudent to make the occasion as important as it might well be.

She was so far successful that she soon found herself *tête-à-tête* with the doctor in his own study. She was no whit dismayed by the pair of human thigh-bones which lay close to his hand, and which, when he was talking in that den of his own, he was in the constant habit of handling with much energy; nor was she frightened out of her propriety even by the little child's skull which grinned at her from off the chimney-piece.

"Doctor," she said, as soon as the first complimentary greetings were over, speaking in her kindest and most would-be-confidential tone, "Doctor, I am still uneasy about that boy of mine, and I have thought it best to come and see you at once, and tell you freely what I think."

The doctor bowed, and said that he was very sorry that she should have any cause for uneasiness about his young friend Frank.

"Indeed, I am very uneasy, doctor; and having, as I do have, such reliance on your prudence, and such perfect confidence in your friendship, I have thought it best to come and speak to you openly:" thereupon the Lady Arabella paused, and the doctor bowed again.

"Nobody knows so well as you do the dreadful state of the squire's affairs."

"Not so very dreadful; not so very dreadful," said the doctor, mildly: "that is, as far as I know."

"Yes they are, doctor; very dreadful; very dreadful indeed. You know how much he owes to this young man: I do not, for the squire never tells anything to me; but I know that it is a very large sum of money; enough to swamp the estate and ruin Frank. Now I call that very dreadful."

"No, no, not ruin him, Lady Arabella; not ruin him, I hope."

"However, I did not come to talk to you about that. As I said before, I know nothing of the squire's affairs, and, as a matter of course, I do not ask you to tell me. But I am sure you will agree with me in this, that, as a mother, I cannot but be interested about my only son," and Lady Arabella put her cambric handkerchief to her eyes.

"Of course you are; of course you are," said the doctor; "and, Lady Arabella, my opinion of Frank is such, that I feel sure that he will do well;" and, in his energy, Dr Thorne brandished one of the thigh-bones almost in the lady's face.

"I hope he will; I am sure I hope he will. But, doctor, he has such dangers to contend with; he is so warm and impulsive that I fear his heart will bring him into trouble. Now, you know, unless Frank marries money he is lost."

The doctor made no answer to this last appeal, but as he sat and listened a slight frown came across his brow.

"He must marry money, doctor. Now we have, you see, with your assistance, contrived to separate him from dear Mary—"

"With my assistance, Lady Arabella! I have given no assistance, nor have I meddled in the matter; nor will I."

"Well, doctor, perhaps not meddled; but you agreed with me, you know, that the two young people had been imprudent."

"I agreed to no such thing, Lady Arabella; never, never. I not only never agreed that Mary had been imprudent, but I will not agree to it now, and will not allow any one to assert it in my presence without contradicting it:" and then the doctor worked away at the thigh-bones in a manner that did rather alarm her ladyship.

"At any rate, you thought that the young people had better be kept apart."

"No; neither did I think that: my niece, I felt sure, was safe from danger. I knew that she would do nothing that would bring either her or me to shame."

"Not to shame," said the lady, apologetically, as it were, using the word perhaps not exactly in the doctor's sense.

"I felt no alarm for her," continued the doctor, "and desired no change. Frank is your son, and it is for you to look to him. You thought proper to do so by desiring Mary to absent herself from Greshamsbury."

"Oh, no, no, no!" said Lady Arabella.

"But you did, Lady Arabella; and as Greshamsbury is your home, neither I nor my niece had any ground of complaint. We acquiesced, not without much suffering, but we did acquiesce; and you, I think, can have no ground of complaint against us."

Lady Arabella had hardly expected that the doctor would reply to her mild and conciliatory exordium with so much sternness. He had yielded so easily to her on the former occasion. She did not comprehend that when she uttered her sentence of exile against Mary, she had given an order which she had the power of enforcing; but that obedience to that order had now placed Mary altogether beyond her jurisdiction. She was, therefore, a little surprised, and for a few moments overawed by the doctor's manner; but she soon recovered herself, remembering, doubtless, that fortune favours none but the brave.

"I make no complaint, Dr Thorne," she said, after assuming a tone more befitting a de Courcy than that hitherto used, "I make no complaint either as regards you or Mary."

"You are very kind, Lady Arabella."

"But I think that it is my duty to put a stop, a peremptory stop to anything like a love affair between my son and your niece."

"I have not the least objection in life. If there is such a love affair, put a stop to it—that is, if you have the power."

Here the doctor was doubtless imprudent. But he had begun to think that he had yielded sufficiently to the lady; and he had begun to resolve, also, that though it would not become him to encourage even the idea of such a marriage, he would make Lady Arabella understand that he thought his niece quite good enough for her son, and that the match, if regarded as imprudent, was to be regarded as equally imprudent on both sides. He would not suffer that Mary and her heart and feelings and interest should be altogether postponed to those of the young heir; and, perhaps, he was unconsciously encouraged in this determination by the reflection that Mary herself might perhaps become a young heiress.

"It is my duty," said Lady Arabella, repeating her words with even a stronger de Courcy intonation; "and your duty also, Dr Thorne."

"My duty!" said he, rising from his chair and leaning on the table with the two thigh-bones. "Lady Arabella, pray understand at once, that I repudiate any such duty, and will have nothing whatever to do with it."

"But you do not mean to say that you will encourage this unfortunate boy to marry your niece?"

"The unfortunate boy, Lady Arabella—whom, by the by, I regard as a very fortunate young man—is your son, not mine. I shall take no steps about his marriage, either one way or the other."

"You think it right, then, that your niece should throw herself in his way?"

"Throw herself in his way! What would you say if I came up to Greshamsbury, and spoke to you of your daughters in such language? What would my dear friend Mr Gresham say, if some neighbour's wife should come and so speak to him? I will tell you what he would say: he would quietly beg her to go back to her own home and meddle only with her own matters."

This was dreadful to Lady Arabella. Even Dr Thorne had never before dared thus to lower her to the level of common humanity, and liken her to any other wife in the countryside. Moreover, she was not quite sure whether he, the parish doctor, was not desiring her, the earl's daughter, to go home and mind her own business. On this first point, however, there seemed to be no room for doubt, of which she gave herself the benefit.

"It would not become me to argue with you, Dr Thorne," she said.

"Not at least on this subject," said he.

"I can only repeat that I mean nothing offensive to our dear Mary; for whom, I think I may say, I have always shown almost a mother's care."

"Neither am I, nor is Mary, ungrateful for the kindness she has received at Greshamsbury."

"But I must do my duty: my own children must be my first consideration."

"Of course they must, Lady Arabella; that's of course."

"And, therefore, I have called on you to say that I think it is imprudent that Beatrice and Mary should be so much together."

The doctor had been standing during the latter part of this conversation, but now he began to walk about, still holding the two bones like a pair of dumb-bells.

"God bless my soul!" he said; "God bless my soul! Why, Lady Arabella, do you suspect your own daughter as well as your own son? Do you think that Beatrice is assisting Mary in preparing this wicked clandestine marriage? I tell you fairly, Lady Arabella, the present tone of your mind is such that I cannot understand it."

"I suspect nobody, Dr Thorne; but young people will be young."

"And old people must be old, I suppose; the more's the pity. Lady Arabella, Mary is the same to me as my own daughter, and owes me the obedience of a child; but as I do not disapprove of your daughter Beatrice as an acquaintance for her, but rather, on the other hand, regard with pleasure their friendship, you cannot expect that I should take any steps to put an end to it."

"But suppose it should lead to renewed intercourse between Frank and Mary?"

"I have no objection. Frank is a very nice young fellow, gentleman-like in his manners, and neighbourly in his disposition."

"Dr Thorne—"

"Lady Arabella—"

"I cannot believe that you really intend to express a wish—"

"You are quite right. I have not intended to express any wish; nor do I intend to do so. Mary is at liberty, within certain bounds—which I am sure she will not pass—to choose her own friends. I think she has not chosen badly as regards Miss Beatrice Gresham; and should she even add Frank Gresham to the number—"

"Friends! why they were more than friends; they were declared lovers."

"I doubt that, Lady Arabella, because I have not heard of it from Mary. But even if it were so, I do not see why I should object."

"Not object!"

"As I said before, Frank is, to my thinking, an excellent young man. Why should I object?"

"Dr Thorne!" said her ladyship, now also rising from her chair in a state of too evident perturbation.

"Why should _I_ object? It is for you, Lady Arabella, to look after your lambs; for me to see that, if possible, no harm shall come to mine. If you think that Mary is an improper acquaintance for your children, it is for you to guide them; for you and their father. Say what you think fit to your own daughter; but pray understand, once for all, that I will allow no one to interfere with my niece."

"Interfere!" said Lady Arabella, now absolutely confused by the severity of the doctor's manner.

"I will allow no one to interfere with her; no one, Lady Arabella. She has suffered very greatly from imputations which you have most unjustly thrown on her. It was, however, your undoubted right to turn her out of your house if you thought fit;—though, as a woman who had known her for so many years, you might, I think, have treated her with more forbearance. That, however, was your right, and you exercised it. There your privilege stops; yes, and must stop, Lady Arabella. You shall not persecute her here, on the only spot of ground she can call her own."

"Persecute her, Dr Thorne! You do not mean to say that I have persecuted her?"

"Ah! but I do mean to say so. You do persecute her, and would continue to do so did I not defend her. It is not sufficient that she is forbidden to enter your domain—and so forbidden with the knowledge of all the country round—but you must come here also with the hope of interrupting all the innocent pleasures of her life. Fearing lest she should be allowed even to speak to your son, to hear a word of him through his own sister, you would put her in prison, tie her up, keep her from the light of day—"

"Dr Thorne! how can you—"

But the doctor was not to be interrupted.

"It never occurs to you to tie him up, to put him in prison. No; he is the heir of Greshamsbury; he is your son, an earl's grandson. It is only natural, after all, that he should throw a few foolish words at the doctor's niece. But she! it is an offence not to be forgiven on her part that she should, however, unwillingly, have been forced to listen to them! Now understand me, Lady Arabella; if any of your family come to my house I shall be delighted to welcome them: if Mary should meet any of them elsewhere I shall be delighted to hear of it. Should she tell me to-morrow that she was engaged to marry Frank, I should talk the matter over with her, quite coolly, solely with a view to her interest, as would be my duty; feeling, at the same time, that Frank would be lucky in having such a wife. Now you know my mind, Lady Arabella. It is so I should do my duty;—you can do yours as you may think fit."

Lady Arabella had by this time perceived that she was not destined on this occasion to gain any great victory. She, however, was angry as well as the doctor. It was not the man's vehemence that provoked her so much as his evident determination to break down the prestige of her rank, and place her on a footing in no respect superior to his own. He had never before been so audaciously arrogant; and, as she moved towards the door, she determined in her wrath that she would never again have confidential intercourse with him in any relation of life whatsoever.

"Dr Thorne," said she. "I think you have forgotten yourself. You must excuse me if I say that after what has passed I—I—I—"

"Certainly," said he, fully understanding what she meant; and bowing low as he opened first the study-door, then the front-door, then the garden-gate.

And then Lady Arabella stalked off, not without full observation from Mrs Yates Umbleby and her friend Miss Gushing, who lived close by.

CHAPTER XXVII

MISS THORNE GOES ON A VISIT

And now began the unpleasant things at Greshamsbury of which we have here told. When Lady Arabella walked away from the doctor's house she resolved that, let it cost what it might, there should be war to the knife between her and him. She had been insulted by him—so at least she said to herself, and so she was prepared to say to others also—and it was not to be borne that a de Courcy should allow her parish doctor to insult her with impunity. She would tell her husband with all the dignity that she could assume, that it had now become absolutely necessary that he should protect his wife by breaking entirely with his unmannered neighbour; and, as regarded the young members of her family, she would use the authority of a mother, and absolutely forbid them to hold any intercourse with Mary Thorne. So resolving, she walked quickly back to her own house.

The doctor, when left alone, was not quite satisfied with the part he had taken in the interview. He had spoken from impulse rather than from judgement, and, as is generally the case with men who do so speak, he had afterwards to acknowledge to himself that he had been imprudent. He accused himself probably of more violence than he had really used, and was therefore unhappy; but, nevertheless, his indignation was not at rest. He was angry with himself; but not on that account the less angry with Lady Arabella. She was cruel, overbearing, and unreasonable; cruel in the most cruel of manners, so he thought; but not on that account was he justified in forgetting the forbearance due from a gentleman to a lady. Mary, moreover, had owed much to the kindness of this woman, and, therefore, Dr Thorne felt that he should have forgiven much.

Thus the doctor walked about his room, much disturbed; now accusing himself for having been so angry with Lady Arabella, and then feeding his own anger by thinking of her misconduct.

The only immediate conclusion at which he resolved was this, that it was unnecessary that he should say anything to Mary on the subject of her ladyship's visit. There was, no doubt, sorrow enough in store for his darling; why should he aggravate it? Lady Arabella would doubtless not stop now in her course; but why should he accelerate the evil which she would doubtless be able to effect?

Lady Arabella, when she returned to the house, allowed no grass to grow under her feet. As she entered the house she desired that Miss Beatrice should be sent to her directly she returned; and she desired also, that as soon as the squire should be in his room a message to that effect might be immediately brought to her.

"Beatrice," she said, as soon as the young lady appeared before her, and in speaking she assumed her firmest tone of authority, "Beatrice, I am sorry, my dear, to say anything that is unpleasant to you, but I must make it a positive request that you will for the future drop all intercourse with Dr Thorne's family."

Beatrice, who had received Lady Arabella's message immediately on entering the house, and had run upstairs imagining that some instant haste was required, now stood before her mother rather out of breath, holding her bonnet by the strings.

"Oh, mamma!" she exclaimed, "what on earth has happened?"

"My dear," said the mother, "I cannot really explain to you what has happened; but I must ask you to give me your positive assurance that you will comply with my request."

"You don't mean that I am not to see Mary any more?"

"Yes, I do, my dear; at any rate, for the present. When I tell you that your brother's interest imperatively demands it, I am sure that you will not refuse me."

Beatrice did not refuse, but she did not appear too willing to comply. She stood silent, leaning against the end of a sofa and twisting her bonnet-strings in her hand.

"Well, Beatrice—"

"But, mamma, I don't understand."

Lady Arabella had said that she could not exactly explain: but she found it necessary to attempt to do so.

"Dr Thorne has openly declared to me that a marriage between poor Frank and Mary is all he could desire for his niece. After such unparalleled audacity as that, even your father will see the necessity of breaking with him."

"Dr Thorne! Oh, mamma, you must have misunderstood him."

"My dear, I am not apt to misunderstand people; especially when I am so much in earnest as I was in talking to Dr Thorne."

"But, mamma, I know so well what Mary herself thinks about it."

"And I know what Dr Thorne thinks about it; he, at any rate, has been candid in what he said; there can be no doubt on earth that he has spoken his true thoughts; there can be no reason to doubt him: of course such a match would be all that he could wish."

"Mamma, I feel sure that there is some mistake."

"Very well, my dear. I know that you are infatuated about these people, and that you are always inclined to contradict what I say to you; but, remember, I expect that you will obey me when I tell you not to go to Dr Thorne's house any more."

"But, mamma—"

"I expect you to obey me, Beatrice. Though you are so prone to contradict, you have never disobeyed me; and I fully trust that you will not do so now."

Lady Arabella had begun by exacting, or trying to exact a promise, but as she found that this was not forthcoming, she thought it better to give up the point without a dispute. It might be that Beatrice would absolutely refuse to pay this respect to her mother's authority, and then where would she have been?

At this moment a servant came up to say that the squire was in his room, and Lady Arabella was opportunely saved the necessity of discussing the matter further with her daughter. "I am now," she said, "going to see your father on the same subject; you may be quite sure, Beatrice, that I should not willingly speak to him on any matter relating to Dr Thorne did I not find it absolutely necessary to do so."

This Beatrice knew was true, and she did therefore feel convinced that something terrible must have happened.

While Lady Arabella opened her budget the squire sat quite silent, listening to her with apparent respect. She found it necessary that her description to him should be much more elaborate than that which she had vouchsafed to her daughter, and, in telling her grievance, she insisted most especially on the personal insult which had been offered to herself.

"After what has now happened," said she, not quite able to repress a tone of triumph as she spoke, "I do expect, Mr Gresham, that you will—will—"

"Will what, my dear?"

"Will at least protect me from the repetition of such treatment."

"You are not afraid that Dr Thorne will come here to attack you? As far as I can understand, he never comes near the place, unless when you send for him."

"No; I do not think that he will come to Greshamsbury any more. I believe I have put a stop to that."

"Then what is it, my dear, that you want me to do?"

Lady Arabella paused a minute before she replied. The game which she now had to play was not very easy; she knew, or thought she knew, that her husband, in his heart of hearts, much preferred his friend to the wife of his bosom, and that he would, if he could, shuffle out of noticing the doctor's iniquities. It behoved her, therefore, to put them forward in such a way that they must be noticed.

"I suppose, Mr Gresham, you do not wish that Frank should marry the girl?"

"I do not think there is the slightest chance of such a thing; and I am quite sure that Dr Thorne would not encourage it."

"But I tell you, Mr Gresham, that he says he will encourage it."

"Oh, you have misunderstood him."

"Of course; I always misunderstand everything. I know that. I misunderstood it when I told you how you would distress yourself if you took those nasty hounds."

"I have had other troubles more expensive than the hounds," said the poor squire, sighing.

"Oh, yes; I know what you mean; a wife and family are expensive, of course. It is a little too late now to complain of that."

"My dear, it is always too late to complain of any troubles when they are no longer to be avoided. We need not, therefore, talk any more about the hounds at present."

"I do not wish to speak of them, Mr Gresham."

"Nor I."

"But I hope you will not think me unreasonable if I am anxious to know what you intend to do about Dr Thorne."

"To do?"

"Yes; I suppose you will do something: you do not wish to see your son marry such a girl as Mary Thorne."

"As far as the girl herself is concerned," said the squire, turning rather red, "I am not sure that he could do much better. I know nothing whatever against Mary. Frank, however, cannot afford to make such a match. It would be his ruin."

"Of course it would; utter ruin; he never could hold up his head again. Therefore it is I ask, What do you intend to do?"

The squire was bothered. He had no intention whatever of doing anything, and no belief in his wife's assertion as to Dr Thorne's iniquity. But he did not know how to get her out of the room. She asked him the same question over and over again, and on each occasion urged on him the heinousness of the insult to which she personally had been subjected; so that at last he was driven to ask her what it was she wished him to do.

"Well, then, Mr Gresham, if you ask me, I must say, that I think you should abstain from any intercourse with Dr Thorne whatever."

"Break off all intercourse with him?"

"Yes."

651

"What do you mean? He has been turned out of this house, and I'm not to go to see him at his own."

"I certainly think that you ought to discontinue your visits to Dr Thorne altogether."

"Nonsense, my dear; absolute nonsense."

"Nonsense! Mr Gresham; it is no nonsense. As you speak in that way, I must let you know plainly what I feel. I am endeavouring to do my duty by my son. As you justly observe, such a marriage as this would be utter ruin to him. When I found that the young people were actually talking of being in love with each other, making vows and all that sort of thing, I did think it time to interfere. I did not, however, turn them out of Greshamsbury as you accuse me of doing. In the kindest possible manner——"

"Well—well—well; I know all that. There, they are gone, and that's enough. I don't complain; surely that ought to be enough."

"Enough! Mr Gresham. No; it is not enough. I find that, in spite of what has occurred, the closest intimacy exists between the two families; that poor Beatrice, who is so very young, and not so prudent as she should be, is made to act as a go-between; and when I speak to the doctor, hoping that he will assist me in preventing this, he not only tells me that he means to encourage Mary in her plans, but positively insults me to my face, laughs at me for being an earl's daughter, and tells me—yes, he absolutely told me—to get out of his house."

Let it be told with some shame as to the squire's conduct, that his first feeling on hearing this was one of envy—of envy and regret that he could not make the same uncivil request. Not that he wished to turn his wife absolutely out of his house; but he would have been very glad to have had the power of dismissing her summarily from his own room. This, however, was at present impossible; so he was obliged to make some mild reply.

"You must have mistaken him, my dear. He could not have intended to say that."

"Oh! of course, Mr Gresham. It is all a mistake, of course. It will be a mistake, only a mistake when you find your son married to Mary Thorne."

"Well, my dear, I cannot undertake to quarrel with Dr Thorne." This was true; for the squire could hardly have quarrelled with Dr Thorne, even had he wished it.

"Then I think it right to tell you that I shall. And, Mr Gresham, I did not expect much co-operation from you; but I did think that you would have shown some little anger when you heard that I had been so ill-treated. I shall, however, know how to take care of myself; and I shall continue to do the best I can to protect Frank from these wicked intrigues."

So saying, her ladyship arose and left the room, having succeeded in destroying the comfort of all our Greshamsbury friends. It was very well for the squire to declare that he would not quarrel with Dr Thorne, and of course he did not do so. But he, himself, had no wish whatever that his son should marry Mary Thorne; and as a falling drop will hollow a stone, so did the continual harping of his wife on the subject give rise to some amount of suspicion in his own mind. Then as to Beatrice, though she had made no promise that she would not again visit Mary, she was by no means prepared to set her mother's authority altogether at defiance; and she also was sufficiently uncomfortable.

Dr Thorne said nothing of the matter to his niece, and she, therefore, would have been absolutely bewildered by Beatrice's absence, had she not received some tidings of what had taken place at Greshamsbury through Patience Oriel. Beatrice and Patience discussed the matter fully, and it was agreed between them that it would be better that Mary should know what sterner orders respecting her had gone forth from the tyrant at Greshamsbury, and that she might understand that Beatrice's absence was compulsory. Patience was thus placed in this position, that on one day she walked and talked with Beatrice, and on the next with Mary; and so matters went on for a while at Greshamsbury—not very pleasantly.

Very unpleasantly and very uncomfortably did the months of May and June pass away. Beatrice and Mary occasionally met, drinking tea together at the parsonage, or in some other of the ordinary meetings of country society; but there were no more confidentially distressing confidential discourses, no more whispering of Frank's name, no more sweet allusions to the inexpediency of a passion, which, according to Beatrice's views, would have been so delightful had it been expedient.

The squire and the doctor also met constantly; there were unfortunately many subjects on which they were obliged to meet. Louis Philippe—or Sir Louis as we must call him—though he had no power over his own property, was wide awake to all the coming privileges of ownership, and he would constantly point out to his guardian the manner in which, according to his ideas, the most should be made of it. The young baronet's ideas of good taste were not of the most refined description, and he did not hesitate to tell Dr Thorne that his, the doctor's, friendship with Mr Gresham must be no bar to his, the baronet's, interest. Sir Louis also had his own lawyer, who gave Dr Thorne to understand that, according to his ideas, the sum due on Mr Gresham's property was too large to be left on its present footing; the title-deeds, he said, should be surrendered or the mortgage foreclosed. All this added to the sadness which now seemed to envelop the village of Greshamsbury.

Early in July, Frank was to come home. The manner in which the comings and goings of "poor Frank" were allowed to disturb the arrangements of all the ladies, and some of the gentlemen, of Greshamsbury was most abominable. And yet it can hardly be said to have been his fault. He would have been only too well pleased had things been allowed to go on after their old fashion. Things were not allowed so to go on. At Christmas Miss Oriel had submitted to be exiled, in order that she might carry Mary away from the presence of the young Bashaw, an arrangement by which all the winter festivities of the poor doctor had been thoroughly sacrificed; and now it began to be said that some similar plan for the summer must be suggested.

It must not be supposed that any direction to this effect was conveyed either to Mary or to the doctor. The suggestion came from them, and was mentioned only to Patience. But Patience, as a matter of course, told Beatrice, and Beatrice told her mother, somewhat triumphantly, hoping thereby to convince the she-dragon of Mary's innocence. Alas! she-dragons are not easily convinced of the innocence of any one. Lady Arabella quite coincided in the propriety of Mary's being sent off,—whither she never inquired,—in order that the coast might be clear for "poor Frank;" but she did not a whit the more abstain from talking of the wicked intrigues of those Thornes. As it turned out, Mary's absence caused her to talk all the more.

The Boxall Hill property, including the house and furniture, had been left to the contractor's son; it being understood that the property would not be at present in his own hands, but that he might inhabit the house if he chose to do so. It would thus be necessary for Lady Scatcherd to find a home for herself, unless she could remain at Boxall Hill by her son's permission. In this position of affairs the doctor had been obliged to make a bargain between them. Sir Louis did wish to have the comfort, or perhaps the honour, of a country house; but he did not wish to have the expense of keeping it up. He was also willing to let his mother live at the house; but not without a consideration. After a prolonged degree of haggling, terms were agreed upon; and a few weeks after her husband's death, Lady Scatcherd found herself alone at Boxall Hill—alone as regards society in the ordinary sense, but not quite alone as concerned her ladyship, for the faithful Hannah was still with her.

The doctor was of course often at Boxall Hill, and never left it without an urgent request from Lady Scatcherd that he would bring his niece over to see her. Now Lady

Scatcherd was no fit companion for Mary Thorne, and though Mary had often asked to be taken to Boxall Hill, certain considerations had hitherto induced the doctor to refuse the request; but there was that about Lady Scatcherd,—a kind of homely honesty of purpose, an absence of all conceit as to her own position, and a strength of womanly confidence in the doctor as her friend, which by degrees won upon his heart. When, therefore, both he and Mary felt that it would be better for her again to absent herself for a while from Greshamsbury, it was, after much deliberation, agreed that she should go on a visit to Boxall Hill.

To Boxall Hill, accordingly, she went, and was received almost as a princess. Mary had all her life been accustomed to women of rank, and had never habituated herself to feel much trepidation in the presence of titled grandees; but she had prepared herself to be more than ordinarily submissive to Lady Scatcherd. Her hostess was a widow, was not a woman of high birth, was a woman of whom her uncle spoke well; and, for all these reasons, Mary was determined to respect her, and pay to her every consideration. But when she settled down in the house she found it almost impossible to do so. Lady Scatcherd treated her as a farmer's wife might have treated some convalescent young lady who had been sent to her charge for a few weeks, in order that she might benefit by the country air. Her ladyship could hardly bring herself to sit still and eat her dinner tranquilly in her guest's presence. And then nothing was good enough for Mary. Lady Scatcherd besought her, almost with tears, to say what she liked best to eat and drink; and was in despair when Mary declared she didn't care, that she liked anything, and that she was in nowise particular in such matters.

"A roast fowl, Miss Thorne?"

"Very nice, Lady Scatcherd."

"And bread sauce?"

"Bread sauce—yes; oh, yes—I like bread sauce,"—and poor Mary tried hard to show a little interest.

"And just a few sausages. We make them all in the house, Miss Thorne; we know what they are. And mashed potatoes—do you like them best mashed or baked?"

Mary finding herself obliged to vote, voted for mashed potatoes.

"Very well. But, Miss Thorne, if you like boiled fowl better, with a little bit of ham, you know, I do hope you'll say so. And there's lamb in the house, quite beautiful; now do 'ee say something; do 'ee, Miss Thorne."

So invoked, Mary felt herself obliged to say something, and declared for the roast fowl and sausages; but she found it very difficult to pay much outward respect to a person who would pay so much outward respect to her. A day or two after her arrival it was decided that she should ride about the place on a donkey; she was accustomed to riding, the doctor having generally taken care that one of his own horses should, when required, consent to carry a lady; but there was no steed at Boxall Hill that she could mount; and when Lady Scatcherd had offered to get a pony for her, she had willingly compromised matters by expressing the delight she would have in making a campaign on a donkey. Upon this, Lady Scatcherd had herself set off in quest of the desired animal, much to Mary's horror; and did not return till the necessary purchase had been effected. Then she came back with the donkey close at her heels, almost holding its collar, and stood there at the hall-door till Mary came to approve.

"I hope she'll do. I don't think she'll kick," said Lady Scatcherd, patting the head of her purchase quite triumphantly.

"Oh, you are so kind, Lady Scatcherd. I'm sure she'll do quite nicely; she seems very quiet," said Mary.

"Please, my lady, it's a he," said the boy who held the halter.

"Oh! a he, is it?" said her ladyship; "but the he-donkeys are quite as quiet as the shes, ain't they?"

"Oh, yes, my lady; a deal quieter, all the world over, and twice as useful."

"I'm so glad of that, Miss Thorne," said Lady Scatcherd, her eyes bright with joy.

And so Mary was established with her donkey, who did all that could be expected from an animal in his position.

"But, dear Lady Scatcherd," said Mary, as they sat together at the open drawing-room window the same evening, "you must not go on calling me Miss Thorne; my name is Mary, you know. Won't you call me Mary?" and she came and knelt at Lady Scatcherd's feet, and took hold of her, looking up into her face.

Lady Scatcherd's cheeks became rather red, as though she was somewhat ashamed of her position.

"You are so very kind to me," continued Mary, "and it seems so cold to hear you call me Miss Thorne."

"Well, Miss Thorne, I'm sure I'd call you anything to please you. Only I didn't know whether you'd like it from me. Else I do think Mary is the prettiest name in all the language."

"I should like it very much."

"My dear Roger always loved that name better than any other; ten times better. I used to wish sometimes that I'd been called Mary."

"Did he! Why?"

"He once had a sister called Mary; such a beautiful creature! I declare I sometimes think you are like her."

"Oh, dear! then she must have been beautiful indeed!" said Mary, laughing.

"She was very beautiful. I just remember her—oh, so beautiful! she was quite a poor girl, you know; and so was I then. Isn't it odd that I should have to be called 'my lady' now? Do you know Miss Thorne—"

"Mary! Mary!" said her guest.

"Ah, yes; but somehow, I hardly like to make so free; but, as I was saying, I do so dislike being called 'my lady:' I always think the people are laughing at me; and so they are."

"Oh, nonsense."

"Yes, they are though: poor dear Roger, he used to call me 'my lady' just to make fun of me; I didn't mind it so much from him. But, Miss Thorne—"

"Mary, Mary, Mary."

"Ah, well! I shall do it in time. But, Miss—Mary, ha! ha! ha! never mind, let me alone. But what I want to say is this: do you think I could drop it? Hannah says, that if I go the right way about it she is sure I can."

"Oh! but, Lady Scatcherd, you shouldn't think of such a thing."

"Shouldn't I now?"

"Oh, no; for your husband's sake you should be proud of it. He gained great honour, you know."

"Ah, well," said she, sighing after a short pause; "if you think it will do him any good, of course I'll put up with it. And then I know Louis would be mad if I talked of such a thing. But, Miss Thorne, dear, a woman like me don't like to have to be made a fool of all the days of her life if she can help it."

"But, Lady Scatcherd," said Mary, when this question of the title had been duly settled, and her ladyship made to understand that she must bear the burden for the rest of her life, "but, Lady Scatcherd, you were speaking of Sir Roger's sister; what became of her?"

"Oh, she did very well at last, as Sir Roger did himself; but in early life she was very unfortunate—just at the time of my marriage with dear Roger—," and then, just as she was about to commence so much as she knew of the history of Mary Scatcherd, she remembered that the author of her sister-in-law's misery had been a Thorne, a brother of the doctor; and, therefore, as she presumed, a relative of her guest; and suddenly she became mute.

"Well," said Mary; "just as you were married, Lady Scatcherd?"

Poor Lady Scatcherd had very little worldly knowledge, and did not in the least know how to turn the conversation or escape from the trouble into which she had fallen. All manner of reflections began to crowd upon her. In her early days she had known very little of the Thornes, nor had she thought much of them since, except as regarded her friend the doctor; but at this moment she began for the first time to remember that she had never heard of more than two brothers in the family. Who then could have been Mary's father? She felt at once that it would be improper for to say anything as to Henry Thorne's terrible faults and sudden fate;—improper also, to say more about Mary Scatcherd; but she was quite unable to drop the matter otherwise than abruptly, and with a start.

"She was very unfortunate, you say, Lady Scatcherd?"

"Yes, Miss Thorne; Mary, I mean—never mind me—I shall do it in time. Yes, she was; but now I think of it, I had better say nothing more about it. There are reasons, and I ought not to have spoken of it. You won't be provoked with me, will you?"

Mary assured her that she would not be provoked, and of course asked no more questions about Mary Scatcherd; nor did she think much more about it. It was not so however with her ladyship, who could not keep herself from reflecting that the old clergyman in the Close at Barchester certainly had but two sons, one of whom was now the doctor at Greshamsbury, and the other of whom had perished so wretchedly at the gate of that farmyard. Who then was the father of Mary Thorne?

The days passed very quietly at Boxall Hill. Every morning Mary went out on her donkey, who justified by his demeanour all that had been said in his praise; then she would read or draw, then walk with Lady Scatcherd, then dine, then walk again; and so the days passed quietly away. Once or twice a week the doctor would come over and drink his tea there, riding home in the cool of the evening. Mary also received one visit from her friend Patience.

So the days passed quietly away till the tranquillity of the house was suddenly broken by tidings from London. Lady Scatcherd received a letter from her son, contained in three lines, in which he intimated that on the following day he meant to honour her with a visit. He had intended, he said, to have gone to Brighton with some friends; but as he felt himself a little out of sorts, he would postpone his marine trip and do his mother the grace of spending a few days with her.

This news was not very pleasant to Mary, by whom it had been understood, as it had also by her uncle, that Lady Scatcherd would have had the house to herself; but as there were no means of preventing the evil, Mary could only inform the doctor, and prepare herself to meet Sir Louis Scatcherd.

CHAPTER XXVIII

THE DOCTOR HEARS SOMETHING TO HIS ADVANTAGE

Sir Louis Scatcherd had told his mother that he was rather out of sorts, and when he reached Boxall Hill it certainly did not appear that he had given any exaggerated statement of his own maladies. He certainly was a good deal out of sorts. He had had more than one attack of delirium tremens since his father's death, and had almost been at death's door.

Nothing had been said about this by Dr Thorne at Boxall Hill; but he was by no means ignorant of his ward's state. Twice he had gone up to London to visit him; twice he had begged him to go down into the country and place himself under his mother's care. On the last occasion, the doctor had threatened him with all manner of pains and penalties: with pains, as to his speedy departure from this world and all its joys; and with penalties, in the shape of poverty if that departure should by any chance be retarded. But these threats had at the moment been in vain, and the doctor had compromised matters by inducing Sir Louis to promise that he would go to Brighton. The baronet, however, who was at length frightened by some renewed attack, gave up his Brighton scheme, and, without any notice to the doctor, hurried down to Boxall Hill.

Mary did not see him on the first day of his coming, but the doctor did. He received such intimation of the visit as enabled him to be at the house soon after the young man's arrival; and, knowing that his assistance might be necessary, he rode over to Boxall Hill. It was a dreadful task to him, this of making the same fruitless endeavour for the son that he had made for the father, and in the same house. But he was bound by every consideration to perform the task. He had promised the father that he would do for the son all that was in his power; and he had, moreover, the consciousness, that should Sir Louis succeed in destroying himself, the next heir to all the property was his own niece, Mary Thorne.

He found Sir Louis in a low, wretched, miserable state. Though he was a drunkard as his father was, he was not at all such a drunkard as was his father. The physical capacities of the men were very different. The daily amount of alcohol which the father had consumed would have burnt up the son in a week; whereas, though the son was continually tipsy, what he swallowed would hardly have had an injurious effect upon the father.

"You are all wrong, quite wrong," said Sir Louis, petulantly; "it isn't that at all. I have taken nothing this week past—literally nothing. I think it's the liver."

Dr Thorne wanted no one to tell him what was the matter with his ward. It was his liver; his liver, and his head, and his stomach, and his heart. Every organ in his body had been destroyed, or was in the course of destruction. His father had killed himself with brandy; the son, more elevated in his tastes, was doing the same thing with curaçoa, maraschino, and cherry-bounce.

"Sir Louis," said the doctor—he was obliged to be much more punctilious with him than he had been with the contractor—"the matter is in your own hands entirely: if you cannot keep your lips from that accursed poison, you have nothing in this world to look forward to; nothing, nothing!"

Mary proposed to return with her uncle to Greshamsbury, and he was at first well inclined that she should do so. But this idea was overruled, partly in compliance with Lady Scatcherd's entreaties, and partly because it would have seemed as though they had both thought the presence of its owner had made the house an unfit habitation for decent people. The doctor therefore returned, leaving Mary there; and Lady Scatcherd busied herself between her two guests.

On the next day Sir Louis was able to come down to a late dinner, and Mary was introduced to him. He had dressed himself in his best array; and as he had—at any rate for the present moment—been frightened out of his libations, he was prepared to make himself as agreeable as possible. His mother waited on him almost as a slave might have done; but she seemed to do so with the fear of a slave rather than the love of a mother. She was fidgety in her attentions, and worried him by endeavouring to make her evening sitting-room agreeable.

But Sir Louis, though he was not very sweetly behaved under these manipulations from his mother's hands, was quite complaisant to Miss Thorne; nay, after the expiration of a week he was almost more than complaisant. He piqued himself on his gallantry, and now found that, in the otherwise dull seclusion of Boxall Hill, he had a good opportunity of exercising it. To do him justice it must be admitted that he would not have been incapable of a decent career had he stumbled upon some girl who could have loved him before he stumbled upon his maraschino bottle. Such might have been the case with many a lost rake. The things that are bad are accepted because the things that are good do not come easily in his way. How many a miserable father reviles with bitterness of spirit the low tastes of his son, who has done nothing to provide his child with higher pleasures!

Sir Louis—partly in the hopes of Mary's smiles, and partly frightened by the doctor's threats—did, for a while, keep himself within decent bounds. He did not usually appear before Mary's eyes till three or four in the afternoon; but when he did come forth, he came forth sober and resolute to please. His mother was delighted, and was not slow to sing his praises; and even the doctor, who now visited Boxall Hill more frequently than ever, began to have some hopes.

One constant subject, I must not say of conversation, on the part of Lady Scatcherd, but rather of declamation, had hitherto been the beauty and manly attributes of Frank Gresham. She had hardly ceased to talk to Mary of the infinite good qualities of the young squire, and especially of his prowess in the matter of Mr Moffat. Mary had listened to all this eloquence, not perhaps with inattention, but without much reply. She had not been exactly sorry to hear Frank talked about; indeed, had she been so minded, she could herself have said something on the same subject; but she did not wish to take Lady Scatcherd altogether into her confidence, and she had been unable to say much about Frank Gresham without doing so. Lady Scatcherd had, therefore, gradually conceived the idea that her darling was not a favourite with her guest.

Now, therefore, she changed the subject; and, as her own son was behaving with such unexampled propriety, she dropped Frank and confined her eulogies to Louis. He had been a little wild, she admitted; young men so often were so; but she hoped that it was now over.

"He does still take a little drop of those French drinks in the morning," said Lady Scatcherd, in her confidence; for she was too honest to be false, even in her own cause. "He does do that, I know: but that's nothing, my dear, to swilling all day; and everything can't be done at once, can it, Miss Thorne?"

On this subject Mary found her tongue loosened. She could not talk about Frank Gresham, but she could speak with hope to the mother of her only son. She could say that Sir Louis was still very young; that there was reason to trust that he might now reform; that his present conduct was apparently good; and that he appeared capable of better things. So much she did say; and the mother took her sympathy for more than it was worth.

On this matter, and on this matter perhaps alone, Sir Louis and Lady Scatcherd were in accord. There was much to recommend Mary to the baronet; not only did he see her to be beautiful, and perceive her to be attractive and ladylike; but she was also the niece of the man who, for the present, held the purse-strings of his wealth. Mary, it is true, had no fortune. But Sir Louis knew that she was acknowledged to be a lady; and he was ambitious that his "lady" should be a lady. There was also much to recommend Mary to the mother, to any mother; and thus it came to pass, that Miss Thorne had no obstacle between her and the dignity of being Lady Scatcherd the second;—no obstacle whatever, if only she could bring herself to wish it.

It was some time—two or three weeks, perhaps—before Mary's mind was first opened to this new brilliancy in her prospects. Sir Louis at first was rather afraid of her, and did not declare his admiration in any very determined terms. He certainly paid her many compliments which, from any one else, she would have regarded as abominable. But she did not expect great things from the baronet's taste: she concluded that he was only doing what he thought a gentleman should do; and she was willing to forgive much for Lady Scatcherd's sake.

His first attempts were, perhaps, more ludicrous than passionate. He was still too much an invalid to take walks, and Mary was therefore saved from his company in her rambles; but he had a horse of his own at Boxall Hill, and had been advised to ride by the doctor. Mary also rode—on a donkey only, it is true—but Sir Louis found himself bound in gallantry to accompany her. Mary's steed had answered every expectation, and proved himself very quiet; so quiet, that without the admonition of a cudgel behind him, he could hardly be persuaded into the demurest trot. Now, as Sir Louis's horse was of a very different mettle, he found it rather difficult not to step faster than his inamorata; and, let it him struggle as he would, was generally so far ahead as to be debarred the delights of conversation.

When for the second time he proposed to accompany her, Mary did what she could to hinder it. She saw that he had been rather ashamed of the manner in which his companion was mounted, and she herself would have enjoyed her ride much more without him. He was an invalid, however; it was necessary to make much of him, and Mary did not absolutely refuse his offer.

"Lady Scatcherd," said he, as they were standing at the door previous to mounting—he always called his mother Lady Scatcherd—"why don't you have a horse for Miss Thorne? This donkey is—is—really is, so very—very—can't go at all, you know?"

Lady Scatcherd began to declare that she would willingly have got a pony if Mary would have let her do so.

"Oh, no, Lady Scatcherd; not on any account. I do like the donkey so much—I do indeed."

"But he won't go," said Sir Louis. "And for a person who rides like you, Miss Thorne—such a horsewoman you know—why, you know, Lady Scatcherd, it's positively ridiculous; d—— absurd, you know."

And then, with an angry look at his mother, he mounted his horse, and was soon leading the way down the avenue.

"Miss Thorne," said he, pulling himself up at the gate, "if I had known that I was to be so extremely happy as to have found you here, I would have brought you down the most beautiful creature, an Arab. She belongs to my friend Jenkins; but I wouldn't have stood at any price in getting her for you. By Jove! if you were on that mare, I'd back you, for style and appearance, against anything in Hyde Park."

The offer of this sporting wager, which naturally would have been very gratifying to Mary, was lost upon her, for Sir Louis had again unwittingly got on in advance, but he stopped himself in time to hear Mary again declare her passion was a donkey.

"If you could only see Jenkins's little mare, Miss Thorne! Only say one word, and she shall be down here before the week's end. Price shall be no obstacle—none whatever. By Jove, what a pair you would be!"

This generous offer was repeated four or five times; but on each occasion Mary only half heard what was said, and on each occasion the baronet was far too much in advance to hear Mary's reply. At last he recollected that he wanted to call on one of the tenants, and begged his companion to allow him to ride on.

"If you at all dislike being left alone, you know—"

"Oh dear no, not at all, Sir Louis. I am quite used to it."

"Because I don't care about it, you know; only I can't make this horse walk the same pace as that brute."

"You mustn't abuse my pet, Sir Louis."

"It's a d—— shame on my mother's part;" said Sir Louis, who, even when in his best behaviour, could not quite give up his ordinary mode of conversation. "When she was fortunate enough to get such a girl as you to come and stay with her, she ought to have had something proper for her to ride upon; but I'll look to it as soon as I am a little stronger, you see if I don't;" and, so saying, Sir Louis trotted off, leaving Mary in peace with her donkey.

Sir Louis had now been living cleanly and forswearing sack for what was to him a very long period, and his health felt the good effects of it. No one rejoiced at this more cordially than did the doctor. To rejoice at it was with him a point of conscience. He could not help telling himself now and again that, circumstanced as he was, he was most specially bound to take joy in any sign of reformation which the baronet might show. Not to do so would be almost tantamount to wishing that he might die in order that Mary might inherit his wealth; and, therefore, the doctor did with all his energy devote himself to the difficult task of hoping and striving that Sir Louis might yet live to enjoy what was his own. But the task was altogether a difficult one, for as Sir Louis became stronger in health, so also did he become more exorbitant in his demands on the doctor's patience, and more repugnant to the doctor's tastes.

In his worst fits of disreputable living he was ashamed to apply to his guardian for money; and in his worst fits of illness he was, through fear, somewhat patient under his doctor's hands; but just at present he had nothing of which to be ashamed, and was not at all patient.

"Doctor,"—said he, one day, at Boxall Hill—"how about those Greshamsbury title-deeds?"

"Oh, that will all be properly settled between my lawyer and your own."

"Oh—ah—yes; no doubt the lawyers will settle it: settle it with a fine bill of costs, of course. But, as Finnie says,"—Finnie was Sir Louis's legal adviser—"I have got a tremen-dously large interest at stake in this matter; eighty thousand pounds is no joke. It ain't eve-everybody that can shell out eighty thousand pounds when they're wanted; and I should like to know how the thing's going on. I've a right to ask, you know; eh, doctor?"

"The title-deeds of a large portion of the Greshamsbury estate will be placed with the mortgage-deeds before the end of next month."

"Oh, that's all right. I choose to know about these things; for though my father did make such a con-found-ed will, that's no reason I shouldn't know how things are going."

"You shall know everything that I know, Sir Louis."

"And now, doctor, what are we to do about money?"

"About money?"

"Yes; money, rhino, ready! 'put money in your purse and cut a dash;' eh, doctor? Not that I want to cut a dash. No, I'm going on the quiet line altogether now: I've done with all that sort of thing."

"I'm heartily glad of it; heartily," said the doctor.

"Yes, I'm not going to make way for my far-away cousin yet; not if I know it, at least. I shall soon be all right now, doctor; shan't I?"

"'All right' is a long word, Sir Louis. But I do hope you will be all right in time, if you will live with decent prudence. You shouldn't take that filth in the morning though."

"Filth in the morning! That's my mother, I suppose! That's her ladyship! She's been talking, has she? Don't you believe her, doctor. There's not a young man in Barsetshire is going more regular, all right within the posts, than I am."

The doctor was obliged to acknowledge that there did seem to be some improvement.

"And now, doctor, how about money? Eh?"

Doctor Thorne, like other guardians similarly circumstanced, began to explain that Sir Louis had already had a good deal of money, and had begun also to promise that more should be forthcoming in the event of good behaviour, when he was somewhat suddenly interrupted by Sir Louis.

"Well, now; I'll tell you what, doctor; I've got a bit of news for you; something that I think will astonish you."

The doctor opened his eyes, and tried to look as though ready to be surprised.

"Something that will really make you look about; and something, too, that will be very much to the hearer's advantage,—as the newspaper advertisements say."

"Something to my advantage?" said the doctor.

"Well, I hope you'll think so. Doctor, what would you think now of my getting mar-ried?"

"I should be delighted to hear of it—more delighted than I can express; that is, of course, if you were to marry well. It was your father's most eager wish that you should marry early."

"That's partly my reason," said the young hypocrite. "But then, if I marry I must have an income fit to live on; eh, doctor?"

The doctor had some fear that his interesting protégée was desirous of a wife for the sake of the income, instead of desiring the income for the sake of the wife. But let the cause be what it would, marriage would probably be good for him; and he had no hesita-tion, therefore, in telling him, that if he married well, he should be put in possession of sufficient income to maintain the new Lady Scatcherd in a manner becoming her dignity.

"As to marrying well," said Sir Louis, "you, I take it, will be be the last man, doctor, to quarrel with my choice."

"Shall I?" said the doctor, smiling.

"Well, you won't disapprove, I guess, as the Yankee says. What would you think of Miss Mary Thorne?"

It must be said in Sir Louis's favour that he had probably no idea whatever of the estimation in which such young ladies as Mary Thorne are held by those who are nearest and dearest to them. He had no sort of conception that she was regarded by her uncle as an inestimable treasure, almost too precious to be rendered up to the arms of any man; and infinitely beyond any price in silver and gold, baronets' incomes of eight or ten thousand a year, and such coins usually current in the world's markets. He was a rich man and a baronet, and Mary was an unmarried girl without a portion. In Sir Louis's estimation he was offering everything, and asking for nothing. He certainly had some idea that girls were apt to be coy, and required a little wooing in the shape of presents, civil speeches—perhaps kisses also. The civil speeches he had, he thought, done, and imagined that they had been well received. The other things were to follow; an Arab pony, for instance,—and the kisses probably with it; and then all these difficulties would be smoothed.

But he did not for a moment conceive that there would be any difficulty with the uncle. How should there be? Was he not a baronet with ten thousand a year coming to him? Had he not everything which fathers want for portionless daughters, and uncles for dependant nieces? Might he not well inform the doctor that he had something to tell him for his advantage?

And yet, to tell the truth, the doctor did not seem to be overjoyed when the announcement was first made to him. He was by no means overjoyed. On the contrary, even Sir Louis could perceive his guardian's surprise was altogether unmixed with delight.

What a question was this that was asked him! What would he think of a marriage between Mary Thorne—his Mary and Sir Louis Scatcherd? Between the alpha of the whole alphabet, and him whom he could not but regard as the omega! Think of it! Why he would think of it as though a lamb and a wolf were to stand at the altar together. Had Sir Louis been a Hottentot, or an Esquimaux, the proposal could not have astonished him more. The two persons were so totally of a different class, that the idea of the one falling in love with the other had never occurred to him. "What would you think of Miss Mary Thorne?" Sir Louis had asked; and the doctor, instead of answering him with ready and pleased alacrity, stood silent, thunderstruck with amazement.

"Well, wouldn't she be a good wife?" said Sir Louis, rather in a tone of disgust at the evident disapproval shown at his choice. "I thought you'd have been so delighted."

"Mary Thorne!" ejaculated the doctor at last. "Have you spoken to my niece about this, Sir Louis?"

"Well, I have and yet I haven't; I haven't, and yet in a manner I have."

"I don't understand you," said the doctor.

"Why, you see, I haven't exactly popped to her yet; but I have been doing the civil; and if she's up to snuff, as I take her to be, she knows very well what I'm after by this time."

Up to snuff! Mary Thorne, his Mary Thorne, up to snuff! To snuff too of such a very disagreeable description!

"I think, Sir Louis, that you are in mistake about this. I think you will find that Mary will not be disposed to avail herself of the great advantages—for great they undoubtedly are—which you are able to offer to your intended wife. If you will take my advice, you will give up thinking of Mary. She would not suit you."

"Not suit me! Oh, but I think she just would. She's got no money, you mean?"

"No, I did not mean that. It will not signify to you whether your wife has money or not. You need not look for money. But you should think of some one more nearly of your own temperament. I am quite sure that my niece would refuse you."

These last words the doctor uttered with much emphasis. His intention was to make the baronet understand that the matter was quite hopeless, and to induce him if possible to drop it on the spot. But he did not know Sir Louis; he ranked him too low in the scale of human beings, and gave him no credit for any strength of character. Sir Louis in his way did love Mary Thorne; and could not bring himself to believe that Mary did not, or at any rate, would not soon return his passion. He was, moreover, sufficiently obstinate, firm we ought perhaps to say,—for his pursuit in this case was certainly not an evil one,—and he at once made up his mind to succeed in spite of the uncle.

"If she consents, however, you will do so too?" asked he.

"It is impossible she should consent," said the doctor.

"Impossible! I don't see anything at all impossible. But if she does?"

"But she won't."

"Very well,—that's to be seen. But just tell me this, if she does, will you consent?"

"The stars would fall first. It's all nonsense. Give it up, my dear friend; believe me you are only preparing unhappiness for yourself;" and the doctor put his hand kindly on the young man's arm. "She will not, cannot accept such an offer."

"Will not! cannot!" said the baronet, thinking over all the reasons which in his estimation could possibly be inducing the doctor to be so hostile to his views, and shaking the hand off his arm. "Will not! cannot! But come, doctor, answer my question fairly. If she'll have me for better or worse, you won't say aught against it; will you?"

"But she won't have you; why should you give her and yourself the pain of a refusal?"

"Oh, as for that, I must stand my chances like another. And as for her, why d——, doctor, you wouldn't have me believe that any young lady thinks it so very dreadful to have a baronet with ten thousand pounds a year at her feet, specially when that same baronet ain't very old, nor yet particularly ugly. I ain't so green as that, doctor."

"I suppose she must go through it, then," said the doctor, musing.

"But, Dr Thorne, I did look for a kinder answer from you, considering all that you so often say about your great friendship with my father. I did think you'd at any rate answer me when I asked you a question."

But the doctor did not want to answer that special question. Could it be possible that Mary should wish to marry this odious man, could such a state of things be imagined to be the case, he would not refuse his consent, infinitely as he would be disgusted by her choice. But he would not give Sir Louis any excuse for telling Mary that her uncle approved of so odious a match.

"I cannot say that in any case I should approve of such a marriage, Sir Louis. I cannot bring myself to say so; for I know it would make you both miserable. But on that matter my niece will choose wholly for herself."

"And about the money, doctor?"

"If you marry a decent woman you shall not want the means of supporting her decently," and so saying the doctor walked away, leaving Sir Louis to his meditations.

CHAPTER XXIX

THE DONKEY RIDE

Sir Louis, when left to himself, was slightly dismayed and somewhat discouraged; but he was not induced to give up his object. The first effort of his mind was made in conjecturing what private motive Dr Thorne could possibly have in wishing to debar his niece from marrying a rich young baronet. That the objection was personal to himself, Sir Louis did not for a moment imagine. Could it be that the doctor did not wish that his niece should be richer, and grander, and altogether bigger than himself? Or was it possible that his guardian was anxious to prevent him from marrying from some view of the reversion of the large fortune? That there was some such reason, Sir Louis was well sure; but let it be what it might, he would get the better of the doctor. "He knew," so he said to himself, "what stuff girls were made of. Baronets did not grow like blackberries." And so, assuring himself with such philosophy, he determined to make his offer.

The time he selected for doing this was the hour before dinner; but on the day on which his conversation with the doctor had taken place, he was deterred by the presence of a strange visitor. To account for this strange visit it will be necessary that we should return to Greshamsbury for a few minutes.

Frank, when he returned home for his summer vacation, found that Mary had again flown; and the very fact of her absence added fuel to the fire of his love, more perhaps than even her presence might have done. For the flight of the quarry ever adds eagerness to the pursuit of the huntsman. Lady Arabella, moreover, had a bitter enemy; a foe, utterly opposed to her side in the contest, where she had once fondly looked for her staunchest ally. Frank was now in the habit of corresponding with Miss Dunstable, and received from her most energetic admonitions to be true to the love which he had sworn. True to it he resolved to be; and therefore, when he found that Mary was flown, he resolved to fly after her.

He did not, however, do this till he had been in a measure provoked to it by it by the sharp-tongued cautions and blunted irony of his mother. It was not enough for her that she had banished Mary out of the parish, and made Dr Thorne's life miserable; not enough that she harassed her husband with harangues on the constant subject of Frank's marrying money, and dismayed Beatrice with invectives against the iniquity of her friend. The snake was so but scotched; to kill it outright she must induce Frank utterly to renounce Miss Thorne.

This task she essayed, but not exactly with success. "Well, mother," said Frank, at last turning very red, partly with shame, and partly with indignation, as he made the frank avowal, "since you press me about it, I tell you fairly that my mind is made up to marry Mary sooner or later, if—"

"Oh, Frank! good heavens! you wicked boy; you are saying this purposely to drive me distracted."

"If," continued Frank, not attending to his mother's interjections, "if she will consent."

"Consent!" said Lady Arabella. "Oh, heavens!" and falling into the corner of the sofa, she buried her face in her handkerchief.

"Yes, mother, if she will consent. And now that I have told you so much, it is only just that I should tell you this also; that as far as I can see at present I have no reason to hope that she will do so."

"Oh, Frank, the girl is doing all she can to catch you," said Lady Arabella,—not prudently.

"No, mother; there you wrong her altogether; wrong her most cruelly."

"You ungracious, wicked boy! you call me cruel!"

"I don't call you cruel; but you wrong her cruelly, most cruelly. When I have spoken to her about this—for I have spoken to her—she has behaved exactly as you would have wanted her to do; but not at all as I wished her. She has given me no encouragement. You have turned her out among you"—Frank was beginning to be very bitter now—"but she has done nothing to deserve it. If there has been any fault it has been mine. But it is well that we should all understand each other. My intention is to marry Mary if I can." And, so speaking, certainly without due filial respect, he turned towards the door.

"Frank," said his mother, raising herself up with energy to make one last appeal. "Frank, do you wish to see me die of a broken heart?"

"You know, mother, I would wish to make you happy, if I could."

"If you wish to see me ever happy again, if you do not wish to see me sink broken-hearted to my grave, you must give up this mad idea, Frank,"—and now all Lady Arabella's energy came out. "Frank there is but one course left open to you. You MUST *marry money*." And then Lady Arabella stood up before her son as Lady Macbeth might have stood, had Lady Macbeth lived to have a son of Frank's years.

"Miss Dunstable, I suppose," said Frank, scornfully. "No, mother; I made an ass, and worse than an ass of myself once in that way, and I won't do it again. I hate money."

"Oh, Frank!"

"I hate money."

"But, Frank, the estate?"

"I hate the estate—at least I shall hate it if I am expected to buy it at such a price as that. The estate is my father's."

"Oh, no, Frank; it is not."

"It is in the sense I mean. He may do with it as he pleases; he will never have a word of complaint from me. I am ready to go into a profession to-morrow. I'll be a lawyer, or a doctor, or an engineer; I don't care what." Frank, in his enthusiasm, probably overlooked some of the preliminary difficulties. "Or I'll take a farm under him, and earn my bread that way; but, mother, don't talk to me any more about marrying money." And, so saying, Frank left the room.

Frank, it will be remembered, was twenty-one when he was first introduced to the reader; he is now twenty-two. It may be said that there was a great difference between his character then and now. A year at that period will make a great difference; but the change has been, not in his character, but in his feelings.

Frank went out from his mother and immediately ordered his black horse to be got ready for him. He would at once go over to Boxall Hill. He went himself to the stables to give his orders; and as he returned to get his gloves and whip he met Beatrice in the corridor.

"Beatrice," said he, "step in here," and she followed him into his room. "I'm not going to bear this any longer; I'm going to Boxall Hill."

"Oh, Frank! how can you be so imprudent?"

"You, at any rate, have some decent feeling for Mary. I believe you have some regard for her; and therefore I tell you. Will you send her any message?"

"Oh, yes; my best, best love; that is if you will see her; but, Frank, you are very foolish, very; and she will be infinitely distressed."

"Do not mention this, that is, not at present; not that I mean to make any secret of it. I shall tell my father everything. I'm off now!" and then, paying no attention to her remonstrance, he turned down the stairs and was soon on horseback.

He took the road to Boxall Hill, but he did not ride very fast: he did not go jauntily as a jolly, thriving wooer; but musingly, and often with diffidence, meditating every now and then whether it would not be better for him to turn back: to turn back—but not from fear of his mother; not from prudential motives; not because that often-repeated lesson as to marrying money was beginning to take effect; not from such causes as these; but because he doubted how he might be received by Mary.

He did, it is true, think something about his worldly prospects. He had talked rather grandiloquently to his mother as to his hating money, and hating the estate. His mother's never-ceasing worldly cares on such subjects perhaps demanded that a little grandiloquence should be opposed to them. But Frank did not hate the estate; nor did he at all hate the position of an English country gentleman. Miss Dunstable's eloquence, however, rang in his ears. For Miss Dunstable had an eloquence of her own, even in her letters. "Never let them talk you out of your own true, honest, hearty feelings," she had said. "Greshamsbury is a very nice place, I am sure; and I hope I shall see it some day; but all its green knolls are not half so nice, should not be half so precious, as the pulses of your own heart. That is your own estate, your own, your very own—your own and another's; whatever may go to the money-lenders, don't send that there. Don't mortgage that, Mr Gresham."

"No," said Frank, pluckily, as he put his horse into a faster trot, "I won't mortgage that. They may do what they like with the estate; but my heart's my own," and so speaking to himself, almost aloud, he turned a corner of the road rapidly and came at once upon the doctor.

"Hallo, doctor! is that you?" said Frank, rather disgusted.

"What! Frank! I hardly expected to meet you here," said Dr Thorne, not much better pleased.

They were now not above a mile from Boxall Hill, and the doctor, therefore, could not but surmise whither Frank was going. They had repeatedly met since Frank's return from Cambridge, both in the village and in the doctor's house; but not a word had been said between them about Mary beyond what the merest courtesy had required. Not that each did not love the other sufficiently to make a full confidence between them desirable to both; but neither had had the courage to speak out.

Nor had either of them the courage to do so now. "Yes," said Frank, blushing, "I am going to Lady Scatcherd's. Shall I find the ladies at home?"

"Yes; Lady Scatcherd is there; but Sir Louis is there also—an invalid: perhaps you would not wish to meet him."

"Oh! I don't mind," said Frank, trying to laugh; "he won't bite, I suppose?"

The doctor longed in his heart to pray to Frank to return with him; not to go and make further mischief; not to do that which might cause a more bitter estrangement between himself and the squire. But he had not the courage to do it. He could not bring himself to accuse Frank of being in love with his niece. So after a few more senseless words on either side, words which each knew to be senseless as he uttered them, they both rode on their own ways.

And then the doctor silently, and almost unconsciously, made such a comparison between Louis Scatcherd and Frank Gresham as Hamlet made between the dead and live king. It was Hyperion to a satyr. Was it not as impossible that Mary should not love the one, as that she should love the other? Frank's offer of his affections had at first probably been but a boyish ebullition of feeling; but if it should now be, that this had grown into a manly and disinterested love, how could Mary remain unmoved? What could her heart want more, better, more beautiful, more rich than such a love as his? Was he not personally all that a girl could like? Were not his disposition, mind, character, acquirements, all such as women most delight to love? Was it not impossible that Mary should be indifferent to him?

So meditated the doctor as he rode along, with only too true a knowledge of human nature. Ah! it was impossible, it was quite impossible that Mary should be indifferent. She had never been indifferent since Frank had uttered his first half-joking word of love. Such things are more important to women than they are to men, to girls than they are to boys. When Frank had first told her that he loved her; aye, months before that, when he merely looked his love, her heart had received the whisper, had acknowledged the glance, unconscious as she was herself, and resolved as she was to rebuke his advances. When, in her hearing, he had said soft nothings to Patience Oriel, a hated, irrepressible tear had gathered in her eye. When he had pressed in his warm, loving grasp the hand which she had offered him as a token of mere friendship, her heart had forgiven him the treachery, nay, almost thanked him for it, before her eyes or her words had been ready to rebuke him. When the rumour of his liaison with Miss Dunstable reached her ears, when she heard of Miss Dunstable's fortune, she had wept, wept outright, in her chamber—wept, as she said to herself, to think that he should be so mercenary; but she had wept, as she should have said to herself, at finding that he was so faithless. Then, when she knew at last that this rumour was false, when she found that she was banished from Greshamsbury for his sake, when she was forced to retreat with her friend Patience, how could she but love him, in that he was not mercenary? How could she not love him in that he was so faithful?

It was impossible that she should not love him. Was he not the brightest and the best of men that she had ever seen, or was like to see?—that she could possibly ever see, she would have said to herself, could she have brought herself to own the truth? And then, when she heard how true he was, how he persisted against father, mother, and sisters, how could it be that that should not be a merit in her eyes which was so great a fault in theirs? When Beatrice, with would-be solemn face, but with eyes beaming with feminine affection, would gravely talk of Frank's tender love as a terrible misfortune, as a misfortune to them all, to Mary herself as well as others, how could Mary do other than love him? "Beatrice is his sister," she would say within her own mind, "otherwise she would never talk like this; were she not his sister, she could not but know the value of such love as this." Ah! yes; Mary did love him; love him with all the strength of her heart; and the strength of her heart was very great. And now by degrees, in those lonely donkey-rides at Boxall Hill, in those solitary walks, she was beginning to own to herself the truth.

And now that she did own it, what should be her course? What should she do, how should she act if this loved one persevered in his love? And, ah! what should she do, how should she act if he did not persevere? Could it be that there should be happiness in store for her? Was it not too clear that, let the matter go how it would, there was no happiness in store for her? Much as she might love Frank Gresham, she could never consent to be his wife unless the squire would smile on her as his daughter-in-law. The squire had been all that was kind, all that was affectionate. And then, too, Lady Arabella! As she thought of the Lady Arabella a sterner form of thought came across her brow. Why should Lady Arabella rob her of her heart's joy? What was Lady Arabella that she, Mary Thorne, need quail before her? Had Lady Arabella stood only in her way, Lady Arabella, flanked by the de Courcy legion, Mary felt that she could have demanded Frank's hand as her own before them all without a blush of shame or a moment's hesitation. Thus, when her heart was all but ready to collapse within her, would she gain some little strength by thinking of the Lady Arabella.

"Please, my lady, here be young squoire Gresham," said one of the untutored servants at Boxall Hill, opening Lady Scatcherd's little parlour door as her ladyship was amusing herself by pulling down and turning, and re-folding, and putting up again, a heap of household linen which was kept in a huge press for the express purpose of supplying her with occupation.

Lady Scatcherd, holding a vast counterpane in her arms, looked back over her shoulders and perceived that Frank was in the room. Down went the counterpane on the ground, and Frank soon found himself in the very position which that useful article had so lately filled.

"Oh! Master Frank! oh, Master Frank!" said her ladyship, almost in an hysterical fit of joy; and then she hugged and kissed him as she had never kissed and hugged her own son since that son had first left the parent nest.

Frank bore it patiently and with a merry laugh. "But, Lady Scatcherd," said he, "what will they all say? you forget I am a man now," and he stooped his head as she again pressed her lips upon his forehead.

"I don't care what none of 'em say," said her ladyship, quite going back to her old days; "I will kiss my own boy; so I will. Eh, but Master Frank, this is good of you. A sight of you is good for sore eyes; and my eyes have been sore enough too since I saw you;" and she put her apron up to wipe away a tear.

"Yes," said Frank, gently trying to disengage himself, but not successfully; "yes, you have had a great loss, Lady Scatcherd. I was so sorry when I heard of your grief."

"You always had a soft, kind heart, Master Frank; so you had. God's blessing on you! What a fine man you have grown! Deary me! Well, it seems as though it were only just t'other day like." And she pushed him a little off from her, so that she might look the better into his face.

"Well. Is it all right? I suppose you would hardly know me again now I've got a pair of whiskers?"

"Know you! I should know you well if I saw but the heel of your foot. Why, what a head of hair you have got, and so dark too! but it doesn't curl as it used once." And she stroked his hair, and looked into his eyes, and put her hand to his cheeks. "You'll think me an old fool, Master Frank: I know that; but you may think what you like. If I live for the next twenty years you'll always be my own boy; so you will."

By degrees, slow degrees, Frank managed to change the conversation, and to induce Lady Scatcherd to speak on some other topic than his own infantine perfections. He affected an indifference as he spoke of her guest, which would have deceived no one but Lady Scatcherd; but her it did deceive; and then he asked where Mary was.

"She's just gone out on her donkey—somewhere about the place. She rides on a donkey mostly every day. But you'll stop and take a bit of dinner with us? Eh, now do 'ee, Master Frank."

But Master Frank excused himself. He did not choose to pledge himself to sit down to dinner with Mary. He did not know in what mood they might return with regard to each other at dinner-time. He said, therefore, that he would walk out and, if possible, find Miss Thorne; and that he would return to the house again before he went.

Lady Scatcherd then began making apologies for Sir Louis. He was an invalid; the doctor had been with him all the morning, and he was not yet out of his room.

These apologies Frank willingly accepted, and then made his way as he could on to the lawn. A gardener, of whom he inquired, offered to go with him in pursuit of Miss Thorne. This assistance, however, he declined, and set forth in quest of her, having learnt what were her most usual haunts. Nor was he directed wrongly; for after walking about twenty minutes, he saw through the trees the legs of a donkey moving on the green-sward, at about two hundred yards from him. On that donkey doubtless sat Mary Thorne.

The donkey was coming towards him; not exactly in a straight line, but so much so as to make it impossible that Mary should not see him if he stood still. He did stand still, and soon emerging from the trees, Mary saw him all but close to her.

Her heart gave a leap within her, but she was so far mistress of herself as to repress any visible sign of outward emotion. She did not fall from her donkey, or scream, or burst into tears. She merely uttered the words, "Mr Gresham!" in a tone of not unnatural surprise.

"Yes," said he, trying to laugh, but less successful than she had been in suppressing a show of feeling. "Mr Gresham! I have come over at last to pay my respects to you. You must have thought me very uncourteous not to do so before."

This she denied. "She had not," she said, "thought him at all uncivil. She had come to Boxall Hill to be out of the way; and, of course, had not expected any such formalities." As she uttered this she almost blushed at the abrupt truth of what she was saying. But she was taken so much unawares that she did not know how to make the truth other than abrupt.

"To be out of the way!" said Frank. "And why should you want to be out of the way?"

"Oh! there were reasons," said she, laughing. "Perhaps I have quarrelled dreadfully with my uncle."

Frank at the present moment had not about him a scrap of badinage. He had not a single easy word at his command. He could not answer her with anything in guise of a joke; so he walked on, not answering at all.

"I hope all my friends at Greshamsbury are well," said Mary. "Is Beatrice quite well?"

"Quite well," said he.

"And Patience?"

"What, Miss Oriel; yes, I believe so. I haven't seen her this day or two." How was it that Mary felt a little flush of joy, as Frank spoke in this indifferent way about Miss Oriel's health?

"I thought she was always a particular friend of yours," said she.

"What! who? Miss Oriel? So she is! I like her amazingly; so does Beatrice." And then he walked about six steps in silence, plucking up courage for the great attempt. He did pluck up his courage and then rushed at once to the attack.

"Mary!" said he, and as he spoke he put his hand on the donkey's neck, and looked tenderly into her face. He looked tenderly, and, as Mary's ear at once told her, his voice sounded more soft than it had ever sounded before. "Mary, do you remember the last time that we were together?"

Mary did remember it well. It was on that occasion when he had treacherously held her hand; on that day when, according to law, he had become a man; when he had outraged all the propriety of the de Courcy interest by offering his love to Mary in Augusta's hearing. Mary did remember it well; but how was she to speak of it? "It was your birthday, I think," said she.

"Yes, it was my birthday. I wonder whether you remember what I said to you then?"

"I remember that you were very foolish, Mr Gresham."

"Mary, I have come to repeat my folly;—that is, if it be folly. I told you then that I loved you, and I dare say that I did so awkwardly, like a boy. Perhaps I may be just as awkward now; but you ought at any rate to believe me when you find that a year has not altered me."

Mary did not think him at all awkward, and she did believe him. But how was she to answer him? She had not yet taught herself what answer she ought to make if he persisted in his suit. She had hitherto been content to run away from him; but she had done so because she would not submit to be accused of the indelicacy of putting herself in his way. She had rebuked him when he first spoke of his love; but she had done so because she looked on what he said as a boy's nonsense. She had schooled herself in obedience to the Greshamsbury doctrines. Was there any real reason, any reason founded on truth and honesty, why she should not be a fitting wife to Frank Gresham,—Francis Newbold Gresham, of Greshamsbury, though he was, or was to be?

He was well born—as well born as any gentleman in England. She was basely born—as basely born as any lady could be. Was this sufficient bar against such a match? Mary felt in her heart that some twelvemonth since, before she knew what little she did now know of her own story, she would have said it was so. And would she indulge her own love by inveigling him she loved into a base marriage? But then reason spoke again. What, after all, was this blood of which she had taught herself to think so much? Would she have been more honest, more fit to grace an honest man's hearthstone, had she been the legitimate descendant of a score of legitimate duchesses? Was it not her first duty to think of him—of what would make him happy? Then of her uncle—what he would approve? Then of herself—what would best become her modesty; her sense of honour? Could it be well that she should sacrifice the happiness of two persons to a theoretic love of pure blood?

So she had argued within herself; not now, sitting on the donkey, with Frank's hand before her on the tame brute's neck; but on other former occasions as she had ridden along demurely among those trees. So she had argued; but she had never brought her arguments to a decision. All manner of thoughts crowded on her to prevent her doing so. She would think of the squire, and resolve to reject Frank; and would then remember Lady Arabella, and resolve to accept him. Her resolutions, however, were most irresolute; and so, when Frank appeared in person before her, carrying his heart in his hand, she did not know what answer to make to him. Thus it was with her as with so many other maidens similarly circumstanced; at last she left it all to chance.

"You ought, at any rate, to believe me," said Frank, "when you find that a year has not altered me."

"A year should have taught you to be wiser," said she. "You should have learnt by this time, Mr Gresham, that your lot and mine are not cast in the same mould; that our stations in life are different. Would your father or mother approve of your even coming here to see me?"

Mary, as she spoke these sensible words, felt that they were "flat, stale, and unprofitable." She felt, also, that they were not true in sense; that they did not come from her heart; that they were not such as Frank deserved at her hands, and she was ashamed of herself.

"My father I hope will approve of it," said he. "That my mother should disapprove of it is a misfortune which I cannot help; but on this point I will take no answer from my father or mother; the question is one too personal to myself. Mary, if you say that you will not, or cannot return my love, I will go away;—not from here only, but from Greshamsbury. My presence shall not banish you from all that you hold dear. If you can honestly say that

I am nothing to you, can be nothing to you, I will then tell my mother that she may be at ease, and I will go away somewhere and get over it as I may." The poor fellow got so far, looking apparently at the donkey's ears, with hardly a gasp of hope in his voice, and he so far carried Mary with him that she also had hardly a gasp of hope in her heart. There he paused for a moment, and then looking up into her face, he spoke but one word more. "But," said he—and there he stopped. It was clearly told in that "but." Thus would he do if Mary would declare that she did not care for him. If, however, she could not bring herself so to declare, then was he ready to throw his father and mother to the winds; then would he stand his ground; then would he look all other difficulties in the face, sure that they might finally be overcome. Poor Mary! the whole onus of settling the matter was thus thrown upon her. She had only to say that he was indifferent to her;—that was all.

If "all the blood of the Howards" had depended upon it, she could not have brought herself to utter such a falsehood. Indifferent to her, as he walked there by her donkey's side, talking thus earnestly of his love for her! Was he not to her like some god come from the heavens to make her blessed? Did not the sun shine upon him with a halo, so that he was bright as an angel? Indifferent to her! Could the open unadulterated truth have been practicable for her, she would have declared her indifference in terms that would truly have astonished him. As it was, she found it easier to say nothing. She bit her lips to keep herself from sobbing. She struggled hard, but in vain, to prevent her hands and feet from trembling. She seemed to swing upon her donkey as though like to fall, and would have given much to be upon her own feet upon the sward.

"*Si la jeunesse savait . . .*" There is so much in that wicked old French proverb! Had Frank known more about a woman's mind—had he, that is, been forty-two instead of twenty-two—he would at once have been sure of his game, and have felt that Mary's silence told him all he wished to know. But then, had he been forty-two instead of twenty-two, he would not have been so ready to risk the acres of Greshamsbury for the smiles of Mary Thorne.

"If you can't say one word to comfort me, I will go," said he, disconsolately. "I made up my mind to tell you this, and so I came over. I told Lady Scatcherd I should not stay,—not even for dinner."

"I did not know you were so hurried," said she, almost in a whisper.

On a sudden he stood still, and pulling the donkey's rein, caused him to stand still also. The beast required very little persuasion to be so guided, and obligingly remained meekly passive.

"Mary, Mary!" said Frank, throwing his arms round her knees as she sat upon her steed, and pressing his face against her body. "Mary, you were always honest; be honest now. I love you with all my heart. Will you be my wife?"

But still Mary said not a word. She no longer bit her lips; she was beyond that, and was now using all her efforts to prevent her tears from falling absolutely on her lover's face. She said nothing. She could no more rebuke him now and send him from her than she could encourage him. She could only sit there shaking and crying and wishing she was on the ground. Frank, on the whole, rather liked the donkey. It enabled him to approach somewhat nearer to an embrace than he might have found practicable had they both been on their feet. The donkey himself was quite at his ease, and looked as though he was approvingly conscious of what was going on behind his ears.

"I have a right to a word, Mary; say 'Go,' and I will leave you at once."

But Mary did not say "Go." Perhaps she would have done so had she been able; but just at present she could say nothing. This came from her having failed to make up her mind in due time as to what course it would best become her to follow.

"One word, Mary; one little word. There, if you will not speak, here is my hand. If you will have it, let it lie in yours;—if not, push it away." So saying, he managed to get the end of his fingers on to her palm, and there it remained unrepulsed. "La jeunesse" was beginning to get a lesson; experience when duly sought after sometimes comes early in life.

In truth Mary had not strength to push the fingers away. "My love, my own, my own!" said Frank, presuming on this very negative sign of acquiescence. "My life, my own one, my own Mary!" and then the hand was caught hold of and was at his lips before an effort could be made to save it from such treatment.

"Mary, look at me; say one word to me."

There was a deep sigh, and then came the one word—"Oh, Frank!"

"Mr Gresham, I hope I have the honour of seeing you quite well," said a voice close to his ear. "I beg to say that you are welcome to Boxall Hill." Frank turned round and instantly found himself shaking hands with Sir Louis Scatcherd.

How Mary got over her confusion Frank never saw, for he had enough to do to get over his own. He involuntarily deserted Mary and began talking very fast to Sir Louis. Sir Louis did not once look at Miss Thorne, but walked back towards the house with Mr Gresham, sulky enough in temper, but still making some effort to do the fine gentleman. Mary, glad to be left alone, merely occupied herself with sitting on the donkey; and the donkey, when he found that the two gentlemen went towards the house, for company's sake and for his stable's sake, followed after them.

Frank stayed but three minutes in the house; gave another kiss to Lady Scatcherd, getting three in return, and thereby infinitely disgusting Sir Louis, shook hands, anything but warmly, with the young baronet, and just felt the warmth of Mary's hand within his own. He felt also the warmth of her eyes' last glance, and rode home a happy man.

CHAPTER XXX

POST PRANDIAL

Frank rode home a happy man, cheering himself, as successful lovers do cheer themselves, with the brilliancy of his late exploit: nor was it till he had turned the corner into the Greshamsbury stables that he began to reflect what he would do next. It was all very well to have induced Mary to allow his three fingers to lie half a minute in her soft hand; the having done so might certainly be sufficient evidence that he had overcome one of the lions in his path; but it could hardly be said that all his difficulties were now smoothed. How was he to make further progress?

To Mary, also, the same ideas no doubt occurred—with many others. But, then, it was not for Mary to make any progress in the matter. To her at least belonged this passive comfort, that at present no act hostile to the de Courcy interest would be expected from her. All that she could do would be to tell her uncle so much as it was fitting that he should know. The doing this would doubtless be in some degree difficult; but it was not probable that there would be much difference, much of anything but loving anxiety for each other, between her and Dr Thorne. One other thing, indeed, she must do; Frank must be made to understand what her birth had been. "This," she said to herself, "will give him an opportunity of retracting what he has done should he choose to avail himself of it. It is well he should have such opportunity."

But Frank had more than this to do. He had told Beatrice that he would make no secret of his love, and he fully resolved to be as good as his word. To his father he owed an unreserved confidence; and he was fully minded to give it. It was, he knew, altogether out of the question that he should at once marry a portionless girl without his father's consent; probably out of the question that he should do so even with it. But he would, at any rate, tell his father, and then decide as to what should be done next. So resolving, he put his black horse into the stable and went in to dinner. After dinner he and his father would be alone.

Yes; after dinner he and his father would be alone. He dressed himself hurriedly, for the dinner-bell was almost on the stroke as he entered the house. He said this to himself once and again; but when the meats and the puddings, and then the cheese, were borne away, as the decanters were placed before his father, and Lady Arabella sipped her one glass of claret, and his sisters ate their portion of strawberries, his pressing anxiety for the coming interview began to wax somewhat dull.

His mother and sisters, however, rendered him no assistance by prolonging their stay. With unwonted assiduity he pressed a second glass of claret on his mother. But Lady Arabella was not only temperate in her habits, but also at the present moment very angry with her son. She thought that he had been to Boxall Hill, and was only waiting a proper moment to cross-question him sternly on the subject. Now she departed, taking her train of daughters with her.

"Give me one big gooseberry," said Nina, as she squeezed herself in under her brother's arm, prior to making her retreat. Frank would willingly have given her a dozen of the biggest, had she wanted them; but having got the one, she squeezed herself out again and scampered off.

The squire was very cheery this evening; from what cause cannot now be said. Perhaps he had succeeded in negotiating a further loan, thus temporarily sprinkling a drop of water over the ever-rising dust of his difficulties.

"Well, Frank, what have you been after to-day? Peter told me you had the black horse out," said he, pushing the decanter to his son. "Take my advice, my boy, and don't give him too much summer road-work. Legs won't stand it, let them be ever so good."

"Why, sir, I was obliged to go out to-day, and therefore, it had to be either the old mare or the young horse."

"Why didn't you take Ramble?" Now Ramble was the squire's own saddle hack, used for farm surveying, and occasionally for going to cover.

"I shouldn't think of doing that, sir."

"My dear boy, he is quite at your service; for goodness' sake do let me have a little wine, Frank—quite at your service; any riding I have now is after the haymakers, and that's all on the grass."

"Thank'ee, sir. Well, perhaps I will take a turn out of Ramble should I want it."

"Do, and pray, pray take care of that black horse's legs. He's turning out more of a horse than I took him to be, and I should be sorry to see him injured. Where have you been to-day?"

"Well, father, I have something to tell you."

"Something to tell me!" and then the squire's happy and gay look, which had been only rendered more happy and more gay by his assumed anxiety about the black horse, gave place to that heaviness of visage which acrimony and misfortune had made so habitual to him. "Something to tell me!" Any grave words like these always presaged some money difficulty to the squire's ears. He loved Frank with the tenderest love. He would have done so under almost any circumstances; but, doubtless, that love had been made more palpable to himself by the fact that Frank had been a good son as regards money—not exigeant as was Lady Arabella, or selfishly reckless as was his nephew Lord Porlock. But now Frank must be in difficulty about money. This was his first idea. "What is it, Frank; you have seldom had anything to say that has not been pleasant for me to hear?" And then the heaviness of visage again gave way for a moment as his eye fell upon his son.

"I have been to Boxall Hill, sir."

The tenor of his father's thoughts was changed in an instant; and the dread of immediate temporary annoyance gave place to true anxiety for his son. He, the squire, had been no party to Mary's exile from his own domain; and he had seen with pain that she had now a second time been driven from her home: but he had never hitherto questioned the expediency of separating his son from Mary Thorne. Alas! it became too necessary—too necessary through his own default—that Frank should marry money!

"At Boxall Hill, Frank! Has that been prudent? Or, indeed, has it been generous to Miss Thorne, who has been driven there, as it were, by your imprudence?"

"Father, it is well that we should understand each other about this—"

"Fill your glass, Frank;" Frank mechanically did as he was told, and passed the bottle.

"I should never forgive myself were I to deceive you, or keep anything from you."

"I believe it is not in your nature to deceive me, Frank."

"The fact is, sir, that I have made up my mind that Mary Thorne shall be my wife—sooner or later that is, unless, of course, she should utterly refuse. Hitherto, she has utterly refused me. I believe I may now say that she has accepted me."

The squire sipped his claret, but at the moment said nothing. There was a quiet, manly, but yet modest determination about his son that he had hardly noticed before. Frank had become legally of age, legally a man, when he was twenty-one. Nature, it seems, had postponed the ceremony till he was twenty-two. Nature often does postpone the ceremony even to a much later age;—sometimes, altogether forgets to accomplish it.

The squire continued to sip his claret; he had to think over the matter a while before he could answer a statement so deliberately made by his son.

"I think I may say so," continued Frank, with perhaps unnecessary modesty. "She is so honest that, had she not intended it, she would have said so honestly. Am I right, father, in thinking that, as regards Mary, personally, you would not reject her as a daughter-in-law?"

"Personally!" said the squire, glad to have the subject presented to him in a view that enabled him to speak out. "Oh, no; personally, I should not object to her, for I love her dearly. She is a good girl. I do believe she is a good girl in every respect. I have always liked her; liked to see her about the house. But—"

"I know what you would say, father." This was rather more than the squire knew himself. "Such a marriage is imprudent."

"It is more than that, Frank; I fear it is impossible."

"Impossible! No, father; it is not impossible."

"It is impossible, Frank, in the usual sense. What are you to live upon? What would you do with your children? You would not wish to see your wife distressed and comfortless."

"No, I should not like to see that."

"You would not wish to begin life as an embarrassed man and end it as a ruined man. If you were now to marry Miss Thorne such would, I fear, doubtless be your lot."

Frank caught at the word "now." "I don't expect to marry immediately. I know that would be imprudent. But I am pledged, father, and I certainly cannot go back. And now that I have told you all this, what is your advice to me?"

The father again sat silent, still sipping his wine. There was nothing in his son that he could be ashamed of, nothing that he could meet with anger, nothing that he could not love; but how should he answer him? The fact was, that the son had more in him than the father; this his mind and spirit were of a calibre not to be opposed successfully by the mind and spirit of the squire.

"Do you know Mary's history?" said Mr Gresham, at last; "the history of her birth?"

"Not a word of it," said Frank. "I did not know she had a history."

"Nor does she know it; at least, I presume not. But you should know it now. And, Frank, I will tell it you; not to turn you from her—not with that object, though I think that, to a certain extent, it should have that effect. Mary's birth was not such as would become your wife and be beneficial to your children."

"If so, father, I should have known that sooner. Why was she brought in here among us?"

"True, Frank. The fault is mine; mine and your mother's. Circumstances brought it about years ago, when it never occurred to us that all this would arise. But I will tell you her history. And, Frank, remember this, though I tell it you as a secret, a secret to be kept from all the world but one, you are quite at liberty to let the doctor know that I have told you. Indeed, I shall be careful to let him know myself should it ever be necessary that he

675

and I should speak together as to this engagement." The squire then told his son the whole story of Mary's birth, as it is known to the reader.

Frank sat silent, looking very blank; he also had, as had every Gresham, a great love for his pure blood. He had said to his mother that he hated money, that he hated the estate; but he would have been very slow to say, even in his warmest opposition to her, that he hated the roll of the family pedigree. He loved it dearly, though he seldom spoke of it;—as men of good family seldom do speak of it. It is one of those possessions which to have is sufficient. A man having it need not boast of what he has, or show it off before the world. But on that account he values it more. He had regarded Mary as a cutting duly taken from the Ullathorne tree; not, indeed, as a grafting branch, full of flower, just separated from the parent stalk, but as being not a whit the less truly endowed with the pure sap of that venerable trunk. When, therefore, he heard her true history he sat awhile dismayed.

"It is a sad story," said the father.

"Yes, sad enough," said Frank, rising from his chair and standing with it before him, leaning on the back of it. "Poor Mary, poor Mary! She will have to learn it some day."

"I fear so, Frank;" and then there was again a few moments' silence.

"To me, father, it is told too late. It can now have no effect on me. Indeed," said he, sighing as he spoke, but still relieving himself by the very sigh, "it could have had no effect had I learned it ever so soon."

"I should have told you before," said the father; "certainly I ought to have done so."

"It would have been no good," said Frank. "Ah, sir, tell me this: who were Miss Dunstable's parents? What was that fellow Moffat's family?"

This was perhaps cruel of Frank. The squire, however, made no answer to the question. "I have thought it right to tell you," said he. "I leave all commentary to yourself. I need not tell you what your mother will think."

"What did she think of Miss Dunstable's birth?" said he, again more bitterly than before. "No, sir," he continued, after a further pause. "All that can make no change; none at any rate now. It can't make my love less, even if it could have prevented it. Nor, even, could it do so—which it can't least, not in the least—but could it do so, it could not break my engagement. I am now engaged to Mary Thorne."

And then he again repeated his question, asking for his father's advice under the present circumstances. The conversation was a very long one, as long as to disarrange all Lady Arabella's plans. She had determined to take her son most stringently to task that very evening; and with this object had ensconced herself in the small drawing-room which had formerly been used for a similar purpose by the august countess herself. Here she now sat, having desired Augusta and Beatrice, as well as the twins, to beg Frank to go to her as soon as he should come out of the dining-room. Poor lady! there she waited till ten o'clock,—tealess. There was not much of the Bluebeard about the squire; but he had succeeded in making it understood through the household that he was not to be interrupted by messages from his wife during the post-prandial hour, which, though no toper, he loved so well.

As a period of twelve months will now have to be passed over, the upshot of this long conversation must be told in as few words as possible. The father found it impracticable to talk his son out of his intended marriage; indeed, he hardly attempted to do so by any direct persuasion. He explained to him that it was impossible that he should marry at once, and suggested that he, Frank, was very young.

"You married, sir, before you were one-and-twenty," said Frank. Yes, and repented before I was two-and-twenty. So did not say the squire.

He suggested that Mary should have time to ascertain what would be her uncle's wishes, and ended by inducing Frank to promise, that after taking his degree in October he would go abroad for some months, and that he would not indeed return to Greshamsbury till he was three-and-twenty.

"He may perhaps forget her," said the father to himself, as this agreement was made between them.

"He thinks that I shall forget her," said Frank to himself at the same time; "but he does not know me."

When Lady Arabella at last got hold of her son she found that the time for her preaching was utterly gone by. He told her, almost with *sang-froid*, what his plans were; and when she came to understand them, and to understand also what had taken place at Boxall Hill, she could not blame the squire for what he had done. She also said to herself, more confidently than the squire had done, that Frank would quite forget Mary before the year was out. "Lord Buckish," said she to herself, rejoicingly, "is now with the ambassador at Paris"—Lord Buckish was her nephew—"and with him Frank will meet women that are really beautiful—women of fashion. When with Lord Buckish he will soon forget Mary Thorne."

But not on this account did she change her resolve to follow up to the furthest point her hostility to the Thornes. She was fully enabled now to do so, for Dr Fillgrave was already reinstalled at Greshamsbury as her medical adviser.

One other short visit did Frank pay to Boxall Hill, and one interview had he with Dr Thorne. Mary told him all she knew of her own sad history, and was answered only by a kiss,—a kiss absolutely not in any way by her to be avoided; the first, the only one, that had ever yet reached her lips from his. And then he went away.

The doctor told him all the story. "Yes," said Frank, "I knew it all before. Dear Mary, dearest Mary! Don't you, doctor, teach yourself to believe that I shall forget her." And then also he went his way from him—went his way also from Greshamsbury, and was absent for the full period of his allotted banishment—twelve months, namely, and a day.

CHAPTER XXXI

THE SMALL END OF THE WEDGE

Frank Gresham was absent from Greshamsbury twelve months and a day: a day is always added to the period of such absences, as shown in the history of Lord Bateman and other noble heroes. We need not detail all the circumstances of his banishment, all the details of the compact that was made. One detail of course was this, that there should be no corresponding; a point to which the squire found some difficulty in bringing his son to assent.

It must not be supposed that Mary Thorne or the doctor were in any way parties to, or privy to these agreements. By no means. The agreements were drawn out, and made, and signed, and sealed at Greshamsbury, and were known of nowhere else. The reader must not imagine that Lady Arabella was prepared to give up her son, if only his love could remain constant for one year. Neither did Lady Arabella consent to any such arrangement, nor did the squire. It was settled rather in this wise: that Frank should be subjected to no torturing process, pestered to give no promises, should in no way be bullied about Mary—that is, not at present—if he would go away for a year. Then, at the end of the year, the matter should again be discussed. Agreeing to this, Frank took his departure, and was absent as per agreement.

What were Mary's fortunes immediately after his departure must be shortly told, and then we will again join some of our Greshamsbury friends at a period about a month before Frank's return.

When Sir Louis saw Frank Gresham standing by Mary's donkey, with his arms round Mary's knees, he began to fear that there must be something in it. He had intended that very day to throw himself at Mary's feet, and now it appeared to his inexperienced eyes as though somebody else had been at the same work before him. This not unnaturally made him cross; so, after having sullenly wished the visitor good-bye, he betook himself to his room, and there drank curaçoa alone, instead of coming down to dinner.

This he did for two or three days, and then, taking heart of grace, he remembered that, after all, he had very many advantages over young Gresham. In the first place, he was a baronet, and could make his wife a "lady." In the next place, Frank's father was alive and like to live, whereas his own was dead. He possessed Boxall Hill in his own right, but his rival had neither house nor land of his own. After all, might it not be possible for him also to put his arm round Mary's knees;—her knees, or her waist, or, perhaps, even her neck? Faint heart never won fair lady. At any rate, he would try.

And he did try. With what result, as regards Mary, need hardly be told. He certainly did not get nearly so far as putting his hand even upon her knee before he was made to understand that it "was no go," as he graphically described it to his mother. He tried once and again. On the first time Mary was very civil, though very determined. On the second, she was more determined, though less civil; and then she told him, that if he pressed her further he would drive her from his mother's house. There was something then about Mary's eye, a fixed composure round her mouth, and an authority in her face, which went far to quell him; and he did not press her again.

He immediately left Boxall Hill, and, returning to London, had more violent recourse to the curaçoa. It was not long before the doctor heard of him, and was obliged to follow him, and then again occurred those frightful scenes in which the poor wretch had to expiate, either in terrible delirium or more terrible prostration of spirits, the vile sin which his father had so early taught him.

Then Mary returned to her uncle's home. Frank was gone, and she therefore could resume her place at Greshamsbury. Yes, she came back to Greshamsbury; but Greshamsbury was by no means the same place that it was formerly. Almost all intercourse was now over between the doctor and the Greshamsbury people. He rarely ever saw the squire, and then only on business. Not that the squire had purposely quarrelled with him; but Dr Thorne himself had chosen that it should be so, since Frank had openly proposed for his niece. Frank was now gone, and Lady Arabella was in arms against him. It should not be said that he kept up any intimacy for the sake of aiding the lovers in their love. No one should rightfully accuse him of inveigling the heir to marry his niece.

Mary, therefore, found herself utterly separated from Beatrice. She was not even able to learn what Beatrice would think, or did think, of the engagement as it now stood. She could not even explain to her friend that love had been too strong for her, and endeavour to get some comfort from that friend's absolution from her sin. This estrangement was now carried so far that she and Beatrice did not even meet on neutral ground. Lady Arabella made it known to Miss Oriel that her daughter could not meet Mary Thorne, even as strangers meet; and it was made known to others also. Mrs Yates Umbleby, and her dear friend Miss Gushing, to whose charming tea-parties none of the Greshamsbury ladies went above once in a twelvemonth, talked through the parish of this distressing difficulty. They would have been so happy to have asked dear Mary Thorne, only the Greshamsbury ladies did not approve.

Mary was thus tabooed from all society in the place in which a twelvemonth since she had been, of all its denizens, perhaps the most courted. In those days, no bevy of Greshamsbury young ladies had fairly represented the Greshamsbury young ladyhood if Mary Thorne was not there. Now she was excluded from all such bevies. Patience did not quarrel with her, certainly;—came to see her frequently;—invited her to walk;—invited her frequently to the parsonage. But Mary was shy of acceding to such invitations, and at last frankly told her friend Patience, that she would not again break bread in Greshamsbury in any house in which she was not thought fit to meet the other guests who habitually resorted there.

In truth, both the doctor and his niece were very sore, but they were of that temperament that keeps all its soreness to itself. Mary walked out by herself boldly, looking at least as though she were indifferent to all the world. She was, indeed, hardly treated. Young ladies' engagements are generally matters of profoundest secrecy, and are hardly known of by their near friends till marriage is a thing settled. But all the world knew of Mary's engagement within a month of that day on which she had neglected to expel Frank's finger from her hand; it had been told openly through the country-side that she had confessed her love for the young squire. Now it is disagreeable for a young lady to walk about under such circumstances, especially so when she has no female friend to keep her in countenance, more especially so when the gentleman is such importance in the neighbourhood as Frank was in that locality. It was a matter of moment to every farmer, and every farmer's wife, which bride Frank should marry of those bespoken for him; Mary, namely, or Money. Every yokel about the place had been made to understand that, by some feminine sleight of hand, the doctor's niece had managed to trap Master Frank, and that Master Frank had been sent out of the way so that he might, if yet possible, break through the trapping. All this made life rather unpleasant for her.

One day, walking solitary in the lanes, she met that sturdy farmer to whose daughter she had in former days been so serviceable. "God bless 'ee, Miss Mary," said he—he always did bid God bless her when he saw her. "And, Miss Mary, to say my mind out freely, thee be quite gude enough for un, quite gude enough; so thee be'st tho'f he were ten squoires." There may, perhaps, have been something pleasant in the heartiness of this; but it was not pleasant to have this heart affair of hers thus publicly scanned and talked over: to have it known to every one that she had set her heart on marrying Frank Gresham, and that all the Greshams had set their hearts on preventing it. And yet she could in nowise help it. No girl could have been more staid and demure, less demonstrative and boastful about her love. She had never yet spoken freely, out of her full heart, to one human being. "Oh, Frank!" All her spoken sin had been contained in that.

But Lady Arabella had been very active. It suited her better that it should be known, far and wide, that a nameless pauper—Lady Arabella only surmised that her foe was nameless; but she did not scruple to declare it—was intriguing to catch the heir of Greshamsbury. None of the Greshams must meet Mary Thorne; that was the edict sent about the country; and the edict was well understood. Those, therefore, were bad days for Miss Thorne.

She had never yet spoken on the matter freely, out of her full heart to one human being. Not to one? Not to him? Not to her uncle? No, not even to him, fully and freely. She had told him that that had passed between Frank and her which amounted, at any rate on his part, to a proposal.

"Well, dearest, and what was your answer?" said her uncle, drawing her close to him, and speaking in his kindest voice.

"I hardly made any answer, uncle."

"You did not reject him, Mary?"

"No, uncle," and then she paused;—he had never known her tremble as she now trembled. "But if you say that I ought, I will," she added, drawing every word from herself with difficulty.

"I say you ought, Mary! Nay; but this question you must answer yourself."

"Must I?" said she, plaintively. And then she sat for the next half hour with her head against his shoulder; but nothing more was said about it. They both acquiesced in the sentence that had been pronounced against them, and went on together more lovingly than before.

The doctor was quite as weak as his niece; nay, weaker. She hesitated fearfully as to what she ought to do: whether she should obey her heart or the dictates of Greshamsbury. But he had other doubts than hers, which nearly set him wild when he strove to bring his mind to a decision. He himself was now in possession—of course as a trustee only—of the title-deeds of the estate; more of the estate, much more, belonged to the heirs under Sir Roger Scatcherd's will than to the squire. It was now more than probable that that heir must be Mary Thorne. His conviction became stronger and stronger that no human efforts would keep Sir Louis in the land of the living till he was twenty-five. Could he, therefore, wisely or honestly, in true friendship to the squire, to Frank, or to his niece, take any steps to separate two persons who loved each other, and whose marriage would in all human probability be so suitable?

And yet he could not bring himself to encourage it then. The idea of "looking after dead men's shoes" was abhorrent to his mind, especially when the man whose death he contemplated had been so trusted to him as had been Sir Louis Scatcherd. He could not speak of the event, even to the squire, as being possible. So he kept his peace from day to day, and gave no counsel to Mary in the matter.

And then he had his own individual annoyances, and very aggravating annoyances they were. The carriage—or rather post-chaise—of Dr Fillgrave was now frequent in Greshamsbury, passing him constantly in the street, among the lanes, and on the high roads. It seemed as though Dr Fillgrave could never get to his patients at the big house without showing himself to his beaten rival, either on his way thither or on his return. This alone would, perhaps, not have hurt the doctor much; but it did hurt him to know that Dr Fillgrave was attending the squire for a little incipient gout, and that dear Nina was in measles under those unloving hands.

And then, also, the old-fashioned phaeton, of old-fashioned old Dr Century was seen to rumble up to the big house, and it became known that Lady Arabella was not very well. "Not very well," when pronounced in a low, grave voice about Lady Arabella, always meant something serious. And, in this case, something serious was meant. Lady Arabella was not only ill, but frightened. It appeared, even to her, that Dr Fillgrave himself hardly knew what he was about, that he was not so sure in his opinion, so confident in himself, as Dr Thorne used to be. How should he be, seeing that Dr Thorne had medically had Lady Arabella in his hands for the last ten years?

If sitting with dignity in his hired carriage, and stepping with authority up the big front steps, would have done anything, Dr Fillgrave might have done much. Lady Arabella was greatly taken with his looks when he first came to her, and it was only when she by degrees perceived that the symptoms, which she knew so well, did not yield to him that she began to doubt those looks.

After a while Dr Fillgrave himself suggested Dr Century. "Not that I fear anything, Lady Arabella," said he,—lying hugely, for he did fear; fear both for himself and for her. "But Dr Century has great experience, and in such a matter, when the interests are so important, one cannot be too safe."

So Dr Century came and toddled slowly into her ladyship's room. He did not say much; he left the talking to his learned brother, who certainly was able to do that part of the business. But Dr Century, though he said very little, looked very grave, and by no means quieted Lady Arabella's mind. She, as she saw the two putting their heads together, already had misgivings that she had done wrong. She knew that she could not be safe without Dr Thorne at her bedside, and she already felt that she had exercised a most injudicious courage in driving him away.

"Well, doctor?" said she, as soon as Dr Century had toddled downstairs to see the squire.

"Oh! we shall be all right, Lady Arabella; all right, very soon. But we must be careful, very careful; I am glad I've had Century here, very; but there's nothing to alter; little or nothing."

There were but few words spoken between Dr Century and the squire; but few as they were, they frightened Mr Gresham. When Dr Fillgrave came down the grand stairs, a servant waited at the bottom to ask him also to go to the squire. Now there never had been much cordiality between the squire and Dr Fillgrave, though Mr Gresham had consented to take a preventative pill from his hands, and the little man therefore swelled himself out somewhat more than ordinarily as he followed the servant.

"Dr Fillgrave," said the squire, at once beginning the conversation, "Lady Arabella, is, I fear, in danger?"

"Well, no; I hope not in danger, Mr Gresham. I certainly believe I may be justified in expressing a hope that she is not in danger. Her state is, no doubt, rather serious—rather serious—as Dr Century has probably told you;" and Dr Fillgrave made a bow to the old man, who sat quiet in one of the dining-room arm-chairs.

"Well, doctor," said the squire, "I have not any grounds on which to doubt your judgement."

Dr Fillgrave bowed, but with the stiffest, slightest inclination which a head could possibly make. He rather thought that Mr Gresham had no ground for doubting his judgement.

"Nor do I."

The doctor bowed, and a little, a very little less stiffly.

"But, doctor, I think that something ought to be done."

The doctor this time did his bowing merely with his eyes and mouth. The former he closed for a moment, the latter he pressed; and then decorously rubbed his hands one over the other.

"I am afraid, Dr Fillgrave, that you and my friend Thorne are not the best friends in the world."

"No, Mr Gresham, no; I may go so far as to say we are not."

"Well, I am sorry for it—"

"Perhaps, Mr Gresham, we need hardly discuss it; but there have been circumstances—"

"I am not going to discuss anything, Dr Fillgrave; I say I am sorry for it, because I believe that prudence will imperatively require Lady Arabella to have Doctor Thorne back again. Now, if you would not object to meet him—"

"Mr Gresham, I beg pardon; I beg pardon, indeed; but you must really excuse me. Doctor Thorne has, in my estimation—"

"But, Doctor Fillgrave—"

"Mr Gresham, you really must excuse me; you really must, indeed. Anything else that I could do for Lady Arabella, I should be most happy to do; but after what has passed, I cannot meet Doctor Thorne; I really cannot. You must not ask me to do so; Mr Gresham. And, Mr Gresham," continued the doctor, "I did understand from Lady Arabella that his— that is, Dr Thorne's—conduct to her ladyship had been such—so very outrageous, I may say, that—that—that—of course, Mr Gresham, you know best; but I did think that Lady Arabella herself was quite unwilling to see Doctor Thorne again;" and Dr Fillgrave looked very big, and very dignified, and very exclusive.

The squire did not ask again. He had no warrant for supposing that Lady Arabella would receive Dr Thorne if he did come; and he saw that it was useless to attempt to overcome the rancour of a man so pig-headed as the little Galen now before him. Other propositions were then broached, and it was at last decided that assistance should be sought for from London, in the person of the great Sir Omicron Pie.

Sir Omicron came, and Drs Fillgrave and Century were there to meet him. When they all assembled in Lady Arabella's room, the poor woman's heart almost sank within her,— as well it might, at such a sight. If she could only reconcile it with her honour, her consistency, with her high de Courcy principles, to send once more for Dr Thorne. Oh, Frank! Frank! to what misery your disobedience brought your mother!

Sir Omicron and the lesser provincial lights had their consultation, and the lesser lights went their way to Barchester and Silverbridge, leaving Sir Omicron to enjoy the hospitality of Greshamsbury.

"You should have Thorne back here, Mr Gresham," said Sir Omicron, almost in a whisper, when they were quite alone. "Doctor Fillgrave is a very good man, and so is Dr Century; very good, I am sure. But Thorne has known her ladyship so long." And then, on the following morning, Sir Omicron also went his way.

And then there was a scene between the squire and her ladyship. Lady Arabella had given herself credit for great good generalship when she found that the squire had been induced to take that pill. We have all heard of the little end of the wedge, and we have most of us an idea that the little end is the difficulty. That pill had been the little end of Lady Arabella's wedge. Up to that period she had been struggling in vain to make a severance between her husband and her enemy. That pill should do the business. She well knew how to make the most of it; to have it published in Greshamsbury that the squire had put his gouty toe into Dr Fillgrave's hands; how to let it be known—especially at that humble house in the corner of the street—that Fillgrave's prescriptions now ran current through the whole establishment. Dr Thorne did hear of it, and did suffer. He had been a true friend to the squire, and he thought the squire should have stood to him more staunchly.

"After all," said he himself, "perhaps it's as well—perhaps it will be best that I should leave this place altogether." And then he thought of Sir Roger and his will, and of Mary and her lover. And then of Mary's birth, and of his own theoretical doctrines as to pure blood. And so his troubles multiplied, and he saw no present daylight through them.

Such had been the way in which Lady Arabella had got in the little end of the wedge. And she would have triumphed joyfully had not her increased doubts and fears as to herself then come in to check her triumph and destroy her joy. She had not yet confessed to any one her secret regret for the friend she had driven away. She hardly yet acknowledged to herself that she did regret him; but she was uneasy, frightened, and in low spirits.

"My dear," said the squire, sitting down by her bedside, "I want to tell you what Sir Omicron said as he went away."

"Well?" said her ladyship, sitting up and looking frightened.

"I don't know how you may take it, Bell; but I think it very good news:" the squire never called his wife Bell, except when he wanted her to be on particularly good terms with him.

"Well?" said she again. She was not over-anxious to be gracious, and did not reciprocate his familiarity.

"Sir Omicron says that you should have Thorne back again, and upon my honour, I cannot but agree with him. Now, Thorne is a clever man, a very clever man; nobody denies that; and then, you know—"

"Why did not Sir Omicron say that to me?" said her ladyship, sharply, all her disposition in Dr Thorne's favour becoming wonderfully damped by her husband's advocacy.

"I suppose he thought it better to say it to me," said the squire, rather curtly.

"He should have spoken to myself," said Lady Arabella, who, though she did not absolutely doubt her husband's word, gave him credit for having induced and led on Sir Omicron to the uttering of this opinion. "Doctor Thorne has behaved to me in so gross, so indecent a manner! And then, as I understand, he is absolutely encouraging that girl—"

"Now, Bell, you are quite wrong—"

"Of course I am; I always am quite wrong."

"Quite wrong in mixing up two things; Doctor Thorne as an acquaintance, and Dr Thorne as a doctor."

"It is dreadful to have him here, even standing in the room with me. How can one talk to one's doctor openly and confidentially when one looks upon him as one's worst enemy?" And Lady Arabella, softening, almost melted into tears.

"My dear, you cannot wonder that I should be anxious for you."

Lady Arabella gave a little snuffle, which might be taken as a not very eloquent expression of thanks for the squire's solicitude, or as an ironical jeer at his want of sincerity.

"And, therefore, I have not lost a moment in telling you what Sir Omicron said. 'You should have Thorne back here;' those were his very words. You can think it over, my dear. And remember this, Bell; if he is to do any good no time should be lost."

And then the squire left the room, and Lady Arabella remained alone, perplexed by many doubts.

CHAPTER XXXII

MR ORIEL

I must now, shortly—as shortly as it is in my power to do it—introduce a new character to my reader. Mention has been made of the rectory of Greshamsbury; but, hitherto, no opportunity has offered itself for the Rev Caleb Oriel to come upon the boards.

Mr Oriel was a man of family and fortune, who, having gone to Oxford with the usual views of such men, had become inoculated there with very High-Church principles, and had gone into orders influenced by a feeling of enthusiastic love for the priesthood. He was by no means an ascetic—such men, indeed, seldom are—nor was he a devotee. He was a man well able, and certainly willing, to do the work of a parish clergyman; and when he became one, he was efficacious in his profession. But it may perhaps be said of him, without speaking slanderously, that his original calling, as a young man, was rather to the outward and visible signs of religion than to its inward and spiritual graces.

He delighted in lecterns and credence-tables, in services at dark hours of winter mornings when no one would attend, in high waistcoats and narrow white neckties, in chanted services and intoned prayers, and in all the paraphernalia of Anglican formalities which have given such offence to those of our brethren who live in daily fear of the scarlet lady. Many of his friends declared that Mr Oriel would sooner or later deliver himself over body and soul to that lady; but there was no need to fear for him: for though sufficiently enthusiastic to get out of bed at five A.M. on winter mornings—he did so, at least, all through his first winter at Greshamsbury—he was not made of that stuff which is necessary for a staunch, burning, self-denying convert. It was not in him to change his very sleek black coat for a Capuchin's filthy cassock, nor his pleasant parsonage for some dirty hole in Rome. And it was better so both for him and others. There are but few, very few, to whom it is given to be a Huss, a Wickliffe, or a Luther; and a man gains but little by being a false Huss, or a false Luther,—and his neighbours gain less.

But certain lengths in self-privation Mr Oriel did go; at any rate, for some time. He eschewed matrimony, imagining that it became him as a priest to do so. He fasted rigorously on Fridays; and the neighbours declared that he scourged himself.

Mr Oriel was, as it has been said, a man of fortune; that is to say, when he came of age he was master of thirty thousand pounds. When he took it into his head to go into the Church, his friends bought for him the next presentation to the living at Greshamsbury; and, a year after his ordination, the living falling in, Mr Oriel brought himself and his sister to the rectory.

Mr Oriel soon became popular. He was a dark-haired, good-looking man, of polished manners, agreeable in society, not given to monkish austerities—except in the matter of Fridays—nor yet to the Low-Church severity of demeanour. He was thoroughly a gentleman, good-humoured, inoffensive, and sociable. But he had one fault: he was not a marrying man.

On this ground there was a feeling against him so strong as almost at one time to throw him into serious danger. It was not only that he should be sworn against matrimony in his individual self—he whom fate had made so able to sustain the weight of a wife and family; but what an example he was setting! If other clergymen all around should declare against wives and families, what was to become of the country? What was to be done in the rural districts? The religious observances, as regards women, of a Brigham Young were hardly so bad as this!

There were around Greshamsbury very many unmarried ladies—I believe there generally are so round most such villages. From the great house he did not receive much annoyance. Beatrice was then only just on the verge of being brought out, and was not perhaps inclined to think very much of a young clergyman; and Augusta certainly intended to fly at higher game. But there were the Miss Athelings, the daughters of a neighbouring clergyman, who were ready to go all lengths with him in High-Church matters, except as that one tremendously papal step of celibacy; and the two Miss Hesterwells, of Hesterwell Park, the younger of whom boldly declared her purpose of civilising the savage; and Mrs Opie Green, a very pretty widow, with a very pretty jointure, who lived in a very pretty house about a mile from Greshamsbury, and who declared her opinion that Mr Oriel was quite right in his view of a clergyman's position. How could a woman, situated as she was, have the comfort of a clergyman's attention if he were to be regarded just as any other man? She could now know in what light to regard Mr Oriel, and would be able without scruple to avail herself of his zeal. So she did avail herself of his zeal,—and that without any scruple.

And then there was Miss Gushing,—a young thing. Miss Gushing had a great advantage over the other competitors for the civilisation of Mr Oriel, namely, in this—that she was able to attend his morning services. If Mr Oriel was to be reached in any way, it was probable that he might be reached in this way. If anything could civilise him, this would do it. Therefore, the young thing, through all one long, tedious winter, tore herself from her warm bed, and was to be seen—no, not seen, but heard—entering Mr Oriel's church at six o'clock. With indefatigable assiduity the responses were made, uttered from under a close bonnet, and out of a dark corner, in an enthusiastically feminine voice, through the whole winter.

Nor did Miss Gushing altogether fail in her object. When a clergyman's daily audience consists of but one person, and that person is a young lady, it is hardly possible that he should not become personally intimate with her; hardly possible that he should not be in some measure grateful. Miss Gushing's responses came from her with such fervour, and she begged for ghostly advice with such eager longing to have her scruples satisfied, that Mr Oriel had nothing for it but to give way to a certain amount of civilisation.

By degrees it came to pass that Miss Gushing could never get her final prayer said, her shawl and boa adjusted, and stow away her nice new Prayer-Book with the red letters inside, and the cross on the back, till Mr Oriel had been into his vestry and got rid of his surplice. And then they met at the church-porch, and naturally walked together till Mr Oriel's cruel gateway separated them. The young thing did sometimes think that, as the parson's civilisation progressed, he might have taken the trouble to walk with her as far as Mr Yates Umbleby's hall door; but she had hope to sustain her, and a firm resolve to merit success, even though she might not attain it.

"Is it not ten thousand pities," she once said to him, "that none here should avail themselves of the inestimable privilege which your coming has conferred upon us? Oh, Mr Oriel, I do so wonder at it! To me it is so delightful! The morning service in the dark church is so beautiful, so touching!"

"I suppose they think it is a bore getting up so early," said Mr Oriel.

"Ah, a bore!" said Miss Gushing, in an enthusiastic tone of depreciation. "How insensate they must be! To me it gives a new charm to life. It quiets one for the day; makes one so much fitter for one's daily trials and daily troubles. Does it not, Mr Oriel?"

"I look upon morning prayer as an imperative duty, certainly."

"Oh, certainly, a most imperative duty; but so delicious at the same time. I spoke to Mrs Umbleby about it, but she said she could not leave the children."

"No: I dare say not," said Mr Oriel.

"And Mr Umbleby said his business kept him up so late at night."

"Very probably. I hardly expect the attendance of men of business."

"But the servants might come, mightn't they, Mr Oriel?"

"I fear that servants seldom can have time for daily prayers in church."

"Oh, ah, no; perhaps not." And then Miss Gushing began to bethink herself of whom should be composed the congregation which it must be presumed that Mr Oriel wished to see around him. But on this matter he did not enlighten her.

Then Miss Gushing took to fasting on Fridays, and made some futile attempts to induce her priest to give her the comfort of confessional absolution. But, unfortunately, the zeal of the master waxed cool as that of the pupil waxed hot; and, at last, when the young thing returned to Greshamsbury from an autumn excursion which she had made with Mrs Umbleby to Weston-super-Mare, she found that the delicious morning services had died a natural death. Miss Gushing did not on that account give up the game, but she was bound to fight with no particular advantage in her favour.

Miss Oriel, though a good Churchwoman, was by no means a convert to her brother's extremist views, and perhaps gave but scanty credit to the Gushings, Athelings, and Opie Greens for the sincerity of their religion. But, nevertheless, she and her brother were staunch friends; and she still hoped to see the day when he might be induced to think that an English parson might get through his parish work with the assistance of a wife better than he could do without such feminine encumbrance. The girl whom she selected for his bride was not the young thing, but Beatrice Gresham.

And at last it seemed probable to Mr Oriel's nearest friends that he was in a fair way to be overcome. Not that he had begun to make love to Beatrice, or committed himself by the utterance of any opinion as to the propriety of clerical marriages; but he daily became looser about his peculiar tenets, raved less immoderately than heretofore as to the atrocity of the Greshamsbury church pews, and was observed to take some opportunities of conversing alone with Beatrice. Beatrice had always denied the imputation—this had usually been made by Mary in their happy days—with vehement asseverations of anger; and Miss Gushing had tittered, and expressed herself as supposing that great people's daughters might be as barefaced as they pleased.

All this had happened previous to the great Greshamsbury feud. Mr Oriel gradually got himself into a way of sauntering up to the great house, sauntering into the drawing-room for the purpose, as I am sure he thought, of talking to Lady Arabella, and then of sauntering home again, having usually found an opportunity for saying a few words to Beatrice during the visit. This went on all through the feud up to the period of Lady Arabella's illness; and then one morning, about a month before the date fixed for Frank's return, Mr Oriel found himself engaged to Miss Beatrice Gresham.

From the day that Miss Gushing heard of it—which was not however for some considerable time after this—she became an Independent Methodist. She could no longer, she said at first, have any faith in any religion; and for an hour or so she was almost tempted to swear that she could no longer have any faith in any man. She had nearly completed a worked cover for a credence-table when the news reached her, as to which, in the young enthusiasm of her heart, she had not been able to remain silent; it had already been promised to Mr Oriel; that promise she swore should not be kept. He was an apostate, she said, from his principles; an utter pervert; a false, designing man, with whom she would never have trusted herself alone on dark mornings had she known that he had such grovelling, worldly inclinations. So Miss Gushing became an Independent Methodist; the credence-table covering was cut up into slippers for the preacher's feet; and the young thing herself, more happy in this direction than she had been in the other, became the arbiter of that preacher's domestic happiness.

But this little history of Miss Gushing's future life is premature. Mr Oriel became engaged demurely, nay, almost silently, to Beatrice, and no one out of their own immediate families was at the time informed of the matter. It was arranged very differently from those two other matches—embryo, or not embryo, those, namely, of Augusta with Mr Moffat, and Frank with Mary Thorne. All Barsetshire had heard of them; but that of Beatrice and Mr Oriel was managed in a much more private manner.

"I do think you are a happy girl," said Patience to her one morning.

"Indeed I am."

"He is so good. You don't know how good he is as yet; he never thinks of himself, and thinks so much of those he loves."

Beatrice took her friend's hand in her own and kissed it. She was full of joy. When a girl is about to be married, when she may lawfully talk of her love, there is no music in her ears so sweet as the praises of her lover.

"I made up my mind from the first that he should marry you."

"Nonsense, Patience."

"I did, indeed. I made up my mind that he should marry; and there were only two to choose from."

"Me and Miss Gushing," said Beatrice, laughing.

"No; not exactly Miss Gushing. I had not many fears for Caleb there."

"I declare she's very pretty," said Beatrice, who could afford to be good-natured. Now Miss Gushing certainly was pretty; and would have been very pretty had her nose not turned up so much, and could she have parted her hair in the centre.

"Well, I am very glad you chose me;—if it was you who chose," said Beatrice, modestly; having, however, in her own mind a strong opinion that Mr Oriel had chosen for himself, and had never had any doubt in the matter. "And who was the other?"

"Can't you guess?"

"I won't guess any more; perhaps Mrs Green."

"Oh, no; certainly not a widow. I don't like widows marrying. But of course you could guess if you would; of course it was Mary Thorne. But I soon saw Mary would not do, for two reasons; Caleb would never have liked her well enough nor would she ever have liked him."

"Not like him! oh I hope she will; I do so love Mary Thorne."

"So do I, dearly; and so does Caleb; but he could never have loved her as he loves you."

"But, Patience, have you told Mary?"

"No, I have told no one, and shall not without your leave."

"Ah, you must tell her. Tell it her with my best, and kindest, warmest love. Tell her how happy I am, and how I long to talk to her. Tell that I will have her for my bridesmaid. Oh! I do hope that before that all this horrid quarrel will be settled."

Patience undertook the commission, and did tell Mary; did give her also the message which Beatrice had sent. And Mary was rejoiced to hear it; for though, as Patience had said of her, she had never herself felt any inclination to fall in love with Mr Oriel, she believed him to be one in whose hands her friend's happiness would be secure. Then, by degrees, the conversation changed from the loves of Mr Oriel and Beatrice to the troubles of Frank Gresham and herself.

"She says, that let what will happen you shall be one of her bridesmaids."

"Ah, yes, dear Trichy! that was settled between us in auld lang syne; but those settlements are all unsettled now, must all be broken. No, I cannot be her bridesmaid; but I shall yet hope to see her once before her marriage."

"And why not be her bridesmaid? Lady Arabella will hardly object to that."

"Lady Arabella!" said Mary, curling her lip with deep scorn. "I do not care that for Lady Arabella," and she let her silver thimble fall from her fingers on to the table. "If Beatrice invited me to her wedding, she might manage as to that; I should ask no question as to Lady Arabella."

"Then why not come to it?"

She remained silent for a while, and then boldly answered. "Though I do not care for Lady Arabella, I do care for Mr Gresham:—and I do care for his son."

"But the squire always loved you."

"Yes, and therefore I will not be there to vex his sight. I will tell you the truth, Patience. I can never be in that house again till Frank Gresham is a married man, or till I am about to be a married woman. I do not think they have treated me well, but I will not treat them ill."

"I am sure you will not do that," said Miss Oriel.

"I will endeavour not to do so; and, therefore, will go to none of their fêtes! No, Patience." And then she turned her head to the arm of the sofa, and silently, without audible sobs, hiding her face, she endeavoured to get rid of her tears unseen. For one moment she had all but resolved to pour out the whole truth of her love into her friend's ears; but suddenly she changed her mind. Why should she talk of her own unhappiness? Why should she speak of her own love when she was fully determined not to speak of Frank's promises.

"Mary, dear Mary."

"Anything but pity, Patience; anything but that," said she, convulsively, swallowing down her sobs, and rubbing away her tears. "I cannot bear that. Tell Beatrice from me, that I wish her every happiness; and, with such a husband, I am sure she will be happy. I wish her every joy; give her my kindest love; but tell her I cannot be at her marriage. Oh, I should so like to see her; not there, you know, but here, in my own room, where I still have liberty to speak."

"But why should you decide now? She is not to be married yet, you know."

"Now, or this day twelvemonth, can make no difference. I will not go into that house again, unless—but never mind; I will not go into it all; never, never again. If I could forgive her for myself, I could not forgive her for my uncle. But tell me, Patience, might not Beatrice now come here? It is so dreadful to see her every Sunday in church and never to speak to her, never to kiss her. She seems to look away from me as though she too had chosen to quarrel with me."

Miss Oriel promised to do her best. She could not imagine, she said, that such a visit could be objected to on such an occasion. She would not advise Beatrice to come without telling her mother; but she could not think that Lady Arabella would be so cruel as to make any objection, knowing, as she could not but know, that her daughter, when married, would be at liberty to choose her own friends.

"Good-bye, Mary," said Patience. "I wish I knew how to say more to comfort you."

"Oh, comfort! I don't want comfort. I want to be let alone."

"That's just it: you are so ferocious in your scorn, so unbending, so determined to take all the punishment that comes in your way."

"What I do take, I'll take without complaint," said Mary; and then they kissed each other and parted.

CHAPTER XXXIII

A MORNING VISIT

It must be remembered that Mary, among her miseries, had to suffer this: that since Frank's departure, now nearly twelve months ago, she had not heard a word about him; or rather, she had only heard that he was very much in love with some lady in London. This news reached her in a manner so circuitous, and from such a doubtful source; it seemed to her to savour so strongly of Lady Arabella's precautions, that she attributed it at once to malice, and blew it to the winds. It might not improbably be the case that Frank was untrue to her; but she would not take it for granted because she was now told so. It was more than probable that he should amuse himself with some one; flirting was his prevailing sin; and if he did flirt, the most would of course be made of it.

But she found it to be very desolate to be thus left alone without a word of comfort or a word of love; without being able to speak to any one of what filled her heart; doubting, nay, more than doubting, being all but sure that her passion must terminate in misery. Why had she not obeyed her conscience and her better instinct in that moment when the necessity for deciding had come upon her? Why had she allowed him to understand that he was master of her heart? Did she not know that there was everything against such a marriage as that which he proposed? Had she not done wrong, very wrong, even to think of it? Had she not sinned deeply, against Mr Gresham, who had ever been so kind to her? Could she hope, was it possible, that a boy like Frank should be true to his first love? And, if he were true, if he were ready to go to the altar with her to-morrow, ought she to allow him to degrade himself by such a marriage?

There was, alas! some truth about the London lady. Frank had taken his degree, as arranged, and had then gone abroad for the winter, doing the fashionable things, going up the Nile, crossing over to Mount Sinai, thence over the long desert to Jerusalem, and home by Damascus, Beyrout, and Constantinople, bringing back a long beard, a red cap, and a chibook, just as our fathers used to go through Italy and Switzerland, and our grandfathers to spend a season in Paris. He had then remained for a couple of months in London, going through all the society which the de Courcys were able to open to him. And it was true that a certain belle of the season, of that season and some others, had been captivated—for the tenth time—by the silken sheen of his long beard. Frank had probably been more demonstrative, perhaps even more susceptible, than he should have been; and hence the rumour, which had all too willingly been forwarded to Greshamsbury.

But young Gresham had also met another lady in London, namely Miss Dunstable. Mary would indeed have been grateful to Miss Dunstable, could she have known all that lady did for her. Frank's love was never allowed to flag. When he spoke of the difficulties in his way, she twitted him by being overcome by straws; and told him that no one was worth having who was afraid of every lion that he met in his path. When he spoke of money, she bade him earn it; and always ended by offering to smooth for him any real difficulty which want of means might put in his way.

"No," Frank used to say to himself, when these offers were made, "I never intended to take her and her money together; and, therefore, I certainly will never take the money alone."

A day or two after Miss Oriel's visit, Mary received the following note from Beatrice.

DEAREST, DEAREST MARY, I shall be so happy to see you, and will come to-morrow at twelve. I have asked mamma, and she says that, for once, she has no objection. You know it is not my fault that I have never been with you; don't you? Frank comes home on the 12th. Mr Oriel wants the wedding to be on the 1st of September; but that seems to be so very, very soon; doesn't it? However, mamma and papa are all on his side. I won't write about this, though, for we shall have such a delicious talk. Oh, Mary! I have been so un-happy without you.

> Ever your own affectionate,
> TRICHY

Monday.

Though Mary was delighted at the idea of once more having her friend in her arms, there was, nevertheless, something in this letter which oppressed her. She could not put up with the idea that Beatrice should have permission given to come to her—just for once. She hardly wished to be seen by permission. Nevertheless, she did not refuse the proffered visit, and the first sight of Beatrice's face, the first touch of the first embrace, dissipated for the moment all her anger.

And then Beatrice fully enjoyed the delicious talk which she had promised herself. Mary let her have her way, and for two hours all the delights and all the duties, all the comforts and all the responsibilities of a parson's wife were discussed with almost equal ardour on both sides. The duties and responsibilities were not exactly those which too often fall to the lot of the mistress of an English vicarage. Beatrice was not doomed to make her husband comfortable, to educate her children, dress herself like a lady, and ex-ercise open-handed charity on an income of two hundred pounds a year. Her duties and responsibilities would have to spread themselves over seven or eight times that amount of worldly burden. Living also close to Greshamsbury, and not far from Courcy Castle, she would have the full advantages and all the privileges of county society. In fact, it was all *couleur de rose*, and so she chatted deliciously with her friend.

But it was impossible that they should separate without something having been said as to Mary's own lot. It would, perhaps, have been better that they should do so; but this was hardly within the compass of human nature.

"And Mary, you know, I shall be able to see you as often as I like;—you and Dr Thorne, too, when I have a house of my own."

Mary said nothing, but essayed to smile. It was but a ghastly attempt.

"You know how happy that will make me," continued Beatrice. "Of course mamma won't expect me to be led by her then: if he likes it, there can be no objection; and he will like it, you may be sure of that."

"You are very kind, Trichy," said Mary; but she spoke in a tone very different from that she would have used eighteen months ago.

"Why, what is the matter, Mary? Shan't you be glad to come to see us?"

"I do not know, dearest; that must depend on circumstances. To see you, you yourself, your own dear, sweet, loving face must always be pleasant to me."

"And shan't you be glad to see him?"

"Yes, certainly, if he loves you."

"Of course he loves me."

"All that alone would be pleasant enough, Trichy. But what if there should be circumstances which should still make us enemies; should make your friends and my friends—friend, I should say, for I have only one—should make them opposed to each other?"

"Circumstances! What circumstances?"

"You are going to be married, Trichy, to the man you love; are you not?"

"Indeed, I am!"

"And it is not pleasant? is it not a happy feeling?"

"Pleasant! happy! yes, very pleasant; very happy. But, Mary, I am not at all in such a hurry as he is," said Beatrice, naturally thinking of her own little affairs.

"And, suppose I should wish to be married to the man that I love?" Mary said this slowly and gravely, and as she spoke she looked her friend full in the face.

Beatrice was somewhat astonished, and for the moment hardly understood. "I am sure I hope you will, some day."

"No, Trichy; no, you hope the other way. I love your brother; I love Frank Gresham; I love him quite as well, quite as warmly, as you love Caleb Oriel."

"Do you?" said Beatrice, staring with all her eyes, and giving one long sigh, as this new subject for sorrow was so distinctly put before her.

"It that so odd?" said Mary. "You love Mr Oriel, though you have been intimate with him hardly more than two years. Is it so odd that I should love your brother, whom I have known almost all my life?"

"But, Mary, I thought it was always understood between us that—that—I mean that you were not to care about him; not in the way of loving him, you know—I thought you always said so—I have always told mamma so as if it came from yourself."

"Beatrice, do not tell anything to Lady Arabella as though it came from me; I do not want anything to be told to her, either of me or from me. Say what you like to me yourself; whatever you say will not anger me. Indeed, I know what you would say—and yet I love you. Oh, I love you, Trichy—Trichy, I do love you so much! Don't turn away from me!"

There was such a mixture in Mary's manner of tenderness and almost ferocity, that poor Beatrice could hardly follow her. "Turn away from you, Mary! no never; but this does make me unhappy."

"It is better that you should know it all, and then you will not be led into fighting my battles again. You cannot fight them so that I should win; I do love your brother; love him truly, fondly, tenderly. I would wish to have him for my husband as you wish to have Mr Oriel."

"But, Mary, you cannot marry him!"

"Why not?" said she, in a loud voice. "Why can I not marry him? If the priest says a blessing over us, shall we not be married as well as you and your husband?"

"But you know he cannot marry unless his wife shall have money."

"Money—money; and he is to sell himself for money? Oh, Trichy! do not you talk about money. It is horrible. But, Trichy, I will grant it—I cannot marry him; but still, I love him. He has a name, a place in the world, and fortune, family, high blood, position, everything. He has all this, and I have nothing. Of course I cannot marry him. But yet I do love him."

"Are you engaged to him, Mary?"

"He is not engaged to me; but I am to him."

"Oh, Mary, that is impossible!"

"It is not impossible: it is the case—I am pledged to him; but he is not pledged to me."

"But, Mary, don't look at me in that way. I do not quite understand you. What is the good of your being engaged if you cannot marry him?"

"Good! there is no good. But can I help it, if I love him? Can I make myself not love him by just wishing it? Oh, I would do it if I could. But now you will understand why I shake my head when you talk of my coming to your house. Your ways and my ways must be different."

Beatrice was startled, and, for a time, silenced. What Mary said of the difference of their ways was quite true. Beatrice had dearly loved her friend, and had thought of her with affection through all this long period in which they had been separated; but she had given her love and her thoughts on the understanding, as it were, that they were in unison as to the impropriety of Frank's conduct.

She had always spoken, with a grave face, of Frank and his love as of a great misfortune, even to Mary herself; and her pity for Mary had been founded on the conviction of her innocence. Now all those ideas had to be altered. Mary owned her fault, confessed herself to be guilty of all that Lady Arabella so frequently laid to her charge, and confessed herself anxious to commit every crime as to which Beatrice had been ever so ready to defend her.

Had Beatrice up to this dreamed that Mary was in love with Frank, she would doubtless have sympathised with her more or less, sooner or later. As it was, is was beyond all doubt that she would soon sympathise with her. But, at the moment, the suddenness of the declaration seemed to harden her heart, and she forgot, as it were, to speak tenderly to her friend.

She was silent, therefore, and dismayed; and looked as though she thought that her ways and Mary's ways must be different.

Mary saw all that was passing in the other's mind: no, not all; all the hostility, the disappointment, the disapproval, the unhappiness, she did see; but not the under-current of love, which was strong enough to well up and drown all these, if only time could be allowed for it to do so.

"I am glad I have told you," said Mary, curbing herself, "for deceit and hypocrisy are detestable."

"It was a misunderstanding, not deceit," said Beatrice.

"Well, now we understand each other; now you know that I have a heart within me, which like those of some others has not always been under my own control. Lady Arabella believes that I am intriguing to be the mistress of Greshamsbury. You, at any rate, will not think that of me. If it could be discovered to-morrow that Frank were not the heir, I might have some chance of happiness."

"But, Mary—"

"Well?"

"You say you love him."

"Yes; I do say so."

"But if he does not love you, will you cease to do so?"

"If I have a fever, I will get rid of it if I can; in such case I must do so, or die."

"I fear," continued Beatrice, "you hardly know, perhaps do not think, what is Frank's real character. He is not made to settle down early in life; even now, I believe he is attached to some lady in London, whom, of course, he cannot marry."

Beatrice said this in perfect trueness of heart. She had heard of Frank's new love-affair, and believing what she had heard, thought it best to tell the truth. But the information was not of a kind to quiet Mary's spirit.

"Very well," said she, "let it be so. I have nothing to say against it."

"But are you not preparing wretchedness and unhappiness for yourself?"

"Very likely."

"Oh, Mary, do not be so cold with me! you know how delighted I should be to have you for a sister-in-law, if only it were possible."

"Yes, Trichy; but it is impossible, is it not? Impossible that Francis Gresham of Gresh-amsbury should disgrace himself by marrying such a poor creature as I am. Of course, I know it; of course, I am prepared for unhappiness and misery. He can amuse himself as he likes with me or others—with anybody. It is his privilege. It is quite enough to say that he is not made for settling down. I know my own position;—and yet I love him."

"But, Mary, has he asked you to be his wife? If so—"

"You ask home-questions, Beatrice. Let me ask you one; has he ever told you that he has done so?"

At this moment Beatrice was not disposed to repeat all that Frank had said. A year ago, before he went away, he had told his sister a score of times that he meant to marry Mary Thorne if she would have him; but Beatrice now looked on all that as idle, boyish vapouring. The pity was, that Mary should have looked on it differently.

"We will each keep our secret," said Mary. "Only remember this: should Frank marry to-morrow, I shall have no ground for blaming him. He is free as far I as am concerned. He can take the London lady if he likes. You may tell him so from me. But, Trichy, what else I have told you, I have told you only."

"Oh, yes!" said Beatrice, sadly; "I shall say nothing of it to anybody. It is very sad, very, very; I was so happy when I came here, and now I am so wretched." This was the end of that delicious talk to which she had looked forward with so much eagerness.

"Don't be wretched about me, dearest; I shall get through it. I sometimes think I was born to be unhappy, and that unhappiness agrees with me best. Kiss me now, Trichy, and don't be wretched any more. You owe it to Mr Oriel to be as happy as the day is long."

And then they parted.

Beatrice, as she went out, saw Dr Thorne in his little shop on the right-hand side of the passage, deeply engaged in some derogatory branch of an apothecary's mechanical trade; mixing a dose, perhaps, for a little child. She would have passed him without speaking if she could have been sure of doing so without notice, for her heart was full, and her eyes were red with tears; but it was so long since she had been in his house that she was more than ordinarily anxious not to appear uncourteous or unkind to him.

"Good morning, doctor," she said, changing her countenance as best she might, and at-tempting a smile.

"Ah, my fairy!" said he, leaving his villainous compounds, and coming out to her; "and you, too, are about to become a steady old lady."

"Indeed, I am not, doctor; I don't mean to be either steady or old for the next ten years. But who has told you? I suppose Mary has been a traitor."

"Well, I will confess, Mary was the traitor. But hadn't I a right to be told, seeing how often I have brought you sugar-plums in my pocket? But I wish you joy with all my heart,—with all my heart. Oriel is an excellent, good fellow."

"Is he not, doctor?"

"An excellent, good fellow. I never heard but of one fault that he had."

"What was that one fault, Doctor Thorne?"

"He thought that clergymen should not marry. But you have cured that, and now he's perfect."

"Thank you, doctor. I declare that you say the prettiest things of all my friends."

"And none of your friends wish prettier things for you. I do congratulate you, Beatrice, and hope you may be happy with the man you have chosen;" and taking both her hands in his, he pressed them warmly, and bade God bless her.

"Oh, doctor! I do so hope the time will come when we shall all be friends again."

"I hope it as well, my dear. But let it come, or let it not come, my regard for you will be the same:" and then she parted from him also, and went her way.

Nothing was spoken of that evening between Dr Thorne and his niece excepting Beatrice's future happiness; nothing, at least, having reference to what had passed that morning. But on the following morning circumstances led to Frank Gresham's name being mentioned.

At the usual breakfast-hour the doctor entered the parlour with a harassed face. He had an open letter in his hand, and it was at once clear to Mary that he was going to speak on some subject that vexed him.

"That unfortunate fellow is again in trouble. Here is a letter from Greyson." Greyson was a London apothecary, who had been appointed as medical attendant to Sir Louis Scatcherd, and whose real business consisted in keeping a watch on the baronet, and reporting to Dr Thorne when anything was very much amiss. "Here is a letter from Greyson; he has been drunk for the last three days, and is now laid up in a terribly nervous state."

"You won't go up to town again; will you, uncle?"

"I hardly know what to do. No, I think not. He talks of coming down here to Greshamsbury."

"Who, Sir Louis?"

"Yes, Sir Louis. Greyson says that he will be down as soon as he can get out of his room."

"What! to this house?"

"What other house can he come to?"

"Oh, uncle! I hope not. Pray, pray do not let him come here."

"I cannot prevent it, my dear. I cannot shut my door on him."

They sat down to breakfast, and Mary gave him his tea in silence. "I am going over to Boxall Hill before dinner," said he. "Have you any message to send to Lady Scatcherd?"

"Message! no, I have no message; not especially: give her my love, of course," she said listlessly. And then, as though a thought had suddenly struck her, she spoke with more energy. "But, couldn't I go to Boxall Hill again? I should be so delighted."

"What! to run away from Sir Louis? No, dearest, we will have no more running away. He will probably also go to Boxall Hill, and he could annoy you much more there than he can here."

"But, uncle, Mr Gresham will be home on the 12th," she said, blushing.

"What! Frank?"

"Yes. Beatrice said he was to be here on the 12th."

"And would you run away from him too, Mary?"

"I do not know: I do not know what to do."

"No; we will have no more running away: I am sorry that you ever did so. It was my fault, altogether my fault; but it was foolish."

"Uncle, I am not happy here." As she said this, she put down the cup which she had held, and, leaning her elbows on the table, rested her forehead on her hands.

"And would you be happier at Boxall Hill? It is not the place makes the happiness."

"No, I know that; it is not the place. I do not look to be happy in any place; but I should be quieter, more tranquil elsewhere than here."

"I also sometimes think that it will be better for us to take up our staves and walk away out of Greshamsbury;—leave it altogether, and settle elsewhere; miles, miles, miles away from here. Should you like that, dearest?"

Miles, miles, miles away from Greshamsbury! There was something in the sound that fell very cold on Mary's ears, unhappy as she was. Greshamsbury had been so dear to her; in spite of all that had passed, was still so dear to her! Was she prepared to take up her staff, as her uncle said, and walk forth from the place with the full understanding that she was to return to it no more; with a mind resolved that there should be an inseparable gulf between her and its inhabitants? Such she knew was the proposed nature of the walking away of which her uncle spoke. So she sat there, resting on her arms, and gave no answer to the question that had been asked her.

"No, we will stay a while yet," said her uncle. "It may come to that, but this is not the time. For one season longer let us face—I will not say our enemies; I cannot call anybody my enemy who bears the name of Gresham." And then he went on for a moment with his breakfast. "So Frank will be here on the 12th?"

"Yes, uncle."

"Well, dearest, I have no questions to ask you: no directions to give. I know how good you are, and how prudent; I am anxious only for your happiness; not at all—"

"Happiness, uncle, is out of the question."

"I hope not. It is never out of the question, never can be out of the question. But, as I was saying, I am quite satisfied your conduct will be good, and, therefore, I have no questions to ask. We will remain here; and, whether good or evil come, we will not be ashamed to show our faces."

She sat for a while again silent, collecting her courage on the subject that was nearest her heart. She would have given the world that he should ask her questions; but she could not bid him to do so; and she found it impossible to talk openly to him about Frank unless he did so. "Will he come here?" at last she said, in a low-toned voice.

"Who? He, Louis? Yes, I think that in all probability he will."

"No; but Frank," she said, in a still lower voice.

"Ah! my darling, that I cannot tell; but will it be well that he should come here?"

"I do not know," she said. "No, I suppose not. But, uncle, I don't think he will come."

She was now sitting on a sofa away from the table, and he got up, sat down beside her, and took her hands in his. "Mary," said he, "you must be strong now; strong to endure, not to attack. I think you have that strength; but, if not, perhaps it will be better that we should go away."

"I will be strong," said she, rising up and going towards the door. "Never mind me, uncle; don't follow me; I will be strong. It will be base, cowardly, mean, to run away; very base in me to make you do so."

"No, dearest, not so; it will be the same to me."

"No," said she, "I will not run away from Lady Arabella. And, as for him—if he loves this other one, he shall hear no reproach from me. Uncle, I will be strong;" and running back to him, she threw her arms round him and kissed him. And, still restraining her tears, she got safely to her bedroom. In what way she may there have shown her strength, it would not be well for us to inquire.

CHAPTER XXXIV

A BAROUCHE AND FOUR ARRIVES AT GRESHAMSBURY

During the last twelve months Sir Louis Scatcherd had been very efficacious in bringing trouble, turmoil, and vexation upon Greshamsbury. Now that it was too late to take steps to save himself, Dr Thorne found that the will left by Sir Roger was so made as to entail upon him duties that he would find it almost impossible to perform. Sir Louis, though his father had wished to make him still a child in the eye of the law, was no child. He knew his own rights and was determined to exact them; and before Sir Roger had been dead three months, the doctor found himself in continual litigation with a low Barchester attorney, who was acting on behalf of his, the doctor's, own ward.

And if the doctor suffered so did the squire, and so did those who had hitherto had the management of the squire's affairs. Dr Thorne soon perceived that he was to be driven into litigation, not only with Mr Finnie, the Barchester attorney, but with the squire himself. While Finnie harassed him, he was compelled to harass Mr Gresham. He was no lawyer himself; and though he had been able to manage very well between the squire and Sir Roger, and had perhaps given himself some credit for his lawyer-like ability in so doing, he was utterly unable to manage between Sir Louis and Mr Gresham.

He had, therefore, to employ a lawyer on his own account, and it seemed probable that the whole amount of Sir Roger's legacy to himself would by degrees be expended in this manner. And then, the squire's lawyers had to take up the matter; and they did so greatly to the detriment of poor Mr Yates Umbleby, who was found to have made a mess of the affairs entrusted to him. Mr Umbleby's accounts were incorrect; his mind was anything but clear, and he confessed, when put to it by the very sharp gentleman that came down from London, that he was "bothered;" and so, after a while, he was suspended from his duties, and Mr Gazebee, the sharp gentleman from London, reigned over the diminished rent-roll of the Greshamsbury estate.

Thus everything was going wrong at Greshamsbury—with the one exception of Mr Oriel and his love-suit. Miss Gushing attributed the deposition of Mr Umbleby to the narrowness of the victory which Beatrice had won in carrying off Mr Oriel. For Miss Gushing was a relation of the Umblebys, and had been for many years one of their family. "If she had only chosen to exert herself as Miss Gresham had done, she could have had Mr Oriel, easily; oh, too easily! but she had despised such work," so she said. "But though she had despised it, the Greshams had not been less irritated, and, therefore, Mr Umbleby had been driven out of his house." We can hardly believe this, as victory generally makes men generous. Miss Gushing, however, stated it as a fact so often that it is probable she was induced to believe it herself.

Thus everything was going wrong at Greshamsbury, and the squire himself was especially a sufferer. Umbleby had at any rate been his own man, and he could do what he liked with him. He could see him when he liked, and where he liked, and how he liked; could scold him if in an ill-humour, and laugh at him when in a good humour. All this Mr Umbleby knew, and bore. But Mr Gazebee was a very different sort of gentleman; he was the junior partner in the firm of Gumption, Gazebee & Gazebee, of Mount Street, a house that never defiled itself with any other business than the agency business, and that in the very highest line. They drew out leases, and managed property both for the Duke of Omnium and Lord de Courcy; and ever since her marriage, it had been one of the objects dearest to Lady Arabella's heart, that the Greshamsbury acres should be superintended by the polite skill and polished legal ability of that all but elegant firm in Mount Street.

The squire had long stood firm, and had delighted in having everything done under his own eye by poor Mr Yates Umbleby. But now, alas! he could stand it no longer. He had put off the evil day as long as he could; he had deferred the odious work of investigation till things had seemed resolved on investigating themselves; and then, when it was absolutely necessary that Mr Umbleby should go, there was nothing for him left but to fall into the ready hands of Messrs Gumption, Gazebee and Gazebee.

It must not be supposed that Messrs Gumption, Gazebee & Gazebee were in the least like the ordinary run of attorneys. They wrote no letters for six-and-eightpence each: they collected no debts, filed no bills, made no charge per folio for "whereases" and "as aforesaids;" they did no dirty work, and probably were as ignorant of the interior of a court of law as any young lady living in their Mayfair vicinity. No; their business was to manage the property of great people, draw up leases, make legal assignments, get the family marriage settlements made, and look after wills. Occasionally, also, they had to raise money; but it was generally understood that this was done by proxy.

The firm had been going on for a hundred and fifty years, and the designation had often been altered; but it always consisted of Gumptions and Gazebees differently arranged, and no less hallowed names had ever been permitted to appear. It had been Gazebee, Gazebee & Gumption; then Gazebee & Gumption; then Gazebee, Gumption & Gumption; then Gumption, Gumption & Gazebee; and now it was Gumption, Gazebee & Gazebee.

Mr Gazebee, the junior member of this firm, was a very elegant young man. While looking at him riding in Rotten Row, you would hardly have taken him for an attorney; and had he heard that you had so taken him, he would have been very much surprised indeed. He was rather bald; not being, as people say, quite so young as he was once. His exact age was thirty-eight. But he had a really remarkable pair of jet-black whiskers, which fully made up for any deficiency as to his head; he had also dark eyes, and a beaked nose, what may be called a distinguished mouth, and was always dressed in fashionable attire. The fact was, that Mr Mortimer Gazebee, junior partner in the firm Gumption, Gazebee & Gazebee, by no means considered himself to be made of that very disagreeable material which mortals call small beer.

When this great firm was applied to, to get Mr Gresham through his difficulties, and when the state of his affairs was made known to them, they at first expressed rather a disinclination for the work. But at last, moved doubtless by their respect for the de Courcy interest, they assented; and Mr Gazebee, junior, went down to Greshamsbury. The poor squire passed many a sad day after that before he again felt himself to be master even of his own domain.

Nevertheless, when Mr Mortimer Gazebee visited Greshamsbury, which he did on more than one or two occasions, he was always received *en grand seigneur*. To Lady Arabella he was by no means an unwelcome guest, for she found herself able, for the first time in her life, to speak confidentially on her husband's pecuniary affairs with the man who had the management of her husband's property. Mr Gazebee also was a pet with Lady de Courcy; and being known to be a fashionable man in London, and quite a different sort of person from poor Mr Umbleby, he was always received with smiles. He had a hundred little ways of making himself agreeable, and Augusta declared to her cousin, the Lady Amelia, after having been acquainted with him for a few months, that he would be a perfect gentleman, only, that his family had never been anything but attorneys. The Lady Amelia smiled in her own peculiarly aristocratic way, shrugged her shoulders slightly, and said, "that Mr Mortimer Gazebee was a very good sort of a person, very." Poor Augusta felt herself snubbed, thinking perhaps of the tailor's son; but as there was never any appeal against the Lady Amelia, she said nothing more at that moment in favour of Mr Mortimer Gazebee.

All these evils—Mr Mortimer Gazebee being the worst of them—had Sir Louis Scatcherd brought down on the poor squire's head. There may be those who will say that the squire had brought them on himself, by running into debt; and so, doubtless, he had; but it was not the less true that the baronet's interference was unnecessary, vexatious, and one might almost say, malicious. His interest would have been quite safe in the doctor's hands, and he had, in fact, no legal right to meddle; but neither the doctor nor the squire could prevent him. Mr Finnie knew very well what he was about, if Sir Louis did not; and so the three went on, each with his own lawyer, and each of them distrustful, unhappy, and ill at ease. This was hard upon the doctor, for he was not in debt, and had borrowed no money.

There was not much reason to suppose that the visit of Sir Louis to Greshamsbury would much improve matters. It must be presumed that he was not coming with any amicable views, but with the object rather of looking after his own; a phrase which was now constantly in his mouth. He might probably find it necessary while looking after his own at Greshamsbury, to say some very disagreeable things to the squire; and the doctor, therefore, hardly expected that the visit would go off pleasantly.

When last we saw Sir Louis, now nearly twelve months since, he was intent on making a proposal of marriage to Miss Thorne. This intention he carried out about two days after Frank Gresham had done the same thing. He had delayed doing so till he had succeeded in purchasing his friend Jenkins's Arab pony, imagining that such a present could not but go far in weaning Mary's heart from her other lover. Poor Mary was put to the trouble of refusing both the baronet and the pony, and a very bad time she had of it while doing so. Sir Louis was a man easily angered, and not very easily pacified, and Mary had to endure a good deal of annoyance; from any other person, indeed, she would have called it impertinence. Sir Louis, however, had to bear his rejection as best he could, and, after a perseverance of three days, returned to London in disgust; and Mary had not seen him since.

Mr Greyson's first letter was followed by a second; and the second was followed by the baronet in person. He also required to be received *en grand seigneur*, perhaps more imperatively than Mr Mortimer Gazebee himself. He came with four posters from the Barchester Station, and had himself rattled up to the doctor's door in a way that took the breath away from all Greshamsbury. Why! the squire himself for a many long year had been contented to come home with a pair of horses; and four were never seen in the place, except when the de Courcys came to Greshamsbury, or Lady Arabella with all her daughters returned from her hard-fought metropolitan campaigns.

Sir Louis, however, came with four, and very arrogant he looked, leaning back in the barouche belonging to the George and Dragon, and wrapped up in fur, although it was now midsummer. And up in the dicky behind was a servant, more arrogant, if possible, than his master—the baronet's own man, who was the object of Dr Thorne's special detestation and disgust. He was a little fellow, chosen originally on account of his light weight on horseback; but if that may be considered a merit, it was the only one he had. His outdoor show dress was a little tight frock-coat, round which a polished strap was always buckled tightly, a stiff white choker, leather breeches, top-boots, and a hat, with a cockade, stuck on one side of his head. His name was Jonah, which his master and his master's friends shortened into Joe; none, however, but those who were very intimate with his master were allowed to do so with impunity.

This Joe was Dr Thorne's special aversion. In his anxiety to take every possible step to keep Sir Louis from poisoning himself, he had at first attempted to enlist the baronet's "own man" in the cause. Joe had promised fairly, but had betrayed the doctor at once, and had become the worst instrument of his master's dissipation. When, therefore, his hat and the cockade were seen, as the carriage dashed up to the door, the doctor's contentment was by no means increased.

Sir Louis was now twenty-three years old, and was a great deal too knowing to allow himself to be kept under the doctor's thumb. It had, indeed, become his plan to rebel against his guardian in almost everything. He had at first been decently submissive, with the view of obtaining increased supplies of ready money; but he had been sharp enough to perceive that, let his conduct be what it would, the doctor would keep him out of debt; but that the doing so took so large a sum that he could not hope for any further advances. In this respect Sir Louis was perhaps more keen-witted than Dr Thorne.

Mary, when she saw the carriage, at once ran up to her own bedroom. The doctor, who had been with her in the drawing-room, went down to meet his ward, but as soon as he saw the cockade he darted almost involuntarily into his shop and shut the door. This protection, however, lasted only for a moment; he felt that decency required him to meet his guest, and so he went forth and faced the enemy.

"I say," said Joe, speaking to Janet, who stood curtsying at the gate, with Bridget, the other maid, behind her, "I say, are there any chaps about the place to take these things— eh? come, look sharp here."

It so happened that the doctor's groom was not on the spot, and "other chaps" the doctor had none.

"Take those things, Bridget," he said, coming forward and offering his hand to the baronet. Sir Louis, when he saw his host, roused himself slowly from the back of his carriage. "How do, doctor?" said he. "What terrible bad roads you have here! and, upon my word, it's as cold as winter:" and, so saying, he slowly proceeded to descend.

Sir Louis was a year older than when we last saw him, and, in his generation, a year wiser. He had then been somewhat humble before the doctor; but now he was determined to let his guardian see that he knew how to act the baronet; that he had acquired the manners of a great man; and that he was not to be put upon. He had learnt some lessons from Jenkins, in London, and other friends of the same sort, and he was about to profit by them.

The doctor showed him to his room, and then proceeded to ask after his health. "Oh, I'm right enough," said Sir Louis. "You mustn't believe all that fellow Greyson tells you: he wants me to take salts and senna, opodeldoc, and all that sort of stuff; looks after his bill, you know—eh? like all the rest of you. But I won't have it;—not at any price; and then he writes to you."

"I'm glad to see you able to travel," said Dr Thorne, who could not force himself to tell his guest that he was glad to see him at Greshamsbury.

"Oh, travel; yes, I can travel well enough. But I wish you had some better sort of trap down in these country parts. I'm shaken to bits. And, doctor, would you tell your people to send that fellow of mine up here with hot water."

So dismissed, the doctor went his way, and met Joe swaggering in one of the passages, while Janet and her colleague dragged along between them a heavy article of baggage.

"Janet," said he, "go downstairs and get Sir Louis some hot water, and Joe, do you take hold of your master's portmanteau."

Joe sulkily did as he was bid. "Seems to me," said he, turning to the girl, and speaking before the doctor was out of hearing, "seems to me, my dear, you be rather short-handed here; lots of work and nothing to get; that's about the ticket, ain't it?" Bridget was too demurely modest to make any answer upon so short an acquaintance; so, putting her end of the burden down at the strange gentleman's door, she retreated into the kitchen.

Sir Louis, in answer to the doctor's inquiries, had declared himself to be all right; but his appearance was anything but all right. Twelve months since, a life of dissipation, or rather, perhaps, a life of drinking, had not had upon him so strong an effect but that some of the salt of youth was still left; some of the freshness of young years might still be seen in his face. But this was now all gone; his eyes were sunken and watery, his cheeks were hollow and wan, his mouth was drawn and his lips dry; his back was even bent, and his legs were unsteady under him, so that he had been forced to step down from his carriage as an old man would do. Alas, alas! he had no further chance now of ever being all right again.

Mary had secluded herself in her bedroom as soon as the carriage had driven up to the door, and there she remained till dinner-time. But she could not shut herself up altogether. It would be necessary that she should appear at dinner; and, therefore, a few minutes before the hour, she crept out into the drawing-room. As she opened the door, she looked in timidly, expecting Sir Louis to be there; but when she saw that her uncle was the only occupant of the room, her brow cleared, and she entered with a quick step.

"He'll come down to dinner; won't he, uncle?"

"Oh, I suppose so."

"What's he doing now?"

"Dressing, I suppose; he's been at it this hour."

"But, uncle—"

"Well?"

"Will he come up after dinner, do you think?"

Mary spoke of him as though he were some wild beast, whom her uncle insisted on having in his house.

"Goodness knows what he will do! Come up? Yes. He will not stay in the dining-room all night."

"But, dear uncle, do be serious."

"Serious!"

"Yes; serious. Don't you think that I might go to bed, instead of waiting?"

The doctor was saved the trouble of answering by the entrance of the baronet. He was dressed in what he considered the most fashionable style of the day. He had on a new dress-coat lined with satin, new dress-trousers, a silk waistcoat covered with chains, a white cravat, polished pumps, and silk stockings, and he carried a scented handkerchief in his hand; he had rings on his fingers, and carbuncle studs in his shirt, and he smelt as sweet as patchouli could make him. But he could hardly do more than shuffle into the room, and seemed almost to drag one of his legs behind him.

Mary, in spite of her aversion, was shocked and distressed when she saw him. He, however, seemed to think himself perfect, and was no whit abashed by the unfavourable reception which twelve months since had been paid to his suit. Mary came up and shook hands with him, and he received her with a compliment which no doubt he thought must be acceptable. "Upon my word, Miss Thorne, every place seems to agree with you; one better than another. You were looking charming at Boxall Hill; but, upon my word, charming isn't half strong enough now."

Mary sat down quietly, and the doctor assumed a face of unutterable disgust. This was the creature for whom all his sympathies had been demanded, all his best energies put in requisition; on whose behalf he was to quarrel with his oldest friends, lose his peace and quietness of life, and exercise all the functions of a loving friend! This was his self-invited guest, whom he was bound to foster, and whom he could not turn from his door.

Then dinner came, and Mary had to put her hand upon his arm. She certainly did not lean upon him, and once or twice felt inclined to give him some support. They reached the dining-room, however, the doctor following them, and then sat down, Janet waiting in the room, as was usual.

"I say, doctor," said the baronet, "hadn't my man better come in and help? He's got nothing to do, you know. We should be more cosy, shouldn't we?"

"Janet will manage pretty well," said the doctor.

"Oh, you'd better have Joe; there's nothing like a good servant at table. I say, Janet, just send that fellow in, will you?"

"We shall do very well without him," said the doctor, becoming rather red about the cheek-bones, and with a slight gleam of determination about the eye. Janet, who saw how matters stood, made no attempt to obey the baronet's order.

"Oh, nonsense, doctor; you think he's an uppish sort of fellow, I know, and you don't like to trouble him; but when I'm near him, he's all right; just send him in, will you?"

"Sir Louis," said the doctor, "I'm accustomed to none but my own old woman here in my own house, and if you will allow me, I'll keep my old ways. I shall be sorry if you are not comfortable." The baronet said nothing more, and the dinner passed off slowly and wearily enough.

When Mary had eaten her fruit and escaped, the doctor got into one arm-chair and the baronet into another, and the latter began the only work of existence of which he knew anything.

"That's good port," said he; "very fair port."

The doctor loved his port wine, and thawed a little in his manner. He loved it not as a toper, but as a collector loves his pet pictures. He liked to talk about it, and think about it; to praise it, and hear it praised; to look at it turned towards the light, and to count over the years it had lain in his cellar.

"Yes," said he, "it's pretty fair wine. It was, at least, when I got it, twenty years ago, and I don't suppose time has hurt it;" and he held the glass up to the window, and looked at the evening light through the ruby tint of the liquid. "Ah, dear, there's not much of it left; more's the pity."

"A good thing won't last for ever. I'll tell you what now; I wish I'd brought down a dozen or two of claret. I've some prime stuff in London; got it from Muzzle & Drug, at ninety-six shillings; it was a great favour, though. I'll tell you what now, I'll send up for a couple of dozen to-morrow. I mustn't drink you out of house, high and dry; must I, doctor?"

The doctor froze immediately.

"I don't think I need trouble you," said he; "I never drink claret, at least not here; and there's enough of the old bin left to last some little time longer yet."

Sir Louis drank two or three glasses of wine very quickly after each other, and they immediately began to tell upon his weak stomach. But before he was tipsy, he became more impudent and more disagreeable.

"Doctor," said he, "when are we to see any of this Greshamsbury money? That's what I want to know."

"Your money is quite safe, Sir Louis; and the interest is paid to the day."

"Interest, yes; but how do I know how long it will be paid? I should like to see the principal. A hundred thousand pounds, or something like it, is a precious large stake to have in one man's hands, and he preciously hard up himself. I'll tell you what, doctor—I shall look the squire up myself."

"Look him up?"

"Yes; look him up; ferret him out; tell him a bit of my mind. I'll thank you to pass the bottle. D—— me doctor; I mean to know how things are going on."

"Your money is quite safe," repeated the doctor, "and, to my mind, could not be better invested."

"That's all very well; d—— well, I dare say, for you and Squire Gresham—"

"What do you mean, Sir Louis?"

"Mean! why I mean that I'll sell the squire up; that's what I mean—hallo—beg pardon. I'm blessed if I haven't broken the water-jug. That comes of having water on the table. Oh, d—— me, it's all over me." And then, getting up, to avoid the flood he himself had caused, he nearly fell into the doctor's arms.

"You're tired with your journey, Sir Louis; perhaps you'd better go to bed."

"Well, I am a bit seedy or so. Those cursed roads of yours shake a fellow so."

The doctor rang the bell, and, on this occasion, did request that Joe might be sent for. Joe came in, and, though he was much steadier than his master, looked as though he also had found some bin of which he had approved.

"Sir Louis wishes to go to bed," said the doctor; "you had better give him your arm."

"Oh, yes; in course I will," said Joe, standing immoveable about half-way between the door and the table.

"I'll just take one more glass of the old port—eh, doctor?" said Sir Louis, putting out his hand and clutching the decanter.

It is very hard for any man to deny his guest in his own house, and the doctor, at the moment, did not know how to do it; so Sir Louis got his wine, after pouring half of it over the table.

"Come in, sir, and give Sir Louis your arm," said the doctor, angrily.

"So I will in course, if my master tells me; but, if you please, Dr Thorne,"—and Joe put his hand up to his hair in a manner that had a great deal more of impudence than reverence in it—"I just want to ax one question: where be I to sleep?"

Now this was a question which the doctor was not prepared to answer on the spur of the moment, however well Janet or Mary might have been able to do so.

"Sleep," said he, "I don't know where you are to sleep, and don't care; ask Janet."

"That's all very well, master—"

"Hold your tongue, sirrah!" said Sir Louis. "What the devil do you want of sleep?—come here," and then, with his servant's help, he made his way up to his bedroom, and was no more heard of that night.

"Did he get tipsy," asked Mary, almost in a whisper, when her uncle joined her in the drawing-room.

"Don't talk of it," said he. "Poor wretch! poor wretch! Let's have some tea now, Molly, and pray don't talk any more about him to-night." Then Mary did make the tea, and did not talk any more about Sir Louis that night.

What on earth were they to do with him? He had come there self-invited; but his connexion with the doctor was such, that it was impossible he should be told to go away, either he himself, or that servant of his. There was no reason to disbelieve him when he declared that he had come down to ferret out the squire. Such was, doubtless, his intention. He would ferret out the squire. Perhaps he might ferret out Lady Arabella also. Frank would be home in a few days; and he, too, might be ferreted out.

But the matter took a very singular turn, and one quite unexpected on the doctor's part. On the morning following the little dinner of which we have spoken, one of the Greshamsbury grooms rode up to the doctor's door with two notes. One was addressed to the doctor in the squire's well-known large handwriting, and the other was for Sir Louis. Each contained an invitation do dinner for the following day; and that to the doctor was in this wise:—

DEAR DOCTOR, Do come and dine here to-morrow, and bring Sir Louis Scatcherd with you. If you're the man I take you to be, you won't refuse me. Lady Arabella sends a note for Sir Louis. There will be nobody here but Oriel, and Mr Gazebee, who is staying in the house.

> Yours ever,
> F. N. GRESHAM.

Greshamsbury, July, 185—.
P.S.—I make a positive request that you'll come, and I think you will hardly refuse me.

The doctor read it twice before he could believe it, and then ordered Janet to take the other note up to Sir Louis. As these invitations were rather in opposition to the then existing Greshamsbury tactics, the cause of Lady Arabella's special civility must be explained.

Mr Mortimer Gazebee was now at the house, and therefore, it must be presumed, that things were not allowed to go on after their old fashion. Mr Gazebee was an acute as well as a fashionable man; one who knew what he was about, and who, moreover, had determined to give his very best efforts on behalf of the Greshamsbury property. His energy, in this respect, will explain itself hereafter. It was not probable that the arrival in the village of such a person as Sir Louis Scatcherd should escape attention. He had heard of it before dinner, and, before the evening was over, had discussed it with Lady Arabella.

Her ladyship was not at first inclined to make much of Sir Louis, and expressed herself as but little inclined to agree with Mr Gazebee when that gentleman suggested that he should be treated with civility at Greshamsbury. But she was at last talked over. She found it pleasant enough to have more to do with the secret management of the estate than Mr Gresham himself; and when Mr Gazebee proved to her, by sundry nods and winks, and subtle allusions to her own infinite good sense, that it was necessary to catch this obscene bird which had come to prey upon the estate, by throwing a little salt upon his tail, she also nodded and winked, and directed Augusta to prepare the salt according to order.

"But won't it be odd, Mr Gazebee, asking him out of Dr Thorne's house?"

"Oh, we must have the doctor, too, Lady Arabella; by all means ask the doctor also."

Lady Arabella's brow grew dark. "Mr Gazebee," she said, "you can hardly believe how that man has behaved to me."

"He is altogether beneath your anger," said Mr Gazebee, with a bow.

"I don't know: in one way he may be, but not in another. I really do not think I can sit down to table with Doctor Thorne."

But, nevertheless, Mr Gazebee gained his point. It was now about a week since Sir Omicron Pie had been at Greshamsbury, and the squire had, almost daily, spoken to his wife as to that learned man's advice. Lady Arabella always answered in the same tone: "You can hardly know, Mr Gresham, how that man has insulted me." But, nevertheless, the physician's advice had not been disbelieved: it tallied too well with her own inward convictions. She was anxious enough to have Doctor Thorne back at her bedside, if she could only get him there without damage to her pride. Her husband, she thought, might probably send the doctor there without absolute permission from herself; in which case she would have been able to scold, and show that she was offended; and, at the same time, profit by what had been done. But Mr Gresham never thought of taking so violent a step as this, and, therefore, Dr Fillgrave still came, and her ladyship's *finesse* was wasted in vain.

But Mr Gazebee's proposition opened a door by which her point might be gained. "Well," said she, at last, with infinite self-denial, "if you think it is for Mr Gresham's advantage, and if he chooses to ask Dr Thorne, I will not refuse to receive him."

Mr Gazebee's next task was to discuss the matter with the squire. Nor was this easy, for Mr Gazebee was no favourite with Mr Gresham. But the task was at last performed successfully. Mr Gresham was so glad at heart to find himself able, once more, to ask his old friend to his own house; and, though it would have pleased him better that this sign of relenting on his wife's part should have reached him by other means, he did not refuse to take advantage of it; and so he wrote the above letter to Dr Thorne.

The doctor, as we have said, read it twice; and he at once resolved stoutly that he would not go.

"Oh, do, do go!" said Mary. She well knew how wretched this feud had made her uncle. "Pray, pray go!"

"Indeed, I will not," said he. "There are some things a man should bear, and some he should not."

"You must go," said Mary, who had taken the note from her uncle's hand, and read it. "You cannot refuse him when he asks you like that."

"It will greatly grieve me; but I must refuse him."

"I also am angry, uncle; very angry with Lady Arabella; but for him, for the squire, I would go to him on my knees if he asked me in that way."

"Yes; and had he asked you, I also would have gone."

"Oh! now I shall be so wretched. It is his invitation, not hers: Mr Gresham could not ask me. As for her, do not think of her; but do, do go when he asks you like that. You will make me so miserable if you do not. And then Sir Louis cannot go without you,"—and Mary pointed upstairs—"and you may be sure that he will go."

"Yes; and make a beast of himself."

This colloquy was cut short by a message praying the doctor to go up to Sir Louis's room. The young man was sitting in his dressing-gown, drinking a cup of coffee at his toilet-table, while Joe was preparing his razor and hot water. The doctor's nose immediately told him that there was more in the coffee-cup than had come out of his own kitchen, and he would not let the offence pass unnoticed.

"Are you taking brandy this morning, Sir Louis?"

"Just a little *chasse-café*," said he, not exactly understanding the word he used. "It's all the go now; and a capital thing for the stomach."

"It's not a capital thing for your stomach;—about the least capital thing you can take; that is, if you wish to live."

"Never mind about that now, doctor, but look here. This is what we call the civil thing—eh?" and he showed the Greshamsbury note. "Not but what they have an object, of course. I understand all that. Lots of girls there—eh?"

The doctor took the note and read it. "It is civil," said he; "very civil."

"Well; I shall go, of course. I don't bear malice because he can't pay me the money he owes me. I'll eat his dinner, and look at the girls. Have you an invite too, doctor?"

"Yes; I have."

"And you'll go?"

"I think not; but that need not deter you. But, Sir Louis—"

"Well! eh! what is it?"

"Step downstairs a moment," said the doctor, turning to the servant, "and wait till you are called for. I wish to speak to your master." Joe, for a moment, looked up at the baronet's face, as though he wanted but the slightest encouragement to disobey the doctor's orders; but not seeing it, he slowly retired, and placed himself, of course, at the keyhole.

And then, the doctor began a long and very useless lecture. The first object of it was to induce his ward not to get drunk at Greshamsbury; but having got so far, he went on, and did succeed in frightening his unhappy guest. Sir Louis did not possess the iron nerves of his father—nerves which even brandy had not been able to subdue. The doctor spoke strongly, very strongly; spoke of quick, almost immediate death in case of further excesses; spoke to him of the certainty there would be that he could not live to dispose of his own property if he could not refrain. And thus he did frighten Sir Louis. The father he had never been able to frighten. But there are men who, though they fear death hugely, fear present suffering more; who, indeed, will not bear a moment of pain if there by any mode of escape. Sir Louis was such: he had no strength of nerve, no courage, no ability to make a resolution and keep it. He promised the doctor that he would refrain; and, as he did so, he swallowed down his cup of coffee and brandy, in which the two articles bore about equal proportions.

The doctor did, at last, make up his mind to go. Whichever way he determined, he found that he was not contented with himself. He did not like to trust Sir Louis by himself, and he did not like to show that he was angry. Still less did he like the idea of breaking bread in Lady Arabella's house till some amends had been made to Mary. But his heart would not allow him to refuse the petition contained in the squire's postscript, and the matter ended in his accepting the invitation.

This visit of his ward's was, in every way, pernicious to the doctor. He could not go about his business, fearing to leave such a man alone with Mary. On the afternoon of the second day, she escaped to the parsonage for an hour or so, and then walked away among the lanes, calling on some of her old friends among the farmers' wives. But even then, the doctor was afraid to leave Sir Louis. What could such a man do, left alone in a village like Greshamsbury? So he stayed at home, and the two together went over their accounts. The baronet was particular about his accounts, and said a good deal as to having Finnie over to Greshamsbury. To this, however, Dr Thorne positively refused his consent.

The evening passed off better than the preceding one; at least the early part of it. Sir Louis did not get tipsy; he came up to tea, and Mary, who did not feel so keenly on the subject as her uncle, almost wished that he had done so. At ten o'clock he went to bed.

But after that new troubles came on. The doctor had gone downstairs into his study to make up some of the time which he had lost, and had just seated himself at his desk, when Janet, without announcing herself, burst into the room; and Bridget, dissolved in hysterical tears, with her apron to her eyes, appeared behind the senior domestic.

"Please, sir," said Janet, driven by excitement much beyond her usual pace of speaking, and becoming unintentionally a little less respectful than usual, "please sir, that 'ere young man must go out of this here house; or else no respectable young 'ooman can't stop here; no, indeed, sir; and we be sorry to trouble you, Dr Thorne; so we be."

"What young man? Sir Louis?" asked the doctor.

"Oh, no! he abides mostly in bed, and don't do nothing amiss; least way not to us. 'Tan't him, sir; but his man."

"Man!" sobbed Bridget from behind. "He an't no man, nor nothing like a man. If Tummas had been here, he wouldn't have dared; so he wouldn't." Thomas was the groom, and, if all Greshamsbury reports were true, it was probable, that on some happy, future day, Thomas and Bridget would become one flesh and one bone.

"Please sir," continued Janet, "there'll be bad work here if that 'ere young man doesn't quit this here house this very night, and I'm sorry to trouble you, doctor; and so I am. But Tom, he be given to fight a'most for nothin'. He's hout now; but if that there young man be's here when Tom comes home, Tom will be punching his head; I know he will."

"He wouldn't stand by and see a poor girl put upon; no more he wouldn't," said Bridget, through her tears.

After many futile inquiries, the doctor ascertained that Mr Jonah had expressed some admiration for Bridget's youthful charms, and had, in the absence of Janet, thrown himself at the lady's feet in a manner which had not been altogether pleasing to her. She had defended herself stoutly and loudly, and in the middle of the row Janet had come down.

"And where is he now?" said the doctor.

"Why, sir," said Janet, "the poor girl was so put about that she did give him one touch across the face with the rolling-pin, and he be all bloody now, in the back kitchen." At hearing this achievement of hers thus spoken of, Bridget sobbed more hysterically than ever; but the doctor, looking at her arm as she held her apron to her face, thought in his heart that Joe must have had so much the worst of it, that there could be no possible need for the interference of Thomas the groom.

And such turned out to be the case. The bridge of Joe's nose was broken; and the doctor had to set it for him in a little bedroom at the village public-house, Bridget having positively refused to go to bed in the same house with so dreadful a character.

"Quiet now, or I'll be serving thee the same way; thee see I've found the trick of it." The doctor could not but hear so much as he made his way into his own house by the back door, after finishing his surgical operation. Bridget was recounting to her champion the fracas that had occurred; and he, as was so natural, was expressing his admiration at her valour.

CHAPTER XXXV

SIR LOUIS GOES OUT TO DINNER

The next day Joe did not make his appearance, and Sir Louis, with many execrations, was driven to the terrible necessity of dressing himself. Then came an unexpected difficulty: how were they to get up to the house? Walking out to dinner, though it was merely through the village and up the avenue, seemed to Sir Louis to be a thing impossible. Indeed, he was not well able to walk at all, and positively declared that he should never be able to make his way over the gravel in pumps. His mother would not have thought half as much of walking from Boxall Hill to Greshamsbury and back again. At last, the one village fly was sent for, and the matter was arranged.

When they reached the house, it was easy to see that there was some unwonted bustle. In the drawing-room there was no one but Mr Mortimer Gazebee, who introduced himself to them both. Sir Louis, who knew that he was only an attorney, did not take much notice of him, but the doctor entered into conversation.

"Have you heard that Mr Gresham has come home?" said Mr Gazebee.

"Mr Gresham! I did not know that he had been away."

"Mr Gresham, junior, I mean." No, indeed; the doctor had not heard. Frank had returned unexpectedly just before dinner, and he was now undergoing his father's smiles, his mother's embraces, and his sisters' questions.

"Quite unexpectedly," said Mr Gazebee. "I don't know what has brought him back before his time. I suppose he found London too hot."

"Deuced hot," said the baronet. "I found it so, at least. I don't know what keeps men in London when it's so hot; except those fellows who have business to do: they're paid for it."

Mr Mortimer Gazebee looked at him. He was managing an estate which owed Sir Louis an enormous sum of money, and, therefore, he could not afford to despise the baronet; but he thought to himself, what a very abject fellow the man would be if he were not a baronet, and had not a large fortune!

And then the squire came in. His broad, honest face was covered with a smile when he saw the doctor.

"Thorne," he said, almost in a whisper, "you're the best fellow breathing; I have hardly deserved this." The doctor, as he took his old friend's hand, could not but be glad that he had followed Mary's counsel.

"So Frank has come home?"

"Oh, yes; quite unexpectedly. He was to have stayed a week longer in London. You would hardly know him if you met him. Sir Louis, I beg your pardon." And the squire went up to his other guest, who had remained somewhat sullenly standing in one corner of the room. He was the man of highest rank present, or to be present, and he expected to be treated as such.

"I am happy to have the pleasure of making your acquaintance, Mr Gresham," said the baronet, intending to be very courteous. "Though we have not met before, I very often see your name in my accounts—ha! ha! ha!" and Sir Louis laughed as though he had said something very good.

The meeting between Lady Arabella and the doctor was rather distressing to the former; but she managed to get over it. She shook hands with him graciously, and said that it was a fine day. The doctor said that it was fine, only perhaps a little rainy. And then they went into different parts of the room.

When Frank came in, the doctor hardly did know him. His hair was darker than it had been, and so was his complexion; but his chief disguise was in a long silken beard, which hung down over his cravat. The doctor had hitherto not been much in favour of long beards, but he could not deny that Frank looked very well with the appendage.

"Oh, doctor, I am so delighted to find you here," said he, coming up to him; "so very, very glad:" and, taking the doctor's arm, he led him away into a window, where they were alone. "And how is Mary?" said he, almost in a whisper. "Oh, I wish she were here! But, doctor, it shall all come in time. But tell me, doctor, there is no news about her, is there?"

"News—what news?"

"Oh, well; no news is good news: you will give her my love, won't you?"

The doctor said that he would. What else could he say? It appeared quite clear to him that some of Mary's fears were groundless.

Frank was again very much altered. It has been said, that though he was a boy at twenty-one, he was a man at twenty-two. But now, at twenty-three, he appeared to be almost a man of the world. His manners were easy, his voice under his control, and words were at his command: he was no longer either shy or noisy; but, perhaps, was open to the charge of seeming, at least, to be too conscious of his own merits. He was, indeed, very handsome; tall, manly, and powerfully built, his form was such as women's eyes have ever loved to look upon. "Ah, if he would but marry money!" said Lady Arabella to herself, taken up by a mother's natural admiration for her son. His sisters clung round him before dinner, all talking to him at once. How proud a family of girls are of one, big, tall, burly brother!

"You don't mean to tell me, Frank, that you are going to eat soup with that beard?" said the squire, when they were seated round the table. He had not ceased to rally his son as to this patriarchal adornment; but, nevertheless, any one could have seen, with half an eye, that he was as proud of it as were the others.

"Don't I, sir? All I require is a relay of napkins for every course:" and he went to work, covering it with every spoonful, as men with beards always do.

"Well, if you like it!" said the squire, shrugging his shoulders.

"But I do like it," said Frank.

"Oh, papa, you wouldn't have him cut it off," said one of the twins. "It is so handsome."

"I should like to work it into a chair-back instead of floss-silk," said the other twin.

"Thank'ee, Sophy; I'll remember you for that."

"Doesn't it look nice, and grand, and patriarchal?" said Beatrice, turning to her neighbour.

"Patriarchal, certainly," said Mr Oriel. "I should grow one myself if I had not the fear of the archbishop before my eyes."

What was next said to him was in a whisper, audible only to himself.

"Doctor, did you know Wildman of the 9th. He was left as surgeon at Scutari for two years. Why, my beard to his is only a little down."

"A little way down, you mean," said Mr Gazebee.

"Yes," said Frank, resolutely set against laughing at Mr Gazebee's pun. "Why, his beard descends to his ankles, and he is obliged to tie it in a bag at night, because his feet get entangled in it when he is asleep!"

"Oh, Frank!" said one of the girls.

This was all very well for the squire, and Lady Arabella, and the girls. They were all delighted to praise Frank, and talk about him. Neither did it come amiss to Mr Oriel and the doctor, who had both a personal interest in the young hero. But Sir Louis did not like it at all. He was the only baronet in the room, and yet nobody took any notice of him. He was seated in the post of honour, next to Lady Arabella; but even Lady Arabella seemed to think more of her own son than of him. Seeing how he was ill-used, he meditated revenge; but not the less did it behove him to make some effort to attract attention.

"Was your ladyship long in London, this season?" said he.

Lady Arabella had not been in London at all this year, and it was a sore subject with her. "No," said she, very graciously; "circumstances have kept us at home."

Sir Louis only understood one description of "circumstances." Circumstances, in his idea, meant the want of money, and he immediately took Lady Arabella's speech as a confession of poverty.

"Ah, indeed! I am very sorry for that; that must be very distressing to a person like your ladyship. But things are mending, perhaps?"

Lady Arabella did not in the least understand him. "Mending!" she said, in her peculiar tone of aristocratic indifference; and then turned to Mr Gazebee, who was on the other side of her.

Sir Louis was not going to stand this. He was the first man in the room, and he knew his own importance. It was not to be borne that Lady Arabella should turn to talk to a dirty attorney, and leave him, a baronet, to eat his dinner without notice. If nothing else would move her, he would let her know who was the real owner of the Greshamsbury title-deeds.

"I think I saw your ladyship out to-day, taking a ride." Lady Arabella had driven through the village in her pony-chair.

"I never ride," said she, turning her head for one moment from Mr Gazebee.

"In the one-horse carriage, I mean, my lady. I was delighted with the way you whipped him up round the corner."

Whipped him up round the corner! Lady Arabella could make no answer to this; so she went on talking to Mr Gazebee. Sir Louis, repulsed, but not vanquished—resolved not to be vanquished by any Lady Arabella—turned his attention to his plate for a minute or two, and then recommenced.

"The honour of a glass of wine with you, Lady Arabella," said he.

"I never take wine at dinner," said Lady Arabella. The man was becoming intolerable to her, and she was beginning to fear that it would be necessary for her to fly the room to get rid of him.

The baronet was again silent for a moment; but he was determined not to be put down.

"This is a nice-looking country about here," said he.

"Yes; very nice," said Mr Gazebee, endeavouring to relieve the lady of the mansion.

"I hardly know which I like best; this, or my own place at Boxall Hill. You have the advantage here in trees, and those sort of things. But, as to the house, why, my box there is very comfortable, very. You'd hardly know the place now, Lady Arabella, if you haven't seen it since my governor bought it. How much do you think he spent about the house and grounds, pineries included, you know, and those sort of things?"

Lady Arabella shook her head.

"Now guess, my lady," said he. But it was not to be supposed that Lady Arabella should guess on such a subject.

"I never guess," said she, with a look of ineffable disgust.

"What do you say, Mr Gazebee?"

"Perhaps a hundred thousand pounds."

"What! for a house! You can't know much about money, nor yet about building, I think, Mr Gazebee."

"Not much," said Mr Gazebee, "as to such magnificent places as Boxall Hill."

"Well, my lady, if you won't guess, I'll tell you. It cost twenty-two thousand four hundred and nineteen pounds four shillings and eightpence. I've all the accounts exact. Now, that's a tidy lot of money for a house for a man to live in."

Sir Louis spoke this in a loud tone, which at least commanded the attention of the table. Lady Arabella, vanquished, bowed her head, and said that it was a large sum; Mr Gazebee went on sedulously eating his dinner; the squire was struck momentarily dumb in the middle of a long chat with the doctor; even Mr Oriel ceased to whisper; and the girls opened their eyes with astonishment. Before the end of his speech, Sir Louis's voice had become very loud.

"Yes, indeed," said Frank; "a very tidy lot of money. I'd have generously dropped the four and eightpence if I'd been the architect."

"It wasn't all one bill; but that's the tot. I can show the bills:" and Sir Louis, well pleased with his triumph, swallowed a glass of wine.

Almost immediately after the cloth was removed, Lady Arabella escaped, and the gentlemen clustered together. Sir Louis found himself next to Mr Oriel, and began to make himself agreeable.

"A very nice girl, Miss Beatrice; very nice."

Now Mr Oriel was a modest man, and, when thus addressed as to his future wife, found it difficult to make any reply.

"You parsons always have your own luck," said Sir Louis. "You get all the beauty, and generally all the money, too. Not much of the latter in this case, though—eh?"

Mr Oriel was dumbfounded. He had never said a word to any creature as to Beatrice's dowry; and when Mr Gresham had told him, with sorrow, that his daughter's portion must be small, he had at once passed away from the subject as one that was hardly fit for conversation, even between him and his future father-in-law; and now he was abruptly questioned on the subject by a man he had never before seen in his life. Of course, he could make no answer.

"The squire has muddled his matters most uncommonly," continued Sir Louis, filling his glass for the second time before he passed the bottle. "What do you suppose now he owes me alone; just at one lump, you know?"

Mr Oriel had nothing for it but to run. He could make no answer, nor would he sit there to hear tidings as to Mr Gresham's embarrassments. So he fairly retreated, without having said one word to his neighbour, finding such discretion to be the only kind of valour left to him.

"What, Oriel! off already?" said the squire. "Anything the matter?"

"Oh, no; nothing particular. I'm not just quite—I think I'll go out for a few minutes."

"See what it is to be in love," said the squire, half-whispering to Dr Thorne. "You're not in the same way, I hope?"

Sir Louis then shifted his seat again, and found himself next to Frank. Mr Gazebee was opposite to him, and the doctor opposite to Frank.

"Parson seems peekish, I think," said the baronet.

"Peekish?" said the squire, inquisitively.

"Rather down on his luck. He's decently well off himself, isn't he?"

There was another pause, and nobody seemed inclined to answer the question.

"I mean, he's got something more than his bare living."

"Oh, yes," said Frank, laughing. "He's got what will buy him bread and cheese when the Rads shut up the Church:—unless, indeed, they shut up the Funds too."

"Ah, there's nothing like land," said Sir Louis: "nothing like the dirty acres; is there, squire?"

"Land is a very good investment, certainly," said Mr Gresham.

"The best going," said the other, who was now, as people say when they mean to be good-natured, slightly under the influence of liquor. "The best going—eh, Gazebee?"

Mr Gazebee gathered himself up, and turned away his head, looking out of the window.

"You lawyers never like to give an opinion without money, ha! ha! ha! Do they, Mr Gresham? You and I have had to pay for plenty of them, and will have to pay for plenty more before they let us alone."

Here Mr Gazebee got up, and followed Mr Oriel out of the room. He was not, of course, on such intimate terms in the house as was Mr Oriel; but he hoped to be forgiven by the ladies in consequence of the severity of the miseries to which he was subjected. He and Mr Oriel were soon to be seen through the dining-room window, walking about the grounds with the two eldest Miss Greshams. And Patience Oriel, who had also been of the party, was also to be seen with the twins. Frank looked at his father with almost a malicious smile, and began to think that he too might be better employed out among the walks. Did he think then of a former summer evening, when he had half broken Mary's heart by walking there too lovingly with Patience Oriel?

Sir Louis, if he continued his brilliant career of success, would soon be left the cock of the walk. The squire, to be sure, could not bolt, nor could the doctor very well; but they might be equally vanquished, remaining there in their chairs. Dr Thorne, during all this time, was sitting with tingling ears. Indeed, it may be said that his whole body tingled. He was in a manner responsible for this horrid scene; but what could he do to stop it? He could not take Sir Louis up bodily and carry him away. One idea did occur to him. The fly had been ordered for ten o'clock. He could rush out and send for it instantly.

"You're not going to leave me?" said the squire, in a voice of horror, as he saw the doctor rising from his chair.

"Oh, no, no, no," said the doctor; and then he whispered the purpose of his mission. "I will be back in two minutes." The doctor would have given twenty pounds to have closed the scene at once; but he was not the man to desert his friend in such a strait as that.

"He's a well-meaning fellow, the doctor," said Sir Louis, when his guardian was out of the room, "very; but he's not up to trap—not at all."

"Up to trap—well, I should say he was; that is, if I know what trap means," said Frank.

"Ah, but that's just the ticket. Do you know? Now I say Dr Thorne's not a man of the world."

"He's about the best man I know, or ever heard of," said the squire. "And if any man ever had a good friend, you have got one in him; and so have I:" and the squire silently drank the doctor's health.

"All very true, I dare say; but yet he's not up to trap. Now look here, squire—"

"If you don't mind, sir," said Frank, "I've got something very particular—perhaps, however—"

"Stay till Thorne returns, Frank."

Frank did stay till Thorne returned, and then escaped.

"Excuse me, doctor," said he, "but I've something very particular to say; I'll explain to-morrow." And then the three were left alone.

Sir Louis was now becoming almost drunk, and was knocking his words together. The squire had already attempted to stop the bottle; but the baronet had contrived to get hold of a modicum of Madeira, and there was no preventing him from helping himself; at least, none at that moment.

"As we were saying about lawyers," continued Sir Louis. "Let's see, what were we saying? Why, squire, it's just here. Those fellows will fleece us both if we don't mind what we are after."

"Never mind about lawyers now," said Dr Thorne, angrily.

"Ah, but I do mind; most particularly. That's all very well for you, doctor; you've nothing to lose. You've no great stake in the matter. Why, now, what sum of money of mine do you think those d—— doctors are handling?"

"D—— doctors!" said the squire in a tone of dismay.

"Lawyers, I mean, of course. Why, now, Gresham; we're all totted now, you see; you're down in my books, I take it, for pretty near a hundred thousand pounds."

"Hold your tongue, sir," said the doctor, getting up.

"Hold my tongue!" said Sir Louis.

"Sir Louis Scatcherd," said the squire, slowly rising from his chair, "we will not, if you please, talk about business at the present moment. Perhaps we had better go to the ladies."

This latter proposition had certainly not come from the squire's heart: going to the ladies was the very last thing for which Sir Louis was now fit. But the squire had said it as being the only recognised formal way he could think of for breaking up the symposium.

"Oh, very well," hiccupped the baronet, "I'm always ready for the ladies," and he stretched out his hand to the decanter to get a last glass of Madeira.

"No," said the doctor, rising stoutly, and speaking with a determined voice. "No; you will have no more wine:" and he took the decanter from him.

"What's all this about?" said Sir Louis, with a drunken laugh.

"Of course he cannot go into the drawing-room, Mr Gresham. If you will leave him here with me, I will stay with him till the fly comes. Pray tell Lady Arabella from me, how sorry I am that this has occurred."

The squire would not leave his friend, and they sat together till the fly came. It was not long, for the doctor had dispatched his messenger with much haste.

"I am so heartily ashamed of myself," said the doctor, almost with tears.

The squire took him by the hand affectionately. "I've seen a tipsy man before to-night," said he.

"Yes," said the doctor, "and so have I, but—" He did not express the rest of his thoughts.

CHAPTER XXXVI

WILL HE COME AGAIN?

Long before the doctor returned home after the little dinner-party above described, Mary had learnt that Frank was already at Greshamsbury. She had heard nothing of him or from him, not a word, nothing in the shape of a message, for twelve months; and at her age twelve months is a long period. Would he come and see her in spite of his mother? Would he send her any tidings of his return, or notice her in any way? If he did not, what would she do? and if he did, what then would she do? It was so hard to resolve; so hard to be deserted; and so hard to dare to wish that she might not be deserted! She continued to say to herself, that it would be better that they should be strangers; and she could hardly keep herself from tears in the fear that they might be so. What chance could there be that he should care for her, after an absence spent in travelling over the world? No; she would forget that affair of his hand; and then, immediately after having so determined, she would confess to herself that it was a thing not to be forgotten, and impossible of oblivion.

On her uncle's return, she would hear some word about him; and so she sat alone, with a book before her, of which she could not read a line. She expected them about eleven, and was, therefore, rather surprised when the fly stopped at the door before nine.

She immediately heard her uncle's voice, loud and angry, calling for Thomas. Both Thomas and Bridget were unfortunately out, being, at this moment, forgetful of all sublunary cares, and seated in happiness under a beech-tree in the park. Janet flew to the little gate, and there found Sir Louis insisting that he would be taken at once to his own mansion at Boxall Hill, and positively swearing that he would no longer submit to the insult of the doctor's surveillance.

In the absence of Thomas, the doctor was forced to apply for assistance to the driver of the fly. Between them the baronet was dragged out of the vehicle, the windows suffered much, and the doctor's hat also. In this way, he was taken upstairs, and was at last put to bed, Janet assisting; nor did the doctor leave the room till his guest was asleep. Then he went into the drawing-room to Mary. It may easily be conceived that he was hardly in a humour to talk much about Frank Gresham.

"What am I to do with him?" said he, almost in tears: "what am I to do with him?"

"Can you not send him to Boxall Hill?" asked Mary.

"Yes; to kill himself there! But it is no matter; he will kill himself somewhere. Oh! what that family have done for me!" And then, suddenly remembering a portion of their doings, he took Mary in his arms, and kissed and blessed her; and declared that, in spite of all this, he was a happy man.

There was no word about Frank that night. The next morning the doctor found Sir Louis very weak, and begging for stimulants. He was worse than weak; he was in such a state of wretched misery and mental prostration; so low in heart, in such collapse of energy and spirit, that Dr Thorne thought it prudent to remove his razors from his reach.

"For God's sake do let me have a little *chasse-café*; I'm always used to it; ask Joe if I'm not! You don't want to kill me, do you?" And the baronet cried piteously, like a child, and, when the doctor left him for the breakfast-table, abjectly implored Janet to get him some curaçoa which he knew was in one of his portmanteaus. Janet, however, was true to her master.

The doctor did give him some wine; and then, having left strict orders as to his treatment—Bridget and Thomas being now both in the house—went forth to some of his too much neglected patients.

Then Mary was again alone, and her mind flew away to her lover. How should she be able to compose herself when she should first see him? See him she must. People cannot live in the same village without meeting. If she passed him at the church-door, as she often passed Lady Arabella, what should she do? Lady Arabella always smiled a peculiar, little, bitter smile, and this, with half a nod of recognition, carried off the meeting. Should she try the bitter smile, the half-nod with Frank? Alas! she knew it was not in her to be so much mistress of her own heart's blood.

As she thus thought, she stood at the drawing-room window, looking out into her garden; and, as she leant against the sill, her head was surrounded by the sweet creepers. "At any rate, he won't come here," she said: and so, with a deep sigh, she turned from the window into the room.

There he was, Frank Gresham himself standing there in her immediate presence, beautiful as Apollo. Her next thought was how she might escape from out of his arms. How it happened that she had fallen into them, she never knew.

"Mary! my own, own love! my own one! sweetest! dearest! best! Mary! dear Mary! have you not a word to say to me?"

No; she had not a word, though her life had depended on it. The exertion necessary for not crying was quite enough for her. This, then, was the bitter smile and the half-nod that was to pass between them; this was the manner in which estrangement was to grow into indifference; this was the mode of meeting by which she was to prove that she was mistress of her conduct, if not her heart! There he held her close bound to his breast, and she could only protect her face, and that all ineffectually, with her hands. "He loves another," Beatrice had said. "At any rate, he will not love me," her own heart had said also. Here was now the answer.

"You know you cannot marry him," Beatrice had said, also. Ah! if that really were so, was not this embrace deplorable for them both? And yet how could she not be happy? She endeavoured to repel him; but with what a weak endeavour! Her pride had been wounded to the core, not by Lady Arabella's scorn, but by the conviction which had grown on her, that though she had given her own heart absolutely away, had parted with it wholly and for ever, she had received nothing in return. The world, her world, would know that she had loved, and loved in vain. But here now was the loved one at her feet; the first moment that his enforced banishment was over, had brought him there. How could she not be happy?

They all said that she could not marry him. Well, perhaps it might be so; nay, when she thought of it, must not that edict too probably be true? But if so, it would not be his fault. He was true to her, and that satisfied her pride. He had taken from her, by surprise, a confession of her love. She had often regretted her weakness in allowing him to do so; but she could not regret it now. She could endure to suffer; nay, it would not be suffering while he suffered with her.

"Not one word, Mary? Then after all my dreams, after all my patience, you do not love me at last?"

Oh, Frank! notwithstanding what has been said in thy praise, what a fool thou art! Was any word necessary for thee? Had not her heart beat against thine? Had she not borne thy caresses? Had there been one touch of anger when she warded off thy threatened kisses? Bridget, in the kitchen, when Jonah became amorous, smashed his nose with the rolling-pin. But when Thomas sinned, perhaps as deeply, she only talked of doing so. Miss Thorne, in the drawing-room, had she needed self-protection, could doubtless have found the means, though the process would probably have been less violent.

At last Mary succeeded in her efforts at enfranchisement, and she and Frank stood at some little distance from each other. She could not but marvel at him. That long, soft beard, which just now had been so close to her face, was all new; his whole look was altered; his mien, and gait, and very voice were not the same. Was this, indeed, the very Frank who had chattered of his boyish love, two years since, in the gardens at Greshamsbury?

"Not one word of welcome, Mary?"

"Indeed, Mr Gresham, you are welcome home."

"Mr Gresham! Tell me, Mary—tell me, at once—has anything happened? I could not ask up there."

"Frank," she said, and then stopped; not being able at the moment to get any further.

"Speak to me honestly, Mary; honestly and bravely. I offered you my hand once before; there it is again. Will you take it?"

She looked wistfully up in his eyes; she would fain have taken it. But though a girl may be honest in such a case, it is so hard for her to be brave.

He still held out his hand. "Mary," said he, "if you can value it, it shall be yours through good fortune or ill fortune. There may be difficulties; but if you can love me, we will get over them. I am a free man; free to do as I please with myself, except so far as I am bound to you. There is my hand. Will you have it?" And then he, too, looked into her eyes, and waited composedly, as though determined to have an answer.

She slowly raised her hand, and, as she did so, her eyes fell to the ground. It then drooped again, and was again raised; and, at last, her light tapering fingers rested on his broad open palm.

They were soon clutched, and the whole hand brought absolutely within his grasp. "There, now you are my own!" he said, "and none of them shall part us; my own Mary, my own wife."

"Oh, Frank, is not this imprudent? Is it not wrong?"

"Imprudent! I am sick of prudence. I hate prudence. And as for wrong—no. I say it is not wrong; certainly not wrong if we love each other. And you do love me, Mary—eh? You do! don't you?"

He would not excuse her, or allow her to escape from saying it in so many words; and when the words did come at last, they came freely. "Yes, Frank, I do love you; if that were all you would have no cause for fear."

"And I will have no cause for fear."

"Ah; but your father, Frank, and my uncle. I can never bring myself to do anything that shall bring either of them to sorrow."

Frank, of course, ran through all his arguments. He would go into a profession, or take a farm and live in it. He would wait; that is, for a few months. "A few months, Frank!" said Mary. "Well, perhaps six." "Oh, Frank!" But Frank would not be stopped. He would do anything that his father might ask him. Anything but the one thing. He would not give up the wife he had chosen. It would not be reasonable, or proper, or righteous that he should be asked to do so; and here he mounted a somewhat high horse.

Mary had no arguments which she could bring from her heart to offer in opposition to all this. She could only leave her hand in his, and feel that she was happier than she had been at any time since the day of that donkey-ride at Boxall Hill.

"But, Mary," continued he, becoming very grave and serious. "We must be true to each other, and firm in this. Nothing that any of them can say shall drive me from my purpose; will you say as much?"

Her hand was still in his, and so she stood, thinking for a moment before she answered him. But she could not do less for him than he was willing to do for her. "Yes," said she— said in a very low voice, and with a manner perfectly quiet—"I will be firm. Nothing that they can say shall shake me. But, Frank, it cannot be soon."

Nothing further occurred in this interview which needs recording. Frank had been three times told by Mary that he had better go before he did go; and, at last, she was obliged to take the matter into her own hands, and lead him to the door.

"You are in a great hurry to get rid of me," said he.

"You have been here two hours, and you must go now; what will they all think?"

"Who cares what they think? Let them think the truth: that after a year's absence, I have much to say to you." However, at last, he did go, and Mary was left alone.

Frank, although he had been so slow to move, had a thousand other things to do, and went about them at once. He was very much in love, no doubt; but that did not interfere with his interest in other pursuits. In the first place, he had to see Harry Baker, and Harry Baker's stud. Harry had been specially charged to look after the black horse during Frank's absence, and the holiday doings of that valuable animal had to be inquired into. Then the kennel of the hounds had to be visited, and—as a matter of second-rate importance—the master. This could not be done on the same day; but a plan for doing so must be concocted with Harry—and then there were two young pointer pups.

Frank, when he left his betrothed, went about these things quite as vehemently as though he were not in love at all; quite as vehemently as though he had said nothing as to going into some profession which must necessarily separate him from horses and dogs. But Mary sat there at her window, thinking of her love, and thinking of nothing else. It was all in all to her now. She had pledged herself not to be shaken from her troth by anything, by any person; and it would behove her to be true to this pledge. True to it, though all the Greshams but one should oppose her with all their power; true to it, even though her own uncle should oppose her.

And how could she have done any other than so pledge herself, invoked to it as she had been? How could she do less for him than he was so anxious to do for her? They would talk to her of maiden delicacy, and tell her that she had put a stain on that snow-white coat of proof, in confessing her love for one whose friends were unwilling to receive her. Let them so talk. Honour, honesty, and truth, out-spoken truth, self-denying truth, and fealty from man to man, are worth more than maiden delicacy; more, at any rate, than the talk of it. It was not for herself that this pledge had been made. She knew her position, and the difficulties of it; she knew also the value of it. He had much to offer, much to give; she had nothing but herself. He had name, and old repute, family, honour, and what eventually would at least be wealth to her. She was nameless, fameless, portionless. He had come there with all his ardour, with the impulse of his character, and asked for her love. It was already his own. He had then demanded her troth, and she acknowledged that he had a right to demand it. She would be his if ever it should be in his power to take her.

But there let the bargain end. She would always remember, that though it was in her power to keep her pledge, it might too probably not be in his power to keep his. That doctrine, laid down so imperatively by the great authorities of Greshamsbury, that edict, which demanded that Frank should marry money, had come home also to her with a certain force. It would be sad that the fame of Greshamsbury should perish, and that the glory should depart from the old house. It might be, that Frank also should perceive that he must marry money. It would be a pity that he had not seen it sooner; but she, at any rate, would not complain.

And so she stood, leaning on the open window, with her book unnoticed lying beside her. The sun had been in the mid-sky when Frank had left her, but its rays were beginning to stream into the room from the west before she moved from her position. Her first thought in the morning had been this: Would he come to see her? Her last now was more soothing to her, less full of absolute fear: Would it be right that he should come again?

The first sounds she heard were the footsteps of her uncle, as he came up to the drawing-room, three steps at a time. His step was always heavy; but when he was disturbed in spirit, it was slow; when merely fatigued in body by ordinary work, it was quick.

"What a broiling day!" he said, and he threw himself into a chair. "For mercy's sake give me something to drink." Now the doctor was a great man for summer-drinks. In his house, lemonade, currant-juice, orange-mixtures, and raspberry-vinegar were used by the quart. He frequently disapproved of these things for his patients, as being apt to disarrange the digestion; but he consumed enough himself to throw a large family into such difficulties.

"Ha—a!" he ejaculated, after a draught; "I'm better now. Well, what's the news?"

"You've been out, uncle; you ought to have the news. How's Mrs Green?"

"Really as bad as ennui and solitude can make her."

"And Mrs Oaklerath?"

"She's getting better, because she has ten children to look after, and twins to suckle. What has he been doing?" And the doctor pointed towards the room occupied by Sir Louis.

Mary's conscience struck her that she had not even asked. She had hardly remembered, during the whole day, that the baronet was in the house. "I do not think he has been doing much," she said. "Janet has been with him all day."

"Has he been drinking?"

"Upon my word, I don't know, uncle. I think not, for Janet has been with him. But, uncle—"

"Well, dear—but just give me a little more of that tipple."

Mary prepared the tumbler, and, as she handed it to him, she said, "Frank Gresham has been here to-day."

The doctor swallowed his draught, and put down the glass before he made any reply, and even then he said but little.

"Oh! Frank Gresham."

"Yes, uncle."

"You thought him looking pretty well?"

"Yes, uncle; he was very well, I believe."

Dr Thorne had nothing more to say, so he got up and went to his patient in the next room.

"If he disapproves of it, why does he not say so?" said Mary to herself. "Why does he not advise me?"

But it was not so easy to give advice while Sir Louis Scatcherd was lying there in that state.

719

CHAPTER XXXVII

SIR LOUIS LEAVES GRESHAMSBURY

Janet had been sedulous in her attentions to Sir Louis, and had not troubled her mistress; but she had not had an easy time of it. Her orders had been, that either she or Thomas should remain in the room the whole day, and those orders had been obeyed.

Immediately after breakfast, the baronet had inquired after his own servant. "His confounded nose must be right by this time, I suppose?"

"It was very bad, Sir Louis," said the old woman, who imagined that it might be difficult to induce Jonah to come into the house again.

"A man in such a place as his has no business to be laid up," said the master, with a whine. "I'll see and get a man who won't break his nose."

Thomas was sent to the inn three or four times, but in vain. The man was sitting up, well enough, in the tap-room; but the middle of his face was covered with streaks of plaster, and he could not bring himself to expose his wounds before his conqueror.

Sir Louis began by ordering the woman to bring him *chasse-café*. She offered him coffee, as much as he would; but no *chasse*. "A glass of port wine," she said, "at twelve o'clock, and another at three had been ordered for him."

"I don't care a —— for the orders," said Sir Louis; "send me my own man." The man was again sent for; but would not come. "There's a bottle of that stuff that I take, in that portmanteau, in the left-hand corner—just hand it to me."

But Janet was not to be done. She would give him no stuff, except what the doctor had ordered, till the doctor came back. The doctor would then, no doubt, give him anything that was proper.

Sir Louis swore a good deal, and stormed as much as he could. He drank, however, his two glasses of wine, and he got no more. Once or twice he essayed to get out of bed and dress; but, at every effort, he found that he could not do it without Joe: and there he was, still under the clothes when the doctor returned.

"I'll tell you what it is," said he, as soon as his guardian entered the room, "I'm not going to be made a prisoner of here."

"A prisoner! no, surely not."

"It seems very much like it at present. Your servant here—that old woman—takes it upon her to say she'll do nothing without your orders."

"Well; she's right there."

"Right! I don't know what you call right; but I won't stand it. You are not going to make a child of me, Dr Thorne; so you need not think it."

And then there was a long quarrel between them, and but an indifferent reconciliation. The baronet said that he would go to Boxall Hill, and was vehement in his intention to do so because the doctor opposed it. He had not, however, as yet ferreted out the squire, or given a bit of his mind to Mr Gazebee, and it behoved him to do this before he took himself off to his own country mansion. He ended, therefore, by deciding to go on the next day but one.

"Let it be so, if you are well enough," said the doctor.

"Well enough!" said the other, with a sneer. "There's nothing to make me ill that I know of. It certainly won't be drinking too much here."

On the next day, Sir Louis was in a different mood, and in one more distressing for the doctor to bear. His compelled abstinence from intemperate drinking had, no doubt, been good for him; but his mind had so much sunk under the pain of the privation, that his state was piteous to behold. He had cried for his servant, as a child cries for its nurse, till at last the doctor, moved to pity, had himself gone out and brought the man in from the public-house. But when he did come, Joe was of but little service to his master, as he was altogether prevented from bringing him either wine or spirits; and when he searched for the liqueur-case, he found that even that had been carried away.

"I believe you want me to die," he said, as the doctor, sitting by his bedside, was trying, for the hundredth time, to make him understand that he had but one chance of living.

The doctor was not the least irritated. It would have been as wise to be irritated by the want of reason in a dog.

"I am doing what I can to save your life," he said calmly; "but, as you said just now, I have no power over you. As long as you are able to move and remain in my house, you certainly shall not have the means of destroying yourself. You will be very wise to stay here for a week or ten days: a week or ten days of healthy living might, perhaps, bring you round."

Sir Louis again declared that the doctor wished him to die, and spoke of sending for his attorney, Finnie, to come to Greshamsbury to look after him.

"Send for him if you choose," said the doctor. "His coming will cost you three or four pounds, but can do no other harm."

"And I will send for Fillgrave," threatened the baronet. "I'm not going to die here like a dog."

It was certainly hard upon Dr Thorne that he should be obliged to entertain such a guest in the house;—to entertain him, and foster him, and care for him, almost as though he were a son. But he had no alternative; he had accepted the charge from Sir Roger, and he must go through with it. His conscience, moreover, allowed him no rest in this matter: it harassed him day and night, driving him on sometimes to great wretchedness. He could not love this incubus that was on his shoulders; he could not do other than be very far from loving him. Of what use or value was he to any one? What could the world make of him that would be good, or he of the world? Was not an early death his certain fate? The earlier it might be, would it not be the better?

Were he to linger on yet for two years longer—and such a space of life was possible for him—how great would be the mischief that he might do; nay, certainly would do! Farewell then to all hopes for Greshamsbury, as far as Mary was concerned. Farewell then to that dear scheme which lay deep in the doctor's heart, that hope that he might, in his niece's name, give back to the son the lost property of the father. And might not one year—six months be as fatal. Frank, they all said, must marry money; and even he—he the doctor himself, much as he despised the idea for money's sake—even he could not but confess that Frank, as the heir to an old, but grievously embarrassed property, had no right to marry, at his early age, a girl without a shilling. Mary, his niece, his own child, would probably be the heiress of this immense wealth; but he could not tell this to Frank; no, nor to Frank's father while Sir Louis was yet alive. What, if by so doing he should achieve this marriage for his niece, and that then Sir Louis should live to dispose of his own? How then would he face the anger of Lady Arabella?

"I will never hanker after a dead man's shoes, neither for myself nor for another," he had said to himself a hundred times; and as often did he accuse himself of doing so. One path, however, was plainly open before him. He would keep his peace as to the will; and would use such efforts as he might use for a son of his own loins to preserve the life that was so valueless. His wishes, his hopes, his thoughts, he could not control; but his conduct was at his own disposal.

"I say, doctor, you don't really think that I'm going to die?" Sir Louis said, when Dr Thorne again visited him.

"I don't think at all; I am sure you will kill yourself if you continue to live as you have lately done."

"But suppose I go all right for a while, and live—live just as you tell me, you know?"

"All of us are in God's hands, Sir Louis. By so doing you will, at any rate, give yourself the best chance."

"Best chance? Why, d——n, doctor! there are fellows have done ten times worse than I; and they are not going to kick. Come, now, I know you are trying to frighten me; ain't you, now?"

"I am trying to do the best I can for you."

"It's very hard on a fellow like me; I have nobody to say a kind word to me; no, not one." And Sir Louis, in his wretchedness, began to weep. "Come, doctor; if you'll put me once more on my legs, I'll let you draw on the estate for five hundred pounds; by G——, I will."

The doctor went away to his dinner, and the baronet also had his in bed. He could not eat much, but he was allowed two glasses of wine, and also a little brandy in his coffee. This somewhat invigorated him, and when Dr Thorne again went to him, in the evening, he did not find him so utterly prostrated in spirit. He had, indeed, made up his mind to a great resolve; and thus unfolded his final scheme for his own reformation:—

"Doctor," he began again, "I believe you are an honest fellow; I do indeed."

Dr Thorne could not but thank him for his good opinion.

"You ain't annoyed at what I said this morning, are you?"

The doctor had forgotten the particular annoyance to which Sir Louis alluded; and informed him that his mind might be at rest on any such matter.

"I do believe you'd be glad to see me well; wouldn't you, now?"

The doctor assured him that such was in very truth the case.

"Well, now, I'll tell you what: I've been thinking about it a great deal to-day; indeed, I have, and I want to do what's right. Mightn't I have a little drop more of that stuff, just in a cup of coffee?"

The doctor poured him out a cup of coffee, and put about a teaspoonful of brandy in it. Sir Louis took it with a disconsolate face, not having been accustomed to such measures in the use of his favourite beverage.

"I do wish to do what's right—I do, indeed; only, you see, I'm so lonely. As to those fellows up in London, I don't think that one of them cares a straw about me."

Dr Thorne was of the same way of thinking, and he said so. He could not but feel some sympathy with the unfortunate man as he thus spoke of his own lot. It was true that he had been thrown on the world without any one to take care of him.

"My dear friend, I will do the best I can in every way; I will, indeed. I do believe that your companions in town have been too ready to lead you astray. Drop them, and you may yet do well."

"May I though, doctor? Well, I will drop them. There's Jenkins; he's the best of them; but even he is always wanting to make money of me. Not but what I'm up to the best of them in that way."

"You had better leave London, Sir Louis, and change your old mode of life. Go to Boxall Hill for a while; for two or three years or so; live with your mother there and take to farming."

"What! farming?"

"Yes; that's what all country gentlemen do: take the land there into your own hand, and occupy your mind upon it."

"Well, doctor, I will—upon one condition."

Dr Thorne sat still and listened. He had no idea what the condition might be, but he was not prepared to promise acquiescence till he heard it.

"You know what I told you once before," said the baronet.

"I don't remember at this moment."

"About my getting married, you know."

The doctor's brow grew black, and promised no help to the poor wretch. Bad in every way, wretched, selfish, sensual, unfeeling, purse-proud, ignorant as Sir Louis Scatcherd was, still, there was left to him the power of feeling something like sincere love. It may be presumed that he did love Mary Thorne, and that he was at the time earnest in declaring, that if she could be given to him, he would endeavour to live according to her uncle's counsel. It was only a trifle he asked; but, alas! that trifle could not be vouchsafed.

"I should much approve of your getting married, but I do not know how I can help you."

"Of course, I mean to Miss Mary: I do love her; I really do, Dr Thorne."

"It is quite impossible, Sir Louis; quite. You do my niece much honour; but I am able to answer for her, positively, that such a proposition is quite out of the question."

"Look here now, Dr Thorne; anything in the way of settlements—"

"I will not hear a word on the subject: you are very welcome to the use of my house as long as it may suit you to remain here; but I must insist that my niece shall not be troubled on this matter."

"Do you mean to say she's in love with that young Gresham?"

This was too much for the doctor's patience. "Sir Louis," said he, "I can forgive you much for your father's sake. I can also forgive something on the score of your own ill health. But you ought to know, you ought by this time to have learnt, that there are some things which a man cannot forgive. I will not talk to you about my niece; and remember this, also, I will not have her troubled by you:" and, so saying, the doctor left him.

On the next day the baronet was sufficiently recovered to be able to resume his braggadocio airs. He swore at Janet; insisted on being served by his own man; demanded in a loud voice, but in vain, that his liqueur-case should be restored to him; and desired that post-horses might be ready for him on the morrow. On that day he got up and ate his dinner in his bedroom. On the next morning he countermanded the horses, informing the doctor that he did so because he had a little bit of business to transact with Squire Gresham before he left the place! With some difficulty, the doctor made him understand that the squire would not see him on business; and it was at last decided, that Mr Gazebee should be invited to call on him at the doctor's house; and this Mr Gazebee agreed to do, in order to prevent the annoyance of having the baronet up at Greshamsbury.

On this day, the evening before Mr Gazebee's visit, Sir Louis condescended to come down to dinner. He dined, however, *tête-à-tête* with the doctor. Mary was not there, nor was anything said as to her absence. Sir Louis Scatcherd never set eyes upon her again.

He bore himself very arrogantly on that evening, having resumed the airs and would-be dignity which he thought belonged to him as a man of rank and property. In his periods of low spirits, he was abject and humble enough; abject, and fearful of the lamentable destiny which at these moments he believed to be in store for him. But it was one of the peculiar symptoms of his state, that as he partially recovered his bodily health, the tone of his mind recovered itself also, and his fears for the time were relieved.

There was very little said between him and the doctor that evening. The doctor sat guarding the wine, and thinking when he should have his house to himself again. Sir Louis sat moody, every now and then uttering some impertinence as to the Greshams and the Greshamsbury property, and, at an early hour, allowed Joe to put him to bed.

The horses were ordered on the next day for three, and, at two, Mr Gazebee came to the house. He had never been there before, nor had he ever met Dr Thorne except at the squire's dinner. On this occasion he asked only for the baronet.

"Ah! ah! I'm glad you're come, Mr Gazebee; very glad," said Sir Louis; acting the part of the rich, great man with all the power he had. "I want to ask you a few questions so as to make it all clear sailing between us."

"As you have asked to see me, I have come, Sir Louis," said the other, putting on much dignity as he spoke. "But would it not be better that any business there may be should be done among the lawyers?"

"The lawyers are very well, I dare say; but when a man has so large a stake at interest as I have in this Greshamsbury property, why, you see, Mr Gazebee, he feels a little inclined to look after it himself. Now, do you know, Mr Gazebee, how much it is that Mr Gresham owes me?"

Mr Gazebee, of course, did know very well; but he was not going to discuss the subject with Sir Louis, if he could help it.

"Whatever claim your father's estate may have on that of Mr Gresham is, as far as I understand, vested in Dr Thorne's hands as trustee. I am inclined to believe that you have not yourself at present any claim on Greshamsbury. The interest, as it becomes due, is paid to Dr Thorne; and if I may be allowed to make a suggestion, I would say that it will not be expedient to make any change in that arrangement till the property shall come into your own hands."

"I differ from you entirely, Mr Gazebee; *in toto*, as we used to say at Eton. What you mean to say is—I can't go to law with Mr Gresham; I'm not so sure of that; but perhaps not. But I can compel Dr Thorne to look after my interests. I can force him to foreclose. And to tell you the truth, Gazebee, unless some arrangement is proposed to me which I shall think advantageous, I shall do so at once. There is near a hundred thousand pounds owing to me; yes to me. Thorne is only a name in the matter. The money is my money; and, by ——, I mean to look after it."

"Have you any doubt, Sir Louis, as to the money being secure?"

"Yes, I have. It isn't so easy to have a hundred thousand pounds secured. The squire is a poor man, and I don't choose to allow a poor man to owe me such a sum as that. Besides, I mean to invest it in land. I tell you fairly, therefore, I shall foreclose."

Mr Gazebee, using all the perspicuity which his professional education had left to him, tried to make Sir Louis understand that he had no power to do anything of the kind.

"No power! Mr Gresham shall see whether I have no power. When a man has a hundred thousand pounds owing to him he ought to have some power; and, as I take it, he has. But we will see. Perhaps you know Finnie, do you?"

Mr Gazebee, with a good deal of scorn in his face, said that he had not that pleasure. Mr Finnie was not in his line.

"Well, you will know him then, and you'll find he's sharp enough; that is, unless I have some offer made to me that I may choose to accept." Mr Gazebee declared that he was not instructed to make any offer, and so he took his leave.

On that afternoon, Sir Louis went off to Boxall Hill, transferring the miserable task of superintending his self-destruction from the shoulders of the doctor to those of his mother. Of Lady Scatcherd, the baronet took no account in his proposed sojourn in the country, nor did he take much of the doctor in leaving Greshamsbury. He again wrapped himself in his furs, and, with tottering steps, climbed up into the barouche which was to carry him away.

"Is my man up behind?" he said to Janet, while the doctor was standing at the little front garden-gate, making his adieux.

"No, sir, he's not up yet," said Janet, respectfully.

"Then send him out, will you? I can't lose my time waiting here all day."

"I shall come over to Boxall Hill and see you," said the doctor, whose heart softened towards the man, in spite of his brutality, as the hour of his departure came.

"I shall be happy to see you if you like to come, of course; that is, in the way of visiting, and that sort of thing. As for doctoring, if I want any I shall send for Fillgrave." Such were his last words as the carriage, with a rush, went off from the door.

The doctor, as he re-entered the house, could not avoid smiling, for he thought of Dr Fillgrave's last patient at Boxall Hill. "It's a question to me," said he to himself, "whether Dr Fillgrave will ever be induced to make another visit to that house, even with the object of rescuing a baronet out of my hands."

"He's gone; isn't he, uncle?" said Mary, coming out of her room.

"Yes, my dear; he's gone, poor fellow."

"He may be a poor fellow, uncle; but he's a very disagreeable inmate in a house. I have not had any dinner these two days."

"And I haven't had what can be called a cup of tea since he's been in the house. But I'll make up for that to-night."

CHAPTER XXXVIII

DE COURCY PRECEPTS AND DE COURCY PRACTICE

There is a mode of novel-writing which used to be much in vogue, but which has now gone out of fashion. It is, nevertheless, one which is very expressive when in good hands, and which enables the author to tell his story, or some portion of his story, with more natural trust than any other, I mean that of familiar letters. I trust I shall be excused if I attempt it as regards this one chapter; though, it may be, that I shall break down and fall into the commonplace narrative, even before the one chapter be completed. The correspondents are the Lady Amelia de Courcy and Miss Gresham. I, of course, give precedence to the higher rank, but the first epistle originated with the latter-named young lady. Let me hope that they will explain themselves.

Miss Gresham to Lady Amelia de Courcy

Greshamsbury House, June, 185—.

MY DEAREST AMELIA, I wish to consult you on a subject which, as you will perceive, is of a most momentous nature. You know how much reliance I place in your judgement and knowledge of what is proper, and, therefore, I write to you before speaking to any other living person on the subject: not even to mamma; for, although her judgement is good too, she has so many cares and troubles, that it is natural that it should be a little warped when the interests of her children are concerned. Now that it is all over, I feel that it may possibly have been so in the case of Mr Moffat.

You are aware that Mr Mortimer Gazebee is now staying here, and that he has been here for nearly two months. He is engaged in managing poor papa's affairs, and mamma, who likes him very much, says that he is a most excellent man of business. Of course, you know that he is the junior partner in the very old firm of Gumption, Gazebee, & Gazebee, who, I understand, do not undertake any business at all, except what comes to them from peers, or commoners of the very highest class.

I soon perceived, dearest Amelia, that Mr Gazebee paid me more than ordinary attention, and I immediately became very guarded in my manner. I certainly liked Mr Gazebee from the first. His manners are quite excellent, his conduct to mamma is charming, and, as regards myself, I must say that there has been nothing in his behaviour of which even *you* could complain.

He has never attempted the slightest familiarity, and I will do him the justice to say, that, though he has been very attentive, he has also been very respectful.

I must confess that, for the last three weeks, I have thought that he meant something. I might, perhaps, have done more to repel him; or I might have consulted you earlier as to the propriety of keeping altogether out of his way. But you know, Amelia, how often these things lead to nothing, and though I thought all along that Mr Gazebee was in earnest, I hardly liked to say anything about it even to you till I was quite certain. If you had advised me, you know, to accept his offer, and if, after that, he had never made it, I should have felt so foolish.

But now he has made it. He came to me yesterday just before dinner, in the little drawing-room, and told me, in the most delicate manner, in words that even you could not have but approved, that his highest ambition was to be thought worthy of my regard, and that he felt for me the warmest love, and the most profound admiration, and the deepest respect. You may say, Amelia, that he is only an attorney, and I believe that he is an attorney; but I am sure you would have esteemed him had you heard the very delicate way in which he expressed his sentiments.

Something had given me a presentiment of what he was going to do when I saw him come into the room, so that I was on my guard. I tried very hard to show no emotion; but I suppose I was a little flurried, as I once detected myself calling him Mr Mortimer: his name, you know, is Mortimer Gazebee. I ought not to have done so, certainly; but it was not so bad as if I had called him Mortimer without the Mr, was it? I don't think there could possibly be a prettier Christian name than Mortimer. Well, Amelia, I allowed him to express himself without interruption. He once attempted to take my hand; but even this was done without any assumption of familiarity; and when he saw that I would not permit it, he drew back, and fixed his eyes on the ground as though he were ashamed even of that.

Of course, I had to give him an answer; and though I had expected that something of this sort would take place, I had not made up my mind on the subject. I would not, certainly, under any circumstances, accept him without consulting you. If I really disliked him, of course there would be no doubt; but I can't say, dearest Amelia, that I do absolutely dislike him; and I really think that we would make each other very happy, if the marriage were suitable as regarded both our positions.

I collected myself as well as I could, and I really do think that you would have said that I did not behave badly, though the position was rather trying. I told him that, of course, I was flattered by his sentiments, though much surprised at hearing them; that since I knew him, I had esteemed and valued him as an acquaintance, but that, looking on him as a man of business, I had never expected anything more. I then endeavoured to explain to him, that I was not perhaps privileged, as some other girls might be, to indulge my own feelings altogether: perhaps that was saying too much, and might make him think that I was in love with him; but, from the way I said it, I don't think he would, for I was very much guarded in my manner, and very collected; and then I told him, that in any proposal of marriage that might be made to me, it would be my duty to consult my family as much, if not more than myself.

He said, of course; and asked whether he might speak to papa. I tried to make him understand, that in talking of my family, I did not exactly mean papa, or even mamma. Of course I was thinking of what was due to the name of Gresham. I know very well what papa would say. He would give his consent in half a minute; he is so broken-hearted by these debts. And, to tell you the truth, Amelia, I think mamma would too. He did not seem quite to comprehend what I meant; but he did say that he knew it was a high ambition to marry into the family of the Greshams. I am sure you would confess that he has the most proper feelings; and as for expressing them no man could do it better.

He owned that it was ambition to ally himself with a family above his own rank in life, and that he looked to doing so as a means of advancing himself. Now this was at any rate honest. That was one of his motives, he said; though, of course, not his first: and then he declared how truly attached he was to me. In answer to this, I remarked, that he had known me only a very short time. This, perhaps, was giving him too much encouragement; but, at that moment, I hardly knew what to say, for I did not wish to hurt his feelings. He then spoke of his income. He has fifteen hundred a year from the business, and that will be greatly increased when his father leaves it; and his father is much older than Mr Gumption, though he is only the second partner. Mortimer Gazebee will be the senior partner himself before very long; and perhaps that does alter his position a little.

He has a very nice place down somewhere in Surrey; I have heard mamma say it is quite a gentleman's place. It is let now; but he will live there when he is married. And he has property of his own besides which he can settle. So, you see, he is quite as well off as Mr Oriel; better, indeed; and if a man is in a profession, I believe it is considered that it does not much matter what. Of course, a clergyman can be a bishop; but then, I think I have heard that one attorney did once become Lord Chancellor. I should have my carriage, you know; I remember his saying that, especially, though I cannot recollect how he brought it in.

I told him, at last, that I was so much taken by surprise that I could not give him an answer then. He was going up to London, he said, on the next day, and might he be permitted to address me on the same subject when he returned? I could not refuse him, you know; and so now I have taken the opportunity of his absence to write to you for your advice. You understand the world so very well, and know so exactly what one ought to do in such a strange position!

I hope I have made it intelligible, at least, as to what I have written about. I have said nothing as to my own feelings, because I wish you to think on the matter without consulting them. If it would be derogatory to accept Mr Gazebee, I certainly would not do so because I happen to like him. If we were to act in that way, what would the world come to, Amelia? Perhaps my ideas may be overstrained; if so, you will tell me.

When Mr Oriel proposed for Beatrice, nobody seemed to make any objection. It all seemed to go as a matter of course. She says that his family is excellent; but as far as I can learn, his grandfather was a general in India, and came home very rich. Mr Gazebee's grandfather was a member of the firm, and so, I believe, was his great-grandfather. Don't you think this ought to count for something? Besides, they have no business except with the most aristocratic persons, such as uncle de Courcy, and the Marquis of Kensington Gore, and that sort. I mention the marquis, because Mr Mortimer Gazebee is there now. And I know that one of the Gumptions was once in Parliament; and I don't think that any of the Oriels ever were. The name of attorney is certainly very bad, is it not, Amelia? but they certainly do not seem to be all the same, and I do think that this ought to make a difference. To hear Mr Mortimer Gazebee talk of some attorney at Barchester, you would say that there is quite as much difference between them as between a bishop and a curate. And so I think there is.

I don't wish at all to speak of my own feelings; but if he were not an attorney, he is, I think, the sort of man I should like. He is very nice in every way, and if you were not told, I don't think you'd know he was an attorney. But, dear Amelia, I will be guided by you altogether. He is certainly much nicer than Mr Moffat, and has a great deal more to say for himself. Of course, Mr Moffat having been in Parliament, and having been taken up by uncle de Courcy, was in a different sphere; but I really felt almost relieved when he behaved in that way. With Mortimer Gazebee, I think it would be different.

I shall wait so impatiently for your answer, so do pray write at once. I hear some people say that these sort of things are not so much thought of now as they were once, and that all manner of marriages are considered to be *comme il faut*. I do not want, you know, to make myself foolish by being too particular. Perhaps all these changes are bad, and I rather think they are; but if the world changes, one must change too; one can't go against the world.

So do write and tell me what you think. Do not suppose that I dislike the man, for I really cannot say that I do. But I would not for anything make an alliance for which any one bearing the name of de Courcy would have to blush.

Always, dearest Amelia,

Your most affectionate cousin,

AUGUSTA GRESHAM.

P.S.—I fear Frank is going to be very foolish with Mary Thorne. You know it is absolutely important that Frank should marry money. It strikes me as quite possible that Mortimer Gazebee may be in Parliament some of these days. He is just the man for it.

Poor Augusta prayed very hard for her husband; but she prayed to a bosom that on this subject was as hard as a flint, and she prayed in vain. Augusta Gresham was twenty-two, Lady Amelia de Courcy was thirty-four; was it likely that Lady Amelia would permit Augusta to marry, the issue having thus been left in her hands? Why should Augusta derogate from her position by marrying beneath herself, seeing that Lady Amelia had spent so many more years in the world without having found it necessary to do so? Augusta's letter was written on two sheets of note-paper, crossed all over; and Lady Amelia's answer was almost equally formidable.

Lady Amelia de Courcy to Miss Augusta Gresham

Courcy Castle, June, 185—.

MY DEAR AUGUSTA, I received your letter yesterday morning, but I have put off answering it till this evening, as I have wished to give it very mature consideration. The question is one which concerns, not only your character, but happiness for life, and nothing less than very mature consideration would justify me in giving a decided opinion on the subject.

In the first place, I may tell you, that I have not a word to say against Mr Mortimer Gazebee. [When Augusta had read as far as this, her heart sank within her; the rest was all leather and prunella; she saw at once that the fiat had gone against her, and that her wish to become Mrs Mortimer Gazebee was not to be indulged.] I have known him for a long time, and I believe him to be a very respectable person, and I have no doubt a good man of business. The firm of Messrs Gumption & Gazebee stands probably quite among the first attorneys in London, and I know that papa has a very high opinion of them.

All of these would be excellent arguments to use in favour of Mr Gazebee as a suitor, had his proposals been made to any one in his own rank of life. But you, in considering the matter, should, I think, look on it in a very different light. The very fact that you pronounce him to be so much superior to other attorneys, shows in how very low esteem you hold the profession in general. It shows also, dear Augusta, how well aware you are that they are a class of people among whom you should not seek a partner for life.

My opinion is, that you should make Mr Gazebee understand—very courteously, of course—that you cannot accept his hand. You observe that he himself confesses, that in marrying you he would seek a wife in a rank above his own. Is it not, therefore, clear, that in marrying him, you would descend to a rank below your own?

I shall be very sorry if this grieves you; but still it will be better that you should bear the grief of overcoming a temporary fancy, than take a step which may so probably make you unhappy; and which some of your friends would certainly regard as disgraceful.

It is not permitted to us, my dear Augusta, to think of ourselves in such matters. As you truly say, if we were to act in that way, what would the world come to? It has been God's pleasure that we should be born with high blood in our veins. This is a great boon which we both value, but the boon has its responsibilities as well as its privileges. It is established by law, that the royal family shall not intermarry with subjects. In our case there is no law, but the necessity is not the less felt; we should not intermarry with those who are probably of a lower rank. Mr Mortimer Gazebee is, after all, only an attorney; and, although you speak of his great-grandfather, he is a man of no blood whatsoever. You must acknowledge that such an admixture should be looked on by a de Courcy, or even by a Gresham, as a pollution. [Here Augusta got very red, and she felt almost inclined to be angry with her cousin.] Beatrice's marriage with Mr Oriel is different; though, remember, I am by no means defending that; it may be good or bad, and I have had no opportunity of inquiring respecting Mr Oriel's family. Beatrice, moreover, has never appeared to me to feel what was due to herself in such matters; but, as I said, her marriage with Mr Oriel is very different. Clergymen—particularly the rectors and vicars of country parishes—do become privileged above other professional men. I could explain why, but it would be too long in a letter.

Your feelings on the subject altogether do you great credit. I have no doubt that Mr Gresham, if asked, would accede to the match; but that is just the reason why he should not be asked. It would not be right that I should say anything against your father to you; but it is impossible for any of us not to see that all through life he has thrown away every advantage, and sacrificed his family. Why is he now in debt, as you say? Why is he not holding the family seat in Parliament? Even though you are his daughter, you cannot but feel that you would not do right to consult him on such a subject.

As to dear aunt, I feel sure, that were she in good health, and left to exercise her own judgement, she would not wish to see you married to the agent for the family estate. For, dear Augusta, that is the real truth. Mr Gazebee often comes here in the way of business; and though papa always receives him as a gentleman—that is, he dines at table and all that—he is not on the same footing in the house as the ordinary guests and friends of the family. How would you like to be received at Courcy Castle in the same way?

You will say, perhaps, that you would still be papa's niece; so you would. But you know how strict in such matters papa is, and you must remember, that the wife always follows the rank of the husband. Papa is accustomed to the strict etiquette of a court, and I am sure that no consideration would induce him to receive the estate-agent in the light of a nephew. Indeed, were you to marry Mr Gazebee, the house to which he belongs would, I imagine, have to give up the management of this property.

Even were Mr Gazebee in Parliament—and I do not see how it is probable that he should get there—it would not make any difference. You must remember, dearest, that I never was an advocate for the Moffat match. I acquiesced in it, because mamma did so. If I could have had my own way, I would adhere to all our old prescriptive principles. Neither money nor position can atone to me for low birth. But the world, alas! is retrograding; and, according to the new-fangled doctrines of the day, a lady of blood is not disgraced by allying herself to a man of wealth, and what may be called quasi-aristocratic position. I wish it were otherwise; but so it is. And, therefore, the match with Mr Moffat was not disgraceful, though it could not be regarded as altogether satisfactory.

But with Mr Gazebee the matter would be altogether different. He is a man earning his bread; honestly, I dare say, but in a humble position. You say he is very respectable: I do not doubt it; and so is Mr Scraggs, the butcher at Courcy. You see, Augusta, to what such arguments reduce you.

I dare say he may be nicer than Mr Moffat, in one way. That is, he may have more small-talk at his command, and be more clever in all those little pursuits and amusements which are valued by ordinary young ladies. But my opinion is, that neither I nor you would be justified in sacrificing ourselves for such amusements. We have high duties before us. It may be that the performance of those duties will prohibit us from taking a part in the ordinary arena of the feminine world. It is natural that girls should wish to marry; and, therefore, those who are weak, take the first that come. Those who have more judgement, make some sort of selection. But the strongest-minded are, perhaps, those who are able to forgo themselves and their own fancies, and to refrain from any alliance that does not tend to the maintenance of high principles. Of course, I speak of those who have blood in their veins. You and I need not dilate as to the conduct of others.

I hope what I have said will convince you. Indeed, I know that it only requires that you and I should have a little cousinly talk on this matter to be quite in accord. You must now remain at Greshamsbury till Mr Gazebee shall return. Immediately that he does so, seek an interview with him; do not wait till he asks for it; then tell him, that when he addressed you, the matter had taken you so much by surprise, that you were not at the moment able to answer him with that decision that the subject demanded. Tell him, that you are flattered—in saying this, however, you must keep a collected countenance, and be very cold in your manner—but that family reasons would forbid you to avail yourself of his offer, even did no other cause prevent it.

And then, dear Augusta, come to us here. I know you will be a little down-hearted after going through this struggle; but I will endeavour to inspirit you. When we are both together, you will feel more sensibly the value of that high position which you will preserve by rejecting Mr Gazebee, and will regret less acutely whatever you may lose.

Your very affectionate cousin,

AMELIA DE COURCY.

P.S.—I am greatly grieved about Frank; but I have long feared that he would do some very silly thing. I have heard lately that Miss Mary Thorne is not even the legitimate niece of your Dr Thorne, but is the daughter of some poor creature who was seduced by the doctor, in Barchester. I do not know how true this may be, but I think your brother should be put on his guard: it might do good.

Poor Augusta! She was in truth to be pitied, for her efforts were made with the intention of doing right according to her lights. For Mr Moffat she had never cared a straw; and when, therefore, she lost the piece of gilding for which she had been instructed by her mother to sell herself, it was impossible to pity her. But Mr Gazebee she would have loved with that sort of love which it was in her power to bestow. With him she would have been happy, respectable, and contented.

She had written her letter with great care. When the offer was made to her, she could not bring herself to throw Lady Amelia to the winds and marry the man, as it were, out of her own head. Lady Amelia had been the tyrant of her life, and so she strove hard to obtain her tyrant's permission. She used all her little cunning in showing that, after all, Mr Gazebee was not so very plebeian. All her little cunning was utterly worthless. Lady Amelia's mind was too strong to be caught with such chaff. Augusta could not serve God and Mammon. She must either be true to the god of her cousin's idolatry, and remain single, or serve the Mammon of her own inclinations, and marry Mr Gazebee.

When refolding her cousin's letter, after the first perusal, she did for a moment think of rebellion. Could she not be happy at the nice place in Surrey, having, as she would have, a carriage, even though all the de Courcys should drop her? It had been put to her that she would not like to be received at Courcy Castle with the scant civility which would be considered due to a Mrs Mortimer Gazebee; but what if she could put up without being received at Courcy Castle at all? Such ideas did float through her mind, dimly.

But her courage failed her. It is so hard to throw off a tyrant; so much easier to yield, when we have been in the habit of yielding. This third letter, therefore, was written; and it is the end of the correspondence.

Miss Augusta Gresham to Lady Amelia de Courcy

Greshamsbury House, July, 185—.

MY DEAREST AMELIA, I did not answer your letter before, because I thought it better to delay doing so till Mr Gazebee had been here. He came the day before yesterday, and yesterday I did, as nearly as possible, what you advised. Perhaps, on the whole, it will be better. As you say, rank has its responsibilities as well as its privileges.

732

I don't quite understand what you mean about clergymen, but we can talk that over when we meet. Indeed, it seems to me that if one is to be particular about family—and I am sure I think we ought—one ought to be so without exception. If Mr Oriel be a *parvenu*, Beatrice's children won't be well born merely because their father was a clergyman, even though he is a rector. Since my former letter, I have heard that Mr Gazebee's great-great-great-grandfather established the firm; and there are many people who were nobodies then who are thought to have good blood in their veins now.

But I do not say this because I differ from you. I agree with you so fully, that I at once made up my mind to reject the man; and, consequently, I have done so.

When I told him I could not accept him from family considerations, he asked me whether I had spoken to papa. I told him, no; and that it would be no good, as I had made up my own mind. I don't think he quite understood me; but it did not perhaps much matter. You told me to be very cold, and I think that perhaps he thought me less gracious than before. Indeed, I fear that when he first spoke, I may seem to have given him too much encouragement. However, it is all over now; quite over! [As Augusta wrote this, she barely managed to save the paper beneath her hand from being moistened with the tear which escaped from her eye.]

I do not mind confessing now, [she continued] at any rate to you, that I did like Mr Gazebee a little. I think his temper and disposition would have suited me. But I am quite satisfied that I have done right. He tried very hard to make me change my mind. That is, he said a great many things as to whether I would not put off my decision. But I was quite firm. I must say that he behaved very well, and that I really do think he liked me honestly and truly; but, of course, I could not sacrifice family considerations on that account.

Yes, rank has its responsibilities as well as its privileges. I will remember that. It is necessary to do so, as otherwise one would be without consolation for what one has to suffer. For I find that one has to suffer, Amelia. I know papa would have advised me to marry this man; and so, I dare say, mamma would, and Frank, and Beatrice, if they knew that I liked him. It would not be so bad if we all thought alike about it; but it is hard to have the responsibilities all on one's own shoulder; is it not?

But I will go over to you, and you will comfort me. I always feel stronger on this subject at Courcy than at Greshamsbury. We will have a long talk about it, and then I shall be happy again. I purpose going on next Friday, if that will suit you and dear aunt. I have told mamma that you all wanted me, and she made no objection. Do write at once, dearest Amelia, for to hear from you now will be my only comfort.

Yours, ever most affectionately and obliged,
AUGUSTA GRESHAM.

P.S.—I told mamma what you said about Mary Thorne, and she said, "Yes; I suppose all the world knows it now; and if all the world did know it, it makes no difference to Frank." She seemed very angry; so you see it was true.

Though, by so doing, we shall somewhat anticipate the end of our story, it may be desirable that the full tale of Mr Gazebee's loves should be told here. When Mary is breaking her heart on her death-bed in the last chapter, or otherwise accomplishing her destiny, we shall hardly find a fit opportunity of saying much about Mr Gazebee and his aristocratic bride.

For he did succeed at last in obtaining a bride in whose veins ran the noble ichor of de Courcy blood, in spite of the high doctrine preached so eloquently by the Lady Amelia. As Augusta had truly said, he had failed to understand her. He was led to think, by her manner of receiving his first proposal—and justly so, enough—that she liked him, and would accept him; and he was, therefore, rather perplexed by his second interview. He tried again and again, and begged permission to mention the matter to Mr Gresham; but Augusta was very firm, and he at last retired in disgust. Augusta went to Courcy Castle, and received from her cousin that consolation and re-strengthening which she so much required.

Four years afterwards—long after the fate of Mary Thorne had fallen, like a thunder-bolt, on the inhabitants of Greshamsbury; when Beatrice was preparing for her second baby, and each of the twins had her accepted lover—Mr Mortimer Gazebee went down to Courcy Castle; of course, on matters of business. No doubt he dined at the table, and all that. We have the word of Lady Amelia, that the earl, with his usual good-nature, allowed him such privileges. Let us hope that he never encroached on them.

But on this occasion, Mr Gazebee stayed a long time at the castle, and singular ru-mours as to the cause of his prolonged visit became current in the little town. No female scion of the present family of Courcy had, as yet, found a mate. We may imagine that eagles find it difficult to pair when they become scarce in their localities; and we all know how hard it has sometimes been to get *comme il faut* husbands when there has been any number of Protestant princesses on hand.

Some such difficulty had, doubtless, brought it about that the countess was still sur-rounded by her full bevy of maidens. Rank has its responsibilities as well as its privileges, and these young ladies' responsibilities seemed to have consisted in rejecting any suitor who may have hitherto kneeled to them. But now it was told through Courcy, that one suitor had kneeled, and not in vain; from Courcy the rumour flew to Barchester, and thence came down to Greshamsbury, startling the inhabitants, and making one poor heart throb with a violence that would have been piteous had it been known. The suitor, so named, was Mr Mortimer Gazebee.

Yes; Mr Mortimer Gazebee had now awarded to him many other privileges than those of dining at the table, and all that. He rode with the young ladies in the park, and they all talked to him very familiarly before company; all except the Lady Amelia. The countess even called him Mortimer, and treated him quite as one of the family.

At last came a letter from the countess to her dear sister Arabella. It should be given at length, but that I fear to introduce another epistle. It is such an easy mode of writing, and facility is always dangerous. In this letter it was announced with much preliminary ambi-guity, that Mortimer Gazebee—who had been found to be a treasure in every way; quite a paragon of men—was about to be taken into the de Courcy bosom as a child of that house. On that day fortnight, he was destined to lead to the altar—the Lady Amelia.

The countess then went on to say, that dear Amelia did not write herself, being so much engaged by her coming duties—the responsibilities of which she doubtless fully realised, as well as the privileges; but she had begged her mother to request that the twins should come and act as bridesmaids on the occasion. Dear Augusta, she knew, was too much occupied in the coming event in Mr Oriel's family to be able to attend.

Mr Mortimer Gazebee was taken into the de Courcy family, and did lead the Lady Amelia to the altar; and the Gresham twins did go there and act as bridesmaids. And, which is much more to say for human nature, Augusta did forgive her cousin, and, after a certain interval, went on a visit to that nice place in Surrey which she had once hoped would be her own home. It would have been a very nice place, Augusta thought, had not Lady Amelia Gazebee been so very economical.

We must presume that there was some explanation between them. If so, Augusta yielded to it, and confessed it to be satisfactory. She had always yielded to her cousin, and loved her with that sort of love which is begotten between fear and respect. Anything was better than quarrelling with her cousin Amelia.

And Mr Mortimer Gazebee did not altogether make a bad bargain. He never received a shilling of dowry, but that he had not expected. Nor did he want it. His troubles arose from the overstrained economy of his noble wife. She would have it, that as she had married a poor man—Mr Gazebee, however, was not a poor man—it behoved her to manage her house with great care. Such a match as that she had made—this she told in confidence to Augusta—had its responsibilities as well as its privileges.

But, on the whole, Mr Gazebee did not repent his bargain; when he asked his friends to dine, he could tell them that Lady Amelia would be very glad to see them; his marriage gave him some éclat at his club, and some additional weight in the firm to which he belonged; he gets his share of the Courcy shooting, and is asked about to Greshamsbury and other Barsetshire houses, not only "to dine at table and all that," but to take his part in whatever delights country society there has to offer. He lives with the great hope that his noble father-in-law may some day be able to bring him into Parliament.

CHAPTER XXXIX

WHAT THE WORLD SAYS ABOUT BLOOD

"Beatrice," said Frank, rushing suddenly into his sister's room, "I want you to do me one especial favour." This was three or four days after Frank had seen Mary Thorne. Since that time he had spoken to none of his family on the subject; but he was only postponing from day to day the task of telling his father. He had now completed his round of visits to the kennel, master huntsman, and stables of the county hunt, and was at liberty to attend to his own affairs. So he had decided on speaking to the squire that very day; but he first made his request to his sister.

"I want you to do me one especial favour." The day for Beatrice's marriage had now been fixed, and it was not to be very distant. Mr Oriel had urged that their honeymoon trip would lose half its delights if they did not take advantage of the fine weather; and Beatrice had nothing to allege in answer. The day had just been fixed, and when Frank ran into her room with his special request, she was not in a humour to refuse him anything.

"If you wish me to be at your wedding, you must do it," said he.

"Wish you to be there! You must be there, of course. Oh, Frank! what do you mean? I'll do anything you ask; if it is not to go to the moon, or anything of that sort."

Frank was too much in earnest to joke. "You must have Mary for one of your brides-maids," he said. "Now, mind; there may be some difficulty, but you must insist on it. I know what has been going on; but it is not to be borne that she should be excluded on such a day as that. You that have been like sisters all your lives till a year ago!"

"But, Frank—"

"Now, Beatrice, don't have any buts; say that you will do it, and it will be done: I am sure Oriel will approve, and so will my father."

"But, Frank, you won't hear me."

"Not if you make objections; I have set my heart on your doing it."

"But I had set my heart on the same thing."

"Well?"

"And I went to Mary on purpose; and told her just as you tell me now, that she must come. I meant to make mamma understand that I could not be happy unless it were so; but Mary positively refused."

"Refused! What did she say?"

"I could not tell you what she said; indeed, it would not be right if I could; but she positively declined. She seemed to feel, that after all that had happened, she never could come to Greshamsbury again."

"Fiddlestick!"

"But, Frank, those are her feelings; and, to tell the truth, I could not combat them. I know she is not happy; but time will cure that. And, to tell you the truth, Frank—"

"It was before I came back that you asked her, was it not?"

"Yes; just the day before you came, I think."

"Well, it's all altered now. I have seen her since that."

"Have you Frank?"

"What do you take me for? Of course, I have. The very first day I went to her. And now, Beatrice, you may believe me or not, as you like; but if I ever marry, I shall marry Mary Thorne; and if ever she marries, I think I may say, she will marry me. At any rate, I have her promise. And now, you cannot be surprised that I should wish her to be at your wedding; or that I should declare, that if she is absent, I will be absent. I don't want any secrets, and you may tell my mother if you like it—and all the de Courcys too, for anything I care."

Frank had ever been used to command his sisters: and they, especially Beatrice, had ever been used to obey. On this occasion, she was well inclined to do so, if she only knew how. She again remembered how Mary had once sworn to be at her wedding, to be near her, and to touch her—even though all the blood of the de Courcys should be crowded before the altar railings.

"I should be so happy that she should be there; but what am I to do, Frank, if she refuses? I have asked her, and she has refused."

"Go to her again; you need not have any scruples with her. Do not I tell you she will be your sister? Not come here again to Greshamsbury! Why, I tell you that she will be living here while you are living there at the parsonage, for years and years to come."

Beatrice promised that she would go to Mary again, and that she would endeavour to talk her mother over if Mary would consent to come. But she could not yet make herself believe that Mary Thorne would ever be mistress of Greshamsbury. It was so indispensably necessary that Frank should marry money! Besides, what were those horrid rumours which were now becoming rife as to Mary's birth; rumours more horrid than any which had yet been heard?

Augusta had said hardly more than the truth when she spoke of her father being broken-hearted by his debts. His troubles were becoming almost too many for him; and Mr Gazebee, though no doubt he was an excellent man of business, did not seem to lessen them. Mr Gazebee, indeed, was continually pointing out how much he owed, and in what a quagmire of difficulties he had entangled himself. Now, to do Mr Yates Umbleby justice, he had never made himself disagreeable in this manner.

Mr Gazebee had been doubtless right, when he declared that Sir Louis Scatcherd had not himself the power to take any steps hostile to the squire; but Sir Louis had also been right, when he boasted that, in spite of his father's will, he could cause others to move in the matter. Others did move, and were moving, and it began to be understood that a moiety, at least, of the remaining Greshamsbury property must be sold. Even this, however, would by no means leave the squire in undisturbed possession of the other moiety. And thus, Mr Gresham was nearly broken-hearted.

Frank had now been at home a week, and his father had not as yet spoken to him about the family troubles; nor had a word as yet been said between them as to Mary Thorne. It had been agreed that Frank should go away for twelve months, in order that he might forget her. He had been away the twelvemonth, and had now returned, not having forgotten her.

It generally happens, that in every household, one subject of importance occupies it at a time. The subject of importance now mostly thought of in the Greshamsbury household, was the marriage of Beatrice. Lady Arabella had to supply the trousseau for her daughter; the squire had to supply the money for the trousseau; Mr Gazebee had the task of obtaining the money for the squire. While this was going on, Mr Gresham was not anxious to talk to his son, either about his own debts or his son's love. There would be time for these things when the marriage-feast should be over.

So thought the father, but the matter was precipitated by Frank. He also had put off the declaration which he had to make, partly from a wish to spare the squire, but partly also with a view to spare himself. We have all some of that cowardice which induces us to postpone an inevitably evil day. At this time the discussions as to Beatrice's wedding were frequent in the house, and at one of them Frank had heard his mother repeat the names of the proposed bridesmaids. Mary's name was not among them, and hence had arisen his attack on his sister.

Lady Arabella had had her reason for naming the list before her son; but she overshot her mark. She wished to show him how totally Mary was forgotten at Greshamsbury; but she only inspired him with a resolve that she should not be forgotten. He accordingly went to his sister; and then, the subject being full on his mind, he resolved at once to discuss it with his father.

"Sir, are you at leisure for five minutes?" he said, entering the room in which the squire was accustomed to sit majestically, to receive his tenants, scold his dependants, and in which, in former happy days, he had always arranged the meets of the Barsetshire hunt.

Mr Gresham was quite at leisure: when was he not so? But had he been immersed in the deepest business of which he was capable, he would gladly have put it aside at his son's instance.

"I don't like to have any secret from you, sir," said Frank; "nor, for the matter of that, from anybody else"—the anybody else was intended to have reference to his mother—"and, therefore, I would rather tell you at once what I have made up my mind to do."

Frank's address was very abrupt, and he felt it was so. He was rather red in the face, and his manner was fluttered. He had quite made up his mind to break the whole affair to his father; but he had hardly made up his mind as to the best mode of doing so.

"Good heavens, Frank! what do you mean? you are not going to do anything rash? What is it you mean, Frank?"

"I don't think it is rash," said Frank.

"Sit down, my boy; sit down. What is it that you say you are going to do?"

"Nothing immediately, sir," said he, rather abashed; "but as I have made up my mind about Mary Thorne,—quite made up my mind, I think it right to tell you."

"Oh, about Mary," said the squire, almost relieved.

And then Frank, in voluble language, which he hardly, however, had quite under his command, told his father all that had passed between him and Mary. "You see, sir," said he, "that it is fixed now, and cannot be altered. Nor must it be altered. You asked me to go away for twelve months, and I have done so. It has made no difference, you see. As to our means of living, I am quite willing to do anything that may be best and most prudent. I was thinking, sir, of taking a farm somewhere near here, and living on that."

The squire sat quite silent for some moments after this communication had been made to him. Frank's conduct, as a son, had been such that he could not find fault with it; and, in this special matter of his love, how was it possible for him to find fault? He himself was almost as fond of Mary as of a daughter; and, though he too would have been desirous that his son should relieve the estate from its embarrassments by a rich marriage, he did not at all share Lady Arabella's feelings on the subject. No Countess de Courcy had ever engraved it on the tablets of his mind that the world would come to ruin if Frank did not marry money. Ruin there was, and would be, but it had been brought about by no sin of Frank's.

"Do you remember about her birth, Frank?" he said, at last.

"Yes, sir; everything. She told me all she knew; and Dr Thorne finished the story."

"And what do you think of it?"

"It is a pity, and a misfortune. It might, perhaps, have been a reason why you or my mother should not have had Mary in the house many years ago; but it cannot make any difference now."

Frank had not meant to lean so heavily on his father; but he did do so. The story had never been told to Lady Arabella; was not even known to her now, positively, and on good authority. But Mr Gresham had always known it. If Mary's birth was so great a stain upon her, why had he brought her into his house among his children?

"It is a misfortune, Frank; a very great misfortune. It will not do for you and me to ignore birth; too much of the value of one's position depends upon it."

"But what was Mr Moffat's birth?" said Frank, almost with scorn; "or what Miss Dunstable's?" he would have added, had it not been that his father had not been concerned in that sin of wedding him to the oil of Lebanon.

"True, Frank. But yet, what you would mean to say is not true. We must take the world as we find it. Were you to marry a rich heiress, were her birth even as low as that of poor Mary—"

"Don't call her poor Mary, father; she is not poor. My wife will have a right to take rank in the world, however she was born."

"Well,—poor in that way. But were she an heiress, the world would forgive her birth on account of her wealth."

"The world is very complaisant, sir."

"You must take it as you find it, Frank. I only say that such is the fact. If Porlock were to marry the daughter of a shoeblack, without a farthing, he would make a *mésalliance*; but if the daughter of the shoeblack had half a million of money, nobody would dream of saying so. I am stating no opinion of my own: I am only giving you the world's opinion."

"I don't give a straw for the world."

"That is a mistake, my boy; you do care for it, and would be very foolish if you did not. What you mean is, that, on this particular point, you value your love more than the world's opinion."

"Well, yes, that is what I mean."

But the squire, though he had been very lucid in his definition, had not got no nearer to his object; had not even yet ascertained what his own object was. This marriage would be ruinous to Greshamsbury; and yet, what was he to say against it, seeing that the ruin had been his fault, and not his son's?

"You could let me have a farm; could you not, sir? I was thinking of about six or seven hundred acres. I suppose it could be managed somehow?"

"A farm?" said the father, abstractedly.

"Yes, sir. I must do something for my living. I should make less of a mess of that than of anything else. Besides, it would take such a time to be an attorney, or a doctor, or anything of that sort."

Do something for his living! And was the heir of Greshamsbury come to this—the heir and only son? Whereas, he, the squire, had succeeded at an earlier age than Frank's to an unembarrassed income of fourteen thousand pounds a year! The reflection was very hard to bear.

"Yes: I dare say you could have a farm:" and then he threw himself back in his chair, closing his eyes. Then, after a while, rose again, and walked hurriedly about the room. "Frank," he said, at last, standing opposite to his son, "I wonder what you think of me?"

"Think of you, sir?" ejaculated Frank.

"Yes; what do you think of me, for having thus ruined you. I wonder whether you hate me?"

Frank, jumping up from his chair, threw his arms round his father's neck. "Hate you, sir? How can you speak so cruelly? You know well that I love you. And, father, do not trouble yourself about the estate for my sake. I do not care for it; I can be just as happy without it. Let the girls have what is left, and I will make my own way in the world, somehow. I will go to Australia; yes, sir, that will be best. I and Mary will both go. Nobody will care about her birth there. But, father, never say, never think, that I do not love you!"

The squire was too much moved to speak at once, so he sat down again, and covered his face with his hands. Frank went on pacing the room, till, gradually, his first idea recovered possession of his mind, and the remembrance of his father's grief faded away. "May I tell Mary," he said at last, "that you consent to our marriage? It will make her so happy."

But the squire was not prepared to say this. He was pledged to his wife to do all that he could to oppose it; and he himself thought, that if anything could consummate the family ruin, it would be this marriage.

"I cannot say that, Frank; I cannot say that. What would you both live on? It would be madness."

"We would go to Australia," answered he, bitterly. "I have just said so."

"Oh, no, my boy; you cannot do that. You must not throw the old place up altogether. There is no other one but you, Frank; and we have lived here now for so many, many years."

"But if we cannot live here any longer, father?"

"But for this scheme of yours, we might do so. I will give up everything to you, the management of the estate, the park, all the land we have in hand, if you will give up this fatal scheme. For, Frank, it is fatal. You are only twenty-three; why should you be in such a hurry to marry?"

"You married at twenty-one, sir."

Frank was again severe on his father, but unwittingly. "Yes, I did," said Mr Gresham; "and see what has come of it! Had I waited ten years longer, how different would everything have been! No, Frank, I cannot consent to such a marriage; nor will your mother."

"It is your consent I ask, sir; and I am asking for nothing but your consent."

"It would be sheer madness; madness for you both. My own Frank, my dear, dear boy, do not drive me to distraction! Give it up for four years."

"Four years!"

"Yes; for four years. I ask it as a personal favour; as an obligation to myself, in order that we may be saved from ruin; you, your mother, and sisters, your family name, and the old house. I do not talk about myself; but were such a marriage to take place, I should be driven to despair."

Frank found it very hard to resist his father, who now had hold of his hand and arm, and was thus half retaining him, and half embracing him. "Frank, say that you will forget this for four years—say for three years."

But Frank would not say so. To postpone his marriage for four years, or for three, seemed to him to be tantamount to giving up Mary altogether; and he would not acknowledge that any one had the right to demand of him to do that.

"My word is pledged, sir," he said.

"Pledged! Pledged to whom?"

"To Miss Thorne."

"But I will see her, Frank;—and her uncle. She was always reasonable. I am sure she will not wish to bring ruin on her old friends at Greshamsbury."

"Her old friends at Greshamsbury have done but little lately to deserve her consideration. She has been treated shamefully. I know it has not been by you, sir; but I must say so. She has already been treated shamefully; but I will not treat her falsely."

"Well, Frank, I can say no more to you. I have destroyed the estate which should have been yours, and I have no right to expect you should regard what I say."

Frank was greatly distressed. He had not any feeling of animosity against his father with reference to the property, and would have done anything to make the squire understand this, short of giving up his engagement to Mary. His feeling rather was, that, as each had a case against the other, they should cry quits; that he should forgive his father for his bad management, on condition that he himself was to be forgiven with regard to his determined marriage. Not that he put it exactly in that shape, even to himself; but could he have unravelled his own thoughts, he would have found that such was the web on which they were based.

"Father, I do regard what you say; but you would not have me be false. Had you doubled the property instead of lessening it, I could not regard what you say any more."

"I should be able to speak in a very different tone; I feel that, Frank."

"Do not feel it any more, sir; say what you wish, as you would have said it under any other circumstances; and pray believe this, the idea never occurs to me, that I have ground of complaint as regards the property; never. Whatever troubles we may have, do not let that trouble you."

Soon after this Frank left him. What more was there that could be said between them? They could not be of one accord; but even yet it might not be necessary that they should quarrel. He went out, and roamed by himself through the grounds, rather more in meditation than was his wont.

If he did marry, how was he to live? He talked of a profession; but had he meant to do as others do, who make their way in professions, he should have thought of that a year or two ago!—or, rather, have done more than think of it. He spoke also of a farm, but even that could not be had in a moment; nor, if it could, would it produce a living. Where was his capital? Where his skill? and he might have asked also, where the industry so necessary for such a trade? He might set his father at defiance, and if Mary were equally headstrong with himself, he might marry her. But, what then?

As he walked slowly about, cutting off the daisies with his stick, he met Mr Oriel, going up to the house, as was now his custom, to dine there and spend the evening, close to Beatrice.

"How I envy you, Oriel!" he said. "What would I not give to have such a position in the world as yours!"

"Thou shalt not covet a man's house, nor his wife," said Mr Oriel; "perhaps it ought to have been added, nor his position."

"It wouldn't have made much difference. When a man is tempted, the Commandments, I believe, do not go for much."

"Do they not, Frank? That's a dangerous doctrine; and one which, if you had my position, you would hardly admit. But what makes you so much out of sorts? Your own position is generally considered about the best which the world has to give."

"Is it? Then let me tell you that the world has very little to give. What can I do? Where can I turn? Oriel, if there be an empty, lying humbug in the world, it is the theory of high birth and pure blood which some of us endeavour to maintain. Blood, indeed! If my father had been a baker, I should know by this time where to look for my livelihood. As it is, I am told of nothing but my blood. Will my blood ever get me half a crown?"

And then the young democrat walked on again in solitude, leaving Mr Oriel in doubt as to the exact line of argument which he had meant to inculcate.

CHAPTER XL

THE TWO DOCTORS CHANGE PATIENTS

Dr Fillgrave still continued his visits to Greshamsbury, for Lady Arabella had not yet mustered the courage necessary for swallowing her pride and sending once more for Dr Thorne. Nothing pleased Dr Fillgrave more than those visits.

He habitually attended grander families, and richer people; but then, he had attended them habitually. Greshamsbury was a prize taken from the enemy; it was his rock of Gibraltar, of which he thought much more than of any ordinary Hampshire or Wiltshire which had always been within his own kingdom.

He was just starting one morning with his post-horses for Greshamsbury, when an impudent-looking groom, with a crooked nose, trotted up to his door. For Joe still had a crooked nose, all the doctor's care having been inefficacious to remedy the evil effects of Bridget's little tap with the rolling-pin. Joe had no written credentials, for his master was hardly equal to writing, and Lady Scatcherd had declined to put herself into further personal communication with Dr Fillgrave; but he had effrontery enough to deliver any message.

"Be you Dr Fillgrave?" said Joe, with one finger just raised to his cocked hat.

"Yes," said Dr Fillgrave, with one foot on the step of the carriage, but pausing at the sight of so well-turned-out a servant. "Yes; I am Dr Fillgrave."

"Then you be to go to Boxall Hill immediately; before anywhere else."

"Boxall Hill!" said the doctor, with a very angry frown.

"Yes; Boxall Hill: my master's place—my master is Sir Louis Scatcherd, baronet. You've heard of him, I suppose?"

Dr Fillgrave had not his mind quite ready for such an occasion. So he withdrew his foot from the carriage step, and rubbing his hands one over another, looked at his own hall door for inspiration. A single glance at his face was sufficient to show that no ordinary thoughts were being turned over within his breast.

"Well!" said Joe, thinking that his master's name had not altogether produced the magic effect which he had expected; remembering, also, how submissive Greyson had always been, who, being a London doctor, must be supposed to be a bigger man than this provincial fellow. "Do you know as how my master is dying, very like, while you stand there?"

"What is your master's disease?" said the doctor, facing Joe, slowly, and still rubbing his hands. "What ails him? What is the matter with him?"

"Oh; the matter with him? Well, to say it out at once then, he do take a drop too much at times, and then he has the horrors—what is it they call it? delicious beam-ends, or something of that sort."

"Oh, ah, yes; I know; and tell me, my man, who is attending him?"

"Attending him? why, I do, and his mother, that is, her ladyship."

"Yes; but what medical attendant: what doctor?"

"Why, there was Greyson, in London, and—"

"Greyson!" and the doctor looked as though a name so medicinally humble had never before struck the tympanum of his ear.

"Yes; Greyson. And then, down at what's the name of the place, there was Thorne."

"Greshamsbury?"

"Yes; Greshamsbury. But he and Thorne didn't hit it off; and so since that he has had no one but myself."

"I will be at Boxall Hill in the course of the morning," said Dr Fillgrave; "or, rather, you may say, that I will be there at once: I will take it in my way." And having thus resolved, he gave his orders that the post-horses should make such a detour as would enable him to visit Boxall Hill on his road. "It is impossible," said he to himself, "that I should be twice treated in such a manner in the same house."

He was not, however, altogether in a comfortable frame of mind as he was driven up to the hall door. He could not but remember the smile of triumph with which his enemy had regarded him in that hall; he could not but think how he had returned fee-less to Barchester, and how little he had gained in the medical world by rejecting Lady Scatcherd's bank-note. However, he also had had his triumphs since that. He had smiled scornfully at Dr Thorne when he had seen him in the Greshamsbury street; and had been able to tell, at twenty houses through the county, how Lady Arabella had at last been obliged to place herself in his hands. And he triumphed again when he found himself really standing by Sir Louis Scatcherd's bedside. As for Lady Scatcherd, she did not even show herself. She kept in her own little room, sending out Hannah to ask him up the stairs; and she only just got a peep at him through the door as she heard the medical creak of his shoes as he again descended.

We need say but little of his visit to Sir Louis. It mattered nothing now, whether it was Thorne, or Greyson, or Fillgrave. And Dr Fillgrave knew that it mattered nothing: he had skill at least for that—and heart enough also to feel that he would fain have been relieved from this task; would fain have left this patient in the hands even of Dr Thorne.

The name which Joe had given to his master's illness was certainly not a false one. He did find Sir Louis "in the horrors." If any father have a son whose besetting sin is a passion for alcohol, let him take his child to the room of a drunkard when possessed by "the horrors." Nothing will cure him if not that.

I will not disgust my reader by attempting to describe the poor wretch in his misery: the sunken, but yet glaring eyes; the emaciated cheeks; the fallen mouth; the parched, sore lips; the face, now dry and hot, and then suddenly clammy with drops of perspiration; the shaking hand, and all but palsied limbs; and worse than this, the fearful mental efforts, and the struggles for drink; struggles to which it is often necessary to give way.

Dr Fillgrave soon knew what was to be the man's fate; but he did what he might to relieve it. There, in one big, best bedroom, looking out to the north, lay Sir Louis Scatcherd, dying wretchedly. There, in the other big, best bedroom, looking out to the south, had died the other baronet about a twelvemonth since, and each a victim to the same sin. To this had come the prosperity of the house of Scatcherd!

And then Dr Fillgrave went on to Greshamsbury. It was a long day's work, both for himself and the horses; but then, the triumph of being dragged up that avenue compensated for both the expense and the labour. He always put on his sweetest smile as he came near the hall door, and rubbed his hands in the most complaisant manner of which he knew. It was seldom that he saw any of the family but Lady Arabella; but then he desired to see none other, and when he left her in a good humour, was quite content to take his glass of sherry and eat his lunch by himself.

On this occasion, however, the servant at once asked him to go into the dining-room, and there he found himself in the presence of Frank Gresham. The fact was, that Lady Arabella, having at last decided, had sent for Dr Thorne; and it had become necessary that some one should be entrusted with the duty of informing Dr Fillgrave. That some one must be the squire, or Frank. Lady Arabella would doubtless have preferred a messenger more absolutely friendly to her own side of the house; but such messenger there was none: she could not send Mr Gazebee to see her doctor, and so, of the two evils, she chose the least.

"Dr Fillgrave," said Frank, shaking hands with him very cordially as he came up, "my mother is so much obliged to you for all your care and anxiety on her behalf! and, so indeed, are we all."

The doctor shook hands with him very warmly. This little expression of a family feeling on his behalf was the more gratifying, as he had always thought that the males of the Greshamsbury family were still wedded to that pseudo-doctor, that half-apothecary who lived in the village.

"It has been awfully troublesome to you, coming over all this way, I am sure. Indeed, money could not pay for it; my mother feels that. It must cut up your time so much."

"Not at all, Mr Gresham; not at all," said the Barchester doctor, rising up on his toes proudly as he spoke. "A person of your mother's importance, you know! I should be happy to go any distance to see her."

"Ah! but, Dr Fillgrave, we cannot allow that."

"Mr Gresham, don't mention it."

"Oh, yes; but I must," said Frank, who thought that he had done enough for civility, and was now anxious to come to the point. "The fact is, doctor, that we are very much obliged for what you have done; but, for the future, my mother thinks she can trust to such assistance as she can get here in the village."

Frank had been particularly instructed to be very careful how he mentioned Dr Thorne's name, and, therefore, cleverly avoided it.

Get what assistance she wanted in the village! What words were those that he heard? "Mr Gresham, eh—hem—perhaps I do not completely—" Yes, alas! he had completely understood what Frank had meant that he should understand. Frank desired to be civil, but he had no idea of beating unnecessarily about the bush on such an occasion as this.

"It's by Sir Omicron's advice, Dr Fillgrave. You see, this man here"—and he nodded his head towards the doctor's house, being still anxious not to pronounce the hideous name—"has known my mother's constitution for so many years."

"Oh, Mr Gresham; of course, if it is wished."

"Yes, Dr Fillgrave, it is wished. Lunch is coming directly:" and Frank rang the bell.

"Nothing, I thank you, Mr Gresham."

"Do take a glass of sherry."

"Nothing at all, I am very much obliged to you."

"Won't you let the horses get some oats?"

"I will return at once, if you please, Mr Gresham." And the doctor did return, taking with him, on this occasion, the fee that was offered to him. His experience had at any rate taught him so much.

But though Frank could do this for Lady Arabella, he could not receive Dr Thorne on her behalf. The bitterness of that interview had to be borne by herself. A messenger had been sent for him, and he was upstairs with her ladyship while his rival was receiving his *congé* downstairs. She had two objects to accomplish, if it might be possible: she had found that high words with the doctor were of no avail; but it might be possible that Frank could be saved by humiliation on her part. If she humbled herself before this man, would he consent to acknowledge that his niece was not the fit bride for the heir of Greshamsbury?

The doctor entered the room where she was lying on her sofa, and walking up to her with a gentle, but yet not constrained step, took the seat beside her little table, just as he had always been accustomed to do, and as though there had been no break in their intercourse.

"Well, doctor, you see that I have come back to you," she said, with a faint smile.

"Or, rather I have come back to you. And, believe me, Lady Arabella, I am very happy to do so. There need be no excuses. You were, doubtless, right to try what other skill could do; and I hope it has not been tried in vain."

She had meant to have been so condescending; but now all that was put quite beyond her power. It was not easy to be condescending to the doctor: she had been trying all her life, and had never succeeded.

"I have had Sir Omicron Pie," she said.

"So I was glad to hear. Sir Omicron is a clever man, and has a good name. I always recommend Sir Omicron myself."

"And Sir Omicron returns the compliment," said she, smiling gracefully, "for he recommends you. He told Mr Gresham that I was very foolish to quarrel with my best friend. So now we are friends again, are we not? You see how selfish I am." And she put out her hand to him.

The doctor took her hand cordially, and assured her that he bore her no ill-will; that he fully understood her conduct—and that he had never accused her of selfishness. This was all very well and very gracious; but, nevertheless, Lady Arabella felt that the doctor kept the upper hand in those sweet forgivenesses. Whereas, she had intended to keep the upper hand, at least for a while, so that her humiliation might be more effective when it did come.

And then the doctor used his surgical lore, as he well knew how to use it. There was an assured confidence about him, an air which seemed to declare that he really knew what he was doing. These were very comfortable to his patients, but they were wanting in Dr Fillgrave. When he had completed his examinations and questions, and she had completed her little details and made her answer, she certainly was more at ease than she had been since the doctor had last left her.

"Don't go yet for a moment," she said. "I have one word to say to you."

He declared that he was not the least in a hurry. He desired nothing better, he said, than to sit there and talk to her. "And I owe you a most sincere apology, Lady Arabella."

"A sincere apology!" said she, becoming a little red. Was he going to say anything about Mary? Was he going to own that he, and Mary, and Frank had all been wrong?

"Yes, indeed. I ought not to have brought Sir Louis Scatcherd here: I ought to have known that he would have disgraced himself."

"Oh! it does not signify," said her ladyship in a tone almost of disappointment. "I had forgotten it. Mr Gresham and you had more inconvenience than we had."

"He is an unfortunate, wretched man—most unfortunate; with an immense fortune which he can never live to possess."

"And who will the money go to, doctor?"

This was a question for which Dr Thorne was hardly prepared. "Go to?" he repeated. "Oh, some member of the family, I believe. There are plenty of nephews and nieces."

"Yes; but will it be divided, or all go to one?"

"Probably to one, I think. Sir Roger had a strong idea of leaving it all in one hand." If it should happen to be a girl, thought Lady Arabella, what an excellent opportunity would that be for Frank to marry money!

"And now, doctor, I want to say one word to you; considering the very long time that we have known each other, it is better that I should be open with you. This estrangement between us and dear Mary has given us all so much pain. Cannot we do anything to put an end to it?"

"Well, what can I say, Lady Arabella? That depends so wholly on yourself."

"If it depends on me, it shall be done at once."

The doctor bowed. And though he could hardly be said to do so stiffly, he did it cold- ly. His bow seemed to say, "Certainly; if you choose to make a proper *amende* it can be done. But I think it is very unlikely that you will do so."

"Beatrice is just going to be married, you know that, doctor." The doctor said that he did know it. "And it will be so pleasant that Mary should make one of us. Poor Beatrice; you don't know what she has suffered."

"Yes," said the doctor, "there has been suffering, I am sure; suffering on both sides."

"You cannot wonder that we should be so anxious about Frank, Dr Thorne; an only son, and the heir to an estate that has been so very long in the family:" and Lady Arabella put her handkerchief to her eyes, as though these facts were in themselves melancholy, and not to be thought of by a mother without some soft tears. "Now I wish you could tell me what your views are, in a friendly manner, between ourselves. You won't find me un- reasonable."

"My views, Lady Arabella?"

"Yes, doctor; about your niece, you know: you must have views of some sort; that's of course. It occurs to me, that perhaps we are all in the dark together. If so, a little candid speaking between you and me may set it all right."

Lady Arabella's career had not hitherto been conspicuous for candour, as far as Dr Thorne had been able to judge of it; but that was no reason why he should not respond to so very becoming an invitation on her part. He had no objection to a little candid speak- ing; at least, so he declared. As to his views with regard to Mary, they were merely these: that he would make her as happy and comfortable as he could while she remained with him; and that he would give her his blessing—for he had nothing else to give her—when she left him;—if ever she should do so.

Now, it will be said that the doctor was not very candid in this; not more so, perhaps, than was Lady Arabella herself. But when one is specially invited to be candid, one is naturally set upon one's guard. Those who by disposition are most open, are apt to become crafty when so admonished. When a man says to you, "Let us be candid with each other," you feel instinctively that he desires to squeeze you without giving a drop of water him- self.

"Yes; but about Frank," said Lady Arabella.

"About Frank!" said the doctor, with an innocent look, which her ladyship could hard- ly interpret.

"What I mean is this: can you give me your word that these young people do not in- tend to do anything rash? One word like that from you will set my mind quite at rest. And then we could be so happy together again."

"Ah! who is to answer for what rash things a young man will do?" said the doctor, smiling.

Lady Arabella got up from the sofa, and pushed away the little table. The man was false, hypocritical, and cunning. Nothing could be made of him. They were all in a conspiracy together to rob her of her son; to make him marry without money! What should she do? Where should she turn for advice or counsel? She had nothing more to say to the doctor; and he, perceiving that this was the case, took his leave. This little attempt to achieve candour had not succeeded.

Dr Thorne had answered Lady Arabella as had seemed best to him on the spur of the moment; but he was by no means satisfied with himself. As he walked away through the gardens, he bethought himself whether it would be better for all parties if he could bring himself to be really candid. Would it not be better for him at once to tell the squire what were the future prospects of his niece, and let the father agree to the marriage, or not agree to it, as he might think fit. But then, if so, if he did do this, would he not in fact say, "There is my niece, there is this girl of whom you have been talking for the last twelve-month, indifferent to what agony of mind you may have occasioned to her; there she is, a probable heiress! It may be worth your son's while to wait a little time, and not cast her off till he shall know whether she be an heiress or no. If it shall turn out that she is rich, let him take her; if not, why, he can desert her then as well as now." He could not bring himself to put his niece into such a position as this. He was anxious enough that she should be Frank Gresham's wife, for he loved Frank Gresham; he was anxious enough, also, that she should give to her husband the means of saving the property of his family. But Frank, though he might find her rich, was bound to take her while she was poor.

Then, also, he doubted whether he would be justified in speaking of this will at all. He almost hated the will for the trouble and vexation it had given him, and the constant stress it had laid on his conscience. He had spoken of it as yet to no one, and he thought that he was resolved not to do so while Sir Louis should yet be in the land of the living.

On reaching home, he found a note from Lady Scatcherd, informing him that Dr Fillgrave had once more been at Boxall Hill, and that, on this occasion, he had left the house without anger.

"I don't know what he has said about Louis," she added, "for, to tell the truth, doctor, I was afraid to see him. But he comes again to-morrow, and then I shall be braver. But I fear that my poor boy is in a bad way."

CHAPTER XLI

DOCTOR THORNE WON'T INTERFERE

At this period there was, as it were, a truce to the ordinary little skirmishes which had been so customary between Lady Arabella and the squire. Things had so fallen out, that they neither of them had much spirit for a contest; and, moreover, on that point which at the present moment was most thought of by both of them, they were strangely in unison. For each of them was anxious to prevent the threatened marriage of their only son.

It must, moreover, be remembered, that Lady Arabella had carried a great point in ousting Mr Yates Umbleby and putting the management of the estate into the hands of her own partisan. But then the squire had not done less in getting rid of Fillgrave and reinstating Dr Thorne in possession of the family invalids. The losses, therefore, had been equal; the victories equal; and there was a mutual object.

And it must be confessed, also, that Lady Arabella's taste for grandeur was on the decline. Misfortune was coming too near to her to leave her much anxiety for the gaieties of a London season. Things were not faring well with her. When her eldest daughter was going to marry a man of fortune, and a member of Parliament, she had thought nothing of demanding a thousand pounds or so for the extraordinary expenses incident to such an occasion. But now, Beatrice was to become the wife of a parish parson, and even that was thought to be a fortunate event; she had, therefore, no heart for splendour.

"The quieter we can do it the better," she wrote to her countess-sister. "Her father wanted to give him at least a thousand pounds; but Mr Gazebee has told me confidentially that it literally cannot be done at the present moment! Ah, my dear Rosina! how things have been managed! If one or two of the girls will come over, we shall all take it as a favour. Beatrice would think it very kind of them. But I don't think of asking you or Amelia." Amelia was always the grandest of the de Courcy family, being almost on an equality with—nay, in some respect superior to—the countess herself. But this, of course, was before the days of the nice place in Surrey.

Such, and so humble being the present temper of the lady of Greshamsbury, it will not be thought surprising that she and Mr Gresham should at last come together in their efforts to reclaim their son.

At first Lady Arabella urged upon the squire the duty of being very peremptory and very angry. "Do as other fathers do in such cases. Make him understand that he will have no allowance to live on." "He understands that well enough," said Mr Gresham.

"Threaten to cut him off with a shilling," said her ladyship, with spirit. "I haven't a shilling to cut him off with," answered the squire, bitterly.

But Lady Arabella herself soon perceived, that this line would not do. As Mr Gresham himself confessed, his own sins against his son had been too great to allow of his taking a high hand with him. Besides, Mr Gresham was not a man who could ever be severe with a son whose individual conduct had been so good as Frank's. This marriage was, in his view, a misfortune to be averted if possible,—to be averted by any possible means; but, as far as Frank was concerned, it was to be regarded rather as a monomania than a crime.

"I did feel so certain that he would have succeeded with Miss Dunstable," said the mother, almost crying.

"I thought it impossible but that at his age a twelvemonth's knocking about the world would cure him," said the father.

"I never heard of a boy being so obstinate about a girl," said the mother. "I'm sure he didn't get it from the de Courcys:" and then, again, they talked it over in all its bearings.

"But what are they to live upon?" said Lady Arabella, appealing, as it were, to some impersonation of reason. "That's what I want him to tell me. What are they to live upon?"

"I wonder whether de Courcy could get him into some embassy?" said the father. "He does talk of a profession."

"What! with the girl and all?" asked Lady Arabella with horror, alarmed at the idea of such an appeal being made to her noble brother.

"No; but before he marries. He might be broken of it that way."

"Nothing will break him," said the wretched mother; "nothing—nothing. For my part, I think that he is possessed. Why was she brought here? Oh, dear! oh, dear! Why was she ever brought into this house?"

This last question Mr Gresham did not think it necessary to answer. That evil had been done, and it would be useless to dispute it. "I'll tell you what I'll do," said he. "I'll speak to the doctor himself."

"It's not the slightest use," said Lady Arabella. "He will not assist us. Indeed, I firmly believe it's all his own doing."

"Oh, nonsense! that really is nonsense, my love."

"Very well, Mr Gresham. What I say is always nonsense, I know; you have always told me so. But yet, see how things have turned out. I knew how it would be when she was first brought into the house." This assertion was rather a stretch on the part of Lady Arabella.

"Well, it is nonsense to say that Frank is in love with the girl at the doctor's bidding."

"I think you know, Mr Gresham, that I don't mean that. What I say is this, that Dr Thorne, finding what an easy fool Frank is—"

"I don't think he's at all easy, my love; and certainly is not a fool."

"Very well, have it your own way. I'll not say a word more. I'm struggling to do my best, and I'm browbeaten on every side. God knows I am not in a state of health to bear it!" And Lady Arabella bowed her head into her pocket-handkerchief.

"I think, my dear, if you were to see Mary herself it might do some good," said the squire, when the violence of his wife's grief had somewhat subsided.

"What! go and call upon this girl?"

"Yes; you can send Beatrice to give her notice, you know. She never was unreasonable, and I do not think that you would find her so. You should tell her, you know—"

"Oh, I should know very well what to tell her, Mr Gresham."

"Yes, my love; I'm sure you would; nobody better. But what I mean is, that if you are to do any good, you should be kind in your manner. Mary Thorne has a spirit that you cannot break. You may perhaps lead, but nobody can drive her."

As this scheme originated with her husband, Lady Arabella could not, of course, confess that there was much in it. But, nevertheless, she determined to attempt it, thinking that if anything could be efficacious for good in their present misfortunes, it would be her own diplomatic powers. It was, therefore, at last settled between them, that he should endeavour to talk over the doctor, and that she would do the same with Mary.

"And then I will speak to Frank," said Lady Arabella. "As yet he has never had the audacity to open his mouth to me about Mary Thorne, though I believe he declares his love openly to every one else in the house."

"And I will get Oriel to speak to him," said the squire.

"I think Patience might do more good. I did once think he was getting fond of Patience, and I was quite unhappy about it then. Ah, dear! I should be almost pleased at that now."

And thus it was arranged that all the artillery of Greshamsbury was to be brought to bear at once on Frank's love, so as to crush it, as it were, by the very weight of metal.

It may be imagined that the squire would have less scruple in addressing the doctor on this matter than his wife would feel; and that his part of their present joint undertaking was less difficult than hers. For he and the doctor had ever been friends at heart. But, nevertheless, he did feel much scruple, as, with his stick in hand, he walked down to the little gate which opened out near the doctor's house.

This feeling was so strong, that he walked on beyond this door to the entrance, thinking of what he was going to do, and then back again. It seemed to be his fate to be depending always on the clemency or consideration of Dr Thorne. At this moment the doctor was imposing the only obstacle which was offered to the sale of a great part of his estate. Sir Louis, through his lawyer, was pressing the doctor to sell, and the lawyer was loudly accusing the doctor of delaying to do so. "He has the management of your property," said Mr Finnie; "but he manages it in the interest of his own friend. It is quite clear, and we will expose it." "By all means," said Sir Louis. "It is a d——d shame, and it shall be exposed." Of all this the squire was aware.

When he reached the doctor's house, he was shown into the drawing-room, and found Mary there alone. It had always been his habit to kiss her forehead when he chanced to meet her about the house at Greshamsbury. She had been younger and more childish then; but even now she was but a child to him, so he kissed her as he had been wont to do. She blushed slightly as she looked up into his face, and said: "Oh, Mr Gresham, I am so glad to see you here again."

As he looked at her he could not but acknowledge that it was natural that Frank should love her. He had never before seen that she was attractive;—had never had an opinion about it. She had grown up as a child under his eye; and as she had not had the name of being especially a pretty child, he had never thought on the subject. Now he saw before him a woman whose every feature was full of spirit and animation; whose eye sparkled with more than mere brilliancy; whose face was full of intelligence; whose very smile was eloquent. Was it to be wondered at that Frank should have learned to love her?

Miss Thorne wanted but one attribute which many consider essential to feminine beauty. She had no brilliancy of complexion, no pearly whiteness, no vivid carnation; nor, indeed, did she possess the dark brilliance of a brunette. But there was a speaking earnestness in her face; an expression of mental faculty which the squire now for the first time perceived to be charming.

And then he knew how good she was. He knew well what was her nature; how generous, how open, how affectionate, and yet how proud! Her pride was her fault; but even that was not a fault in his eyes. Out of his own family there was no one whom he had loved, and could love, as he loved her. He felt, and acknowledged that no man could have a better wife. And yet he was there with the express object of rescuing his son from such a marriage!

"You are looking very well, Mary," he said, almost involuntarily. "Am I?" she answered, smiling. "It's very nice at any rate to be complimented. Uncle never pays me any compliments of that sort."

In truth, she was looking well. She would say to herself over and over again, from morning to night, that Frank's love for her would be, must be, unfortunate; could not lead to happiness. But, nevertheless, it did make her happy. She had before his return made up her mind to be forgotten, and it was so sweet to find that he had been so far from forgetting her. A girl may scold a man in words for rashness in his love, but her heart never scolds him for such an offence as that. She had not been slighted, and her heart, therefore, still rose buoyant within her breast.

The doctor entered the room. As the squire's visit had been expected by him, he had of course not been out of the house. "And now I suppose I must go," said Mary; "for I know you are going to talk about business. But, uncle, Mr Gresham says I'm looking very well. Why have you not been able to find that out?"

"She's a dear, good girl," said the squire, as the door shut behind her; "a dear good girl;" and the doctor could not fail to see that his eyes were filled with tears.

"I think she is," said he, quietly. And then they both sat silent, as though each was waiting to hear whether the other had anything more to say on that subject. The doctor, at any rate, had nothing more to say.

"I have come here specially to speak to you about her," said the squire.

"About Mary?"

"Yes, doctor; about her and Frank: something must be done, some arrangement made: if not for our sakes, at least for theirs."

"What arrangement, squire?"

"Ah! that is the question. I take it for granted that either Frank or Mary has told you that they have engaged themselves to each other."

"Frank told me so twelve months since."

"And has not Mary told you?"

"Not exactly that. But, never mind; she has, I believe, no secret from me. Though I have said but little to her, I think I know it all."

"Well, what then?"

The doctor shook his head and put up his hands. He had nothing to say; no proposition to make; no arrangement to suggest. The thing was so, and he seemed to say that, as far as he was concerned, there was an end of it.

The squire sat looking at him, hardly knowing how to proceed. It seemed to him, that the fact of a young man and a young lady being in love with each other was not a thing to be left to arrange itself, particularly, seeing the rank of life in which they were placed. But the doctor seemed to be of a different opinion.

"But, Dr Thorne, there is no man on God's earth who knows my affairs as well as you do; and in knowing mine, you know Frank's. Do you think it possible that they should marry each other?"

"Possible; yes, it is possible. You mean, will it be prudent?"

"Well, take it in that way; would it not be most imprudent?"

"At present, it certainly would be. I have never spoken to either of them on the subject; but I presume they do not think of such a thing for the present."

"But, doctor—" The squire was certainly taken aback by the coolness of the doctor's manner. After all, he, the squire, was Mr Gresham of Greshamsbury, generally acknowledged to be the first commoner in Barsetshire; after all, Frank was his heir, and, in process of time, he would be Mr Gresham of Greshamsbury. Crippled as the estate was, there would be something left, and the rank at any rate remained. But as to Mary, she was not

752

even the doctor's daughter. She was not only penniless, but nameless, fatherless, worse than motherless! It was incredible that Dr Thorne, with his generally exalted ideas as to family, should speak in this cold way as to a projected marriage between the heir of Greshamsbury and his brother's bastard child!

"But, doctor," repeated the squire.

The doctor put one leg over the other, and began to rub his calf. "Squire," said he. "I think I know all that you would say, all that you mean. And you don't like to say it, because you would not wish to pain me by alluding to Mary's birth."

"But, independently of that, what would they live on?" said the squire, energetically. "Birth is a great thing, a very great thing. You and I think exactly alike about that, so we need have no dispute. You are quite as proud of Ullathorne as I am of Greshamsbury."

"I might be if it belonged to me."

"But you are. It is no use arguing. But, putting that aside altogether, what would they live on? If they were to marry, what would they do? Where would they go? You know what Lady Arabella thinks of such things; would it be possible that they should live up at the house with her? Besides, what a life would that be for both of them! Could they live here? Would that be well for them?"

The squire looked at the doctor for an answer; but he still went on rubbing his calf. Mr Gresham, therefore, was constrained to continue his expostulation.

"When I am dead there will still, I hope, be something;—something left for the poor fellow. Lady Arabella and the girls would be better off, perhaps, than now, and I sometimes wish, for Frank's sake, that the time had come."

The doctor could not now go on rubbing his leg. He was moved to speak, and declared that, of all events, that was the one which would be furthest from Frank's heart. "I know no son," said he, "who loves his father more dearly than he does."

"I do believe it," said the squire; "I do believe it. But yet, I cannot but feel that I am in his way."

"No, squire, no; you are in no one's way. You will find yourself happy with your son yet, and proud of him. And proud of his wife, too. I hope so, and I think so: I do, indeed, or I should not say so, squire; we will have many a happy day yet together, when we shall talk of all these things over the dining-room fire at Greshamsbury."

The squire felt it kind in the doctor that he should thus endeavour to comfort him; but he could not understand, and did not inquire, on what basis these golden hopes was founded. It was necessary, however, to return to the subject which he had come to discuss. Would the doctor assist him in preventing this marriage? That was now the one thing necessary to be kept in view.

"But, doctor, about the young people; of course they cannot marry, you are aware of that."

"I don't know that exactly."

"Well, doctor, I must say I thought you would feel it."

"Feel what, squire?"

"That, situated as they are, they ought not to marry."

"That is quite another question. I have said nothing about that either to you or to anybody else. The truth is, squire, I have never interfered in this matter one way or the other; and I have no wish to do so now."

"But should you not interfere? Is not Mary the same to you as your own child?"

Dr Thorne hardly knew how to answer this. He was aware that his argument about not interfering was in fact absurd. Mary could not marry without his interference; and had it been the case that she was in danger of making an improper marriage, of course he would interfere. His meaning was, that he would not at the present moment express any opinion;

he would not declare against a match which might turn out to be in every way desirable; nor, if he spoke in favour of it, could he give his reasons for doing so. Under these circumstances, he would have wished to say nothing, could that only have been possible.

But as it was not possible, and as he must say something, he answered the squire's last question by asking another. "What is your objection, squire?"

"Objection! Why, what on earth would they live on?"

"Then I understand, that if that difficulty were over, you would not refuse your consent merely because of Mary's birth?"

This was a manner in which the squire had by no means expected to have the affair presented to him. It seemed so impossible that any sound-minded man should take any but his view of the case, that he had not prepared himself for argument. There was every objection to his son marrying Miss Thorne; but the fact of their having no income between them, did certainly justify him in alleging that first.

"But that difficulty can't be got over, doctor. You know, however, that it would be cause of grief to us all to see Frank marry much beneath his station; that is, I mean, in family. You should not press me to say this, for you know that I love Mary dearly."

"But, my dear friend, it is necessary. Wounds sometimes must be opened in order that they may be healed. What I mean is this;—and, squire, I'm sure I need not say to you that I hope for an honest answer,—were Mary Thorne an heiress; had she, for instance, such wealth as that Miss Dunstable that we hear of; in that case would you object to the match?"

When the doctor declared that he expected an honest answer the squire listened with all his ears; but the question, when finished, seemed to have no bearing on the present case.

"Come, squire, speak your mind faithfully. There was some talk once of Frank's marrying Miss Dunstable; did you mean to object to that match?"

"Miss Dunstable was legitimate; at least, I presume so."

"Oh, Mr Gresham! has it come to that? Miss Dunstable, then, would have satisfied your ideas of high birth?"

Mr Gresham was rather posed, and regretted, at the moment, his allusion to Miss Dunstable's presumed legitimacy. But he soon recovered himself. "No," said he, "it would not. And I am willing to admit, as I have admitted before, that the undoubted advantages arising from wealth are taken by the world as atoning for what otherwise would be a *mésalliance*. But—"

"You admit that, do you? You acknowledge that as your conviction on the subject?"

"Yes. But—" The squire was going on to explain the propriety of this opinion, but the doctor uncivilly would not hear him.

"Then squire, I will not interfere in this matter one way or the other."

"How on earth can such an opinion—"

"Pray excuse me, Mr Gresham; but my mind is now quite made up. It was very nearly so before. I will do nothing to encourage Frank, nor will I say anything to discourage Mary."

"That is the most singular resolution that a man of sense like you ever came to."

"I can't help it, squire; it is my resolution."

"But what has Miss Dunstable's fortune to do with it?"

"I cannot say that it has anything; but, in this matter, I will not interfere."

The squire went on for some time, but it was all to no purpose; and at last he left the house, considerably in dudgeon. The only conclusion to which he could come was, that Dr Thorne had thought the chance on his niece's behalf too good to be thrown away, and had, therefore, resolved to act in this very singular way.

"I would not have believed it of him, though all Barsetshire had told me," he said to himself as he entered the great gates; and he went on repeating the same words till he found himself in his own room. "No, not if all Barsetshire had told me!"

He did not, however, communicate the ill result of his visit to the Lady Arabella.

CHAPTER XLII

WHAT CAN YOU GIVE IN RETURN?

In spite of the family troubles, these were happy days for Beatrice. It so seldom happens that young ladies on the eve of their marriage have their future husbands living near them. This happiness was hers, and Mr Oriel made the most of it. She was constantly being coaxed down to the parsonage by Patience, in order that she might give her opinion, in private, as to some domestic arrangement, some piece of furniture, or some new carpet; but this privacy was always invaded. What Mr Oriel's parishioners did in these halcyon days, I will not ask. His morning services, however, had been altogether given up, and he had provided himself with a very excellent curate.

But one grief did weigh heavily on Beatrice. She continually heard her mother say things which made her feel that it would be more than ever impossible that Mary should be at her wedding; and yet she had promised her brother to ask her. Frank had also repeated his threat, that if Mary were not present, he would absent himself.

Beatrice did what most girls do in such a case; what all would do who are worth anything; she asked her lover's advice.

"Oh! but Frank can't be in earnest," said the lover. "Of course he'll be at our wedding."

"You don't know him, Caleb. He is so changed that no one hardly would know him. You can't conceive how much in earnest he is, how determined and resolute. And then, I should like to have Mary so much if mamma would let her come."

"Ask Lady Arabella," said Caleb.

"Well, I suppose I must do that; but I know what she'll say, and Frank will never believe that I have done my best." Mr Oriel comforted her with such little whispered consolations as he was able to afford, and then she went away on her errand to her mother.

She was indeed surprised at the manner in which her prayer was received. She could hardly falter forth her petition; but when she had done so, Lady Arabella answered in this wise:—

"Well my dear, I have no objection, none the least; that is, of course, if Mary is disposed to behave herself properly."

"Oh, mamma! of course she will," said Beatrice; "she always did and always does."

"I hope she will, my love. But, Beatrice, when I say that I shall be glad to see her, of course I mean under certain conditions. I never disliked Mary Thorne, and if she would only let Frank understand that she will not listen to his mad proposals, I should be delighted to see her at Greshamsbury just as she used to be."

Beatrice could say nothing in answer to this; but she felt very sure that Mary, let her intention be what it might, would not undertake to make Frank understand anything at anybody's bidding.

"I will tell you what I will do, my dear," continued Lady Arabella; "I will call on Mary myself."

"What! at Dr Thorne's house?"

"Yes; why not? I have been at Dr Thorne's house before now." And Lady Arabella could not but think of her last visit thither, and the strong feeling she had, as she came out, that she would never again enter those doors. She was, however, prepared to do anything on behalf of her rebellious son.

"Oh, yes! I know that, mamma."

"I will call upon her, and if I can possibly manage it, I will ask her myself to make one of your party. If so, you can go to her afterwards and make your own arrangements. Just write her a note, my dear, and say that I will call to-morrow at twelve. It might fluster her if I were to go in without notice."

Beatrice did as she was bid, but with a presentiment that no good would come of it. The note was certainly unnecessary for the purpose assigned by Lady Arabella, as Mary was not given to be flustered by such occurrences; but, perhaps, it was as well that it was written, as it enabled her to make up her mind steadily as to what information should be given, and what should not be given to her coming visitor.

On the next morning, at the appointed hour, Lady Arabella walked down to the doctor's house. She never walked about the village without making some little disturbance among the inhabitants. With the squire, himself, they were quite familiar, and he could appear and reappear without creating any sensation; but her ladyship had not made herself equally common in men's sight. Therefore, when she went in at the doctor's little gate, the fact was known through all Greshamsbury in ten minutes, and before she had left the house, Mrs Umbleby and Miss Gushing had quite settled between them what was the exact cause of the very singular event.

The doctor, when he had heard what was going to happen, carefully kept out of the way: Mary, therefore, had the pleasure of receiving Lady Arabella alone. Nothing could exceed her ladyship's affability. Mary thought that it perhaps might have savoured less of condescension; but then, on this subject, Mary was probably prejudiced. Lady Arabella smiled and simpered, and asked after the doctor, and the cat, and Janet, and said everything that could have been desired by any one less unreasonable than Mary Thorne.

"And now, Mary, I'll tell you why I have called." Mary bowed her head slightly, as much to say, that she would be glad to receive any information that Lady Arabella could give her on that subject. "Of course you know that Beatrice is going to be married very shortly."

Mary acknowledged that she had heard so much.

"Yes: we think it will be in September—early in September—and that is coming very soon now. The poor girl is anxious that you should be at her wedding." Mary turned slightly red; but she merely said, and that somewhat too coldly, that she was much indebted to Beatrice for her kindness.

"I can assure you, Mary, that she is very fond of you, as much so as ever; and so, indeed, am I, and all of us are so. You know that Mr Gresham was always your friend."

"Yes, he always was, and I am grateful to Mr Gresham," answered Mary. It was well for Lady Arabella that she had her temper under command, for had she spoken her mind out there would have been very little chance left for reconciliation between her and Mary.

"Yes, indeed he was; and I think we all did what little we could to make you welcome at Greshamsbury, Mary, till those unpleasant occurrences took place."

757

"What occurrences, Lady Arabella?"

"And Beatrice is so very anxious on this point," said her ladyship, ignoring for the moment Mary's question. "You two have been so much together, that she feels she cannot be quite happy if you are not near her when she is being married."

"Dear Beatrice!" said Mary, warmed for the moment to an expression of genuine feeling.

"She came to me yesterday, begging that I would waive any objection I might have to your being there. I have made her no answer yet. What answer do you think I ought to make her?"

Mary was astounded at this question, and hesitated in her reply. "What answer ought you to make her?" she said.

"Yes, Mary. What answer do you think I ought to give? I wish to ask you the question, as you are the person the most concerned."

Mary considered for a while, and then did give her opinion on the matter in a firm voice. "I think you should tell Beatrice, that as you cannot at present receive me cordially in your house, it will be better that you should not be called on to receive me at all."

This was certainly not the sort of answer that Lady Arabella expected, and she was now somewhat astounded in her turn. "But, Mary," she said, "I should be delighted to receive you cordially if I could do so."

"But it seems you cannot, Lady Arabella; and so there must be an end of it."

"Oh, but I do not know that:" and she smiled her sweetest smile. "I do not know that. I want to put an end to all this ill-feeling if I can. It all depends upon one thing, you know."

"Does it, Lady Arabella?"

"Yes, upon one thing. You won't be angry if I ask you another question—eh, Mary?"

"No; at least I don't think I will."

"Is there any truth in what we hear about your being engaged to Frank?"

Mary made no immediate answer to this, but sat quite silent, looking Lady Arabella in the face; not but that she had made up her mind as to what answer she would give, but the exact words failed her at the moment.

"Of course you must have heard of such a rumour," continued Lady Arabella.

"Oh, yes, I have heard of it."

"Yes, and you have noticed it, and I must say very properly. When you went to Boxall Hill, and before that with Miss Oriel's to her aunt's, I thought you behaved extremely well." Mary felt herself glow with indignation, and began to prepare words that should be sharp and decisive. "But, nevertheless, people talk; and Frank, who is still quite a boy" (Mary's indignation was not softened by this allusion to Frank's folly), "seems to have got some nonsense in his head. I grieve to say it, but I feel myself in justice bound to do so, that in this matter he has not acted as well as you have done. Now, therefore, I merely ask you whether there is any truth in the report. If you tell me that there is none, I shall be quite contented."

"But it is altogether true, Lady Arabella; I am engaged to Frank Gresham."

"Engaged to be married to him?"

"Yes; engaged to be married to him."

What was to say or do now? Nothing could be more plain, more decided, or less embarrassed with doubt than Mary's declaration. And as she made it she looked her visitor full in the face, blushing indeed, for her cheeks were now suffused as well as her forehead; but boldly, and, as it were, with defiance.

"And you tell me so to my face, Miss Thorne?"

"And why not? Did you not ask me the question; and would you have me answer you with a falsehood? I am engaged to him. As you would put the question to me, what other answer could I make? The truth is, that I am engaged to him."

The decisive abruptness with which Mary declared her own iniquity almost took away her ladyship's breath. She had certainly believed that they were engaged, and had hardly hoped that Mary would deny it; but she had not expected that the crime would be acknowledged, or, at any rate, if acknowledged, that the confession would be made without some show of shame. On this Lady Arabella could have worked; but there was no such expression, nor was there the slightest hesitation. "I am engaged to Frank Gresham," and having so said, Mary looked her visitor full in the face.

"Then it is indeed impossible that you should be received at Greshamsbury."

"At present, quite so, no doubt: in saying so, Lady Arabella, you only repeat the answer I made to your first question. I can now go to Greshamsbury only in one light: that of Mr Gresham's accepted daughter-in-law."

"And that is perfectly out of the question; altogether out of the question, now and for ever."

"I will not dispute with you about that; but, as I said before, my being at Beatrice's wedding is not to be thought of."

Lady Arabella sat for a while silent, that she might meditate, if possible, calmly as to what line of argument she had now better take. It would be foolish in her, she thought, to return home, having merely expressed her anger. She had now an opportunity of talking to Mary which might not again occur: the difficulty was in deciding in what special way she should use the opportunity. Should she threaten, or should she entreat? To do her justice, it should be stated, that she did actually believe that the marriage was all but impossible; she did not think that it could take place. But the engagement might be the ruin of her son's prospects, seeing how he had before him one imperative, one immediate duty—that of marrying money.

Having considered all this as well as her hurry would allow her, she determined first to reason, then to entreat, and lastly, if necessary, to threaten.

"I am astonished! you cannot be surprised at that, Miss Thorne: I am astonished at hearing so singular a confession made."

"Do you think my confession singular, or is it the fact of my being engaged to your son?"

"We will pass over that for the present. But do let me ask you, do you think it possible, I say possible, that you and Frank should be married?"

"Oh, certainly; quite possible."

"Of course you know that he has not a shilling in the world."

"Nor have I, Lady Arabella."

"Nor will he have were he to do anything so utterly hostile to his father's wishes. The property, you are aware, is altogether at Mr Gresham's disposal."

"I am aware of nothing about the property, and can say nothing about it except this, that it has not been, and will not be inquired after by me in this matter. If I marry Frank Gresham, it will not be for the property. I am sorry to make such an apparent boast, but you force me to do it."

"On what then are you to live? You are too old for love in a cottage, I suppose?"

"Not at all too old; Frank, you know is 'still quite a boy.'"

Impudent hussy! forward, ill-conditioned saucy minx! such were the epithets which rose to Lady Arabella's mind; but she politely suppressed them.

"Miss Thorne, this subject is of course to me very serious; very ill-adapted for jesting. I look upon such a marriage as absolutely impossible."

"I do not know what you mean by impossible, Lady Arabella."

"I mean, in the first place, that you two could not get yourselves married."

"Oh, yes; Mr Oriel would manage that for us. We are his parishioners, and he would be bound to do it."

"I beg your pardon; I believe that under all the circumstances it would be illegal."

Mary smiled; but she said nothing. "You may laugh, Miss Thorne, but I think you will find that I am right. There are still laws to prevent such fearful distress as would be brought about by such a marriage."

"I hope that nothing I shall do will bring distress on the family."

"Ah, but it would; don't you know that it would? Think of it, Miss Thorne. Think of Frank's state, and of his father's state. You know enough of that, I am sure, to be well aware that Frank is not in a condition to marry without money. Think of the position which Mr Gresham's only son should hold in the county; think of the old name, and the pride we have in it; you have lived among us enough to understand all this; think of these things, and then say whether it is possible such a marriage should take place without family distress of the deepest kind. Think of Mr Gresham; if you truly love my son, you could not wish to bring on him all this misery and ruin."

Mary now was touched, for there was truth in what Lady Arabella said. But she had no power of going back; her troth was plighted, and nothing that any human being could say should shake her from it. If he, indeed, chose to repent, that would be another thing.

"Lady Arabella," she said, "I have nothing to say in favour of this engagement, except that he wishes it."

"And is that a reason, Mary?"

"To me it is; not only a reason, but a law. I have given him my promise."

"And you will keep your promise even to his own ruin?"

"I hope not. Our engagement, unless he shall choose to break it off, must necessarily be a long one; but the time will come—"

"What! when Mr Gresham is dead?"

"Before that, I hope."

"There is no probability of it. And because he is headstrong, you, who have always had credit for so much sense, will hold him to this mad engagement?"

"No, Lady Arabella; I will not hold him to anything to which he does not wish to be held. Nothing that you can say shall move me: nothing that anybody can say shall induce me to break my promise to him. But a word from himself will do it. One look will be sufficient. Let him give me to understand, in any way, that his love for me is injurious to him—that he has learnt to think so—and then I will renounce my part in this engagement as quickly as you could wish it."

There was much in this promise, but still not so much as Lady Arabella wished to get. Mary, she knew, was obstinate, but yet reasonable; Frank, she thought, was both obstinate and unreasonable. It might be possible to work on Mary's reason, but quite impossible to touch Frank's irrationality. So she persevered—foolishly.

"Miss Thorne—that, is, Mary, for I still wish to be thought your friend—"

"I will tell you the truth, Lady Arabella: for some considerable time past I have not thought you so."

"Then you have wronged me. But I will go on with what I was saying. You quite acknowledge that this is a foolish affair?"

"I acknowledge no such thing."

"Something very much like it. You have not a word in its defence."

"Not to you: I do not choose to be put on my defence by you."

"I don't know who has more right; however, you promise that if Frank wishes it, you will release him from his engagement."

"Release him! It is for him to release me, that is, if he wishes it."

"Very well; at any rate, you give him permission to do so. But will it not be more honourable for you to begin?"

"No; I think not."

"Ah, but it would. If he, in his position, should be the first to speak, the first to suggest that this affair between you is a foolish one, what would people say?"

"They would say the truth."

"And what would you yourself say?"

"Nothing."

"What would he think of himself?"

"Ah, that I do not know. It is according as that may be, that he will or will not act at your bidding."

"Exactly; and because you know him to be high-minded, because you think that he, having so much to give, will not break his word to you—to you who have nothing to give in return—it is, therefore, that you say that the first step must be taken by him. Is that noble?"

Then Mary rose from her seat, for it was no longer possible for her to speak what it was in her to say, sitting there leisurely on her sofa. Lady Arabella's worship of money had not hitherto been so brought forward in the conversation as to give her unpardonable offence; but now she felt that she could no longer restrain her indignation. "To you who have nothing to give in return!" Had she not given all that she possessed? Had she not emptied his store into his lap? that heart of hers, beating with such genuine life, capable of such perfect love, throbbing with so grand a pride; had she not given that? And was it not that, between him and her, more than twenty Greshamsburys, nobler than any pedigree? "To you who have nothing to give," indeed! This to her who was so ready to give everything!

"Lady Arabella," she said, "I think that you do not understand me, and that it is not likely that you should. If so, our further talking will be worse than useless. I have taken no account of what will be given between your son and me in your sense of the word giving. But he has professed to—to love me"—as she spoke, she still looked on the lady's face, but her eyelashes for a moment screened her eyes, and her colour was a little heightened—"and I have acknowledged that I also love him, and so we are engaged. To me my promise is sacred. I will not be threatened into breaking it. If, however, he shall wish to change his mind, he can do so. I will not upbraid him; will not, if I can help it, think harshly of him. So much you may tell him if it suits you; but I will not listen to your calculations as to how much or how little each of us may have to give to the other."

She was still standing when she finished speaking, and so she continued to stand. Her eyes were fixed on Lady Arabella, and her position seemed to say that sufficient words had been spoken, and that it was time that her ladyship should go; and so Lady Arabella felt it. Gradually she also rose; slowly, but tacitly, she acknowledged that she was in the presence of a spirit superior to her own; and so she took her leave.

"Very well," she said, in a tone that was intended to be grandiloquent, but which failed grievously; "I will tell him that he has your permission to think a second time on this matter. I do not doubt but that he will do so." Mary would not condescend to answer, but curtsied low as her visitor left the room. And so the interview was over.

The interview was over, and Mary was alone. She remained standing as long as she heard the footsteps of Frank's mother on the stairs; not immediately thinking of what had passed, but still buoying herself up with her hot indignation, as though her work with Lady Arabella was not yet finished; but when the footfall was no longer heard, and the sound of the closing door told her that she was in truth alone, she sank back in her seat, and, covering her face with her hands, burst into bitter tears.

All that doctrine about money was horrible to her; that insolent pretence, that she had caught at Frank because of his worldly position, made her all but ferocious; but Lady Arabella had not the less spoken much that was true. She did think of the position which the heir of Greshamsbury should hold in the county, and of the fact that a marriage would mar that position so vitally; she did think of the old name, and the old Gresham pride; she did think of the squire and his deep distress: it was true that she had lived among them long enough to understand these things, and to know that it was not possible that this marriage should take place without deep family sorrow.

And then she asked herself whether, in consenting to accept Frank's hand, she had adequately considered this; and she was forced to acknowledge that she had not considered it. She had ridiculed Lady Arabella for saying that Frank was still a boy; but was it not true that his offer had been made with a boy's energy, rather than a man's forethought? If so, if she had been wrong to accede to that offer when made, would she not be doubly wrong to hold him to it now that she saw their error?

It was doubtless true that Frank himself could not be the first to draw back. What would people say of him? She could now calmly ask herself the question that had so angered her when asked by Lady Arabella. If he could not do it, and if, nevertheless, it behoved them to break off this match, by whom was it to be done if not by her? Was not Lady Arabella right throughout, right in her conclusions, though so foully wrong in her manner of drawing them?

And then she did think for one moment of herself. "You who have nothing to give in return!" Such had been Lady Arabella's main accusation against her. Was it in fact true that she had nothing to give? Her maiden love, her feminine pride, her very life, and spirit, and being—were these things nothing? Were they to be weighed against pounds sterling per annum? and, when so weighed, were they ever to kick the beam like feathers? All these things had been nothing to her when, without reflection, governed wholly by the impulse of the moment, she had first allowed his daring hand to lie for an instant in her own. She had thought nothing of these things when that other suitor came, richer far than Frank, to love whom it was as impossible to her as it was not to love him.

Her love had been pure from all such thoughts; she was conscious that it ever would be pure from them. Lady Arabella was unable to comprehend this, and, therefore, was Lady Arabella so utterly distasteful to her.

Frank had once held her close to his warm breast; and her very soul had thrilled with joy to feel that he so loved her,—with a joy which she had hardly dared to acknowledge. At that moment, her maidenly efforts had been made to push him off, but her heart had grown to his. She had acknowledged him to be master of her spirit; her bosom's lord; the man whom she had been born to worship; the human being to whom it was for her to link her destiny. Frank's acres had been of no account; nor had his want of acres. God had brought them two together that they should love each other; that conviction had satisfied her, and she had made it a duty to herself that she would love him with her very soul. And now she was called upon to wrench herself asunder from him because she had nothing to give in return!

Well, she would wrench herself asunder, as far as such wrenching might be done compatibly with her solemn promise. It might be right that Frank should have an opportunity offered him, so that he might escape from his position without disgrace. She would endeavour to give him this opportunity. So, with one deep sigh, she arose, took herself pen, ink, and paper, and sat herself down again so that the wrenching might begin.

And then, for a moment, she thought of her uncle. Why had he not spoken to her of all this? Why had he not warned her? He who had ever been so good to her, why had he now failed her so grievously? She had told him everything, had had no secret from him; but he had never answered her a word. "He also must have known," she said to herself, piteously, "he also must have known that I could give nothing in return." Such accusation, however, availed her not at all, so she sat down and slowly wrote her letter.

"Dearest Frank," she began. She had at first written "dear Mr Gresham;" but her heart revolted against such useless coldness. She was not going to pretend she did not love him. DEAREST FRANK, Your mother has been here talking to me about our engagement. I do not generally agree with her about such matters; but she has said some things to-day which I cannot but acknowledge to be true. She says, that our marriage would be distressing to your father, injurious to all your family, and ruinous to yourself. If this be so, how can I, who love you, wish for such a marriage?

> I remember my promise, and have kept it. I would not yield to your mother when she desired me to disclaim our engagement. But I do think it will be more prudent if you will consent to forget all that has passed between us—not, perhaps, to forget it; that may not be possible for us—but to let it pass by as though it had never been. If so, if you think so, dear Frank, do not have any scruples on my account. What will be best for you, must be best for me. Think what a reflection it would ever be to me, to have been the ruin of one that I love so well.
>
> Let me have but one word to say that I am released from my promise, and I will tell my uncle that the matter between us is over. It will be painful for us at first; those occasional meetings which must take place will distress us, but that will wear off. We shall always think well of each other, and why should we not be friends? This, doubtless, cannot be done without inward wounds; but such wounds are in God's hands, and He can cure them.
>
> I know what your first feelings will be on reading this letter; but do not answer it in obedience to first feelings. Think over it, think of your father, and all you owe him, of your old name, your old family, and of what the world expects from you. [Mary was forced to put her hand to her eyes, to save her paper from her falling tears, as she found herself thus repeating, nearly word for word, the arguments that had been used by Lady Arabella.] Think of these things, coolly, if you can, but, at any rate, without passion: and then let me have one word in answer. One word will suffice.
>
> I have but to add this: do not allow yourself to think that my heart will ever reproach you. It cannot reproach you for doing that which I myself suggest. [Mary's logic in this was very false; but she was not herself aware of it.] I will never reproach you either in word or thought; and as for all others, it seems to me that the world agrees that we have hitherto been wrong. The world, I hope, will be satisfied when we have obeyed it.
>
> God bless you, dearest Frank! I shall never call you so again; but it would be a pretence were I to write otherwise in this letter. Think of this, and then let me have one line.
> > Your affectionate friend,
> > MARY THORNE.

P.S.—Of course I cannot be at dear Beatrice's marriage; but when they come back to the parsonage, I shall see her. I am sure they will both be happy, because they are so good. I need hardly say that I shall think of them on their wedding day.

When she had finished her letter, she addressed it plainly, in her own somewhat bold handwriting, to Francis N. Gresham, Jun., Esq., and then took it herself to the little village post-office. There should be nothing underhand about her correspondence: all the Greshamsbury world should know of it—that world of which she had spoken in her letter—if that world so pleased. Having put her penny label on it, she handed it, with an open brow and an unembarrassed face, to the baker's wife, who was Her Majesty's postmistress at Greshamsbury; and, having so finished her work, she returned to see the table prepared for her uncle's dinner. "I will say nothing to him," said she to herself, "till I get the answer. He will not talk to me about it, so why should I trouble him?"

CHAPTER XLIII

THE RACE OF SCATCHERD BECOMES EXTINCT

It will not be imagined, at any rate by feminine readers, that Mary's letter was written off at once, without alterations and changes, or the necessity for a fair copy. Letters from one young lady to another are doubtless written in this manner, and even with them it might sometimes be better if more patience had been taken; but with Mary's first letter to her lover—her first love-letter, if love-letter it can be called—much more care was used. It was copied and re-copied, and when she returned from posting it, it was read and re-read.

"It is very cold," she said to herself; "he will think I have no heart, that I have never loved him!" And then she all but resolved to run down to the baker's wife, and get back her letter, that she might alter it. "But it will be better so," she said again. "If I touched his feelings now, he would never bring himself to leave me. It is right that I should be cold to him. I should be false to myself if I tried to move his love—I, who have nothing to give him in return for it." And so she made no further visit to the post-office, and the letter went on its way.

We will now follow its fortunes for a short while, and explain how it was that Mary received no answer for a week; a week, it may well be imagined, of terrible suspense to her. When she took it to the post-office, she doubtless thought that the baker's wife had nothing to do but to send it up to the house at Greshamsbury, and that Frank would receive it that evening, or, at latest, early on the following morning. But this was by no means so. The epistle was posted on a Friday afternoon, and it behoved the baker's wife to send it into Silverbridge—Silverbridge being the post-town—so that all due formalities, as ordered by the Queen's Government, might there be perfected. Now, unfortunately, the post-boy had taken his departure before Mary reached the shop, and it was not, therefore, dispatched till Saturday. Sunday was always a *dies non* with the Greshamsbury Mercury, and, consequently, Frank's letter was not delivered at the house till Monday morning; at which time Mary had for two long days been waiting with weary heart for the expected answer.

Now Frank had on that morning gone up to London by the early train, with his future brother-in-law, Mr Oriel. In order to accomplish this, they had left Greshamsbury for Barchester exactly as the postboy was leaving Silverbridge for Greshamsbury.

"I should like to wait for my letters," Mr Oriel had said, when the journey was being discussed.

"Nonsense," Frank had answered. "Who ever got a letter that was worth waiting for?" and so Mary was doomed to a week of misery.

When the post-bag arrived at the house on Monday morning, it was opened as usual by the squire himself at the breakfast-table. "Here is a letter for Frank," said he, "posted in the village. You had better send it to him:" and he threw the letter across the table to Beatrice.

"It's from Mary," said Beatrice, out loud, taking the letter up and examining the address. And having said so, she repented what she had done, as she looked first at her father and then at her mother.

A cloud came over the squire's brow as for a minute he went on turning over the letters and newspapers. "Oh, from Mary Thorne, is it?" he said. "Well, you had better send it to him."

"Frank said that if any letters came they were to be kept," said his sister Sophy. "He told me so particularly. I don't think he likes having letters sent after him."

"You had better send that one," said the squire.

"Mr Oriel is to have all his letters addressed to Long's Hotel, Bond Street, and this one can very well be sent with them," said Beatrice, who knew all about it, and intended herself to make a free use of the address.

"Yes, you had better send it," said the squire; and then nothing further was said at the table. But Lady Arabella, though she said nothing, had not failed to mark what had passed. Had she asked for the letter before the squire, he would probably have taken possession of it himself; but as soon as she was alone with Beatrice, she did demand it. "I shall be writing to Frank myself," she said, "and will send it to him." And so, Beatrice, with a heavy heart, gave it up.

The letter lay before Lady Arabella's eyes all that day, and many a wistful glance was cast at it. She turned it over and over, and much she desired to know its contents; but she did not dare to break the seal of her son's letter. All that day it lay upon her desk, and all the next, for she could hardly bring herself to part with it; but on the Wednesday it was sent—sent with these lines from herself:—

"Dearest, dearest Frank, I send you a letter which has come by the post from Mary Thorne. I do not know what it may contain; but before you correspond with her, pray, pray think of what I said to you. For my sake, for your father's, for your own, pray think of it."

That was all, but it was enough to make her word to Beatrice true. She did send it to Frank enclosed in a letter from herself. We must reserve to the next chapter what had taken place between Frank and his mother; but, for the present, we will return to the doctor's house.

Mary said not a word to him about the letter; but, keeping silent on the subject, she felt wretchedly estranged from him. "Is anything the matter, Mary?" he said to her on the Sunday afternoon.

"No, uncle," she answered, turning away her head to hide her tears.

"Ah, but there is something; what is it, dearest?"

"Nothing—that is, nothing that one can talk about."

"What Mary! Be unhappy and not to talk about it to me? That's something new, is it not?"

"One has presentiments sometimes, and is unhappy without knowing why. Besides, you know—"

"I know! What do I know? Do I know anything that will make my pet happier?" and he took her in his arms as they sat together on the sofa. Her tears were now falling fast, and she no longer made an effort to hide them. "Speak to me, Mary; this is more than a presentiment. What is it?"

"Oh, uncle—"

"Come, love, speak to me; tell me why you are grieving."

"Oh, uncle, why have you not spoken to me? Why have you not told me what to do? Why have you not advised me? Why are you always so silent?"

"Silent about what?"

"You know, uncle, you know; silent about him; silent about Frank."

Why, indeed? What was he to say to this? It was true that he had never counselled her; never shown her what course she should take; had never even spoken to her about her lover. And it was equally true that he was not now prepared to do so, even in answer to such an appeal as this. He had a hope, a strong hope, more than a hope, that Mary's love would yet be happy; but he could not express or explain his hope; nor could he even acknowledge to himself a wish that would seem to be based on the death of him whose life he was bound, if possible, to preserve.

"My love," he said, "it is a matter in which you must judge for yourself. Did I doubt your conduct, I should interfere; but I do not."

"Conduct! Is conduct everything? One may conduct oneself excellently, and yet break one's heart."

This was too much for the doctor; his sternness and firmness instantly deserted him. "Mary," he said, "I will do anything that you would have me. If you wish it, I will make arrangements for leaving this place at once."

"Oh, no," she said, plaintively.

"When you tell me of a broken heart, you almost break my own. Come to me, darling; do not leave me so. I will say all that I can say. I have thought, do still think, that circumstances will admit of your marriage with Frank if you both love each other, and can both be patient."

"You think so," said she, unconsciously sliding her hand into his, as though to thank him by its pressure for the comfort he was giving her.

"I do think so now more than ever. But I only think so; I have been unable to assure you. There, darling, I must not say more; only that I cannot bear to see you grieving, I would not have said this:" and then he left her, and nothing more was spoken on the subject.

If you can be patient! Why, a patience of ten years would be as nothing to her. Could she but live with the knowledge that she was first in his estimation, dearest in his heart; could it be also granted to her to feel that she was regarded as his equal, she could be patient for ever. What more did she want than to know and feel this? Patient, indeed!

But what could these circumstances be to which her uncle had alluded? "I do think that circumstances will admit of your marriage." Such was his opinion, and she had never known him to be wrong. Circumstances! What circumstances? Did he perhaps mean that Mr Gresham's affairs were not so bad as they had been thought to be? If so, that alone would hardly alter the matter, for what could she give in return? "I would give him the world for one word of love," she said to herself, "and never think that he was my debtor. Ah! how beggarly the heart must be that speculates on such gifts as those!"

But there was her uncle's opinion: he still thought that they might be married. Oh, why had she sent her letter? and why had she made it so cold? With such a letter as that before him, Frank could not do other than consent to her proposal. And then, why did he not at least answer it?

On the Sunday afternoon there arrived at Greshamsbury a man and a horse from Box-all Hill, bearing a letter from Lady Scatcherd to Dr Thorne, earnestly requesting the doctor's immediate attendance. "I fear everything is over with poor Louis," wrote the un-happy mother. "It has been very dreadful. Do come to me; I have no other friend, and I am nearly worn through with it. The man from the city"—she meant Dr Fillgrave—"comes every day, and I dare say he is all very well, but he has never done much good. He has not had spirit enough to keep the bottle from him; and it was that, and that only, that most behoved to be done. I doubt you won't find him in this world when you arrive here."

Dr Thorne started immediately. Even though he might have to meet Dr Fillgrave, he could not hesitate, for he went not as a doctor to the dying man, but as the trustee under Sir Roger's will. Moreover, as Lady Scatcherd had said, he was her only friend, and he could not desert her at such a moment for an army of Fillgraves. He told Mary he should not return that night; and taking with him a small saddle-bag, he started at once for Boxall Hill.

As he rode up to the hall door, Dr Fillgrave was getting into his carriage. They had never met so as to speak to each other since that memorable day, when they had their fa-mous passage of arms in the hall of that very house before which they both now stood. But, at the present moment, neither of them was disposed to renew the fight.

"What news of your patient, Dr Fillgrave?" said our doctor, still seated on his sweating horse, and putting his hand lightly to his hat.

Dr Fillgrave could not refrain from one moment of supercilious disdain: he gave one little chuck to his head, one little twist to his neck, one little squeeze to his lips, and then the man within him overcame the doctor. "Sir Louis is no more," he said.

"God's will be done!" said Dr Thorne.

"His death is a release; for his last days have been very frightful. Your coming, Dr Thorne, will be a comfort to Lady Scatcherd." And then Dr Fillgrave, thinking that even the present circumstances required no further condescension, ensconced himself in the carriage.

"His last days have been very dreadful! Ah, me, poor fellow! Dr Fillgrave, before you go, allow me to say this: I am quite aware that when he fell into your hands, no medical skill in the world could save him."

Dr Fillgrave bowed low from the carriage, and after this unwonted exchange of cour-tesies, the two doctors parted, not to meet again—at any rate, in the pages of this novel. Of Dr Fillgrave, let it now be said, that he grows in dignity as he grows in years, and that he is universally regarded as one of the celebrities of the city of Barchester.

Lady Scatcherd was found sitting alone in her little room on the ground-floor. Even Hannah was not with her, for Hannah was now occupied upstairs. When the doctor en-tered the room, which he did unannounced, he found her seated on a chair, with her back against one of the presses, her hands clasped together over her knees, gazing into vacancy. She did not ever hear him or see him as he approached, and his hand had slightly touched her shoulder before she knew that she was not alone. Then, she looked up at him with a face so full of sorrow, so worn with suffering, that his own heart was racked to see her.

"It is all over, my friend," said he. "It is better so; much better so."

She seemed at first hardly to understand him, but still regarding him with that wan face, shook her head slowly and sadly. One might have thought that she was twenty years older than when Dr Thorne last saw her.

He drew a chair to her side, and sitting by her, took her hand in his. "It is better so, La-dy Scatcherd; better so," he repeated. "The poor lad's doom had been spoken, and it is well for him, and for you, that it should be over."

"They are both gone now," said she, speaking very low; "both gone now. Oh, doctor! To be left alone here, all alone!"

He said some few words trying to comfort her; but who can comfort a widow bereaved of her child? Who can console a heart that has lost all that it possessed? Sir Roger had not been to her a tender husband; but still he had been the husband of her love. Sir Louis had not been to her an affectionate son; but still he had been her child, her only child. Now they were both gone. Who can wonder that the world should be a blank to her?

Still the doctor spoke soothing words, and still he held her hand. He knew that his words could not console her; but the sounds of his kindness at such desolate moments are, to such minds as hers, some alleviation of grief. She hardly answered him, but sat there staring out before her, leaving her hand passively to him, and swaying her head backwards and forwards as though her grief were too heavy to be borne.

At last, her eye rested on an article which stood upon the table, and she started up impetuously from her chair. She did this so suddenly, that the doctor's hand fell beside him before he knew that she had risen. The table was covered with all those implements which become so frequent about a house when severe illness is an inhabitant there. There were little boxes and apothecaries' bottles, cups and saucers standing separate, and bowls, in which messes have been prepared with the hope of suiting a sick man's failing appetite. There was a small saucepan standing on a plate, a curiously shaped glass utensil left by the doctor, and sundry pieces of flannel, which had been used in rubbing the sufferer's limbs. But in the middle of the débris stood one black bottle, with head erect, unsuited to the companionship in which it was found.

"There," she said, rising up, and seizing this in a manner that would have been ridiculous had it not been so truly tragic. "There, that has robbed me of everything—of all that I ever possessed; of husband and child; of the father and son; that has swallowed them both—murdered them both! Oh, doctor! that such a thing as that should cause such bitter sorrow! I have hated it always, but now—Oh, woe is me! weary me!" And then she let the bottle drop from her hand as though it were too heavy for her.

"This comes of their barro-niting," she continued. "If they had let him alone, he would have been here now, and so would the other one. Why did they do it? why did they do it? Ah, doctor! people such as us should never meddle with them above us. See what has come of it; see what has come of it!"

The doctor could not remain with her long, as it was necessary that he should take upon himself the direction of the household, and give orders for the funeral. First of all, he had to undergo the sad duty of seeing the corpse of the deceased baronet. This, at any rate, may be spared to my readers. It was found to be necessary that the interment should be made very quickly, as the body was already nearly destroyed by alcohol. Having done all this, and sent back his horse to Greshamsbury, with directions that clothes for a journey might be sent to him, and a notice that he should not be home for some days, he again returned to Lady Scatcherd.

Of course he could not but think much of the immense property which was now, for a short time, altogether in his own hands. His resolution was soon made to go at once to London and consult the best lawyer he could find—or the best dozen lawyers should such be necessary—as to the validity of Mary's claims. This must be done before he said a word to her or to any of the Gresham family; but it must be done instantly, so that all suspense might be at an end as soon as possible. He must, of course, remain with Lady Scatcherd till the funeral should be over; but when that office should be complete, he would start instantly for London.

In resolving to tell no one as to Mary's fortune till after he had fortified himself with legal warranty, he made one exception. He thought it rational that he should explain to Lady Scatcherd who was now the heir under her husband's will; and he was the more inclined to do so, from feeling that the news would probably be gratifying to her. With this view, he had once or twice endeavoured to induce her to talk about the property, but she had been unwilling to do so. She seemed to dislike all allusions to it, and it was not till she had incidentally mentioned the fact that she would have to look for a home, that he was able to fix her to the subject. This was on the evening before the funeral; on the afternoon of which day he intended to proceed to London.

"It may probably be arranged that you may continue to live here," said the doctor.

"I don't wish it at all," said she, rather sharply. "I don't wish to have any arrangements made. I would not be indebted to any of them for anything. Oh, dear! if money could make it all right, I should have enough of that."

"Indebted to whom, Lady Scatcherd? Who do you think will be the owner of Boxall Hill?"

"Indeed, then, Dr Thorne, I don't much care: unless it be yourself, it won't be any friend of mine, or any one I shall care to make a friend of. It isn't so easy for an old woman like me to make new friends."

"Well, it certainly won't belong to me."

"I wish it did, with all my heart. But even then, I would not live here. I have had too many troubles here to wish to see more."

"That shall be just as you like, Lady Scatcherd; but you will be surprised to hear that the place will—at least I think it will—belong to a friend of yours: to one to whom you have been very kind."

"And who is he, doctor? Won't it go to some of those Americans? I am sure I never did anything kind to them; though, indeed, I did love poor Mary Scatcherd. But that's years upon years ago, and she is dead and gone now. Well, I begrudge nothing to Mary's children. As I have none of my own, it is right they should have the money. It has not made me happy; I hope it may do so to them."

"The property will, I think, go to Mary Scatcherd's eldest child. It is she whom you have known as Mary Thorne."

"Doctor!" And then Lady Scatcherd, as she made the exclamation, put both her hands down to hold her chair, as though she feared the weight of her surprise would topple her off her seat.

"Yes; Mary Thorne—my Mary—to whom you have been so good, who loves you so well; she, I believe, will be Sir Roger's heiress. And it was so that Sir Roger intended on his deathbed, in the event of poor Louis's life being cut short. If this be so, will you be ashamed to stay here as the guest of Mary Thorne? She has not been ashamed to be your guest."

But Lady Scatcherd was now too much interested in the general tenor of the news which she had heard to care much about the house which she was to inhabit in future. Mary Thorne, the heiress of Boxall Hill! Mary Thorne, the still living child of that poor creature who had so nearly died when they were all afflicted with their early grief! Well; there was consolation, there was comfort in this. There were but three people left in the world that she could love: her foster-child, Frank Gresham—Mary Thorne, and the doctor. If the money went to Mary, it would of course go to Frank, for she now knew that they loved each other; and if it went to them, would not the doctor have his share also; such share as he might want? Could she have governed the matter, she would have given it all to Frank; and now it would be as well bestowed.

Yes; there was consolation in this. They both sat up more than half the night talking over it, and giving and receiving explanations. If only the council of lawyers would not be adverse! That was now the point of suspense.

The doctor, before he left her, bade her hold her peace, and say nothing of Mary's fortune to any one till her rights had been absolutely acknowledged. "It will be nothing not to have it," said the doctor; "but it would be very bad to hear it was hers, and then to lose it."

On the next morning, Dr Thorne deposited the remains of Sir Louis in the vault prepared for the family in the parish church. He laid the son where a few months ago he had laid the father,—and so the title of Scatcherd became extinct. Their race of honour had not been long.

After the funeral, the doctor hurried up to London, and there we will leave him.

CHAPTER XLIV

SATURDAY EVENING AND SUNDAY MORNING

We must now go back a little and describe how Frank had been sent off on special business to London. The household at Greshamsbury was at this time in but a doleful state. It seemed to be pervaded, from the squire down to the scullery-maid, with a feeling that things were not going well; and men and women, in spite of Beatrice's coming marriage, were grim-visaged, and dolorous. Mr Mortimer Gazebee, rejected though he had been, still went and came, talking much to the squire, much also to her ladyship, as to the ill-doings which were in the course of projection by Sir Louis; and Frank went about the house with clouded brow, as though finally resolved to neglect his one great duty.

Poor Beatrice was robbed of half her joy: over and over again her brother asked her whether she had yet seen Mary, and she was obliged as often to answer that she had not. Indeed, she did not dare to visit her friend, for it was hardly possible that they should sympathise with each other. Mary was, to say the least, stubborn in her pride; and Beatrice, though she could forgive her friend for loving her brother, could not forgive the obstinacy with which Mary persisted in a course which, as Beatrice thought, she herself knew to be wrong.

And then Mr Gazebee came down from town, with an intimation that it behoved the squire himself to go up that he might see certain learned pundits, and be badgered in his own person at various dingy, dismal chambers in Lincoln's Inn Fields, the Temple, and Gray's Inn Lane. It was an invitation exactly of that sort which a good many years ago was given to a certain duck.

"Will you, will you—will you, will you—come and be killed?" Although Mr Gazebee urged the matter with such eloquence, the squire remained steady to his objection, and swam obstinately about his Greshamsbury pond in any direction save that which seemed to lead towards London.

This occurred on the very evening of that Friday which had witnessed the Lady Arabella's last visit to Dr Thorne's house. The question of the squire's necessary journey to the great fountains of justice was, of course, discussed between Lady Arabella and Mr Gazebee; and it occurred to the former, full as she was of Frank's iniquity and of Mary's obstinacy, that if Frank were sent up in lieu of his father, it would separate them at least for a while. If she could only get Frank away without seeing his love, she might yet so work upon him, by means of the message which Mary had sent, as to postpone, if not break off, this hateful match. It was inconceivable that a youth of twenty-three, and such a youth as Frank, should be obstinately constant to a girl possessed of no great beauty—so argued Lady Arabella to herself—and who had neither wealth, birth, nor fashion to recommend her.

And thus it was at last settled—the squire being a willing party to the agreement—that Frank should go up and be badgered in lieu of his father. At his age it was possible to make it appear a thing desirable, if not necessary—on account of the importance conveyed—to sit day after day in the chambers of Messrs Slow & Bidewhile, and hear musty law talk, and finger dusty law parchments. The squire had made many visits to Messrs Slow & Bidewhile, and he knew better. Frank had not hitherto been there on his own bottom, and thus he fell easily into the trap.

Mr Oriel was also going to London, and this was another reason for sending Frank. Mr Oriel had business of great importance, which it was quite necessary that he should execute before his marriage. How much of this business consisted in going to his tailor, buying a wedding-ring, and purchasing some other more costly present for Beatrice, we need not here inquire. But Mr Oriel was quite on Lady Arabella's side with reference to this mad engagement, and as Frank and he were now fast friends, some good might be done in that way. "If we all caution him against it, he can hardly withstand us all!" said Lady Arabella to herself.

The matter was broached to Frank on the Saturday evening, and settled between them all the same night. Nothing, of course, was at that moment said about Mary; but Lady Arabella was too full of the subject to let him go to London without telling him that Mary was ready to recede if only he would allow her to do so. About eleven o'clock, Frank was sitting in his own room, conning over the difficulties of the situation—thinking of his father's troubles, and his own position—when he was roused from his reverie by a slight tap at the door.

"Come in," said he, somewhat loudly. He thought it was one of his sisters, who were apt to visit him at all hours and for all manner of reasons; and he, though he was usually gentle to them, was not at present exactly in a humour to be disturbed.

The door gently opened, and he saw his mother standing hesitating in the passage.

"Can I come in, Frank?" said she.

"Oh, yes, mother; by all means:" and then, with some surprise marked in his countenance, he prepared a seat for her. Such a visit as this from Lady Arabella was very unusual; so much so, that he had probably not seen her in his own room since the day when he first left school. He had nothing, however, to be ashamed of; nothing to conceal, unless it were an open letter from Miss Dunstable which he had in his hand when she entered, and which he somewhat hurriedly thrust into his pocket.

"I wanted to say a few words to you, Frank, before you start for London about this business." Frank signified by a gesture, that he was quite ready to listen to her.

"I am so glad to see your father putting the matter into your hands. You are younger than he is; and then—I don't know why, but somehow your father has never been a good man of business—everything has gone wrong with him."

"Oh, mother! do not say anything against him."

"No, Frank, I will not; I do not wish it. Things have been unfortunate, certainly. Ah me! I little thought when I married—but I don't mean to complain—I have excellent children, and I ought to be thankful for that."

Frank began to fear that no good could be coming when his mother spoke in that strain. "I will do the best I can," said he, "up in town. I can't help thinking myself that Mr Gazebee might have done as well, but—"

"Oh, dear no; by no means. In such cases the principal must show himself. Besides, it is right you should know how matters stand. Who is so much interested in it as you are? Poor Frank! I so often feel for you when I think how the property has dwindled."

"Pray do not mind me, mother. Why should you talk of it as my matter while my father is not yet forty-five? His life, so to speak, is as good as mine. I can do very well without it; all I want is to be allowed to settle to something."

"You mean a profession."

"Yes; something of that sort."

"They are so slow, dear Frank. You, who speak French so well—I should think my brother might get you in as attaché to some embassy."

"That wouldn't suit me at all," said Frank.

"Well, we'll talk about that some other time. But I came about something else, and I do hope you will hear me."

Frank's brow again grew black, for he knew that his mother was about to say something which it would be disagreeable for him to hear.

"I was with Mary, yesterday."

"Well, mother?"

"Don't be angry with me, Frank; you can't but know that the fate of an only son must be a subject of anxiety to a mother." Ah! how singularly altered was Lady Arabella's tone since first she had taken upon herself to discuss the marriage prospects of her son! Then how autocratic had she been as she sent him away, bidding him, with full command, to throw himself into the golden embraces of Miss Dunstable! But now, how humble, as she came suppliantly to his room, craving that she might have leave to whisper into his ears a mother's anxious fears! Frank had laughed at her stern behests, though he had half obeyed them; but he was touched to the heart by her humility.

He drew his chair nearer to her, and took her by the hand. But she, disengaging hers, parted the hair from off his forehead, and kissed his brow. "Oh, Frank," she said, "I have been so proud of you, am still so proud of you. It will send me to my grave if I see you sink below your proper position. Not that it will be your fault. I am sure it will not be your fault. Only circumstanced as you are, you should be doubly, trebly, careful. If your father had not—"

"Do not speak against my father."

"No, Frank; I will not—no, I will not; not another word. And now, Frank—"

Before we go on we must say one word further as to Lady Arabella's character. It will probably be said that she was a consummate hypocrite; but at the present moment she was not hypocritical. She did love her son; was anxious—very, very anxious for him; was proud of him, and almost admired the very obstinacy which so vexed her to her inmost soul. No grief would be to her so great as that of seeing him sink below what she conceived to be his position. She was as genuinely motherly, in wishing that he should marry money, as another woman might be in wishing to see her son a bishop; or as the Spartan matron, who preferred that her offspring should return on his shield, to hearing that he had come back whole in limb but tainted in honour. When Frank spoke of a profession, she instantly thought of what Lord de Courcy might do for him. If he would not marry money, he might, at any rate, be an attaché at an embassy. A profession—hard work, as a doctor, or as an engineer—would, according to her ideas, degrade him; cause him to sink below his proper position; but to dangle at a foreign court, to make small talk at the evening parties of a lady ambassadress, and occasionally, perhaps, to write demi-official notes containing demi-official tittle-tattle; this would be in proper accordance with the high honour of a Gresham of Greshamsbury.

We may not admire the direction taken by Lady Arabella's energy on behalf of her son, but that energy was not hypocritical.

"And now, Frank—" She looked wistfully into his face as she addressed him, as though half afraid to go on, and begging that he would receive with complaisance whatever she found herself forced to say.

"Well, mother?"

"I was with Mary, yesterday."

"Yes, yes; what then? I know what your feelings are with regard to her."

"No, Frank; you wrong me. I have no feelings against her—none, indeed; none but this: that she is not fit to be your wife."

"I think her fit."

"Ah, yes; but how fit? Think of your position, Frank, and what means you have of keeping her. Think what you are. Your father's only son; the heir to Greshamsbury. If Greshamsbury be ever again more than a name, it is you that must redeem it. Of all men living you are the least able to marry a girl like Mary Thorne."

"Mother, I will not sell myself for what you call my position."

"Who asks you? I do not ask you; nobody asks you. I do not want you to marry any one. I did think once—but let that pass. You are now twenty-three. In ten years' time you will still be a young man. I only ask you to wait. If you marry now, that is, marry such a girl as Mary Thorne—"

"Such a girl! Where shall I find such another?"

"I mean as regards money, Frank; you know I mean that; how are you to live? Where are you to go? And then, her birth. Oh, Frank, Frank!"

"Birth! I hate such pretence. What was—but I won't talk about it. Mother, I tell you my word is pledged, and on no account will I be induced to break it."

"Ah, that's just it; that's just the point. Now, Frank, listen to me. Pray listen to me patiently for one minute. I do not ask much of you."

Frank promised that he would listen patiently; but he looked anything but patient as he said so.

"I have seen Mary, as it was certainly my duty to do. You cannot be angry with me for that."

"Who said that I was angry, mother?"

"Well, I have seen her, and I must own, that though she was not disposed to be courteous to me, personally, she said much that marked her excellent good sense. But the gist of it was this; that as she had made you a promise, nothing should turn her from that promise but your permission."

"And do you think—"

"Wait a moment, Frank, and listen to me. She confessed that this marriage was one which would necessarily bring distress on all your family; that it was one which would probably be ruinous to yourself; that it was a match which could not be approved of: she did, indeed; she confessed all that. 'I have nothing', she said—those were her own words—'I have nothing to say in favour of this engagement, except that he wishes it.' That is what she thinks of it herself. 'His wishes are not a reason; but a law,' she said—"

"And, mother, would you have me desert such a girl as that?"

"It is not deserting, Frank: it would not be deserting: you would be doing that which she herself approves of. She feels the impropriety of going on; but she cannot draw back because of her promise to you. She thinks that she cannot do it, even though she wishes it."

"Wishes it! Oh, mother!"

"I do believe she does, because she has sense to feel the truth of all that your friends say. Oh, Frank, I will go on my knees to you if you will listen to me."

"Oh, mother! mother! mother!"

"You should think twice, Frank, before you refuse the only request your mother ever made you. And why do I ask you? why do I come to you thus? Is it for my own sake? Oh, my boy! my darling boy! will you lose everything in life, because you love the child with whom you have played as a child?"

"Whose fault is it that we were together as children? She is now more than a child. I look on her already as my wife."

"But she is not your wife, Frank; and she knows that she ought not to be. It is only because you hold her to it that she consents to be so."

"Do you mean to say that she does not love me?"

Lady Arabella would probably have said this, also, had she dared; but she felt, that in doing so, she would be going too far. It was useless for her to say anything that would be utterly contradicted by an appeal to Mary herself.

"No, Frank; I do not mean to say that you do not love her. What I do mean is this: that it is not becoming in you to give up everything—not only yourself, but all your family—for such a love as this; and that she, Mary herself, acknowledges this. Every one is of the same opinion. Ask your father: I need not say that he would agree with you about everything if he could. I will not say the de Courcys."

"Oh, the de Courcys!"

"Yes, they are my relations; I know that." Lady Arabella could not quite drop the tone of bitterness which was natural to her in saying this. "But ask your sisters; ask Mr Oriel, whom you esteem so much; ask your friend Harry Baker."

Frank sat silent for a moment or two while his mother, with a look almost of agony, gazed into his face. "I will ask no one," at last he said.

"Oh, my boy! my boy!"

"No one but myself can know my own heart."

"And you will sacrifice all to such a love as that, all; her, also, whom you say that you so love? What happiness can you give her as your wife? Oh, Frank! is that the only answer you will make your mother on her knees?

"Oh, mother! mother!"

"No, Frank, I will not let you ruin yourself; I will not let you destroy yourself. Promise this, at least, that you will think of what I have said."

"Think of it! I do think of it."

"Ah, but think of it in earnest. You will be absent now in London; you will have the business of the estate to manage; you will have heavy cares upon your hands. Think of it as a man, and not as a boy."

"I will see her to-morrow before I go."

"No, Frank, no; grant me that trifle, at any rate. Think upon this without seeing her. Do not proclaim yourself so weak that you cannot trust yourself to think over what your mother says to you without asking her leave. Though you be in love, do not be childish with it. What I have told you as coming from her is true, word for word; if it were not, you would soon learn so. Think now of what I have said, and of what she says, and when you come back from London, then you can decide."

To so much Frank consented after some further parley; namely, that he would proceed to London on the following Monday morning without again seeing Mary. And in the meantime, she was waiting with sore heart for his answer to that letter that was lying, and was still to lie for so many hours, in the safe protection of the Silverbridge postmistress.

It may seem strange; but, in truth, his mother's eloquence had more effect on Frank than that of his father: and yet, with his father he had always sympathised. But his mother had been energetic; whereas, his father, if not lukewarm, had, at any rate, been timid. "I will ask no one," Frank had said in the strong determination of his heart; and yet the words were hardly out of his mouth before he bethought himself that he would talk the thing over with Harry Baker. "Not," said he to himself, "that I have any doubt; I have no doubt; but I hate to have all the world against me. My mother wishes me to ask Harry Baker. Harry is a good fellow, and I will ask him." And with this resolve he betook himself to bed.

The following day was Sunday. After breakfast Frank went with the family to church, as was usual; and there, as usual, he saw Mary in Dr Thorne's pew. She, as she looked at him, could not but wonder why he had not answered the letter which was still at Silverbridge; and he endeavoured to read in her face whether it was true, as his mother had told him, that she was quite ready to give him up. The prayers of both of them were disturbed, as is so often the case with the prayers of other anxious people.

There was a separate door opening from the Greshamsbury pew out into the Greshamsbury grounds, so that the family were not forced into unseemly community with the village multitude in going to and from their prayers; for the front door of the church led out into a road which had no connexion with the private path. It was not unusual with Frank and his father to go round, after the service, to the chief entrance, so that they might speak to their neighbours, and get rid of some of the exclusiveness which was intended for them. On this morning the squire did so; but Frank walked home with his mother and sisters, so that Mary saw no more of him.

I have said that he walked home with his mother and his sisters; but he rather followed in their path. He was not inclined to talk much, at least, not to them; and he continued asking himself the question—whether it could be possible that he was wrong in remaining true to his promise? Could it be that he owed more to his father and his mother, and what they chose to call his position, than he did to Mary?

After church, Mr Gazebee tried to get hold of him, for there was much still to be said, and many hints to be given, as to how Frank should speak, and, more especially, as to how he should hold his tongue among the learned pundits in and about Chancery Lane. "You must be very wide awake with Messrs Slow & Bideawhile," said Mr Gazebee. But Frank would not hearken to him just at that moment. He was going to ride over to Harry Baker, so he put Mr Gazebee off till the half-hour before dinner,—or else the half-hour after tea.

On the previous day he had received a letter from Miss Dunstable, which he had hitherto read but once. His mother had interrupted him as he was about to refer to it; and now, as his father's nag was being saddled—he was still prudent in saving the black horse—he again took it out.

Miss Dunstable had written in an excellent humour. She was in great distress about the oil of Lebanon, she said. "I have been trying to get a purchaser for the last two years; but my lawyer won't let me sell it, because the would-be purchasers offer a thousand pounds or so less than the value. I would give ten to be rid of the bore; but I am as little able to act myself as Sancho was in his government. The oil of Lebanon! Did you hear anything of it when you were in those parts? I thought of changing the name to 'London particular;' but my lawyer says the brewers would bring an action against me.

"I was going down to your neighbourhood—to your friend the duke's, at least. But I am prevented by my poor doctor, who is so weak that I must take him to Malvern. It is a great bore; but I have the satisfaction that I do my duty by him!

"Your cousin George is to be married at last. So I hear, at least. He loves wisely, if not well; for his widow has the name of being prudent and fairly well to do in the world. She has got over the caprices of her youth. Dear Aunt de Courcy will be so delighted. I might perhaps have met her at Gatherum Castle. I do so regret it.

"Mr Moffat has turned up again. We all thought you had finally extinguished him. He left a card the other day, and I have told the servant always to say that I am at home, and that you are with me. He is going to stand for some borough in the west of Ireland. He's used to shillelaghs by this time.

"By the by, I have a *cadeau* for a friend of yours. I won't tell you what it is, nor permit you to communicate the fact. But when you tell me that in sending it I may fairly congratulate her on having so devoted a slave as you, it shall be sent.

"If you have nothing better to do at present, do come and see my invalid at Malvern. Perhaps you might have a mind to treat for the oil of Lebanon. I'll give you all the assistance I can in cheating my lawyers."

There was not much about Mary in this; but still, the little that was said made him again declare that neither father nor mother should move him from his resolution. "I will write to her and say that she may send her present when she pleases. Or I will run down to Malvern for a day. It will do me good to see her." And so resolved, he rode away to Mill Hill, thinking, as he went, how he would put the matter to Harry Baker.

Harry was at home; but we need not describe the whole interview. Had Frank been asked beforehand, he would have declared, that on no possible subject could he have had the slightest hesitation in asking Harry any question, or communicating to him any tidings. But when the time came, he found that he did hesitate much. He did not want to ask his friend if he should be wise to marry Mary Thorne. Wise or not, he was determined to do that. But he wished to be quite sure that his mother was wrong in saying that all the world would dissuade him from it. Miss Dunstable, at any rate, did not do so.

At last, seated on a stile at the back of the Mill Hill stables, while Harry stood close before him with both his hands in his pockets, he did get his story told. It was by no means the first time that Harry Baker had heard about Mary Thorne, and he was not, therefore, so surprised as he might have been, had the affair been new to him. And thus, standing there in the position we have described, did Mr Baker, junior, give utterance to such wisdom as was in him on this subject.

"You see, Frank, there are two sides to every question; and, as I take it, fellows are so apt to go wrong because they are so fond of one side, they won't look at the other. There's no doubt about it, Lady Arabella is a very clever woman, and knows what's what; and there's no doubt about this either, that you have a very ticklish hand of cards to play."

"I'll play it straightforward; that's my game" said Frank.

"Well and good, my dear fellow. That's the best game always. But what is straightforward? Between you and me, I fear there's no doubt that your father's property has got into a deuce of a mess."

"I don't see that that has anything to do with it."

"Yes, but it has. If the estate was all right, and your father could give you a thousand a year to live on without feeling it, and if your eldest child would be cock-sure of Greshamsbury, it might be very well that you should please yourself as to marrying at once. But that's not the case; and yet Greshamsbury is too good a card to be flung away."

"I could fling it away to-morrow," said Frank.

"Ah! you think so," said Harry the Wise. "But if you were to hear to-morrow that Sir Louis Scatcherd were master of the whole place, and be d—— to him, you would feel very uncomfortable." Had Harry known how near Sir Louis was to his last struggle, he would not have spoken of him in this manner. "That's all very fine talk, but it won't bear wear and tear. You do care for Greshamsbury if you are the fellow I take you to be: care for it very much; and you care too for your father being Gresham of Greshamsbury."

"This won't affect my father at all."

"Ah, but it will affect him very much. If you were to marry Miss Thorne to-morrow, there would at once be an end to any hope of your saving the property."

"And do you mean to say I'm to be a liar to her for such reasons as that? Why, Harry, I should be as bad as Moffat. Only it would be ten times more cowardly, as she has no brother."

"I must differ from you there altogether; but mind, I don't mean to say anything. Tell me that you have made up your mind to marry her, and I'll stick to you through thick and thin. But if you ask my advice, why, I must give it. It is quite a different affair to that of Moffat's. He had lots of tin, everything he could want, and there could be no reason why he should not marry,—except that he was a snob, of whom your sister was well quit. But this is very different. If I, as your friend, were to put it to Miss Thorne, what do you think she would say herself?"

"She would say whatever she thought best for me."

"Exactly: because she is a trump. And I say the same. There can be no doubt about it, Frank, my boy: such a marriage would be very foolish for you both; very foolish. Nobody can admire Miss Thorne more than I do; but you oughtn't to be a marrying man for the next ten years, unless you get a fortune. If you tell her the truth, and if she's the girl I take her to be, she'll not accuse you of being false. She'll peak for a while; and so will you, old chap. But others have had to do that before you. They have got over it, and so will you."

Such was the spoken wisdom of Harry Baker, and who can say that he was wrong? Frank sat a while on his rustle seat, paring his nails with his penknife, and then looking up, he thus thanked his friend:—

"I'm sure you mean well, Harry; and I'm much obliged to you. I dare say you're right too. But, somehow, it doesn't come home to me. And what is more, after what has passed, I could not tell her that I wish to part from her. I could not do it. And besides, I have that sort of feeling, that if I heard she was to marry any one else, I am sure I should blow his brains out. Either his or my own."

"Well, Frank, you may count on me for anything, except the last proposition:" and so they shook hands, and Frank rode back to Greshamsbury.

CHAPTER XLV

LAW BUSINESS IN LONDON

On the Monday morning at six o'clock, Mr Oriel and Frank started together; but early as it was, Beatrice was up to give them a cup of coffee, Mr Oriel having slept that night in the house. Whether Frank would have received his coffee from his sister's fair hands had not Mr Oriel been there, may be doubted. He, however, loudly asserted that he should not have done so, when she laid claim to great merit for rising in his behalf.

Mr Oriel had been specially instigated by Lady Arabella to use the opportunity of their joint journey, for pointing out to Frank the iniquity as well as madness of the course he was pursuing; and he had promised to obey her ladyship's behests. But Mr Oriel was perhaps not an enterprising man, and was certainly not a presumptuous one. He did intend to do as he was bid; but when he began, with the object of leading up to the subject of Frank's engagement, he always softened down into some much easier enthusiasm in the matter of his own engagement with Beatrice. He had not that perspicuous, but not over-sensitive strength of mind which had enabled Harry Baker to express his opinion out at once; and boldly as he did it, yet to do so without offence.

Four times before the train arrived in London, he made some little attempt; but four times he failed. As the subject was matrimony, it was his easiest course to begin about himself; but he never could get any further.

"No man was ever more fortunate in a wife than I shall be," he said, with a soft, euphuistic self-complacency, which would have been silly had it been adopted to any other person than the bride's brother. His intention, however, was very good, for he meant to show, that in his case marriage was prudent and wise, because his case differed so widely from that of Frank.

"Yes," said Frank. "She is an excellent good girl:" he had said it three times before, and was not very energetic.

"Yes, and so exactly suited to me; indeed, all that I could have dreamed of. How very well she looked this morning! Some girls only look well at night. I should not like that at all."

"You mustn't expect her to look like that always at six o'clock A.M.," said Frank, laughing. "Young ladies only take that trouble on very particular occasions. She wouldn't have come down like that if my father or I had been going alone. No, and she won't do so for you in a couple of years' time."

"Oh, but she's always nice. I have seen her at home as much almost as you could do; and then she's so sincerely religious."

"Oh, yes, of course; that is, I am sure she is," said Frank, looking solemn as became him.

"She's made to be a clergyman's wife."

"Well, so it seems," said Frank.

"A married life is, I'm sure, the happiest in the world—if people are only in a position to marry," said Mr Oriel, gradually drawing near to the accomplishment of his design.

"Yes; quite so. Do you know, Oriel, I never was so sleepy in my life. What with all that fuss of Gazebee's, and one thing and another, I could not get to bed till one o'clock; and then I couldn't sleep. I'll take a snooze now, if you won't think it uncivil." And then, putting his feet upon the opposite seat, he settled himself comfortably to his rest. And so Mr Oriel's last attempt for lecturing Frank in the railway-carriage faded away and was annihilated.

By twelve o'clock Frank was with Messrs Slow & Bideawhile. Mr Bideawhile was engaged at the moment, but he found the managing Chancery clerk to be a very chatty gentleman. Judging from what he saw, he would have said that the work to be done at Messrs Slow & Bideawhile's was not very heavy.

"A singular man that Sir Louis," said the Chancery clerk.

"Yes; very singular," said Frank.

"Excellent security, excellent; no better; and yet he will foreclose; but you see he has no power himself. But the question is, can the trustee refuse? Then, again, trustees are so circumscribed nowadays that they are afraid to do anything. There has been so much said lately, Mr Gresham, that a man doesn't know where he is, or what he is doing. Nobody trusts anybody. There have been such terrible things that we can't wonder at it. Only think of the case of those Hills! How can any one expect that any one else will ever trust a lawyer again after that? But that's Mr Bideawhile's bell. How can any one expect it? He will see you now, I dare say, Mr Gresham."

So it turned out, and Frank was ushered into the presence of Mr Bideawhile. He had got his lesson by heart, and was going to rush into the middle of his subject; such a course, however, was not in accordance with Mr Bideawhile's usual practice. Mr Bideawhile got up from his large wooden-seated Windsor chair, and, with a soft smile, in which, however, was mingled some slight dash of the attorney's acuteness, put out his hand to his young client; not, indeed, as though he were going to shake hands with him, but as though the hand were some ripe fruit all but falling, which his visitor might take and pluck if he thought proper. Frank took hold of the hand, which returned him no pressure, and then let it go again, not making any attempt to gather the fruit.

"I have come up to town, Mr Bideawhile, about this mortgage," commenced Frank.

"Mortgage—ah, sit down, Mr Gresham; sit down. I hope your father is quite well?"

"Quite well, thank you."

"I have a great regard for your father. So I had for your grandfather; a very good man indeed. You, perhaps, don't remember him, Mr Gresham?"

"He died when I was only a year old."

"Oh, yes; no, you of course, can't remember him; but I do, well: he used to be very fond of some port wine I had. I think it was '11;' and if I don't mistake, I have a bottle or two of it yet; but it is not worth drinking now. Port wine, you know, won't keep beyond a certain time. That was very good wine. I don't exactly remember what it stood me a dozen then; but such wine can't be had now. As for the Madeira, you know there's an end of that. Do you drink Madeira, Mr Gresham?"

"No," said Frank, "not very often."

"I'm sorry for that, for it's a fine wine; but then there's none of it left, you know. I have a few dozen, I'm told they're growing pumpkins where the vineyards were. I wonder what they do with all the pumpkins they grow in Switzerland! You've been in Switzerland, Mr Gresham?"

Frank said he had been in Switzerland.

"It's a beautiful country; my girls made me go there last year. They said it would do me good; but then you know, they wanted to see it themselves; ha! ha! ha! However, I believe I shall go again this autumn. That is to Aix, or some of those places; just for three weeks. I can't spare any more time, Mr Gresham. Do you like that dining at the *tables d'hôte*?"

"Pretty well, sometimes."

"One would get tired of it—eh! But they gave us capital dinners at Zurich. I don't think much of their soup. But they had fish, and about seven kinds of meats and poultry, and three or four puddings, and things of that sort. Upon my word, I thought we did very well, and so did my girls, too. You see a great many ladies travelling now."

"Yes," said Frank; "a great many."

"Upon my word, I think they are right; that is, if they can afford time. I can't afford time. I'm here every day till five, Mr Gresham; then I go out and dine in Fleet Street, and then back to work till nine."

"Dear me! that's very hard."

"Well, yes it is hard work. My boys don't like it; but I manage it somehow. I get down to my little place in the country on Saturday. I shall be most happy to see you there next Saturday."

Frank, thinking it would be outrageous on his part to take up much of the time of the gentleman who was constrained to work so unreasonably hard, began again to talk about his mortgages, and, in so doing, had to mention the name of Mr Yates Umbleby.

"Ah, poor Umbleby!" said Mr Bideawhile; "what is he doing now? I am quite sure your father was right, or he wouldn't have done it; but I used to think that Umbleby was a decent sort of man enough. Not so grand, you know, as your Gazebees and Gumptions— eh, Mr Gresham? They do say young Gazebee is thinking of getting into Parliament. Let me see: Umbleby married—who was it he married? That was the way your father got hold of him; not your father, but your grandfather. I used to know all about it. Well, I was sorry for Umbleby. He has got something, I suppose—eh?"

Frank said that he believed Mr Yates Umbleby had something wherewith to keep the wolf from the door.

"So you have got Gazebee down there now? Gumption, Gazebee & Gazebee: very good people, I'm sure; only, perhaps, they have a little too much on hand to do your father justice."

"But about Sir Louis, Mr Bideawhile."

"Well, about Sir Louis; a very bad sort of fellow, isn't he? Drinks—eh? I knew his father a little. He was a rough diamond, too. I was once down in Northamptonshire, about some railway business; let me see; I almost forget whether I was with him, or against him. But I know he made sixty thousand pounds by one hour's work; sixty thousand pounds! And then he got so mad with drinking that we all thought—"

And so Mr Bideawhile went on for two hours, and Frank found no opportunity of saying one word about the business which had brought him up to town. What wonder that such a man as this should be obliged to stay at his office every night till nine o'clock?

During these two hours, a clerk had come in three or four times, whispering something to the lawyer, who, on the last of such occasions, turned to Frank, saying, "Well, perhaps that will do for to-day. If you'll manage to call to-morrow, say about two, I will have the whole thing looked up; or, perhaps Wednesday or Thursday would suit you better." Frank, declaring that the morrow would suit him very well, took his departure, wondering much at the manner in which business was done at the house of Messrs Slow & Bideawhile.

When he called the next day, the office seemed to be rather disturbed, and he was shown quickly into Mr Bideawhile's room. "Have you heard this?" said that gentleman, putting a telegram into his hands. It contained tidings of the death of Sir Louis Scatcherd. Frank immediately knew that these tidings must be of importance to his father; but he had no idea how vitally they concerned his own more immediate interests.

"Dr Thorne will be up in town on Thursday evening after the funeral," said the talkative clerk. "And nothing of course can be done till he comes," said Mr Bideawhile. And so Frank, pondering on the mutability of human affairs, again took his departure.

He could do nothing now but wait for Dr Thorne's arrival, and so he amused himself in the interval by running down to Malvern, and treating with Miss Dunstable in person for the oil of Lebanon. He went down on the Wednesday, and thus, failed to receive, on the Thursday morning, Mary's letter, which reached London on that day. He returned, however, on the Friday, and then got it; and perhaps it was well for Mary's happiness that he had seen Miss Dunstable in the interval. "I don't care what your mother says," said she, with emphasis. "I don't care for any Harry, whether it be Harry Baker, or old Harry himself. You made her a promise, and you are bound to keep it; if not on one day, then on another. What! because you cannot draw back yourself, get out of it by inducing her to do so! Aunt de Courcy herself could not improve upon that." Fortified in this manner, he returned to town on the Friday morning, and then got Mary's letter. Frank also got a note from Dr Thorne, stating that he had taken up his temporary domicile at the Gray's Inn Coffee-house, so as to be near the lawyers.

It has been suggested that the modern English writers of fiction should among them keep a barrister, in order that they may be set right on such legal points as will arise in their little narratives, and thus avoid that exposure of their own ignorance of the laws, which, now, alas! they too often make. The idea is worthy of consideration, and I can only say, that if such an arrangement can be made, and if a counsellor adequately skilful can be found to accept the office, I shall be happy to subscribe my quota; it would be but a modest tribute towards the cost.

But as the suggestion has not yet been carried out, and as there is at present no learned gentleman whose duty would induce him to set me right, I can only plead for mercy if I be wrong allotting all Sir Roger's vast possessions in perpetuity to Miss Thorne, alleging also, in excuse, that the course of my narrative absolutely demands that she shall be ultimately recognised as Sir Roger's undoubted heiress.

Such, after a not immoderate delay, was the opinion expressed to Dr Thorne by his law advisers; and such, in fact, turned out to be the case. I will leave the matter so, hoping that my very absence of defence may serve to protect me from severe attack. If under such a will as that described as having been made by Sir Roger, Mary would not have been the heiress, that will must have been described wrongly.

But it was not quite at once that those tidings made themselves absolutely certain to Dr Thorne's mind; nor was he able to express any such opinion when he first met Frank in London. At that time Mary's letter was in Frank's pocket; and Frank, though his real business appertained much more to the fact of Sir Louis's death, and the effect that would immediately have on his father's affairs, was much more full of what so much more nearly concerned himself. "I will show it Dr Thorne himself," said he, "and ask him what he thinks."

Dr Thorne was stretched fast asleep on the comfortless horse-hair sofa in the dingy sitting-room at the Gray's Inn Coffee-house when Frank found him. The funeral, and his journey to London, and the lawyers had together conquered his energies, and he lay and snored, with nose upright, while heavy London summer flies settled on his head and face, and robbed his slumbers of half their charms.

"I beg your pardon," said he, jumping up as though he had been detected in some disgraceful act. "Upon my word, Frank, I beg your pardon; but—well, my dear fellow, all well at Greshamsbury—eh?" and as he shook himself, he made a lunge at one uncommonly disagreeable fly that had been at him for the last ten minutes. It is hardly necessary to say that he missed his enemy.

"I should have been with you before, doctor, but I was down at Malvern."

"At Malvern, eh? Ah! so Oriel told me. The death of poor Sir Louis was very sudden—was it not?"

"Very."

"Poor fellow—poor fellow! His fate has for some time been past hope. It is a madness, Frank; the worst of madness. Only think of it—father and son! And such a career as the father had—such a career as the son might have had!"

"It has been very quickly run," said Frank.

"May it be all forgiven him! I sometimes cannot but believe in a special Providence. That poor fellow was not able, never would have been able, to make proper use of the means which fortune had given him. I hope they may fall into better hands. There is no use in denying it, his death will be an immense relief to me, and a relief also to your father. All this law business will now, of course, be stopped. As for me, I hope I may never be a trustee again."

Frank had put his hand four or five times into his breast-pocket, and had as often taken out and put back again Mary's letter before he could find himself able to bring Dr Thorne to the subject. At last there was a lull in the purely legal discussion, caused by the doctor intimating that he supposed Frank would now soon return to Greshamsbury.

"Yes; I shall go to-morrow morning."

"What! so soon as that? I counted on having you one day in London with me."

"No, I shall go to-morrow. I'm not fit for company for any one. Nor am I fit for anything. Read that, doctor. It's no use putting it off any longer. I must get you to talk this over with me. Just read that, and tell me what you think about it. It was written a week ago, when I was there, but somehow I have only got it to-day." And putting the letter into the doctor's hands, he turned away to the window, and looked out among the Holborn omnibuses. Dr Thorne took the letter and read it. Mary, after she had written it, had bewailed to herself that the letter was cold; but it had not seemed cold to her lover, nor did it appear so to her uncle. When Frank turned round from the window, the doctor's handkerchief was up to his eyes; who, in order to hide the tears that were there, was obliged to go through a rather violent process of blowing his nose.

"Well," he said, as he gave back the letter to Frank.

Well! what did well mean? Was it well? or would it be well were he, Frank, to comply with the suggestion made to him by Mary?

"It is impossible," he said, "that matters should go on like that. Think what her sufferings must have been before she wrote that. I am sure she loves me."

"I think she does," said the doctor.

"And it is out of the question that she should be sacrificed; nor will I consent to sacrifice my own happiness. I am quite willing to work for my bread, and I am sure that I am able. I will not submit to— Doctor, what answer do you think I ought to give to that letter? There can be no person so anxious for her happiness as you are—except myself." And as he asked the question, he again put into the doctor's hand, almost unconsciously, the letter which he had still been holding in his own.

The doctor turned it over and over, and then opened it again.

"What answer ought I to make to it?" demanded Frank, with energy.

"You see, Frank, I have never interfered in this matter, otherwise than to tell you the whole truth about Mary's birth."

"Oh, but you must interfere: you should say what you think."

"Circumstanced as you are now—that is, just at the present moment—you could hardly marry immediately."

"Why not let me take a farm? My father could, at any rate, manage a couple of thousand pounds or so for me to stock it. That would not be asking much. If he could not give it me, I would not scruple to borrow so much elsewhere." And Frank bethought him of all Miss Dunstable's offers.

"Oh, yes; that could be managed."

"Then why not marry immediately; say in six months or so? I am not unreasonable; though, Heaven knows, I have been kept in suspense long enough. As for her, I am sure she must be suffering frightfully. You know her best, and, therefore, I ask you what answer I ought to make: as for myself, I have made up my own mind; I am not a child, nor will I let them treat me as such."

Frank, as he spoke, was walking rapidly about the room; and he brought out his different positions, one after the other, with a little pause, while waiting for the doctor's answer. The doctor was sitting, with the letter still in his hands, on the head of the sofa, turning over in his mind the apparent absurdity of Frank's desire to borrow two thousand pounds for a farm, when, in all human probability, he might in a few months be in possession of almost any sum he should choose to name. And yet he would not tell him of Sir Roger's will. "If it should turn out to be all wrong?" said he to himself.

"Do you wish me to give her up?" said Frank, at last.

"No. How can I wish it? How can I expect a better match for her? Besides, Frank, I love no man in the world so well as I do you."

"Then you will help me?"

"What! against your father?"

"Against! no, not against anybody. But will you tell Mary that she has your consent?"

"I think she knows that."

"But you have never said anything to her."

"Look here, Frank; you ask me for my advice, and I will give it you: go home; though, indeed, I would rather you went anywhere else."

"No, I must go home; and I must see her."

"Very well, go home: as for seeing Mary, I think you had better put it off for a fortnight."

"Quite impossible."

"Well, that's my advice. But, at any rate, make up your mind to nothing for a fortnight. Wait for one fortnight, and I then will tell you plainly—you and her too—what I think you ought to do. At the end of a fortnight come to me, and tell the squire that I will take it as a great kindness if he will come with you. She has suffered, terribly, terribly; and it is necessary that something should be settled. But a fortnight more can make no great difference."

"And the letter?"

"Oh! there's the letter."

"But what shall I say? Of course I shall write to-night."

"Tell her to wait a fortnight. And, Frank, mind you bring your father with you."

Frank could draw nothing further from his friend save constant repetitions of this charge to him to wait a fortnight,—just one other fortnight.

"Well, I will come to you at any rate," said Frank; "and, if possible, I will bring my father. But I shall write to Mary to-night."

On the Saturday morning, Mary, who was then nearly broken-hearted at her lover's silence, received a short note:—

MY OWN MARY, I shall be home to-morrow. I will by no means release you from your promise. Of course you will perceive that I only got your letter to-day.

> Your own dearest,
>   FRANK.

P.S.—You will have to call me so hundreds and hundreds of times yet.

Short as it was, this sufficed Mary. It is one thing for a young lady to make prudent, heart-breaking suggestions, but quite another to have them accepted. She did call him dearest Frank, even on that one day, almost as often as he had desired her.

CHAPTER XLVI

OUR PET FOX FINDS A TAIL

Frank returned home, and his immediate business was of course with his father, and with Mr Gazebee, who was still at Greshamsbury.

"But who is the heir?" asked Mr Gazebee, when Frank had explained that the death of Sir Louis rendered unnecessary any immediate legal steps.

"Upon my word I don't know," said Frank.

"You saw Dr Thorne," said the squire. "He must have known."

"I never thought of asking him," said Frank, naïvely.

Mr Gazebee looked rather solemn. "I wonder at that," said he; "for everything now depends on the hands the property will go into. Let me see; I think Sir Roger had a married sister. Was not that so, Mr Gresham?" And then it occurred for the first time, both to the squire and to his son, that Mary Thorne was the eldest child of this sister. But it never occurred to either of them that Mary could be the baronet's heir.

Dr Thorne came down for a couple of days before the fortnight was over to see his patients, and then returned again to London. But during this short visit he was utterly dumb on the subject of the heir. He called at Greshamsbury to see Lady Arabella, and was even questioned by the squire on the subject. But he obstinately refused to say more than that nothing certain could be known for yet a few days.

Immediately after his return, Frank saw Mary, and told her all that had happened. "I cannot understand my uncle," said she, almost trembling as she stood close to him in her own drawing-room. "He usually hates mysteries, and yet now he is so mysterious. He told me, Frank—that was after I had written that unfortunate letter—"

"Unfortunate, indeed! I wonder what you really thought of me when you were writing it?"

"If you had heard what your mother said, you would not be surprised. But, after that, uncle said—"

"Said what?"

"He seemed to think—I don't remember what it was he said. But he said, he hoped that things might yet turn out well; and then I was almost sorry that I had written the letter."

"Of course you were sorry, and so you ought to have been. To say that you would never call me Frank again!"

"I didn't exactly say that."

"I have told him I will wait a fortnight, and so I will. After that, I shall take the matter into my own hands."

It may be well supposed that Lady Arabella was not well pleased to learn that Frank and Mary had been again together; and, in the agony of her spirit, she did say some ill-natured things before Augusta, who had now returned from Courcy Castle, as to the gross impropriety of Mary's conduct. But to Frank she said nothing.

Nor was there much said between Frank and Beatrice. If everything could really be settled at the end of that fortnight which was to witness the disclosure of the doctor's mystery, there would still be time to arrange that Mary should be at the wedding. "It shall be settled then," he said to himself; "and if it be settled, my mother will hardly venture to exclude my affianced bride from the house." It was now the beginning of August, and it wanted yet a month to the Oriel wedding.

But though he said nothing to his mother or to Beatrice, he did say much to his father. In the first place, he showed him Mary's letter. "If your heart be not made of stone it will be softened by that," he said. Mr Gresham's heart was not of stone, and he did acknowledge that the letter was a very sweet letter. But we know how the drop of water hollows stone. It was not by the violence of his appeal that Frank succeeded in obtaining from his father a sort of half-consent that he would no longer oppose the match; but by the assiduity with which the appeal was repeated. Frank, as we have said, had more stubbornness of will than his father; and so, before the fortnight was over, the squire had been talked over, and promised to attend at the doctor's bidding.

"I suppose you had better take the Hazlehurst farm," said he to his son, with a sigh. "It joins the park and the home-fields, and I will give you up them also. God knows, I don't care about farming any more—or about anything else either."

"Don't say that, father."

"Well, well! But, Frank, where will you live? The old house is big enough for us all. But how would Mary get on with your mother?"

At the end of his fortnight, true to his time, the doctor returned to the village. He was a bad correspondent; and though he had written some short notes to Mary, he had said no word to her about his business. It was late in the evening when he got home, and it was understood by Frank and the squire that they were to be with him on the following morning. Not a word had been said to Lady Arabella on the subject.

It was late in the evening when he got home, and Mary waited for him with a heart almost sick with expectation. As soon as the fly had stopped at the little gate she heard his voice, and heard at once that it was quick, joyful, and telling much of inward satisfaction. He had a good-natured word for Janet, and called Thomas an old blunder-head in a manner that made Bridget laugh outright.

"He'll have his nose put out of joint some day; won't he?" said the doctor. Bridget blushed and laughed again, and made a sign to Thomas that he had better look to his face.

Mary was in his arms before he was yet within the door. "My darling," said he, tenderly kissing her. "You are my own darling yet awhile."

"Of course I am. Am I not always to be so?"

"Well, well; let me have some tea, at any rate, for I'm in a fever of thirst. They may call that tea at the Junction if they will; but if China were sunk under the sea it would make no difference to them."

Dr Thorne always was in a fever of thirst when he got home from the railway, and always made complaint as to the tea at the Junction. Mary went about her usual work with almost more than her usual alacrity, and so they were soon seated in the drawing-room together.

She soon found that his manner was more than ordinarily kind to her; and there was moreover something about him which seemed to make him sparkle with contentment, but he said no word about Frank, nor did he make any allusion to the business which had taken him up to town.

"Have you got through all your work?" she said to him once.

"Yes, yes; I think all."

"And thoroughly?"

"Yes; thoroughly, I think. But I am very tired, and so are you too, darling, with waiting for me."

"Oh, no, I am not," said she, as she went on continually filling his cup; "but I am so happy to have you home again. You have been away so much lately."

"Ah, yes; well I suppose I shall not go away any more now. It will be somebody else's turn now."

"Uncle, I think you're going to take up writing mystery romances, like Mrs Radcliffe's."

"Yes; and I'll begin to-morrow, certainly with— But, Mary, I will not say another word to-night. Give me a kiss, dearest, and I'll go."

Mary did kiss him, and he did go. But as she was still lingering in the room, putting away a book, or a reel of thread, and then sitting down to think what the morrow would bring forth, the doctor again came into the room in his dressing-gown, and with the slippers on.

"What, not gone yet?" said he.

"No, not yet; I'm going now."

"You and I, Mary, have always affected a good deal of indifference as to money, and all that sort of thing."

"I won't acknowledge that it has been an affectation at all," she answered.

"Perhaps not; but we have often expressed it, have we not?"

"I suppose, uncle, you think that we are like the fox that lost his tail, or rather some unfortunate fox that might be born without one."

"I wonder how we should either of us bear it if we found ourselves suddenly rich. It would be a great temptation—a sore temptation. I fear, Mary, that when poor people talk disdainfully of money, they often are like your fox, born without a tail. If nature suddenly should give that beast a tail, would he not be prouder of it than all the other foxes in the wood?"

"Well, I suppose he would. That's the very meaning of the story. But how moral you've become all of a sudden at twelve o'clock at night! Instead of being Mrs Radcliffe, I shall think you're Mr Æsop."

He took up the article which he had come to seek, and kissing her again on the forehead, went away to his bed-room without further speech. "What can he mean by all this about money?" said Mary to herself. "It cannot be that by Sir Louis's death he will get any of all this property;" and then she began to bethink herself whether, after all, she would wish him to be a rich man. "If he were very rich, he might do something to assist Frank; and then—"

There never was a fox yet without a tail who would not be delighted to find himself suddenly possessed of that appendage. Never; let the untailed fox have been ever so sincere in his advice to his friends! We are all of us, the good and the bad, looking for tails—for one tail, or for more than one; we do so too often by ways that are mean enough: but perhaps there is no tail-seeker more mean, more sneakingly mean than he who looks out to adorn his bare back with a tail by marriage.

The doctor was up very early the next morning, long before Mary was ready with her teacups. He was up, and in his own study behind the shop, arranging dingy papers, pulling about tin boxes which he had brought down with him from London, and piling on his writing-table one set of documents in one place, and one in another. "I think I understand it all," said he; "but yet I know I shall be bothered. Well, I never will be anybody's trustee again. Let me see!" and then he sat down, and with bewildered look recapitulated to himself sundry heavy items. "What those shares are really worth I cannot understand, and nobody seems able to tell one. They must make it out among them as best they can. Let me see; that's Boxall Hill, and this is Greshamsbury. I'll put a newspaper over Greshamsbury, or the squire will know it!" and then, having made his arrangements, he went to his breakfast.

I know I am wrong, my much and truly honoured critic, about these title-deeds and documents. But when we've got that barrister in hand, then if I go wrong after that, let the blame be on my own shoulders—or on his.

The doctor ate his breakfast quickly; and did not talk much to his niece. But what he did say was of a nature to make her feel strangely happy. She could not analyse her own feelings, or give a reason for her own confidence; but she certainly did feel, and even trust, that something was going to happen after breakfast which would make her more happy than she had been for many months.

"Janet," said he, looking at his watch, "if Mr Gresham and Mr Frank call, show them into my study. What are you going to do with yourself, my dear?"

"I don't know, uncle; you are so mysterious, and I am in such a twitter, that I don't know what to do. Why is Mr Gresham coming here—that is, the squire?"

"Because I have business with him about the Scatcherd property. You know that he owed Sir Louis money. But don't go out, Mary. I want you to be in the way if I should have to call for you. You can stay in the drawing-room, can't you?"

"Oh, yes, uncle; or here."

"No, dearest; go into the drawing-room." Mary obediently did as she was bid; and there she sat, for the next three hours, wondering, wondering, wondering. During the greater part of that time, however, she well knew that Mr Gresham, senior, and Mr Gresham, junior, were both with her uncle, below.

At eleven o'clock the doctor's visitors came. He had expected them somewhat earlier, and was beginning to become fidgety. He had so much on his hands that he could not sit still for a moment till he had, at any rate, commenced it. The expected footsteps were at last heard on the gravel-path, and a moment or two afterwards Janet ushered the father and son into the room.

The squire did not look very well. He was worn and sorrowful, and rather pale. The death of his young creditor might be supposed to have given him some relief from his more pressing cares, but the necessity of yielding to Frank's wishes had almost more than balanced this. When a man has daily to reflect that he is poorer than he was the day before, he soon becomes worn and sorrowful.

But Frank was well; both in health and spirits. He also felt as Mary did, that the day was to bring forth something which should end his present troubles; and he could not but be happy to think that he could now tell Dr Thorne that his father's consent to his marriage had been given.

The doctor shook hands with them both, and then they sat down. They were all rather constrained in their manner; and at first it seemed that nothing but little speeches of compliment were to be made. At last, the squire remarked that Frank had been talking to him about Miss Thorne.

"About Mary?" said the doctor.

"Yes; about Mary," said the squire, correcting himself. It was quite unnecessary that he should use so cold a name as the other, now that he had agreed to the match.

"Well!" said Dr Thorne.

"I suppose it must be so, doctor. He has set his heart upon it, and God knows, I have nothing to say against her—against her personally. No one could say a word against her. She is a sweet, good girl, excellently brought up; and, as for myself, I have always loved her." Frank drew near to his father, and pressed his hand against the squire's arm, by way of giving him, in some sort, a filial embrace for his kindness.

"Thank you, squire, thank you," said the doctor. "It is very good of you to say that. She is a good girl, and if Frank chooses to take her, he will, in my estimation, have made a good choice."

"Chooses!" said Frank, with all the enthusiasm of a lover.

The squire felt himself perhaps a little ruffled at the way in which the doctor received his gracious intimation; but he did now show it as he went on. "They cannot, you know, doctor, look to be rich people—"

"Ah! well, well," interrupted the doctor.

"I have told Frank so, and I think that you should tell Mary. Frank means to take some land into his hand, and he must farm it as a farmer. I will endeavour to give him three, or perhaps four hundred a year. But you know better—"

"Stop, squire; stop a minute. We will talk about that presently. This death of poor Sir Louis will make a difference."

"Not permanently," said the squire mournfully.

"And now, Frank," said the doctor, not attending to the squire's last words, "what do you say?"

"What do I say? I say what I said to you in London the other day. I believe Mary loves me; indeed, I won't be affected—I know she does. I have loved her—I was going to say always; and, indeed, I almost might say so. My father knows that this is no light fancy of mine. As to what he says about our being poor, why—"

The doctor was very arbitrary, and would hear neither of them on this subject.

"Mr Gresham," said he, interrupting Frank, "of course I am well aware how very little suited Mary is by birth to marry your only son."

"It is too late to think about it now," said the squire.

"It is not too late for me to justify myself," replied the doctor. "We have long known each other, Mr Gresham, and you said here the other day, that this is a subject as to which we have been both of one mind. Birth and blood are very valuable gifts."

"I certainly think so," said the squire; "but one can't have everything."

"No; one can't have everything."

"If I am satisfied in that matter—" began Frank.

"Stop a moment, my dear boy," said the doctor. "As your father says, one can't have everything. My dear friend—" and he gave his hand to the squire—"do not be angry if I alluded for a moment to the estate. It has grieved me to see it melting away—the old family acres that have so long been the heritage of the Greshams."

"We need not talk about that now, Dr Thorne," said Frank, in an almost angry tone.

"But I must, Frank, for one moment, to justify myself. I could not have excused myself in letting Mary think that she could become your wife if I had not hoped that good might come of it."

"Well; good will come of it," said Frank, who did not quite understand at what the doctor was driving.

"I hope so. I have had much doubt about this, and have been sorely perplexed; but now I do hope so. Frank—Mr Gresham—" and then Dr Thorne rose from his chair; but was, for a moment, unable to go on with his tale.

"We will hope that it is all for the best," said the squire.

"I am sure it is," said Frank.

"Yes; I hope it is. I do think it is; I am sure it is, Frank. Mary will not come to you empty-handed. I wish for your sake—yes, and for hers too—that her birth were equal to her fortune, as her worth is superior to both. Mr Gresham, this marriage will, at any rate, put an end to your pecuniary embarrassments—unless, indeed, Frank should prove a hard creditor. My niece is Sir Roger Scatcherd's heir."

The doctor, as soon as he made the announcement, began to employ himself sedulously about the papers on the table; which, in the confusion caused by his own emotion, he transferred hither and thither in such a manner as to upset all his previous arrangements. "And now," he said, "I might as well explain, as well as I can, of what that fortune consists. Here, this is—no—"

"But, Dr Thorne," said the squire, now perfectly pale, and almost gasping for breath, "what is it you mean?"

"There's not a shadow of doubt," said the doctor. "I've had Sir Abraham Haphazard, and Sir Rickety Giggs, and old Neversaye Die, and Mr Snilam; and they are all of the same opinion. There is not the smallest doubt about it. Of course, she must administer, and all that; and I'm afraid there'll be a very heavy sum to pay for the tax; for she cannot inherit as a niece, you know. Mr Snilam pointed that out particularly. But, after all that, there'll be—I've got it down on a piece of paper, somewhere—three grains of blue pill. I'm really so bothered, squire, with all these papers, and all those lawyers, that I don't know whether I'm sitting or standing. There's ready money enough to pay all the tax and all the debts. I know that, at any rate."

"You don't mean to say that Mary Thorne is now possessed of all Sir Roger Scatcherd's wealth?" at last ejaculated the squire.

"But that's exactly what I do mean to say," said the doctor, looking up from his papers with a tear in his eye, and a smile on his mouth; "and what is more, squire, you owe her at the present moment exactly—I've got that down too, somewhere, only I am so bothered with all these papers. Come, squire, when do you mean to pay her? She's in a great hurry, as young ladies are when they want to get married."

The doctor was inclined to joke if possible, so as to carry off, as it were, some of the great weight of obligation which it might seem that he was throwing on the father and son; but the squire was by no means in a state to understand a joke: hardly as yet in a state to comprehend what was so very serious in this matter.

"Do you mean that Mary is the owner of Boxall Hill?" said he.

"Indeed, I do," said the doctor; and he was just going to add, "and of Greshamsbury also," but he stopped himself.

"What, the whole property there?"

"That's only a small portion," said the doctor. "I almost wish it were all, for then I should not be so bothered. Look here; these are the Boxall Hill title-deeds; that's the simplest part of the whole affair; and Frank may go and settle himself there to-morrow if he pleases."

"Stop a moment, Dr Thorne," said Frank. These were the only words which he had yet uttered since the tidings had been conveyed to him.

"And these, squire, are the Greshamsbury papers:" and the doctor, with considerable ceremony, withdrew the covering newspapers. "Look at them; there they all are once again. When I suggested to Mr Snilam that I supposed they might now all go back to the Greshamsbury muniment room, I thought he would have fainted. As I cannot return them to you, you will have to wait till Frank shall give them up."

"But, Dr Thorne," said Frank.

"Well, my boy."

"Does Mary know all about this?"

"Not a word of it. I mean that you shall tell her."

"Perhaps, under such very altered circumstances—"

"Eh?"

"The change is so great and so sudden, so immense in its effects, that Mary may perhaps wish—"

"Wish! wish what? Wish not to be told of it at all?"

"I shall not think of holding her to her engagement—that is, if—I mean to say, she should have time at any rate for consideration."

"Oh, I understand," said the doctor. "She shall have time for consideration. How much shall we give her, squire? three minutes? Go up to her Frank: she is in the drawing-room."

Frank went to the door, and then hesitated, and returned. "I could not do it," said he. "I don't think that I understand it all yet. I am so bewildered that I could not tell her;" and he sat down at the table, and began to sob with emotion.

"And she knows nothing of it?" said the squire.

"Not a word. I thought that I would keep the pleasure of telling her for Frank."

"She should not be left in suspense," said the squire.

"Come, Frank, go up to her," again urged the doctor. "You've been ready enough with your visits when you knew that you ought to stay away."

"I cannot do it," said Frank, after a pause of some moments; "nor is it right that I should. It would be taking advantage of her."

"Go to her yourself, doctor; it is you that should do it," said the squire.

After some further slight delay, the doctor got up, and did go upstairs. He, even, was half afraid of the task. "It must be done," he said to himself, as his heavy steps mounted the stairs. "But how to tell it?"

When he entered, Mary was standing half-way up the room, as though she had risen to meet him. Her face was troubled, and her eyes were almost wild. The emotion, the hopes, the fears of that morning had almost been too much for her. She had heard the murmuring of the voices in the room below, and had known that one of them was that of her lover. Whether that discussion was to be for her good or ill she did not know; but she felt that further suspense would almost kill her. "I could wait for years," she said to herself, "if I did but know. If I lost him, I suppose I should bear it, if I did but know."—Well; she was going to know.

Her uncle met her in the middle of the room. His face was serious, though not sad; too serious to confirm her hopes at that moment of doubt. "What is it, uncle?" she said, taking one of his hands between both of her own. "What is it? Tell me." And as she looked up into his face with her wild eyes, she almost frightened him.

"Mary," he said gravely, "you have heard much, I know, of Sir Roger Scatcherd's great fortune."

"Yes, yes, yes!"

"Now that poor Sir Louis is dead—"

"Well, uncle, well?"

"It has been left—"

"To Frank! to Mr Gresham, to the squire!" exclaimed Mary, who felt, with an agony of doubt, that this sudden accession of immense wealth might separate her still further from her lover.

"No, Mary, not to the Greshams; but to yourself."

"To me!" she cried, and putting both her hands to her forehead, she seemed to be holding her temples together. "To me!"

"Yes, Mary; it is all your own now. To do as you like best with it all—all. May God, in His mercy, enable you to bear the burden, and lighten for you the temptation!"

She had so far moved as to find the nearest chair, and there she was now seated, staring at her uncle with fixed eyes. "Uncle," she said, "what does it mean?" Then he came, and sitting beside her, he explained, as best he could, the story of her birth, and her kinship with the Scatcherds. "And where is he, uncle?" she said. "Why does he not come to me?"

"I wanted him to come, but her refused. They are both there now, the father and son; shall I fetch them?"

"Fetch them! whom? The squire? No, uncle; but may we go to them?"

"Surely, Mary."

"But, uncle—"

"Yes, dearest."

"Is it true? are you sure? For his sake, you know; not for my own. The squire, you know—Oh, uncle! I cannot go."

"They shall come to you."

"No—no. I have gone to him such hundreds of times; I will never allow that he shall be sent to me. But, uncle, is it true?"

The doctor, as he went downstairs, muttered something about Sir Abraham Haphazard, and Sir Rickety Giggs; but these great names were much thrown away upon poor Mary. The doctor entered the room first, and the heiress followed him with downcast eyes and timid steps. She was at first afraid to advance, but when she did look up, and saw Frank standing alone by the window, her lover restored her courage, and rushing up to him, she threw herself into his arms. "Oh, Frank; my own Frank! my own Frank! we shall never be separated now."

CHAPTER XLVII

HOW THE BRIDE WAS RECEIVED, AND WHO WERE ASKED TO THE WEDDING

And thus after all did Frank perform his great duty; he did marry money; or rather, as the wedding has not yet taken place, and is, indeed, as yet hardly talked of, we should more properly say that he had engaged himself to marry money. And then, such a quantity of money! The Scatcherd wealth greatly exceeded the Dunstable wealth; so that our hero may be looked on as having performed his duties in a manner deserving the very highest commendation from all classes of the de Courcy connexion.

And he received it. But that was nothing. That *he* should be fêted by the de Courcys and Greshams, now that he was about to do his duty by his family in so exemplary a manner: that he should be patted on the back, now that he no longer meditated that vile crime which had been so abhorrent to his mother's soul; this was only natural; this is hardly worthy of remark. But there was another to be fêted, another person to be made a personage, another blessed human mortal about to do her duty by the family of Gresham in a manner that deserved, and should receive, Lady Arabella's warmest caresses.

Dear Mary! It was, indeed, not singular that she should be prepared to act so well, seeing that in early youth she had had the advantage of an education in the Greshamsbury nursery; but not on that account was it the less fitting that her virtue should be acknowledged, eulogised, nay, all but worshipped.

How the party at the doctor's got itself broken up, I am not prepared to say. Frank, I know, stayed and dined there, and his poor mother, who would not retire to rest till she had kissed him, and blessed him, and thanked him for all he was doing for the family, was kept waiting in her dressing-room till a very unreasonable hour of the night.

It was the squire who brought the news up to the house. "Arabella," he said, in a low, but somewhat solemn voice, "you will be surprised at the news I bring you. Mary Thorne is the heiress to all the Scatcherd property!"

"Oh, heavens! Mr Gresham."

"Yes, indeed," continued the squire. "So it is; it is very, very—" But Lady Arabella had fainted. She was a woman who generally had her feelings and her emotions much under her own control; but what she now heard was too much for her. When she came to her senses, the first words that escaped her lips were, "Dear Mary!"

But the household had to sleep on the news before it could be fully realised. The squire was not by nature a mercenary man. If I have at all succeeded in putting his character before the reader, he will be recognised as one not over attached to money for money's sake.

But things had gone so hard with him, the world had become so rough, so ungracious, so full of thorns, the want of means had become an evil so keenly felt in every hour, that it cannot be wondered at that his dreams that night should be of a golden elysium. The wealth was not coming to him. True. But his chief sorrow had been for his son. Now that son would be his only creditor. It was as though mountains of marble had been taken from off his bosom.

But Lady Arabella's dreams flew away at once into the seventh heaven. Sordid as they certainly were, they were not absolutely selfish. Frank would now certainly be the first commoner in Barsetshire; of course he would represent the county; of course there would be the house in town; it wouldn't be her house, but she was contented that the grandeur should be that of her child. He would have heaven knows what to spend per annum. And that it should come through Mary Thorne! What a blessing she had allowed Mary to be brought into the Greshamsbury nursery! Dear Mary!

"She will of course be one now," said Beatrice to her sister. With her, at the present moment, "one" of course meant one of the bevy that was to attend her at the altar. "Oh dear! how nice! I shan't know what to say to her to-morrow. But I know one thing."

"What is that?" asked Augusta.

"She will be as mild and as meek as a little dove. If she and the doctor had lost every shilling in the world, she would have been as proud as an eagle." It must be acknowledged that Beatrice had had the wit to read Mary's character aright.

But Augusta was not quite pleased with the whole affair. Not that she begrudged her brother his luck, or Mary her happiness. But her ideas of right and wrong—perhaps we should rather say Lady Amelia's ideas—would not be fairly carried out.

"After all, Beatrice, this does not alter her birth. I know it is useless saying anything to Frank."

"Why, you wouldn't break both their hearts now?"

"I don't want to break their hearts, certainly. But there are those who put their dearest and warmest feelings under restraint rather than deviate from what they know to be proper." Poor Augusta! she was the stern professor of the order of this philosophy; the last in the family who practised with unflinching courage its cruel behests; the last, always excepting the Lady Amelia.

And how slept Frank that night? With him, at least, let us hope, nay, let us say boldly, that his happiest thoughts were not of the wealth which he was to acquire. But yet it would be something to restore Boxall Hill to Greshamsbury; something to give back to his father those rumpled vellum documents, since the departure of which the squire had never had a happy day; nay, something to come forth again to his friends as a gay, young country squire, instead of as a farmer, clod-compelling for his bread. We would not have him thought to be better than he was, nor would we wish him to make him of other stuff than nature generally uses. His heart did exult at Mary's wealth; but it leaped higher still when he thought of purer joys.

And what shall we say of Mary's dreams? With her, it was altogether what she should give, not at all what she should get. Frank had loved her so truly when she was so poor, such an utter castaway; Frank, who had ever been the heir of Greshamsbury! Frank, who with his beauty, and spirit, and his talents might have won the smiles of the richest, the grandest, the noblest! What lady's heart would not have rejoiced to be allowed to love her Frank? But he had been true to her through everything. Ah! how often she thought of that hour, when suddenly appearing before her, he had strained her to his breast, just as she had resolved how best to bear the death-like chill of his supposed estrangements! She was always thinking of that time. She fed her love by recurring over and over to the altered feeling of that moment. Any now she could pay him for his goodness. Pay him! No, that would be a base word, a base thought. Her payment must be made, if God would so grant it, in many, many years to come. But her store, such as it was, should be emptied into his lap. It was soothing to her pride that she would not hurt him by her love, that she would bring no injury to the old house. "Dear, dear Frank" she murmured, as her waking dreams, conquered at last by sleep, gave way to those of the fairy world.

But she thought not only of Frank; dreamed not only of him. What had he not done for her, that uncle of hers, who had been more loving to her than any father! How was he, too, to be paid? Paid, indeed! Love can only be paid in its own coin: it knows of no other legal tender. Well, if her home was to be Greshamsbury, at any rate she would not be separated from him.

What the doctor dreamed of that, neither he or any one ever knew. "Why, uncle, I think you've been asleep," said Mary to him that evening as he moved for a moment uneasily on the sofa. He had been asleep for the last three-quarters of an hour;—but Frank, his guest, had felt no offence. "No, I've not been exactly asleep," said he; "but I'm very tired. I wouldn't do it all again, Frank, to double the money. You haven't got any more tea, have you, Mary?"

On the following morning, Beatrice was of course with her friend. There was no awkwardness between them in meeting. Beatrice had loved her when she was poor, and though they had not lately thought alike on one very important subject, Mary was too gracious to impute that to Beatrice as a crime.

"You will be one now, Mary; of course you will."

"If Lady Arabella will let me come."

"Oh, Mary; let you! Do you remember what you said once about coming, and being near me? I have so often thought of it. And now, Mary, I must tell you about Caleb;" and the young lady settled herself on the sofa, so as to have a comfortable long talk. Beatrice had been quite right. Mary was as meek with her, and as mild as a dove.

And then Patience Oriel came. "My fine, young, darling, magnificent, overgrown heiress," said Patience, embracing her. "My breath deserted me, and I was nearly stunned when I heard of it. How small we shall all be, my dear! I am quite prepared to toady to you immensely; but pray be a little gracious to me, for the sake of auld lang syne."

Mary gave a long, long kiss. "Yes, for auld lang syne, Patience; when you took me away under your wing to Richmond." Patience also had loved her when she was in her trouble, and that love, too, should never be forgotten.

But the great difficulty was Lady Arabella's first meeting with her. "I think I'll go down to her after breakfast," said her ladyship to Beatrice, as the two were talking over the matter while the mother was finishing her toilet.

"I am sure she will come up if you like it, mamma."

"She is entitled to every courtesy—as Frank's accepted bride, you know," said Lady Arabella. "I would not for worlds fail in any respect to her for his sake."

"He will be glad enough for her to come, I am sure," said Beatrice. "I was talking with Caleb this morning, and he says—"

The matter was of importance, and Lady Arabella gave it her most mature consideration. The manner of receiving into one's family an heiress whose wealth is to cure all one's difficulties, disperse all one's troubles, give a balm to all the wounds of misfortune, must, under any circumstances, be worthy of much care. But when that heiress has been already treated as Mary had been treated!

"I must see her, at any rate, before I go to Courcy." said Lady Arabella.

"Are you going to Courcy, mamma?"

"Oh, certainly; yes, I must see my sister-in-law now. You don't seem to realise the importance, my dear, of Frank's marriage. He will be in a great hurry about it, and, indeed, I cannot blame him. I expect that they will all come here."

"Who, mamma? the de Courcys?"

"Yes, of course. I shall be very much surprised if the earl does not come now. And I must consult my sister-in-law as to asking the Duke of Omnium."

Poor Mary!

"And I think it will perhaps be better," continued Lady Arabella, "that we should have a larger party than we intended at your affair. The countess, I'm sure, would come now. We couldn't put it off for ten days; could we, dear?"

"Put it off ten days!"

"Yes; it would be convenient."

"I don't think Mr Oriel would like that at all, mamma. You know he has made all his arrangements for his Sundays—"

Pshaw! The idea of the parson's Sundays being allowed to have any bearing on such a matter as Frank's wedding would now become! Why, they would have—how much? Between twelve and fourteen thousand a year! Lady Arabella, who had made her calculations a dozen times during the night, had never found it to be much less than the larger sum. Mr Oriel's Sundays, indeed!

After much doubt, Lady Arabella acceded to her daughter's suggestion, that Mary should be received at Greshamsbury instead of being called on at the doctor's house. "If you think she won't mind the coming up first," said her ladyship. "I certainly could receive her better here. I should be more—more—more able, you know, to express what I feel. We had better go into the big drawing-room to-day, Beatrice. Will you remember to tell Mrs Richards?"

"Oh, certainly," was Mary's answer when Beatrice, with a voice a little trembling, proposed to her to walk up to the house. "Certainly I will, if Lady Arabella will receive me;— only one thing, Trichy."

"What's that, dearest?"

"Frank will think that I come after him."

"Never mind what he thinks. To tell you the truth, Mary, I often call upon Patience for the sake of finding Caleb. That's all fair now, you know."

Mary very quietly put on her straw bonnet, and said she was ready to go up to the house. Beatrice was a little fluttered, and showed it. Mary was, perhaps, a good deal fluttered, but she did not show it. She had thought a good deal of her first interview with Lady Arabella, of her first return to the house; but she had resolved to carry herself as though the matter were easy to her. She would not allow it to be seen that she felt that she brought with her to Greshamsbury, comfort, ease, and renewed opulence.

So she put on her straw bonnet and walked up with Beatrice. Everybody about the place had already heard the news. The old woman at the lodge curtsied low to her; the gardener, who was mowing the lawn. The butler, who opened the front door—he must have been watching Mary's approach—had manifestly put on a clean white neckcloth for the occasion.

"God bless you once more, Miss Thorne!" said the old man, in a half-whisper. Mary was somewhat troubled, for everything seemed, in a manner, to bow down before her. And why should not everything bow down before her, seeing that she was in truth the owner of Greshamsbury?

And then a servant in livery would open the big drawing-room door. This rather upset both Mary and Beatrice. It became almost impossible for Mary to enter the room just as she would have done two years ago; but she got through the difficulty with much self-control.

"Mamma, here's Mary," said Beatrice.

Nor was Lady Arabella quite mistress of herself, although she had studied minutely how to bear herself.

"Oh, Mary, my dear Mary; what can I say to you?" and then, with a handkerchief to her eyes, she ran forward and hid her face on Miss Thorne's shoulders. "What can I say—can you forgive me my anxiety for my son?"

"How do you do, Lady Arabella?" said Mary.

"My daughter! my child! my Frank's own bride! Oh, Mary! oh, my child! If I have seemed unkind to you, it has been through love to him."

"All these things are over now," said Mary. "Mr Gresham told me yesterday that I should be received as Frank's future wife; and so, you see, I have come." And then she slipped through Lady Arabella's arms, and sat down, meekly down, on a chair. In five minutes she had escaped with Beatrice into the school-room, and was kissing the children, and turning over the new trousseau. They were, however, soon interrupted, and there was, perhaps, some other kissing besides that of the children.

"You have no business in here at all, Frank," said Beatrice. "Has he, Mary?"

"None in the world, I should think."

"See what he has done to my poplin; I hope you won't have your things treated so cruelly. He'll be careful enough about them."

"Is Oriel a good hand at packing up finery—eh, Beatrice?" asked Frank.

"He is, at any rate, too well-behaved to spoil it." Thus Mary was again made at home in the household of Greshamsbury.

Lady Arabella did not carry out her little plan of delaying the Oriel wedding. Her idea had been to add some grandeur to it, in order to make it a more fitting precursor of that other greater wedding which was to follow so soon in its wake. But this, with the assistance of the countess, she found herself able to do without interfering with poor Mr Oriel's Sunday arrangements. The countess herself, with the Ladies Alexandrina and Margaretta, now promised to come, even to this first affair; and for the other, the whole de Courcy family would turn out, count and countess, lords and ladies, Honourable Georges and Honourable Johns. What honour, indeed, could be too great to show to a bride who had fourteen thousand a year in her own right, or to a cousin who had done his duty by securing such a bride to himself!

"If the duke be in the country, I am sure he will be happy to come," said the countess. "Of course, he will be talking to Frank about politics. I suppose the squire won't expect Frank to belong to the old school now."

"Frank, of course, will judge for himself, Rosina;—with his position, you know!" And so things were settled at Courcy Castle.

And then Beatrice was wedded and carried off to the Lakes. Mary, as she had promised, did stand near her; but not exactly in the gingham frock of which she had once spoken. She wore on that occasion— But it will be too much, perhaps, to tell the reader what she wore as Beatrice's bridesmaid, seeing that a couple of pages, at least, must be devoted to her marriage-dress, and seeing, also, that we have only a few pages to finish everything; the list of visitors, the marriage settlements, the dress, and all included.

It was in vain that Mary endeavoured to repress Lady Arabella's ardour for grand doings. After all, she was to be married from the doctor's house, and not from Greshamsbury, and it was the doctor who should have invited the guests; but, in this matter, he did not choose to oppose her ladyship's spirit, and she had it all her own way.

"What can I do?" said he to Mary. "I have been contradicting her in everything for the last two years. The least we can do is to let her have her own way now in a trifle like this."

But there was one point on which Mary would let nobody have his or her own way; on which the way to be taken was very manifestly to be her own. This was touching the marriage settlements. It must not be supposed, that if Beatrice were married on a Tuesday, Mary could be married on the Tuesday week following. Ladies with twelve thousand a year cannot be disposed of in that way: and bridegrooms who do their duty by marrying money often have to be kept waiting. It was spring, the early spring, before Frank was made altogether a happy man.

But a word about the settlements. On this subject the doctor thought he would have been driven mad. Messrs Slow & Bideawhile, as the lawyers of the Greshamsbury family—it will be understood that Mr Gazebee's law business was of quite a different nature, and his work, as regarded Greshamsbury, was now nearly over—Messrs Slow & Bideawhile declared that it would never do for them to undertake alone to draw out the settlements. An heiress, such as Mary, must have lawyers of her own; half a dozen at least, according to the apparent opinion of Messrs Slow & Bideawhile. And so the doctor had to go to other lawyers, and they had again to consult Sir Abraham, and Mr Snilam on a dozen different heads.

If Frank became tenant in tail, in right of his wife, but under his father, would he be able to grant leases for more than twenty-one years? and, if so, to whom would the right of trover belong? As to flotsam and jetsam—there was a little property, Mr Critic, on the sea-shore—that was a matter that had to be left unsettled at the last. Such points as these do take a long time to consider. All this bewildered the doctor sadly, and Frank himself began to make accusations that he was to be done out of his wife altogether.

But, as we have said, there was one point on which Mary would have her own way. The lawyers might tie up as they would on her behalf all the money, and shares, and mortgages which had belonged to the late Sir Roger, with this exception, all that had ever appertained to Greshamsbury should belong to Greshamsbury again; not in perspective, not to her children, or to her children's children, but at once. Frank should be lord of Boxall Hill in his own right; and as to those other *liens* on Greshamsbury, let Frank manage that with his father as he might think fit. She would only trouble herself to see that he was empowered to do as he did think fit.

"But," argued the ancient, respectable family attorney to the doctor, "that amounts to two-thirds of the whole estate. Two-thirds, Dr Thorne! It is preposterous; I should almost say impossible." And the scanty hairs on the poor man's head almost stood on end as he thought of the outrageous manner in which the heiress prepared to sacrifice herself.

"It will all be the same in the end," said the doctor, trying to make things smooth. "Of course, their joint object will be to put the Greshamsbury property together again."

"But, my dear sir,"—and then, for twenty minutes, the lawyer went on proving that it would by no means be the same thing; but, nevertheless, Mary Thorne did have her own way.

In the course of the winter, Lady de Courcy tried very hard to induce the heiress to visit Courcy Castle, and this request was so backed by Lady Arabella, that the doctor said he thought she might as well go there for three or four days. But here, again, Mary was obstinate.

"I don't see it at all," she said. "If you make a point of it, or Frank, or Mr Gresham, I will go; but I can't see any possible reason." The doctor, when so appealed to, would not absolutely say that he made a point of it, and Mary was tolerably safe as regarded Frank or the squire. If she went, Frank would be expected to go, and Frank disliked Courcy Castle almost more than ever. His aunt was now more than civil to him, and, when they were together, never ceased to compliment him on the desirable way in which he had done his duty by his family.

And soon after Christmas a visitor came to Mary, and stayed a fortnight with her: one whom neither she nor the doctor had expected, and of whom they had not much more than heard. This was the famous Miss Dunstable. "Birds of a feather flock together," said Mrs Rantaway—late Miss Gushing—when she heard of the visit. "The railway man's niece—if you can call her a niece—and the quack's daughter will do very well together, no doubt."

"At any rate, they can count their money-bags," said Mrs Umbleby.

And in fact, Mary and Miss Dunstable did get on very well together; and Miss Dunstable made herself quite happy at Greshamsbury, although some people—including Mrs Rantaway—contrived to spread a report, that Dr Thorne, jealous of Mary's money, was going to marry her.

"I shall certainly come and see you turned off," said Miss Dunstable, taking leave of her new friend. Miss Dunstable, it must be acknowledged, was a little too fond of slang; but then, a lady with her fortune, and of her age, may be fond of almost whatever she pleases.

And so by degrees the winter wore away—very slowly to Frank, as he declared often enough; and slowly, perhaps, to Mary also, though she did not say so. The winter wore away, and the chill, bitter, windy, early spring came round. The comic almanacs give us dreadful pictures of January and February; but, in truth, the months which should be made to look gloomy in England are March and April. Let no man boast himself that he has got through the perils of winter till at least the seventh of May.

It was early in April, however, that the great doings were to be done at Greshamsbury. Not exactly on the first. It may be presumed, that in spite of the practical, common-sense spirit of the age, very few people do choose to have themselves united on that day. But some day in the first week of that month was fixed for the ceremony, and from the end of February all through March, Lady Arabella worked and strove in a manner that entitled her to profound admiration.

It was at last settled that the breakfast should be held in the large dining-room at Greshamsbury. There was a difficulty about it which taxed Lady Arabella to the utmost, for, in making the proposition, she could not but seem to be throwing some slight on the house in which the heiress had lived. But when the affair was once opened to Mary, it was astonishing how easy it became.

"Of course," said Mary, "all the rooms in our house would not hold half the people you are talking about—if they must come."

Lady Arabella looked so beseechingly, nay, so piteously, that Mary had not another word to say. It was evident that they must all come: the de Courcys to the fifth generation; the Duke of Omnium himself, and others in concatenation accordingly.

"But will your uncle be angry if we have the breakfast up here? He has been so very handsome to Frank, that I wouldn't make him angry for all the world."

"If you don't tell him anything about it, Lady Arabella, he'll think that it is all done properly. He will never know, if he's not told, that he ought to give the breakfast, and not you."

"Won't he, my dear?" And Lady Arabella looked her admiration for this very talented suggestion. And so that matter was arranged. The doctor never knew, till Mary told him some year or so afterwards, that he had been remiss in any part of his duty.

And who was asked to the wedding? In the first place, we have said that the Duke of Omnium was there. This was, in fact, the one circumstance that made this wedding so superior to any other that had ever taken place in that neighbourhood. The Duke of Omnium never went anywhere; and yet he went to Mary's wedding! And Mary, when the ceremony was over, absolutely found herself kissed by a duke. "Dearest Mary!" exclaimed Lady Arabella, in her ecstasy of joy, when she saw the honour that was done to her daughter-in-law.

"I hope we shall induce you to come to Gatherum Castle soon," said the duke to Frank. "I shall be having a few friends there in the autumn. Let me see; I declare, I have not seen you since you were good enough to come to my collection. Ha! ha! ha! It wasn't bad fun, was it?" Frank was not very cordial with his answer. He had not quite reconciled himself to the difference of his position. When he was treated as one of the "collection" at Gatherum Castle, he had not married money.

It would be vain to enumerate all the de Courcys that were there. There was the earl, looking very gracious, and talking to the squire about the county. And there was Lord Porlock, looking very ungracious, and not talking to anybody about anything. And there was the countess, who for the last week past had done nothing but pat Frank on the back whenever she could catch him. And there were the Ladies Alexandrina, Margaretta, and Selina, smiling at everybody. And the Honourable George, talking in whispers to Frank about his widow—"Not such a catch as yours, you know; but something extremely snug;—and have it all my own way, too, old fellow, or I shan't come to the scratch." And the Honourable John prepared to toady Frank about his string of hunters; and the Lady Amelia, by herself, not quite contented with these democratic nuptials—"After all, she is so absolutely nobody; absolutely, absolutely," she said confidentially to Augusta, shaking her head. But before Lady Amelia had left Greshamsbury, Augusta was quite at a loss to understand how there could be need for so much conversation between her cousin and Mr Mortimer Gazebee.

And there were many more de Courcys, whom to enumerate would be much too long.

And the bishop of the diocese, and Mrs Proudie were there. A hint had even been given, that his lordship would himself condescend to perform the ceremony, if this should be wished; but that work had already been anticipated by a very old friend of the Greshams. Archdeacon Grantly, the rector of Plumstead Episcopi, had long since undertaken this part of the business; and the knot was eventually tied by the joint efforts of himself and Mr Oriel. Mrs Grantly came with him, and so did Mrs Grantly's sister, the new dean's wife. The dean himself was at the time unfortunately absent at Oxford.

And all the Bakers and the Jacksons were there. The last time they had all met together under the squire's roof, was on the occasion of Frank's coming of age. The present gala doings were carried on a very different spirit. That had been a very poor affair, but this was worthy of the best days of Greshamsbury.

Occasion also had been taken of this happy moment to make up, or rather to get rid of the last shreds of the last feud that had so long separated Dr Thorne from his own relatives. The Thornes of Ullathorne had made many overtures in a covert way. But our doctor had contrived to reject them. "They would not receive Mary as their cousin," said he, "and I will go nowhere that she cannot go." But now all this was altered. Mrs Gresham would certainly be received in any house in the county. And thus, Mr Thorne of Ullathorne, an amiable, popular old bachelor, came to the wedding; and so did his maiden sister, Miss Monica Thorne, than whose no kinder heart glowed through all Barsetshire.

"My dear," said she to Mary, kissing her, and offering her some little tribute, "I am very glad to make your acquaintance; very. It was not her fault," she added, speaking to herself. "And now that she will be a Gresham, that need not be any longer thought of." Nevertheless, could Miss Thorne have spoken her inward thoughts out loud, she would have declared, that Frank would have done better to have borne his poverty than marry wealth without blood. But then, there are but few so stanch as Miss Thorne; perhaps none in that county—always excepting Lady Amelia.

And Miss Dunstable, also, was a bridesmaid. "Oh, no" said she, when asked; "you should have them young and pretty." But she gave way when she found that Mary did not flatter her by telling her that she was either the one or the other. "The truth is," said Miss Dunstable, "I have always been a little in love with your Frank, and so I shall do it for his sake." There were but four: the other two were the Gresham twins. Lady Arabella exerted herself greatly in framing hints to induce Mary to ask some of the de Courcy ladies to do her so much honour; but on this head Mary would please herself. "Rank," said she to Beatrice, with a curl on her lip, "has its drawbacks—and must put up with them."

And now I find that I have not one page—not half a page—for the wedding-dress. But what matters? Will it not be all found written in the columns of the *Morning Post*?

And thus Frank married money, and became a great man. Let us hope that he will be a happy man. As the time of the story has been brought down so near to the present era, it is not practicable for the novelist to tell much of his future career. When I last heard from Barsetshire, it seemed to be quite settled that he is to take the place of one of the old members at the next election; and they say, also, that there is no chance of any opposition. I have heard, too, that there have been many very private consultations between him and various gentlemen of the county, with reference to the hunt; and the general feeling is said to be that the hounds should go to Boxall Hill.

At Boxall Hill the young people established themselves on their return from the Continent. And that reminds me that one word must be said of Lady Scatcherd.

"You will always stay here with us," said Mary to her, caressing her ladyship's rough hand, and looking kindly into that kind face.

But Lady Scatcherd would not consent to this. "I will come and see you sometimes, and then I shall enjoy myself. Yes, I will come and see you, and my own dear boy." The affair was ended by her taking Mrs Opie Green's cottage, in order that she might be near the doctor; Mrs Opie Green having married—somebody.

And of whom else must we say a word? Patience, also, of course, got a husband—or will do so. Dear Patience! it would be a thousand pities that so good a wife should be lost to the world. Whether Miss Dunstable will ever be married, or Augusta Gresham, or Mr Moffat, or any of the tribe of the de Courcys—except Lady Amelia—I cannot say. They have all of them still their future before them. That Bridget was married to Thomas—that I am able to assert; for I know that Janet was much put out by their joint desertion.

Lady Arabella has not yet lost her admiration for Mary, and Mary, in return, behaves admirably. Another event is expected, and her ladyship is almost as anxious about that as she was about the wedding. "A matter, you know, of such importance in the county!" she whispered to Lady de Courcy.

Nothing can be more happy than the intercourse between the squire and his son. What their exact arrangements are, we need not specially inquire; but the demon of pecuniary embarrassment has lifted his black wings from the demesne of Greshamsbury.

And now we have but one word left for the doctor. "If you don't come and dine with me," said the squire to him, when they found themselves both deserted, "mind I shall come and dine with you." And on this principle they seem to act. Dr Thorne continues to extend his practice, to the great disgust of Dr Fillgrave; and when Mary suggested to him that he should retire, he almost boxed her ears. He knows the way, however, to Boxall Hill as well as he ever did, and is willing to acknowledge, that the tea there is almost as good as it ever was at Greshamsbury.

FRAMLEY
PARSONAGE

CHAPTER I.

"OMNES OMNIA BONA DICERE."

When young Mark Robarts was leaving college, his father might well declare that all men began to say all good things to him, and to extol his fortune in that he had a son blessed with so excellent a disposition.

This father was a physician living at Exeter. He was a gentleman possessed of no private means, but enjoying a lucrative practice, which had enabled him to maintain and educate a family with all the advantages which money can give in this country. Mark was his eldest son and second child; and the first page or two of this narrative must be consumed in giving a catalogue of the good things which chance and conduct together had heaped upon this young man's head.

His first step forward in life had arisen from his having been sent, while still very young, as a private pupil to the house of a clergyman, who was an old friend and intimate friend of his father's. This clergyman had one other, and only one other, pupil—the young Lord Lufton; and between the two boys, there had sprung up a close alliance.

While they were both so placed, Lady Lufton had visited her son, and then invited young Robarts to pass his next holidays at Framley Court. This visit was made; and it ended in Mark going back to Exeter with a letter full of praise from the widowed peeress. She had been delighted, she said, in having such a companion for her son, and expressed a hope that the boys might remain together during the course of their education. Dr. Robarts was a man who thought much of the breath of peers and peeresses, and was by no means inclined to throw away any advantage which might arise to his child from such a friendship. When, therefore, the young lord was sent to Harrow, Mark Robarts went there also.

That the lord and his friend often quarrelled, and occasionally fought,—the fact even that for one period of three months they never spoke to each other—by no means interfered with the doctor's hopes. Mark again and again stayed a fortnight at Framley Court, and Lady Lufton always wrote about him in the highest terms.

And then the lads went together to Oxford, and here Mark's good fortune followed him, consisting rather in the highly respectable manner in which he lived, than in any wonderful career of collegiate success. His family was proud of him, and the doctor was always ready to talk of him to his patients; not because he was a prizeman, and had gotten medals and scholarships, but on account of the excellence of his general conduct. He lived with the best set—he incurred no debts—he was fond of society, but able to avoid low society—liked his glass of wine, but was never known to be drunk; and, above all things, was one of the most popular men in the university.

Then came the question of a profession for this young Hyperion, and on this subject, Dr. Robarts was invited himself to go over to Framley Court to discuss the matter with Lady Lufton. Dr. Robarts returned with a very strong conception that the Church was the profession best suited to his son.

Lady Lufton had not sent for Dr. Robarts all the way from Exeter for nothing. The living of Framley was in the gift of the Lufton family, and the next presentation would be in Lady Lufton's hands, if it should fall vacant before the young lord was twenty-five years of age, and in the young lord's hands if it should fall afterwards. But the mother and the heir consented to give a joint promise to Dr. Robarts. Now, as the present incumbent was over seventy, and as the living was worth £900 a year, there could be no doubt as to the eligibility of the clerical profession.

And I must further say, that the dowager and the doctor were justified in their choice by the life and principles of the young man—as far as any father can be justified in choosing such a profession for his son, and as far as any lay impropriator can be justified in making such a promise. Had Lady Lufton had a second son, that second son would probably have had the living, and no one would have thought it wrong;—certainly not if that second son had been such a one as Mark Robarts.

Lady Lufton herself was a woman who thought much on religious matters, and would by no means have been disposed to place any one in a living, merely because such a one had been her son's friend. Her tendencies were High Church, and she was enabled to perceive that those of young Mark Robarts ran in the same direction. She was very desirous that her son should make an associate of his clergyman, and by this step she would insure, at any rate, that. She was anxious that the parish vicar should be one with whom she could herself fully co-operate, and was perhaps unconsciously wishful that he might in some measure be subject to her influence. Should she appoint an elder man, this might probably not be the case to the same extent; and should her son have the gift, it might probably not be the case at all. And therefore it was resolved that the living should be given to young Robarts.

He took his degree—not with any brilliancy, but quite in the manner that his father desired; he then travelled for eight or ten months with Lord Lufton and a college don, and almost immediately after his return home was ordained.

The living of Framley is in the diocese of Barchester; and, seeing what were Mark's hopes with reference to that diocese, it was by no means difficult to get him a curacy within it. But this curacy he was not allowed long to fill. He had not been in it above a twelvemonth, when poor old Dr. Stopford, the then vicar of Framley, was gathered to his fathers, and the full fruition of his rich hopes fell upon his shoulders.

But even yet more must be told of his good fortune before we can come to the actual incidents of our story. Lady Lufton, who, as I have said, thought much of clerical matters, did not carry her High Church principles so far as to advocate celibacy for the clergy. On the contrary, she had an idea that a man could not be a good parish parson without a wife. So, having given to her favourite a position in the world, and an income sufficient for a gentleman's wants, she set herself to work to find him a partner in those blessings.

And here also, as in other matters, he fell in with the views of his patroness—not, however, that they were declared to him in that marked manner in which the affair of the living had been broached. Lady Lufton was much too highly gifted with woman's craft for that. She never told the young vicar that Miss Monsell accompanied her ladyship's married daughter to Framley Court expressly that he, Mark, might fall in love with her; but such was in truth the case.

Lady Lufton had but two children. The eldest, a daughter, had been married some four or five years to Sir George Meredith, and this Miss Monsell was a dear friend of hers. And now looms before me the novelist's great difficulty. Miss Monsell,—or, rather, Mrs. Mark Robarts,—must be described. As Miss Monsell, our tale will have to take no prolonged note of her. And yet we will call her Fanny Monsell, when we declare that she was one of the pleasantest companions that could be brought near to a man, as the future partner of his home, and owner of his heart. And if high principles without asperity, female gentleness without weakness, a love of laughter without malice, and a true loving heart, can qualify a woman to be a parson's wife, then was Fanny Monsell qualified to fill that station.

In person she was somewhat larger than common. Her face would have been beautiful but that her mouth was large. Her hair, which was copious, was of a bright brown; her eyes also were brown, and, being so, were the distinctive feature of her face, for brown eyes are not common. They were liquid, large, and full either of tenderness or of mirth. Mark Robarts still had his accustomed luck, when such a girl as this was brought to Framley for his wooing.

And he did woo her—and won her. For Mark himself was a handsome fellow. At this time the vicar was about twenty-five years of age, and the future Mrs. Robarts was two or three years younger. Nor did she come quite empty-handed to the vicarage. It cannot be said that Fanny Monsell was an heiress, but she had been left with a provision of some few thousand pounds. This was so settled, that the interest of his wife's money paid the heavy insurance on his life which young Robarts effected, and there was left to him, over and above, sufficient to furnish his parsonage in the very best style of clerical comfort,— and to start him on the road of life rejoicing.

So much did Lady Lufton do for her *protégé*, and it may well be imagined that the Devonshire physician, sitting meditative over his parlour fire, looking back, as men will look back on the upshot of their life, was well contented with that upshot, as regarded his eldest offshoot, the Rev. Mark Robarts, the vicar of Framley.

But little has as yet been said, personally, as to our hero himself, and perhaps it may not be necessary to say much. Let us hope that by degrees he may come forth upon the canvas, showing to the beholder the nature of the man inwardly and outwardly. Here it may suffice to say that he was no born heaven's cherub, neither was he a born fallen devil's spirit. Such as his training made him, such he was. He had large capabilities for good—and aptitudes also for evil, quite enough: quite enough to make it needful that he should repel temptation as temptation only can be repelled. Much had been done to spoil him, but in the ordinary acceptation of the word he was not spoiled. He had too much tact, too much common sense, to believe himself to be the paragon which his mother thought him. Self-conceit was not, perhaps, his greatest danger. Had he possessed more of it, he might have been a less agreeable man, but his course before him might on that account have been the safer.

In person he was manly, tall, and fair-haired, with a square forehead, denoting intelligence rather than thought, with clear white hands, filbert nails, and a power of dressing himself in such a manner that no one should ever observe of him that his clothes were either good or bad, shabby or smart.

Such was Mark Robarts when at the age of twenty-five, or a little more, he married Fanny Monsell. The marriage was celebrated in his own church, for Miss Monsell had no home of her own, and had been staying for the last three months at Framley Court. She was given away by Sir George Meredith, and Lady Lufton herself saw that the wedding was what it should be, with almost as much care as she had bestowed on that of her own daughter. The deed of marrying, the absolute tying of the knot, was performed by the Very Reverend the Dean of Barchester, an esteemed friend of Lady Lufton's. And Mrs. Arabin, the dean's wife, was of the party, though the distance from Barchester to Framley is long, and the roads deep, and no railway lends its assistance. And Lord Lufton was there of course; and people protested that he would surely fall in love with one of the four beautiful bridesmaids, of whom Blanche Robarts, the vicar's second sister, was by common acknowledgment by far the most beautiful.

And there was there another and a younger sister of Mark's—who did not officiate at the ceremony, though she was present—and of whom no prediction was made, seeing that she was then only sixteen, but of whom mention is made here, as it will come to pass that my readers will know her hereafter. Her name was Lucy Robarts.

And then the vicar and his wife went off on their wedding tour, the old curate taking care of the Framley souls the while.

And in due time they returned; and after a further interval, in due course, a child was born to them; and then another; and after that came the period at which we will begin our story. But before doing so, may I not assert that all men were right in saying all manner of good things to the Devonshire physician, and in praising his luck in having such a son?

"You were up at the house to-day, I suppose?" said Mark to his wife, as he sat stretching himself in an easy chair in the drawing-room, before the fire, previously to his dressing for dinner. It was a November evening, and he had been out all day, and on such occasions the aptitude for delay in dressing is very powerful. A strong-minded man goes direct from the hall-door to his chamber without encountering the temptation of the drawing-room fire.

"No; but Lady Lufton was down here."

"Full of arguments in favour of Sarah Thompson?"

"Exactly so, Mark."

"And what did you say about Sarah Thompson?"

"Very little as coming from myself; but I did hint that you thought, or that I thought that you thought, that one of the regular trained schoolmistresses would be better."

"But her ladyship did not agree?"

"Well, I won't exactly say that;—though I think that perhaps she did not."

"I am sure she did not. When she has a point to carry, she is very fond of carrying it."

"But then, Mark, her points are generally so good."

"But, you see, in this affair of the school she is thinking more of her *protégée* than she does of the children."

"Tell her that, and I am sure she will give way."

And then again they were both silent. And the vicar having thoroughly warmed himself, as far as this might be done by facing the fire, turned round and began the operation *à tergo*.

"Come, Mark, it is twenty minutes past six. Will you go and dress?"

"I'll tell you what, Fanny: she must have her way about Sarah Thompson. You can see her to-morrow and tell her so."

"I am sure, Mark, I would not give way, if I thought it wrong. Nor would she expect it."

"If I persist this time, I shall certainly have to yield the next; and then the next may probably be more important."

"But if it's wrong, Mark?"

"I didn't say it was wrong. Besides, if it is wrong, wrong in some infinitesimal degree, one must put up with it. Sarah Thompson is very respectable; the only question is whether she can teach."

The young wife, though she did not say so, had some idea that her husband was in error. It is true that one must put up with wrong, with a great deal of wrong. But no one need put up with wrong that he can remedy. Why should he, the vicar, consent to receive an incompetent teacher for the parish children, when he was able to procure one that was competent? In such a case,—so thought Mrs. Robarts to herself,—she would have fought the matter out with Lady Lufton.

On the next morning, however, she did as she was bid, and signified to the dowager that all objection to Sarah Thompson would be withdrawn.

"Ah! I was sure he would agree with me," said her ladyship, "when he learned what sort of person she is. I know I had only to explain;"—and then she plumed her feathers, and was very gracious; for, to tell the truth, Lady Lufton did not like to be opposed in things which concerned the parish nearly.

"And, Fanny," said Lady Lufton, in her kindest manner, "you are not going anywhere on Saturday, are you?"

"No, I think not."

"Then you must come to us. Justinia is to be here, you know"—Lady Meredith was named Justinia—"and you and Mr. Robarts had better stay with us till Monday. He can have the little book-room all to himself on Sunday. The Merediths go on Monday; and Justinia won't be happy if you are not with her."

It would be unjust to say that Lady Lufton had determined not to invite the Robartses if she were not allowed to have her own way about Sarah Thompson. But such would have been the result. As it was, however, she was all kindness; and when Mrs. Robarts made some little excuse, saying that she was afraid she must return home in the evening, because of the children, Lady Lufton declared that there was room enough at Framley Court for baby and nurse, and so settled the matter in her own way, with a couple of nods and three taps of her umbrella.

This was on a Tuesday morning, and on the same evening, before dinner, the vicar again seated himself in the same chair before the drawing-room fire, as soon as he had seen his horse led into the stable.

"Mark," said his wife, "the Merediths are to be at Framley on Saturday and Sunday; and I have promised that we will go up and stay over till Monday."

"You don't mean it! Goodness gracious, how provoking!"

"Why? I thought you wouldn't mind it. And Justinia would think it unkind if I were not there."

"You can go, my dear, and of course will go. But as for me, it is impossible."

"But why, love?"

"Why? Just now, at the school-house, I answered a letter that was brought to me from Chaldicotes. Sowerby insists on my going over there for a week or so; and I have said that I would."

"Go to Chaldicotes for a week, Mark?"

"I believe I have even consented to ten days."

"And be away two Sundays?"

"No, Fanny, only one. Don't be so censorious."

"Don't call me censorious, Mark; you know I am not so. But I am so sorry. It is just what Lady Lufton won't like. Besides, you were away in Scotland two Sundays last month."

"In September, Fanny. And that is being censorious."

"Oh, but, Mark, dear Mark; don't say so. You know I don't mean it. But Lady Lufton does not like those Chaldicotes people. You know Lord Lufton was with you the last time you were there; and how annoyed she was!"

"Lord Lufton won't be with me now, for he is still in Scotland. And the reason why I am going is this: Harold Smith and his wife will be there, and I am very anxious to know more of them. I have no doubt that Harold Smith will be in the government some day, and I cannot afford to neglect such a man's acquaintance."

"But, Mark, what do you want of any government?"

"Well, Fanny, of course I am bound to say that I want nothing; neither in one sense do I; but nevertheless, I shall go and meet the Harold Smiths."

"Could you not be back before Sunday?"

"I have promised to preach at Chaldicotes. Harold Smith is going to lecture at Barchester, about the Australasian archipelago, and I am to preach a charity sermon on the same subject. They want to send out more missionaries."

"A charity sermon at Chaldicotes!"

"And why not? The house will be quite full, you know; and I dare say the Arabins will be there."

"I think not; Mrs. Arabin may get on with Mrs. Harold Smith, though I doubt that; but I'm sure she's not fond of Mrs. Smith's brother. I don't think she would stay at Chaldicotes."

"And the bishop will probably be there for a day or two."

"That is much more likely, Mark. If the pleasure of meeting Mrs. Proudie is taking you to Chaldicotes, I have not a word more to say."

"I am not a bit more fond of Mrs. Proudie than you are, Fanny," said the vicar, with something like vexation in the tone of his voice, for he thought that his wife was hard upon him. "But it is generally thought that a parish clergyman does well to meet his bishop now and then. And as I was invited there, especially to preach while all these people are staying at the place, I could not well refuse." And then he got up, and taking his candlestick, escaped to his dressing-room.

"But what am I to say to Lady Lufton?" his wife said to him, in the course of the evening.

"Just write her a note, and tell her that you find I had promised to preach at Chaldicotes next Sunday. You'll go, of course?"

"Yes: but I know she'll be annoyed. You were away the last time she had people there."

"It can't be helped. She must put it down against Sarah Thompson. She ought not to expect to win always."

"I should not have minded it, if she had lost, as you call it, about Sarah Thompson. That was a case in which you ought to have had your own way."

"And this other is a case in which I shall have it. It's a pity that there should be such a difference; isn't it?"

Then the wife perceived that, vexed as she was, it would be better that she should say nothing further; and before she went to bed, she wrote the note to Lady Lufton, as her husband recommended.

CHAPTER II.

THE FRAMLEY SET, AND THE CHALDICOTES SET.

It will be necessary that I should say a word or two of some of the people named in the few preceding pages, and also of the localities in which they lived.

Of Lady Lufton herself enough, perhaps, has been written to introduce her to my readers. The Framley property belonged to her son; but as Lufton Park—an ancient ramshackle place in another county—had heretofore been the family residence of the Lufton family, Framley Court had been apportioned to her for her residence for life. Lord Lufton himself was still unmarried; and as he had no establishment at Lufton Park—which indeed had not been inhabited since his grandfather died—he lived with his mother when it suited him to live anywhere in that neighbourhood. The widow would fain have seen more of him than he allowed her to do. He had a shooting-lodge in Scotland, and apartments in London, and a string of horses in Leicestershire—much to the disgust of the county gentry around him, who held that their own hunting was as good as any that England could afford. His lordship, however, paid his subscription to the East Barsetshire pack, and then thought himself at liberty to follow his own pleasure as to his own amusement.

Framley itself was a pleasant country place, having about it nothing of seignorial dignity or grandeur, but possessing everything necessary for the comfort of country life. The house was a low building of two stories, built at different periods, and devoid of all pretensions to any style of architecture; but the rooms, though not lofty, were warm and comfortable, and the gardens were trim and neat beyond all others in the county. Indeed, it was for its gardens only that Framley Court was celebrated.

Village there was none, properly speaking. The high road went winding about through the Framley paddocks, shrubberies, and wood-skirted home fields, for a mile and a half, not two hundred yards of which ran in a straight line; and there was a cross-road which passed down through the domain, whereby there came to be a locality called Framley Cross. Here stood the "Lufton Arms," and here, at Framley Cross, the hounds occasionally would meet; for the Framley woods were drawn in spite of the young lord's truant disposition; and then, at the Cross also, lived the shoemaker, who kept the post-office.

Framley church was distant from this just a quarter of a mile, and stood immediately opposite to the chief entrance to Framley Court. It was but a mean, ugly building, having been erected about a hundred years since, when all churches then built were made to be mean and ugly; nor was it large enough for the congregation, some of whom were thus driven to the dissenting chapels, the Sions and Ebenezers, which had got themselves established on each side of the parish, in putting down which Lady Lufton thought that her pet parson was hardly as energetic as he might be. It was, therefore, a matter near to Lady Lufton's heart to see a new church built, and she was urgent in her eloquence, both with her son and with the vicar, to have this good work commenced.

Beyond the church, but close to it, were the boys' school and girls' school, two distinct buildings, which owed their erection to Lady Lufton's energy; then came a neat little grocer's shop, the neat grocer being the clerk and sexton, and the neat grocer's wife, the pew-opener in the church. Podgens was their name, and they were great favourites with her ladyship, both having been servants up at the house.

And here the road took a sudden turn to the left, turning, as it were, away from Framley Court; and just beyond the turn was the vicarage, so that there was a little garden path running from the back of the vicarage grounds into the churchyard, cutting the Podgenses off into an isolated corner of their own;—from whence, to tell the truth, the vicar would have been glad to banish them and their cabbages, could he have had the power to do so. For has not the small vineyard of Naboth been always an eyesore to neighbouring potentates?

The potentate in this case had as little excuse as Ahab, for nothing in the parsonage way could be more perfect than his parsonage. It had all the details requisite for the house of a moderate gentleman with moderate means, and none of those expensive superfluities which immoderate gentlemen demand, or which themselves demand—immoderate means. And then the gardens and paddocks were exactly suited to it; and everything was in good order;—not exactly new, so as to be raw and uncovered, and redolent of workmen; but just at that era of their existence in which newness gives way to comfortable homeliness.

Other village at Framley there was none. At the back of the Court, up one of those cross-roads, there was another small shop or two, and there was a very neat cottage residence, in which lived the widow of a former curate, another *protégé* of Lady Lufton's; and there was a big, staring brick house, in which the present curate lived; but this was a full mile distant from the church, and farther from Framley Court, standing on that cross-road which runs from Framley Cross in a direction away from the mansion. This gentleman, the Rev. Evan Jones, might, from his age, have been the vicar's father; but he had been for many years curate of Framley; and though he was personally disliked by Lady Lufton, as being Low Church in his principles, and unsightly in his appearance, nevertheless, she would not urge his removal. He had two or three pupils in that large brick house, and if turned out from these and from his curacy, might find it difficult to establish himself elsewhere. On this account mercy was extended to the Rev. E. Jones, and, in spite of his red face and awkward big feet, he was invited to dine at Framley Court, with his plain daughter, once in every three months.

Over and above these, there was hardly a house in the parish of Framley, outside the bounds of Framley Court, except those of farmers and farm labourers; and yet the parish was of large extent.

Framley is in the eastern division of the county of Barsetshire, which, as all the world knows, is, politically speaking, as true blue a county as any in England. There have been backslidings even here, it is true; but then, in what county have there not been such backslidings? Where, in these pinchbeck days, can we hope to find the old agricultural virtue in all its purity? But, among those backsliders, I regret to say, that men now reckon Lord Lufton. Not that he is a violent Whig, or perhaps that he is a Whig at all. But he jeers and sneers at the old county doings; declares, when solicited on the subject, that, as far as he is concerned, Mr. Bright may sit for the county, if he pleases; and alleges, that being unfortunately a peer, he has no right even to interest himself in the question. All this is deeply regretted, for, in the old days, there was no portion of the county more decidedly true blue than that Framley district; and, indeed, up to the present day, the dowager is able to give an occasional helping hand.

Chaldicotes is the seat of Nathaniel Sowerby, Esq., who, at the moment supposed to be now present, is one of the members for the Western Division of Barsetshire. But this Western Division can boast none of the fine political attributes which grace its twin brother. It is decidedly Whig, and is almost governed in its politics by one or two great Whig families.

It has been said that Mark Robarts was about to pay a visit to Chaldicotes, and it has been hinted that his wife would have been as well pleased had this not been the case. Such was certainly the fact; for she, dear, prudent, excellent wife as she was, knew that Mr. Sowerby was not the most eligible friend in the world for a young clergyman, and knew, also, that there was but one other house in the whole county the name of which was so distasteful to Lady Lufton. The reasons for this were, I may say, manifold. In the first place, Mr. Sowerby was a Whig, and was seated in Parliament mainly by the interest of that great Whig autocrat the Duke of Omnium, whose residence was more dangerous even than that of Mr. Sowerby, and whom Lady Lufton regarded as an impersonation of Lucifer upon earth. Mr. Sowerby, too, was unmarried—as indeed, also, was Lord Lufton, much to his mother's grief. Mr. Sowerby, it is true, was fifty, whereas the young lord was as yet only twenty-six, but, nevertheless, her ladyship was becoming anxious on the subject. In her mind, every man was bound to marry as soon as he could maintain a wife; and she held an idea—a quite private tenet, of which she was herself but imperfectly conscious—that men in general were inclined to neglect this duty for their own selfish gratifications, that the wicked ones encouraged the more innocent in this neglect, and that many would not marry at all, were not an unseen coercion exercised against them by the other sex. The Duke of Omnium was the very head of all such sinners, and Lady Lufton greatly feared that her son might be made subject to the baneful Omnium influence, by means of Mr. Sowerby and Chaldicotes.

And then Mr. Sowerby was known to be a very poor man, with a very large estate. He had wasted, men said, much on electioneering, and more in gambling. A considerable portion of his property had already gone into the hands of the duke, who, as a rule, bought up everything around him that was to be purchased. Indeed it was said of him by his enemies, that so covetous was he of Barsetshire property, that he would lead a young neighbour on to his ruin, in order that he might get his land. What—oh! what if he should come to be possessed in this way of any of the fair acres of Framley Court? What if he should become possessed of them all? It can hardly be wondered at that Lady Lufton should not like Chaldicotes.

The Chaldicotes set, as Lady Lufton called them, were in every way opposed to what a set should be according to her ideas. She liked cheerful, quiet, well-to-do people, who loved their Church, their country, and their Queen, and who were not too anxious to make a noise in the world. She desired that all the farmers round her should be able to pay their rents without trouble, that all the old women should have warm flannel petticoats, that the working men should be saved from rheumatism by healthy food and dry houses, that they should all be obedient to their pastors and masters—temporal as well as spiritual. That was her idea of loving her country. She desired also that the copses should be full of pheasants, the stubble-field of partridges, and the gorse covers of foxes;—in that way, also, she loved her country. She had ardently longed, during that Crimean war, that the Russians might be beaten—but not by the French, to the exclusion of the English, as had seemed to her to be too much the case; and hardly by the English under the dictatorship of

Lord Palmerston. Indeed, she had had but little faith in that war after Lord Aberdeen had been expelled. If, indeed, Lord Derby could have come in!

But now as to this Chaldicotes set. After all, there was nothing so very dangerous about them; for it was in London, not in the country, that Mr. Sowerby indulged, if he did indulge, his bachelor mal-practices. Speaking of them as a set, the chief offender was Mr. Harold Smith, or perhaps his wife. He also was a member of Parliament, and, as many thought, a rising man. His father had been for many years a debater in the House, and had held high office. Harold, in early life, had intended himself for the cabinet; and if working hard at his trade could ensure success, he ought to obtain it sooner or later. He had already filled more than one subordinate station, had been at the Treasury, and for a month or two at the Admiralty, astonishing official mankind by his diligence. Those last-named few months had been under Lord Aberdeen, with whom he had been forced to retire. He was a younger son, and not possessed of any large fortune. Politics as a profession was therefore of importance to him. He had in early life married a sister of Mr. Sowerby; and as the lady was some six or seven years older than himself, and had brought with her but a scanty dowry, people thought that in this matter Mr. Harold Smith had not been perspicacious. Mr. Harold Smith was not personally a popular man with any party, though some judged him to be eminently useful. He was laborious, well-informed, and, on the whole, honest; but he was conceited, long-winded, and pompous.

Mrs. Harold Smith was the very opposite of her lord. She was a clever, bright woman, good-looking for her time of life—and she was now over forty—with a keen sense of the value of all worldly things, and a keen relish for all the world's pleasures. She was neither laborious, nor well-informed, nor perhaps altogether honest—what woman ever understood the necessity or recognized the advantage of political honesty?—but then she was neither dull nor pompous, and if she was conceited, she did not show it. She was a disappointed woman, as regards her husband; seeing that she had married him on the speculation that he would at once become politically important; and as yet Mr. Smith had not quite fulfilled the prophecies of his early life.

And Lady Lufton, when she spoke of the Chaldicotes set, distinctly included, in her own mind, the Bishop of Barchester, and his wife and daughter. Seeing that Bishop Proudie was, of course, a man much addicted to religion and to religious thinking, and that Mr. Sowerby himself had no peculiar religious sentiments whatever, there would not at first sight appear to be ground for much intercourse, and perhaps there was not much of such intercourse; but Mrs. Proudie and Mrs. Harold Smith were firm friends of four or five years' standing—ever since the Proudies came into the diocese; and therefore the bishop was usually taken to Chaldicotes whenever Mrs. Smith paid her brother a visit. Now Bishop Proudie was by no means a High Church dignitary, and Lady Lufton had never forgiven him for coming into that diocese. She had, instinctively, a high respect for the episcopal office; but of Bishop Proudie himself she hardly thought better than she did of Mr. Sowerby, or of that fabricator of evil, the Duke of Omnium. Whenever Mr. Robarts would plead that in going anywhere he would have the benefit of meeting the bishop, Lady Lufton would slightly curl her upper lip. She could not say in words, that Bishop Proudie—bishop as he certainly must be called—was no better than he ought to be; but by that curl of her lip she did explain to those who knew her that such was the inner feeling of her heart.

And then it was understood—Mark Robarts, at least, had so heard, and the information soon reached Framley Court—that Mr. Supplehouse was to make one of the Chaldicotes party. Now Mr. Supplehouse was a worse companion for a gentlemanlike, young, High Church, conservative county parson than even Harold Smith. He also was in Parliament, and had been extolled during the early days of that Russian war by some portion of the metropolitan daily press, as the only man who could save the country. Let him be in the ministry, the *Jupiter* had said, and there would be some hope of reform, some chance that England's ancient glory would not be allowed in these perilous times to go headlong to oblivion. And upon this the ministry, not anticipating much salvation from Mr. Supplehouse, but willing, as they usually are, to have the *Jupiter* at their back, did send for that gentleman, and gave him some footing among them. But how can a man born to save a nation, and to lead a people, be content to fill the chair of an under-secretary? Supplehouse was not content, and soon gave it to be understood that his place was much higher than any yet tendered to him. The seals of high office, or war to the knife, was the alternative which he offered to a much-belaboured Head of Affairs—nothing doubting that the Head of Affairs would recognize the claimant's value, and would have before his eyes a wholesome fear of the *Jupiter*. But the Head of Affairs, much belaboured as he was, knew that he might pay too high even for Mr. Supplehouse and the *Jupiter*; and the saviour of the nation was told that he might swing his tomahawk. Since that time he had been swinging his tomahawk, but not with so much effect as had been anticipated. He also was very intimate with Mr. Sowerby, and was decidedly one of the Chaldicotes set.

And there were many others included in the stigma whose sins were political or religious rather than moral. But they were gall and wormwood to Lady Lufton, who regarded them as children of the Lost One, and who grieved with a mother's grief when she knew that her son was among them, and felt all a patron's anger when she heard that her clerical *protégé* was about to seek such society. Mrs. Robarts might well say that Lady Lufton would be annoyed.

"You won't call at the house before you go, will you?" the wife asked on the following morning. He was to start after lunch on that day, driving himself in his own gig, so as to reach Chaldicotes, some twenty-four miles distant, before dinner.

"No, I think not. What good should I do?"

"Well, I can't explain; but I think I should call: partly, perhaps, to show her that as I had determined to go, I was not afraid of telling her so."

"Afraid! That's nonsense, Fanny. I'm not afraid of her. But I don't see why I should bring down upon myself the disagreeable things she will say. Besides, I have not time. I must walk up and see Jones about the duties; and then, what with getting ready, I shall have enough to do to get off in time."

He paid his visit to Mr. Jones, the curate, feeling no qualms of conscience there, as he rather boasted of all the members of Parliament he was going to meet, and of the bishop who would be with them. Mr. Evan Jones was only his curate, and in speaking to him on the matter he could talk as though it were quite the proper thing for a vicar to meet his bishop at the house of a county member. And one would be inclined to say that it was proper: only why could he not talk of it in the same tone to Lady Lufton? And then, having kissed his wife and children, he drove off, well pleased with his prospect for the coming ten days, but already anticipating some discomfort on his return.

On the three following days, Mrs. Robarts did not meet her ladyship. She did not exactly take any steps to avoid such a meeting, but she did not purposely go up to the big house. She went to her school as usual, and made one or two calls among the farmers' wives, but put no foot within the Framley Court grounds. She was braver than her husband, but even she did not wish to anticipate the evil day.

On the Saturday, just before it began to get dusk, when she was thinking of preparing for the fatal plunge, her friend, Lady Meredith, came to her.

"So, Fanny, we shall again be so unfortunate as to miss Mr. Robarts," said her ladyship.

"Yes. Did you ever know anything so unlucky? But he had promised Mr. Sowerby before he heard that you were coming. Pray do not think that he would have gone away had he known it."

"We should have been sorry to keep him from so much more amusing a party."

"Now, Justinia, you are unfair. You intend to imply that he has gone to Chaldicotes, because he likes it better than Framley Court; but that is not the case. I hope Lady Lufton does not think that it is."

Lady Meredith laughed as she put her arm round her friend's waist. "Don't lose your eloquence in defending him to me," she said. "You'll want all that for my mother."

"But is your mother angry?" asked Mrs. Robarts, showing by her countenance, how eager she was for true tidings on the subject.

"Well, Fanny, you know her ladyship as well as I do. She thinks so very highly of the vicar of Framley, that she does begrudge him to those politicians at Chaldicotes."

"But, Justinia, the bishop is to be there, you know."

"I don't think that that consideration will at all reconcile my mother to the gentleman's absence. He ought to be very proud, I know, to find that he is so much thought of. But come, Fanny, I want you to walk back with me, and you can dress at the house. And now we'll go and look at the children."

After that, as they walked together to Framley Court, Mrs. Robarts made her friend promise that she would stand by her if any serious attack were made on the absent clergyman.

"Are you going up to your room at once?" said the vicar's wife, as soon as they were inside the porch leading into the hall. Lady Meredith immediately knew what her friend meant, and decided that the evil day should not be postponed. "We had better go in and have it over," she said, "and then we shall be comfortable for the evening." So the drawing-room door was opened, and there was Lady Lufton alone upon the sofa.

"Now, mamma," said the daughter, "you mustn't scold Fanny much about Mr. Robarts. He has gone to preach a charity sermon before the bishop, and under those circumstances, perhaps, he could not refuse." This was a stretch on the part of Lady Meredith—put in with much good nature, no doubt; but still a stretch; for no one had supposed that the bishop would remain at Chaldicotes for the Sunday.

"How do you do, Fanny?" said Lady Lufton, getting up. "I am not going to scold her; and I don't know how you can talk such nonsense, Justinia. Of course, we are very sorry not to have Mr. Robarts; more especially as he was not here the last Sunday that Sir George was with us. I do like to see Mr. Robarts in his own church, certainly; and I don't like any other clergyman there as well. If Fanny takes that for scolding, why—"

"Oh! no, Lady Lufton; and it's so kind of you to say so. But Mr. Robarts was so sorry that he had accepted this invitation to Chaldicotes, before he heard that Sir George was coming, and—"

"Oh, I know that Chaldicotes has great attractions which we cannot offer," said Lady Lufton.

"Indeed, it was not that. But he was asked to preach, you know; and Mr. Harold Smith—" Poor Fanny was only making it worse. Had she been worldly wise, she would have accepted the little compliment implied in Lady Lufton's first rebuke, and then have held her peace.

"Oh, yes; the Harold Smiths! They are irresistible, I know. How could any man refuse to join a party, graced both by Mrs. Harold Smith and Mrs. Proudie—even though his duty should require him to stay away?"

"Now, mamma—" said Justinia.

"Well, my dear, what am I to say? You would not wish me to tell a fib. I don't like Mrs. Harold Smith—at least, what I hear of her; for it has not been my fortune to meet her since her marriage. It may be conceited; but to own the truth, I think that Mr. Robarts would be better off with us at Framley than with the Harold Smiths at Chaldicotes,—even though Mrs. Proudie be thrown into the bargain."

It was nearly dark, and therefore the rising colour in the face of Mrs. Robarts could not be seen. She, however, was too good a wife to hear these things said without some anger within her bosom. She could blame her husband in her own mind; but it was intolerable to her that others should blame him in her hearing.

"He would undoubtedly be better off," she said; "but then, Lady Lufton, people can't always go exactly where they will be best off. Gentlemen sometimes must—"

"Well—well, my dear, that will do. He has not taken you, at any rate; and so we will forgive him." And Lady Lufton kissed her. "As it is,"—and she affected a low whisper between the two young wives—"as it is, we must e'en put up with poor old Evan Jones. He is to be here to-night, and we must go and dress to receive him."

And so they went off. Lady Lufton was quite good enough at heart to like Mrs. Robarts all the better for standing up for her absent lord.

CHAPTER III.

CHALDICOTES.

Chaldicotes is a house of much more pretension than Framley Court. Indeed, if one looks at the ancient marks about it, rather than at those of the present day, it is a place of very considerable pretension. There is an old forest, not altogether belonging to the property, but attached to it, called the Chace of Chaldicotes. A portion of this forest comes up close behind the mansion, and of itself gives a character and celebrity to the place. The Chace of Chaldicotes—the greater part of it, at least—is, as all the world knows, Crown property, and now, in these utilitarian days, is to be disforested. In former times it was a great forest, stretching half across the country, almost as far as Silverbridge; and there are bits of it, here and there, still to be seen at intervals throughout the whole distance; but the larger remaining portion, consisting of aged hollow oaks, centuries old, and wide-spreading withered beeches, stands in the two parishes of Chaldicotes and Uffley. People still come from afar to see the oaks of Chaldicotes, and to hear their feet rustle among the thick autumn leaves. But they will soon come no longer. The giants of past ages are to give way to wheat and turnips; a ruthless Chancellor of the Exchequer, disregarding old associations and rural beauty, requires money returns from the lands; and the Chace of Chaldicotes is to vanish from the earth's surface.

Some part of it, however, is the private property of Mr. Sowerby, who hitherto, through all his pecuniary distresses, has managed to save from the axe and the auction-mart that portion of his paternal heritage. The house of Chaldicotes is a large stone building, probably of the time of Charles the Second. It is approached on both fronts by a heavy double flight of stone steps. In the front of the house a long, solemn, straight avenue through a double row of lime-trees, leads away to lodge-gates, which stand in the centre of the village of Chaldicotes; but to the rear the windows open upon four different vistas, which run down through the forest: four open green rides, which all converge together at a large iron gateway, the barrier which divides the private grounds from the Chace. The Sowerbys, for many generations, have been rangers of the Chace of Chaldicotes, thus having almost as wide an authority over the Crown forest as over their own. But now all this is to cease, for the forest will be disforested.

It was nearly dark as Mark Robarts drove up through the avenue of lime-trees to the hall-door; but it was easy to see that the house, which was dead and silent as the grave through nine months of the year, was now alive in all its parts. There were lights in many of the windows, and a noise of voices came from the stables, and servants were moving about, and dogs barked, and the dark gravel before the front steps was cut up with many a coach-wheel.

"Oh, be that you, sir, Mr. Robarts?" said a groom, taking the parson's horse by the head, and touching his own hat. "I hope I see your reverence well?"

"Quite well, Bob, thank you. All well at Chaldicotes?"

"Pretty bobbish, Mr. Robarts. Deal of life going on here now, sir. The bishop and his lady came this morning."

"Oh—ah—yes! I understood they were to be here. Any of the young ladies?"

"One young lady. Miss Olivia, I think they call her, your reverence."

"And how's Mr. Sowerby?"

"Very well, your reverence. He, and Mr. Harold Smith, and Mr. Fothergill—that's the duke's man of business, you know—is getting off their horses now in the stable-yard there."

"Home from hunting—eh, Bob?"

"Yes, sir, just home, this minute." And then Mr. Robarts walked into the house, his portmanteau following on a footboy's shoulder.

It will be seen that our young vicar was very intimate at Chaldicotes; so much so that the groom knew him, and talked to him about the people in the house. Yes; he was intimate there: much more than he had given the Framley people to understand. Not that he had wilfully and overtly deceived any one; not that he had ever spoken a false word about Chaldicotes. But he had never boasted at home that he and Sowerby were near allies. Neither had he told them there how often Mr. Sowerby and Lord Lufton were together in London. Why trouble women with such matters? Why annoy so excellent a woman as Lady Lufton?

And then Mr. Sowerby was one whose intimacy few young men would wish to reject. He was fifty, and had lived, perhaps, not the most salutary life; but he dressed young, and usually looked well. He was bald, with a good forehead, and sparkling moist eyes. He was a clever man, and a pleasant companion, and always good-humoured when it so suited him. He was a gentleman, too, of high breeding and good birth, whose ancestors had been known in that county—longer, the farmers around would boast, than those of any other landowner in it, unless it be the Thornes of Ullathorne, or perhaps the Greshams of Greshamsbury—much longer than the De Courcys at Courcy Castle. As for the Duke of Omnium, he, comparatively speaking, was a new man.

And then he was a member of Parliament, a friend of some men in power, and of others who might be there; a man who could talk about the world as one knowing the matter of which he talked. And moreover, whatever might be his ways of life at other times, when in the presence of a clergyman he rarely made himself offensive to clerical tastes. He neither swore, nor brought his vices on the carpet, nor sneered at the faith of the Church. If he was no churchman himself, he at least knew how to live with those who were.

How was it possible that such a one as our vicar should not relish the intimacy of Mr. Sowerby? It might be very well, he would say to himself, for a woman like Lady Lufton to turn up her nose at him—for Lady Lufton, who spent ten months of the year at Framley Court, and who during those ten months, and for the matter of that, during the two months also which she spent in London, saw no one out of her own set. Women did not understand such things, the vicar said to himself; even his own wife—good, and nice, and sensible, and intelligent as she was—even she did not understand that a man in the world must meet all sorts of men; and that in these days it did not do for a clergyman to be a hermit.

'Twas thus that Mark Robarts argued when he found himself called upon to defend himself before the bar of his own conscience for going to Chaldicotes and increasing his intimacy with Mr. Sowerby. He did know that Mr. Sowerby was a dangerous man; he was aware that he was over head and ears in debt, and that he had already entangled young Lord Lufton in some pecuniary embarrassment; his conscience did tell him that it would be well for him, as one of Christ's soldiers, to look out for companions of a different stamp. But nevertheless he went to Chaldicotes, not satisfied with himself indeed, but repeating to himself a great many arguments why he should be so satisfied.

He was shown into the drawing-room at once, and there he found Mrs. Harold Smith, with Mrs. and Miss Proudie, and a lady whom he had never before seen, and whose name he did not at first hear mentioned.

"Is that Mr. Robarts?" said Mrs. Harold Smith, getting up to greet him, and screening her pretended ignorance under the veil of the darkness. "And have you really driven over four-and-twenty miles of Barsetshire roads on such a day as this to assist us in our little difficulties? Well, we can promise you gratitude at any rate."

And then the vicar shook hands with Mrs. Proudie, in that deferential manner which is due from a vicar to his bishop's wife; and Mrs. Proudie returned the greeting with all that smiling condescension which a bishop's wife should show to a vicar. Miss Proudie was not quite so civil. Had Mr. Robarts been still unmarried, she also could have smiled sweetly; but she had been exercising smiles on clergymen too long to waste them now on a married parish parson.

"And what are the difficulties, Mrs. Smith, in which I am to assist you?"

"We have six or seven gentlemen here, Mr. Robarts, and they always go out hunting before breakfast, and they never come back—I was going to say—till after dinner. I wish it were so, for then we should not have to wait for them."

"Excepting Mr. Supplehouse, you know," said the unknown lady, in a loud voice.

"And he is generally shut up in the library, writing articles."

"He'd be better employed if he were trying to break his neck like the others," said the unknown lady.

"Only he would never succeed," said Mrs. Harold Smith. "But perhaps, Mr. Robarts, you are as bad as the rest; perhaps you, too, will be hunting to-morrow."

"My dear Mrs. Smith!" said Mrs. Proudie, in a tone denoting slight reproach, and modified horror.

"Oh! I forgot. No, of course, you won't be hunting, Mr. Robarts; you'll only be wishing that you could."

"Why can't he?" said the lady with the loud voice.

"My dear Miss Dunstable! a clergyman hunt, while he is staying in the same house with the bishop? Think of the proprieties!"

"Oh—ah! The bishop wouldn't like it—wouldn't he? Now, do tell me, sir, what would the bishop do to you if you did hunt?"

"It would depend upon his mood at the time, madam," said Mr. Robarts. "If that were very stern, he might perhaps have me beheaded before the palace gates."

Mrs. Proudie drew herself up in her chair, showing that she did not like the tone of the conversation; and Miss Proudie fixed her eyes vehemently on her book, showing that Miss Dunstable and her conversation were both beneath her notice.

"If these gentlemen do not mean to break their necks to-night," said Mrs. Harold Smith, "I wish they'd let us know it. It's half-past six already."

And then Mr. Robarts gave them to understand that no such catastrophe could be looked for that day, as Mr. Sowerby and the other sportsmen were within the stable-yard when he entered the door.

"Then, ladies, we may as well dress," said Mrs. Harold Smith. But as she moved towards the door, it opened, and a short gentleman, with a slow, quiet step, entered the room; but was not yet to be distinguished through the dusk by the eyes of Mr. Robarts. "Oh! bishop, is that you?" said Mrs. Smith. "Here is one of the luminaries of your diocese." And then the bishop, feeling through the dark, made his way up to the vicar and shook him cordially by the hand. "He was delighted to meet Mr. Robarts at Chaldicotes," he said—"quite delighted. Was he not going to preach on behalf of the Papuan Mission next Sunday? Ah! so he, the bishop, had heard. It was a good work, an excellent work." And then Dr. Proudie expressed himself as much grieved that he could not remain at Chaldicotes, and hear the sermon. It was plain that his bishop thought no ill of him on account of his intimacy with Mr. Sowerby. But then he felt in his own heart that he did not much regard his bishop's opinion.

"Ah, Robarts, I'm delighted to see you," said Mr. Sowerby, when they met on the drawing-room rug before dinner. "You know Harold Smith? Yes, of course you do. Well, who else is there? Oh! Supplehouse. Mr. Supplehouse, allow me to introduce to you my friend Mr. Robarts. It is he who will extract the five-pound note out of your pocket next Sunday for these poor Papuans whom we are going to Christianize. That is, if Harold Smith does not finish the work out of hand at his Saturday lecture. And, Robarts, you have seen the bishop, of course:" this he said in a whisper. "A fine thing to be a bishop, isn't it? I wish I had half your chance. But, my dear fellow, I've made such a mistake; I haven't got a bachelor parson for Miss Proudie. You must help me out, and take her in to dinner." And then the great gong sounded, and off they went in pairs.

At dinner Mark found himself seated between Miss Proudie and the lady whom he had heard named as Miss Dunstable. Of the former he was not very fond, and, in spite of his host's petition, was not inclined to play bachelor parson for her benefit. With the other lady he would willingly have chatted during the dinner, only that everybody else at table seemed to be intent on doing the same thing. She was neither young, nor beautiful, nor peculiarly ladylike; yet she seemed to enjoy a popularity which must have excited the envy of Mr. Supplehouse, and which certainly was not altogether to the taste of Mrs. Proudie—who, however, fêted her as much as did the others. So that our clergyman found himself unable to obtain more than an inconsiderable share of the lady's attention.

"Bishop," said she, speaking across the table, "we have missed you so all day! we have had no one on earth to say a word to us."

"My dear Miss Dunstable, had I known that— But I really was engaged on business of some importance."

"I don't believe in business of importance; do you, Mrs. Smith?"

"Do I not?" said Mrs. Smith. "If you were married to Mr. Harold Smith for one week, you'd believe in it."

"Should I, now? What a pity that I can't have that chance of improving my faith! But you are a man of business, also, Mr. Supplehouse; so they tell me." And she turned to her neighbour on her right hand.

"I cannot compare myself to Harold Smith," said he. "But perhaps I may equal the bishop."

"What does a man do, now, when he sits himself down to business? How does he set about it? What are his tools? A quire of blotting paper, I suppose, to begin with?"

"That depends, I should say, on his trade. A shoemaker begins by waxing his thread."

"And Mr. Harold Smith—?"

"By counting up his yesterday's figures, generally, I should say; or else by unrolling a ball of red tape. Well-docketed papers and statistical facts are his forte."

"And what does a bishop do? Can you tell me that?"

"He sends forth to his clergy either blessings or blowings-up, according to the state of his digestive organs. But Mrs. Proudie can explain all that to you with the greatest accuracy."

"Can she, now? I understand what you mean, but I don't believe a word of it. The bishop manages his own affairs himself, quite as much as you do, or Mr. Harold Smith."

"I, Miss Dunstable?"

"Yes, you."

"But I, unluckily, have not a wife to manage them for me."

"Then you should not laugh at those who have, for you don't know what you may come to yourself, when you're married."

Mr. Supplehouse began to make a pretty speech, saying that he would be delighted to incur any danger in that respect to which he might be subjected by the companionship of Miss Dunstable. But before he was half through it, she had turned her back upon him, and begun a conversation with Mark Robarts.

"Have you much work in your parish, Mr. Robarts?" she asked. Now, Mark was not aware that she knew his name, or the fact of his having a parish, and was rather surprised by the question. And he had not quite liked the tone in which she had seemed to speak of the bishop and his work. His desire for her further acquaintance was therefore somewhat moderated, and he was not prepared to answer her question with much zeal.

"All parish clergymen have plenty of work, if they choose to do it."

"Ah, that is it; is it not, Mr. Robarts? If they choose to do it? A great many do—many that I know, do; and see what a result they have. But many neglect it—and see what a result *they* have. I think it ought to be the happiest life that a man can lead, that of a parish clergyman, with a wife and family, and a sufficient income."

"I think it is," said Mark Robarts, asking himself whether the contentment accruing to him from such blessings had made him satisfied at all points. He had all these things of which Miss Dunstable spoke, and yet he had told his wife, the other day, that he could not afford to neglect the acquaintance of a rising politician like Harold Smith.

"What I find fault with is this," continued Miss Dunstable, "that we expect clergymen to do their duty, and don't give them a sufficient income—give them hardly any income at all. Is it not a scandal, that an educated gentleman with a family should be made to work half his life, and perhaps the whole, for a pittance of seventy pounds a year?"

Mark said that it was a scandal, and thought of Mr. Evan Jones and his daughter;—and thought also of his own worth, and his own house, and his own nine hundred a year.

"And yet you clergymen are so proud—aristocratic would be the genteel word, I know—that you won't take the money of common, ordinary poor people. You must be paid from land and endowments, from tithe and church property. You can't bring yourself to work for what you earn, as lawyers and doctors do. It is better that curates should starve than undergo such ignominy as that."

"It is a long subject, Miss Dunstable."

"A very long one; and that means that I am not to say any more about it."

"I did not mean that exactly."

"Oh! but you did though, Mr. Robarts. And I can take a hint of that kind when I get it. You clergymen like to keep those long subjects for your sermons, when no one can answer you. Now if I have a longing heart's desire for anything at all in this world, it is to be able to get up into a pulpit, and preach a sermon."

"You can't conceive how soon that appetite would pall upon you, after its first indulgence."

"That would depend upon whether I could get people to listen to me. It does not pall upon Mr. Spurgeon, I suppose." Then her attention was called away by some question from Mr. Sowerby, and Mark Robarts found himself bound to address his conversation to Miss Proudie. Miss Proudie, however, was not thankful, and gave him little but monosyllables for his pains.

"Of course you know Harold Smith is going to give us a lecture about these islanders," Mr. Sowerby said to him, as they sat round the fire over their wine after dinner. Mark said that he had been so informed, and should be delighted to be one of the listeners.

"You are bound to do that, as he is going to listen to you the day afterwards—or, at any rate, to pretend to do so, which is as much as you will do for him. It'll be a terrible bore—the lecture, I mean, not the sermon." And he spoke very low into his friend's ear. "Fancy having to drive ten miles after dusk, and ten miles back, to hear Harold Smith talk for two hours about Borneo! One must do it, you know."

"I daresay it will be very interesting."

"My dear fellow, you haven't undergone so many of these things as I have. But he's right to do it. It's his line of life; and when a man begins a thing he ought to go on with it. Where's Lufton all this time?"

"In Scotland, when I last heard from him; but he's probably at Melton now."

"It's deuced shabby of him, not hunting here in his own county. He escapes all the bore of going to lectures, and giving feeds to the neighbours; that's why he treats us so. He has no idea of his duty, has he?"

"Lady Lufton does all that, you know."

"I wish I'd a Mrs. Sowerby *mère* to do it for me. But then Lufton has no constituents to look after—lucky dog! By-the-by, has he spoken to you about selling that outlying bit of land of his in Oxfordshire? It belongs to the Lufton property, and yet it doesn't. In my mind it gives more trouble than it's worth."

Lord Lufton had spoken to Mark about this sale, and had explained to him that such a sacrifice was absolutely necessary, in consequence of certain pecuniary transactions between him, Lord Lufton, and Mr. Sowerby. But it was found impracticable to complete the business without Lady Lufton's knowledge, and her son had commissioned Mr. Robarts not only to inform her ladyship, but to talk her over, and to appease her wrath. This commission he had not yet attempted to execute, and it was probable that this visit to Chaldicotes would not do much to facilitate the business.

"They are the most magnificent islands under the sun," said Harold Smith to the bishop.

"Are they, indeed!" said the bishop, opening his eyes wide, and assuming a look of intense interest.

"And the most intelligent people."

"Dear me!" said the bishop.

"All they want is guidance, encouragement, instruction—"

"And Christianity," suggested the bishop.

"And Christianity, of course," said Mr. Smith, remembering that he was speaking to a dignitary of the Church. It was well to humour such people, Mr. Smith thought. But the Christianity was to be done in the Sunday sermon, and was not part of his work.

"And how do you intend to begin with them?" asked Mr. Supplehouse, the business of whose life it had been to suggest difficulties.

"Begin with them—oh—why—it's very easy to begin with them. The difficulty is to go on with them, after the money is all spent. We'll begin by explaining to them the benefits of civilization."

"Capital plan!" said Mr. Supplehouse. "But how do you set about it, Smith?"

"How do we set about it? How did we set about it with Australia and America? It is very easy to criticize; but in such matters the great thing is to put one's shoulder to the wheel."

"We sent our felons to Australia," said Supplehouse, "and they began the work for us. And as to America, we exterminated the people instead of civilizing them."

"We did not exterminate the inhabitants of India," said Harold Smith, angrily.

"Nor have we attempted to Christianize them, as the bishop so properly wishes to do with your islanders."

"Supplehouse, you are not fair," said Mr. Sowerby, "neither to Harold Smith nor to us;—you are making him rehearse his lecture, which is bad for him; and making us hear the rehearsal, which is bad for us."

"Supplehouse belongs to a clique which monopolizes the wisdom of England," said Harold Smith; "or, at any rate, thinks that it does. But the worst of them is that they are given to talk leading articles."

"Better that, than talk articles which are not leading," said Mr. Supplehouse. "Some first-class official men do that."

"Shall I meet you at the duke's next week, Mr. Robarts?" said the bishop to him, soon after they had gone into the drawing-room.

Meet him at the duke's!—the established enemy of Barsetshire mankind, as Lady Lufton regarded his grace! No idea of going to the duke's had ever entered our hero's mind; nor had he been aware that the duke was about to entertain any one.

"No, my lord; I think not. Indeed, I have no acquaintance with his grace."

"Oh—ah! I did not know. Because Mr. Sowerby is going; and so are the Harold Smiths, and, I think, Mr. Supplehouse. An excellent man is the duke;—that is, as regards all the county interests," added the bishop, remembering that the moral character of his bachelor grace was not the very best in the world.

And then his lordship began to ask some questions about the church affairs of Framley, in which a little interest as to Framley Court was also mixed up, when he was interrupted by a rather sharp voice, to which he instantly attended.

"Bishop," said the rather sharp voice; and the bishop trotted across the room to the back of the sofa, on which his wife was sitting. "Miss Dunstable thinks that she will be able to come to us for a couple of days, after we leave the duke's."

"I shall be delighted above all things," said the bishop, bowing low to the dominant lady of the day. For be it known to all men, that Miss Dunstable was the great heiress of that name.

"Mrs. Proudie is so very kind as to say that she will take me in, with my poodle, parrot, and pet old woman."

"I tell Miss Dunstable that we shall have quite room for any of her suite," said Mrs. Proudie. "And that it will give us no trouble."

"'The labour we delight in physics pain,'" said the gallant bishop, bowing low, and putting his hand upon his heart.

In the meantime, Mr. Fothergill had got hold of Mark Robarts. Mr. Fothergill was a gentleman, and a magistrate of the county, but he occupied the position of managing man on the Duke of Omnium's estates. He was not exactly his agent; that is to say, he did not receive his rents; but he "managed" for him, saw people, went about the county, wrote letters, supported the electioneering interest, did popularity when it was too much trouble for the duke to do it himself, and was, in fact, invaluable. People in West Barsetshire would often say that they did not know what *on earth* the duke would do, if it were not for Mr. Fothergill. Indeed, Mr. Fothergill was useful to the duke.

"Mr. Robarts," he said, "I am very happy to have the pleasure of meeting you—very happy, indeed. I have often heard of you from our friend Sowerby."

Mark bowed, and said that he was delighted to have the honour of making Mr. Fothergill's acquaintance.

"I am commissioned by the Duke of Omnium," continued Mr. Fothergill, "to say how glad he will be if you will join his grace's party at Gatherum Castle, next week. The bishop will be there, and indeed nearly the whole set who are here now. The duke would have written when he heard that you were to be at Chaldicotes; but things were hardly quite arranged then, so his grace has left it for me to tell you how happy he will be to make your acquaintance in his own house. I have spoken to Sowerby," continued Mr. Fothergill, "and he very much hopes that you will be able to join us."

Mark felt that his face became red when this proposition was made to him. The party in the county to which he properly belonged—he and his wife, and all that made him happy and respectable—looked upon the Duke of Omnium with horror and amazement; and now he had absolutely received an invitation to the duke's house! A proposition was made to him that he should be numbered among the duke's friends!

And though in one sense he was sorry that the proposition was made to him, yet in another he was proud of it. It is not every young man, let his profession be what it may, who can receive overtures of friendship from dukes without some elation. Mark, too, had risen in the world, as far as he had yet risen, by knowing great people; and he certainly had an ambition to rise higher. I will not degrade him by calling him a tuft-hunter; but he undoubtedly had a feeling that the paths most pleasant for a clergyman's feet were those which were trodden by the great ones of the earth.

Nevertheless, at the moment he declined the duke's invitation. He was very much flattered, he said, but the duties of his parish would require him to return direct from Chaldicotes to Framley.

"You need not give me an answer to-night, you know," said Mr. Fothergill. "Before the week is past, we will talk it over with Sowerby and the bishop. It will be a thousand pities, Mr. Robarts, if you will allow me to say so, that you should neglect such an opportunity of knowing his grace."

When Mark went to bed, his mind was still set against going to the duke's; but, nevertheless, he did feel that it was a pity that he should not do so. After all, was it necessary that he should obey Lady Lufton in all things?

CHAPTER IV.

A MATTER OF CONSCIENCE.

It is no doubt very wrong to long after a naughty thing. But nevertheless we all do so. One may say that hankering after naughty things is the very essence of the evil into which we have been precipitated by Adam's fall. When we confess that we are all sinners, we confess that we all long after naughty things.

And ambition is a great vice—as Mark Antony told us a long time ago—a great vice, no doubt, if the ambition of the man be with reference to his own advancement, and not to the advancement of others. But then, how many of us are there who are not ambitious in this vicious manner?

And there is nothing viler than the desire to know great people—people of great rank, I should say; nothing worse than the hunting of titles and worshipping of wealth. We all know this, and say it every day of our lives. But presuming that a way into the society of Park Lane was open to us, and a way also into that of Bedford Row, how many of us are there who would prefer Bedford Row because it is so vile to worship wealth and title?

I am led into these rather trite remarks by the necessity of putting forward some sort of excuse for that frame of mind in which the Rev. Mark Robarts awoke on the morning after his arrival at Chaldicotes. And I trust that the fact of his being a clergyman will not be allowed to press against him unfairly. Clergymen are subject to the same passions as other men; and, as far as I can see, give way to them, in one line or in another, almost as frequently. Every clergyman should, by canonical rule, feel a personal disinclination to a bishopric; but yet we do not believe that such personal disinclination is generally very strong.

Mark's first thoughts when he woke on that morning flew back to Mr. Fothergill's invitation. The duke had sent a special message to say how peculiarly glad he, the duke, would be to make acquaintance with him, the parson! How much of this message had been of Mr. Fothergill's own manufacture, that Mark Robarts did not consider.

He had obtained a living at an age when other young clergymen are beginning to think of a curacy, and he had obtained such a living as middle-aged parsons in their dreams regard as a possible Paradise for their old years. Of course he thought that all these good things had been the results of his own peculiar merits. Of course he felt that he was different from other parsons,—more fitted by nature for intimacy with great persons, more urbane, more polished, and more richly endowed with modern clerical well-to-do aptitudes. He was grateful to Lady Lufton for what she had done for him; but perhaps not so grateful as he should have been.

At any rate he was not Lady Lufton's servant, nor even her dependant. So much he had repeated to himself on many occasions, and had gone so far as to hint the same idea to his wife. In his career as parish priest he must in most things be the judge of his own actions—and in many also it was his duty to be the judge of those of his patroness. The fact of Lady Lufton having placed him in the living, could by no means make her the proper judge of his actions. This he often said to himself; and he said as often that Lady Lufton certainly had a hankering after such a judgment-seat.

Of whom generally did prime ministers and official bigwigs think it expedient to make bishops and deans? Was it not, as a rule, of those clergymen who had shown themselves able to perform their clerical duties efficiently, and able also to take their place with ease in high society? He was very well off certainly at Framley; but he could never hope for anything beyond Framley, if he allowed himself to regard Lady Lufton as a bugbear. Putting Lady Lufton and her prejudices out of the question, was there any reason why he ought not to accept the duke's invitation? He could not see that there was any such reason. If any one could be a better judge on such a subject than himself, it must be his bishop. And it was clear that the bishop wished him to go to Gatherum Castle.

The matter was still left open to him. Mr. Fothergill had especially explained that; and therefore his ultimate decision was as yet within his own power. Such a visit would cost him some money, for he knew that a man does not stay at great houses without expense; and then, in spite of his good income, he was not very flush of money. He had been down this year with Lord Lufton in Scotland. Perhaps it might be more prudent for him to return home.

But then an idea came to him that it behoved him as a man and a priest to break through that Framley thraldom under which he felt that he did to a certain extent exist. Was it not the fact that he was about to decline this invitation from fear of Lady Lufton? and if so, was that a motive by which he ought to be actuated? It was incumbent on him to rid himself of that feeling. And in this spirit he got up and dressed.

There was hunting again on that day; and as the hounds were to meet near Chaldicotes, and to draw some coverts lying on the verge of the Chace, the ladies were to go in carriages through the drives of the forest, and Mr. Robarts was to escort them on horseback. Indeed it was one of those hunting-days got up rather for the ladies than for the sport. Great nuisances they are to steady, middle-aged hunting men; but the young fellows like them because they have thereby an opportunity of showing off their sporting finery, and of doing a little flirtation on horseback. The bishop, also, had been minded to be of the party; so, at least, he had said on the previous evening; and a place in one of the carriages had been set apart for him: but since that, he and Mrs. Proudie had discussed the matter in private, and at breakfast his lordship declared that he had changed his mind.

Mr. Sowerby was one of those men who are known to be very poor—as poor as debt can make a man—but who, nevertheless, enjoy all the luxuries which money can give. It was believed that he could not live in England out of jail but for his protection as a member of Parliament; and yet it seemed that there was no end to his horses and carriages, his servants and retinue. He had been at this work for a great many years, and practice, they say, makes perfect. Such companions are very dangerous. There is no cholera, no yellow-fever, no small-pox more contagious than debt. If one lives habitually among embarrassed men, one catches it to a certainty. No one had injured the community in this way more fatally than Mr. Sowerby. But still he carried on the game himself; and now on this morning carriages and horses thronged at his gate, as though he were as substantially rich as his friend the Duke of Omnium.

"Robarts, my dear fellow," said Mr. Sowerby, when they were well under way down one of the glades of the forest,—for the place where the hounds met was some four or five miles from the house of Chaldicotes,—"ride on with me a moment. I want to speak to you; and if I stay behind we shall never get to the hounds." So Mark, who had come expressly to escort the ladies, rode on alongside of Mr. Sowerby in his pink coat.

"My dear fellow, Fothergill tells me that you have some hesitation about going to Gatherum Castle."

"Well, I did decline, certainly. You know I am not a man of pleasure, as you are. I have some duties to attend to."

"Gammon!" said Mr. Sowerby; and as he said it he looked with a kind of derisive smile into the clergyman's face.

"It is easy enough to say that, Sowerby; and perhaps I have no right to expect that you should understand me."

"Ah, but I do understand you; and I say it is gammon. I would be the last man in the world to ridicule your scruples about duty, if this hesitation on your part arose from any such scruple. But answer me honestly, do you not know that such is not the case?"

"I know nothing of the kind."

"Ah, but I think you do. If you persist in refusing this invitation will it not be because you are afraid of making Lady Lufton angry? I do not know what there can be in that woman that she is able to hold both you and Lufton in leading-strings."

Robarts, of course, denied the charge and protested that he was not to be taken back to his own parsonage by any fear of Lady Lufton. But though he made such protest with warmth, he knew that he did so ineffectually. Sowerby only smiled and said that the proof of the pudding was in the eating.

"What is the good of a man keeping a curate if it be not to save him from that sort of drudgery?" he asked.

"Drudgery! If I were a drudge how could I be here to-day?"

"Well, Robarts, look here. I am speaking now, perhaps, with more of the energy of an old friend than circumstances fully warrant; but I am an older man than you, and as I have a regard for you I do not like to see you throw up a good game when it is in your hands."

"Oh, as far as that goes, Sowerby, I need hardly tell you that I appreciate your kindness."

"If you are content," continued the man of the world, "to live at Framley all your life, and to warm yourself in the sunshine of the dowager there, why, in such case, it may perhaps be useless for you to extend the circle of your friends; but if you have higher ideas than these, I think you will be very wrong to omit the present opportunity of going to the duke's. I never knew the duke go so much out of his way to be civil to a clergyman as he has done in this instance."

"I am sure I am very much obliged to him."

"The fact is, that you may, if you please, make yourself popular in the county; but you cannot do it by obeying all Lady Lufton's behests. She is a dear old woman, I am sure."

"She is, Sowerby; and you would say so, if you knew her."

"I don't doubt it; but it would not do for you or me to live exactly according to her ideas. Now, here, in this case, the bishop of the diocese is to be one of the party, and he has, I believe, already expressed a wish that you should be another."

"He asked me if I were going."

"Exactly; and Archdeacon Grantly will be there."

"Will he?" asked Mark. Now, that would be a great point gained, for Archdeacon Grantly was a close friend of Lady Lufton.

"So I understand from Fothergill. Indeed, it will be very wrong of you not to go, and I tell you so plainly; and what is more, when you talk about your duty—you having a curate as you have—why, it is gammon." These last words he spoke looking back over his shoulder as he stood up in his stirrups, for he had caught the eye of the huntsman, who was surrounded by his hounds, and was now trotting on to join him.

During a great portion of the day, Mark found himself riding by the side of Mrs. Proudie, as that lady leaned back in her carriage. And Mrs. Proudie smiled on him graciously, though her daughter would not do so. Mrs. Proudie was fond of having an attendant clergyman; and as it was evident that Mr. Robarts lived among nice people— titled dowagers, members of Parliament, and people of that sort—she was quite willing to instal him as a sort of honorary chaplain *pro tem*.

"I'll tell you what we have settled, Mrs. Harold Smith and I," said Mrs. Proudie to him. "This lecture at Barchester will be so late on Saturday evening, that you had all better come and dine with us."

Mark bowed and thanked her, and declared that he should be very happy to make one of such a party. Even Lady Lufton could not object to this, although she was not especially fond of Mrs. Proudie.

"And then they are to sleep at the hotel. It will really be too late for ladies to think of going back so far at this time of the year. I told Mrs. Harold Smith, and Miss Dunstable, too, that we could manage to make room at any rate for them. But they will not leave the other ladies; so they go to the hotel for that night. But, Mr. Robarts, the bishop will never allow you to stay at the inn, so of course you will take a bed at the palace."

It immediately occurred to Mark that as the lecture was to be given on Saturday evening, the next morning would be Sunday; and, on that Sunday, he would have to preach at Chaldicotes. "I thought they were all going to return the same night," said he.

"Well, they did intend it; but you see Mrs. Smith is afraid."

"I should have to get back here on the Sunday morning, Mrs. Proudie."

"Ah, yes, that is bad—very bad, indeed. No one dislikes any interference with the Sabbath more than I do. Indeed, if I am particular about anything it is about that. But some works are works of necessity, Mr. Robarts; are they not? Now you must necessarily be back at Chaldicotes on Sunday morning!" And so the matter was settled. Mrs. Proudie was very firm in general in the matter of Sabbath-day observances; but when she had to deal with such persons as Mrs. Harold Smith, it was expedient that she should give way a little. "You can start as soon as it's daylight, you know, if you like it, Mr. Robarts," said Mrs. Proudie.

There was not much to boast of as to the hunting, but it was a very pleasant day for the ladies. The men rode up and down the grass roads through the Chace, sometimes in the greatest possible hurry as though they never could go quick enough; and then the coachmen would drive very fast also, though they did not know why, for a fast pace of movement is another of those contagious diseases. And then again the sportsmen would move at an undertaker's pace, when the fox had traversed and the hounds would be at a loss to know which was the hunt and which was the heel; and then the carriage also would go slowly, and the ladies would stand up and talk. And then the time for lunch came; and altogether the day went by pleasantly enough.

"And so that's hunting, is it?" said Miss Dunstable.

"Yes, that's hunting," said Mr. Sowerby.

"I did not see any gentleman do anything that I could not do myself, except there was one young man slipped off into the mud; and I shouldn't like that."

"But there was no breaking of bones, was there, my dear?" said Mrs. Harold Smith.

"And nobody caught any foxes," said Miss Dunstable. "The fact is, Mrs. Smith, that I don't think much more of their sport than I do of their business. I shall take to hunting a pack of hounds myself after this."

"Do, my dear, and I'll be your whipper-in. I wonder whether Mrs. Proudie would join us."

"I shall be writing to the duke to-night," said Mr. Fothergill to Mark, as they were all riding up to the stable-yard together. "You will let me tell his grace that you will accept his invitation—will you not?"

"Upon my word, the duke is very kind," said Mark.

"He is very anxious to know you, I can assure you," said Fothergill.

What could a young flattered fool of a parson do, but say that he would go? Mark did say that he would go; and in the course of the evening his friend Mr. Sowerby congratulated him, and the bishop joked with him and said that he knew that he would not give up good company so soon; and Miss Dunstable said she would make him her chaplain as soon as Parliament would allow quack doctors to have such articles—an allusion which Mark did not understand, till he learned that Miss Dunstable was herself the proprietress of the celebrated Oil of Lebanon, invented by her late respected father, and patented by him with such wonderful results in the way of accumulated fortune; and Mrs. Proudie made him quite one of their party, talking to him about all manner of church subjects; and then at last, even Miss Proudie smiled on him, when she learned that he had been thought worthy of a bed at a duke's castle. And all the world seemed to be open to him.

But he could not make himself happy that evening. On the next morning he must write to his wife; and he could already see the look of painful sorrow which would fall upon his Fanny's brow when she learned that her husband was going to be a guest at the Duke of Omnium's. And he must tell her to send him money, and money was scarce. And then, as to Lady Lufton, should he send her some message, or should he not? In either case he must declare war against her. And then did he not owe everything to Lady Lufton? And thus in spite of all his triumphs he could not get himself to bed in a happy frame of mind.

On the next day, which was Friday, he postponed the disagreeable task of writing. Saturday would do as well; and on Saturday morning, before they all started for Barchester, he did write. And his letter ran as follows:—

Chaldicotes, — November, 185—.

DEAREST LOVE,—You will be astonished when I tell you how gay we all are here, and what further dissipations are in store for us. The Arabins, as you supposed, are not of our party; but the Proudies are,—as you supposed also. Your suppositions are always right. And what will you think when I tell you that I am to sleep at the palace on Saturday? You know that there is to be a lecture in Barchester on that day. Well; we must all go, of course, as Harold Smith, one of our set here, is to give it. And now it turns out that we cannot get back the same night because there is no moon; and Mrs. Bishop would not allow that my cloth should be contaminated by an hotel;—very kind and considerate, is it not? But I have a more astounding piece of news for you than this. There is to be a great party at Gatherum Castle next week, and they have talked me over into accepting an invitation which the duke sent expressly to me. I refused at first; but everybody here said that my doing so would be so strange; and then they all wanted to know my reason. When I came to render it, I did not know what reason I had to give. The bishop is going, and he thought it very odd that I should not go also, seeing that I was asked.

> I know what my own darling will think, and I know that she will not be pleased, and I must put off my defence till I return to her from this ogre-land,—if ever I do get back alive. But joking apart, Fanny, I think that I should have been wrong to stand out, when so much was said about it. I should have been seeming to take upon myself to sit in judgment upon the duke. I doubt if there be a single clergyman in the diocese, under fifty years

of age, who would have refused the invitation under such circumstances,—unless it be Crawley, who is so mad on the subject that he thinks it almost wrong to take a walk out of his own parish.

I must stay at Gatherum Castle over Sunday week—indeed, we only go there on Friday. I have written to Jones about the duties. I can make it up to him, as I know he wishes to go into Wales at Christmas. My wanderings will all be over then, and he may go for a couple of months if he pleases. I suppose you will take my classes in the school on Sunday, as well as your own; but pray make them have a good fire. If this is too much for you, make Mrs. Podgens take the boys. Indeed I think that will be better.

Of course you will tell her ladyship of my whereabouts. Tell her from me, that as regards the bishop, as well as regarding another great personage, the colour has been laid on perhaps a little too thickly. Not that Lady Lufton would ever like him. Make her understand that my going to the duke's has almost become a matter of conscience with me. I have not known how to make it appear that it would be right for me to refuse, without absolutely making a party matter of it. I saw that it would be said, that I, coming from Lady Lufton's parish, could not go to the Duke of Omnium's. This I did not choose.

I find that I shall want a little more money before I leave here, five or ten pounds—say ten pounds. If you cannot spare it, get it from Davis. He owes me more than that, a good deal.

And now, God bless and preserve you, my own love. Kiss my darling bairns for papa, and give them my blessing.

Always and ever your own,
M. R.

And then there was written, on an outside scrap which was folded round the full-written sheet of paper, "Make it as smooth at Framley Court as possible."

However strong, and reasonable, and unanswerable the body of Mark's letter may have been, all his hesitation, weakness, doubt, and fear, were expressed in this short postscript.

CHAPTER V.

AMANTIUM IRÆ AMORIS INTEGRATIO.

And now, with my reader's consent, I will follow the postman with that letter to Framley; not by its own circuitous route indeed, or by the same mode of conveyance; for that letter went into Barchester by the Courcy night mail-cart, which, on its road, passes through the villages of Uffley and Chaldicotes, reaching Barchester in time for the up mail-train to London. By that train, the letter was sent towards the metropolis as far as the junction of the Barset branch line, but there it was turned in its course, and came down again by the main line as far as Silverbridge; at which place, between six and seven in the morning, it was shouldered by the Framley footpost messenger, and in due course delivered at the Framley Parsonage exactly as Mrs. Robarts had finished reading prayers to the four servants. Or, I should say rather, that such would in its usual course have been that letter's destiny. As it was, however, it reached Silverbridge on Sunday, and lay there till the Monday, as the Framley people have declined their Sunday post. And then again, when the letter was delivered at the parsonage, on that wet Monday morning, Mrs. Robarts was not at home. As we are all aware, she was staying with her ladyship at Framley Court.

"Oh, but it's mortial wet," said the shivering postman as he handed in that and the vicar's newspaper. The vicar was a man of the world, and took the *Jupiter*.

"Come in, Robin postman, and warm theeself awhile," said Jemima the cook, pushing a stool a little to one side, but still well in front of the big kitchen fire.

"Well, I dudna jist know how it'll be. The wery 'edges 'as eyes and tells on me in Silverbridge, if I so much as stops to pick a blackberry."

"There bain't no hedges here, mon, nor yet no blackberries; so sit thee down and warm theeself. That's better nor blackberries I'm thinking," and she handed him a bowl of tea with a slice of buttered toast.

Robin postman took the proffered tea, put his dripping hat on the ground, and thanked Jemima cook. "But I dudna jist know how it'll be," said he; "only it do pour so tarnation heavy." Which among us, O my readers, could have withstood that temptation?

Such was the circuitous course of Mark's letter; but as it left Chaldicotes on Saturday evening, and reached Mrs. Robarts on the following morning, or would have done, but for that intervening Sunday, doing all its peregrinations during the night, it may be held that its course of transport was not inconveniently arranged. We, however, will travel by a much shorter route.

Robin, in the course of his daily travels, passed, first the post-office at Framley, then the Framley Court back entrance, and then the vicar's house, so that on this wet morning Jemima cook was not able to make use of his services in transporting this letter back to her mistress; for Robin had got another village before him, expectant of its letters.

"Why didn't thee leave it, mon, with Mr. Applejohn at the Court?" Mr. Applejohn was the butler who took the letter-bag. "Thee know'st as how missus was there."

And then Robin, mindful of the tea and toast, explained to her courteously how the law made it imperative on him to bring the letter to the very house that was indicated, let the owner of the letter be where she might; and he laid down the law very satisfactorily with sundry long-worded quotations. Not to much effect, however, for the housemaid called him an oaf; and Robin would decidedly have had the worst of it had not the gardener come in and taken his part. "They women knows nothin', and understands nothin'," said the gardener. "Give us hold of the letter. I'll take it up to the house. It's the master's fist." And then Robin postman went on one way, and the gardener, he went the other. The gardener never disliked an excuse for going up to the Court gardens, even on so wet a day as this.

Mrs. Robarts was sitting over the drawing-room fire with Lady Meredith, when her husband's letter was brought to her. The Framley Court letter-bag had been discussed at breakfast; but that was now nearly an hour since, and Lady Lufton, as was her wont, was away in her own room writing her own letters, and looking after her own matters: for Lady Lufton was a person who dealt in figures herself, and understood business almost as well as Harold Smith. And on that morning she also had received a letter which had displeased her not a little. Whence arose this displeasure neither Mrs. Robarts nor Lady Meredith knew; but her ladyship's brow had grown black at breakfast time; she had bundled up an ominous-looking epistle into her bag without speaking of it, and had left the room immediately that breakfast was over.

"There's something wrong," said Sir George.

"Mamma does fret herself so much about Ludovic's money matters," said Lady Meredith. Ludovic was Lord Lufton,—Ludovic Lufton, Baron Lufton of Lufton, in the county of Oxfordshire.

"And yet I don't think Lufton gets much astray," said Sir George, as he sauntered out of the room. "Well, Justy; we'll put off going then till to-morrow; but remember, it must be the first train." Lady Meredith said she would remember, and then they went into the drawing-room, and there Mrs. Robarts received her letter.

Fanny, when she read it, hardly at first realized to herself the idea that her husband, the clergyman of Framley, the family clerical friend of Lady Lufton's establishment, was going to stay with the Duke of Omnium. It was so thoroughly understood at Framley Court that the duke and all belonging to him was noxious and damnable. He was a Whig, he was a bachelor, he was a gambler, he was immoral in every way, he was a man of no church principle, a corrupter of youth, a sworn foe of young wives, a swallower up of small men's patrimonies; a man whom mothers feared for their sons, and sisters for their brothers; and worse again, whom fathers had cause to fear for their daughters, and brothers for their sisters;—a man who, with his belongings, dwelt, and must dwell, poles asunder from Lady Lufton and her belongings!

And it must be remembered that all these evil things were fully believed by Mrs. Robarts. Could it really be that her husband was going to dwell in the halls of Apollyon, to shelter himself beneath the wings of this very Lucifer? A cloud of sorrow settled upon her face, and then she read the letter again very slowly, not omitting the tell-tale postscript.

"Oh, Justinia!" at last she said.

"What, have you got bad news, too?"

"I hardly know how to tell you what has occurred. There; I suppose you had better read it;" and she handed her husband's epistle to Lady Meredith,—keeping back, however, the postscript.

"What on earth will her ladyship say now?" said Lady Meredith, as she folded the paper, and replaced it in the envelope.

"What had I better do, Justinia? how had I better tell her?" And then the two ladies put their heads together, bethinking themselves how they might best deprecate the wrath of Lady Lufton. It had been arranged that Mrs. Robarts should go back to the parsonage after lunch, and she had persisted in her intention after it had been settled that the Merediths were to stay over that evening. Lady Meredith now advised her friend to carry out this determination without saying anything about her husband's terrible iniquities, and then to send the letter up to Lady Lufton as soon as she reached the parsonage. "Mamma will never know that you received it here," said Lady Meredith.

But Mrs. Robarts would not consent to this. Such a course seemed to her to be cowardly. She knew that her husband was doing wrong; she felt that he knew it himself; but still it was necessary that she should defend him. However terrible might be the storm, it must break upon her own head. So she at once went up and tapped at Lady Lufton's private door; and as she did so Lady Meredith followed her.

"Come in," said Lady Lufton, and the voice did not sound soft and pleasant. When they entered, they found her sitting at her little writing table, with her head resting on her arm, and that letter which she had received that morning was lying open on the table before her. Indeed there were two letters now there, one from a London lawyer to herself, and the other from her son to that London lawyer. It needs only be explained that the subject of those letters was the immediate sale of that outlying portion of the Lufton property in Oxfordshire, as to which Mr. Sowerby once spoke. Lord Lufton had told the lawyer that the thing must be done at once, adding that his friend Robarts would have explained the whole affair to his mother. And then the lawyer had written to Lady Lufton, as indeed was necessary; but unfortunately Lady Lufton had not hitherto heard a word of the matter.

In her eyes the sale of family property was horrible; the fact that a young man with some fifteen or twenty thousand a year should require subsidiary money was horrible; that her own son should have not written to her himself was horrible; and it was also horrible that her own pet, the clergyman whom she had brought there to be her son's friend, should be mixed up in the matter,—should be cognizant of it while she was not cognizant,—should be employed in it as a go-between and agent in her son's bad courses. It was all horrible, and Lady Lufton was sitting there with a black brow and an uneasy heart. As regarded our poor parson, we may say that in this matter he was blameless, except that he had hitherto lacked the courage to execute his friend's commission.

"What is it, Fanny?" said Lady Lufton as soon as the door was opened; "I should have been down in half-an-hour, if you wanted me, Justinia."

"Fanny has received a letter which makes her wish to speak to you at once," said Lady Meredith. "What letter, Fanny?"

Poor Fanny's heart was in her mouth; she held it in her hand, but had not quite made up her mind whether she would show it bodily to Lady Lufton.

"From Mr. Robarts," she said.

"Well; I suppose he is going to stay another week at Chaldicotes. For my part I should be as well pleased;" and Lady Lufton's voice was not friendly, for she was thinking of that farm in Oxfordshire. The imprudence of the young is very sore to the prudence of their elders. No woman could be less covetous, less grasping than Lady Lufton; but the sale of a portion of the old family property was to her as the loss of her own heart's blood.

"Here is the letter, Lady Lufton; perhaps you had better read it;" and Fanny handed it to her, again keeping back the postscript. She had read and re-read the letter downstairs, but could not make out whether her husband had intended her to show it. From the line of the argument she thought that he must have done so. At any rate he said for himself more than she could say for him, and so, probably, it was best that her ladyship should see it.

Lady Lufton took it, and read it, and her face grew blacker and blacker. Her mind was set against the writer before she began it, and every word in it tended to make her feel more estranged from him. "Oh, he is going to the palace, is he?—well; he must choose his own friends. Harold Smith one of his party! It's a pity, my dear, he did not see Miss Proudie before he met you, he might have lived to be the bishop's chaplain. Gatherum Castle! You don't mean to tell me that he is going there? Then I tell you fairly, Fanny, that I have done with him."

"Oh, Lady Lufton, don't say that," said Mrs. Robarts, with tears in her eyes.

"Mamma, mamma, don't speak in that way," said Lady Meredith.

"But my dear, what am I to say? I must speak in that way. You would not wish me to speak falsehoods, would you? A man must choose for himself, but he can't live with two different sets of people; at least, not if I belong to one and the Duke of Omnium to the other. The bishop going indeed! If there be anything that I hate it is hypocrisy."

"There is no hypocrisy in that, Lady Lufton."

"But I say there is, Fanny. Very strange, indeed! 'Put off his defence!' Why should a man need any defence to his wife if he acts in a straightforward way? His own language condemns him: 'Wrong to stand out!' Now, will either of you tell me that Mr. Robarts would really have thought it wrong to refuse that invitation? I say that that is hypocrisy. There is no other word for it."

By this time the poor wife, who had been in tears, was wiping them away and preparing for action. Lady Lufton's extreme severity gave her courage. She knew that it behoved her to fight for her husband when he was thus attacked. Had Lady Lufton been moderate in her remarks Mrs. Robarts would not have had a word to say.

"My husband may have been ill-judged," she said, "but he is no hypocrite."

"Very well, my dear, I dare say you know better than I; but to me it looks extremely like hypocrisy: eh, Justinia?"

"Oh, mamma, do be moderate."

"Moderate! That's all very well. How is one to moderate one's feelings when one has been betrayed?"

"You do not mean that Mr. Robarts has betrayed you?" said the wife.

"Oh, no; of course not." And then she went on reading the letter: "'Seem to have been standing in judgment upon the duke.' Might he not use the same argument as to going into any house in the kingdom, however infamous? We must all stand in judgment one upon another in that sense. 'Crawley!' Yes; if he were a little more like Mr. Crawley it would be a good thing for me, and for the parish, and for you too, my dear. God forgive me for bringing him here; that's all."

"Lady Lufton, I must say that you are very hard upon him—very hard. I did not expect it from such a friend."

"My dear, you ought to know me well enough to be sure that I shall speak my mind. 'Written to Jones'—yes; it is easy enough to write to poor Jones. He had better write to Jones, and bid him do the whole duty. Then he can go and be the duke's domestic chaplain."

"I believe my husband does as much of his own duty as any clergyman in the whole diocese," said Mrs. Robarts, now again in tears.

"And you are to take his work in the school; you and Mrs. Podgens. What with his curate and his wife and Mrs. Podgens, I don't see why he should come back at all."

"Oh, mamma," said Justinia, "pray, pray don't be so harsh to her."

"Let me finish it, my dear;—oh, here I come. 'Tell her ladyship my whereabouts.' He little thought you'd show me this letter."

"Didn't he?" said Mrs. Robarts, putting out her hand to get it back, but in vain. "I thought it was for the best; I did indeed."

"I had better finish it now, if you please. What is this? How does he dare send his ribald jokes to me in such a matter? No, I do not suppose I ever shall like Dr. Proudie; I have never expected it. A matter of conscience with him! Well—well, well. Had I not read it myself, I could not have believed it of him. I would not positively have believed it. 'Coming from my parish he could not go to the Duke of Omnium!' And it is what I would wish to have said. People fit for this parish should not be fit for the Duke of Omnium's house. And I had trusted that he would have this feeling more strongly than any one else in it. I have been deceived—that's all."

"He has done nothing to deceive you, Lady Lufton."

"I hope he will not have deceived you, my dear. 'More money;' yes, it is probable that he will want more money. There is your letter, Fanny. I am very sorry for it. I can say nothing more." And she folded up the letter and gave it back to Mrs. Robarts.

"I thought it right to show it you," said Mrs. Robarts.

"It did not much matter whether you did or no; of course I must have been told."

"He especially begs me to tell you."

"Why, yes; he could not very well have kept me in the dark in such a matter. He could not neglect his own work, and go and live with gamblers and adulterers at the Duke of Omnium's without my knowing it."

And now Fanny Robarts's cup was full, full to the overflowing. When she heard these words she forgot all about Lady Lufton, all about Lady Meredith, and remembered only her husband,—that he was her husband, and, in spite of his faults, a good and loving husband;—and that other fact also she remembered, that she was his wife.

"Lady Lufton," she said, "you forget yourself in speaking in that way of my husband."

"What!" said her ladyship; "you are to show me such a letter as that, and I am not to tell you what I think?"

"Not if you think such hard things as that. Even you are not justified in speaking to me in that way, and I will not hear it."

"Heighty-tighty!" said her ladyship.

"Whether or no he is right in going to the Duke of Omnium's, I will not pretend to judge. He is the judge of his own actions, and neither you nor I."

"And when he leaves you with the butcher's bill unpaid and no money to buy shoes for the children, who will be the judge then?"

"Not you, Lady Lufton. If such bad days should ever come—and neither you nor I have a right to expect them—I will not come to you in my troubles; not after this."

"Very well, my dear. You may go to the Duke of Omnium if that suits you better."

"Fanny, come away," said Lady Meredith. "Why should you try to anger my mother?"

"I don't want to anger her; but I won't hear him abused in that way without speaking up for him. If I don't defend him, who will? Lady Lufton has said terrible things about him; and they are not true."

"Oh, Fanny!" said Justinia.

"Very well, very well!" said Lady Lufton. "This is the sort of return that one gets."

"I don't know what you mean by return, Lady Lufton: but would you wish me to stand by quietly and hear such things said of my husband? He does not live with such people as you have named. He does not neglect his duties. If every clergyman were as much in his parish, it would be well for some of them. And in going to such a house as the Duke of Omnium's it does make a difference that he goes there in company with the bishop. I can't explain why, but I know that it does."

"Especially when the bishop is coupled up with the devil, as Mr. Robarts has done," said Lady Lufton; "he can join the duke with them and then they'll stand for the three Graces, won't they, Justinia?" And Lady Lufton laughed a bitter little laugh at her own wit.

"I suppose I may go now, Lady Lufton."

"Oh, yes, certainly, my dear."

"I am sorry if I have made you angry with me; but I will not allow any one to speak against Mr. Robarts without answering them. You have been very unjust to him; and even though I do anger you, I must say so."

"Come, Fanny; this is too bad," said Lady Lufton. "You have been scolding me for the last half-hour because I would not congratulate you on this new friend that your husband has made, and now you are going to begin it all over again. That is more than I can stand. If you have nothing else particular to say, you might as well leave me." And Lady Lufton's face as she spoke was unbending, severe, and harsh.

Mrs. Robarts had never before been so spoken to by her old friend; indeed she had never been so spoken to by any one, and she hardly knew how to bear herself.

"Very well, Lady Lufton," she said; "then I will go. Good-bye."

"Good-bye," said Lady Lufton, and turning herself to her table she began to arrange her papers. Fanny had never before left Framley Court to go back to her own parsonage without a warm embrace. Now she was to do so without even having her hand taken. Had it come to this, that there was absolutely to be a quarrel between them,—a quarrel for ever?

"Fanny is going, you know, mamma," said Lady Meredith. "She will be home before you are down again."

"I cannot help it, my dear. Fanny must do as she pleases. I am not to be the judge of her actions. She has just told me so."

Mrs. Robarts had said nothing of the kind, but she was far too proud to point this out. So with a gentle step she retreated through the door, and then Lady Meredith, having tried what a conciliatory whisper with her mother would do, followed her. Alas, the conciliatory whisper was altogether ineffectual!

The two ladies said nothing as they descended the stairs, but when they had regained the drawing-room they looked with blank horror into each other's faces. What were they to do now? Of such a tragedy as this they had had no remotest preconception. Was it absolutely the case that Fanny Robarts was to walk out of Lady Lufton's house as a declared enemy,—she who, before her marriage as well as since, had been almost treated as an adopted daughter of the family?

"Oh, Fanny, why did you answer my mother in that way?" said Lady Meredith. "You saw that she was vexed. She had other things to vex her besides this about Mr. Robarts."

"And would not you answer any one who attacked Sir George?"

"No, not my own mother. I would let her say what she pleased, and leave Sir George to fight his own battles."

"Ah, but it is different with you. You are her daughter, and Sir George—she would not dare to speak in that way as to Sir George's doings."

"Indeed she would, if it pleased her. I am sorry I let you go up to her."

"It is as well that it should be over, Justinia. As those are her thoughts about Mr. Robarts, it is quite as well that we should know them. Even for all that I owe to her, and all the love I bear to you, I will not come to this house if I am to hear my husband abused;—not into any house."

"My dearest Fanny, we all know what happens when two angry people get together."

"I was not angry when I went up to her; not in the least."

"It is no good looking back. What are we to do now, Fanny?"

"I suppose I had better go home," said Mrs. Robarts. "I will go and put my things up, and then I will send James for them."

"Wait till after lunch, and then you will be able to kiss my mother before you leave us."

"No, Justinia; I cannot wait. I must answer Mr. Robarts by this post, and I must think what I have to say to him. I could not write that letter here, and the post goes at four." And Mrs. Robarts got up from her chair, preparatory to her final departure.

"I shall come to you before dinner," said Lady Meredith; "and if I can bring you good tidings, I shall expect you to come back here with me. It is out of the question that I should go away from Framley leaving you and my mother at enmity with each other."

To this Mrs. Robarts made no answer; and in a very few minutes afterwards she was in her own nursery, kissing her children, and teaching the elder one to say something about papa. But, even as she taught him, the tears stood in her eyes, and the little fellow knew that everything was not right.

And there she sat till about two, doing little odds and ends of things for the children, and allowing that occupation to stand as an excuse to her for not commencing her letter. But then there remained only two hours to her, and it might be that the letter would be difficult in the writing—would require thought and changes, and must needs be copied, perhaps more than once. As to the money, that she had in the house—as much, at least, as Mark now wanted, though the sending of it would leave her nearly penniless. She could, however, in case of personal need, resort to Davis as desired by him.

So she got out her desk in the drawing-room and sat down and wrote her letter. It was difficult, though she found that it hardly took so long as she expected. It was difficult, for she felt bound to tell him the truth; and yet she was anxious not to spoil all his pleasure among his friends. She told him, however, that Lady Lufton was very angry, "unreasonably angry, I must say," she put in, in order to show that she had not sided against him. "And indeed we have quite quarrelled, and this has made me unhappy, as it will you, dearest; I know that. But we both know how good she is at heart, and Justinia thinks that she had other things to trouble her; and I hope it will all be made up before you come home; only, dearest Mark, pray do not be longer than you said in your last letter." And then there were three or four paragraphs about the babies and two about the schools, which I may as well omit.

She had just finished her letter, and was carefully folding it for its envelope, with the two whole five-pound notes imprudently placed within it, when she heard a footstep on the gravel path which led up from a small wicket to the front-door. The path ran near the drawing-room window, and she was just in time to catch a glimpse of the last fold of a passing cloak. "It is Justinia," she said to herself; and her heart became disturbed at the idea of again discussing the morning's adventure. "What am I to do," she had said to herself before, "if she wants me to beg her pardon? I will not own before her that he is in the wrong."

And then the door opened—for the visitor made her entrance without the aid of any servant—and Lady Lufton herself stood before her. "Fanny," she said at once, "I have come to beg your pardon."

"Oh, Lady Lufton!"

"I was very much harassed when you came to me just now;—by more things than one, my dear. But, nevertheless, I should not have spoken to you of your husband as I did, and so I have come to beg your pardon."

Mrs. Robarts was past answering by the time that this was said,—past answering at least in words; so she jumped up and, with her eyes full of tears, threw herself into her old friend's arms. "Oh, Lady Lufton!" she sobbed forth again.

"You will forgive me, won't you?" said her ladyship, as she returned her young friend's caress. "Well, that's right. I have not been at all happy since you left my den this morning, and I don't suppose you have. But, Fanny, dearest, we love each other too well and know each other too thoroughly, to have a long quarrel, don't we?"

"Oh, yes, Lady Lufton."

"Of course we do. Friends are not to be picked up on the road-side every day; nor are they to be thrown away lightly. And now sit down, my love, and let us have a little talk. There, I must take my bonnet off. You have pulled the strings so that you have almost choked me." And Lady Lufton deposited her bonnet on the table and seated herself comfortably in the corner of the sofa.

"My dear," she said, "there is no duty which any woman owes to any other human being at all equal to that which she owes to her husband, and, therefore, you were quite right to stand up for Mr. Robarts this morning."

Upon this Mrs. Robarts said nothing, but she got her hand within that of her ladyship and gave it a slight squeeze.

"And I loved you for what you were doing all the time. I did, my dear; though you were a little fierce, you know. Even Justinia admits that, and she has been at me ever since you went away. And indeed, I did not know that it was in you to look in that way out of those pretty eyes of yours."

"Oh, Lady Lufton!"

"But I looked fierce enough too myself, I dare say; so we'll say nothing more about that; will we? But now, about this good man of yours?"

"Dear Lady Lufton, you must forgive him."

"Well: as you ask me, I will. We'll have nothing more said about the duke, either now or when he comes back; not a word. Let me see—he's to be back;—when is it?"

"Wednesday week, I think."

"Ah, Wednesday. Well, tell him to come and dine up at the house on Wednesday. He'll be in time, I suppose, and there shan't be a word said about this horrid duke."

"I am so much obliged to you, Lady Lufton."

"But look here, my dear; believe me, he's better off without such friends."

"Oh, I know he is; much better off."

"Well, I'm glad you admit that, for I thought you seemed to be in favour of the duke."

"Oh, no, Lady Lufton."

"That's right, then. And now, if you'll take my advice, you'll use your influence, as a good, dear sweet wife as you are, to prevent his going there any more. I'm an old woman and he is a young man, and it's very natural that he should think me behind the times. I'm not angry at that. But he'll find that it's better for him, better for him in every way, to stick to his old friends. It will be better for his peace of mind, better for his character as a clergyman, better for his pocket, better for his children and for you,—and better for his eternal welfare. The duke is not such a companion as he should seek;—nor if he is sought, should he allow himself to be led away."

And then Lady Lufton ceased, and Fanny Robarts kneeling at her feet sobbed, with her face hidden on her friend's knees. She had not a word now to say as to her husband's capability of judging for himself.

"And now I must be going again; but Justinia has made me promise,—promise, mind you, most solemnly, that I would have you back to dinner to-night,—by force if necessary. It was the only way I could make my peace with her; so you must not leave me in the lurch." Of course, Fanny said that she would go and dine at Framley Court.

"And you must not send that letter, by any means," said her ladyship as she was leaving the room, poking with her umbrella at the epistle, which lay directed on Mrs. Robarts's desk. "I can understand very well what it contains. You must alter it altogether, my dear." And then Lady Lufton went.

Mrs. Robarts instantly rushed to her desk and tore open her letter. She looked at her watch and it was past four. She had hardly begun another when the postman came. "Oh, Mary," she said, "do make him wait. If he'll wait a quarter of an hour I'll give him a shilling."

"There's no need of that, ma'am. Let him have a glass of beer."

"Very well, Mary; but don't give him too much, for fear he should drop the letters about. I'll be ready in ten minutes."

And in five minutes she had scrawled a very different sort of a letter. But he might want the money immediately, so she would not delay it for a day.

CHAPTER VI.

MR. HAROLD SMITH'S LECTURE.

On the whole the party at Chaldicotes was very pleasant, and the time passed away quickly enough. Mr. Robarts's chief friend there, independently of Mr. Sowerby, was Miss Dunstable, who seemed to take a great fancy to him, whereas she was not very accessible to the blandishments of Mr. Supplehouse, nor more specially courteous even to her host than good manners required of her. But then Mr. Supplehouse and Mr. Sowerby were both bachelors, while Mark Robarts was a married man.

With Mr. Sowerby Robarts had more than one communication respecting Lord Lufton and his affairs, which he would willingly have avoided had it been possible. Sowerby was one of those men who are always mixing up business with pleasure, and who have usually some scheme in their mind which requires forwarding. Men of this class have, as a rule, no daily work, no regular routine of labour; but it may be doubted whether they do not toil much more incessantly than those who have.

"Lufton is so dilatory," Mr. Sowerby said. "Why did he not arrange this at once, when he promised it? And then he is so afraid of that old woman at Framley Court. Well, my dear fellow, say what you will; she is an old woman and she'll never be younger. But do write to Lufton and tell him that this delay is inconvenient to me; he'll do anything for you, I know."

Mark said that he would write, and, indeed, did do so; but he did not at first like the tone of the conversation into which he was dragged. It was very painful to him to hear Lady Lufton called an old woman, and hardly less so to discuss the propriety of Lord Lufton's parting with his property. This was irksome to him, till habit made it easy. But by degrees his feelings became less acute, and he accustomed himself to his friend Sowerby's mode of talking.

And then on the Saturday afternoon they all went over to Barchester. Harold Smith during the last forty-eight hours had become crammed to overflowing with Sarawak, Labuan, New Guinea, and the Salomon Islands. As is the case with all men labouring under temporary specialities, he for the time had faith in nothing else, and was not content that any one near him should have any other faith. They called him Viscount Papua and Baron Borneo; and his wife, who headed the joke against him, insisted on her title. Miss Dunstable swore that she would wed none but a South Sea islander; and to Mark was offered the income and duties of Bishop of Spices. Nor did the Proudie family set themselves against these little sarcastic quips with any overwhelming severity. It is sweet to unbend oneself at the proper opportunity, and this was the proper opportunity for Mrs.

Proudie's unbending. No mortal can be seriously wise at all hours; and in these happy hours did that usually wise mortal, the bishop, lay aside for awhile his serious wisdom.

"We think of dining at five to-morrow, my Lady Papua," said the facetious bishop; "will that suit his lordship and the affairs of State? he! he! he!" And the good prelate laughed at the fun.

How pleasantly young men and women of fifty or thereabouts can joke and flirt and poke their fun about, laughing and holding their sides, dealing in little innuendoes and rejoicing in nicknames when they have no Mentors of twenty-five or thirty near them to keep them in order. The vicar of Framley might perhaps have been regarded as such a Mentor, were it not for that capability of adapting himself to the company immediately around him on which he so much piqued himself. He therefore also talked to my Lady Papua, and was jocose about the Baron,—not altogether to the satisfaction of Mr. Harold Smith himself.

For Mr. Harold Smith was in earnest and did not quite relish these jocundities. He had an idea that he could in about three months talk the British world into civilizing New Guinea, and that the world of Barsetshire would be made to go with him by one night's efforts. He did not understand why others should be less serious, and was inclined to resent somewhat stiffly the amenities of our friend Mark.

"We must not keep the Baron waiting," said Mark, as they were preparing to start for Barchester.

"I don't know what you mean by the Baron, sir," said Harold Smith. "But perhaps the joke will be against you, when you are getting up into your pulpit to-morrow and sending the hat round among the clodhoppers of Chaldicotes."

"Those who live in glass houses shouldn't throw stones; eh, Baron?" said Miss Dunstable. "Mr. Robarts's sermon will be too near akin to your lecture to allow of his laughing."

"If we can do nothing towards instructing the outer world till it's done by the parsons," said Harold Smith, "the outer world will have to wait a long time, I fear."

"Nobody can do anything of that kind short of a member of Parliament and a would-be minister," whispered Mrs. Harold.

And so they were all very pleasant together, in spite of a little fencing with edge-tools; and at three o'clock the *cortége* of carriages started for Barchester, that of the bishop, of course, leading the way. His lordship, however, was not in it.

"Mrs. Proudie, I'm sure you'll let me go with you," said Miss Dunstable, at the last moment, as she came down the big stone steps. "I want to hear the rest of that story about Mr. Slope."

Now this upset everything. The bishop was to have gone with his wife, Mrs. Smith, and Mark Robarts; and Mr. Sowerby had so arranged matters that he could have accompanied Miss Dunstable in his phaeton. But no one ever dreamed of denying Miss Dunstable anything. Of course Mark gave way; but it ended in the bishop declaring that he had no special predilection for his own carriage, which he did in compliance with a glance from his wife's eye. Then other changes of course followed, and, at last, Mr. Sowerby and Harold Smith were the joint occupants of the phaeton.

The poor lecturer, as he seated himself, made some remark such as those he had been making for the last two days—for out of a full heart the mouth speaketh. But he spoke to an impatient listener. "D—— the South Sea islanders," said Mr. Sowerby. "You'll have it all your own way in a few minutes, like a bull in a china-shop; but for Heaven's sake let us have a little peace till that time comes." It appeared that Mr. Sowerby's little plan of having Miss Dunstable for his companion was not quite insignificant; and, indeed, it may be said that but few of his little plans were so. At the present moment he flung himself back

844

in the carriage and prepared for sleep. He could further no plan of his by a *tête-à-tête* conversation with his brother-in-law.

And then Mrs. Proudie began her story about Mr. Slope, or rather recommenced it. She was very fond of talking about this gentleman, who had once been her pet chaplain but was now her bitterest foe; and in telling the story, she had sometimes to whisper to Miss Dunstable, for there were one or two fie-fie little anecdotes about a married lady, not altogether fit for young Mr. Robarts's ears. But Mrs. Harold Smith insisted on having them out loud, and Miss Dunstable would gratify that lady in spite of Mrs. Proudie's winks.

"What, kissing her hand, and he a clergyman!" said Miss Dunstable. "I did not think they ever did such things, Mr. Robarts."

"Still waters run deepest," said Mrs. Harold Smith.

"Hush-h-h," looked, rather than spoke, Mrs. Proudie. "The grief of spirit which that bad man caused me nearly broke my heart, and all the while, you know, he was courting—" and then Mrs. Proudie whispered a name.

"What, the dean's wife!" shouted Miss Dunstable, in a voice which made the coachman of the next carriage give a chuck to his horses as he overheard her.

"The archdeacon's sister-in-law!" screamed Mrs. Harold Smith.

"What might he not have attempted next?" said Miss Dunstable.

"She wasn't the dean's wife then, you know," said Mrs. Proudie, explaining.

"Well, you've a gay set in the chapter, I must say," said Miss Dunstable. "You ought to make one of them in Barchester, Mr. Robarts."

"Only perhaps Mrs. Robarts might not like it," said Mrs. Harold Smith.

"And then the schemes which he tried on with the bishop!" said Mrs. Proudie.

"It's all fair in love and war, you know," said Miss Dunstable.

"But he little knew whom he had to deal with when he began that," said Mrs. Proudie.

"The bishop was too many for him," suggested Mrs. Harold Smith, very maliciously.

"If the bishop was not, somebody else was; and he was obliged to leave Barchester in utter disgrace. He has since married the wife of some tallow-chandler."

"The wife!" said Miss Dunstable. "What a man!"

"Widow, I mean; but it's all one to him."

"The gentleman was clearly born when Venus was in the ascendant," said Mrs. Smith. "You clergymen usually are, I believe, Mr. Robarts." So that Mrs. Proudie's carriage was by no means the dullest as they drove into Barchester that day; and by degrees our friend Mark became accustomed to his companions, and before they reached the palace he acknowledged to himself that Miss Dunstable was very good fun.

We cannot linger over the bishop's dinner, though it was very good of its kind; and as Mr. Sowerby contrived to sit next to Miss Dunstable, thereby overturning a little scheme made by Mr. Supplehouse, he again shone forth in unclouded good humour. But Mr. Harold Smith became impatient immediately on the withdrawal of the cloth. The lecture was to begin at seven, and according to his watch that hour had already come. He declared that Sowerby and Supplehouse were endeavouring to delay matters in order that the Barchesterians might become vexed and impatient; and so the bishop was not allowed to exercise his hospitality in true episcopal fashion.

"You forget, Sowerby," said Supplehouse, "that the world here for the last fortnight has been looking forward to nothing else."

"The world shall be gratified at once," said Mrs. Harold, obeying a little nod from Mrs. Proudie. "Come, my dear," and she took hold of Miss Dunstable's arm, "don't let us keep Barchester waiting. We shall be ready in a quarter-of-an-hour, shall we not, Mrs. Proudie?" and so they sailed off.

"And we shall have time for one glass of claret," said the bishop.

"There; that's seven by the cathedral," said Harold Smith, jumping up from his chair as he heard the clock. "If the people have come it would not be right in me to keep them waiting, and I shall go."

"Just one glass of claret, Mr. Smith, and we'll be off," said the bishop.

"Those women will keep me an hour," said Harold, filling his glass, and drinking it standing. "They do it on purpose." He was thinking of his wife, but it seemed to the bishop as though his guest were actually speaking of Mrs. Proudie.

It was rather late when they all found themselves in the big room of the Mechanics' Institute; but I do not know whether this on the whole did them any harm. Most of Mr. Smith's hearers, excepting the party from the palace, were Barchester tradesmen with their wives and families; and they waited, not impatiently, for the big people. And then the lecture was gratis, a fact which is always borne in mind by an Englishman when he comes to reckon up and calculate the way in which he is treated. When he pays his money, then he takes his choice; he may be impatient or not as he likes. His sense of justice teaches him so much, and in accordance with that sense he usually acts.

So the people on the benches rose graciously when the palace party entered the room. Seats for them had been kept in the front. There were three arm-chairs, which were filled, after some little hesitation, by the bishop, Mrs. Proudie, and Miss Dunstable—Mrs. Smith positively declining to take one of them; though, as she admitted, her rank as Lady Papua of the islands did give her some claim. And this remark, as it was made quite out loud, reached Mr. Smith's ears as he stood behind a little table on a small raised dais, holding his white kid gloves; and it annoyed him and rather put him out. He did not like that joke about Lady Papua.

And then the others of the party sat upon a front bench covered with red cloth. "We shall find this very hard and very narrow about the second hour," said Mr. Sowerby, and Mr. Smith on his dais again overheard the words, and dashed his gloves down to the table. He felt that all the room would hear it.

And there were one or two gentlemen on the second seat who shook hands with some of our party. There was Mr. Thorne of Ullathorne, a good-natured old bachelor, whose residence was near enough to Barchester to allow of his coming in without much personal inconvenience; and next to him was Mr. Harding, an old clergyman of the chapter, with whom Mrs. Proudie shook hands very graciously, making way for him to seat himself close behind her if he would so please. But Mr. Harding did not so please. Having paid his respects to the bishop he returned quietly to the side of his old friend Mr. Thorne, thereby angering Mrs. Proudie, as might easily be seen by her face. And Mr. Chadwick also was there, the episcopal man of business for the diocese; but he also adhered to the two gentlemen above named.

And now that the bishop and the ladies had taken their places, Mr. Harold Smith relifted his gloves and again laid them down, hummed three times distinctly, and then began.

"It was," he said, "the most peculiar characteristic of the present era in the British islands that those who were high placed before the world in rank, wealth, and education were willing to come forward and give their time and knowledge without fee or reward, for the advantage and amelioration of those who did not stand so high in the social scale." And then he paused for a moment, during which Mrs. Smith remarked to Miss Dunstable that that was pretty well for a beginning; and Miss Dunstable replied, "that as for herself she felt very grateful to rank, wealth, and education." Mr. Sowerby winked to Mr. Supplehouse, who opened his eyes very wide and shrugged his shoulders. But the Barchesterians took it all in good part and gave the lecturer the applause of their hands and feet.

And then, well pleased, he recommenced—"I do not make these remarks with reference to myself—"

"I hope he's not going to be modest," said Miss Dunstable.

"It will be quite new if he is," replied Mrs. Smith.

"—so much as to many noble and talented lords and members of the Lower House who have lately from time to time devoted themselves to this good work." And then he went through a long list of peers and members of Parliament, beginning, of course, with Lord Boanerges, and ending with Mr. Green Walker, a young gentleman who had lately been returned by his uncle's interest for the borough of Crewe Junction, and had immediately made his entrance into public life by giving a lecture on the grammarians of the Latin language as exemplified at Eton school.

"On the present occasion," Mr. Smith continued, "our object is to learn something as to those grand and magnificent islands which lie far away, beyond the Indies, in the Southern Ocean; the lands of which produce rich spices and glorious fruits, and whose seas are imbedded with pearls and corals,—Papua and the Philippines, Borneo and the Moluccas. My friends, you are familiar with your maps, and you know the track which the equator makes for itself through those distant oceans." And then many heads were turned down, and there was a rustle of leaves; for not a few of those "who stood not so high in the social scale" had brought their maps with them, and refreshed their memories as to the whereabouts of these wondrous islands.

And then Mr. Smith also, with a map in his hand, and pointing occasionally to another large map which hung against the wall, went into the geography of the matter. "We might have found that out from our atlases, I think, without coming all the way to Barchester," said that unsympathizing helpmate, Mrs. Harold, very cruelly—most illogically too, for there be so many things which we could find out ourselves by search, but which we never do find out unless they be specially told us; and why should not the latitude and longitude of Labuan be one—or rather two of these things?

And then, when he had duly marked the path of the line through Borneo, Celebes, and Gilolo, through the Macassar strait and the Molucca passage, Mr. Harold Smith rose to a higher flight. "But what," said he, "avails all that God can give to man, unless man will open his hand to receive the gift? And what is this opening of the hand but the process of civilization—yes, my friends, the process of civilization? These South Sea islanders have all that a kind Providence can bestow on them; but that all is as nothing without education. That education and that civilization it is for you to bestow upon them—yes, my friends, for you; for you, citizens of Barchester as you are." And then he paused again, in order that the feet and hands might go to work. The feet and hands did go to work, during which Mr. Smith took a slight drink of water.

He was now quite in his element and had got into the proper way of punching the table with his fists. A few words dropping from Mr. Sowerby did now and again find their way to his ears, but the sound of his own voice had brought with it the accustomed charm, and he ran on from platitude to truism, and from truism back to platitude, with an eloquence that was charming to himself.

"Civilization," he exclaimed, lifting up his eyes and hands to the ceiling. "Oh, civilization—"

"There will not be a chance for us now for the next hour and a half," said Mr. Supplehouse, groaning.

Harold Smith cast one eye down at him, but it immediately flew back to the ceiling.

"Oh, civilization! thou that ennoblest mankind and makest him equal to the gods, what is like unto thee?" Here Mrs. Proudie showed evident signs of disapprobation, which no doubt would have been shared by the bishop, had not that worthy prelate been asleep. But Mr. Smith continued unobservant; or, at any rate, regardless.

"What is like unto thee? Thou art the irrigating stream which makest fertile the barren plain. Till thou comest all is dark and dreary; but at thy advent the noontide sun shines out, the earth gives forth her increase; the deep bowels of the rocks render up their tribute. Forms which were dull and hideous become endowed with grace and beauty, and vegetable existence rises to the scale of celestial life. Then, too, Genius appears clad in a panoply of translucent armour, grasping in his hand the whole terrestrial surface, and making every rood of earth subservient to his purposes;—Genius, the child of civilization, the mother of the Arts!"

The last little bit, taken from the Pedigree of Progress, had a great success, and all Barchester went to work with its hands and feet;—all Barchester, except that ill-natured aristocratic front-row together with the three arm-chairs at the corner of it. The aristocratic front-row felt itself to be too intimate with civilization to care much about it; and the three arm-chairs, or rather that special one which contained Mrs. Proudie, considered that there was a certain heathenness, a pagan sentimentality almost amounting to infidelity, contained in the lecturer's remarks, with which she, a pillar of the Church, could not put up, seated as she was now in public conclave.

"It is to civilization that we must look," continued Mr. Harold Smith, descending from poetry to prose as a lecturer well knows how, and thereby showing the value of both— "for any material progress in these islands; and—"

"And to Christianity," shouted Mrs. Proudie, to the great amazement of the assembled people and to the thorough wakening of the bishop, who, jumping up in his chair at the sound of the well-known voice, exclaimed, "Certainly, certainly."

"Hear, hear, hear," said those on the benches who particularly belonged to Mrs. Proudie's school of divinity in the city, and among the voices was distinctly heard that of a new verger in whose behalf she had greatly interested herself.

"Oh, yes, Christianity of course," said Harold Smith, upon whom the interruption did not seem to operate favourably.

"Christianity and Sabbath-day observance," exclaimed Mrs. Proudie, who, now that she had obtained the ear of the public, seemed well inclined to keep it. "Let us never forget that these islanders can never prosper unless they keep the Sabbath holy."

Poor Mr. Smith, having been so rudely dragged from his high horse, was never able to mount it again, and completed the lecture in a manner not at all comfortable to himself. He had there, on the table before him, a huge bundle of statistics with which he had meant to convince the reason of his hearers after he had taken full possession of their feelings. But they fell very dull and flat. And at the moment when he was interrupted he was about to explain that that material progress to which he had alluded could not be attained without money; and that it behoved them, the people of Barchester before him, to come forward with their purses like men and brothers. He did also attempt this; but from the moment of that fatal onslaught from the arm-chair, it was clear to him and to every one else, that Mrs. Proudie was now the hero of the hour. His time had gone by, and the people of Barchester did not care a straw for his appeal.

From these causes the lecture was over full twenty minutes earlier than any one had expected, to the great delight of Messrs. Sowerby and Supplehouse, who, on that evening, moved and carried a vote of thanks to Mrs. Proudie. For they had gay doings yet before they went to their beds.

"Robarts, here one moment," Mr. Sowerby said, as they were standing at the door of the Mechanics' Institute. "Don't you go off with Mr. and Mrs. Bishop. We are going to have a little supper at the Dragon of Wantly, and after what we have gone through upon my word we want it. You can tell one of the palace servants to let you in."

Mark considered the proposal wistfully. He would fain have joined the supper-party had he dared; but he, like many others of his cloth, had the fear of Mrs. Proudie before his eyes.

And a very merry supper they had; but poor Mr. Harold Smith was not the merriest of the party.

CHAPTER VII.

SUNDAY MORNING.

It was, perhaps, quite as well on the whole for Mark Robarts, that he did not go to that supper party. It was eleven o'clock before they sat down, and nearly two before the gentlemen were in bed. It must be remembered that he had to preach, on the coming Sunday morning, a charity sermon on behalf of a mission to Mr. Harold Smith's islanders; and, to tell the truth, it was a task for which he had now very little inclination.

When first invited to do this, he had regarded the task seriously enough, as he always did regard such work, and he completed his sermon for the occasion before he left Framley; but, since that, an air of ridicule had been thrown over the whole affair, in which he had joined without much thinking of his own sermon, and this made him now heartily wish that he could choose a discourse upon any other subject.

He knew well that the very points on which he had most insisted, were those which had drawn most mirth from Miss Dunstable and Mrs. Smith, and had oftenest provoked his own laughter; and how was he now to preach on those matters in a fitting mood, knowing, as he would know, that those two ladies would be looking at him, would endeavour to catch his eye, and would turn him into ridicule as they had already turned the lecturer?

In this he did injustice to one of the ladies, unconsciously. Miss Dunstable, with all her aptitude for mirth, and we may almost fairly say for frolic, was in no way inclined to ridicule religion or anything which she thought to appertain to it. It may be presumed that among such things she did not include Mrs. Proudie, as she was willing enough to laugh at that lady; but Mark, had he known her better, might have been sure that she would have sat out his sermon with perfect propriety.

As it was, however, he did feel considerable uneasiness; and in the morning he got up early with the view of seeing what might be done in the way of emendation. He cut out those parts which referred most specially to the islands,—he rejected altogether those names over which they had all laughed together so heartily,—and he inserted a string of general remarks, very useful, no doubt, which he flattered himself would rob his sermon of all similarity to Harold Smith's lecture. He had, perhaps, hoped, when writing it, to create some little sensation; but now he would be quite satisfied if it passed without remark.

But his troubles for that Sunday were destined to be many. It had been arranged that the party at the hotel should breakfast at eight, and start at half-past eight punctually, so as to enable them to reach Chaldicotes in ample time to arrange their dresses before they went to church. The church stood in the grounds, close to that long formal avenue of lime-trees, but within the front gates. Their walk, therefore, after reaching Mr. Sowerby's house, would not be long.

Mrs. Proudie, who was herself an early body, would not hear of her guest—and he a clergyman—going out to the inn for his breakfast on a Sunday morning. As regarded that Sabbath-day journey to Chaldicotes, to that she had given her assent, no doubt with much uneasiness of mind; but let them have as little desecration as possible. It was, therefore, an understood thing that he was to return with his friends; but he should not go without the advantage of family prayers and family breakfast. And so Mrs. Proudie on retiring to rest gave the necessary orders, to the great annoyance of her household.

To the great annoyance, at least, of her servants! The bishop himself did not make his appearance till a much later hour. He in all things now supported his wife's rule; in all things, now, I say; for there had been a moment, when in the first flush and pride of his episcopacy other ideas had filled his mind. Now, however, he gave no opposition to that good woman with whom Providence had blessed him; and in return for such conduct that good woman administered in all things to his little personal comforts. With what surprise did the bishop now look back upon that unholy war which he had once been tempted to wage against the wife of his bosom?

Nor did any of the Miss Proudies show themselves at that early hour. They, perhaps, were absent on a different ground. With them Mrs. Proudie had not been so successful as with the bishop. They had wills of their own which became stronger and stronger every day. Of the three with whom Mrs. Proudie was blessed one was already in a position to exercise that will in a legitimate way over a very excellent young clergyman in the diocese, the Rev. Optimus Grey; but the other two, having as yet no such opening for their powers of command, were perhaps a little too much inclined to keep themselves in practice at home.

But at half-past seven punctually Mrs. Proudie was there, and so was the domestic chaplain; so was Mr. Robarts, and so were the household servants,—all excepting one lazy recreant. "Where is Thomas?" said she of the Argus eyes, standing up with her book of family prayers in her hand. "So please you, ma'am, Tummas be bad with the tooth-ache." "Tooth-ache!" exclaimed Mrs. Proudie; but her eyes said more terrible things than that. "Let Thomas come to me before church." And then they proceeded to prayers. These were read by the chaplain, as it was proper and decent that they should be; but I cannot but think that Mrs. Proudie a little exceeded her office in taking upon herself to pronounce the blessing when the prayers were over. She did it, however, in a clear, sonorous voice, and perhaps with more personal dignity than was within the chaplain's compass.

Mrs. Proudie was rather stern at breakfast, and the vicar of Framley felt an unaccountable desire to get out of the house. In the first place she was not dressed with her usual punctilious attention to the proprieties of her high situation. It was evident that there was to be a further toilet before she sailed up the middle of the cathedral choir. She had on a large loose cap with no other strings than those which were wanted for tying it beneath her chin, a cap with which the household and the chaplain were well acquainted, but which seemed ungracious in the eyes of Mr. Robarts after all the well-dressed holiday doings of the last week. She wore also a large, loose, dark-coloured wrapper, which came well up round her neck, and which was not buoyed out, as were her dresses in general, with an under mechanism of petticoats. It clung to her closely, and added to the inflexibility of her general appearance. And then she had encased her feet in large carpet slippers, which no doubt were comfortable, but which struck her visitor as being strange and unsightly.

"Do you find a difficulty in getting your people together for early morning prayers?" she said, as she commenced her operations with the teapot.

"I can't say that I do," said Mark. "But then we are seldom so early as this."

"Parish clergymen should be early, I think," said she. "It sets a good example in the village."

"I am thinking of having morning prayers in the church," said Mr. Robarts.

"That's nonsense," said Mrs. Proudie, "and usually means worse than nonsense. I know what that comes to. If you have three services on Sunday and domestic prayers at home, you do very well." And so saying she handed him his cup.

"But I have not three services on Sunday, Mrs. Proudie."

"Then I think you should have. Where can the poor people be so well off on Sundays as in church? The bishop intends to express a very strong opinion on this subject in his next charge; and then I am sure you will attend to his wishes."

To this Mark made no answer, but devoted himself to his egg.

"I suppose you have not a very large establishment at Framley?" asked Mrs. Proudie.

"What, at the parsonage?"

"Yes; you live at the parsonage, don't you?"

"Certainly—well; not very large, Mrs. Proudie; just enough to do the work, make things comfortable, and look after the children."

"It is a very fine living," said she; "very fine. I don't remember that we have anything so good ourselves,—except it is Plumstead, the archdeacon's place. He has managed to butter his bread pretty well."

"His father was Bishop of Barchester."

"Oh, yes, I know all about him. Only for that he would barely have risen to be an archdeacon, I suspect. Let me see; yours is £800, is it not, Mr. Robarts? And you such a young man! I suppose you have insured your life highly."

"Pretty well, Mrs. Proudie."

"And then, too, your wife had some little fortune, had she not? We cannot all fall on our feet like that; can we, Mr. White?" and Mrs. Proudie in her playful way appealed to the chaplain.

Mrs. Proudie was an imperious woman; but then so also was Lady Lufton; and it may therefore be said that Mr. Robarts ought to have been accustomed to feminine domination; but as he sat there munching his toast he could not but make a comparison between the two. Lady Lufton in her little attempts sometimes angered him; but he certainly thought, comparing the lay lady and the clerical together, that the rule of the former was the lighter and the pleasanter. But then Lady Lufton had given him a living and a wife, and Mrs. Proudie had given him nothing.

Immediately after breakfast Mr. Robarts escaped to the Dragon of Wantly, partly because he had had enough of the matutinal Mrs. Proudie, and partly also in order that he might hurry his friends there. He was already becoming fidgety about the time, as Harold Smith had been on the preceding evening, and he did not give Mrs. Smith credit for much punctuality. When he arrived at the inn he asked if they had done breakfast, and was immediately told that not one of them was yet down. It was already half-past eight, and they ought to be now under weigh on the road.

He immediately went to Mr. Sowerby's room, and found that gentleman shaving himself. "Don't be a bit uneasy," said Mr. Sowerby. "You and Smith shall have my phaeton, and those horses will take you there in an hour. Not, however, but what we shall all be in time. We'll send round to the whole party and ferret them out." And then Mr. Sowerby, having evoked manifold aid with various peals of the bell, sent messengers, male and female, flying to all the different rooms.

"I think I'll hire a gig and go over at once," said Mark. "It would not do for me to be late, you know."

"It won't do for any of us to be late; and it's all nonsense about hiring a gig. It would be just throwing a sovereign away, and we should pass you on the road. Go down and see that the tea is made, and all that; and make them have the bill ready; and, Robarts, you may pay it too, if you like it. But I believe we may as well leave that to Baron Borneo—eh?"

And then Mark did go down and make the tea, and he did order the bill; and then he walked about the room, looking at his watch, and nervously waiting for the footsteps of his friends. And as he was so employed, he bethought himself whether it was fit that he should be so doing on a Sunday morning; whether it was good that he should be waiting there, in painful anxiety, to gallop over a dozen miles in order that he might not be too late with his sermon; whether his own snug room at home, with Fanny opposite to him, and his bairns crawling on the floor, with his own preparations for his own quiet service, and the warm pressure of Lady Lufton's hand when that service should be over, was not better than all this.

He could not afford not to know Harold Smith, and Mr. Sowerby, and the Duke of Omnium, he had said to himself. He had to look to rise in the world, as other men did. But what pleasure had come to him as yet from these intimacies? How much had he hitherto done towards his rising? To speak the truth he was not over well pleased with himself, as he made Mrs. Harold Smith's tea and ordered Mr. Sowerby's mutton-chops on that Sunday morning.

At a little after nine they all assembled; but even then he could not make the ladies understand that there was any cause for hurry; at least Mrs. Smith, who was the leader of the party, would not understand it. When Mark again talked of hiring a gig, Miss Dunstable indeed said that she would join him; and seemed to be so far earnest in the matter that Mr. Sowerby hurried through his second egg in order to prevent such a catastrophe. And then Mark absolutely did order the gig; whereupon Mrs. Smith remarked that in such case she need not hurry herself; but the waiter brought up word that all the horses of the hotel were out, excepting one pair, neither of which could go in single harness. Indeed, half of their stable establishment was already secured by Mr. Sowerby's own party.

"Then let me have the pair," said Mark, almost frantic with delay.

"Nonsense, Robarts; we are ready now. He won't want them, James. Come, Supplehouse, have you done?"

"Then I am to hurry myself, am I?" said Mrs. Harold Smith. "What changeable creatures you men are! May I be allowed half a cup more tea, Mr. Robarts?"

Mark, who was now really angry, turned away to the window. There was no charity in these people, he said to himself. They knew the nature of his distress, and yet they only laughed at him. He did not, perhaps, reflect that he had assisted in the joke against Harold Smith on the previous evening.

"James," said he, turning to the waiter, "let me have that pair of horses immediately, if you please."

"Yes, sir; round in fifteen minutes, sir: only Ned, sir, the post-boy, sir; I fear he's at his breakfast, sir; but we'll have him here in less than no time, sir!"

But before Ned and the pair were there, Mrs. Smith had absolutely got her bonnet on, and at ten they started. Mark did share the phaeton with Harold Smith, but the phaeton did not go any faster than the other carriages. They led the way, indeed, but that was all; and when the vicar's watch told him that it was eleven, they were still a mile from Chaldicotes' gate, although the horses were in a lather of steam; and they had only just entered the village when the church bells ceased to be heard.

"Come, you are in time, after all," said Harold Smith. "Better time than I was last night." Robarts could not explain to him that the entry of a clergyman into church, of a clergyman who is going to assist in the service, should not be made at the last minute, that it should be staid and decorous, and not done in scrambling haste, with running feet and scant breath.

"I suppose we'll stop here, sir," said the postilion, as he pulled up his horses short at the church-door, in the midst of the people who were congregated together ready for the service. But Mark had not anticipated being so late, and said at first that it was necessary that he should go on to the house; then, when the horses had again begun to move, he remembered that he could send for his gown, and as he got out of the carriage he gave his orders accordingly. And now the other two carriages were there, and so there was a noise and confusion at the door—very unseemly, as Mark felt it; and the gentlemen spoke in loud voices, and Mrs. Harold Smith declared that she had no prayer-book, and was much too tired to go in at present;—she would go home and rest herself, she said. And two other ladies of the party did so also, leaving Miss Dunstable to go alone;—for which, however, she did not care one button. And then one of the party, who had a nasty habit of swearing, cursed at something as he walked in close to Mark's elbow; and so they made their way up the church as the absolution was being read, and Mark Robarts felt thoroughly ashamed of himself. If his rising in the world brought him in contact with such things as these, would it not be better for him that he should do without rising?

His sermon went off without any special notice. Mrs. Harold Smith was not there, much to his satisfaction; and the others who were did not seem to pay any special attention to it. The subject had lost its novelty, except with the ordinary church congregation, the farmers and labourers of the parish; and the "quality" in the squire's great pew were content to show their sympathy by a moderate subscription. Miss Dunstable, however, gave a ten-pound note, which swelled up the sum total to a respectable amount—for such a place as Chaldicotes.

"And now I hope I may never hear another word about New Guinea," said Mr. Sowerby, as they all clustered round the drawing-room fire after church. "That subject may be regarded as having been killed and buried; eh, Harold?"

"Certainly murdered last night," said Mrs. Harold, "by that awful woman, Mrs. Proudie."

"I wonder you did not make a dash at her and pull her out of the arm-chair," said Miss Dunstable. "I was expecting it, and thought that I should come to grief in the scrimmage."

"I never knew a lady do such a brazen-faced thing before," said Miss Kerrigy, a travelling friend of Miss Dunstable's.

"Nor I—never; in a public place, too," said Dr. Easyman, a medical gentleman, who also often accompanied her.

"As for brass," said Mr. Supplehouse, "she would never stop at anything for want of that. It is well that she has enough, for the poor bishop is but badly provided."

"I hardly heard what it was she did say," said Harold Smith; "so I could not answer her, you know. Something about Sundays, I believe."

"She hoped you would not put the South Sea islanders up to Sabbath travelling," said Mr. Sowerby.

"And specially begged that you would establish Lord's-day schools," said Mrs. Smith; and then they all went to work and picked Mrs. Proudie to pieces from the top ribbon of her cap down to the sole of her slipper.

"And then she expects the poor parsons to fall in love with her daughters. That's the hardest thing of all," said Miss Dunstable.

But, on the whole, when our vicar went to bed he did not feel that he had spent a profitable Sunday.

CHAPTER VIII.

GATHERUM CASTLE.

On the Tuesday morning Mark did receive his wife's letter and the ten-pound note, whereby a strong proof was given of the honesty of the post-office people in Barsetshire. That letter, written as it had been in a hurry, while Robin post-boy was drinking a single mug of beer,—well, what of it if it was half filled a second time?—was nevertheless eloquent of his wife's love and of her great triumph.

> I have only half a moment to send you the money [she said], for the postman is here waiting. When I see you I'll explain why I am so hurried. Let me know that you get it safe. It is all right now, and Lady Lufton was here not a minute ago. She did not quite like it; about Gatherum Castle I mean; but you'll hear <u>nothing about it</u>. Only remember that <u>you must dine</u> at Framley Court on Wednesday week. <u>I have promised for you.</u> You will: won't you, dearest? I shall come and fetch you away if you attempt to stay longer than you have said. But I'm sure you won't. God bless you, my own one! Mr. Jones gave us the same sermon he preached the second Sunday after Easter. Twice in the same year is too often. God bless you! The children <u>are quite well</u>. Mark sends a big kiss.—Your own F.

Robarts, as he read this letter and crumpled the note up into his pocket, felt that it was much more satisfactory than he deserved. He knew that there must have been a fight, and that his wife, fighting loyally on his behalf, had got the best of it; and he knew also that her victory had not been owing to the goodness of her cause. He frequently declared to himself that he would not be afraid of Lady Lufton; but nevertheless these tidings that no reproaches were to be made to him afforded him great relief.

On the following Friday they all went to the duke's, and found that the bishop and Mrs. Proudie were there before them; as were also sundry other people, mostly of some note, either in the estimation of the world at large or of that of West Barsetshire. Lord Boanerges was there, an old man who would have his own way in everything, and who was regarded by all men—apparently even by the duke himself—as an intellectual king, by no means of the constitutional kind,—as an intellectual emperor, rather, who took upon himself to rule all questions of mind without the assistance of any ministers whatever. And Baron Brawl was of the party, one of her Majesty's puisne judges, as jovial a guest as ever entered a country house; but given to be rather sharp withal in his jovialities. And there was Mr. Green Walker, a young but rising man, the same who lectured not long since on a popular subject to his constituents at the Crewe Junction. Mr. Green Walker was a nephew of the Marchioness of Hartletop, and the Marchioness of Hartletop was a friend of the Duke of Omnium's. Mr. Mark Robarts was certainly elated when he ascertained who composed the company of which he had been so earnestly pressed to make a portion. Would it have been wise in him to forego this on account of the prejudices of Lady Lufton?

As the guests were so many and so great, the huge front portals of Gatherum Castle were thrown open, and the vast hall, adorned with trophies—with marble busts from Italy and armour from Wardour Street,—was thronged with gentlemen and ladies, and gave forth unwonted echoes to many a footstep. His grace himself, when Mark arrived there with Sowerby and Miss Dunstable—for in this instance Miss Dunstable did travel in the phaeton while Mark occupied a seat in the dicky—his grace himself was at this moment in the drawing-room, and nothing could exceed his urbanity.

"Oh, Miss Dunstable," he said, taking that lady by the hand, and leading her up to the fire, "now I feel for the first time that Gatherum Castle has not been built for nothing."

"Nobody ever supposed it was, your grace," said Miss Dunstable. "I am sure the architect did not think so when his bill was paid." And Miss Dunstable put her toes up on the fender to warm them with as much self-possession as though her father had been a duke also, instead of a quack doctor.

"We have given the strictest orders about the parrot," said the duke—

"Ah! but I have not brought him after all," said Miss Dunstable.

—"and I have had an aviary built on purpose,—just such as parrots are used to in their own country. Well, Miss Dunstable, I do call that unkind. Is it too late to send for him?"

"He and Dr. Easyman are travelling together. The truth was, I could not rob the doctor of his companion."

"Why? I have had another aviary built for him. I declare, Miss Dunstable, the honour you are doing me is shorn of half its glory. But the poodle—I still trust in the poodle."

"And your grace's trust shall not in that respect be in vain. Where is he, I wonder?" And Miss Dunstable looked round as though she expected that somebody would certainly have brought her dog in after her. "I declare I must go and look for him,—only think if they were to put him among your grace's dogs,—how his morals would be destroyed!"

"Miss Dunstable, is that intended to be personal?" But the lady had turned away from the fire, and the duke was able to welcome his other guests.

This he did with much courtesy. "Sowerby," he said, "I am glad to find that you have survived the lecture. I can assure you I had fears for you."

"I was brought back to life after considerable delay by the administration of tonics at the Dragon of Wantly. Will your grace allow me to present to you Mr. Robarts, who on that occasion was not so fortunate. It was found necessary to carry him off to the palace, where he was obliged to undergo very vigorous treatment."

And then the duke shook hands with Mr. Robarts, assuring him that he was most happy to make his acquaintance. He had often heard of him since he came into the county; and then he asked after Lord Lufton, regretting that he had been unable to induce his lordship to come to Gatherum Castle.

"But you had a diversion at the lecture, I am told," continued the duke. "There was a second performer, was there not, who almost eclipsed poor Harold Smith?" And then Mr. Sowerby gave an amusing sketch of the little Proudie episode.

"It has, of course, ruined your brother-in-law for ever as a lecturer," said the duke, laughing.

"If so, we shall feel ourselves under the deepest obligations to Mrs. Proudie," said Mr. Sowerby. And then Harold Smith himself came up and received the duke's sincere and hearty congratulations on the success of his enterprise at Barchester.

Mark Robarts had now turned away, and his attention was suddenly arrested by the loud voice of Miss Dunstable, who had stumbled across some very dear friends in her passage through the rooms, and who by no means hid from the public her delight upon the occasion.

"Well—well—well!" she exclaimed, and then she seized upon a very quiet-looking, well-dressed, attractive young woman who was walking towards her, in company with a gentleman. The gentleman and lady, as it turned out, were husband and wife. "Well—well—well! I hardly hoped for this." And then she took hold of the lady and kissed her enthusiastically, and after that grasped both the gentleman's hands, shaking them stoutly.

"And what a deal I shall have to say to you!" she went on. "You'll upset all my other plans. But, Mary, my dear, how long are you going to stay here? I go—let me see—I forget when, but it's all put down in a book upstairs. But the next stage is at Mrs. Proudie's. I shan't meet you there, I suppose. And now, Frank, how's the governor?"

The gentleman called Frank declared that the governor was all right—"mad about the hounds, of course, you know."

"Well, my dear, that's better than the hounds being mad about him, like the poor gentleman they've put into a statue. But talking of hounds, Frank, how badly they manage their foxes at Chaldicotes! I was out hunting all one day—"

"You out hunting!" said the lady called Mary.

"And why shouldn't I go out hunting? I'll tell you what, Mrs. Proudie was out hunting, too. But they didn't catch a single fox; and, if you must have the truth, it seemed to me to be rather slow."

"You were in the wrong division of the county," said the gentleman called Frank.

"Of course I was. When I really want to practise hunting I'll go to Greshamsbury; not a doubt about that."

"Or to Boxall Hill," said the lady; "you'll find quite as much zeal there as at Greshamsbury."

"And more discretion, you should add," said the gentleman.

"Ha! ha! ha!" laughed Miss Dunstable; "your discretion indeed! But you have not told me a word about Lady Arabella."

"My mother is quite well," said the gentleman.

"And the doctor? By-the-by, my dear, I've had such a letter from the doctor; only two days ago. I'll show it you upstairs to-morrow. But mind, it must be a positive secret. If he goes on in this way he'll get himself into the Tower, or Coventry, or a blue-book, or some dreadful place."

"Why; what has he said?"

"Never you mind, Master Frank: I don't mean to show you the letter, you may be sure of that. But if your wife will swear three times on a poker and tongs that she won't reveal, I'll show it to her. And so you are quite settled at Boxall Hill, are you?"

"Frank's horses are settled; and the dogs nearly so," said Frank's wife; "but I can't boast much of anything else yet."

"Well, there's a good time coming. I must go and change my things now. But, Mary, mind you get near me this evening; I have such a deal to say to you." And then Miss Dunstable marched out of the room.

All this had been said in so loud a voice that it was, as a matter of course, overheard by Mark Robarts—that part of the conversation of course I mean which had come from Miss Dunstable. And then Mark learned that this was young Frank Gresham of Boxall Hill, son of old Mr. Gresham of Greshamsbury. Frank had lately married a great heiress; a greater heiress, men said, even than Miss Dunstable; and as the marriage was hardly as yet more than six months old the Barsetshire world was still full of it.

"The two heiresses seem to be very loving, don't they?" said Mr. Supplehouse. "Birds of a feather flock together, you know. But they did say some little time ago that young Gresham was to have married Miss Dunstable himself."

"Miss Dunstable! why she might almost be his mother," said Mark.

"That makes but little difference. He was obliged to marry money, and I believe there is no doubt that he did at one time propose to Miss Dunstable."

"I have had a letter from Lufton," Mr. Sowerby said to him the next morning. "He declares that the delay was all your fault. You were to have told Lady Lufton before he did anything, and he was waiting to write about it till he heard from you. It seems that you never said a word to her ladyship on the subject."

"I never did, certainly. My commission from Lufton was to break the matter to her when I found her in a proper humour for receiving it. If you knew Lady Lufton as well as I do, you would know that it is not every day that she would be in a humour for such tidings."

"And so I was to be kept waiting indefinitely because you two between you were afraid of an old woman! However I have not a word to say against her, and the matter is settled now."

"Has the farm been sold?"

"Not a bit of it. The dowager could not bring her mind to suffer such profanation for the Lufton acres, and so she sold five thousand pounds out of the funds and sent the money to Lufton as a present;—sent it to him without saying a word, only hoping that it would suffice for his wants. I wish I had a mother, I know."

Mark found it impossible at the moment to make any remark upon what had been told him, but he felt a sudden qualm of conscience and a wish that he was at Framley instead of at Gatherum Castle at the present moment. He knew a good deal respecting Lady Lufton's income and the manner in which it was spent. It was very handsome for a single lady, but then she lived in a free and open-handed style; her charities were noble; there was no reason why she should save money, and her annual income was usually spent within the year. Mark knew this, and he knew also that nothing short of an impossibility to maintain them would induce her to lessen her charities. She had now given away a portion of her principal to save the property of her son—her son, who was so much more opulent than herself,—upon whose means, too, the world made fewer effectual claims.

And Mark knew, too, something of the purpose for which this money had gone. There had been unsettled gambling claims between Sowerby and Lord Lufton, originating in affairs of the turf. It had now been going on for four years, almost from the period when Lord Lufton had become of age. He had before now spoken to Robarts on the matter with much bitter anger, alleging that Mr. Sowerby was treating him unfairly, nay, dishonestly—that he was claiming money that was not due to him; and then he declared more than once that he would bring the matter before the Jockey Club. But Mark, knowing that Lord Lufton was not clear-sighted in these matters, and believing it to be impossible that Mr. Sowerby should actually endeavour to defraud his friend, had smoothed down the young lord's anger, and recommended him to get the case referred to some private arbiter. All this had afterwards been discussed between Robarts and Mr. Sowerby himself, and hence had originated their intimacy. The matter was so referred, Mr. Sowerby naming the referee; and Lord Lufton, when the matter was given against him, took it easily. His anger was over by that time. "I've been clean done among them," he said to Mark, laughing; "but it does not signify; a man must pay for his experience. Of course, Sowerby thinks it all right;

I am bound to suppose so." And then there had been some further delay as to the amount, and part of the money had been paid to a third person, and a bill had been given, and heaven and the Jews only know how much money Lord Lufton had paid in all; and now it was ended by his handing over to some wretched villain of a money-dealer, on behalf of Mr. Sowerby, the enormous sum of five thousand pounds, which had been deducted from the means of his mother, Lady Lufton!

Mark, as he thought of all this, could not but feel a certain animosity against Mr. Sowerby—could not but suspect that he was a bad man. Nay, must he not have known that he was very bad? And yet he continued walking with him through the duke's grounds, still talking about Lord Lufton's affairs, and still listening with interest to what Sowerby told him of his own.

"No man was ever robbed as I have been," said he. "But I shall win through yet, in spite of them all. But those Jews, Mark"—he had become very intimate with him in these latter days—"whatever you do, keep clear of them. Why, I could paper a room with their signatures; and yet I never had a claim upon one of them, though they always have claims on me!"

I have said above that this affair of Lord Lufton's was ended; but it now appeared to Mark that it was not *quite* ended. "Tell Lufton, you know," said Sowerby, "that every bit of paper with his name has been taken up, except what that ruffian Tozer has. Tozer may have one bill, I believe,—something that was not given up when it was renewed. But I'll make my lawyer Gumption get that up. It may cost ten pounds or twenty pounds, not more. You'll remember that when you see Lufton, will you?"

"You'll see Lufton in all probability before I shall."

"Oh, did I not tell you? He's going to Framley Court at once; you'll find him there when you return."

"Find him at Framley!"

"Yes; this little *cadeau* from his mother has touched his filial heart. He is rushing home to Framley to pay back the dowager's hard moidores in soft caresses. I wish I had a mother; I know that."

And Mark still felt that he feared Mr. Sowerby, but he could not make up his mind to break away from him.

And there was much talk of politics just then at the castle. Not that the duke joined in it with any enthusiasm. He was a Whig—a huge mountain of a colossal Whig—all the world knew that. No opponent would have dreamed of tampering with his whiggery, nor would any brother Whig have dreamed of doubting it. But he was a Whig who gave very little practical support to any set of men, and very little practical opposition to any other set. He was above troubling himself with such sublunar matters. At election time he supported, and always carried, Whig candidates; and in return he had been appointed lord lieutenant of the county by one Whig minister, and had received the Garter from another. But these things were matters of course to a Duke of Omnium. He was born to be a lord lieutenant and a knight of the Garter.

But not the less on account of his apathy, or rather quiescence, was it thought that Gatherum Castle was a fitting place in which politicians might express to each other their present hopes and future aims, and concoct together little plots in a half-serious and half-mocking way. Indeed it was hinted that Mr. Supplehouse and Harold Smith, with one or two others, were at Gatherum for this express purpose. Mr. Fothergill, too, was a noted politician, and was supposed to know the duke's mind well; and Mr. Green Walker, the nephew of the marchioness, was a young man whom the duke desired to have brought forward. Mr. Sowerby also was the duke's own member, and so the occasion suited well for the interchange of a few ideas.

The then prime minister, angry as many men were with him, had not been altogether unsuccessful. He had brought the Russian war to a close, which, if not glorious, was at any rate much more so than Englishmen at one time had ventured to hope. And he had had wonderful luck in that Indian mutiny. It is true that many of those even who voted with him would declare that this was in no way attributable to him. Great men had risen in India and done all that. Even his minister there, the governor whom he had sent out, was not allowed in those days any credit for the success which was achieved under his orders. There was great reason to doubt the man at the helm. But nevertheless he had been lucky. There is no merit in a public man like success!

But now, when the evil days were well nigh over, came the question whether he had not been too successful. When a man has nailed fortune to his chariot-wheels he is apt to travel about in rather a proud fashion. There are servants who think that their masters cannot do without them; and the public also may occasionally have some such servant. What if this too successful minister were one of them!

And then a discreet, commonplace, zealous member of the Lower House does not like to be jeered at, when he does his duty by his constituents and asks a few questions. An all-successful minister who cannot keep his triumph to himself, but must needs drive about in a proud fashion, laughing at commonplace zealous members—laughing even occasionally at members who are by no means commonplace, which is outrageous!—may it not be as well to ostracize him for awhile?

"Had we not better throw in our shells against him?" says Mr. Harold Smith.

"Let us throw in our shells, by all means," says Mr. Supplehouse, mindful as Juno of his despised charms. And when Mr. Supplehouse declares himself an enemy, men know how much it means. They know that that much-belaboured head of affairs must succumb to the terrible blows which are now in store for him. "Yes, we will throw in our shells." And Mr. Supplehouse rises from his chair with gleaming eyes. "Has not Greece as noble sons as him? ay, and much nobler, traitor that he is. We must judge a man by his friends," says Mr. Supplehouse; and he points away to the East, where our dear allies the French are supposed to live, and where our head of affairs is supposed to have too close an intimacy.

They all understand this, even Mr. Green Walker. "I don't know that he is any good to any of us at all, now," says the talented member for the Crewe Junction. "He's a great deal too uppish to suit my book; and I know a great many people that think so too. There's my uncle—"

"He's the best fellow in the world," said Mr. Fothergill, who felt, perhaps, that that coming revelation about Mr. Green Walker's uncle might not be of use to them; "but the fact is one gets tired of the same man always. One does not like partridge every day. As for me, I have nothing to do with it myself; but I would certainly like to change the dish."

"If we're merely to do as we are bid, and have no voice of our own, I don't see what's the good of going to the shop at all," said Mr. Sowerby.

"Not the least use," said Mr. Supplehouse. "We are false to our constituents in submitting to such a dominion."

"Let's have a change, then," said Mr. Sowerby. "The matter's pretty much in our own hands."

"Altogether," said Mr. Green Walker. "That's what my uncle always says."

"The Manchester men will only be too happy for the chance," said Harold Smith.

"And as for the high and dry gentlemen," said Mr. Sowerby, "it's not very likely that they will object to pick up the fruit when we shake the tree."

"As to picking up the fruit, that's as may be," said Mr. Supplehouse. Was he not the man to save the nation; and if so, why should he not pick up the fruit himself? Had not the greatest power in the country pointed him out as such a saviour? What though the country at the present moment needed no more saving, might there not, nevertheless, be a good time coming? Were there not rumours of other wars still prevalent—if indeed the actual war then going on was being brought to a close without his assistance by some other species of salvation? He thought of that country to which he had pointed, and of that friend of his enemies, and remembered that there might be still work for a mighty saviour. The public mind was now awake, and understood what it was about. When a man gets into his head an idea that the public voice calls for him, it is astonishing how great becomes his trust in the wisdom of the public. *Vox populi vox Dei.* "Has it not been so always?" he says to himself, as he gets up and as he goes to bed. And then Mr. Supplehouse felt that he was the master mind there at Gatherum Castle, and that those there were all puppets in his hand. It is such a pleasant thing to feel that one's friends are puppets, and that the strings are in one's own possession. But what if Mr. Supplehouse himself were a puppet?

Some months afterwards, when the much-belaboured head of affairs was in very truth made to retire, when unkind shells were thrown in against him in great numbers, when he exclaimed, "*Et tu, Brute!*" till the words were stereotyped upon his lips, all men in all places talked much about the great Gatherum Castle confederation. The Duke of Omnium, the world said, had taken into his high consideration the state of affairs, and seeing with his eagle's eye that the welfare of his countrymen at large required that some great step should be initiated, he had at once summoned to his mansion many members of the Lower House, and some also of the House of Lords,—mention was here especially made of the all-venerable and all-wise Lord Boanerges; and men went on to say that there, in deep conclave, he had made known to them his views. It was thus agreed that the head of affairs, Whig as he was, must fall. The country required it, and the duke did his duty. This was the beginning, the world said, of that celebrated confederation, by which the ministry was overturned, and—as the *Goody Twoshoes* added,—the country saved. But the *Jupiter* took all the credit to itself; and the *Jupiter* was not far wrong. All the credit was due to the *Jupiter*—in that, as in everything else.

In the meantime the Duke of Omnium entertained his guests in the quiet princely style, but did not condescend to have much conversation on politics either with Mr. Supplehouse or with Mr. Harold Smith. And as for Lord Boanerges, he spent the morning on which the above-described conversation took place in teaching Miss Dunstable to blow soap-bubbles on scientific principles.

"Dear, dear!" said Miss Dunstable, as sparks of knowledge came flying in upon her mind. "I always thought that a soap-bubble was a soap-bubble, and I never asked the reason why. One doesn't, you know, my lord."

"Pardon me, Miss Dunstable," said the old lord, "one does; but nine hundred and ninety-nine do not."

"And the nine hundred and ninety-nine have the best of it," said Miss Dunstable. "What pleasure can one have in a ghost after one has seen the phosphorus rubbed on?"

"Quite true, my dear lady. 'If ignorance be bliss, 'tis folly to be wise.' It all lies in the 'if.'"

Then Miss Dunstable began to sing:—

> "'What tho' I trace each herb and flower
> That sips the morning dew—'

—you know the rest, my lord." Lord Boanerges did know almost everything, but he did not know that; and so Miss Dunstable went on:—

> "'Did I not own Jehovah's power
> How vain were all I knew.'"

"Exactly, exactly, Miss Dunstable," said his lordship; "but why not own the power and trace the flower as well? perhaps one might help the other."

Upon the whole I am afraid that Lord Boanerges got the best of it. But then that is his line. He has been getting the best of it all his life.

It was observed by all that the duke was especially attentive to young Mr. Frank Gresham, the gentleman on whom and on whose wife Miss Dunstable had seized so vehemently. This Mr. Gresham was the richest commoner in the county, and it was rumoured that at the next election he would be one of the members for the East Riding. Now the duke had little or nothing to do with the East Riding, and it was well known that young Gresham would be brought forward as a strong conservative. But, nevertheless, his acres were so extensive and his money so plentiful that he was worth a duke's notice. Mr. Sowerby also was almost more than civil to him, as was natural, seeing that this very young man by a mere scratch of his pen could turn a scrap of paper into a bank-note of almost fabulous value.

"So you have the East Barsetshire hounds at Boxall Hill; have you not?" said the duke.

"The hounds are there," said Frank. "But I am not the master."

"Oh! I understood—"

"My father has them. But he finds Boxall Hill more centrical than Greshamsbury. The dogs and horses have to go shorter distances."

"Boxall Hill is very centrical."

"Oh, exactly!"

"And your young gorse coverts are doing well?"

"Pretty well—gorse won't thrive everywhere, I find. I wish it would."

"That's just what I say to Fothergill; and then where there's much woodland you can't get the vermin to leave it."

"But we haven't a tree at Boxall Hill," said Mrs. Gresham.

"Ah, yes; you're new there, certainly; you've enough of it at Greshamsbury in all conscience. There's a larger extent of wood there than we have; isn't there, Fothergill?"

Mr. Fothergill said that the Greshamsbury woods were very extensive, but that, perhaps, he thought—

"Oh, ah! I know," said the duke. "The Black Forest in its old days was nothing to Gatherum woods, according to Fothergill. And then again, nothing in East Barsetshire could be equal to anything in West Barsetshire. Isn't that it; eh, Fothergill?"

Mr. Fothergill professed that he had been brought up in that faith and intended to die in it.

"Your exotics at Boxall Hill are very fine, magnificent!" said Mr. Sowerby.

"I'd sooner have one full-grown oak standing in its pride alone," said young Gresham, rather grandiloquently, "than all the exotics in the world."

"They'll come in due time," said the duke.

"But the due time won't be in my days. And so they're going to cut down Chaldicotes forest, are they, Mr. Sowerby?"

"Well, I can't tell you that. They are going to disforest it. I have been ranger since I was twenty-two, and I don't yet know whether that means cutting down."

"Not only cutting down, but rooting up," said Mr. Fothergill.

"It's a murderous shame," said Frank Gresham; "and I will say one thing, I don't think any but a Whig government would do it."

"Ha, ha, ha!" laughed his grace. "At any rate I'm sure of this," he said, "that if a conservative government did do so, the Whigs would be just as indignant as you are now."

"I'll tell you what you ought to do, Mr. Gresham," said Sowerby: "put in an offer for the whole of the West Barsetshire crown property; they will be very glad to sell it."

"And we should be delighted to welcome you on this side of the border," said the duke.

Young Gresham did feel rather flattered. There were not many men in the county to whom such an offer could be made without an absurdity. It might be doubted whether the duke himself could purchase the Chace of Chaldicotes with ready money; but that he, Gresham, could do so—he and his wife between them—no man did doubt. And then Mr. Gresham thought of a former day when he had once been at Gatherum Castle. He had been poor enough then, and the duke had not treated him in the most courteous manner in the world. How hard it is for a rich man not to lean upon his riches! harder, indeed, than for a camel to go through the eye of a needle.

All Barsetshire knew—at any rate all West Barsetshire—that Miss Dunstable had been brought down in those parts in order that Mr. Sowerby might marry her. It was not sur-mised that Miss Dunstable herself had had any previous notice of this arrangement, but it was supposed that the thing would turn out as a matter of course. Mr. Sowerby had no money, but then he was witty, clever, good-looking, and a member of Parliament. He lived before the world, represented an old family, and had an old place. How could Miss Dunstable possibly do better? She was not so young now, and it was time that she should look about her.

The suggestion as regarded Mr. Sowerby was certainly true, and was not the less so as regarded some of Mr. Sowerby's friends. His sister, Mrs. Harold Smith, had devoted her-self to the work, and with this view had run up a dear friendship with Miss Dunstable. The bishop had intimated, nodding his head knowingly, that it would be a very good thing. Mrs. Proudie had given in her adherence. Mr. Supplehouse had been made to understand that it must be a case of "Paws off" with him, as long as he remained in that part of the world; and even the duke himself had desired Fothergill to manage it.

"He owes me an enormous sum of money," said the duke, who held all Mr. Sowerby's title-deeds, "and I doubt whether the security will be sufficient."

"Your grace will find the security quite sufficient," said Mr. Fothergill; "but neverthe-less it would be a good match."

"Very good," said the duke. And then it became Mr. Fothergill's duty to see that Mr. Sowerby and Miss Dunstable became man and wife as speedily as possible.

Some of the party, who were more wide awake than others, declared that he had made the offer; others, that he was just going to do so; and one very knowing lady went so far at one time as to say that he was making it at that moment. Bets also were laid as to the la-dy's answer, as to the terms of the settlement, and as to the period of the marriage,—of all which poor Miss Dunstable of course knew nothing.

Mr. Sowerby, in spite of the publicity of his proceedings, proceeded in the matter very well. He said little about it to those who joked with him, but carried on the fight with what best knowledge he had in such matters. But so much it is given to us to declare with cer-tainty, that he had not proposed on the evening previous to the morning fixed for the departure of Mark Robarts.

During the last two days Mr. Sowerby's intimacy with Mark had grown warmer and warmer. He had talked to the vicar confidentially about the doings of these bigwigs now present at the castle, as though there were no other guest there with whom he could speak in so free a manner. He confided, it seemed, much more in Mark than in his brother-in-law, Harold Smith, or in any of his brother members of Parliament, and had altogether opened his heart to him in this affair of his anticipated marriage. Now Mr. Sowerby was a man of mark in the world, and all this flattered our young clergyman not a little.

On that evening before Robarts went away Sowerby asked him to come up into his bedroom when the whole party was breaking up, and there got him into an easy-chair while he, Sowerby, walked up and down the room.

"You can hardly tell, my dear fellow," said he, "the state of nervous anxiety in which this puts me."

"Why don't you ask her and have done with it? She seems to me to be fond of your society."

"Ah, it is not that only; there are wheels within wheels;" and then he walked once or twice up and down the room, during which Mark thought that he might as well go to bed.

"Not that I mind telling you everything," said Sowerby. "I am infernally hard up for a little ready money just at the present moment. It may be, and indeed I think it will be, the case that I shall be ruined in this matter for the want of it."

"Could not Harold Smith give it you?"

"Ha, ha, ha! you don't know Harold Smith. Did you ever hear of his lending a man a shilling in his life?"

"Or Supplehouse?"

"Lord love you! You see me and Supplehouse together here, and he comes and stays at my house, and all that; but Supplehouse and I are no friends. Look you here, Mark—I would do more for your little finger than for his whole hand, including the pen which he holds in it. Fothergill indeed might—but then I know Fothergill is pressed himself at the present moment. It is deuced hard, isn't it? I must give up the whole game if I can't put my hand upon £400 within the next two days."

"Ask her for it, herself."

"What, the woman I wish to marry! No, Mark, I'm not quite come to that. I would sooner lose her than that."

Mark sat silent, gazing at the fire and wishing that he was in his own bedroom. He had an idea that Mr. Sowerby wished him to produce this £400; and he knew also that he had not £400 in the world, and that if he had he would be acting very foolishly to give it to Mr. Sowerby. But nevertheless he felt half fascinated by the man, and half afraid of him.

"Lufton owes it to me to do more than this," continued Mr. Sowerby; "but then Lufton is not here."

"Why, he has just paid five thousand pounds for you."

"Paid five thousand pounds for me! Indeed he has done no such thing: not a sixpence of it came into my hands. Believe me, Mark, you don't know the whole of that yet. Not that I mean to say a word against Lufton. He is the soul of honour; though so deucedly dilatory in money matters. He thought he was right all through that affair, but no man was ever so confoundedly wrong. Why, don't you remember that that was the very view you took of it yourself?"

"I remember saying that I thought he was mistaken."

"Of course he was mistaken. And dearly the mistake cost me. I had to make good the money for two or three years. And my property is not like his—I wish it were."

"Marry Miss Dunstable, and that will set it all right for you."

"Ah! so I would if I had this money. At any rate I would bring it to the point. Now, I tell you what, Mark; if you'll assist me at this strait I'll never forget it. And the time will come round when I may be able to do something for you."

"I have not got a hundred, no, not fifty pounds by me in the world."

"Of course you've not. Men don't walk about the streets with £400 in their pockets. I don't suppose there's a single man here in the house with such a sum at his bankers', unless it be the duke."

"What is it you want then?"

"Why, your name, to be sure. Believe me, my dear fellow, I would not ask you really to put your hand into your pocket to such a tune as that. Allow me to draw on you for that amount at three months. Long before that time I shall be flush enough." And then, before Mark could answer, he had a bill stamp and pen and ink out on the table before him, and was filling in the bill as though his friend had already given his consent.

"Upon my word, Sowerby, I had rather not do that."

"Why! what are you afraid of?"—Mr. Sowerby asked this very sharply. "Did you ever hear of my having neglected to take up a bill when it fell due?" Robarts thought that he had heard of such a thing; but in his confusion he was not exactly sure, and so he said nothing.

"No, my boy; I have not come to that. Look here: just you write, 'Accepted, Mark Robarts,' across that, and then you shall never hear of the transaction again;—and you will have obliged me for ever."

"As a clergyman it would be wrong of me," said Robarts.

"As a clergyman! Come, Mark! If you don't like to do as much as that for a friend, say so; but don't let us have that sort of humbug. If there be one class of men whose names would be found more frequent on the backs of bills in the provincial banks than another, clergymen are that class. Come, old fellow, you won't throw me over when I am so hard pushed."

Mark Robarts took the pen and signed the bill. It was the first time in his life that he had ever done such an act. Sowerby then shook him cordially by the hand, and he walked off to his own bedroom a wretched man.

CHAPTER IX.

THE VICAR'S RETURN.

The next morning Mr. Robarts took leave of all his grand friends with a heavy heart. He had lain awake half the night thinking of what he had done and trying to reconcile himself to his position. He had not well left Mr. Sowerby's room before he felt certain that at the end of three months he would again be troubled about that £400. As he went along the passage all the man's known antecedents crowded upon him much quicker than he could remember them when seated in that arm-chair with the bill stamp before him, and the pen and ink ready to his hand. He remembered what Lord Lufton had told him—how he had complained of having been left in the lurch; he thought of all the stories current through the entire county as to the impossibility of getting money from Chaldicotes; he brought to mind the known character of the man, and then he knew that he must prepare himself to make good a portion at least of that heavy payment.

Why had he come to this horrid place? Had he not everything at home at Framley which the heart of man could desire? No; the heart of man can desire deaneries—the heart, that is, of the man vicar; and the heart of the man dean can desire bishoprics; and before the eyes of the man bishop does there not loom the transcendental glory of Lambeth? He had owned to himself that he was ambitious; but he had to own to himself now also that he had hitherto taken but a sorry path towards the object of his ambition.

On the next morning at breakfast-time, before his horse and gig arrived for him, no one was so bright as his friend Sowerby. "So you are off, are you?" said he.

"Yes, I shall go this morning."

"Say everything that's kind from me to Lufton. I may possibly see him out hunting; otherwise we shan't meet till the spring. As to my going to Framley, that's out of the question. Her ladyship would look for my tail, and swear that she smelt brimstone. By-bye, old fellow!"

The German student when he first made his bargain with the devil felt an indescribable attraction to his new friend; and such was the case now with Robarts. He shook Sowerby's hand very warmly, said that he hoped he should meet him soon somewhere, and professed himself specially anxious to hear how that affair with the lady came off. As he had made his bargain—as he had undertaken to pay nearly half-a-year's income for his dear friend—ought he not to have as much value as possible for his money? If the dear friendship of this flash member of Parliament did not represent that value, what else did do so? But then he felt, or fancied that he felt, that Mr. Sowerby did not care for him so much this morning as he had done on the previous evening. "By-bye," said Mr. Sowerby, but he spoke no word as to such future meetings, nor did he even promise to write. Mr. Sowerby probably had many things on his mind; and it might be that it behoved him, having finished one piece of business, immediately to look to another.

The sum for which Robarts had made himself responsible—which he so much feared that he would be called upon to pay—was very nearly half-a-year's income; and as yet he had not put by one shilling since he had been married. When he found himself settled in his parsonage, he found also that all the world regarded him as a rich man. He had taken the dictum of all the world as true, and had set himself to work to live comfortably. He had no absolute need of a curate; but he could afford the £70—as Lady Lufton had said rather injudiciously; and by keeping Jones in the parish he would be acting charitably to a brother clergyman, and would also place himself in a more independent position. Lady Lufton had wished to see her pet clergyman well-to-do and comfortable; but now, as matters had turned out, she much regretted this affair of the curate. Mr. Jones, she said to herself, more than once, must be made to depart from Framley.

He had given his wife a pony-carriage, and for himself he had a saddle-horse, and a second horse for his gig. A man in his position, well-to-do as he was, required as much as that. He had a footman also, and a gardener, and a groom. The two latter were absolutely necessary, but about the former there had been a question. His wife had been decidedly hostile to the footman; but, in all such matters as that, to doubt is to be lost. When the footman had been discussed for a week it became quite clear to the master that he also was a necessary.

As he drove home that morning he pronounced to himself the doom of that footman, and the doom also of that saddle-horse. They at any rate should go. And then he would spend no more money in trips to Scotland; and above all, he would keep out of the bedrooms of impoverished members of Parliament at the witching hour of midnight. Such resolves did he make to himself as he drove home; and bethought himself wearily how that £400 might be made to be forthcoming. As to any assistance in the matter from Sowerby,—of that he gave himself no promise.

But he almost felt himself happy again as his wife came out into the porch to meet him, with a silk shawl over her head, and pretending to shiver as she watched him descending from his gig.

"My dear old man," she said, as she led him into the warm drawing-room with all his wrappings still about him, "you must be starved." But Mark during the whole drive had been thinking too much of that transaction in Mr. Sowerby's bedroom to remember that the air was cold. Now he had his arm round his own dear Fanny's waist; but was he to tell her of that transaction? At any rate he would not do it now, while his two boys were in his arms, rubbing the moisture from his whiskers with their kisses. After all, what is there equal to that coming home?

"And so Lufton is here. I say, Frank, gently, old boy,"—Frank was his eldest son— "you'll have baby into the fender."

"Let me take baby; it's impossible to hold the two of them, they are so strong," said the proud mother. "Oh, yes, he came home early yesterday."

"Have you seen him?"

"He was here yesterday, with her ladyship; and I lunched there to-day. The letter came, you know, in time to stop the Merediths. They don't go till to-morrow, so you will meet them after all. Sir George is wild about it, but Lady Lufton would have her way. You never saw her in such a state as she is."

"Good spirits, eh?"

"I should think so. All Lord Lufton's horses are coming, and he's to be here till March."

"Till March!"

"So her ladyship whispered to me. She could not conceal her triumph at his coming. He's going to give up Leicestershire this year altogether. I wonder what has brought it all about?" Mark knew very well what had brought it about; he had been made acquainted, as the reader has also, with the price at which Lady Lufton had purchased her son's visit. But no one had told Mrs. Robarts that the mother had made her son a present of five thousand pounds.

"She's in a good humour about everything now," continued Fanny; "so you need say nothing at all about Gatherum Castle."

"But she was very angry when she first heard it; was she not?"

"Well, Mark, to tell the truth, she was; and we had quite a scene there up in her own room up-stairs,—Justinia and I. She had heard something else that she did not like at the same time; and then—but you know her way. She blazed up quite hot."

"And said all manner of horrid things about me."

"About the duke she did. You know she never did like the duke; and for the matter of that, neither do I. I tell you that fairly, Master Mark!"

"The duke is not so bad as he's painted."

"Ah, that's what you say about another great person. However, he won't come here to trouble us, I suppose. And then I left her, not in the best temper in the world; for I blazed up too, you must know."

"I am sure you did," said Mark, pressing his arm round her waist.

"And then we were going to have a dreadful war, I thought; and I came home and wrote such a doleful letter to you. But what should happen when I had just closed it, but in came her ladyship—all alone, and—. But I can't tell you what she did or said, only she behaved beautifully; just like herself too; so full of love and truth and honesty. There's nobody like her, Mark; and she's better than all the dukes that ever wore—whatever dukes do wear."

"Horns and hoofs; that's their usual apparel, according to you and Lady Lufton," said he, remembering what Mr. Sowerby had said of himself.

"You may say what you like about me, Mark, but you shan't abuse Lady Lufton. And if horns and hoofs mean wickedness and dissipation, I believe it's not far wrong. But get off your big coat and make yourself comfortable." And that was all the scolding that Mark Robarts got from his wife on the occasion of his great iniquity.

"I will certainly tell her about this bill transaction," he said to himself; "but not to-day; not till after I have seen Lufton."

That evening they dined at Framley Court, and there they met the young lord; they found also Lady Lufton still in high good-humour. Lord Lufton himself was a fine, bright-looking young man; not so tall as Mark Robarts, and with perhaps less intelligence marked on his face; but his features were finer, and there was in his countenance a thorough appearance of good-humour and sweet temper. It was, indeed, a pleasant face to look upon, and dearly Lady Lufton loved to gaze at it.

"Well, Mark, so you have been among the Philistines?" that was his lordship's first remark. Robarts laughed as he took his friend's hands, and bethought himself how truly that was the case; that he was, in very truth, already "himself in bonds under Philistian yoke." Alas, alas, it is very hard to break asunder the bonds of the latter-day Philistines. When a Samson does now and then pull a temple down about their ears, is he not sure to be engulfed in the ruin with them? There is no horse-leech that sticks so fast as your latter-day Philistine.

"So you have caught Sir George, after all," said Lady Lufton; and that was nearly all she did say in allusion to his absence. There was afterwards some conversation about the lecture, and from her ladyship's remarks, it certainly was apparent that she did not like the people among whom the vicar had been lately staying; but she said no word that was personal to him himself, or that could be taken as a reproach. The little episode of Mrs. Proudie's address in the lecture-room had already reached Framley, and it was only to be expected that Lady Lufton should enjoy the joke. She would affect to believe that the body of the lecture had been given by the bishop's wife; and afterwards, when Mark described her costume at that Sunday morning breakfast-table, Lady Lufton would assume that such had been the dress in which she had exercised her faculties in public.

"I would have given a five-pound note to have heard it," said Sir George.

"So would not I," said Lady Lufton. "When one hears of such things described so graphically as Mr. Robarts now tells it, one can hardly help laughing. But it would give me great pain to see the wife of one of our bishops place herself in such a situation. For he is a bishop after all."

"Well, upon my word, my lady, I agree with Meredith," said Lord Lufton. "It must have been good fun. As it did happen, you know,—as the Church was doomed to the disgrace, I should like to have heard it."

"I know you would have been shocked, Ludovic."

"I should have got over that in time, mother. It would have been like a bull-fight I suppose—horrible to see no doubt, but extremely interesting. And Harold Smith, Mark; what did he do all the while?"

"It didn't take so very long, you know," said Robarts.

"And the poor bishop," said Lady Meredith; "how did he look? I really do pity him."

"Well, he was asleep, I think."

"What, slept through it all?" said Sir George.

"It awakened him; and then he jumped up and said something."

"What, out loud too?"

"Only one word or so."

"What a disgraceful scene!" said Lady Lufton. "To those who remember the good old man who was in the diocese before him it is perfectly shocking. He confirmed you, Ludovic, and you ought to remember him. It was over at Barchester, and you went and lunched with him afterwards."

"I do remember; and especially this, that I never ate such tarts in my life, before or since. The old man particularly called my attention to them, and seemed remarkably pleased that I concurred in his sentiments. There are no such tarts as those going in the palace now, I'll be bound."

"Mrs. Proudie will be very happy to do her best for you if you will go and try," said Sir George.

"I beg that he will do no such thing," said Lady Lufton, and that was the only severe word she said about any of Mark's visitings.

As Sir George Meredith was there, Robarts could say nothing then to Lord Lufton about Mr. Sowerby and Mr. Sowerby's money affairs; but he did make an appointment for a *tête-à-tête* on the next morning.

"You must come down and see my nags, Mark; they came to-day. The Merediths will be off at twelve, and then we can have an hour together." Mark said he would, and then went home with his wife under his arm.

"Well, now, is not she kind?" said Fanny, as soon as they were out on the gravel together.

"She is kind; kinder than I can tell you just at present. But did you ever know anything so bitter as she is to the poor bishop? And really the bishop is not so bad."

"Yes; I know something much more bitter; and that is what she thinks of the bishop's wife. And you know, Mark, it was so unladylike, her getting up in that way. What must the people of Barchester think of her?"

"As far as I could see the people of Barchester liked it."

"Nonsense, Mark; they could not. But never mind that now. I want you to own that she is good." And then Mrs. Robarts went on with another long eulogy on the dowager. Since that affair of the pardon-begging at the parsonage Mrs. Robarts hardly knew how to think well enough of her friend. And the evening had been so pleasant after the dreadful storm and threatenings of hurricanes; her husband had been so well received after his lapse of judgment; the wounds that had looked so sore had been so thoroughly healed, and everything was so pleasant. How all of this would have been changed had she known of that little bill!

At twelve the next morning the lord and the vicar were walking through the Framley stables together. Quite a commotion had been made there, for the larger portion of these buildings had of late years seldom been used. But now all was crowding and activity. Seven or eight very precious animals had followed Lord Lufton from Leicestershire, and all of them required dimensions that were thought to be rather excessive by the Framley old-fashioned groom. My lord, however, had a head man of his own who took the matter quite into his own hands.

Mark, priest as he was, was quite worldly enough to be fond of a good horse; and for some little time allowed Lord Lufton to descant on the merit of this four-year-old filly, and that magnificent Rattlebones colt, out of a Mousetrap mare; but he had other things that lay heavy on his mind, and after bestowing half an hour on the stud, he contrived to get his friend away to the shrubbery walks.

"So you have settled with Sowerby," Robarts began by saying.

"Settled with him; yes, but do you know the price?"

"I believe that you have paid five thousand pounds."

"Yes, and about three before; and that in a matter in which I did not really owe one shilling. Whatever I do in future, I'll keep out of Sowerby's grip."

"But you don't think he has been unfair to you."

"Mark, to tell you the truth I have banished the affair from my mind, and don't wish to take it up again. My mother has paid the money to save the property, and of course I must pay her back. But I think I may promise that I will not have any more money dealings with Sowerby. I will not say that he is dishonest, but at any rate he is sharp."

"Well, Lufton; what will you say when I tell you that I have put my name to a bill for him, for four hundred pounds?"

"Say; why I should say—; but you're joking; a man in your position would never do such a thing."

"But I have done it."

Lord Lufton gave a long low whistle.

"He asked me the last night that I was there, making a great favour of it, and declaring that no bill of his had ever yet been dishonoured."

Lord Lufton whistled again. "No bill of his dishonoured! Why the pocket-books of the Jews are stuffed full of his dishonoured papers! And you have really given him your name for four hundred pounds?"

"I have certainly."

"At what date?"

"Three months."

"And have you thought where you are to get the money?"

"I know very well that I can't get it; not at least by that time. The bankers must renew it for me, and I must pay it by degrees. That is, if Sowerby really does not take it up."

"It is just as likely that he will take up the national debt."

Robarts then told him about the projected marriage with Miss Dunstable, giving it as his opinion that the lady would probably accept the gentleman.

"Not at all improbable," said his lordship, "for Sowerby is an agreeable fellow; and if it be so, he will have all that he wants for life. But his creditors will gain nothing. The duke, who has his title-deeds, will doubtless get his money, and the estate will in fact belong to the wife. But the small fry, such as you, will not get a shilling."

Poor Mark! He had had an inkling of this before; but it had hardly presented itself to him in such certain terms. It was, then, a positive fact, that in punishment for his weakness in having signed that bill he would have to pay, not only four hundred pounds, but four hundred pounds with interest, and expenses of renewal, and commission, and bill stamps. Yes; he had certainly got among the Philistines during that visit of his to the duke. It began to appear to him pretty clearly that it would have been better for him to have relinquished altogether the glories of Chaldicotes and Gatherum Castle.

And now, how was he to tell his wife?

CHAPTER X.

LUCY ROBARTS.

And now how was he to tell his wife? That was the consideration heavy on Mark Robarts' mind when last we left him; and he turned the matter often in his thoughts before he could bring himself to a resolution. At last he did do so, and one may say that it was not altogether a bad one, if only he could carry it out.

He would ascertain in what bank that bill of his had been discounted. He would ask Sowerby, and if he could not learn from him, he would go to the three banks in Barchester. That it had been taken to one of them he felt tolerably certain. He would explain to the manager his conviction that he would have to make good the amount, his inability to do so at the end of the three months, and the whole state of his income; and then the banker would explain to him how the matter might be arranged. He thought that he could pay £50 every three months with interest. As soon as this should have been concerted with the banker, he would let his wife know all about it. Were he to tell her at the present moment, while the matter was all unsettled, the intelligence would frighten her into illness.

But on the next morning there came to him tidings by the hands of Robin postman, which for a long while upset all his plans. The letter was from Exeter. His father had been taken ill, and had very quickly been pronounced to be in danger. That evening—the evening on which his sister wrote—the old man was much worse, and it was desirable that Mark should go off to Exeter as quickly as possible. Of course he went to Exeter—again leaving the Framley souls at the mercy of the Welsh Low Churchman. Framley is only four miles from Silverbridge, and at Silverbridge he was on the direct road to the west. He was therefore at Exeter before nightfall on that day.

But nevertheless he arrived there too late to see his father again alive. The old man's illness had been sudden and rapid, and he expired without again seeing his eldest son. Mark arrived at the house of mourning just as they were learning to realize the full change in their position.

The doctor's career had been on the whole successful, but nevertheless he did not leave behind him as much money as the world had given him credit for possessing. Who ever does? Dr. Robarts had educated a large family, had always lived with every comfort, and had never possessed a shilling but what he had earned himself. A physician's fees come in, no doubt, with comfortable rapidity as soon as rich old gentlemen and middle-aged ladies begin to put their faith in him; but fees run out almost with equal rapidity when a wife and seven children are treated to everything that the world considers most desirable. Mark, we have seen, had been educated at Harrow and Oxford, and it may be said, therefore, that he had received his patrimony early in life. For Gerald Robarts, the second brother, a commission had been bought in a crack regiment. He also had been lucky, having lived and become a captain in the Crimea; and the purchase-money was lodged for his majority. And John Robarts, the youngest, was a clerk in the Petty Bag Office, and was already assistant private secretary to the Lord Petty Bag himself—a place of considerable trust, if not hitherto of large emolument; and on his education money had been spent freely, for in these days a young man cannot get into the Petty Bag Office without knowing at least three modern languages; and he must be well up in trigonometry too, in bible theology, or in one dead language—at his option.

And the doctor had four daughters. The two elder were married, including that Blanche with whom Lord Lufton was to have fallen in love at the vicar's wedding. A Devonshire squire had done this in the lord's place; but on marrying her it was necessary that he should have a few thousand pounds, two or three perhaps, and the old doctor had managed that they should be forthcoming. The elder also had not been sent away from the paternal mansion quite empty-handed. There were, therefore, at the time of the doctor's death two children left at home, of whom one only, Lucy, the younger, will come much across us in the course of our story.

Mark stayed for ten days at Exeter, he and the Devonshire squire having been named as executors in the will. In this document it was explained that the doctor trusted that provision had been made for most of his children. As for his dear son Mark, he said, he was aware that he need be under no uneasiness. On hearing this read Mark smiled sweetly, and looked very gracious; but, nevertheless, his heart did sink somewhat within him, for there had been a hope that a small windfall, coming now so opportunely, might enable him to rid himself at once of that dreadful Sowerby incubus. And then the will went on to declare that Mary, and Gerald, and Blanche, had also, by God's providence, been placed beyond want. And here, looking into the squire's face, one might have thought that his heart fell a little also; for he had not so full a command of his feelings as his brother-in-law, who had been so much more before the world. To John, the assistant private secretary, was left a legacy of a thousand pounds; and to Jane and Lucy certain sums in certain four per cents., which were quite sufficient to add an efficient value to the hands of those young ladies in the eyes of most prudent young would-be Benedicts. Over and beyond this there was nothing but the furniture, which he desired might be sold, and the proceeds divided among them all. It might come to sixty or seventy pounds a piece, and pay the expenses incidental on his death.

And then all men and women there and thereabouts said that old Dr. Robarts had done well. His life had been good and prosperous, and his will was just. And Mark, among others, so declared,—and was so convinced in spite of his own little disappointment. And on the third morning after the reading of the will Squire Crowdy, of Creamclotted Hall, altogether got over his grief, and said that it was all right. And then it was decided that Jane should go home with him,—for there was a brother squire who, it was thought, might have an eye to Jane;—and Lucy, the younger, should be taken to Framley Parsonage. In a fortnight from the receipt of that letter Mark arrived at his own house with his sister Lucy under his wing.

All this interfered greatly with Mark's wise resolution as to the Sowerby-bill incubus. In the first place he could not get to Barchester as soon as he had intended, and then an idea came across him that possibly it might be well that he should borrow the money of his brother John, explaining the circumstances, of course, and paying him due interest. But he had not liked to broach the subject when they were there in Exeter, standing, as it were, over their father's grave, and so the matter was postponed. There was still ample time for arrangement before the bill would come due, and he would not tell Fanny till he had made up his mind what that arrangement would be. It would kill her, he said to himself over and over again, were he to tell her of it without being able to tell her also that the means of liquidating the debt were to be forthcoming.

And now I must say a word about Lucy Robarts. If one might only go on without those descriptions, how pleasant it would all be! But Lucy Robarts has to play a forward part in this little drama, and those who care for such matters must be made to understand something of her form and likeness. When last we mentioned her as appearing, though not in any prominent position, at her brother's wedding, she was only sixteen; but now, at the time of her father's death, somewhat over two years having since elapsed, she was nearly nineteen. Laying aside for the sake of clearness that indefinite term of girl—for girls are girls from the age of three up to forty-three, if not previously married—dropping that generic word, we may say that then, at that wedding of her brother, she was a child; and now, at the death of her father, she was a woman.

Nothing, perhaps, adds so much to womanhood, turns the child so quickly into a woman, as such death-bed scenes as these. Hitherto but little had fallen to Lucy to do in the way of woman's duties. Of money transactions she had known nothing, beyond a jocose attempt to make her annual allowance of twenty-five pounds cover all her personal wants—an attempt which was made jocose by the loving bounty of her father. Her sister, who was three years her elder—for John came in between them—had managed the house; that is, she had made the tea and talked to the housekeeper about the dinners. But Lucy had sat at her father's elbow, had read to him of evenings when he went to sleep, had brought him his slippers and looked after the comforts of his easy-chair. All this she had done as a child; but when she stood at the coffin head, and knelt at the coffin side, then she was a woman.

She was smaller in stature than either of her three sisters, to all of whom had been acceded the praise of being fine women—a eulogy which the people of Exeter, looking back at the elder sisters, and the general remembrance of them which pervaded the city, were not willing to extend to Lucy. "Dear—dear!" had been said of her; "poor Lucy is not like a Robarts at all; is she, now, Mrs. Pole?"—for as the daughters had become fine women, so had the sons grown into stalwart men. And then Mrs. Pole had answered: "Not a bit; is she, now? Only think what Blanche was at her age. But she has fine eyes, for all that; and they do say she is the cleverest of them all."

And that, too, is so true a description of her, that I do not know that I can add much to it. She was not like Blanche; for Blanche had a bright complexion, and a fine neck, and a noble bust, *et vera incessu patuit Dea*—a true goddess, that is, as far as the eye went. She had a grand idea, moreover, of an apple-pie, and had not reigned eighteen months at Creamclotted Hall before she knew all the mysteries of pigs and milk, and most of those appertaining to cider and green geese.

Lucy had no neck at all worth speaking of,—no neck, I mean, that ever produced eloquence; she was brown, too, and had addicted herself in nowise, as she undoubtedly should have done, to larder utility. In regard to the neck and colour, poor girl, she could not help herself; but in that other respect she must be held as having wasted her opportunities.

But then what eyes she had! Mrs. Pole was right there. They flashed upon you—not always softly; indeed not often softly, if you were a stranger to her; but whether softly or savagely, with a brilliancy that dazzled you as you looked at them. And who shall say of what colour they were? Green probably, for most eyes are green—green or grey, if green be thought uncomely for an eye-colour. But it was not their colour, but their fire, which struck one with such surprise.

LUCY ROBARTS.

Lucy Robarts was thoroughly a brunette. Sometimes the dark tint of her cheek was exquisitely rich and lovely, and the fringes of her eyes were long and soft, and her small teeth, which one so seldom saw, were white as pearls, and her hair, though short, was beautifully soft—by no means black, but yet of so dark a shade of brown. Blanche, too, was noted for fine teeth. They were white and regular and lofty as a new row of houses in a French city. But then when she laughed she was all teeth; as she was all neck when she sat at the piano. But Lucy's teeth!—it was only now and again, when in some sudden burst of wonder she would sit for a moment with her lips apart, that the fine finished lines and dainty pearl-white colour of that perfect set of ivory could be seen. Mrs. Pole would have said a word of her teeth also, but that to her they had never been made visible.

"But they do say that she is the cleverest of them all," Mrs. Pole had added, very properly. The people of Exeter had expressed such an opinion, and had been quite just in doing so. I do not know how it happens, but it always does happen, that everybody in every small town knows which is the brightest-witted in every family. In this respect Mrs. Pole had only expressed public opinion, and public opinion was right. Lucy Robarts was blessed with an intelligence keener than that of her brothers or sisters.

"To tell the truth, Mark, I admire Lucy more than I do Blanche." This had been said by Mrs. Robarts within a few hours of her having assumed that name. "She's not a beauty, I know, but yet I do."

"My dearest Fanny!" Mark had answered in a tone of surprise.

"I do then; of course people won't think so; but I never seem to care about regular beauties. Perhaps I envy them too much."

What Mark said next need not be repeated, but everybody may be sure that it contained some gross flattery for his young bride. He remembered this, however, and had always called Lucy his wife's pet. Neither of the sisters had since that been at Framley; and though Fanny had spent a week at Exeter on the occasion of Blanche's marriage, it could hardly be said that she was very intimate with them. Nevertheless, when it became expedient that one of them should go to Framley, the remembrance of what his wife had said immediately induced Mark to make the offer to Lucy; and Jane, who was of a kindred soul with Blanche, was delighted to go to Creamclotted Hall. The acres of Heavybed House, down in that fat Totnes country, adjoined those of Creamclotted Hall, and Heavybed House still wanted a mistress.

Fanny was delighted when the news reached her. It would of course be proper that one of his sisters should live with Mark under their present circumstances, and she was happy to think that that quiet little bright-eyed creature was to come and nestle with her under the same roof. The children should so love her—only not quite so much as they loved mamma; and the snug little room that looks out over the porch, in which the chimney never smokes, should be made ready for her; and she should be allowed her share of driving the pony—which was a great sacrifice of self on the part of Mrs. Robarts—and Lady Lufton's best good-will should be bespoken. In fact, Lucy was not unfortunate in the destination that was laid out for her.

Lady Lufton had of course heard of the doctor's death, and had sent all manner of kind messages to Mark, advising him not to hurry home by any means until everything was settled at Exeter. And then she was told of the new-comer that was expected in the parish. When she heard that it was Lucy, the younger, she also was satisfied; for Blanche's charms, though indisputable, had not been altogether to her taste. If a second Blanche were to arrive there what danger might there not be for young Lord Lufton!

"Quite right," said her ladyship, "just what he ought to do. I think I remember the young lady; rather small, is she not, and very retiring?"

"Rather small and very retiring. What a description!" said Lord Lufton.

875

"Never mind, Ludovic; some young ladies must be small, and some at least ought to be retiring. We shall be delighted to make her acquaintance."

"I remember your other sister-in-law very well," said Lord Lufton. "She was a beautiful woman."

"I don't think you will consider Lucy a beauty," said Mrs. Robarts.

"Small, retiring, and—" so far Lord Lufton had gone, when Mrs. Robarts finished by the word, "plain." She had liked Lucy's face, but she had thought that others probably did not do so.

"Upon my word," said Lady Lufton, "you don't deserve to have a sister-in-law. I remember her very well, and can say that she is not plain. I was very much taken with her manner at your wedding, my dear; and thought more of her than I did of the beauty, I can tell you."

"I must confess I do not remember her at all," said his lordship. And so the conversation ended.

And then at the end of the fortnight Mark arrived with his sister. They did not reach Framley till long after dark—somewhere between six and seven—and by this time it was December. There was snow on the ground, and frost in the air, and no moon, and cautious men when they went on the roads had their horses' shoes cocked. Such being the state of the weather Mark's gig had been nearly filled with cloaks and shawls when it was sent over to Silverbridge. And a cart was sent for Lucy's luggage, and all manner of preparations had been made. Three times had Fanny gone herself to see that the fire burned brightly in the little room over the porch, and at the moment that the sound of the wheels was heard she was engaged in opening her son's mind as to the nature of an aunt. Hitherto papa and mamma and Lady Lufton were all that he had known, excepting, of course, the satellites of the nursery.

And then in three minutes Lucy was standing by the fire. Those three minutes had been taken up in embraces between the husband and the wife. Let who would be brought as a visitor to the house, after a fortnight's absence, she would kiss him before she welcomed any one else. But then she turned to Lucy, and began to assist her with her cloaks.

"Oh, thank you," said Lucy; "I'm not cold,—not very at least. Don't trouble yourself: I can do it." But here she had made a false boast, for her fingers had been so numbed that she could not do nor undo anything.

They were all in black, of course; but the sombreness of Lucy's clothes struck Fanny much more than her own. They seemed to have swallowed her up in their blackness, and to have made her almost an emblem of death. She did not look up, but kept her face turned towards the fire, and seemed almost afraid of her position.

"She may say what she likes, Fanny," said Mark, "but she is very cold. And so am I,— cold enough. You had better go up with her to her room. We won't do much in the dressing way to-night; eh, Lucy?"

In the bedroom Lucy thawed a little, and Fanny, as she kissed her, said to herself that she had been wrong as to that word "plain." Lucy, at any rate, was not plain.

"You will be used to us soon," said Fanny, "and then I hope we shall make you comfortable." And she took her sister-in-law's hand and pressed it.

Lucy looked up at her, and her eyes then were tender enough. "I am sure I shall be happy here," she said, "with you. But—but—dear papa!" And then they got into each other's arms, and had a great bout of kissing and crying. "Plain," said Fanny to herself, as at last she got her guest's hair smoothed and the tears washed from her eyes—"plain! She has the loveliest countenance that I ever looked at in my life!"

"Your sister is quite beautiful," she said to Mark, as they talked her over alone before they went to sleep that night.

"No, she's not beautiful; but she's a very good girl, and clever enough too, in her sort of way."

"I think her perfectly lovely. I never saw such eyes in my life before."

"I'll leave her in your hands then; you shall get her a husband."

"That mayn't be so easy. I don't think she'd marry anybody."

"Well, I hope not. But she seems to me to be exactly cut out for an old maid;—to be aunt Lucy for ever and ever to your bairns."

"And so she shall, with all my heart. But I don't think she will, very long. I have no doubt she will be hard to please; but if I were a man I should fall in love with her at once. Did you ever observe her teeth, Mark?"

"I don't think I ever did."

"You wouldn't know whether any one had a tooth in their head, I believe."

"No one except you, my dear; and I know all yours by heart."

"You are a goose."

"And a very sleepy one; so, if you please, I'll go to roost." And thus there was nothing more said about Lucy's beauty on that occasion.

For the first two days Mrs. Robarts did not make much of her sister-in-law. Lucy, indeed, was not demonstrative; and she was, moreover, one of those few persons—for they are very few—who are contented to go on with their existence without making themselves the centre of any special outward circle. To the ordinary run of minds it is impossible not to do this. A man's own dinner is to himself so important that he cannot bring himself to believe that it is a matter utterly indifferent to every one else. A lady's collection of baby-clothes, in early years, and of house linen and curtain-fringes in later life, is so very interesting to her own eyes, that she cannot believe but what other people will rejoice to behold it. I would not, however, be held as regarding this tendency as evil. It leads to conversation of some sort among people, and perhaps to a kind of sympathy. Mrs. Jones will look at Mrs. White's linen-chest, hoping that Mrs. White may be induced to look at hers. One can only pour out of a jug that which is in it. For the most of us, if we do not talk of ourselves, or at any rate of the individual circles of which we are the centres, we can talk of nothing. I cannot hold with those who wish to put down the insignificant chatter of the world. As for myself, I am always happy to look at Mrs. Jones's linen, and never omit an opportunity of giving her the details of my own dinners.

But Lucy Robarts had not this gift. She had come there as a stranger into her sister-in-law's house, and at first seemed as though she would be contented in simply having her corner in the drawing-room and her place at the parlour-table. She did not seem to need the comforts of condolence and open-hearted talking. I do not mean to say that she was moody, that she did not answer when she was spoken to, or that she took no notice of the children; but she did not at once throw herself and all her hopes and sorrows into Fanny's heart, as Fanny would have had her do.

Mrs. Robarts herself was what we call demonstrative. When she was angry with Lady Lufton she showed it. And as since that time her love and admiration for Lady Lufton had increased, she showed that also. When she was in any way displeased with her husband, she could not hide it, even though she tried to do so, and fancied herself successful;—no more than she could hide her warm, constant, overflowing woman's love. She could not walk through a room hanging on her husband's arm without seeming to proclaim to every one there that she thought him the best man in it. She was demonstrative, and therefore she was the more disappointed in that Lucy did not rush at once with all her cares into her open heart.

"She is so quiet," Fanny said to her husband.

"That's her nature," said Mark. "She always was quiet as a child. While we were smashing everything, she would never crack a teacup."

"I wish she would break something now," said Fanny, "and then perhaps we should get to talk about it." But she did not on this account give over loving her sister-in-law. She probably valued her the more, unconsciously, for not having those aptitudes with which she herself was endowed.

And then after two days Lady Lufton called; of course it may be supposed that Fanny had said a good deal to her new inmate about Lady Lufton. A neighbour of that kind in the country exercises so large an influence upon the whole tenor of one's life, that to abstain from such talk is out of the question. Mrs. Robarts had been brought up almost under the dowager's wing, and of course she regarded her as being worthy of much talking. Do not let persons on this account suppose that Mrs. Robarts was a tuft-hunter, or a toad-eater. If they do not see the difference they have yet got to study the earliest principles of human nature.

Lady Lufton called, and Lucy was struck dumb. Fanny was particularly anxious that her ladyship's first impression should be favourable, and to effect this, she especially endeavoured to throw the two together during that visit. But in this she was unwise. Lady Lufton, however, had woman-craft enough not to be led into any egregious error by Lucy's silence.

"And what day will you come and dine with us?" said Lady Lufton, turning expressly to her old friend Fanny.

"Oh, do you name the day. We never have many engagements, you know."

"Will Thursday do, Miss Robarts? You will meet nobody you know, only my son; so you need not regard it as going out. Fanny here will tell you that stepping over to Framley Court is no more going out, than when you go from one room to another in the parsonage. Is it, Fanny?"

Fanny laughed and said that that stepping over to Framley Court certainly was done so often that perhaps they did not think so much about it as they ought to do.

"We consider ourselves a sort of happy family here, Miss Robarts, and are delighted to have the opportunity of including you in the ménage."

Lucy gave her ladyship one of her sweetest smiles, but what she said at that moment was inaudible. It was plain, however, that she could not bring herself even to go as far as Framley Court for her dinner just at present. "It was very kind of Lady Lufton," she said to Fanny; "but it was so very soon, and—and—and if they would only go without her, she would be so happy." But as the object was to go with her—expressly to take her there—the dinner was adjourned for a short time—*sine die*.

CHAPTER XI.

GRISELDA GRANTLY.

It was nearly a month after this that Lucy was first introduced to Lord Lufton, and then it was brought about only by accident. During that time Lady Lufton had been often at the parsonage, and had in a certain degree learned to know Lucy; but the stranger in the parish had never yet plucked up courage to accept one of the numerous invitations that had reached her. Mr. Robarts and his wife had frequently been at Framley Court, but the dreaded day of Lucy's initiation had not yet arrived.

She had seen Lord Lufton in church, but hardly so as to know him, and beyond that she had not seen him at all. One day, however—or rather, one evening, for it was already dusk—he overtook her and Mrs. Robarts on the road walking towards the vicarage. He had his gun on his shoulder, three pointers were at his heels, and a gamekeeper followed a little in the rear.

"How are you, Mrs. Robarts?" he said, almost before he had overtaken them. "I have been chasing you along the road for the last half mile. I never knew ladies walk so fast."

"We should be frozen if we were to dawdle about as you gentlemen do," and then she stopped and shook hands with him. She forgot at the moment that Lucy and he had not met, and therefore she did not introduce them.

"Won't you make me known to your sister-in-law?" said he, taking off his hat, and bowing to Lucy. "I have never yet had the pleasure of meeting her, though we have been neighbours for a month and more."

Fanny made her excuses and introduced them, and then they went on till they came to Framley Gate, Lord Lufton talking to them both, and Fanny answering for the two, and there they stopped for a moment.

"I am surprised to see you alone," Mrs. Robarts had just said; "I thought that Captain Culpepper was with you."

"The captain has left me for this one day. If you'll whisper I'll tell you where he has gone. I dare not speak it out loud, even to the woods."

"To what terrible place can he have taken himself? I'll have no whisperings about such horrors."

"He has gone to—to—but you'll promise not to tell my mother?"

"Not tell your mother! Well, now you have excited my curiosity! where can he be?"

"Do you promise, then?"

"Oh, yes! I will promise, because I am sure Lady Lufton won't ask me as to Captain Culpepper's whereabouts. We won't tell; will we, Lucy?"

"He has gone to Gatherum Castle for a day's pheasant-shooting. Now, mind, you must not betray us. Her ladyship supposes that he is shut up in his room with a toothache. We did not dare to mention the name to her."

And then it appeared that Mrs. Robarts had some engagement which made it necessary that she should go up and see Lady Lufton, whereas Lucy was intending to walk on to the parsonage alone.

"And I have promised to go to your husband," said Lord Lufton; "or rather to your husband's dog, Ponto. And I will do two other good things—I will carry a brace of pheasants with me, and protect Miss Robarts from the evil spirits of the Framley roads." And so Mrs. Robarts turned in at the gate, and Lucy and his lordship walked off together.

Lord Lufton, though he had never before spoken to Miss Robarts, had already found out that she was by no means plain. Though he had hardly seen her except at church, he had already made himself certain that the owner of that face must be worth knowing, and was not sorry to have the present opportunity of speaking to her. "So you have an unknown damsel shut up in your castle," he had once said to Mrs. Robarts. "If she be kept a prisoner much longer, I shall find it my duty to come and release her by force of arms." He had been there twice with the object of seeing her, but on both occasions Lucy had managed to escape. Now we may say she was fairly caught, and Lord Lufton, taking a pair of pheasants from the gamekeeper, and swinging them over his shoulder, walked off with his prey.

"You have been here a long time," he said, "without our having had the pleasure of seeing you."

"Yes, my lord," said Lucy. Lords had not been frequent among her acquaintance hitherto.

"I tell Mrs. Robarts that she has been confining you illegally, and that we shall release you by force or stratagem."

"I—I—I have had a great sorrow lately."

"Yes, Miss Robarts; I know you have; and I am only joking, you know. But I do hope that now you will be able to come amongst us. My mother is so anxious that you should do so."

"I am sure she is very kind, and you also—my lord."

"I never knew my own father," said Lord Lufton, speaking gravely. "But I can well understand what a loss you have had." And then, after pausing a moment, he continued, "I remember Dr. Robarts well."

"Do you, indeed?" said Lucy, turning sharply towards him, and speaking now with some animation in her voice. Nobody had yet spoken to her about her father since she had been at Framley. It had been as though the subject were a forbidden one. And how frequently is this the case! When those we love are dead, our friends dread to mention them, though to us who are bereaved no subject would be so pleasant as their names. But we rarely understand how to treat our own sorrow or those of others.

There was once a people in some land—and they may be still there for what I know—who thought it sacrilegious to stay the course of a raging fire. If a house were being burned, burn it must, even though there were facilities for saving it. For who would dare to interfere with the course of the god? Our idea of sorrow is much the same. We think it wicked, or at any rate heartless, to put it out. If a man's wife be dead, he should go about lugubrious, with long face, for at least two years, or perhaps with full length for eighteen months, decreasing gradually during the other six. If he be a man who can quench his sorrow—put out his fire as it were—in less time than that, let him at any rate not show his power!

"Yes: I remember him," continued Lord Lufton. "He came twice to Framley while I was a boy, consulting with my mother about Mark and myself,—whether the Eton flog-gings were not more efficacious than those at Harrow. He was very kind to me, forebod-foreboding all manner of good things on my behalf."

"He was very kind to every one," said Lucy.

"I should think he would have been—a kind, good, genial man—just the man to be adored by his own family."

"Exactly; and so he was. I do not remember that I ever heard an unkind word from him. There was not a harsh tone in his voice. And he was generous as the day." Lucy, we have said, was not generally demonstrative, but now, on this subject, and with this abso-lute stranger, she became almost eloquent.

"I do not wonder that you should feel his loss, Miss Robarts."

"Oh, I do feel it. Mark is the best of brothers, and, as for Fanny, she is too kind and too good to me. But I had always been specially my father's friend. For the last year or two we had lived so much together!"

"He was an old man when he died, was he not?"

"Just seventy, my lord."

"Ah, then he was old. My mother is only fifty, and we sometimes call her the old woman. Do you think she looks older than that? We all say that she makes herself out to be so much more ancient than she need do."

"Lady Lufton does not dress young."

"That is it. She never has, in my memory. She always used to wear black when I first recollect her. She has given that up now; but she is still very sombre; is she not?"

"I do not like ladies to dress very young, that is, ladies of—of—"

"Ladies of fifty, we will say?"

"Very well; ladies of fifty, if you like it."

"Then I am sure you will like my mother."

They had now turned up through the parsonage wicket, a little gate that opened into the garden at a point on the road nearer than the chief entrance.

"I suppose I shall find Mark up at the house?" said he.

"I daresay you will, my lord."

"Well, I'll go round this way, for my business is partly in the stable. You see I am quite at home here, though you never have seen me before. But, Miss Robarts, now that the ice is broken, I hope that we may be friends." He then put out his hand, and when she gave him hers he pressed it almost as an old friend might have done.

And, indeed, Lucy had talked to him almost as though he were an old friend. For a mi-nute or two she had forgotten that he was a lord and a stranger—had forgotten also to be stiff and guarded as was her wont. Lord Lufton had spoken to her as though he had really cared to know her; and she, unconsciously, had been taken by the compliment. Lord Luf-ton, indeed, had not thought much about it—excepting as thus, that he liked the glance of a pair of bright eyes, as most other young men do like it. But, on this occasion, the even-ing had been so dark, that he had hardly seen Lucy's eyes at all.

"Well, Lucy, I hope you liked your companion," Mrs. Robarts said, as the three of them clustered round the drawing-room fire before dinner.

"Oh, yes; pretty well," said Lucy.

"That is not at all complimentary to his lordship."

"I did not mean to be complimentary, Fanny."

"Lucy is a great deal too matter-of-fact for compliments," said Mark.

"What I meant was, that I had no great opportunity for judging, seeing that I was only with Lord Lufton for about ten minutes."

"Ah! but there are girls here who would give their eyes for ten minutes of Lord Lufton to themselves. You do not know how he's valued. He has the character of being always able to make himself agreeable to ladies at half a minute's warning."

"Perhaps he had not the half-minute's warning in this case," said Lucy,—hypocrite that she was.

"Poor Lucy," said her brother; "he was coming up to see Ponto's shoulder, and I am afraid he was thinking more about the dog than you."

"Very likely," said Lucy; and then they went in to dinner.

Lucy had been a hypocrite, for she had confessed to herself, while dressing, that Lord Lufton had been very pleasant; but then it is allowed to young ladies to be hypocrites when the subject under discussion is the character of a young gentleman.

Soon after that, Lucy did dine at Framley Court. Captain Culpepper, in spite of his enormity with reference to Gatherum Castle, was still staying there, as was also a clergyman from the neighbourhood of Barchester with his wife and daughter. This was Archdeacon Grantly, a gentleman whom we have mentioned before, and who was as well known in the diocese as the bishop himself,—and more thought about by many clergymen than even that illustrious prelate.

Miss Grantly was a young lady not much older than Lucy Robarts, and she also was quiet, and not given to much talking in open company. She was decidedly a beauty, but somewhat statuesque in her loveliness. Her forehead was high and white, but perhaps too like marble to gratify the taste of those who are fond of flesh and blood. Her eyes were large and exquisitely formed, but they seldom showed much emotion. She, indeed, was impassive herself, and betrayed but little of her feelings. Her nose was nearly Grecian, not coming absolutely in a straight line from her forehead, but doing so nearly enough to entitle it to be considered as classical. Her mouth, too, was very fine—artists, at least, said so, and connoisseurs in beauty; but to me she always seemed as though she wanted fulness of lip. But the exquisite symmetry of her cheek and chin and lower face no man could deny. Her hair was light, and being always dressed with considerable care, did not detract from her appearance; but it lacked that richness which gives such luxuriance to feminine loveliness. She was tall and slight, and very graceful in her movements; but there were those who thought that she wanted the ease and *abandon* of youth. They said that she was too composed and stiff for her age, and that she gave but little to society beyond the beauty of her form and face.

There can be no doubt, however, that she was considered by most men and women to be the beauty of Barsetshire, and that gentlemen from neighbouring counties would come many miles through dirty roads on the mere hope of being able to dance with her. Whatever attractions she may have lacked, she had at any rate created for herself a great reputation. She had spent two months of the last spring in London, and even there she had made a sensation; and people had said that Lord Dumbello, Lady Hartletop's eldest son, had been peculiarly struck with her.

It may be imagined that the archdeacon was proud of her, and so indeed was Mrs. Grantly—more proud, perhaps, of her daughter's beauty, than so excellent a woman should have allowed herself to be of such an attribute. Griselda—that was her name—was now an only daughter. One sister she had had, but that sister had died. There were two brothers also left, one in the Church and the other in the army. That was the extent of the archdeacon's family, and as the archdeacon was a very rich man—he was the only child of his father, who had been Bishop of Barchester for a great many years; and in those years it had been worth a man's while to be Bishop of Barchester—it was supposed that Miss Grantly would have a large fortune. Mrs. Grantly, however, had been heard to say, that she was in no hurry to see her daughter established in the world;—ordinary young ladies are merely married, but those of real importance are established:—and this, if anything, added to the value of the prize. Mothers sometimes depreciate their wares by an undue solicitude to dispose of them.

But to tell the truth openly and at once—a virtue for which a novelist does not receive very much commendation—Griselda Grantly was, to a certain extent, already given away. Not that she, Griselda, knew anything about it, or that the thrice happy gentleman had been made aware of his good fortune; nor even had the archdeacon been told. But Mrs. Grantly and Lady Lufton had been closeted together more than once, and terms had been signed and sealed between them. Not signed on parchment, and sealed with wax, as is the case with treaties made by kings and diplomats,—to be broken by the same; but signed with little words, and sealed with certain pressings of the hand,—a treaty which between two such contracting parties would be binding enough. And by the terms of this treaty Griselda Grantly was to become Lady Lufton.

Lady Lufton had hitherto been fortunate in her matrimonial speculations. She had selected Sir George for her daughter, and Sir George, with the utmost good nature, had fallen in with her views. She had selected Fanny Monsell for Mr. Robarts, and Fanny Monsell had not rebelled against her for a moment. There was a prestige of success about her doings, and she felt almost confident that her dear son Ludovic must fall in love with Griselda.

As to the lady herself, nothing, Lady Lufton thought, could be much better than such a match for her son. Lady Lufton, I have said, was a good churchwoman, and the archdeacon was the very type of that branch of the Church which she venerated. The Grantlys, too, were of a good family,—not noble, indeed; but in such matters Lady Lufton did not want everything. She was one of those persons who, in placing their hopes at a moderate pitch, may fairly trust to see them realized. She would fain that her son's wife should be handsome; this she wished for his sake, that he might be proud of his wife, and because men love to look on beauty. But she was afraid of vivacious beauty, of those soft, sparkling feminine charms which are spread out as lures for all the world, soft dimples, laughing eyes, luscious lips, conscious smiles, and easy whispers. What if her son should bring her home a rattling, rapid-spoken, painted piece of Eve's flesh such as this? Would not the glory and joy of her life be over, even though such child of their first mother should have come forth to the present day ennobled by the blood of two dozen successive British peers?

And then, too, Griselda's money would not be useless. Lady Lufton, with all her high-flown ideas, was not an imprudent woman. She knew that her son had been extravagant, though she did not believe that he had been reckless; and she was well content to think that some balsam from the old bishop's coffers should be made to cure the slight wounds which his early imprudence might have inflicted on the carcase of the family property. And thus, in this way, and for these reasons, Griselda Grantly had been chosen out from all the world to be the future Lady Lufton.

Lord Lufton had met Griselda more than once already; had met her before these high contracting parties had come to any terms whatsoever, and had evidently admired her. Lord Dumbello had remained silent one whole evening in London with ineffable disgust, because Lord Lufton had been rather particular in his attentions; but then Lord Dumbello's muteness was his most eloquent mode of expression. Both Lady Hartletop and Mrs. Grantly, when they saw him, knew very well what he meant. But that match would not exactly have suited Mrs. Grantly's views. The Hartletop people were not in her line. They belonged altogether to another set, being connected, as we have heard before, with the Omnium interest—"those *horrid* Gatherum people," as Lady Lufton would say to her, raising her hands and eyebrows, and shaking her head. Lady Lufton probably thought that they ate babies in pies during their midnight orgies at Gatherum Castle; and that widows were kept in cells, and occasionally put on racks for the amusement of the duke's guests.

When the Robarts's party entered the drawing-room the Grantlys were already there, and the archdeacon's voice sounded loud and imposing in Lucy's ears, as she heard him speaking while she was yet on the threshold of the door.

"My dear Lady Lufton, I would believe anything on earth about her—anything. There is nothing too outrageous for her. Had she insisted on going there with the bishop's apron on, I should not have been surprised." And then they all knew that the archdeacon was talking about Mrs. Proudie, for Mrs. Proudie was his bugbear.

Lady Lufton after receiving her guests introduced Lucy to Griselda Grantly. Miss Grantly smiled graciously, bowed slightly, and then remarked in the lowest voice possible that it was exceedingly cold. A low voice, we know, is an excellent thing in woman.

Lucy, who thought that she was bound to speak, said that it was cold, but that she did not mind it when she was walking. And then Griselda smiled again, somewhat less graciously than before, and so the conversation ended. Miss Grantly was the elder of the two, and having seen most of the world, should have been the best able to talk, but perhaps she was not very anxious for a conversation with Miss Robarts.

"So, Robarts, I hear that you have been preaching at Chaldicotes," said the archdeacon, still rather loudly. "I saw Sowerby the other day, and he told me that you gave them the fag end of Mrs. Proudie's lecture."

"It was ill-natured of Sowerby to say the fag end," said Robarts. "We divided the matter into thirds. Harold Smith took the first part, I the last—"

"And the lady the intervening portion. You have electrified the county between you; but I am told that she had the best of it."

"I was so sorry that Mr. Robarts went there," said Lady Lufton, as she walked into the dining-room leaning on the archdeacon's arm.

"I am inclined to think he could not very well have helped himself," said the archdeacon, who was never willing to lean heavily on a brother parson, unless on one who had utterly and irrevocably gone away from his side of the Church.

"Do you think not, archdeacon?"

"Why, no: Sowerby is a friend of Lufton's—"

"Not particularly," said poor Lady Lufton, in a deprecating tone.

"Well, they have been intimate; and Robarts, when he was asked to preach at Chaldicotes, could not well refuse."

"But then he went afterwards to Gatherum Castle. Not that I am vexed with him at all now, you understand. But it is such a dangerous house, you know."

"So it is.—But the very fact of the duke's wishing to have a clergyman there, should always be taken as a sign of grace, Lady Lufton. The air was impure, no doubt; but it was less impure with Robarts there than it would have been without him. But, gracious heavens! what blasphemy have I been saying about impure air? Why, the bishop was there!"

"Yes, the bishop was there," said Lady Lufton, and they both understood each other thoroughly.

Lord Lufton took out Mrs. Grantly to dinner, and matters were so managed that Miss Grantly sat on his other side. There was no management apparent in this to anybody; but there she was, while Lucy was placed between her brother and Captain Culpepper. Captain Culpepper was a man with an enormous moustache, and a great aptitude for slaughtering game; but as he had no other strong characteristics, it was not probable that he would make himself very agreeable to poor Lucy.

She had seen Lord Lufton once, for two minutes, since the day of that walk, and then he had addressed her quite like an old friend. It had been in the parsonage drawing-room, and Fanny had been there. Fanny now was so well accustomed to his lordship, that she thought but little of this, but to Lucy it had been very pleasant. He was not forward or familiar, but kind, and gentle, and pleasant; and Lucy did feel that she liked him.

Now, on this evening, he had hitherto hardly spoken to her; but then she knew that there were other people in the company to whom he was bound to speak. She was not exactly humble-minded in the usual sense of the word; but she did recognize the fact that her position was less important than that of other people there, and that therefore it was probable that to a certain extent she would be overlooked. But not the less would she have liked to occupy the seat to which Miss Grantly had found her way. She did not want to flirt with Lord Lufton; she was not such a fool as that; but she would have liked to have heard the sound of his voice close to her ear, instead of that of Captain Culpepper's knife and fork.

This was the first occasion on which she had endeavoured to dress herself with care since her father had died; and now, sombre though she was in her deep mourning, she did look very well.

"There is an expression about her forehead that is full of poetry," Fanny had said to her husband.

"Don't you turn her head, Fanny, and make her believe that she is a beauty," Mark had answered.

"I doubt it is not so easy to turn her head, Mark. There is more in Lucy than you imagine, and so you will find out before long." It was thus that Mrs. Robarts prophesied about her sister-in-law. Had she been asked she might perhaps have said that Lucy's presence would be dangerous to the Grantly interest at Framley Court.

Lord Lufton's voice was audible enough as he went on talking to Miss Grantly—his voice, but not his words. He talked in such a way that there was no appearance of whispering, and yet the person to whom he spoke, and she only, could hear what he said. Mrs. Grantly the while conversed constantly with Lucy's brother, who sat at Lucy's left hand. She never lacked for subjects on which to speak to a country clergyman of the right sort, and thus Griselda was left quite uninterrupted.

But Lucy could not but observe that Griselda herself seemed to have very little to say,—or at any rate to say very little. Every now and then she did open her mouth, and some word or brace of words would fall from it. But for the most part she seemed to be content in the fact that Lord Lufton was paying her attention. She showed no animation, but sat there still and graceful, composed and classical, as she always was. Lucy, who could not keep her ears from listening or her eyes from looking, thought that had she been there she would have endeavoured to take a more prominent part in the conversation. But then Griselda Grantly probably knew much better than Lucy did how to comport herself in such a situation. Perhaps it might be that young men, such as Lord Lufton, liked to hear the sound of their own voices.

"Immense deal of game about here," Captain Culpepper said to her towards the end of the dinner. It was the second attempt he had made; on the former he had asked her whether she knew any of the fellows of the 9th.

"Is there?" said Lucy. "Oh! I saw Lord Lufton the other day with a great armful of pheasants."

"An armful! Why we had seven cartloads the other day at Gatherum."

"Seven carts full of pheasants!" said Lucy, amazed.

"That's not so much. We had eight guns, you know. Eight guns will do a deal of work when the game has been well got together. They manage all that capitally at Gatherum. Been at the duke's, eh?"

Lucy had heard the Framley report as to Gatherum Castle, and said with a sort of shudder that she had never been at that place. After this, Captain Culpepper troubled her no further.

When the ladies had taken themselves to the drawing-room Lucy found herself hardly better off than she had been at the dinner-table. Lady Lufton and Mrs. Grantly got themselves on to a sofa together, and there chatted confidentially into each other's ears. Her ladyship had introduced Lucy and Miss Grantly, and then she naturally thought that the young people might do very well together. Mrs. Robarts did attempt to bring about a joint conversation, which should include the three, and for ten minutes or so she worked hard at it. But it did not thrive. Miss Grantly was monosyllabic, smiling, however, at every monosyllable; and Lucy found that nothing would occur to her at that moment worthy of being spoken. There she sat, still and motionless, afraid to take up a book, and thinking in her heart how much happier she would have been at home at the parsonage. She was not made for society; she felt sure of that; and another time she would let Mark and Fanny come to Framley Court by themselves.

And then the gentlemen came in, and there was another stir in the room. Lady Lufton got up and bustled about; she poked the fire and shifted the candles, spoke a few words to Dr. Grantly, whispered something to her son, patted Lucy on the cheek, told Fanny, who was a musician, that they would have a little music, and ended by putting her two hands on Griselda's shoulders and telling her that the fit of her frock was perfect. For Lady Lufton, though she did dress old herself, as Lucy had said, delighted to see those around her neat and pretty, jaunty and graceful.

"Dear Lady Lufton!" said Griselda, putting up her hand so as to press the end of her ladyship's fingers. It was the first piece of animation she had shown, and Lucy Robarts watched it all.

And then there was music. Lucy neither played nor sang; Fanny did both, and for an amateur did both well. Griselda did not sing, but she played; and did so in a manner that showed that neither her own labour nor her father's money had been spared in her instruction. Lord Lufton sang also, a little, and Captain Culpepper a very little; so that they got up a concert among them. In the meantime the doctor and Mark stood talking together on the rug before the fire; the two mothers sat contented, watching the billings and the cooings of their offspring—and Lucy sat alone, turning over the leaves of a book of pictures. She made up her mind fully, then and there, that she was quite unfitted by disposition for such work as this. She cared for no one, and no one cared for her. Well, she must go through with it now; but another time she would know better. With her own book and a fireside she never felt herself to be miserable as she was now.

She had turned her back to the music, for she was sick of seeing Lord Lufton watch the artistic motion of Miss Grantly's fingers, and was sitting at a small table as far away from the piano as a long room would permit, when she was suddenly roused from a reverie of self-reproach by a voice close behind her: "Miss Robarts," said the voice, "why have you cut us all?" and Lucy felt that though she heard the words plainly, nobody else did. Lord Lufton was now speaking to her as he had before spoken to Miss Grantly.

"I don't play, my lord," said Lucy, "nor yet sing."

"That would have made your company so much more valuable to us, for we are terribly badly off for listeners. Perhaps you don't like music?"

"I do like it,—sometimes very much."

"And when are the sometimes? But we shall find it all out in time. We shall have unravelled all your mysteries, and read all your riddles, by—when shall I say?—by the end of the winter. Shall we not?"

"I do not know that I have got any mysteries."

"Oh, but you have! It is very mysterious in you to come and sit here, with your back to us all—"

"Oh, Lord Lufton; if I have done wrong—!" and poor Lucy almost started from her chair, and a deep flush came across her dark cheek.

"No—no; you have done no wrong. I was only joking. It is we who have done wrong in leaving you to yourself—you who are the greatest stranger among us."

"I have been very well, thank you. I don't care about being left alone. I have always been used to it."

"Ah! but we must break you of the habit. We won't allow you to make a hermit of yourself. But the truth is, Miss Robarts, you don't know us yet, and therefore you are not quite happy among us."

"Oh! yes, I am; you are all very good to me."

"You must let us be good to you. At any rate, you must let me be so. You know, don't you, that Mark and I have been dear friends since we were seven years old. His wife has been my sister's dearest friend almost as long; and now that you are with them, you must be a dear friend too. You won't refuse the offer; will you?"

"Oh, no," she said, quite in a whisper; and, indeed, she could hardly raise her voice above a whisper, fearing that tears would fall from her tell-tale eyes.

"Dr. and Mrs. Grantly will have gone in a couple of days, and then we must get you down here. Miss Grantly is to remain for Christmas, and you two must become bosom friends."

Lucy smiled, and tried to look pleased, but she felt that she and Griselda Grantly could never be bosom friends—could never have anything in common between them. She felt sure that Griselda despised her, little, brown, plain, and unimportant as she was. She herself could not despise Griselda in turn; indeed she could not but admire Miss Grantly's great beauty and dignity of demeanour; but she knew that she could never love her. It is hardly possible that the proud-hearted should love those who despise them; and Lucy Robarts was very proud-hearted.

"Don't you think she is very handsome?" said Lord Lufton.

"Oh, very," said Lucy. "Nobody can doubt that."

"Ludovic," said Lady Lufton—not quite approving of her son's remaining so long at the back of Lucy's chair—"won't you give us another song? Mrs. Robarts and Miss Grantly are still at the piano."

"I have sung away all that I knew, mother. There's Culpepper has not had a chance yet. He has got to give us his dream—how he 'dreamt that he dwelt in marble halls!'"

"I sang that an hour ago," said the captain, not over pleased.

"But you certainly have not told us how 'your little lovers came!'"

The captain, however, would not sing any more. And then the party was broken up, and the Robartses went home to their parsonage.

CHAPTER XII.

THE LITTLE BILL.

Lucy, during those last fifteen minutes of her sojourn in the Framley Court drawing-room, somewhat modified the very strong opinion she had before formed as to her unfitness for such society. It was very pleasant sitting there in that easy chair, while Lord Lufton stood at the back of it saying nice, soft, good-natured words to her. She was sure that in a little time she could feel a true friendship for him, and that she could do so without any risk of falling in love with him. But then she had a glimmering of an idea that such a friendship would be open to all manner of remarks, and would hardly be compatible with the world's ordinary ways. At any rate it would be pleasant to be at Framley Court, if he would come and occasionally notice her. But she did not admit to herself that such a visit would be intolerable if his whole time were devoted to Griselda Grantly. She neither admitted it, nor thought it; but nevertheless, in a strange unconscious way, such a feeling did find entrance in her bosom.

And then the Christmas holidays passed away. How much of this enjoyment fell to her share, and how much of this suffering she endured, we will not attempt accurately to describe. Miss Grantly remained at Framley Court up to Twelfth Night, and the Robartses also spent most of the season at the house. Lady Lufton, no doubt, had hoped that everything might have been arranged on this occasion in accordance with her wishes, but such had not been the case. Lord Lufton had evidently admired Miss Grantly very much; indeed, he had said so to his mother half-a-dozen times; but it may almost be questioned whether the pleasure Lady Lufton derived from this was not more than neutralized by an opinion he once put forward that Griselda Grantly wanted some of the fire of Lucy Robarts.

"Surely, Ludovic, you would never compare the two girls," said Lady Lufton.

"Of course not. They are the very antipodes to each other. Miss Grantly would probably be more to my taste; but then I am wise enough to know that it is so because my taste is a bad taste."

"I know no man with a more accurate or refined taste in such matters," said Lady Lufton. Beyond this she did not dare to go. She knew very well that her strategy would be vain should her son once learn that she had a strategy. To tell the truth, Lady Lufton was becoming somewhat indifferent to Lucy Robarts. She had been very kind to the little girl; but the little girl seemed hardly to appreciate the kindness as she should do—and then Lord Lufton would talk to Lucy, "which was so unnecessary, you know;" and Lucy had got into a way of talking quite freely with Lord Lufton, having completely dropped that short, spasmodic, ugly exclamation of "my lord."

And so the Christmas festivities were at an end, and January wore itself away. During the greater part of this month Lord Lufton did not remain at Framley, but was nevertheless in the county, hunting with the hounds of both divisions, and staying at various houses. Two or three nights he spent at Chaldicotes; and one—let it only be told in an under voice—at Gatherum Castle! Of this he said nothing to Lady Lufton. "Why make her unhappy?" as he said to Mark. But Lady Lufton knew it, though she said not a word to him—knew it, and was unhappy. "If he would only marry Griselda, there would be an end of that danger," she said to herself.

But now we must go back for a while to the vicar and his little bill. It will be remembered, that his first idea with reference to that trouble, after the reading of his father's will, was to borrow the money from his brother John. John was down at Exeter at the time, and was to stay one night at the parsonage on his way to London. Mark would broach the matter to him on the journey, painful though it would be to him to tell the story of his own folly to a brother so much younger than himself, and who had always looked up to him, clergyman and full-blown vicar as he was, with a deference greater than that which such difference in age required.

The story was told, however; but was told all in vain, as Mark found out before he reached Framley. His brother John immediately declared that he would lend him the money, of course—eight hundred, if his brother wanted it. He, John, confessed that, as regarded the remaining two, he should like to feel the pleasure of immediate possession. As for interest, he would not take any—take interest from a brother! of course not. Well, if Mark made such a fuss about it, he supposed he must take it; but would rather not. Mark should have his own way, and do just what he liked.

This was all very well, and Mark had fully made up his mind that his brother should not be kept long out of his money. But then arose the question, how was that money to be reached? He, Mark, was executor, or one of the executors under his father's will, and, therefore, no doubt, could put his hand upon it; but his brother wanted five months of being of age, and could not therefore as yet be put legally in possession of the legacy.

"That's a bore," said the assistant private secretary to the Lord Petty Bag, thinking, perhaps, as much of his own immediate wish for ready cash as he did of his brother's necessities. Mark felt that it was a bore, but there was nothing more to be done in that direction. He must now find out how far the bankers could assist him.

Some week or two after his return to Framley he went over to Barchester, and called there on a certain Mr. Forrest, the manager of one of the banks, with whom he was acquainted; and with many injunctions as to secrecy told this manager the whole of his story. At first he concealed the name of his friend Sowerby, but it soon appeared that no such concealment was of any avail. "That's Sowerby, of course," said Mr. Forrest. "I know you are intimate with him; and all his friends go through that, sooner or later."

It seemed to Mark as though Mr. Forrest made very light of the whole transaction.

"I cannot possibly pay the bill when it falls due," said Mark.

"Oh, no, of course not," said Mr. Forrest. "It's never very convenient to hand out four hundred pounds at a blow. Nobody will expect you to pay it!"

"But I suppose I shall have to do it sooner or later?"

"Well, that's as may be. It will depend partly on how you manage with Sowerby, and partly on the hands it gets into. As the bill has your name on it, they'll have patience as long as the interest is paid, and the commissions on renewal. But no doubt it will have to be met some day by somebody."

Mr. Forrest said that he was sure that the bill was not in Barchester; Mr. Sowerby would not, he thought, have brought it to a Barchester bank. The bill was probably in London, but doubtless would be sent to Barchester for collection. "If it comes in my way," said Mr. Forrest, "I will give you plenty of time, so that you may manage about the renewal with Sowerby. I suppose he'll pay the expense of doing that."

Mark's heart was somewhat lighter as he left the bank. Mr. Forrest had made so little of the whole transaction that he felt himself justified in making little of it also. "It may be as well," said he to himself, as he drove home, "not to tell Fanny anything about it till the three months have run round. I must make some arrangement then." And in this way his mind was easier during the last of those three months than it had been during the two former. That feeling of over-due bills, of bills coming due, of accounts overdrawn, of tradesmen unpaid, of general money cares, is very dreadful at first; but it is astonishing how soon men get used to it. A load which would crush a man at first becomes, by habit, not only endurable, but easy and comfortable to the bearer. The habitual debtor goes along jaunty and with elastic step, almost enjoying the excitement of his embarrassments. There was Mr. Sowerby himself; who ever saw a cloud on his brow? It made one almost in love with ruin to be in his company. And even now, already, Mark Robarts was thinking to himself quite comfortably about this bill;—how very pleasantly those bankers managed these things. Pay it! No; no one will be so unreasonable as to expect you to do that! And then Mr. Sowerby certainly was a pleasant fellow, and gave a man something in return for his money. It was still a question with Mark whether Lord Lufton had not been too hard on Sowerby. Had that gentleman fallen across his clerical friend at the present moment, he might no doubt have gotten from him an acceptance for another four hundred pounds.

One is almost inclined to believe that there is something pleasurable in the excitement of such embarrassments, as there is also in the excitement of drink. But then, at last, the time does come when the excitement is over, and when nothing but the misery is left. If there be an existence of wretchedness on earth it must be that of the elderly, worn-out roué, who has run this race of debt and bills of accommodation and acceptances,—of what, if we were not in these days somewhat afraid of good broad English, we might call lying and swindling, falsehood and fraud—and who, having ruined all whom he should have loved, having burnt up every one who would trust him much, and scorched all who would trust him a little, is at last left to finish his life with such bread and water as these men get, without one honest thought to strengthen his sinking heart, or one honest friend to hold his shivering hand! If a man could only think of that, as he puts his name to the first little bill, as to which he is so good-naturedly assured that it can easily be renewed!

When the three months had nearly run out, it so happened that Robarts met his friend Sowerby. Mark had once or twice ridden with Lord Lufton as far as the meet of the hounds, and may, perhaps, have gone a field or two farther on some occasions. The reader must not think that he had taken to hunting, as some parsons do; and it is singular enough that whenever they do so they always show a special aptitude for the pursuit, as though hunting were an employment peculiarly congenial with a cure of souls in the country. Such a thought would do our vicar injustice. But when Lord Lufton would ask him what on earth could be the harm of riding along the roads to look at the hounds, he hardly knew what sensible answer to give his lordship. It would be absurd to say that his time would be better employed at home in clerical matters, for it was notorious that he had not clerical pursuits for the employment of half his time. In this way, therefore, he had got into a habit of looking at the hounds, and keeping up his acquaintance in the county, meeting Lord Dumbello, Mr. Green Walker, Harold Smith, and other such like sinners; and on one such occasion, as the three months were nearly closing, he did meet Mr. Sowerby.

"Look here, Sowerby; I want to speak to you for half a moment. What are you doing about that bill?"

"Bill—bill! what bill?—which bill? The whole bill, and nothing but the bill. That seems to be the conversation now-a-days of all men, morning, noon, and night."

"Don't you know the bill I signed for you for four hundred pounds?"

"Did you, though? Was not that rather green of you?"

This did seem strange to Mark. Could it really be the fact that Mr. Sowerby had so many bills flying about that he had absolutely forgotten that occurrence in the Gatherum Castle bedroom? And then to be called green by the very man whom he had obliged!

"Perhaps I was," said Mark, in a tone that showed that he was somewhat piqued. "But all the same I should be glad to know how it will be taken up."

"Oh, Mark, what a ruffian you are to spoil my day's sport in this way. Any man but a parson would be too good a Christian for such intense cruelty. But let me see—four hundred pounds? Oh, yes—Tozer has it."

"And what will Tozer do with it?"

"Make money of it; whatever way he may go to work he will do that."

"But will Tozer bring it to me on the 20th?"

"Oh, Lord, no! Upon my word, Mark, you are deliciously green. A cat would as soon think of killing a mouse directly she got it into her claws. But, joking apart, you need not trouble yourself. Maybe you will hear no more about it; or, perhaps, which no doubt is more probable, I may have to send it to you to be renewed. But you need do nothing till you hear from me or somebody else."

"Only do not let any one come down upon me for the money."

"There is not the slightest fear of that. Tally-ho, old fellow! He's away. Tally-ho! right over by Gossetts' barn. Come along, and never mind Tozer—'Sufficient for the day is the evil thereof.'" And away they both went together, parson and member of Parliament.

And then again on that occasion Mark went home with a sort of feeling that the bill did not matter. Tozer would manage it somehow; and it was quite clear that it would not do to tell his wife of it just at present.

On the 21st of that month of February, however, he did receive a reminder that the bill and all concerning it had not merely been a farce. This was a letter from Mr. Sowerby, dated from Chaldicotes, though not bearing the Barchester post-mark, in which that gentleman suggested a renewal—not exactly of the old bill, but of a new one. It seemed to Mark that the letter had been posted in London. If I give it entire, I shall, perhaps, most quickly explain its purport:

Chaldicotes,—20th February, 185—.

MY DEAR MARK,—"Lend not thy name to the money-dealers, for the same is a destruction and a snare." If that be not in the Proverbs, it ought to be. Tozer has given me certain signs of his being alive and strong this cold weather. As we can neither of us take up that bill for £400 at the moment, we must renew it, and pay him his commission and interest, with all the rest of his perquisites, and pickings, and stealings—from all which, I can assure you, Tozer does not keep his hands as he should do. To cover this and some other little outstanding trifles, I have filled in the new bill for £500, making it due 23rd of May next. Before that time, a certain accident will, I trust, have occurred to your impoverished friend. By-the-by, I never told you how she went off from Gatherum Castle, the morning after you left us, with the Greshams. Cart-ropes would not hold her, even though the duke held them; which he did, with all the strength of his ducal hands. She would go to meet some doctor of theirs, and so I was put off for that time; but I think that the matter stands in a good train.

Do not lose a post in sending back the bill accepted, as Tozer may annoy you—nay, undoubtedly will, if the matter be not in his hand, duly signed by both of us, the day after to-morrow. He is an ungrateful brute; he has lived on me for these eight years, and would not let me off a single squeeze now to save my life. But I am specially anxious to save you from the annoyance and cost of lawyers' letters; and if delayed, it might get into the papers.

Put it under cover to me, at No. 7, Duke Street, St. James's. I shall be in town by that time.

Good-bye, old fellow. That was a decent brush we had the other day from Cobbold's Ashes. I wish I could get that brown horse from you. I would not mind going to a hundred and thirty.

Yours ever,
N. SOWERBY.

When Mark had read it through he looked down on his table to see whether the old bill had fallen from the letter; but no, there was no enclosure, and had been no enclosure but the new bill. And then he read the letter through again, and found that there was no word about the old bill,—not a syllable, at least, as to its whereabouts. Sowerby did not even say that it would remain in his own hands.

Mark did not in truth know much about such things. It might be that the very fact of his signing this second document would render that first document null and void; and from Sowerby's silence on the subject, it might be argued that this was so well known to be the case, that he had not thought of explaining it. But yet Mark could not see how this should be so.

But what was he to do? That threat of cost and lawyers, and specially of the newspapers, did have its effect upon him—as no doubt it was intended to do. And then he was utterly dumfounded by Sowerby's impudence in drawing on him for £500 instead of £400, "covering," as Sowerby so good-humouredly said, "sundry little outstanding trifles."

But at last he did sign the bill, and sent it off, as Sowerby had directed. What else was he to do?

Fool that he was. A man always can do right, even though he has done wrong before. But that previous wrong adds so much difficulty to the path—a difficulty which increases in tremendous ratio, till a man at last is choked in his struggling, and is drowned beneath the waters.

And then he put away Sowerby's letter carefully, locking it up from his wife's sight. It was a letter that no parish clergyman should have received. So much he acknowledged to himself. But nevertheless it was necessary that he should keep it. And now again for a few hours this affair made him very miserable.

CHAPTER XIII.

DELICATE HINTS.

Lady Lufton had been greatly rejoiced at that good deed which her son did in giving up his Leicestershire hunting, and coming to reside for the winter at Framley. It was proper, and becoming, and comfortable in the extreme. An English nobleman ought to hunt in the county where he himself owns the fields over which he rides; he ought to receive the respect and honour due to him from his own tenants; he ought to sleep under a roof of his own, and he ought also—so Lady Lufton thought—to fall in love with a young embryo bride of his own mother's choosing.

And then it was so pleasant to have him there in the house. Lady Lufton was not a woman who allowed her life to be what people in common parlance call dull. She had too many duties, and thought too much of them, to allow of her suffering from tedium and *ennui*. But nevertheless the house was more joyous to her when he was there. There was a reason for some little gaiety, which would never have been attracted thither by herself, but which, nevertheless, she did enjoy when it was brought about by his presence. She was younger and brighter when he was there, thinking more of the future and less of the past. She could look at him, and that alone was happiness to her. And then he was pleasant-mannered with her; joking with her on her little old-world prejudices in a tone that was musical to her ear as coming from him; smiling on her, reminding her of those smiles which she had loved so dearly when as yet he was all her own, lying there in his little bed beside her chair. He was kind and gracious to her, behaving like a good son, at any rate while he was there in her presence. When we add, to this, her fears that he might not be so perfect in his conduct when absent, we may well imagine that Lady Lufton was pleased to have him there at Framley Court.

She had hardly said a word to him as to that five thousand pounds. Many a night, as she lay thinking on her pillow, she said to herself that no money had ever been better expended, since it had brought him back to his own house. He had thanked her for it in his own open way, declaring that he would pay it back to her during the coming year, and comforting her heart by his rejoicing that the property had not been sold.

"I don't like the idea of parting with an acre of it," he had said.

"Of course not, Ludovic. Never let the estate decrease in your hands. It is only by such resolutions as that that English noblemen and English gentlemen can preserve their country. I cannot bear to see property changing hands."

"Well, I suppose it's a good thing to have land in the market sometimes, so that the millionnaires may know what to do with their money."

"God forbid that yours should be there!" And the widow made a little mental prayer that her son's acres might be protected from the millionnaires and other Philistines.

"Why, yes: I don't exactly want to see a Jew tailor investing his earnings at Lufton," said the lord.

"Heaven forbid!" said the widow.

All this, as I have said, was very nice. It was manifest to her ladyship, from his lordship's way of talking, that no vital injury had as yet been done: he had no cares on his mind, and spoke freely about the property: but nevertheless there were clouds even now, at this period of bliss, which somewhat obscured the brilliancy of Lady Lufton's sky. Why was Ludovic so slow in that affair of Griselda Grantly? why so often in these latter winter days did he saunter over to the parsonage? And then that terrible visit to Gatherum Castle!

What actually did happen at Gatherum Castle, she never knew. We, however, are more intrusive, less delicate in our inquiries, and we can say. He had a very bad day's sport with the West Barsetshire. The county is altogether short of foxes, and some one who understands the matter must take that point up before they can do any good. And after that he had had rather a dull dinner with the duke. Sowerby had been there, and in the evening he and Sowerby had played billiards. Sowerby had won a pound or two, and that had been the extent of the damage done.

But those saunterings over to the parsonage might be more dangerous. Not that it ever occurred to Lady Lufton as possible that her son should fall in love with Lucy Robarts. Lucy's personal attractions were not of a nature to give ground for such a fear as that. But he might turn the girl's head with his chatter; she might be fool enough to fancy any folly; and, moreover, people would talk. Why should he go to the parsonage now more frequently than he had ever done before Lucy came there?

And then her ladyship, in reference to the same trouble, hardly knew how to manage her invitations to the parsonage. These hitherto had been very frequent, and she had been in the habit of thinking that they could hardly be too much so; but now she was almost afraid to continue the custom. She could not ask the parson and his wife without Lucy; and when Lucy was there, her son would pass the greater part of the evening in talking to her, or playing chess with her. Now this did disturb Lady Lufton not a little.

And then Lucy took it all so quietly. On her first arrival at Framley she had been so shy, so silent, and so much awestruck by the grandeur of Framley Court, that Lady Lufton had sympathized with her and encouraged her. She had endeavoured to moderate the blaze of her own splendour, in order that Lucy's unaccustomed eyes might not be dazzled. But all this was changed now. Lucy could listen to the young lord's voice by the hour together—without being dazzled in the least.

Under these circumstances two things occurred to her. She would speak either to her son or to Fanny Robarts, and by a little diplomacy have this evil remedied. And then she had to determine on which step she would take.

"Nothing could be more reasonable than Ludovic." So at least she said to herself over and over again. But then Ludovic understood nothing about such matters; and he had, moreover, a habit, inherited from his father, of taking the bit between his teeth whenever he suspected interference. Drive him gently without pulling his mouth about, and you might take him anywhere, almost at any pace; but a smart touch, let it be ever so slight, would bring him on his haunches, and then it might be a question whether you could get him another mile that day. So that on the whole Lady Lufton thought that the other plan would be the best. I have no doubt that Lady Lufton was right.

She got Fanny up into her own den one afternoon, and seated her discreetly in an easy arm-chair, making her guest take off her bonnet, and showing by various signs that the visit was regarded as one of great moment.

894

"Fanny," she said, "I want to speak to you about something that is important and necessary to mention, and yet it is a very delicate affair to speak of." Fanny opened her eyes, and said that she hoped that nothing was wrong.

"No, my dear, I think nothing is wrong: I hope so, and I think I may say I'm sure of it; but then it's always well to be on one's guard."

"Yes, it is," said Fanny, who knew that something unpleasant was coming—something as to which she might probably be called upon to differ from her ladyship. Mrs. Robarts' own fears, however, were running entirely in the direction of her husband;—and, indeed, Lady Lufton had a word or two to say on that subject also, only not exactly now. A hunting parson was not at all to her taste; but that matter might be allowed to remain in abeyance for a few days.

"Now, Fanny, you know that we have all liked your sister-in-law, Lucy, very much." And then Mrs. Robarts' mind was immediately opened, and she knew the rest as well as though it had all been spoken. "I need hardly tell you that, for I am sure we have shown it."

"You have, indeed, as you always do."

"And you must not think that I am going to complain," continued Lady Lufton.

"I hope there is nothing to complain of," said Fanny, speaking by no means in a defiant tone, but humbly as it were, and deprecating her ladyship's wrath. Fanny had gained one signal victory over Lady Lufton, and on that account, with a prudence equal to her generosity, felt that she could afford to be submissive. It might, perhaps, not be long before she would be equally anxious to conquer again.

"Well, no; I don't think there is," said Lady Lufton. "Nothing to complain of; but a little chat between you and me may, perhaps, set matters right, which, otherwise, might become troublesome."

"Is it about Lucy?"

"Yes, my dear—about Lucy. She is a very nice, good girl, and a credit to her father—"

"And a great comfort to us," said Fanny.

"I am sure she is: she must be a very pleasant companion to you, and so useful about the children; but—" And then Lady Lufton paused for a moment; for she, eloquent and discreet as she always was, felt herself rather at a loss for words to express her exact meaning.

"I don't know what I should do without her," said Fanny, speaking with the object of assisting her ladyship in her embarrassment.

"But the truth is this: she and Lord Lufton are getting into the way of being too much together—of talking to each other too exclusively. I am sure you must have noticed it, Fanny. It is not that I suspect any evil. I don't think that I am suspicious by nature."

"Oh! no," said Fanny.

"But they will each of them get wrong ideas about the other, and about themselves. Lucy will, perhaps, think that Ludovic means more than he does, and Ludovic will—" But it was not quite so easy to say what Ludovic might do or think; but Lady Lufton went on: "I am sure that you understand me, Fanny, with your excellent sense and tact. Lucy is clever, and amusing, and all that; and Ludovic, like all young men, is perhaps ignorant that his attentions may be taken to mean more than he intends—"

"You don't think that Lucy is in love with him?"

"Oh dear, no—nothing of the kind. If I thought it had come to that, I should recommend that she should be sent away altogether. I am sure she is not so foolish as that."

"I don't think there is anything in it at all, Lady Lufton."

"I don't think there is, my dear, and therefore I would not for worlds make any suggestion about it to Lord Lufton. I would not let him suppose that I suspected Lucy of being so imprudent. But still, it may be well that you should just say a word to her. A little management now and then, in such matters, is so useful."

"But what shall I say to her?"

"Just explain to her that any young lady who talks so much to the same young gentleman will certainly be observed—that people will accuse her of setting her cap at Lord Lufton. Not that I suspect her—I give her credit for too much proper feeling: I know her education has been good, and her principles are upright. But people will talk of her. You must understand that, Fanny, as well as I do."

Fanny could not help meditating whether proper feeling, education, and upright principles did forbid Lucy Robarts to fall in love with Lord Lufton; but her doubts on this subject, if she held any, were not communicated to her ladyship. It had never entered into her mind that a match was possible between Lord Lufton and Lucy Robarts, nor had she the slightest wish to encourage it now that the idea was suggested to her. On such a matter she could sympathize with Lady Lufton, though she did not completely agree with her as to the expediency of any interference. Nevertheless, she at once offered to speak to Lucy.

"I don't think that Lucy has any idea in her head upon the subject," said Mrs. Robarts.

"I dare say not—I don't suppose she has. But young ladies sometimes allow themselves to fall in love, and then to think themselves very ill-used, just because they have had no idea in their head."

"I will put her on her guard if you wish it, Lady Lufton."

"Exactly, my dear; that is just it. Put her on her guard—that is all that is necessary. She is a dear, good, clever girl, and it would be very sad if anything were to interrupt our comfortable way of getting on with her."

Mrs. Robarts knew to a nicety the exact meaning of this threat. If Lucy would persist in securing to herself so much of Lord Lufton's time and attention, her visits to Framley Court must become less frequent. Lady Lufton would do much, very much, indeed, for her friends at the parsonage; but not even for them could she permit her son's prospects in life to be endangered.

There was nothing more said between them, and Mrs. Robarts got up to take her leave, having promised to speak to Lucy.

"You manage everything so perfectly," said Lady Lufton, as she pressed Mrs. Robarts' hand, "that I am quite at ease now that I find you will agree with me." Mrs. Robarts did not exactly agree with her ladyship, but she hardly thought it worth her while to say so.

Mrs. Robarts immediately started off on her walk to her own home, and when she had got out of the grounds into the road, where it makes a turn towards the parsonage, nearly opposite to Podgens' shop, she saw Lord Lufton on horseback, and Lucy standing beside him. It was already nearly five o'clock, and it was getting dusk; but as she approached, or rather as she came suddenly within sight of them, she could see that they were in close conversation. Lord Lufton's face was towards her, and his horse was standing still; he was leaning over towards his companion, and the whip, which he held in his right hand, hung almost over her arm and down her back, as though his hand had touched and perhaps rested on her shoulder. She was standing by his side, looking up into his face, with one gloved hand resting on the horse's neck. Mrs. Robarts, as she saw them, could not but own that there might be cause for Lady Lufton's fears.

But then Lucy's manner, as Mrs. Robarts approached, was calculated to dissipate any such fears, and to prove that there was no ground for them. She did not move from her position, or allow her hand to drop, or show that she was in any way either confused or conscious. She stood her ground, and when her sister-in-law came up was smiling and at her ease.

"Lord Lufton wants me to learn to ride," said she.

"To learn to ride!" said Fanny, not knowing what answer to make to such a proposition.

"Yes," said he. "This horse would carry her beautifully: he is as quiet as a lamb, and I made Gregory go out with him yesterday with a sheet hanging over him like a lady's habit, and the man got up into a lady's saddle."

"I think Gregory would make a better hand of it than Lucy."

"The horse cantered with him as though he had carried a lady all his life, and his mouth is like velvet; indeed, that is his fault—he is too soft-mouthed."

"I suppose that's the same sort of thing as a man being soft-hearted," said Lucy.

"Exactly: you ought to ride them both with a very light hand. They are difficult cattle to manage, but very pleasant when you know how to do it."

"But you see I don't know how to do it," said Lucy.

"As regards the horse, you will learn in two days, and I do hope you will try. Don't you think it will be an excellent thing for her, Mrs. Robarts?"

"Lucy has got no habit," said Mrs. Robarts, making use of the excuse common on all such occasions.

"There is one of Justinia's in the house, I know. She always leaves one here, in order that she may be able to ride when she comes."

"She would not think of taking such a liberty with Lady Meredith's things," said Fanny, almost frightened at the proposal.

"Of course it is out of the question, Fanny," said Lucy, now speaking rather seriously. "In the first place, I would not take Lord Lufton's horse; in the second place, I would not take Lady Meredith's habit; in the third place, I should be a great deal too much frightened; and, lastly, it is quite out of the question for a great many other very good reasons."

"Nonsense," said Lord Lufton.

"A great deal of nonsense," said Lucy, laughing, "but all of it of Lord Lufton's talking. But we are getting cold—are we not, Fanny?—so we will wish you good-night." And then the two ladies shook hands with him, and walked on towards the parsonage.

That which astonished Mrs. Robarts the most in all this was the perfectly collected manner in which Lucy spoke and conducted herself. This connected, as she could not but connect it, with the air of chagrin with which Lord Lufton received Lucy's decision, made it manifest to Mrs. Robarts that Lord Lufton was annoyed because Lucy would not consent to learn to ride; whereas she, Lucy herself, had given her refusal in a firm and decided tone, as though resolved that nothing more should be said about it.

They walked on in silence for a minute or two, till they reached the parsonage gate, and then Lucy said, laughing, "Can't you fancy me sitting on that great big horse? I wonder what Lady Lufton would say if she saw me there, and his lordship giving me my first lesson?"

"I don't think she would like it," said Fanny.

"I'm sure she would not. But I will not try her temper in that respect. Sometimes I fancy that she does not even like seeing Lord Lufton talking to me."

"She does not like it, Lucy, when she sees him flirting with you."

This Mrs. Robarts said rather gravely, whereas Lucy had been speaking in a half-bantering tone. As soon as even the word flirting was out of Fanny's mouth, she was conscious that she had been guilty of an injustice in using it. She had wished to say something which would convey to her sister-in-law an idea of what Lady Lufton would dislike; but in doing so, she had unintentionally brought against her an accusation.

"Flirting, Fanny!" said Lucy, standing still in the path, and looking up into her companion's face with all her eyes. "Do you mean to say that I have been flirting with Lord Lufton?"

"I did not say that."

"Or that I have allowed him to flirt with me?"

"I did not mean to shock you, Lucy."

"What did you mean, Fanny?"

"Why, just this: that Lady Lufton would not be pleased if he paid you marked attentions, and if you received them;—just like that affair of the riding; it was better to decline it."

"Of course I declined it; of course I never dreamt of accepting such an offer. Go riding about the country on his horses! What have I done, Fanny, that you should suppose such a thing?"

"You have done nothing, dearest."

"Then why did you speak as you did just now?"

"Because I wished to put you on your guard. You know, Lucy, that I do not intend to find fault with you; but you may be sure, as a rule, that intimate friendships between young gentlemen and young ladies are dangerous things."

They then walked up to the hall-door in silence. When they had reached it, Lucy stood in the doorway instead of entering it, and said, "Fanny, let us take another turn together, if you are not tired."

"No, I'm not tired."

"It will be better that I should understand you at once,"—and then they again moved away from the house. "Tell me truly now, do you think that Lord Lufton and I have been flirting?"

"I do think that he is a little inclined to flirt with you."

"And Lady Lufton has been asking you to lecture me about it?"

Poor Mrs. Robarts hardly knew what to say. She thought well of all the persons concerned, and was very anxious to behave well by all of them;—was particularly anxious to create no ill feeling, and wished that everybody should be comfortable, and on good terms with everybody else. But yet the truth was forced out of her when this question was asked so suddenly.

"Not to lecture you, Lucy," she said at last.

"Well, to preach to me, or to talk to me, or to give me a lesson; to say something that shall drive me to put my back up against Lord Lufton?"

"To caution you, dearest. Had you heard what she said, you would hardly have felt angry with Lady Lufton."

"Well, to caution me. It is such a pleasant thing for a girl to be cautioned against falling in love with a gentleman, especially when the gentleman is very rich, and a lord, and all that sort of thing!"

"Nobody for a moment attributes anything wrong to you, Lucy."

"Anything wrong—no. I don't know whether it would be anything wrong, even if I were to fall in love with him. I wonder whether they cautioned Griselda Grantly when she was here? I suppose when young lords go about, all the girls are cautioned as a matter of course. Why do they not label him 'dangerous'?" And then again they were silent for a moment, as Mrs. Robarts did not feel that she had anything further to say on the matter.

"'Poison' should be the word with any one so fatal as Lord Lufton; and he ought to be made up of some particular colour, for fear he should be swallowed in mistake."

"You will be safe, you see," said Fanny, laughing, "as you have been specially cautioned as to this individual bottle."

"Ah! but what's the use of that after I have had so many doses? It is no good telling me about it now, when the mischief is done,—after I have been taking it for I don't know how long. Dear! dear! dear! and I regarded it as a mere commonplace powder, good for the complexion. I wonder whether it's too late, or whether there's any antidote?"

Mrs. Robarts did not always quite understand her sister-in-law, and now she was a little at a loss. "I don't think there's much harm done yet on either side," she said, cheerily.

"Ah! you don't know, Fanny. But I do think that if I die—as I shall—I feel I shall;—and if so, I do think it ought to go very hard with Lady Lufton. Why didn't she label him 'dangerous' in time?" And then they went into the house and up to their own rooms.

It was difficult for any one to understand Lucy's state of mind at present, and it can hardly be said that she understood it herself. She felt that she had received a severe blow in having been thus made the subject of remark with reference to Lord Lufton. She knew that her pleasant evenings at Framley Court were now over, and that she could not again talk to him in an unrestrained tone and without embarrassment. She had felt the air of the whole place to be very cold before her intimacy with him, and now it must be cold again. Two homes had been open to her, Framley Court and the parsonage; and now, as far as comfort was concerned, she must confine herself to the latter. She could not again be comfortable in Lady Lufton's drawing-room.

But then she could not help asking herself whether Lady Lufton was not right. She had had courage enough, and presence of mind, to joke about the matter when her sister-in-law spoke to her, and yet she was quite aware that it was no joking matter. Lord Lufton had not absolutely made love to her, but he had latterly spoken to her in a manner which she knew was not compatible with that ordinary comfortable masculine friendship with the idea of which she had once satisfied herself. Was not Fanny right when she said that intimate friendships of that nature were dangerous things?

Yes, Lucy, very dangerous. Lucy, before she went to bed that night, had owned to herself that they were so; and lying there with sleepless eyes and a moist pillow, she was driven to confess that the label would in truth be now too late, that the caution had come to her after the poison had been swallowed. Was there any antidote? That was all that was left for her to consider. But, nevertheless, on the following morning she could appear quite at her ease. And when Mark had left the house after breakfast, she could still joke with Fanny as to Lady Lufton's poison cupboard.

CHAPTER XIV.

MR. CRAWLEY OF HOGGLESTOCK.

And then there was that other trouble in Lady Lufton's mind, the sins, namely, of her selected parson. She had selected him, and she was by no means inclined to give him up, even though his sins against parsondom were grievous. Indeed she was a woman not prone to give up anything, and of all things not prone to give up a *protégé*. The very fact that she herself had selected him was the strongest argument in his favour.

But his sins against parsondom were becoming very grievous in her eyes, and she was at a loss to know what steps to take. She hardly dared to take him to task, him himself. Were she to do so, and should he then tell her to mind her own business—as he probably might do, though not in those words—there would be a schism in the parish; and almost anything would be better than that. The whole work of her life would be upset, all the outlets of her energy would be impeded if not absolutely closed, if a state of things were to come to pass in which she and the parson of her parish should not be on good terms.

But what was to be done? Early in the winter he had gone to Chaldicotes and to Gatherum Castle, consorting with gamblers, Whigs, atheists, men of loose pleasure, and Proudieites. That she had condoned; and now he was turning out a hunting parson on her hands. It was all very well for Fanny to say that he merely looked at the hounds as he rode about his parish. Fanny might be deceived. Being his wife, it might be her duty not to see her husband's iniquities. But Lady Lufton could not be deceived. She knew very well in what part of the county Cobbold's Ashes lay. It was not in Framley parish, nor in the next parish to it. It was half-way across to Chaldicotes—in the western division; and she had heard of that run in which two horses had been killed, and in which Parson Robarts had won such immortal glory among West Barsetshire sportsmen. It was not easy to keep Lady Lufton in the dark as to matters occurring in her own county.

All these things she knew, but as yet had not noticed, grieving over them in her own heart the more on that account. Spoken grief relieves itself; and when one can give counsel, one always hopes at least that that counsel will be effective. To her son she had said, more than once, that it was a pity that Mr. Robarts should follow the hounds.—"The world has agreed that it is unbecoming in a clergyman," she would urge, in her deprecatory tone. But her son would by no means give her any comfort. "He doesn't hunt, you know—not as I do," he would say. "And if he did, I really don't see the harm of it. A man must have some amusement, even if he be an archbishop." "He has amusement at home," Lady Lufton would answer. "What does his wife do—and his sister?" This allusion to Lucy, however, was very soon dropped.

Lord Lufton would in no wise help her. He would not even passively discourage the vicar, or refrain from offering to give him a seat in going to the meets. Mark and Lord Lufton had been boys together, and his lordship knew that Mark in his heart would enjoy a brush across the country quite as well as he himself; and then what was the harm of it?

Lady Lufton's best aid had been in Mark's own conscience. He had taken himself to task more than once, and had promised himself that he would not become a sporting parson. Indeed, where would be his hopes of ulterior promotion, if he allowed himself to degenerate so far as that? It had been his intention, in reviewing what he considered to be the necessary proprieties of clerical life, in laying out his own future mode of living, to assume no peculiar sacerdotal strictness; he would not be known as a denouncer of dancing or of card-tables, of theatres or of novel-reading; he would take the world around him as he found it, endeavouring by precept and practice to lend a hand to the gradual amelioration which Christianity is producing; but he would attempt no sudden or majestic reforms. Cake and ale would still be popular, and ginger be hot in the mouth, let him preach ever so—let him be never so solemn a hermit; but a bright face, a true trusting heart, a strong arm, and an humble mind, might do much in teaching those around him that men may be gay and yet not profligate, that women may be devout and yet not dead to the world.

Such had been his ideas as to his own future life; and though many would think that as a clergyman he should have gone about his work with more serious devotion of thought, nevertheless there was some wisdom in them;—some folly also, undoubtedly, as appeared by the troubles into which they led him.

"I will not affect to think that to be bad," said he to himself, "which in my heart of hearts does not seem to be bad." And thus he resolved that he might live without contamination among hunting squires. And then, being a man only too prone by nature to do as others did around him, he found by degrees that that could hardly be wrong for him which he admitted to be right for others.

But still his conscience upbraided him, and he declared to himself more than once that after this year he would hunt no more. And then his own Fanny would look at him on his return home on those days in a manner that cut him to the heart. She would say nothing to him. She never inquired in a sneering tone, and with angry eyes, whether he had enjoyed his day's sport; but when he spoke of it, she could not answer him with enthusiasm; and in other matters which concerned him she was always enthusiastic.

After a while, too, he made matters worse, for about the end of March he did another very foolish thing. He almost consented to buy an expensive horse from Sowerby—an animal which he by no means wanted, and which, if once possessed, would certainly lead him into further trouble. A gentleman, when he has a good horse in his stable, does not like to leave him there eating his head off. If he be a gig-horse, the owner of him will be keen to drive a gig; if a hunter, the happy possessor will wish to be with a pack of hounds.

"Mark," said Sowerby to him one day, when they were out together, "this brute of mine is so fresh, I can hardly ride him; you are young and strong; change with me for an hour or so." And then they did change, and the horse on which Robarts found himself mounted went away with him beautifully.

"He's a splendid animal," said Mark, when they again met.

"Yes, for a man of your weight. He's thrown away upon me;—too much of a horse for my purposes. I don't get along now quite as well as I used to do. He is a nice sort of hunter; just rising six, you know."

How it came to pass that the price of the splendid animal was mentioned between them, I need not describe with exactness. But it did come to pass that Mr. Sowerby told the parson that the horse should be his for £130.

"And I really wish you'd take him," said Sowerby. "It would be the means of partially relieving my mind of a great weight."

Mark looked up into his friend's face with an air of surprise, for he did not at the moment understand how this should be the case.

"I am afraid, you know, that you will have to put your hand into your pocket sooner or later about that accursed bill—" Mark shrank as the profane word struck his ears—"and I should be glad to think that you had got something in hand in the way of value."

"Do you mean that I shall have to pay the whole sum of £500?"

"Oh! dear, no; nothing of the kind. But something I dare say you will have to pay: if you like to take Dandy for a hundred and thirty, you can be prepared for that amount when Tozer comes to you. The horse is dog cheap, and you will have a long day for your money."

Mark at first declared, in a quiet, determined tone, that he did not want the horse; but it afterwards appeared to him that if it were so fated that he must pay a portion of Mr. Sowerby's debts, he might as well repay himself to any extent within his power. It would be as well perhaps that he should take the horse and sell him. It did not occur to him that by so doing he would put it in Mr. Sowerby's power to say that some valuable consideration had passed between them with reference to this bill, and that he would be aiding that gentleman in preparing an inextricable confusion of money-matters between them. Mr. Sowerby well knew the value of this. It would enable him to make a plausible story, as he had done in that other case of Lord Lufton.

"Are you going to have Dandy?" Sowerby said to him again.

"I can't say that I will just at present," said the parson. "What should I want of him now the season's over?"

"Exactly, my dear fellow; and what do I want of him now the season's over? If it were the beginning of October instead of the end of March, Dandy would be up at two hundred and thirty instead of one: in six months' time that horse will be worth anything you like to ask for him. Look at his bone."

The vicar did look at his bones, examining the brute in a very knowing and unclerical manner. He lifted the animal's four feet, one after another, handling the frogs, and measuring with his eye the proportion of the parts; he passed his hand up and down the legs, spanning the bones of the lower joint; he peered into his eyes, took into consideration the width of his chest, the dip of his back, the form of his ribs, the curve of his haunches, and his capabilities for breathing when pressed by work. And then he stood away a little, eyeing him from the side, and taking in a general idea of the form and make of the whole. "He seems to stand over a little, I think," said the parson.

"It's the lie of the ground. Move him about, Bob. There now, let him stand there."

"He's not perfect," said Mark. "I don't quite like his heels; but no doubt he's a nicish cut of a horse."

"I rather think he is. If he were perfect, as you say, he would not be going into your stables for a hundred and thirty. Do you ever remember to have seen a perfect horse?"

"Your mare Mrs. Gamp was as nearly perfect as possible."

"Even Mrs. Gamp had her faults. In the first place she was a bad feeder. But one certainly doesn't often come across anything much better than Mrs. Gamp." And thus the matter was talked over between them with much stable conversation, all of which tended to make Sowerby more and more oblivious of his friend's sacred profession, and perhaps to make the vicar himself too frequently oblivious of it also. But no: he was not oblivious of it. He was even mindful of it; but mindful of it in such a manner that his thoughts on the subject were nowadays always painful.

MR. CRAWLEY OF HOGGLESTOCK.

There is a parish called Hogglestock lying away quite in the northern extremity of the eastern division of the county—lying also on the borders of the western division. I almost fear that it will become necessary, before this history be completed, to provide a map of Barsetshire for the due explanation of all these localities. Framley is also in the northern portion of the county, but just to the south of the grand trunk line of railway from which the branch to Barchester strikes off at a point some thirty miles nearer to London. The station for Framley Court is Silverbridge, which is, however, in the western division of the county. Hogglestock is to the north of the railway, the line of which, however, runs through a portion of the parish, and it adjoins Framley, though the churches are as much as seven miles apart. Barsetshire, taken altogether, is a pleasant green tree-becrowded county, with large bosky hedges, pretty damp deep lanes, and roads with broad grass margins running along them. Such is the general nature of the county; but just up in its northern extremity this nature alters. There it is bleak and ugly, with low artificial hedges and without wood; not uncultivated, as it is all portioned out into new-looking large fields, bearing turnips and wheat and mangel, all in due course of agricultural rotation; but it has none of the special beauties of English cultivation. There is not a gentleman's house in the parish of Hogglestock besides that of the clergyman; and this, though it is certainly the house of a gentleman, can hardly be said to be fit to be so. It is ugly, and straight, and small. There is a garden attached to the house, half in front of it and half behind; but this garden, like the rest of the parish, is by no means ornamental, though sufficiently useful. It produces cabbages, but no trees: potatoes of, I believe, an excellent description, but hardly any flowers, and nothing worthy of the name of a shrub. Indeed the whole parish of Hogglestock should have been in the adjoining county, which is by no means so attractive as Barsetshire;—a fact well known to those few of my readers who are well acquainted with their own country.

Mr. Crawley, whose name has been mentioned in these pages, was the incumbent of Hogglestock. On what principle the remuneration of our parish clergymen was settled when the original settlement was made, no deepest, keenest lover of middle-aged ecclesiastical black-letter learning can, I take it, now say. That the priests were to be paid from tithes of the parish produce, out of which tithes certain other good things were to be bought and paid for, such as church repairs and education, of so much the most of us have an inkling. That a rector, being a big sort of parson, owned the tithes of his parish in full,—or at any rate that part of them intended for the clergyman,—and that a vicar was somebody's deputy, and therefore entitled only to little tithes, as being a little body: of so much we that are simple in such matters have a general idea. But one cannot conceive that even in this way any approximation could have been made, even in those old mediæval days, towards a fair proportioning of the pay to the work. At any rate, it is clear enough that there is no such approximation now.

And what a screech would there not be among the clergy of the Church, even in these reforming days, if any over-bold reformer were to suggest that such an approximation should be attempted? Let those who know clergymen, and like them, and have lived with them, only fancy it! Clergymen to be paid, not according to the temporalities of any living which they may have acquired either by merit or favour, but in accordance with the work to be done! O Doddington! and O Stanhope, think of this, if an idea so sacrilegious can find entrance into your warm ecclesiastical bosoms! Ecclesiastical work to be bought and paid for according to its quantity and quality!

But, nevertheless, one may prophesy that we Englishmen must come to this, disagreeable as the idea undoubtedly is. Most pleasant-minded churchmen feel, I think, on this subject pretty much in the same way. Our present arrangement of parochial incomes is beloved as being time-honoured, gentlemanlike, English, and picturesque. We would fain adhere to it closely as long as we can, but we know that we do so by the force of our prejudices, and not by that of our judgment. A time-honoured, gentlemanlike, English, pictur-picturesque arrangement is so far very delightful. But are there not other attributes very desirable—nay, absolutely necessary—in respect to which this time-honoured, picturesque arrangement is so very deficient?

How pleasant it was, too, that one bishop should be getting fifteen thousand a year and another with an equal cure of parsons only four! That a certain prelate could get twenty thousand one year and his successor in the same diocese only five the next! There was something in it pleasant, and picturesque; it was an arrangement endowed with feudal charms, and the change which they have made was distasteful to many of us. A bishop with a regular salary, and no appanage of land and land-bailiffs, is only half a bishop. Let any man prove to me the contrary ever so thoroughly—let me prove it to my own self ever so often—my heart in this matter is not thereby a whit altered. One liked to know that there was a dean or two who got his three thousand a year, and that old Dr. Purple held four stalls, one of which was golden, and the other three silver-gilt! Such knowledge was always pleasant to me! A golden stall! How sweet is the sound thereof to church-loving ears!

But bishops have been shorn of their beauty, and deans are in their decadence. A utilitarian age requires the fatness of the ecclesiastical land, in order that it may be divided out into small portions of provender, on which necessary working clergymen may live,—into portions so infinitesimally small that working clergymen can hardly live. And the full-blown rectors and vicars, with full-blown tithes—with tithes when too full-blown for strict utilitarian principles—will necessarily follow. Stanhope and Doddington must bow their heads, with such compensation for temporal rights as may be extracted,—but probably without such compensation as may be desired. In other trades, professions, and lines of life, men are paid according to their work. Let it be so in the Church. Such will sooner or later be the edict of a utilitarian, reforming, matter-of-fact House of Parliament.

I have a scheme of my own on the subject, which I will not introduce here, seeing that neither men nor women would read it. And with reference to this matter, I will only here further explain that all these words have been brought about by the fact, necessary to be here stated, that Mr. Crawley only received one hundred and thirty pounds a year for performing the whole parochial duty of the parish of Hogglestock. And Hogglestock is a large parish. It includes two populous villages, abounding in brickmakers, a race of men very troublesome to a zealous parson who won't let men go rollicking to the devil without interference. Hogglestock has full work for two men; and yet all the funds therein applicable to parson's work is this miserable stipend of one hundred and thirty pounds a year. It is a stipend neither picturesque, nor time-honoured, nor feudal, for Hogglestock takes rank only as a perpetual curacy.

Mr. Crawley has been mentioned before as a clergyman of whom Mr. Robarts said, that he almost thought it wrong to take a walk out of his own parish. In so saying Mark Robarts of course burlesqued his brother parson; but there can be no doubt that Mr. Crawley was a strict man,—a strict, stern, unpleasant man, and one who feared God and his own conscience. We must say a word or two of Mr. Crawley and his concerns.

He was now some forty years of age, but of these he had not been in possession even of his present benefice for more than four or five. The first ten years of his life as a clergyman had been passed in performing the duties and struggling through the life of a curate in a bleak, ugly, cold parish on the northern coast of Cornwall. It had been a weary life and a fearful struggle, made up of duties ill requited and not always satisfactorily performed, of love and poverty, of increasing cares, of sickness, debt, and death. For Mr. Crawley had married almost as soon as he was ordained, and children had been born to him in that chill, comfortless Cornish cottage. He had married a lady well educated and softly nurtured, but not dowered with worldly wealth. They two had gone forth determined to fight bravely together; to disregard the world and the world's ways, looking only to God and to each other for their comfort. They would give up ideas of gentle living, of soft raiment, and delicate feeding. Others,—those that work with their hands, even the bettermost of such workers—could live in decency and health upon even such provision as he could earn as a clergyman. In such manner would they live, so poorly and so decently, working out their work, not with their hands but with their hearts.

And so they had established themselves, beginning the world with one bare-footed little girl of fourteen to aid them in their small household matters; and for a while they had both kept heart, loving each other dearly, and prospering somewhat in their work. But a man who has once walked the world as a gentleman knows not what it is to change his position, and place himself lower down in the social rank. Much less can he know what it is so to put down the woman whom he loves. There are a thousand things, mean and trifling in themselves, which a man despises when he thinks of them in his philosophy, but to dispense with which puts his philosophy to so stern a proof. Let any plainest man who reads this think of his usual mode of getting himself into his matutinal garments, and confess how much such a struggle would cost him.

And then children had come. The wife of the labouring man does rear her children, and often rears them in health, without even so many appliances of comfort as found their way into Mrs. Crawley's cottage; but the task to her was almost more than she could accomplish. Not that she ever fainted or gave way: she was made of the sterner metal of the two, and could last on while he was prostrate.

And sometimes he was prostrate—prostrate in soul and spirit. Then would he complain with bitter voice, crying out that the world was too hard for him, that his back was broken with his burden, that his God had deserted him. For days and days, in such moods, he would stay within his cottage, never darkening the door or seeing other face than those of his own inmates. Those days were terrible both to him and her. He would sit there unwashed, with his unshorn face resting on his hand, with an old dressing-gown hanging loose about him, hardly tasting food, seldom speaking, striving to pray, but striving so frequently in vain. And then he would rise from his chair, and, with a burst of frenzy, call upon his Creator to remove him from this misery.

In these moments she never deserted him. At one period they had had four children, and though the whole weight of this young brood rested on her arms, on her muscles, on her strength of mind and body, she never ceased in her efforts to comfort him. Then at length, falling utterly upon the ground, he would pour forth piteous prayers for mercy, and, after a night of sleep, would once more go forth to his work.

But she never yielded to despair: the struggle was never beyond her powers of endurance. She had possessed her share of woman's loveliness, but that was now all gone. Her colour quickly faded, and the fresh, soft tints soon deserted her face and forehead. She became thin, and rough, and almost haggard: thin, till her cheek-bones were nearly pressing through her skin, till her elbows were sharp, and her finger-bones as those of a skeleton. Her eye did not lose its lustre, but it became unnaturally bright, prominent, and too large for her wan face. The soft brown locks which she had once loved to brush back, scorning, as she would boast to herself, to care that they should be seen, were now sparse enough and all untidy and unclean. It was matter of little thought now whether they were seen or no. Whether he could be made fit to go into his pulpit—whether they might be fed—those four innocents—and their backs kept from the cold wind—that was now the matter of her thought.

And then two of them died, and she went forth herself to see them laid under the frost-bound sod, lest he should faint in his work over their graves. For he would ask aid from no man—such at least was his boast through all.

Two of them died, but their illness had been long; and then debts came upon them. Debt, indeed, had been creeping on them with slow but sure feet during the last five years. Who can see his children hungry, and not take bread if it be offered? Who can see his wife lying in sharpest want, and not seek a remedy if there be a remedy within reach? So debt had come upon them, and rude men pressed for small sums of money—for sums small to the world, but impossibly large to them. And he would hide himself within there, in that cranny of an inner chamber—hide himself with deep shame from the world, with shame, and a sinking heart, and a broken spirit.

But had such a man no friend? it will be said. Such men, I take it, do not make many friends. But this man was not utterly friendless. Almost every year one visit was paid to him in his Cornish curacy by a brother clergyman, an old college friend, who, as far as might in him lie, did give aid to the curate and his wife. This gentleman would take up his abode for a week at a farmer's in the neighbourhood, and though he found Mr. Crawley in despair, he would leave him with some drops of comfort in his soul. Nor were the benefits in this respect all on one side. Mr. Crawley, though at some periods weak enough for himself, could be strong for others; and, more than once, was strong to the great advantage of this man whom he loved. And then, too, pecuniary assistance was forthcoming—in those earlier years not in great amount, for this friend was not then among the rich ones of the earth—but in amount sufficient for that moderate hearth, if only its acceptance could have been managed. But in that matter there were difficulties without end. Of absolute money tenders Mr. Crawley would accept none. But a bill here and there was paid, the wife assisting; and shoes came for Kate—till Kate was placed beyond the need of shoes; and cloth for Harry and Frank found its way surreptitiously in beneath the cover of that wife's solitary trunk—cloth with which those lean fingers worked garments for the two boys, to be worn—such was God's will—only by the one.

Such were Mr. and Mrs. Crawley in their Cornish curacy, and during their severest struggles. To one who thinks that a fair day's work is worth a fair day's wages, it seems hard enough that a man should work so hard and receive so little. There will be those who think that the fault was all his own in marrying so young. But still there remains that question, Is not a fair day's work worth a fair day's wages? This man did work hard—at a task perhaps the hardest of any that a man may do; and for ten years he earned some seventy pounds a year. Will any one say that he received fair wages for his fair work, let him be married or single? And yet there are so many who would fain pay their clergy, if they only knew how to apply their money! But that is a long subject, as Mr. Robarts had told Miss Dunstable.

Such was Mr. Crawley in his Cornish curacy.

CHAPTER XV.

LADY LUFTON'S AMBASSADOR.

And then, in the days which followed, that friend of Mr. Crawley's, whose name, by-the-by, is yet to be mentioned, received quick and great promotion. Mr. Arabin by name he was then;—Dr. Arabin afterwards, when that quick and great promotion reached its climax. He had been simply a Fellow of Lazarus in those former years. Then he became Vicar of St. Ewold's, in East Barsetshire, and had not yet got himself settled there when he married the Widow Bold, a widow with belongings in land and funded money, and with but one small baby as an encumbrance. Nor had he even yet married her,—had only engaged himself so to do, when they made him Dean of Barchester—all which may be read in the diocesan and county chronicles.

And now that he was wealthy, the new dean did contrive to pay the debts of his poor friend, some lawyer of Camelford assisting him. It was but a paltry schedule after all, amounting in the total to something not much above a hundred pounds. And then, in the course of eighteen months, this poor piece of preferment fell in the dean's way, this incumbency of Hogglestock with its stipend reaching one hundred and thirty pounds a year. Even that was worth double the Cornish curacy, and there was, moreover, a house attached to it. Poor Mrs. Crawley, when she heard of it, thought that their struggles of poverty were now well nigh over. What might not be done with a hundred and thirty pounds by people who had lived for ten years on seventy?

And so they moved away out of that cold, bleak country, carrying with them their humble household gods, and settled themselves in another country, cold and bleak also, but less terribly so than the former. They settled themselves, and again began their struggles against man's hardness and the devil's zeal. I have said that Mr. Crawley was a stern, unpleasant man; and it certainly was so. The man must be made of very sterling stuff, whom continued and undeserved misfortune does not make unpleasant. This man had so far succumbed to grief, that it had left upon him its marks, palpable and not to be effaced. He cared little for society, judging men to be doing evil who did care for it. He knew as a fact, and believed with all his heart, that these sorrows had come to him from the hand of God, and that they would work for his weal in the long run; but not the less did they make him morose, silent, and dogged. He had always at his heart a feeling that he and his had been ill-used, and too often solaced himself, at the devil's bidding, with the conviction that eternity would make equal that which life in this world had made so unequal;—the last bait that with which the devil angles after those who are struggling to elude his rod and line.

The Framley property did not run into the parish of Hogglestock; but nevertheless Lady Lufton did what she could in the way of kindness to these new-comers. Providence had not supplied Hogglestock with a Lady Lufton, or with any substitute in the shape of lord or lady, squire or squiress. The Hogglestock farmers, male and female, were a rude, rough set, not bordering in their social rank on the farmer gentle; and Lady Lufton, knowing this, and hearing something of these Crawleys from Mrs. Arabin, the dean's wife, trimmed her lamps, so that they should shed a wider light, and pour forth some of their influence on that forlorn household.

And as regards Mrs. Crawley, Lady Lufton by no means found that her work and good-will were thrown away. Mrs. Crawley accepted her kindness with thankfulness, and returned to some of the softnesses of life under her hand. As for dining at Framley Court, that was out of the question. Mr. Crawley, she knew, would not hear of it, even if other things were fitting and appliances were at command. Indeed Mrs. Crawley at once said that she felt herself unfit to go through such a ceremony with anything like comfort. The dean, she said, would talk of their going to stay at the deanery; but she thought it quite impossible that either of them should endure even that. But, all the same, Lady Lufton was a comfort to her; and the poor woman felt that it was well to have a lady near her in case of need.

The task was much harder with Mr. Crawley, but even with him it was not altogether unsuccessful. Lady Lufton talked to him of his parish and of her own; made Mark Robarts go to him, and by degrees did something towards civilizing him. Between him and Robarts too there grew up an intimacy rather than a friendship. Robarts would submit to his opinion on matters of ecclesiastical and even theological law, would listen to him with patience, would agree with him where he could, and differ from him mildly when he could not. For Robarts was a man who made himself pleasant to all men. And thus, under Lady Lufton's wing, there grew up a connection between Framley and Hogglestock, in which Mrs. Robarts also assisted.

And now that Lady Lufton was looking about her, to see how she might best bring proper clerical influence to bear upon her own recreant fox-hunting parson, it occurred to her that she might use Mr. Crawley in the matter. Mr. Crawley would certainly be on her side as far as opinion went, and would have no fear as to expressing his opinion to his brother clergyman. So she sent for Mr. Crawley.

In appearance he was the very opposite to Mark Robarts. He was a lean, slim, meagre man, with shoulders slightly curved, and pale, lank, long locks of ragged hair; his forehead was high, but his face was narrow; his small grey eyes were deeply sunken in his head, his nose was well-formed, his lips thin, and his mouth expressive. Nobody could look at him without seeing that there was a purpose and a meaning in his countenance. He always wore, in summer and winter, a long dusky gray coat, which buttoned close up to his neck and descended almost to his heels. He was full six feet high, but being so slight in build, he looked as though he were taller.

He came at once at Lady Lufton's bidding, putting himself into the gig beside the servant, to whom he spoke no single word during the journey. And the man, looking into his face, was struck with taciturnity. Now Mark Robarts would have talked with him the whole way from Hogglestock to Framley Court; discoursing partly as to horses and land, but partly also as to higher things.

And then Lady Lufton opened her mind and told her griefs to Mr. Crawley, urging, however, through the whole length of her narrative, that Mr. Robarts was an excellent parish clergyman,—"just such a clergyman in his church as I would wish him to be," she explained, with the view of saving herself from an expression of any of Mr. Crawley's special ideas as to church teaching, and of confining him to the one subject-matter in hand; "but he got this living so young, Mr. Crawley, that he is hardly quite as steady as I could wish him to be. It has been as much my fault as his own in placing him in such a position so early in life."

"I think it has," said Mr. Crawley, who might perhaps be a little sore on such a subject.

"Quite so, quite so," continued her ladyship, swallowing down with a gulp a certain sense of anger. "But that is done now, and is past cure. That Mr. Robarts will become a credit to his profession, I do not doubt, for his heart is in the right place and his sentiments are good; but I fear that at present he is succumbing to temptation."

"I am told that he hunts two or three times a week. Everybody round us is talking about it."

"No, Mr. Crawley; not two or three times a week; very seldom above once, I think. And then I do believe he does it more with the view of being with Lord Lufton than any-thing else."

"I cannot see that that would make the matter better," said Mr. Crawley.

"It would show that he was not strongly imbued with a taste which I cannot but regard as vicious in a clergyman."

"It must be vicious in all men," said Mr. Crawley. "It is in itself cruel, and leads to idleness and profligacy."

Again Lady Lufton made a gulp. She had called Mr. Crawley thither to her aid, and felt that it would be inexpedient to quarrel with him. But she did not like to be told that her son's amusement was idle and profligate. She had always regarded hunting as a proper pursuit for a country gentleman. It was, indeed, in her eyes one of the peculiar institutions of country life in England, and it may be almost said that she looked upon the Barsetshire hunt as something sacred. She could not endure to hear that a fox was trapped, and al-lowed her turkeys to be purloined without a groan. Such being the case, she did not like being told that it was vicious, and had by no means wished to consult Mr. Crawley on that matter. But nevertheless, she swallowed down her wrath.

"It is at any rate unbecoming in a clergyman," she said; "and as I know that Mr. Robarts places a high value on your opinion, perhaps you will not object to advise him to discontinue it. He might possibly feel aggrieved were I to interfere personally on such a question."

"I have no doubt he would," said Mr. Crawley. "It is not within a woman's province to give counsel to a clergyman on such a subject, unless she be very near and very dear to him—his wife, or mother, or sister."

"As living in the same parish, you know, and being, perhaps—" the leading person in it, and the one who naturally rules the others. Those would have been the fitting words for the expression of her ladyship's ideas; but she remembered herself, and did not use them. She had made up her mind that, great as her influence ought to be, she was not the proper person to speak to Mr. Robarts as to his pernicious, unclerical habits, and she would not now depart from her resolve by attempting to prove that she was the proper person.

"Yes," said Mr. Crawley, "just so. All that would entitle him to offer you his counsel if he thought that your mode of life was such as to require it, but could by no means justify you in addressing yourself to him."

This was very hard upon Lady Lufton. She was endeavouring with all her woman's strength to do her best, and endeavouring so to do it that the feelings of the sinner might be spared; and yet the ghostly comforter whom she had evoked to her aid, treated her as though she were arrogant and overbearing. She acknowledged the weakness of her own position with reference to her parish clergyman by calling in the aid of Mr. Crawley; and under such circumstances, he might, at any rate, have abstained from throwing that weak-ness in her teeth.

"Well, sir; I hope my mode of life may not require it; but that is not exactly to the point: what I wish to know is, whether you will speak to Mr. Robarts?"

"Certainly I will," said he.

"Then I shall be much obliged to you. But, Mr. Crawley, pray—pray, remember this: I would not on any account wish that you should be harsh with him. He is an excellent young man, and—"

"Lady Lufton, if I do this, I can only do it in my own way, as best I may, using such words as God may give me at the time. I hope that I am harsh to no man; but it is worse than useless, in all cases, to speak anything but the truth."

"Of course—of course."

"If the ears be too delicate to hear the truth, the mind will be too perverse to profit by it." And then Mr. Crawley got up to take his leave.

But Lady Lufton insisted that he should go with her to luncheon. He hummed and ha'd and would fain have refused, but on this subject she was peremptory. It might be that she was unfit to advise a clergyman as to his duties, but in a matter of hospitality she did know what she was about. Mr. Crawley should not leave the house without refreshment. As to this, she carried her point; and Mr. Crawley—when the matter before him was cold roast-beef and hot potatoes, instead of the relative position of a parish priest and his parishioner—became humble, submissive, and almost timid. Lady Lufton recommended Madeira instead of Sherry, and Mr. Crawley obeyed at once, and was, indeed, perfectly unconscious of the difference. Then there was a basket of seakale in the gig for Mrs. Crawley; that he would have left behind had he dared, but he did not dare. Not a word was said to him as to the marmalade for the children which was hidden under the seakale, Lady Lufton feeling well aware that that would find its way to its proper destination without any necessity for his co-operation. And then Mr. Crawley returned home in the Framley Court gig.

Three or four days after this he walked over to Framley Parsonage. This he did on a Saturday, having learned that the hounds never hunted on that day; and he started early, so that he might be sure to catch Mr. Robarts before he went out on his parish business. He was quite early enough to attain this object, for when he reached the parsonage door at about half-past nine, the vicar, with his wife and sister, were just sitting down to breakfast.

"Oh, Crawley," said Robarts, before the other had well spoken, "you are a capital fellow;" and then he got him into a chair, and Mrs. Robarts had poured him out tea, and Lucy had surrendered to him a knife and plate, before he knew under what guise to excuse his coming among them.

"I hope you will excuse this intrusion," at last he muttered; "but I have a few words of business to which I will request your attention presently."

"Certainly," said Robarts, conveying a broiled kidney on to the plate before Mr. Crawley; "but there is no preparation for business like a good breakfast. Lucy, hand Mr. Crawley the buttered toast. Eggs, Fanny; where are the eggs?" And then John, in livery, brought in the fresh eggs. "Now we shall do. I always eat my eggs while they're hot, Crawley, and I advise you to do the same."

To all this Mr. Crawley said very little, and he was not at all at home under the circumstances. Perhaps a thought did pass across his brain, as to the difference between the meal which he had left on his own table, and that which he now saw before him; and as to any cause which might exist for such difference. But, if so, it was a very fleeting thought, for he had far other matter now fully occupying his mind. And then the breakfast was over, and in a few minutes the two clergymen found themselves together in the parsonage study.

"Mr. Robarts," began the senior, when he had seated himself uncomfortably on one of the ordinary chairs at the farther side of the well-stored library table, while Mark was sitting at his ease in his own arm-chair by the fire, "I have called upon you on an unpleasant business."

Mark's mind immediately flew off to Mr. Sowerby's bill, but he could not think it possible that Mr. Crawley could have had anything to do with that.

"But as a brother clergyman, and as one who esteems you much and wishes you well, I have thought myself bound to take this matter in hand."

"What matter is it, Crawley?"

"Mr. Robarts, men say that your present mode of life is one that is not befitting a soldier in Christ's army."

"Men say so! what men?"

"The men around you, of your own neighbourhood; those who watch your life, and know all your doings; those who look to see you walking as a lamp to guide their feet, but find you consorting with horse-jockeys and hunters, galloping after hounds, and taking your place among the vainest of worldly pleasure-seekers. Those who have a right to expect an example of good living, and who think that they do not see it."

Mr. Crawley had gone at once to the root of the matter, and in doing so had certainly made his own task so much the easier. There is nothing like going to the root of the matter at once when one has on hand an unpleasant piece of business.

"And have such men deputed you to come here?"

"No one has or could depute me. I have come to speak my own mind, not that of any other. But I refer to what those around you think and say, because it is to them that your duties are due. You owe it to those around you to live a godly, cleanly life;—as you owe it also, in a much higher way, to your Father who is in heaven. I now make bold to ask you whether you are doing your best to lead such a life as that?" And then he remained silent, waiting for an answer.

He was a singular man; so humble and meek, so unutterably inefficient and awkward in the ordinary intercourse of life, but so bold and enterprising, almost eloquent, on the one subject which was the work of his mind! As he sat there, he looked into his companion's face from out his sunken grey eyes with a gaze which made his victim quail. And then repeated his words: "I now make bold to ask you, Mr. Robarts, whether you are doing your best to lead such a life as may become a parish clergyman among his parishioners?" And again he paused for an answer.

"There are but few of us," said Mark in a low tone, "who could safely answer that question in the affirmative."

"But are there many, think you, among us who would find the question so unanswerable as yourself? And even were there many, would you, young, enterprising, and talented as you are, be content to be numbered among them? Are you satisfied to be a castaway after you have taken upon yourself Christ's armour? If you will say so, I am mistaken in you, and will go my way." There was again a pause, and then he went on. "Speak to me, my brother, and open your heart if it be possible." And rising from his chair, he walked across the room, and laid his hand tenderly on Mark's shoulder.

Mark had been sitting lounging in his chair, and had at first, for a moment only, thought to brazen it out. But all idea of brazening had now left him. He had raised himself from his comfortable ease, and was leaning forward with his elbow on the table; but now, when he heard these words, he allowed his head to sink upon his arms, and he buried his face between his hands.

"It is a terrible falling off," continued Crawley: "terrible in the fall, but doubly terrible through that difficulty of returning. But it cannot be that it should content you to place yourself as one among those thoughtless sinners, for the crushing of whose sin you have been placed here among them. You become a hunting parson, and ride with a happy mind among blasphemers and mocking devils—you, whose aspirations were so high, who have spoken so often and so well of the duties of a minister of Christ; you, who can argue in your pride as to the petty details of your Church, as though the broad teachings of its great and simple lessons were not enough for your energies! It cannot be that I have had a hyp-ocrite beside me in all those eager controversies!"

"Not a hypocrite—not a hypocrite," said Mark, in a tone which was almost reduced to sobbing.

"But a castaway! Is it so that I must call you? No, Mr. Robarts, not a castaway; neither a hypocrite, nor a castaway; but one who in walking has stumbled in the dark and bruised his feet among the stones. Henceforth let him take a lantern in his hand, and look warily to his path, and walk cautiously among the thorns and rocks,—cautiously, but yet boldly, with manly courage, but Christian meekness, as all men should walk on their pilgrimage through this vale of tears." And then without giving his companion time to stop him he hurried out of the room, and from the house, and without again seeing any others of the family, stalked back on his road to Hogglestock, thus tramping fourteen miles through the deep mud in performance of the mission on which he had been sent.

It was some hours before Mr. Robarts left his room. As soon as he found that Crawley was really gone, and that he should see him no more, he turned the lock of his door, and sat himself down to think over his present life. At about eleven his wife knocked, not knowing whether that other strange clergyman were there or no, for none had seen his departure. But Mark, answering cheerily, desired that he might be left to his studies.

Let us hope that his thoughts and mental resolves were then of service to him.

CHAPTER XVI.

MRS. PODGENS' BABY.

The hunting season had now nearly passed away, and the great ones of the Barsetshire world were thinking of the glories of London. Of these glories Lady Lufton always thought with much inquietude of mind. She would fain have remained throughout the whole year at Framley Court, did not certain grave considerations render such a course on her part improper in her own estimation. All the Lady Luftons of whom she had heard, dowager and ante-dowager, had always had their seasons in London, till old age had incapacitated them for such doings—sometimes for clearly long after the arrival of such period. And then she had an idea, perhaps not altogether erroneous, that she annually imported back with her into the country somewhat of the passing civilization of the times:— may we not say an idea that certainly was not erroneous? for how otherwise is it that the forms of new caps and remodelled shapes for women's waists find their way down into agricultural parts, and that the rural eye learns to appreciate grace and beauty? There are those who think that remodelled waists and new caps had better be kept to the towns; but such people, if they would follow out their own argument, would wish to see ploughboys painted with ruddle and milkmaids covered with skins.

For these and other reasons Lady Lufton always went to London in April, and stayed there till the beginning of June. But for her this was usually a period of penance. In London she was no very great personage. She had never laid herself out for greatness of that sort, and did not shine as a lady-patroness or state secretary in the female cabinet of fashion. She was dull and listless, and without congenial pursuits in London, and spent her happiest moments in reading accounts of what was being done at Framley, and in writing orders for further local information of the same kind.

But on this occasion there was a matter of vital import to give an interest of its own to her visit to town. She was to entertain Griselda Grantly, and as far as might be possible to induce her son to remain in Griselda's society. The plan of the campaign was to be as follows:—Mrs. Grantly and the archdeacon were in the first place to go up to London for a month, taking Griselda with them; and then, when they returned to Plumstead, Griselda was to go to Lady Lufton. This arrangement was not at all points agreeable to Lady Lufton, for she knew that Mrs. Grantly did not turn her back on the Hartletop people quite as cordially as she should do, considering the terms of the Lufton-Grantly family treaty. But then Mrs. Grantly might have alleged in excuse the slow manner in which Lord Lufton proceeded in the making and declaring of his love, and the absolute necessity which there is for two strings to one's bow, when one string may be in any way doubtful. Could it be possible that Mrs. Grantly had heard anything of that unfortunate Platonic friendship with Lucy Robarts?

There came a letter from Mrs. Grantly just about the end of March, which added much to Lady Lufton's uneasiness, and made her more than ever anxious to be herself on the scene of action and to have Griselda in her own hands. After some communications of mere ordinary importance with reference to the London world in general and the Lufton-Grantly world in particular, Mrs. Grantly wrote confidentially about her daughter:

"It would be useless to deny," she said, with a mother's pride and a mother's humility, "that she is very much admired. She is asked out a great deal more than I can take her, and to houses to which I myself by no means wish to go. I could not refuse her as to Lady Hartletop's first ball, for there will be nothing else this year like them; and of course when with you, dear Lady Lufton, that house will be out of the question. So indeed would it be with me, were I myself only concerned. The duke was there, of course, and I really wonder Lady Hartletop should not be more discreet in her own drawing-room when all the world is there. It is clear to me that Lord Dumbello admires Griselda much more than I could wish. She, dear girl, has such excellent sense that I do not think it likely that her head should be turned by it; but with how many girls would not the admiration of such a man be irresistible? The marquis, you know, is very feeble, and I am told that since this rage for building has come on, the Lancashire property is over two hundred thousand a year!! I do not think that Lord Dumbello has said much to her. Indeed it seems to me that he never does say much to any one. But he always stands up to dance with her, and I see that he is uneasy and fidgety when she stands up with any other partner whom he could care about. It was really embarrassing to see him the other night at Miss Dunstable's, when Griselda was dancing with a certain friend of ours. But she did look very well that evening, and I have seldom seen her more animated!"

All this, and a great deal more of the same sort in the same letter, tended to make Lady Lufton anxious to be in London. It was quite certain—there was no doubt of that, at any rate—that Griselda would see no more of Lady Hartletop's meretricious grandeur when she had been transferred to Lady Lufton's guardianship. And she, Lady Lufton, did wonder that Mrs. Grantly should have taken her daughter to such a house. All about Lady Hartletop was known to all the world. It was known that it was almost the only house in London at which the Duke of Omnium was constantly to be met. Lady Lufton herself would almost as soon think of taking a young girl to Gatherum Castle; and on these accounts she did feel rather angry with her friend Mrs. Grantly. But then perhaps she did not sufficiently calculate that Mrs. Grantly's letter had been written purposely to produce such feelings—with the express view of awakening her ladyship to the necessity of action. Indeed in such a matter as this Mrs. Grantly was a more able woman than Lady Lufton—more able to see her way and to follow it out. The Lufton-Grantly alliance was in her mind the best, seeing that she did not regard money as everything. But failing that, the Hartletop-Grantly alliance was not bad. Regarding it as a second string to her bow, she thought that it was not at all bad.

Lady Lufton's reply was very affectionate. She declared how happy she was to know that Griselda was enjoying herself; she insinuated that Lord Dumbello was known to the world as a fool, and his mother as—being not a bit better than she ought to be; and then she added that circumstances would bring herself up to town four days sooner than she had expected, and that she hoped her dear Griselda would come to her at once. Lord Lufton, she said, though he would not sleep in Bruton Street—Lady Lufton lived in Bruton Street—had promised to pass there as much of his time as his parliamentary duties would permit.

O Lady Lufton! Lady Lufton! did it not occur to you, when you wrote those last words, intending that they should have so strong an effect on the mind of your correspondent, that you were telling a—tarradiddle? Was it not the case that you had said to your son, in your own dear, kind, motherly way: "Ludovic, we shall see something of you in Bruton Street this year, shall we not? Griselda Grantly will be with me, and we must not let her be dull—must we?" And then had he not answered, "Oh, of course, mother," and sauntered out of the room, not altogether graciously? Had he, or you, said a word about his parliamentary duties? Not a word! O Lady Lufton! have you not now written a tarradiddle to your friend?

In these days we are becoming very strict about truth with our children; terribly strict occasionally, when we consider the natural weakness of the moral courage at the ages of ten, twelve, and fourteen. But I do not know that we are at all increasing the measure of strictness with which we, grown-up people, regulate our own truth and falsehood. Heaven forbid that I should be thought to advocate falsehood in children; but an untruth is more pardonable in them than in their parents. Lady Lufton's tarradiddle was of a nature that is usually considered excusable—at least with grown people; but, nevertheless, she would have been nearer to perfection could she have confined herself to the truth. Let us suppose that a boy were to write home from school, saying that another boy had promised to come and stay with him, that other having given no such promise—what a very naughty boy would that first boy be in the eyes of his pastors and masters!

That little conversation between Lord Lufton and his mother—in which nothing was said about his lordship's parliamentary duties—took place on the evening before he started for London. On that occasion he certainly was not in his best humour, nor did he behave to his mother in his kindest manner. He had then left the room when she began to talk about Miss Grantly; and once again in the course of the evening, when his mother, not very judiciously, said a word or two about Griselda's beauty, he had remarked that she was no conjuror, and would hardly set the Thames on fire.

"If she were a conjuror!" said Lady Lufton, rather piqued, "I should not now be going to take her out in London. I know many of those sort of girls whom you call conjurors; they can talk for ever, and always talk either loudly or in a whisper. I don't like them, and I am sure that you do not in your heart."

"Oh, as to liking them in my heart—that is being very particular."

"Griselda Grantly is a lady, and as such I shall be happy to have her with me in town. She is just the girl that Justinia will like to have with her."

"Exactly," said Lord Lufton. "She will do exceedingly well for Justinia."

Now this was not good-natured on the part of Lord Lufton; and his mother felt it the more strongly, inasmuch as it seemed to signify that he was setting his back up against the Lufton-Grantly alliance. She had been pretty sure that he would do so in the event of his suspecting that a plot was being laid to catch him; and now it almost appeared that he did suspect such a plot. Why else that sarcasm as to Griselda doing very well for his sister?

And now we must go back and describe a little scene at Framley which will account for his lordship's ill-humour and suspicions, and explain how it came to pass that he so snubbed his mother. This scene took place about ten days after the evening on which Mrs. Robarts and Lucy were walking together in the parsonage garden, and during those ten days Lucy had not once allowed herself to be entrapped into any special conversation with the young peer. She had dined at Framley Court during that interval, and had spent a second evening there; Lord Lufton had also been up at the parsonage on three or four occasions, and had looked for her in her usual walks; but, nevertheless, they had never come together in their old familiar way, since the day on which Lady Lufton had hinted her fears to Mrs. Robarts.

Lord Lufton had very much missed her. At first he had not attributed this change to a purposed scheme of action on the part of any one; nor, indeed, had he much thought about it, although he had felt himself to be annoyed. But as the period fixed for his departure grew near, it did occur to him as very odd that he should never hear Lucy's voice unless when she said a few words to his mother, or to her sister-in-law. And then he made up his mind that he would speak to her before he went, and that the mystery should be explained to him.

And he carried out his purpose, calling at the parsonage on one special afternoon; and it was on the evening of the same day that his mother sang the praises of Griselda Grantly so inopportunely. Robarts, he knew, was then absent from home, and Mrs. Robarts was with his mother down at the house, preparing lists of the poor people to be specially attended to in Lady Lufton's approaching absence. Taking advantage of this, he walked boldly in through the parsonage garden; asked the gardener, with an indifferent voice, whether either of the ladies were at home, and then caught poor Lucy exactly on the door-step of the house.

"Were you going in or out, Miss Robarts?"

"Well, I was going out," said Lucy; and she began to consider how best she might get quit of any prolonged encounter.

"Oh, going out, were you? I don't know whether I may offer to—"

"Well, Lord Lufton, not exactly, seeing that I am about to pay a visit to our near neighbour, Mrs. Podgens. Perhaps you have no particular call towards Mrs. Podgens' just at present, or to her new baby?"

"And have you any very particular call that way?"

"Yes, and especially to Baby Podgens. Baby Podgens is a real little duck—only just two days old." And Lucy, as she spoke, progressed a step or two, as though she were determined not to remain there talking on the doorstep.

A slight cloud came across his brow as he saw this, and made him resolve that she should not gain her purpose. He was not going to be foiled in that way by such a girl as Lucy Robarts. He had come there to speak to her, and speak to her he would. There had been enough of intimacy between them to justify him in demanding, at any rate, as much as that.

"Miss Robarts," he said, "I am starting for London to-morrow, and if I do not say good-bye to you now, I shall not be able to do so at all."

"Good-bye, Lord Lufton," she said, giving him her hand, and smiling on him with her old genial, good-humoured, racy smile. "And mind you bring into Parliament that law which you promised me for defending my young chickens."

He took her hand, but that was not all that he wanted. "Surely Mrs. Podgens and her baby can wait ten minutes. I shall not see you again for months to come, and yet you seem to begrudge me two words."

"Not two hundred if they can be of any service to you," said she, walking cheerily back into the drawing-room; "only I did not think it worth while to waste your time, as Fanny is not here."

She was infinitely more collected, more master of herself than he was. Inwardly, she did tremble at the idea of what was coming, but outwardly she showed no agitation—none as yet; if only she could so possess herself as to refrain from doing so, when she heard what he might have to say to her.

He hardly knew what it was for the saying of which he had so resolutely come thither. He had by no means made up his mind that he loved Lucy Robarts; nor had he made up his mind that, loving her, he would, or that, loving her, he would not, make her his wife. He had never used his mind in the matter in any way, either for good or evil. He had learned to like her and to think that she was very pretty. He had found out that it was very pleasant to talk to her; whereas, talking to Griselda Grantly, and, indeed, to some other young ladies of his acquaintance, was often hard work. The half-hours which he had spent with Lucy had always been satisfactory to him. He had found himself to be more bright with her than with other people, and more apt to discuss subjects worth discussing; and thus it had come about that he thoroughly liked Lucy Robarts. As to whether his affection was Platonic or anti-Platonic he had never asked himself; but he had spoken words to her, shortly before that sudden cessation of their intimacy, which might have been taken as anti-Platonic by any girl so disposed to regard them. He had not thrown himself at her feet, and declared himself to be devoured by a consuming passion; but he had touched her hand as lovers touch those of women whom they love; he had had his confidences with her, talking to her of his own mother, of his sister, and of his friends; and he had called her his own dear friend Lucy.

All this had been very sweet to her, but very poisonous also. She had declared to herself very frequently that her liking for this young nobleman was as purely a feeling of mere friendship as was that of her brother; and she had professed to herself that she would give the lie to the world's cold sarcasms on such subjects. But she had now acknowledged that the sarcasms of the world on that matter, cold though they may be, are not the less true; and having so acknowledged, she had resolved that all close alliance between herself and Lord Lufton must be at an end. She had come to a conclusion, but he had come to none; and in this frame of mind he was now there with the object of reopening that dangerous friendship which she had had the sense to close.

"And so you are going to-morrow?" she said, as soon as they were both within the drawing-room.

"Yes: I'm off by the early train to-morrow morning, and Heaven knows when we may meet again."

"Next winter, shall we not?"

"Yes, for a day or two, I suppose. I do not know whether I shall pass another winter here. Indeed, one can never say where one will be."

"No, one can't; such as you, at least, cannot. I am not of a migratory tribe myself."

"I wish you were."

"I'm not a bit obliged to you. Your nomade life does not agree with young ladies."

"I think they are taking to it pretty freely, then. We have unprotected young women all about the world."

"And great bores you find them, I suppose?"

"No; I like it. The more we can get out of old-fashioned grooves the better I am pleased. I should be a radical to-morrow—a regular man of the people,—only I should break my mother's heart."

"Whatever you do, Lord Lufton, do not do that."

"That is why I have liked you so much," he continued, "because you get out of the grooves."

"Do I?"

"Yes; and go along by yourself, guiding your own footsteps; not carried hither and thither, just as your grandmother's old tramway may chance to take you."

"Do you know I have a strong idea that my grandmother's old tramway will be the safest and the best after all? I have not left it very far, and I certainly mean to go back to it."

"That's impossible! An army of old women, with coils of ropes made out of time-honoured prejudices, could not drag you back."

"No, Lord Lufton, that is true. But one—" and then she stopped herself. She could not tell him that one loving mother, anxious for her only son, had sufficed to do it. She could not explain to him that this departure from the established tramway had already broken her own rest, and turned her peaceful happy life into a grievous battle.

"I know that you are trying to go back," he said. "Do you think that I have eyes and cannot see? Come, Lucy, you and I have been friends, and we must not part in this way. My mother is a paragon among women. I say it in earnest;—a paragon among women: and her love for me is the perfection of motherly love."

"It is, it is; and I am so glad that you acknowledge it."

"I should be worse than a brute did I not do so; but, nevertheless, I cannot allow her to lead me in all things. Were I to do so, I should cease to be a man."

"Where can you find any one who will counsel you so truly?"

"But, nevertheless, I must rule myself. I do not know whether my suspicions may be perfectly just, but I fancy that she has created this estrangement between you and me. Has it not been so?"

"Certainly not by speaking to me," said Lucy, blushing ruby-red through every vein of her deep-tinted face. But though she could not command her blood, her voice was still under her control—her voice and her manner.

"But has she not done so? You, I know, will tell me nothing but the truth."

"I will tell you nothing on this matter, Lord Lufton, whether true or false. It is a subject on which it does not concern me to speak."

"Ah! I understand," he said; and rising from his chair, he stood against the chimney-piece with his back to the fire. "She cannot leave me alone to choose for myself my own friends, and my own—;" but he did not fill up the void.

"But why tell me this, Lord Lufton?"

"No! I am not to choose my own friends, though they be among the best and purest of God's creatures. Lucy, I cannot think that you have ceased to have a regard for me. That you had a regard for me, I am sure."

She felt that it was almost unmanly of him thus to seek her out, and hunt her down, and then throw upon her the whole weight of the explanation that his coming thither made necessary. But, nevertheless, the truth must be told, and with God's help she would find strength for the telling of it.

"Yes, Lord Lufton, I had a regard for you—and have. By that word you mean something more than the customary feeling of acquaintance which may ordinarily prevail between a gentleman and lady of different families, who have known each other so short a time as we have done."

"Yes, something much more," said he, with energy.

"Well, I will not define the much—something closer than that."

"Yes, and warmer, and dearer, and more worthy of two human creatures who value each other's minds and hearts."

"Some such closer regard I have felt for you—very foolishly. Stop! You have made me speak, and do not interrupt me now. Does not your conscience tell you that in doing so I have unwisely deserted those wise old grandmother's tramways of which you spoke just now? It has been pleasant to me to do so. I have liked the feeling of independence with which I have thought that I might indulge in an open friendship with such as you are. And your rank, so different from my own, has doubtless made this more attractive."

"Nonsense!"

"Ah! but it has. I know it now. But what will the world say of me as to such an alliance?"

"The world!"

"Yes, the world! I am not such a philosopher as to disregard it, though you may afford to do so. The world will say that I, the parson's sister, set my cap at the young lord, and that the young lord had made a fool of me."

"The world shall say no such thing!" said Lord Lufton, very imperiously.

"Ah! but it will. You can no more stop it, than King Canute could the waters. Your mother has interfered wisely to spare me from this; and the only favour that I can ask you is, that you will spare me also." And then she got up as though she intended at once to walk forth to her visit to Mrs. Podgens' baby.

"Stop, Lucy!" he said, putting himself between her and the door.

"It must not be Lucy any longer, Lord Lufton; I was madly foolish when I first allowed it."

"By heavens! but it shall be Lucy—Lucy before all the world. My Lucy, my own Lucy—my heart's best friend, and chosen love. Lucy, there is my hand. How long you may have had my heart, it matters not to say now."

The game was at her feet now, and no doubt she felt her triumph. Her ready wit and speaking lip, not her beauty, had brought him to her side; and now he was forced to acknowledge that her power over him had been supreme. Sooner than leave her he would risk all. She did feel her triumph; but there was nothing in her face to tell him that she did so.

As to what she would now do she did not for a moment doubt. He had been precipitated into the declaration he had made, not by his love, but by his embarrassment. She had thrown in his teeth the injury which he had done her, and he had then been moved by his generosity to repair that injury by the noblest sacrifice which he could make. But Lucy Robarts was not the girl to accept a sacrifice.

He had stepped forward as though he were going to clasp her round the waist, but she receded, and got beyond the reach of his hand. "Lord Lufton!" she said, "when you are more cool you will know that this is wrong. The best thing for both of us now is to part."

"Not the best thing, but the very worst, till we perfectly understand each other."

"Then perfectly understand me, that I cannot be your wife."

"Lucy! do you mean that you cannot learn to love me?"

"I mean that I shall not try. Do not persevere in this, or you will have to hate yourself for your own folly."

"But I will persevere till you accept my love, or say with your hand on your heart that you cannot and will not love me."

"Then I must beg you to let me go," and having so said, she paused while he walked once or twice hurriedly up and down the room. "And, Lord Lufton," she continued, "if you will leave me now, the words that you have spoken shall be as though they had never been uttered."

"I care not who knows that they have been uttered. The sooner that they are known to all the world, the better I shall be pleased, unless indeed—"

"Think of your mother, Lord Lufton."

"What can I do better than give her as a daughter the best and sweetest girl I have ever met? When my mother really knows you, she will love you as I do. Lucy, say one word to me of comfort."

"I will say no word to you that shall injure your future comfort. It is impossible that I should be your wife."

"Do you mean that you cannot love me?"

"You have no right to press me any further," she said; and sat down upon the sofa, with an angry frown upon her forehead.

"By heavens," he said, "I will take no such answer from you till you put your hand up-on your heart, and say that you cannot love me."

"Oh, why should you press me so, Lord Lufton?"

"Why! because my happiness depends upon it; because it behoves me to know the very truth. It has come to this, that I love you with my whole heart, and I must know how your heart stands towards me."

She had now again risen from the sofa, and was looking steadily in his face.

"Lord Lufton," she said, "I cannot love you," and as she spoke she did put her hand, as he had desired, upon her heart.

"Then God help me! for I am very wretched. Good-bye, Lucy," and he stretched out his hand to her.

"Good-bye, my lord. Do not be angry with me."

"No, no, no!" and without further speech he left the room and the house, and hurried home. It was hardly surprising that he should that evening tell his mother that Griselda Grantly would be a companion sufficiently good for his sister. He wanted no such companion.

And when he was well gone—absolutely out of sight from the window—Lucy walked steadily up to her room, locked the door, and then threw herself on the bed. Why—oh! why had she told such a falsehood? Could anything justify her in a lie? Was it not a lie—knowing as she did that she loved him with all her loving heart?

But, then, his mother! and the sneers of the world, which would have declared that she had set her trap, and caught the foolish young lord! Her pride would not have submitted to that. Strong as her love was, yet her pride was, perhaps, stronger—stronger at any rate during that interview.

But how was she to forgive herself the falsehood she had told?

CHAPTER XVII.

MRS. PROUDIE'S CONVERSAZIONE.

It was grievous to think of the mischief and danger into which Griselda Grantly was brought by the worldliness of her mother in those few weeks previous to Lady Lufton's arrival in town—very grievous, at least, to her ladyship, as from time to time she heard of what was done in London. Lady Hartletop's was not the only objectionable house at which Griselda was allowed to reap fresh fashionable laurels. It had been stated openly in the *Morning Post* that that young lady had been the most admired among the beautiful at one of Miss Dunstable's celebrated *soirées*, and then she was heard of as gracing the drawing-room at Mrs. Proudie's conversazione.

Of Miss Dunstable herself Lady Lufton was not able openly to allege any evil. She was acquainted, Lady Lufton knew, with very many people of the right sort, and was the dear friend of Lady Lufton's highly conservative and not very distant neighbours, the Greshams. But then she was also acquainted with so many people of the bad sort. Indeed, she was intimate with everybody, from the Duke of Omnium to old Dowager Lady Goodygaffer, who had represented all the cardinal virtues for the last quarter of a century. She smiled with equal sweetness on treacle and on brimstone; was quite at home at Exeter Hall, having been consulted—so the world said, probably not with exact truth—as to the selection of more than one disagreeably Low Church bishop; and was not less frequent in her attendance at the ecclesiastical doings of a certain terrible prelate in the Midland counties, who was supposed to favour stoles and vespers, and to have no proper Protestant hatred for auricular confession and fish on Fridays. Lady Lufton, who was very staunch, did not like this, and would say of Miss Dunstable that it was impossible to serve both God and Mammon.

But Mrs. Proudie was much more objectionable to her. Seeing how sharp was the feud between the Proudies and the Grantlys down in Barsetshire, how absolutely unable they had always been to carry a decent face towards each other in church matters, how they headed two parties in the diocese, which were, when brought together, as oil and vinegar, in which battles the whole Lufton influence had always been brought to bear on the Grantly side;—seeing all this, I say, Lady Lufton was surprised to hear that Griselda had been taken to Mrs. Proudie's evening exhibition. "Had the archdeacon been consulted about it," she said to herself, "this would never have happened." But there she was wrong, for in matters concerning his daughter's introduction to the world the archdeacon never interfered.

On the whole, I am inclined to think that Mrs. Grantly understood the world better than did Lady Lufton. In her heart of hearts Mrs. Grantly hated Mrs. Proudie—that is, with that sort of hatred one Christian lady allows herself to feel towards another. Of course Mrs. Grantly forgave Mrs. Proudie all her offences, and wished her well, and was at peace with her, in the Christian sense of the word, as with all other women. But under this forbearance and meekness, and perhaps, we may say, wholly unconnected with it, there was certainly a current of antagonistic feeling which, in the ordinary unconsidered language of every day, men and women do call hatred. This raged and was strong throughout the whole year in Barsetshire, before the eyes of all mankind. But, nevertheless, Mrs. Grantly took Griselda to Mrs. Proudie's evening parties in London.

In these days Mrs. Proudie considered herself to be by no means the least among bishops' wives. She had opened the season this year in a new house in Gloucester Place, at which the reception rooms, at any rate, were all that a lady bishop could desire. Here she had a front drawing-room of very noble dimensions, a second drawing-room rather noble also, though it had lost one of its back corners awkwardly enough, apparently in a jostle with the neighbouring house; and then there was a third—shall we say drawing-room, or closet?—in which Mrs. Proudie delighted to be seen sitting, in order that the world might know that there was a third room; altogether a noble suite, as Mrs. Proudie herself said in confidence to more than one clergyman's wife from Barsetshire. "A noble suite, indeed, Mrs. Proudie!" the clergymen's wives from Barsetshire would usually answer.

For some time Mrs. Proudie was much at a loss to know by what sort of party or entertainment she would make herself famous. Balls and suppers were of course out of the question. She did not object to her daughters dancing all night at other houses—at least, of late she had not objected, for the fashionable world required it, and the young ladies had perhaps a will of their own—but dancing at her house—absolutely under the shade of the bishop's apron—would be a sin and a scandal. And then as to suppers—of all modes in which one may extend one's hospitality to a large acquaintance, they are the most costly.

"It is horrid to think that we should go out among our friends for the mere sake of eating and drinking," Mrs. Proudie would say to the clergymen's wives from Barsetshire. "It shows such a sensual propensity."

"Indeed it does, Mrs. Proudie; and is so vulgar too!" those ladies would reply.

But the elder among them would remember with regret the unsparing, open-handed hospitality of Barchester palace in the good old days of Bishop Grantly—God rest his soul! One old vicar's wife there was whose answer had not been so courteous—

"When we are hungry, Mrs. Proudie," she had said, "we do all have sensual propensities."

"It would be much better, Mrs. Athill, if the world would provide for all that at home," Mrs. Proudie had rapidly replied; with which opinion I must here profess that I cannot by any means bring myself to coincide.

But a conversazione would give play to no sensual propensity, nor occasion that intolerable expense which the gratification of sensual propensities too often produces. Mrs. Proudie felt that the word was not all that she could have desired. It was a little faded by old use and present oblivion, and seemed to address itself to that portion of the London world that is considered blue, rather than fashionable. But, nevertheless, there was a spirituality about it which suited her, and one may also say an economy. And then as regarded fashion, it might perhaps not be beyond the power of a Mrs. Proudie to regild the word with a newly burnished gilding. Some leading person must produce fashion at first hand, and why not Mrs. Proudie?

Her plan was to set the people by the ears talking, if talk they would, or to induce them to show themselves there inert if no more could be got from them. To accommodate with chairs and sofas as many as the furniture of her noble suite of rooms would allow, especially with the two chairs and padded bench against the wall in the back closet—the small inner drawing-room, as she would call it to the clergymen's wives from Barsetshire—and to let the others stand about upright, or "group themselves," as she described it. Then four times during the two hours' period of her conversazione tea and cake were to be handed round on salvers. It is astonishing how far a very little cake will go in this way, particularly if administered tolerably early after dinner. The men can't eat it, and the women, having no plates and no table, are obliged to abstain. Mrs. Jones knows that she cannot hold a piece of crumbly cake in her hand till it be consumed without doing serious injury to her best dress. When Mrs. Proudie, with her weekly books before her, looked into the financial upshot of her conversazione, her conscience told her that she had done the right thing.

Going out to tea is not a bad thing, if one can contrive to dine early, and then be allowed to sit round a big table with a tea urn in the middle. I would, however, suggest that breakfast cups should always be provided for the gentlemen. And then with pleasant neighbours,—or more especially with a pleasant neighbour,—the affair is not, according to my taste, by any means the worst phase of society. But I do dislike that handing round, unless it be of a subsidiary thimbleful when the business of the social intercourse has been dinner.

And indeed this handing round has become a vulgar and an intolerable nuisance among us second-class gentry with our eight hundred a year—there or thereabouts;— doubly intolerable as being destructive of our natural comforts, and a wretchedly vulgar aping of men with large incomes. The Duke of Omnium and Lady Hartletop are undoubtedly wise to have everything handed round. Friends of mine who occasionally dine at such houses tell me that they get their wine quite as quickly as they can drink it, that their mutton is brought to them without delay, and that the potato-bearer follows quick upon the heels of carnifer. Nothing can be more comfortable, and we may no doubt acknowledge that these first-class grandees do understand their material comforts. But we of the eight hundred can no more come up to them in this than we can in their opera-boxes and equipages. May I not say that the usual tether of this class, in the way of carnifers, cup-bearers, and the rest, does not reach beyond neat-handed Phyllis and the greengrocer? and that Phyllis, neat-handed as she probably is, and the greengrocer, though he be ever so active, cannot administer a dinner to twelve people who are prohibited by a Medo-Persian law from all self-administration whatever? And may I not further say that the lamentable consequence to us eight hundreders dining out among each other is this, that we too often get no dinner at all. Phyllis, with the potatoes, cannot reach us till our mutton is devoured, or in a lukewarm state past our power of managing; and Ganymede, the greengrocer, though we admire the skill of his necktie and the whiteness of his unexceptionable gloves, fails to keep us going in Sherry.

Seeing a lady the other day in this strait, left without a small modicum of stimulus which was no doubt necessary for her good digestion, I ventured to ask her to drink wine with me. But when I bowed my head at her, she looked at me with all her eyes, struck with amazement. Had I suggested that she should join me in a wild Indian war-dance, with nothing on but my paint, her face could not have shown greater astonishment. And yet I should have thought she might have remembered the days when Christian men and women used to drink wine with each other.

God be with the good old days when I could hobnob with my friend over the table as often as I was inclined to lift my glass to my lips, and make a long arm for a hot potato whenever the exigencies of my plate required it.

I think it may be laid down as a rule in affairs of hospitality, that whatever extra luxury or grandeur we introduce at our tables when guests are with us, should be introduced for the advantage of the guest and not for our own. If, for instance, our dinner be served in a manner different from that usual to us, it should be so served in order that our friends may with more satisfaction eat our repast than our everyday practice would produce on them. But the change should by no means be made to their material detriment in order that our fashion may be acknowledged. Again, if I decorate my sideboard and table, wishing that the eyes of my visitors may rest on that which is elegant and pleasant to the sight, I act in that matter with a becoming sense of hospitality; but if my object be to kill Mrs. Jones with envy at the sight of all my silver trinkets, I am a very mean-spirited fellow. This, in a broad way, will be acknowledged; but if we would bear in mind the same idea at all times,—on occasions when the way perhaps may not be so broad, when more thinking may be required to ascertain what is true hospitality,—I think we of the eight hundred would make a greater advance towards really entertaining our own friends than by any rearrangement of the actual meats and dishes which we set before them.

Knowing as we do, that the terms of the Lufton-Grantly alliance had been so solemnly ratified between the two mothers, it is perhaps hardly open to us to suppose that Mrs. Grantly was induced to take her daughter to Mrs. Proudie's by any knowledge which she may have acquired that Lord Dumbello had promised to grace the bishop's assembly. It is certainly the fact that high contracting parties do sometimes allow themselves a latitude which would be considered dishonest by contractors of a lower sort; and it may be possible that the archdeacon's wife did think of that second string with which her bow was furnished. Be that as it may, Lord Dumbello was at Mrs. Proudie's, and it did so come to pass that Griselda was seated at the corner of a sofa close to which was a vacant space in which his lordship could—"group himself."

They had not been long there before Lord Dumbello did group himself. "Fine day," he said, coming up and occupying the vacant position by Miss Grantly's elbow.

"We were driving to-day, and we thought it rather cold," said Griselda.

"Deuced cold," said Lord Dumbello, and then he adjusted his white cravat and touched up his whiskers. Having got so far, he did not proceed to any other immediate conversational efforts; nor did Griselda. But he grouped himself again as became a marquis, and gave very intense satisfaction to Mrs. Proudie.

"This is so kind of you, Lord Dumbello," said that lady, coming up to him and shaking his hand warmly; "so very kind of you to come to my poor little tea-party."

"Uncommonly pleasant, I call it," said his lordship. "I like this sort of thing—no trouble, you know."

"No; that is the charm of it: isn't it? no trouble, or fuss, or parade. That's what I always say. According to my ideas, society consists in giving people facility for an interchange of thoughts—what we call conversation."

"Aw, yes, exactly."

"Not in eating and drinking together—eh, Lord Dumbello? And yet the practice of our lives would seem to show that the indulgence of those animal propensities can alone suffice to bring people together. The world in this has surely made a great mistake."

"I like a good dinner all the same," said Lord Dumbello.

"Oh, yes, of course—of course. I am by no means one of those who would pretend to preach that our tastes have not been given to us for our enjoyment. Why should things be nice if we are not to like them?"

"A man who can really give a good dinner has learned a great deal," said Lord Dumbello, with unusual animation.

"An immense deal. It is quite an art in itself; and one which I, at any rate, by no means despise. But we cannot always be eating—can we?"

"No," said Lord Dumbello, "not always." And he looked as though he lamented that his powers should be so circumscribed.

And then Mrs. Proudie passed on to Mrs. Grantly. The two ladies were quite friendly in London; though down in their own neighbourhood they waged a war so internecine in its nature. But nevertheless Mrs. Proudie's manner might have showed to a very close observer that she knew the difference between a bishop and an archdeacon. "I am so delighted to see you," said she. "No, don't mind moving; I won't sit down just at present. But why didn't the archdeacon come?"

"It was quite impossible; it was indeed," said Mrs. Grantly. "The archdeacon never has a moment in London that he can call his own."

"You don't stay up very long, I believe."

"A good deal longer than we either of us like, I can assure you. London life is a perfect nuisance to me."

"But people in a certain position must go through with it, you know," said Mrs. Proudie. "The bishop, for instance, must attend the House."

"Must he?" asked Mrs. Grantly, as though she were not at all well informed with reference to this branch of a bishop's business. "I am very glad that archdeacons are under no such liability."

"Oh, no; there's nothing of that sort," said Mrs. Proudie, very seriously. "But how uncommonly well Miss Grantly is looking! I do hear that she has quite been admired."

This phrase certainly was a little hard for the mother to bear. All the world had acknowledged, so Mrs. Grantly had taught herself to believe, that Griselda was undoubtedly the beauty of the season. Marquises and lords were already contending for her smiles, and paragraphs had been written in newspapers as to her profile. It was too hard to be told, after that, that her daughter had been "quite admired." Such a phrase might suit a pretty little red-cheeked milkmaid of a girl.

"She cannot, of course, come near your girls in that respect," said Mrs. Grantly, very quietly. Now the Miss Proudies had not elicited from the fashionable world any very loud encomiums on their beauty. Their mother felt the taunt in its fullest force, but she would not essay to do battle on the present arena. She jotted down the item in her mind, and kept it over for Barchester and the chapter. Such debts as those she usually paid on some day, if the means of doing so were at all within her power.

"But there is Miss Dunstable, I declare," she said, seeing that that lady had entered the room; and away went Mrs. Proudie to welcome her distinguished guest.

"And so this is a conversazione, is it?" said that lady, speaking, as usual, not in a suppressed voice. "Well, I declare, it's very nice. It means conversation, don't it, Mrs. Proudie?"

"Ha, ha, ha! Miss Dunstable, there is nobody like you, I declare."

"Well, but don't it? and tea and cake? and then, when we're tired of talking, we go away,—isn't that it?"

"But you must not be tired for these three hours yet."

"Oh, I'm never tired of talking; all the world knows that. How do, bishop? A very nice sort of thing this conversazione, isn't it now?"

The bishop rubbed his hands together and smiled, and said that he thought it was rather nice.

"Mrs. Proudie is so fortunate in all her little arrangements," said Miss Dunstable.

"Yes, yes," said the bishop. "I think she is happy in these matters. I do flatter myself that she is so. Of course, Miss Dunstable, you are accustomed to things on a much grander scale."

"I! Lord bless you, no! Nobody hates grandeur so much as I do. Of course I must do as I am told. I must live in a big House, and have three footmen six feet high. I must have a coachman with a top-heavy wig, and horses so big that they frighten me. If I did not, I should be made out a lunatic and declared unable to manage my own affairs. But as for grandeur, I hate it. I certainly think that I shall have some of these conversaziones. I wonder whether Mrs. Proudie will come and put me up to a wrinkle or two."

The bishop again rubbed his hands, and said that he was sure she would. He never felt quite at his ease with Miss Dunstable, as he rarely could ascertain whether or no she was earnest in what she was saying. So he trotted off, muttering some excuse as he went, and Miss Dunstable chuckled with an inward chuckle at his too evident bewilderment. Miss Dunstable was by nature kind, generous, and open-hearted; but she was living now very much with people on whom kindness, generosity, and open-heartedness were thrown away. She was clever also, and could be sarcastic; and she found that those qualities told better in the world around her than generosity and an open heart. And so she went on from month to month, and year to year, not progressing in a good spirit as she might have done, but still carrying within her bosom a warm affection for those she could really love. And she knew that she was hardly living as she should live,—that the wealth which she affected to despise was eating into the soundness of her character, not by its splendour, but by the style of life which it had seemed to produce as a necessity. She knew that she was gradually becoming irreverent, scornful, and prone to ridicule; but yet, knowing this and hating it, she hardly knew how to break from it.

She had seen so much of the blacker side of human nature that blackness no longer startled her as it should do. She had been the prize at which so many ruined spendthrifts had aimed; so many pirates had endeavoured to run her down while sailing in the open waters of life, that she had ceased to regard such attempts on her money-bags as unmanly or over-covetous. She was content to fight her own battle with her own weapons, feeling secure in her own strength of purpose and strength of wit.

Some few friends she had whom she really loved,—among whom her inner self could come out and speak boldly what it had to say with its own true voice. And the woman who thus so spoke was very different from that Miss Dunstable whom Mrs. Proudie courted, and the Duke of Omnium fêted, and Mrs. Harold Smith claimed as her bosom friend. If only she could find among such one special companion on whom her heart might rest, who would help her to bear the heavy burdens of her world! But where was she to find such a friend?—she with her keen wit, her untold money, and loud laughing voice. Everything about her was calculated to attract those whom she could not value, and to scare from her the sort of friend to whom she would fain have linked her lot.

And then she met Mrs. Harold Smith, who had taken Mrs. Proudie's noble suite of rooms in her tour for the evening, and was devoting to them a period of twenty minutes. "And so I may congratulate you," Miss Dunstable said eagerly to her friend.

"No, in mercy's name do no such thing, or you may too probably have to uncongratulate me again; and that will be so unpleasant."

"But they told me that Lord Brock had sent for him yesterday." Now at this period Lord Brock was Prime Minister.

"So he did, and Harold was with him backwards and forwards all the day. But he can't shut his eyes and open his mouth, and see what God will send him, as a wise and prudent man should do. He is always for bargaining, and no Prime Minister likes that."

"I would not be in his shoes if, after all, he has to come home and say that the bargain is off."

"Ha, ha, ha! Well, I should not take it very quietly. But what can we poor women do, you know? When it is settled, my dear, I'll send you a line at once." And then Mrs. Harold

Smith finished her course round the rooms, and regained her carriage within the twenty minutes.

"Beautiful profile, has she not?" said Miss Dunstable, somewhat later in the evening, to Mrs. Proudie. Of course, the profile spoken of belonged to Miss Grantly.

"Yes, it is beautiful, certainly," said Mrs. Proudie. "The pity is that it means nothing."

"The gentlemen seem to think that it means a good deal."

"I am not sure of that. She has no conversation, you see; not a word. She has been sitting there with Lord Dumbello at her elbow for the last hour, and yet she has hardly opened her mouth three times."

"But, my dear Mrs. Proudie, who on earth could talk to Lord Dumbello?"

Mrs. Proudie thought that her own daughter Olivia would undoubtedly be able to do so, if only she could get the opportunity. But, then, Olivia had so much conversation.

And while the two ladies were yet looking at the youthful pair, Lord Dumbello did speak again. "I think I have had enough of this now," said he, addressing himself to Griselda.

"I suppose you have other engagements," said she.

"Oh, yes; and I believe I shall go to Lady Clantelbrocks." And then he took his departure. No other word was spoken that evening between him and Miss Grantly beyond those given in this chronicle, and yet the world declared that he and that young lady had passed the evening in so close a flirtation as to make the matter more than ordinarily particular; and Mrs. Grantly, as she was driven home to her lodgings, began to have doubts in her mind whether it would be wise to discountenance so great an alliance as that which the head of the great Hartletop family now seemed so desirous to establish. The prudent mother had not yet spoken a word to her daughter on these subjects, but it might soon become necessary to do so. It was all very well for Lady Lufton to hurry up to town, but of what service would that be, if Lord Lufton were not to be found in Bruton Street?

CHAPTER XVIII.

THE NEW MINISTER'S PATRONAGE.

At that time, just as Lady Lufton was about to leave Framley for London, Mark Robarts received a pressing letter, inviting him also to go up to the metropolis for a day or two—not for pleasure, but on business. The letter was from his indefatigable friend Sowerby.

"My dear Robarts," the letter ran:—

> I have just heard that poor little Burslem, the Barsetshire prebendary, is dead. We must all die some day, you know,—as you have told your parishioners from the Framley pulpit more than once, no doubt. The stall must be filled up, and why should not you have it as well as another? It is six hundred a year and a house. Little Burslem had nine, but the good old times are gone. Whether the house is letable or not under the present ecclesiastical régime, I do not know. It used to be so, for I remember Mrs. Wiggins, the tallow-chandler's widow, living in old Stanhope's house.
>
> Harold Smith has just joined the Government as Lord Petty Bag, and could, I think, at the present moment get this for asking. He cannot well refuse me, and, if you will say the word, I will speak to him. You had better come up yourself; but say the word "Yes," or "No," by the wires.
>
> If you say "Yes," as of course you will, do not fail to come up. You will find me at the "Travellers," or at the House. The stall will just suit you,—will give you no trouble, improve your position, and give some little assistance towards bed and board, and rack and manger.
>
> Yours ever faithfully,
> N. SOWERBY.

Singularly enough, I hear that your brother is private secretary to the new Lord Petty Bag. I am told that his chief duty will consist in desiring the servants to call my sister's carriage. I have only seen Harold once since he accepted office; but my Lady Petty Bag says that he has certainly grown an inch since that occurrence.

This was certainly very good-natured on the part of Mr. Sowerby, and showed that he had a feeling within his bosom that he owed something to his friend the parson for the injury he had done him. And such was in truth the case. A more reckless being than the member for West Barsetshire could not exist. He was reckless for himself, and reckless for all others with whom he might be concerned. He could ruin his friends with as little remorse as he had ruined himself. All was fair game that came in the way of his net. But, nevertheless, he was good-natured, and willing to move heaven and earth to do a friend a good turn, if it came in his way to do so.

He did really love Mark Robarts as much as it was given him to love any among his acquaintance. He knew that he had already done him an almost irreparable injury, and might very probably injure him still deeper before he had done with him. That he would undoubtedly do so, if it came in his way, was very certain. But then, if it also came in his way to repay his friend by any side blow, he would also undoubtedly do that. Such an occasion had now come, and he had desired his sister to give the new Lord Petty Bag no rest till he should have promised to use all his influence in getting the vacant prebend for Mark Robarts.

This letter of Sowerby's Mark immediately showed to his wife. How lucky, thought he to himself, that not a word was said in it about those accursed money transactions! Had he understood Sowerby better he would have known that that gentleman never said anything about money transactions until it became absolutely necessary. "I know you don't like Mr. Sowerby," he said; "but you must own that this is very good-natured."

"It is the character I hear of him that I don't like," said Mrs. Robarts.

"But what shall I do now, Fanny? As he says, why should not I have the stall as well as another?"

"I suppose it would not interfere with your parish?" she asked.

"Not in the least, at the distance at which we are. I did think of giving up old Jones; but if I take this, of course I must keep a curate."

His wife could not find it in her heart to dissuade him from accepting promotion when it came in his way—what vicar's wife would have so persuaded her husband? But yet she did not altogether like it. She feared that Greek from Chaldicotes, even when he came with the present of a prebendal stall in his hands. And then what would Lady Lufton say?

"And do you think that you must go up to London, Mark?"

"Oh, certainly; that is, if I intend to accept Harold Smith's kind offices in the matter."

"I suppose it will be better to accept them," said Fanny, feeling perhaps that it would be useless in her to hope that they should not be accepted.

"Prebendal stalls, Fanny, don't generally go begging long among parish clergymen. How could I reconcile it to the duty I owe to my children to refuse such an increase to my income?" And so it was settled that he should at once drive to Silverbridge and send off a message by telegraph, and that he should himself proceed to London on the following day. "But you must see Lady Lufton first, of course," said Fanny, as soon as all this was settled.

Mark would have avoided this if he could have decently done so, but he felt that it would be impolitic, as well as indecent. And why should he be afraid to tell Lady Lufton that he hoped to receive this piece of promotion from the present government? There was nothing disgraceful in a clergyman becoming a prebendary of Barchester. Lady Lufton herself had always been very civil to the prebendaries, and especially to little Dr. Burslem, the meagre little man who had just now paid the debt of nature. She had always been very fond of the chapter, and her original dislike to Bishop Proudie had been chiefly founded on his interference with the cathedral clergy,—on his interference, or on that of his wife or chaplain. Considering these things Mark Robarts tried to make himself believe that Lady Lufton would be delighted at his good fortune. But yet he did not believe it. She at any rate would revolt from the gift of the Greek of Chaldicotes.

"Oh, indeed," she said, when the vicar had with some difficulty explained to her all the circumstances of the case. "Well, I congratulate you, Mr. Robarts, on your powerful new patron."

"You will probably feel with me, Lady Lufton, that the benefice is one which I can hold without any detriment to me in my position here at Framley," said he, prudently resolving to let the slur upon his friends pass by unheeded.

"Well, I hope so. Of course, you are a very young man, Mr. Robarts, and these things have generally been given to clergymen more advanced in life."

"But you do not mean to say that you think I ought to refuse it?"

"What my advice to you might be if you really came to me for advice, I am hardly prepared to say at so very short a notice. You seem to have made up your mind, and therefore I need not consider it. As it is, I wish you joy, and hope that it may turn out to your advantage in every way."

"You understand, Lady Lufton, that I have by no means got it as yet."

"Oh, I thought it had been offered to you: I thought you spoke of this new minister as having all that in his own hand."

"Oh, dear, no. What may be the amount of his influence in that respect I do not at all know. But my correspondent assures me—"

"Mr. Sowerby, you mean. Why don't you call him by his name?"

"Mr. Sowerby assures me that Mr. Smith will ask for it; and thinks it most probable that his request will be successful."

"Oh, of course. Mr. Sowerby and Mr. Harold Smith together would no doubt be successful in anything. They are the sort of men who are successful nowadays. Well, Mr. Robarts, I wish you joy." And she gave him her hand in token of her sincerity.

Mark took her hand, resolving to say nothing further on that occasion. That Lady Lufton was not now cordial with him, as she used to be, he was well aware; and sooner or later he was determined to have the matter out with her. He would ask her why she now so constantly met him with a taunt, and so seldom greeted him with that kind old affectionate smile which he knew and appreciated so well. That she was honest and true, he was quite sure. If he asked her the question plainly, she would answer him openly. And if he could induce her to say that she would return to her old ways, return to them she would in a hearty manner. But he could not do this just at present. It was but a day or two since Mr. Crawley had been with him; and was it not probable that Mr. Crawley had been sent thither by Lady Lufton? His own hands were not clean enough for a remonstrance at the present moment. He would cleanse them, and then he would remonstrate.

"Would you like to live part of the year in Barchester?" he said to his wife and sister that evening.

"I think that two houses are only a trouble," said his wife. "And we have been very happy here."

"I have always liked a cathedral town," said Lucy; "and I am particularly fond of the close."

"And Barchester-close is the closest of all closes," said Mark. "There is not a single house within the gateways that does not belong to the chapter."

"But if we are to keep up two houses, the additional income will soon be wasted," said Fanny prudently.

"The thing would be, to let the house furnished every summer," said Lucy.

"But I must take my residence as the terms come," said the vicar; "and I certainly should not like to be away from Framley all the winter; I should never see anything of Lufton." And perhaps he thought of his hunting, and then thought again of that cleansing of his hands.

"I should not a bit mind being away during the winter," said Lucy, thinking of what the last winter had done for her.

"But where on earth should we find money to furnish one of those large, old-fashioned houses? Pray, Mark, do not do anything rash." And the wife laid her hand affectionately on her husband's arm. In this manner the question of the prebend was discussed between them on the evening before he started for London.

Success had at last crowned the earnest effort with which Harold Smith had carried on the political battle of his life for the last ten years. The late Lord Petty Bag had resigned in disgust, having been unable to digest the Prime Minister's ideas on Indian Reform, and Mr. Harold Smith, after sundry hitches in the business, was installed in his place. It was said that Harold Smith was not exactly the man whom the Premier would himself have chosen for that high office; but the Premier's hands were a good deal tied by circumstances. The last great appointment he had made had been terribly unpopular,—so much so as to subject him, popular as he undoubtedly was himself, to a screech from the whole nation. The *Jupiter*, with withering scorn, had asked whether vice of every kind was to be considered, in these days of Queen Victoria, as a passport to the cabinet. Adverse members of both Houses had arrayed themselves in a pure panoply of morality, and thundered forth their sarcasms with the indignant virtue and keen discontent of political Juvenals; and even his own friends had held up their hands in dismay. Under these circumstances he had thought himself obliged in the present instance to select a man who would not be especially objectionable to any party. Now Harold Smith lived with his wife, and his circumstances were not more than ordinarily embarrassed. He kept no race-horses; and, as Lord Brock now heard for the first time, gave lectures in provincial towns on popular subjects. He had a seat which was tolerably secure, and could talk to the House by the yard if required to do so. Moreover, Lord Brock had a great idea that the whole machinery of his own ministry would break to pieces very speedily. His own reputation was not bad, but it was insufficient for himself and that lately selected friend of his. Under all these circumstances combined, he chose Harold Smith to fill the vacant office of Lord Petty Bag.

And very proud the Lord Petty Bag was. For the last three or four months, he and Mr. Supplehouse had been agreeing to consign the ministry to speedy perdition. "This sort of dictatorship will never do," Harold Smith had himself said, justifying that future vote of his as to want of confidence in the Queen's government. And Mr. Supplehouse in this matter had fully agreed with him. He was a Juno whose form that wicked old Paris had utterly despised, and he, too, had quite made up his mind as to the lobby in which he would be found when that day of vengeance should arrive. But now things were much altered in Harold Smith's views. The Premier had shown his wisdom in seeking for new strength where strength ought to be sought, and introducing new blood into the body of his ministry. The people would now feel fresh confidence, and probably the House also. As to Mr. Supplehouse—he would use all his influence on Supplehouse. But, after all, Mr. Supplehouse was not everything.

On the morning after our vicar's arrival in London he attended at the Petty Bag office. It was situated in the close neighbourhood of Downing Street and the higher governmental gods; and though the building itself was not much, seeing that it was shored up on one side, that it bulged out in the front, was foul with smoke, dingy with dirt, and was devoid of any single architectural grace or modern scientific improvement, nevertheless its position gave it a status in the world which made the clerks in the Lord Petty Bag's office quite respectable in their walk in life. Mark had seen his friend Sowerby on the previous evening, and had then made an appointment with him for the following morning at the new minister's office. And now he was there a little before his time, in order that he might have a few moments' chat with his brother.

When Mark found himself in the private secretary's room he was quite astonished to see the change in his brother's appearance which the change in his official rank had produced. Jack Robarts had been a well-built, straight-legged, lissome young fellow, pleasant to the eye because of his natural advantages, but rather given to a harum-skarum style of gait, and occasionally careless, not to say slovenly, in his dress. But now he was the very pink of perfection. His jaunty frock-coat fitted him to perfection; not a hair of his head was out of place; his waistcoat and trousers were glossy and new, and his umbrella, which stood in the umbrella-stand in the corner, was tight, and neat, and small, and natty.

"Well, John, you've become quite a great man," said his brother.

"I don't know much about that," said John; "but I find that I have an enormous deal of fagging to go through."

"Do you mean work? I thought you had about the easiest berth in the whole Civil Service."

"Ah! that's just the mistake that people make. Because we don't cover whole reams of foolscap paper at the rate of fifteen lines to a page, and five words to a line, people think that we private secretaries have got nothing to do. Look here," and he tossed over scornfully a dozen or so of little notes. "I tell you what, Mark; it is no easy matter to manage the patronage of a cabinet minister. Now I am bound to write to every one of these fellows a letter that will please him; and yet I shall refuse to every one of them the request which he asks."

"That must be difficult."

"Difficult is no word for it. But, after all, it consists chiefly in the knack of the thing. One must have the wit 'from such a sharp and waspish word as No to pluck the sting.' I do it every day, and I really think that the people like it."

"Perhaps your refusals are better than other people's acquiescences."

"I don't mean that at all. We private secretaries have all to do the same thing. Now, would you believe it? I have used up three lifts of note-paper already in telling people that there is no vacancy for a lobby messenger in the Petty Bag office. Seven peeresses have asked for it for their favourite footmen. But there—there's the Lord Petty Bag!"

A bell rang and the private secretary, jumping up from his note-paper, tripped away quickly to the great man's room.

"He'll see you at once," said he, returning. "Buggins, show the Reverend Mr. Robarts to the Lord Petty Bag."

Buggins was the messenger for whose not vacant place all the peeresses were striving with so much animation. And then Mark, following Buggins for two steps, was ushered into the next room.

If a man be altered by becoming a private secretary, he is much more altered by being made a cabinet minister. Robarts, as he entered the room, could hardly believe that this was the same Harold Smith whom Mrs. Proudie bothered so cruelly in the lecture-room at Barchester. Then he was cross, and touchy, and uneasy, and insignificant. Now, as he stood smiling on the hearthrug of his official fireplace, it was quite pleasant to see the kind, patronizing smile which lighted up his features. He delighted to stand there, with his hands in his trousers' pocket, the great man of the place, conscious of his lordship, and feeling himself every inch a minister. Sowerby had come with him, and was standing a little in the background, from which position he winked occasionally at the parson over the minister's shoulder.

"Ah, Robarts, delighted to see you. How odd, by-the-by, that your brother should be my private secretary!" Mark said that it was a singular coincidence.

"A very smart young fellow, and, if he minds himself, he'll do well."

"I'm quite sure he'll do well," said Mark.

"Ah! well, yes; I think he will. And now, what can I do for you, Robarts?"

Hereupon Mr. Sowerby struck in, making it apparent by his explanation that Mr. Robarts himself by no means intended to ask for anything; but that, as his friends had thought that this stall at Barchester might be put into his hands with more fitness than in those of any other clergyman of the day, he was willing to accept the piece of preferment from a man whom he respected so much as he did the new Lord Petty Bag.

The minister did not quite like this, as it restricted him from much of his condescension, and robbed him of the incense of a petition which he had expected Mark Robarts would make to him. But, nevertheless, he was very gracious.

"He could not take upon himself to declare," he said, "what might be Lord Brock's pleasure with reference to the preferment at Barchester which was vacant. He had certainly already spoken to his lordship on the subject, and had perhaps some reason to believe that his own wishes would be consulted. No distinct promise had been made, but he might perhaps go so far as to say that he expected such result. If so, it would give him the greatest pleasure in the world to congratulate Mr. Robarts on the possession of the stall—a stall which he was sure Mr. Robarts would fill with dignity, piety, and brotherly love." And then, when he had finished, Mr. Sowerby gave a final wink, and said that he regarded the matter as settled.

"No, not settled, Nathaniel," said the cautious minister.

"It's the same thing," rejoined Sowerby. "We all know what all that flummery means. Men in office, Mark, never do make a distinct promise,—not even to themselves of the leg of mutton which is roasting before their kitchen fires. It is so necessary in these days to be safe; is it not, Harold?"

"Most expedient," said Harold Smith, shaking his head wisely. "Well, Robarts, who is it now?" This he said to his private secretary, who came to notice the arrival of some bigwig. "Well, yes. I will say good morning, with your leave, for I am a little hurried. And remember, Mr. Robarts, I will do what I can for you; but you must distinctly understand that there is no promise."

"Oh, no promise at all," said Sowerby—"of course not." And then, as he sauntered up Whitehall towards Charing Cross, with Robarts on his arm, he again pressed upon him the sale of that invaluable hunter, who was eating his head off his shoulders in the stable at Chaldicotes.

CHAPTER XIX.

MONEY DEALINGS.

Mr. Sowerby, in his resolution to obtain this good gift for the Vicar of Framley, did not depend quite alone on the influence of his near connection with the Lord Petty Bag. He felt the occasion to be one on which he might endeavour to move even higher powers than that, and therefore he had opened the matter to the duke—not by direct application, but through Mr. Fothergill. No man who understood matters ever thought of going direct to the duke in such an affair as that. If one wanted to speak about a woman or a horse or a picture the duke could, on occasions, be affable enough.

But through Mr. Fothergill the duke was approached. It was represented, with some cunning, that this buying over of the Framley clergyman from the Lufton side would be a praiseworthy spoiling of the Amalekites. The doing so would give the Omnium interest a hold even in the cathedral close. And then it was known to all men that Mr. Robarts had considerable influence over Lord Lufton himself. So guided, the Duke of Omnium did say two words to the Prime Minister, and two words from the duke went a great way, even with Lord Brock. The upshot of all this was, that Mark Robarts did get the stall; but he did not hear the tidings of his success till some days after his return to Framley.

Mr. Sowerby did not forget to tell him of the great effort—the unusual effort, as he of Chaldicotes called it—which the duke had made on the subject. "I don't know when he has done such a thing before," said Sowerby; "and you may be quite sure of this, he would not have done it now, had you not gone to Gatherum Castle when he asked you: indeed, Fothergill would have known that it was vain to attempt it. And I'll tell you what, Mark— it does not do for me to make little of my own nest, but I truly believe the duke's word will be more efficacious than the Lord Petty Bag's solemn adjuration."

Mark, of course, expressed his gratitude in proper terms, and did buy the horse for a hundred and thirty pounds. "He's as well worth it," said Sowerby, "as any animal that ever stood on four legs; and my only reason for pressing him on you is, that when Tozer's day does come round, I know you will have to stand to us to something about that tune." It did not occur to Mark to ask him why the horse should not be sold to some one else, and the money forthcoming in the regular way. But this would not have suited Mr. Sowerby.

Mark knew that the beast was good, and as he walked to his lodgings was half proud of his new possession. But then, how would he justify it to his wife, or how introduce the animal into his stables without attempting any justification in the matter? And yet, looking to the absolute amount of his income, surely he might feel himself entitled to buy a new horse when it suited him. He wondered what Mr. Crawley would say when he heard of the new purchase. He had lately fallen into a state of much wondering as to what his friends and neighbours would say about him.

He had now been two days in town, and was to go down after breakfast on the following morning so that he might reach home by Friday afternoon. But on that evening, just as he was going to bed, he was surprised by Lord Lufton coming into the coffee-room at his hotel. He walked in with a hurried step, his face was red, and it was clear that he was very angry.

"Robarts," said he, walking up to his friend and taking the hand that was extended to him, "do you know anything about this man, Tozer?"

"Tozer—what Tozer? I have heard Sowerby speak of such a man."

"Of course you have. If I do not mistake you have written to me about him yourself."

"Very probably. I remember Sowerby mentioning the man with reference to your affairs. But why do you ask me?"

"This man has not only written to me, but has absolutely forced his way into my rooms when I was dressing for dinner; and absolutely had the impudence to tell me that if I did not honour some bill which he holds for eight hundred pounds he would proceed against me."

"But you settled all that matter with Sowerby?"

"I did settle it at a very great cost to me. Sooner than have a fuss I paid him through the nose—like a fool that I was—everything that he claimed. This is an absolute swindle, and if it goes on I will expose it as such."

Robarts looked round the room, but luckily there was not a soul in it but themselves. "You do not mean to say that Sowerby is swindling you?" said the clergyman.

"It looks very like it," said Lord Lufton; "and I tell you fairly that I am not in a humour to endure any more of this sort of thing. Some years ago I made an ass of myself through that man's fault. But four thousand pounds should have covered the whole of what I really lost. I have now paid more than three times that sum; and, by heavens! I will not pay more without exposing the whole affair."

"But, Lufton, I do not understand. What is this bill?—has it your name to it?"

"Yes, it has: I'll not deny my name, and if there be absolute need I will pay it; but if I do so, my lawyer shall sift it, and it shall go before a jury."

"But I thought all those bills were paid?"

"I left it to Sowerby to get up the old bills when they were renewed, and now one of them that has in truth been already honoured is brought against me."

Mark could not but think of the two documents which he himself had signed, and both of which were now undoubtedly in the hands of Tozer, or of some other gentleman of the same profession;—which both might be brought against him, the second as soon as he should have satisfied the first. And then he remembered that Sowerby had said something to him about an outstanding bill, for the filling up of which some trifle must be paid, and of this he reminded Lord Lufton.

"And do you call eight hundred pounds a trifle? If so, I do not."

"They will probably make no such demand as that."

"But I tell you they do make such a demand, and have made it. The man whom I saw, and who told me that he was Tozer's friend, but who was probably Tozer himself, positively swore to me that he would be obliged to take legal proceedings if the money were not forthcoming within a week or ten days. When I explained to him that it was an old bill that had been renewed, he declared that his friend had given full value for it."

"Sowerby said that you would probably have to pay ten pounds to redeem it. I should offer the man some such sum as that."

"My intention is to offer the man nothing, but to leave the affair in the hands of my lawyer with instructions to him to spare none;—neither myself nor any one else. I am not going to allow such a man as Sowerby to squeeze me like an orange."

"But, Lufton, you seem as though you were angry with me."

"No, I am not. But I think it is as well to caution you about this man; my transactions with him lately have chiefly been through you, and therefore—"

"But they have only been so through his and your wish: because I have been anxious to oblige you both. I hope you don't mean to say that I am concerned in these bills."

"I know that you are concerned in bills with him."

"Why, Lufton, am I to understand, then, that you are accusing me of having any interest in these transactions which you have called swindling?"

"As far as I am concerned there has been swindling, and there is swindling going on now."

"But you do not answer my question. Do you bring any accusation against me? If so, I agree with you that you had better go to your lawyer."

"I think that is what I shall do."

"Very well. But upon the whole, I never heard of a more unreasonable man, or of one whose thoughts are more unjust than yours. Solely with the view of assisting you, and solely at your request, I spoke to Sowerby about these money transactions of yours. Then at his request, which originated out of your request, he using me as his ambassador to you, as you had used me as yours to him, I wrote and spoke to you. And now this is the upshot."

"I bring no accusation against you, Robarts; but I know you have dealings with this man. You have told me so yourself."

"Yes, at his request to accommodate him, I have put my name to a bill."

"Only to one?"

"Only to one; and then to that same renewed, or not exactly to that same, but to one which stands for it. The first was for four hundred pounds; the last for five hundred."

"All which you will have to make good, and the world will of course tell you that you have paid that price for this stall at Barchester."

This was terrible to be borne. He had heard much lately which had frightened and scared him, but nothing so terrible as this; nothing which so stunned him, or conveyed to his mind so frightful a reality of misery and ruin. He made no immediate answer, but standing on the hearthrug with his back to the fire, looked up the whole length of the room. Hitherto his eyes had been fixed upon Lord Lufton's face, but now it seemed to him as though he had but little more to do with Lord Lufton. Lord Lufton and Lord Lufton's mother were neither now to be counted among those who wished him well. Upon whom indeed could he now count, except that wife of his bosom upon whom he was bringing all this wretchedness?

In that moment of agony ideas ran quickly through his brain. He would immediately abandon this preferment at Barchester, of which it might be said with so much colour that he had bought it. He would go to Harold Smith, and say positively that he declined it. Then he would return home and tell his wife all that had occurred;—tell the whole also to Lady Lufton, if that might still be of any service. He would make arrangement for the payment of both those bills as they might be presented, asking no questions as to the justice of the claim, making no complaint to any one, not even to Sowerby. He would put half his income, if half were necessary, into the hands of Forrest the banker, till all was paid. He would sell every horse he had. He would part with his footman and groom, and at any rate strive like a man to get again a firm footing on good ground. Then, at that moment, he loathed with his whole soul the position in which he found himself placed, and his own folly which had placed him there. How could he reconcile it to his conscience that he was there in London with Sowerby and Harold Smith, petitioning for Church preferment to a man who should have been altogether powerless in such a matter, buying horses, and arranging about past due bills? He did not reconcile it to his conscience. Mr. Crawley had been right when he told him that he was a castaway.

Lord Lufton, whose anger during the whole interview had been extreme, and who had become more angry the more he talked, had now walked once or twice up and down the room; and as he so walked the idea did occur to him that he had been unjust. He had come there with the intention of exclaiming against Sowerby, and of inducing Robarts to convey to that gentleman, that if he, Lord Lufton, were made to undergo any further annoyance about this bill, the whole affair should be thrown into the lawyer's hands; but instead of doing this, he had brought an accusation against Robarts. That Robarts had latterly become Sowerby's friend rather than his own in all these horrid money dealings, had galled him; and now he had expressed himself in terms much stronger than he had intended to use.

"As to you personally, Mark," he said, coming back to the spot on which Robarts was standing, "I do not wish to say anything that shall annoy you."

"You have said quite enough, Lord Lufton."

"You cannot be surprised that I should be angry and indignant at the treatment I have received."

"You might, I think, have separated in your mind those who have wronged you, if there has been such wrong, from those who have only endeavoured to do your will and pleasure for you. That I, as a clergyman, have been very wrong in taking any part whatsoever in these matters, I am well aware. That as a man I have been outrageously foolish in lending my name to Mr. Sowerby, I also know well enough: it is perhaps as well that I should be told of this somewhat rudely; but I certainly did not expect the lesson to come from you."

"Well, there has been mischief enough. The question is, what we had better now both do?"

"You have said what you mean to do. You will put the affair into the hands of your lawyer."

"Not with any object of exposing you."

"Exposing me, Lord Lufton! Why, one would think that I had had the handling of your money."

"You will misunderstand me. I think no such thing. But do you not know yourself that if legal steps be taken in this wretched affair, your arrangements with Sowerby will be brought to light?"

"My arrangements with Sowerby will consist in paying or having to pay, on his account, a large sum of money, for which I have never had and shall never have any consideration whatever."

"And what will be said about this stall at Barchester?"

"After the charge which you brought against me just now, I shall decline to accept it."

At this moment three or four other gentlemen entered the room, and the conversation between our two friends was stopped. They still remained standing near the fire, but for a few minutes neither of them said anything. Robarts was waiting till Lord Lufton should go away, and Lord Lufton had not yet said that which he had come to say. At last he spoke again, almost in a whisper: "I think it will be best to ask Sowerby to come to my rooms tomorrow, and I think also that you should meet him there."

"I do not see any necessity for my presence," said Robarts. "It seems probable that I shall suffer enough for meddling with your affairs, and I will do so no more."

"Of course I cannot make you come; but I think it will be only just to Sowerby, and it will be a favour to me."

Robarts again walked up and down the room for half-a-dozen times, trying to resolve what it would most become him to do in the present emergency. If his name were dragged before the courts,—if he should be shown up in the public papers as having been engaged in accommodation bills, that would certainly be ruinous to him. He had already learned from Lord Lufton's innuendoes what he might expect to hear as the public version of his share in these transactions! And then his wife,—how would she bear such exposure?

"I will meet Mr. Sowerby at your rooms to-morrow, on one condition," he at last said.

"And what is that?"

"That I receive your positive assurance that I am not suspected by you of having had any pecuniary interest whatever in any money matters with Mr. Sowerby, either as concerns your affairs or those of anybody else."

"I have never suspected you of any such thing. But I have thought that you were compromised with him."

"And so I am—I am liable for these bills. But you ought to have known, and do know, that I have never received a shilling on account of such liability. I have endeavoured to oblige a man whom I regarded first as your friend, and then as my own; and this has been the result."

Lord Lufton did at last give him the assurance that he desired, as they sat with their heads together over one of the coffee-room tables; and then Robarts promised that he would postpone his return to Framley till the Saturday, so that he might meet Sowerby at Lord Lufton's chambers in the Albany on the following afternoon. As soon as this was arranged, Lord Lufton took his leave and went his way.

After that poor Mark had a very uneasy night of it. It was clear enough that Lord Lufton had thought, if he did not still think, that the stall at Barchester was to be given as pecuniary recompense in return for certain money accommodation to be afforded by the nominee to the dispenser of this patronage. Nothing on earth could be worse than this. In the first place it would be simony; and then it would be simony beyond all description mean and simoniacal. The very thought of it filled Mark's soul with horror and dismay. It might be that Lord Lufton's suspicions were now at rest; but others would think the same thing, and their suspicions it would be impossible to allay; those others would consist of the outer world, which is always so eager to gloat over the detected vice of a clergyman.

And then that wretched horse which he had purchased, and the purchase of which should have prohibited him from saying that nothing of value had accrued to him in these transactions with Mr. Sowerby! what was he to do about that? And then of late he had been spending, and had continued to spend, more money than he could well afford. This very journey of his up to London would be most imprudent, if it should become necessary for him to give up all hope of holding the prebend. As to that he had made up his mind; but then again he unmade it, as men always do in such troubles. That line of conduct which he had laid down for himself in the first moments of his indignation against Lord Lufton, by adopting which he would have to encounter poverty, and ridicule, and discomfort, the annihilation of his high hopes, and the ruin of his ambition—that, he said to himself over and over again, would now be the best for him. But it is so hard for us to give up our high hopes, and willingly encounter poverty, ridicule, and discomfort!

On the following morning, however, he boldly walked down to the Petty Bag office, determined to let Harold Smith know that he was no longer desirous of the Barchester stall. He found his brother there, still writing artistic notes to anxious peeresses on the subject of Buggins' non-vacant situation; but the great man of the place, the Lord Petty Bag himself, was not there. He might probably look in when the House was beginning to sit, perhaps at four or a little after; but he certainly would not be at the office in the morning. The functions of the Lord Petty Bag he was no doubt performing elsewhere. Perhaps he had carried his work home with him—a practice which the world should know is not uncommon with civil servants of exceeding zeal.

Mark did think of opening his heart to his brother, and of leaving his message with him. But his courage failed him, or perhaps it might be more correct to say that his prudence prevented him. It would be better for him, he thought, to tell his wife before he told any one else. So he merely chatted with his brother for half an hour and then left him.

The day was very tedious till the hour came at which he was to attend at Lord Lufton's rooms; but at last it did come, and just as the clock struck, he turned out of Piccadilly into the Albany. As he was going across the court before he entered the building, he was greeted by a voice just behind him.

"As punctual as the big clock on Barchester tower," said Mr. Sowerby. "See what it is to have a summons from a great man, Mr. Prebendary."

He turned round and extended his hand mechanically to Mr. Sowerby, and as he looked at him he thought he had never before seen him so pleasant in appearance, so free from care, and so joyous in demeanour.

"You have heard from Lord Lufton," said Mark in a voice that was certainly very lugubrious.

"Heard from him! oh, yes, of course I have heard from him. I'll tell you what it is, Mark," and he now spoke almost in a whisper as they walked together along the Albany passage, "Lufton is a child in money matters—a perfect child. The dearest, finest fellow in the world, you know; but a very baby in money matters." And then they entered his lordship's rooms.

Lord Lufton's countenance also was lugubrious enough, but this did not in the least abash Sowerby, who walked quickly up to the young lord with his gait perfectly self-possessed and his face radiant with satisfaction.

"Well, Lufton, how are you?" said he. "It seems that my worthy friend Tozer has been giving you some trouble?"

Then Lord Lufton with a face by no means radiant with satisfaction again began the story of Tozer's fraudulent demand upon him. Sowerby did not interrupt him, but listened patiently to the end;—quite patiently, although Lord Lufton, as he made himself more and more angry by the history of his own wrongs, did not hesitate to pronounce certain threats against Mr. Sowerby, as he had pronounced them before against Mark Robarts. He would not, he said, pay a shilling, except through his lawyer; and he would instruct his lawyer, that before he paid anything, the whole matter should be exposed openly in court. He did not care, he said, what might be the effect on himself or any one else. He was determined that the whole case should go to a jury.

"To grand jury, and special jury, and common jury, and Old Jewry, if you like," said Sowerby. "The truth is, Lufton, you lost some money, and as there was some delay in paying it, you have been harassed."

"I have paid more than I lost three times over," said Lord Lufton, stamping his foot.

"I will not go into that question now. It was settled, as I thought, some time ago by persons to whom you yourself referred it. But will you tell me this: Why on earth should Robarts be troubled in this matter? What has he done?"

"Well, I don't know. He arranged the matter with you."

"No such thing. He was kind enough to carry a message from you to me, and to convey back a return message from me to you. That has been his part in it."

"You don't suppose that I want to implicate him: do you?"

"I don't think you want to implicate any one, but you are hot-headed and difficult to deal with, and very irrational into the bargain. And, what is worse, I must say you are a little suspicious. In all this matter I have harassed myself greatly to oblige you, and in return I have got more kicks than halfpence."

"Did not you give this bill to Tozer—the bill which he now holds?"

"In the first place he does not hold it; and in the next place I did not give it to him. These things pass through scores of hands before they reach the man who makes the application for payment."

"And who came to me the other day?"

"That, I take it, was Tom Tozer, a brother of our Tozer's."

"Then he holds the bill, for I saw it with him."

"Wait a moment; that is very likely. I sent you word that you would have to pay for taking it up. Of course they don't abandon those sort of things without some consideration."

"Ten pounds, you said," observed Mark.

"Ten or twenty; some such sum as that. But you were hardly so soft as to suppose that the man would ask for such a sum. Of course he would demand the full payment. There is the bill, Lord Lufton," and Sowerby, producing a document, handed it across the table to his lordship. "I gave five-and-twenty pounds for it this morning."

Lord Lufton took the paper and looked at it. "Yes," said he, "that's the bill. What am I to do with it now?"

"Put it with the family archives," said Sowerby,—"or behind the fire, just which you please."

"And is this the last of them? Can no other be brought up?"

"You know better than I do what paper you may have put your hand to. I know of no other. At the last renewal that was the only outstanding bill of which I was aware."

"And you have paid five-and-twenty pounds for it?"

"I have. Only that you have been in such a tantrum about it, and would have made such a noise this afternoon if I had not brought it, I might have had it for fifteen or twenty. In three or four days they would have taken fifteen."

"The odd ten pounds does not signify, and I'll pay you the twenty-five, of course," said Lord Lufton, who now began to feel a little ashamed of himself.

"You may do as you please about that."

"Oh! it's my affair, as a matter of course. Any amount of that kind I don't mind," and he sat down to fill in a cheque for the money.

"Well, now, Lufton, let me say a few words to you," said Sowerby, standing with his back against the fireplace, and playing with a small cane which he held in his hand. "For heaven's sake try and be a little more charitable to those around you. When you become fidgety about anything, you indulge in language which the world won't stand, though men who know you as well as Robarts and I may consent to put up with it. You have accused me, since I have been here, of all manner of iniquity—"

"Now, Sowerby—"

"My dear fellow, let me have my say out. You have accused me, I say, and I believe that you have accused him. But it has never occurred to you, I daresay, to accuse yourself."

"Indeed it has."

"Of course you have been wrong in having to do with such men as Tozer. I have also been very wrong. It wants no great moral authority to tell us that. Pattern gentlemen don't have dealings with Tozer, and very much the better they are for not having them. But a man should have back enough to bear the weight which he himself puts on it. Keep away from Tozer, if you can, for the future; but if you do deal with him, for heaven's sake keep your temper."

"That's all very fine, Sowerby; but you know as well as I do—"

"I know this," said the devil, quoting Scripture, as he folded up the check for twenty-five pounds, and put it in his pocket, "that when a man sows tares, he won't reap wheat, and it's no use to expect it. I am tough in these matters, and can bear a great deal—that is, if I be not pushed too far," and he looked full into Lord Lufton's face as he spoke; "but I think you have been very hard upon Robarts."

"Never mind me, Sowerby; Lord Lufton and I are very old friends."

"And may therefore take a liberty with each other. Very well. And now I've done my sermon. My dear dignitary, allow me to congratulate you. I hear from Fothergill that that little affair of yours has been definitely settled."

Mark's face again became clouded. "I rather think," said he, "that I shall decline the presentation."

"Decline it!" said Sowerby, who, having used his utmost efforts to obtain it, would have been more absolutely offended by such vacillation on the vicar's part than by any personal abuse which either he or Lord Lufton could heap upon him.

"I think I shall," said Mark.

"And why?"

Mark looked up at Lord Lufton, and then remained silent for a moment.

"There can be no occasion for such a sacrifice under the present circumstances," said his lordship.

"And under what circumstances could there be occasion for it?" asked Sowerby. "The Duke of Omnium has used some little influence to get the place for you as a parish clergyman belonging to his county, and I should think it monstrous if you were now to reject it."

And then Robarts openly stated the whole of his reasons, explaining exactly what Lord Lufton had said with reference to the bill transactions, and to the allegation which would be made as to the stall having been given in payment for the accommodation.

"Upon my word that's too bad," said Sowerby.

"Now, Sowerby, I won't be lectured," said Lord Lufton.

"I have done my lecture," said he, aware, perhaps, that it would not do for him to push his friend too far, "and I shall not give a second. But, Robarts, let me tell you this: as far as I know, Harold Smith has had little or nothing to do with the appointment. The duke has told the Prime Minister that he was very anxious that a parish clergyman from the county should go into the chapter, and then, at Lord Brock's request, he named you. If under those circumstances you talk of giving it up, I shall believe you to be insane. As for the bill which you accepted for me, you need have no uneasiness about it. The money will be ready; but of course, when that time comes, you will let me have the hundred and thirty for—"

And then Mr. Sowerby took his leave, having certainly made himself master of the occasion. If a man of fifty have his wits about him, and be not too prosy, he can generally make himself master of the occasion, when his companions are under thirty.

Robarts did not stay at the Albany long after him, but took his leave, having received some assurances of Lord Lufton's regret for what had passed and many promises of his friendship for the future. Indeed Lord Lufton was a little ashamed of himself. "And as for the prebend, after what has passed, of course you must accept it." Nevertheless his lordship had not omitted to notice Mr. Sowerby's hint about the horse and the hundred and thirty pounds.

Robarts, as he walked back to his hotel, thought that he certainly would accept the Barchester promotion, and was very glad that he had said nothing on the subject to his brother. On the whole his spirits were much raised. That assurance of Sowerby's about the bill was very comforting to him; and strange to say, he absolutely believed it. In truth Sowerby had been so completely the winning horse at the late meeting, that both Lord Lufton and Robarts were inclined to believe almost anything he said;—which was not always the case with either of them.

CHAPTER XX.

HAROLD SMITH IN THE CABINET.

For a few days the whole Harold Smith party held their heads very high. It was not only that their man had been made a cabinet minister; but a rumour had got abroad that Lord Brock, in selecting him, had amazingly strengthened his party, and done much to cure the wounds which his own arrogance and lack of judgment had inflicted on the body politic of his government. So said the Harold-Smithians, much elated. And when we consider what Harold had himself achieved, we need not be surprised that he himself was somewhat elated also.

It must be a proud day for any man when he first walks into a cabinet. But when a humble-minded man thinks of such a phase of life, his mind becomes lost in wondering what a cabinet is. Are they gods that attend there or men? Do they sit on chairs, or hang about on clouds? When they speak, is the music of the spheres audible in their Olympian mansion, making heaven drowsy with its harmony? In what way do they congregate? In what order do they address each other? Are the voices of all the deities free and equal? Is plodding Themis from the Home Department, or Ceres from the Colonies, heard with as rapt attention as powerful Pallas of the Foreign Office, the goddess that is never seen without her lance and helmet? Does our Whitehall Mars make eyes there at bright young Venus of the Privy Seal, disgusting that quaint tinkering Vulcan, who is blowing his bellows at our Exchequer, not altogether unsuccessfully? Old Saturn of the Woolsack sits there mute, we will say, a relic of other days, as seated in this divan. The hall in which he rules is now elsewhere. Is our Mercury of the Post Office ever ready to fly nimbly from globe to globe, as great Jove may order him, while Neptune, unaccustomed to the waves, offers needful assistance to the Apollo of the India Board? How Juno sits apart, glum and huffy, uncared for, Council President though she be, great in name, but despised among gods—that we can guess. If Bacchus and Cupid share Trade and the Board of Works between them, the fitness of things will have been as fully consulted as is usual. And modest Diana of the Petty Bag, latest summoned to these banquets of ambrosia,—does she not cling retiring near the doors, hardly able as yet to make her low voice heard among her brother deities? But Jove, great Jove—old Jove, the King of Olympus, hero among gods and men, how does he carry himself in these councils summoned by his voice? Does he lie there at his ease, with his purple cloak cut from the firmament around his shoulders? Is his thunderbolt ever at his hand to reduce a recreant god to order? Can he proclaim silence in that immortal hall? Is it not there, as elsewhere, in all places, and among all nations, that a king of gods and a king of men is and will be king, rules and will rule, over those who are smaller than himself?

Harold Smith, when he was summoned to the august hall of divine councils, did feel himself to be a proud man; but we may perhaps conclude that at the first meeting or two he did not attempt to take a very leading part. Some of my readers may have sat at vestries, and will remember how mild, and for the most part, mute, is a new-comer at their board. He agrees generally, with abated enthusiasm; but should he differ, he apologizes for the liberty. But anon, when the voices of his colleagues have become habitual in his ears—when the strangeness of the room is gone, and the table before him is known and trusted—he throws off his awe and dismay, and electrifies his brotherhood by the vehemence of his declamation and the violence of his thumping. So let us suppose it will be with Harold Smith, perhaps in the second or third season of his cabinet practice. Alas! alas! that such pleasures should be so fleeting!

And then, too, there came upon him a blow which somewhat modified his triumph—a cruel, dastard blow, from a hand which should have been friendly to him, from one to whom he had fondly looked to buoy him up in the great course that was before him. It had been said by his friends that in obtaining Harold Smith's services the Prime Minister had infused new young healthy blood into his body. Harold himself had liked the phrase, and had seen at a glance how it might have been made to tell by some friendly Supplehouse or the like. But why should a Supplehouse out of Elysium be friendly to a Harold Smith within it? Men lapped in Elysium, steeped to the neck in bliss, must expect to see their friends fall off from them. Human nature cannot stand it. If I want to get anything from my old friend Jones, I like to see him shoved up into a high place. But if Jones, even in his high place, can do nothing for me, then his exaltation above my head is an insult and an injury. Who ever believes his own dear intimate companion to be fit for the highest promotion? Mr. Supplehouse had known Mr. Smith too closely to think much of his young blood.

Consequently, there appeared an article in the *Jupiter*, which was by no means complimentary to the ministry in general. It harped a good deal on the young blood view of the question, and seemed to insinuate that Harold Smith was not much better than diluted water. "The Prime Minister," the article said, "having lately recruited his impaired vigour by a new infusion of aristocratic influence of the highest moral tone, had again added to himself another tower of strength chosen from among the people. What might he not hope, now that he possessed the services of Lord Brittleback and Mr. Harold Smith! Renovated in a Medea's caldron of such potency, all his effete limbs—and it must be acknowledged that some of them had become very effete—would come forth young and round and robust. A new energy would diffuse itself through every department; India would be saved and quieted; the ambition of France would be tamed; even-handed reform would remodel our courts of law and parliamentary elections; and Utopia would be realized. Such, it seems, is the result expected in the ministry from Mr. Harold Smith's young blood!"

This was cruel enough, but even this was hardly so cruel as the words with which the article ended. By that time irony had been dropped, and the writer spoke out earnestly his opinion upon the matter. "We beg to assure Lord Brock," said the article, "that such alliances as these will not save him from the speedy fall with which his arrogance and want of judgment threaten to overwhelm it. As regards himself we shall be sorry to hear of his resignation. He is in many respects the best statesman that we possess for the emergencies of the present period. But if he be so ill-judged as to rest on such men as Mr. Harold Smith and Lord Brittleback for his assistants in the work which is before him, he must not expect that the country will support him. Mr. Harold Smith is not made of the stuff from which cabinet ministers should be formed."

Mr. Harold Smith, as he read this, seated at his breakfast-table, recognized, or said that he recognized, the hand of Mr. Supplehouse in every touch. That phrase about the effete limbs was Supplehouse all over, as was also the realization of Utopia. "When he wants to be witty, he always talks about Utopia," said Mr. Harold Smith—to himself: for Mrs. Harold was not usually present in the flesh at these matutinal meals.

And then he went down to his office, and saw in the glance of every man that he met an announcement that that article in the *Jupiter* had been read. His private secretary tittered in evident allusion to the article, and the way in which Buggins took his coat made it clear that it was well known in the messengers' lobby. "He won't have to fill up my vacancy when I go," Buggins was saying to himself. And then in the course of the morning came the cabinet council, the second that he had attended, and he read in the countenance of every god and goddess there assembled that their chief was thought to have made another mistake. If Mr. Supplehouse could have been induced to write in another strain, then indeed that new blood might have been felt to have been efficacious.

All this was a great drawback to his happiness, but still it could not rob him of the fact of his position. Lord Brock could not ask him to resign because the *Jupiter* had written against him; nor was Lord Brock the man to desert a new colleague for such a reason. So Harold Smith girded his loins, and went about the duties of the Petty Bag with new zeal. "Upon my word, the *Jupiter* is right," said young Robarts to himself, as he finished his fourth dozen of private notes explanatory of everything in and about the Petty Bag Office. Harold Smith required that his private secretary's notes should be so terribly precise.

But nevertheless, in spite of his drawbacks, Harold Smith was happy in his new honours, and Mrs. Harold Smith enjoyed them also. She certainly, among her acquaintance, did quiz the new cabinet minister not a little, and it may be a question whether she was not as hard upon him as the writer in the *Jupiter*. She whispered a great deal to Miss Dunstable about new blood, and talked of going down to Westminster Bridge to see whether the Thames were really on fire. But though she laughed, she triumphed, and though she flattered herself that she bore her honours without any outward sign, the world knew that she was triumphing, and ridiculed her elation.

About this time she also gave a party—not a pure-minded conversazione like Mrs. Proudie, but a downright wicked worldly dance, at which there were fiddles, ices, and champagne sufficient to run away with the first quarter's salary accruing to Harold from the Petty Bag Office. To us this ball is chiefly memorable from the fact that Lady Lufton was among the guests. Immediately on her arrival in town she received cards from Mrs. H. Smith for herself and Griselda, and was about to send back a reply at once declining the honour. What had she to do at the house of Mr. Sowerby's sister? But it so happened that at that moment her son was with her, and as he expressed a wish that she should go, she yielded. Had there been nothing in his tone of persuasion more than ordinary,—had it merely had reference to herself,—she would have smiled on him for his kind solicitude, have made out some occasion for kissing his forehead as she thanked him, and would still have declined. But he had reminded her both of himself and Griselda. "You might as well go, mother, for the sake of meeting me," he said; "Mrs. Harold caught me the other day, and would not liberate me till I had given her a promise."

"That is an attraction certainly," said Lady Lufton. "I do like going to a house when I know that you will be there."

"And now that Miss Grantly is with you—you owe it to her to do the best you can for her."

"I certainly do, Ludovic; and I have to thank you for reminding me of my duty so gallantly." And so she said that she would go to Mrs. Harold Smith's. Poor lady! She gave much more weight to those few words about Miss Grantly than they deserved. It rejoiced her heart to think that her son was anxious to meet Griselda—that he should perpetrate this little *ruse* in order to gain his wish. But he had spoken out of the mere emptiness of his mind, without thought of what he was saying, excepting that he wished to please his mother.

But nevertheless he went to Mrs. Harold Smith's, and when there he did dance more than once with Griselda Grantly—to the manifest discomfiture of Lord Dumbello. He came in late, and at the moment Lord Dumbello was moving slowly up the room, with Griselda on his arm, while Lady Lufton was sitting near looking on with unhappy eyes. And then Griselda sat down, and Lord Dumbello stood mute at her elbow.

"Ludovic," whispered his mother, "Griselda is absolutely bored by that man, who follows her like a ghost. Do go and rescue her."

He did go and rescue her, and afterwards danced with her for the best part of an hour consecutively. He knew that the world gave Lord Dumbello the credit of admiring the young lady, and was quite alive to the pleasure of filling his brother nobleman's heart with jealousy and anger. Moreover, Griselda was in his eyes very beautiful, and had she been one whit more animated, or had his mother's tactics been but a thought better concealed, Griselda might have been asked that night to share the vacant throne at Lufton, in spite of all that had been said and sworn in the drawing-room of Framley Parsonage.

It must be remembered that our gallant, gay Lothario had passed some considerable number of days with Miss Grantly in his mother's house, and the danger of such contiguity must be remembered also. Lord Lufton was by no means a man capable of seeing beauty unmoved or of spending hours with a young lady without some approach to tenderness. Had there been no such approach, it is probable that Lady Lufton would not have pursued the matter. But, according to her ideas on such subjects, her son Ludovic had on some occasions shown quite sufficient partiality for Miss Grantly to justify her in her hopes, and to lead her to think that nothing but opportunity was wanted. Now, at this ball of Mrs. Smith's, he did, for a while, seem to be taking advantage of such opportunity, and his mother's heart was glad. If things should turn out well on this evening she would forgive Mrs. Harold Smith all her sins.

And for a while it looked as though things would turn out well. Not that it must be supposed that Lord Lufton had come there with any intention of making love to Griselda, or that he ever had any fixed thought that he was doing so. Young men in such matters are so often without any fixed thoughts! They are such absolute moths. They amuse themselves with the light of the beautiful candle, fluttering about, on and off, in and out of the flame with dazzled eyes, till in a rash moment they rush in too near the wick, and then fall with singed wings and crippled legs, burnt up and reduced to tinder by the consuming fire of matrimony. Happy marriages, men say, are made in heaven, and I believe it. Most marriages are fairly happy, in spite of Sir Cresswell Cresswell; and yet how little care is taken on earth towards such a result!

"I hope my mother is using you well?" said Lord Lufton to Griselda, as they were standing together in a doorway between the dances.

"Oh, yes: she is very kind."

"You have been rash to trust yourself in the hands of so very staid and demure a person. And, indeed, you owe your presence here at Mrs. Harold Smith's first cabinet ball altogether to me. I don't know whether you are aware of that."

"Oh, yes: Lady Lufton told me."

"And are you grateful or otherwise? Have I done you an injury or a benefit? Which do you find best, sitting with a novel in the corner of a sofa in Bruton Street, or pretending to dance polkas here with Lord Dumbello?"

"I don't know what you mean. I haven't stood up with Lord Dumbello all the evening. We were going to dance a quadrille, but we didn't."

"Exactly; just what I say;—pretending to do it. Even that's a good deal for Lord Dumbello; isn't it?" And then Lord Lufton, not being a pretender himself, put his arm round her waist, and away they went up and down the room, and across and about, with an energy which showed that what Griselda lacked in her tongue she made up with her feet. Lord Dumbello, in the meantime, stood by, observant, thinking to himself that Lord Lufton was a glib-tongued, empty-headed ass, and reflecting that if his rival were to break the tendons of his leg in one of those rapid evolutions, or suddenly come by any other dreadful misfortune, such as the loss of all his property, absolute blindness, or chronic lumbago, it would only serve him right. And in that frame of mind he went to bed, in spite of the prayer which no doubt he said as to his forgiveness of other people's trespasses.

And then, when they were again standing, Lord Lufton, in the little intervals between his violent gasps for fresh breath, asked Griselda if she liked London. "Pretty well," said Griselda, gasping also a little herself.

"I am afraid—you were very dull—down at Framley."

"Oh, no;—I liked it—particularly."

"It was a great bore when you went—away, I know. There wasn't a soul—about the house worth speaking to." And they remained silent for a minute till their lungs had become quiescent.

"Not a soul," he continued—not of falsehood prepense, for he was not in fact thinking of what he was saying. It did not occur to him at the moment that he had truly found Griselda's going a great relief, and that he had been able to do more in the way of conversation with Lucy Robarts in one hour than with Miss Grantly during a month of intercourse in the same house. But, nevertheless, we should not be hard upon him. All is fair in love and war; and if this was not love, it was the usual thing that stands as a counterpart for it.

"Not a soul," said Lord Lufton. "I was very nearly hanging myself in the park next morning;—only it rained."

"What nonsense! You had your mother to talk to."

"Oh, my mother,—yes; and you may tell me too, if you please, that Captain Culpepper was there. I do love my mother dearly; but do you think that she could make up for your absence?" And his voice was very tender, and so were his eyes.

"And Miss Robarts; I thought you admired her very much?"

"What, Lucy Robarts?" said Lord Lufton, feeling that Lucy's name was more than he at present knew how to manage. Indeed that name destroyed all the life there was in that little flirtation. "I do like Lucy Robarts, certainly. She is very clever; but it so happened that I saw little or nothing of her after you were gone."

To this Griselda made no answer, but drew herself up, and looked as cold as Diana when she froze Orion in the cave. Nor could she be got to give more than monosyllabic answers to the three or four succeeding attempts at conversation which Lord Lufton made. And then they danced again, but Griselda's steps were by no means so lively as before.

What took place between them on that occasion was very little more than what has been here related. There may have been an ice or a glass of lemonade into the bargain, and perhaps the faintest possible attempt at hand-pressing. But if so, it was all on one side. To such overtures as that Griselda Grantly was as cold as any Diana.

But little as all this was, it was sufficient to fill Lady Lufton's mind and heart. No mother with six daughters was ever more anxious to get them off her hands, than Lady Lufton was to see her son married,—married, that is, to some girl of the right sort. And now it really did seem as though he were actually going to comply with her wishes. She had watched him during the whole evening, painfully endeavouring not to be observed in doing so. She had seen Lord Dumbello's failure and wrath, and she had seen her son's victory and pride. Could it be the case that he had already said something, which was still allowed to be indecisive only through Griselda's coldness? Might it not be the case, that by some judicious aid on her part, that indecision might be turned into certainty, and that coldness into warmth? But then any such interference requires so delicate a touch,—as Lady Lufton was well aware.

"Have you had a pleasant evening?" Lady Lufton said, when she and Griselda were seated together with their feet on the fender of her ladyship's dressing-room. Lady Lufton had especially invited her guest into this, her most private sanctum, to which as a rule none had admittance but her daughter, and sometimes Fanny Robarts. But to what sanctum might not such a daughter-in-law as Griselda have admittance?

"Oh, yes—very," said Griselda.

"It seemed to me that you bestowed most of your smiles upon Ludovic." And Lady Lufton put on a look of good pleasure that such should have been the case.

"Oh! I don't know," said Griselda: "I did dance with him two or three times."

"Not once too often to please me, my dear. I like to see Ludovic dancing with my friends."

"I am sure I am very much obliged to you, Lady Lufton."

"Not at all, my dear. I don't know where he could get so nice a partner." And then she paused a moment, not feeling how far she might go. In the meantime Griselda sat still, staring at the hot coals. "Indeed, I know that he admires you very much," continued Lady Lufton.

"Oh! no, I am sure he doesn't," said Griselda; and then there was another pause.

"I can only say this," said Lady Lufton, "that if he does do so—and I believe he does— it would give me very great pleasure. For you know, my dear, that I am very fond of you myself."

"Oh! thank you," said Griselda, and stared at the coals more perseveringly than before.

"He is a young man of a most excellent disposition—though he is my own son, I will say that—and if there should be anything between you and him—"

"There isn't, indeed, Lady Lufton."

"But if there ever should be, I should be delighted to think that Ludovic had made so good a choice."

"But there will never be anything of the sort, I'm sure, Lady Lufton. He is not thinking of such a thing in the least."

"Well, perhaps he may, some day. And now, good-night, my dear."

"Good-night, Lady Lufton." And Griselda kissed her with the utmost composure, and betook herself to her own bedroom. Before she retired to sleep she looked carefully to her different articles of dress, discovering what amount of damage the evening's wear and tear might have inflicted.

CHAPTER XXI.

WHY PUCK, THE PONY, WAS BEATEN.

Mark Robarts returned home the day after the scene at the Albany, considerably relieved in spirit. He now felt that he might accept the stall without discredit to himself as a clergyman in doing so. Indeed, after what Mr. Sowerby had said, and after Lord Lufton's assent to it, it would have been madness, he considered, to decline it. And then, too, Mr. Sowerby's promise about the bills was very comfortable to him. After all, might it not be possible that he might get rid of all these troubles with no other drawback than that of having to pay £130 for a horse that was well worth the money?

On the day after his return he received proper authentic tidings of his presentation to the prebend. He was, in fact, already prebendary, or would be as soon as the dean and chapter had gone through the form of instituting him in his stall. The income was already his own; and the house also would be given up to him in a week's time—a part of the arrangement with which he would most willingly have dispensed had it been at all possible to do so. His wife congratulated him nicely, with open affection, and apparent satisfaction at the arrangement. The enjoyment of one's own happiness at such windfalls depends so much on the free and freely expressed enjoyment of others! Lady Lufton's congratulations had nearly made him throw up the whole thing; but his wife's smiles re-encouraged him; and Lucy's warm and eager joy made him feel quite delighted with Mr. Sowerby and the Duke of Omnium. And then that splendid animal, Dandy, came home to the parsonage stables, much to the delight of the groom and gardener, and of the assistant stable boy who had been allowed to creep into the establishment, unawares as it were, since "master" had taken so keenly to hunting. But this satisfaction was not shared in the drawing-room. The horse was seen on his first journey round to the stable gate, and questions were immediately asked. It was a horse, Mark said, "which he had bought from Mr. Sowerby some little time since with the object of obliging him. He, Mark, intended to sell him again, as soon as he could do so judiciously." This, as I have said above, was not satisfactory. Neither of the two ladies at Framley Parsonage knew much about horses, or of the manner in which one gentleman might think it proper to oblige another by purchasing the superfluities of his stable; but they did both feel that there were horses enough in the parsonage stable without Dandy, and that the purchasing of a hunter with the view of immediately selling him again, was, to say the least of it, an operation hardly congenial with the usual tastes and pursuits of a clergyman.

"I hope you did not give very much money for him, Mark," said Fanny.

"Not more than I shall get again," said Mark; and Fanny saw from the form of his countenance that she had better not pursue the subject any further at that moment.

"I suppose I shall have to go into residence almost immediately," said Mark, recurring to the more agreeable subject of the stall.

"And shall we all have to go and live at Barchester at once?" asked Lucy.

"The house will not be furnished, will it, Mark?" said his wife. "I don't know how we shall get on."

"Don't frighten yourselves. I shall take lodgings in Barchester."

"And we shall not see you all the time," said Mrs. Robarts with dismay. But the prebendary explained that he would be backwards and forwards at Framley every week, and that in all probability he would only sleep at Barchester on the Saturdays and Sundays—and, perhaps, not always then.

"It does not seem very hard work, that of a prebendary," said Lucy.

"But it is very dignified," said Fanny. "Prebendaries are dignitaries of the Church—are they not, Mark?"

"Decidedly," said he; "and their wives also, by special canon law. The worst of it is that both of them are obliged to wear wigs."

"Shall you have a hat, Mark, with curly things at the side, and strings through to hold them up?" asked Lucy.

"I fear that does not come within my perquisites."

"Nor a rosette? Then I shall never believe that you are a dignitary. Do you mean to say that you will wear a hat like a common parson—like Mr. Crawley, for instance?"

"Well—I believe I may give a twist to the leaf; but I am by no means sure till I shall have consulted the dean in chapter."

And thus at the parsonage they talked over the good things that were coming to them, and endeavoured to forget the new horse, and the hunting boots that had been used so often during the last winter, and Lady Lufton's altered countenance. It might be that the evils would vanish away, and the good things alone remain to them.

It was now the month of April, and the fields were beginning to look green, and the wind had got itself out of the east and was soft and genial, and the early spring flowers were showing their bright colours in the parsonage garden, and all things were sweet and pleasant. This was a period of the year that was usually dear to Mrs. Robarts. Her husband was always a better parson when the warm months came than he had been during the winter. The distant county friends whom she did not know and of whom she did not approve went away when the spring came, leaving their houses innocent and empty. The parish duty was better attended to, and perhaps domestic duties also. At such period he was a pattern parson and a pattern husband, atoning to his own conscience for past shortcomings by present zeal. And then, though she had never acknowledged it to herself, the absence of her dear friend Lady Lufton was perhaps in itself not disagreeable. Mrs. Robarts did love Lady Lufton heartily; but it must be acknowledged of her ladyship, that, with all her good qualities, she was inclined to be masterful. She liked to rule, and she made people feel that she liked it. Mrs. Robarts would never have confessed that she laboured under a sense of thraldom; but perhaps she was mouse enough to enjoy the temporary absence of her kind-hearted cat. When Lady Lufton was away Mrs. Robarts herself had more play in the parish.

And Mark also was not unhappy, though he did not find it practicable immediately to turn Dandy into money. Indeed, just at this moment, when he was a good deal over at Barchester, going through those deep mysteries and rigid ecclesiastical examinations which are necessary before a clergyman can become one of a chapter, Dandy was rather a thorn in his side. Those wretched bills were to come due early in May, and before the end of April Sowerby wrote to him saying that he was doing his utmost to provide for the evil day; but that if the price of Dandy could be remitted to him *at once*, it would greatly facilitate his object. Nothing could be more different than Mr. Sowerby's tone about money at different times. When he wanted to raise the wind, everything was so important; haste and superhuman efforts, and men running to and fro with blank acceptances in their hands, could alone stave off the crack of doom; but at other times, when retaliatory applications were made to him, he could prove with the easiest voice and most jaunty manner that everything was quite serene. Now, at this period, he was in that mood of superhuman efforts, and he called loudly for the hundred and thirty pounds for Dandy. After what had passed, Mark could not bring himself to say that he would pay nothing till the bills were safe; and therefore with the assistance of Mr. Forrest of the Bank, he did remit the price of Dandy to his friend Sowerby in London.

And Lucy Robarts—we must now say a word of her. We have seen how, on that occasion, when the world was at her feet, she had sent her noble suitor away, not only dismissed, but so dismissed that he might be taught never again to offer to her the sweet incense of his vows. She had declared to him plainly that she did not love him and could not love him, and had thus thrown away not only riches and honour and high station, but more than that—much worse than that—she had flung away from her the lover to whose love her warm heart clung. That her love did cling to him, she knew even then, and owned more thoroughly as soon as he was gone. So much her pride had done for her, and that strong resolve that Lady Lufton should not scowl on her and tell her that she had entrapped her son.

I know it will be said of Lord Lufton himself that, putting aside his peerage and broad acres, and handsome, sonsy face, he was not worth a girl's care and love. That will be said because people think that heroes in books should be so much better than heroes got up for the world's common wear and tear. I may as well confess that of absolute, true heroism there was only a moderate admixture in Lord Lufton's composition; but what would the world come to if none but absolute true heroes were to be thought worthy of women's love? What would the men do? and what—oh! what would become of the women? Lucy Robarts in her heart did not give her dismissed lover credit for much more heroism than did truly appertain to him;—did not, perhaps, give him full credit for a certain amount of heroism which did really appertain to him; but, nevertheless, she would have been very glad to take him could she have done so without wounding her pride.

That girls should not marry for money we are all agreed. A lady who can sell herself for a title or an estate, for an income or a set of family diamonds, treats herself as a farmer treats his sheep and oxen—makes hardly more of herself, of her own inner self, in which are comprised a mind and soul, than the poor wretch of her own sex who earns her bread in the lowest stage of degradation. But a title, and an estate, and an income, are matters which will weigh in the balance with all Eve's daughters—as they do with all Adam's sons. Pride of place, and the power of living well in front of the world's eye, are dear to us all;—are, doubtless, intended to be dear. Only in acknowledging so much, let us remember that there are prices at which these good things may be too costly. Therefore, being desirous, too, of telling the truth in this matter, I must confess that Lucy did speculate with some regret on what it would have been to be Lady Lufton. To have been the wife of such a man, the owner of such a heart, the mistress of such a destiny—what more or what better could the world have done for her? And now she had thrown all that aside because she would not endure that Lady Lufton should call her a scheming, artful girl! Actuated by that fear she had repulsed him with a falsehood, though the matter was one on which it was so terribly expedient that she should tell the truth.

And yet she was cheerful with her brother and sister-in-law. It was when she was quite alone, at night in her own room, or in her solitary walks, that a single silent tear would gather in the corner of her eye and gradually moisten her eyelids. "She never told her love," nor did she allow concealment to "feed on her damask cheek." In all her employments, in her ways about the house, and her accustomed quiet mirth, she was the same as ever. In this she showed the peculiar strength which God had given her. But not the less did she in truth mourn for her lost love and spoiled ambition.

"We are going to drive over to Hogglestock this morning," Fanny said one day at breakfast. "I suppose, Mark, you won't go with us?"

"Well, no; I think not. The pony-carriage is wretched for three."

"Oh, as for that, I should have thought the new horse might have been able to carry you as far as that. I heard you say you wanted to see Mr. Crawley."

"So I do; and the new horse, as you call him, shall carry me there to-morrow. Will you say that I'll be over about twelve o'clock?"

"You had better say earlier, as he is always out about the parish."

"Very well, say eleven. It is parish business about which I am going, so it need not irk his conscience to stay in for me."

"Well, Lucy, we must drive ourselves, that's all. You shall be charioteer going, and then we'll change coming back." To all which Lucy agreed, and as soon as their work in the school was over they started.

Not a word had been spoken between them about Lord Lufton since that evening, now more than a month ago, on which they had been walking together in the garden. Lucy had so demeaned herself on that occasion as to make her sister-in-law quite sure that there had been no love passages up to that time; and nothing had since occurred which had created any suspicion in Mrs. Robarts' mind. She had seen at once that all the close intimacy between them was over, and thought that everything was as it should be.

"Do you know, I have an idea," she said in the pony-carriage that day, "that Lord Lufton will marry Griselda Grantly." Lucy could not refrain from giving a little check at the reins which she was holding, and she felt that the blood rushed quickly to her heart. But she did not betray herself. "Perhaps he may," she said, and then gave the pony a little touch with her whip.

"Oh, Lucy, I won't have Puck beaten. He was going very nicely."

"I beg Puck's pardon. But you see when one is trusted with a whip one feels such a longing to use it."

"Oh, but you should keep it still. I feel almost certain that Lady Lufton would like such a match."

"I daresay she might. Miss Grantly will have a large fortune, I believe."

"It is not that altogether: but she is the sort of young lady that Lady Lufton likes. She is ladylike and very beautiful—"

"Come, Fanny!"

"I really think she is; not what I should call lovely, you know, but very beautiful. And then she is quiet and reserved; she does not require excitement, and I am sure is conscientious in the performance of her duties."

"Very conscientious, I have no doubt," said Lucy, with something like a sneer in her tone. "But the question, I suppose, is, whether Lord Lufton likes her."

"I think he does,—in a sort of way. He did not talk to her so much as he did to you—"

"Ah! that was all Lady Lufton's fault, because she didn't have him properly labelled."

"There does not seem to have been much harm done?"

"Oh! by God's mercy, very little. As for me, I shall get over it in three or four years I don't doubt—that's if I can get ass's milk and change of air."

"We'll take you to Barchester for that. But as I was saying, I really do think Lord Lufton likes Griselda Grantly."

"Then I really do think that he has uncommon bad taste," said Lucy, with a reality in her voice differing much from the tone of banter she had hitherto used.

"What, Lucy!" said her sister-in-law, looking at her. "Then I fear we shall really want the ass's milk."

"Perhaps, considering my position, I ought to know nothing of Lord Lufton, for you say that it is very dangerous for young ladies to know young gentlemen. But I do know enough of him to understand that he ought not to like such a girl as Griselda Grantly. He ought to know that she is a mere automaton, cold, lifeless, spiritless, and even vapid. There is, I believe, nothing in her mentally, whatever may be her moral excellences. To me she is more absolutely like a statue than any other human being I ever saw. To sit still and be admired is all that she desires; and if she cannot get that, to sit still and not be admired would almost suffice for her. I do not worship Lady Lufton as you do; but I think quite well enough of her to wonder that she should choose such a girl as that for her son's wife. That she does wish it, I do not doubt. But I shall indeed be surprised if he wishes it also." And then as she finished her speech, Lucy again flogged the pony. This she did in vexation, because she felt that the tell-tale blood had suffused her face.

"Why, Lucy, if he were your brother you could not be more eager about it."

"No, I could not. He is the only man friend with whom I was ever intimate, and I cannot bear to think that he should throw himself away. It's horridly improper to care about such a thing, I have no doubt."

"I think we might acknowledge that if he and his mother are both satisfied, we may be satisfied also."

"I shall not be satisfied. It's no use your looking at me, Fanny. You will make me talk of it, and I won't tell a lie on the subject. I do like Lord Lufton very much; and I do dislike Griselda Grantly almost as much. Therefore I shall not be satisfied if they become man and wife. However, I do not suppose that either of them will ask my consent; nor is it probable that Lady Lufton will do so." And then they went on for perhaps a quarter of a mile without speaking.

"Poor Puck!" at last Lucy said. "He shan't be whipped any more, shall he, because Miss Grantly looks like a statue? And, Fanny, don't tell Mark to put me into a lunatic asylum. I also know a hawk from a heron, and that's why I don't like to see such a very unfitting marriage." There was then nothing more said on the subject, and in two minutes they arrived at the house of the Hogglestock clergyman.

Mrs. Crawley had brought two children with her when she came from the Cornish curacy to Hogglestock, and two other babies had been added to her cares since then. One of these was now ill with croup, and it was with the object of offering to the mother some comfort and solace, that the present visit was made. The two ladies got down from their carriage, having obtained the services of a boy to hold Puck, and soon found themselves in Mrs. Crawley's single sitting-room. She was sitting there with her foot on the board of a child's cradle, rocking it, while an infant about three months old was lying in her lap. For the elder one, who was the sufferer, had in her illness usurped the baby's place. Two other children, considerably older, were also in the room. The eldest was a girl, perhaps nine years of age, and the other a boy three years her junior. These were standing at their father's elbow, who was studiously endeavouring to initiate them in the early mysteries of grammar. To tell the truth Mrs. Robarts would much have preferred that Mr. Crawley had not been there, for she had with her and about her certain contraband articles, presents for the children, as they were to be called, but in truth relief for that poor, much-tasked mother, which they knew it would be impossible to introduce in Mr. Crawley's presence.

She, as we have said, was not quite so gaunt, not altogether so haggard as in the latter of those dreadful Cornish days. Lady Lufton and Mrs. Arabin between them, and the scanty comfort of their improved, though still wretched income, had done something towards bringing her back to the world in which she had lived in the soft days of her childhood. But even the liberal stipend of a hundred and thirty pounds a-year—liberal according to the scale by which the incomes of clergymen in some of our new districts are now apportioned—would not admit of a gentleman with his wife and four children living with the ordinary comforts of an artisan's family. As regards the mere eating and drinking, the amounts of butcher's meat and tea and butter, they of course were used in quantities which any artisan would have regarded as compatible only with demi-starvation. Better clothing for her children was necessary, and better clothing for him. As for her own raiment, the wives of few artisans would have been content to put up with Mrs. Crawley's best gown. The stuff of which it was made had been paid for by her mother when she with much difficulty bestowed upon her daughter her modest wedding *trousseau.*

Lucy had never seen Mrs. Crawley. These visits to Hogglestock were not frequent, and had generally been made by Lady Lufton and Mrs. Robarts together. It was known that they were distasteful to Mr. Crawley, who felt a savage satisfaction in being left to himself. It may almost be said of him that he felt angry with those who relieved him, and he had certainly never as yet forgiven the Dean of Barchester for paying his debts. The dean had also given him his present living; and consequently his old friend was not now so dear to him as when in old days he would come down to that farm-house, almost as penniless as the curate himself. Then they would walk together for hours along the rock-bound shore, listening to the waves, discussing deep polemical mysteries, sometimes with hot fury, then again with tender, loving charity, but always with a mutual acknowledgment of each other's truth. Now they lived comparatively near together, but no opportunities arose for such discussions. At any rate once a quarter Mr. Crawley was pressed by his old friend to visit him at the deanery, and Dr. Arabin had promised that no one else should be in the house if Mr. Crawley objected to society. But this was not what he wanted. The finery and grandeur of the deanery, and the comfort of that warm, snug library, would silence him at once. Why did not Dr. Arabin come out there to Hogglestock, and tramp with him through the dirty lanes as they used to tramp? Then he could have enjoyed himself; then he could have talked; then old days would have come back to them. But now!—"Arabin always rides on a sleek, fine horse, now-a-days," he once said to his wife with a sneer. His poverty had been so terrible to himself that it was not in his heart to love a rich friend.

CHAPTER XXII.

HOGGLESTOCK PARSONAGE.

At the end of the last chapter, we left Lucy Robarts waiting for an introduction to Mrs. Crawley, who was sitting with one baby in her lap while she was rocking another who lay in a cradle at her feet. Mr. Crawley, in the meanwhile, had risen from his seat with his finger between the leaves of an old grammar out of which he had been teaching his two elder children. The whole Crawley family was thus before them when Mrs. Robarts and Lucy entered the sitting-room.

"This is my sister-in-law, Lucy," said Mrs. Robarts. "Pray don't move now, Mrs. Crawley; or if you do, let me take baby." And she put out her arms and took the infant into them, making him quite at home there; for she had work of this kind of her own, at home, which she by no means neglected, though the attendance of nurses was more plentiful with her than at Hogglestock.

Mrs. Crawley did get up, and told Lucy that she was glad to see her, and Mr. Crawley came forward, grammar in hand, looking humble and meek. Could we have looked into the innermost spirit of him and his life's partner, we should have seen that mixed with the pride of his poverty there was some feeling of disgrace that he was poor, but that with her, regarding this matter, there was neither pride nor shame. The realities of life had become so stern to her that the outward aspects of them were as nothing. She would have liked a new gown because it would have been useful; but it would have been nothing to her if all the county knew that the one in which she went to church had been turned three times. It galled him, however, to think that he and his were so poorly dressed.

"I am afraid you can hardly find a chair, Miss Robarts," said Mr. Crawley.

"Oh, yes; there is nothing here but this young gentleman's library," said Lucy, moving a pile of ragged, coverless books on to the table. "I hope he'll forgive me for moving them."

"They are not Bob's,—at least, not the most of them,—but mine," said the girl.

"But some of them are mine," said the boy; "ain't they, Grace?"

"And are you a great scholar?" asked Lucy, drawing the child to her.

"I don't know," said Grace, with a sheepish face. "I am in Greek Delectus and the irregular verbs."

"Greek Delectus and the irregular verbs!" And Lucy put up her hands with astonishment.

"And she knows an ode of Horace all by heart," said Bob.

"An ode of Horace!" said Lucy, still holding the young shamefaced female prodigy close to her knees.

"It is all that I can give them," said Mr. Crawley, apologetically. "A little scholarship is the only fortune that has come in my way, and I endeavour to share that with my children."

"I believe men say that it is the best fortune any of us can have," said Lucy, thinking, however, in her own mind, that Horace and the irregular Greek verbs savoured too much of precocious forcing in a young lady of nine years old. But, nevertheless, Grace was a pretty, simple-looking girl, and clung to her ally closely, and seemed to like being fondled. So that Lucy anxiously wished that Mr. Crawley could be got rid of and the presents produced.

"I hope you have left Mr. Robarts quite well," said Mr. Crawley, with a stiff, ceremonial voice, differing very much from that in which he had so energetically addressed his brother clergyman when they were alone together in the study at Framley.

"He is quite well, thank you. I suppose you have heard of his good fortune?"

"Yes; I have heard of it," said Mr. Crawley, gravely. "I hope that his promotion may tend in every way to his advantage here and hereafter."

It seemed, however, to be manifest from the manner in which he expressed his kind wishes, that his hopes and expectations did not go hand-in-hand together.

"By-the-by, he desired us to say that he will call here to-morrow; at about eleven, didn't he say, Fanny?"

"Yes; he wishes to see you about some parish business, I think," said Mrs. Robarts, looking up for a moment from the anxious discussion in which she was already engaged with Mrs. Crawley on nursery matters.

"Pray tell him," said Mr. Crawley, "that I shall be happy to see him; though, perhaps, now that new duties have been thrown upon him, it will be better that I should visit him at Framley."

"His new duties do not disturb him much as yet," said Lucy. "And his riding over here will be no trouble to him."

"Yes; there he has the advantage over me. I unfortunately have no horse."

And then Lucy began petting the little boy, and by degrees slipped a small bag of gingerbread-nuts out of her muff into his hands. She had not the patience necessary for waiting, as had her sister-in-law.

The boy took the bag, peeped into it, and then looked up into her face.

"What is that, Bob?" said Mr. Crawley.

"Gingerbread," faltered Bobby, feeling that a sin had been committed, though, probably, feeling also that he himself could hardly as yet be accounted as deeply guilty.

"Miss Robarts," said the father, "we are very much obliged to you; but our children are hardly used to such things."

"I am a lady with a weak mind, Mr. Crawley, and always carry things of this sort about with me when I go to visit children; so you must forgive me, and allow your little boy to accept them."

"Oh, certainly. Bob, my child, give the bag to your mamma, and she will let you and Grace have them, one at a time." And then the bag in a solemn manner was carried over to their mother, who, taking it from her son's hands, laid it high on a bookshelf.

"And not one now?" said Lucy Robarts, very piteously. "Don't be so hard, Mr. Crawley,—not upon them, but upon me. May I not learn whether they are good of their kind?"

"I am sure they are very good; but I think their mamma will prefer their being put by for the present."

This was very discouraging to Lucy. If one small bag of gingerbread-nuts created so great a difficulty, how was she to dispose of the pot of guava jelly and box of bonbons, which were still in her muff; or how distribute the packet of oranges with which the pony-carriage was laden? And there was jelly for the sick child, and chicken broth, which was, indeed, another jelly; and, to tell the truth openly, there was also a joint of fresh pork and a basket of eggs from the Framley Parsonage farmyard, which Mrs. Robarts was to introduce, should she find herself capable of doing so; but which would certainly be cast out with utter scorn by Mr. Crawley, if tendered in his immediate presence. There had also been a suggestion as to adding two or three bottles of port; but the courage of the ladies had failed them on that head, and the wine was not now added to their difficulties.

Lucy found it very difficult to keep up a conversation with Mr. Crawley—the more so, as Mrs. Robarts and Mrs. Crawley presently withdrew into a bedroom, taking the two younger children with them. "How unlucky," thought Lucy, "that she has not got my muff with her!" But the muff lay in her lap, ponderous with its rich enclosures.

"I suppose you will live in Barchester for a portion of the year now," said Mr. Crawley.

"I really do not know as yet; Mark talks of taking lodgings for his first month's residence."

"But he will have the house, will he not?"

"Oh, yes; I suppose so."

"I fear he will find it interfere with his own parish—with his general utility there: the schools, for instance."

"Mark thinks that, as he is so near, he need not be much absent from Framley, even during his residence. And then Lady Lufton is so good about the schools."

"Ah! yes; but Lady Lufton is not a clergyman, Miss Robarts."

It was on Lucy's tongue to say that her ladyship was pretty nearly as bad, but she stopped herself.

At this moment Providence sent great relief to Miss Robarts in the shape of Mrs. Crawley's red-armed maid-of-all-work, who, walking up to her master, whispered into his ear that he was wanted. It was the time of day at which his attendance was always required in his parish school; and that attendance being so punctually given, those who wanted him looked for him there at this hour, and if he were absent, did not scruple to send for him.

"Miss Robarts, I am afraid you must excuse me," said he, getting up and taking his hat and stick. Lucy begged that she might not be at all in the way, and already began to speculate how she might best unload her treasures. "Will you make my compliments to Mrs. Robarts, and say that I am sorry to miss the pleasure of wishing her good-bye? But I shall probably see her as she passes the school-house." And then, stick in hand, he walked forth, and Lucy fancied that Bobby's eyes immediately rested on the bag of gingerbread-nuts.

"Bob," said she, almost in a whisper, "do you like sugar-plums?"

"Very much indeed," said Bob, with exceeding gravity, and with his eye upon the window to see whether his father had passed.

"Then come here," said Lucy. But as she spoke the door again opened, and Mr. Crawley reappeared. "I have left a book behind me," he said; and, coming back through the room, he took up the well-worn prayer-book which accompanied him in all his wanderings through the parish. Bobby, when he saw his father, had retreated a few steps back, as also did Grace, who, to confess the truth, had been attracted by the sound of sugar-plums, in spite of the irregular verbs. And Lucy withdrew her hand from her muff, and looked guilty. Was she not deceiving the good man—nay, teaching his own children to deceive him? But there are men made of such stuff that an angel could hardly live with them without some deceit.

"Papa's gone now," whispered Bobby; "I saw him turn round the corner." He, at any rate, had learned his lesson—as it was natural that he should do.

Some one else, also, had learned that papa was gone; for while Bob and Grace were still counting the big lumps of sugar-candy, each employed the while for inward solace with an inch of barley-sugar, the front-door opened, and a big basket, and a bundle done up in a kitchen-cloth, made surreptitious entrance into the house, and were quickly unpacked by Mrs. Robarts herself on the table in Mrs. Crawley's bedroom.

"I did venture to bring them," said Fanny, with a look of shame, "for I know how a sick child occupies the whole house."

"Ah! my friend," said Mrs. Crawley, taking hold of Mrs. Robarts' arm and looking into her face, "that sort of shame is over with me. God has tried us with want, and for my children's sake I am glad of such relief."

"But will he be angry?"

"I will manage it. Dear Mrs. Robarts, you must not be surprised at him. His lot is sometimes very hard to bear: such things are so much worse for a man than for a woman."

Fanny was not quite prepared to admit this in her own heart, but she made no reply on that head. "I am sure I hope we may be able to be of use to you," she said, "if you will only look upon me as an old friend, and write to me if you want me. I hesitate to come frequently for fear that I should offend him."

And then, by degrees, there was confidence between them, and the poverty-stricken helpmate of the perpetual curate was able to speak of the weight of her burden to the well-to-do young wife of the Barchester prebendary. "It was hard," the former said, "to feel herself so different from the wives of other clergymen around her—to know that they lived softly, while she, with all the work of her hands, and unceasing struggle of her energies, could hardly manage to place wholesome food before her husband and children. It was a terrible thing—a grievous thing to think of, that all the work of her mind should be given up to such subjects as these. But, nevertheless, she could bear it," she said, "as long as he would carry himself like a man, and face his lot boldly before the world." And then she told how he had been better there at Hogglestock than in their former residence down in Cornwall, and in warm language she expressed her thanks to the friend who had done so much for them.

"Mrs. Arabin told me that she was so anxious you should go to them," said Mrs. Robarts.

"Ah, yes; but that I fear is impossible. The children, you know, Mrs. Robarts."

"I would take care of two of them for you."

"Oh, no; I could not punish you for your goodness in that way. But he would not go. He could go and leave me at home. Sometimes I have thought that it might be so, and I have done all in my power to persuade him. I have told him that if he could mix once more with the world, with the clerical world, you know, that he would be better fitted for the performance of his own duties. But he answers me angrily, that it is impossible—that his coat is not fit for the dean's table," and Mrs. Crawley almost blushed as she spoke of such a reason.

"What! with an old friend like Dr. Arabin? Surely that must be nonsense."

"I know that it is. The dean would be glad to see him with any coat. But the fact is that he cannot bear to enter the house of a rich man unless his duty calls him there."

"But surely that is a mistake?"

"It is a mistake. But what can I do? I fear that he regards the rich as his enemies. He is pining for the solace of some friend to whom he could talk—for some equal, with a mind educated like his own, to whose thoughts he could listen, and to whom he could speak his own thoughts. But such a friend must be equal, not only in mind, but in purse; and where can he ever find such a man as that?"

"But you may get better preferment."

"Ah, no; and if he did, we are hardly fit for it now. If I could think that I could educate my children; if I could only do something for my poor Grace—"

In answer to this Mrs. Robarts said a word or two, but not much. She resolved, however, that if she could get her husband's leave, something should be done for Grace. Would it not be a good work? and was it not incumbent on her to make some kindly use of all the goods with which Providence had blessed herself?

And then they went back to the sitting-room, each again with a young child in her arms, Mrs. Crawley having stowed away in the kitchen the chicken broth and the leg of pork and the supply of eggs. Lucy had been engaged the while with the children, and when the two married ladies entered, they found that a shop had been opened at which all manner of luxuries were being readily sold and purchased at marvellously easy prices; the guava jelly was there, and the oranges, and the sugar-plums, red and yellow and striped; and, moreover, the gingerbread had been taken down in the audacity of their commercial speculations, and the nuts were spread out upon a board, behind which Lucy stood as shop-girl, disposing of them for kisses.

"Mamma, mamma," said Bobby, running up to his mother, "you must buy something of her," and he pointed with his fingers at the shop-girl. "You must give her two kisses for that heap of barley-sugar." Looking at Bobby's mouth at the time, one would have said that his kisses might be dispensed with.

When they were again in the pony-carriage, behind the impatient Puck, and were well away from the door, Fanny was the first to speak.

"How very different those two are," she said; "different in their minds and in their spirit!"

"But how much higher toned is her mind than his! How weak he is in many things, and how strong she is in everything! How false is his pride, and how false his shame!"

"But we must remember what he has to bear. It is not every one that can endure such a life as his without false pride and false shame."

"But she has neither," said Lucy.

"Because you have one hero in a family, does that give you a right to expect another?" said Mrs. Robarts. "Of all my own acquaintance, Mrs. Crawley, I think, comes nearest to heroism."

And then they passed by the Hogglestock school, and Mr. Crawley, when he heard the noise of the wheels, came out.

"You have been very kind," said he, "to remain so long with my poor wife."

"We had a great many things to talk about, after you went."

"It is very kind of you, for she does not often see a friend, now-a-days. Will you have the goodness to tell Mr. Robarts that I shall be here at the school, at eleven o'clock to-morrow?"

And then he bowed, taking off his hat to them, and they drove on.

"If he really does care about her comfort, I shall not think so badly of him," said Lucy.

CHAPTER XXIII.

THE TRIUMPH OF THE GIANTS.

And now about the end of April news arrived almost simultaneously in all quarters of the habitable globe that was terrible in its import to one of the chief persons of our history;—some may think to the chief person in it. All high parliamentary people will doubtless so think, and the wives and daughters of such. The Titans warring against the gods had been for awhile successful. Typhœus and Mimas, Porphyrion and Rhœcus, the giant brood of old, steeped in ignorance and wedded to corruption, had scaled the heights of Olympus, assisted by that audacious flinger of deadly ponderous missiles, who stands ever ready armed with his terrific sling—Supplehouse, the Enceladus of the press. And in this universal cataclasm of the starry councils, what could a poor Diana do, Diana of the Petty Bag, but abandon her pride of place to some rude Orion? In other words, the ministry had been compelled to resign, and with them Mr. Harold Smith.

"And so poor Harold is out, before he has well tasted the sweets of office," said Sowerby, writing to his friend the parson; "and as far as I know, the only piece of Church patronage which has fallen in the way of the ministry since he joined it, has made its way down to Framley—to my great joy and contentment." But it hardly tended to Mark's joy and contentment on the same subject that he should be so often reminded of the benefit conferred upon him.

Terrible was this break-down of the ministry, and especially to Harold Smith, who to the last had had confidence in that theory of new blood. He could hardly believe that a large majority of the House should vote against a government which he had only just joined. "If we are to go on in this way," he said to his young friend Green Walker, "the Queen's government cannot be carried on." That alleged difficulty as to carrying on the Queen's government has been frequently mooted in late years since a certain great man first introduced the idea. Nevertheless, the Queen's government is carried on, and the propensity and aptitude of men for this work seems to be not at all on the decrease. If we have but few young statesmen, it is because the old stagers are so fond of the rattle of their harness.

"I really do not see how the Queen's government is to be carried on," said Harold Smith to Green Walker, standing in a corner of one of the lobbies of the House of Commons on the first of those days of awful interest, in which the Queen was sending for one crack statesman after another; and some anxious men were beginning to doubt whether or no we should, in truth, be able to obtain the blessing of another cabinet. The gods had all vanished from their places. Would the giants be good enough to do anything for us or no?

There were men who seemed to think that the giants would refuse to do anything for us. "The House will now be adjourned over till Monday, and I would not be in her Majesty's shoes for something," said Mr. Harold Smith.

"By Jove! no," said Green Walker, who in these days was a stanch Harold Smithian, having felt a pride in joining himself on as a substantial support to a cabinet minister. Had he contented himself with being merely a Brockite, he would have counted as nobody. "By Jove! no," and Green Walker opened his eyes and shook his head, as he thought of the perilous condition in which her Majesty must be placed. "I happen to know that Lord —— won't join them unless he has the Foreign Office," and he mentioned some hundred-handed Gyas supposed to be of the utmost importance to the counsels of the Titans.

"And that, of course, is impossible. I don't see what on earth they are to do. There's Sidonia; they do say that he's making some difficulty now." Now Sidonia was another giant, supposed to be very powerful.

"We all know that the Queen won't see him," said Green Walker, who, being a member of Parliament for the Crewe Junction, and nephew to Lady Hartletop, of course had perfectly correct means of ascertaining what the Queen would do, and what she would not.

"The fact is," said Harold Smith, recurring again to his own situation as an ejected god, "that the House does not in the least understand what it is about;—doesn't know what it wants. The question I should like to ask them is this: do they intend that the Queen shall have a government, or do they not? Are they prepared to support such men as Sidonia and Lord De Terrier? If so, I am their obedient humble servant; but I shall be very much surprised, that's all." Lord De Terrier was at this time recognized by all men as the leader of the giants.

"And so shall I,—deucedly surprised. They can't do it, you know. There are the Manchester men. I ought to know something about them down in my country; and I say they can't support Lord De Terrier. It wouldn't be natural."

"Natural! Human nature has come to an end, I think," said Harold Smith, who could hardly understand that the world should conspire to throw over a government which he had joined, and that, too, before the world had waited to see how much he would do for it; "the fact is this, Walker, we have no longer among us any strong feeling of party."

"No, not a d——," said Green Walker, who was very energetic in his present political aspirations.

"And till we can recover that, we shall never be able to have a government firm-seated and sure-handed. Nobody can count on men from one week to another. The very members who in one month place a minister in power, are the very first to vote against him in the next."

"We must put a stop to that sort of thing, otherwise we shall never do any good."

"I don't mean to deny that Brock was wrong with reference to Lord Brittleback. I think that he was wrong, and I said so all through. But, heavens on earth—!" and instead of completing his speech Harold Smith turned away his head, and struck his hands together in token of his astonishment at the fatuity of the age. What he probably meant to express was this: that if such a good deed as that late appointment made at the Petty Bag Office were not held sufficient to atone for that other evil deed to which he had alluded, there would be an end of all justice in sublunary matters. Was no offence to be forgiven, even when so great virtue had been displayed?

"I attribute it all to Supplehouse," said Green Walker, trying to console his friend.

"Yes," said Harold Smith, now verging on the bounds of parliamentary eloquence, although he still spoke with bated breath, and to one solitary hearer. "Yes; we are becoming the slaves of a mercenary and irresponsible press—of one single newspaper. There is a man endowed with no great talent, enjoying no public confidence, untrusted as a politician, and unheard of even as a writer by the world at large, and yet, because he is on the staff of the *Jupiter*, he is able to overturn the government and throw the whole country into dismay. It is astonishing to me that a man like Lord Brock should allow himself to be so timid." And nevertheless it was not yet a month since Harold Smith had been counselling with Supplehouse how a series of strong articles in the *Jupiter*, together with the expected support of the Manchester men, might probably be effective in hurling the minister from his seat. But at that time the minister had not revigorated himself with young blood. "How the Queen's government is to be carried on, that is the question now," Harold Smith repeated. A difficulty which had not caused him much dismay at that period, about a month since, to which we have alluded.

At this moment Sowerby and Supplehouse together joined them, having come out of the House, in which some unimportant business had been completed after the minister's notice of adjournment.

"Well, Harold," said Sowerby, "what do you say to your governor's statement?"

"I have nothing to say to it," said Harold Smith, looking up very solemnly from under the penthouse of his hat, and, perhaps, rather savagely. Sowerby had supported the government at the late crisis; but why was he now seen herding with such a one as Supplehouse?

"He did it pretty well, I think," said Sowerby.

"Very well, indeed," said Supplehouse; "as he always does those sort of things. No man makes so good an explanation of circumstances, or comes out with so telling a personal statement. He ought to keep himself in reserve for those sort of things."

"And who in the meantime is to carry on the Queen's government?" said Harold Smith, looking very stern.

"That should be left to men of lesser mark," said he of the *Jupiter*. "The points as to which one really listens to a minister, the subjects about which men really care, are always personal. How many of us are truly interested as to the best mode of governing India? But in a question touching the character of a prime minister we all muster together like bees round a sounding cymbal."

"That arises from envy, malice, and all uncharitableness," said Harold Smith.

"Yes; and from picking and stealing, evil speaking, lying, and slandering," said Mr. Sowerby.

"We are so prone to desire and covet other men's places," said Supplehouse.

"Some men are so," said Sowerby; "but it is the evil speaking, lying, and slandering, which does the mischief. Is it not, Harold?"

"And in the meantime how is the Queen's government to be carried on?" said Mr. Green Walker.

On the following morning it was known that Lord De Terrier was with the Queen at Buckingham Palace, and at about twelve a list of the new ministry was published, which must have been in the highest degree satisfactory to the whole brood of giants. Every son of Tellus was included in it, as were also very many of the daughters. But then, late in the afternoon, Lord Brock was again summoned to the palace, and it was thought in the West End among the clubs that the gods had again a chance. "If only," said the *Purist*, an evening paper which was supposed to be very much in the interest of Mr. Harold Smith, "if only Lord Brock can have the wisdom to place the right men in the right places. It was only the other day that he introduced Mr. Smith into his government. That this was a step in the right direction every one has acknowledged, though unfortunately it was made too late to prevent the disturbance which has since occurred. It now appears probable that his lordship will again have an opportunity of selecting a list of statesmen with the view of carrying on the Queen's government; and it is to be hoped that such men as Mr. Smith may be placed in situations in which their talents, industry, and acknowledged official aptitudes, may be of permanent service to the country."

Supplehouse, when he read this at the club with Mr. Sowerby at his elbow, declared that the style was too well marked to leave any doubt as to the author; but we ourselves are not inclined to think that Mr. Harold Smith wrote the article himself, although it may be probable that he saw it in type.

But the *Jupiter* the next morning settled the whole question, and made it known to the world that, in spite of all the sendings and re-sendings, Lord Brock and the gods were permanently out, and Lord De Terrier and the giants permanently in. That fractious giant who would only go to the Foreign Office had, in fact, gone to some sphere of much less important duty, and Sidonia, in spite of the whispered dislike of an illustrious personage, opened the campaign with all the full appanages of a giant of the highest standing. "We hope," said the *Jupiter*, "that Lord Brock may not yet be too old to take a lesson. If so, the present decision of the House of Commons, and we may say of the country also, may teach him not to put his trust in such princes as Lord Brittleback, or such broken reeds as Mr. Harold Smith." Now this parting blow we always thought to be exceedingly unkind, and altogether unnecessary, on the part of Mr. Supplehouse.

"My dear," said Mrs. Harold, when she first met Miss Dunstable after the catastrophe was known, "how am I possibly to endure this degradation?" And she put her deeply-laced handkerchief up to her eyes.

"Christian resignation," suggested Miss Dunstable.

"Fiddlestick!" said Mrs. Harold Smith. "You millionnaires always talk of Christian resignation, because you never are called on to resign anything. If I had any Christian resignation, I shouldn't have cared for such pomps and vanities. Think of it, my dear; a cabinet minister's wife for only three weeks!"

"How does poor Mr. Smith endure it?"

"What? Harold? He only lives on the hope of vengeance. When he has put an end to Mr. Supplehouse, he will be content to die."

And then there were further explanations in both Houses of Parliament, which were altogether satisfactory. The high-bred, courteous giants assured the gods that they had piled Pelion on Ossa and thus climbed up into power, very much in opposition to their own good-wills; for they, the giants themselves, preferred the sweets of dignified retirement. But the voice of the people had been too strong for them; the effort had been made, not by themselves, but by others, who were determined that the giants should be at the head of affairs. Indeed, the spirit of the times was so clearly in favour of giants that there had been no alternative. So said Briareus to the Lords, and Orion to the Commons. And then the gods were absolutely happy in ceding their places; and so far were they from any uncelestial envy or malice which might not be divine, that they promised to give the giants all the assistance in their power in carrying on the work of government; upon which the giants declared how deeply indebted they would be for such valuable counsel and friendly assistance. All this was delightful in the extreme; but not the less did ordinary men seem to expect that the usual battle would go on in the old customary way. It is easy to love one's enemy when one is making fine speeches; but so difficult to do so in the actual everyday work of life.

But there was and always has been this peculiar good point about the giants, that they are never too proud to follow in the footsteps of the gods. If the gods, deliberating painfully together, have elaborated any skilful project, the giants are always willing to adopt it as their own, not treating the bantling as a foster-child, but praising it and pushing it so that men should regard it as the undoubted offspring of their own brains. Now just at this time

963

there had been a plan much thought of for increasing the number of the bishops. Good active bishops were very desirable, and there was a strong feeling among certain excellent churchmen that there could hardly be too many of them. Lord Brock had his measure cut and dry. There should be a Bishop of Westminster to share the Herculean toils of the metropolitan prelate, and another up in the North to Christianize the mining interests and wash white the blackamoors of Newcastle: Bishop of Beverley he should be called. But, in opposition to this, the giants, it was known, had intended to put forth the whole measure of their brute force. More curates, they said, were wanting, and district incumbents; not more bishops rolling in carriages. That bishops should roll in carriages was very good; but of such blessings the English world for the present had enough. And therefore Lord Brock and the gods had had much fear as to their little project.

But now, immediately on the accession of the giants, it was known that the bishop bill was to be gone on with immediately. Some small changes would be effected so that the bill should be gigantic rather than divine; but the result would be altogether the same. It must, however, be admitted that bishops appointed by ourselves may be very good things, whereas those appointed by our adversaries will be anything but good. And, no doubt, this feeling went a long way with the giants. Be that as it may, the new bishop bill was to be their first work of government, and it was to be brought forward and carried, and the new prelates selected and put into their chairs all at once,—before the grouse should begin to crow and put an end to the doings of gods as well as giants.

Among other minor effects arising from this decision was the following, that Archdeacon and Mrs. Grantly returned to London, and again took the lodgings in which they had before been staying. On various occasions also during the first week of this second sojourn, Dr. Grantly might be seen entering the official chambers of the First Lord of the Treasury. Much counsel was necessary among high churchmen of great repute before any fixed resolution could wisely be made in such a matter as this; and few churchmen stood in higher repute than the Archdeacon of Barchester. And then it began to be rumoured in the world that the minister had disposed at any rate of the see of Westminster.

This present time was a very nervous one for Mrs. Grantly. What might be the aspirations of the archdeacon himself, we will not stop to inquire. It may be that time and experience had taught him the futility of earthly honours, and made him content with the comfortable opulence of his Barsetshire rectory. But there is no theory of church discipline which makes it necessary that a clergyman's wife should have an objection to a bishopric. The archdeacon probably was only anxious to give a disinterested aid to the minister, but Mrs. Grantly did long to sit in high places, and be at any rate equal to Mrs. Proudie. It was for her children, she said to herself, that she was thus anxious,—that they should have a good position before the world, and the means of making the best of themselves. "One is able to do nothing, you know, shut up there, down at Plumstead," she had remarked to Lady Lufton on the occasion of her first visit to London, and yet the time was not long past when she had thought that rectory house at Plumstead to be by no means insufficient or contemptible.

And then there came a question whether or no Griselda should go back to her mother; but this idea was very strongly opposed by Lady Lufton, and ultimately with success. "I really think the dear girl is very happy with me," said Lady Lufton; "and if ever she is to belong to me more closely, it will be so well that we should know and love one another."

To tell the truth, Lady Lufton had been trying hard to know and love Griselda, but hitherto she had scarcely succeeded to the full extent of her wishes. That she loved Griselda was certain,—with that sort of love which springs from a person's volition and not from the judgment. She had said all along to herself and others that she did love Griselda Grantly. She had admired the young lady's face, liked her manner, approved of her fortune and family, and had selected her for a daughter-in-law in a somewhat impetuous manner. Therefore she loved her. But it was by no means clear to Lady Lufton that she did as yet know her young friend. The match was a plan of her own, and therefore she stuck to it as warmly as ever, but she began to have some misgivings whether or no the dear girl would be to her herself all that she had dreamed of in a daughter-in-law.

"But, dear Lady Lufton," said Mrs. Grantly, "is it not possible that we may put her affections to too severe a test? What, if she should learn to regard him, and then—"

"Ah! if she did, I should have no fear of the result. If she showed anything like love for Ludovic, he would be at her feet in a moment. He is impulsive, but she is not."

"Exactly, Lady Lufton. It is his privilege to be impulsive and to sue for her affection, and hers to have her love sought for without making any demonstration. It is perhaps the fault of young ladies of the present day that they are too impulsive. They assume privileges which are not their own, and thus lose those which are."

"Quite true! I quite agree with you. It is probably that very feeling that has made me think so highly of Griselda. But then—" But then a young lady, though she need not jump down a gentleman's throat, or throw herself into his face, may give some signs that she is made of flesh and blood; especially when her papa and mamma and all belonging to her are so anxious to make the path of her love run smooth. That was what was passing through Lady Lufton's mind; but she did not say it all; she merely looked it.

"I don't think she will ever allow herself to indulge in an unauthorized passion," said Mrs. Grantly.

"I am sure she will not," said Lady Lufton, with ready agreement, fearing perhaps in her heart that Griselda would never indulge in any passion, authorized or unauthorized.

"I don't know whether Lord Lufton sees much of her now," said Mrs. Grantly, thinking perhaps of that promise of Lady Lufton's with reference to his lordship's spare time.

"Just lately, during these changes, you know, everybody has been so much engaged. Ludovic has been constantly at the House, and then men find it so necessary to be at their clubs just now."

"Yes, yes, of course," said Mrs. Grantly, who was not at all disposed to think little of the importance of the present crisis, or to wonder that men should congregate together when such deeds were to be done as those which now occupied the breasts of the Queen's advisers. At last, however, the two mothers perfectly understood each other. Griselda was still to remain with Lady Lufton; and was to accept her ladyship's son, if he could only be induced to exercise his privilege of asking her; but in the meantime, as this seemed to be doubtful, Griselda was not to be debarred from her privilege of making what use she could of any other string which she might have to her bow.

"But, mamma," said Griselda, in a moment of unwatched intercourse between the mother and daughter, "is it really true that they are going to make papa a bishop?"

"We can tell nothing as yet, my dear. People in the world are talking about it. Your papa has been a good deal with Lord De Terrier."

"And isn't he prime minister?"

"Oh, yes; I am happy to say that he is."

"I thought the prime minister could make any one a bishop that he chooses,—any clergyman, that is."

"But there is no see vacant," said Mrs. Grantly.

"Then there isn't any chance," said Griselda, looking very glum.

"They are going to have an Act of Parliament for making two more bishops. That's what they are talking about at least. And if they do—"

"Papa will be Bishop of Westminster—won't he? And we shall live in London?"

"But you must not talk about it, my dear."

"No, I won't. But, mamma, a Bishop of Westminster will be higher than a Bishop of Barchester; won't he? I shall so like to be able to snub those Miss Proudies." It will therefore be seen that there were matters on which even Griselda Grantly could be animated. Like the rest of her family she was devoted to the Church.

Late on that afternoon the archdeacon returned home to dine in Mount Street, having spent the whole of the day between the Treasury chambers, a meeting of Convocation, and his club. And when he did get home it was soon manifest to his wife that he was not laden with good news.

"It is almost incredible," he said, standing with his back to the drawing-room fire.

"What is incredible?" said his wife, sharing her husband's anxiety to the full.

"If I had not learned it as fact, I would not have believed it, even of Lord Brock," said the archdeacon.

"Learned what?" said the anxious wife.

"After all, they are going to oppose the bill."

"Impossible!" said Mrs. Grantly.

"But they are."

"The bill for the two new bishops, archdeacon? oppose their own bill!"

"Yes—oppose their own bill. It is almost incredible; but so it is. Some changes have been forced upon us; little things which they had forgotten—quite minor matters; and they now say that they will be obliged to divide against us on these twopenny-halfpenny, hair-splitting points. It is Lord Brock's own doing too, after all that he said about abstaining from factious opposition to the government."

"I believe there is nothing too bad or too false for that man," said Mrs. Grantly.

"After all they said, too, when they were in power themselves, as to the present government opposing the cause of religion! They declare now that Lord De Terrier cannot be very anxious about it, as he had so many good reasons against it a few weeks ago. Is it not dreadful that there should be such double-dealing in men in such positions?"

"It is sickening," said Mrs. Grantly.

And then there was a pause between them as each thought of the injury that was done to them.

"But, archdeacon—"

"Well?"

"Could you not give up those small points and shame them into compliance?"

"Nothing would shame them."

"But would it not be well to try?"

The game was so good a one, and the stake so important, that Mrs. Grantly felt that it would be worth playing for to the last.

"It is no good."

"But I certainly would suggest it to Lord De Terrier. I am sure the country would go along with him; at any rate the Church would."

"It is impossible," said the archdeacon. "To tell the truth, it did occur to me. But some of them down there seemed to think that it would not do."

Mrs. Grantly sat awhile on the sofa, still meditating in her mind whether there might not yet be some escape from so terrible a downfall.

"But, archdeacon—"

"I'll go upstairs and dress," said he, in despondency.

"But, archdeacon, surely the present ministry may have a majority on such a subject as that; I thought they were sure of a majority now."

"No; not sure."

"But at any rate the chances are in their favour? I do hope they'll do their duty, and exert themselves to keep their members together."

And then the archdeacon told out the whole of the truth.

"Lord De Terrier says that under the present circumstances he will not bring the matter forward this session at all. So we had better go back to Plumstead."

Mrs. Grantly then felt that there was nothing further to be said, and it will be proper that the historian should drop a veil over their sufferings.

CHAPTER XXIV.

MAGNA EST VERITAS.

It was made known to the reader that in the early part of the winter Mr. Sowerby had a scheme for retrieving his lost fortunes, and setting himself right in the world, by marrying that rich heiress, Miss Dunstable. I fear my friend Sowerby does not, at present, stand high in the estimation of those who have come on with me thus far in this narrative. He has been described as a spendthrift and gambler, and as one scarcely honest in his extravagance and gambling. But nevertheless there are worse men than Mr. Sowerby, and I am not prepared to say that, should he be successful with Miss Dunstable, that lady would choose by any means the worst of the suitors who are continually throwing themselves at her feet. Reckless as this man always appeared to be, reckless as he absolutely was, there was still within his heart a desire for better things, and in his mind an understanding that he had hitherto missed the career of an honest English gentleman. He was proud of his position as member for his county, though hitherto he had done so little to grace it; he was proud of his domain at Chaldicotes, though the possession of it had so nearly passed out of his own hands; he was proud of the old blood that flowed in his veins; and he was proud also of that easy, comfortable, gay manner, which went so far in the world's judgment to atone for his extravagance and evil practices. If only he could get another chance, as he now said to himself, things should go very differently with him. He would utterly forswear the whole company of Tozers. He would cease to deal in bills, and to pay heaven only knows how many hundred per cent. for his moneys. He would no longer prey upon his friends, and would redeem his title-deeds from the clutches of the Duke of Omnium. If only he could get another chance!

Miss Dunstable's fortune would do all this and ever so much more, and then, moreover, Miss Dunstable was a woman whom he really liked. She was not soft, feminine, or pretty, nor was she very young; but she was clever, self-possessed, and quite able to hold her own in any class; and as to age, Mr. Sowerby was not very young himself. In making such a match he would have no cause of shame. He could speak of it before his friends without fear of their grimaces, and ask them to his house, with the full assurance that the head of his table would not disgrace him. And then as the scheme grew clearer and clearer to him, he declared to himself that if he should be successful, he would use her well, and not rob her of her money—beyond what was absolutely necessary.

He had intended to have laid his fortunes at her feet at Chaldicotes; but the lady had been coy. Then the deed was to have been done at Gatherum Castle, but the lady ran away from Gatherum Castle just at the time on which he had fixed. And since that, one circumstance after another had postponed the affair in London, till now at last he was resolved that he would know his fate, let it be what it might. If he could not contrive that things should speedily be arranged, it might come to pass that he would be altogether debarred from presenting himself to the lady as Mr. Sowerby of Chaldicotes. Tidings had reached him, through Mr. Fothergill, that the duke would be glad to have matters arranged; and Mr. Sowerby well knew the meaning of that message.

Mr. Sowerby was not fighting this campaign alone, without the aid of any ally. Indeed, no man ever had a more trusty ally in any campaign than he had in this. And it was this ally, the only faithful comrade that clung to him through good and ill during his whole life, who first put it into his head that Miss Dunstable was a woman and might be married.

"A hundred needy adventurers have attempted it, and failed already," Mr. Sowerby had said, when the plan was first proposed to him.

"But, nevertheless, she will some day marry some one; and why not you as well as another?" his sister had answered. For Mrs. Harold Smith was the ally of whom I have spoken.

Mrs. Harold Smith, whatever may have been her faults, could boast of this virtue— that she loved her brother. He was probably the only human being that she did love. Children she had none; and as for her husband, it had never occurred to her to love him. She had married him for a position; and being a clever woman, with a good digestion and command of her temper, had managed to get through the world without much of that unhappiness which usually follows ill-assorted marriages. At home she managed to keep the upper hand, but she did so in an easy, good-humoured way that made her rule bearable; and away from home she assisted her lord's political standing, though she laughed more keenly than any one else at his foibles. But the lord of her heart was her brother; and in all his scrapes, all his extravagances, and all his recklessness, she had ever been willing to assist him. With the view of doing this she had sought the intimacy of Miss Dunstable, and for the last year past had indulged every caprice of that lady. Or rather, she had had the wit to learn that Miss Dunstable was to be won, not by the indulgence of caprices, but by free and easy intercourse, with a dash of fun, and, at any rate, a semblance of honesty. Mrs. Harold Smith was not, perhaps, herself very honest by disposition; but in these latter days she had taken up a theory of honesty for the sake of Miss Dunstable—not altogether in vain, for Miss Dunstable and Mrs. Harold Smith were certainly very intimate.

"If I am to do it at all, I must not wait any longer," said Mr. Sowerby to his sister a day or two after the final break-down of the gods. The affection of the sister for the brother may be imagined from the fact that at such a time she could give up her mind to such a subject. But, in truth, her husband's position as a cabinet minister was as nothing to her compared with her brother's position as a county gentleman.

"One time is as good as another," said Mrs. Harold Smith.

"You mean that you would advise me to ask her at once."

"Certainly. But you must remember, Nat, that you will have no easy task. It will not do for you to kneel down and swear that you love her."

"If I do it at all, I shall certainly do it without kneeling—you may be sure of that, Harriet."

"Yes, and without swearing that you love her. There is only one way in which you can be successful with Miss Dunstable—you must tell her the truth."

"What!—tell her that I am ruined, horse, foot, and dragoons, and then bid her help me out of the mire?"

"Exactly: that will be your only chance, strange as it may appear."

"This is very different from what you used to say, down at Chaldicotes."

"So it is; but I know her much better than I did when we were there. Since then I have done but little else than study the freaks of her character. If she really likes you—and I think she does—she could forgive you any other crime but that of swearing that you loved her."

"I should hardly know how to propose without saying something about it."

"But you must say nothing—not a word; you must tell her that you are a gentleman of good blood and high station, but sadly out at elbows."

"She knows that already."

"Of course she does; but she must know it as coming directly from your own mouth. And then tell her that you propose to set yourself right by marrying her—by marrying her for the sake of her money."

"That will hardly win her, I should say."

"If it does not, no other way, that I know of, will do so. As I told you before, it will be no easy task. Of course you must make her understand that her happiness shall be cared for; but that must not be put prominently forward as your object. Your first object is her money, and your only chance for success is in telling the truth."

"It is very seldom that a man finds himself in such a position as that," said Sowerby, walking up and down his sister's room; "and, upon my word, I don't think I am up to the task. I should certainly break down. I don't believe there's a man in London could go to a woman with such a story as that, and then ask her to marry him."

"If you cannot, you may as well give it up," said Mrs. Harold Smith. "But if you can do it—if you can go through with it in that manner—my own opinion is that your chance of success would not be bad. The fact is," added the sister after awhile, during which her brother was continuing his walk and meditating on the difficulties of his position—"the fact is, you men never understand a woman; you give her credit neither for her strength, nor for her weakness. You are too bold, and too timid: you think she is a fool and tell her so, and yet never can trust her to do a kind action. Why should she not marry you with the intention of doing you a good turn? After all, she would lose very little: there is the estate, and if she redeemed it, it would belong to her as well as to you."

"It would be a good turn, indeed. I fear I should be too modest to put it to her in that way."

"Her position would be much better as your wife than it is at present. You are good-humoured and good-tempered, you would intend to treat her well, and, on the whole, she would be much happier as Mrs. Sowerby, of Chaldicotes, than she can be in her present position."

"If she cared about being married, I suppose she could be a peer's wife to-morrow."

"But I don't think she cares about being a peer's wife. A needy peer might perhaps win her in the way that I propose to you; but then a needy peer would not know how to set about it. Needy peers have tried—half a dozen I have no doubt—and have failed, because they have pretended that they were in love with her. It may be difficult, but your only chance is to tell her the truth."

"And where shall I do it?"

"Here if you choose; but her own house will be better."

"But I never can see her there—at least, not alone. I believe that she never is alone. She always keeps a lot of people round her in order to stave off her lovers. Upon my word, Harriet, I think I'll give it up. It is impossible that I should make such a declaration to her as that you propose."

"Faint heart, Nat—you know the rest."

"But the poet never alluded to such wooing as that you have suggested. I suppose I had better begin with a schedule of my debts, and make reference, if she doubts me, to Fothergill, the sheriff's officers, and the Tozer family."

"She will not doubt you, on that head; nor will she be a bit surprised."

Then there was again a pause, during which Mr. Sowerby still walked up and down the room, thinking whether or no he might possibly have any chance of success in so hazardous an enterprise.

"I tell you what, Harriet," at last he said; "I wish you'd do it for me."

"Well," said she, "if you really mean it, I will make the attempt."

"I am sure of this, that I shall never make it myself. I positively should not have the courage to tell her in so many words, that I wanted to marry her for her money."

"Well, Nat, I will attempt it. At any rate, I am not afraid of her. She and I are excellent friends, and, to tell the truth, I think I like her better than any other woman that I know; but I never should have been intimate with her, had it not been for your sake."

"And now you will have to quarrel with her, also for my sake?"

"Not at all. You'll find that whether she accedes to my proposition or not, we shall continue friends. I do not think that she would die for me—nor I for her. But as the world goes we suit each other. Such a little trifle as this will not break our loves."

And so it was settled. On the following day Mrs. Harold Smith was to find an opportunity of explaining the whole matter to Miss Dunstable, and was to ask that lady to share her fortune—some incredible number of thousands of pounds—with the bankrupt member for West Barsetshire, who in return was to bestow on her—himself and his debts.

Mrs. Harold Smith had spoken no more than the truth in saying that she and Miss Dunstable suited one another. And she had not improperly described their friendship. They were not prepared to die, one for the sake of the other. They had said nothing to each other of mutual love and affection. They never kissed, or cried, or made speeches, when they met or when they parted. There was no great benefit for which either had to be grateful to the other; no terrible injury which either had forgiven. But they suited each other; and this, I take it, is the secret of most of our pleasantest intercourse in the world.

And it was almost grievous that they should suit each other, for Miss Dunstable was much the worthier of the two, had she but known it herself. It was almost to be lamented that she should have found herself able to live with Mrs. Harold Smith on terms that were perfectly satisfactory to herself. Mrs. Harold Smith was worldly, heartless—to all the world but her brother—and, as has been above hinted, almost dishonest. Miss Dunstable was not worldly, though it was possible that her present style of life might make her so; she was affectionate, fond of truth, and prone to honesty, if those around would but allow her to exercise it. But she was fond of ease and humour, sometimes of wit that might almost be called broad, and she had a thorough love of ridiculing the world's humbugs. In all these propensities Mrs. Harold Smith indulged her.

Under these circumstances they were now together almost every day. It had become quite a habit with Mrs. Harold Smith to have herself driven early in the forenoon to Miss Dunstable's house; and that lady, though she could never be found alone by Mr. Sowerby, was habitually so found by his sister. And after that they would go out together, or each separately, as fancy or the business of the day might direct them. Each was easy to the other in this alliance, and they so managed that they never trod on each other's corns.

On the day following the agreement made between Mr. Sowerby and Mrs. Harold Smith, that lady as usual called on Miss Dunstable, and soon found herself alone with her friend in a small room which the heiress kept solely for her own purposes. On special occasions persons of various sorts were there admitted; occasionally a parson who had a church to build, or a dowager laden with the last morsel of town slander, or a poor author who could not get due payment for the efforts of his brain, or a poor governess on whose feeble stamina the weight of the world had borne too hardly. But men who by possibility could be lovers did not make their way thither, nor women who could be bores. In these latter days, that is, during the present London season, the doors of it had been oftener opened to Mrs. Harold Smith than to any other person.

And now the effort was to be made with the object of which all this intimacy had been effected. As she came thither in her carriage, Mrs. Harold Smith herself was not altogether devoid of that sinking of the heart which is so frequently the forerunner of any difficult and hazardous undertaking. She had declared that she would feel no fear in making the little proposition. But she did feel something very like it; and when she made her entrance into the little room she certainly wished that the work was done and over.

"How is poor Mr. Smith to-day?" asked Miss Dunstable, with an air of mock condolence, as her friend seated herself in her accustomed easy-chair. The downfall of the gods was as yet a history hardly three days old, and it might well be supposed that the late lord of the Petty Bag had hardly recovered from his misfortune.

"Well, he is better, I think, this morning; at least I should judge so from the manner in which he confronted his eggs. But still I don't like the way he handles the carving-knife. I am sure he is always thinking of Mr. Supplehouse at those moments."

"Poor man! I mean Supplehouse. After all, why shouldn't he follow his trade as well as another? Live and let live, that's what I say."

"Ay, but it's kill and let kill with him. That is what Horace says. However, I am tired of all that now, and I came here to-day to talk about something else."

"I rather like Mr. Supplehouse myself," exclaimed Miss Dunstable. "He never makes any bones about the matter. He has a certain work to do, and a certain cause to serve—namely, his own; and in order to do that work, and serve that cause, he uses such weapons as God has placed in his hands."

"That's what the wild beasts do."

"And where will you find men honester than they? The tiger tears you up because he is hungry and wants to eat you. That's what Supplehouse does. But there are so many among us tearing up one another without any excuse of hunger. The mere pleasure of destroying is reason enough."

"Well, my dear, my mission to you to-day is certainly not one of destruction, as you will admit when you hear it. It is one, rather, very absolutely of salvation. I have come to make love to you."

"Then the salvation, I suppose, is not for myself," said Miss Dunstable.

It was quite clear to Mrs. Harold Smith that Miss Dunstable had immediately understood the whole purport of this visit, and that she was not in any great measure surprised. It did not seem from the tone of the heiress's voice, or from the serious look which at once settled on her face, that she would be prepared to give a very ready compliance. But then great objects can only be won with great efforts.

"That's as may be," said Mrs. Harold Smith. "For you and another also, I hope. But I trust, at any rate, that I may not offend you?"

"Oh, laws, no; nothing of that kind ever offends me now."

"Well, I suppose you're used to it."

"Like the eels, my dear. I don't mind it the least in the world—only sometimes, you know, it is a little tedious."

"I'll endeavour to avoid that, so I may as well break the ice at once. You know enough of Nathaniel's affairs to be aware that he is not a very rich man."

"Since you do ask me about it, I suppose there's no harm in saying that I believe him to be a very poor man."

"Not the least harm in the world, but just the reverse. Whatever may come of this, my wish is that the truth should be told scrupulously on all sides; the truth, the whole truth, and nothing but the truth."

"*Magna est veritas*," said Miss Dunstable. "The Bishop of Barchester taught me as much Latin as that at Chaldicotes; and he did add some more, but there was a long word, and I forgot it."

"The bishop was quite right, my dear, I'm sure. But if you go to your Latin, I'm lost. As we were just now saying, my brother's pecuniary affairs are in a very bad state. He has a beautiful property of his own, which has been in the family for I can't say how many centuries—long before the Conquest, I know."

"I wonder what my ancestors were then?"

"It does not much signify to any of us," said Mrs. Harold Smith, with a moral shake of her head, "what our ancestors were; but it's a sad thing to see an old property go to ruin."

"Yes, indeed; we none of us like to see our property going to ruin, whether it be old or new. I have some of that sort of feeling already, although mine was only made the other day out of an apothecary's shop."

"God forbid that I should ever help you to ruin it," said Mrs. Harold Smith. "I should be sorry to be the means of your losing a ten-pound note."

"*Magna est veritas*, as the dear bishop said," exclaimed Miss Dunstable. "Let us have the truth, the whole truth, and nothing but the truth, as we agreed just now."

Mrs. Harold Smith did begin to find that the task before her was difficult. There was a hardness about Miss Dunstable when matters of business were concerned on which it seemed almost impossible to make any impression. It was not that she had evinced any determination to refuse the tender of Mr. Sowerby's hand; but she was so painfully resolute not to have dust thrown in her eyes! Mrs. Harold Smith had commenced with a mind fixed upon avoiding what she called humbug; but this sort of humbug had become so prominent a part of her usual rhetoric, that she found it very hard to abandon it.

"And that's what I wish," said she. "Of course my chief object is to secure my brother's happiness."

"That's very unkind to poor Mr. Harold Smith."

"Well, well, well—you know what I mean."

"Yes, I think I do know what you mean. Your brother is a gentleman of good family, but of no means."

"Not quite so bad as that."

"Of embarrassed means, then, or anything that you will; whereas I am a lady of no family, but of sufficient wealth. You think that if you brought us together and made a match of it, it would be a very good thing for—for whom?" said Miss Dunstable.

"Yes, exactly," said Mrs. Harold Smith.

"For which of us? Remember the bishop now and his nice little bit of Latin."

"For Nathaniel then," said Mrs. Harold Smith, boldly. "It would be a very good thing for him." And a slight smile came across her face as she said it. "Now that's honest, or the mischief is in it."

"Yes, that's honest enough. And did he send you here to tell me this?"

"Well, he did that, and something else."

"And now let's have the something else. The really important part, I have no doubt, has been spoken."

"No, by no means, by no means all of it. But you are so hard on one, my dear, with your running after honesty, that one is not able to tell the real facts as they are. You make one speak in such a bald, naked way."

"Ah, you think that anything naked must be indecent; even truth."

"I think it is more proper-looking, and better suited, too, for the world's work, when it goes about with some sort of a garment on it. We are so used to a leaven of falsehood in all we hear and say, now-a-days, that nothing is more likely to deceive us than the absolute truth. If a shopkeeper told me that his wares were simply middling, of course, I should think that they were not worth a farthing. But all that has nothing to do with my poor brother. Well, what was I saying?"

"You were going to tell me how well he would use me, no doubt."

"Something of that kind."

"That he wouldn't beat me; or spend all my money if I managed to have it tied up out of his power; or look down on me with contempt because my father was an apothecary! Was not that what you were going to say?"

"I was going to tell you that you might be more happy as Mrs. Sowerby of Chaldicotes than you can be as Miss Dunstable—"

"Of Mount Lebanon. And had Mr. Sowerby no other message to send?—nothing about love, or anything of that sort? I should like, you know, to understand what his feelings are before I take such a leap."

"I do believe he has as true a regard for you as any man of his age ever does have—"

"For any woman of mine. That is not putting it in a very devoted way certainly; but I am glad to see that you remember the bishop's maxim."

"What would you have me say? If I told you that he was dying for love, you would say, I was trying to cheat you; and now because I don't tell you so, you say that he is wanting in devotion. I must say you are hard to please."

"Perhaps I am, and very unreasonable into the bargain. I ought to ask no questions of the kind when your brother proposes to do me so much honour. As for my expecting the love of a man who condescends to wish to be my husband, that, of course, would be monstrous. What right can I have to think that any man should love me? It ought to be enough for me to know that as I am rich, I can get a husband. What business can such as I have to inquire whether the gentleman who would so honour me really would like my company, or would only deign to put up with my presence in his household?"

"Now, my dear Miss Dunstable—"

"Of course I am not such an ass as to expect that any gentleman should love me; and I feel that I ought to be obliged to your brother for sparing me the string of complimentary declarations which are usual on such occasions. He, at any rate, is not tedious—or rather you on his behalf; for no doubt his own time is so occupied with his parliamentary duties that he cannot attend to this little matter himself. I do feel grateful to him; and perhaps nothing more will be necessary than to give him a schedule of the property, and name an early day for putting him in possession."

Mrs. Smith did feel that she was rather badly used. This Miss Dunstable, in their mutual confidences, had so often ridiculed the love-making grimaces of her mercenary suitors—had spoken so fiercely against those who had persecuted her, not because they had desired her money, but on account of their ill-judgment in thinking her to be a fool—that Mrs. Smith had a right to expect that the method she had adopted for opening the negotiation would be taken in a better spirit. Could it be possible, after all, thought Mrs. Smith to herself, that Miss Dunstable was like other women, and that she did like to have men kneeling at her feet? Could it be the case that she had advised her brother badly, and that it would have been better for him to have gone about his work in the old-fashioned way? "They are very hard to manage," said Mrs. Harold Smith to herself, thinking of her own sex.

"He was coming here himself," said she, "but I advised him not to do so."

"That was so kind of you."

"I thought that I could explain to you more openly and more freely, what his intentions really are."

"Oh! I have no doubt that they are honourable," said Miss Dunstable. "He does not want to deceive me in that way, I am quite sure."

It was impossible to help laughing, and Mrs. Harold Smith did laugh. "Upon my word, you would provoke a saint," said she.

"I am not likely to get into any such company by the alliance that you are now suggesting to me. There are not many saints usually at Chaldicotes, I believe;—always excepting my dear bishop and his wife."

"But, my dear, what am I to say to Nathaniel?"

"Tell him, of course, how much obliged to him I am."

"Do listen to me one moment. I daresay that I have done wrong to speak to you in such a bold, unromantic way."

"Not at all. The truth, the whole truth, and nothing but the truth. That's what we agreed upon. But one's first efforts in any line are always apt to be a little uncouth."

"I will send Nathaniel to you himself."

"No, do not do so. Why torment either him or me? I do like your brother; in a certain way I like him much. But no earthly consideration would induce me to marry him. Is it not so glaringly plain that he would marry me for my money only, that you have not even dared to suggest any other reason?"

"Of course it would have been nonsense to say that he had no regard whatever towards your money."

"Of course it would—absolute nonsense. He is a poor man with a good position, and he wants to marry me because I have got that which he wants. But, my dear, I do not want that which he has got, and therefore the bargain would not be a fair one."

"But he would do his very best to make you happy."

"I am so much obliged to him; but you see, I am very happy as I am. What should I gain?"

"A companion whom you confess that you like."

"Ah! but I don't know that I should like too much even of such a companion as your brother. No, my dear—it won't do. Believe me when I tell you, once for all, that it won't do."

"Do you mean, then, Miss Dunstable, that you'll never marry?"

"To-morrow—if I met any one that I fancied, and he would have me. But I rather think that any that I may fancy won't have me. In the first place, if I marry any one, the man must be quite indifferent to money."

"Then you'll not find him in this world, my dear."

"Very possibly not," said Miss Dunstable.

All that was further said upon the subject need not be here repeated. Mrs. Harold Smith did not give up her cause quite at once, although Miss Dunstable had spoken so plainly. She tried to explain how eligible would be her friend's situation as mistress of Chaldicotes, when Chaldicotes should owe no penny to any man: and went so far as to hint that the master of Chaldicotes, if relieved of his embarrassments and known as a rich man, might in all probability be found worthy of a peerage when the gods should return to Olympus. Mr. Harold Smith, as a cabinet minister, would, of course, do his best. But it was all of no use. "It's not my destiny," said Miss Dunstable, "and therefore do not press it any longer."

"But we shall not quarrel," said Mrs. Harold Smith, almost tenderly.

"Oh, no—why should we quarrel?"

"And you won't look glum at my brother?"

975

"Why should I look glum at him? But, Mrs. Smith, I'll do more than not looking glum at him. I do like you, and I do like your brother, and if I can in any moderate way assist him in his difficulties, let him tell me so."

Soon after this, Mrs. Harold Smith went her way. Of course, she declared in a very strong manner that her brother could not think of accepting from Miss Dunstable any such pecuniary assistance as that offered—and, to give her her due, such was the feeling of her mind at the moment; but as she went to meet her brother and gave him an account of this interview, it did occur to her that possibly Miss Dunstable might be a better creditor than the Duke of Omnium for the Chaldicotes property.

CHAPTER XXV.

NON-IMPULSIVE.

It cannot be held as astonishing, that that last decision on the part of the giants in the matter of the two bishoprics should have disgusted Archdeacon Grantly. He was a politician, but not a politician as they were. As is the case with all exoteric men, his political eyes saw a short way only, and his political aspirations were as limited. When his friends came into office, that bishop bill, which as the original product of his enemies had been regarded by him as being so pernicious—for was it not about to be made law in order that other Proudies and such like might be hoisted up into high places and large incomes, to the terrible detriment of the Church?—that bishop bill, I say, in the hands of his friends, had appeared to him to be a means of almost national salvation. And then, how great had been the good fortune of the giants in this matter! Had they been the originators of such a measure they would not have had a chance of success; but now—now that the two bishops were falling into their mouths out of the weak hands of the gods, was not their success ensured? So Dr. Grantly had girded up his loins and marched up to the fight, almost regretting that the triumph would be so easy. The subsequent failure was very trying to his temper as a party man.

It always strikes me that the supporters of the Titans are in this respect much to be pitied. The giants themselves, those who are actually handling Pelion and breaking their shins over the lower rocks of Ossa, are always advancing in some sort towards the councils of Olympus. Their highest policy is to snatch some ray from heaven. Why else put Pelion on Ossa, unless it be that a furtive hand, making its way through Jove's windows, may pluck forth a thunderbolt or two, or some article less destructive, but of manufacture equally divine? And in this consists the wisdom of the higher giants—that, in spite of their mundane antecedents, theories, and predilections, they can see that articles of divine manufacture are necessary. But then they never carry their supporters with them. Their whole army is an army of martyrs. "For twenty years I have stuck to them, and see how they have treated me!" Is not that always the plaint of an old giant-slave? "I have been true to my party all my life, and where am I now?" he says. Where, indeed, my friend? Looking about you, you begin to learn that you cannot describe your whereabouts. I do not marvel at that. No one finds himself planted at last in so terribly foul a morass, as he would fain stand still for ever on dry ground.

Dr. Grantly was disgusted; and although he was himself too true and thorough in all his feelings, to be able to say aloud that any Giant was wrong, still he had a sad feeling within his heart that the world was sinking from under him. He was still sufficiently exoteric to think that a good stand-up fight in a good cause was a good thing. No doubt he did wish to be Bishop of Westminster, and was anxious to compass that preferment by any means that might appear to him to be fair. And why not? But this was not the end of his aspirations. He wished that the giants might prevail in everything, in bishoprics as in all other matters; and he could not understand that they should give way on the very first appearance of a skirmish. In his open talk he was loud against many a god; but in his heart of hearts he was bitter enough against both Porphyrion and Orion.

"My dear doctor, it would not do;—not in this session; it would not indeed." So had spoken to him a half-fledged but especially esoteric young monster-cub at the Treasury, who considered himself as up to all the dodges of his party, and regarded the army of martyrs who supported it as a rather heavy, but very useful collection of fogeys. Dr. Grantly had not cared to discuss the matter with the half-fledged monster-cub. The best licked of all the monsters, the Giant most like a god of them all, had said a word or two to him; and he also had said a word or two to that Giant. Porphyrion had told him that the bishop bill would not do; and he, in return, speaking with warm face, and blood in his cheeks, had told Porphyrion that he saw no reason why the bill should not do. The courteous Giant had smiled as he shook his ponderous head, and then the archdeacon had left him, unconsciously shaking some dust from his shoes, as he paced the passages of the Treasury chambers for the last time. As he walked back to his lodgings in Mount Street, many thoughts, not altogether bad in their nature, passed through his mind. Why should he trouble himself about a bishopric? Was he not well as he was, in his rectory down at Plumstead? Might it not be ill for him at his age to transplant himself into new soil, to engage in new duties, and live among new people? Was he not useful at Barchester, and respected also; and might it not be possible, that up there at Westminster, he might be regarded merely as a tool with which other men could work? He had not quite liked the tone of that specially esoteric young monster-cub, who had clearly regarded him as a distinguished fogey from the army of martyrs. He would take his wife back to Barsetshire, and there live contented with the good things which Providence had given him.

Those high political grapes had become sour, my sneering friends will say. Well? Is it not a good thing that grapes should become sour which hang out of reach? Is he not wise who can regard all grapes as sour which are manifestly too high for his hand? Those grapes of the Treasury bench, for which gods and giants fight, suffering so much when they are forced to abstain from eating, and so much more when they do eat,—those grapes are very sour to me. I am sure that they are indigestible, and that those who eat them undergo all the ills which the Revalenta Arabica is prepared to cure. And so it was now with the archdeacon. He thought of the strain which would have been put on his conscience had he come up there to sit in London as Bishop of Westminster; and in this frame of mind he walked home to his wife.

During the first few moments of his interview with her all his regrets had come back upon him. Indeed, it would have hardly suited for him then to have preached this new doctrine of rural contentment. The wife of his bosom, whom he so fully trusted—had so fully loved—wished for grapes that hung high upon the wall, and he knew that it was past his power to teach her at the moment to drop her ambition. Any teaching that he might effect in that way, must come by degrees. But before many minutes were over he had told her of her fate and of his own decision. "So we had better go back to Plumstead," he said; and she had not dissented.

"I am sorry for poor Griselda's sake," Mrs. Grantly had remarked later in the evening, when they were again together.

"But I thought she was to remain with Lady Lufton?"

"Well; so she will, for a little time. There is no one with whom I would so soon trust her out of my own care as with Lady Lufton. She is all that one can desire."

"Exactly; and as far as Griselda is concerned, I cannot say that I think she is to be pitied."

"Not to be pitied, perhaps," said Mrs. Grantly. "But, you see, archdeacon, Lady Lufton, of course, has her own views."

"Her own views?"

"It is hardly any secret that she is very anxious to make a match between Lord Lufton and Griselda. And though that might be a very proper arrangement if it were fixed—"

"Lord Lufton marry Griselda!" said the archdeacon, speaking quick and raising his eyebrows. His mind had as yet been troubled by but few thoughts respecting his child's future establishment. "I had never dreamt of such a thing."

"But other people have done more than dream of it, archdeacon. As regards the match itself, it would, I think, be unobjectionable. Lord Lufton will not be a very rich man, but his property is respectable, and as far as I can learn his character is on the whole good. If they like each other, I should be contented with such a marriage. But, I must own, I am not quite satisfied at the idea of leaving her all alone with Lady Lufton. People will look on it as a settled thing, when it is not settled—and very probably may not be settled; and that will do the poor girl harm. She is very much admired; there can be no doubt of that; and Lord Dumbello—"

The archdeacon opened his eyes still wider. He had had no idea that such a choice of sons-in-law was being prepared for him; and, to tell the truth, was almost bewildered by the height of his wife's ambition. Lord Lufton, with his barony and twenty thousand a year, might be accepted as just good enough; but failing him there was an embryo marquis, whose fortune would be more than ten times as great, all ready to accept his child! And then he thought, as husbands sometimes will think, of Susan Harding as she was when he had gone a-courting to her under the elms before the house in the warden's garden at Barchester, and of dear old Mr. Harding, his wife's father, who still lived in humble lodgings in that city; and as he thought, he wondered at and admired the greatness of that lady's mind.

"I never can forgive Lord De Terrier," said the lady, connecting various points together in her own mind.

"That's nonsense," said the archdeacon. "You must forgive him."

"And I must confess that it annoys me to leave London at present."

"It can't be helped," said the archdeacon, somewhat gruffly; for he was a man who, on certain points, chose to have his own way—and had it.

"Oh, no: I know it can't be helped," said Mrs. Grantly, in a tone which implied a deep injury. "I know it can't be helped. Poor Griselda!" And then they went to bed.

On the next morning Griselda came to her, and in an interview that was strictly private, her mother said more to her than she had ever yet spoken, as to the prospects of her future life. Hitherto, on this subject, Mrs. Grantly had said little or nothing. She would have been well pleased that her daughter should have received the incense of Lord Lufton's vows—or, perhaps, as well pleased had it been the incense of Lord Dumbello's vows—without any interference on her part. In such case her child, she knew, would have told her with quite sufficient eagerness, and the matter in either case would have been arranged as a very pretty love match. She had no fear of any impropriety or of any rashness on Griselda's part. She had thoroughly known her daughter when she boasted that Griselda would never indulge in an unauthorized passion. But as matters now stood, with those two strings to her bow, and with that Lufton-Grantly alliance treaty in existence—of which she, Griselda herself, knew nothing—might it not be possible that the poor child should stumble through want of adequate direction? Guided by these thoughts, Mrs. Grantly had resolved to say a few words before she left London. So she wrote a line to her daughter, and Griselda reached Mount Street at two o'clock in Lady Lufton's carriage, which, during the interview, waited for her at the beer-shop round the corner.

"And papa won't be Bishop of Westminster?" said the young lady, when the doings of the giants had been sufficiently explained to make her understand that all those hopes were over.

"No, my dear; at any rate not now."

"What a shame! I thought it was all settled. What's the good, mamma, of Lord De Terrier being prime minister, if he can't make whom he likes a bishop?"

"I don't think that Lord De Terrier has behaved at all well to your father. However, that's a long question, and we can't go into it now."

"How glad those Proudies will be!"

Griselda would have talked by the hour on this subject had her mother allowed her, but it was necessary that Mrs. Grantly should go to other matters. She began about Lady Lufton, saying what a dear woman her ladyship was; and then went on to say that Griselda was to remain in London as long as it suited her friend and hostess to stay there with her; but added, that this might probably not be very long, as it was notorious that Lady Lufton, when in London, was always in a hurry to get back to Framley.

"But I don't think she is in such a hurry this year, mamma," said Griselda, who in the month of May preferred Bruton Street to Plumstead, and had no objection whatever to the coronet on the panels of Lady Lufton's coach.

And then Mrs. Grantly commenced her explanation—very cautiously. "No, my dear, I daresay she is not in such a hurry this year,—that is, as long as you remain with her."

"I am sure she is very kind."

"She is very kind, and you ought to love her very much. I know I do. I have no friend in the world for whom I have a greater regard than for Lady Lufton. It is that which makes me so happy to leave you with her."

"All the same, I wish that you and papa had remained up; that is, if they had made papa a bishop."

"It's no good thinking of that now, my dear. What I particularly wanted to say to you was this: I think you should know what are the ideas which Lady Lufton entertains."

"Her ideas!" said Griselda, who had never troubled herself much in thinking about other people's thoughts.

"Yes, Griselda. While you were staying down at Framley Court, and also, I suppose, since you have been up here in Bruton Street, you must have seen a good deal of—Lord Lufton."

"He doesn't come very often to Bruton Street,—that is to say, not *very* often."

"H-m," ejaculated Mrs. Grantly, very gently. She would willingly have repressed the sound altogether, but it had been too much for her. If she found reason to think that Lady Lufton was playing her false, she would immediately take her daughter away, break up the treaty, and prepare for the Hartletop alliance. Such were the thoughts that ran through her mind. But she knew all the while that Lady Lufton was not false. The fault was not with Lady Lufton; nor, perhaps, altogether with Lord Lufton. Mrs. Grantly had understood the full force of the complaint which Lady Lufton had made against her daughter; and though she had of course defended her child, and on the whole had defended her successfully, yet she confessed to herself that Griselda's chance of a first-rate establishment would be better if she were a little more impulsive. A man does not wish to marry a statue, let the statue be ever so statuesque. She could not teach her daughter to be impulsive, any more than she could teach her to be six feet high; but might it not be possible to teach her to seem so? The task was a very delicate one, even for a mother's hand.

"Of course he cannot be at home now as much as he was down in the country, when he was living in the same house," said Mrs. Grantly, whose business it was to take Lord Lufton's part at the present moment. "He must be at his club, and at the House of Lords, and in twenty places."

"He is very fond of going to parties, and he dances beautifully."

"I am sure he does. I have seen as much as that myself, and I think I know some one with whom he likes to dance." And the mother gave her daughter a loving little squeeze.

"Do you mean me, mamma?"

"Yes, I do mean you, my dear. And is it not true? Lady Lufton says that he likes dancing with you better than with any one else in London."

"I don't know," said Griselda, looking down upon the ground.

Mrs. Grantly thought that this upon the whole was rather a good opening. It might have been better. Some point of interest more serious in its nature than that of a waltz might have been found on which to connect her daughter's sympathies with those of her future husband. But any point of interest was better than none; and it is so difficult to find points of interest in persons who by their nature are not impulsive.

"Lady Lufton says so, at any rate," continued Mrs. Grantly, ever so cautiously. "She thinks that Lord Lufton likes no partner better. What do you think yourself, Griselda?"

"I don't know, mamma."

"But young ladies must think of such things, must they not?"

"Must they, mamma?"

"I suppose they do, don't they? The truth is, Griselda, that Lady Lufton thinks that if— Can you guess what it is she thinks?"

"No, mamma." But that was a fib on Griselda's part.

"She thinks that my Griselda would make the best possible wife in the world for her son; and I think so too. I think that her son will be a very fortunate man if he can get such a wife. And now what do you think, Griselda?"

"I don't think anything, mamma."

But that would not do. It was absolutely necessary that she should think, and absolutely necessary that her mother should tell her so. Such a degree of unimpulsiveness as this would lead to—heaven knows what results! Lufton-Grantly treaties and Hartletop interests would be all thrown away upon a young lady who would not think anything of a noble suitor sighing for her smiles. Besides, it was not natural. Griselda, as her mother knew, had never been a girl of headlong feeling; but still she had had her likes and her dislikes. In that matter of the bishopric she was keen enough; and no one could evince a deeper interest in the subject of a well-made new dress than Griselda Grantly. It was not possible that she should be indifferent as to her future prospects, and she must know that those prospects depended mainly on her marriage. Her mother was almost angry with her, but nevertheless she went on very gently:

"You don't think anything! But, my darling, you must think. You must make up your mind what would be your answer if Lord Lufton were to propose to you. That is what Lady Lufton wishes him to do."

"But he never will, mamma."

"And if he did?"

"But I'm sure he never will. He doesn't think of such a thing at all—and—and—"

"And what, my dear?"

"I don't know, mamma."

"Surely you can speak out to me, dearest! All I care about is your happiness. Both Lady Lufton and I think that it would be a happy marriage if you both cared for each other enough. She thinks that he is fond of you. But if he were ten times Lord Lufton I would not tease you about it if I thought that you could not learn to care about him. What was it you were going to say, my dear?"

"Lord Lufton thinks a great deal more of Lucy Robarts than he does of—of—of any one else, I believe," said Griselda, showing now some little animation by her manner, "dumpy little black thing that she is."

"Lucy Robarts!" said Mrs. Grantly, taken by surprise at finding that her daughter was moved by such a passion as jealousy, and feeling also perfectly assured that there could not be any possible ground for jealousy in such a direction as that. "Lucy Robarts, my dear! I don't suppose Lord Lufton ever thought of speaking to her, except in the way of civility."

"Yes, he did, mamma! Don't you remember at Framley?"

Mrs. Grantly began to look back in her mind, and she thought she did remember having once observed Lord Lufton talking in rather a confidential manner with the parson's sister. But she was sure that there was nothing in it. If that was the reason why Griselda was so cold to her proposed lover, it would be a thousand pities that it should not be removed.

"Now you mention her, I do remember the young lady," said Mrs. Grantly, "a dark girl, very low, and without much figure. She seemed to me to keep very much in the background."

"I don't know much about that, mamma."

"As far as I saw her, she did. But, my dear Griselda, you should not allow yourself to think of such a thing. Lord Lufton, of course, is bound to be civil to any young lady in his mother's house, and I am quite sure that he has no other idea whatever with regard to Miss Robarts. I certainly cannot speak as to her intellect, for I do not think she opened her mouth in my presence; but—"

"Oh! she has plenty to say for herself, when she pleases. She's a sly little thing."

"But, at any rate, my dear, she has no personal attractions whatever, and I do not at all think that Lord Lufton is a man to be taken by—by—by anything that Miss Robarts might do or say."

As those words "personal attractions" were uttered, Griselda managed so to turn her neck as to catch a side view of herself in one of the mirrors on the wall, and then she bridled herself up, and made a little play with her eyes, and looked, as her mother thought, very well. "It is all nothing to me, mamma, of course," she said.

"Well, my dear, perhaps not. I don't say that it is. I do not wish to put the slightest constraint upon your feelings. If I did not have the most thorough dependence on your good sense and high principles, I should not speak to you in this way. But as I have, I thought it best to tell you that both Lady Lufton and I should be well pleased if we thought that you and Lord Lufton were fond of each other."

"I am sure he never thinks of such a thing, mamma."

"And as for Lucy Robarts, pray get that idea out of your head; if not for your sake, then for his. You should give him credit for better taste."

But it was not so easy to take anything out of Griselda's head that she had once taken into it. "As for tastes, mamma, there is no accounting for them," she said; and then the colloquy on that subject was over. The result of it on Mrs. Grantly's mind was a feeling amounting almost to a conviction in favour of the Dumbello interest.

CHAPTER XXVI.

IMPULSIVE.

I trust my readers will all remember how Puck the pony was beaten during that drive to Hogglestock. It may be presumed that Puck himself on that occasion did not suffer much. His skin was not so soft as Mrs. Robarts's heart. The little beast was full of oats and all the good things of this world, and therefore, when the whip touched him, he would dance about and shake his little ears, and run on at a tremendous pace for twenty yards, making his mistress think that he had endured terrible things. But, in truth, during those whippings Puck was not the chief sufferer.

Lucy had been forced to declare—forced by the strength of her own feelings, and by the impossibility of assenting to the propriety of a marriage between Lord Lufton and Miss Grantly—, she had been forced to declare that she did care about Lord Lufton as much as though he were her brother. She had said all this to herself,—nay, much more than this—very often. But now she had said it out loud to her sister-in-law; and she knew that what she had said was remembered, considered, and had, to a certain extent, become the cause of altered conduct. Fanny alluded very seldom to the Luftons in casual conversation, and never spoke about Lord Lufton, unless when her husband made it impossible that she should not speak of him. Lucy had attempted on more than one occasion to remedy this, by talking about the young lord in a laughing and, perhaps, half-jeering way; she had been sarcastic as to his hunting and shooting, and had boldly attempted to say a word in joke about his love for Griselda. But she felt that she had failed; that she had failed altogether as regarded Fanny; and that as to her brother, she would more probably be the means of opening his eyes, than have any effect in keeping them closed. So she gave up her efforts and spoke no further word about Lord Lufton. Her secret had been told, and she knew that it had been told.

At this time the two ladies were left a great deal alone together in the drawing-room at the parsonage; more, perhaps, than had ever yet been the case since Lucy had been there. Lady Lufton was away, and therefore the almost daily visit to Framley Court was not made; and Mark in these days was a great deal at Barchester, having, no doubt, very onerous duties to perform before he could be admitted as one of that chapter. He went into, what he was pleased to call residence, almost at once. That is, he took his month of preaching, aiding also in some slight and very dignified way, in the general Sunday morning services. He did not exactly live at Barchester, because the house was not ready. That at least was the assumed reason. The chattels of Dr. Stanhope, the late prebendary, had not been as yet removed, and there was likely to be some little delay, creditors asserting their right to them. This might have been very inconvenient to a gentleman anxiously expecting the excellent house which the liberality of past ages had provided for his use; but it was not so felt by Mr. Robarts. If Dr. Stanhope's family or creditors would keep the house for the next twelve months, he would be well pleased. And by this arrangement he was enabled to get through his first month of absence from the church of Framley without any notice from Lady Lufton, seeing that Lady Lufton was in London all the time. This also was convenient, and taught our young prebendary to look on his new preferment more favourably than he had hitherto done.

Fanny and Lucy were thus left much alone: and as out of the full head the mouth speaks, so is the full heart more prone to speak at such periods of confidence as these. Lucy, when she first thought of her own state, determined to endow herself with a powerful gift of reticence. She would never tell her love, certainly; but neither would she let concealment feed on her damask cheek, nor would she ever be found for a moment sitting like Patience on a monument. She would fight her own fight bravely within her own bosom, and conquer her enemy altogether. She would either preach, or starve, or weary her love into subjection, and no one should be a bit the wiser. She would teach herself to shake hands with Lord Lufton without a quiver, and would be prepared to like his wife amazingly—unless indeed that wife should be Griselda Grantly. Such were her resolutions; but at the end of the first week they were broken into shivers and scattered to the winds.

They had been sitting in the house together the whole of one wet day; and as Mark was to dine in Barchester with the dean, they had had dinner early, eating with the children almost in their laps. It is so that ladies do, when their husbands leave them to themselves. It was getting dusk towards evening, and they were still sitting in the drawing-room, the children now having retired, when Mrs. Robarts for the fifth time since her visit to Hogglestock began to express her wish that she could do some good to the Crawleys,—to Grace Crawley in particular, who, standing up there at her father's elbow, learning Greek irregular verbs, had appeared to Mrs. Robarts to be an especial object of pity.

"I don't know how to set about it," said Mrs. Robarts.

Now any allusion to that visit to Hogglestock always drove Lucy's mind back to the consideration of the subject which had most occupied it at the time. She at such moments remembered how she had beaten Puck, and how in her half-bantering but still too serious manner she had apologized for doing so, and had explained the reason. And therefore she could not interest herself about Grace Crawley as vividly as she should have done.

"No; one never does," she said.

"I was thinking about it all that day as I drove home," said Fanny. "The difficulty is this: What can we do with her?"

"Exactly," said Lucy, remembering the very point of the road at which she had declared that she did like Lord Lufton very much.

"If we could have her here for a month or so and then send her to school;—but I know Mr. Crawley would not allow us to pay for her schooling."

"I don't think he would," said Lucy, with her thoughts far removed from Mr. Crawley and his daughter Grace.

"And then we should not know what to do with her; should we?"

"No; you would not."

"It would never do to have the poor girl about the house here, with no one to teach her anything. Mark would not teach her Greek verbs, you know."

"I suppose not."

"Lucy, you are not attending to a word I say to you, and I don't think you have for the last hour. I don't believe you know what I am talking about."

"Oh, yes, I do—Grace Crawley; I'll try and teach her if you like, only I don't know anything myself."

"That's not what I mean at all, and you know I would not ask you to take such a task as that on yourself. But I do think you might talk it over with me."

"Might I? very well; I will. What is it? Oh, Grace Crawley—you want to know who is to teach her the irregular Greek verbs. Oh dear, Fanny, my head does ache so: pray don't be angry with me." And then Lucy, throwing herself back on the sofa, put one hand up painfully to her forehead, and altogether gave up the battle.

Mrs. Robarts was by her side in a moment. "Dearest Lucy, what is it makes your head ache so often now? you used not to have those headaches."

"It's because I'm growing stupid: never mind. We will go on about poor Grace. It would not do to have a governess, would it?"

"I can see that you are not well, Lucy," said Mrs. Robarts, with a look of deep concern. "What is it, dearest? I can see that something is the matter."

"Something the matter! No, there's not; nothing worth talking of. Sometimes I think I'll go back to Devonshire and live there. I could stay with Blanche for a time, and then get a lodging in Exeter."

"Go back to Devonshire!" and Mrs. Robarts looked as though she thought that her sister-in-law was going mad. "Why do you want to go away from us? This is to be your own, own home, always now."

"Is it? Then I am in a bad way. Oh dear, oh dear, what a fool I am! What an idiot I've been! Fanny, I don't think I can stay here; and I do so wish I'd never come. I do—I do—I do, though you look at me so horribly," and jumping up she threw herself into her sister-in-law's arms and began kissing her violently. "Don't pretend to be wounded, for you know that I love you. You know that I could live with you all my life, and think you were perfect—as you are; but—"

"Has Mark said anything?"

"Not a word,—not a ghost of a syllable. It is not Mark; oh, Fanny!"

"I am afraid I know what you mean," said Mrs. Robarts in a low tremulous voice, and with deep sorrow painted on her face.

"Of course you do; of course you know; you have known it all along: since that day in the pony-carriage. I knew that you knew it. You do not dare to mention his name: would not that tell me that you know it? And I, I am hypocrite enough for Mark; but my hypocrisy won't pass muster before you. And, now, had I not better go to Devonshire?"

"Dearest, dearest Lucy."

"Was I not right about that labelling? O heavens! what idiots we girls are! That a dozen soft words should have bowled me over like a ninepin, and left me without an inch of ground to call my own. And I was so proud of my own strength; so sure that I should never be missish, and spoony, and sentimental! I was so determined to like him as Mark does, or you—"

"I shall not like him at all if he has spoken words to you that he should not have spoken."

"But he has not." And then she stopped a moment to consider. "No, he has not. He never said a word to me that would make you angry with him if you knew of it. Except, perhaps, that he called me Lucy; and that was my fault, not his."

"Because you talked of soft words."

"Fanny, you have no idea what an absolute fool I am, what an unutterable ass. The soft words of which I tell you were of the kind which he speaks to you when he asks you how the cow gets on which he sent you from Ireland, or to Mark about Ponto's shoulder. He told me that he knew papa, and that he was at school with Mark, and that as he was such good friends with you here at the parsonage, he must be good friends with me too. No; it has not been his fault. The soft words which did the mischief were such as those. But how well his mother understood the world! In order to have been safe, I should not have dared to look at him."

"But, dearest Lucy—"

"I know what you are going to say, and I admit it all. He is no hero. There is nothing on earth wonderful about him. I never heard him say a single word of wisdom, or utter a thought that was akin to poetry. He devotes all his energies to riding after a fox or killing poor birds, and I never heard of his doing a single great action in my life. And yet—"

Fanny was so astounded by the way her sister-in-law went on, that she hardly knew how to speak. "He is an excellent son, I believe," at last she said.

"Except when he goes to Gatherum Castle. I'll tell you what he has: he has fine straight legs, and a smooth forehead, and a good-humoured eye, and white teeth. Was it possible to see such a catalogue of perfections, and not fall down, stricken to the very bone? But it was not that that did it all, Fanny. I could have stood against that. I think I could at least. It was his title that killed me. I had never spoken to a lord before. Oh, me! what a fool, what a beast I have been!" And then she burst out into tears.

Mrs. Robarts, to tell the truth, could hardly understand poor Lucy's ailment. It was evident enough that her misery was real; but yet she spoke of herself and her sufferings with so much irony, with so near an approach to joking, that it was very hard to tell how far she was in earnest. Lucy, too, was so much given to a species of badinage which Mrs. Robarts did not always quite understand, that the latter was afraid sometimes to speak out what came uppermost to her tongue. But now that Lucy was absolutely in tears, and was almost breathless with excitement, she could not remain silent any longer. "Dearest Lucy, pray do not speak in that way; it will all come right. Things always do come right when no one has acted wrongly."

"Yes, when nobody has done wrongly. That's what papa used to call begging the question. But I'll tell you what, Fanny; I will not be beaten. I will either kill myself or get through it. I am so heartily self-ashamed that I owe it to myself to fight the battle out."

"To fight what battle, dearest?"

"This battle. Here, now, at the present moment, I could not meet Lord Lufton. I should have to run like a scared fowl if he were to show himself within the gate; and I should not dare to go out of the house, if I knew that he was in the parish."

"I don't see that, for I am sure you have not betrayed yourself."

"Well, no; as for myself, I believe I have done the lying and the hypocrisy pretty well. But, dearest Fanny, you don't know half; and you cannot and must not know."

"But I thought you said there had been nothing whatever between you."

"Did I? Well, to you I have not said a word that was not true. I said that he had spoken nothing that it was wrong for him to say. It could not be wrong—. But never mind. I'll tell you what I mean to do. I have been thinking of it for the last week—only I shall have to tell Mark."

"If I were you I would tell him all."

"What, Mark! If you do, Fanny, I'll never, never, never speak to you again. Would you—when I have given you all my heart in true sisterly love?"

Mrs. Robarts had to explain that she had not proposed to tell anything to Mark herself, and was persuaded, moreover, to give a solemn promise that she would not tell anything to him unless specially authorized to do so.

"I'll go into a home, I think," continued Lucy. "You know what those homes are?" Mrs. Robarts assured her that she knew very well, and then Lucy went on: "A year ago I should have said that I was the last girl in England to think of such a life, but I do believe now that it would be the best thing for me. And then I'll starve myself, and flog myself, and in that way I'll get back my own mind and my own soul."

"Your own soul, Lucy!" said Mrs. Robarts, in a tone of horror.

"Well, my own heart, if you like it better; but I hate to hear myself talking about hearts. I don't care for my heart. I'd let it go—with this young popinjay lord or anyone else, so that I could read, and talk, and walk, and sleep, and eat, without always feeling that I was wrong here—here—here," and she pressed her hand vehemently against her side. "What is it that I feel, Fanny? Why am I so weak in body that I cannot take exercise? Why cannot I keep my mind on a book for one moment? Why can I not write two sentences together? Why should every mouthful that I eat stick in my throat? Oh, Fanny, is it his legs, think you, or is it his title?"

Through all her sorrow,—and she was very sorrowful,—Mrs. Robarts could not help smiling. And, indeed, there was every now and then something even in Lucy's look that was almost comic. She acted the irony so well with which she strove to throw ridicule on herself! "Do laugh at me," she said. "Nothing on earth will do me so much good as that; nothing, unless it be starvation and a whip. If you would only tell me that I must be a sneak and an idiot to care for a man because he is good-looking and a lord!"

"But that has not been the reason. There is a great deal more in Lord Lufton than that; and since I must speak, dear Lucy, I cannot but say that I should not wonder at your being in love with him, only—only that—"

"Only what? Come, out with it. Do not mince matters, or think that I shall be angry with you because you scold me."

"Only that I should have thought that you would have been too guarded to have—have cared for any gentleman till—till he had shown that he cared for you."

"Guarded! Yes, that's it; that's just the word. But it's he that should have been guarded. He should have had a fire-guard hung before him—or a love-guard, if you will. Guarded! Was I not guarded, till you all would drag me out? Did I want to go there? And when I was there, did I not make a fool of myself, sitting in a corner, and thinking how much better placed I should have been down in the servants' hall. Lady Lufton—she dragged me out, and then cautioned me, and then, then— Why is Lady Lufton to have it all her own way? Why am I to be sacrificed for her? I did not want to know Lady Lufton, or any one belonging to her."

"I cannot think that you have any cause to blame Lady Lufton, nor, perhaps, to blame anybody very much."

"Well, no, it has been all my own fault; though for the life of me, Fanny, going back and back, I cannot see where I took the first false step. I do not know where I went wrong. One wrong thing I did, and it is the only thing that I do not regret."

"What was that, Lucy?"

"I told him a lie."

Mrs. Robarts was altogether in the dark, and feeling that she was so, she knew that she could not give counsel as a friend or a sister. Lucy had begun by declaring—so Mrs. Robarts thought—that nothing had passed between her and Lord Lufton but words of most trivial import, and yet she now accused herself of falsehood, and declared that that falsehood was the only thing which she did not regret!

"I hope not," said Mrs. Robarts. "If you did, you were very unlike yourself."

"But I did, and were he here again, speaking to me in the same way, I should repeat it. I know I should. If I did not, I should have all the world on me. You would frown on me, and be cold. My darling Fanny, how would you look if I really displeasured you?"

"I don't think you will do that, Lucy."

"But if I told him the truth I should, should I not? Speak now. But no, Fanny, you need not speak. It was not the fear of you; no, nor even of her: though Heaven knows that her terrible glumness would be quite unendurable."

"I cannot understand you, Lucy. What truth or what untruth can you have told him if, as you say, there has been nothing between you but ordinary conversation?"

Lucy then got up from the sofa, and walked twice the length of the room before she spoke. Mrs. Robarts had all the ordinary curiosity—I was going to say, of a woman, but I mean to say, of humanity; and she had, moreover, all the love of a sister. She was both curious and anxious, and remained sitting where she was, silent, and with her eyes fixed on her companion.

"Did I say so?" Lucy said at last. "No, Fanny; you have mistaken me: I did not say that. Ah, yes, about the cow and the dog. All that was true. I was telling you of what his soft words had been while I was becoming such a fool. Since that he has said more."

"What more has he said, Lucy?"

"I yearn to tell you, if only I can trust you;" and Lucy knelt down at the feet of Mrs. Robarts, looking up into her face and smiling through the remaining drops of her tears. "I would fain tell you, but I do not know you yet,—whether you are quite true. I could be true,—true against all the world, if my friend told me. I will tell you, Fanny, if you say that you can be true. But if you doubt yourself, if you must whisper all to Mark—then let us be silent."

There was something almost awful in this to Mrs. Robarts. Hitherto, since their marriage, hardly a thought had passed through her mind which she had not shared with her husband. But now all this had come upon her so suddenly, that she was unable to think whether it would be well that she should become the depositary of such a secret,—not to be mentioned to Lucy's brother, not to be mentioned to her own husband. But who ever yet was offered a secret and declined it? Who at least ever declined a love secret? What sister could do so? Mrs. Robarts therefore gave the promise, smoothing Lucy's hair as she did so, and kissing her forehead and looking into her eyes, which, like a rainbow, were the brighter for her tears. "And what has he said to you, Lucy?"

"What? Only this, that he asked me to be his wife."

"Lord Lufton proposed to you?"

"Yes; proposed to me. It is not credible, is it? You cannot bring yourself to believe that such a thing happened, can you?" And Lucy rose again to her feet, as the idea of the scorn with which she felt that others would treat her—with which she herself treated herself—made the blood rise to her cheek. "And yet it is not a dream. I think that it is not a dream. I think that he really did."

"Think, Lucy!"

"Well, I may say that I am sure."

"A gentleman would not make you a formal proposal, and leave you in doubt as to what he meant."

"Oh dear, no. There was no doubt at all of that kind; none in the least. Mr. Smith in asking Miss Jones to do him the honour of becoming Mrs. Smith never spoke more plainly. I was alluding to the possibility of having dreamt it all."

"Lucy!"

"Well, it was not a dream. Here, standing here, on this very spot—on that flower of the carpet—he begged me a dozen times to be his wife. I wonder whether you and Mark would let me cut it out and keep it."

"And what answer did you make to him?"

"I lied to him and told him that I did not love him."

"You refused him?"

"Yes; I refused a live lord. There is some satisfaction in having that to think of, is there not? Fanny, was I wicked to tell that falsehood?"

"And why did you refuse him?"

"Why? Can you ask? Think what it would have been to go down to Framley Court, and to tell her ladyship in the course of conversation that I was engaged to her son. Think of Lady Lufton. But yet it was not that, Fanny. Had I thought that it was good for him, that he would not have repented, I would have braved anything—for his sake. Even your frown, for you would have frowned. You would have thought it sacrilege for me to marry Lord Lufton! You know you would."

Mrs. Robarts hardly knew how to say what she thought, or indeed what she ought to think. It was a matter on which much meditation would be required before she could give advice, and there was Lucy expecting counsel from her at that very moment. If Lord Lufton really loved Lucy Robarts, and was loved by Lucy Robarts, why should not they two become man and wife? And yet she did feel that it would be—perhaps not sacrilege, as Lucy had said, but something almost as troublesome. What would Lady Lufton say, or think, or feel? What would she say, and think, and feel as to that parsonage from which so deadly a blow would fall upon her? Would she not accuse the vicar and the vicar's wife of the blackest ingratitude? Would life be endurable at Framley under such circumstances as those?

"What you tell me so surprises me, that I hardly as yet know how to speak about it," said Mrs. Robarts.

"It was amazing, was it not? He must have been insane at the time; there can be no other excuse made for him. I wonder whether there is anything of that sort in the family?"

"What; madness?" said Mrs. Robarts, quite in earnest.

"Well, don't you think he must have been mad when such an idea as that came into his head? But you don't believe it; I can see that. And yet it is as true as heaven. Standing exactly here, on this spot, he said that he would persevere till I accepted his love. I wonder what made me specially observe that both his feet were within the lines of that division."

"And you would not accept his love?"

"No; I would have nothing to say to it. Look you, I stood here, and putting my hand upon my heart,—for he bade me to do that,—I said that I could not love him."

"And what then?"

"He went away,—with a look as though he were heart-broken. He crept away slowly, saying that he was the most wretched soul alive. For a minute I believed him, and could almost have called him back. But, no, Fanny; do not think that I am over proud, or conceited about my conquest. He had not reached the gate before he was thanking God for his escape."

"That I do not believe."

"But I do; and I thought of Lady Lufton too. How could I bear that she should scorn me, and accuse me of stealing her son's heart? I know that it is better as it is; but tell me— is a falsehood always wrong, or can it be possible that the end should justify the means? Ought I to have told him the truth, and to have let him know that I could almost kiss the ground on which he stood?"

This was a question for the doctors which Mrs. Robarts would not take upon herself to answer. She would not make that falsehood matter of accusation, but neither would she pronounce for it any absolution. In that matter Lucy must regulate her own conscience. "And what shall I do next?" said Lucy, still speaking in a tone that was half tragic and half jeering.

"Do?" said Mrs. Robarts.

"Yes, something must be done. If I were a man I should go to Switzerland, of course; or, as the case is a bad one, perhaps as far as Hungary. What is it that girls do? they don't die now-a-days, I believe."

"Lucy, I do not believe that you care for him one jot. If you were in love you would not speak of it like that."

"There, there. That's my only hope. If I could laugh at myself till it had become incredible to you, I also, by degrees, should cease to believe that I had cared for him. But, Fanny, it is very hard. If I were to starve, and rise before daybreak, and pinch myself, or do some nasty work,—clean the pots and pans and the candlesticks; that I think would do the most good. I have got a piece of sack-cloth, and I mean to wear that, when I have made it up."

"You are joking now, Lucy, I know."

"No, by my word; not in the spirit of what I am saying. How shall I act upon my heart, if I do not do it through the blood and the flesh?"

"Do you not pray that God will give you strength to bear these troubles?"

"But how is one to word one's prayer, or how even to word one's wishes? I do not know what is the wrong that I have done. I say it boldly; in this matter I cannot see my own fault. I have simply found that I have been a fool."

It was now quite dark in the room, or would have been so to any one entering it afresh. They had remained there talking till their eyes had become accustomed to the gloom, and would still have remained, had they not suddenly been disturbed by the sound of a horse's feet.

"There is Mark," said Fanny, jumping up and running to the bell, that lights might be ready when he should enter.

"I thought he remained in Barchester to-night."

"And so did I; but he said it might be doubtful. What shall we do if he has not dined?"

That, I believe, is always the first thought in the mind of a good wife when her husband returns home. Has he had his dinner? What can I give him for dinner? Will he like his dinner? Oh dear, oh dear! there is nothing in the house but cold mutton. But on this occasion the lord of the mansion had dined, and came home radiant with good-humour, and owing, perhaps, a little of his radiance to the dean's claret. "I have told them," said he, "that they may keep possession of the house for the next two months, and they have agreed to that arrangement."

"That is very pleasant," said Mrs. Robarts.

"And I don't think we shall have so much trouble about the dilapidations after all."

"I am very glad of that," said Mrs. Robarts. But nevertheless she was thinking much more of Lucy than of the house in Barchester Close.

"You won't betray me," said Lucy, as she gave her sister-in-law a parting kiss at night.

"No; not unless you give me permission."

"Ah; I shall never do that."

CHAPTER XXVII.

SOUTH AUDLEY STREET.

The Duke of Omnium had notified to Mr. Fothergill his wish that some arrangement should be made about the Chaldicotes mortgages, and Mr. Fothergill had understood what the duke meant as well as though his instructions had been written down with all a lawyer's verbosity. The duke's meaning was this, that Chaldicotes was to be swept up and garnered, and made part and parcel of the Gatherum property. It had seemed to the duke that that affair between his friend and Miss Dunstable was hanging fire, and, therefore, it would be well that Chaldicotes should be swept up and garnered. And, moreover, tidings had come into the western division of the county that young Frank Gresham of Boxall Hill was in treaty with the Government for the purchase of all that Crown property called the Chace of Chaldicotes. It had been offered to the duke, but the duke had given no definite answer. Had he got his money back from Mr. Sowerby, he could have forestalled Mr. Gresham; but now that did not seem to be probable, and his grace was resolved that either the one property or the other should be duly garnered. Therefore Mr. Fothergill went up to town, and therefore Mr. Sowerby was, most unwillingly, compelled to have a business interview with Mr. Fothergill. In the meantime, since last we saw him, Mr. Sowerby had learned from his sister the answer which Miss Dunstable had given to his proposition, and knew that he had no further hope in that direction.

There was no further hope thence of absolute deliverance, but there had been a tender of money services. To give Mr. Sowerby his due, he had at once declared that it would be quite out of the question that he should now receive any assistance of that sort from Miss Dunstable; but his sister had explained to him that it would be a mere business transaction; that Miss Dunstable would receive her interest; and that, if she would be content with four per cent., whereas the duke received five, and other creditors six, seven, eight, ten, and heaven only knows how much more, it might be well for all parties. He, himself, understood, as well as Fothergill had done, what was the meaning of the duke's message. Chaldicotes was to be gathered up and garnered, as had been done with so many another fair property lying in those regions. It was to be swallowed whole, and the master was to walk out from his old family hall, to leave the old woods that he loved, to give up utterly to another the parks and paddocks and pleasant places which he had known from his earliest infancy, and owned from his earliest manhood.

There can be nothing more bitter to a man than such a surrender. What, compared to this, can be the loss of wealth to one who has himself made it, and brought it together, but has never actually seen it with his bodily eyes? Such wealth has come by one chance, and goes by another: the loss of it is part of the game which the man is playing; and if he cannot lose as well as win, he is a poor, weak, cowardly creature. Such men, as a rule, do know how to bear a mind fairly equal to adversity. But to have squandered the acres which have descended from generation to generation; to be the member of one's family that has ruined that family; to have swallowed up in one's own maw all that should have graced one's children, and one's grandchildren! It seems to me that the misfortunes of this world can hardly go beyond that!

Mr. Sowerby, in spite of his recklessness and that dare-devil gaiety which he knew so well how to wear and use, felt all this as keenly as any man could feel it. It had been absolutely his own fault. The acres had come to him all his own, and now, before his death, every one of them would have gone bodily into that greedy maw. The duke had bought up nearly all the debts which had been secured upon the property, and now could make a clean sweep of it. Sowerby, when he received that message from Mr. Fothergill, knew well that this was intended; and he knew well also, that when once he should cease to be Mr. Sowerby of Chaldicotes, he need never again hope to be returned as member for West Barsetshire. This world would for him be all over. And what must such a man feel when he reflects that this world is for him all over?

On the morning in question he went to his appointment, still bearing a cheerful countenance. Mr. Fothergill, when in town on such business as this, always had a room at his service in the house of Messrs. Gumption and Gagebee, the duke's London law agents, and it was thither that Mr. Sowerby had been summoned. The house of business of Messrs. Gumption and Gagebee was in South Audley Street; and it may be said that there was no spot on the whole earth which Mr. Sowerby so hated as he did the gloomy, dingy back sitting-room up-stairs in that house. He had been there very often, but had never been there without annoyance. It was a horrid torture-chamber, kept for such dread purposes as these, and no doubt had been furnished, and papered, and curtained with the express object of finally breaking down the spirits of such poor country gentlemen as chanced to be involved. Everything was of a brown crimson,—of a crimson that had become brown. Sunlight, real genial light of the sun, never made its way there, and no amount of candles could illumine the gloom of that brownness. The windows were never washed; the ceiling was of a dark brown; the old Turkey carpet was thick with dust, and brown withal. The ungainly office-table, in the middle of the room, had been covered with black leather, but that was now brown. There was a bookcase full of dingy brown law books in a recess on one side of the fireplace, but no one had touched them for years, and over the chimney-piece hung some old legal pedigree table, black with soot. Such was the room which Mr. Fothergill always used in the business house of Messrs. Gumption and Gagebee, in South Audley Street, near to Park Lane.

I once heard this room spoken of by an old friend of mine, one Mr. Gresham of Greshamsbury, the father of Frank Gresham, who was now about to purchase that part of the Chace of Chaldicotes which belonged to the Crown. He also had had evil days, though now happily they were past and gone; and he, too, had sat in that room, and listened to the voice of men who were powerful over his property, and intended to use that power. The idea which he left on my mind was much the same as that which I had entertained, when a boy, of a certain room in the castle of Udolpho. There was a chair in that Udolpho room in which those who sat were dragged out limb by limb, the head one way and the legs another; the fingers were dragged off from the hands, and the teeth out from the jaws, and the hair off the head, and the flesh from the bones, and the joints from their sockets, till there was nothing left but a lifeless trunk seated in the chair. Mr. Gresham, as he told me, always sat in the same seat, and the tortures he suffered when so seated, the dislocations of his property which he was forced to discuss, the operations on his very self which he was forced to witness, made me regard that room as worse than the chamber of Udolpho. He, luckily—a rare instance of good fortune—had lived to see all his bones and joints put together again, and flourishing soundly; but he never could speak of the room without horror.

"No consideration on earth," he once said to me, very solemnly,—"I say none, should make me again enter that room." And indeed this feeling was so strong with him, that from the day when his affairs took a turn he would never even walk down South Audley Street. On the morning in question into this torture-chamber Mr. Sowerby went, and there, after some two or three minutes, he was joined by Mr. Fothergill.

Mr. Fothergill was, in one respect, like to his friend Sowerby. He enacted two altogether different persons on occasions which were altogether different. Generally speaking, with the world at large, he was a jolly, rollicking, popular man, fond of eating and drinking, known to be devoted to the duke's interests, and supposed to be somewhat unscrupulous, or at any rate hard, when they were concerned; but in other respects a good-natured fellow; and there was a report about that he had once lent somebody money, without charging him interest or taking security. On the present occasion Sowerby saw at a glance that he had come thither with all the aptitudes and appurtenances of his business about him. He walked into the room with a short, quick step; there was no smile on his face as he shook hands with his old friend; he brought with him a box laden with papers and parchments, and he had not been a minute in the room before he was seated in one of the old dingy chairs.

"How long have you been in town, Fothergill?" said Sowerby, still standing with his back against the chimney. He had resolved on only one thing—that nothing should induce him to touch, look at, or listen to any of those papers. He knew well enough that no good would come of that. He also had his own lawyer, to see that he was pilfered according to rule.

"How long? Since the day before yesterday. I never was so busy in my life. The duke, as usual, wants to have everything done at once."

"If he wants to have all that I owe him paid at once, he is like to be out in his reckoning."

"Ah, well; I'm glad you are ready to come quickly to business, because it's always best. Won't you come and sit down here?"

"No, thank you; I'll stand."

"But we shall have to go through these figures, you know."

"Not a figure, Fothergill. What good would it do? None to me, and none to you either, as I take it; if there is anything wrong, Potter's fellows will find it out. What is it the duke wants?"

"Well; to tell the truth, he wants his money."

"In one sense, and that the main sense, he has got it. He gets his interest regularly, does not he?"

"Pretty well for that, seeing how times are. But, Sowerby, that's nonsense. You understand the duke as well as I do, and you know very well what he wants. He has given you time, and if you had taken any steps towards getting the money, you might have saved the property."

"A hundred and eighty thousand pounds! What steps could I take to get that? Fly a bill, and let Tozer have it to get cash on it in the City!"

"We hoped you were going to marry."

"That's all off."

"Then I don't think you can blame the duke for looking for his own. It does not suit him to have so large a sum standing out any longer. You see, he wants land, and will have it. Had you paid off what you owed him, he would have purchased the Crown property; and now, it seems, young Gresham has bid against him, and is to have it. This has riled him, and I may as well tell you fairly, that he is determined to have either money or marbles."

"You mean that I am to be dispossessed."

"Well, yes; if you choose to call it so. My instructions are to foreclose at once."

"Then I must say the duke is treating me most uncommonly ill."

"Well, Sowerby, I can't see it."

"I can, though. He has his money like clock-work; and he has bought up these debts from persons who would have never disturbed me as long as they got their interest."

"Haven't you had the seat?"

"The seat! and is it expected that I am to pay for that?"

"I don't see that any one is asking you to pay for it. You are like a great many other people that I know. You want to eat your cake and have it. You have been eating it for the last twenty years, and now you think yourself very ill-used because the duke wants to have his turn."

"I shall think myself very ill-used if he sells me out—worse than ill-used. I do not want to use strong language, but it will be more than ill-usage. I can hardly believe that he really means to treat me in that way."

"It is very hard that he should want his own money!"

"It is not his money that he wants. It is my property."

"And has he not paid for it? Have you not had the price of your property? Now, Sowerby, it is of no use for you to be angry; you have known for the last three years what was coming on you as well as I did. Why should the duke lend you money without an object? Of course he has his own views. But I do say this; he has not hurried you; and had you been able to do anything to save the place you might have done it. You have had time enough to look about you."

Sowerby still stood in the place in which he had first fixed himself, and now for awhile he remained silent. His face was very stern, and there was in his countenance none of those winning looks which often told so powerfully with his young friends,—which had caught Lord Lufton and had charmed Mark Robarts. The world was going against him, and things around him were coming to an end. He was beginning to perceive that he had in truth eaten his cake, and that there was now little left for him to do,—unless he chose to blow out his brains. He had said to Lord Lufton that a man's back should be broad enough for any burden with which he himself might load it. Could he now boast that his back was broad enough and strong enough for this burden? But he had even then, at that bitter moment, a strong remembrance that it behoved him still to be a man. His final ruin was coming on him, and he would soon be swept away out of the knowledge and memory of those with whom he had lived. But, nevertheless, he would bear himself well to the last. It was true that he had made his own bed, and he understood the justice which required him to lie upon it.

During all this time Fothergill occupied himself with the papers. He continued to turn over one sheet after another, as though he were deeply engaged in money considerations and calculations. But, in truth, during all that time he did not read a word. There was nothing there for him to read. The reading and the writing, and the arithmetic in such matters, are done by underlings—not by such big men as Mr. Fothergill. His business was to tell Sowerby that he was to go. All those records there were of very little use. The duke had the power; Sowerby knew that the duke had the power; and Fothergill's business was to explain that the duke meant to exercise his power. He was used to the work, and went on turning over the papers and pretending to read them, as though his doing so were of the greatest moment.

"I shall see the duke myself," Mr. Sowerby said at last, and there was something almost dreadful in the sound of his voice.

"You know that the duke won't see you on a matter of this kind. He never speaks to anyone about money; you know that as well as I do."

"By ——, but he shall speak to me. Never speak to anyone about money! Why is he ashamed to speak of it when he loves it so dearly? He shall see me."

"I have nothing further to say, Sowerby. Of course I shan't ask his grace to see you; and if you force your way in on him you know what will happen. It won't be my doing if he is set against you. Nothing that you say to me in that way,—nothing that anybody ever says,—goes beyond myself."

"I shall manage the matter through my own lawyer," said Sowerby; and then he took his hat, and, without uttering another word, left the room.

We know not what may be the nature of that eternal punishment to which those will be doomed who shall be judged to have been evil at the last; but methinks that no more terrible torment can be devised than the memory of self-imposed ruin. What wretchedness can exceed that of remembering from day to day that the race has been all run, and has been altogether lost; that the last chance has gone, and has gone in vain; that the end has come, and with it disgrace, contempt, and self-scorn—disgrace that never can be redeemed, contempt that never can be removed, and self-scorn that will eat into one's vitals for ever?

Mr. Sowerby was now fifty; he had enjoyed his chances in life; and as he walked back, up South Audley Street, he could not but think of the uses he had made of them. He had fallen into the possession of a fine property on the attainment of his manhood; he had been endowed with more than average gifts of intellect; never-failing health had been given to him, and a vision fairly clear in discerning good from evil; and now to what a pass had he brought himself!

And that man Fothergill had put all this before him in so terribly clear a light! Now that the day for his final demolishment had arrived, the necessity that he should be demolished—finished away at once, out of sight and out of mind—had not been softened, or, as it were, half hidden, by any ambiguous phrase. "You have had your cake, and eaten it—eaten it greedily. Is not that sufficient for you? Would you eat your cake twice? Would you have a succession of cakes? No, my friend; there is no succession of these cakes for those who eat them greedily. Your proposition is not a fair one, and we who have the whip-hand of you will not listen to it. Be good enough to vanish. Permit yourself to be swept quietly into the dunghill. All that there was about you of value has departed from you; and allow me to say that you are now—rubbish." And then the ruthless besom comes with irresistible rush, and the rubbish is swept into the pit, there to be hidden for ever from the sight.

And the pity of it is this—that a man, if he will only restrain his greed, may eat his cake and yet have it; ay, and in so doing will have twice more the flavour of the cake than he who with gourmandizing maw will devour his dainty all at once. Cakes in this world will grow by being fed on, if only the feeder be not too insatiate. On all which wisdom Mr. Sowerby pondered with sad heart and very melancholy mind as he walked away from the premises of Messrs. Gumption and Gagebee.

His intention had been to go down to the House after leaving Mr. Fothergill, but the prospect of immediate ruin had been too much for him, and he knew that he was not fit to be seen at once among the haunts of men. And he had intended also to go down to Barchester early on the following morning—only for a few hours, that he might make further arrangements respecting that bill which Robarts had accepted for him. That bill—the second one—had now become due, and Mr. Tozer had been with him.

"Now it ain't no use in life, Mr. Sowerby," Tozer had said. "I ain't got the paper myself, nor didn't 'old it, not two hours. It went away through Tom Tozer; you knows that, Mr. Sowerby, as well as I do."

Now, whenever Tozer, Mr. Sowerby's Tozer, spoke of Tom Tozer, Mr. Sowerby knew that seven devils were being evoked, each worse than the first devil. Mr. Sowerby did feel something like sincere regard, or rather love, for that poor parson whom he had inveigled into mischief, and would fain save him, if it were possible, from the Tozer fang. Mr. Forrest, of the Barchester bank, would probably take up that last five hundred pound bill, on behalf of Mr. Robarts,—only it would be needful that he, Sowerby, should run down and see that this was properly done. As to the other bill—the former and lesser one—as to that, Mr. Tozer would probably be quiet for a while.

Such had been Sowerby's programme for these two days; but now—what further possibility was there now that he should care for Robarts, or any other human being; he that was to be swept at once into the dung-heap?

In this frame of mind he walked up South Audley Street, and crossed one side of Grosvenor Square, and went almost mechanically into Green Street. At the farther end of Green Street, near to Park Lane, lived Mr. and Mrs. Harold Smith.

CHAPTER XXVIII.

DR. THORNE.

When Miss Dunstable met her friends, the Greshams—young Frank Gresham and his wife—at Gatherum Castle, she immediately asked after one Dr. Thorne, who was Mrs. Gresham's uncle. Dr. Thorne was an old bachelor, in whom both as a man and a doctor Miss Dunstable was inclined to place much confidence. Not that she had ever entrusted the cure of her bodily ailments to Dr. Thorne—for she kept a doctor of her own, Dr. Easyman, for this purpose—and it may moreover be said that she rarely had bodily ailments requiring the care of any doctor. But she always spoke of Dr. Thorne among her friends as a man of wonderful erudition and judgment; and had once or twice asked and acted on his advice in matters of much moment. Dr. Thorne was not a man accustomed to the London world; he kept no house there, and seldom even visited the metropolis; but Miss Dunstable had known him at Greshamsbury, where he lived, and there had for some months past grown up a considerable intimacy between them. He was now staying at the house of his niece, Mrs. Gresham; but the chief reason of his coming up had been a desire expressed by Miss Dunstable, that he should do so. She had wished for his advice; and at the instigation of his niece he had visited London and given it.

The special piece of business as to which Dr. Thorne had thus been summoned from the bedsides of his country patients, and especially from the bedside of Lady Arabella Gresham, to whose son his niece was married, related to certain large money interests, as to which one might have imagined that Dr. Thorne's advice would not be peculiarly valuable. He had never been much versed in such matters on his own account, and was knowing neither in the ways of the share market, nor in the prices of land. But Miss Dunstable was a lady accustomed to have her own way, and to be indulged in her own wishes without being called on to give adequate reasons for them.

"My dear," she had said to young Mrs. Gresham, "if your uncle don't come up to London now, when I make such a point of it, I shall think that he is a bear and a savage; and I certainly will never speak to him again,—or to Frank—or to you; so you had better see to it." Mrs. Gresham had not probably taken her friend's threat as meaning quite all that it threatened. Miss Dunstable habitually used strong language; and those who knew her well, generally understood when she was to be taken as expressing her thoughts by figures of speech. In this instance she had not meant it all; but, nevertheless, Mrs. Gresham had used violent influence in bringing the poor doctor up to London.

"Besides," said Miss Dunstable, "I have resolved on having the doctor at my conversazione, and if he won't come of himself, I shall go down and fetch him. I have set my heart on trumping my dear friend Mrs. Proudie's best card; so I mean to get everybody!"

The upshot of all this was, that the doctor did come up to town, and remained the best part of a week at his niece's house in Portman Square—to the great disgust of the Lady Arabella, who conceived that she must die if neglected for three days. As to the matter of business, I have no doubt but that he was of great use. He was possessed of common sense and an honest purpose; and I am inclined to think that they are often a sufficient counterpoise to a considerable amount of worldly experience. If one could have the worldly experience also—! True! but then it is so difficult to get everything. But with that special matter of business we need not have any further concern. We will presume it to have been discussed and completed, and will now dress ourselves for Miss Dunstable's conversazione.

But it must not be supposed that she was so poor in genius as to call her party openly by a name borrowed for the nonce from Mrs. Proudie. It was only among her specially intimate friends, Mrs. Harold Smith and some few dozen others, that she indulged in this little joke. There had been nothing in the least pretentious about the card with which she summoned her friends to her house on this occasion. She had merely signified in some ordinary way, that she would be glad to see them as soon after nine o'clock on Thursday evening, the —— instant, as might be convenient. But all the world understood that all the world was to be gathered together at Miss Dunstable's house on the night in question,— that an effort was to be made to bring together people of all classes, gods and giants, saints and sinners, those rabid through the strength of their morality, such as our dear friend Lady Lufton, and those who were rabid in the opposite direction, such as Lady Hartletop, the Duke of Omnium, and Mr. Sowerby. An orthodox martyr had been caught from the East, and an oily latter-day St. Paul from the other side of the water—to the horror and amazement of Archdeacon Grantly, who had come up all the way from Plumstead to be present on the occasion. Mrs. Grantly also had hankered to be there; but when she heard of the presence of the latter-day St. Paul, she triumphed loudly over her husband, who had made no offer to take her. That Lords Brock and De Terrier were to be at the gathering was nothing. The pleasant king of the gods and the courtly chief of the giants could shake hands with each other in any house with the greatest pleasure; but men were to meet who, in reference to each other, could shake nothing but their heads or their fists. Supplehouse was to be there, and Harold Smith, who now hated his enemy with a hatred surpassing that of women—or even of politicians. The minor gods, it was thought, would congregate together in one room, very bitter in their present state of banishment; and the minor giants in another, terribly loud in their triumph. That is the fault of the giants, who, otherwise, are not bad fellows; they are unable to endure the weight of any temporary success. When attempting Olympus—and this work of attempting is doubtless their natural condition—they scratch and scramble, diligently using both toes and fingers, with a mixture of good-humoured virulence and self-satisfied industry that is gratifying to all parties. But whenever their efforts are unexpectedly, and for themselves unfortunately successful, they are so taken aback that they lose the power of behaving themselves with even gigantesque propriety.

Such, so great and so various, was to be the intended gathering at Miss Dunstable's house. She herself laughed, and quizzed herself—speaking of the affair to Mrs. Harold Smith as though it were an excellent joke, and to Mrs. Proudie as though she were simply emulous of rivalling those world-famous assemblies in Gloucester Place; but the town at large knew that an effort was being made, and it was supposed that even Miss Dunstable was somewhat nervous. In spite of her excellent joking it was presumed that she would be unhappy if she failed.

To Mrs. Frank Gresham she did speak with some little seriousness. "But why on earth should you give yourself all this trouble?" that lady had said, when Miss Dunstable owned that she was doubtful, and unhappy in her doubts, as to the coming of one of the great colleagues of Mr. Supplehouse. "When such hundreds are coming, big wigs and little wigs of all shades, what can it matter whether Mr. Towers be there or not?"

But Miss Dunstable had answered almost with a screech,—"My dear, it will be nothing without him. You don't understand; but the fact is, that Tom Towers is everybody and everything at present."

And then, by no means for the first time, Mrs. Gresham began to lecture her friend as to her vanity; in answer to which lecture Miss Dunstable mysteriously hinted, that if she were only allowed her full swing on this occasion,—if all the world would now indulge her, she would— She did not quite say what she would do, but the inference drawn by Mrs. Gresham was this: that if the incense now offered on the altar of Fashion were accepted, Miss Dunstable would at once abandon the pomps and vanities of this wicked world, and all the sinful lusts of the flesh.

"But the doctor will stay, my dear? I hope I may look on that as fixed."

Miss Dunstable, in making this demand on the doctor's time, showed an energy quite equal to that with which she invoked the gods that Tom Towers might not be absent. Now, to tell the truth, Dr. Thorne had at first thought it very unreasonable that he should be asked to remain up in London in order that he might be present at an evening party, and had for a while pertinaciously refused; but when he learned that three or four prime ministers were expected, and that it was possible that even Tom Towers might be there in the flesh, his philosophy also had become weak, and he had written to Lady Arabella to say that his prolonged absence for two days further must be endured, and that the mild tonics, morning and evening, might be continued.

But why should Miss Dunstable be so anxious that Dr. Thorne should be present on this grand occasion? Why, indeed, should she be so frequently inclined to summon him away from his country practice, his compounding board, and his useful ministrations to rural ailments? The doctor was connected with her by no ties of blood. Their friendship, intimate as it was, had as yet been but of short date. She was a very rich woman, capable of purchasing all manner of advice and good counsel, whereas he was so far from being rich, that any continued disturbance to his practice might be inconvenient to him. Nevertheless, Miss Dunstable seemed to have no more compunction in making calls upon his time, than she might have felt had he been her brother. No ideas on this matter suggested themselves to the doctor himself. He was a simple-minded man, taking things as they came, and especially so taking things that came pleasantly. He liked Miss Dunstable, and was gratified by her friendship, and did not think of asking himself whether she had a right to put him to trouble and inconvenience. But such ideas did occur to Mrs. Gresham, the doctor's niece. Had Miss Dunstable any object, and if so, what object? Was it simply veneration for the doctor, or was it caprice? Was it eccentricity—or could it possibly be love?

In speaking of the ages of these two friends it may be said in round terms that the lady was well past forty, and that the gentleman was well past fifty. Under such circumstances could it be love? The lady, too, was one who had had offers almost by the dozen,—offers from men of rank, from men of fashion, and from men of power; from men endowed with personal attractions, with pleasant manners, with cultivated tastes, and with eloquent tongues. Not only had she loved none such, but by none such had she been cajoled into an idea that it was possible that she could love them. That Dr. Thorne's tastes were cultivated, and his manners pleasant, might probably be admitted by three or four old friends in the country who valued him; but the world in London, that world to which Miss Dunstable was accustomed, and which was apparently becoming dearer to her day by day, would not have regarded the doctor as a man likely to become the object of a lady's passion.

But nevertheless the idea did occur to Mrs. Gresham. She had been brought up at the elbow of this country practitioner; she had lived with him as though she had been his daughter; she had been for years the ministering angel of his household; and, till her heart had opened to the natural love of womanhood, all her closest sympathies had been with him. In her eyes the doctor was all but perfect; and it did not seem to her to be out of the question that Miss Dunstable should have fallen in love with her uncle.

Miss Dunstable once said to Mrs. Harold Smith that it was possible that she might marry, the only condition then expressed being this, that the man elected should be one who was quite indifferent as to money. Mrs. Harold Smith, who, by her friends, was presumed to know the world with tolerable accuracy, had replied that such a man Miss Dunstable would never find in this world. All this had passed in that half comic vein of banter which Miss Dunstable so commonly used when conversing with such friends as Mrs. Harold Smith; but she had spoken words of the same import more than once to Mrs. Gresham; and Mrs. Gresham, putting two and two together as women do, had made four of the little sum; and, as the final result of the calculation, determined that Miss Dunstable would marry Dr. Thorne if Dr. Thorne would ask her.

And then Mrs. Gresham began to bethink herself of two other questions. Would it be well that her uncle should marry Miss Dunstable? and if so, would it be possible to induce him to make such a proposition? After the consideration of many pros and cons, and the balancing of very various arguments, Mrs. Gresham thought that the arrangement on the whole might not be a bad one. For Miss Dunstable she herself had a sincere affection, which was shared by her husband. She had often grieved at the sacrifices Miss Dunstable made to the world, thinking that her friend was falling into vanity, indifference, and an ill mode of life; but such a marriage as this would probably cure all that. And then as to Dr. Thorne himself, to whose benefit were of course applied Mrs. Gresham's most earnest thoughts in this matter, she could not but think that he would be happier married than he was single. In point of temper, no woman could stand higher than Miss Dunstable; no one had ever heard of her being in an ill humour; and then though Mrs. Gresham was gifted with a mind which was far removed from being mercenary, it was impossible not to feel that some benefit must accrue from the bride's wealth. Mary Thorne, the present Mrs. Frank Gresham, had herself been a great heiress. Circumstances had weighted her hand with enormous possessions, and hitherto she had not realized the truth of that lesson which would teach us to believe that happiness and riches are incompatible. Therefore she resolved that it might be well if the doctor and Miss Dunstable were brought together.

But could the doctor be induced to make such an offer? Mrs. Gresham acknowledged a terrible difficulty in looking at the matter from that point of view. Her uncle was fond of Miss Dunstable; but she was sure that an idea of such a marriage had never entered his head; that it would be very difficult—almost impossible—to create such an idea; and that if the idea were there, the doctor could hardly be instigated to make the proposition. Looking at the matter as a whole, she feared that the match was not practicable.

On the day of Miss Dunstable's party, Mrs. Gresham and her uncle dined together alone in Portman Square. Mr. Gresham was not yet in Parliament, but an almost immediate vacancy was expected in his division of the county, and it was known that no one could stand against him with any chance of success. This threw him much among the politicians of his party—those giants, namely, whom it would be his business to support—and on this account he was a good deal away from his own house at the present moment.

"Politics make a terrible demand on a man's time," he said to his wife; and then went down to dine at his club in Pall Mall with sundry other young philogeants. On men of that class politics do make a great demand—at the hour of dinner and thereabouts.

"What do you think of Miss Dunstable?" said Mrs. Gresham to her uncle, as they sat together over their coffee. She added nothing to the question, but asked it in all its baldness.

"Think about her!" said the doctor. "Well, Mary; what do you think about her? I dare say we think the same."

"But that's not the question. What do you think about her? Do you think she's honest?"

"Honest? Oh, yes, certainly—very honest, I should say."

"And good-tempered?"

"Uncommonly good-tempered."

"And affectionate?"

"Well; yes,—and affectionate. I should certainly say that she is affectionate."

"I'm sure she's clever."

"Yes, I think she's clever."

"And, and—and womanly in her feelings." Mrs. Gresham felt that she could not quite say lady-like, though she would fain have done so had she dared.

"Oh, certainly," said the doctor. "But, Mary, why are you dissecting Miss Dunstable's character with so much ingenuity?"

"Well, uncle, I will tell you why; because—" and Mrs. Gresham, while she was speaking, got up from her chair, and going round the table to her uncle's side, put her arm round his neck till her face was close to his, and then continued speaking as she stood behind him out of his sight—"because—I think that Miss Dunstable is—is very fond of you; and that it would make her happy if you would—ask her to be your wife."

"Mary!" said the doctor, turning round with an endeavour to look his niece in the face.

"I am quite in earnest, uncle—quite in earnest. From little things that she has said, and little things that I have seen, I do believe what I now tell you."

"And you want me to—"

"Dear uncle; my own one darling uncle, I want you only to do that which will make you—make you happy. What is Miss Dunstable to me compared to you?" And then she stooped down and kissed him.

The doctor was apparently too much astounded by the intimation given him to make any further immediate reply. His niece, seeing this, left him that she might go and dress; and when they met again in the drawing-room Frank Gresham was with them.

CHAPTER XXIX.

MISS DUNSTABLE AT HOME.

Miss Dunstable did not look like a love-lorn maiden, as she stood in a small ante-chamber at the top of her drawing-room stairs receiving her guests. Her house was one of those abnormal mansions, which are to be seen here and there in London, built in compliance rather with the rules of rural architecture, than with those which usually govern the erection of city streets and town terraces. It stood back from its brethren, and alone, so that its owner could walk round it. It was approached by a short carriageway; the chief door was in the back of the building; and the front of the house looked on to one of the parks. Miss Dunstable in procuring it had had her usual luck. It had been built by an eccentric millionaire at an enormous cost; and the eccentric millionaire, after living in it for twelve months, had declared that it did not possess a single comfort, and that it was deficient in most of those details which, in point of house accommodation, are necessary to the very existence of man. Consequently the mansion was sold, and Miss Dunstable was the purchaser. Cranbourn House it had been named, and its present owner had made no change in this respect; but the world at large very generally called it Ointment Hall, and Miss Dunstable herself as frequently used that name for it as any other. It was impossible to quiz Miss Dunstable with any success, because she always joined in the joke herself.

Not a word further had passed between Mrs. Gresham and Dr. Thorne on the subject of their last conversation; but the doctor as he entered the lady's portals amongst a tribe of servants and in a glare of light, and saw the crowd before him and the crowd behind him, felt that it was quite impossible that he should ever be at home there. It might be all right that a Miss Dunstable should live in this way, but it could not be right that the wife of Dr. Thorne should so live. But all this was a matter of the merest speculation, for he was well aware—as he said to himself a dozen times—that his niece had blundered strangely in her reading of Miss Dunstable's character.

When the Gresham party entered the ante-room into which the staircase opened, they found Miss Dunstable standing there surrounded by a few of her most intimate allies. Mrs. Harold Smith was sitting quite close to her; Dr. Easyman was reclining on a sofa against the wall, and the lady who habitually lived with Miss Dunstable was by his side. One or two others were there also, so that a little running conversation was kept up, in order to relieve Miss Dunstable of the tedium which might otherwise be engendered by the work she had in hand. As Mrs. Gresham, leaning on her husband's arm, entered the room, she saw the back of Mrs. Proudie, as that lady made her way through the opposite door, leaning on the arm of the bishop.

Mrs. Harold Smith had apparently recovered from the annoyance which she must no doubt have felt when Miss Dunstable so utterly rejected her suit on behalf of her brother. If any feeling had existed, even for a day, calculated to put a stop to the intimacy between the two ladies, that feeling had altogether died away, for Mrs. Harold Smith was conversing with her friend, quite in the old way. She made some remark on each of the guests as they passed by, and apparently did so in a manner satisfactory to the owner of the house, for Miss Dunstable answered with her kindest smiles, and in that genial, happy tone of voice which gave its peculiar character to her good humour:

"She is quite convinced that you are a mere plagiarist in what you are doing," said Mrs. Harold Smith, speaking of Mrs. Proudie.

"And so I am. I don't suppose there can be anything very original now-a-days about an evening party."

"But she thinks you are copying her."

"And why not? I copy everybody that I see, more or less. You did not at first begin to wear big petticoats out of your own head? If Mrs. Proudie has any such pride as that, pray don't rob her of it. Here's the doctor and the Greshams. Mary, my darling, how are you?" and in spite of all her grandeur of apparel, Miss Dunstable took hold of Mrs. Gresham and kissed her—to the disgust of the dozen-and-a-half of the distinguished fashionable world who were passing up the stairs behind.

The doctor was somewhat repressed in his mode of address by the communication which had so lately been made to him. Miss Dunstable was now standing on the very top of the pinnacle of wealth, and seemed to him to be not only so much above his reach, but also so far removed from his track in life, that he could not in any way put himself on a level with her. He could neither aspire so high nor descend so low; and thinking of this he spoke to Miss Dunstable as though there were some great distance between them,—as though there had been no hours of intimate friendship down at Greshamsbury. There had been such hours, during which Miss Dunstable and Dr. Thorne had lived as though they belonged to the same world: and this at any rate may be said of Miss Dunstable, that she had no idea of forgetting them.

Dr. Thorne merely gave her his hand, and then prepared to pass on.

"Don't go, doctor," she said; "for heaven's sake, don't go yet. I don't know when I may catch you if you get in there. I shan't be able to follow you for the next two hours. Lady Meredith, I am so much obliged to you for coming—your mother will be here, I hope. Oh, I am so glad! From her you know that is quite a favour. You, Sir George, are half a sinner yourself, so I don't think so much about it."

"Oh, quite so," said Sir George; "perhaps rather the largest half."

"The men divide the world into gods and giants," said Miss Dunstable. "We women have our divisions also. We are saints or sinners according to our party. The worst of it is, that we rat almost as often as you do." Whereupon Sir George laughed and passed on.

"I know, doctor, you don't like this kind of thing," she continued, "but there is no reason why you should indulge yourself altogether in your own way, more than another—is there, Frank?"

"I am not so sure but he does like it," said Mr. Gresham. "There are some of your reputed friends whom he owns that he is anxious to see."

"Are there? Then there is some hope of his ratting too. But he'll never make a good staunch sinner; will he, Mary? You're too old to learn new tricks; eh, doctor?"

"I am afraid I am," said the doctor, with a faint laugh.

"Does Dr. Thorne rank himself among the army of saints?" asked Mrs. Harold Smith.

"Decidedly," said Miss Dunstable. "But you must always remember that there are saints of different orders; are there not, Mary? and nobody supposes that the Franciscans and the Dominicans agree very well together. Dr. Thorne does not belong to the school of St. Proudie, of Barchester; he would prefer the priestess whom I see coming round the corner of the staircase, with a very famous young novice at her elbow."

"From all that I can hear, you will have to reckon Miss Grantly among the sinners," said Mrs. Harold Smith—seeing that Lady Lufton with her young friend was approaching—"unless, indeed, you can make a saint of Lady Hartletop."

And then Lady Lufton entered the room, and Miss Dunstable came forward to meet her with more quiet respect in her manner than she had as yet shown to many of her guests. "I am much obliged to you for coming, Lady Lufton," she said, "and the more so, for bringing Miss Grantly with you."

Lady Lufton uttered some pretty little speech, during which Dr. Thorne came up and shook hands with her; as did also Frank Gresham and his wife. There was a county acquaintance between the Framley people and the Greshamsbury people, and therefore there was a little general conversation before Lady Lufton passed out of the small room into what Mrs. Proudie would have called the noble suite of apartments. "Papa will be here," said Miss Grantly; "at least so I understand. I have not seen him yet myself."

"Oh, yes, he has promised me," said Miss Dunstable; "and the archdeacon, I know, will keep his word. I should by no means have the proper ecclesiastical balance without him."

"Papa always does keep his word," said Miss Grantly, in a tone that was almost severe. She had not at all understood poor Miss Dunstable's little joke, or at any rate she was too dignified to respond to it.

"I understand that old Sir John is to accept the Chiltern Hundreds at once," said Lady Lufton, in a half whisper to Frank Gresham. Lady Lufton had always taken a keen interest in the politics of East Barsetshire, and was now desirous of expressing her satisfaction that a Gresham should again sit for the county. The Greshams had been old county members in Barsetshire, time out of mind.

"Oh, yes; I believe so," said Frank, blushing. He was still young enough to feel almost ashamed of putting himself forward for such high honours.

"There will be no contest, of course," said Lady Lufton, confidentially. "There seldom is in East Barsetshire, I am happy to say. But if there were, every tenant at Framley would vote on the right side; I can assure you of that. Lord Lufton was saying so to me only this morning."

Frank Gresham made a pretty little speech in reply, such as young sucking politicians are expected to make; and this, with sundry other small courteous murmurings, detained the Lufton party for a minute or two in the ante-chamber. In the meantime the world was pressing on and passing through to the four or five large reception-rooms—the noble suite, which was already piercing poor Mrs. Proudie's heart with envy to the very core. "These are the sort of rooms," she said to herself unconsciously, "which ought to be provided by the country for the use of its bishops."

"But the people are not brought enough together," she said to her lord.

"No, no; I don't think they are," said the bishop.

"And that is so essential for a conversazione," continued Mrs. Proudie. "Now in Gloucester Place—." But we will not record all her adverse criticisms, as Lady Lufton is waiting for us in the ante-room.

And now another arrival of moment had taken place;—an arrival indeed of very great moment. To tell the truth, Miss Dunstable's heart had been set upon having two special persons; and though no stone had been left unturned,—no stone which could be turned with discretion,—she was still left in doubt as to both these two wondrous potentates. At the very moment of which we are now speaking, light and airy as she appeared to be—for it was her character to be light and airy—her mind was torn with doubts. If the wished-for two would come, her evening would be thoroughly successful; but if not, all her trouble would have been thrown away, and the thing would have been a failure; and there were circumstances connected with the present assembly which made Miss Dunstable very anxious that she should not fail. That the two great ones of the earth were Tom Towers of the *Jupiter*, and the Duke of Omnium, need hardly be expressed in words.

And now, at this very moment, as Lady Lufton was making her civil speeches to young Gresham, apparently in no hurry to move on, and while Miss Dunstable was endeavouring to whisper something into the doctor's ear, which would make him feel himself at home in this new world, a sound was heard which made that lady know that half her wish had at any rate been granted to her. A sound was heard—but only by her own and one other attentive pair of ears. Mrs. Harold Smith had also caught the name, and knew that the duke was approaching.

There was great glory and triumph in this; but why had his grace come at so unchancy a moment? Miss Dunstable had been fully aware of the impropriety of bringing Lady Lufton and the Duke of Omnium into the same house at the same time; but when she had asked Lady Lufton, she had been led to believe that there was no hope of obtaining the duke; and then, when that hope had dawned upon her, she had comforted herself with the reflection that the two suns, though they might for some few minutes be in the same hemisphere, could hardly be expected to clash, or come across each other's orbits. Her rooms were large and would be crowded; the duke would probably do little more than walk through them once, and Lady Lufton would certainly be surrounded by persons of her own class. Thus Miss Dunstable had comforted herself. But now all things were going wrong, and Lady Lufton would find herself in close contiguity to the nearest representative of Satanic agency, which, according to her ideas, was allowed to walk this nether English world of ours. Would she scream? or indignantly retreat out of the house?—or would she proudly raise her head, and with outstretched hand and audible voice, boldly defy the devil and all his works? In thinking of these things as the duke approached Miss Dunstable almost lost her presence of mind.

But Mrs. Harold Smith did not lose hers. "So here at last is the duke," she said, in a tone intended to catch the express attention of Lady Lufton.

Mrs. Smith had calculated that there might still be time for her ladyship to pass on and avoid the interview. But Lady Lufton, if she heard the words, did not completely understand them. At any rate they did not convey to her mind at the moment the meaning they were intended to convey. She paused to whisper a last little speech to Frank Gresham, and then looking round, found that the gentleman who was pressing against her dress was—the Duke of Omnium!

On this great occasion, when the misfortune could no longer be avoided, Miss Dunstable was by no means beneath herself or her character. She deplored the calamity, but she now saw that it was only left to her to make the best of it. The duke had honoured her by coming to her house, and she was bound to welcome him, though in doing so she should bring Lady Lufton to her last gasp.

"Duke," she said, "I am greatly honoured by this kindness on the part of your grace. I hardly expected that you would be so good to me."

"The goodness is all on the other side," said the duke, bowing over her hand.

And then in the usual course of things this would have been all. The duke would have walked on and shown himself, would have said a word or two to Lady Hartletop, to the bishop, to Mr. Gresham, and such like, and would then have left the rooms by another way, and quietly escaped. This was the duty expected from him, and this he would have done, and the value of the party would have been increased thirty per cent. by such doing; but now, as it was, the news-mongers of the West End were likely to get much more out of him.

Circumstances had so turned out that he had absolutely been pressed close against Lady Lufton, and she, when she heard the voice, and was made positively acquainted with the fact of the great man's presence by Miss Dunstable's words, turned round quickly, but still with much feminine dignity, removing her dress from the contact. In doing this she was brought absolutely face to face with the duke, so that each could not but look full at the other. "I beg your pardon," said the duke. They were the only words that had ever passed between them, nor have they spoken to each other since; but simple as they were, accompanied by the little by-play of the speakers, they gave rise to a considerable amount of ferment in the fashionable world. Lady Lufton, as she retreated back on to Dr. Easyman, curtseyed low; she curtseyed low and slowly, and with a haughty arrangement of her drapery that was all her own; but the curtsey, though it was eloquent, did not say half so much,—did not reprobate the habitual iniquities of the duke with a voice nearly as potent as that which was expressed in the gradual fall of her eye and the gradual pressure of her lips. When she commenced her curtsey she was looking full in her foe's face. By the time that she had completed it her eyes were turned upon the ground, but there was an ineffable amount of scorn expressed in the lines of her mouth. She spoke no word, and retreated, as modest virtue and feminine weakness must ever retreat, before barefaced vice and virile power; but nevertheless she was held by all the world to have had the best of the encounter. The duke, as he begged her pardon, wore in his countenance that expression of modified sorrow which is common to any gentleman who is supposed by himself to have incommoded a lady. But over and above this,—or rather under it,—there was a slight smile of derision, as though it were impossible for him to look upon the bearing of Lady Lufton without some amount of ridicule. All this was legible to eyes so keen as those of Miss Dunstable and Mrs. Harold Smith, and the duke was known to be a master of this silent inward sarcasm; but even by them,—by Miss Dunstable and Mrs. Harold Smith,—it was admitted that Lady Lufton had conquered. When her ladyship again looked up, the duke had passed on; she then resumed the care of Miss Grantly's hand, and followed in among the company.

"That is what I call unfortunate," said Miss Dunstable, as soon as both belligerents had departed from the field of battle. "The fates sometimes will be against one."

"But they have not been at all against you here," said Mrs. Harold Smith. "If you could arrive at her ladyship's private thoughts to-morrow morning, you would find her to be quite happy in having met the duke. It will be years before she has done boasting of her triumph, and it will be talked of by the young ladies of Framley for the next three generations."

The Gresham party, including Dr. Thorne, had remained in the ante-chamber during the battle. The whole combat did not occupy above two minutes, and the three of them were hemmed off from escape by Lady Lufton's retreat into Dr. Easyman's lap; but now they, too, essayed to pass on.

"What, you will desert me," said Miss Dunstable. "Very well; but I shall find you out by-and-by. Frank, there is to be some dancing in one of the rooms,—just to distinguish the affair from Mrs. Proudie's conversazione. It would be stupid, you know, if all conversaziones were alike; wouldn't it? So I hope you will go and dance."

"There will, I presume, be another variation at feeding time," said Mrs. Harold Smith.

"Oh, yes; certainly; I am the most vulgar of all wretches in that respect. I do love to set people eating and drinking.—Mr. Supplehouse, I am delighted to see you; but do tell me—" and then she whispered with great energy into the ear of Mr. Supplehouse, and Mr. Supplehouse again whispered into her ear. "You think he will, then?" said Miss Dunstable.

Mr. Supplehouse assented; he did think so; but he had no warrant for stating the circumstance as a fact. And then he passed on, hardly looking at Mrs. Harold Smith as he passed.

"What a hang-dog countenance he has," said that lady.

"Ah! you're prejudiced, my dear, and no wonder; as for myself I always liked Supplehouse. He means mischief; but then mischief is his trade, and he does not conceal it. If I were a politician I should as soon think of being angry with Mr. Supplehouse for turning against me as I am now with a pin for pricking me. It's my own awkwardness, and I ought to have known how to use the pin more craftily."

"But you must detest a man who professes to stand by his party, and then does his best to ruin it."

"So many have done that, my dear; and with much more success than Mr. Supplehouse! All is fair in love and war,—why not add politics to the list? If we could only agree to do that, it would save us from such a deal of heartburning, and would make none of us a bit the worse."

Miss Dunstable's rooms, large as they were—"a noble suite of rooms certainly, though perhaps a little too—too—too scattered, we will say, eh, bishop?"—were now nearly full, and would have been inconveniently crowded, were it not that many who came only remained for half-an-hour or so. Space, however, had been kept for the dancers—much to Mrs. Proudie's consternation. Not that she disapproved of dancing in London, as a rule; but she was indignant that the laws of a conversazione, as re-established by herself in the fashionable world, should be so violently infringed.

"Conversaziones will come to mean nothing," she said to the bishop, putting great stress on the latter word, "nothing at all, if they are to be treated in this way."

"No, they won't; nothing in the least," said the bishop.

"Dancing may be very well in its place," said Mrs. Proudie.

"I have never objected to it myself; that is, for the laity," said the bishop.

"But when people profess to assemble for higher objects," said Mrs. Proudie, "they ought to act up to their professions."

"Otherwise they are no better than hypocrites," said the bishop.

"A spade should be called a spade," said Mrs. Proudie.

"Decidedly," said the bishop, assenting.

"And when I undertook the trouble and expense of introducing conversaziones," continued Mrs. Proudie, with an evident feeling that she had been ill-used, "I had no idea of seeing the word so—so—so misinterpreted;" and then observing certain desirable acquaintances at the other side of the room, she went across, leaving the bishop to fend for himself.

Lady Lufton, having achieved her success, passed on to the dancing, whither it was not probable that her enemy would follow her, and she had not been there very long before she was joined by her son. Her heart at the present moment was not quite satisfied at the state of affairs with reference to Griselda. She had gone so far as to tell her young friend what were her own wishes; she had declared her desire that Griselda should become her daughter-in-law; but in answer to this Griselda herself had declared nothing. It was, to be sure, no more than natural that a young lady so well brought up as Miss Grantly should show no signs of a passion till she was warranted in showing them by the proceedings of the gentleman; but notwithstanding this—fully aware as she was of the propriety of such reticence—Lady Lufton did think that to her Griselda might have spoken some word evincing that the alliance would be satisfactory to her. Griselda, however, had spoken no such word, nor had she uttered a syllable to show that she would accept Lord Lufton if he did offer. Then again she had uttered no syllable to show that she would not accept him; but, nevertheless, although she knew that the world had been talking about her and Lord Dumbello, she stood up to dance with the future marquess on every possible occasion. All this did give annoyance to Lady Lufton, who began to bethink herself that if she could not quickly bring her little plan to a favourable issue, it might be well for her to wash her hands of it. She was still anxious for the match on her son's account. Griselda would, she did not doubt, make a good wife; but Lady Lufton was not so sure as she once had been that she herself would be able to keep up so strong a feeling for her daughter-in-law as she had hitherto hoped to do.

"Ludovic, have you been here long?" she said, smiling as she always did smile when her eyes fell upon her son's face.

"This instant arrived; and I hurried on after you, as Miss Dunstable told me that you were here. What a crowd she has! Did you see Lord Brock?"

"I did not observe him."

"Or Lord De Terrier? I saw them both in the centre room."

"Lord De Terrier did me the honour of shaking hands with me as I passed through."

"I never saw such a mixture of people. There is Mrs. Proudie going out of her mind because you are all going to dance."

"The Miss Proudies dance," said Griselda Grantly.

"But not at conversaziones. You don't see the difference. And I saw Spermoil there, looking as pleased as Punch. He had quite a circle of his own round him, and was chattering away as though he were quite accustomed to the wickednesses of the world."

"There certainly are people here whom one would not have wished to meet, had one thought of it," said Lady Lufton, mindful of her late engagement.

"But it must be all right, for I walked up the stairs with the archdeacon. That is an absolute proof, is it not, Miss Grantly?"

"I have no fears. When I am with your mother I know I must be safe."

"I am not so sure of that," said Lord Lufton, laughing. "Mother, you hardly know the worst of it yet. Who is here, do you think?"

"I know whom you mean; I have seen him," said Lady Lufton, very quietly.

"We came across him just at the top of the stairs," said Griselda, with more animation in her face than ever Lord Lufton had seen there before.

"What; the duke?"

"Yes, the duke," said Lady Lufton. "I certainly should not have come had I expected to be brought in contact with that man. But it was an accident, and on such an occasion as this it could not be helped."

Lord Lufton at once perceived, by the tone of his mother's voice and by the shades of her countenance that she had absolutely endured some personal encounter with the duke, and also that she was by no means so indignant at the occurrence as might have been expected. There she was, still in Miss Dunstable's house, and expressing no anger as to Miss Dunstable's conduct. Lord Lufton could hardly have been more surprised had he seen the duke handing his mother down to supper; he said, however, nothing further on the subject.

"Are you going to dance, Ludovic?" said Lady Lufton.

"Well, I am not sure that I do not agree with Mrs. Proudie in thinking that dancing would contaminate a conversazione. What are your ideas, Miss Grantly?"

Griselda was never very good at a joke, and imagined that Lord Lufton wanted to escape the trouble of dancing with her. This angered her. For the only species of love-making, or flirtation, or sociability between herself as a young lady, and any other self as a young gentleman, which recommended itself to her taste, was to be found in the amusement of dancing. She was altogether at variance with Mrs. Proudie on this matter, and gave Miss Dunstable great credit for her innovation. In society Griselda's toes were more serviceable to her than her tongue, and she was to be won by a rapid twirl much more probably than by a soft word. The offer of which she would approve would be conveyed by two all but breathless words during a spasmodic pause in a waltz; and then as she lifted up her arm to receive the accustomed support at her back, she might just find power enough to say, "You—must ask—papa." After that she would not care to have the affair mentioned till everything was properly settled.

"I have not thought about it," said Griselda, turning her face away from Lord Lufton.

It must not, however, be supposed that Miss Grantly had not thought about Lord Lufton, or that she had not considered how great might be the advantage of having Lady Lufton on her side if she made up her mind that she did wish to become Lord Lufton's wife. She knew well that now was her time for a triumph, now in this very first season of her acknowledged beauty; and she knew also that young, good-looking bachelor lords do not grow on hedges like blackberries. Had Lord Lufton offered to her, she would have accepted him at once without any remorse as to the greater glories which might appertain to a future Marchioness of Hartletop. In that direction she was not without sufficient wisdom. But then Lord Lufton had not offered to her, nor given any signs that he intended to do so; and to give Griselda Grantly her due, she was not a girl to make a first overture. Neither had Lord Dumbello offered; but he had given signs,—dumb signs, such as birds give to each other, quite as intelligible as verbal signs to a girl who preferred the use of her toes to that of her tongue.

"I have not thought about it," said Griselda, very coldly, and at that moment a gentleman stood before her and asked her hand for the next dance. It was Lord Dumbello; and Griselda, making no reply except by a slight bow, got up and put her hand within her partner's arm.

"Shall I find you here, Lady Lufton, when we have done?" she said; and then started off among the dancers. When the work before one is dancing the proper thing for a gentleman to do is, at any rate, to ask a lady; this proper thing Lord Lufton had omitted, and now the prize was taken away from under his very nose.

There was clearly an air of triumph about Lord Dumbello as he walked away with the beauty. The world had been saying that Lord Lufton was to marry her, and the world had also been saying that Lord Dumbello admired her. Now this had angered Lord Dumbello, and made him feel as though he walked about, a mark of scorn, as a disappointed suitor. Had it not been for Lord Lufton, perhaps he would not have cared so much for Griselda Grantly; but circumstances had so turned out that he did care for her, and felt it to be incumbent upon him as the heir to a marquisate to obtain what he wanted, let who would have a hankering after the same article. It is in this way that pictures are so well sold at auctions; and Lord Dumbello regarded Miss Grantly as being now subject to the auctioneer's hammer, and conceived that Lord Lufton was bidding against him. There was, therefore, an air of triumph about him as he put his arm round Griselda's waist and whirled her up and down the room in obedience to the music.

Lady Lufton and her son were left together looking at each other. Of course he had intended to ask Griselda to dance, but it cannot be said that he very much regretted his disappointment. Of course also Lady Lufton had expected that her son and Griselda would stand up together, and she was a little inclined to be angry with her *protégée*.

"I think she might have waited a minute," said Lady Lufton.

"But why, mother? There are certain things for which no one ever waits: to give a friend, for instance, the first passage through a gate out hunting, and such like. Miss Grantly was quite right to take the first that offered."

Lady Lufton had determined to learn what was to be the end of this scheme of hers. She could not have Griselda always with her, and if anything were to be arranged it must be arranged now, while both of them were in London. At the close of the season Griselda would return to Plumstead, and Lord Lufton would go—nobody as yet knew where. It would be useless to look forward to further opportunities. If they did not contrive to love each other now, they would never do so. Lady Lufton was beginning to fear that her plan would not work, but she made up her mind that she would learn the truth then and there,—at least as far as her son was concerned.

"Oh, yes; quite so;—if it is equal to her with which she dances," said Lady Lufton.

"Quite equal, I should think—unless it be that Dumbello is longer-winded than I am."

"I am sorry to hear you speak of her in that way, Ludovic."

"Why sorry, mother?"

"Because I had hoped—that you and she would have liked each other." This she said in a serious tone of voice, tender and sad, looking up into his face with a plaintive gaze, as though she knew that she were asking of him some great favour.

"Yes, mother, I have known that you have wished that."

"You have known it, Ludovic!"

"Oh, dear, yes; you are not at all sharp at keeping your secrets from me. And, mother, at one time, for a day or so, I thought that I could oblige you. You have been so good to me, that I would almost do anything for you."

"Oh, no, no, no," she said, deprecating his praise, and the sacrifice which he seemed to offer of his own hopes and aspirations. "I would not for worlds have you do so for my sake. No mother ever had a better son, and my only ambition is for your happiness."

"But, mother, she would not make me happy. I was mad enough for a moment to think that she could do so—for a moment I did think so. There was one occasion on which I would have asked her to take me, but—"

"But what, Ludovic?"

"Never mind; it passed away; and now I shall never ask her. Indeed I do not think she would have me. She is ambitious, and flying at higher game than I am. And I must say this for her, that she knows well what she is doing, and plays her cards as though she had been born with them in her hand."

"You will never ask her?"

"No, mother; had I done so, it would have been for love of you—only for love of you."

"I would not for worlds that you should do that."

"Let her have Dumbello; she will make an excellent wife for him, just the wife that he will want. And you, you will have been so good to her in assisting her to such a matter."

"But, Ludovic, I am so anxious to see you settled."

"All in good time, mother!"

"Ah, but the good time is passing away. Years run so very quickly. I hope you think about marrying, Ludovic."

"But, mother, what if I brought you a wife that you did not approve?"

"I will approve of any one that you love; that is—"

"That is, if you love her also; eh, mother?"

"But I rely with such confidence on your taste. I know that you can like no one that is not lady-like and good."

"Lady-like and good! Will that suffice?" said he, thinking of Lucy Robarts.

"Yes; it will suffice, if you love her. I don't want you to care for money. Griselda will have a fortune that would have been convenient; but I do not wish you to care for that." And thus, as they stood together in Miss Dunstable's crowded room, the mother and son settled between themselves that the Lufton-Grantly alliance treaty was not to be ratified. "I suppose I must let Mrs. Grantly know," said Lady Lufton to herself, as Griselda returned to her side. There had not been above a dozen words spoken between Lord Dumbello and his partner, but that young lady also had now fully made up her mind that the treaty above mentioned should never be brought into operation.

We must go back to our hostess, whom we should not have left for so long a time, seeing that this chapter is written to show how well she could conduct herself in great emergencies. She had declared that after awhile she would be able to leave her position near the entrance door, and find out her own peculiar friends among the crowd; but the opportunity for doing so did not come till very late in the evening. There was a continuation of arrivals; she was wearied to death with making little speeches, and had more than once declared that she must depute Mrs. Harold Smith to take her place.

That lady stuck to her through all her labours with admirable constancy, and made the work bearable. Without some such constancy on a friend's part, it would have been unbearable. And it must be acknowledged that this was much to the credit of Mrs. Harold Smith. Her own hopes with reference to the great heiress had all been shattered, and her answer had been given to her in very plain language. But, nevertheless, she was true to her friendship, and was almost as willing to endure fatigue on the occasion as though she had a sister-in-law's right in the house.

At about one o'clock her brother came. He had not yet seen Miss Dunstable since the offer had been made, and had now with difficulty been persuaded by his sister to show himself.

"What can be the use?" said he. "The game is up with me now;"—meaning, poor, ruined ne'er-do-well, not only that that game with Miss Dunstable was up, but that the great game of his whole life was being brought to an uncomfortable termination.

"Nonsense," said his sister. "Do you mean to despair because a man like the Duke of Omnium wants his money? What has been good security for him will be good security for another;" and then Mrs. Harold Smith made herself more agreeable than ever to Miss Dunstable.

When Miss Dunstable was nearly worn out, but was still endeavouring to buoy herself up by a hope of the still-expected great arrival—for she knew that the hero would show himself only at a very late hour if it were to be her good fortune that he showed himself at all—Mr. Sowerby walked up the stairs. He had schooled himself to go through this ordeal with all the cool effrontery which was at his command; but it was clearly to be seen that all his effrontery did not stand him in sufficient stead, and that the interview would have been embarrassing had it not been for the genuine good-humour of the lady.

"Here is my brother," said Mrs. Harold Smith, showing by the tremulousness of the whisper that she looked forward to the meeting with some amount of apprehension.

"How do you do, Mr. Sowerby?" said Miss Dunstable, walking almost into the doorway to welcome him. "Better late than never."

"I have only just got away from the House," said he, as he gave her his hand.

"Oh, I know well that you are *sans reproche* among senators;—as Mr. Harold Smith is *sans peur*;—eh, my dear?"

"I must confess that you have contrived to be uncommonly severe upon them both," said Mrs. Harold, laughing; "and as regards poor Harold, most undeservedly so: Nathaniel is here, and may defend himself."

"And no one is better able to do so on all occasions. But, my dear Mr. Sowerby, I am dying of despair. Do you think he'll come?"

"He? who?"

"You stupid man—as if there were more than one he! There were two, but the other has been."

"Upon my word, I don't understand," said Mr. Sowerby, now again at his ease. "But can I do anything? shall I go and fetch any one? Oh, Tom Towers! I fear I can't help you. But here he is at the foot of the stairs!" And then Mr. Sowerby stood back with his sister to make way for the great representative man of the age.

"Angels and ministers of grace, assist me!" said Miss Dunstable. "How on earth am I to behave myself? Mr. Sowerby, do you think that I ought to kneel down? My dear, will he have a reporter at his back in the royal livery?" And then Miss Dunstable advanced two or three steps—not into the doorway, as she had done for Mr. Sowerby—put out her hand, and smiled her sweetest on Mr. Towers, of the *Jupiter*.

"Mr. Towers," she said, "I am delighted to have this opportunity of seeing you in my own house."

"Miss Dunstable, I am immensely honoured by the privilege of being here," said he.

"The honour done is all conferred on me," and she bowed and curtseyed with very stately grace. Each thoroughly understood the badinage of the other; and then, in a few moments, they were engaged in very easy conversation.

"By-the-by, Sowerby, what do you think of this threatened dissolution?" said Tom Towers.

"We are all in the hands of Providence," said Mr. Sowerby, striving to take the matter without any outward show of emotion. But the question was one of terrible import to him, and up to this time he had heard of no such threat. Nor had Mrs. Harold Smith, nor Miss Dunstable, nor had a hundred others who now either listened to the vaticinations of Mr. Towers, or to the immediate report made of them. But it is given to some men to originate such tidings, and the performance of the prophecy is often brought about by the authority of the prophet. On the following morning the rumour that there would be a dissolution was current in all high circles. "They have no conscience in such matters; no conscience whatever," said a small god, speaking of the giants,—a small god, whose constituency was expensive.

Mr. Towers stood there chatting for about twenty minutes, and then took his departure without making his way into the room. He had answered the purpose for which he had been invited, and left Miss Dunstable in a happy frame of mind.

"I am very glad that he came," said Mrs. Harold Smith, with an air of triumph.

"Yes, I am glad," said Miss Dunstable, "though I am thoroughly ashamed that I should be so. After all, what good has he done to me or to any one?" And having uttered this moral reflection, she made her way into the rooms, and soon discovered Dr. Thorne standing by himself against the wall.

"Well, doctor," she said, "where are Mary and Frank? You do not look at all comfortable, standing here by yourself."

"I am quite as comfortable as I expected, thank you," said he. "They are in the room somewhere, and, as I believe, equally happy."

"That's spiteful in you, doctor, to speak in that way. What would you say if you were called on to endure all that I have gone through this evening?"

"There is no accounting for tastes, but I presume you like it."

"I am not so sure of that. Give me your arm, and let me get some supper. One always likes the idea of having done hard work, and one always likes to have been successful."

"We all know that virtue is its own reward," said the doctor.

"Well, that is something hard upon me," said Miss Dunstable, as she sat down to table. "And you really think that no good of any sort can come from my giving such a party as this?"

"Oh, yes; some people, no doubt, have been amused."

"It is all vanity in your estimation," said Miss Dunstable; "vanity and vexation of spirit. Well; there is a good deal of the latter, certainly. Sherry, if you please. I would give anything for a glass of beer, but that is out of the question. Vanity and vexation of spirit! And yet I meant to do good."

"Pray, do not suppose that I am condemning you, Miss Dunstable."

"Ah, but I do suppose it. Not only you, but another also, whose judgment I care for perhaps more than yours; and that, let me tell you, is saying a great deal. You do condemn me, Dr. Thorne, and I also condemn myself. It is not that I have done wrong, but the game is not worth the candle."

"Ah; that's the question."

"The game is not worth the candle. And yet it was a triumph to have both the duke and Tom Towers. You must confess that I have not. managed badly."

Soon after that the Greshams went away, and in an hour's time or so, Miss Dunstable was allowed to drag herself to her own bed.

That is the great question to be asked on all such occasions, "Is the game worth the candle?"

CHAPTER XXX.

THE GRANTLY TRIUMPH.

It has been mentioned cursorily—the reader, no doubt, will have forgotten it—that Mrs. Grantly was not specially invited by her husband to go up to town with a view of being present at Miss Dunstable's party. Mrs. Grantly said nothing on the subject, but she was somewhat chagrined; not on account of the loss she sustained with reference to that celebrated assembly, but because she felt that her daughter's affairs required the supervision of a mother's eye. She also doubted the final ratification of that Lufton-Grantly treaty, and, doubting it, she did not feel quite satisfied that her daughter should be left in Lady Lufton's hands. She had said a word or two to the archdeacon before he went up, but only a word or two, for she hesitated to trust him in so delicate a matter. She was, therefore, not a little surprised at receiving, on the second morning after her husband's departure, a letter from him desiring her immediate presence in London. She was surprised; but her heart was filled rather with hope than dismay, for she had full confidence in her daughter's discretion.

On the morning after the party, Lady Lufton and Griselda had breakfasted together as usual, but each felt that the manner of the other was altered. Lady Lufton thought that her young friend was somewhat less attentive, and perhaps less meek in her demeanour, than usual; and Griselda felt that Lady Lufton was less affectionate. Very little, however, was said between them, and Lady Lufton expressed no surprise when Griselda begged to be left alone at home, instead of accompanying her ladyship when the carriage came to the door.

Nobody called in Bruton Street that afternoon—no one, at least, was let in—except the archdeacon. He came there late in the day, and remained with his daughter till Lady Lufton returned. Then he took his leave, with more abruptness than was usual with him, and without saying anything special to account for the duration of his visit. Neither did Griselda say anything special; and so the evening wore away, each feeling in some unconscious manner that she was on less intimate terms with the other than had previously been the case.

On the next day also Griselda would not go out, but at four o'clock a servant brought a letter to her from Mount Street. Her mother had arrived in London and wished to see her at once. Mrs. Grantly sent her love to Lady Lufton, and would call at half-past five, or at any later hour at which it might be convenient for Lady Lufton to see her. Griselda was to stay and dine in Mount Street; so said the letter. Lady Lufton declared that she would be very happy to see Mrs. Grantly at the hour named; and then, armed with this message, Griselda started for her mother's lodgings.

"I'll send the carriage for you," said Lady Lufton. "I suppose about ten will do."

"Thank you," said Griselda, "that will do very nicely;" and then she went.

Exactly at half-past five Mrs. Grantly was shown into Lady Lufton's drawing-room. Her daughter did not come with her, and Lady Lufton could see by the expression of her friend's face that business was to be discussed. Indeed, it was necessary that she herself should discuss business, for Mrs. Grantly must now be told that the family treaty could not be ratified. The gentleman declined the alliance, and poor Lady Lufton was uneasy in her mind at the nature of the task before her.

"Your coming up has been rather unexpected," said Lady Lufton, as soon as her friend was seated on the sofa.

"Yes, indeed; I got a letter from the archdeacon only this morning, which made it absolutely necessary that I should come."

"No bad news, I hope?" said Lady Lufton.

"No; I can't call it bad news. But, dear Lady Lufton, things won't always turn out exactly as one would have them."

"No, indeed," said her ladyship, remembering that it was incumbent on her to explain to Mrs. Grantly now at this present interview the tidings with which her mind was fraught. She would, however, let Mrs. Grantly first tell her own story, feeling, perhaps, that the one might possibly bear upon the other.

"Poor dear Griselda!" said Mrs. Grantly, almost with a sigh. "I need not tell you, Lady Lufton, what my hopes were regarding her."

"Has she told you anything—anything that—"

"She would have spoken to you at once—and it was due to you that she should have done so—but she was timid; and not unnaturally so. And then it was right that she should see her father and me before she quite made up her own mind. But I may say that it is settled now."

"What is settled?" asked Lady Lufton.

"Of course it is impossible for any one to tell beforehand how these things will turn out," continued Mrs. Grantly, beating about the bush rather more than was necessary. "The dearest wish of my heart was to see her married to Lord Lufton. I should so much have wished to have her in the same county with me, and such a match as that would have fully satisfied my ambition."

"Well, I should rather think it might!" Lady Lufton did not say this out loud, but she thought it. Mrs. Grantly was absolutely speaking of a match between her daughter and Lord Lufton as though she would have displayed some amount of Christian moderation in putting up with it! Griselda Grantly might be a very nice girl; but even she—so thought Lady Lufton at the moment—might possibly be priced too highly.

"Dear Mrs. Grantly," she said, "I have foreseen for the last few days that our mutual hopes in this respect would not be gratified. Lord Lufton, I think;—but perhaps it is not necessary to explain— Had you not come up to town I should have written to you,—probably to-day. Whatever may be dear Griselda's fate in life, I sincerely hope that she may be happy."

"I think she will," said Mrs. Grantly, in a tone that expressed much satisfaction.

"Has—has anything—"

"Lord Dumbello proposed to Griselda the other night, at Miss Dunstable's party," said Mrs. Grantly, with her eyes fixed upon the floor, and assuming on the sudden much meekness in her manner; "and his lordship was with the archdeacon yesterday, and again this morning. I fancy he is in Mount Street at the present moment."

"Oh, indeed!" said Lady Lufton. She would have given worlds to have possessed at the moment sufficient self-command to have enabled her to express in her tone and manner unqualified satisfaction at the tidings. But she had not such self-command, and was painfully aware of her own deficiency.

"Yes," said Mrs. Grantly. "And as it is all so far settled, and as I know you are so kindly anxious about dear Griselda, I thought it right to let you know at once. Nothing can be more upright, honourable, and generous, than Lord Dumbello's conduct; and, on the whole, the match is one with which I and the archdeacon cannot but be contented."

"It is certainly a great match," said Lady Lufton. "Have you seen Lady Hartletop yet?"

Now Lady Hartletop could not be regarded as an agreeable connection, but this was the only word which escaped from Lady Lufton that could be considered in any way disparaging, and, on the whole, I think that she behaved well.

"Lord Dumbello is so completely his own master that that has not been necessary," said Mrs. Grantly. "The marquis has been told, and the archdeacon will see him either tomorrow or the day after."

There was nothing left for Lady Lufton but to congratulate her friend, and this she did in words perhaps not very sincere, but which, on the whole, were not badly chosen.

"I am sure I hope she will be very happy," said Lady Lufton, "and I trust that the alliance"—the word was very agreeable to Mrs. Grantly's ear—"will give unalloyed gratification to you and to her father. The position which she is called to fill is a very splendid one, but I do not think that it is above her merits."

This was very generous, and so Mrs. Grantly felt it. She had expected that her news would be received with the coldest shade of civility, and she was quite prepared to do battle if there were occasion. But she had no wish for war, and was almost grateful to Lady Lufton for her cordiality.

"Dear Lady Lufton," she said, "it is so kind of you to say so. I have told no one else, and of course would tell no one till you knew it. No one has known her and understood her so well as you have done. And I can assure you of this: that there is no one to whose friendship she looks forward in her new sphere of life with half so much pleasure as she does to yours."

Lady Lufton did not say much further. She could not declare that she expected much gratification from an intimacy with the future Marchioness of Hartletop. The Hartletops and Luftons must, at any rate for her generation, live in a world apart, and she had now said all that her old friendship with Mrs. Grantly required. Mrs. Grantly understood all this quite as well as did Lady Lufton; but then Mrs. Grantly was much the better woman of the world.

It was arranged that Griselda should come back to Bruton Street for that night, and that her visit should then be brought to a close.

"The archdeacon thinks that for the present I had better remain up in town," said Mrs. Grantly, "and under the very peculiar circumstances Griselda will be—perhaps more comfortable with me."

To this Lady Lufton entirely agreed; and so they parted, excellent friends, embracing each other in a most affectionate manner.

That evening Griselda did return to Bruton Street, and Lady Lufton had to go through the further task of congratulating her. This was the more disagreeable of the two, especially so as it had to be thought over beforehand. But the young lady's excellent good sense and sterling qualities made the task comparatively an easy one. She neither cried, nor was impassioned, nor went into hysterics, nor showed any emotion. She did not even talk of her noble Dumbello—her generous Dumbello. She took Lady Lufton's kisses almost in

silence, thanked her gently for her kindness, and made no allusion to her own future grandeur.

"I think I should like to go to bed early," she said, "as I must see to my packing up."

"Richards will do all that for you, my dear."

"Oh, yes, thank you, nothing can be kinder than Richards. But I'll just see to my own
dresses." And so she went to bed early.

Lady Lufton did not see her son for the next two days, but when she did, of course she
said a word or two about Griselda.

"You have heard the news, Ludovic?" she asked.

"Oh, yes: it's at all the clubs. I have been overwhelmed with presents of willow
branches."

"You, at any rate, have got nothing to regret," she said.

"Nor you either, mother. I am sure that you do not think you have. Say that you do not
regret it. Dearest mother, say so for my sake. Do you not know in your heart of hearts that
she was not suited to be happy as my wife,—or to make me happy?"

"Perhaps not," said Lady Lufton, sighing. And then she kissed her son, and declared to
herself that no girl in England could be good enough for him.

CHAPTER XXXI.

SALMON FISHING IN NORWAY.

Lord Dumbello's engagement with Griselda Grantly was the talk of the town for the next ten days. It formed, at least, one of two subjects which monopolized attention, the other being that dreadful rumour, first put in motion by Tom Towers at Miss Dunstable's party, as to a threatened dissolution of Parliament.

"Perhaps, after all, it will be the best thing for us," said Mr. Green Walker, who felt himself to be tolerably safe at Crewe Junction.

"I regard it as a most wicked attempt," said Harold Smith, who was not equally secure in his own borough, and to whom the expense of an election was disagreeable. "It is done in order that they may get time to tide over the autumn. They won't gain ten votes by a dissolution, and less than forty would hardly give them a majority. But they have no sense of public duty—none whatever. Indeed, I don't know who has."

"No, by Jove; that's just it. That's what my aunt Lady Hartletop says; there is no sense of duty left in the world. By-the-by, what an uncommon fool Dumbello is making himself!" And then the conversation went off to that other topic.

Lord Lufton's joke against himself about the willow branches was all very well, and nobody dreamed that his heart was sore in that matter. The world was laughing at Lord Dumbello for what it chose to call a foolish match, and Lord Lufton's friends talked to him about it as though they had never suspected that he could have made an ass of himself in the same direction; but, nevertheless, he was not altogether contented. He by no means wished to marry Griselda; he had declared to himself a dozen times since he had first suspected his mother's manœuvres, that no consideration on earth should induce him to do so; he had pronounced her to be cold, insipid, and unattractive in spite of her beauty; and yet he felt almost angry that Lord Dumbello should have been successful. And this, too, was the more inexcusable, seeing that he had never forgotten Lucy Robarts, had never ceased to love her, and that, in holding those various conversations within his own bosom, he was as loud in Lucy's favour as he was in dispraise of Griselda.

"Your hero, then," I hear some well-balanced critic say, "is not worth very much."

In the first place Lord Lufton is not my hero; and in the next place, a man may be very imperfect and yet worth a great deal. A man may be as imperfect as Lord Lufton, and yet worthy of a good mother and a good wife. If not, how many of us are unworthy of the mothers and wives we have! It is my belief that few young men settle themselves down to the work of the world, to the begetting of children, and carving and paying and struggling and fretting for the same, without having first been in love with four or five possible mothers for them, and probably with two or three at the same time. And yet these men are, as a rule, worthy of the excellent wives that ultimately fall to their lot. In this way Lord Lufton had, to a certain extent, been in love with Griselda. There had been one moment in his life in which he would have offered her his hand, had not her discretion been so excellent; and though that moment never returned, still he suffered from some feeling akin to disappointment when he learned that Griselda had been won and was to be worn. He was, then, a dog in the manger, you will say. Well; and are we not all dogs in the manger, more or less actively? Is not that manger-doggishness one of the most common phases of the human heart?

But not the less was Lord Lufton truly in love with Lucy Robarts. Had he fancied that any Dumbello was carrying on a siege before that fortress, his vexation would have manifested itself in a very different manner. He could joke about Griselda Grantly with a frank face and a happy tone of voice; but had he heard of any tidings of a similar import with reference to Lucy, he would have been past all joking, and I much doubt whether it would not even have affected his appetite.

"Mother," he said to Lady Lufton a day or two after the declaration of Griselda's engagement, "I am going to Norway to fish."

"To Norway,—to fish!"

"Yes. We've got rather a nice party. Clontarf is going, and Culpepper—"

"What, that horrid man!"

"He's an excellent hand at fishing;—and Haddington Peebles, and—and—there'll be six of us altogether; and we start this day week."

"That's rather sudden, Ludovic."

"Yes, it is sudden; but we're sick of London. I should not care to go so soon myself, but Clontarf and Culpepper say that the season is early this year. I must go down to Framley before I start—about my horses; and therefore I came to tell you that I shall be there to-morrow."

"At Framley to-morrow! If you could put it off for three days I should be going myself."

But Lord Lufton could not put it off for three days. It may be that on this occasion he did not wish for his mother's presence at Framley while he was there; that he conceived that he should be more at his ease in giving orders about his stable if he were alone while so employed. At any rate he declined her company, and on the following morning did go down to Framley by himself.

"Mark," said Mrs. Robarts, hurrying into her husband's book-room about the middle of the day, "Lord Lufton is at home. Have you heard it?"

"What! here at Framley?"

"He is over at Framley Court; so the servants say. Carson saw him in the paddock with some of the horses. Won't you go and see him?"

"Of course I will," said Mark, shutting up his papers. "Lady Lufton can't be here, and if he is alone he will probably come and dine."

"I don't know about that," said Mrs. Robarts, thinking of poor Lucy.

"He is not in the least particular. What does for us will do for him. I shall ask him, at any rate." And without further parley the clergyman took up his hat and went off in search of his friend.

Lucy Robarts had been present when the gardener brought in tidings of Lord Lufton's arrival at Framley, and was aware that Fanny had gone to tell her husband.

"He won't come here, will he?" she said, as soon as Mrs. Robarts returned.

"I can't say," said Fanny. "I hope not. He ought not to do so, and I don't think he will. But Mark says that he will ask him to dinner."

"Then, Fanny, I must be taken ill. There is nothing else for it."

"I don't think he will come. I don't think he can be so cruel. Indeed, I feel sure that he won't; but I thought it right to tell you."

Lucy also conceived that it was improbable that Lord Lufton should come to the parsonage under the present circumstances; and she declared to herself that it would not be possible that she should appear at table if he did do so; but, nevertheless, the idea of his being at Framley was, perhaps, not altogether painful to her. She did not recognize any pleasure as coming to her from his arrival, but still there was something in his presence which was, unconsciously to herself, soothing to her feelings. But that terrible question remained;—how was she to act if it should turn out that he was coming to dinner?

"If he does come, Fanny," she said, solemnly, after a pause, "I must keep to my own room, and leave Mark to think what he pleases. It will be better for me to make a fool of myself there, than in his presence in the drawing-room."

Mark Robarts took his hat and stick and went over at once to the home paddock, in which he knew that Lord Lufton was engaged with the horses and grooms. He also was in no supremely happy frame of mind, for his correspondence with Mr. Tozer was on the increase. He had received notice from that indefatigable gentleman that certain "overdue bills" were now lying at the bank in Barchester, and were very desirous of his, Mr. Robarts's, notice. A concatenation of certain peculiarly unfortunate circumstances made it indispensably necessary that Mr. Tozer should be repaid, without further loss of time, the various sums of money which he had advanced on the credit of Mr. Robarts's name, &c. &c. &c. No absolute threat was put forth, and, singular to say, no actual amount was named. Mr. Robarts, however, could not but observe, with a most painfully accurate attention, that mention was made, not of an overdue bill, but of overdue bills. What if Mr. Tozer were to demand from him the instant repayment of nine hundred pounds? Hitherto he had merely written to Mr. Sowerby, and he might have had an answer from that gentleman this morning, but no such answer had as yet reached him. Consequently he was not, at the present moment, in a very happy frame of mind.

He soon found himself with Lord Lufton and the horses. Four or five of them were being walked slowly about the paddock in the care of as many men or boys, and the sheets were being taken off them—off one after another, so that their master might look at them with the more accuracy and satisfaction. But though Lord Lufton was thus doing his duty, and going through his work, he was not doing it with his whole heart,—as the head groom perceived very well. He was fretful about the nags, and seemed anxious to get them out of his sight as soon as he had made a decent pretext of looking at them.

"How are you, Lufton?" said Robarts, coming forward. "They told me that you were down, and so I came across at once."

"Yes; I only got here this morning, and should have been over with you directly. I am going to Norway for six weeks or so, and it seems that the fish are so early this year, that we must start at once. I have a matter on which I want to speak to you before I leave; and, indeed, it was that which brought me down more than anything else."

There was something hurried and not altogether easy about his manner as he spoke, which struck Robarts, and made him think that this promised matter to be spoken of would not be agreeable in discussion. He did not know whether Lord Lufton might not again be mixed up with Tozer and the bills.

"You will dine with us to-day," he said, "if, as I suppose, you are all alone."

"Yes, I am all alone."

"Then you'll come?"

"Well, I don't quite know. No, I don't think I can go over to dinner. Don't look so disgusted. I'll explain it all to you just now."

What could there be in the wind; and how was it possible that Tozer's bill should make it inexpedient for Lord Lufton to dine at the parsonage? Robarts, however, said nothing further about it at the moment, but turned off to look at the horses.

"They are an uncommonly nice set of animals," said he.

"Well, yes; I don't know. When a man has four or five horses to look at, somehow or other he never has one fit to go. That chestnut mare is a picture, now that nobody wants her; but she wasn't able to carry me well to hounds a single day last winter. Take them in, Pounce; that'll do."

"Won't your lordship run your eye over the old black 'oss?" said Pounce, the head groom, in a melancholy tone; "he's as fine, sir—as fine as a stag."

"To tell you the truth, I think they're too fine; but that'll do; take them in. And now, Mark, if you're at leisure, we'll take a turn round the place."

Mark, of course, was at leisure, and so they started on their walk.

"You're too difficult to please about your stable," Robarts began.

"Never mind the stable now," said Lord Lufton. "The truth is, I am not thinking about it. Mark," he then said, very abruptly, "I want you to be frank with me. Has your sister ever spoken to you about me?"

"My sister; Lucy?"

"Yes; your sister Lucy."

"No, never; at least nothing especial; nothing that I can remember at this moment."

"Nor your wife?"

"Spoken about you!—Fanny? Of course she has, in an ordinary way. It would be impossible that she should not. But what do you mean?"

"Have either of them told you that I made an offer to your sister?"

"That you made an offer to Lucy?"

"Yes, that I made an offer to Lucy."

"No; nobody has told me so. I have never dreamed of such a thing; nor, as far as I believe, have they. If anybody has spread such a report, or said that either of them have hinted at such a thing, it is a base lie. Good heavens! Lufton, for what do you take them?"

"But I did," said his lordship.

"Did what?" said the parson.

"I did make your sister an offer."

"You made Lucy an offer of marriage!"

"Yes, I did;—in as plain language as a gentleman could use to a lady."

"And what answer did she make?"

"She refused me. And now, Mark, I have come down here with the express purpose of making that offer again. Nothing could be more decided than your sister's answer. It struck me as being almost uncourteously decided. But still it is possible that circumstances may have weighed with her, which ought not to weigh with her. If her love be not given to any one else, I may still have a chance of it. It's the old story of faint heart, you know: at any rate, I mean to try my luck again; and thinking over it with deliberate purpose, I have come to the conclusion that I ought to tell you before I see her."

Lord Lufton in love with Lucy! As these words repeated themselves over and over again within Mark Robarts's mind, his mind added to them notes of surprise without end. How had it possibly come about,—and why? In his estimation his sister Lucy was a very simple girl—not plain indeed, but by no means beautiful; certainly not stupid, but by no means brilliant. And then, he would have said, that of all men whom he knew, Lord Lufton would have been the last to fall in love with such a girl as his sister. And now, what was he to say or do? What views was he bound to hold? In what direction should he act? There was Lady Lufton on the one side, to whom he owed everything. How would life be possible to him in that parsonage—within a few yards of her elbow—if he consented to receive Lord Lufton as the acknowledged suitor of his sister? It would be a great match for Lucy, doubtless; but— Indeed, he could not bring himself to believe that Lucy could in truth become the absolute reigning queen of Framley Court.

"Do you think that Fanny knows anything of all this?" he said, after a moment or two.

"I cannot possibly tell. If she does it is not with my knowledge. I should have thought that you could best answer that."

"I cannot answer it at all," said Mark. "I, at least, have had no remotest idea of such a thing."

"Your ideas of it now need not be at all remote," said Lord Lufton, with a faint smile; "and you may know it as a fact. I did make her an offer of marriage; I was refused; I am going to repeat it; and I am now taking you into my confidence, in order that, as her brother, and as my friend, you may give me such assistance as you can." They then walked on in silence for some yards, after which Lord Lufton added: "And now I'll dine with you to-day if you wish it."

Mr. Robarts did not know what to say; he could not bethink himself what answer duty required of him. He had no right to interfere between his sister and such a marriage, if she herself should wish it; but still there was something terrible in the thought of it! He had a vague conception that it must come to evil; that the project was a dangerous one; and that it could not finally result happily for any of them. What would Lady Lufton say? That undoubtedly was the chief source of his dismay.

"Have you spoken to your mother about this?" he said.

"My mother? no; why speak to her till I know my fate? A man does not like to speak much of such matters if there be a probability of his being rejected. I tell you because I do not like to make my way into your house under a false pretence."

"But what would Lady Lufton say?"

"I think it probable that she would be displeased on the first hearing it; that in four-and-twenty hours she would be reconciled; and that after a week or so Lucy would be her dearest favourite and the prime minister of all her machinations. You don't know my mother as well as I do. She would give her head off her shoulders to do me a pleasure."

"And for that reason," said Mark Robarts, "you ought, if possible, to do her pleasure."

"I cannot absolutely marry a wife of her choosing, if you mean that," said Lord Lufton.

They went on walking about the garden for an hour, but they hardly got any farther than the point to which we have now brought them. Mark Robarts could not make up his mind on the spur of the moment; nor, as he said more than once to Lord Lufton, could he be at all sure that Lucy would in any way be guided by him. It was, therefore, at last settled between them that Lord Lufton should come to the parsonage immediately after breakfast on the following morning. It was agreed also that the dinner had better not come off, and Robarts promised that he would, if possible, have determined by the morning as to what advice he would give his sister.

He went direct home to the parsonage from Framley Court, feeling that he was altogether in the dark till he should have consulted his wife. How would he feel if Lucy were to become Lady Lufton? and how would he look Lady Lufton in the face in telling her that such was to be his sister's destiny? On returning home he immediately found his wife, and had not been closeted with her five minutes before he knew, at any rate, all that she knew.

"And you mean to say that she does love him?" said Mark.

"Indeed she does; and is it not natural that she should? When I saw them so much together I feared that she would. But I never thought that he would care for her."

Even Fanny did not as yet give Lucy credit for half her attractiveness. After an hour's talking the interview between the husband and wife ended in a message to Lucy, begging her to join them both in the book-room.

"Aunt Lucy," said a chubby little darling, who was taken up into his aunt's arms as he spoke, "papa and mamma 'ant 'oo in te tuddy, and I musn't go wis 'oo."

Lucy, as she kissed the boy and pressed his face against her own, felt that her blood was running quick to her heart.

"Musn't 'oo go wis me, my own one?" she said, as she put her playfellow down; but she played with the child only because she did not wish to betray even to him that she was hardly mistress of herself. She knew that Lord Lufton was at Framley; she knew that her brother had been to him; she knew that a proposal had been made that he should come there that day to dinner. Must it not therefore be the case that this call to a meeting in the study had arisen out of Lord Lufton's arrival at Framley? and yet, how could it have done so? Had Fanny betrayed her in order to prevent the dinner invitation? It could not be possible that Lord Lufton himself should have spoken on the subject! And then she again stooped to kiss the child, rubbed her hands across her forehead to smooth her hair, and erase, if that might be possible, the look of care which she wore, and then descended slowly to her brother's sitting-room.

Her hand paused for a second on the door ere she opened it, but she had resolved that, come what might, she would be brave. She pushed it open and walked in with a bold front, with eyes wide open, and a slow step.

"Frank says that you want me," she said.

Mr. Robarts and Fanny were both standing up by the fireplace, and each waited a second for the other to speak when Lucy entered the room; and then Fanny began,—

"Lord Lufton is here, Lucy."

"Here! Where? At the parsonage?"

"No, not at the parsonage; but over at Framley Court," said Mark.

"And he promises to call here after breakfast to-morrow," said Fanny. And then again there was a pause. Mrs. Robarts hardly dared to look Lucy in the face. She had not betrayed her trust, seeing that the secret had been told to Mark, not by her, but by Lord Lufton; but she could not but feel that Lucy would think that she had betrayed it.

"Very well," said Lucy, trying to smile; "I have no objection in life."

"But, Lucy, dear,"—and now Mrs. Robarts put her arm round her sister-in-law's waist,—"he is coming here especially to see you."

"Oh; that makes a difference. I am afraid that I shall be—engaged."

"He has told everything to Mark," said Mrs. Robarts.

Lucy now felt that her bravery was almost deserting her. She hardly knew which way to look or how to stand. Had Fanny told everything also? There was so much that Fanny knew that Lord Lufton could not have known. But, in truth, Fanny had told all—the whole story of Lucy's love, and had described the reasons which had induced her to reject her suitor; and had done so in words which, had Lord Lufton heard them, would have made him twice as passionate in his love.

And then it certainly did occur to Lucy to think why Lord Lufton should have come to Framley and told all this history to her brother. She attempted for a moment to make herself believe that she was angry with him for doing so. But she was not angry. She had not time to argue much about it, but there came upon her a gratified sensation of having been remembered, and thought of, and—loved. Must it not be so? Could it be possible that he himself would have told this tale to her brother, if he did not still love her? Fifty times she had said to herself that his offer had been an affair of the moment, and fifty times she had been unhappy in so saying. But this new coming of his could not be an affair of the moment. She had been the dupe, she had thought, of an absurd passion on her own part; but now—how was it now? She did not bring herself to think that she should ever be Lady Lufton. She had still, in some perversely obstinate manner, made up her mind against that result. But yet, nevertheless, it did in some unaccountable manner satisfy her to feel that Lord Lufton had himself come down to Framley and himself told this story.

"He has told everything to Mark," said Mrs. Robarts; and then again there was a pause for a moment, during which these thoughts passed through Lucy's mind.

"Yes," said Mark, "he has told me all, and he is coming here to-morrow morning that he may receive an answer from yourself."

"What answer?" said Lucy, trembling.

"Nay, dearest; who can say that but yourself?" and her sister-in-law, as she spoke, pressed close against her. "You must say that yourself."

Mrs. Robarts in her long conversation with her husband had pleaded strongly on Lucy's behalf, taking, as it were, a part against Lady Lufton. She had said that if Lord Lufton persevered in his suit, they at the parsonage could not be justified in robbing Lucy of all that she had won for herself, in order to do Lady Lufton's pleasure.

"But she will think," said Mark, "that we have plotted and intrigued for this. She will call us ungrateful, and will make Lucy's life wretched." To which the wife had answered, that all that must be left in God's hands. They had not plotted or intrigued. Lucy, though loving the man in her heart of hearts, had already once refused him, because she would not be thought to have snatched at so great a prize. But if Lord Lufton loved her so warmly that he had come down there in this manner, on purpose, as he himself had put it, that he might learn his fate, then—so argued Mrs. Robarts—they two, let their loyalty to Lady Lufton be ever so strong, could not justify it to their consciences to stand between Lucy and her lover. Mark had still somewhat demurred to this, suggesting how terrible would be their plight if they should now encourage Lord Lufton, and if he, after such encouragement, when they should have quarrelled with Lady Lufton, should allow himself to be led away from his engagement by his mother. To which Fanny had answered that justice was justice, and that right was right. Everything must be told to Lucy, and she must judge for herself.

"But I do not know what Lord Lufton wants," said Lucy, with her eyes fixed upon the ground, and now trembling more than ever. "He did come to me, and I did give him an answer."

"And is that answer to be final?" said Mark,—somewhat cruelly, for Lucy had not yet been told that her lover had made any repetition of his proposal. Fanny, however, determined that no injustice should be done, and therefore she at last continued the story.

"We know that you did give him an answer, dearest; but gentlemen sometimes will not put up with one answer on such a subject. Lord Lufton has declared to Mark that he means to ask again. He has come down here on purpose to do so."

"And Lady Lufton—" said Lucy, speaking hardly above a whisper, and still hiding her face as she leaned against her sister's shoulder.

"Lord Lufton has not spoken to his mother about it," said Mark; and it immediately became clear to Lucy, from the tone of her brother's voice, that he, at least, would not be pleased, should she accept her lover's vow.

"You must decide out of your own heart, dear," said Fanny, generously. "Mark and I know how well you have behaved, for I have told him everything." Lucy shuddered and leaned closer against her sister as this was said to her. "I had no alternative, dearest, but to tell him. It was best so; was it not? But nothing has been told to Lord Lufton. Mark would not let him come here to-day, because it would have flurried you, and he wished to give you time to think. But you can see him to-morrow morning,—can you not? and then answer him."

Lucy now stood perfectly silent, feeling that she dearly loved her sister-in-law for her sisterly kindness—for that sisterly wish to promote a sister's love; but still there was in her mind a strong resolve not to allow Lord Lufton to come there under the idea that he would be received as a favoured lover. Her love was powerful, but so also was her pride; and she could not bring herself to bear the scorn which would lay in Lady Lufton's eyes. "His mother will despise me, and then he will despise me too," she said to herself; and with a strong gulp of disappointed love and ambition she determined to persist.

"Shall we leave you now, dear; and speak of it again to-morrow morning, before he comes?" said Fanny.

"That will be the best," said Mark. "Turn it in your mind every way to-night. Think of it when you have said your prayers—and, Lucy, come here to me;"—then, taking her in his arms, he kissed her with a tenderness that was not customary with him towards her. "It is fair," said he, "that I should tell you this: that I have perfect confidence in your judgment and feeling; and that I will stand by you as your brother in whatever decision you may come to. Fanny and I both think that you have behaved excellently, and are both of us sure that you will do what is best. Whatever you do I will stick to you;—and so will Fanny."

"Dearest, dearest Mark!"

"And now we will say nothing more about it till to-morrow morning," said Fanny.

But Lucy felt that this saying nothing more about it till to-morrow morning would be tantamount to an acceptance on her part of Lord Lufton's offer. Mrs. Robarts knew, and Mr. Robarts also now knew, the secret of her heart; and if, such being the case, she allowed Lord Lufton to come there with the acknowledged purpose of pleading his own suit, it would be impossible for her not to yield. If she were resolved that she would not yield, now was the time for her to stand her ground and make her fight.

"Do not go, Fanny; at least not quite yet," she said.

"Well, dear?"

"I want you to stay while I tell Mark. He must not let Lord Lufton come here to-morrow."

"Not let him!" said Mrs. Robarts.

Mr. Robarts said nothing, but he felt that his sister was rising in his esteem from minute to minute.

"No; Mark must bid him not come. He will not wish to pain me when it can do no good. Look here, Mark;" and she walked over to her brother, and put both her hands upon his arm. "I do love Lord Lufton. I had no such meaning or thought when I first knew him. But I do love him—I love him dearly;—almost as well as Fanny loves you, I suppose. You may tell him so if you think proper—nay, you must tell him so, or he will not understand me. But tell him this, as coming from me: that I will never marry him, unless his mother asks me."

"She will not do that, I fear," said Mark, sorrowfully.

"No; I suppose not," said Lucy, now regaining all her courage. "If I thought it probable that she should wish me to be her daughter-in-law, it would not be necessary that I should make such a stipulation. It is because she will not wish it; because she would regard me as unfit to—to—to mate with her son. She would hate me, and scorn me; and then he would begin to scorn me, and perhaps would cease to love me. I could not bear her eye upon me, if she thought that I had injured her son. Mark, you will go to him now; will you not? and explain this to him;—as much of it as is necessary. Tell him, that if his mother asks me I will—consent. But that as I know that she never will, he is to look upon all that he has said as forgotten. With me it shall be the same as though it were forgotten."

Such was her verdict, and so confident were they both of her firmness—of her obstinacy Mark would have called it on any other occasion,—that they, neither of them, sought to make her alter it.

"You will go to him now,—this afternoon; will you not?" she said; and Mark promised that he would. He could not but feel that he himself was greatly relieved. Lady Lufton might probably hear that her son had been fool enough to fall in love with the parson's sister, but under existing circumstances she could not consider herself aggrieved either by the parson or by his sister. Lucy was behaving well, and Mark was proud of her. Lucy was behaving with fierce spirit, and Fanny was grieving for her.

"I'd rather be by myself till dinner-time," said Lucy, as Mrs. Robarts prepared to go with her out of the room. "Dear Fanny, don't look unhappy; there's nothing to make us unhappy. I told you I should want goat's milk, and that will be all."

Robarts, after sitting for an hour with his wife, did return again to Framley Court; and, after a considerable search, found Lord Lufton returning home to a late dinner.

"Unless my mother asks her," said he, when the story had been told him. "That is nonsense. Surely you told her that such is not the way of the world."

Robarts endeavoured to explain to him that Lucy could not endure to think that her husband's mother should look on her with disfavour.

"Does she think that my mother dislikes her—her specially?" asked Lord Lufton.

No; Robarts could not suppose that that was the case; but Lady Lufton might probably think that a marriage with a clergyman's sister would be a mésalliance.

"That is out of the question," said Lord Lufton; "as she has especially wanted me to marry a clergyman's daughter for some time past. But, Mark, it is absurd talking about my mother. A man in these days is not to marry as his mother bids him."

Mark could only assure him, in answer to all this, that Lucy was very firm in what she was doing, that she had quite made up her mind, and that she altogether absolved Lord Lufton from any necessity to speak to his mother, if he did not think well of doing so. But all this was to very little purpose.

"She does love me then?" said Lord Lufton.

"Well," said Mark, "I will not say whether she does or does not. I can only repeat her own message. She cannot accept you, unless she does so at your mother's request." And having said that again, he took his leave, and went back to the parsonage.

Poor Lucy, having finished her interview with so much dignity, having fully satisfied her brother, and declined any immediate consolation from her sister-in-law, betook herself to her own bed-room. She had to think over what she had said and done, and it was necessary that she should be alone to do so. It might be that, when she came to reconsider the matter, she would not be quite so well satisfied as was her brother. Her grandeur of demeanour and slow propriety of carriage lasted her till she was well into her own room. There are animals who, when they are ailing in any way, contrive to hide themselves, ashamed, as it were, that the weakness of their suffering should be witnessed. Indeed, I am not sure whether all dumb animals do not do so more or less; and in this respect Lucy was like a dumb animal. Even in her confidences with Fanny she made a joke of her own misfortunes, and spoke of her heart ailments with self-ridicule. But now, having walked up the staircase with no hurried step, and having deliberately locked the door, she turned herself round to suffer in silence and solitude—as do the beasts and birds.

She sat herself down on a low chair, which stood at the foot of her bed, and, throwing back her head, held her handkerchief across her eyes and forehead, holding it tight in both her hands; and then she began to think. She began to think and also to cry, for the tears came running down from beneath the handkerchief; and low sobs were to be heard,—only that the animal had taken itself off, to suffer in solitude.

Had she not thrown from her all her chances of happiness? Was it possible that he should come to her yet again,—a third time? No; it was not possible. The very mode and pride of this, her second rejection of him, made it impossible. In coming to her determination, and making her avowal, she had been actuated by the knowledge that Lady Lufton would regard such a marriage with abhorrence. Lady Lufton would not and could not ask her to condescend to be her son's bride. Her chance of happiness, of glory, of ambition, of love, was all gone. She had sacrificed everything, not to virtue, but to pride; and she had sacrificed not only herself, but him. When first he came there—when she had meditated over his first visit—she had hardly given him credit for deep love; but now—there could be no doubt that he loved her now. After his season in London, his days and nights passed with all that was beautiful, he had returned there, to that little country parsonage, that he might again throw himself at her feet. And she—she had refused to see him, though she loved him with all her heart; she had refused to see him, because she was so vile a coward that she could not bear the sour looks of an old woman!

"I will come down directly," she said, when Fanny at last knocked at the door, begging to be admitted. "I won't open it, love, but I will be with you in ten minutes; I will, indeed." And so she was; not, perhaps, without traces of tears, discernible by the experienced eye of Mrs. Robarts, but yet with a smooth brow, and voice under her own command.

"I wonder whether she really loves him," Mark said to his wife that night.

"Love him!" his wife had answered; "indeed she does; and, Mark, do not be led away by the stern quiet of her demeanour. To my thinking she is a girl who might almost die for love."

On the next day Lord Lufton left Framley; and started, according to his arrangements, for the Norway salmon fishing.

CHAPTER XXXII.

THE GOAT AND COMPASSES.

Harold Smith had been made unhappy by that rumour of a dissolution; but the misfortune to him would be as nothing compared to the severity with which it would fall on Mr. Sowerby. Harold Smith might or might not lose his borough, but Mr. Sowerby would undoubtedly lose his county; and, in losing that, he would lose everything. He felt very certain now that the duke would not support him again, let who would be master of Chaldicotes; and as he reflected on these things he found it very hard to keep up his spirits.

Tom Towers, it seems, had known all about it, as he always does. The little remark which had dropped from him at Miss Dunstable's, made, no doubt, after mature deliberation, and with profound political motives, was the forerunner, only by twelve hours, of a very general report that the giants were going to the country. It was manifest that the giants had not a majority in Parliament, generous as had been the promises of support disinterestedly made to them by the gods. This indeed was manifest, and therefore they were going to the country, although they had been deliberately warned by a very prominent scion of Olympus that if they did do so that disinterested support must be withdrawn. This threat did not seem to weigh much, and by two o'clock on the day following Miss Dunstable's party, the fiat was presumed to have gone forth. The rumour had begun with Tom Towers, but by that time it had reached Buggins at the Petty Bag Office.

"It won't make no difference to hus, sir; will it, Mr. Robarts?" said Buggins, as he leaned respectfully against the wall near the door, in the room of the private secretary at that establishment.

A good deal of conversation, miscellaneous, special, and political, went on between young Robarts and Buggins in the course of the day; as was natural, seeing that they were thrown in these evil times very much upon each other. The Lord Petty Bag of the present ministry was not such a one as Harold Smith. He was a giant indifferent to his private notes, and careless as to the duties even of patronage; he rarely visited the office, and as there were no other clerks in the establishment—owing to a root and branch reform carried out in the short reign of Harold Smith—to whom could young Robarts talk, if not to Buggins?

"No; I suppose not," said Robarts, as he completed on his blotting-paper an elaborate picture of a Turk seated on his divan.

"'Cause, you see, sir, we're in the Upper 'Ouse, now;—as I always thinks we hought to be. I don't think it ain't constitutional for the Petty Bag to be in the Commons, Mr. Robarts. Hany ways, it never usen't."

"They're changing all those sort of things now-a-days, Buggins," said Robarts, giving the final touch to the Turk's smoke.

"Well; I'll tell you what it is, Mr. Robarts: I think I'll go. I can't stand all these changes. I'm turned of sixty now, and don't want any 'stifflicates. I think I'll take my pension and walk. The hoffice ain't the same place at all since it come down among the Commons." And then Buggins retired sighing, to console himself with a pot of porter behind a large open office ledger, set up on end on a small table in the little lobby outside the private secretary's room. Buggins sighed again as he saw that the date made visible in the open book was almost as old as his own appointment; for such a book as this lasted long in the Petty Bag Office. A peer of high degree had been Lord Petty Bag in those days; one whom a messenger's heart could respect with infinite veneration, as he made his unaccustomed visits to the office with much solemnity—perhaps four times during the season. The Lord Petty Bag then was highly regarded by his staff, and his coming among them was talked about for some hours previously and for some days afterwards; but Harold Smith had bustled in and out like the managing clerk in a Manchester house. "The service is going to the dogs," said Buggins to himself, as he put down the porter pot and looked up over the book at a gentleman who presented himself at the door.

"Mr. Robarts in his room?" said Buggins, repeating the gentleman's words. "Yes, Mr. Sowerby; you'll find him there; first door to the left." And then, remembering that the visitor was a county member—a position which Buggins regarded as next to that of a peer—he got up, and, opening the private secretary's door, ushered in the visitor.

Young Robarts and Mr. Sowerby had, of course, become acquainted in the days of Harold Smith's reign. During that short time the member for East Barset had on most days dropped in at the Petty Bag Office for a minute or two, finding out what the energetic cabinet minister was doing, chatting on semi-official subjects, and teaching the private secretary to laugh at his master. There was nothing, therefore, in his present visit which need appear to be singular, or which required any immediate special explanation. He sat himself down in his ordinary way, and began to speak of the subject of the day.

"We're all to go," said Sowerby.

"So I hear," said the private secretary. "It will give me no trouble, for, as the respectable Buggins says, we're in the Upper House now."

"What a delightful time those lucky dogs of lords do have!" said Sowerby. "No constituents, no turning out, no fighting, no necessity for political opinions,—and, as a rule, no such opinions at all!"

"I suppose you're tolerably safe in East Barsetshire?" said Robarts. "The duke has it pretty much his own way there."

"Yes; the duke does have it pretty much his own way. By-the-by, where is your brother?"

"At home," said Robarts; "at least I presume so."

"At Framley or at Barchester? I believe he was in residence at Barchester not long since."

"He's at Framley now, I know. I got a letter only yesterday from his wife, with a commission. He was there, and Lord Lufton had just left."

"Yes; Lufton was down. He started for Norway this morning. I want to see your brother. You have not heard from him yourself, have you?"

"No; not lately. Mark is a bad correspondent. He would not do at all for a private secretary."

"At any rate, not to Harold Smith. But you are sure I should not catch him at Barchester?"

"Send down by telegraph, and he would meet you."

"I don't want to do that. A telegraph message makes such a fuss in the country, frightening people's wives, and setting all the horses about the place galloping."

"What is it about?"

"Nothing of any great consequence. I didn't know whether he might have told you. I'll write down by to-night's post, and then he can meet me at Barchester to-morrow. Or do you write. There's nothing I hate so much as letter-writing;—just tell him that I called, and that I shall be much obliged if he can meet me at the Dragon of Wantly—say at two to-morrow. I will go down by the express."

Mark Robarts, in talking over this coming money trouble with Sowerby, had once mentioned that if it were necessary to take up the bill for a short time he might be able to borrow the money from his brother. So much of the father's legacy still remained in the hands of the private secretary as would enable him to produce the amount of the latter bill, and there could be no doubt that he would lend it if asked. Mr. Sowerby's visit to the Petty Bag Office had been caused by a desire to learn whether any such request had been made,—and also by a half-formed resolution to make the request himself if he should find that the clergyman had not done so. It seemed to him to be a pity that such a sum should be lying about, as it were, within reach, and that he should not stoop to put his hands upon it. Such abstinence would be so contrary to all the practice of his life that it was as difficult to him as it is for a sportsman to let pass a cock-pheasant. But yet something like remorse touched his heart as he sat there balancing himself on his chair in the private secretary's room, and looking at the young man's open face.

"Yes; I'll write to him," said John Robarts; "but he hasn't said anything to me about anything particular."

"Hasn't he? It does not much signify. I only mentioned it because I thought I understood him to say that he would." And then Mr. Sowerby went on swinging himself. How was it that he felt so averse to mention that little sum of £500 to a young man like John Robarts, a fellow without wife or children or calls on him of any sort, who would not even be injured by the loss of the money, seeing that he had an ample salary on which to live? He wondered at his own weakness. The want of the money was urgent on him in the extreme. He had reasons for supposing that Mark would find it very difficult to renew the bills, but he, Sowerby, could stop their presentation if he could get this money at once into his own hands.

"Can I do anything for you?" said the innocent lamb, offering his throat to the butcher.

But some unwonted feeling numbed the butcher's fingers, and blunted his knife. He sat still for half a minute after the question, and then jumping from his seat, declined the offer. "No, no; nothing, thank you. Only write to Mark, and say that I shall be there to-morrow," and then, taking his hat, he hurried out of the office. "What an ass I am," he said to himself as he went: "as if it were of any use now to be particular!"

He then got into a cab and had himself driven half way up Portman Street towards the New Road, and walking from thence a few hundred yards down a cross-street he came to a public-house. It was called the "Goat and Compasses,"—a very meaningless name, one would say; but the house boasted of being a place of public entertainment very long established on that site, having been a tavern out in the country in the days of Cromwell. At that time the pious landlord, putting up a pious legend for the benefit of his pious customers, had declared that—"God encompasseth us." The "Goat and Compasses" in these days does quite as well; and, considering the present character of the house, was perhaps less unsuitable than the old legend.

"Is Mr. Austen here?" asked Mr. Sowerby of the man at the bar.

"Which on 'em? Not Mr. John; he ain't here. Mr. Tom is in—the little room on the left-hand side." The man whom Mr. Sowerby would have preferred to see was the elder brother, John; but as he was not to be found, he did go into the little room. In that room he found—Mr. Austen, Junior, according to one arrangement of nomenclature, and Mr. Tom Tozer according to another. To gentlemen of the legal profession he generally chose to introduce himself as belonging to the respectable family of the Austens; but among his intimates he had always been—Tozer.

Mr. Sowerby, though he was intimate with the family, did not love the Tozers; but he especially hated Tom Tozer. Tom Tozer was a bull-necked, beetle-browed fellow, the expression of whose face was eloquent with acknowledged roguery. "I am a rogue," it seemed to say. "I know it; all the world knows it: but you're another. All the world don't know that, but I do. Men are all rogues, pretty nigh. Some are soft rogues, and some are 'cute rogues. I am a 'cute one; so mind your eye." It was with such words that Tom Tozer's face spoke out; and though a thorough liar in his heart, he was not a liar in his face.

"Well, Tozer," said Mr. Sowerby, absolutely shaking hands with the dirty miscreant, "I wanted to see your brother."

"John ain't here, and ain't like; but it's all as one."

"Yes, yes; I suppose it is. I know you two hunt in couples."

"I don't know what you mean about hunting, Mr. Sowerby. You gents 'as all the hunting, and we poor folk 'as all the work. I hope you're going to make up this trifle of money we're out of so long."

"It's about that I've called. I don't know what you call long, Tozer; but the last bill was only dated in February."

"It's overdue; ain't it?"

"Oh, yes; it's overdue. There's no doubt about that."

"Well; when a bit of paper is come round, the next thing is to take it up. Them's my ideas. And to tell you the truth, Mr. Sowerby, we don't think as 'ow you've been treating us just on the square lately. In that matter of Lord Lufton's you was down on us uncommon."

"You know I couldn't help myself."

"Well; and we can't help ourselves now. That's where it is, Mr. Sowerby. Lord love you; we know what's what, we do. And so, the fact is we're uncommon low as to the ready just at present, and we must have them few hundred pounds. We must have them at once, or we must sell up that clerical gent. I'm dashed if it ain't as hard to get money from a parson as it is to take a bone from a dog. 'E's 'ad 'is account, no doubt, and why don't 'e pay?"

Mr. Sowerby had called with the intention of explaining that he was about to proceed to Barchester on the following day with the express view of "making arrangements" about this bill; and had he seen John Tozer, John would have been compelled to accord to him some little extension of time. Both Tom and John knew this; and, therefore, John—the soft-hearted one—kept out of the way. There was no danger that Tom would be weak; and, after some half-hour of parley, he was again left by Mr. Sowerby, without having evinced any symptom of weakness.

"It's the dibs as we want, Mr. Sowerby; that's all," were the last words which he spoke as the member of Parliament left the room.

Mr. Sowerby then got into another cab, and had himself driven to his sister's house. It is a remarkable thing with reference to men who are distressed for money—distressed as was now the case with Mr. Sowerby—that they never seem at a loss for small sums, or deny themselves those luxuries which small sums purchase. Cabs, dinners, wine, theatres, and new gloves are always at the command of men who are drowned in pecuniary embarrassments, whereas those who don't owe a shilling are so frequently obliged to go without them! It would seem that there is no gratification so costly as that of keeping out of debt. But then it is only fair that, if a man has a hobby, he should pay for it.

Any one else would have saved his shilling, as Mrs. Harold Smith's house was only just across Oxford Street, in the neighbourhood of Hanover Square; but Mr. Sowerby never thought of this. He had never saved a shilling in his life, and it did not occur to him to begin now. He had sent word to her to remain at home for him, and he now found her waiting.

"Harriet," said he, throwing himself back into an easy chair, "the game is pretty well up at last."

"Nonsense," said she. "The game is not up at all if you have the spirit to carry it on."

"I can only say that I got a formal notice this morning from the duke's lawyer, saying that he meant to foreclose at once;—not from Fothergill, but from those people in South Audley Street."

"You expected that," said his sister.

"I don't see how that makes it any better; besides, I am not quite sure that I did expect it; at any rate I did not feel certain. There is no doubt now."

"It is better that there should be no doubt. It is much better that you should know on what ground you have to stand."

"I shall soon have no ground to stand on, none at least of my own,—not an acre," said the unhappy man, with great bitterness in his tone.

"You can't in reality be poorer now than you were last year. You have not spent anything to speak of. There can be no doubt that Chaldicotes will be ample to pay all you owe the duke."

"It's as much as it will; and what am I to do then? I almost think more of the seat than I do of Chaldicotes."

"You know what I advise," said Mrs. Smith. "Ask Miss Dunstable to advance the money on the same security which the duke holds. She will be as safe then as he is now. And if you can arrange that, stand for the county against him; perhaps you may be beaten."

"I shouldn't have a chance."

"But it would show that you are not a creature in the duke's hands. That's my advice," said Mrs. Smith, with much spirit; "and if you wish, I'll broach it to Miss Dunstable, and ask her to get her lawyer to look into it."

"If I had done this before I had run my head into that other absurdity!"

"Don't fret yourself about that; she will lose nothing by such an investment, and therefore you are not asking any favour of her. Besides, did she not make the offer? and she is just the woman to do this for you now, because she refused to do that other thing for you yesterday. You understand most things, Nathaniel; but I am not sure that you understand women; not, at any rate, such a woman as her."

It went against the grain with Mr. Sowerby, this seeking of pecuniary assistance from the very woman whose hand he had attempted to gain about a fortnight since; but he allowed his sister to prevail. What could any man do in such straits that would not go against the grain? At the present moment he felt in his mind an infinite hatred against the duke, Mr. Fothergill, Gumption and Gagebee, and all the tribes of Gatherum Castle and South Audley Street; they wanted to rob him of that which had belonged to the Sowerbys before the name of Omnium had been heard of in the county, or in England! The great leviathan of the deep was anxious to swallow him up as a prey! He was to be swallowed up, and made away with, and put out of sight, without a pang of remorse! Any measure which could now present itself as the means of staving off so evil a day would be acceptable; and therefore he gave his sister the commission of making this second proposal to Miss Dunstable. In cursing the duke—for he did curse the duke lustily—it hardly occurred to him to think that, after all, the duke only asked for his own.

THE GOAT AND COMPASSES.

As for Mrs. Harold Smith, whatever may be the view taken of her general character as a wife and a member of society, it must be admitted that as a sister she had virtues.

CHAPTER XXXIII.

CONSOLATION.

On the next day, at two o'clock punctually, Mark Robarts was at the "Dragon of Want-ly," walking up and down the very room in which the party had breakfasted after Harold Smith's lecture, and waiting for the arrival of Mr. Sowerby. He had been very well able to divine what was the business on which his friend wished to see him, and he had been ra-ther glad than otherwise to receive the summons. Judging of his friend's character by what he had hitherto seen, he thought that Mr. Sowerby would have kept out of the way, unless he had it in his power to make some provision for these terrible bills. So he walked up and down the dingy room, impatient for the expected arrival, and thought himself wickedly ill-used in that Mr. Sowerby was not there when the clock struck a quarter to three. But when the clock struck three, Mr. Sowerby was there, and Mark Robarts's hopes were nearly at an end.

"Do you mean that they will demand nine hundred pounds?" said Robarts, standing up and glaring angrily at the member of Parliament.

"I fear that they will," said Sowerby. "I think it is best to tell you the worst, in order that we may see what can be done."

"I can do nothing, and will do nothing," said Robarts. "They may do what they choose—what the law allows them."

And then he thought of Fanny and his nursery, and Lucy refusing in her pride Lord Lufton's offer, and he turned away his face that the hard man of the world before him might not see the tear gathering in his eye.

"But, Mark, my dear fellow—" said Sowerby, trying to have recourse to the power of his cajoling voice.

Robarts, however, would not listen.

"Mr. Sowerby," said he, with an attempt at calmness which betrayed itself at every syl-lable, "it seems to me that you have robbed me. That I have been a fool, and worse than a fool, I know well; but—but—but I thought that your position in the world would guaran-tee me from such treatment as this."

Mr. Sowerby was by no means without feeling, and the words which he now heard cut him very deeply—the more so because it was impossible that he should answer them with an attempt at indignation. He had robbed his friend, and, with all his wit, knew no words at the present moment sufficiently witty to make it seem that he had not done so.

"Robarts," said he, "you may say what you like to me now; I shall not resent it."

"Who would care for your resentment?" said the clergyman, turning on him with ferocity. "The resentment of a gentleman is terrible to a gentleman; and the resentment of one just man is terrible to another. Your resentment!"—and then he walked twice the length of the room, leaving Sowerby dumb in his seat. "I wonder whether you ever thought of my wife and children when you were plotting this ruin for me!" And then again he walked the room.

"I suppose you will be calm enough presently to speak of this with some attempt to make a settlement?"

"No; I will make no such attempt. These friends of yours, you tell me, have a claim on me for nine hundred pounds, of which they demand immediate payment. You shall be asked in a court of law how much of that money I have handled. You know that I have never touched—have never wanted to touch—one shilling. I will make no attempt at any settlement. My person is here, and there is my house. Let them do their worst."

"But, Mark—"

"Call me by my name, sir, and drop that affectation of regard. What an ass I have been to be so cozened by a sharper!"

Sowerby had by no means expected this. He had always known that Robarts possessed what he, Sowerby, would have called the spirit of a gentleman. He had regarded him as a bold, open, generous fellow, able to take his own part when called on to do so, and by no means disinclined to speak his own mind; but he had not expected from him such a torrent of indignation, or thought that he was capable of such a depth of anger.

"If you use such language as that, Robarts, I can only leave you."

"You are welcome. Go. You tell me that you are the messenger of these men who intend to work nine hundred pounds out of me. You have done your part in the plot, and have now brought their message. It seems to me that you had better go back to them. As for me, I want my time to prepare my wife for the destiny before her."

"Robarts, you will be sorry some day for the cruelty of your words."

"I wonder whether you will ever be sorry for the cruelty of your doings, or whether these things are really a joke to you."

"I am at this moment a ruined man," said Sowerby. "Everything is going from me,—my place in the world, the estate of my family, my father's house, my seat in Parliament, the power of living among my countrymen, or, indeed, of living anywhere;—but all this does not oppress me now so much as the misery which I have brought upon you." And then Sowerby also turned away his face, and wiped from his eyes tears which were not artificial.

Robarts was still walking up and down the room, but it was not possible for him to continue his reproaches after this. This is always the case. Let a man endure to heap contumely on his own head, and he will silence the contumely of others—for the moment. Sowerby, without meditating on the matter, had had some inkling of this, and immediately saw that there was at last an opening for conversation.

"You are unjust to me," said he, "in supposing that I have now no wish to save you. It is solely in the hope of doing so that I have come here."

"And what is your hope? That I should accept another brace of bills, I suppose."

"Not a brace; but one renewed bill for—"

"Look here, Mr. Sowerby. On no earthly consideration that can be put before me will I again sign my name to any bill in the guise of an acceptance. I have been very weak, and am ashamed of my weakness; but so much strength as that, I hope, is left to me. I have been very wicked, and am ashamed of my wickedness; but so much right principle as that, I hope, remains. I will put my name to no other bill; not for you, not even for myself."

"But, Robarts, under your present circumstances that will be madness."

"Then I will be mad."

"Have you seen Forrest? If you will speak to him I think you will find that everything can be accommodated."

"I already owe Mr. Forrest a hundred and fifty pounds, which I obtained from him when you pressed me for the price of that horse, and I will not increase the debt. What a fool I was again there. Perhaps you do not remember that, when I agreed to buy the horse, the price was to be my contribution to the liquidation of these bills."

"I do remember it; but I will tell you how that was."

"It does not signify. It has been all of a piece."

"But listen to me. I think you would feel for me if you knew all that I have gone through. I pledge you my solemn word that I had no intention of asking you for the money when you took the horse;—indeed I had not. But you remember that affair of Lufton's, when he came to you at your hotel in London and was so angry about an outstanding bill."

"I know that he was very unreasonable as far as I was concerned."

"He was so; but that makes no difference. He was resolved, in his rage, to expose the whole affair; and I saw that, if he did so, it would be most injurious to you, seeing that you had just accepted your stall at Barchester." Here the poor prebendary winced terribly. "I moved heaven and earth to get up that bill. Those vultures stuck to their prey when they found the value which I attached to it, and I was forced to raise above a hundred pounds at the moment to obtain possession of it, although every shilling absolutely due on it had long since been paid. Never in my life did I wish to get money as I did to raise that hundred and twenty pounds; and as I hope for mercy in my last moments, I did that for your sake. Lufton could not have injured me in that matter."

"But you told him that you got it for twenty-five pounds."

"Yes, I told him so. I was obliged to tell him that, or I should have apparently condemned myself by showing how anxious I was to get it. And you know I could not have explained all this before him and you. You would have thrown up the stall in disgust."

Would that he had! That was Mark's wish now,—his futile wish. In what a slough of despond had he come to wallow in consequence of his folly on that night at Gatherum Castle! He had then done a silly thing, and was he now to rue it by almost total ruin? He was sickened also with all these lies. His very soul was dismayed by the dirt through which he was forced to wade. He had become unconsciously connected with the lowest dregs of mankind, and would have to see his name mingled with theirs in the daily newspapers. And for what had he done this? Why had he thus filed his mind and made himself a disgrace to his cloth? In order that he might befriend such a one as Mr. Sowerby!

"Well," continued Sowerby, "I did get the money, but you would hardly believe the rigour of the pledge which was exacted from me for repayment. I got it from Harold Smith, and never, in my worst straits, will I again look to him for assistance. I borrowed it only for a fortnight; and in order that I might repay it, I was obliged to ask you for the price of the horse. Mark, it was on your behalf that I did all this,—indeed it was."

"And now I am to repay you for your kindness by the loss of all that I have in the world."

"If you will put the affair into the hands of Mr. Forrest, nothing need be touched,—not a hair of a horse's back; no, not though you should be obliged to pay the whole amount yourself, gradually out of your income. You must execute a series of bills, falling due quarterly, and then—"

"I will execute no bill, I will put my name to no paper in the matter; as to that my mind is fully made up. They may come and do their worst."

Mr. Sowerby persevered for a long time, but he was quite unable to move the parson from this position. He would do nothing towards making what Mr. Sowerby called an arrangement, but persisted that he would remain at home at Framley, and that any one who had a claim upon him might take legal steps.

"I shall do nothing myself," he said; "but if proceedings against me be taken, I shall prove that I have never had a shilling of the money." And in this resolution he quitted the Dragon of Wantly.

Mr. Sowerby at one time said a word as to the expediency of borrowing that sum of money from John Robarts; but as to this Mark would say nothing. Mr. Sowerby was not the friend with whom he now intended to hold consultation in such matters. "I am not at present prepared," he said, "to declare what I may do; I must first see what steps others take." And then he took his hat and went off; and mounting his horse in the yard of the Dragon of Wantly—that horse which he had now so many reasons to dislike—he slowly rode back home.

Many thoughts passed through his mind during that ride, but only one resolution obtained for itself a fixture there. He must now tell his wife everything. He would not be so cruel as to let it remain untold until a bailiff were at the door, ready to walk him off to the county gaol, or until the bed on which they slept was to be sold from under them. Yes, he would tell her everything,—immediately, before his resolution could again have faded away. He got off his horse in the yard, and seeing his wife's maid at the kitchen door, desired her to beg her mistress to come to him in the book-room. He would not allow one half-hour to pass towards the waning of his purpose. If it be ordained that a man shall drown, had he not better drown and have done with it?

Mrs. Robarts came to him in his room, reaching him in time to touch his arm as he entered it.

"Mary says you want me. I have been gardening, and she caught me just as I came in."

"Yes, Fanny, I do want you. Sit down for a moment." And walking across the room, he placed his whip in its proper place.

"Oh, Mark, is there anything the matter?"

"Yes, dearest; yes. Sit down, Fanny; I can talk to you better if you will sit."

But she, poor lady, did not wish to sit. He had hinted at some misfortune, and therefore she felt a longing to stand by him and cling to him.

"Well, there; I will if I must; but, Mark, do not frighten me. Why is your face so very wretched?"

"Fanny, I have done very wrong," he said. "I have been very foolish. I fear that I have brought upon you great sorrow and trouble." And then he leaned his head upon his hand and turned his face away from her.

"Oh, Mark, dearest Mark, my own Mark! what is it?" and then she was quickly up from her chair, and went down on her knees before him. "Do not turn from me. Tell me, Mark! tell me, that we may share it."

"Yes, Fanny, I must tell you now; but I hardly know what you will think of me when you have heard it."

"I will think that you are my own husband, Mark; I will think that—that chiefly, whatever it may be." And then she caressed his knees, and looked up in his face, and, getting hold of one of his hands, pressed it between her own. "Even if you have been foolish, who should forgive you if I cannot?"

And then he told it her all, beginning from that evening when Mr. Sowerby had got him into his bedroom, and going on gradually, now about the bills, and now about the horses, till his poor wife was utterly lost in the complexity of the accounts. She could by no means follow him in the details of his story; nor could she quite sympathize with him in his indignation against Mr. Sowerby, seeing that she did not comprehend at all the nature of the renewing of a bill. The only part to her of importance in the matter was the amount of money which her husband would be called upon to pay;—that and her strong hope, which was already a conviction, that he would never again incur such debts.

"And how much is it, dearest, altogether?"

"These men claim nine hundred pounds of me."

"Oh, dear! that is a terrible sum."

"And then there is the hundred and fifty which I have borrowed from the bank—the price of the horse, you know; and there are some other debts,—not a great deal, I think; but people will now look for every shilling that is due to them. If I have to pay it all, it will be twelve or thirteen hundred pounds."

"That will be as much as a year's income, Mark; even with the stall."

That was the only word of reproach she said,—if that could be called a reproach.

"Yes," he said; "and it is claimed by men who will have no pity in exacting it at any sacrifice, if they have the power. And to think that I should have incurred all this debt without having received anything for it. Oh, Fanny, what will you think of me!"

But she swore to him that she would think nothing of it;—that she would never bear it in her mind against him,—that it could have no effect in lessening her trust in him. Was he not her husband? She was so glad she knew it, that she might comfort him. And she did comfort him, making the weight seem lighter and lighter on his shoulders as he talked of it. And such weights do thus become lighter. A burden that will crush a single pair of shoulders will, when equally divided—when shared by two, each of whom is willing to take the heavier part—become light as a feather. Is not that sharing of the mind's burdens one of the chief purposes for which a man wants a wife? For there is no folly so great as keeping one's sorrows hidden.

And this wife cheerfully, gladly, thankfully took her share. To endure with her lord all her lord's troubles was easy to her; it was the work to which she had pledged herself. But to have thought that her lord had troubles not communicated to her—that would have been to her the one thing not to be borne.

And then they discussed their plans;—what mode of escape they might have out of this terrible money difficulty. Like a true woman, Mrs. Robarts proposed at once to abandon all superfluities. They would sell all their horses; they would not sell their cows, but would sell the butter that came from them; they would sell the pony-carriage, and get rid of the groom. That the footman must go was so much a matter of course, that it was hardly mentioned. But then, as to that house at Barchester, the dignified prebendal mansion in the close—might they not be allowed to leave it unoccupied for one year longer,—perhaps to let it? The world of course must know of their misfortune; but if that misfortune was faced bravely, the world would be less bitter in its condemnation. And then, above all things, everything must be told to Lady Lufton.

"You may, at any rate, believe this, Fanny," said he, "that for no consideration which can be offered to me will I ever put my name to another bill."

The kiss with which she thanked him for this was as warm and generous as though he had brought to her that day news of the brightest; and when he sat, as he did that evening, discussing it all, not only with his wife, but with Lucy, he wondered how it was that his troubles were now so light.

Whether or no a man should have his own private pleasures, I will not now say; but it never can be worth his while to keep his sorrows private.

CHAPTER XXXIV.

LADY LUFTON IS TAKEN BY SURPRISE.

Lord Lufton, as he returned to town, found some difficulty in resolving what step he would next take. Sometimes, for a minute or two, he was half inclined to think—or rather to say to himself—that Lucy was perhaps not worth the trouble which she threw in his way. He loved her very dearly, and would willingly make her his wife, he thought or said at such moments; but— Such moments, however, were only moments. A man in love seldom loves less because his love becomes difficult. And thus, when those moments were over, he would determine to tell his mother at once, and urge her to signify her consent to Miss Robarts. That she would not be quite pleased he knew; but if he were firm enough to show that he had a will of his own in this matter, she would probably not gainsay him. He would not ask this humbly, as a favour, but request her ladyship to go through the ceremony as though it were one of those motherly duties which she as a good mother could not hesitate to perform on behalf of her son. Such was the final resolve with which he reached his chambers in the Albany.

On the next day he did not see his mother. It would be well, he thought, to have his interview with her immediately before he started for Norway, so that there might be no repetition of it; and it was on the day before he did start that he made his communication, having invited himself to breakfast in Brook Street on the occasion.

"Mother," he said, quite abruptly, throwing himself into one of the dining-room arm-chairs, "I have a thing to tell you."

His mother at once knew that the thing was important, and with her own peculiar motherly instinct imagined that the question to be discussed had reference to matrimony. Had her son desired to speak to her about money, his tone and look would have been different; as would also have been the case—in a different way—had he entertained any thought of a pilgrimage to Pekin, or a prolonged fishing excursion to the Hudson Bay territories.

"A thing, Ludovic! well; I am quite at liberty."

"I want to know what you think of Lucy Robarts?"

Lady Lufton became pale and frightened, and the blood ran cold to her heart. She had feared more than rejoiced in conceiving that her son was about to talk of love, but she had feared nothing so bad as this. "What do I think of Lucy Robarts?" she said, repeating her son's words in a tone of evident dismay.

"Yes, mother; you have said once or twice lately that you thought I ought to marry, and I am beginning to think so too. You selected one clergyman's daughter for me, but that lady is going to do much better with herself—"

"Indeed she is not," said Lady Lufton sharply.

"And therefore I rather think I shall select for myself another clergyman's sister. You don't dislike Miss Robarts, I hope?"

"Oh, Ludovic!"

It was all that Lady Lufton could say at the spur of the moment.

"Is there any harm in her? Have you any objection to her? Is there anything about her that makes her unfit to be my wife?"

For a moment or two Lady Lufton sat silent, collecting her thoughts. She thought that there was very great objection to Lucy Robarts, regarding her as the possible future Lady Lufton. She could hardly have stated all her reasons, but they were very cogent. Lucy Robarts had, in her eyes, neither beauty, nor style, nor manner, nor even the education which was desirable. Lady Lufton was not herself a worldly woman. She was almost as far removed from being so as a woman could be in her position. But, nevertheless, there were certain worldly attributes which she regarded as essential to the character of any young lady who might be considered fit to take the place which she herself had so long filled. It was her desire in looking for a wife for her son to combine these with certain moral excellences which she regarded as equally essential. Lucy Robarts might have the moral excellences, or she might not; but as to the other attributes Lady Lufton regarded her as altogether deficient. She could never look like a Lady Lufton, or carry herself in the county as a Lady Lufton should do. She had not that quiet personal demeanour—that dignity of repose—which Lady Lufton loved to look upon in a young married woman of rank. Lucy, she would have said, could be nobody in a room except by dint of her tongue, whereas Griselda Grantly would have held her peace for a whole evening, and yet would have impressed everybody by the majesty of her presence. Then again Lucy had no money—and, again, Lucy was only the sister of her own parish clergyman. People are rarely prophets in their own country, and Lucy was no prophet at Framley; she was none, at least, in the eyes of Lady Lufton. Once before, as may be remembered, she had had fears on this subject—fears, not so much for her son, whom she could hardly bring herself to suspect of such a folly, but for Lucy, who might be foolish enough to fancy that the lord was in love with her. Alas! alas! her son's question fell upon the poor woman at the present moment with the weight of a terrible blow.

"Is there anything about her which makes her unfit to be my wife?"

Those were her son's last words.

"Dearest Ludovic, dearest Ludovic!" and she got up and came over to him, "I do think so; I do, indeed."

"Think what?" said he, in a tone that was almost angry.

"I do think that she is unfit to be your wife. She is not of that class from which I would wish to see you choose."

"She is of the same class as Griselda Grantly."

"No, dearest. I think you are in error there. The Grantlys have moved in a different sphere of life. I think you must feel that they are—"

"Upon my word, mother, I don't. One man is Rector of Plumstead, and the other is Vicar of Framley. But it is no good arguing that. I want you to take to Lucy Robarts. I have come to you on purpose to ask it of you as a favour."

"Do you mean as your wife, Ludovic?"

"Yes; as my wife."

"Am I to understand that you are—are engaged to her?"

"Well, I cannot say that I am—not actually engaged to her. But you may take this for granted, that, as far as it lies in my power, I intend to become so. My mind is made up, and I certainly shall not alter it."

"And the young lady knows all this?"

"Certainly."

"Horrid, sly, detestable, underhand girl," Lady Lufton said to herself, not being by any means brave enough to speak out such language before her son. What hope could there be if Lord Lufton had already committed himself by a positive offer? "And her brother, and Mrs. Robarts; are they aware of it?"

"Yes; both of them."

"And both approve of it?"

"Well, I cannot say that. I have not seen Mrs. Robarts, and do not know what may be her opinion. To speak my mind honestly about Mark, I do not think he does cordially approve. He is afraid of you, and would be desirous of knowing what you think."

"I am glad, at any rate, to hear that," said Lady Lufton, gravely. "Had he done anything to encourage this, it would have been very base." And then there was another short period of silence.

Lord Lufton had determined not to explain to his mother the whole state of the case. He would not tell her that everything depended on her word—that Lucy was ready to marry him only on condition that she, Lady Lufton, would desire her to do so. He would not let her know that everything depended on her—according to Lucy's present verdict. He had a strong disinclination to ask his mother's permission to get married; and he would have to ask it were he to tell her the whole truth. His object was to make her think well of Lucy, and to induce her to be kind, and generous, and affectionate down at Framley. Then things would all turn out comfortably when he again visited that place, as he intended to do on his return from Norway. So much he thought it possible he might effect, relying on his mother's probable calculation that it would be useless for her to oppose a measure which she had no power of stopping by authority. But were he to tell her that she was to be the final judge, that everything was to depend on her will, then, so thought Lord Lufton, that permission would in all probability be refused.

"Well, mother, what answer do you intend to give me?" he said. "My mind is positively made up. I should not have come to you had not that been the case. You will now be going down home, and I would wish you to treat Lucy as you yourself would wish to treat any girl to whom you knew that I was engaged."

"But you say that you are not engaged."

"No, I am not; but I have made my offer to her, and I have not been rejected. She has confessed that she—loves me,—not to myself, but to her brother. Under these circumstances, may I count upon your obliging me?"

There was something in his manner which almost frightened his mother, and made her think that there was more behind than was told to her. Generally speaking, his manner was open, gentle, and unguarded; but now he spoke as though he had prepared his words, and was resolved on being harsh as well as obstinate.

"I am so much taken by surprise, Ludovic, that I can hardly give you an answer. If you ask me whether I approve of such a marriage, I must say that I do not; I think that you would be throwing yourself away in marrying Miss Robarts."

"That is because you do not know her."

"May it not be possible that I know her better than you do, dear Ludovic? You have been flirting with her—"

"I hate that word; it always sounds to me to be vulgar."

"I will say making love to her, if you like it better; and gentlemen under these circumstances will sometimes become infatuated."

"You would not have a man marry a girl without making love to her. The fact is, mother, that your tastes and mine are not exactly the same; you like silent beauty, whereas I like talking beauty, and then—"

"Do you call Miss Robarts beautiful?"

"Yes, I do; very beautiful; she has the beauty that I admire. Good-bye now, mother; I shall not see you again before I start. It will be no use writing, as I shall be away so short a time, and I don't quite know where we shall be. I shall come down to Framley immediately I return, and shall learn from you how the land lies. I have told you my wishes, and you will consider how far you think it right to fall in with them." He then kissed her, and without waiting for her reply he took his leave.

Poor Lady Lufton, when she was left to herself, felt that her head was going round and round. Was this to be the end of all her ambition,—of all her love for her son? and was this to be the result of all her kindness to the Robartses? She almost hated Mark Robarts as she reflected that she had been the means of bringing him and his sister to Framley. She thought over all his sins, his absences from the parish, his visit to Gatherum Castle, his dealings with reference to that farm which was to have been sold, his hunting, and then his acceptance of that stall, given, as she had been told, through the Omnium interest. How could she love him at such a moment as this? And then she thought of his wife. Could it be possible that Fanny Robarts, her own friend Fanny, would be so untrue to her as to lend any assistance to such a marriage as this; as not to use all her power in preventing it? She had spoken to Fanny on this very subject,—not fearing for her son, but with a general idea of the impropriety of intimacies between such girls as Lucy and such men as Lord Lufton, and then Fanny had agreed with her. Could it be possible that even she must be regarded as an enemy?

And then by degrees Lady Lufton began to reflect what steps she had better take. In the first place, should she give in at once, and consent to the marriage? The only thing quite certain to her was this, that life would be not worth having if she were forced into a permanent quarrel with her son. Such an event would probably kill her. When she read of quarrels in other noble families—and the accounts of such quarrels will sometimes, unfortunately, force themselves upon the attention of unwilling readers—she would hug herself, with a spirit that was almost pharisaical, reflecting that her destiny was not like that of others. Such quarrels and hatreds between fathers and daughters, and mothers and sons, were in her eyes disreputable to all the persons concerned. She had lived happily with her husband, comfortably with her neighbours, respectably with the world, and, above all things, affectionately with her children. She spoke everywhere of Lord Lufton as though he were nearly perfect,—and in so speaking, she had not belied her convictions. Under these circumstances, would not any marriage be better than a quarrel?

But then, again, how much of the pride of her daily life would be destroyed by such a match as that! And might it not be within her power to prevent it without any quarrel? That her son would be sick of such a chit as Lucy before he had been married to her six months—of that Lady Lufton entertained no doubt, and therefore her conscience would not be disquieted in disturbing the consummation of an arrangement so pernicious. It was evident that the matter was not considered as settled even by her son; and also evident that he regarded the matter as being in some way dependent on his mother's consent. On the whole, might it not be better for her—better for them all—that she should think wholly of her duty, and not of the disagreeable results to which that duty might possibly lead? It could not be her duty to accede to such an alliance; and therefore she would do her best to prevent it. Such, at least, should be her attempt in the first instance.

Having so decided, she next resolved on her course of action. Immediately on her arrival at Framley, she would send for Lucy Robarts, and use all her eloquence—and perhaps also a little of that stern dignity for which she was so remarkable—in explaining to that young lady how very wicked it was on her part to think of forcing herself into such a family as that of the Luftons. She would explain to Lucy that no happiness could come of it, that people placed by misfortune above their sphere are always miserable; and, in short, make use of all those excellent moral lessons which are so customary on such occasions. The morality might, perhaps, be thrown away; but Lady Lufton depended much on her dignified sternness. And then, having so resolved, she prepared for her journey home.

Very little had been said at Framley Parsonage about Lord Lufton's offer after the departure of that gentleman; very little, at least, in Lucy's presence. That the parson and his wife should talk about it between themselves was a matter of course; but very few words were spoken on the matter either by or to Lucy. She was left to her own thoughts, and possibly to her own hopes.

And then other matters came up at Framley which turned the current of interest into other tracks. In the first place there was the visit made by Mr. Sowerby to the Dragon of Wantly, and the consequent revelation made by Mark Robarts to his wife. And while that latter subject was yet new, before Fanny and Lucy had as yet made up their minds as to all the little economies which might be practised in the household without serious detriment to the master's comfort, news reached them that Mrs. Crawley of Hogglestock had been stricken with fever. Nothing of the kind could well be more dreadful than this. To those who knew the family it seemed impossible that their most ordinary wants could be supplied if that courageous head were even for a day laid low; and then the poverty of poor Mr. Crawley was such that the sad necessities of a sick bed could hardly be supplied without assistance.

"I will go over at once," said Fanny.

"My dear!" said her husband, "it is typhus, and you must first think of the children. I will go."

"What on earth could you do, Mark?" said his wife. "Men on such occasions are almost worse than useless; and then they are so much more liable to infection."

"I have no children, nor am I a man," said Lucy, smiling; "for both of which exemptions I am thankful. I will go, and when I come back I will keep clear of the bairns."

So it was settled, and Lucy started in the pony-carriage, carrying with her such things from the parsonage storehouse as were thought to be suitable to the wants of the sick lady at Hogglestock. When she arrived there, she made her way into the house, finding the door open, and not being able to obtain the assistance of the servant girl in ushering her in. In the parlour she found Grace Crawley, the eldest child, sitting demurely in her mother's chair nursing an infant. She, Grace herself, was still a young child, but not the less, on this occasion of well-understood sorrow, did she go through her task not only with zeal but almost with solemnity. Her brother, a boy of six years old, was with her, and he had the care of another baby. There they sat in a cluster, quiet, grave, and silent, attending on themselves, because it had been willed by fate that no one else should attend on them.

"How is your mamma, dear Grace?" said Lucy, walking up to her, and holding out her hand.

"Poor mamma is very ill, indeed," said Grace.

"And papa is very unhappy," said Bobby, the boy.

"I can't get up because of baby," said Grace; "but Bobby can go and call papa out."

"I will knock at the door," said Lucy, and so saying she walked up to the bedroom door, and tapped against it lightly. She repeated this for the third time before she was summoned in by a low hoarse voice, and then on entering she saw Mr. Crawley standing by the bedside with a book in his hand. He looked at her uncomfortably, in a manner which seemed to show that he was annoyed by this intrusion, and Lucy was aware that she had disturbed him while at prayers by the bedside of his wife. He came across the room, however, and shook hands with her, and answered her inquiries in his ordinary grave and solemn voice.

"Mrs. Crawley is very ill," he said, "very ill. God has stricken us heavily, but His will be done. But you had better not go to her, Miss Robarts. It is typhus."

The caution, however, was too late; for Lucy was already by the bedside, and had taken the hand of the sick woman, which had been extended on the coverlid to greet her. "Dear Miss Robarts," said a weak voice; "this is very good of you; but it makes me unhappy to see you here."

Lucy lost no time in taking sundry matters into her own hands, and ascertaining what was most wanted in that wretched household. For it was wretched enough. Their only servant, a girl of sixteen, had been taken away by her mother as soon as it became known that Mrs. Crawley was ill with fever. The poor mother, to give her her due, had promised to come down morning and evening herself, to do such work as might be done in an hour or so; but she could not, she said, leave her child to catch the fever. And now, at the period of Lucy's visit, no step had been taken to procure a nurse, Mr. Crawley having resolved to take upon himself the duties of that position. In his absolute ignorance of all sanatory measures, he had thrown himself on his knees to pray; and if prayers—true prayers—might succour his poor wife, of such succour she might be confident. Lucy, however, thought that other aid also was wanting to her.

"If you can do anything for us," said Mrs. Crawley, "let it be for the poor children."

"I will have them all moved from this till you are better," said Lucy, boldly.

"Moved!" said Mr. Crawley, who even now—even in his present strait—felt a repugnance to the idea that any one should relieve him of any portion of his burden.

"Yes," said Lucy; "I am sure it will be better that you should lose them for a week or two, till Mrs. Crawley may be able to leave her room."

"But where are they to go?" said he, very gloomily.

As to this Lucy was not as yet able to say anything. Indeed when she left Framley Parsonage there had been no time for discussion. She would go back and talk it all over with Fanny, and find out in what way the children might be best put out of danger. Why should they not all be harboured at the parsonage, as soon as assurance could be felt that they were not tainted with the poison of the fever? An English lady of the right sort will do all things but one for a sick neighbour; but for no neighbour will she wittingly admit contagious sickness within the precincts of her own nursery.

Lucy unloaded her jellies and her febrifuges, Mr. Crawley frowning at her bitterly the while. It had come to this with him, that food had been brought into his house, as an act of charity, in his very presence, and in his heart of hearts he disliked Lucy Robarts in that she had brought it. He could not cause the jars and the pots to be replaced in the pony-carriage, as he would have done had the position of his wife been different. In her state it would have been barbarous to refuse them, and barbarous also to have created the *fracas* of a refusal; but each parcel that was introduced was an additional weight laid on the sore withers of his pride, till the total burden became almost intolerable. All this his wife saw and recognized even in her illness, and did make some slight ineffectual efforts to give him ease; but Lucy in her new power was ruthless, and the chicken to make the chicken-broth was taken out of the basket under his very nose.

But Lucy did not remain long. She had made up her mind what it behoved her to do herself, and she was soon ready to return to Framley. "I shall be back again, Mr. Crawley," she said, "probably this evening, and I shall stay with her till she is better." "Nurses don't want rooms," she went on to say, when Mr. Crawley muttered something as to there being no bed-chamber. "I shall make up some sort of a litter near her; you'll see that I shall be very snug." And then she got into the pony-chaise, and drove herself home.

CHAPTER XXXV.

THE STORY OF KING COPHETUA.

Lucy as she drove herself home had much as to which it was necessary that she should arouse her thoughts. That she would go back and nurse Mrs. Crawley through her fever she was resolved. She was free agent enough to take so much on herself, and to feel sure that she could carry it through. But how was she to redeem her promise about the children? Twenty plans ran through her mind, as to farm-houses in which they might be placed, or cottages which might be hired for them; but all these entailed the want of money; and at the present moment, were not all the inhabitants of the parsonage pledged to a dire economy? This use of the pony-carriage would have been illicit under any circumstances less pressing than the present, for it had been decided that the carriage, and even poor Puck himself, should be sold. She had, however, given her promise about the children, and though her own stock of money was very low, that promise should be redeemed.

When she reached the parsonage she was of course full of her schemes, but she found that another subject of interest had come up in her absence, which prevented her from obtaining the undivided attention of her sister-in-law to her present plans. Lady Lufton had returned that day, and immediately on her return had sent up a note addressed to Miss Lucy Robarts, which note was in Fanny's hands when Lucy stepped out of the pony-carriage. The servant who brought it had asked for an answer, and a verbal answer had been sent, saying that Miss Robarts was away from home, and would herself send a reply when she returned. It cannot be denied that the colour came to Lucy's face, and that her hand trembled when she took the note from Fanny in the drawing-room. Everything in the world to her might depend on what that note contained; and yet she did not open it at once, but stood with it in her hand, and when Fanny pressed her on the subject, still endeavoured to bring back the conversation to the subject of Mrs. Crawley.

But yet her mind was intent on the letter, and she had already augured ill from the handwriting and even from the words of the address. Had Lady Lufton intended to be propitious, she would have directed her letter to Miss Robarts, without the Christian name; so at least argued Lucy,—quite unconsciously, as one does argue in such matters. One forms half the conclusions of one's life without any distinct knowledge that the premises have even passed through one's mind.

They were now alone together, as Mark was out.

"Won't you open her letter?" said Mrs. Robarts.

"Yes, immediately; but, Fanny, I must speak to you about Mrs. Crawley first. I must go back there this evening, and stay there; I have promised to do so, and shall certainly keep my promise. I have promised also that the children shall be taken away, and we must arrange about that. It is dreadful, the state she is in. There is no one to see to her but Mr. Crawley, and the children are altogether left to themselves."

"Do you mean that you are going back to stay?"

"Yes, certainly; I have made a distinct promise that I would do so. And about the children; could not you manage for the children, Fanny,—not perhaps in the house; at least not at first perhaps?" And yet during all the time that she was thus speaking and pleading for the Crawleys, she was endeavouring to imagine what might be the contents of that letter which she held between her fingers.

"And is she so very ill?" asked Mrs. Robarts.

"I cannot say how ill she may be, except this, that she certainly has typhus fever. They have had some doctor or doctor's assistant from Silverbridge; but it seems to me that they are greatly in want of better advice."

"But, Lucy, will you not read your letter? It is astonishing to me that you should be so indifferent about it."

Lucy was anything but indifferent, and now did proceed to tear the envelope. The note was very short, and ran in these words,—

MY DEAR MISS ROBARTS,—I am particularly anxious to see you, and shall feel much obliged to you if you can step over to me here, at Framley Court. I must apologize for taking this liberty with you, but you will probably feel that an interview here would suit us both better than one at the parsonage. Truly yours,   M. LUFTON.

"There; I am in for it now," said Lucy, handing the note over to Mrs. Robarts. "I shall have to be talked to as never poor girl was talked to before; and when one thinks of what I have done, it is hard."

"Yes; and of what you have not done."

"Exactly; and of what I have not done. But I suppose I must go," and she proceeded to re-tie the strings of her bonnet, which she had loosened.

"Do you mean that you are going over at once?"

"Yes; immediately. Why not? it will be better to have it over, and then I can go to the Crawleys. But, Fanny, the pity of it is that I know it all as well as though it had been already spoken; and what good can there be in my having to endure it? Can't you fancy the tone in which she will explain to me the conventional inconveniences which arose when King Cophetua would marry the beggar's daughter? how she will explain what Griselda went through;—not the archdeacon's daughter, but the other Griselda?"

"But it all came right with her."

"Yes; but then I am not Griselda, and she will explain how it would certainly all go wrong with me. But what's the good when I know it all beforehand? Have I not desired King Cophetua to take himself and sceptre elsewhere?"

And then she started, having first said another word or two about the Crawley children, and obtained a promise of Puck and the pony-carriage for the afternoon. It was also almost agreed that Puck on his return to Framley should bring back the four children with him; but on this subject it was necessary that Mark should be consulted. The present scheme was to prepare for them a room outside the house, once the dairy, at present occupied by the groom and his wife; and to bring them into the house as soon as it was manifest that there was no danger from infection. But all this was to be matter for deliberation.

Fanny wanted her to send over a note, in reply to Lady Lufton's, as harbinger of her coming; but Lucy marched off, hardly answering this proposition.

"What's the use of such a deal of ceremony?" she said. "I know she's at home; and if she is not, I shall only lose ten minutes in going." And so she went, and on reaching the door of Framley Court house found that her ladyship was at home. Her heart almost came to her mouth as she was told so, and then, in two minutes' time, she found herself in the little room upstairs. In that little room we found ourselves once before,—you, and I, O my reader;—but Lucy had never before visited that hallowed precinct. There was something in its air calculated to inspire awe in those who first saw Lady Lufton sitting bolt upright in the cane-bottomed arm-chair, which she always occupied when at work at her books and papers; and this she knew when she determined to receive Lucy in that apartment. But there was there another arm-chair, an easy, cozy chair, which stood by the fireside; and for those who had caught Lady Lufton napping in that chair of an afternoon, some of this awe had perhaps been dissipated.

"Miss Robarts," she said, not rising from her chair, but holding out her hand to her visitor; "I am much obliged to you for having come over to me here. You, no doubt, are aware of the subject on which I wish to speak to you, and will agree with me that it is better that we should meet here than over at the parsonage."

In answer to which Lucy merely bowed her head, and took her seat on the chair which had been prepared for her.

"My son," continued her ladyship, "has spoken to me on the subject of—I think I understand, Miss Robarts, that there has been no engagement between you and him?"

"None whatever," said Lucy. "He made me an offer and I refused him." This she said very sharply;—more so undoubtedly than the circumstances required; and with a brusqueness that was injudicious as well as uncourteous. But at the moment, she was thinking of her own position with reference to Lady Lufton—not to Lord Lufton; and of her feelings with reference to the lady—not to the gentleman.

"Oh," said Lady Lufton, a little startled by the manner of the communication. "Then I am to understand that there is nothing now going on between you and my son;—that the whole affair is over?"

"That depends entirely upon you."

"On me! does it?"

"I do not know what your son may have told you, Lady Lufton. For myself, I do not care to have any secrets from you in this matter; and as he has spoken to you about it, I suppose that such is his wish also. Am I right in presuming that he has spoken to you on the subject?"

"Yes, he has; and it is for that reason that I have taken the liberty of sending for you."

"And may I ask what he has told you? I mean, of course, as regards myself," said Lucy.

Lady Lufton, before she answered this question, began to reflect that the young lady was taking too much of the initiative in this conversation, and was, in fact, playing the game in her own fashion, which was not at all in accordance with those motives which had induced Lady Lufton to send for her.

"He has told me that he made you an offer of marriage," replied Lady Lufton; "a matter which, of course, is very serious to me, as his mother; and I have thought, therefore, that I had better see you, and appeal to your own good sense and judgment and high feeling. Of course you are aware—"

Now was coming the lecture to be illustrated by King Cophetua and Griselda, as Lucy had suggested to Mrs. Robarts; but she succeeded in stopping it for awhile.

"And did Lord Lufton tell you what was my answer?"

"Not in words. But you yourself now say that you refused him; and I must express my admiration for your good—"

"Wait half a moment, Lady Lufton. Your son did make me an offer. He made it to me in person, up at the parsonage, and I then refused him;—foolishly, as I now believe, for I dearly love him. But I did so from a mixture of feelings which I need not, perhaps, explain; that most prominent, no doubt, was a fear of your displeasure. And then he came again, not to me but to my brother, and urged his suit to him. Nothing can have been kinder to me, more noble, more loving, more generous, than his conduct. At first I thought, when he was speaking to myself, that he was led on thoughtlessly to say all that he did say. I did not trust his love, though I saw that he did trust it himself. But I could not but trust it when he came again—to my brother, and made his proposal to him. I don't know whether you will understand me, Lady Lufton; but a girl placed as I am feels ten times more assurance in such a tender of affection as that, than in one made to herself, at the spur of the moment, perhaps. And then you must remember that I—I myself—I loved him from the first. I was foolish enough to think that I could know him and not love him."

"I saw all that going on," said Lady Lufton, with a certain assumption of wisdom about her; "and took steps which I hoped would have put a stop to it in time."

"Everybody saw it. It was a matter of course," said Lucy, destroying her ladyship's wisdom at a blow. "Well; I did learn to love him, not meaning to do so; and I do love him with all my heart. It is no use my striving to think that I do not; and I could stand with him at the altar to-morrow and give him my hand, feeling that I was doing my duty by him, as a woman should do. And now he has told you of his love, and I believe in that as I do in my own—" And then for a moment she paused.

"But, my dear Miss Robarts—" began Lady Lufton.

Lucy, however, had now worked herself up into a condition of power, and would not allow her ladyship to interrupt her in her speech.

"I beg your pardon, Lady Lufton; I shall have done directly, and then I will hear you. And so my brother came to me, not urging this suit, expressing no wish for such a marriage, but allowing me to judge for myself, and proposing that I should see your son again on the following morning. Had I done so, I could not but have accepted him. Think of it, Lady Lufton. How could I have done other than accept him, seeing that in my heart I had accepted his love already?"

"Well?" said Lady Lufton, not wishing now to put in any speech of her own.

"I did not see him—I refused to do so—because I was a coward. I could not endure to come into this house as your son's wife, and be coldly looked on by your son's mother. Much as I loved him, much as I do love him, dearly as I prize the generous offer which he came down here to repeat to me, I could not live with him to be made the object of your scorn. I sent him word, therefore, that I would have him when you would ask me, and not before."

And then, having thus pleaded her cause—and pleaded as she believed the cause of her lover also—she ceased from speaking, and prepared herself to listen to the story of King Cophetua.

But Lady Lufton felt considerable difficulty in commencing her speech. In the first place she was by no means a hard-hearted or a selfish woman; and were it not that her own son was concerned, and all the glory which was reflected upon her from her son, her sympathies would have been given to Lucy Robarts. As it was, she did sympathize with her, and admire her, and to a certain extent like her. She began also to understand what it was that had brought about her son's love, and to feel that but for certain unfortunate concomitant circumstances the girl before her might have made a fitting Lady Lufton. Lucy had grown bigger in her eyes while sitting there and talking, and had lost much of that missish want of importance—that lack of social weight which Lady Lufton in her own opinion had always imputed to her. A girl that could thus speak up and explain her own position now, would be able to speak up and explain her own, and perhaps some other positions at any future time.

But not for all or any of these reasons did Lady Lufton think of giving way. The power of making or marring this marriage was placed in her hands, as was very fitting, and that power it behoved her to use, as best she might use it, to her son's advantage. Much as she might admire Lucy, she could not sacrifice her son to that admiration. The unfortunate concomitant circumstances still remained, and were of sufficient force, as she thought, to make such a marriage inexpedient. Lucy was the sister of a gentleman, who by his peculiar position as parish clergyman of Framley was unfitted to be the brother-in-law of the owner of Framley. Nobody liked clergymen better than Lady Lufton, or was more willing to live with them on terms of affectionate intimacy, but she could not get over the feeling that the clergyman of her own parish,—or of her son's,—was a part of her own establishment, of her own appanage,—or of his,—and that it could not be well that Lord Lufton should marry among his own—dependants. Lady Lufton would not have used the word, but she did think it. And then, too, Lucy's education had been so deficient. She had had no one about her in early life accustomed to the ways of,—of what shall I say, without making Lady Lufton appear more worldly than she was? Lucy's wants in this respect, not to be defined in words, had been exemplified by the very way in which she had just now stated her case. She had shown talent, good temper, and sound judgment; but there had been no quiet, no repose about her. The species of power in young ladies which Lady Lufton most admired was the *vis inertiæ* belonging to beautiful and dignified reticence; of this poor Lucy had none. Then, too, she had no fortune, which, though a minor evil, was an evil; and she had no birth, in the high-life sense of the word, which was a greater evil. And then, though her eyes had sparkled when she confessed her love, Lady Lufton was not prepared to admit that she was possessed of positive beauty. Such were the unfortunate concomitant circumstances which still induced Lady Lufton to resolve that the match must be marred.

But the performance of her part in this play was much more difficult than she had imagined, and she found herself obliged to sit silent for a minute or two, during which, however, Miss Robarts made no attempt at further speech.

"I am greatly struck," Lady Lufton said at last, "by the excellent sense you have displayed in the whole of this affair; and you must allow me to say, Miss Robarts, that I now regard you with very different feelings from those which I entertained when I left London." Upon this Lucy bowed her head, slightly but very stiffly; acknowledging rather the former censure implied than the present eulogium expressed.

"But my feelings," continued Lady Lufton, "my strongest feelings in this matter, must be those of a mother. What might be my conduct if such a marriage did take place, I need not now consider. But I must confess that I should think such a marriage very—very ill-judged. A better hearted young man than Lord Lufton does not exist, nor one with better principles, or a deeper regard for his word; but he is exactly the man to be mistaken in any hurried outlook as to his future life. Were you and he to become man and wife, such a marriage would tend to the happiness neither of him nor of you."

It was clear that the whole lecture was now coming; and as Lucy had openly declared her own weakness, and thrown all the power of decision into the hands of Lady Lufton, she did not see why she should endure this.

"We need not argue about that, Lady Lufton," she said. "I have told you the only circumstances under which I would marry your son; and you, at any rate, are safe."

"No; I was not wishing to argue," answered Lady Lufton, almost humbly; "but I was desirous of excusing myself to you, so that you should not think me cruel in withholding my consent. I wished to make you believe that I was doing the best for my son."

"I am sure that you think you are, and therefore no excuse is necessary."

"No; exactly; of course it is a matter of opinion, and I do think so. I cannot believe that this marriage would make either of you happy, and therefore I should be very wrong to express my consent."

"Then, Lady Lufton," said Lucy, rising from her chair, "I suppose we have both now said what is necessary, and I will therefore wish you good-bye."

"Good-bye, Miss Robarts. I wish I could make you understand how very highly I regard your conduct in this matter. It has been above all praise, and so I shall not hesitate to say when speaking of it to your relatives." This was disagreeable enough to Lucy, who cared but little for any praise which Lady Lufton might express to her relatives in this matter. "And pray," continued Lady Lufton, "give my best love to Mrs. Robarts, and tell her that I shall hope to see her over here very soon, and Mr. Robarts also. I would name a day for you all to dine, but perhaps it will be better that I should have a little talk with Fanny first."

Lucy muttered something, which was intended to signify that any such dinner-party had better not be made up with the intention of including her, and then took her leave. She had decidedly had the best of the interview, and there was a consciousness of this in her heart as she allowed Lady Lufton to shake hands with her. She had stopped her antagonist short on each occasion on which an attempt had been made to produce the homily which had been prepared, and during the interview had spoken probably three words for every one which her ladyship had been able to utter. But, nevertheless, there was a bitter feeling of disappointment about her heart as she walked back home; and a feeling, also, that she herself had caused her own unhappiness. Why should she have been so romantic and chivalrous and self-sacrificing, seeing that her romance and chivalry had all been to his detriment as well as to hers,—seeing that she sacrificed him as well as herself? Why should she have been so anxious to play into Lady Lufton's hands? It was not because she thought it right, as a general social rule, that a lady should refuse a gentleman's hand, unless the gentleman's mother were a consenting party to the marriage. She would have held any such doctrine as absurd. The lady, she would have said, would have had to look to her own family and no further. It was not virtue but cowardice which had influenced her, and she had none of that solace which may come to us in misfortune from a consciousness that our own conduct has been blameless. Lady Lufton had inspired her with awe, and any such feeling on her part was mean, ignoble, and unbecoming the spirit with which she wished to think that she was endowed. That was the accusation which she brought against herself, and it forbade her to feel any triumph as to the result of her interview.

When she reached the parsonage, Mark was there, and they were of course expecting her. "Well," said she, in her short, hurried manner, "is Puck ready again? I have no time to lose, and I must go and pack up a few things. Have you settled about the children, Fanny?"

"Yes; I will tell you directly; but you have seen Lady Lufton?"

"Seen her! Oh, yes, of course I have seen her. Did she not send for me? and in that case it was not on the cards that I should disobey her."

"And what did she say?"

"How green you are, Mark; and not only green, but impolite also, to make me repeat the story of my own disgrace. Of course she told me that she did not intend that I should marry my lord, her son; and of course I said that under those circumstances I should not think of doing such a thing."

"Lucy, I cannot understand you," said Fanny, very gravely. "I am sometimes inclined to doubt whether you have any deep feeling in the matter or not. If you have, how can you bring yourself to joke about it?"

"Well, it is singular; and sometimes I doubt myself whether I have. I ought to be pale, ought I not? and very thin, and to go mad by degrees? I have not the least intention of doing anything of the kind, and, therefore, the matter is not worth any further notice."

"But was she civil to you, Lucy?" asked Mark; "civil in her manner, you know?"

"Oh, uncommonly so. You will hardly believe it, but she actually asked me to dine. She always does, you know, when she wants to show her good-humour. If you'd broken your leg, and she wished to commiserate you, she'd ask you to dinner."

"I suppose she meant to be kind," said Fanny, who was not disposed to give up her old friend, though she was quite ready to fight Lucy's battle, if there were any occasion for a battle to be fought.

"Lucy is so perverse," said Mark, "that it is impossible to learn from her what really has taken place."

"Upon my word, then, you know it all as well as I can tell you. She asked me if Lord Lufton had made me an offer. I said, yes. She asked next, if I meant to accept it. Not without her approval, I said. And then she asked us all to dinner. That is exactly what took place, and I cannot see that I have been perverse at all." After that she threw herself into a chair, and Mark and Fanny stood looking at each other.

"Mark," she said, after a while, "don't be unkind to me. I make as little of it as I can, for all our sakes. It is better so, Fanny, than that I should go about moaning, like a sick cow;" and then they looked at her, and saw that the tears were already brimming over from her eyes.

"Dearest, dearest Lucy," said Fanny, immediately going down on her knees before her, "I won't be unkind to you again." And then they had a great cry together.

CHAPTER XXXVI.

KIDNAPPING AT HOGGLESTOCK.

The great cry, however, did not take long, and Lucy was soon in the pony-carriage again. On this occasion her brother volunteered to drive her, and it was now understood that he was to bring back with him all the Crawley children. The whole thing had been arranged; the groom and his wife were to be taken into the house, and the big bedroom across the yard, usually occupied by them, was to be converted into a quarantine hospital until such time as it might be safe to pull down the yellow flag. They were about half way on their road to Hogglestock when they were overtaken by a man on horseback, whom, when he came up beside them, Mr. Robarts recognized as Dr. Arabin, Dean of Barchester, and head of the chapter to which he himself belonged. It immediately appeared that the dean also was going to Hogglestock, having heard of the misfortune that had befallen his friends there; he had, he said, started as soon as the news reached him, in order that he might ascertain how best he might render assistance. To effect this he had undertaken a ride of nearly forty miles, and explained that he did not expect to reach home again much before midnight.

"You pass by Framley?" said Robarts.

"Yes, I do," said the dean.

"Then of course you will dine with us as you go home; you and your horse also, which will be quite as important." This having been duly settled, and the proper ceremony of introduction having taken place between the dean and Lucy, they proceeded to discuss the character of Mr. Crawley.

"I have known him all my life," said the dean, "having been at school and college with him, and for years since that I was on terms of the closest intimacy with him; but in spite of that, I do not know how to help him in his need. A prouder-hearted man I never met, or one less willing to share his sorrows with his friends."

"I have often heard him speak of you," said Mark.

"One of the bitterest feelings I have is that a man so dear to me should live so near to me, and that I should see so little of him. But what can I do? He will not come to my house; and when I go to his he is angry with me because I wear a shovel hat and ride on horseback."

"I should leave my hat and my horse at the borders of the last parish," said Lucy, timidly.

"Well; yes, certainly; one ought not to give offence even in such matters as that; but my coat and waistcoat would then be equally objectionable. I have changed,—in outward matters I mean,—and he has not. That irritates him, and unless I could be what I was in the old days, he will not look at me with the same eyes;" and then he rode on, in order, as he said, that the first pang of the interview might be over before Robarts and his sister came upon the scene.

Mr. Crawley was standing before his door, leaning over the little wooden railing, when the dean trotted up on his horse. He had come out after hours of close watching to get a few mouthfuls of the sweet summer air, and as he stood there he held the youngest of his children in his arms. The poor little baby sat there, quiet indeed, but hardly happy. This father, though he loved his offspring with an affection as intense as that which human nature can supply, was not gifted with the knack of making children fond of him; for it is hardly more than a knack, that aptitude which some men have of gaining the good graces of the young. Such men are not always the best fathers or the safest guardians; but they carry about with them a certain duc ad me which children recognize, and which in three minutes upsets all the barriers between five and five-and-forty. But Mr. Crawley was a stern man, thinking ever of the souls and minds of his bairns—as a father should do; and thinking also that every season was fitted for operating on these souls and minds—as, perhaps, he should not have done either as a father or as a teacher. And consequently his children avoided him when the choice was given them, thereby adding fresh wounds to his torn heart, but by no means quenching any of the great love with which he regarded them.

He was standing there thus with a placid little baby in his arms—a baby placid enough, but one that would not kiss him eagerly, and stroke his face with her soft little hands, as he would have had her do—when he saw the dean coming towards him. He was sharp-sighted as a lynx out in the open air, though now obliged to pore over his well-fingered books with spectacles on his nose; and thus he knew his friend from a long distance, and had time to meditate the mode of his greeting. He too doubtless had come, if not with jelly and chicken, then with money and advice;—with money and advice such as a thriving dean might offer to a poor brother clergyman; and Mr. Crawley, though no husband could possibly be more anxious for a wife's safety than he was, immediately put his back up and began to bethink himself how these tenders might be rejected.

"How is she?" were the first words which the dean spoke as he pulled up his horse close to the little gate, and put out his hand to take that of his friend.

"How are you, Arabin?" said he. "It is very kind of you to come so far, seeing how much there is to keep you at Barchester. I cannot say that she is any better, but I do not know that she is worse. Sometimes I fancy that she is delirious, though I hardly know. At any rate her mind wanders, and then after that she sleeps."

"But is the fever less?"

"Sometimes less and sometimes more, I imagine."

"And the children?"

"Poor things; they are well as yet."

"They must be taken from this, Crawley, as a matter of course."

Mr. Crawley fancied that there was a tone of authority in the dean's advice, and immediately put himself into opposition.

"I do not know how that may be; I have not yet made up my mind."

"But, my dear Crawley—"

"Providence does not admit of such removals in all cases," said he. "Among the poorer classes the children must endure such perils."

"In many cases it is so," said the dean, by no means inclined to make an argument of it at the present moment; "but in this case they need not. You must allow me to make arrangements for sending for them, as of course your time is occupied here."

Miss Robarts, though she had mentioned her intention of staying with Mrs. Crawley, had said nothing of the Framley plan with reference to the children.

"What you mean is that you intend to take the burden off my shoulders—in fact, to pay for them. I cannot allow that, Arabin. They must take the lot of their father and their mother, as it is proper that they should do."

Again the dean had no inclination for arguing, and thought it might be well to let the question of the children drop for a little while.

"And is there no nurse with her?" said he.

"No, no; I am seeing to her myself at the present moment. A woman will be here just now."

"What woman?"

"Well; her name is Mrs. Stubbs; she lives in the parish. She will put the younger children to bed, and—and—but it's no use troubling you with all that. There was a young lady talked of coming, but no doubt she has found it too inconvenient. It will be better as it is."

"You mean Miss Robarts; she will be here directly; I passed her as I came here;" and as Dr. Arabin was yet speaking, the noise of the carriage wheels was heard upon the road.

"I will go in now," said Mr. Crawley, "and see if she still sleeps;" and then he entered the house, leaving the dean at the door still seated upon his horse. "He will be afraid of the infection, and I will not ask him to come in," said Mr. Crawley to himself.

"I shall seem to be prying into his poverty, if I enter unasked," said the dean to himself. And so he remained there till Puck, now acquainted with the locality, stopped at the door.

"Have you not been in?" said Robarts.

"No; Crawley has been at the door talking to me; he will be here directly, I suppose;" and then Mark Robarts also prepared himself to wait till the master of the house should reappear.

But Lucy had no such punctilious misgivings; she did not much care now whether she offended Mr. Crawley or no. Her idea was to place herself by the sick woman's bedside, and to send the four children away;—with their father's consent if it might be; but certainly without it if that consent were withheld. So she got down from the carriage, and taking certain packages in her hand made her way direct into the house.

"There's a big bundle under the seat, Mark," she said; "I'll come and fetch it directly, if you'll drag it out."

For some five minutes the two dignitaries of the Church remained at the door, one on his cob and the other in his low carriage, saying a few words to each other and waiting till some one should again appear from the house. "It is all arranged, indeed it is," were the first words which reached their ears, and these came from Lucy. "There will be no trouble at all, and no expense, and they shall all come back as soon as Mrs. Crawley is able to get out of bed."

"But, Miss Robarts, I can assure—" That was Mr. Crawley's voice, heard from him as he followed Miss Robarts to the door; but one of the elder children had then called him into the sick room, and Lucy was left to do her worst.

"Are you going to take the children back with you?" said the dean.

"Yes; Mrs. Robarts has prepared for them."

"You can take greater liberties with my friend here than I can."

"It is all my sister's doing," said Robarts. "Women are always bolder in such matters than men." And then Lucy reappeared, bringing Bobby with her, and one of the younger children.

"Do not mind what he says," said she, "but drive away when you have got them all. Tell Fanny I have put into the basket what things I could find, but they are very few. She must borrow things for Grace from Mrs. Granger's little girl"—(Mrs. Granger was the wife of a Framley farmer);—"and, Mark, turn Puck's head round, so that you may be off in a moment. I'll have Grace and the other one here directly." And then, leaving her brother to pack Bobby and his little sister on the back part of the vehicle, she returned to her business in the house. She had just looked in at Mrs. Crawley's bed, and finding her awake, had smiled on her, and deposited her bundle in token of her intended stay, and then, without speaking a word, had gone on her errand about the children. She had called to Grace to show her where she might find such things as were to be taken to Framley, and having explained to the bairns, as well as she might, the destiny which immediately awaited them, prepared them for their departure without saying a word to Mr. Crawley on the subject. Bobby and the elder of the two infants were stowed away safely in the back part of the carriage, where they allowed themselves to be placed without saying a word. They opened their eyes and stared at the dean, who sat by on his horse, and assented to such orders as Mr. Robarts gave them,—no doubt with much surprise, but nevertheless in absolute silence.

"Now, Grace, be quick, there's a dear," said Lucy, returning with the infant in her arms. "And, Grace, mind you are very careful about baby; and bring the basket; I'll give it you when you are in." Grace and the other child were then packed on to the other seat, and a basket with children's clothes put in on the top of them. "That'll do, Mark; good-bye; tell Fanny to be sure and send the day after to-morrow, and not to forget—" and then she whispered into her brother's ear an injunction about certain dairy comforts which might not be spoken of in the hearing of Mr. Crawley. "Good-bye, dears; mind you are good children; you shall hear about mamma the day after to-morrow," said Lucy; and Puck, admonished by a sound from his master's voice, began to move just as Mr. Crawley reappeared at the house door.

"Oh, oh, stop!" he said. "Miss Robarts, you really had better not—"

"Go on, Mark," said Lucy, in a whisper, which, whether audible or not by Mr. Crawley, was heard very plainly by the dean. And Mark, who had slightly arrested Puck by the reins on the appearance of Mr. Crawley, now touched the impatient little beast with his whip; and the vehicle with its freight darted off rapidly, Puck shaking his head and going away with a tremendously quick short trot which soon separated Mr. Crawley from his family.

"Miss Robarts," he began, "this step has been taken altogether without—"

"Yes," said she, interrupting him. "My brother was obliged to return at once. The children, you know, will remain all together at the parsonage; and that, I think, is what Mrs. Crawley will best like. In a day or two they will be under Mrs. Robarts's own charge."

"But, my dear Miss Robarts, I had no intention whatever of putting the burden of my family on the shoulders of another person. They must return to their own home immediately—that is, as soon as they can be brought back."

"I really think Miss Robarts has managed very well," said the dean. "Mrs. Crawley must be so much more comfortable to think that they are out of danger."

"And they will be quite comfortable at the parsonage," said Lucy.

"I do not at all doubt that," said Mr. Crawley; "but too much of such comforts will unfit them for their home; and—and I could have wished that I had been consulted more at leisure before the proceeding had been taken."

"It was arranged, Mr. Crawley, when I was here before, that the children had better go away," pleaded Lucy.

"I do not remember agreeing to such a measure, Miss Robarts; however— I suppose they cannot be had back to-night?"

"No, not to-night," said Lucy. "And now I will go in to your wife." And then she returned to the house, leaving the two gentlemen at the door. At this moment a labourer's boy came sauntering by, and the dean, obtaining possession of his services for the custody of his horse, was able to dismount and put himself on a more equal footing for conversation with his friend.

"Crawley," said he, putting his hand affectionately on his friend's shoulder, as they both stood leaning on the little rail before the door; "that is a good girl—a very good girl."

"Yes," said he slowly; "she means well."

"Nay, but she does well; she does excellently. What can be better than her conduct now? While I was meditating how I might possibly assist your wife in this strait—"

"I want no assistance; none, at least, from man," said Crawley, bitterly.

"Oh, my friend, think of what you are saying! Think of the wickedness which must accompany such a state of mind! Have you ever known any man able to walk alone, without assistance from his brother men?"

Mr. Crawley did not make any immediate answer, but putting his arms behind his back and closing his hands, as was his wont when he walked alone thinking of the general bitterness of his lot in life, began to move slowly along the road in front of his house. He did not invite the other to walk with him, but neither was there anything in his manner which seemed to indicate that he had intended to be left to himself. It was a beautiful summer afternoon, at that delicious period of the year when summer has just burst forth from the growth of spring; when the summer is yet but three days old, and all the various shades of green which nature can put forth are still in their unsoiled purity of freshness. The apple blossoms were on the trees, and the hedges were sweet with May. The cuckoo at five o'clock was still sounding his soft summer call with unabated energy, and even the common grasses of the hedgerows were sweet with the fragrance of their new growth. The foliage of the oaks was complete, so that every bough and twig was clothed; but the leaves did not yet hang heavy in masses, and the bend of every bough and the tapering curve of every twig were visible through their light green covering. There is no time of the year equal in beauty to the first week in summer; and no colour which nature gives, not even the gorgeous hues of autumn, which can equal the verdure produced by the first warm suns of May.

Hogglestock, as has been explained, has little to offer in the way of landskip beauty, and the clergyman's house at Hogglestock was not placed on a green slopy bank of land, retired from the road, with its windows opening on to a lawn, surrounded by shrubs, with a view of the small church tower seen through them; it had none of that beauty which is so common to the cozy houses of our spiritual pastors in the agricultural parts of England. Hogglestock Parsonage stood bleak beside the road, with no pretty paling lined inside by hollies and laburnum, Portugal laurels and rose-trees. But, nevertheless, even Hogglestock was pretty now. There were apple-trees there covered with blossom, and the hedgerows were in full flower. There were thrushes singing, and here and there an oak-tree stood in the roadside, perfect in its solitary beauty.

"Let us walk on a little," said the dean. "Miss Robarts is with her now, and you will be better for leaving the room for a few minutes."

"No," said he; "I must go back; I cannot leave that young lady to do my work."

"Stop, Crawley!" And the dean, putting his hand upon him, stayed him in the road. "She is doing her own work, and if you were speaking of her with reference to any other household than your own, you would say so. Is it not a comfort to you to know that your wife has a woman near her at such a time as this; and a woman, too, who can speak to her as one lady does to another?"

"These are comforts which we have no right to expect. I could not have done much for poor Mary; but what a man could have done should not have been wanting."

"I am sure of it; I know it well. What any man could do by himself you would do—excepting one thing." And the dean as he spoke looked full into the other's face.

"And what is there I would not do?" said Crawley.

"Sacrifice your own pride."

"My pride?"

"Yes; your own pride."

"I have had but little pride this many a day. Arabin, you do not know what my life has been. How is a man to be proud who—" And then he stopped himself, not wishing to go through the catalogue of those grievances, which, as he thought, had killed the very germs of pride within him, or to insist by spoken words on his poverty, his wants, and the injustice of his position. "No; I wish I could be proud; but the world has been too heavy to me, and I have forgotten all that."

"How long have I known you, Crawley?"

"How long? Ah dear! a life-time nearly, now."

"And we were like brothers once."

"Yes; we were equal as brothers then—in our fortunes, our tastes, and our modes of life."

"And yet you would begrudge me the pleasure of putting my hand in my pocket, and relieving the inconveniences which have been thrown on you, and those you love better than yourself, by the chances of your fate in life."

"I will live on no man's charity," said Crawley, with an abruptness which amounted almost to an expression of anger.

"And is not that pride?"

"No—yes;—it is a species of pride, but not that pride of which you spoke. A man cannot be honest if he have not some pride. You yourself;—would you not rather starve than become a beggar?"

"I would rather beg than see my wife starve," said Arabin.

Crawley when he heard these words turned sharply round, and stood with his back to the dean, with his hands still behind him, and with his eyes fixed upon the ground.

"But in this case there is no question of begging," continued the dean. "I, out of those superfluities which it has pleased God to put at my disposal, am anxious to assist the needs of those whom I love."

"She is not starving," said Crawley, in a voice very bitter, but still intended to be exculpatory of himself.

"No, my dear friend; I know she is not, and do not you be angry with me because I have endeavoured to put the matter to you in the strongest language I could use."

"You look at it, Arabin, from one side only; I can only look at it from the other. It is very sweet to give; I do not doubt that. But the taking of what is given is very bitter. Gift bread chokes in a man's throat and poisons his blood, and sits like lead upon the heart. You have never tried it."

"But that is the very fault for which I blame you. That is the pride which I say you ought to sacrifice."

"And why should I be called on to do so? Is not the labourer worthy of his hire? Am I not able to work, and willing? Have I not always had my shoulder to the collar, and is it right that I should now be contented with the scraps from a rich man's kitchen? Arabin, you and I were equal once and we were then friends, understanding each other's thoughts and sympathizing with each other's sorrows. But it cannot be so now."

"If there be such inability, it is all with you."

"It is all with me,—because in our connection the pain would all be on my side. It would not hurt you to see me at your table with worn shoes and a ragged shirt. I do not think so meanly of you as that. You would give me your feast to eat though I were not clad a tithe as well as the menial behind your chair. But it would hurt me to know that there were those looking at me who thought me unfit to sit in your rooms."

"That is the pride of which I speak;—false pride."

"Call it so if you will; but, Arabin, no preaching of yours can alter it. It is all that is left to me of my manliness. That poor broken reed who is lying there sick,—who has sacrificed all the world to her love for me,—who is the mother of my children, and the partner of my sorrows and the wife of my bosom,—even she cannot change me in this, though she pleads with the eloquence of all her wants. Not even for her can I hold out my hand for a dole."

They had now come back to the door of the house, and Mr. Crawley, hardly conscious of what he was doing, was preparing to enter.

"Will Mrs. Crawley be able to see me if I come in?" said the dean.

"Oh, stop; no; you had better not do so," said Mr. Crawley. "You, no doubt, might be subject to infection, and then Mrs. Arabin would be frightened."

"I do not care about it in the least," said the dean.

"But it is of no use; you had better not. Her room, I fear, is quite unfit for you to see; and the whole house, you know, may be infected."

Dr. Arabin by this time was in the sitting-room; but seeing that his friend was really anxious that he should not go farther, he did not persist.

"It will be a comfort to us, at any rate, to know that Miss Robarts is with her."

"The young lady is very good—very good indeed," said Crawley; "but I trust she will return to her home to-morrow. It is impossible that she should remain in so poor a house as mine. There will be nothing here of all the things that she will want."

The dean thought that Lucy Robarts's wants during her present occupation of nursing would not be so numerous as to make her continued sojourn in Mrs. Crawley's sick room impossible, and therefore took his leave with a satisfied conviction that the poor lady would not be left wholly to the somewhat unskilful nursing of her husband.

CHAPTER XXXVII.

MR. SOWERBY WITHOUT COMPANY.

And now there were going to be wondrous doings in West Barsetshire, and men's minds were much disturbed. The fiat had gone forth from the high places, and the Queen had dissolved her faithful Commons. The giants, finding that they could effect little or nothing with the old House, had resolved to try what a new venture would do for them, and the hubbub of a general election was to pervade the country. This produced no inconsiderable irritation and annoyance, for the House was not as yet quite three years old; and members of Parliament, though they naturally feel a constitutional pleasure in meeting their friends and in pressing the hands of their constituents, are, nevertheless, so far akin to the lower order of humanity that they appreciate the danger of losing their seats; and the certainty of a considerable outlay in their endeavours to retain them is not agreeable to the legislative mind.

Never did the old family fury between the gods and giants rage higher than at the present moment. The giants declared that every turn which they attempted to take in their country's service had been thwarted by faction, in spite of those benign promises of assistance made to them only a few weeks since by their opponents; and the gods answered by asserting that they were driven to this opposition by the Bœotian fatuity of the giants. They had no doubt promised their aid, and were ready to give it to measures that were decently prudent; but not to a bill enabling government at its will to pension aged bishops! No; there must be some limit to their tolerance, and when such attempts as these were made that limit had been clearly passed.

All this had taken place openly only a day or two after that casual whisper dropped by Tom Towers at Miss Dunstable's party—by Tom Towers, that most pleasant of all pleasant fellows. And how should he have known it,—he who flutters from one sweetest flower of the garden to another,

> "Adding sugar to the pink, and honey to the rose,
> So loved for what he gives, but taking nothing as he goes"?

But the whisper had grown into a rumour, and the rumour into a fact, and the political world was in a ferment. The giants, furious about their bishops' pension bill, threatened the House—most injudiciously; and then it was beautiful to see how indignant members got up, glowing with honesty, and declared that it was base to conceive that any gentleman in that House could be actuated in his vote by any hopes or fears with reference to his seat. And so matters grew from bad to worse, and these contending parties never hit at each other with such envenomed wrath as they did now;—having entered the ring together so lately with such manifold promises of good-will, respect, and forbearance! But going from the general to the particular, we may say that nowhere was a deeper consternation spread than in the electoral division of West Barsetshire. No sooner had the tidings of the dissolution reached the county than it was known that the duke intended to change his nominee. Mr. Sowerby had now sat for the division since the Reform Bill! He had become one of the county institutions, and by the dint of custom and long establishment had been borne with and even liked by the county gentlemen, in spite of his well-known pecuniary irregularities. Now all this was to be changed. No reason had as yet been publicly given, but it was understood that Lord Dumbello was to be returned, although he did not own an acre of land in the county. It is true that rumour went on to say that Lord Dumbello was about to form close connections with Barsetshire. He was on the eve of marrying a young lady, from the other division indeed, and was now engaged, so it was said, in completing arrangements with the government for the purchase of that noble crown property usually known as the Chace of Chaldicotes. It was also stated—this statement, however, had hitherto been only announced in confidential whispers—that Chaldicotes House itself would soon become the residence of the marquis. The duke was claiming it as his own—would very shortly have completed his claims and taken possession;—and then, by some arrangement between them, it was to be made over to Lord Dumbello.

But very contrary rumours to these got abroad also. Men said—such as dared to oppose the duke, and some few also who did not dare to oppose him when the day of battle came—that it was beyond his grace's power to turn Lord Dumbello into a Barsetshire magnate. The crown property—such men said—was to fall into the hands of young Mr. Gresham, of Boxall Hill, in the other division, and that the terms of purchase had been already settled. And as to Mr. Sowerby's property and the house of Chaldicotes—these opponents of the Omnium interest went on to explain—it was by no means as yet so certain that the duke would be able to enter it and take possession. The place was not to be given up to him quietly. A great fight would be made, and it was beginning to be believed that the enormous mortgages would be paid off by a lady of immense wealth. And then a dash of romance was not wanting to make these stories palatable. This lady of immense wealth had been courted by Mr. Sowerby, had acknowledged her love,—but had refused to marry him on account of his character. In testimony of her love, however, she was about to pay all his debts.

It was soon put beyond a rumour, and became manifest enough, that Mr. Sowerby did not intend to retire from the county in obedience to the duke's behests. A placard was posted through the whole division in which no allusion was made by name to the duke, but in which Mr. Sowerby warned his friends not to be led away by any report that he intended to retire from the representation of West Barsetshire. "He had sat," the placard said, "for the same county during the full period of a quarter of a century, and he would not lightly give up an honour that had been extended to him so often and which he prized so dearly. There were but few men now in the House whose connection with the same body of constituents had remained unbroken so long as had that which bound him to West Barsetshire; and he confidently hoped that that connection might be continued through another period of coming years till he might find himself in the glorious position of being the father of the county members of the House of Commons." The placard said much more than this, and hinted at sundry and various questions, all of great interest to the county; but it did not say one word of the Duke of Omnium, though every one knew what the duke was supposed to be doing in the matter. He was, as it were, a great Llama, shut up in a holy of holies, inscrutable, invisible, inexorable,—not to be seen by men's eyes or heard by their ears, hardly to be mentioned by ordinary men at such periods as these without an inward quaking. But nevertheless, it was he who was supposed to rule them. Euphemism required that his name should be mentioned at no public meetings in connection with the coming election; but, nevertheless, most men in the county believed that he could send his dog up to the House of Commons as member for West Barsetshire if it so pleased him.

It was supposed, therefore, that our friend Sowerby would have no chance; but he was lucky in finding assistance in a quarter from which he certainly had not deserved it. He had been a staunch friend of the gods during the whole of his political life,—as, indeed, was to be expected, seeing that he had been the duke's nominee; but, nevertheless, on the present occasion, all the giants connected with the county came forward to his rescue. They did not do this with the acknowledged purpose of opposing the duke; they declared that they were actuated by a generous disinclination to see an old county member put from his seat;—but the world knew that the battle was to be waged against the great Llama. It was to be a contest between the powers of aristocracy and the powers of oligarchy, as those powers existed in West Barsetshire,—and, it may be added, that democracy would have very little to say to it, on one side or on the other. The lower order of voters, the small farmers and tradesmen, would no doubt range themselves on the side of the duke, and would endeavour to flatter themselves that they were thereby furthering the views of the liberal side; but they would in fact be led to the poll by an old-fashioned, time-honoured adherence to the will of their great Llama; and by an apprehension of evil if that Llama should arise and shake himself in his wrath. What might not come to the county if the Llama were to walk himself off, he with his satellites and armies and courtiers? There he was, a great Llama; and though he came among them but seldom, and was scarcely seen when he did come, nevertheless—and not the less but rather the more—was obedience to him considered as salutary and opposition regarded as dangerous. A great rural Llama is still sufficiently mighty in rural England.

But the priest of the temple, Mr. Fothergill, was frequent enough in men's eyes, and it was beautiful to hear with how varied a voice he alluded to the things around him and to the changes which were coming. To the small farmers, not only on the Gatherum property but on others also, he spoke of the duke as a beneficent influence, shedding prosperity on all around him, keeping up prices by his presence, and forbidding the poor rates to rise above one and fourpence in the pound by the general employment which he occasioned. Men must be mad, he thought, who would willingly fly in the duke's face. To the squires from a distance he declared that no one had a right to charge the duke with any interference;—as far, at least, as he knew the duke's mind. People would talk of things of which they understood nothing. Could any one say that he had traced a single request for a vote home to the duke? All this did not alter the settled conviction on men's minds; but it had its effect, and tended to increase the mystery in which the duke's doings were enveloped. But to his own familiars, to the gentry immediately around him, Mr. Fothergill merely winked his eye. They knew what was what, and so did he. The duke had never been bit yet in such matters, and Mr. Fothergill did not think that he would now submit himself to any such operation.

I never heard in what manner and at what rate Mr. Fothergill received remuneration for the various services performed by him with reference to the duke's property in Barsetshire; but I am very sure that, whatever might be the amount, he earned it thoroughly. Never was there a more faithful partisan, or one who, in his partisanship, was more discreet. In this matter of the coming election he declared that he himself,—personally, on his own hook,—did intend to bestir himself actively on behalf of Lord Dumbello. Mr. Sowerby was an old friend of his, and a very good fellow. That was true. But all the world must admit that Sowerby was not in the position which a county member ought to occupy.

He was a ruined man, and it would not be for his own advantage that he should be maintained in a position which was fit only for a man of property. He knew—he, Fothergill—that Mr. Sowerby must abandon all right and claim to Chaldicotes; and if so, what would be more absurd than to acknowledge that he had a right and claim to the seat in Parliament? As to Lord Dumbello, it was probable that he would soon become one of the largest landowners in the county; and, as such, who could be more fit for the representation? Beyond this, Mr. Fothergill was not ashamed to confess—so he said—that he hoped to hold Lord Dumbello's agency. It would be compatible with his other duties, and therefore, as a matter of course, he intended to support Lord Dumbello;—he himself, that is. As to the duke's mind in the matter—! But I have already explained how Mr. Fothergill disposed of that.

In these days, Mr. Sowerby came down to his own house—for ostensibly it was still his own house—but he came very quietly, and his arrival was hardly known in his own village. Though his placard was stuck up so widely, he himself took no electioneering steps; none, at least, as yet. The protection against arrest which he derived from Parliament would soon be over, and those who were most bitter against the duke averred that steps would be taken to arrest him, should he give sufficient opportunity to the myrmidons of the law. That he would, in such case, be arrested was very likely; but it was not likely that this would be done in any way at the duke's instance. Mr. Fothergill declared indignantly that this insinuation made him very angry; but he was too prudent a man to be very angry at anything, and he knew how to make capital on his own side of charges such as these which overshot their own mark.

Mr. Sowerby came down very quietly to Chaldicotes, and there he remained for a couple of days, quite alone. The place bore a very different aspect now to that which we noticed when Mark Robarts drove up to it, in the early pages of this little narrative. There were no lights in the windows now, and no voices came from the stables; no dogs barked, and all was dead and silent as the grave. During the greater portion of those two days he sat alone within the house, almost unoccupied. He did not even open his letters, which lay piled on a crowded table in the small breakfast parlour in which he sat; for the letters of such men come in piles, and there are few of them which are pleasant in the reading. There he sat, troubled with thoughts which were sad enough, now and then moving to and fro the house, but for the most part occupied in thinking over the position to which he had brought himself. What would he be in the world's eye, if he ceased to be the owner of Chaldicotes, and ceased also to be the member for his county? He had lived ever before the world, and, though always harassed by encumbrances, had been sustained and comforted by the excitement of a prominent position. His debts and difficulties had hitherto been bearable, and he had borne them with ease so long that he had almost taught himself to think that they would never be unendurable. But now,—

The order for foreclosing had gone forth, and the harpies of the law, by their present speed in sticking their claws into the carcase of his property, were atoning to themselves for the delay with which they had hitherto been compelled to approach their prey. And the order as to his seat had gone forth also. That placard had been drawn up by the combined efforts of his sister, Miss Dunstable, and a certain well-known electioneering agent, named Closerstill, presumed to be in the interest of the giants. But poor Sowerby had but little confidence in the placard. No one knew better than he how great was the duke's power.

He was hopeless, therefore, as he walked about through those empty rooms, thinking of his past life and of that life which was to come. Would it not be well for him that he were dead, now that he was dying to all that had made the world pleasant! We see and hear of such men as Mr. Sowerby, and are apt to think that they enjoy all that the world can give, and that they enjoy that all without payment either in care or labour; but I doubt that, with even the most callous of them, their periods of wretchedness must be frequent, and that wretchedness very intense. Salmon and lamb in February and green pease and new potatoes in March can hardly make a man happy, even though nobody pays for them; and the feeling that one is an *antecedentem scelestum* after whom a sure, though lame, Nemesis is hobbling, must sometimes disturb one's slumbers. On the present occasion Scelestus felt that his Nemesis had overtaken him. Lame as she had been, and swift as he had run, she had mouthed him at last, and there was nothing left for him but to listen to the "whoop" set up at the sight of his own death-throes.

It was a melancholy, dreary place now, that big house of Chaldicotes; and though the woods were all green with their early leaves, and the gardens thick with flowers, they also were melancholy and dreary. The lawns were untrimmed and weeds were growing through the gravel, and here and there a cracked Dryad, tumbled from her pedestal and sprawling in the grass, gave a look of disorder to the whole place. The wooden trellis-work was shattered here and bending there, the standard rose-trees were stooping to the ground, and the leaves of the winter still encumbered the borders. Late in the evening of the second day Mr. Sowerby strolled out, and went through the gardens into the wood. Of all the inanimate things of the world this wood of Chaldicotes was the dearest to him. He was not a man to whom his companions gave much credit for feelings or thoughts akin to poetry, but here, out in the Chace, his mind would be almost poetical. While wandering among the forest trees, he became susceptible of the tenderness of human nature: he would listen to the birds singing, and pick here and there a wild flower on his path. He would watch the decay of the old trees and the progress of the young, and make pictures in his eyes of every turn in the wood. He would mark the colour of a bit of road as it dipped into a dell, and then, passing through a water-course, rose brown, rough, irregular, and beautiful against the bank on the other side. And then he would sit and think of his old family: how they had roamed there time out of mind in those Chaldicotes woods, father and son and grandson in regular succession, each giving them over, without blemish or decrease, to his successor. So he would sit; and so he did sit even now, and, thinking of these things, wished that he had never been born.

It was dark night when he returned to the house, and as he did so he resolved that he would quit the place altogether, and give up the battle as lost. The duke should take it and do as he pleased with it; and as for the seat in Parliament, Lord Dumbello, or any other equally gifted young patrician, might hold it for him. He would vanish from the scene and betake himself to some land from whence he would be neither heard nor seen, and there—starve. Such were now his future outlooks into the world; and yet, as regards health and all physical capacities, he knew that he was still in the prime of his life. Yes; in the prime of his life! But what could he do with what remained to him of such prime? How could he turn either his mind or his strength to such account as might now be serviceable? How could he, in his sore need, earn for himself even the barest bread? Would it not be better for him that he should die? Let not any one covet the lot of a spendthrift, even though the days of his early pease and champagne seem to be unnumbered; for that lame Nemesis will surely be up before the game has been all played out.

When Mr. Sowerby reached his house he found that a message by telegraph had arrived for him in his absence. It was from his sister, and it informed him that she would be with him that night. She was coming down by the mail train, had telegraphed to Barchester for post-horses, and would be at Chaldicotes about two hours after midnight. It was therefore manifest enough that her business was of importance.

Exactly at two the Barchester post-chaise did arrive, and Mrs. Harold Smith, before she retired to her bed, was closeted for about an hour with her brother.

"Well," she said, the following morning, as they sat together at the breakfast-table, "what do you say to it now? If you accept her offer you should be with her lawyer this afternoon."

"I suppose I must accept it," said he.

"Certainly, I think so. No doubt it will take the property out of your own hands as completely as though the duke had it, but it will leave you the house, at any rate, for your life."

"What good will the house be, when I can't keep it up?"

"But I am not so sure of that. She will not want more than her fair interest; and as it will be thoroughly well managed, I should think that there would be something over—something enough to keep up the house. And then, you know, we must have some place in the country."

"I tell you fairly, Harriet, that I will have nothing further to do with Harold in the way of money."

"Ah! that was because you would go to him. Why did you not come to me? And then, Nathaniel, it is the only way in which you can have a chance of keeping the seat. She is the queerest woman I ever met, but she seems resolved on beating the duke."

"I do not quite understand it, but I have not the slightest objection."

"She thinks that he is interfering with young Gresham about the crown property. I had no idea that she had so much business at her fingers' ends. When I first proposed the matter she took it up quite as a lawyer might, and seemed to have forgotten altogether what occurred about that other matter."

"I wish I could forget it also," said Mr. Sowerby.

"I really think that she does. When I was obliged to make some allusion to it—at least I felt myself obliged, and was sorry afterwards that I did—she merely laughed—a great loud laugh as she always does, and then went on about the business. However, she was clear about this, that all the expenses of the election should be added to the sum to be advanced by her, and that the house should be left to you without any rent. If you choose to take the land round the house you must pay for it, by the acre, as the tenants do. She was as clear about it all as though she had passed her life in a lawyer's office."

My readers will now pretty well understand what last step that excellent sister, Mrs. Harold Smith, had taken on her brother's behalf, nor will they be surprised to learn that in the course of the day Mr. Sowerby hurried back to town and put himself into communication with Miss Dunstable's lawyer.

CHAPTER XXXVIII.

IS THERE CAUSE OR JUST IMPEDIMENT?

I now purpose to visit another country house in Barsetshire, but on this occasion our sojourn shall be in the eastern division, in which, as in every other county in England, electioneering matters are paramount at the present moment. It has been mentioned that Mr. Gresham, junior, young Frank Gresham as he was always called, lived at a place called Boxall Hill. This property had come to his wife by will, and he was now settled there,—seeing that his father still held the family seat of the Greshams at Greshamsbury.

At the present moment Miss Dunstable was staying at Boxall Hill with Mrs. Frank Gresham. They had left London,—as, indeed, all the world had done, to the terrible dismay of the London tradesmen. This dissolution of Parliament was ruining everybody except the country publicans, and had of course destroyed the London season among other things.

Mrs. Harold Smith had only just managed to catch Miss Dunstable before she left London; but she did do so, and the great heiress had at once seen her lawyers, and instructed them how to act with reference to the mortgages on the Chaldicotes property. Miss Dunstable was in the habit of speaking of herself and her own pecuniary concerns as though she herself were rarely allowed to meddle in their management; but this was one of those small jokes which she ordinarily perpetrated; for in truth few ladies, and perhaps not many gentlemen, have a more thorough knowledge of their own concerns or a more potent voice in their own affairs, than was possessed by Miss Dunstable. Circumstances had lately brought her much into Barsetshire and she had there contracted very intimate friendships. She was now disposed to become, if possible, a Barsetshire proprietor, and with this view had lately agreed with young Mr. Gresham that she would become the purchaser of the Crown property. As, however, the purchase had been commenced in his name, it was so to be continued; but now, as we are aware, it was rumoured that, after all, the duke, or, if not the duke, then the Marquis of Dumbello, was to be the future owner of the Chace. Miss Dunstable, however, was not a person to give up her object if she could attain it, nor, under the circumstances, was she at all displeased at finding herself endowed with the power of rescuing the Sowerby portion of the Chaldicotes property from the duke's clutches. Why had the duke meddled with her, or with her friend, as to the other property? Therefore it was arranged that the full amount due to the duke on mortgage should be ready for immediate payment; but it was arranged also that the security as held by Miss Dunstable should be very valid.

Miss Dunstable, at Boxall Hill or at Greshamsbury, was a very different person from Miss Dunstable in London; and it was this difference which so much vexed Mrs. Gresham; not that her friend omitted to bring with her into the country her London wit and aptitude for fun, but that she did not take with her up to town the genuine goodness and love of honesty which made her loveable in the country. She was as it were two persons, and Mrs. Gresham could not understand that any lady should permit herself to be more worldly at one time of the year than at another—or in one place than in any other.

"Well, my dear, I am heartily glad we've done with that," Miss Dunstable said to her, as she sat herself down to her desk in the drawing-room on the first morning after her arrival at Boxall Hill.

"What does 'that' mean?" said Mrs. Gresham.

"Why, London and smoke and late hours, and standing on one's legs for four hours at a stretch on the top of one's own staircase, to be bowed at by any one who chooses to come. That's all done—for one year, at any rate."

"You know you like it."

"No, Mary; that's just what I don't know. I don't know whether I like it or not. Sometimes, when the spirit of that dearest of all women, Mrs. Harold Smith, is upon me, I think that I do like it; but then again, when other spirits are on me, I think that I don't."

"And who are the owners of the other spirits?"

"Oh! you are one, of course. But you are a weak little thing, by no means able to contend with such a Samson as Mrs. Harold. And then you are a little given to wickedness yourself, you know. You've learned to like London well enough since you sat down to the table of Dives. Your uncle,—he's the real impracticable, unapproachable Lazarus who declares that he can't come down because of the big gulf. I wonder how he'd behave, if somebody left him ten thousand a year?"

"Uncommonly well, I am sure."

"Oh, yes; he is a Lazarus now, so of course we are bound to speak well of him; but I should like to see him tried. I don't doubt but what he'd have a house in Belgrave Square, and become noted for his little dinners before the first year of his trial was over."

"Well, and why not? You would not wish him to be an anchorite?"

"I am told that he is going to try his luck,—not with ten thousand a year, but with one or two."

"What do you mean?"

"Jane tells me that they all say at Greshamsbury that he is going to marry Lady Scatcherd." Now Lady Scatcherd was a widow living in those parts; an excellent woman, but one not formed by nature to grace society of the highest order.

"What!" exclaimed Mrs. Gresham, rising up from her chair while her eyes flashed with anger at such a rumour.

"Well, my dear, don't eat me. I don't say it is so; I only say that Jane said so."

"Then you ought to send Jane out of the house."

"You may be sure of this, my dear: Jane would not have told me if somebody had not told her."

"And you believed it?"

"I have said nothing about that."

"But you look as if you had believed it."

"Do I? Let us see what sort of a look it is, this look of faith." And Miss Dunstable got up and went to the glass over the fire-place. "But, Mary, my dear, ain't you old enough to know that you should not credit people's looks? You should believe nothing now-a-days; and I did not believe the story about poor Lady Scatcherd. I know the doctor well enough to be sure that he is not a marrying man."

"What a nasty, hackneyed, false phrase that is—that of a marrying man! It sounds as though some men were in the habit of getting married three or four times a month."

"It means a great deal all the same. One can tell very soon whether a man is likely to marry or no."

"And can one tell the same of a woman?"

"The thing is so different. All unmarried women are necessarily in the market; but if they behave themselves properly they make no signs. Now there was Griselda Grantly; of course she intended to get herself a husband, and a very grand one she has got; but she always looked as though butter would not melt in her mouth. It would have been very wrong to call her a marrying girl."

"Oh, of course she was," says Mrs. Gresham, with that sort of acrimony which one pretty young woman so frequently expresses with reference to another. "But if one could always tell of a woman, as you say you can of a man, I should be able to tell of you. Now, I wonder whether you are a marrying woman? I have never been able to make up my mind yet."

Miss Dunstable remained silent for a few moments, as though she were at first minded to take the question as being, in some sort, one made in earnest; but then she attempted to laugh it off. "Well, I wonder at that," said she, "as it was only the other day I told you how many offers I had refused."

"Yes; but you did not tell me whether any had been made that you meant to accept."

"None such was ever made to me. Talking of that, I shall never forget your cousin, the Honourable George."

"He is not my cousin."

"Well, your husband's. It would not be fair to show a man's letters; but I should like to show you his."

"You are determined, then, to remain single?"

"I didn't say that. But why do you cross-question me so?"

"Because I think so much about you. I am afraid that you will become so afraid of men's motives as to doubt that any one can be honest. And yet sometimes I think you would be a happier woman and a better woman, if you were married."

"To such an one as the Honourable George, for instance?"

"No, not to such an one as him; you have probably picked out the worst."

"Or to Mr. Sowerby?"

"Well, no; not to Mr. Sowerby, either. I would not have you marry any man that looked to you for your money principally."

"And how is it possible that I should expect any one to look to me principally for any-thing else? You don't see my difficulty, my dear? If I had only five hundred a year, I might come across some decent middle-aged personage, like myself, who would like me, myself, pretty well, and would like my little income—pretty well also. He would not tell me any violent lie, and perhaps no lie at all. I should take to him in the same sort of way, and we might do very well. But, as it is, how is it possible that any disinterested person should learn to like me? How could such a man set about it? If a sheep have two heads, is not the fact of the two heads the first and, indeed, only thing which the world regards in that sheep? Must it not be so as a matter of course? I am a sheep with two heads. All this money which my father put together, and which has been growing since like grass under May showers, has turned me into an abortion. I am not the giantess eight feet high, or the dwarf that stands in the man's hand,—"

"Or the two-headed sheep—"

"But I am the unmarried woman with—half a dozen millions of money—as I believe some people think. Under such circumstances have I a fair chance of getting my own sweet bit of grass to nibble, like any ordinary animal with one head? I never was very beautiful, and I am not more so now than I was fifteen years ago."

"I am quite sure it is not that which hinders it. You would not call yourself plain; and even plain women are married every day, and are loved, too, as well as pretty women."

"Are they? Well, we won't say more about that; but I don't expect a great many lovers on account of my beauty. If ever you hear of such an one, mind you tell me."

It was almost on Mrs. Gresham's tongue to say that she did know of one such—meaning her uncle. But in truth, she did not know any such thing; nor could she boast to herself that she had good grounds for feeling that it was so—certainly none sufficient to justify her in speaking of it. Her uncle had said no word to her on the matter, and had been confused and embarrassed when the idea of such a marriage was hinted to him. But, nevertheless, Mrs. Gresham did think that each of these two was well inclined to love the other, and that they would be happier together than they would be single. The difficulty, however, was very great, for the doctor would be terribly afraid of being thought covetous in regard to Miss Dunstable's money; and it would hardly be expected that she should be induced to make the first overture to the doctor.

"My uncle would be the only man that I can think of that would be at all fit for you," said Mrs. Gresham, boldly.

"What, and rob poor Lady Scatcherd!" said Miss Dunstable.

"Oh, very well. If you choose to make a joke of his name in that way, I have done."

"Why, God bless the girl! what does she want me to say? And as for joking, surely that is innocent enough. You're as tender about the doctor as though he were a girl of seventeen."

"It's not about him; but it's such a shame to laugh at poor dear Lady Scatcherd. If she were to hear it she'd lose all comfort in having my uncle near her."

"And I'm to marry him, so that she may be safe with her friend!"

"Very well; I have done." And Mrs. Gresham, who had already got up from her seat, employed herself very sedulously in arranging flowers which had been brought in for the drawing-room tables. Thus they remained silent for a minute or two, during which she began to reflect that, after all, it might probably be thought that she also was endeavouring to catch the great heiress for her uncle.

"And now you are angry with me," said Miss Dunstable.

"No, I am not."

"Oh, but you are. Do you think I'm such a fool as not to see when a person's vexed? You wouldn't have twitched that geranium's head off if you'd been in a proper frame of mind."

"I don't like that joke about Lady Scatcherd."

"And is that all, Mary? Now do try and be true, if you can. You remember the bishop? *Magna est veritas.*"

"The fact is you've got into such a way of being sharp, and saying sharp things among your friends up in London, that you can hardly answer a person without it."

"Can't I? Dear, dear, what a Mentor you are, Mary! No poor lad that ever ran up from Oxford for a spree in town got so lectured for his dissipation and iniquities as I do. Well, I beg Dr. Thorne's pardon, and Lady Scatcherd's, and I won't be sharp any more; and I will—let me see, what was it I was to do? Marry him myself, I believe; was not that it?"

"No; you're not half good enough for him."

"I know that. I'm quite sure of that. Though I am so sharp, I'm very humble. You can't accuse me of putting any very great value on myself."

"Perhaps not as much as you ought to do—on yourself."

"Now, what do you mean, Mary? I won't be bullied and teased, and have innuendos thrown out at me, because you've got something on your mind, and don't quite dare to speak it out. If you have got anything to say, say it."

But Mrs. Gresham did not choose to say it at that moment. She held her peace, and went on arranging her flowers—now with a more satisfied air, and without destruction to the geraniums. And when she had grouped her bunches properly she carried the jar from one part of the room to another, backwards and forwards, trying the effect of the colours, as though her mind was quite intent upon her flowers, and was for the moment wholly unoccupied with any other subject.

But Miss Dunstable was not the woman to put up with this. She sat silent in her place, while her friend made one or two turns about the room; and then she got up from her seat also. "Mary," she said, "give over about those wretched bits of green branches and leave the jars where they are. You're trying to fidget me into a passion."

"Am I?" said Mrs. Gresham, standing opposite to a big bowl, and putting her head a little on one side, as though she could better look at her handiwork in that position.

"You know you are; and it's all because you lack courage to speak out. You didn't begin at me in this way for nothing."

"I do lack courage. That's just it," said Mrs. Gresham, still giving a twist here and a set there to some of the small sprigs which constituted the background of her bouquet. "I do lack courage—to have ill motives imputed to me. I was thinking of saying something, and I am afraid, and therefore I will not say it. And now, if you like, I will be ready to take you out in ten minutes."

But Miss Dunstable was not going to be put off in this way. And to tell the truth, I must admit that her friend Mrs. Gresham was not using her altogether well. She should either have held her peace on the matter altogether,—which would probably have been her wiser course,—or she should have declared her own ideas boldly, feeling secure in her own conscience as to her own motives. "I shall not stir from this room," said Miss Dunstable, "till I have had this matter out with you. And as for imputations,—my imputing bad motives to you,—I don't know how far you may be joking, and saying what you call sharp things to me; but you have no right to think that I should think evil of you. If you really do think so, it is treason to the love I have for you. If I thought that you thought so, I could not remain in the house with you. What! you are not able to know the difference which one makes between one's real friends and one's mock friends! I don't believe it of you, and I know you are only striving to bully me." And Miss Dunstable now took her turn of walking up and down the room.

"Well, she shan't be bullied," said Mrs. Gresham, leaving her flowers, and putting her arm round her friend's waist;—"at least, not here, in this house, although she is sometimes such a bully herself."

"Mary, you have gone too far about this to go back. Tell me what it was that was on your mind, and as far as it concerns me, I will answer you honestly."

Mrs. Gresham now began to repent that she had made her little attempt. That uttering of hints in a half-joking way was all very well, and might possibly bring about the desired result, without the necessity of any formal suggestion on her part; but now she was so brought to book that she must say something formal. She must commit herself to the expression of her own wishes, and to an expression also of an opinion as to what had been the wishes of her friend; and this she must do without being able to say anything as to the wishes of that third person.

"Well," she said, "I suppose you know what I meant."

"I suppose I did," said Miss Dunstable; "but it is not at all the less necessary that you should say it out. I am not to commit myself by my interpretation of your thoughts, while you remain perfectly secure in having only hinted your own. I hate hints, as I do—the mischief. I go in for the bishop's doctrine. *Magna est veritas.*"

"Well, I don't know," said Mrs. Gresham.

"Ah! but I do," said Miss Dunstable. "And therefore go on, or for ever hold your peace."

"That's just it," said Mrs. Gresham.

"What's just it?" said Miss Dunstable.

"The quotation out of the Prayer Book which you finished just now. 'If any of you know cause or just impediment why these two persons should not be joined together in holy matrimony, ye are to declare it. This is the first time of asking.' Do you know any cause, Miss Dunstable?"

"Do you know any, Mrs. Gresham?"

"None, on my honour!" said the younger lady, putting her hand upon her breast.

"Ah! but do you not?" and Miss Dunstable caught hold of her arm, and spoke almost abruptly in her energy.

"No, certainly not. What impediment? If I did, I should not have broached the subject. I declare I think you would both be very happy together. Of course, there is one impediment; we all know that. That must be your look out."

"What do you mean? What impediment?"

"Your own money."

"Psha! Did you find that an impediment in marrying Frank Gresham?"

"Ah! the matter was so different there. He had much more to give than I had, when all was counted. And I had no money when we—when we were first engaged." And the tears came into her eyes as she thought of the circumstances of her early love;—all of which have been narrated in the county chronicles of Barsetshire, and may now be read by men and women interested therein.

"Yes; yours was a love match. I declare, Mary, I often think that you are the happiest woman of whom I ever heard; to have it all to give, when you were so sure that you were loved while you yet had nothing."

"Yes; I was sure," and she wiped the sweet tears from her eyes, as she remembered a certain day when a certain youth had come to her, claiming all kinds of privileges in a very determined manner. She had been no heiress then. "Yes; I was sure. But now with you, dear, you can't make yourself poor again. If you can trust no one—"

"I can. I can trust him. As regards that I do trust him altogether. But how can I tell that he would care for me?"

"Do you not know that he likes you?"

"Ah, yes; and so he does Lady Scatcherd."

"Miss Dunstable!"

"And why not Lady Scatcherd, as well as me? We are of the same kind—come from the same class."

"Not quite that, I think."

"Yes, from the same class; only I have managed to poke myself up among dukes and duchesses, whereas she has been content to remain where God placed her. Where I beat her in art, she beats me in nature."

"You know you are talking nonsense."

"I think that we are both doing that—absolute nonsense; such as schoolgirls of eighteen talk to each other. But there is a relief in it; is there not? It would be a terrible curse to have to talk sense always. Well, that's done; and now let us go out."

Mrs. Gresham was sure after this that Miss Dunstable would be a consenting party to the little arrangement which she contemplated. But of that she had felt but little doubt for some considerable time past. The difficulty lay on the other side, and all that she had as yet done was to convince herself that she would be safe in assuring her uncle of success if he could be induced to take the enterprise in hand. He was to come to Boxall Hill that evening, and to remain there for a day or two. If anything could be done in the matter, now would be the time for doing it. So at least thought Mrs. Gresham.

The doctor did come, and did remain for the allotted time at Boxall Hill; but when he left, Mrs. Gresham had not been successful. Indeed, he did not seem to enjoy his visit as was usual with him; and there was very little of that pleasant friendly intercourse which for some time past had been customary between him and Miss Dunstable. There were no passages of arms between them; no abuse from the doctor against the lady's London gaiety; no raillery from the lady as to the doctor's country habits. They were very courteous to each other, and, as Mrs. Gresham thought, too civil by half; nor, as far as she could see, did they ever remain alone in each other's company for five minutes at a time during the whole period of the doctor's visit. What, thought Mrs. Gresham to herself,—what if she had set these two friends at variance with each other, instead of binding them together in the closest and most durable friendship!

But still she had an idea that, as she had begun to play this game, she must play it out. She felt conscious that what she had done must do evil, unless she could so carry it on as to make it result in good. Indeed, unless she could so manage, she would have done a manifest injury to Miss Dunstable in forcing her to declare her thoughts and feelings. She had already spoken to her uncle in London, and though he had said nothing to show that he approved of her plan, neither had he said anything to show that he disapproved it. Therefore she had hoped through the whole of those three days that he would make some sign,—at any rate to her; that he would in some way declare what were his own thoughts on this matter. But the morning of his departure came, and he had declared nothing.

"Uncle," she said, in the last five minutes of his sojourn there, after he had already taken leave of Miss Dunstable and shaken hands with Mrs. Gresham, "have you ever thought of what I said to you up in London?"

"Yes, Mary; of course I have thought about it. Such an idea as that, when put into a man's head, will make itself thought about."

"Well; and what next? Do talk to me about it. Do not be so hard and unlike yourself."

"I have very little to say about it."

"I can tell you this for certain, you may if you like."

"Mary! Mary!"

"I would not say so if I were not sure that I should not lead you into trouble."

"You are foolish in wishing this, my dear; foolish in trying to tempt an old man into a folly."

"Not foolish if I know that it will make you both happier."

He made her no further reply, but stooping down that she might kiss him, as was his wont, went his way, leaving her almost miserable in the thought that she had troubled all these waters to no purpose. What would Miss Dunstable think of her? But on that afternoon Miss Dunstable seemed to be as happy and even-tempered as ever.

CHAPTER XXXIX.

HOW TO WRITE A LOVE LETTER.

Dr. Thorne, in the few words which he spoke to his niece before he left Boxall Hill, had called himself an old man; but he was as yet on the right side of sixty by five good years, and bore about with him less of the marks of age than most men of fifty-five do bear. One would have said in looking at him that there was no reason why he should not marry if he found that such a step seemed good to him; and looking at the age of the proposed bride, there was nothing unsuitable in that respect.

But nevertheless he felt almost ashamed of himself, in that he allowed himself even to think of the proposition which his niece had made. He mounted his horse that day at Boxall Hill—for he made all his journeys about the county on horseback—and rode slowly home to Greshamsbury, thinking not so much of the suggested marriage as of his own folly in thinking of it. How could he be such an ass at his time of life as to allow the even course of his way to be disturbed by any such idea? Of course he could not propose to himself such a wife as Miss Dunstable without having some thoughts as to her wealth; and it had been the pride of his life so to live that the world might know that he was indifferent about money. His profession was all in all to him,—the air which he breathed as well as the bread which he ate; and how could he follow his profession if he made such a marriage as this? She would expect him to go to London with her; and what would he become, dangling at her heels there, known only to the world as the husband of the richest woman in the town? The kind of life was one which would be unsuitable to him;—and yet, as he rode home, he could not resolve to rid himself of the idea. He went on thinking of it, though he still continued to condemn himself for keeping it in his thoughts. That night at home he would make up his mind, so he declared to himself; and would then write to his niece begging her to drop the subject. Having so far come to a resolution he went on meditating what course of life it might be well for him to pursue if he and Miss Dunstable should, after all, become man and wife.

There were two ladies whom it behoved him to see on the day of his arrival—whom, indeed, he generally saw every day except when absent from Greshamsbury. The first of these—first in the general consideration of the people of the place—was the wife of the squire, Lady Arabella Gresham, a very old patient of the doctor's. Her it was his custom to visit early in the afternoon; and then, if he were able to escape the squire's daily invitation to dinner, he customarily went to the other, Lady Scatcherd, when the rapid meal in his own house was over. Such, at least, was his summer practice.

"Well, doctor, how are they at Boxall Hill?" said the squire, waylaying him on the gravel sweep before the door. The squire was very hard set for occupation in these summer months.

"Quite well, I believe."

"I don't know what's come to Frank. I think he hates this place now. He's full of the election, I suppose."

"Oh, yes; he told me to say he should be over here soon. Of course there'll be no contest, so he need not trouble himself."

"Happy dog, isn't he, doctor? to have it all before him instead of behind him. Well, well; he's as good a lad as ever lived,—as ever lived. And let me see; Mary's time—" And then there were a few very important words spoken on that subject.

"I'll just step up to Lady Arabella now," said the doctor.

"She's as fretful as possible," said the squire. "I've just left her."

"Nothing special the matter, I hope?"

"No, I think not; nothing in your way, that is; only specially cross, which always comes in my way. You'll stop and dine to-day, of course?"

"Not to-day, squire."

"Nonsense; you will. I have been quite counting on you. I have a particular reason for wanting to have you to-day,—a most particular reason." But the squire always had his particular reasons.

"I'm very sorry, but it is impossible to-day. I shall have a letter to write that I must sit down to seriously. Shall I see you when I come down from her ladyship?"

The squire turned away sulkily, almost without answering him, for he now had no prospect of any alleviation to the tedium of the evening; and the doctor went up-stairs to his patient.

For Lady Arabella, though it cannot be said that she was ill, was always a patient. It must not be supposed that she kept her bed and swallowed daily doses, or was prevented from taking her share in such prosy gaieties as came from time to time in the way of her prosy life; but it suited her turn of mind to be an invalid and to have a doctor; and as the doctor whom her good fates had placed at her elbow thoroughly understood her case, no great harm was done.

"It frets me dreadfully that I cannot get to see Mary," Lady Arabella said, as soon as the first ordinary question as to her ailments had been asked and answered.

"She's quite well and will be over to see you before long."

"Now I beg that she won't. She never thinks of coming when there can be no possible objection, and travelling, at the present moment, would be—" Whereupon the Lady Arabella shook her head very gravely. "Only think of the importance of it, doctor," she said. "Remember the enormous stake there is to be considered."

"It would not do her a ha'porth of harm if the stake were twice as large."

"Nonsense, doctor, don't tell me; as if I didn't know myself. I was very much against her going to London this spring, but of course what I said was overruled. It always is. I do believe Mr. Gresham went over to Boxall Hill, on purpose to induce her to go. But what does he care? He's fond of Frank; but he never thinks of looking beyond the present day. He never did, as you know well enough, doctor."

"The trip did her all the good in the world," said Dr. Thorne, preferring anything to a conversation respecting the squire's sins.

"I very well remember that when I was in that way it wasn't thought that such trips would do me any good. But, perhaps, things are altered since then."

"Yes, they are," said the doctor. "We don't interfere so much now-a-days."

"I know I never asked for such amusements when so much depended on quietness. I remember before Frank was born—and, indeed, when all of them were born— But as you say, things were different then; and I can easily believe that Mary is a person quite determined to have her own way."

"Why, Lady Arabella, she would have stayed at home without wishing to stir if Frank had done so much as hold up his little finger."

"So did I always. If Mr. Gresham made the slightest hint I gave way. But I really don't see what one gets in return for such implicit obedience. Now this year, doctor, of course I should have liked to have been up in London for a week or two. You seemed to think yourself that I might as well see Sir Omicron."

"There could be no possible objection, I said."

"Well; no; exactly; and as Mr. Gresham knew I wished it, I think he might as well have offered it. I suppose there can be no reason now about money."

"But I understood that Mary specially asked you and Augusta?"

"Yes; Mary was very good. She did ask me. But I know very well that Mary wants all the room she has got in London. The house is not at all too large for herself. And, for the matter of that, my sister, the countess, was very anxious that I should be with her. But one does like to be independent if one can, and for one fortnight I do think that Mr. Gresham might have managed it. When I knew that he was so dreadfully out at elbows I never troubled him about it,—though, goodness knows, all that was never my fault."

"The squire hates London. A fortnight there in warm weather would nearly be the death of him."

"He might at any rate have paid me the compliment of asking me. The chances are ten to one I should not have gone. It is that indifference that cuts me so. He was here just now, and, would you believe it?—"

But the doctor was determined to avoid further complaint for the present day. "I wonder what you would feel, Lady Arabella, if the squire were to take it into his head to go away and amuse himself, leaving you at home. There are worse men than Mr. Gresham, if you will believe me." All this was an allusion to Earl de Courcy, her ladyship's brother, as Lady Arabella very well understood; and the argument was one which was very often used to silence her.

"Upon my word, then, I should like it better than his hanging about here doing nothing but attend to those nasty dogs. I really sometimes think that he has no spirit left."

"You are mistaken there, Lady Arabella," said the doctor, rising with his hat in his hand and making his escape without further parley.

As he went home he could not but think that that phase of married life was not a very pleasant one. Mr. Gresham and his wife were supposed by the world to live on the best of terms. They always inhabited the same house, went out together when they did go out, always sat in their respective corners in the family pew, and in their wildest dreams after the happiness of novelty never thought of Sir Cresswell Cresswell. In some respects— with regard, for instance, to the continued duration of their joint domesticity at the family mansion of Greshamsbury—they might have been taken for a pattern couple. But yet, as far as the doctor could see, they did not seem to add much to the happiness of each other. They loved each other, doubtless, and had either of them been in real danger, that danger would have made the other miserable; but yet it might well be a question whether either would not be more comfortable without the other.

The doctor, as was his custom, dined at five, and at seven he went up to the cottage of his old friend Lady Scatcherd. Lady Scatcherd was not a refined woman, having in her early days been a labourer's daughter and having then married a labourer. But her husband had risen in the world—as has been told in those chronicles before mentioned,—and his widow was now Lady Scatcherd with a pretty cottage and a good jointure. She was in all things the very opposite to Lady Arabella Gresham; nevertheless, under the doctor's auspices, the two ladies were in some measure acquainted with each other. Of her married life, also, Dr. Thorne had seen something, and it may be questioned whether the memory of that was more alluring than the reality now existing at Greshamsbury.

Of the two women Dr. Thorne much preferred his humbler friend, and to her he made his visits not in the guise of a doctor, but as a neighbour. "Well, my lady," he said, as he sat down by her on a broad garden seat—all the world called Lady Scatcherd "my lady,"—"and how do these long summer days agree with you? Your roses are twice better out than any I see up at the big house."

"You may well call them long, doctor. They're long enough surely."

"But not too long. Come, now, I won't have you complaining. You don't mean to tell me that you have anything to make you wretched? You had better not, for I won't believe you."

"Eh; well; wretched! I don't know as I'm wretched. It'd be wicked to say that, and I with such comforts about me."

"I think it would, almost." The doctor did not say this harshly, but in a soft, friendly tone, and pressing her hand gently as he spoke.

"And I didn't mean to be wicked. I'm very thankful for everything—leastways, I always try to be. But, doctor, it is so lonely like."

"Lonely! not more lonely than I am."

"Oh, yes; you're different. You can go everywheres. But what can a lone woman do? I'll tell you what, doctor; I'd give it all up to have Roger back with his apron on and his pick in his hand. How well I mind his look when he'd come home o' nights."

"And yet it was a hard life you had then, eh, old woman? It would be better for you to be thankful for what you've got."

"I am thankful. Didn't I tell you so before?" said she, somewhat crossly. "But it's a sad life, this living alone. I declares I envy Hannah, 'cause she's got Jemima to sit in the kitchen with her. I want her to sit with me sometimes, but she won't."

"Ah! but you shouldn't ask her. It's letting yourself down."

"What do I care about down or up? It makes no difference, as he's gone. If he had lived one might have cared about being up, as you call it. Eh, deary; I'll be going after him before long, and it will be no matter then."

"We shall all be going after him, sooner or later; that's sure enough."

"Eh, dear, that's true, surely. It's only a span long, as Parson Oriel tells us when he gets romantic in his sermons. But it's a hard thing, doctor, when two is married, as they can't have their span, as he calls it, out together. Well, I must only put up with it, I suppose, as others does. Now, you're not going, doctor? You'll stop and have a dish of tea with me. You never see such cream as Hannah has from the Alderney cow. Do'ey now, doctor."

But the doctor had his letter to write, and would not allow himself to be tempted even by the promise of Hannah's cream. So he went his way, angering Lady Scatcherd by his departure as he had before angered the squire, and thinking as he went which was most unreasonable in her wretchedness, his friend Lady Arabella, or his friend Lady Scatcherd. The former was always complaining of an existing husband who never refused her any moderate request; and the other passed her days in murmuring at the loss of a dead husband, who in his life had ever been to her imperious and harsh, and had sometimes been cruel and unjust.

The doctor had his letter to write, but even yet he had not quite made up his mind what he would put into it; indeed, he had not hitherto resolved to whom it should be written. Looking at the matter as he had endeavoured to look at it, his niece, Mrs. Gresham, would be his correspondent; but if he brought himself to take this jump in the dark, in that case he would address himself direct to Miss Dunstable.

He walked home, not by the straightest road, but taking a considerable curve, round by narrow lanes, and through thick flower-laden hedges,—very thoughtful. He was told that she wished to marry him; and was he to think only of himself? And as to that pride of his about money, was it in truth a hearty, manly feeling; or was it a false pride, of which it behoved him to be ashamed as it did of many cognate feelings? If he acted rightly in this matter, why should he be afraid of the thoughts of any one? A life of solitude was bitter enough, as poor Lady Scatcherd had complained. But then, looking at Lady Scatcherd, and looking also at his other near neighbour, his friend the squire, there was little thereabouts to lead him on to matrimony. So he walked home slowly through the lanes, very meditative, with his hands behind his back.

Nor when he got home was he much more inclined to any resolute line of action. He might have drunk his tea with Lady Scatcherd, as well as have sat there in his own drawing-room, drinking it alone; for he got no pen and paper, and he dawdled over his teacup with the utmost dilatoriness, putting off, as it were, the evil day. To only one thing was he fixed—to this, namely, that that letter should be written before he went to bed.

Having finished his tea, which did not take place till near eleven, he went downstairs to an untidy little room which lay behind his depôt of medicines, and in which he was wont to do his writing; and herein he did at last set himself down to his work. Even at that moment he was in doubt. But he would write his letter to Miss Dunstable and see how it looked. He was almost determined not to send it; so, at least, he said to himself: but he could do no harm by writing it. So he did write it, as follows:—

Greshamsbury, — June, 185—.

My dear Miss Dunstable,—

When he had got so far, he leaned back in his chair and looked at the paper. How on earth was he to find words to say that which he now wished to have said? He had never written such a letter in his life, or anything approaching to it, and now found himself overwhelmed with a difficulty of which he had not previously thought. He spent another half-hour in looking at the paper, and was at last nearly deterred by this new difficulty. He would use the simplest, plainest language, he said to himself over and over again; but it is not always easy to use simple, plain language,—by no means so easy as to mount on stilts, and to march along with sesquipedalian words, with pathos, spasms, and notes of interjection. But the letter did at last get itself written, and there was not a note of interjection in it.

MY DEAR MISS DUNSTABLE,—I think it right to confess that I should not be now writing this letter to you, had I not been led to believe by other judgment than my own that the proposition which I am going to make would be regarded by you with favour. Without such other judgment I should, I own, have feared that the great disparity between you and me in regard to money would have given to such a proposition an appearance of being false and mercenary. All I ask of you now, with confidence, is to acquit me of such fault as that. When you have read so far you will understand what I mean. We have known each other now somewhat intimately, though indeed not very long, and I have sometimes fancied that you were almost as well pleased to be with me as I have been to be with you. If I have been wrong in this, tell me so simply, and I will endeavour to let our friendship run on as though this letter had not been written. But if I have been right, and if it be possible that you can think that a union between us will make us both happier than we are single, I will plight you my word and troth with good faith, and will do what an old man may do to make the burden of the world lie light upon your shoulders. Looking at my age

I can hardly keep myself from thinking that I am an old fool: but I try to reconcile myself to that by remembering that you yourself are no longer a girl. You see that I pay you no compliments, and that you need expect none from me.

> I do not know that I could add anything to the truth of this, if I were to write three times as much. All that is necessary is, that you should know what I mean. If you do not believe me to be true and honest already, nothing that I can write will make you believe it.
> God bless you. I know you will not keep me long in suspense for an answer.
> > Affectionately your friend,
> > THOMAS THORNE.

When he had finished he meditated again for another half-hour whether it would not be right that he should add something about her money. Would it not be well for him to tell her—it might be said in a postscript—that with regard to all her wealth she would be free to do what she chose? At any rate he owed no debts for her to pay, and would still have his own income, sufficient for his own purposes. But about one o'clock he came to the conclusion that it would be better to leave the matter alone. If she cared for him, and could trust him, and was worthy also that he should trust her, no omission of such a statement would deter her from coming to him: and if there were no such trust, it would not be created by any such assurance on his part. So he read the letter over twice, sealed it, and took it up, together with his bed candle, into his bed-room. Now that the letter was written it seemed to be a thing fixed by fate that it must go. He had written it that he might see how it looked when written; but now that it was written, there remained no doubt but that it must be sent. So he went to bed, with the letter on the toilette-table beside him; and early in the morning—so early as to make it seem that the importance of the letter had disturbed his rest—he sent it off by a special messenger to Boxall Hill.

"I'se wait for an answer?" said the boy.

"No," said the doctor: "leave the letter, and come away."

The breakfast hour was not very early at Boxall Hill in these summer months. Frank Gresham, no doubt, went round his farm before he came in for prayers, and his wife was probably looking to the butter in the dairy. At any rate, they did not meet till near ten, and therefore, though the ride from Greshamsbury to Boxall Hill was nearly two hours' work, Miss Dunstable had her letter in her own room before she came down.

She read it in silence as she was dressing, while the maid was with her in the room; but she made no sign which could induce her Abigail to think that the epistle was more than ordinarily important. She read it, and then quietly refolding it and placing it in the envelope, she put it down on the table at which she was sitting. It was full fifteen minutes afterwards that she begged her servant to see if Mrs. Gresham were still in her own room. "Because I want to see her for five minutes, alone, before breakfast," said Miss Dunstable.

"You traitor; you false, black traitor!" were the first words which Miss Dunstable spoke when she found herself alone with her friend.

"Why, what's the matter?"

"I did not think there was so much mischief in you, nor so keen and commonplace a desire for match-making. Look here. Read the first four lines; not more, if you please; the rest is private. Whose is the other judgment of whom your uncle speaks in his letter?"

"Oh, Miss Dunstable! I must read it all."

"Indeed you'll do no such thing. You think it's a love-letter, I dare say; but indeed there's not a word about love in it."

"I know he has offered. I shall be so glad, for I know you like him."

"He tells me that I am an old woman, and insinuates that I may probably be an old fool."

"I am sure he does not say that."

"Ah! but I'm sure that he does. The former is true enough, and I never complain of the truth. But as to the latter, I am by no means so certain that it is true—not in the sense that he means it."

"Dear, dearest woman, don't go on in that way now. Do speak out to me, and speak without jesting."

"Whose was the other judgment to whom he trusts so implicitly? Tell me that."

"Mine, mine, of course. No one else can have spoken to him about it. Of course I talked to him."

"And what did you tell him?"

"I told him—"

"Well, out with it. Let me have the real facts. Mind, I tell you fairly that you had no right to tell him anything. What passed between us, passed in confidence. But let us hear what you did say."

"I told him that you would have him if he offered." And Mrs. Gresham, as she spoke, looked into her friend's face doubtingly, not knowing whether in very truth Miss Dunstable were pleased with her or displeased. If she were displeased, then how had her uncle been deceived!

"You told him that as a fact?"

"I told him that I thought so."

"Then I suppose I am bound to have him," said Miss Dunstable, dropping the letter on to the floor in mock despair.

"My dear, dear, dearest woman!" said Mrs. Gresham, bursting into tears, and throwing herself on to her friend's neck.

"Mind you are a dutiful niece," said Miss Dunstable. "And now let me go and finish dressing."

In the course of the afternoon, an answer was sent back to Greshamsbury, in these words:—

DEAR DR. THORNE,—I do and will trust you in everything; and it shall be as you would have it. Mary writes to you; but do not believe a word she says. I never will again, for she has behaved so bad in this matter.   Yours affectionately and very truly,

MARTHA DUNSTABLE.

"And so I am going to marry the richest woman in England," said Dr. Thorne to himself, as he sat down that day to his mutton-chop.

CHAPTER XL.

INTERNECINE.

It must be conceived that there was some feeling of triumph at Plumstead Episcopi, when the wife of the rector returned home with her daughter, the bride elect of the Lord Dumbello. The heir of the Marquis of Hartletop was, in wealth, the most considerable unmarried young nobleman of the day; he was noted, too, as a man difficult to be pleased, as one who was very fine and who gave himself airs,—and to have been selected as the wife of such a man as this was a great thing for the daughter of a parish clergyman. We have seen in what manner the happy girl's mother communicated the fact to Lady Lufton, hiding, as it were, her pride under a veil; and we have seen also how meekly the happy girl bore her own great fortune, applying herself humbly to the packing of her clothes, as though she ignored her own glory.

But nevertheless there was triumph at Plumstead Episcopi. The mother, when she returned home, began to feel that she had been thoroughly successful in the great object of her life. While she was yet in London she had hardly realized her satisfaction, and there were doubts then whether the cup might not be dashed from her lips before it was tasted. It might be that even the son of the Marquis of Hartletop was subject to parental authority, and that barriers should spring up between Griselda and her coronet; but there had been nothing of the kind. The archdeacon had been closeted with the marquis, and Mrs. Grantly had been closeted with the marchioness; and though neither of those noble persons had expressed themselves gratified by their son's proposed marriage, so also neither of them had made any attempt to prevent it. Lord Dumbello was a man who had a will of his own,—as the Grantlys boasted amongst themselves. Poor Griselda! the day may perhaps come when this fact of her lord's masterful will may not to her be matter of much boasting. But in London, as I was saying, there had been no time for an appreciation of the family joy. The work to be done was nervous in its nature, and self-glorification might have been fatal; but now, when they were safe at Plumstead, the great truth burst upon them in all its splendour.

Mrs. Grantly had but one daughter, and the formation of that child's character and her establishment in the world had been the one main object of the mother's life. Of Griselda's great beauty the Plumstead household had long been conscious; of her discretion also, of her conduct, and of her demeanour there had been no doubt. But the father had sometimes hinted to the mother that he did not think that Grizzy was quite so clever as her brothers. "I don't agree with you at all," Mrs. Grantly had answered. "Besides, what you call cleverness is not at all necessary in a girl; she is perfectly ladylike; even you won't deny that."

The archdeacon had never wished to deny it, and was now fain to admit that what he had called cleverness was not necessary in a young lady.

At this period of the family glory the archdeacon himself was kept a little in abeyance, and was hardly allowed free intercourse with his own magnificent child. Indeed, to give him his due, it must be said of him that he would not consent to walk in the triumphal procession which moved with stately step, to and fro, through the Barchester regions. He kissed his daughter and blessed her, and bade her love her husband and be a good wife; but such injunctions as these, seeing how splendidly she had done her duty in securing to herself a marquis, seemed out of place and almost vulgar. Girls about to marry curates or sucking barristers should be told to do their duty in that station of life to which God might be calling them; but it seemed to be almost an impertinence in a father to give such an injunction to a future marchioness.

"I do not think that you have any ground for fear on her behalf," said Mrs. Grantly, "seeing in what way she has hitherto conducted herself."

"She has been a good girl," said the archdeacon, "but she is about to be placed in a position of great temptation."

"She has a strength of mind suited for any position," replied Mrs. Grantly, vaingloriously.

But nevertheless even the archdeacon moved about through the close at Barchester with a somewhat prouder step since the tidings of this alliance had become known there. The time had been—in the latter days of his father's lifetime—when he was the greatest man of the close. The dean had been old and infirm, and Dr. Grantly had wielded the bishop's authority. But since that things had altered. A new bishop had come there, absolutely hostile to him. A new dean had also come, who was not only his friend, but the brother-in-law of his wife; but even this advent had lessened the authority of the archdeacon. The vicars choral did not hang upon his words as they had been wont to do, and the minor canons smiled in return to his smile less obsequiously when they met him in the clerical circles of Barchester. But now it seemed that his old supremacy was restored to him. In the minds of many men an archdeacon, who was the father-in-law of a marquis, was himself as good as any bishop. He did not say much of his new connection to others beside the dean, but he was conscious of the fact, and conscious also of the reflected glory which shone around his own head.

But as regards Mrs. Grantly it may be said that she moved in an unending procession of stately ovation. It must not be supposed that she continually talked to her friends and neighbours of Lord Dumbello and the marchioness. She was by far too wise for such folly as that. The coming alliance having been once announced, the name of Hartletop was hardly mentioned by her out of her own domestic circle. But she assumed, with an ease that was surprising even to herself, the airs and graces of a mighty woman. She went through her work of morning calls as though it were her business to be affable to the country gentry. She astonished her sister, the dean's wife, by the simplicity of her grandeur; and condescended to Mrs. Proudie in a manner which nearly broke that lady's heart. "I shall be even with her yet," said Mrs. Proudie to herself, who had contrived to learn various very deleterious circumstances respecting the Hartletop family since the news about Lord Dumbello and Griselda had become known to her.

Griselda herself was carried about in the procession, taking but little part in it of her own, like an Eastern god. She suffered her mother's caresses and smiled in her mother's face as she listened to her own praises, but her triumph was apparently within. To no one did she say much on the subject, and greatly disgusted the old family housekeeper by declining altogether to discuss the future Dumbello *ménage*. To her aunt, Mrs. Arabin, who strove hard to lead her into some open-hearted speech as to her future aspirations, she was perfectly impassive. "Oh, yes, aunt, of course," and "I'll think about it, aunt Eleanor," or "Of course I shall do that if Lord Dumbello wishes it." Nothing beyond this could be got from her; and so, after half-a-dozen ineffectual attempts, Mrs. Arabin abandoned the matter.

But then there arose the subject of clothes—of the wedding *trousseau*! Sarcastic people are wont to say that the tailor makes the man. Were I such a one, I might certainly assert that the milliner makes the bride. As regarding her bridehood, in distinction either to her girlhood or her wifehood—as being a line of plain demarcation between those two periods of a woman's life—the milliner does do much to make her. She would be hardly a bride if the *trousseau* were not there. A girl married without some such appendage would seem to pass into the condition of a wife without any such line of demarcation. In that moment in which she finds herself in the first fruition of her marriage finery she becomes a bride; and in that other moment, when she begins to act upon the finest of these things as clothes to be packed up, she becomes a wife.

When this subject was discussed Griselda displayed no lack of a becoming interest. She went to work steadily, slowly, and almost with solemnity, as though the business in hand were one which it would be wicked to treat with impatience. She even struck her mother with awe by the grandeur of her ideas and the depth of her theories. Nor let it be supposed that she rushed away at once to the consideration of the great fabric which was to be the ultimate sign and mark of her status, the quintessence of her briding, the outer veil, as it were, of the tabernacle—namely, her wedding-dress. As a great poet works himself up by degrees to that inspiration which is necessary for the grand turning point of his epic, so did she slowly approach the hallowed ground on which she would sit, with her ministers around her, when about to discuss the nature, the extent, the design, the colouring, the structure, and the ornamentation of that momentous piece of apparel. No; there was much indeed to be done before she came to this; and as the poet, to whom I have already alluded, first invokes his muse, and then brings his smaller events gradually out upon his stage, so did Miss Grantly with sacred fervour ask her mother's aid, and then prepare her list of all those articles of under-clothing which must be the substratum for the visible magnificence of her *trousseau*.

Money was no object. We all know what that means; and frequently understand, when the words are used, that a blaze of splendour is to be attained at the cheapest possible price. But, in this instance, money was no object;—such an amount of money, at least, as could by any possibility be spent on a lady's clothes, independently of her jewels. With reference to diamonds and such like, the archdeacon at once declared his intention of taking the matter into his own hands—except in so far as Lord Dumbello, or the Hartletop interest, might be pleased to participate in the selection. Nor was Mrs. Grantly sorry for such a decision. She was not an imprudent woman, and would have dreaded the responsibility of trusting herself on such an occasion among the dangerous temptations of a jeweller's shop. But as far as silks and satins went—in the matter of French bonnets, muslins, velvets, hats, riding-habits, artificial flowers, head-gilding, curious nettings, enamelled buckles, golden tagged bobbins, and mechanical petticoats—as regarded shoes, and gloves, and corsets, and stockings, and linen, and flannel, and calico—money, I may conscientiously assert, was no object. And, under these circumstances, Griselda Grantly went to work with a solemn industry and a steady perseverance that was beyond all praise.

"I hope she will be happy," Mrs. Arabin said to her sister, as the two were sitting together in the dean's drawing-room.

"Oh, yes; I think she will. Why should she not?" said the mother.

"Oh, no; I know of no reason. But she is going up into a station so much above her own in the eyes of the world that one cannot but feel anxious for her."

"I should feel much more anxious if she were going to marry a poor man," said Mrs. Grantly. "It has always seemed to me that Griselda was fitted for a high position; that nature intended her for rank and state. You see that she is not a bit elated. She takes it all as if it were her own by right. I do not think that there is any danger that her head will be turned, if you mean that."

"I was thinking rather of her heart," said Mrs. Arabin.

"She never would have taken Lord Dumbello without loving him," said Mrs. Grantly, speaking rather quickly.

"That is not quite what I mean either, Susan. I am sure she would not have accepted him had she not loved him. But it is so hard to keep the heart fresh among all the grandeurs of high rank; and it is harder for a girl to do so who has not been born to it, than for one who has enjoyed it as her birthright."

"I don't quite understand about fresh hearts," said Mrs. Grantly, pettishly. "If she does her duty, and loves her husband, and fills the position in which God has placed her with propriety, I don't know that we need look for anything more. I don't at all approve of the plan of frightening a young girl when she is making her first outset into the world."

"No; I would not frighten her. I think it would be almost difficult to frighten Griselda."

"I hope it would. The great matter with a girl is whether she has been brought up with proper notions as to a woman's duty. Of course it is not for me to boast on this subject. Such as she is, I, of course, am responsible. But I must own that I do not see occasion to wish for any change." And then the subject was allowed to drop.

Among those of her relations who wondered much at the girl's fortune, but allowed themselves to say but little, was her grandfather, Mr. Harding. He was an old clergyman, plain and simple in his manners, and not occupying a very prominent position, seeing that he was only precentor to the chapter. He was loved by his daughter, Mrs. Grantly, and was treated by the archdeacon, if not invariably with the highest respect, at least always with consideration and regard. But, old and plain as he was, the young people at Plumstead did not hold him in any great reverence. He was poorer than their other relatives, and made no attempt to hold his head high in Barsetshire circles. Moreover, in these latter days, the home of his heart had been at the deanery. He had, indeed, a lodging of his own in the city, but was gradually allowing himself to be weaned away from it. He had his own bedroom in the dean's house, his own arm-chair in the dean's library, and his own corner on a sofa in Mrs. Dean's drawing-room. It was not, therefore, necessary that he should interfere greatly in this coming marriage; but still it became his duty to say a word of congratulation to his granddaughter,—and perhaps to say a word of advice.

"Grizzy, my dear," he said to her—he always called her Grizzy, but the endearment of the appellation had never been appreciated by the young lady—"come and kiss me, and let me congratulate you on your great promotion. I do so very heartily."

"Thank you, grandpapa," she said, touching his forehead with her lips, thus being, as it were, very sparing with her kiss. But those lips now were august and reserved for nobler foreheads than that of an old cathedral hack. For Mr. Harding still chanted the Litany from Sunday to Sunday, unceasingly, standing at that well-known desk in the cathedral choir; and Griselda had a thought in her mind that when the Hartletop people should hear of the practice they would not be delighted. Dean and archdeacon might be very well, and if her grandfather had even been a prebendary, she might have put up with him; but he had, she thought, almost disgraced his family in being, at his age, one of the working menial clergy of the cathedral. She kissed him, therefore, sparingly, and resolved that her words with him should be few.

"You are going to be a great lady, Grizzy," said he.

"Umph!" said she.

What was she to say when so addressed?

"And I hope you will be happy,—and make others happy."

"I hope I shall," said she.

"But always think most about the latter, my dear. Think about the happiness of those around you, and your own will come without thinking. You understand that; do you not?"

"Oh, yes, I understand," she said.

As they were speaking Mr. Harding still held her hand, but Griselda left it with him unwillingly, and therefore ungraciously, looking as though she were dragging it from him.

"And Grizzy—I believe it is quite as easy for a rich countess to be happy, as for a dairymaid—"

Griselda gave her head a little chuck which was produced by two different operations of her mind. The first was a reflection that her grandpapa was robbing her of her rank. She was to be a rich marchioness. And the second was a feeling of anger at the old man for comparing her lot to that of a dairymaid.

"Quite as easy, I believe," continued he; "though others will tell you that it is not so. But with the countess as with the dairymaid, it must depend on the woman herself. Being a countess—that fact alone won't make you happy."

"Lord Dumbello at present is only a viscount," said Griselda. "There is no earl's title in the family."

"Oh! I did not know," said Mr. Harding, relinquishing his granddaughter's hand; and, after that, he troubled her with no further advice.

Both Mrs. Proudie and the bishop had called at Plumstead since Mrs. Grantly had come back from London, and the ladies from Plumstead, of course, returned the visit. It was natural that the Grantlys and Proudies should hate each other. They were essentially church people, and their views on all church matters were antagonistic. They had been compelled to fight for supremacy in the diocese, and neither family had so conquered the other as to have become capable of magnanimity and good-humour. They did hate each other, and this hatred had, at one time, almost produced an absolute disseverance of even the courtesies which are so necessary between a bishop and his clergy. But the bitterness of this rancour had been overcome, and the ladies of the families had continued on visiting terms.

But now this match was almost more than Mrs. Proudie could bear. The great disappointment which, as she well knew, the Grantlys had encountered in that matter of the proposed new bishopric had for the moment mollified her. She had been able to talk of poor dear Mrs. Grantly! "She is heartbroken, you know, in this matter, and the repetition of such misfortunes is hard to bear," she had been heard to say, with a complacency which had been quite becoming to her. But now that complacency was at an end. Olivia Proudie had just accepted a widowed preacher at a district church in Bethnal Green,—a man with three children, who was dependent on pew-rents; and Griselda Grantly was engaged to the eldest son of the Marquis of Hartletop! When women are enjoined to forgive their enemies it cannot be intended that such wrongs as these should be included.

But Mrs. Proudie's courage was nothing daunted. It may be boasted of her that nothing could daunt her courage. Soon after her return to Barchester, she and Olivia—Olivia being very unwilling—had driven over to Plumstead, and, not finding the Grantlys at home, had left their cards; and now, at a proper interval, Mrs. Grantly and Griselda returned the visit. It was the first time that Miss Grantly had been seen by the Proudie ladies since the fact of her engagement had become known.

The first bevy of compliments that passed might be likened to a crowd of flowers on a hedge rosebush. They were beautiful to the eye but were so closely environed by thorns that they could not be plucked without great danger. As long as the compliments were allowed to remain on the hedge—while no attempt was made to garner them and realize their fruits for enjoyment—they did no mischief; but the first finger that was put forth for such a purpose was soon drawn back, marked with spots of blood.

"Of course it is a great match for Griselda," said Mrs. Grantly, in a whisper the meekness of which would have disarmed an enemy whose weapons were less firmly clutched than those of Mrs. Proudie; "but, independently of that, the connection is one which is gratifying in many ways."

"Oh, no doubt," said Mrs. Proudie.

"Lord Dumbello is so completely his own master," continued Mrs. Grantly, and a slight, unintended semi-tone of triumph mingled itself with the meekness of that whisper.

"And is likely to remain so, from all I hear," said Mrs. Proudie, and the scratched hand was at once drawn back.

"Of course the estab—," and then Mrs. Proudie, who was blandly continuing her list of congratulations, whispered her sentence close into the ear of Mrs. Grantly, so that not a word of what she said might be audible by the young people.

"I never heard a word of it," said Mrs. Grantly, gathering herself up, "and I don't believe it."

"Oh, I may be wrong; and I'm sure I hope so. But young men will be young men, you know;—and children will take after their parents. I suppose you will see a great deal of the Duke of Omnium now."

But Mrs. Grantly was not a woman to be knocked down and trampled on without resistance; and though she had been lacerated by the rosebush she was not as yet placed altogether *hors de combat*. She said some word about the Duke of Omnium very tranquilly, speaking of him merely as a Barsetshire proprietor, and then, smiling with her sweetest smile, expressed a hope that she might soon have the pleasure of becoming acquainted with Mr. Tickler; and as she spoke she made a pretty little bow towards Olivia Proudie. Now Mr. Tickler was the worthy clergyman attached to the district church at Bethnal Green.

"He'll be down here in August," said Olivia, boldly, determined not to be shamefaced about her love affairs.

"You'll be starring it about the Continent by that time, my dear," said Mrs. Proudie to Griselda. "Lord Dumbello is well known at Homburg and Ems, and places of that sort; so you will find yourself quite at home."

"We are going to Rome," said Griselda, majestically.

"I suppose Mr. Tickler will come into the diocese soon," said Mrs. Grantly. "I remember hearing him very favourably spoken of by Mr. Slope, who was a friend of his."

Nothing short of a fixed resolve on the part of Mrs. Grantly that the time had now come in which she must throw away her shield and stand behind her sword, declare war to the knife, and neither give nor take quarter, could have justified such a speech as this. Any allusion to Mr. Slope acted on Mrs. Proudie as a red cloth is supposed to act on a bull; but when that allusion connected the name of Mr. Slope in a friendly bracket with that of Mrs. Proudie's future son-in-law it might be certain that the effect would be terrific. And there was more than this: for that very Mr. Slope had once entertained audacious hopes—hopes not thought to be audacious by the young lady herself—with reference to Miss Olivia Proudie. All this Mrs. Grantly knew, and, knowing it, still dared to mention his name.

The countenance of Mrs. Proudie became darkened with black anger, and the polished smile of her company manners gave place before the outraged feelings of her nature.

"The man you speak of, Mrs. Grantly," said she, "was never known as a friend by Mr. Tickler."

"Oh, indeed," said Mrs. Grantly. "Perhaps I have made a mistake. I am sure I have heard Mr. Slope mention him."

"When Mr. Slope was running after your sister, Mrs. Grantly, and was encouraged by her as he was, you perhaps saw more of him than I did."

"Mrs. Proudie, that was never the case."

"I have reason to know that the archdeacon conceived it to be so, and that he was very unhappy about it." Now this, unfortunately, was a fact which Mrs. Grantly could not deny.

"The archdeacon may have been mistaken about Mr. Slope," she said, "as were some other people at Barchester. But it was you, I think, Mrs. Proudie, who were responsible for bringing him here."

Mrs. Grantly, at this period of the engagement, might have inflicted a fatal wound by referring to poor Olivia's former love affairs, but she was not destitute of generosity. Even in the extremest heat of the battle she knew how to spare the young and tender.

"When I came here, Mrs. Grantly, I little dreamed what a depth of wickedness might be found in the very close of a cathedral city," said Mrs. Proudie.

"Then, for dear Olivia's sake, pray do not bring poor Mr. Tickler to Barchester."

"Mr. Tickler, Mrs. Grantly, is a man of assured morals and of a highly religious tone of thinking. I wish every one could be so safe as regards their daughters' future prospects as I am."

"Yes, I know he has the advantage of being a family man," said Mrs. Grantly, getting up. "Good morning, Mrs. Proudie; good day, Olivia."

"A great deal better that than—" But the blow fell upon the empty air; for Mrs. Grantly had already escaped on to the staircase while Olivia was ringing the bell for the servant to attend the front-door.

Mrs. Grantly, as she got into her carriage, smiled slightly, thinking of the battle, and as she sat down she gently pressed her daughter's hand. But Mrs. Proudie's face was still dark as Acheron when her enemy withdrew, and with angry tone she sent her daughter to her work. "Mr. Tickler will have great reason to complain if, in your position, you indulge such habits of idleness," she said. Therefore I conceive that I am justified in saying that in that encounter Mrs. Grantly was the conqueror.

CHAPTER XLI.

DON QUIXOTE.

On the day on which Lucy had her interview with Lady Lufton the dean dined at Framley Parsonage. He and Robarts had known each other since the latter had been in the diocese, and now, owing to Mark's preferment in the chapter, had become almost intimate. The dean was greatly pleased with the manner in which poor Mr. Crawley's children had been conveyed away from Hogglestock, and was inclined to open his heart to the whole Framley household. As he still had to ride home he could only allow himself to remain half an hour after dinner, but in that half-hour he said a great deal about Crawley, complimented Robarts on the manner in which he was playing the part of the Good Samaritan, and then by degrees informed him that it had come to his, the dean's, ears, before he left Barchester, that a writ was in the hands of certain persons in the city, enabling them to seize—he did not know whether it was the person or the property of the vicar of Framley.

The fact was that these tidings had been conveyed to the dean with the express intent that he might put Robarts on his guard; but the task of speaking on such a subject to a brother clergyman had been so unpleasant to him that he had been unable to introduce it till the last five minutes before his departure.

"I hope you will not put it down as an impertinent interference," said the dean, apologizing.

"No," said Mark; "no, I do not think that." He was so sad at heart that he hardly knew how to speak of it.

"I do not understand much about such matters," said the dean; "but I think, if I were you, I should go to a lawyer. I should imagine that anything so terribly disagreeable as an arrest might be avoided."

"It is a hard case," said Mark, pleading his own cause. "Though these men have this claim against me I have never received a shilling either in money or money's worth."

"And yet your name is to the bills!" said the dean.

"Yes, my name is to the bills, certainly, but it was to oblige a friend."

And then the dean, having given his advice, rode away. He could not understand how a clergyman, situated as was Mr. Robarts, could find himself called upon by friendship to attach his name to accommodation bills which he had not the power of liquidating when due!

On that evening they were both wretched enough at the parsonage. Hitherto Mark had hoped that perhaps, after all, no absolutely hostile steps would be taken against him with reference to these bills. Some unforeseen chance might occur in his favour, or the persons holding them might consent to take small instalments of payment from time to time; but now it seemed that the evil day was actually coming upon him at a blow. He had no longer any secrets from his wife. Should he go to a lawyer? and if so, to what lawyer? And when he had found his lawyer, what should he say to him? Mrs. Robarts at one time suggested that everything should be told to Lady Lufton. Mark, however, could not bring himself to do that. "It would seem," he said, "as though I wanted her to lend me the money."

On the following morning Mark did ride into Barchester, dreading, however, lest he should be arrested on his journey, and he did see a lawyer. During his absence two calls were made at the parsonage—one by a very rough-looking individual, who left a suspicious document in the hands of the servant, purporting to be an invitation—not to dinner—dinner—from one of the judges of the land; and the other call was made by Lady Lufton in person.

Mrs. Robarts had determined to go down to Framley Court on that day. In accordance with her usual custom she would have been there within an hour or two of Lady Lufton's return from London, but things between them were not now as they usually had been. This affair of Lucy's must make a difference, let them both resolve to the contrary as they might. And, indeed, Mrs. Robarts had found that the closeness of her intimacy with Framley Court had been diminishing from day to day since Lucy had first begun to be on friendly terms with Lord Lufton. Since that she had been less at Framley Court than usual; she had heard from Lady Lufton less frequently by letter during her absence than she had done in former years, and was aware that she was less implicitly trusted with all the affairs of the parish. This had not made her angry, for she was in a manner conscious that it must be so. It made her unhappy, but what could she do? She could not blame Lucy, nor could she blame Lady Lufton. Lord Lufton she did blame, but she did so in the hearing of no one but her husband.

Her mind, however, was made up to go over and bear the first brunt of her ladyship's arguments, when she was stopped by her ladyship's arrival. If it were not for this terrible matter of Lucy's love—a matter on which they could not now be silent when they met—there would be twenty subjects of pleasant, or, at any rate, not unpleasant conversation. But even then there would be those terrible bills hanging over her conscience, and almost crushing her by their weight. At the moment in which Lady Lufton walked up to the drawing-room window, Mrs. Robarts held in her hand that ominous invitation from the judge. Would it not be well that she should make a clean breast of it all, disregarding what her husband had said? It might be well: only this—she had never yet done anything in opposition to her husband's wishes. So she hid the slip within her desk, and left the matter open to consideration.

The interview commenced with an affectionate embrace, as was a matter of course. "Dear Fanny," and "Dear Lady Lufton," was said between them with all the usual warmth. And then the first inquiry was made about the children, and the second about the school. For a minute or two Mrs. Robarts thought that, perhaps, nothing was to be said about Lucy. If it pleased Lady Lufton to be silent she, at least, would not commence the subject.

Then there was a word or two spoken about Mrs. Podgens' baby, after which Lady Lufton asked whether Fanny were alone.

"Yes," said Mrs. Robarts. "Mark has gone over to Barchester."

"I hope he will not be long before he lets me see him. Perhaps he can call to-morrow. Would you both come and dine to-morrow?"

"Not to-morrow, I think, Lady Lufton; but Mark, I am sure, will go over and call."

"And why not come to dinner? I hope there is to be no change among us, eh, Fanny?" and Lady Lufton as she spoke looked into the other's face in a manner which almost made

Mrs. Robarts get up and throw herself on her old friend's neck. Where was she to find a friend who would give her such constant love as she had received from Lady Lufton? And who was kinder, better, more honest than she?

"Change! no, I hope not, Lady Lufton;" and as she spoke the tears stood in her eyes.

"Ah, but I shall think there is if you will not come to me as you used to do. You always used to come and dine with me the day I came home, as a matter of course."

What could she say, poor woman, to this?

"We were all in confusion yesterday about poor Mrs. Crawley, and the dean dined here; he had been over at Hogglestock to see his friend."

"I have heard of her illness, and will go over and see what ought to be done. Don't you go, do you hear, Fanny? You with your young children! I should never forgive you if you did."

And then Mrs. Robarts explained how Lucy had gone there, had sent the four children back to Framley, and was herself now staying at Hogglestock with the object of nursing Mrs. Crawley. In telling the story she abstained from praising Lucy with all the strong language which she would have used had not Lucy's name and character been at the present moment of peculiar import to Lady Lufton; but nevertheless she could not tell it without dwelling much on Lucy's kindness. It would have been ungenerous to Lady Lufton to make much of Lucy's virtue at this present moment, but unjust to Lucy to make nothing of it.

"And she is actually with Mrs. Crawley now?" asked Lady Lufton.

"Oh, yes; Mark left her there yesterday afternoon."

"And the four children are all here in the house?"

"Not exactly in the house—that is, not as yet. We have arranged a sort of quarantine hospital over the coach-house."

"What, where Stubbs lives?"

"Yes; Stubbs and his wife have come into the house, and the children are to remain up there till the doctor says that there is no danger of infection. I have not even seen my visitors myself as yet," said Mrs. Robarts with a slight laugh.

"Dear me!" said Lady Lufton. "I declare you have been very prompt. And so Miss Robarts is over there! I should have thought Mr. Crawley would have made a difficulty about the children."

"Well, he did; but they kidnapped them,—that is, Lucy and Mark did. The dean gave me such an account of it. Lucy brought them out by twos and packed them in the pony-carriage, and then Mark drove off at a gallop while Mr. Crawley stood calling to them in the road. The dean was there at the time and saw it all."

"That Miss Lucy of yours seems to be a very determined young lady when she takes a thing into her head," said Lady Lufton, now sitting down for the first time.

"Yes, she is," said Mrs. Robarts, having laid aside all her pleasant animation, for the discussion which she dreaded was now at hand.

"A very determined young lady," continued Lady Lufton. "Of course, my dear Fanny, you know all this about Ludovic and your sister-in-law?"

"Yes, she has told me about it."

"It is very unfortunate—very."

"I do not think Lucy has been to blame," said Mrs. Robarts; and as she spoke the blood was already mounting to her cheeks.

"Do not be too anxious to defend her, my dear, before any one accuses her. Whenever a person does that it looks as though their cause were weak."

"But my cause is not weak as far as Lucy is concerned; I feel quite sure that she has not been to blame."

"I know how obstinate you can be, Fanny, when you think it necessary to dub yourself any one's champion. Don Quixote was not a better knight-errant than you are. But is it not a pity to take up your lance and shield before an enemy is within sight or hearing? But that was ever the way with your Don Quixotes."

"Perhaps there may be an enemy in ambush." That was Mrs. Robarts' thought to herself, but she did not dare to express it, so she remained silent.

"My only hope is," continued Lady Lufton, "that when my back is turned you fight as gallantly for me."

"Ah, you are never under a cloud, like poor Lucy."

"Am I not? But, Fanny, you do not see all the clouds. The sun does not always shine for any of us, and the down-pouring rain and the heavy wind scatter also my fairest flowers,—as they have done hers, poor girl. Dear Fanny, I hope it may be long before any cloud comes across the brightness of your heaven. Of all the creatures I know you are the one most fitted for quiet continued sunshine."

And then Mrs. Robarts did get up and embrace her friend, thus hiding the tears which were running down her face. Continued sunshine indeed! A dark spot had already gathered on her horizon which was likely to fall in a very waterspout of rain. What was to come of that terrible notice which was now lying in the desk under Lady Lufton's very arm?

"But I am not come here to croak like an old raven," continued Lady Lufton, when she had brought this embrace to an end. "It is probable that we all may have our sorrows; but I am quite sure of this,—that if we endeavour to do our duties honestly, we shall all find our consolation and all have our joys also. And now, my dear, let you and I say a few words about this unfortunate affair. It would not be natural if we were to hold our tongues to each other; would it?"

"I suppose not," said Mrs. Robarts.

"We should always be conceiving worse than the truth,—each as to the other's thoughts. Now, some time ago, when I spoke to you about your sister-in-law and Ludovic—I daresay you remember—"

"Oh, yes, I remember."

"We both thought then that there would really be no danger. To tell you the plain truth I fancied, and indeed hoped, that his affections were engaged elsewhere; but I was altogether wrong then; wrong in thinking it, and wrong in hoping it."

Mrs. Robarts knew well that Lady Lufton was alluding to Griselda Grantly, but she conceived that it would be discreet to say nothing herself on that subject at present. She remembered, however, Lucy's flashing eye when the possibility of Lord Lufton making such a marriage was spoken of in the pony-carriage, and could not but feel glad that Lady Lufton had been disappointed.

"I do not at all impute any blame to Miss Robarts for what has occurred since," continued her ladyship. "I wish you distinctly to understand that."

"I do not see how any one could blame her. She has behaved so nobly."

"It is of no use inquiring whether any one can. It is sufficient that I do not."

"But I think that is hardly sufficient," said Mrs. Robarts, pertinaciously.

"Is it not?" asked her ladyship, raising her eyebrows.

"No. Only think what Lucy has done and is doing. If she had chosen to say that she would accept your son I really do not know how you could have justly blamed her. I do not by any means say that I would have advised such a thing."

"I am glad of that, Fanny."

"I have not given any advice; nor is it needed. I know no one more able than Lucy to see clearly, by her own judgment, what course she ought to pursue. I should be afraid to

1090

advise one whose mind is so strong, and who, of her own nature, is so self-denying as she is. She is sacrificing herself now, because she will not be the means of bringing trouble and dissension between you and your son. If you ask me, Lady Lufton, I think you owe her a deep debt of gratitude. I do, indeed. And as for blaming her—what has she done that you possibly could blame?"

"Don Quixote on horseback!" said Lady Lufton. "Fanny, I shall always call you Don Quixote, and some day or other I will get somebody to write your adventures. But the truth is this, my dear: there has been imprudence. You may call it mine, if you will—though I really hardly see how I am to take the blame. I could not do other than ask Miss Robarts to my house, and I could not very well turn my son out of it. In point of fact, it has been the old story."

"Exactly; the story that is as old as the world, and which will continue as long as people are born into it. It is a story of God's own telling!"

"But, my dear child, you do not mean that every young gentleman and every young lady should fall in love with each other directly they meet! Such a doctrine would be very inconvenient."

"No, I do not mean that. Lord Lufton and Miss Grantly did not fall in love with each other, though you meant them to do so. But was it not quite as natural that Lord Lufton and Lucy should do so instead?"

"It is generally thought, Fanny, that young ladies should not give loose to their affections until they have been certified of their friends' approval."

"And that young gentlemen of fortune may amuse themselves as they please! I know that is what the world teaches, but I cannot agree to the justice of it. The terrible suffering which Lucy has to endure makes me cry out against it. She did not seek your son. The moment she began to suspect that there might be danger she avoided him scrupulously. She would not go down to Framley Court, though her not doing so was remarked by yourself. She would hardly go out about the place lest she should meet him. She was contented to put herself altogether in the background till he should have pleased to leave the place. But he—he came to her here, and insisted on seeing her. He found her when I was out, and declared himself determined to speak to her. What was she to do? She did try to escape, but he stopped her at the door. Was it her fault that he made her an offer?"

"My dear, no one has said so."

"Yes, but you do say so when you tell me that young ladies should not give play to their affections without permission. He persisted in saying to her, here, all that it pleased him, though she implored him to be silent. I cannot tell the words she used, but she did implore him."

"I do not doubt that she behaved well."

"But he—he persisted, and begged her to accept his hand. She refused him then, Lady Lufton—not as some girls do, with a mock reserve, not intending to be taken at their words—but steadily, and, God forgive her, untruly. Knowing what your feelings would be, and knowing what the world would say, she declared to him that he was indifferent to her. What more could she do in your behalf?" And then Mrs. Robarts paused.

"I shall wait till you have done, Fanny."

"You spoke of girls giving loose to their affections. She did not do so. She went about her work exactly as she had done before. She did not even speak to me of what had passed—not then, at least. She determined that it should all be as though it had never been. She had learned to love your son; but that was her misfortune and she would get over it as she might. Tidings came to us here that he was engaged, or about to engage himself, to Miss Grantly."

"Those tidings were untrue."

"Yes, we know that now; but she did not know it then. Of course she could not but suffer; but she suffered within herself." Mrs. Robarts, as she said this, remembered the pony-carriage and how Puck had been beaten. "She made no complaint that he had ill-treated her—not even to herself. She had thought it right to reject his offer; and there, as far as he was concerned, was to be an end of it."

"That would be a matter of course, I should suppose."

"But it was not a matter of course, Lady Lufton. He returned from London to Framley on purpose to repeat his offer. He sent for her brother— You talk of a young lady waiting for her friends' approval. In this matter who would be Lucy's friends?"

"You and Mr. Robarts, of course."

"Exactly; her only friends. Well, Lord Lufton sent for Mark and repeated his offer to him. Mind you, Mark had never heard a word of this before, and you may guess whether or no he was surprised. Lord Lufton repeated his offer in the most formal manner and claimed permission to see Lucy. She refused to see him. She has never seen him since that day when, in opposition to all her efforts, he made his way into this room. Mark,—as I think very properly,—would have allowed Lord Lufton to come up here. Looking at both their ages and position he could have had no right to forbid it. But Lucy positively refused to see your son, and sent him a message instead, of the purport of which you are now aware—that she would never accept him unless she did so at your request."

"It was a very proper message."

"I say nothing about that. Had she accepted him I would not have blamed her:—and so I told her, Lady Lufton."

"I cannot understand your saying that, Fanny."

"Well; I did say so. I don't want to argue now about myself,—whether I was right or wrong, but I did say so. Whatever sanction I could give she would have had. But she again chose to sacrifice herself, although I believe she regards him with as true a love as ever a girl felt for a man. Upon my word I don't know that she is right. Those considerations for the world may perhaps be carried too far."

"I think that she was perfectly right."

"Very well, Lady Lufton; I can understand that. But after such sacrifice on her part—a sacrifice made entirely to you—how can you talk of 'not blaming her'? Is that the language in which you speak of those whose conduct from first to last has been superlatively excellent? If she is open to blame at all, it is—it is—"

But here Mrs. Robarts stopped herself. In defending her sister she had worked herself almost into a passion; but such a state of feeling was not customary to her, and now that she had spoken her mind she sank suddenly into silence.

"It seems to me, Fanny, that you almost regret Miss Robarts' decision," said Lady Lufton.

"My wish in this matter is for her happiness, and I regret anything that may mar it."

"You think nothing then of our welfare, and yet I do not know to whom I might have looked for hearty friendship and for sympathy in difficulties, if not to you?"

Poor Mrs. Robarts was almost upset by this. A few months ago, before Lucy's arrival, she would have declared that the interests of Lady Lufton's family would have been paramount with her, after and next to those of her own husband. And even now, it seemed to argue so black an ingratitude on her part—this accusation that she was indifferent to them! From her childhood upwards she had revered and loved Lady Lufton, and for years had taught herself to regard her as an epitome of all that was good and gracious in woman. Lady Lufton's theories of life had been accepted by her as the right theories, and those whom Lady Lufton had liked she had liked. But now it seemed that all these ideas which it had taken a life to build up were to be thrown to the ground, because she was bound to defend a sister-in-law whom she had only known for the last eight months. It was not that she regretted a word that she had spoken on Lucy's behalf. Chance had thrown her and Lucy together, and, as Lucy was her sister, she should receive from her a sister's treatment. But she did not the less feel how terrible would be the effect of any disseverance from Lady Lufton.

"Oh, Lady Lufton," she said, "do not say that."

"But, Fanny, dear, I must speak as I find. You were talking about clouds just now, and do you think that all this is not a cloud in my sky? Ludovic tells me that he is attached to Miss Robarts, and you tell me that she is attached to him; and I am called upon to decide between them. Her very act obliges me to do so."

"Dear Lady Lufton," said Mrs. Robarts, springing from her seat. It seemed to her at the moment as though the whole difficulty were to be solved by an act of grace on the part of her old friend.

"And yet I cannot approve of such a marriage," said Lady Lufton.

Mrs. Robarts returned to her seat, saying nothing further.

"Is not that a cloud on one's horizon?" continued her ladyship. "Do you think that I can be basking in the sunshine while I have such a weight upon my heart as that? Ludovic will soon be home, but instead of looking to his return with pleasure I dread it. I would prefer that he should remain in Norway. I would wish that he should stay away for months. And, Fanny, it is a great addition to my misfortune to feel that you do not sympathize with me."

Having said this, in a slow, sorrowful, and severe tone, Lady Lufton got up and took her departure. Of course Mrs. Robarts did not let her go without assuring her that she did sympathize with her,—did love her as she ever had loved her. But wounds cannot be cured as easily as they may be inflicted, and Lady Lufton went her way with much real sorrow at her heart. She was proud and masterful, fond of her own way, and much too careful of the worldly dignities to which her lot had called her: but she was a woman who could cause no sorrow to those she loved without deep sorrow to herself.

CHAPTER XLII.

TOUCHING PITCH.

In these hot midsummer days, the end of June and the beginning of July, Mr. Sowerby had but an uneasy time of it. At his sister's instance, he had hurried up to London, and there had remained for days in attendance on the lawyers. He had to see new lawyers, Miss Dunstable's men of business, quiet old cautious gentlemen whose place of business was in a dark alley behind the Bank, Messrs. Slow and Bideawhile by name, who had no scruple in detaining him for hours while they or their clerks talked to him about anything or about nothing. It was of vital consequence to Mr. Sowerby that this business of his should be settled without delay, and yet these men, to whose care this settling was now confided, went on as though law processes were a sunny bank on which it delighted men to bask easily. And then, too, he had to go more than once to South Audley Street, which was a worse infliction; for the men in South Audley Street were less civil now than had been their wont. It was well understood there that Mr. Sowerby was no longer a client of the duke's, but his opponent; no longer his nominee and dependant, but his enemy in the county. "Chaldicotes," as old Mr. Gumption remarked to young Mr. Gagebee; "Chaldicotes, Gagebee, is a cooked goose, as far as Sowerby is concerned. And what difference could it make to him whether the duke is to own it or Miss Dunstable? For my part I cannot understand how a gentleman like Sowerby can like to see his property go into the hands of a gallipot wench whose money still smells of bad drugs. And nothing can be more ungrateful," he said, "than Sowerby's conduct. He has held the county for five-and-twenty years without expense; and now that the time for payment has come, he begrudges the price." He called it no better than cheating, he did not—he, Mr. Gumption. According to his ideas Sowerby was attempting to cheat the duke. It may be imagined, therefore, that Mr. Sowerby did not feel any very great delight in attending at South Audley Street.

And then rumour was spread about among all the bill-discounting leeches that blood was once more to be sucked from the Sowerby carcase. The rich Miss Dunstable had taken up his affairs; so much as that became known in the purlieus of the Goat and Compasses. Tom Tozer's brother declared that she and Sowerby were going to make a match of it, and that any scrap of paper with Sowerby's name on it would become worth its weight in bank-notes; but Tom Tozer himself—Tom, who was the real hero of the family—pooh-poohed at this, screwing up his nose, and alluding in most contemptuous terms to his brother's softness. He knew better—as was indeed the fact. Miss Dunstable was buying up the squire, and by jingo she should buy them up—them, the Tozers, as well as others! They knew their value, the Tozers did;—whereupon they became more than ordinarily active.

From them and all their brethren Mr. Sowerby at this time endeavoured to keep his distance, but his endeavours were not altogether effectual. Whenever he could escape for a day or two from the lawyers he ran down to Chaldicotes; but Tom Tozer in his perseverance followed him there, and boldly sent in his name by the servant at the front-door.

"Mr. Sowerby is not just at home at the present moment," said the well-trained domestic.

"I'll wait about then," said Tom, seating himself on an heraldic stone griffin which flanked the big stone steps before the house. And in this way Mr. Tozer gained his purpose. Sowerby was still contesting the county, and it behoved him not to let his enemies say that he was hiding himself. It had been a part of his bargain with Miss Dunstable that he should contest the county. She had taken it into her head that the duke had behaved badly, and she had resolved that he should be made to pay for it. "The duke," she said, "had meddled long enough;" she would now see whether the Chaldicotes interest would not suffice of itself to return a member for the county, even in opposition to the duke. Mr. Sowerby himself was so harassed at the time, that he would have given way on this point if he had had the power; but Miss Dunstable was determined, and he was obliged to yield to her. In this manner Mr. Tom Tozer succeeded and did make his way into Mr. Sowerby's presence—of which intrusion one effect was the following letter from Mr. Sowerby to his friend Mark Robarts:—

Chaldicotes, July, 185—.

MY DEAR ROBARTS,—I am so harassed at the present moment by an infinity of troubles of my own that I am almost callous to those of other people. They say that prosperity makes a man selfish. I have never tried that, but I am quite sure that adversity does so. Nevertheless I am anxious about those bills of yours—

"Bills of mine!" said Robarts to himself, as he walked up and down the shrubbery path at the parsonage, reading this letter. This happened a day or two after his visit to the lawyer at Barchester.

—and would rejoice greatly if I thought that I could save you from any further annoyance about them. That kite, Tom Tozer, has just been with me, and insists that both of them shall be paid. He knows—no one better—that no consideration was given for the latter. But he knows also that the dealing was not with him, nor even with his brother, and he will be prepared to swear that he gave value for both. He would swear anything for five hundred pounds—or for half the money, for that matter. I do not think that the father of mischief ever let loose upon the world a greater rascal than Tom Tozer. He declares that nothing shall induce him to take one shilling less than the whole sum of nine hundred pounds. He has been brought to this by hearing that my debts are about to be paid. Heaven help me! The meaning of that is that these wretched acres, which are now mortgaged to one millionnaire, are to change hands and be mortgaged to another instead. By this exchange I may possibly obtain the benefit of having a house to live in for the next twelve months, but no other. Tozer, however, is altogether wrong in his scent; and the worst of it is that his malice will fall on you rather than on me.

> What I want you to do is this: let us pay him one hundred pounds between us. Though I sell the last sorry jade of a horse I have, I will make up fifty; and I know you can, at any rate, do as much as that. Then do you accept a bill, conjointly with me, for eight hundred. It shall be done in Forrest's presence, and handed to him; and you shall receive back the two old bills into your own hands at the same time. This new bill should be

timed to run ninety days; and I will move heaven and earth during that time to have it included in the general schedule of my debts which are to be secured on the Chaldicotes property.

The meaning of which was that Miss Dunstable was to be cozened into paying the money under an idea that it was part of the sum covered by the existing mortgage.

What you said the other day at Barchester, as to never executing another bill, is very well as regards future transactions. Nothing can be wiser than such a resolution. But it would be folly—worse than folly—if you were to allow your furniture to be seized when the means of preventing it are so ready to your hand. By leaving the new bill in Forrest's hands you may be sure that you are safe from the claws of such birds of prey as these Tozers. Even if I cannot get it settled when the three months are over, Forrest will enable you to make any arrangement that may be most convenient.

For Heaven's sake, my dear fellow, do not refuse this. You can hardly conceive how it weighs upon me, this fear that bailiffs should make their way into your wife's drawing-room. I know you think ill of me, and I do not wonder at it. But you would be less inclined to do so if you knew how terribly I am punished. Pray let me hear that you will do as I counsel you.
Yours always faithfully,
N. SOWERBY.

In answer to which the parson wrote a very short reply:—

Framley, July, 185—.

MY DEAR SOWERBY,— I will sign no more bills on any consideration.

Yours truly,
MARK ROBARTS.

And then having written this, and having shown it to his wife, he returned to the shrubbery walk and paced it up and down, looking every now and then to Sowerby's letter as he thought over all the past circumstances of his friendship with that gentleman. That the man who had written this letter should be his friend—that very fact was a disgrace to him. Sowerby so well knew himself and his own reputation, that he did not dare to suppose that his own word would be taken for anything,—not even when the thing promised was an act of the commonest honesty. "The old bills shall be given back into your own hands," he had declared with energy, knowing that his friend and correspondent would not feel himself secure against further fraud under any less stringent guarantee. This gentleman, this county member, the owner of Chaldicotes, with whom Mark Robarts had been so anxious to be on terms of intimacy, had now come to such a phase of life that he had given over speaking of himself as an honest man. He had become so used to suspicion that he argued of it as of a thing of course. He knew that no one could trust either his spoken or his written word, and he was content to speak and to write without attempt to hide this conviction.

And this was the man whom he had been so glad to call his friend; for whose sake he had been willing to quarrel with Lady Lufton, and at whose instance he had unconsciously abandoned so many of the best resolutions of his life. He looked back now, as he walked there slowly, still holding the letter in his hand, to the day when he had stopped at the school-house and written his letter to Mr. Sowerby, promising to join the party at Chaldicotes. He had been so eager then to have his own way, that he would not permit himself to go home and talk the matter over with his wife. He thought also of the manner in which he had been tempted to the house of the Duke of Omnium, and the conviction on his mind at the time that his giving way to that temptation would surely bring him to evil. And then he remembered the evening in Sowerby's bedroom, when the bill had been brought out, and he had allowed himself to be persuaded to put his name upon it;—not because he was willing in this way to assist his friend, but because he was unable to refuse. He had lacked the courage to say, "No," though he knew at the time how gross was the error which he was committing. He had lacked the courage to say, "No," and hence had come upon him and on his household all this misery and cause for bitter repentance.

I have written much of clergymen, but in doing so I have endeavoured to portray them as they bear on our social life rather than to describe the mode and working of their professional careers. Had I done the latter I could hardly have steered clear of subjects on which it has not been my intention to pronounce an opinion, and I should either have laden my fiction with sermons or I should have degraded my sermons into fiction. Therefore I have said but little in my narrative of this man's feelings or doings as a clergyman.

But I must protest against its being on this account considered that Mr. Robarts was indifferent to the duties of his clerical position. He had been fond of pleasure and had given way to temptation,—as is so customarily done by young men of six-and-twenty, who are placed beyond control and who have means at command. Had he remained as a curate till that age, subject in all his movements to the eye of a superior, he would, we may say, have put his name to no bills, have ridden after no hounds, have seen nothing of the iniquities of Gatherum Castle. There are men of twenty-six as fit to stand alone as ever they will be—fit to be prime ministers, heads of schools, judges on the bench—almost fit to be bishops; but Mark Robarts had not been one of them. He had within him many aptitudes for good, but not the strengthened courage of a man to act up to them. The stuff of which his manhood was to be formed had been slow of growth, as it is with many men; and, consequently, when temptation was offered to him, he had fallen.

But he deeply grieved over his own stumbling, and from time to time, as his periods of penitence came upon him, he resolved that he would once more put his shoulder to the wheel as became one who fights upon earth that battle for which he had put on his armour. Over and over again did he think of those words of Mr. Crawley, and now as he walked up and down the path, crumpling Mr. Sowerby's letter in his hand, he thought of them again—"It is a terrible falling off; terrible in the fall, but doubly terrible through that difficulty of returning." Yes; that is a difficulty which multiplies itself in a fearful ratio as one goes on pleasantly running down the path—whitherward? Had it come to that with him that he could not return—that he could never again hold up his head with a safe conscience as the pastor of his parish! It was Sowerby who had led him into this misery, who had brought on him this ruin? But then had not Sowerby paid him? Had not that stall which he now held in Barchester been Sowerby's gift? He was a poor man now—a distressed, poverty-stricken man; but nevertheless he wished with all his heart that he had never become a sharer in the good things of the Barchester chapter.

"I shall resign the stall," he said to his wife that night. "I think I may say that I have made up my mind as to that."

"But, Mark, will not people say that it is odd?"

"I cannot help it—they must say it. Fanny, I fear that we shall have to bear the saying of harder words than that."

"Nobody can ever say that you have done anything that is unjust or dishonourable. If there are such men as Mr. Sowerby—"

"The blackness of his fault will not excuse mine." And then again he sat silent, hiding his eyes, while his wife, sitting by him, held his hand.

"Don't make yourself wretched, Mark. Matters will all come right yet. It cannot be that the loss of a few hundred pounds should ruin you."

"It is not the money—it is not the money!"

"But you have done nothing wrong, Mark."

"How am I to go into the church, and take my place before them all, when every one will know that bailiffs are in the house?" And then, dropping his head on to the table, he sobbed aloud.

Mark Robarts' mistake had been mainly this,—he had thought to touch pitch and not to be defiled. He, looking out from his pleasant parsonage into the pleasant upper ranks of the world around him, had seen that men and things in those quarters were very engaging. His own parsonage, with his sweet wife, were exceedingly dear to him, and Lady Lufton's affectionate friendship had its value; but were not these things rather dull for one who had lived in the best sets at Harrow and Oxford;—unless, indeed, he could supplement them with some occasional bursts of more lively life? Cakes and ale were as pleasant to his palate as to the palates of those with whom he had formerly lived at college. He had the same eye to look at a horse, and the same heart to make him go across a country, as they. And then, too, he found that men liked him,—men and women also; men and women who were high in worldly standing. His ass's ears were tickled, and he learned to fancy that he was intended by nature for the society of high people. It seemed as though he were following his appointed course in meeting men and women of the world at the houses of the fashionable and the rich. He was not the first clergyman that had so lived and had so prospered. Yes, clergymen had so lived, and had done their duties in their sphere of life altogether to the satisfaction of their countrymen—and of their sovereigns. Thus Mark Robarts had determined that he would touch pitch, and escape defilement if that were possible. With what result those who have read so far will have perceived.

Late on the following afternoon who should drive up to the parsonage door but Mr. Forrest, the bank manager from Barchester—Mr. Forrest, to whom Sowerby had always pointed as the *Deus ex machinâ* who, if duly invoked, could relieve them all from their present troubles, and dismiss the whole Tozer family—not howling into the wilderness, as one would have wished to do with that brood of Tozers, but so gorged with prey that from them no further annoyance need be dreaded? All this Mr. Forrest could do; nay, more, most willingly would do! Only let Mark Robarts put himself into the banker's hand, and blandly sign what documents the banker might desire.

"This is a very unpleasant affair," said Mr. Forrest as soon as they were closeted together in Mark's book-room. In answer to which observation the parson acknowledged that it was a very unpleasant affair.

"Mr. Sowerby has managed to put you into the hands of about the worst set of rogues now existing, in their line of business, in London."

"So I supposed; Curling told me the same." Curling was the Barchester attorney whose aid he had lately invoked.

"Curling has threatened them that he will expose their whole trade; but one of them who was down here, a man named Tozer, replied, that you had much more to lose by exposure than he had. He went further and declared that he would defy any jury in England to refuse him his money. He swore that he discounted both bills in the regular way of business; and, though this is of course false, I fear that it will be impossible to prove it so. He well knows that you are a clergyman, and that, therefore, he has a stronger hold on you than on other men."

"The disgrace shall fall on Sowerby," said Robarts, hardly actuated at the moment by any strong feeling of Christian forgiveness.

"I fear, Mr. Robarts, that he is somewhat in the condition of the Tozers. He will not feel it as you will do."

"I must bear it, Mr. Forrest, as best I may."

"Will you allow me, Mr. Robarts, to give you my advice? Perhaps I ought to apologize for intruding it upon you; but as the bills have been presented and dishonoured across my counter, I have, of necessity, become acquainted with the circumstances."

"I am sure I am very much obliged to you," said Mark.

"You must pay this money, or, at any rate, the most considerable portion of it;—the whole of it, indeed, with such deduction as a lawyer may be able to induce these hawks to make on the sight of the ready money. Perhaps £750 or £800 may see you clear of the whole affair."

"But I have not a quarter of that sum lying by me."

"No, I suppose not; but what I would recommend is this: that you should borrow the money from the bank, on your own responsibility,—with the joint security of some friend who may be willing to assist you with his name. Lord Lufton probably would do it."

"No, Mr. Forrest—"

"Listen to me first, before you make up your mind. If you took this step, of course you would do so with the fixed intention of paying the money yourself,—without any further reliance on Sowerby or on any one else."

"I shall not rely on Mr. Sowerby again; you may be sure of that."

"What I mean is that you must teach yourself to recognize the debt as your own. If you can do that, with your income you can surely pay it, with interest, in two years. If Lord Lufton will assist you with his name I will so arrange the bills that the payments shall be made to fall equally over that period. In that way the world will know nothing about it, and in two years' time you will once more be a free man. Many men, Mr. Robarts, have bought their experience much dearer than that, I can assure you."

"Mr. Forrest, it is quite out of the question."

"You mean that Lord Lufton will not give you his name."

"I certainly shall not ask him; but that is not all. In the first place my income will not be what you think it, for I shall probably give up the prebend at Barchester."

"Give up the prebend! give up six hundred a year!"

"And, beyond this, I think I may say that nothing shall tempt me to put my name to another bill. I have learned a lesson which I hope I may never forget."

"Then what do you intend to do?"

"Nothing!"

"Then those men will sell every stick of furniture about the place. They know that your property here is enough to secure all that they claim."

"If they have the power, they must sell it."

"And all the world will know the facts."

"So it must be. Of the faults which a man commits he must bear the punishment. If it were only myself!"

"That's where it is, Mr. Robarts. Think what your wife will have to suffer in going through such misery as that! You had better take my advice. Lord Lufton, I am sure—"

But the very name of Lord Lufton, his sister's lover, again gave him courage. He thought, too, of the accusations which Lord Lufton had brought against him on that night when he had come to him in the coffee-room of the hotel, and he felt that it was impossible that he should apply to him for such aid. It would be better to tell all to Lady Lufton! That she would relieve him, let the cost to herself be what it might, he was very sure. Only this;—that in looking to her for assistance he would be forced to bite the dust in very deed.

"Thank you, Mr. Forrest, but I have made up my mind. Do not think that I am the less obliged to you for your disinterested kindness,—for I know that it is disinterested; but this I think I may confidently say, that not even to avert so terrible a calamity will I again put my name to any bill. Even if you could take my own promise to pay without the addition of any second name, I would not do it."

There was nothing for Mr. Forrest to do under such circumstances but simply to drive back to Barchester. He had done the best for the young clergyman according to his lights, and perhaps, in a worldly view, his advice had not been bad. But Mark dreaded the very name of a bill. He was as a dog that had been terribly scorched, and nothing should again induce him to go near the fire.

"Was not that the man from the bank?" said Fanny, coming into the room when the sound of the wheels had died away.

"Yes; Mr. Forrest."

"Well, dearest?"

"We must prepare ourselves for the worst."

"You will not sign any more papers, eh, Mark?"

"No; I have just now positively refused to do so."

"Then I can bear anything. But, dearest, dearest Mark, will you not let me tell Lady Lufton?"

Let them look at the matter in any way the punishment was very heavy.

CHAPTER XLIII.

IS SHE NOT INSIGNIFICANT?

And now a month went by at Framley without any increase of comfort to our friends there, and also without any absolute development of the ruin which had been daily expected at the parsonage. Sundry letters had reached Mr. Robarts from various personages acting in the Tozer interest, all of which he referred to Mr. Curling, of Barchester. Some of these letters contained prayers for the money, pointing out how an innocent widow lady had been induced to invest her all on the faith of Mr. Robarts' name, and was now starving in a garret, with her three children, because Mr. Robarts would not make good his own undertakings. But the majority of them were filled with threats;—only two days longer would be allowed and then the sheriff's officers would be enjoined to do their work; then one day of grace would be added, at the expiration of which the dogs of war would be unloosed. These, as fast as they came, were sent to Mr. Curling, who took no notice of them individually, but continued his endeavour to prevent the evil day. The second bill Mr. Robarts would take up—such was Mr. Curling's proposition; and would pay by two instalments of £250 each, the first in two months, and the second in four. If this were acceptable to the Tozer interest—well; if it were not, the sheriff's officers must do their worst and the Tozer interest must look for what it could get. The Tozer interest would not declare itself satisfied with these terms, and so the matter went on. During which the roses faded from day to day on the cheeks of Mrs. Robarts, as under such circumstances may easily be conceived.

In the meantime Lucy still remained at Hogglestock and had there become absolute mistress of the house. Poor Mrs. Crawley had been at death's door; for some days she was delirious, and afterwards remained so weak as to be almost unconscious; but now the worst was over, and Mr. Crawley had been informed, that as far as human judgment might pronounce, his children would not become orphans nor would he become a widower. During these weeks Lucy had not once been home nor had she seen any of the Framley people. "Why should she incur the risk of conveying infection for so small an object?" as she herself argued, writing by letters, which were duly fumigated before they were opened at the parsonage. So she remained at Hogglestock, and the Crawley children, now admitted to all the honours of the nursery, were kept at Framley. They were kept at Framley, although it was expected from day to day that the beds on which they lay would be seized for the payment of Mr. Sowerby's debts.

Lucy, as I have said, became mistress of the house at Hogglestock and made herself absolutely ascendant over Mr. Crawley. Jellies, and broth, and fruit, and even butter, came from Lufton Court, which she displayed on the table, absolutely on the cloth before him, and yet he bore it. I cannot say that he partook of these delicacies with any freedom himself, but he did drink his tea when it was given to him although it contained Framley cream;—and, had he known it, Bohea itself from the Framley chest. In truth, in these days, he had given himself over to the dominion of this stranger; and he said nothing beyond, "Well, well," with two uplifted hands, when he came upon her as she was sewing the buttons on to his own shirts—sewing on the buttons and perhaps occasionally applying her needle elsewhere,—not without utility.

He said to her at this period very little in the way of thanks. Some protracted conversations they did have, now and again, during the long evenings; but even in these he did not utter many words as to their present state of life. It was on religion chiefly that he spoke, not lecturing her individually, but laying down his ideas as to what the life of a Christian should be, and especially what should be the life of a minister. "But though I can see this, Miss Robarts," he said, "I am bound to say that no one has fallen off so frequently as myself. I have renounced the devil and all his works; but it is by word of mouth only—by word of mouth only. How shall a man crucify the old Adam that is within him, unless he throw himself prostrate in the dust and acknowledge that all his strength is weaker than water?" To this, often as it might be repeated, she would listen patiently, comforting him by such words as her theology would supply; but then, when this was over, she would again resume her command and enforce from him a close obedience to her domestic behests.

At the end of the month Lord Lufton came back to Framley Court. His arrival there was quite unexpected; though, as he pointed out when his mother expressed some surprise, he had returned exactly at the time named by him before he started.

"I need not say, Ludovic, how glad I am to have you," said she, looking to his face and pressing his arm; "the more so, indeed, seeing that I hardly expected it."

He said nothing to his mother about Lucy the first evening, although there was some conversation respecting the Robarts family.

"I am afraid Mr. Robarts has embarrassed himself," said Lady Lufton, looking very seriously. "Rumours reach me which are most distressing. I have said nothing to anybody as yet—not even to Fanny; but I can see in her face, and hear in the tones of her voice, that she is suffering some great sorrow."

"I know all about it," said Lord Lufton.

"You know all about it, Ludovic?"

"Yes; it is through that precious friend of mine, Mr. Sowerby, of Chaldicotes. He has accepted bills for Sowerby; indeed, he told me so."

"What business had he at Chaldicotes? What had he to do with such friends as that? I do not know how I am to forgive him."

"It was through me that he became acquainted with Sowerby. You must remember that, mother."

"I do not see that that is any excuse. Is he to consider that all your acquaintances must necessarily be his friends also? It is reasonable to suppose that you in your position must live occasionally with a great many people who are altogether unfit companions for him as a parish clergyman. He will not remember this, and he must be taught it. What business had he to go to Gatherum Castle?"

"He got his stall at Barchester by going there."

"He would be much better without his stall, and Fanny has the sense to know this. What does he want with two houses? Prebendal stalls are for older men than he—for men who have earned them, and who at the end of their lives want some ease. I wish with all my heart that he had never taken it."

"Six hundred a year has its charms all the same," said Lufton, getting up and strolling out of the room.

"If Mark really be in any difficulty," he said, later in the evening, "we must put him on his legs."

"You mean, pay his debts?"

"Yes; he has no debts except these acceptances of Sowerby's."

"How much will it be, Ludovic?"

"A thousand pounds, perhaps, more or less. I'll find the money, mother; only I shan't be able to pay you quite as soon as I intended." Whereupon his mother got up, and throwing her arms round his neck declared that she would never forgive him if he ever said a word more about her little present to him. I suppose there is no pleasure a mother can have more attractive than giving away her money to an only son.

Lucy's name was first mentioned at breakfast the next morning. Lord Lufton had made up his mind to attack his mother on the subject early in the morning—before he went up to the parsonage; but as matters turned out Miss Robarts' doings were necessarily brought under discussion without reference to Lord Lufton's special aspirations regarding her. The fact of Mrs. Crawley's illness had been mentioned, and Lady Lufton had stated how it had come to pass that all the Crawleys' children were at the parsonage.

"I must say that Fanny has behaved excellently," said Lady Lufton. "It was just what might have been expected from her. And indeed," she added, speaking in an embarrassed tone, "so has Miss Robarts. Miss Robarts has remained at Hogglestock and nursed Mrs. Crawley through the whole."

"Remained at Hogglestock—through the fever!" exclaimed his lordship.

"Yes, indeed," said Lady Lufton.

"And is she there now?"

"Oh, yes; I am not aware that she thinks of leaving just yet."

"Then I say that it is a great shame—a scandalous shame!"

"But, Ludovic, it was her own doing."

"Oh, yes; I understand. But why should she be sacrificed? Were there no nurses in the country to be hired, but that she must go and remain there for a month at the bedside of a pestilent fever? There is no justice in it."

"Justice, Ludovic? I don't know about justice, but there was great Christian charity. Mrs. Crawley has probably owed her life to Miss Robarts."

"Has she been ill? Is she ill? I insist upon knowing whether she is ill. I shall go over to Hogglestock myself immediately after breakfast."

To this Lady Lufton made no reply. If Lord Lufton chose to go to Hogglestock she could not prevent him. She thought, however, that it would be much better that he should stay away. He would be quite as open to the infection as Lucy Robarts; and, moreover, Mrs. Crawley's bedside would be as inconvenient a place as might be selected for any interview between two lovers. Lady Lufton felt at the present moment that she was cruelly treated by circumstances with reference to Miss Robarts. Of course it would have been her part to lessen, if she could do so without injustice, that high idea which her son entertained of the beauty and worth of the young lady; but, unfortunately, she had been compelled to praise her and to load her name with all manner of eulogy. Lady Lufton was essentially a true woman, and not even with the object of carrying out her own views in so important a matter would she be guilty of such deception as she might have practised by simply holding her tongue; but nevertheless she could hardly reconcile herself to the necessity of singing Lucy's praises.

After breakfast Lady Lufton got up from her chair, but hung about the room without making any show of leaving. In accordance with her usual custom she would have asked her son what he was going to do; but she did not dare so to inquire now. Had he not declared, only a few minutes since, whither he would go? "I suppose I shall see you at lunch?" at last she said.

"At lunch? Well, I don't know. Look here, mother. What am I to say to Miss Robarts when I see her?" and he leaned with his back against the chimney-piece as he interrogated his mother.

"What are you to say to her, Ludovic?"

"Yes; what am I to say,—as coming from you? Am I to tell her that you will receive her as your daughter-in-law?"

"Ludovic, I have explained all that to Miss Robarts herself."

"Explained what?"

"I have told her that I did not think that such a marriage would make either you or her happy."

"And why have you told her so? Why have you taken upon yourself to judge for me in such a matter, as though I were a child? Mother, you must unsay what you have said."

Lord Lufton, as he spoke, looked full into his mother's face; and he did so, not as though he were begging from her a favour, but issuing to her a command. She stood near him, with one hand on the breakfast-table, gazing at him almost furtively, not quite daring to meet the full view of his eye. There was only one thing on earth which Lady Lufton feared, and that was her son's displeasure. The sun of her earthly heaven shone upon her through the medium of his existence. If she were driven to quarrel with him, as some ladies of her acquaintance were driven to quarrel with their sons, the world to her would be over. Not but what facts might be so strong as to make it absolutely necessary that she should do this. As some people resolve that, under certain circumstances, they will commit suicide, so she could see that, under certain circumstances, she must consent even to be separated from him. She would not do wrong,—not that which she knew to be wrong,—even for his sake. If it were necessary that all her happiness should collapse and be crushed in ruin around her, she must endure it, and wait God's time to relieve her from so dark a world. The light of the sun was very dear to her, but even that might be purchased at too dear a cost.

"I told you before, mother, that my choice was made, and I asked you then to give your consent; you have now had time to think about it, and therefore I have come to ask you again. I have reason to know that there will be no impediment to my marriage if you will frankly hold out your hand to Lucy."

The matter was altogether in Lady Lufton's hands, but, fond as she was of power, she absolutely wished that it were not so. Had her son married without asking her and then brought Lucy home as his wife, she would undoubtedly have forgiven him; and much as she might have disliked the match, she would, ultimately, have embraced the bride. But now she was compelled to exercise her judgment. If he married imprudently, it would be her doing. How was she to give her expressed consent to that which she believed to be wrong?

"Do you know anything against her; any reason why she should not be my wife?" continued he.

"If you mean as regards her moral conduct, certainly not," said Lady Lufton. "But I could say as much as that in favour of a great many young ladies whom I should regard as very ill suited for such a marriage."

"Yes; some might be vulgar, some might be ill-tempered, some might be ugly; others might be burdened with disagreeable connections. I can understand that you should object to a daughter-in-law under any of these circumstances. But none of these things can be said of Miss Robarts. I defy you to say that she is not in all respects what a lady should be."

But her father was a doctor of medicine, she is the sister of the parish clergyman, she is only five feet two in height, and is so uncommonly brown! Had Lady Lufton dared to give a catalogue of her objections, such would have been its extent and nature. But she did not dare to do this.

"I cannot say, Ludovic, that she is possessed of all that you should seek in a wife." Such was her answer.

"Do you mean that she has not got money?"

"No, not that; I should be very sorry to see you making money your chief object, or indeed any essential object. If it chanced that your wife did have money, no doubt you would find it a convenience. But pray understand me, Ludovic; I would not for a moment advise you to subject your happiness to such a necessity as that. It is not because she is without fortune—"

"Then why is it? At breakfast you were singing her praises, and saying how excellent she is."

"If I were forced to put my objection into one word, I should say—" and then she paused, hardly daring to encounter the frown which was already gathering itself on her son's brow.

"You would say what?" said Lord Lufton, almost roughly.

"Don't be angry with me, Ludovic; all that I think, and all that I say on this subject, I think and say with only one object—that of your happiness. What other motive can I have for anything in this world?" And then she came close to him and kissed him.

"But tell me, mother, what is this objection; what is this terrible word that is to sum up the list of all poor Lucy's sins, and prove that she is unfit for married life?"

"Ludovic, I did not say that. You know that I did not."

"What is the word, mother?"

And then at last Lady Lufton spoke it out. "She is—insignificant. I believe her to be a very good girl, but she is not qualified to fill the high position to which you would exalt her."

"Insignificant!"

"Yes, Ludovic, I think so."

"Then, mother, you do not know her. You must permit me to say that you are talking of a girl whom you do not know. Of all the epithets of opprobrium which the English language could give you, that would be nearly the last which she would deserve."

"I have not intended any opprobrium."

"Insignificant!"

"Perhaps you do not quite understand me, Ludovic."

"I know what insignificant means, mother."

"I think that she would not worthily fill the position which your wife should take in the world."

"I understand what you say."

"She would not do you honour at the head of your table."

"Ah, I understand. You want me to marry some bouncing Amazon, some pink and white giantess of fashion who would frighten the little people into their proprieties."

"Oh, Ludovic! you are intending to laugh at me now."

"I was never less inclined to laugh in my life—never, I can assure you. And now I am more certain than ever that your objection to Miss Robarts arises from your not knowing her. You will find, I think, when you do know her, that she is as well able to hold her own as any lady of your acquaintance;—ay, and to maintain her husband's position, too. I can assure you that I shall have no fear of her on that score."

"I think, dearest, that perhaps you hardly—"

"I think this, mother, that in such a matter as this I must choose for myself. I have chosen; and I now ask you, as my mother, to go to her and bid her welcome. Dear mother, I will own this, that I should not be happy if I thought that you did not love my wife." These last words he said in a tone of affection that went to his mother's heart, and then he left the room.

Poor Lady Lufton, when she was alone, waited till she heard her son's steps retreating through the hall, and then betook herself up-stairs to her customary morning work. She sat down at last as though about so to occupy herself; but her mind was too full to allow of her taking up her pen. She had often said to herself, in days which to her were not as yet long gone by, that she would choose a bride for her son, and that then she would love the chosen one with all her heart. She would dethrone herself in favour of this new queen, sinking with joy into her dowager state, in order that her son's wife might shine with the greater splendour. The fondest day-dreams of her life had all had reference to the time when her son should bring home a new Lady Lufton, selected by herself from the female excellence of England, and in which she might be the first to worship her new idol. But could she dethrone herself for Lucy Robarts? Could she give up her chair of state in order to place thereon the little girl from the parsonage? Could she take to her heart, and treat with absolute loving confidence, with the confidence of an almost idolatrous mother, that little chit who, a few months since, had sat awkwardly in one corner of her drawing-room, afraid to speak to any one? And yet it seemed that it must come to this—to this—or else those day-dreams of hers would in nowise come to pass.

She sat herself down, trying to think whether it were possible that Lucy might fill the throne; for she had begun to recognize it as probable that her son's will would be too strong for her; but her thoughts would fly away to Griselda Grantly. In her first and only matured attempt to realize her day-dreams, she had chosen Griselda for her queen. She had failed there, seeing that the fates had destined Miss Grantly for another throne;—for another and a higher one, as far as the world goes. She would have made Griselda the wife of a baron, but fate was about to make that young lady the wife of a marquis. Was there cause of grief in this? Did she really regret that Miss Grantly, with all her virtues, should be made over to the house of Hartletop? Lady Lufton was a woman who did not bear disappointment lightly; but nevertheless she did almost feel herself to have been relieved from a burden when she thought of the termination of the Lufton-Grantly marriage treaty. What if she had been successful, and, after all, the prize had been other than she had expected? She was sometimes prone to think that that prize was not exactly all that she had once hoped. Griselda looked the very thing that Lady Lufton wanted for a queen;—but how would a queen reign who trusted only to her looks? In that respect it was perhaps well for her that destiny had interposed. Griselda, she was driven to admit, was better suited to Lord Dumbello than to her son.

But still—such a queen as Lucy! Could it ever come to pass that the lieges of the kingdom would bow the knee in proper respect before so puny a sovereign? And then there was that feeling which, in still higher quarters, prevents the marriage of princes with the most noble of their people. Is it not a recognized rule of these realms that none of the blood royal shall raise to royal honours those of the subjects who are by birth un-royal! Lucy was a subject of the house of Lufton in that she was the sister of the parson and a resident denizen of the parsonage. Presuming that Lucy herself might do for queen— granting that she might have some faculty to reign, the crown having been duly placed on her brow—how, then, about that clerical brother near the throne? Would it not come to this, that there would no longer be a queen at Framley?

And yet she knew that she must yield. She did not say so to herself. She did not as yet acknowledge that she must put out her hand to Lucy, calling her by name as her daughter. She did not absolutely say as much to her own heart;—not as yet. But she did begin to bethink herself of Lucy's high qualities, and to declare to herself that the girl, if not fit to be a queen, was at any rate fit to be a woman. That there was a spirit within that body, insignificant though the body might be, Lady Lufton was prepared to admit. That she had acquired the power—the chief of all powers in this world—of sacrificing herself for the sake of others; that, too, was evident enough. That she was a good girl, in the usual accep-tation of the word good, Lady Lufton had never doubted. She was ready-witted too, prompt in action, gifted with a certain fire. It was that gift of fire which had won for her, so unfortunately, Lord Lufton's love. It was quite possible for her also to love Lucy Robarts; Lady Lufton admitted that to herself;—but then who could bow the knee before her, and serve her as a queen? Was it not a pity that she should be so insignificant?

But, nevertheless, we may say that as Lady Lufton sate that morning in her own room for two hours without employment, the star of Lucy Robarts was gradually rising in the firmament. After all, love was the food chiefly necessary for the nourishment of Lady Lufton,—the only food absolutely necessary. She was not aware of this herself, nor prob-ably would those who knew her best have so spoken of her. They would have declared that family pride was her daily pabulum, and she herself would have said so too, calling it, however, by some less offensive name. Her son's honour, and the honour of her house!—of those she would have spoken as the things dearest to her in this world. And this was partly true, for had her son been dishonoured, she would have sunk with sorrow to the grave. But the one thing necessary to her daily life was the power of loving those who were near to her.

Lord Lufton, when he left the dining-room, intended at once to go up to the parsonage, but he first strolled round the garden in order that he might make up his mind what he would say there. He was angry with his mother, having not had the wit to see that she was about to give way and yield to him, and he was determined to make it understood that in this matter he would have his own way. He had learned that which it was necessary that he should know as to Lucy's heart, and such being the case he would not conceive it pos-sible that he should be debarred by his mother's opposition. "There is no son in England loves his mother better than I do," he said to himself; "but there are some things which a man cannot stand. She would have married me to that block of stone if I would have let her; and now, because she is disappointed there— Insignificant! I never in my life heard anything so absurd, so untrue, so uncharitable, so— She'd like me to bring a dragon home, I suppose. It would serve her right if I did,—some creature that would make the house intolerable to her." "She must do it though," he said again, "or she and I will quarrel," and then he turned off towards the gate, preparing to go to the parsonage.

"My lord, have you heard what has happened?" said the gardener, coming to him at the gate. The man was out of breath and almost overwhelmed by the greatness of his own tidings.

"No; I have heard nothing. What is it?"

"The bailiffs have taken possession of everything at the parsonage."

CHAPTER XLIV.

THE PHILISTINES AT THE PARSONAGE.

It has been already told how things went on between the Tozers, Mr. Curling, and Mark Robarts during that month. Mr. Forrest had drifted out of the business altogether, as also had Mr. Sowerby, as far as any active participation in it went. Letters came frequently from Mr. Curling to the parsonage, and at last came a message by special mission to say that the evil day was at hand. As far as Mr. Curling's professional experience would enable him to anticipate or foretell the proceedings of such a man as Tom Tozer, he thought that the sheriff's officers would be at Framley Parsonage on the following morning. Mr. Curling's experience did not mislead him in this respect.

"And what will you do, Mark?" said Fanny, speaking through her tears, after she had read the letter which her husband handed to her.

"Nothing. What can I do? They must come."

"Lord Lufton came to-day. Will you not go to him?"

"No. If I were to do so it would be the same as asking him for the money."

"Why not borrow it of him, dearest? Surely it would not be so much for him to lend."

"I could not do it. Think of Lucy, and how she stands with him. Besides I have already had words with Lufton about Sowerby and his money matters. He thinks that I am to blame, and he would tell me so; and then there would be sharp things said between us. He would advance me the money if I pressed for it, but he would do so in a way that would make it impossible that I should take it."

There was nothing more then to be said. If she had had her own way Mrs. Robarts would have gone at once to Lady Lufton, but she could not induce her husband to sanction such a proceeding. The objection to seeking assistance from her ladyship was as strong as that which prevailed as to her son. There had already been some little beginning of ill-feeling, and under such circumstances it was impossible to ask for pecuniary assistance. Fanny, however, had a prophetic assurance that assistance out of these difficulties must in the end come to them from that quarter, or not come at all; and she would fain, had she been allowed, make everything known at the big house.

On the following morning they breakfasted at the usual hour, but in great sadness. A maid-servant, whom Mrs. Robarts had brought with her when she married, told her that a rumour of what was to happen had reached the kitchen. Stubbs, the groom, had been in Barchester on the preceding day, and, according to his account—so said Mary—everybody in the city was talking about it. "Never mind, Mary," said Mrs. Robarts, and Mary replied, "Oh, no, of course not, ma'am."

In these days Mrs. Robarts was ordinarily very busy, seeing that there were six children in the house, four of whom had come to her but ill supplied with infantine belongings; and now, as usual, she went about her work immediately after breakfast. But she moved about the house very slowly, and was almost unable to give her orders to the servants, and spoke sadly to the children who hung about her wondering what was the matter. Her husband at the same time took himself to his book-room, but when there did not attempt any employment. He thrust his hands into his pockets, and, leaning against the fire-place, fixed his eyes upon the table before him without looking at anything that was on it; it was impossible for him to betake himself to his work. Remember what is the ordinary labour of a clergyman in his study, and think how fit he must have been for such employment! What would have been the nature of a sermon composed at such a moment, and with what satisfaction could he have used the sacred volume in referring to it for his arguments? He, in this respect, was worse off than his wife; she did employ herself, but he stood there without moving, doing nothing, with fixed eyes, thinking what men would say of him.

Luckily for him this state of suspense was not long, for within half an hour of his leaving the breakfast-table the footman knocked at his door—that footman with whom at the beginning of his difficulties he had made up his mind to dispense, but who had been kept on because of the Barchester prebend.

"If you please, your reverence, there are two men outside," said the footman.

Two men! Mark knew well enough what men they were, but he could hardly take the coming of two such men to his quiet country parsonage quite as a matter of course.

"Who are they, John?" said he, not wishing any answer, but because the question was forced upon him.

"I'm afeard they're—bailiffs, sir."

"Very well, John; that will do; of course they must do what they please about the place."

And then, when the servant left him, he still stood without moving, exactly as he had stood before. There he remained for ten minutes, but the time went by very slowly. When about noon some circumstance told him what was the hour, he was astonished to find that the day had not nearly passed away.

And then another tap was struck on the door,—a sound which he well recognized,—and his wife crept silently into the room. She came close up to him before she spoke, and put her arm within his:

"Mark," she said, "the men are here; they are in the yard."

"I know it," he answered gruffly.

"Will it be better that you should see them, dearest?"

"See them; no; what good can I do by seeing them? But I shall see them soon enough; they will be here, I suppose, in a few minutes."

"They are taking an inventory, cook says; they are in the stable now."

"Very well; they must do as they please; I cannot help them."

"Cook says that if they are allowed their meals and some beer, and if nobody takes anything away, they will be quite civil."

"Civil! But what does it matter? Let them eat and drink what they please, as long as the food lasts. I don't suppose the butcher will send you more."

"But, Mark, there's nothing due to the butcher,—only the regular monthly bill."

"Very well; you'll see."

"Oh, Mark, don't look at me in that way. Do not turn away from me. What is to comfort us if we do not cling to each other now?"

"Comfort us! God help you! I wonder, Fanny, that you can bear to stay in the room with me."

"Mark, dearest Mark, my own dear, dearest husband! who is to be true to you, if I am not? You shall not turn from me. How can anything like this make a difference between you and me?" And then she threw her arms round his neck and embraced him.

It was a terrible morning to him, and one of which every incident will dwell on his memory to the last day of his life. He had been so proud in his position—had assumed to himself so prominent a standing—had contrived, by some trick which he had acquired, to carry his head so high above the heads of neighbouring parsons. It was this that had taken him among great people, had introduced him to the Duke of Omnium, had procured for him the stall at Barchester. But how was he to carry his head now? What would the Arabins and Grantlys say? How would the bishop sneer at him, and Mrs. Proudie and her daughters tell of him in all their quarters? How would Crawley look at him—Crawley, who had already once had him on the hip? The stern severity of Crawley's face loomed upon him now. Crawley, with his children half naked, and his wife a drudge, and himself half starved, had never had a bailiff in his house at Hogglestock! And then his own curate, Evans, whom he had patronized, and treated almost as a dependant—how was he to look his curate in the face and arrange with him for the sacred duties of the next Sunday?

His wife still stood by him, gazing into his face; and as he looked at her and thought of her misery, he could not control his heart with reference to the wrongs which Sowerby had heaped on him. It was Sowerby's falsehood and Sowerby's fraud which had brought upon him and his wife this terrible anguish. "If there be justice on earth he will suffer for it yet," he said at last, not speaking intentionally to his wife, but unable to repress his feelings.

"Do not wish him evil, Mark; you may be sure he has his own sorrows."

"His own sorrows! No; he is callous to such misery as this. He has become so hardened in dishonesty that all this is mirth to him. If there be punishment in heaven for falsehood—"

"Oh, Mark, do not curse him!"

"How am I to keep myself from cursing when I see what he has brought upon you?"

"'Vengeance is mine, saith the Lord,'" answered the young wife, not with solemn, preaching accent, as though bent on reproof, but with the softest whisper into his ear. "Leave that to Him, Mark; and for us, let us pray that He may soften the hearts of us all;—of him who has caused us to suffer, and of our own."

Mark was not called upon to reply to this, for he was again disturbed by a servant at the door. It was the cook this time herself, who had come with a message from the men of the law. And she had come, be it remembered, not from any necessity that she as cook should do this line of work; for the footman, or Mrs. Robarts' maid, might have come as well as she. But when things are out of course servants are always out of course also. As a rule, nothing will induce a butler to go into a stable, or persuade a housemaid to put her hand to a frying-pan. But now that this new excitement had come upon the household—seeing that the bailiffs were in possession, and that the chattels were being entered in a catalogue, everybody was willing to do everything—everything but his or her own work. The gardener was looking after the dear children; the nurse was doing the rooms before the bailiffs should reach them; the groom had gone into the kitchen to get their lunch ready for them; and the cook was walking about with an inkstand, obeying all the orders of these great potentates. As far as the servants were concerned, it may be a question whether the coming of the bailiffs had not hitherto been regarded as a treat.

"If you please, ma'am," said Jemima cook, "they wishes to know in which room you'd be pleased to have the inmintory took fust. 'Cause, ma'am, they wouldn't disturb you nor master more than can be avoided. For their line of life, ma'am, they is very civil—very civil indeed."

"I suppose they may go into the drawing-room," said Mrs. Robarts, in a sad low voice. All nice women are proud of their drawing-rooms, and she was very proud of hers. It had been furnished when money was plenty with them, immediately after their marriage, and everything in it was pretty, good, and dear to her. O ladies, who have drawing-rooms in which the things are pretty, good, and dear to you, think of what it would be to have two bailiffs rummaging among them with pen and inkhorn, making a catalogue preparatory to a sheriff's auction; and all without fault or extravagance of your own! There were things there that had been given to her by Lady Lufton, by Lady Meredith, and other friends, and the idea did occur to her that it might be possible to save them from contamination; but she would not say a word, lest by so saying she might add to Mark's misery.

"And then the dining-room," said Jemima cook, in a tone almost of elation.

"Yes; if they please."

"And then master's book-room here; or perhaps the bedrooms, if you and master be still here."

"Any way they please, cook; it does not much signify," said Mrs. Robarts. But for some days after that Jemima was by no means a favourite with her.

The cook was hardly out of the room before a quick footstep was heard on the gravel before the window, and the hall door was immediately opened.

"Where is your master?" said the well-known voice of Lord Lufton; and then in half a minute he also was in the book-room.

"Mark, my dear fellow, what's all this?" said he, in a cheery tone and with a pleasant face. "Did not you know that I was here? I came down yesterday; landed from Hamburg only yesterday morning. How do you do, Mrs. Robarts? This is a terrible bore, isn't it?"

Robarts, at the first moment, hardly knew how to speak to his old friend. He was struck dumb by the disgrace of his position; the more so as his misfortune was one which it was partly in the power of Lord Lufton to remedy. He had never yet borrowed money since he had filled a man's position, but he had had words about money with the young peer, in which he knew that his friend had wronged him; and for this double reason he was now speechless.

"Mr. Sowerby has betrayed him," said Mrs. Robarts, wiping the tears from her eyes. Hitherto she had said no word against Sowerby, but now it was necessary to defend her husband.

"No doubt about it. I believe he has always betrayed every one who has ever trusted him. I told you what he was, some time since; did I not? But, Mark, why on earth have you let it go so far as this? Would not Forrest help you?"

"Mr. Forrest wanted him to sign more bills, and he would not do that," said Mrs. Robarts, sobbing.

"Bills are like dram-drinking," said the discreet young lord: "when one once begins, it is very hard to leave off. Is it true that the men are here now, Mark?"

"Yes, they are in the next room."

"What, in the drawing-room?"

"They are making out a list of the things," said Mrs. Robarts.

"We must stop that at any rate," said his lordship, walking off towards the scene of the operations; and as he left the room Mrs. Robarts followed him, leaving her husband by himself.

"Why did you not send down to my mother?" said he, speaking hardly above a whisper, as they stood together in the hall.

"He would not let me."

"But why not go yourself? or why not have written to me,—considering how intimate we are?"

Mrs. Robarts could not explain to him that the peculiar intimacy between him and Lucy must have hindered her from doing so, even if otherwise it might have been possible; but she felt such was the case.

"Well, my men, this is bad work you're doing here," said he, walking into the drawing-room. Whereupon the cook curtseyed low, and the bailiffs, knowing his lordship, stopped from their business and put their hands to their foreheads. "You must stop this, if you please,—at once. Come, let's go out into the kitchen, or some place outside. I don't like to see you here with your big boots and the pen and ink among the furniture."

"We ain't a-done no harm, my lord, so please your lordship," said Jemima cook.

"And we is only a-doing our bounden dooties," said one of the bailiffs.

"As we is sworn to do, so please your lordship," said the other.

"And is wery sorry to be unconwenient, my lord, to any gen'leman or lady as is a gen'leman or lady. But accidents will happen, and then what can the likes of us do?" said the first.

"Because we is sworn, my lord," said the second. But, nevertheless, in spite of their oaths, and in spite also of the stern necessity which they pleaded, they ceased their operations at the instance of the peer. For the name of a lord is still great in England.

"And now leave this, and let Mrs. Robarts go into her drawing-room."

"And, please your lordship, what is we to do? Who is we to look to?"

In satisfying them absolutely on this point Lord Lufton had to use more than his influence as a peer. It was necessary that he should have pen and paper. But with pen and paper he did satisfy them;—satisfy them so far that they agreed to return to Stubbs' room, the former hospital, due stipulation having been made for the meals and beer, and there await the order to evacuate the premises which would no doubt, under his lordship's influence, reach them on the following day. The meaning of all which was that Lord Lufton had undertaken to bear upon his own shoulder the whole debt due by Mr. Robarts.

And then he returned to the book-room where Mark was still standing almost on the spot in which he had placed himself immediately after breakfast. Mrs. Robarts did not return, but went up among the children to counter-order such directions as she had given for the preparation of the nursery for the Philistines. "Mark," he said, "do not trouble yourself about this more than you can help. The men have ceased doing anything, and they shall leave the place to-morrow morning."

"And how will the money—be paid?" said the poor clergyman.

"Do not bother yourself about that at present. It shall so be managed that the burden shall fall ultimately on yourself—not on any one else. But I am sure it must be a comfort to you to know that your wife need not be driven out of her drawing-room."

"But, Lufton, I cannot allow you—after what has passed—and at the present moment—"

"My dear fellow, I know all about it, and I am coming to that just now. You have employed Curling, and he shall settle it; and upon my word, Mark, you shall pay the bill. But, for the present emergency, the money is at my banker's."

"But, Lufton—"

"And to deal honestly, about Curling's bill I mean, it ought to be as much my affair as your own. It was I that brought you into this mess with Sowerby, and I know now how unjust about it I was to you up in London. But the truth is that Sowerby's treachery had nearly driven me wild. It has done the same to you since, I have no doubt."

"He has ruined me," said Robarts.

"No, he has not done that. No thanks to him though; he would not have scrupled to do it had it come in his way. The fact is, Mark, that you and I cannot conceive the depth of fraud in such a man as that. He is always looking for money; I believe that in all his hours of most friendly intercourse,—when he is sitting with you over your wine, and riding beside you in the field,—he is still thinking how he can make use of you to tide him over some difficulty. He has lived in that way till he has a pleasure in cheating, and has become so clever in his line of life that if you or I were with him again to-morrow he would again get the better of us. He is a man that must be absolutely avoided; I, at any rate, have learned to know so much."

In the expression of which opinion Lord Lufton was too hard upon poor Sowerby; as indeed we are all apt to be too hard in forming an opinion upon the rogues of the world. That Mr. Sowerby had been a rogue, I cannot deny. It is roguish to lie, and he had been a great liar. It is roguish to make promises which the promiser knows he cannot perform, and such had been Mr. Sowerby's daily practice. It is roguish to live on other men's money, and Mr. Sowerby had long been doing so. It is roguish, at least so I would hold it, to deal willingly with rogues; and Mr. Sowerby had been constant in such dealings. I do not know whether he had not at times fallen even into more palpable roguery than is proved by such practices as those enumerated. Though I have for him some tender feeling, knowing that there was still a touch of gentle bearing round his heart, an abiding taste for better things within him, I cannot acquit him from the great accusation. But, for all that, in spite of his acknowledged roguery, Lord Lufton was too hard upon him in his judgment. There was yet within him the means of repentance, could a *locus penitentiæ* have been supplied to him. He grieved bitterly over his own ill doings, and knew well what changes gentlehood would have demanded from him. Whether or no he had gone too far for all changes—whether the *locus penitentiæ* was for him still a possibility—that was between him and a higher power.

"I have no one to blame but myself," said Mark, still speaking in the same heart-broken tone and with his face averted from his friend.

The debt would now be paid, and the bailiffs would be expelled; but that would not set him right before the world. It would be known to all men—to all clergymen in the diocese—that the sheriff's officers had been in charge of Framley Parsonage, and he could never again hold up his head in the close of Barchester.

"My dear fellow, if we were all to make ourselves miserable for such a trifle as this—" said Lord Lufton, putting his arm affectionately on his friend's shoulder.

"But we are not all clergymen," said Mark, and as he spoke he turned away to the window and Lord Lufton knew that the tears were on his cheek.

Nothing was then said between them for some moments, after which Lord Lufton again spoke,—

"Mark, my dear fellow!"

"Well," said Mark, with his face still turned towards the window.

"You must remember one thing; in helping you over this stile, which will be really a matter of no inconvenience to me, I have a better right than that even of an old friend; I look upon you now as my brother-in-law."

Mark turned slowly round, plainly showing the tears upon his face.

"Do you mean," said he, "that anything more has taken place?"

"I mean to make your sister my wife; she sent me word by you to say that she loved me, and I am not going to stand upon any nonsense after that. If she and I are both willing no one alive has a right to stand between us; and, by heavens, no one shall. I will do nothing secretly, so I tell you that, exactly as I have told her ladyship."

"But what does she say?"

"She says nothing; but it cannot go on like that. My mother and I cannot live here together if she opposes me in this way. I do not want to frighten your sister by going over to her at Hogglestock, but I expect you to tell her so much as I now tell you, as coming from me; otherwise she will think that I have forgotten her."

"She will not think that."

"She need not; good-bye, old fellow. I'll make it all right between you and her ladyship about this affair of Sowerby's."

And then he took his leave and walked off to settle about the payment of the money.

"Mother," said he to Lady Lufton that evening, "you must not bring this affair of the bailiffs up against Robarts. It has been more my fault than his."

Hitherto not a word had been spoken between Lady Lufton and her son on the subject. She had heard with terrible dismay of what had happened, and had heard also that Lord Lufton had immediately gone to the parsonage. It was impossible, therefore, that she should now interfere. That the necessary money would be forthcoming she was aware, but that would not wipe out the terrible disgrace attached to an execution in a clergyman's house. And then, too, he was her clergyman,—her own clergyman, selected, and appointed, and brought to Framley by herself, endowed with a wife of her own choosing, filled with good things by her own hand! It was a terrible misadventure, and she began to repent that she had ever heard the name of Robarts. She would not, however, have been slow to put forth the hand to lessen the evil by giving her own money, had this been either necessary or possible. But how could she interfere between Robarts and her son, especially when she remembered the proposed connection between Lucy and Lord Lufton?

"Your fault, Ludovic?"

"Yes, mother. It was I who introduced him to Mr. Sowerby; and, to tell the truth, I do not think he would ever have been intimate with Sowerby if I had not given him some sort of a commission with reference to money matters then pending between Mr. Sowerby and me. They are all over now,—thanks to you, indeed."

"Mr. Robarts' character as a clergyman should have kept him from such troubles, if no other feeling did so."

"At any rate, mother, oblige me by letting it pass by."

"Oh, I shall say nothing to him."

"You had better say something to her, or otherwise it will be strange; and even to him I would say a word or two,—a word in kindness, as you so well know how. It will be easier to him in that way, than if you were to be altogether silent."

No further conversation took place between them at the time, but later in the evening she brushed her hand across her son's forehead, sweeping the long silken hairs into their place, as she was wont to do when moved by any special feeling of love. "Ludovic," she said, "no one, I think, has so good a heart as you. I will do exactly as you would have me about this affair of Mr. Robarts and the money." And then there was nothing more said about it.

CHAPTER XLV.

PALACE BLESSINGS.

And now, at this period, terrible rumours found their way into Barchester, and flew about the cathedral towers and round the cathedral door; ay, and into the canons' houses and the humbler sitting-rooms of the vicars choral. Whether they made their way from thence up to the bishop's palace, or whether they descended from the palace to the close, I will not pretend to say. But they were shocking, unnatural, and no doubt grievous to all those excellent ecclesiastical hearts which cluster so thickly in those quarters.

The first of these had reference to the new prebendary, and to the disgrace which he had brought on the chapter; a disgrace, as some of them boasted, which Barchester had never known before. This, however, like most other boasts, was hardly true; for within but a very few years there had been an execution in the house of a late prebendary, old Dr. Stanhope; and on that occasion the doctor himself had been forced to fly away to Italy, starting in the night, lest he also should fall into the hands of the Philistines, as well as his chairs and tables.

"It is a scandalous shame," said Mrs. Proudie, speaking not of the old doctor, but of the new offender; "a scandalous shame: and it would only serve him right if the gown were stripped from his back."

"I suppose his living will be sequestrated," said a young minor canon who attended much to the ecclesiastical injunctions of the lady of the diocese, and was deservedly held in high favour. If Framley were sequestrated, why should not he, as well as another, undertake the duty—with such stipend as the bishop might award?

"I am told that he is over head and ears in debt," said the future Mrs. Tickler, "and chiefly for horses which he has bought and not paid for."

"I see him riding very splendid animals when he comes over for the cathedral duties," said the minor canon.

"The sheriff's officers are in the house at present, I am told," said Mrs. Proudie.

"And is not he in jail?" said Mrs. Tickler.

"If not, he ought to be," said Mrs. Tickler's mother.

"And no doubt soon will be," said the minor canon; "for I hear that he is linked up with a most discreditable gang of persons."

This was what was said in the palace on that heading; and though, no doubt, more spirit and poetry was displayed there than in the houses of the less gifted clergy, this shows the manner in which the misfortune of Mr. Robarts was generally discussed. Nor, indeed, had he deserved any better treatment at their hands. But his name did not run the gauntlet for the usual nine days; nor, indeed, did his fame endure at its height for more than two. This sudden fall was occasioned by other tidings of a still more distressing nature; by a rumour which so affected Mrs. Proudie that it caused, as she said, her blood to creep. And she was very careful that the blood of others should creep also, if the blood of others was equally sensitive. It was said that Lord Dumbello had jilted Miss Grantly.

From what adverse spot in the world these cruel tidings fell upon Barchester I have never been able to discover. We know how quickly rumour flies, making herself common through all the cities. That Mrs. Proudie should have known more of the facts connected with the Hartletop family than any one else in Barchester was not surprising, seeing that she was so much more conversant with the great world in which such people lived. She knew, and was therefore correct enough in declaring, that Lord Dumbello had already jilted one other young lady—the Lady Julia Mac Mull, to whom he had been engaged three seasons back, and that therefore his character in such matters was not to be trusted. That Lady Julia had been a terrible flirt and greatly given to waltzing with a certain German count, with whom she had since gone off—that, I suppose, Mrs. Proudie did not know, much as she was conversant with the great world,—seeing that she said nothing about it to any of her ecclesiastical listeners on the present occasion.

"It will be a terrible warning, Mrs. Quiverful, to us all; a most useful warning to us—not to trust to the things of this world. I fear they made no inquiry about this young nobleman before they agreed that his name should be linked with that of their daughter." This she said to the wife of the present warden of Hiram's Hospital, a lady who had received favours from her, and was therefore bound to listen attentively to her voice.

"But I hope it may not be true," said Mrs. Quiverful, who, in spite of the allegiance due by her to Mrs. Proudie, had reasons of her own for wishing well to the Grantly family.

"I hope so, indeed," said Mrs. Proudie, with a slight tinge of anger in her voice; "but I fear that there is no doubt. And I must confess that it is no more than we had a right to expect. I hope that it may be taken by all of us as a lesson, and an ensample, and a teaching of the Lord's mercy. And I wish you would request your husband—from me, Mrs. Quiverful—to dwell on this subject in morning and evening lecture at the hospital on Sabbath next, showing how false is the trust which we put in the good things of this world;" which behest, to a certain extent, Mr. Quiverful did obey, feeling that a quiet life in Barchester was of great value to him; but he did not go so far as to caution his hearers, who consisted of the aged bedesmen of the hospital, against matrimonial projects of an ambitious nature.

In this case, as in all others of the kind, the report was known to all the chapter before it had been heard by the archdeacon or his wife. The dean heard it, and disregarded it; as did also the dean's wife—at first; and those who generally sided with the Grantlys in the diocesan battles pooh-poohed the tidings, saying to each other that both the archdeacon and Mrs. Grantly were very well able to take care of their own affairs. But dripping water hollows a stone; and at last it was admitted on all sides that there was ground for fear,—on all sides, except at Plumstead.

"I am sure there is nothing in it; I really am sure of it," said Mrs. Arabin, whispering to her sister; "but after turning it over in my mind, I thought it right to tell you. And yet I don't know now but I am wrong."

"Quite right, dearest Eleanor," said Mrs. Grantly. "And I am much obliged to you. But we understand it, you know. It comes, of course, like all other Christian blessings, from the palace." And then there was nothing more said about it between Mrs. Grantly and her sister.

But on the following morning there arrived a letter by post, addressed to Mrs. Grantly, bearing the postmark of Littlebath. The letter ran:—

MADAM, It is known to the writer that Lord Dumbello has arranged with certain friends how he may escape from his present engagement. I think, therefore, that it is my duty as a Christian to warn you of this.

Yours truly,
A WELLWISHER.

Now it had happened that the embryo Mrs. Tickler's most intimate bosom friend and confidante was known at Plumstead to live at Littlebath, and it had also happened—most unfortunately—that the embryo Mrs. Tickler, in the warmth of her neighbourly regard, had written a friendly line to her friend Griselda Grantly, congratulating her with all female sincerity on her splendid nuptials with the Lord Dumbello.

"It is not her natural hand," said Mrs. Grantly, talking the matter over with her husband, "but you may be sure it has come from her. It is a part of the new Christianity which we learn day by day from the palace teaching."

But these things had some effect on the archdeacon's mind. He had learned lately the story of Lady Julia Mac Mull, and was not sure that his son-in-law—as ought to be about to be—had been entirely blameless in that matter. And then in these days Lord Dumbello made no great sign. Immediately on Griselda's return to Plumstead he had sent her a magnificent present of emeralds, which, however, had come to her direct from the jewellers, and might have been—and probably was—ordered by his man of business. Since that he had neither come, nor sent, nor written. Griselda did not seem to be in any way annoyed by this absence of the usual sign of love, and went on steadily with her great duties. "Nothing," as she told her mother, "had been said about writing, and, therefore, she did not expect it." But the archdeacon was not quite at his ease. "Keep Dumbello up to his P's and Q's, you know," a friend of his had whispered to him at his club. By heavens, yes. The archdeacon was not a man to bear with indifference a wrong in such a quarter. In spite of his clerical profession, few men were more inclined to fight against personal wrongs—and few men more able.

"Can there be anything wrong, I wonder?" said he to his wife. "Is it worth while that I should go up to London?" But Mrs. Grantly attributed it all to the palace doctrine. What could be more natural, looking at all the circumstances of the Tickler engagement? She therefore gave her voice against any steps being taken by the archdeacon.

A day or two after that Mrs. Proudie met Mrs. Arabin in the close and condoled with her openly on the termination of the marriage treaty;—quite openly, for Mrs. Tickler—as she was to be—was with her mother, and Mrs. Arabin was accompanied by her sister-in-law, Mary Bold.

"It must be very grievous to Mrs. Grantly, very grievous indeed," said Mrs. Proudie, "and I sincerely feel for her. But, Mrs. Arabin, all these lessons are sent to us for our eternal welfare."

"Of course," said Mrs. Arabin. "But as to this special lesson, I am inclined to doubt that it—"

"Ah-h! I fear it is too true. I fear there is no room for doubt. Of course you are aware that Lord Dumbello is off for the Continent."

Mrs. Arabin was not aware of it, and she was obliged to admit as much.

"He started four days ago, by way of Boulogne," said Mrs. Tickler, who seemed to be very well up in the whole affair. "I am so sorry for poor dear Griselda. I am told she has got all her things. It is such a pity, you know."

"But why should not Lord Dumbello come back from the Continent?" said Miss Bold, very quietly.

"Why not, indeed? I'm sure I hope he may," said Mrs. Proudie. "And no doubt he will, some day. But if he be such a man as they say he is, it is really well for Griselda that she should be relieved from such a marriage. For, after all, Mrs. Arabin, what are the things of this world?—dust beneath our feet, ashes between our teeth, grass cut for the oven, vanity, vexation, and nothing more!"—well pleased with which variety of Christian metaphors Mrs. Proudie walked on, still muttering, however, something about worms and grubs, by which she intended to signify her own species and the Dumbello and Grantly sects of it in particular.

This now had gone so far that Mrs. Arabin conceived herself bound in duty to see her sister, and it was then settled in consultation at Plumstead that the archdeacon should call officially at the palace and beg that the rumour might be contradicted. This he did early on the next morning and was shown into the bishop's study, in which he found both his lordship and Mrs. Proudie. The bishop rose to greet him with special civility, smiling his very sweetest on him, as though of all his clergy the archdeacon were the favourite; but Mrs. Proudie wore something of a gloomy aspect, as though she knew that such a visit at such an hour must have reference to some special business. The morning calls made by the archdeacon at the palace in the way of ordinary civility were not numerous.

On the present occasion he dashed at once into his subject. "I have called this morning, Mrs. Proudie," said he, "because I wish to ask a favour from you." Whereupon Mrs. Proudie bowed.

"Mrs. Proudie will be most happy, I am sure," said the bishop.

"I find that some foolish people have been talking in Barchester about my daughter," said the archdeacon; "and I wish to ask Mrs. Proudie—"

Most women under such circumstances would have felt the awkwardness of their situation, and would have prepared to eat their past words with wry faces. But not so Mrs. Proudie. Mrs. Grantly had had the imprudence to throw Mr. Slope in her face—there, in her own drawing-room, and she was resolved to be revenged. Mrs. Grantly, too, had ridiculed the Tickler match, and no too great niceness should now prevent Mrs. Proudie from speaking her mind about the Dumbello match.

"A great many people are talking about her, I am sorry to say," said Mrs. Proudie; "but, poor dear, it is not her fault. It might have happened to any girl; only, perhaps, a little more care—; you'll excuse me, Dr. Grantly."

"I have come here to allude to a report which has been spread about in Barchester, that the match between Lord Dumbello and my daughter has been broken off; and—"

"Everybody in Barchester knows it, I believe," said Mrs. Proudie.

—"and," continued the archdeacon, "to request that that report may be contradicted."

"Contradicted! Why, he has gone right away,—out of the country!"

"Never mind where he has gone to, Mrs. Proudie; I beg that the report may be contradicted."

"You'll have to go round to every house in Barchester then," said she.

"By no means," replied the archdeacon. "And perhaps it may be right that I should explain to the bishop that I came here because—"

"The bishop knows nothing about it," said Mrs. Proudie.

"Nothing in the world," said his lordship. "And I am sure I hope that the young lady may not be disappointed."

—"because the matter was so distinctly mentioned to Mrs. Arabin by yourself yesterday."

"Distinctly mentioned! Of course it was distinctly mentioned. There are some things which can't be kept under a bushel, Dr. Grantly; and this seems to be one of them. Your going about in this way won't make Lord Dumbello marry the young lady."

That was true; nor would it make Mrs. Proudie hold her tongue. Perhaps the archdeacon was wrong in his present errand, and so he now began to bethink himself. "At any rate," said he, "when I tell you that there is no ground whatever for such a report you will do me the kindness to say that, as far as you are concerned, it shall go no further. I think, my lord, I am not asking too much in asking that."

"The bishop knows nothing about it," said Mrs. Proudie again.

"Nothing at all," said the bishop.

"And as I must protest that I believe the information which has reached me on this head," said Mrs. Proudie, "I do not see how it is possible that I should contradict it. I can easily understand your feelings, Dr. Grantly. Considering your daughter's position the match was, as regards earthly wealth, a very great one. I do not wonder that you should be grieved at its being broken off; but I trust that this sorrow may eventuate in a blessing to you and to Miss Griselda. These worldly disappointments are precious balms, and I trust you know how to accept them as such."

The fact was that Dr. Grantly had done altogether wrong in coming to the palace. His wife might have some chance with Mrs. Proudie, but he had none. Since she had come to Barchester he had had only two or three encounters with her, and in all of these he had gone to the wall. His visits to the palace always resulted in his leaving the presence of the inhabitants in a frame of mind by no means desirable, and he now found that he had to do so once again. He could not compel Mrs. Proudie to say that the report was untrue; nor could he condescend to make counter hits at her about her own daughter, as his wife would have done. And thus, having utterly failed, he got up and took his leave.

But the worst of the matter was, that, in going home, he could not divest his mind of the idea that there might be some truth in the report. What if Lord Dumbello had gone to the Continent resolved to send back from thence some reason why it was impossible that he should make Miss Grantly his wife? Such things had been done before now by men in his rank. Whether or no Mrs. Tickler had been the letter-writing wellwisher from Littlebath, or had induced her friend to be so, it did seem manifest to him, Dr. Grantly, that Mrs. Proudie absolutely believed the report which she promulgated so diligently. The wish might be father to the thought, no doubt; but that the thought was truly there, Dr. Grantly could not induce himself to disbelieve.

His wife was less credulous, and to a certain degree comforted him; but that evening he received a letter which greatly confirmed the suspicions set on foot by Mrs. Proudie, and even shook his wife's faith in Lord Dumbello. It was from a mere acquaintance, who in the ordinary course of things would not have written to him. And the bulk of the letter referred to ordinary things, as to which the gentleman in question would hardly have thought of giving himself the trouble to write a letter. But at the end of the note he said,—

"Of course you are aware that Dumbello is off to Paris; I have not heard whether the exact day of his return is fixed."

"It is true then," said the archdeacon, striking the library table with his hand, and becoming absolutely white about the mouth and jaws.

"It cannot be," said Mrs. Grantly; but even she was now trembling.

"If it be so I'll drag him back to England by the collar of his coat, and disgrace him before the steps of his father's hall."

And the archdeacon as he uttered the threat looked his character as an irate British father much better than he did his other character as a clergyman of the Church of England. The archdeacon had been greatly worsted by Mrs. Proudie, but he was a man who knew how to fight his battles among men,—sometimes without too close a regard to his cloth.

"Had Lord Dumbello intended any such thing he would have written, or got some friend to write by this time," said Mrs. Grantly. "It is quite possible that he might wish to be off, but he would be too chary of his name not to endeavour to do so with decency."

Thus the matter was discussed, and it appeared to them both to be so serious that the archdeacon resolved to go at once to London. That Lord Dumbello had gone to France he did not doubt; but he would find some one in town acquainted with the young man's intentions, and he would, no doubt, be able to hear when his return was expected. If there were real reason for apprehension he would follow the runagate to the Continent, but he would not do this without absolute knowledge. According to Lord Dumbello's present engagements he was bound to present himself in August next at Plumstead Episcopi, with the view of then and there taking Griselda Grantly in marriage; but if he kept his word in this respect no one had a right to quarrel with him for going to Paris in the meantime. Most expectant bridegrooms would, no doubt, under such circumstances have declared their intentions to their future brides; but if Lord Dumbello were different from others, who had a right on that account to be indignant with him? He was unlike other men in other things; and especially unlike other men in being the eldest son of the Marquis of Hartletop. It would be all very well for Tickler to proclaim his whereabouts from week to week; but the eldest son of a marquis might find it inconvenient to be so precise! Nevertheless the archdeacon thought it only prudent to go up to London.

"Susan," said the archdeacon to his wife, just as he was starting;—at this moment neither of them were in the happiest spirits,—"I think I would say a word of caution to Griselda."

"Do you feel so much doubt about it as that?" said Mrs. Grantly. But even she did not dare to put a direct negative to this proposal, so much had she been moved by what she had heard!

"I think I would do so, not frightening her more than I could help. It will lessen the blow if it be that the blow is to fall."

"It will kill me," said Mrs. Grantly; "but I think that she will be able to bear it."

On the next morning Mrs. Grantly, with much cunning preparation, went about the task which her husband had left her to perform. It took her long to do, for she was very cunning in the doing of it; but at last it dropped from her in words that there was a possibility—a bare possibility—that some disappointment might even yet be in store for them.

"Do you mean, mamma, that the marriage will be put off?"

"I don't mean to say that I think it will; God forbid! but it is just possible. I daresay that I am very wrong to tell you of this, but I know that you have sense enough to bear it. Papa has gone to London and we shall hear from him soon."

"Then, mamma, I had better give them orders not to go on with the marking."

CHAPTER XLVI.

LADY LUFTON'S REQUEST.

The bailiffs on that day had their meals regular,—and their beer, which state of things, together with an absence of all duty in the way of making inventories and the like, I take to be the earthly paradise of bailiffs; and on the next morning they walked off with civil speeches and many apologies as to their intrusion. "They was very sorry," they said, "to have troubled a gen'leman as were a gen'leman, but in their way of business what could they do?" To which one of them added a remark that, "business is business." This statement I am not prepared to contradict, but I would recommend all men in choosing a profession to avoid any that may require an apology at every turn;—either an apology or else a somewhat violent assertion of right. Each younger male reader may perhaps reply that he has no thought of becoming a sheriff's officer; but then are there not other cognate lines of life to which perhaps the attention of some such may be attracted?

On the evening of the day on which they went Mark received a note from Lady Lufton begging him to call early on the following morning, and immediately after breakfast he went across to Framley Court. It may be imagined that he was not in a very happy frame of mind, but he felt the truth of his wife's remark that the first plunge into cold water was always the worst. Lady Lufton was not a woman who would continually throw his disgrace into his teeth, however terribly cold might be the first words with which she spoke of it. He strove hard as he entered her room to carry his usual look and bearing, and to put out his hand to greet her with his customary freedom, but he knew that he failed. And it may be said that no good man who has broken down in his goodness can carry the disgrace of his fall without some look of shame. When a man is able to do that, he ceases to be in any way good.

"This has been a distressing affair," said Lady Lufton after her first salutation.

"Yes, indeed," said he. "It has been very sad for poor Fanny."

"Well; we must all have our little periods of grief; and it may perhaps be fortunate if none of us have worse than this. She will not complain, herself, I am sure."

"She complain!"

"No, I am sure she will not. And now all I've got to say, Mr. Robarts, is this: I hope you and Lufton have had enough to do with black sheep to last you your lives; for I must protest that your late friend Mr. Sowerby is a black sheep."

In no possible way could Lady Lufton have alluded to the matter with greater kindness than in thus joining Mark's name with that of her son. It took away all the bitterness of the rebuke, and made the subject one on which even he might have spoken without difficulty.

But now, seeing that she was so gentle to him, he could not but lean the more hardly on himself.

"I have been very foolish," said he, "very foolish and very wrong, and very wicked."

"Very foolish, I believe, Mr. Robarts—to speak frankly and once for all; but, as I also believe, nothing worse. I thought it best for both of us that we should just have one word about it, and now I recommend that the matter be never mentioned between us again."

"God bless you, Lady Lufton," he said. "I think no man ever had such a friend as you are."

She had been very quiet during the interview, and almost subdued, not speaking with the animation that was usual to her; for this affair with Mr. Robarts was not the only one she had to complete that day, nor, perhaps, the one most difficult of completion. But she cheered up a little under the praise now bestowed on her, for it was the sort of praise she loved best. She did hope, and, perhaps, flatter herself, that she was a good friend.

"You must be good enough, then, to gratify my friendship by coming up to dinner this evening; and Fanny, too, of course. I cannot take any excuse, for the matter is completely arranged. I have a particular reason for wishing it." These last violent injunctions had been added because Lady Lufton had seen a refusal rising in the parson's face. Poor Lady Lufton! Her enemies—for even she had enemies—used to declare of her, that an invitation to dinner was the only method of showing itself of which her good-humour was cognizant. But let me ask of her enemies whether it is not as good a method as any other known to be extant? Under such orders as these obedience was of course a necessity, and he promised that he, with his wife, would come across to dinner. And then, when he went away, Lady Lufton ordered her carriage.

During these doings at Framley, Lucy Robarts still remained at Hogglestock, nursing Mrs. Crawley. Nothing occurred to take her back to Framley, for the same note from Fanny which gave her the first tidings of the arrival of the Philistines told her also of their departure—and also of the source from whence relief had reached them. "Don't come, therefore, for that reason," said the note, "but, nevertheless, do come as quickly as you can, for the whole house is sad without you."

On the morning after the receipt of this note Lucy was sitting, as was now usual with her, beside an old arm-chair to which her patient had lately been promoted. The fever had gone, and Mrs. Crawley was slowly regaining her strength—very slowly, and with frequent caution from the Silverbridge doctor that any attempt at being well too fast might again precipitate her into an abyss of illness and domestic inefficiency.

"I really think I can get about to-morrow," said she; "and then, dear Lucy, I need not keep you longer from your home."

"You are in a great hurry to get rid of me, I think. I suppose Mr. Crawley has been complaining again about the cream in his tea." Mr. Crawley had on one occasion stated his assured conviction that surreptitious daily supplies were being brought into the house, because he had detected the presence of cream instead of milk in his own cup. As, however, the cream had been going for sundry days before this, Miss Robarts had not thought much of his ingenuity in making the discovery.

"Ah, you do not know how he speaks of you when your back is turned."

"And how does he speak of me? I know you would not have the courage to tell me the whole."

"No, I have not; for you would think it absurd coming from one who looks like him. He says that if he were to write a poem about womanhood, he would make you the heroine."

"With a cream-jug in my hand, or else sewing buttons on to a shirt-collar. But he never forgave me about the mutton broth. He told me, in so many words, that I was a— storyteller. And for the matter of that, my dear, so I was."

"He told me that you were an angel."

"Goodness gracious!"

"A ministering angel. And so you have been. I can almost feel it in my heart to be glad that I have been ill, seeing that I have had you for my friend."

"But you might have had that good fortune without the fever."

"No, I should not. In my married life I have made no friends till my illness brought you to me; nor should I ever really have known you but for that. How should I get to know any one?"

"You will now, Mrs. Crawley; will you not? Promise that you will. You will come to us at Framley when you are well? You have promised already, you know."

"You made me do so when I was too weak to refuse."

"And I shall make you keep your promise too. He shall come, also, if he likes; but you shall come whether he likes or no. And I won't hear a word about your old dresses. Old dresses will wear as well at Framley as at Hogglestock."

From all which it will appear that Mrs. Crawley and Lucy Robarts had become very intimate during this period of the nursing; as two women always will, or, at least should do, when shut up for weeks together in the same sick room.

The conversation was still going on between them when the sound of wheels was heard upon the road. It was no highway that passed before the house, and carriages of any sort were not frequent there.

"It is Fanny, I am sure," said Lucy, rising from her chair.

"There are two horses," said Mrs. Crawley, distinguishing the noise with the accurate sense of hearing which is always attached to sickness; "and it is not the noise of the pony-carriage."

"It is a regular carriage," said Lucy, speaking from the window, "and stopping here. It is somebody from Framley Court, for I know the servant."

As she spoke a blush came to her forehead. Might it not be Lord Lufton, she thought to herself,—forgetting at the moment that Lord Lufton did not go about the country in a close chariot with a fat footman. Intimate as she had become with Mrs. Crawley she had said nothing to her new friend on the subject of her love affair.

The carriage stopped and down came the footman, but nobody spoke to him from the inside.

"He has probably brought something from Framley," said Lucy, having cream and such like matters in her mind; for cream and such like matters had come from Framley Court more than once during her sojourn there. "And the carriage, probably, happened to be coming this way."

But the mystery soon elucidated itself partially, or, perhaps, became more mysterious in another way. The red-armed little girl who had been taken away by her frightened mother in the first burst of the fever had now returned to her place, and at the present moment entered the room, with awestruck face, declaring that Miss Robarts was to go at once to the big lady in the carriage.

"I suppose it's Lady Lufton," said Mrs. Crawley.

Lucy's heart was so absolutely in her mouth that any kind of speech was at the moment impossible to her. Why should Lady Lufton have come thither to Hogglestock, and why should she want to see her, Lucy Robarts, in the carriage? Had not everything between them been settled? And yet—! Lucy, in the moment for thought that was allowed to her, could not determine what might be the probable upshot of such an interview. Her chief feeling was a desire to postpone it for the present instant. But the red-armed little girl would not allow that.

"You are to come at once," said she.

And then Lucy, without having spoken a word, got up and left the room. She walked downstairs, along the little passage, and out through the small garden, with firm steps, but hardly knowing whither she went, or why. Her presence of mind and self-possession had all deserted her. She knew that she was unable to speak as she should do; she felt that she would have to regret her present behaviour, but yet she could not help herself. Why should Lady Lufton have come to her there? She went on, and the big footman stood with the carriage door open. She stepped up almost unconsciously, and, without knowing how she got there, she found herself seated by Lady Lufton.

To tell the truth her ladyship also was a little at a loss to know how she was to carry through her present plan of operations. The duty of beginning, however, was clearly with her, and therefore, having taken Lucy by the hand, she spoke.

"Miss Robarts," she said, "my son has come home. I don't know whether you are aware of it."

She spoke with a low, gentle voice, not quite like herself, but Lucy was much too confused to notice this.

"I was not aware of it," said Lucy.

She had, however, been so informed in Fanny's letter, but all that had gone out of her head.

"Yes; he has come back. He has been in Norway, you know,—fishing."

"Yes," said Lucy.

"I am sure you will remember all that took place when you came to me, not long ago, in my little room upstairs at Framley Court."

In answer to which, Lucy, quivering in every nerve, and wrongly thinking that she was visibly shaking in every limb, timidly answered that she did remember. Why was it that she had then been so bold, and now was so poor a coward?

"Well, my dear, all that I said to you then I said to you thinking that it was for the best. You, at any rate, will not be angry with me for loving my own son better than I love any one else."

"Oh, no," said Lucy.

"He is the best of sons, and the best of men, and I am sure that he will be the best of husbands."

Lucy had an idea, by instinct, however, rather than by sight, that Lady Lufton's eyes were full of tears as she spoke. As for herself she was altogether blinded and did not dare to lift her face or to turn her head. As for the utterance of any sound, that was quite out of the question.

"And now I have come here, Lucy, to ask you to be his wife."

She was quite sure that she heard the words. They came plainly to her ears, leaving on her brain their proper sense, but yet she could not move or make any sign that she had understood them. It seemed as though it would be ungenerous in her to take advantage of such conduct and to accept an offer made with so much self-sacrifice. She had not time at the first moment to think even of his happiness, let alone her own, but she thought only of the magnitude of the concession which had been made to her. When she had constituted Lady Lufton the arbiter of her destiny she had regarded the question of her love as decided against herself. She had found herself unable to endure the position of being Lady Lufton's daughter-in-law while Lady Lufton would be scorning her, and therefore she had given up the game. She had given up the game, sacrificing herself, and, as far as it might be a sacrifice, sacrificing him also. She had been resolute to stand to her word in this respect, but she had never allowed herself to think it possible that Lady Lufton should comply with the conditions which she, Lucy, had laid upon her. And yet such was the case, as she so plainly heard. "And now I have come here, Lucy, to ask you to be his wife."

How long they sat together silent, I cannot say; counted by minutes the time would not probably have amounted to many, but to each of them the duration seemed considerable. Lady Lufton, while she was speaking, had contrived to get hold of Lucy's hand, and she sat, still holding it, trying to look into Lucy's face,—which, however, she could hardly see, so much was it turned away. Neither, indeed, were Lady Lufton's eyes perfectly dry. No answer came to her question, and therefore, after a while, it was necessary that she should speak again.

"Must I go back to him, Lucy, and tell him that there is some other objection—something besides a stern old mother; some hindrance, perhaps, not so easily overcome?"

"No," said Lucy, and it was all which at the moment she could say.

"What shall I tell him, then? Shall I say yes—simply yes?"

"Simply yes," said Lucy.

"And as to the stern old mother who thought her only son too precious to be parted with at the first word—is nothing to be said to her?"

"Oh, Lady Lufton!"

"No forgiveness to be spoken, no sign of affection to be given? Is she always to be regarded as stern and cross, vexatious and disagreeable?"

Lucy slowly turned round her head and looked up into her companion's face. Though she had as yet no voice to speak of affection she could fill her eyes with love, and in that way make to her future mother all the promises that were needed.

"Lucy, dearest Lucy, you must be very dear to me now." And then they were in each other's arms, kissing each other.

Lady Lufton now desired her coachman to drive up and down for some little space along the road while she completed her necessary conversation with Lucy. She wanted at first to carry her back to Framley that evening, promising to send her again to Mrs. Crawley on the following morning—"till some permanent arrangement could be made," by which Lady Lufton intended the substitution of a regular nurse for her future daughter-in-law, seeing that Lucy Robarts was now invested in her eyes with attributes which made it unbecoming that she should sit in attendance at Mrs. Crawley's bedside. But Lucy would not go back to Framley on that evening; no, nor on the next morning. She would be so glad if Fanny would come to her there, and then she would arrange about going home.

"But, Lucy, dear, what am I to say to Ludovic? Perhaps you would feel it awkward if he were to come to see you here."

"Oh, yes, Lady Lufton; pray tell him not to do that."

"And is that all that I am to tell him?"

"Tell him—tell him—He won't want you to tell him anything;—only I should like to be quiet for a day, Lady Lufton."

"Well, dearest, you shall be quiet; the day after to-morrow then.—Mind we must not spare you any longer, because it will be right that you should be at home now. He would think it very hard if you were to be so near, and he was not to be allowed to look at you. And there will be some one else who will want to see you. I shall want to have you very near to me, for I shall be wretched, Lucy, if I cannot teach you to love me." In answer to which Lucy did find voice enough to make sundry promises.

And then she was put out of the carriage at the little wicket gate, and Lady Lufton was driven back to Framley. I wonder whether the servant when he held the door for Miss Robarts was conscious that he was waiting on his future mistress. I fancy that he was, for these sort of people always know everything, and the peculiar courtesy of his demeanour as he let down the carriage steps was very observable.

Lucy felt almost beside herself as she returned upstairs, not knowing what to do, or how to look, and with what words to speak. It behoved her to go at once to Mrs. Crawley's room, and yet she longed to be alone. She knew that she was quite unable either to conceal her thoughts or express them; nor did she wish at the present moment to talk to any one about her happiness,—seeing that she could not at the present moment talk to Fanny Robarts. She went, however, without delay into Mrs. Crawley's room, and with that little eager way of speaking quickly which is so common with people who know that they are confused, said that she feared she had been a very long time away.

"And was it Lady Lufton?"

"Yes; it was Lady Lufton."

"Why, Lucy; I did not know that you and her ladyship were such friends."

"She had something particular she wanted to say," said Lucy, avoiding the question, and avoiding also Mrs. Crawley's eyes; and then she sat down in her usual chair.

"It was nothing unpleasant, I hope."

"No, nothing at all unpleasant; nothing of that kind.—Oh, Mrs. Crawley, I'll tell you some other time, but pray do not ask me now." And then she got up and escaped, for it was absolutely necessary that she should be alone.

When she reached her own room—that in which the children usually slept—she made a great effort to compose herself, but not altogether successfully. She got out her paper and blotting-book intending, as she said to herself, to write to Fanny, knowing, however, that the letter when written would be destroyed; but she was not able even to form a word. Her hand was unsteady and her eyes were dim and her thoughts were incapable of being fixed. She could only sit, and think, and wonder, and hope; occasionally wiping the tears from her eyes, and asking herself why her present frame of mind was so painful to her? During the last two or three months she had felt no fear of Lord Lufton, had always carried herself before him on equal terms, and had been signally capable of doing so when he made his declaration to her at the parsonage; but now she looked forward with an undefined dread to the first moment in which she should see him.

And then she thought of a certain evening she had passed at Framley Court, and acknowledged to herself that there was some pleasure in looking back to that. Griselda Grantly had been there, and all the constitutional powers of the two families had been at work to render easy a process of love-making between her and Lord Lufton. Lucy had seen and understood it all, without knowing that she understood it, and had, in a certain degree, suffered from beholding it. She had placed herself apart, not complaining—painfully conscious of some inferiority, but, at the same time, almost boasting to herself that in her own way she was the superior. And then he had come behind her chair, whispering to her, speaking to her his first words of kindness and good-nature, and she had resolved that she would be his friend—his friend, even though Griselda Grantly might be his wife. What those resolutions were worth had soon become manifest to her. She had soon confessed to herself the result of that friendship, and had determined to bear her punishment with courage. But now—

She sate so for about an hour, and would fain have so sat out the day. But as this could not be, she got up, and having washed her face and eyes returned to Mrs. Crawley's room. There she found Mr. Crawley also, to her great joy, for she knew that while he was there no questions would be asked of her. He was always very gentle to her, treating her with an old-fashioned polished respect—except when compelled on that one occasion by his sense of duty to accuse her of mendacity respecting the purveying of victuals—, but he had never become absolutely familiar with her as his wife had done; and it was well for her now that he had not done so, for she could not have talked about Lady Lufton.

In the evening, when the three were present, she did manage to say that she expected Mrs. Robarts would come over on the following day.

"We shall part with you, Miss Robarts, with the deepest regret," said Mr. Crawley; "but we would not on any account keep you longer. Mrs. Crawley can do without you now. What she would have done, had you not come to us, I am at a loss to think."

"I did not say that I should go," said Lucy.

"But you will," said Mrs. Crawley. "Yes, dear, you will. I know that it is proper now that you should return. Nay, but we will not have you any longer. And the poor dear children, too,—they may return. How am I to thank Mrs. Robarts for what she has done for us?"

It was settled that if Mrs. Robarts came on the following day Lucy should go back with her; and then, during the long watches of the night—for on this last night Lucy would not leave the bed-side of her new friend till long after the dawn had broken—she did tell Mrs. Crawley what was to be her destiny in life. To herself there seemed nothing strange in her new position; but to Mrs. Crawley it was wonderful that she—she, poor as she was—should have an embryo peeress at her bedside, handing her her cup to drink, and smoothing her pillow that she might be at rest. It was strange, and she could hardly maintain her accustomed familiarity. Lucy felt this, at the moment.

"It must make no difference, you know," said she, eagerly; "none at all, between you and me. Promise me that it shall make no difference."

The promise was, of course, exacted; but it was not possible that such a promise should be kept.

Very early on the following morning—so early that it woke her while still in her first sleep—there came a letter for her from the parsonage. Mrs. Robarts had written it, after her return home from Lady Lufton's dinner.

The letter said:—

MY OWN OWN DARLING, How am I to congratulate you, and be eager enough in wishing you joy? I do wish you joy, and am so very happy. I write now chiefly to say that I shall be over with you about twelve to-morrow, and that I <u>must</u> bring you away with me. If I did not some one else, by no means so trustworthy, would insist on doing it.

But this, though it was thus stated to be the chief part of the letter, and though it might be so in matter, was by no means so in space. It was very long, for Mrs. Robarts had sat writing it till past midnight.

> I will not say anything about him [she went on to say, after two pages had been filled with his name], but I must tell you how beautifully she has behaved. You will own that she is a dear woman; will you not?

Lucy had already owned it many times since the visit of yesterday, and had declared to herself, as she has continued to declare ever since, that she had never doubted it.

> She took us by surprise when we got into the drawing-room before dinner, and she told us first of all that she had been to see you at Hogglestock. Lord Lufton, of course, could not keep the secret, but brought it out instantly. I can't tell you now how he told it all, but I am sure you will believe that he did it in the best possible manner. He took my hand and pressed it half a dozen times, and I thought he was going to do something else; but he did not, so you need not be jealous. And she was so nice to Mark, saying such things in praise of you, and paying all manner of compliments to your father. But Lord Lufton scolded her immensely for not bringing you. He said

it was lackadaisical and nonsensical; but I could see how much he loved her for what she had done; and she could see it too, for I know her ways, and know that she was delighted with him. She could not keep her eyes off him all the evening, and certainly I never did see him look so well.

And then while Lord Lufton and Mark were in the dining-room, where they remained a terribly long time, she would make me go through the house that she might show me your rooms, and explain how you were to be mistress there. She has got it all arranged to perfection, and I am sure she has been thinking about it for years. Her great fear at present is that you and he should go and live at Lufton. If you have any gratitude in you, either to her or me, you will not let him do this. I consoled her by saying that there are not two stones upon one another at Lufton as yet; and I believe such is the case. Besides, everybody says that it is the ugliest spot in the world. She went on to declare, with tears in her eyes, that if you were content to remain at Framley, she would never interfere in anything. I do think that she is the best woman that ever lived.

So much as I have given of this letter formed but a small portion of it, but it comprises all that it is necessary that we should know. Exactly at twelve o'clock on that day Puck the pony appeared, with Mrs. Robarts and Grace Crawley behind him, Grace having been brought back as being capable of some service in the house. Nothing that was confidential, and very little that was loving, could be said at the moment, because Mr. Crawley was there, waiting to bid Miss Robarts adieu; and he had not as yet been informed of what was to be the future fate of his visitor. So they could only press each other's hands and embrace, which to Lucy was almost a relief; for even to her sister-in-law she hardly as yet knew how to speak openly on this subject.

"May God Almighty bless you, Miss Robarts," said Mr. Crawley, as he stood in his dingy sitting-room ready to lead her out to the pony-carriage. "You have brought sunshine into this house, even in the time of sickness, when there was no sunshine; and He will bless you. You have been the Good Samaritan, binding up the wounds of the afflicted, pouring in oil and balm. To the mother of my children you have given life, and to me you have brought light, and comfort, and good words,—making my spirit glad within me as it had not been gladdened before. All this hath come of charity, which vaunteth not itself and is not puffed up. Faith and hope are great and beautiful, but charity exceedeth them all." And having so spoken, instead of leading her out, he went away and hid himself.

How Puck behaved himself as Fanny drove him back to Framley, and how those two ladies in the carriage behaved themselves—of that, perhaps, nothing further need be said.

CHAPTER XLVII.

NEMESIS.

But in spite of all these joyful tidings it must, alas! be remembered that Pœna, that just but Rhadamanthine goddess, whom we moderns ordinarily call Punishment, or Nemesis when we wish to speak of her goddess-ship, very seldom fails to catch a wicked man though she have sometimes a lame foot of her own, and though the wicked man may possibly get a start of her. In this instance the wicked man had been our unfortunate friend Mark Robarts; wicked in that he had wittingly touched pitch, gone to Gatherum Castle, ridden fast mares across the country to Cobbold's Ashes, and fallen very imprudently among the Tozers; and the instrument used by Nemesis was Mr. Tom Towers of the *Jupiter*, than whom, in these our days, there is no deadlier scourge in the hands of that goddess.

In the first instance, however, I must mention, though I will not relate, a little conversation which took place between Lady Lufton and Mr. Robarts. That gentleman thought it right to say a few words more to her ladyship respecting those money transactions. He could not but feel, he said, that he had received that prebendal stall from the hands of Mr. Sowerby; and under such circumstances, considering all that had happened, he could not be easy in his mind as long as he held it. What he was about to do would, he was aware, delay considerably his final settlement with Lord Lufton; but Lufton, he hoped, would pardon that, and agree with him as to the propriety of what he was about to do.

On the first blush of the thing Lady Lufton did not quite go along with him. Now that Lord Lufton was to marry the parson's sister it might be well that the parson should be a dignitary of the Church; and it might be well, also, that one so nearly connected with her son should be comfortable in his money matters. There loomed also, in the future, some distant possibility of higher clerical honours for a peer's brother-in-law; and the top rung of the ladder is always more easily attained when a man has already ascended a step or two. But, nevertheless, when the matter came to be fully explained to her, when she saw clearly the circumstances under which the stall had been conferred, she did agree that it had better be given up.

And well for both of them it was—well for them all at Framley—that this conclusion had been reached before the scourge of Nemesis had fallen. Nemesis, of course, declared that her scourge had produced the resignation; but it was generally understood that this was a false boast, for all clerical men at Barchester knew that the stall had been restored to the chapter, or, in other words, into the hands of the Government, before Tom Towers had twirled the fatal lash above his head. But the manner of the twirling was as follows:—

It is with difficulty enough [said the article in the *Jupiter*], that the Church of England maintains at the present moment that ascendancy among the religious sects of this country which it so loudly claims. And perhaps it is rather from an old-fashioned and time-honoured affection for its standing than from any intrinsic merits of its own that some such general acknowledgment of its ascendancy is still allowed to prevail. If, however, the patrons and clerical members of this Church are bold enough to disregard all general rules of decent behaviour, we think we may predict that this chivalrous feeling will be found to give way. From time to time we hear of instances of such imprudence, and are made to wonder at the folly of those who are supposed to hold the State Church in the greatest reverence.

Among those positions of dignified ease to which fortunate clergymen may be promoted are the stalls of the canons or prebendaries in our cathedrals. Some of these, as is well known, carry little or no emolument with them, but some are rich in the good things of this world. Excellent family houses are attached to them, with we hardly know what domestic privileges, and clerical incomes, moreover, of an amount which, if divided, would make glad the hearts of many a hard-working clerical slave. Reform has been busy even among these stalls, attaching some amount of work to the pay, and paring off some superfluous wealth from such of them as were over full; but reform has been lenient with them, acknowledging that it was well to have some such places of comfortable and dignified retirement for those who have worn themselves out in the hard work of their profession. There has of late prevailed a taste for the appointment of young bishops, produced no doubt by a feeling that bishops should be men fitted to get through really hard work; but we have never heard that young prebendaries were considered desirable. A clergyman selected for such a position should, we have always thought, have earned an evening of ease by a long day of work, and should, above all things, be one whose life has been, and therefore in human probability will be, so decorous as to be honourable to the cathedral of his adoption.

We were, however, the other day given to understand that one of these luxurious benefices, belonging to the cathedral of Barchester, had been bestowed on the Rev. Mark Robarts, the vicar of a neighbouring parish, on the understanding that he should hold the living and the stall together; and on making further inquiry we were surprised to learn that this fortunate gentleman is as yet considerably under thirty years of age. We were desirous, however, of believing that his learning, his piety, and his conduct, might be of a nature to add peculiar grace to his chapter, and therefore, though almost unwillingly, we were silent. But now it has come to our ears, and, indeed, to the ears of all the world, that this piety and conduct are sadly wanting; and judging of Mr. Robarts by his life and associates, we are inclined to doubt even the learning. He has at this moment, or at any rate had but a few days since, an execution in his parsonage house at Framley, on the suit of certain most disreputable bill discounters in London; and probably would have another execution in his other house in Barchester close, but for the fact that he has never thought it necessary to go into residence.

Then followed some very stringent, and, no doubt, much-needed advice to those clerical members of the Church of England who are supposed to be mainly responsible for the conduct of their brethren; and the article ended as follows:—

Many of these stalls are in the gift of the respective deans and chapters, and in such cases the dean and chapters are bound to see that proper persons are appointed; but in other instances the power of selection is vested in the Crown, and then an equal responsibility rests on the government of the day. Mr. Robarts, we learn, was appointed to the stall in Barchester by the late Prime Minister, and we really think that a grave censure rests on him for the manner in which his patronage has been exercised. It may be impossible that he should himself in all such cases satisfy himself by personal inquiry. But our government is altogether conducted on the footing of vicarial responsibility. *Quod facit per alium, facit per se*, is in a special manner true of our ministers, and any man who rises to high position among them must abide by the danger thereby incurred. In this peculiar case we are informed that the recommendation was made by a very recently admitted member of the Cabinet, to whose appointment we alluded at the time as a great mistake. The gentleman in question held no high individual office of his own; but evil such as this which has now been done at Barchester, is exactly the sort of mischief which follows the exaltation of unfit men to high positions, even though no great scope for executive failure may be placed within their reach.

If Mr. Robarts will allow us to tender to him our advice, he will lose no time in going through such ceremony as may be necessary again to place the stall at the disposal of the Crown!

I may here observe that poor Harold Smith, when he read this, writhing in agony, declared it to be the handiwork of his hated enemy, Mr. Supplehouse. He knew the mark; so, at least, he said; but I myself am inclined to believe that his animosity misled him. I think that one greater than Mr. Supplehouse had taken upon himself the punishment of our poor vicar.

This was very dreadful to them all at Framley, and, when first read, seemed to crush them to atoms. Poor Mrs. Robarts, when she heard it, seemed to think that for them the world was over. An attempt had been made to keep it from her, but such attempts always fail, as did this. The article was copied into all the good-natured local newspapers, and she soon discovered that something was being hidden. At last it was shown to her by her husband, and then for a few hours she was annihilated; for a few days she was unwilling to show herself; and for a few weeks she was very sad. But after that the world seemed to go on much as it had done before; the sun shone upon them as warmly as though the article had not been written; and not only the sun of heaven, which, as a rule, is not limited in his shining by any display of pagan thunder, but also the genial sun of their own sphere, the warmth and light of which were so essentially necessary to their happiness. Neighbouring rectors did not look glum, nor did the rectors' wives refuse to call. The people in the shops at Barchester did not regard her as though she were a disgraced woman, though it must be acknowledged that Mrs. Proudie passed her in the close with the coldest nod of recognition.

On Mrs. Proudie's mind alone did the article seem to have any enduring effect. In one respect it was, perhaps, beneficial; Lady Lufton was at once induced by it to make common cause with her own clergyman, and thus the remembrance of Mr. Robarts' sins passed away the quicker from the minds of the whole Framley Court household.

And, indeed, the county at large was not able to give to the matter that undivided attention which would have been considered its due at periods of no more than ordinary interest. At the present moment preparations were being made for a general election, and although no contest was to take place in the eastern division, a very violent fight was being carried on in the west; and the circumstances of that fight were so exciting that Mr. Robarts and his article were forgotten before their time. An edict had gone forth from Gatherum Castle directing that Mr. Sowerby should be turned out, and an answering note of defiance had been sounded from Chaldicotes, protesting on behalf of Mr. Sowerby, that the duke's behest would not be obeyed.

There are two classes of persons in this realm who are constitutionally inefficient to take any part in returning members to Parliament—peers, namely, and women; and yet it was soon known through the whole length and breadth of the county that the present electioneering fight was being carried on between a peer and a woman. Miss Dunstable had been declared the purchaser of the Chace of Chaldicotes, as it were, just in the very nick of time; which purchase—so men in Barsetshire declared, not knowing anything of the facts—would have gone altogether the other way, had not the giants obtained temporary supremacy over the gods. The duke was a supporter of the gods, and therefore, so Mr. Fothergill hinted, his money had been refused. Miss Dunstable was prepared to beard this ducal friend of the gods in his own county, and therefore her money had been taken. I am inclined, however, to think that Mr. Fothergill knew nothing about it, and to opine that Miss Dunstable, in her eagerness for victory, offered to the Crown more money than the property was worth in the duke's opinion, and that the Crown took advantage of her anxiety, to the manifest profit of the public at large.

And it soon became known also that Miss Dunstable was, in fact, the proprietor of the whole Chaldicotes estate, and that in promoting the success of Mr. Sowerby as a candidate for the county, she was standing by her own tenant. It also became known, in the course of the battle, that Miss Dunstable had herself at last succumbed, and that she was about to marry Dr. Thorne of Greshamsbury, or the "Greshamsbury apothecary," as the adverse party now delighted to call him. "He has been little better than a quack all his life," said Dr. Fillgrave, the eminent physician of Barchester, "and now he is going to marry a quack's daughter." By which, and the like to which, Dr. Thorne did not allow himself to be much annoyed.

But all this gave rise to a very pretty series of squibs arranged between Mr. Fothergill and Mr. Closerstill, the electioneering agent. Mr. Sowerby was named "the lady's pet," and descriptions were given of the lady who kept this pet, which were by no means flattering to Miss Dunstable's appearance, or manners, or age. And then the western division of the county was asked in a grave tone—as counties and boroughs are asked by means of advertisements stuck up on blind walls and barn doors—whether it was fitting and proper that it should be represented by a woman. Upon which the county was again asked whether it was fitting and proper that it should be represented by a duke. And then the question became more personal as against Miss Dunstable, and inquiry was urged whether the county would not be indelibly disgraced if it were not only handed over to a woman, but handed over to a woman who sold the oil of Lebanon. But little was got by this move, for an answering placard explained to the unfortunate county how deep would be its shame if it allowed itself to become the appanage of any peer, but more especially of a peer who was known to be the most immoral lord that ever disgraced the benches of the upper house.

And so the battle went on very prettily, and, as money was allowed to flow freely, the West Barsetshire world at large was not ill satisfied. It is wonderful how much disgrace of that kind a borough or county can endure without flinching; and wonderful, also, seeing how supreme is the value attached to the constitution by the realm at large, how very little the principles of that constitution are valued by the people in detail. The duke, of course, did not show himself. He rarely did on any occasion, and never on such occasions as this; but Mr. Fothergill was to be seen everywhere. Miss Dunstable, also, did not hide her light under a bushel; though I here declare, on the faith of an historian, that the rumour spread abroad of her having made a speech to the electors from the top of the porch over the hotel-door at Courcy was not founded on fact. No doubt she was at Courcy, and her carriage stopped at the hotel; but neither there nor elsewhere did she make any public exhibition. "They must have mistaken me for Mrs. Proudie," she said, when the rumour reached her ears.

But there was, alas! one great element of failure on Miss Dunstable's side of the battle. Mr. Sowerby himself could not be induced to fight it as became a man. Any positive injunctions that were laid upon him he did, in a sort, obey. It had been a part of the bargain that he should stand the contest, and from that bargain he could not well go back; but he had not the spirit left to him for any true fighting on his own part. He could not go up on the hustings, and there defy the duke. Early in the affair Mr. Fothergill challenged him to do so, and Mr. Sowerby never took up the gauntlet.

"We have heard," said Mr. Fothergill, in that great speech which he made at the Omnium Arms at Silverbridge—"we have heard much during this election of the Duke of Omnium, and of the injuries which he is supposed to have inflicted on one of the candidates. The duke's name is very frequent in the mouths of the gentlemen,—and of the lady,—who support Mr. Sowerby's claims. But I do not think that Mr. Sowerby himself has dared to say much about the duke. I defy Mr. Sowerby to mention the duke's name upon the hustings."

And it so happened that Mr. Sowerby never did mention the duke's name.

It is ill fighting when the spirit is gone, and Mr. Sowerby's spirit for such things was now well nigh broken. It is true that he had escaped from the net in which the duke, by Mr. Fothergill's aid, had entangled him; but he had only broken out of one captivity into another. Money is a serious thing; and when gone cannot be had back by a shuffle in the game, or a fortunate blow with the battledore, as may political power, or reputation, or fashion. One hundred thousand pounds gone, must remain as gone, let the person who claims to have had the honour of advancing it be Mrs. B. or my Lord C. No lucky dodge can erase such a claim from the things that be—unless, indeed, such dodge be possible as Mr. Sowerby tried with Miss Dunstable. It was better for him, undoubtedly, to have the lady for a creditor than the duke, seeing that it was possible for him to live as a tenant in his own old house under the lady's reign. But this he found to be a sad enough life, after all that was come and gone.

The election on Miss Dunstable's part was lost. She carried on the contest nobly, fighting it to the last moment, and sparing neither her own money nor that of her antagonist; but she carried it on unsuccessfully. Many gentlemen did support Mr. Sowerby because they were willing enough to emancipate their county from the duke's thraldom; but Mr. Sowerby was felt to be a black sheep, as Lady Lufton had called him, and at the close of the election he found himself banished from the representation of West Barsetshire;—banished for ever, after having held the county for five-and-twenty years.

Unfortunate Mr. Sowerby! I cannot take leave of him here without some feeling of regret, knowing that there was that within him which might, under better guidance, have produced better things. There are men, even of high birth, who seem as though they were born to be rogues; but Mr. Sowerby was, to my thinking, born to be a gentleman. That he had not been a gentleman—that he had bolted from his appointed course, going terribly on the wrong side of the posts—let us all acknowledge. It is not a gentlemanlike deed, but a very blackguard action, to obtain a friend's acceptance to a bill in an unguarded hour of social intercourse. That and other similar doings have stamped his character too plainly. But, nevertheless, I claim a tear for Mr. Sowerby, and lament that he has failed to run his race discreetly, in accordance with the rules of the Jockey Club.

He attempted that plan of living as a tenant in his old house at Chaldicotes and of making a living out of the land which he farmed; but he soon abandoned it. He had no aptitude for such industry, and could not endure his altered position in the county. He soon relinquished Chaldicotes of his own accord, and has vanished away, as such men do vanish—not altogether without necessary income; to which point in the final arrangement of their joint affairs, Mrs. Thorne's man of business—if I may be allowed so far to anticipate—paid special attention.

And thus Lord Dumbello, the duke's nominee, got in, as the duke's nominee had done for very many years past. There was no Nemesis here—none as yet. Nevertheless, she with the lame foot will assuredly catch him, the duke, if it be that he deserve to be caught. With us his grace's appearance has been so unfrequent that I think we may omit to make any further inquiry as to his concerns.

One point, however, is worthy of notice, as showing the good sense with which we manage our affairs here in England. In an early portion of this story the reader was introduced to the interior of Gatherum Castle, and there saw Miss Dunstable entertained by the duke in the most friendly manner. Since those days the lady has become the duke's neighbour, and has waged a war with him, which he probably felt to be very vexatious. But, nevertheless, on the next great occasion at Gatherum Castle, Doctor and Mrs. Thorne were among the visitors, and to no one was the duke more personally courteous than to his opulent neighbour, the late Miss Dunstable.

CHAPTER XLVIII.

HOW THEY WERE ALL MARRIED, HAD TWO CHILDREN, AND LIVED HAPPY EVER AFTER.

Dear, affectionate, sympathetic readers, we have four couple of sighing lovers with whom to deal in this our last chapter, and I, as leader of the chorus, disdain to press you further with doubts as to the happiness of any of that quadrille. They were all made happy, in spite of that little episode which so lately took place at Barchester; and in telling of their happiness—shortly, as is now necessary—we will take them chronologically, giving precedence to those who first appeared at the hymeneal altar.

In July, then, at the cathedral, by the father of the bride, assisted by his examining chaplain, Olivia Proudie, the eldest daughter of the Bishop of Barchester, was joined in marriage to the Rev. Tobias Tickler, incumbent of the Trinity district church in Bethnal Green. Of the bridegroom, in this instance, our acquaintance has been so short, that it is not, perhaps, necessary to say much. When coming to the wedding he proposed to bring his three darling children with him; but in this measure he was, I think prudently, stopped by advice, rather strongly worded, from his future valued mother-in-law. Mr. Tickler was not an opulent man, nor had he hitherto attained any great fame in his profession; but, at the age of forty-three he still had sufficient opportunity before him, and now that his merit has been properly viewed by high ecclesiastical eyes the refreshing dew of deserved promotion will no doubt fall upon him. The marriage was very smart, and Olivia carried herself through the trying ordeal with an excellent propriety of conduct.

Up to that time, and even for a few days longer, there was doubt at Barchester as to that strange journey which Lord Dumbello undoubtedly did take to France. When a man so circumstanced will suddenly go to Paris, without notice given even to his future bride, people must doubt; and grave were the apprehensions expressed on this occasion by Mrs. Proudie, even at her child's wedding-breakfast. "God bless you, my dear children," she said, standing up at the head of her table as she addressed Mr. Tickler and his wife; "when I see your perfect happiness—perfect, that is, as far as human happiness can be made perfect in this vale of tears—and think of the terrible calamity which has fallen on our unfortunate neighbours, I cannot but acknowledge His infinite mercy and goodness. The Lord giveth, and the Lord taketh away." By which she intended, no doubt, to signify that whereas Mr. Tickler had been given to her Olivia, Lord Dumbello had been taken away from the archdeacon's Griselda. The happy couple then went in Mrs. Proudie's carriage to the nearest railway station but one, and from thence proceeded to Malvern, and there spent the honeymoon.

And a great comfort it was, I am sure, to Mrs. Proudie when authenticated tidings reached Barchester that Lord Dumbello had returned from Paris, and that the Hartletop-Grantly alliance was to be carried to its completion. She still, however, held her opinion—whether correctly or not, who shall say?—that the young lord had intended to escape. "The archdeacon has shown great firmness in the way in which he has done it," said Mrs. Proudie; "but whether he has consulted his child's best interests in forcing her into a marriage with an unwilling husband, I for one must take leave to doubt. But then, unfortunately, we all know how completely the archdeacon is devoted to worldly matters."

In this instance the archdeacon's devotion to worldly matters was rewarded by that success which he no doubt desired. He did go up to London, and did see one or two of Lord Dumbello's friends. This he did, not obtrusively, as though in fear of any falsehood or vacillation on the part of the viscount, but with that discretion and tact for which he has been so long noted. Mrs. Proudie declares that during the few days of his absence from Barsetshire he himself crossed to France and hunted down Lord Dumbello at Paris. As to this I am not prepared to say anything; but I am quite sure, as will be all those who knew the archdeacon, that he was not a man to see his daughter wronged as long as any measure remained by which such wrong might be avoided.

But, be that as it may—that mooted question as to the archdeacon's journey to Paris—Lord Dumbello was forthcoming at Plumstead on the 5th of August, and went through his work like a man. The Hartletop family, when the alliance was found to be unavoidable, endeavoured to arrange that the wedding should be held at Hartletop Priory, in order that the clerical dust and dinginess of Barchester Close might not soil the splendour of the marriage gala doings; for, to tell the truth, the Hartletopians, as a rule, were not proud of their new clerical connections. But on this subject Mrs. Grantly was very properly inexorable; nor, when an attempt was made on the bride to induce her to throw over her mamma at the last moment and pronounce for herself that she would be married at the priory, was it attended with any success. The Hartletopians knew nothing of the Grantly fibre and calibre, or they would have made no such attempt. The marriage took place at Plumstead, and on the morning of the day Lord Dumbello posted over from Barchester to the rectory. The ceremony was performed by the archdeacon, without assistance, although the dean, and the precentor, and two other clergymen, were at the ceremony. Griselda's propriety of conduct was quite equal to that of Olivia Proudie; indeed, nothing could exceed the statuesque grace and fine aristocratic bearing with which she carried herself on the occasion. The three or four words which the service required of her she said with ease and dignity; there was neither sobbing nor crying to disturb the work or embarrass her friends, and she signed her name in the church books as "Griselda Grantly" without a tremor—and without a regret.

Mrs. Grantly kissed her and blessed her in the hall as she was about to step forward to her travelling carriage, leaning on her father's arm, and the child put up her face to her mother for a last whisper. "Mamma," she said, "I suppose Jane can put her hand at once on the moire antique when we reach Dover?" Mrs. Grantly smiled and nodded, and again blessed her child. There was not a tear shed—at least, not then—nor a sign of sorrow to cloud for a moment the gay splendour of the day. But the mother did bethink herself, in the solitude of her own room, of those last words, and did acknowledge a lack of something for which her heart had sighed. She had boasted to her sister that she had nothing to regret as to her daughter's education; but now, when she was alone after her success, did she feel that she could still support herself with that boast? For, be it known, Mrs. Grantly had a heart within her bosom and a faith within her heart. The world, it is true, had pressed upon her sorely with all its weight of accumulated clerical wealth, but it had not utterly crushed her—not her, but only her child. For the sins of the father, are they not visited on the third and fourth generation?

But if any such feeling of remorse did for awhile mar the fulness of Mrs. Grantly's joy, it was soon dispelled by the perfect success of her daughter's married life. At the end of the autumn the bride and bridegroom returned from their tour, and it was evident to all the circle at Hartletop Priory that Lord Dumbello was by no means dissatisfied with his bargain. His wife had been admired everywhere to the top of his bent. All the world at Ems, and at Baden, and at Nice, had been stricken by the stately beauty of the young viscountess. And then, too, her manner, style, and high dignity of demeanour altogether supported the reverential feeling which her grace and form at first inspired. She never derogated from her husband's honour by the fictitious liveliness of gossip, or allowed any one to forget the peeress in the woman. Lord Dumbello soon found that his reputation for discretion was quite safe in her hands, and that there were no lessons as to conduct in which it was necessary that he should give instruction.

Before the winter was over she had equally won the hearts of all the circle at Hartletop Priory. The duke was there and declared to the marchioness that Dumbello could not possibly have done better. "Indeed, I do not think he could," said the happy mother. "She sees all that she ought to see, and nothing that she ought not."

And then, in London, when the season came, all men sang all manner of praises in her favour, and Lord Dumbello was made aware that he was reckoned among the wisest of his age. He had married a wife who managed everything for him, who never troubled him, whom no woman disliked, and whom every man admired. As for feast of reason and for flow of soul, is it not a question whether any such flows and feasts are necessary between a man and his wife? How many men can truly assert that they ever enjoy connubial flows of soul, or that connubial feasts of reason are in their nature enjoyable? But a handsome woman at the head of your table, who knows how to dress, and how to sit, and how to get in and out of her carriage—who will not disgrace her lord by her ignorance, or fret him by her coquetry, or disparage him by her talent—how beautiful a thing it is! For my own part I think that Griselda Grantly was born to be the wife of a great English peer.

"After all, then," said Miss Dunstable, speaking of Lady Dumbello—she was Mrs. Thorne at this time—"after all, there is some truth in what our quaint latter-day philosopher tells us—'Great are thy powers, O Silence!'"

The marriage of our old friends Dr. Thorne and Miss Dunstable was the third on the list, but that did not take place till the latter end of September. The lawyers on such an occasion had no inconsiderable work to accomplish, and though the lady was not coy, nor the gentleman slow, it was not found practicable to arrange an earlier wedding. The ceremony was performed at St. George's, Hanover Square, and was not brilliant in any special degree. London at the time was empty, and the few persons whose presence was actually necessary were imported from the country for the occasion. The bride was given away by Dr. Easyman, and the two bridesmaids were ladies who had lived with Miss Dunstable as companions. Young Mr. Gresham and his wife were there, as was also Mrs. Harold Smith, who was not at all prepared to drop her old friend in her new sphere of life.

"We shall call her Mrs. Thorne instead of Miss Dunstable, and I really think that that will be all the difference," said Mrs. Harold Smith.

To Mrs. Harold Smith that probably was all the difference, but it was not so to the persons most concerned.

According to the plan of life arranged between the doctor and his wife she was still to keep up her house in London, remaining there during such period of the season as she might choose, and receiving him when it might appear good to him to visit her; but he was to be the master in the country. A mansion at the Chace was to be built, and till such time as that was completed, they would keep on the old house at Greshamsbury. Into this, small as it was, Mrs. Thorne,—in spite of her great wealth,—did not disdain to enter. But subsequent circumstances changed their plans. It was found that Mr. Sowerby could not or would not live at Chaldicotes; and, therefore, in the second year of their marriage, that place was prepared for them. They are now well known to the whole county as Dr. and Mrs. Thorne of Chaldicotes,—of Chaldicotes, in distinction to the well-known Thornes of Ullathorne in the eastern division. Here they live respected by their neighbours, and on terms of alliance both with the Duke of Omnium and with Lady Lufton. "Of course those dear old avenues will be very sad to me," said Mrs. Harold Smith, when at the end of a London season she was invited down to Chaldicotes; and as she spoke she put her handkerchief up to her eyes.

"Well, dear, what can I do?" said Mrs. Thorne. "I can't cut them down; the doctor would not let me."

"Oh, no," said Mrs. Harold Smith, sighing; and in spite of her feelings she did visit Chaldicotes.

But it was October before Lord Lufton was made a happy man;—that is, if the fruition of his happiness was a greater joy than the anticipation of it. I will not say that the happiness of marriage is like the Dead Sea fruit,—an apple which, when eaten, turns to bitter ashes in the mouth. Such pretended sarcasm would be very false. Nevertheless, is it not the fact that the sweetest morsel of love's feast has been eaten, that the freshest, fairest blush of the flower has been snatched and has passed away, when the ceremony at the altar has been performed, and legal possession has been given? There is an aroma of love, an undefinable delicacy of flavour, which escapes and is gone before the church portal is left, vanishing with the maiden name, and incompatible with the solid comfort appertaining to the rank of wife. To love one's own spouse, and to be loved by her, is the ordinary lot of man, and is a duty exacted under penalties. But to be allowed to love youth and beauty that is not one's own—to know that one is loved by a soft being who still hangs cowering from the eye of the world as though her love were all but illicit—can it be that a man is made happy when a state of anticipation such as this is brought to a close? No; when the husband walks back from the altar, he has already swallowed the choicest dainties of his banquet. The beef and pudding of married life are then in store for him;—or perhaps only the bread and cheese. Let him take care lest hardly a crust remain,—or perhaps not a crust.

But before we finish, let us go back for one moment to the dainties,—to the time before the beef and pudding were served,—while Lucy was still at the parsonage, and Lord Lufton still staying at Framley Court. He had come up one morning, as was now frequently his wont, and, after a few minutes' conversation, Mrs. Robarts had left the room,—as not unfrequently on such occasions was her wont. Lucy was working and continued her work, and Lord Lufton for a moment or two sat looking at her; then he got up abruptly, and standing before her, thus questioned her:—

"Lucy," said he.

"Well, what of Lucy now? Any particular fault this morning?"

"Yes, a most particular fault. When I asked you, here, in this room, on this very spot, whether it was possible that you should love me—why did you say that it was impossible?"

Lucy, instead of answering at the moment, looked down upon the carpet, to see if his memory were as good as hers. Yes; he was standing on the exact spot where he had stood before. No spot in all the world was more frequently clear before her own eyes.

"Do you remember that day, Lucy?" he said again.

"Yes, I remember it," she said.

"Why did you say it was impossible?"

"Did I say impossible?"

She knew that she had said so. She remembered how she had waited till he had gone, and that then, going to her own room, she had reproached herself with the cowardice of the falsehood. She had lied to him then; and now—how was she punished for it?

"Well, I suppose it was possible," she said.

"But why did you say so when you knew it would make me so miserable?"

"Miserable! nay, but you went away happy enough! I thought I had never seen you look better satisfied."

"Lucy!"

"You had done your duty and had had such a lucky escape! What astonishes me is that you should have ever come back again. But the pitcher may go to the well once too often, Lord Lufton."

"But will you tell me the truth now?"

"What truth?"

"That day, when I came to you,—did you love me at all then?"

"We'll let bygones be bygones, if you please."

"But I swear you shall tell me. It was such a cruel thing to answer me as you did, unless you meant it. And yet you never saw me again till after my mother had been over for you to Mrs. Crawley's."

"It was absence that made me—care for you."

"Lucy, I swear I believe you loved me then."

"Ludovic, some conjuror must have told you that."

She was standing as she spoke, and, laughing at him, she held up her hands and shook her head. But she was now in his power, and he had his revenge,—his revenge for her past falsehood and her present joke. How could he be more happy when he was made happy by having her all his own, than he was now?

And in these days there again came up that petition as to her riding—with very different result now than on that former occasion. There were ever so many objections, then. There was no habit, and Lucy was—or said that she was—afraid; and then, what would Lady Lufton say? But now Lady Lufton thought it would be quite right; only were they quite sure about the horse? Was Ludovic certain that the horse had been ridden by a lady? And Lady Meredith's habits were dragged out as a matter of course, and one of them chipped and snipped and altered, without any compunction. And as for fear, there could be no bolder horsewoman than Lucy Robarts. It was quite clear to all Framley that riding was the very thing for her. "But I never shall be happy, Ludovic, till you have got a horse properly suited for her," said Lady Lufton.

And then, also, came the affair of her wedding garments, of her *trousseau*,—as to which I cannot boast that she showed capacity or steadiness at all equal to that of Lady Dumbello. Lady Lufton, however, thought it a very serious matter; and as, in her opinion, Mrs. Robarts did not go about it with sufficient energy, she took the matter mainly into her own hands, striking Lucy dumb by her frowns and nods, deciding on everything herself, down to the very tags of the boot-ties.

"My dear, you really must allow me to know what I am about;" and Lady Lufton patted her on the arm as she spoke. "I did it all for Justinia, and she never had reason to regret a single thing that I bought. If you'll ask her, she'll tell you so."

Lucy did not ask her future sister-in-law, seeing that she had no doubt whatever as to her future mother-in-law's judgment on the articles in question. Only the money! And what could she want with six dozen pocket-handkerchiefs all at once? There was no question of Lord Lufton's going out as governor-general to India! But twelve dozen pocket-handkerchiefs had not been too many for Griselda's imagination.

And Lucy would sit alone in the drawing-room at Framley Court, filling her heart with thoughts of that evening when she had first sat there. She had then resolved, painfully, with inward tears, with groanings of her spirit, that she was wrongly placed in being in that company. Griselda Grantly had been there, quite at her ease, petted by Lady Lufton, admired by Lord Lufton; while she had retired out of sight, sore at heart, because she felt herself to be no fit companion to those around her. Then he had come to her, making matters almost worse by talking to her, bringing the tears into her eyes by his good-nature, but still wounding her by the feeling that she could not speak to him at her ease.

But things were at a different pass with her now. He had chosen her—her out of all the world, and brought her there to share with him his own home, his own honours, and all that he had to give. She was the apple of his eye, and the pride of his heart. And the stern mother, of whom she had stood so much in awe, who at first had passed her by as a thing not to be noticed, and had then sent out to her that she might be warned to keep herself aloof, now hardly knew in what way she might sufficiently show her love, regard, and solicitude.

I must not say that Lucy was not proud in these moments—that her heart was not elated at these thoughts. Success does beget pride, as failure begets shame. But her pride was of that sort which is in no way disgraceful to either man or woman, and was accompanied by pure true love, and a full resolution to do her duty in that state of life to which it had pleased her God to call her. She did rejoice greatly to think that she had been chosen, and not Griselda. Was it possible that having loved she should not so rejoice, or that, rejoicing, she should not be proud of her love?

They spent the whole winter abroad, leaving the dowager Lady Lufton to her plans and preparations for their reception at Framley Court; and in the following spring they appeared in London, and there set up their staff. Lucy had some inner tremblings of the spirit, and quiverings about the heart, at thus beginning her duty before the great world, but she said little or nothing to her husband on the matter. Other women had done as much before her time, and by courage had gone through with it. It would be dreadful enough, that position in her own house with lords and ladies bowing to her, and stiff members of Parliament for whom it would be necessary to make small talk; but, nevertheless, it was to be endured. The time came, and she did endure it. The time came, and before the first six weeks were over she found that it was easy enough. The lords and ladies got into their proper places and talked to her about ordinary matters in a way that made no effort necessary, and the members of Parliament were hardly more stiff than the clergymen she had known in the neighbourhood of Framley.

She had not been long in town before she met Lady Dumbello. At this interview also she had to overcome some little inward emotion. On the few occasions on which she had met Griselda Grantly at Framley they had not much progressed in friendship, and Lucy had felt that she had been despised by the rich beauty. She also in her turn had disliked, if she had not despised, her rival. But how would it be now? Lady Dumbello could hardly despise her, and yet it did not seem possible that they should meet as friends. They did meet, and Lucy came forward with a pretty eagerness to give her hand to Lady Lufton's late favourite. Lady Dumbello smiled slightly—the same old smile which had come across her face when they two had been first introduced in the Framley drawing-room; the same smile without the variation of a line,—took the offered hand, muttered a word or two, and then receded. It was exactly as she had done before. She had never despised Lucy Robarts. She had accorded to the parson's sister the amount of cordiality with which she usually received her acquaintance; and now she could do no more for the peer's wife. Lady Dumbello and Lady Lufton have known each other ever since, and have occasionally visited at each other's houses, but the intimacy between them has never gone beyond this.

The dowager came up to town for about a month, and while there was contented to fill a second place. She had no desire to be the great lady in London. But then came the trying period when they commenced their life together at Framley Court. The elder lady formally renounced her place at the top of the table,—formally persisted in renouncing it though Lucy with tears implored her to resume it. She said also, with equal formality—repeating her determination over and over again to Mrs. Robarts with great energy—that she would in no respect detract by interference of her own from the authority of the proper mistress of the house; but, nevertheless, it is well known to every one at Framley that old Lady Lufton still reigns paramount in the parish.

"Yes, my dear; the big room looking into the little garden to the south was always the nursery; and if you ask my advice, it will still remain so. But, of course, any room you please—"

And the big room looking into the little garden to the south is still the nursery at Framley Court.

Five Novels by Thomas Hardy - Far From The Madding Crowd, The Return of the Native, The Mayor of Casterbridge, Tess of the d'Urbervilles, Jude the Obscure (complete and unabridged)
Thomas Hardy
Benediction Classics, 2013
1114 pages
ISBN: 978-1-78139-356-7

Available from www.amazon.com, www.amazon.co.uk

Thomas Hardy, (1840 - 1928) was an English novelist and poet. He was highly critical of Victorian society and focussed mainly on the declining rural communities.

E M Forster - Collected Works, including A Room with a View, Howards End, The Longest Journey, Where Angels Fear to Tread and The Celestial Omnibus and other Stories
E M Forster
Oxford City Press, 2013
808 pages
ISBN: 978-1-78139-373-4

Available from www.amazon.com, www.amazon.co.uk

Edward Morgan Forster (1879 - 1970) is best known for his beautiful novels - ironic with delicious plots, highlighting the hypocrisy and discrimination in early 20th-century British society.

Make Way for Lucia - The Complete Mapp & Lucia -
Queen Lucia, Miss Mapp including 'The Male Imperson-
ator', Lucia in London, Mapp and Lucia, Lucia's
Progress (also known as The Worshipful Lucia), & Trou-
ble for Lucia
E F Benson
Benediction Classics, 2012
1052 pages
ISBN: 978-1-78139-148-8

Available from www.amazon.com, www.amazon.co.uk

Make way for Lucia is a series of novels written by E.F Benson. They feature hilarious incidents in the lives of upper-middle class people in the 1920s and '30s.
The characters vie for social standing in an extremely snobby world. In the series
the two main characters - sophisticated Lucia and frumpy Miss Mapp compete
with each other and have to extricate themselves from a series of social disasters
in comical style. The novels are: Queen Lucia (1920) Miss Mapp (1922) The
Male Impersonator (a short story) Lucia in London (1927) Mapp and Lucia
(1931) Lucia's Progress (1935) (published in the U.S. as The Worshipful Lucia)
Trouble for Lucia (1939)

Jerome K Jerome, Collected Works (complete and
unabridged), including: Three Men in a Boat (To Say
Nothing of the Dog) (illustrated), Three Men on the
Bummel, Idle Thoughts of an Idle Fellow, Second
Thoughts of an Idle Fellow, Told After Supper, Diary
of a Pilgrimage, The Philosopher's Joke, All Roads
Lead to Calvary and Sketches in Lavender, Blue and
Green
Jerome K Jerome
Benediction Classics, 2013
968 pages
ISBN: 978-1-78139-358-1

Available from www.amazon.com, www.amazon.co.uk

Jerome K Jerome is best known for his hilarious book "Three Men in a Boat"
charting the misadventures of the author and his friends on a boating trip up the
Thames. The book started off as a serious Travel Book, but morphed into a very
funny book and a social commentary. This book collects nine of his best known
and loved works into a single volume.

Also from Benediction Books …
Wandering Between Two Worlds: Essays on Faith and Art
Anita Mathias
Benediction Books, 2007
152 pages
ISBN: 0955373700

Available from www.amazon.com, www.amazon.co.uk

In these wide-ranging lyrical essays, Anita Mathias writes, in lush, lovely prose, of her naughty Catholic childhood in Jamshedpur, India; her large, eccentric family in Mangalore, a sea-coast town converted by the Portuguese in the sixteenth century; her rebellion and atheism as a teenager in her Himalayan boarding school, run by German missionary nuns, St. Mary's Convent, Nainital; and her abrupt religious conversion after which she entered Mother Teresa's convent in Calcutta as a novice. Later rich, elegant essays explore the dualities of her life as a writer, mother, and Christian in the United States-- Domesticity and Art, Writing and Prayer, and the experience of being "an alien and stranger" as an immigrant in America, sensing the need for roots.

About the Author

Anita Mathias is the author of *Wandering Between Two Worlds: Essays on Faith and Art*. She has a B.A. and M.A. in English from Somerville College, Oxford University, and an M.A. in Creative Writing from the Ohio State University, USA. Anita won a National Endowment of the Arts fellowship in Creative Non-fiction in 1997. She lives in Oxford, England with her husband, Roy, and her daughters, Zoe and Irene.

Anita's website:
 http://www.anitamathias.com, and
Anita's blog Dreaming Beneath the Spires:
 http://dreamingbeneaththespires.blogspot.com

The Church That Had Too Much
Anita Mathias
Benediction Books, 2010
52 pages
ISBN: 9781849026567

Available from www.amazon.com, www.amazon.co.uk

The Church That Had Too Much was very well-intentioned. She wanted to love God, she wanted to love people, but she was both hampered by her muchness and the abundance of her possessions, and beset by ambition, power struggles and snobbery. Read about the surprising way The Church That Had Too Much began to resolve her problems in this deceptively simple and enchanting fable.

About the Author

Anita Mathias is the author of *Wandering Between Two Worlds: Essays on Faith and Art*. She has a B.A. and M.A. in English from Somerville College, Oxford University, and an M.A. in Creative Writing from the Ohio State University, USA. Anita won a National Endowment of the Arts fellowship in Creative Non-fiction in 1997. She lives in Oxford, England with her husband, Roy, and her daughters, Zoe and Irene.

Anita's website:
    http://www.anitamathias.com, and
Anita's blog Dreaming Beneath the Spires:
    http://dreamingbeneaththespires.blogspot.com